RUDYARD KIPLING

*The Complete Children's
Short Stories*

RUDYARD KIPLING

The Complete Children's Short Stories

Wordsworth Editions

This edition published in 2004 by Wordsworth Editions Limited
8B East Street, Ware, Hertfordshire SG12 9HJ

ISBN 1 84022 057 0

Text © Wordsworth Editions Limited 2004

Wordsworth® is a registered trademark of
Wordsworth Editions Limited

Typeset by Antony Gray
Printed in Great Britain by
Mackays of Chatham, Chatham, Kent

CONTENTS

THE JUNGLE BOOK

Contents

Preface

The demands made by a work of this nature upon the generosity of specialists are very numerous, and the Editor would be wanting in all title to the generous treatment he has received were he not willing to make the fullest possible acknowledgement of his indebtedness.

His thanks are due in the first place to the scholarly and accomplished Bahadur Shah, baggage elephant 174 on the Indian Register, who, with his amiable sister Pudmini, most courteously supplied the history of 'Toomai of the Elephants' and much of the information contained in 'Her Majesty's Servants'. The adventures of Mowgli were collected at various times and in various places from a multitude of informants, most of whom desire to preserve the strictest anonymity. Yet, at this distance, the Editor feels at liberty to thank a Hindu gentleman of the old rock, an esteemed resident of the upper slopes of Jakko, for his convincing if somewhat caustic estimate of the national characteristics of his caste – the Presbytes. Sahi, a savant of infinite research and industry, a member of the recently disbanded Seeonee Pack, and an artist well known at most of the local fairs of Southern India, where his muzzled dance with his master attracts the youth, beauty, and culture of many villages, have contributed most valuable data on people, manners, and customs. These have been freely drawn upon, in the stories of 'Tiger! Tiger!', 'Kaa's Hunting', and 'Mowgli's Brothers'. For the outlines of 'Rikki-tikki-tavi' the Editor stands indebted to one of the leading herpetologists of Upper India, a fearless and independent investigator who, resolving 'not to live but know', lately sacrificed his life through over-application to the study of our Eastern Thanatophidia. A happy accident of travel enabled the Editor, when a passenger on the *Empress of India*, to be of some slight assistance to a fellow-passenger. How richly his poor services were repaid, readers of 'The White Seal' may judge for themselves.

Mowgli's Brothers

Now Chil the Kite brings home the night
   That Mang the Bat sets free –
The herds are shut in byre and hut,
   For loosed till dawn are we.
This is the hour of pride and power,
   Talon and tush and claw.
Oh, hear the call! – Good hunting all
   That keep the Jungle Law!

Night Song in the Jungle

It was seven o'clock of a very warm evening in the Seeonee hills when Father Wolf woke up from his day's rest, scratched himself, yawned, and spread out his paws one after the other to get rid of the sleepy feeling in their tips. Mother Wolf lay with her big grey nose dropped across her four tumbling, squealing cubs, and the moon shone into the mouth of the cave where they all lived. 'Augrh!' said Father Wolf, 'it is time to hunt again'; and he was going to spring downhill when a little shadow with a bushy tail crossed the threshold and whined: 'Good luck go with you, O Chief of the Wolves; and good luck and strong white teeth go with the noble children, that they may never forget the hungry in this world.'

It was the jackal – Tabaqui, the Dish-licker – and the wolves of India despise Tabaqui because he runs about making mischief, and telling tales, and eating rags and pieces of leather from the village rubbish-heaps. But they are afraid of him too, because Tabaqui, more than anyone else in the Jungle, is apt to go mad, and then he forgets that he was ever afraid of anyone, and runs through the forest biting everything in his way. Even the tiger runs and hides when little Tabaqui goes mad, for madness is the most disgraceful thing that can overtake a wild creature. We call it hydrophobia, but they call it *dewanee* – the madness – and run.

'Enter, then, and look,' said Father Wolf stiffly; 'but there is no food here.'

'For a wolf, no,' said Tabaqui; 'but for so mean a person as myself a dry bone is a good feast. Who are we, the *Gidur-log* [the Jackal People], to pick and choose?' He scuttled to the back of the cave, where he found the bone of a buck with some meat on it, and sat cracking the end merrily.

'All thanks for this good meal,' he said, licking his lips. 'How beautiful are the noble children! How large are their eyes! And so young too! Indeed, indeed, I might have remembered that the children of Kings are men from the beginning.'

Now, Tabaqui knew as well as anyone else that there is nothing so unlucky as to compliment children to their faces; and it pleased him to see Mother and Father Wolf look uncomfortable.

Tabaqui sat still, rejoicing in the mischief that he had made: then he said spitefully:

'Shere Khan, the Big One, has shifted his hunting-grounds. He will hunt among these hills for the next moon, so he has told me.'

Shere Khan was the tiger who lived near the Waingunga River, twenty miles away.

'He has no right!' Father Wolf began angrily – 'By the Law of the Jungle he has no right to change his quarters without due warning. He will frighten every head of game within ten miles, and I – I have to kill for two, these days.'

'His mother did not call him Lungri [the Lame One] for nothing,' said Mother Wolf quietly. 'He has been lame in one foot from his birth. That is why he has only killed cattle. Now the villagers of the Waingunga are angry with him, and he has come here to make *our* villagers angry. They will scour the Jungle for him when he is far away, and we and our children must run when the grass is set alight. Indeed, we are very grateful to Shere Khan!'

'Shall I tell him of your gratitude?' said Tabaqui.

'Out!' snapped Father Wolf. 'Out and hunt with thy master. Thou hast done harm enough for one night.'

'I go,' said Tabaqui quietly. 'Ye can hear Shere Khan below in the thickets. I might have saved myself the message.'

Father Wolf listened, and below in the valley that ran down to a little river, he heard the dry, angry, snarly, singsong whine of a tiger who has caught nothing and does not care if all the Jungle knows it.

'The fool!' said Father Wolf. 'To begin a night's work with that noise! Does he think that our buck are like his fat Waingunga bullocks?'

'H'sh! It is neither bullock nor buck he hunts tonight,' said Mother Wolf. 'It is Man.' The whine had changed to a sort of humming purr that seemed to come from every quarter of the compass. It was the noise that bewilders woodcutters and gypsies sleeping in the open, and makes them run sometimes into the very mouth of the tiger.

'Man!' said Father Wolf, showing all his white teeth. 'Faugh! Are there not enough beetles and frogs in the tanks that he must eat Man, and on our ground too?'

The Law of the Jungle, which never orders anything without a reason, forbids every beast to eat Man except when he is killing to show his children how to kill, and then he must hunt outside the hunting-grounds of his pack or tribe. The real reason for this is that man-killing means, sooner or later, the arrival of white men on elephants, with guns, and hundreds of brown

Good luck go with you, O Chief of the Wolves

men with gongs and rockets and torches. Then everybody in the Jungle suffers. The reason the beasts give among themselves is that Man is the weakest and most defenceless of all living things, and it is unsportsmanlike to touch him. They say too – and it is true – that man-eaters become mangy, and lose their teeth.

The purr grew louder, and ended in the full-throated 'Aaarh!' of the tiger's charge.

Then there was a howl – an untigerish howl – from Shere Khan. 'He has missed,' said Mother Wolf. 'What is it?'

Father Wolf ran out a few paces and heard Shere Khan muttering and mumbling savagely, as he tumbled about in the scrub.

'The fool has had no more sense than to jump at a woodcutter's camp-fire, and has burned his feet,' said Father Wolf, with a grunt. 'Tabaqui is with him.'

'Something is coming uphill,' said Mother Wolf, twitching one ear. 'Get ready.'

The bushes rustled a little in the thicket, and Father Wolf dropped with his haunches under him, ready for his leap. Then, if you had been watching, you would have seen the most wonderful thing in the world – the wolf checked in mid-spring. He made his bound before he saw what it was he was jumping at, and then he tried to stop himself. The result was that he shot up straight into the air for four or five feet, landing almost where he left ground.

'Man!' he snapped. 'A man's cub. Look!'

Directly in front of him, holding on by a low branch, stood a naked brown baby who could just walk – as soft and as dimpled a little atom as ever came to a wolf's cave at night. He looked up into Father Wolf's face, and laughed.

'Is that a man's cub?' said Mother Wolf. 'I have never seen one. Bring it here.'

A wolf accustomed to moving his own cubs can, if necessary, mouth an egg without breaking it, and though Father Wolf's jaws closed right on the child's back not a tooth even scratched the skin, as he laid it down among the cubs.

'How little! How naked, and – how bold!' said Mother Wolf softly. The baby was pushing his way between the cubs to get close to the warm hide. 'Ahai! He is taking his meal with the others. And so this is a man's cub. Now, was there ever a wolf that could boast of a man's cub among her children?'

'I have heard now and again of such a thing, but never in our Pack or in my time,' said Father Wolf. 'He is altogether without hair, and I could kill him with a touch of my foot. But see, he looks up and is not afraid.'

The moonlight was blocked out of the mouth of the cave, for Shere Khan's great square head and shoulders were thrust into the entrance. Tabaqui, behind him, was squeaking: 'My lord, my lord, it went in here!'

'Shere Khan does us great honour,' said Father Wolf, but his eyes were very angry. 'What does Shere Khan need?'

'My quarry. A man's cub went this way,' said Shere Khan. 'Its parents have run off. Give it to me.'

Shere Khan had jumped at a woodcutter's camp-fire, as Father Wolf had said, and was furious from the pain of his burned feet. But Father Wolf knew that the mouth of the cave was too narrow for a tiger to come in by. Even where he was, Shere Khan's shoulders and forepaws were cramped for want of room, as a man's would be if he tried to fight in a barrel.

'The Wolves are a free people,' said Father Wolf. 'They take orders from the Head of the Pack, and not from any striped cattle-killer. The man's cub is ours – to kill if we choose.'

'Ye choose and ye do not choose! What talk is this of choosing? By the bull that I killed, am I to stand nosing into your dog's den for my fair dues? It is I, Shere Khan, who speak!'

The tiger's roar filled the cave with thunder. Mother Wolf shook herself clear of the cubs and sprang forward, her eyes, like two green moons in the darkness, facing the blazing eyes of Shere Khan.

'And it is I, Raksha [The Demon], who answer. The man's cub is mine, Lungri – mine to me! He shall not be killed. He shall live to run with the Pack and to hunt with the Pack; and in the end, look you, hunter of little naked cubs – frog-eater – fish-killer – he shall hunt *thee*! Now get hence, or by the Sambhur that I killed (*I* eat no starved cattle), back thou goest to thy mother, burned beast of the Jungle, lamer than ever thou camest into the world! Go!'

Father Wolf looked on amazed. He had almost forgotten the days when he won Mother Wolf in fair fight from five other wolves, when she ran in the

The tiger's roar filled the cave with thunder

Pack and was not called The Demon for compliment's sake. Shere Khan might have faced Father Wolf, but he could not stand up against Mother Wolf, for he knew that where he was she had all the advantage of the ground, and would fight to the death.

So he backed out of the cave-mouth growling, and when he was clear he shouted: 'Each dog barks in his own yard! We will see what the Pack will say to this fostering of man-cubs. The cub is mine, and to my teeth he will come in the end, O bush-tailed thieves!'

Mother Wolf threw herself down panting among the cubs, and Father Wolf said to her gravely: 'Shere Khan speaks this much truth. The cub must be shown to the Pack. Wilt thou still keep him, Mother?'

'Keep him!' she gasped. 'He came naked, by night, alone and very hungry; yet he was not afraid! Look, he has pushed one of my babes to one side already. And that lame butcher would have killed him and would have run off to the Waingunga while the villagers here hunted through all our lairs in revenge! Keep him? Assuredly I will keep him. Lie still, little frog. O thou Mowgli – for Mowgli the Frog I will call thee – the time will come when thou wilt hunt Shere Khan as he has hunted thee.'

'But what will our Pack say?' said Father Wolf.

The Law of the Jungle lays down very clearly that any wolf may, when he marries, withdraw from the Pack he belongs to; but as soon as his cubs are old enough to stand on their feet he must bring them to the Pack Council, which is generally held once a month at full moon, in order that the other wolves may identify them. After that inspection the cubs are free to run where they please, and until they have killed their first buck no excuse is accepted if a grown wolf of the Pack kills one of them. The punishment is death where the murderer can be found; and if you think for a minute you will see that this must be so.

Father Wolf waited till his cubs could run a little, and then on the night of the Pack Meeting took them and Mowgli and Mother Wolf to the Council Rock – a hilltop covered with stones and boulders where a hundred wolves could hide. Akela, the great grey Lone Wolf who led all the Pack by strength and cunning, lay out at full length on his rock, and below him sat forty or more wolves of every size and colour, from badger-coloured veterans who could handle a buck alone, to young black three-year-olds who thought they could. The Lone Wolf had led them for a year now. He had fallen twice into a wolf-trap in his youth, and once he had been beaten and left for dead; so he knew the manners and customs of men. There was very little talking at the Rock. The cubs tumbled over each other in the centre of the circle where their mothers and fathers sat, and now and again a senior wolf would go quietly up to a cub, look at him carefully, and return to his place on noiseless feet. Sometimes a mother would push her cub far out into the moonlight, to be sure that he had not been overlooked. Akela from his rock would cry: 'Ye know the Law – ye know the Law. Look well, O Wolves!' and the anxious mothers would take up the call: 'Look – look well, O Wolves!'

At last – and Mother Wolf's neck-bristles lifted as the time came – Father Wolf pushed 'Mowgli the Frog', as they called him, into the centre, where he sat laughing and playing with some pebbles that glistened in the moonlight.

Akela never raised his head from his paws, but went on with the monotonous cry: 'Look well!' A muffled roar came up from behind the rocks – the voice of Shere Khan crying: 'The cub is mine. Give him to me. What have the Free People to do with a man's cub?' Akela never even twitched his ears: all he said was: 'Look well, O Wolves! What have the Free People to do with the orders of any save the Free People? Look well!'

There was a chorus of deep growls, and a young wolf in his fourth year flung back Shere Khan's question to Akela: 'What have the Free People to do with a man's cub?' Now, the Law of the Jungle lays down that if there is any dispute as to the right of a cub to be accepted by the Pack, he must be spoken for by at least two members of the Pack who are not his father and mother.

'Who speaks for this cub?' said Akela. 'Among the Free People who speaks?' There was no answer, and Mother Wolf got ready for what she knew would be her last fight, if things came to fighting.

Then the only other creature who is allowed at the Pack Council – Baloo, the sleepy brown bear who teaches the wolf-cubs the Law of the Jungle: old Baloo, who can come and go where he pleases because he eats only nuts and roots and honey – rose up on his hindquarters and grunted.

'The man's cub – the man's cub?' he said. '*I* speak for the man's cub. There is no harm in a man's cub. I have no gift of words, but I speak the

The Meeting at the Council Rock

truth. Let him run with the Pack, and be entered with the others. I myself will teach him.'

'We need yet another,' said Akela. 'Baloo has spoken, and he is our teacher for the young cubs. Who speaks besides Baloo?'

A black shadow dropped down into the circle. It was Bagheera the Black Panther, inky black all over, but with the panther markings showing up in certain lights like the pattern of watered silk. Everybody knew Bagheera, and nobody cared to cross his path; for he was as cunning as Tabaqui, as bold as the wild buffalo, and as reckless as the wounded elephant. But he had a voice as soft as wild honey dripping from a tree, and a skin softer than down.

'O Akela, and ye the Free People,' he purred, 'I have no right in your assembly; but the Law of the Jungle says that if there is a doubt which is not a killing matter in regard to a new cub, the life of that cub may be bought at a price. And the Law does not say who may or may not pay that price. Am I right?'

'Good! good!' said the young wolves, who are always hungry. 'Listen to Bagheera. The cub can be bought for a price. It is the Law.'

'Knowing that I have no right to speak here, I ask your leave.'

'Speak then,' cried twenty voices.

'To kill a naked cub is shame. Besides, he may make better sport for you when he is grown. Baloo has spoken in his behalf. Now to Baloo's word I will add one bull, and a fat one, newly killed, not half a mile from here, if ye will accept the man's cub according to the Law. Is it difficult?'

There was a clamour of scores of voices, saying: 'What matter? He will die in the winter rains. He will scorch in the sun. What harm can a naked frog do us? Let him run with the Pack. Where is the bull, Bagheera? Let him be accepted.' And then came Akela's deep bay, crying: 'Look well – look well, O Wolves!'

Mowgli was still deeply interested in the pebbles and he did not notice when the wolves came and looked at him one by one. At last they all went down the hill for the dead bull, and only Akela, Bagheera, Baloo, and Mowgli's own wolves were left. Shere Khan roared still in the night, for he was very angry that Mowgli had not been handed over to him.

'Ay, roar well,' said Bagheera, under his whiskers; 'for the time comes when this naked thing will make thee roar to another tune, or I know nothing of Man.'

'It was well done,' said Akela. 'Men and their cubs are very wise. He may be a help in time.'

'Truly, a help in time of need; for none can hope to lead the Pack for ever,' said Bagheera.

Akela said nothing. He was thinking of the time that comes to every leader of every pack when his strength goes from him and he gets feebler and feebler, till at last he is killed by the wolves and a new leader comes up – to be killed in his turn.

'Take him away,' he said to Father Wolf, 'and train him as befits one of the Free People.'

And that is how Mowgli was entered into the Seeonee Wolf Pack at the price of a bull and on Baloo's good word.

*　　*　　*

Now you must be content to skip ten or eleven whole years, and only guess at all the wonderful life that Mowgli led among the wolves, because if it were written out it would fill ever so many books. He grew up with the cubs, though they, of course, were grown wolves almost before he was a child, and Father Wolf taught him his business, and the meaning of things in the Jungle, till every rustle in the grass, every breath of the warm night air, every note of the owls above his head, every scratch of a bat's claws as it roosted for a while in a tree, and every splash of every little fish jumping in a pool, meant just as much to him as the work of his office means to a business man. When he was not learning, he sat out in the sun and slept, and ate and went to sleep again; when he felt dirty or hot he swam in the forest pools; and when he wanted honey (Baloo told him that honey and nuts were just as pleasant to eat as raw meat) he climbed up for it, and that Bagheera showed him how to do. Bagheera would lie out on a branch and call, 'Come along, Little Brother,' and at first Mowgli would cling like the sloth, but afterward he would fling himself through the branches almost as boldly as the grey ape. He took his place at the Council Rock, too, when the Pack met, and there he discovered

Bagheera would lie out on a branch and call, 'Come along, Little Brother,'

that if he stared hard at any wolf, the wolf would be forced to drop his eyes, and so he used to stare for fun. At other times he would pick the long thorns out of the pads of his friends, for wolves suffer terribly from thorns and burrs in their coats. He would go down the hillside into the cultivated lands by night, and look very curiously at the villagers in their huts, but he had a mistrust of men because Bagheera showed him a square box with a drop-gate so cunningly hidden in the Jungle that he nearly walked into it, and told him that it was a trap. He loved better than anything else to go with Bagheera into the dark warm heart of the forest, to sleep all through the drowsy day, and at night to see how Bagheera did his killing. Bagheera killed right and left as he felt hungry, and so did Mowgli – with one exception. As soon as he was old enough to understand things, Bagheera told him that he must never touch cattle because he had been bought into the Pack at the price of a bull's life. 'All the Jungle is thine,' said Bagheera, 'and thou canst kill everything that thou art strong enough to kill; but for the sake of the bull that bought thee thou must never kill or eat any cattle young or old. That is the Law of the Jungle.' Mowgli obeyed faithfully.

And he grew and grew strong as a boy must grow who does not know that he is learning any lessons, and who has nothing in the world to think of except things to eat.

Mother Wolf told him once or twice that Shere Khan was not a creature to be trusted, and that some day he must kill Shere Khan; but though a young wolf would have remembered that advice every hour, Mowgli forgot it because he was only a boy – though he would have called himself a wolf if he had been able to speak in any human tongue.

Shere Khan was always crossing his path in the Jungle, for as Akela grew older and feebler the lame tiger had come to be great friends with the younger wolves of the Pack, who followed him for scraps, a thing that Akela would never have allowed if he had dared to push his authority to the proper bounds. Then Shere Khan would flatter them and wonder that such fine young hunters were content to be led by a dying wolf and a man's cub. 'They tell me,' Shere Khan would say, 'that at Council ye dare not look him between the eyes'; and the young wolves would growl and bristle.

Bagheera, who had eyes and ears everywhere, knew something of this, and once or twice he told Mowgli in so many words that Shere Khan would kill him some day; and Mowgli would laugh and answer: 'I have the Pack and I have thee; and Baloo, though he is so lazy, might strike a blow or two for my sake. Why should I be afraid?'

It was one very warm day that a new notion came to Bagheera – born of something that he had heard. Perhaps Ikki the Porcupine had told him; but he said to Mowgli when they were deep in the Jungle, as the boy lay with his head on Bagheera's beautiful black skin: 'Little Brother, how often have I told thee that Shere Khan is thy enemy?'

'As many times as there are nuts on that palm,' said Mowgli, who, naturally, could not count. 'What of it? I am sleepy, Bagheera, and Shere Khan is all long tail and loud talk – like Mao, the Peacock.'

'But this is no time for sleeping. Baloo knows it; I know it; the Pack know it; and even the foolish, foolish deer know. Tabaqui has told thee, too.'

'Ho! ho!' said Mowgli. 'Tabaqui came to me not long ago with some rude talk that I was a naked man's cub and not fit to dig pig-nuts; but I caught Tabaqui by the tail and swung him twice against a palm tree to teach him better manners.'

'That was foolishness; for though Tabaqui is a mischief-maker, he would have told thee of something that concerned thee closely. Open those eyes, Little Brother. Shere Khan dare not kill thee in the Jungle; but remember, Akela is very old, and soon the day comes when he cannot kill his buck, and then he will be leader no more. Many of the wolves that looked thee over when thou wast brought to the Council first are old too, and the young wolves believe, as Shere Khan has taught them, that a man-cub has no place with the Pack. In a little time thou wilt be a man.'

'And what is a man that he should not run with his brothers?' said Mowgli. 'I was born in the Jungle. I have obeyed the Law of the Jungle, and there is no wolf of ours from whose paws I have not pulled a thorn. Surely they are my brothers!'

Bagheera stretched himself at full length and half shut his eyes. 'Little Brother,' said he, 'feel under my jaw.'

Mowgli put up his strong brown hand, and just under Bagheera's silky chin, where the giant rolling muscles were all hid by the glossy hair, he came upon a little bald spot.

'There is no one in the Jungle that knows that I, Bagheera, carry that mark – the mark of the collar; and yet, Little Brother, I was born among men, and it was among men that my mother died – in the cages of the King's Palace at Oodeypore. It was because of this that I paid the price for thee at the Council when thou wast a little naked cub. Yes, I too was born among men. I had never seen the Jungle. They fed me behind bars from an iron pan till one night I felt that I was Bagheera – the Panther – and no man's plaything, and I broke the silly lock with one blow of my paw and came away; and because I had learned the ways of men, I became more terrible in the Jungle than Shere Khan. Is it not so?'

'Yes,' said Mowgli; 'all the Jungle fear Bagheera – all except Mowgli.'

'Oh, *thou* art a man's cub,' said the Black Panther, very tenderly; 'and even as I returned to my Jungle, so thou must go back to men at last – to the men who are thy brothers – if thou art not killed in the Council.'

'But why – but why should any wish to kill me?' said Mowgli.

'Look at me,' said Bagheera; and Mowgli looked at him steadily between the eyes. The big panther turned his head away in half a minute.

'*That* is why,' he said, shifting his paw on the leaves. 'Not even I can look thee between the eyes, and I was born among men, and I love thee, Little Brother. The others they hate thee because their eyes cannot meet thine – because thou art wise – because thou hast pulled out thorns from their feet – because thou art a man.'

'I did not know these things,' said Mowgli sullenly; and he frowned under his heavy black eyebrows.

'What is the Law of the Jungle? Strike first and then give tongue. By thy very carelessness they know that thou art a man. But be wise. It is in my heart that when Akela misses his next kill – and at each hunt it costs him more to pin the buck – the Pack will turn against him and against thee. They will hold a Jungle Council at the Rock, and then – and then – I have it!' said Bagheera, leaping up. 'Go thou down quickly to the men's huts in the valley, and take some of the Red Flower which they grow there, so that when the time comes thou mayest have even a stronger friend than I or Baloo or those of the Pack that love thee. Get the Red Flower.'

By Red Flower Bagheera meant fire, only no creature in the Jungle will call fire by its proper name. Every beast lives in deadly fear of it, and invents a hundred ways of describing it.

'The Red Flower?' said Mowgli. 'That grows outside their huts in the twilight. I will get some.'

'There speaks the man's cub,' said Bagheera proudly. 'Remember that it grows in little pots. Get one swiftly, and keep it by thee for time of need.'

'Good!' said Mowgli. 'I go. But art thou sure, O my Bagheera' – he slipped his arm round the splendid neck, and looked deep into the big eyes – 'art thou sure that all this is Shere Khan's doing?'

'By the Broken Lock that freed me, I am sure, Little Brother.'

'Then, by the Bull that bought me, I will pay Shere Khan full tale for this, and it may be a little over,' said Mowgli; and he bounded away.

'That is a man. That is all a man,' said Bagheera to himself, lying down again. 'Oh, Shere Khan, never was a blacker hunting than that frog-hunt of thine ten years ago!'

Mowgli was far and far through the forest, running hard, and his heart was hot in him. He came to the cave as the evening mist rose, and drew breath, and looked down the valley. The cubs were out, but Mother Wolf, at the back of the cave, knew by his breathing that something was troubling her frog.

'What is it, Son?' she said.

'Some bat's chatter of Shere Khan,' he called back. 'I hunt among the ploughed fields tonight,' and he plunged downward through the bushes, to the stream at the bottom of the valley. There he checked, for he heard the yell of the Pack hunting, heard the bellow of a hunted sambhur, and the snort as the buck turned at bay. Then there were wicked, bitter howls from the young wolves: 'Akela! Akela! Let the Lone Wolf show his strength. Room for the leader of the Pack! Spring, Akela!'

The Lone Wolf must have sprung and missed his hold, for Mowgli heard the snap of his teeth and then a yelp as the sambhur knocked him over with his forefoot.

He did not wait for anything more, but dashed on; and the yells grew fainter behind him as he ran into the crop-lands where the villagers lived.

'Bagheera spoke truth,' he panted, as he nestled down in some cattle-fodder by the window of a hut. 'Tomorrow is one day both for Akela and for me.'

Then he pressed his face close to the window and watched the fire on the hearth. He saw the husbandman's wife get up and feed it in the night with black lumps; and when the morning came and the mists were all white and cold, he saw the man's child pick up a wicker pot plastered inside with earth, fill it with lumps of red-hot charcoal, put it under his blanket, and go out to tend the cows in the byre.

'Is that all?' said Mowgli. 'If a cub can do it, there is nothing to fear'; so he strode round the corner and met the boy, took the pot from his hand, and disappeared into the mist while the boy howled with fear.

'They are very like me,' said Mowgli, blowing into the pot, as he had seen the woman do. 'This thing will die if I do not give it things to eat'; and he dropped twigs and dried bark on the red stuff. Halfway up the hill he met Bagheera with the morning dew shining like moonstones on his coat.

'Akela has missed,' said the Panther. 'They would have killed him last night, but they needed thee also. They were looking for thee on the hill.'

'I was among the ploughed lands. I am ready. See!' Mowgli held up the fire-pot.

'Good! Now, I have seen men thrust a dry branch into that stuff, and presently the Red Flower blossomed at the end of it. Art thou not afraid?'

'No. Why should I fear? I remember now – if it is not a dream – how, before I was a Wolf, I lay beside the Red Flower, and it was warm and pleasant.'

All that day Mowgli sat in the cave tending his fire-pot and dipping dry branches into it to see how they looked. He found a branch that satisfied him, and in the evening when Tabaqui came to the cave and told him rudely enough that he was wanted at the Council Rock, he laughed till Tabaqui ran away. Then Mowgli went to the Council, still laughing.

Akela the Lone Wolf lay by the side of his rock as a sign that the leadership of the Pack was open, and Shere Khan with his following of scrap-fed wolves walked to and fro openly, being flattered. Bagheera lay close to Mowgli, and the fire-pot was between Mowgli's knees. When they were all gathered together, Shere Khan began to speak – a thing he would never have dared to do when Akela was in his prime.

'He has no right,' whispered Bagheera. 'Say so. He is a dog's son. He will be frightened.'

Mowgli sprang to his feet. 'Free People,' he cried, 'does Shere Khan lead the Pack? What has a tiger to do with our leadership?'

'Seeing that the leadership is yet open, and being asked to speak – ' Shere Khan began.

'By whom?' said Mowgli. 'Are we *all* jackals, to fawn on this cattle-butcher? The leadership of the Pack is with the Pack alone.'

There were yells of 'Silence, thou man's cub!' 'Let him speak. He has kept our Law'; and at last the seniors of the Pack thundered: 'Let the Dead Wolf speak.' When a leader of the Pack has missed his kill, he is called the Dead Wolf as long as he lives, which is not long, as a rule.

Akela raised his old head wearily – 'Free People, and ye too, jackals of Shere Khan, for many seasons I have led ye to and from the kill, and in all my time not one has been trapped or maimed. Now I have missed my kill. Ye know how that plot was made. Ye know how ye brought me up to an untried buck to make my weakness known. It was cleverly done. Your right is to kill me here on the Council Rock now. Therefore, I ask, who comes to make an end of the Lone Wolf? For it is my right, by the Law of the Jungle, that ye come one by one.'

There was a long hush, for no single wolf cared to fight Akela to the death. Then Shere Khan roared: 'Bah! what have we to do with this toothless fool? He is doomed to die! It is the man-cub who has lived too long. Free People, he was my meat from the first. Give him to me. I am weary of this man-wolf folly. He has troubled the Jungle for ten seasons. Give me the man-cub, or I will hunt here always, and not give you one bone. He is a man, a man's child, and from the marrow of my bones I hate him!'

Then more than half the Pack yelled: 'A man! a man! What has a man to do with us? Let him go to his own place.'

'And turn all the people of the villages against us?' clamoured Shere Khan. 'No; give him to me. He is a man, and none of us can look him between the eyes.'

Akela lifted his head again, and said: 'He has eaten our food. He has slept with us. He has driven game for us. He has broken no word of the Law of the Jungle.'

'Also, I paid for him with a bull when he was accepted. The worth of a bull is little, but Bagheera's honour is something that he will perhaps fight for,' said Bagheera, in his gentlest voice.

'A bull paid ten years ago!' the Pack snarled. 'What do we care for bones ten years old?'

'Or for a pledge?' said Bagheera, his white teeth bared under his lip. 'Well are ye called the Free People!'

'No man's cub can run with the people of the Jungle,' howled Shere Khan. 'Give him to me!'

'He is our brother in all but blood,' Akela went on; 'and ye would kill him here! In truth, I have lived too long. Some of ye are eaters of cattle, and of others I have heard that, under Shere Khan's teaching, ye go by dark night and snatch children from the villager's doorstep. Therefore I know ye to be cowards, and it is to cowards I speak. It is certain that I must die, and my life is of no worth, or I would offer that in the Man-cub's place. But for the sake of the Honour of the Pack – a little matter that by being without a leader ye have forgotten – I promise that if ye let the Man-cub go to his own place, I will not, when my time comes to die, bare one tooth against ye. I will die without fighting. That will at least save the Pack three lives. More I cannot do; but if ye will, I can save ye the shame that comes of killing a brother against whom there is no fault – a brother spoken for and bought into the Pack according to the Law of the Jungle.'

'He is a man – a man – a man!' snarled the Pack; and most of the wolves began to gather round Shere Khan, whose tail was beginning to switch.

'Now the business is in thy hands,' said Bagheera to Mowgli. '*We* can do no more except fight.'

Mowgli stood upright – the fire-pot in his hands. Then he stretched out his arms, and yawned in the face of the Council; but he was furious with rage and sorrow, for, wolflike, the wolves had never told him how they hated him. 'Listen, you!' he cried. 'There is no need for this dog's jabber. Ye have told me so often tonight that I am a man (and indeed I would have been a wolf with you to my life's end), that I feel your words are true. So I do not call ye my brothers any more, but *sag* [dogs], as a man should. What ye will do, and what ye will not do, is not yours to say. That matter is with me; and that we may see the matter more plainly, I, the man, have brought here a little of the Red Flower which ye, dogs, fear.'

He flung the fire-pot on the ground, and some of the red coals lit a tuft of dried moss that flared up, as all the Council drew back in terror before the leaping flames.

Mowgli thrust his dead branch into the fire till the twigs lit and crackled, and whirled it above his head among the cowering wolves.

'Thou art the master,' said Bagheera, in an undertone. 'Save Akela from the death. He was ever thy friend.'

Akela, the grim old wolf who had never asked for mercy in his life, gave one piteous look at Mowgli as the boy stood all naked, his long black hair tossing over his shoulders in the light of the blazing branch that made the shadows jump and quiver.

'Good!' said Mowgli, staring round slowly. 'I see that ye are dogs. I go from you to my own people – if they be my own people. The Jungle is shut to me, and I must forget your talk and your companionship; but I will be more merciful than ye are. Because I was all but your brother in blood, I promise that when I am a man among men I will not betray ye to men as ye have betrayed me.' He kicked the fire with his foot, and the sparks flew up. 'There shall be no war between any of us and the Pack. But here is a debt to pay before I go.' He strode forward to where Shere Khan sat blinking stupidly at the flames, and caught him by the tuft on his chin. Bagheera followed in case of accidents. 'Up, dog!' Mowgli cried. 'Up, when a man speaks, or I will set that coat ablaze!'

Shere Khan's ears lay flat back on his head, and he shut his eyes, for the blazing branch was very near.

'This cattle-killer said he would kill me in the Council because he had not killed me when I was a cub. Thus and thus, then, do we beat dogs when we are men. Stir a whisker, Lungri, and I ram the Red Flower down thy gullet!' He beat Shere Khan over the head with the branch, and the tiger whimpered and whined in an agony of fear.

'Pah! Singed jungle-cat – go now! But remember when next I come to the Council Rock, as a man should come, it will be with Shere Khan's hide on my head. For the rest, Akela goes free to live as he pleases. Ye will *not* kill him, because that is not my will. Nor do I think that ye will sit here any longer, lolling out your tongues as though ye were somebodies, instead of dogs whom I drive out – thus! Go!' The fire was burning furiously at the end of the branch, and Mowgli struck right and left round the circle, and the wolves ran howling with the sparks burning their fur. At last there were only Akela, Bagheera, and perhaps ten wolves that had taken Mowgli's part. Then something began to hurt Mowgli inside him, as he had never been hurt in his life before, and he caught his breath and sobbed, and the tears ran down his face.

'What is it? What is it?' he said. 'I do not wish to leave the Jungle, and I do not know what this is. Am I dying, Bagheera?'

'No, Little Brother. Those are only tears such as men use,' said Bagheera. 'Now I know thou art a man, and a man's cub no longer. The Jungle is shut indeed to thee henceforward. Let them fall, Mowgli. They are only tears.' So Mowgli sat and cried as though his heart would break; and he had never cried in all his life before.

'Now,' he said, 'I will go to men. But first I must say farewell to my mother'; and he went to the cave where she lived with Father Wolf, and he cried on her coat, while the four cubs howled miserably.

'Ye will not forget me?' said Mowgli.

'Never while we can follow a trail,' said the cubs. 'Come to the foot of the hill when thou art a man, and we will talk to thee; and we will come into the crop-lands to play with thee by night.'

'Come soon!' said Father Wolf. 'Oh, wise little frog, come again soon; for we be old, thy mother and I.'

'Come soon,' said Mother Wolf, 'little naked son of mine; for, listen, child of man, I loved thee more than ever I loved my cubs.'

'I will surely come,' said Mowgli; 'and when I come it will be to lay out Shere Khan's hide upon the Council Rock. Do not forget me! Tell them in the Jungle never to forget me!'

The dawn was beginning to break when Mowgli went down the hillside alone, to meet those mysterious things that are called men.

Hunting Song of the Seeonee Pack

As the dawn was breaking the sambhur belled
    Once, twice and again!
And a doe leaped up, and a doe leaped up
From the pond in the wood where the wild deer sup.
This I, scouting alone, beheld,
    Once, twice and again!

As the dawn was breaking the sambhur belled
    Once, twice and again!
And a wolf stole back, and a wolf stole back
To carry the word to the waiting pack,
And we sought and we found and we bayed on his track
    Once, twice and again!

As the dawn was breaking the Wolf Pack yelled
    Once, twice and again!
Feet in the Jungle that leave no mark!
Eyes that can see in the dark – the dark!
Tongue – give tongue to it! Hark! O, hark!
    Once, twice and again!

Kaa's Hunting

His spots are the joy of the Leopard: his horns are the
                          Buffalo's pride.
Be clean, for the strength of the hunter is known by the
                          gloss of his hide.
If ye find that the bullock can toss you, or the heavy-browed
                          sambhur can gore;
Ye need not stop work to inform us: we knew it ten seasons before.
Oppress not the cubs of the stranger, but hail them as
                          Sister and Brother,
For though they are little and fubsy, it may be the Bear
                          is their mother.
'There is none like to me!' says the Cub in the pride of
                          his earliest kill;
But the Jungle is large and the Cub he is small. Let him
                          think and be still.
                              Maxims of Baloo

All that is told here happened some time before Mowgli was turned out of the Seeonee Wolf Pack, or revenged himself on Shere Khan the tiger. It was in the days when Baloo was teaching him the Law of the Jungle. The big, serious, old brown bear was delighted to have so quick a pupil, for the young wolves will only learn as much of the Law of the Jungle as applies to their own pack and tribe, and run away as soon as they can repeat the Hunting Verse – 'Feet that make no noise; eyes that can see in the dark; ears that can hear the winds in their lairs, and sharp white teeth, all these things are the marks of our brothers except Tabaqui the Jackal and the Hyaena whom we hate.' But Mowgli, as a man-cub, had to learn a great deal more than this.

Sometimes Bagheera, the Black Panther, would come lounging through the Jungle to see how his pet was getting on, and would purr with his head against a tree while Mowgli recited the day's lesson to Baloo. The boy could climb almost as well as he could swim, and swim almost as well as he could run; so Baloo, the Teacher of the Law, taught him the Wood and Water Laws; how to tell a rotten branch from a sound one; how to speak politely to the wild bees when he came upon a hive of them fifty feet above ground; what to say to Mang the Bat when he disturbed him in the branches at midday; and how to warn the water-snakes in the pools before he splashed down among them. None of the Jungle People like being disturbed, and all are very ready to fly at an intruder. Then, too, Mowgli was taught the Stranger's Hunting Call, which must be repeated aloud till it is answered, whenever one of the Jungle People hunts outside his own grounds. It means, translated: 'Give me leave to hunt here because I am hungry'; and the answer is: 'Hunt then for food, but not for pleasure.'

All this will show you how much Mowgli had to learn by heart, and he grew very tired of saying the same thing over a hundred times; but, as Baloo said to Bagheera, one day when Mowgli had been cuffed and run off in a temper: 'A Man-cub is a Man-cub, and he must learn *all* the Law of the Jungle.'

'But think how small he is,' said the Black Panther, who would have spoiled Mowgli if he had had his own way. 'How can his little head carry all thy long talk?'

'Is there anything in the Jungle too little to be killed? No. That is why I teach him these things, and that is why I hit him, very softly, when he forgets.'

'Softly! What dost thou know of softness, old Iron-feet?' Bagheera grunted. 'His face is all bruised today by thy – softness. Ugh!'

'Better he should be bruised from head to foot by me who love him than that he should come to harm through ignorance,' Baloo answered very earnestly. 'I am now teaching him the Master Words of the Jungle that shall protect him with the birds and the Snake People, and all that hunt on four feet, except his own pack. He can now claim protection, if he will only remember the words, from all in the Jungle. Is not that worth a little beating?'

'Well, look to it then that thou dost not kill the Man-cub. He is no tree-trunk to sharpen thy blunt claws upon. But what are those Master Words? I am more likely to give help than to ask it' – Bagheera stretched out one paw and admired the steel-blue, ripping-chisel talons at the end of it – 'still I should like to know.'

'I will call Mowgli and he shall say them – if he will. Come, Little Brother!'

'My head is ringing like a bee-tree,' said a sullen little voice over their heads, and Mowgli slid down a tree-trunk very angry and indignant, adding as he reached the ground: 'I come for Bagheera and not for *thee*, fat old Baloo!'

'That is all one to me,' said Baloo, though he was hurt and grieved. 'Tell Bagheera, then, the Master Words of the Jungle that I have taught thee this day.'

'Master Words for which people?' said Mowgli, delighted to show off. 'The Jungle has many tongues. *I* know them all.'

'A little thou knowest, but not much. See, O Bagheera, they never thank their teacher. Not one small wolfling has ever come back to thank old Baloo for his teachings. Say the word for the Hunting People, then – great scholar.'

'We be of one blood, ye and I,' said Mowgli, giving the words the Bear accent which all the Hunting People use.

'Good. Now for the birds.'

Mowgli repeated, with the Kite's whistle at the end of the sentence.

'Now for the Snake People,' said Bagheera.

The answer was a perfectly indescribable hiss, and Mowgli kicked up his feet behind, clapped his hands together to applaud himself, and jumped on to Bagheera's back, where he sat sideways, drumming with his heels on the glossy skin and making the worst faces he could think of at Baloo.

'There – there! That was worth a little bruise,' said the brown bear tenderly. 'Some day thou wilt remember me.' Then he turned aside to tell Bagheera how he had begged the Master Words from Hathi the Wild Elephant, who knows all about these things, and how Hathi had taken Mowgli down to a pool to get the Snake Word from a water-snake, because Baloo could not pronounce it, and how Mowgli was now reasonably safe against all accidents in the Jungle, because neither snake, bird, nor beast would hurt him.

'No one, then, is to be feared,' Baloo wound up, patting his big furry stomach with pride.

'Except his own tribe,' said Bagheera, under his breath; and then aloud to Mowgli: 'Have a care for my ribs, Little Brother! What is all this dancing up and down?'

Mowgli had been trying to make himself heard by pulling at Bagheera's shoulder-fur and kicking hard. When the two listened to him he was shouting at the top of his voice: 'And so I shall have a tribe of my own, and lead them through the branches all day long.'

'What is this new folly, little dreamer of dreams?' said Bagheera.

'Yes, and throw branches and dirt at old Baloo,' Mowgli went on. 'They have promised me this. Ah!'

'*Whoof!*' Baloo's big paw scooped Mowgli off Bagheera's back, and as the boy lay between the big forepaws he could see the Bear was angry.

'Mowgli,' said Baloo, 'thou hast been talking with the *Bandar-log* – the Monkey People.'

Mowgli looked at Bagheera to see if the Panther was angry too, and Bagheera's eyes were as hard as jade stones.

'Thou hast been with the Monkey People – the grey apes – the people without a Law – the eaters of everything. That is great shame.'

'When Baloo hurt my head,' said Mowgli (he was still on his back), 'I went away, and the grey apes came down from the trees and had pity on me. No one else cared.' He snuffled a little.

'The pity of the Monkey People!' Baloo snorted. 'The stillness of the mountain stream! The cool of the summer sun! And then, Man-cub?'

'And then, and then, they gave me nuts and pleasant things to eat, and they – they carried me in their arms up to the top of the trees and said I was their blood-brother except that I had no tail, and should be their leader someday.'

'They have *no* leader,' said Bagheera. 'They lie. They have always lied.'

'They were very kind and bade me come again. Why have I never been taken among the Monkey People? They stand on their feet as I do. They do not hit me with hard paws. They play all day. Let me get up! Bad Baloo, let me up! I will play with them again.'

'Listen, Man-cub,' said the Bear, and his voice rumbled like thunder on a hot night. 'I have taught thee all the Law of the Jungle for all the peoples of the Jungle – except the Monkey Folk who live in the trees. They have no Law. They are outcasts. They have no speech of their own, but use the stolen words which they overhear when they listen, and peep, and wait up above in the branches. Their way is not our way. They are without leaders. They have no remembrance. They boast and chatter and pretend that they are a great people about to do great affairs in the Jungle, but the falling of a nut turns their minds to laughter and all is forgotten. We of the Jungle have no dealings with them. We do not drink where the monkeys drink; we do not go where the monkeys go; we do not hunt where they hunt; we do not die where they die. Hast thou ever heard me speak of the *Bandar-log*, till today?'

'No,' said Mowgli in a whisper, for the forest was very still now Baloo had finished.

'The Jungle People put them out of their mouths and out of their minds. They are very many, evil, dirty, shameless, and they desire, if they have any fixed desire, to be noticed by the Jungle People. But we do *not* notice them even when they throw nuts and filth on our heads.'

He had hardly spoken when a shower of nuts and twigs spattered down through the branches; and they could hear coughings and howlings and angry jumpings high up in the air among the thin branches.

'The Monkey People are forbidden,' said Baloo, 'forbidden to the Jungle People. Remember.'

'Forbidden,' said Bagheera; 'but I still think Baloo should have warned thee against them.'

'I – I? How was I to guess he would play with such dirt? The Monkey People! Faugh!'

A fresh shower came down on their heads and the two trotted away, taking Mowgli with them. What Baloo had said about the monkeys was perfectly true. They belonged to the tree-tops, and as beasts very seldom look up, there was no occasion for the monkeys and the Jungle People to cross each other's path. But whenever they found a sick wolf, or a wounded tiger, or bear, the monkeys would torment him, and would throw sticks and nuts at any beast for fun and in the hope of being noticed. Then they would howl and shriek senseless songs, and invite the Jungle People to climb up their trees and fight them, or would start furious battles over nothing among themselves, and leave the dead monkeys where the Jungle People could see them. They were always just going to have a leader, and laws and customs of their own, but they never did, because their memories would not hold over from day to day, and so they compromised things by making up a saying: 'What the *Bandar-log* think now the Jungle will think later,' and that comforted them a great deal. None of the beasts could reach them, but on the other hand none of the beasts would notice them, and that was why they were so pleased when Mowgli came to play with them, and they heard how angry Baloo was.

They never meant to do any more – the *Bandar-log* never mean anything at all; but one of them invented what seemed to him a brilliant idea, and he told all the others that Mowgli would be a useful person to keep in the tribe, because he could weave sticks together for protection from the wind; so, if they caught him, they could make him teach them. Of course, Mowgli, as a woodcutter's child, inherited all sorts of instincts, and used to make little huts of fallen branches without thinking how he came to do it, and the Monkey People, watching in the trees, considered his play most wonderful. This time, they said, they were really going to have a leader and become the wisest people in the Jungle – so wise that everyone else would notice and envy them. Therefore they followed Baloo and Bagheera and Mowgli through the Jungle very quietly till it was time for the midday nap, and Mowgli, who was very much ashamed of himself, slept between the Panther and the Bear, resolving to have no more to do with the Monkey People.

The next thing he remembered was feeling hands on his legs and arms – hard, strong, little hands – and then a swash of branches in his face, and then he was staring down through the swaying boughs as Baloo woke the Jungle with his deep cries and Bagheera bounded up the trunk with every tooth bared. The *Bandar-log* howled with triumph and scuffled away to the upper branches where Bagheera dared not follow, shouting: 'He has noticed us! Bagheera has noticed us. All the Jungle People admire us for our skill and our cunning.' Then they began their flight; and the flight of the Monkey People through tree-land is one of the things nobody can describe. They have their regular roads and crossroads, up hills and down hills, all laid out from fifty to seventy or a hundred feet above ground, and by these they can travel even at night if necessary. Two of the strongest monkeys caught Mowgli under the arms and swung off with him through the tree-tops, twenty feet at a bound. Had they been alone they could have gone twice as fast, but the boy's weight held them back. Sick and giddy as Mowgli was he could not help enjoying the wild rush, though the glimpses of earth far down below frightened him, and the terrible check and jerk at the end of the swing over nothing but empty air brought his heart between his teeth. His escort would rush him up a tree till he felt the thinnest topmost branches crackle and bend under them, and then with a cough and a whoop would fling themselves into the air outward and downward, and bring up, hanging by their hands or their feet to the lower limbs of the next tree. Sometimes he could see for miles and miles across the still green Jungle, as a man on the top of a mast can see for miles across the sea, and then the branches and leaves would lash him across the face, and he and his two guards would be almost down to earth again. So, bounding and crashing and whooping and yelling, the whole tribe of *Bandar-log* swept along the tree-roads with Mowgli their prisoner.

For a time he was afraid of being dropped: then he grew angry but knew better than to struggle, and then he began to think. The first thing was to send back word to Baloo and Bagheera, for, at the pace the monkeys were going, he knew his friends would be left far behind. It was useless to look down, for he could only see the top-sides of the branches, so he stared upward and saw, far away in the blue, Chil the Kite balancing and wheeling as he kept watch over the Jungle waiting for things to die. Chil saw that the monkeys were carrying something, and dropped a few hundred yards to find out whether their load was good to eat. He whistled with surprise when he saw Mowgli being dragged up to a tree-top and heard him give the Kite call for – 'We be of one blood, thou and I.' The waves of the branches closed over the boy, but Chil balanced away to the next tree in time to see the little brown face come up again. 'Mark my trail,' Mowgli shouted. 'Tell Baloo of the Seeonee Pack and Bagheera of the Council Rock.'

'In whose name, Brother?' Chil had never seen Mowgli before, though of course he had heard of him.

'Mowgli, the Frog. Man-cub they call me! Mark my tra–il!'

The last words were shrieked as he was being swung through the air, but Chil nodded and rose up till he looked no bigger than a speck of dust, and there he hung, watching with his telescope eyes the swaying of the tree-tops as Mowgli's escort whirled along.

'They never go far,' he said with a chuckle. 'They never do what they set out to do. Always pecking at new things are the *Bandar-log*. This time, if I have any eyesight, they have pecked down trouble for themselves, for Baloo is no fledgling and Bagheera can, as I know, kill more than goats.'

So he rocked on his wings, his feet gathered up under him, and waited.

Meantime, Baloo and Bagheera were furious with rage and grief. Bagheera climbed as he had never climbed before, but the thin branches broke beneath his weight, and he slipped down, his claws full of bark.

'Why didst thou not warn the Man-cub?' he roared to poor Baloo, who had set off at a clumsy trot in the hope of overtaking the monkeys. 'What was the use of half slaying him with blows if thou didst not warn him?'

'Haste! Oh, haste! We – we may catch them yet!' Baloo panted.

'At that speed! It would not tire a wounded cow. Teacher of the Law – cub-beater – a mile of that rolling to and fro would burst thee open. Sit still and think! Make a plan. This is no time for chasing. They may drop him if we follow too close.'

'*Arrula! Whoo!* They may have dropped him already, being tired of carrying him. Who can trust the *Bandar-log*? Put dead bats on my head! Give me black bones to eat! Roll me into the hives of the wild bees that I may be stung to death, and bury me with the Hyaena, for I am the most miserable of bears! *Arrulala! Wahooa!* Oh, Mowgli, Mowgli! why did I not warn thee against the Monkey Folk instead of breaking thy head? Now perhaps I may have knocked the day's lesson out of his mind, and he will be alone in the Jungle without the Master Words.'

Baloo clasped his paws over his ears and rolled to and fro moaning.

'At least he gave me all the Words correctly a little time ago,' said Bagheera impatiently. 'Baloo, thou hast neither memory nor respect. What would the Jungle think if I, the Black Panther, curled myself up like Ikki the Porcupine, and howled?'

'What do I care what the Jungle thinks? He may be dead by now.'

'Unless and until they drop him from the branches in sport, or kill him out of idleness, I have no fear for the Man-cub. He is wise and well taught, and above all he has the eyes that make the Jungle People afraid. But (and it is a great evil) he is in the power of the *Bandar-log*, and they, because they live in trees, have no fear of any of our people.' Bagheera licked one forepaw thoughtfully.

'Fool that I am! Oh, fat, brown, root-digging fool that I am,' said Baloo, uncurling himself with a jerk, 'it is true what Hathi the Wild Elephant says: "*To each his own fear*"; and they, the *Bandar-log*, fear Kaa the Rock Snake. He can climb as well as they can. He steals the young monkeys in the night. The whisper of his name makes their wicked tails cold. Let us go to Kaa.'

'What will he do for us? He is not of our tribe, being footless – and with most evil eyes,' said Bagheera.

'He is very old and very cunning. Above all, he is always hungry,' said Baloo hopefully. 'Promise him many goats.'

'He sleeps for a full month after he has once eaten. He may be asleep now, and even were he awake what if he would rather kill his own goats?' Bagheera, who did not know much about Kaa, was naturally suspicious.

'Then in that case, thou and I together, old hunter, might make him see reason.' Here Baloo rubbed his faded brown shoulder against the Panther, and they went off to look for Kaa the Rock Python.

They found him stretched out on a warm ledge in the afternoon sun, admiring his beautiful new coat, for he had been in retirement for the last ten days, changing his skin, and now he was very splendid – darting his big blunt-nosed head along the ground, and twisting the thirty feet of his body into fantastic knots and curves, and licking his lips as he thought of his dinner to come.

'He has not eaten,' said Baloo, with a grunt of relief, as soon as he saw the beautifully mottled brown-and-yellow jacket. 'Be careful, Bagheera! He is always a little blind after he has changed his skin, and very quick to strike.'

Kaa was not a poison-snake – in fact he rather despised the poison-snakes as cowards – but his strength lay in his hug, and when he had once lapped his huge coils round anybody there was no more to be said. 'Good hunting!' cried Baloo, sitting up on his haunches. Like all snakes of his breed, Kaa was rather deaf, and did not hear the call at first. Then he curled up ready for any accident, his head lowered.

'Good hunting for us all!' he answered. 'Oho, Baloo, what dost thou do here? Good hunting, Bagheera! One of us at least needs food. Is there any news of game afoot? A doe now, or even a young buck? I am as empty as a dried well.'

'We are hunting,' said Baloo carelessly. He knew that you must not hurry Kaa. He is too big.

'Give me permission to come with you,' said Kaa. 'A blow more or less is nothing to thee, Bagheera or Baloo, but I – I have to wait and wait for days in a wood-path and climb half a night on the mere chance of a young ape. Psshaw! The branches are not what they were when I was young. Rotten twigs and dry boughs are they all.'

'Maybe thy great weight has something to do with the matter,' said Baloo.

'I am a fair length – a fair length,' said Kaa, with a little pride. 'But for all that, it is the fault of this new-grown timber. I came very near to falling on my last hunt – very near indeed – and the noise of my slipping, for my tail was not tight wrapped round the tree, waked the *Bandar-log*, and they called me most evil names.'

'Footless, yellow earthworm,' said Bagheera under his whiskers, as though he were trying to remember something.

'Sssss! Have they ever called me *that*?' said Kaa.

'Something of that kind it was that they shouted to us last moon, but we never noticed them. They will say anything – even that thou hast lost all thy teeth, and wilt not face anything bigger than a kid, because (they are indeed shameless, these *Bandar-log*) – because thou art afraid of the he-goat's horns,' Bagheera went on sweetly.

Now a snake, especially a wary old python like Kaa, very seldom shows that he is angry, but Baloo and Bagheera could see the big swallowing-muscles on either side of Kaa's throat ripple and bulge.

'The *Bandar-log* have shifted their grounds,' he said quietly. 'When I came up into the sun today I heard them whooping among the tree-tops.'

'It – it is the *Bandar-log* that we follow now,' said Baloo; but the words stuck in his throat, for that was the first time in his memory that one of the Jungle People had owned to being interested in the doings of the monkeys.

'Beyond doubt then it is no small thing that takes two such hunters – leaders in their own Jungle I am certain – on the trail of the *Bandar-log*,' Kaa replied courteously, as he swelled with curiosity.

'Indeed,' Baloo began, 'I am no more than the old and sometimes very foolish Teacher of the Law to the Seeonee wolf-cubs, and Bagheera here – '

'Is Bagheera,' said the Black Panther, and his jaws shut with a snap, for he did not believe in being humble. 'The trouble is this, Kaa. Those nut-stealers and pickers of palm-leaves have stolen away our Man-cub, of whom thou hast perhaps heard.'

'I heard some news from Ikki (his quills make him presumptuous) of a man-thing that was entered into a wolf-pack, but I did not believe. Ikki is full of stories half heard and very badly told.'

'But it is true. He is such a Man-cub as never was,' said Baloo. 'The best and wisest and boldest of Man-cubs – my own pupil, who shall make the name of Baloo famous through all the jungles; and besides, I – we – love him, Kaa.'

'Tss! Tss!' said Kaa, shaking his head to and fro. 'I also have known what love is. There are tales I could tell that – '

'That need a clear night when we are all well fed to praise properly,' said Bagheera quickly. 'Our Man-cub is in the hands of the *Bandar-log* now, and we know that of all the Jungle People they fear Kaa alone.'

'They fear me alone. They have good reason,' said Kaa. 'Chattering, foolish, vain – vain, foolish, and chattering, are the monkeys. But a man-thing in their hands is in no good luck. They grow tired of the nuts they pick, and throw them down. They carry a branch half a day, meaning to do great things with it, and then they snap it in two. That man-thing is not to be envied. They called me also – "yellow fish", was it not?'

'Worm – worm – earthworm,' said Bagheera, 'as well as other things which I cannot now say for shame.'

'We must remind them to speak well of their master. Aaa-ssh! We must help their wandering memories. Now, whither went they with the cub?'

'The Jungle alone knows. Toward the sunset, I believe,' said Baloo. 'We had thought that thou wouldst know, Kaa.'

'I? How? I take them when they come in my way, but I do not hunt the *Bandar-log*, or frogs – or green scum on a water-hole for that matter.'

'Up, Up! Up, Up! Hillo! Illo! Illo! Look up, Baloo of the Seeonee Wolf Pack!'

Baloo looked up to see where the voice came from, and there was Chil the Kite, sweeping down with the sun shining on the upturned flanges of his wings. It was near Chil's bedtime, but he had ranged all over the Jungle looking for the Bear and had missed him in the thick foliage.

'What is it?' said Baloo.

'I have seen Mowgli among the *Bandar-log*. He bade me tell you. I watched. The *Bandar-log* have taken him beyond the river to the monkey city – to the Cold Lairs. They may stay there for a night, or ten nights, or an hour. I have told the bats to watch through the dark time. That is my message. Good hunting, all you below!'

'Full gorge and a deep sleep to you, Chil,' cried Bagheera. 'I will remember thee in my next kill, and put aside the head for thee alone, O best of kites!'

'It is nothing. It is nothing. The boy held the Master Word. I could have done no less,' and Chil circled up again to his roost.

'He has not forgotten to use his tongue,' said Baloo, with a chuckle of pride. 'To think of one so young remembering the Master Word for the birds too while he was being pulled across-trees!'

'It was most firmly driven into him,' said Bagheera. 'But I am proud of him, and now we must go to the Cold Lairs.'

They all knew where that place was, but few of the Jungle People ever went there, because what they called the Cold Lairs was an old deserted city, lost and buried in the Jungle, and beasts seldom use a place that men have once used. The wild boar will, but the hunting tribes do not. Besides, the monkeys lived there as much as they could be said to live anywhere, and no self-respecting animal would come within eyeshot of it except in times of drought, when the half-ruined tanks and reservoirs held a little water.

'It is half a night's journey – at full speed,' said Bagheera, and Baloo looked very serious. 'I will go as fast as I can,' he said anxiously.

'We dare not wait for thee. Follow, Baloo. We must go on the quick-foot – Kaa and I.'

'Feet or no feet, I can keep abreast of all thy four,' said Kaa shortly. Baloo made one effort to hurry, but had to sit down panting, and so they left him to come on later, while Bagheera hurried forward, at the quick panther-canter. Kaa said nothing, but, strive as Bagheera might, the huge Rock Python held level with him. When they came to a hill-stream, Bagheera gained, because he bounded across while Kaa swam, his head and two feet of his neck clearing the water, but on level ground Kaa made up the distance.

'By the Broken Lock that freed me,' said Bagheera, when twilight had fallen, 'thou art no slow goer!'

'I am hungry,' said Kaa. 'Besides, they called me speckled frog.'

'Worm – earthworm, and yellow to boot.'

'All one. Let us go on,' and Kaa seemed to pour himself along the ground, finding the shortest road with his steady eyes, and keeping to it.

In the Cold Lairs the Monkey People were not thinking of Mowgli's friends at all. They had brought the boy to the Lost City, and were very pleased with themselves for the time. Mowgli had never seen an Indian city before, and though this was almost a heap of ruins it seemed very wonderful and splendid. Some king had built it long ago on a little hill. You could still trace the stone causeways that led up to the ruined gates where the last splinters of wood hung to the worn, rusted hinges. Trees had grown into and out of the walls; the battlements were tumbled down and decayed, and wild creepers hung out of the windows of the towers on the walls in bushy hanging clumps.

A great roofless palace crowned the hill, and the marble of the courtyards and the fountains was split, and stained with red and green, and the very cobblestones in the courtyard where the king's elephants used to live had been thrust up and apart by grasses and young trees. From the palace you could see the rows and rows of roofless houses that made up the city looking like empty honeycombs filled with blackness; the shapeless block of stone that had been an idol, in the square where four roads met; the pits and dimples at street-corners where the public wells once stood, and the shattered domes of temples with wild figs sprouting on their sides. The monkeys called the place their city, and pretended to despise the Jungle People because they lived in the forest. And yet they never knew what the buildings were made for nor how to use them. They would sit in circles on the hall of the king's council chamber, and scratch for fleas and pretend to be men; or they would run in and out of the roofless houses and collect pieces of plaster and old bricks in a corner, and forget where they had hidden them, and fight and cry in scuffling crowds, and then break off to play up and down the terraces of the king's garden, where they would shake the rose trees and the oranges in sport to see the fruit and flowers fall. They explored all the passages and dark tunnels in the palace and the hundreds of little dark rooms, but they never remembered what they had seen and what they had not; and so drifted about in ones and twos or crowds telling each other that they were doing as men did. They drank at the tanks and made the water all muddy, and then they fought over it, and then they would all rush together in mobs and shout: 'There is no one in the Jungle so wise and good and clever and strong and gentle as the *Bandar-log*.' Then all would begin again till they grew tired of the city and went back to the tree-tops, hoping the Jungle People would notice them.

Mowgli, who had been trained under the Law of the Jungle, did not like or understand this kind of life. The monkeys dragged him into the Cold Lairs late in the afternoon, and instead of going to sleep, as Mowgli would have done after a long journey, they joined hands and danced about and sang their foolish songs. One of the monkeys made a speech and told his companions that Mowgli's capture marked a new thing in the history of the *Bandar-log*, for Mowgli was going to show them how to weave sticks and canes together as a protection against rain and cold. Mowgli picked up some creepers and began to work them in and out, and the monkeys tried to imitate; but in a very few minutes they lost interest and began to pull their friends' tails or jump up and down on all fours, coughing.

'I wish to eat,' said Mowgli. 'I am a stranger in this part of the Jungle. Bring me food, or give me leave to hunt here.'

Twenty or thirty monkeys bounded away to bring him nuts and wild pawpaws; but they fell to fighting on the road, and it was too much trouble to go back with what was left of the fruit. Mowgli was sore and angry as well as hungry, and he roamed through the empty city giving the Stranger's Hunting Call from time to time, but no one answered him, and Mowgli felt that he had reached a very bad place indeed. 'All that Baloo has said about the *Bandar-log* is true,' he thought to himself. 'They have no Law, no Hunting Call, and no leaders – nothing but foolish words and little picking thievish hands. So if I am starved or killed here, it will be all my own fault. But I must try to return to my own Jungle. Baloo will surely beat me, but that is better than chasing silly rose leaves with the *Bandar-log*.'

No sooner had he walked to the city wall than the monkeys pulled him back, telling him that he did not know how happy he was, and pinching him to make him grateful. He set his teeth and said nothing, but went with the shouting monkeys to a terrace above the red sandstone reservoirs that were half-full of rain-water. There was a ruined summerhouse of white marble in the centre of the terrace, built for queens dead a hundred years ago. The domed roof had half fallen in and blocked up the underground passage from the palace by which the queens used to enter; but the walls were made of screens of marble tracery – beautiful milk-white fretwork, set with agates and cornelians and jasper and lapis lazuli, and as the moon came up behind the hill it shone through the open-work, casting shadows on the ground like black velvet embroidery. Sore, sleepy, and hungry as he was, Mowgli could not help laughing when the *Bandar-log* began, twenty at a time, to tell him how great and wise and strong and gentle they were, and how foolish he was to wish to leave them. 'We are great. We are free. We are wonderful. We are the most wonderful people in all the Jungle! We all say so, and so it must be true,' they shouted. 'Now, as you are a new listener and can carry our words back to the Jungle People so that they may notice us in future, we will tell you all about our most excellent selves.' Mowgli made no objection, and the monkeys gathered by hundreds and hundreds on the terrace to listen to their own speakers singing the praises of the *Bandar-log*, and whenever a speaker stopped for want of breath they would all shout together: 'This is true; we all say so.' Mowgli nodded and blinked, and said 'Yes' when they asked him a question, and his head spun with the noise. 'Tabaqui the Jackal must have bitten all these people,' he said to himself, 'and now they have the madness. Certainly this is *dewanee*, the madness. Do they never go to sleep? Now there is a cloud coming to cover that moon. If it were only a big enough cloud I might try to run away in the darkness. But I am tired.'

That same cloud was being watched by two good friends in the ruined ditch below the city wall, for Bagheera and Kaa, knowing well how dangerous the Monkey People were in large numbers, did not wish to run any risks. The monkeys never fight unless they are a hundred to one, and few in the Jungle care for those odds.

'I will go to the west wall,' Kaa whispered, 'and come down swiftly with the slope of the ground in my favour. They will not throw themselves upon *my* back in their hundreds, but – '

'I know it,' said Bagheera. 'Would that Baloo were here; but we must do what we can. When that cloud covers the moon I shall go to the terrace. They hold some sort of council there over the boy.'

'Good hunting!' said Kaa grimly, and glided away to the west wall. That happened to be the least ruined of any, and the big snake was delayed a while before he could find a way up the stones. The cloud hid the moon, and as Mowgli wondered what would come next he heard Bagheera's light feet on the terrace. The Black Panther had raced up the slope almost without a sound and was striking – he knew better than to waste time in biting – right and left among the monkeys, who were seated round Mowgli in circles fifty and sixty deep. There was a howl of fright and rage, and then as Bagheera tripped on the rolling kicking bodies beneath him, a monkey shouted: 'There is only one here! Kill him! Kill!' A scuffling mass of monkeys, biting, scratching, tearing, and pulling, closed over Bagheera, while five or six laid hold of Mowgli, dragged him up the wall of the summerhouse and pushed him through the hole of the broken dome. A man-trained boy would have been badly bruised, for the fall was a good fifteen feet, but Mowgli fell as Baloo had taught him to fall, and landed on his feet.

'Stay there,' shouted the monkeys, 'till we have killed thy friends, and later we will play with thee – if the Poison People leave thee alive.'

'We be of one blood, ye and I,' said Mowgli, quickly giving the Snake's Call. He could hear rustling and hissing in the rubbish all round him and gave the Call a second time, to make sure.

'Even ssso! Down hoods all!' said half a dozen low voices (every ruin in India becomes sooner or later a dwelling-place of snakes, and the old summerhouse was alive with cobras). 'Stand still, Little Brother, for thy feet may do us harm.'

Mowgli stood as quietly as he could, peering through the open-work and listening to the furious din of the fight round the Black Panther – the yells and chatterings and scufflings, and Bagheera's deep, hoarse cough as he backed and bucked and twisted and plunged under the heaps of his enemies. For the first time since he was born, Bagheera was fighting for his life.

'Baloo must be at hand; Bagheera would not have come alone,' Mowgli thought; and then he called aloud: 'To the tank, Bagheera! Roll to the water-tanks. Roll and plunge! Get to the water!'

Bagheera heard, and the cry that told him Mowgli was safe gave him new courage. He worked his way desperately, inch by inch, straight for the reservoirs, hitting in silence. Then from the ruined wall nearest the Jungle rose up the rumbling war-shout of Baloo. The old bear had done his best, but he could not come before. 'Bagheera,' he shouted, 'I am here. I climb! I haste! *Ahuwora!* The stones slip under my feet! Wait my coming, O most infamous *Bandar-log*!' He panted up the terrace only to disappear to the head in a wave of monkeys, but he threw himself squarely on his haunches, and, spreading out his forepaws, hugged as many as he could hold, and then began to hit with a regular *bat-bat-bat*, like the flipping strokes of a paddle-wheel. A crash and a splash told Mowgli that Bagheera had fought his way to the tank where the monkeys could not follow. The panther lay gasping for breath, his head just out of water, while the monkeys stood three deep on the red steps, dancing up and down with rage, ready to spring upon him from all sides if he came out to help Baloo. It was then that Bagheera lifted up his dripping chin, and in despair gave the Snake's Call for protection – 'We be of one blood, ye and I' – for he believed that Kaa had turned tail at the last minute. Even Baloo, half smothered under the monkeys on the edge of the terrace, could not help chuckling as he heard the Black Panther asking for help.

Kaa had only just worked his way over the west wall, landing with a wrench that dislodged a coping-stone into the ditch. He had no intention of losing any advantage of the ground, and coiled and uncoiled himself once or twice, to be sure that every foot of his long body was in working order. All that while the fight with Baloo went on, and the monkeys yelled in the tank around Bagheera, and Mang the Bat, flying to and fro, carried the news of the great battle over the Jungle, till even Hathi the Wild Elephant trumpeted, and, far away, scattered bands of the Monkey Folk woke and came leaping along the tree-roads to help their comrades in the Cold Lairs, and the noise of the fight roused all the day-birds for miles round. Then Kaa came straight, quickly, and anxious to kill. The fighting-strength of a python is in the driving blow of his head backed by all the strength and weight of his body. If you can imagine a lance, or a battering-ram, or a hammer weighing nearly half a ton driven by a cool, quiet mind living in the handle of it, you can roughly imagine what Kaa was like when he fought. A python four or five feet long can knock a man down if he hits him fairly in the chest, and Kaa was thirty feet long, as you know. His first stroke was delivered into the heart of the crowd round Baloo – was sent home with shut mouth in silence, and there was no need of a second. The monkeys scattered with cries of – 'Kaa! It is Kaa! Run! Run!'

Generations of monkeys had been scared into good behaviour by the stories their elders told them of Kaa, the night-thief, who could slip along the branches as quietly as moss grows, and steal away the strongest monkey that ever lived; of old Kaa, who could make himself look so like a dead branch or a rotten stump that the wisest were deceived, till the branch caught them. Kaa was everything that the monkeys feared in the Jungle, for none of them knew the limits of his power, none of them could look him in the face, and none had ever come alive out of his hug. And so they ran, stammering with terror, to the walls and the roofs of the houses, and Baloo drew a deep breath of relief. His fur was much thicker than Bagheera's, but he had suffered sorely in the fight. Then Kaa opened his mouth for the first time and spoke one long hissing word, and the faraway monkeys, hurrying to the defence of the Cold Lairs, stayed where they were, cowering, till the loaded branches bent and crackled under them. The monkeys on the walls and the empty houses stopped their cries, and in the stillness that fell upon the city Mowgli heard Bagheera shaking his wet sides as he came up from the tank. Then the clamour broke out again. The monkeys leaped higher up the walls; they clung round the necks of the big stone idols and shrieked as they skipped along the battlements, while Mowgli, dancing in the summerhouse, put his eye to the screen-work and hooted owl-fashion between his front teeth, to show his derision and contempt.

'Get the Man-cub out of that trap; I can do no more,' Bagheera gasped. 'Let us take the Man-cub and go. They may attack again.'

'They will not move till I order them. Stay you sssso!' Kaa hissed, and the city was silent once more. 'I could not come before, Brother, but I *think* I heard thee call' – this was to Bagheera.

'I – I may have cried out in the battle,' Bagheera answered. 'Baloo, art thou hurt?'

'I am not sure that they have not pulled me into a hundred little bearlings,' said Baloo gravely, shaking one leg after the other. 'Wow! I am sore. Kaa, we owe thee, I think, our lives – Bagheera and I.'

'No matter. Where is the Manling?'

'Here, in a trap. I cannot climb out,' cried Mowgli. The curve of the broken dome was above his head.

'Take him away. He dances like Mao the Peacock. He will crush our young,' said the cobras inside.

'Hah!' said Kaa, with a chuckle, 'he has friends everywhere, this Manling. Stand back, Manling; and hide you, O Poison People. I break down the wall.'

Kaa looked carefully till he found a discoloured crack in the marble tracery showing a weak spot, made two or three light taps with his head to get the distance, and then, lifting up six feet of his body clear of the ground, sent home half a dozen full-power, smashing blows, nose-first. The screen-work broke and fell away in a cloud of dust and rubbish, and Mowgli leaped through the opening and flung himself between Baloo and Bagheera – an arm round each big neck.

'Art thou hurt?' said Baloo, hugging him softly.

'I am sore, hungry, and not a little bruised; but, oh, they have handled ye grievously, my Brothers! Ye bleed.'

'Others also,' said Bagheera, licking his lips, and looking at the monkey-dead on the terrace and round the tank.

'It is nothing, it is nothing, if thou art safe, O my pride of all little frogs!' whimpered Baloo.

'Of that we shall judge later,' said Bagheera, in a dry voice that Mowgli did not at all like. 'But here is Kaa, to whom we owe the battle and thou owest thy life. Thank him according to our customs, Mowgli.'

Mowgli turned and saw the great python's head swaying a foot above his own.

'So this is the Manling,' said Kaa. 'Very soft is his skin, and he is not so unlike the *Bandar-log*. Have a care, Manling, that I do not mistake thee for a monkey some twilight when I have newly changed my coat.'

'We be of one blood, thou and I,' Mowgli answered. 'I take my life from thee, tonight. My kill shall be thy kill if ever thou art hungry, O Kaa.'

'All thanks, Little Brother,' said Kaa, though his eyes twinkled. 'And what may so bold a hunter kill? I ask that I may follow when next he goes abroad.'

'I kill nothing – I am too little – but I drive goats toward such as can use them. When thou art empty come to me and see if I speak the truth. I have some skill in these' – he held out his hands – 'and if ever thou art in a trap, I may pay the debt which I owe to thee, to Bagheera, and to Baloo, here. Good hunting to ye all, my masters.'

'Well said,' growled Baloo, for Mowgli had returned thanks very prettily. The python dropped his head lightly for a minute on Mowgli's shoulder. 'A brave heart and a courteous tongue,' said he. 'They shall carry thee far through the Jungle, Manling. But now go hence quickly with thy friends. Go and sleep, for the moon sets, and what follows it is not well that thou shouldst see.'

The moon was sinking behind the hills, and the lines of trembling monkeys huddled together on the walls and battlements looked like ragged, shaky fringes of things. Baloo went down to the tank for a drink, and Bagheera began to put his fur in order, as Kaa glided out into the centre of the terrace and brought his jaws together with a ringing snap that drew all the monkeys' eyes upon him.

'The moon sets,' he said. 'Is there yet light to see?'

From the walls came a moan like the wind in the tree-tops: 'We see, O Kaa.'

'Good. Begins now the Dance – the Dance of the Hunger of Kaa. Sit still and watch.'

He turned twice or thrice in a big circle, weaving his head from right to left. Then he began making loops and figures of eight with his body, and soft, oozy triangles that melted into squares and five-sided figures, and coiled mounds, never resting, never hurrying, and never stopping his low, humming song. It grew darker and darker, till at last the dragging, shifting coils disappeared, but they could hear the rustle of the scales.

Baloo and Bagheera stood still as stone, growling in their throats, their neck-hair bristling, and Mowgli watched and wondered.

'*Bandar-log*,' said the voice of Kaa at last, 'can ye stir foot or hand without my order? Speak!'

'Without thy order we cannot stir foot or hand, O Kaa!'

'Good! Come all one pace closer to me.'

The lines of the monkeys swayed forward helplessly, and Baloo and Bagheera took one stiff step forward with them.

'Closer!' hissed Kaa, and they all moved again.

Mowgli laid his hands on Baloo and Bagheera to get them away, and the two great beasts started as though they had been waked from a dream.

'Keep thy hand on my shoulder,' Bagheera whispered. 'Keep it there, or I must go back – must go back to Kaa. *Aah!*'

'It is only old Kaa making circles on the dust,' said Mowgli; 'let us go'; and the three slipped off through a gap in the walls to the Jungle.

'*Whoof!*' said Baloo, when he stood under the still trees again. 'Never more will I make an ally of Kaa,' and he shook himself all over.

'He knows more than we,' said Bagheera, trembling. 'In a little time, had I stayed, I should have walked down his throat.'

'Many will walk by that road before the moon rises again,' said Baloo. 'He will have good hunting – after his own fashion.'

'But what was the meaning of it all?' said Mowgli, who did not know anything of a python's powers of fascination. 'I saw no more than a big snake making foolish circles till the dark came. And his nose was all sore. Ho! Ho!'

'Mowgli,' said Bagheera angrily, 'his nose was sore on *thy* account; as my ears and sides and paws and Baloo's neck and shoulders are bitten on *thy* account. Neither Baloo nor Bagheera will be able to hunt with pleasure for many days.'

'It is nothing,' said Baloo; 'we have the Man-cub again.'

'True; but he has cost us heavily in time which might have been spent in good hunting, in wounds, in hair – I am half plucked along my back – and, last of all, in honour. For, remember, Mowgli, I, who am the Black Panther, was forced to call upon Kaa for protection, and Baloo and I were both made stupid as little birds by the Hunger Dance. All this, Man-cub, came of thy playing with the *Bandar-log*.'

'True; it is true,' said Mowgli sorrowfully. 'I am an evil Man-cub, and my stomach is sad in me.'

'*Mf!* What says the Law of the Jungle, Baloo?'

Baloo did not wish to bring Mowgli into any more trouble, but he could not tamper with the Law, so he mumbled: 'Sorrow never stays punishment. But remember, Bagheera, he is very little.'

'I will remember; but he has done mischief, and blows must be dealt now. Mowgli, hast thou anything to say?'

'Nothing. I did wrong. Baloo and thou are wounded. It is just.'

Bagheera gave him half a dozen love-taps; from a panther's point of view they would hardly have waked one of his own cubs, but for a seven-year-old boy they amounted to as severe a beating as you could wish to avoid. When it was all over Mowgli sneezed, and picked himself up without a word.

'Now,' said Bagheera, 'jump on my back, Little Brother, and we will go home.'

One of the beauties of Jungle Law is that punishment settles all scores. There is no nagging afterward.

Mowgli laid his head down on Bagheera's back and slept so deeply that he never waked when he was put down by Mother Wolf's side in the home-cave.

Road Song of the Bandar-log

Here we go in a flung festoon,
Halfway up to the jealous moon!
Don't you envy our pranceful bands?
Don't you wish you had extra hands?
Wouldn't you like if your tails were – *so* –
Curved in the shape of a Cupid's bow?
　　Now you're angry, but – never mind,
　　Brother, thy tail hangs down behind!

Here we sit in a branchy row,
Thinking of beautiful things we know;
Dreaming of deeds that we mean to do,
All complete, in a minute or two –
Something noble and grand and good,
Won by merely wishing we could.
　　Now we're going to – never mind,
　　Brother, thy tail hangs down behind!

All the talk we ever have heard
Uttered by bat or beast or bird –
Hide or fin or scale or feather –
Jabber it quickly and all together!
Excellent! Wonderful! Once again!
Now we are talking just like men.
　　Let's pretend we are . . . never mind,
　　Brother, thy tail hangs down behind!
　　This is the way of the Monkey-kind.

Then join our leaping lines that scumfish through the pines,
That rocket by where, light and high, the wild grape swings.
By the rubbish in our wake, and the noble noise we make,
Be sure, be sure, we're going to do some splendid things!

'Tiger! Tiger!'

What of the hunting, hunter bold?
Brother, the watch was long and cold.
What of the quarry ye went to kill?
Brother, he crops in the Jungle still.
Where is the power that made your pride?
Brother, it ebbs from my flank and side.
Where is the haste that ye hurry by?
Brother, I go to my lair – to die!

Now we must go back to the first tale. When Mowgli left the wolf's cave after the fight with the Pack at the Council Rock, he went down to the ploughed lands where the villagers lived, but he would not stop there because it was too near to the Jungle, and he knew that he had made at least one bad enemy at the Council. So he hurried on, keeping to the rough road that ran down the valley, and followed it at a steady jog-trot for nearly twenty miles, till he came to a country that he did not know. The valley opened out into a great plain dotted over with rocks and cut up by ravines. At one end stood a little village, and at the other the thick Jungle came down in a sweep to the grazing-grounds, and stopped there as though it had been cut off with a hoe. All over the plain, cattle and buffaloes were grazing, and when the little boys in charge of the herds saw Mowgli they shouted and ran away, and the yellow pariah dogs that hang about every Indian village barked. Mowgli walked on, for he was feeling hungry, and when he came to the village gate he saw the big thornbush that was drawn up before the gate at twilight pushed to one side.

'Umph!' he said, for he had come across more than one such barricade in his night rambles after things to eat. 'So men are afraid of the People of the Jungle here also.' He sat down by the gate, and when a man came out he stood up, opened his mouth, and pointed down it to show that he wanted food. The man stared, and ran back up the one street of the village shouting for the priest, who was a big, fat man dressed in white, with a red-and-yellow mark on his forehead. The priest came to the gate, and with him at least a hundred people, who stared and talked and shouted and pointed at Mowgli.

'They have no manners, these Men Folk,' said Mowgli to himself. 'Only the grey ape would behave as they do.' So he threw back his long hair and frowned at the crowd.

'What is there to be afraid of?' said the priest. 'Look at the marks on his arms and legs. They are the bites of wolves. He is but a wolf-child run away from the Jungle.'

Of course, in playing together, the cubs had often nipped Mowgli harder than they intended, and there were white scars all over his arms and legs. But he would have been the last person in the world to call these bites, for he knew what real biting meant.

'*Arré! Arré!*' said two or three women together. 'To be bitten by wolves, poor child! He is a handsome boy. He has eyes like red fire. By my honour, Messua, he is not unlike thy boy that was taken by the tiger.'

'Let me look,' said a woman with heavy copper rings on her wrists and ankles, and she peered at Mowgli under the palm of her hand. 'Indeed he is not. He is thinner, but he has the very look of my boy.'

The priest was a clever man, and he knew that Messua was wife to the richest villager in the place. So he looked up at the sky for a minute, and said solemnly: 'What the Jungle has taken the Jungle has restored. Take the boy into thy house, my sister, and forget not to honour the priest who sees so far into the lives of men.'

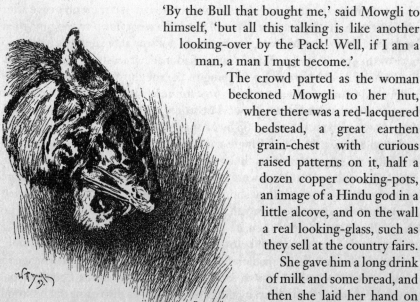

'By the Bull that bought me,' said Mowgli to himself, 'but all this talking is like another looking-over by the Pack! Well, if I am a man, a man I must become.'

The crowd parted as the woman beckoned Mowgli to her hut, where there was a red-lacquered bedstead, a great earthen grain-chest with curious raised patterns on it, half a dozen copper cooking-pots, an image of a Hindu god in a little alcove, and on the wall a real looking-glass, such as they sell at the country fairs.

She gave him a long drink of milk and some bread, and then she laid her hand on his head and looked into his eyes; for she thought that perhaps he might be her real son come back from the Jungle where the tiger had taken him. So she said: 'Nathoo, O Nathoo!' Mowgli did not show that he knew the name. 'Dost thou not remember the day when I gave thee thy new shoes?' She touched his foot, and it was almost as hard as horn. 'No,' she said sorrowfully, 'those feet have never worn shoes, but thou art very like my Nathoo, and thou shalt be my son.'

Mowgli was uneasy, because he had never been under a roof before; but as he looked at the thatch, he saw that he could tear it out any time if he wanted to get away, and that the window had no fastenings. 'What is the good of a man,' he said to himself at last, 'if he does not understand man's talk? Now I am as silly and dumb as a man would be with us in the Jungle. I must learn their talk.'

It was not for fun that he had learned while he was with the wolves to imitate the challenge of bucks in the Jungle and the grunt of the little wild pig. So as soon as Messua pronounced a word Mowgli would imitate it almost perfectly, and before dark he had learned the names of many things in the hut.

There was a difficulty at bedtime, because Mowgli would not sleep under anything that looked so like a panther-trap as that hut, and when they shut the door he went through the window. 'Give him his will,' said Messua's husband. 'Remember he can never till now have slept on a bed. If he is indeed sent in the place of our son he will not run away.'

So Mowgli stretched himself in some long, clean grass at the edge of the field, but before he had closed his eyes a soft grey nose poked him under the chin.

'Phew!' said Grey Brother (he was the eldest of Mother Wolf's cubs). 'This is a poor reward for following thee twenty miles. Thou smellest of wood-smoke and cattle – altogether like a man already. Wake, Little Brother; I bring news.'

'Are all well in the Jungle?' said Mowgli, hugging him.

'All except the wolves that were burned with the Red Flower. Now, listen. Shere Khan has gone away to hunt far off till his coat grows again, for he is badly singed. When he returns he swears that he will lay thy bones in the Waingunga.'

'There are two words to that. I also have made a little promise. But news is always good. I am tired tonight – very tired with new things, Grey Brother – but bring me the news always.'

'Thou wilt not forget that thou art a wolf? Men will not make thee forget?' said Grey Brother anxiously.

'Never. I will always remember that I love thee and all in our cave; but also I will always remember that I have been cast out of the Pack.'

'And that thou mayest be cast out of another pack. Men are only men, Little Brother, and their talk is like the talk of frogs in a pond. When I come

Wake, Little Brother; I bring news

down here again, I will wait for thee in the bamboos at the edge of the grazing-ground.'

For three months after that night Mowgli hardly ever left the village gate, he was so busy learning the ways and customs of men. First he had to wear a cloth round him, which annoyed him horribly; and then he had to learn about money, which he did not in the least understand, and about ploughing, of which he did not see the use. Then the little children in the village made him very angry. Luckily, the Law of the Jungle had taught him to keep his temper, for in the Jungle life and food depend on keeping your temper; but when they made fun of him because he would not play games or fly kites, or because he mispronounced some word, only the knowledge that it was unsportsmanlike to kill little naked cubs kept him from picking them up and breaking them in two.

He did not know his own strength in the least. In the Jungle he knew he was weak compared with the beasts, but in the village people said that he was as strong as a bull.

And Mowgli had not the faintest idea of the difference that caste makes between man and man. When the potter's donkey slipped in the clay-pit, Mowgli hauled it out by the tail, and helped to stack the pots for their journey to the market at Khanhiwara. That was very shocking, too, for the potter is a low-caste man, and his donkey is worse. When the priest scolded him,

Mowgli threatened to put him on the donkey, too, and the priest told Messua's husband that Mowgli had better be set to work as soon as possible; and the village headman told Mowgli that he would have to go out with the buffaloes next day, and herd them while they grazed. No one was more pleased than Mowgli; and that night, because he had been appointed, as it were, a servant of the village, he went off to a circle that met every evening on a masonry platform under a great fig tree. It was the village club, and the headman and the watchman and the barber (who knew all the gossip of the village), and old Buldeo, the village hunter, who owned a Tower musket, met and smoked. The monkeys sat and talked in the upper branches, and there was a hole under the platform where a cobra lived, and he had his little platter of milk every night because he was sacred; and the old men sat around the tree and talked, and pulled at the big hookahs [water-pipes], till far into the night. They told wonderful tales of gods and men and ghosts; and Buldeo told even more wonderful ones of the ways of beasts in the Jungle, till the eyes of the children sitting outside the circle bulged out of their heads. Most of the tales were about animals, for the Jungle was always at their door. The deer and the wild pig grubbed up their crops, and now and again the tiger carried off a man at twilight, within sight of the village gates.

Mowgli, who, naturally, knew something about what they were talking of, had to cover his face not to show that he was laughing, while Buldeo, the Tower musket across his knees, climbed on from one wonderful story to another, and Mowgli's shoulders shook.

Buldeo was explaining how the tiger that had carried away Messua's son was a ghost-tiger, and his body was inhabited by the ghost of a wicked old moneylender, who had died some years ago. 'And I know that this is true,' he said, 'because Purun Dass always limped from the blow that he got in a riot when his account-books were burned, and the tiger that I speak of, *he* limps, too, for the tracks of his pads are unequal.'

'True, true; that must be the truth,' said the greybeards, nodding together.

'Are all these tales such cobwebs and moon-talk?' said Mowgli. 'That tiger limps because he was born lame, as everyone knows. To talk of the soul of a moneylender in a beast that never had the courage of a jackal is child's talk.'

Buldeo was speechless with surprise for a moment, and the headman stared.

'Oho! It is the Jungle brat, is it?' said Buldeo. 'If thou art so wise, better bring his hide to Khanhiwara, for the Government has set a hundred rupees on his life. Better still, do not talk when thy elders speak.'

Mowgli rose to go. 'All the evening I have lain here listening,' he called back over his shoulder, 'and, except once or twice, Buldeo has not said one word of truth concerning the Jungle, which is at his very doors. How, then, shall I believe the tales of ghosts and gods and goblins which he says he has seen?'

'It is full time that boy went to herding,' said the headman, while Buldeo puffed and snorted at Mowgli's impertinence.

'Are all these tales such cobwebs and moon-talk?' said Mowgli.

The custom of most Indian villages is for a few boys to take the cattle and buffaloes out to graze in the early morning, and bring them back at night; and the very cattle that would trample a white man to death allow themselves to be banged and bullied and shouted at by children that hardly come up to their noses. So long as the boys keep with the herds they are safe, for not even the tiger will charge a mob of cattle. But if they straggle to pick flowers or hunt lizards, they are sometimes carried off. Mowgli went through the village street in the dawn, sitting on the back of Rama, the great herd bull; and the slaty-blue buffaloes, with their long, backwards-sweeping horns and savage eyes, rose out of their byres, one by one, and followed him, and Mowgli made it very clear to the children with him that he was the master. He beat the buffaloes with a long, polished bamboo, and told Kamya, one of the boys, to graze the cattle by themselves, while he went on with the buffaloes, and to be very careful not to stray away from the herd.

An Indian grazing-ground is all rocks and scrub and tussocks and little ravines, among which the herds scatter and disappear. The buffaloes gener- ally keep to the pools and muddy places, where they lie wallowing or basking in the warm mud for hours. Mowgli drove them on to the edge of the plain where the Waingunga River came out of the Jungle; then he dropped from Rama's neck, trotted off to a bamboo clump, and found Grey Brother. 'Ah!' said Grey Brother. 'I have waited here very many days. What is the meaning of this cattle-herding work?'

'It is an order,' said Mowgli. 'I am a village herd for a while. What news of Shere Khan?'

'He has come back to this country, and has waited here a long time for thee. Now he has gone off again, for the game is scarce. But he means to kill thee.'

'Very good,' said Mowgli. 'So long as he is away do thou or one of the four brothers sit on that rock, so that I can see thee as I come out of the village. When he comes back wait for me in the ravine by the *dhâk* tree in the centre of the plain. We need not walk into Shere Khan's mouth.'

Then Mowgli picked out a shady place, and lay down and slept while the buffaloes grazed round him. Herding in India is one of the laziest things in the world. The cattle move and crunch, and lie down, and move on again, and they do not even low. They only grunt, and the buffaloes very seldom say anything, but get down into the muddy pools one after another, and work their way into the mud till only their noses and staring china-blue eyes show above the surface, and there they lie like logs. The sun makes the rocks dance in the heat, and the herd-children hear one kite (never any more) whistling almost out of sight overhead, and they know that if they died, or a cow died, that kite would sweep down, and the next kite miles away would see him drop and would follow, and the next, and the next, and almost before they were dead there would be a score of hungry kites come out of nowhere. Then they sleep and wake and sleep again, and weave little baskets of dried grass and put grasshoppers in them; or catch two praying-mantises and make them fight; or string a necklace of red and black Jungle-nuts; or watch a lizard basking on a rock, or a snake hunting a frog near the wallows. Then they sing long, long songs with odd native quavers at the end of them, and the day seems longer than most people's whole lives, and perhaps they make a mud castle with mud figures of men and horses and buffaloes, and put reeds into the men's hands, and pretend that they are kings and the figures are their armies, or that they are gods to be worshipped. Then evening comes, and the children call, and the buffaloes lumber up out of the sticky mud with noises like gunshots going off one after the other, and they all string across the grey plain back to the twinkling village lights.

Day after day Mowgli would lead the buffaloes out to their wallows, and day after day he would see Grey Brother's back a mile and a half away across the plain (so he knew that Shere Khan had not come back), and day after day he would lie on the grass listening to the noises round him, and dreaming of old days in the Jungle. If Shere Khan had made a false step with his lame paw up in the Jungles by the Waingunga, Mowgli would have heard him in those long, still mornings.

At last a day came when he did not see Grey Brother at the signal-place, and he laughed and headed the buffaloes for the ravine by the *dhâk* tree, which was all covered with golden-red flowers. There sat Grey Brother, every bristle on his back lifted.

'He has hidden for a month to throw thee off thy guard. He crossed the ranges last night with Tabaqui, hotfoot on thy trail,' said the wolf, panting.

Mowgli frowned. 'I am not afraid of Shere Khan, but Tabaqui is very cunning.'

'Have no fear,' said Grey Brother, licking his lips a little. 'I met Tabaqui in the dawn. Now he is telling all his wisdom to the kites, but he told *me* everything before I broke his back. Shere Khan's plan is to wait for thee at the village gate this evening – for thee and for no one else. He is lying up now in the big dry ravine of the Waingunga.'

'Has he eaten today, or does he hunt empty?' said Mowgli, for the answer meant life or death to him.

'He killed at dawn – a pig – and he has drunk too. Remember, Shere Khan could never fast, even for the sake of revenge.'

'Oh! Fool, fool! What a cub's cub it is! Eaten and drunk too, and he thinks that I shall wait till he has slept! Now, where does he lie up? If there were but ten of us we might pull him down as he lies. These buffaloes will not charge unless they wind him, and I cannot speak their language. Can we get behind his track so that they may smell it?'

'He swam far down the Waingunga to cut that off,' said Grey Brother.

'Tabaqui told him that, I know. He would never have thought of it alone.' Mowgli stood with his finger in his mouth, thinking. 'The big ravine of the Waingunga. That opens out on the plain not half a mile from here. I can take the herd round through the Jungle to the head of the ravine and then sweep down – but he would slink out at the foot. We must block that end. Grey Brother, canst thou cut the herd in two for me?'

'Not I, perhaps – but I have brought a wise helper.' Grey Brother trotted off and dropped into a hole. Then there lifted up a huge grey head that Mowgli knew well, and the hot air was filled with the most desolate cry of all the Jungle – the hunting-howl of a wolf at midday.

'Akela! Akela!' said Mowgli, clapping his hands. 'I might have known that thou wouldst not forget me. We have a big work in hand. Cut the herd in two, Akela. Keep the cows and calves together, and the bulls and the plough-buffaloes by themselves.'

The two wolves ran, ladies'-chain fashion, in and out of the herd, which snorted and threw up its head, and separated into two clumps. In one the cow-buffaloes stood, with their calves in the centre, and glared and pawed, ready, if a wolf would only stay still, to charge down and trample the life out of him. In the other the bulls and the young bulls snorted and stamped; but, though they looked more imposing, they were much less dangerous, for they had no calves to protect. No six men could have divided the herd so neatly.

'What orders?' panted Akela. 'They are trying to join again.'

Mowgli slipped on to Rama's back. 'Drive the bulls away to the left, Akela. Grey Brother, when we are gone, hold the cows together, and drive them into the foot of the ravine.'

'How far?' said Grey Brother, panting and snapping.

'Till the sides are higher than Shere Khan can jump,' shouted Mowgli.

'Keep them there till we come down.' The bulls swept off as Akela bayed, and Grey Brother stopped in front of the cows. They charged down on him, and he ran just before them to the foot of the ravine, as Akela drove the bulls far to the left.

'Well done! Another charge and they are fairly started. Careful, now – careful, Akela. A snap too much, and the bulls will charge. *Huyah!* This is wilder work than driving black-buck. Didst thou think these creatures could move so swiftly?' Mowgli called.

'I have – have hunted these too in my time,' gasped Akela in the dust. 'Shall I turn them into the Jungle?'

'Ay, turn! Swiftly turn them! Rama is mad with rage. Oh, if I could only tell him what I need of him today!'

The bulls were turned to the right this time, and crashed into the standing thicket. The other herd-children, watching with the cattle half a mile away, hurried to the village as fast as their legs could carry them, crying that the buffaloes had gone mad and run away.

But Mowgli's plan was simple enough. All he wanted to do was to make a big circle uphill and get at the head of the ravine, and then take the bulls down it and catch Shere Khan between the bulls and the cows; for he knew that after a meal and a full drink Shere Khan would not be in any condition to fight or to clamber up the sides of the ravine. He was soothing the buffaloes now by voice, and Akela had dropped far to the rear, only whimpering once or twice to hurry the rearguard. It was a long, long circle, for they did not wish to get too near the ravine and give Shere Khan warning. At last Mowgli rounded up the bewildered herd at the head of the ravine on a grassy patch that sloped steeply down to the ravine itself. From that height you could see across the tops of the trees down to the plain below; but what Mowgli looked at was the sides of the ravine, and he saw with a great deal of satisfaction that they ran nearly straight up and down, while the vines and creepers that hung over them would give no foothold to a tiger who wanted to get out.

'Let them breathe, Akela,' he said, holding up his hand. 'They have not winded him yet. Let them breathe. I must tell Shere Khan who comes. We have him in the trap.'

He put his hands to his mouth and shouted down the ravine – it was almost like shouting down a tunnel – and the echoes jumped from rock to rock.

After a long time there came back the drawling, sleepy snarl of a full-fed tiger just wakened.

'Who calls?' said Shere Khan, and a splendid peacock fluttered up out of the ravine screeching.

'I, Mowgli. Cattle thief, it is time to come to the Council Rock! Down – hurry them down, Akela! Down, Rama, down!'

The herd paused for an instant at the edge of the slope, but Akela gave tongue in the full hunting-yell, and they pitched over one after the other, just as steamers shoot rapids, the sand and stones spurting up round them. Once started, there was no chance of stopping, and before they were fairly in the bed of the ravine Rama winded Shere Khan and bellowed.

'Ha! Ha!' said Mowgli, on his back. 'Now thou knowest!' and the torrent of black horns, foaming muzzles, and staring eyes whirled down the ravine like boulders in flood-time; the weaker buffaloes being shouldered out to the sides of the ravine, where they tore through the creepers. They knew what the business was before them – the terrible charge of the buffalo-herd, against which no tiger can hope to stand. Shere Khan heard the thunder of their hoofs, picked himself up, and lumbered down the ravine, looking from side to side for some way of escape; but the walls of the ravine were straight, and he had to keep on, heavy with his dinner and his drink, willing to do anything rather than fight. The herd splashed through the pool he had just left, bellowing till the narrow cut rang. Mowgli heard an answering bellow from the foot of the ravine, saw Shere Khan turn (the tiger knew if the worst came to the worst it was better to meet the bulls than the cows with their calves), and then Rama tripped, stumbled, and went on again over something soft, and, with the bulls at his heels, crashed full into the other herd, while the weaker buffaloes were lifted clean off their feet by the shock of the meeting. That charge carried both herds out into the plain, goring and stamping and snorting. Mowgli watched his time, and slipped off Rama's neck, laying about him right and left with his stick.

'Quick, Akela! Break them up. Scatter them, or they will be fighting one another. Drive them away, Akela. *Hai*, Rama! *Hai! hai! hai!* my children. Softly now, softly! It is all over.'

Akela and Grey Brother ran to and fro nipping the buffaloes' legs, and though the herd wheeled once to charge up the ravine again, Mowgli managed to turn Rama, and the others followed him to the wallows.

Shere Khan needed no more trampling. He was dead, and the kites were coming for him already.

'Brothers, that was a dog's death,' said Mowgli, feeling for the knife he always carried in a sheath round his neck now that he lived with men. 'But he would never have shown fight. His hide will look well on the Council Rock. We must get to work swiftly.'

A boy trained among men would never have dreamed of skinning a ten-foot tiger alone, but Mowgli knew better than anyone else how an animal's skin is fitted on, and how it can be taken off. But it was hard work, and Mowgli slashed and tore and grunted for an hour, while the wolves lolled out their tongues, or came forward and tugged as he ordered them.

Presently a hand fell on his shoulder, and looking up he saw Buldeo with the Tower musket. The children had told the village about the buffalo stampede, and Buldeo went out angrily, only too anxious to correct Mowgli for not taking better care of the herd. The wolves dropped out of sight as soon as they saw the man coming.

'What is this folly?' said Buldeo angrily. 'To think that thou canst skin a tiger! Where did the buffaloes kill him? It is the Lame Tiger, too, and there is a hundred rupees on his head. Well, well, we will overlook thy letting the herd run off, and perhaps I will give thee one of the rupees of the reward when I have taken the skin to Khanhiwara.' He fumbled in his waist-cloth for flint and steel, and stooped down to singe Shere Khan's whiskers. Most native hunters singe a tiger's whiskers to prevent his ghost haunting them.

'Hum!' said Mowgli, half to himself as he ripped back the skin of a forepaw. 'So thou wilt take the hide to Khanhiwara for the reward, and perhaps give me one rupee? Now it is in my mind that I need the skin for my own use. Heh! old man, take away that fire!'

'What talk is this to the chief hunter of the village? Thy luck and the stupidity of thy buffaloes have helped thee to this kill. The tiger has just fed, or he would have gone twenty miles by this time. Thou canst not even skin him properly, little beggar-brat, and forsooth I, Buldeo, must be told not to singe his whiskers. Mowgli, I will not give thee one anna of the reward, but only a very big beating. Leave the carcass!'

'By the Bull that bought me,' said Mowgli, who was trying to get at the shoulder, 'must I stay babbling to an old ape all noon? Here, Akela, this man plagues me.'

Buldeo, who was still stooping over Shere Khan's head, found himself sprawling on the grass, with a grey wolf standing over him, while Mowgli went on skinning as though he were alone in all India.

'Ye–es,' he said, between his teeth. 'Thou art altogether right, Buldeo. Thou wilt never give me one anna of the reward. There is an old war between this lame tiger and myself – a very old war, and – I have won.'

To do Buldeo justice, if he had been ten years younger he would have taken his chance with Akela had he met the wolf in the woods; but a wolf who obeyed the orders of this boy who had private wars with man-eating tigers was not a common animal. It was sorcery, magic of the worst kind, thought Buldeo, and he wondered whether the amulet round his neck would protect him. He lay as still as still, expecting every minute to see Mowgli turn into a tiger, too.

'Maharajah! Great King!' he said at last, in a husky whisper.

'Yes,' said Mowgli, without turning his head, chuckling a little.

'I am an old man. I did not know that thou wast anything more than a herd-boy. May I rise up and go away, or will thy servant tear me to pieces?'

'Go, and peace go with thee. Only, another time do not meddle with my game. Let him go, Akela.'

Buldeo hobbled away to the village as fast as he could, looking back over his shoulder in case Mowgli should change into something terrible. When he got to the village he told a tale of magic and enchantment and sorcery that made the priest look very grave.

Mowgli went on with his work, but it was nearly twilight before he and the wolves had drawn the great gay skin clear of the body.

He lay as still as still, expecting every minute to see Mowgli turn into a tiger, too.

'Now we must hide this and take the buffaloes home! Help me to herd them, Akela.'

The herd rounded up in the misty twilight, and when they got near the village Mowgli saw lights, and heard the conches and bells blowing and banging. Half the village seemed to be waiting for him by the gate. 'That is because I have killed Shere Khan,' he said to himself; but a shower of stones whistled about his ears, and the villagers shouted: 'Sorcerer! Wolf's brat! Jungle-demon! Go away! Get hence quickly, or the priest will turn thee into a wolf again. Shoot, Buldeo, shoot!'

The old Tower musket went off with a bang, and a young buffalo bellowed in pain.

'More sorcery!' shouted the villagers. 'He can turn bullets. Buldeo, that was *thy* buffalo.'

'Now what is this?' said Mowgli, bewildered, as the stones flew thicker.

'They are not unlike the Pack, these brothers of thine,' said Akela, sitting down composedly. 'It is in my head that, if bullets mean anything, they would cast thee out.'

'Wolf! Wolf's cub! Go away!' shouted the priest, waving a sprig of the sacred *tulsi* plant.

'Again? Last time it was because I was a man. This time it is because I am a wolf. Let us go, Akela.'

A woman – it was Messua – ran across to the herd, and cried: 'Oh, my son, my son! They say thou art a sorcerer who can turn himself into a beast at will.

I do not believe, but go away or they will kill thee. Buldeo says thou art a wizard, but I know thou hast avenged Nathoo's death.'

'Come back, Messua!' shouted the crowd. 'Come back, or we will stone thee.'

Mowgli laughed a little short ugly laugh, for a stone had hit him in the mouth. 'Run back, Messua. This is one of the foolish tales they tell under the big tree at dusk. I have at least paid for thy son's life. Farewell; and run quickly, for I shall send the herd in more swiftly than their brickbats. I am no wizard, Messua. Farewell!'

'Now, once more, Akela,' he cried. 'Bring the herd in.'

The buffaloes were anxious enough to get to the village. They hardly needed Akela's yell, but charged through the gate like a whirlwind, scattering the crowd right and left.

'Keep count!' shouted Mowgli scornfully. 'It may be that I have stolen one of them. Keep count, for I will do your herding no more. Fare you well, children of men, and thank Messua that I do not come in with my wolves and hunt you up and down your street.'

He turned on his heel and walked away with the Lone Wolf; and as he looked up at the stars he felt happy. 'No more sleeping in traps for me, Akela. Let us get Shere Khan's skin and go away. No; we will not hurt the village, for Messua was kind to me.'

When the moon rose over the plain, making it look all milky, the horrified villagers saw Mowgli, with two wolves at his heels and a bundle on his head, trotting across at the steady wolf's trot that eats up the long miles like fire. Then they banged the temple bells and blew the conches louder than ever;

When the moon rose over the plain the villagers saw Mowgli, with two wolves at his heels and a bundle on his head

and Messua cried, and Buldeo embroidered the story of his adventures in the Jungle, till he ended by saying that Akela stood up on his hind legs and talked like a man.

The moon was just going down when Mowgli and the two wolves came to the hill of the Council Rock, and they stopped at Mother Wolf's cave.

'They have cast me out from the Man Pack, Mother,' shouted Mowgli, 'but I come with the hide of Shere Khan to keep my word.' Mother Wolf walked stiffly from the cave with the cubs behind her, and her eyes glowed as she saw the skin.

'I told him on that day, when he crammed his head and shoulders into this cave, hunting for thy life, Little Frog – I told him that the hunter would be the hunted. It is well done.'

'Little Brother, it is well done,' said a deep voice in the thicket. 'We were lonely in the Jungle without thee,' and Bagheera came running to Mowgli's bare feet. They clambered up the Council Rock together, and Mowgli spread the skin out on the flat stone where Akela used to sit, and pegged it down with four slivers of bamboo, and Akela lay down upon it, and called the old call to the Council, 'Look – look well, O Wolves!' exactly as he had called when Mowgli was first brought there.

Ever since Akela had been deposed, the Pack had been without a leader, hunting and fighting at their own pleasure. But they answered the call from habit, and some of them were lame from the traps they had fallen into, and some limped from shot-wounds, and some were mangy from eating bad food, and many were missing; but they came to the Council Rock, all that were left of them, and saw Shere Khan's striped hide on the rock, and the huge claws dangling at the end of the empty, dangling feet. It was then that Mowgli made up a song without any rhymes, a song that came up into his throat all by itself, and he shouted it aloud, leaping up and down on the rattling skin, and beating time with his heels till he had no more breath left, while Grey Brother and Akela howled between the verses.

'Look well, O Wolves! Have I kept my word?' said Mowgli when he had finished; and the wolves bayed, 'Yes,' and one tattered wolf howled: 'Lead us again, O Akela. Lead us again, O Man-cub, for we be sick of this lawlessness, and we would be the Free People once more.'

'Nay,' purred Bagheera, 'that may not be. When ye are full-fed, the madness may come upon ye again. Not for nothing are ye called the Free People. Ye fought for freedom, and it is yours. Eat it, O Wolves.'

'Man Pack and Wolf Pack have cast me out,' said Mowgli. 'Now I will hunt alone in the Jungle.'

'And we will hunt with thee,' said the four cubs.

So Mowgli went away and hunted with the four cubs in the Jungle from that day on. But he was not always alone, because years afterward he became a man and married.

But that is a story for grown-ups.

*They clambered up the Council Rock together, and Mowgli spread the skin out on
the flat stone where Akela used to sit*

Mowgli's Song

THAT HE SANG AT THE COUNCIL ROCK
WHEN HE DANCED ON SHERE KHAN'S HIDE

The Song of Mowgli – I, Mowgli, am singing. Let the Jungle listen
to the things I have done.

Shere Khan said he would kill – would kill! At the gates in the
twilight he would kill Mowgli, the Frog!

He ate and he drank. Drink deep, Shere Khan, for when wilt thou
drink again? Sleep and dream of the kill.

I am alone on the grazing-grounds. Grey Brother, come to me!
Come to me, Lone Wolf, for there is big game afoot.

Bring up the great bull-buffaloes, the blue-skinned herd-bulls with
the angry eyes. Drive them to and fro as I order.

Sleepest thou still, Shere Khan? Wake, oh, wake! Here come I, and
the bulls are behind.

Rama, the King of the Buffaloes, stamped with his foot. Waters of
the Waingunga, whither went Shere Khan?

He is not Ikki to dig holes, nor Mao, the Peacock, that he should fly.
He is not Mang, the Bat, to hang in the branches. Little bamboos
that creak together, tell me where he ran.

Ow! He is there. *Ahoo!* He is there. Under the feet of Rama lies the
Lame One! Up, Shere Khan! Up and kill! Here is meat; break the
necks of the bulls!

Hsh! He is asleep. We will not wake him, for his strength is very
great. The kites have come down to see it. The black ants have
come up to know it. There is a great assembly in his honour.

Alala! I have no cloth to wrap me. The kites will see that I am naked.
I am ashamed to meet all these people.

Lend me thy coat, Shere Khan. Lend me thy gay striped coat that I
may go to the Council Rock.

By the Bull that bought me, I have made a promise – a little promise.
Only thy coat is lacking before I keep my word.

With the knife – with the knife that men use – with the knife of the
hunter, the man, I will stoop down for my gift.

Waters of the Waingunga, bear witness that Shere Khan gives me
his coat for the love that he bears me. Pull, Grey Brother! Pull,
Akela! Heavy is the hide of Shere Khan.

The Man Pack are angry. They throw stones and talk child's talk. My mouth is bleeding. Let us run away.

Through the night, through the hot night, run swiftly with me, my brothers. We will leave the lights of the village and go to the low moon.

Waters of the Waingunga, the Man Pack have cast me out. I did them no harm, but they were afraid of me. Why?

Wolf Pack, ye have cast me out too. The Jungle is shut to me and the village gates are shut. Why?

As Mang flies between the beasts and the birds, so fly I between the village and the Jungle. Why?

I dance on the hide of Shere Khan, but my heart is very heavy. My mouth is cut and wounded with the stones from the village, but my heart is very light because I have come back to the Jungle. Why?

These two things fight together in me as the snakes fight in the spring.

The water comes out of my eyes; yet I laugh while it falls. Why?

I am two Mowglis, but the hide of Shere Khan is under my feet.

All the Jungle knows that I have killed Shere Khan. Look – look well, O Wolves!

Ahae! My heart is heavy with the things that I do not understand.

The White Seal

Oh! hush thee, my baby, the night is behind us,
    And black are the waters that sparkled so green.
The moon, o'er the combers, looks downward to find us
    At rest in the hollows that rustle between.
Where billow meets billow, there soft be thy pillow;
    Ah, weary wee flipperling, curl at thy ease!
The storm shall not wake thee, nor shark overtake thee,
    Asleep in the arms of the slow-swinging seas.

Seal Lullaby

All these things happened several years ago at a place called Novastoshnah, or North-East Point, on the Island of St Paul, away and away in the Bering Sea. Limmershin, the Winter Wren, told me the tale when he was blown on to the rigging of a steamer going to Japan, and I took him down into my cabin and warmed and fed him for a couple of days till he was fit to fly back to St Paul's again. Limmershin is a very odd little bird, but he knows how to tell the truth.

Nobody comes to Novastoshnah except on business, and the only people who have regular business there are the seals. They come in the summer months by hundreds and hundreds of thousands out of the cold grey sea; for Novastoshnah Beach has the finest accommodation for seals of any place in all the world.

Sea Catch knew that, and every spring would swim from whatever place he happened to be in – would swim like a torpedo-boat straight for Novastoshnah, and spend a month fighting with his companions for a good place on the rocks as close to the sea as possible. Sea Catch was fifteen years old, a huge grey fur-seal with almost a mane on his shoulders, and long, wicked dog-teeth. When he heaved himself up on his front flippers he stood more than four feet clear of the ground, and his weight, if anyone had been bold enough to weigh him, was nearly seven hundred pounds. He was scarred all over with the marks of savage fights, but he was always ready for just one fight more. He would put his head on one side, as though he were afraid to look his enemy in the face; then he would shoot it out like lightning, and when the big teeth were firmly fixed on the other seal's neck, the other seal might get away if he could, but Sea Catch would not help him.

Yet Sea Catch never chased a beaten seal, for that was against the Rules of the Beach. He only wanted room by the sea for his nursery; but as there were forty or fifty thousand other seals hunting for the same thing each spring, the whistling, bellowing, roaring, and blowing on the beach were something frightful.

From a little hill called Hutchinson's Hill you could look over three and a half miles of ground covered with fighting seals; and the surf was dotted all over with the heads of seals hurrying to land and begin their share of the fighting. They fought in the breakers, they fought in the sand, and they fought on the smooth-worn basalt rocks of the nurseries; for they were just as stupid and unaccommodating as men. Their wives never came to the island until late in May or early in June, for they did not care to be torn to pieces; and the young two-, three-, and four-year-old seals who had not begun housekeeping went inland about half a mile through the ranks of the fighters and played about on the sand-dunes in droves and legions, and rubbed off every single green thing that grew. They were called the holluschickie – the bachelors – and there were perhaps two or three hundred thousand of them at Novastoshnah alone.

Sea Catch had just finished his forty-fifth fight one spring when Matkah, his soft, sleek, gentle-eyed wife, came up out of the sea, and he caught her by the scruff of the neck and dumped her down on his reservation, saying gruffly: 'Late, as usual. Where *have* you been?'

It was not the fashion for Sea Catch to eat anything during the four months he stayed on the beaches, and so his temper was generally bad. Matkah knew better than to answer back. She looked round and cooed: 'How thoughtful of you! You've taken the old place again.'

'I should think I had,' said Sea Catch. 'Look at me!'

He was scratched and bleeding in twenty places; one eye was almost blind, and his sides were torn to ribbons.

'Oh, you men, you men!' Matkah said, fanning herself with her hind flipper. 'Why can't you be sensible and settle your places quietly? You look as though you had been fighting with the Killer Whale.'

'I haven't been doing anything *but* fight since the middle of May. The beach is disgracefully crowded this season. I've met at least a hundred seals from Lukannon Beach, house-hunting. Why can't people stay where they belong?'

'I've often thought we should be much happier if we hauled out at Otter Island instead of this crowded place,' said Matkah.

'Bah! Only the holluschickie go to Otter Island. If we went there they would say we were afraid. We must preserve appearances, my dear.'

Sea Catch sunk his head proudly between his fat shoulders and pretended to go to sleep for a few minutes, but all the time he was keeping a sharp look-out for a fight. Now that all the seals and their wives were on the land, you could hear their clamour miles out to sea above the loudest gales. At the lowest counting there were over a million seals on the beach – old seals, mother seals, tiny babies, and holluschickie, fighting, scuffling, bleating, crawling, and playing together – going down to the sea and coming up from it in gangs and regiments, lying over every foot of ground as far as the eye could reach, and skirmishing about in brigades through the fog. It is nearly always foggy at Novastoshnah, except when the sun comes out and makes everything look all pearly and rainbow-coloured for a little while.

Kotick, Matkah's baby, was born in the middle of that confusion, and he was all head and shoulders, with pale, watery-blue eyes, as tiny seals must be; but there was something about his coat that made his mother look at him very closely.

'Sea Catch,' she said at last, 'our baby's going to be white!'

'Empty clam-shells and dry seaweed!' snorted Sea Catch. 'There never has been such a thing in the world as a white seal.'

'I can't help that,' said Matkah; 'there's going to be now'; and she sang the low, crooning seal-song that all the mother seals sing to their babies:

> You mustn't swim till you're six weeks old,
>   Or your head will be sunk by your heels;
> And summer gales and Killer Whales
>   Are bad for baby seals.
>
> Are bad for baby seals, dear rat,
>   As bad as bad can be;
> But splash and grow strong,
> And you can't be wrong,
>   Child of the Open Sea!

Of course the little fellow did not understand the words at first. He paddled and scrambled about by his mother's side, and learned to scuffle out of the way when his father was fighting with another seal, and the two rolled and roared up and down the slippery rocks. Matkah used to go to sea to get things to eat, and the baby was fed only once in two days; but then he ate all he could, and thrived upon it.

The first thing he did was to crawl inland, and there he met tens of thousands of babies of his own age, and they played together like puppies, went to sleep on the clean sand, and played again. The old people in the nurseries took no notice of them, and the holluschickie kept to their own grounds, so the babies had a beautiful playtime.

When Matkah came back from her deep-sea fishing she would go straight to their playground and call as a sheep calls for a lamb, and wait until she heard Kotick bleat. Then she would take the straightest of straight lines in his direction, striking out with her fore flippers and knocking the youngsters head over heels right and left. There were always a few hundred mothers hunting for their children through the playgrounds, and the babies were kept lively; but, as Matkah told Kotick, 'So long as you don't lie in muddy water and get mange, or rub the hard sand into a cut or scratch, and so long as you never go swimming when there is a heavy sea, nothing will hurt you here.'

Little seals can no more swim than little children, but they are unhappy till they learn. The first time that Kotick went down to the sea a wave carried him out beyond his depth, and his big head sank and his little hind flippers flew up exactly as his mother had told him in the song, and if the next wave had not thrown him back again he would have drowned.

After that he learned to lie in a beach-pool and let the wash of the waves just cover him and lift him up while he paddled, but he always kept his eye open for big waves that might hurt. He was two weeks learning to use his flippers; and all that while he floundered in and out of the water, and coughed and grunted and crawled up the beach and took catnaps on the sand, and went back again, until at last he found that he truly belonged to the water.

Then you can imagine the times that he had with his companions, ducking under the rollers; or coming in on top of a comber and landing with a swash and a splutter as the big wave went whirling far up the beach; or standing up on his tail and scratching his head as the old people did; or playing 'I'm the King of the Castle' on slippery, weedy rocks that just stuck out of the wash. Now and then he would see a thin fin, like a big shark's fin, drifting along close to shore, and he knew that that was the Killer Whale,

the Grampus, who eats young seals when he can get them; and Kotick
would head for the beach like an arrow, and the fin would jig off slowly, as
if it were looking for nothing at all.

Late in October the seals began to leave St Paul's for the deep sea, by
families and tribes, and there was no more fighting over the nurseries, and the
holluschickie played anywhere they liked. 'Next year,' said Matkah to Kotick,
'you will be a holluschickie; but this year you must learn how to catch fish.'

They set out together across the Pacific, and Matkah showed Kotick how
to sleep on his back with his flippers tucked down by his side and his little
nose just out of the water. No cradle is so comfortable as the long, rocking
swell of the Pacific. When Kotick felt his skin tingle all over, Matkah told him
he was learning the 'feel of the water', and that tingly, prickly feelings meant
bad weather coming, and he must swim hard and get away.

'In a little time,' she said, 'you'll know where to swim to, but just now we'll
follow Sea Pig, the Porpoise, for he is very wise.' A school of porpoises were
ducking and tearing through the water, and little Kotick followed them as fast
as he could. 'How do you know where to go to?' he panted. The leader of the
school rolled his white eyes, and ducked under. 'My tail tingles, youngster,'
he said. 'That means there's a gale behind me. Come along! When you're
south of the Sticky Water [he meant the Equator], and your tail tingles, that
means there's a gale in front of you and you must head north. Come along!
The water feels bad here.'

This was one of the very many things that Kotick learned, and he was
always learning. Matkah taught him to follow the cod and the halibut along
the under-sea banks, and wrench the rockling out of his hole among the
weeds; how to skirt the wrecks lying a hundred fathoms below water, and dart
like a rifle-bullet in at one porthole and out at another as the fishes ran; how
to dance on the top of the waves when the lightning was racing all over the
sky, and wave his flipper politely to the stumpy-tailed Albatross and the Man-
of-war Hawk as they went down the wind; how to jump three or four feet
clear of the water, like a dolphin, flippers close to the side and tail curved; to
leave the flying-fish alone because they are all bony; to take the shoulder-
piece out of a cod at full speed ten fathoms deep; and never to stop and look
at a boat or a ship, but particularly a row-boat. At the end of six months, what
Kotick did not know about deep-sea fishing was not worth the knowing, and
all that time he never set flipper on dry ground.

One day, however, as he was lying half asleep in the warm water somewhere off the Island of Juan Fernandez, he felt faint and lazy all over, just as
human people do when the spring is in their legs, and he remembered the
good firm beaches of Novastoshnah seven thousand miles away, the games
his companions played, the smell of the seaweed, the seal roar, and the
fighting. That very minute he turned north, swimming steadily, and as he
went on he met scores of his mates, all bound for the same place, and they
said: 'Greeting, Kotick! This year we are all holluschickie, and we can dance

the Fire Dance in the breakers off Lukannon and play on the new grass. But where did you get that coat?'

Kotick's fur was almost pure white now, and though he felt very proud of it, he only said: 'Swim quickly! My bones are aching for the land.' And so they all came to the beaches where they had been born, and heard the old seals, their fathers, fighting in the rolling mist.

That night Kotick danced the Fire Dance with the yearling seals. The sea is full of fire on summer nights all the way down from Novastoshnah to Lukannon, and each seal leaves a wake like burning oil behind him, and a flaming flash when he jumps, and the waves break in great phosphorescent streaks and swirls. Then they went inland to the holluschickie grounds, and rolled up and down in the new wild wheat, and told stories of what they had done while they had been at sea. They talked about the Pacific as boys would talk about a wood that they had been nutting in, and if anyone had understood them, he could have gone away and made such a chart of that ocean as never was. The three- and four-year-old holluschickie romped down from Hutchinson's Hill, crying: 'Out of the way, youngsters! The sea is deep, and you don't know all that's in it yet. Wait till you've rounded the Horn. Hi, you yearling, where did you get that white coat?'

'I didn't get it,' said Kotick; 'it grew.' And just as he was going to roll the speaker over, a couple of black-haired men with flat red faces came from behind a sand-dune, and Kotick, who had never seen a man before, coughed and lowered his head. The holluschickie just bundled off a few yards and sat staring stupidly. The men were no less than Kerick Booterin, the chief of the seal-hunters on the island, and Patalamon, his son. They came from the little village not half a mile from the seal-nurseries, and they were deciding what seals they would drive up to the killing-pens (for the seals were driven just like sheep), to be turned into sealskin jackets later on.

'Ho!' said Patalamon. 'Look! There's a white seal!'

Kerick Booterin turned nearly white under his oil and smoke, for he was an Aleut, and Aleuts are not clean people. Then he began to mutter a prayer. 'Don't touch him, Patalamon. There has never been a white seal since – since I was born. Perhaps it is old Zaharrof's ghost. He was lost last year in the big gale.'

'I'm not going near him,' said Patalamon. 'He's unlucky. Do you really think he is old Zaharrof come back? I owe him for some gulls' eggs.'

'Don't look at him,' said Kerick. 'Head off that drove of four-year-olds. The men ought to skin two hundred today, but it's the beginning of the season, and they are new to the work. A hundred will do. Quick!'

Patalamon rattled a pair of seal's shoulder-bones in front of a herd of holluschickie, and they stopped dead, puffing and blowing. Then he stepped near, and the seals began to move, and Kerick headed them inland, and they never tried to get back to their companions. Hundreds and hundreds of thousands of seals watched them being driven, but they went on playing just

the same. Kotick was the only one who asked questions, and none of his companions could tell him anything, except that the men always drove seals in that way for six weeks or two months of every year.

'I am going to follow,' he said, and his eyes nearly popped out of his head as he shuffled along in the wake of the herd.

'The white seal is coming after us,' cried Patalamon. 'That's the first time a seal has ever come to the killing-grounds alone.'

'Hsh! Don't look behind you,' said Kerick. 'It *is* Zaharrof's ghost! I must speak to the priest about this.'

The distance to the killing-grounds was only half a mile, but it took an hour to cover, because if the seals went too fast Kerick knew that they would get heated and then their fur would come off in patches when they were skinned. So they went on very slowly, past Sea-Lion's Neck, past Webster House, till they came to the Salt House just beyond the sight of the seals on the beach. Kotick followed, panting and wondering. He thought that he was at the world's end, but the roar of the seal-nurseries behind him sounded as loud as the roar of a train in a tunnel. Then Kerick sat down on the moss and pulled out a heavy pewter watch and let the drove cool off for thirty minutes, and Kotick could hear the fog-dew dripping from the brim of his cap. Then ten or twelve men, each with an iron-bound club three or four feet long, came up, and Kerick pointed out one or two of the drove that were bitten by their companions or were too hot, and the men kicked those aside with their heavy boots made of the skin of a walrus's throat, and then Kerick said: 'Let go!' and then the men clubbed the seals on the head as fast as they could.

Ten minutes later little Kotick did not recognise his friends any more, for their skins were ripped off from the nose to the hind flippers – whipped off and thrown down on the ground in a pile.

That was enough for Kotick. He turned and galloped (a seal can gallop very swiftly for a short time) back to the sea, his little new moustache bristling with horror. At Sea-Lion's Neck, where the great sea-lions sit on the edge of the surf, he flung himself flipper over head into the cool water, and rocked there, gasping miserably. 'What's here?' said a sea-lion gruffly; for as a rule the sea-lions keep themselves to themselves.

'*Scoochnie! Ochen Scoochnie!* [I'm lonesome, very lonesome!]' said Kotick. 'They're killing all the holluschickie on *all* the beaches!'

The sea-lion turned his head inshore. 'Nonsense!' he said; 'your friends are making as much noise as ever. You must have seen old Kerick polishing off a drove. He's done that for thirty years.'

'It's horrible,' said Kotick, backing water as a wave went over him, and steadying himself with a screw-stroke of his flippers that brought him up all standing within three inches of a jagged edge of rock.

'Well done for a yearling!' said the sea-lion, who could appreciate good swimming. 'I suppose it *is* rather awful from your way of looking at it; but if you seals will come here year after year, of course the men get to know of it, and unless you can find an island where no men ever come, you will always be driven.'

'Isn't there any such island?' began Kotick.

'I've followed the *poltoos* [the halibut] for twenty years, and I can't say I've found it yet. But look here – you seem to have a fondness for talking to your betters; suppose you go to Walrus Islet and talk to Sea Vitch. He may know something. Don't flounce off like that. It's a six-mile swim, and if I were you I should haul out and take a nap first, little one.'

Kotick thought that that was good advice, so he swam round to his own beach, hauled out, and slept for half an hour, twitching all over, as seals will. Then he headed straight for Walrus Islet, a little low sheet of rocky island almost due north-east from Novastoshnah, all ledges of rocks and gulls' nests, where the walrus herded by themselves.

He landed close to old Sea Vitch – the big, ugly, bloated, pimpled, fat-necked, long-tusked walrus of the North Pacific, who has no manners except when he is asleep – as he was then, with his hind flippers half in and half out of the surf.

'Wake up!' barked Kotick, for the gulls were making a great noise.

'Hah! Ho! Hmph! What's that?' said Sea Vitch, and he struck the next walrus a blow with his tusks and waked him up, and the next struck the next, and so on till they were all awake and staring in every direction but the right one.

'Hi! It's me,' said Kotick, bobbing in the surf and looking like a little white slug.

'Well! May I be – skinned!' said Sea Vitch, and they all looked at Kotick as you can fancy a club full of drowsy old gentlemen would look at a little boy. Kotick did not care to hear any more about skinning just then; he had seen enough of it; so he called out: 'Isn't there any place for seals to go where men don't ever come?'

'Go and find out,' said Sea Vitch, shutting his eyes. 'Run away. We're busy here.'

Kotick made his dolphin-jump in the air and shouted as loud as he could: 'Clam-eater! Clam-eater!' He knew that Sea Vitch never caught a fish in his life, but always rooted for clams and seaweeds, though he pretended to be a very terrible person. Naturally the Chickies and the Gooverooskies and the Epatkas, the Burgomaster Gulls and the Kittiwakes and the Puffins, who are always looking for a chance to be rude, took up the cry, and – so Limmershin told me – for nearly five minutes you could not have heard a gun fired on Walrus Islet. All the population was yelling and screaming: 'Clam-eater! *Stareek!* [old man!]' while Sea Vitch rolled from side to side grunting and coughing.

'*Now* will you tell?' said Kotick, all out of breath.

'Go and ask Sea Cow,' said Sea Vitch. 'If he is living still, he'll be able to tell you.'

'How shall I know Sea Cow when I meet him?' said Kotick, sheering off.

'He's the only thing in the sea uglier than Sea Vitch,' screamed a Burgomaster Gull, wheeling under Sea Vitch's nose. 'Uglier, and with worse manners! *Stareek!*'

Kotick swam back to Novastoshnah, leaving the gulls to scream. There he found that no one sympathised with him in his little attempts to discover a quiet place for the seals. They told him that men had always driven the holluschickie – it was part of the day's work – and that if he did not like to see ugly things he should not have gone to the killing-grounds. But none of the other seals had seen the killing, and that made the difference between him and his friends. Besides, Kotick was a white seal.

'What you must do,' said old Sea Catch, after he had heard his son's adventures, 'is to grow up and be a big seal like your father, and have a nursery on the beach, and then they will leave you alone. In another five years you ought to be able to fight for yourself.' Even gentle Matkah, his mother, said: 'You will never be able to stop the killing. Go and play in the sea, Kotick.' And Kotick went off and danced the Fire Dance with a very heavy little heart.

That autumn he left the beach as soon as he could, and set off alone because of a notion in his bullet-head. He was going to find Sea Cow, if there was such a person in the sea, and he was going to find a quiet island with good firm beaches for seals to live on, where men could not get at them. So he explored and explored by himself from the North to the South Pacific, swimming as much as three hundred miles in a day and a night. He met with more adventures than can be told, and narrowly escaped being caught by the Basking Shark, and the Spotted Shark, and the Hammerhead, and he met all the untrustworthy ruffians that loaf up and down the seas, and the heavy polite fish, and the scarlet-spotted scallops that are moored in one place for hundreds of years, and grow very proud of it; but he never met Sea Cow, and he never found an island that he could fancy.

If the beach was good and hard, with a slope behind it for seals to play on, there was always the smoke of a whaler on the horizon, boiling down blubber, and Kotick knew what *that* meant. Or else he could see that seals had once visited the island and been killed off, and Kotick knew that where men had come once they would come again.

He picked up with an old stumpy-tailed albatross, who told him that Kerguelen Island was the very place for peace and quiet, and when Kotick went down there he was all but smashed to pieces against some wicked black cliffs in a heavy sleet-storm with lightning and thunder. Yet as he pulled out against the gale he could see that even there had once been a seal-nursery. And so it was in all the other islands that he visited.

Limmershin gave a long list of them, for he said that Kotick spent five seasons exploring, with a four months' rest each year at Novastoshnah, when the holluschickie used to make fun of him and his imaginary islands. He went to the Galapagos, a horrid dry place on the Equator, where he was nearly baked to death; he went to the Georgia Islands, the South Orkneys, Emerald Island, Little Nightingale Island, Gough's Island, Bouvet's Island, the Crossets, and even to a little speck of an island south of the Cape of Good Hope. But everywhere the People of the Sea told him the same things. Seals had come to those islands once upon a time, but men had killed them all off. Even when he swam thousands of miles out of the Pacific, and got to a place called Cape Corrientes (that was when he was coming back from Gough's Island), he found a few hundred mangy seals on a rock, and they told him that men came there too.

That nearly broke his heart, and he headed round the Horn back to his own beaches; and on his way north he hauled out on an island full of green trees, where he found an old, old seal who was dying, and Kotick caught fish for him, and told him all his sorrows. 'Now,' said Kotick, 'I am going back to Novastoshnah, and if I am driven to the killing-pens with the holluschickie I shall not care.'

The old seal said: 'Try once more. I am the last of the Lost Rookery of Masafuera, and in the days when men killed us by the hundred thousand there was a story on the beaches that some day a white seal would come out of the north and lead the seal people to a quiet place. I am old and I shall never live to see that day, but others will. Try once more.'

And Kotick curled up his moustache (it was a beauty), and said: 'I am the only white seal that has ever been born on the beaches, and I am the only seal, black or white, who ever thought of looking for new islands.'

That cheered him immensely; and when he came back to Novastoshnah that summer, Matkah, his mother, begged him to marry and settle down, for he was no longer a holluschick, but a full-grown sea-catch, with a curly white mane on his shoulders, as heavy, as big, and as fierce as his father. 'Give me another season,' he said. 'Remember, Mother, it is always the seventh wave that goes farthest up the beach.'

Curiously enough, there was another seal who thought that she would put off marrying till the next year, and Kotick danced the Fire Dance with her all down Lukannon Beach the night before he set off on his last exploration.

This time he went westward, because he had fallen on the trail of a great shoal of halibut, and he needed at least one hundred pounds of fish a day to keep him in good condition. He chased them till he was tired, and then he curled himself up and went to sleep on the hollows of the groundswell that sets in to Copper Island. He knew the coast perfectly well, so about midnight, when he felt himself gently bumped on a weed-bed, he said, 'Hm, tide's running strong tonight,' and turning over under water opened his eyes slowly and stretched. Then he jumped like a cat, for he saw huge things nosing about in the shoal water and browsing on the heavy fringes of the weeds.

'By the Great Combers of Magellan!' he said, beneath his moustache. 'Who in the Deep Sea are these people?'

They were like no walrus, sea-lion, seal, bear, whale, shark, fish, squid, or scallop that Kotick had ever seen before. They were between twenty and thirty feet long, and they had no hind flippers, but a shovel-like tail that looked as if it had been whittled out of wet leather. Their heads were the most foolish-looking things you ever saw, and they balanced on the ends of their tails in deep water when they weren't grazing, bowing solemnly to one another and waving their front flippers as a fat man waves his arm.

'Ahem!' said Kotick. 'Good sport, gentlemen?' The big things answered by bowing and waving their flippers like the Frog-Footman. When they began feeding again Kotick saw that their upper lip was split into two pieces that they could twitch apart about a foot and bring together again with a whole bushel of seaweed between the splits. They tucked the stuff into their mouths and chomped solemnly.

'Messy style of feeding, that,' said Kotick. They bowed again, and Kotick began to lose his temper. 'Very good,' he said. 'If you do happen to have an extra joint in your front flipper you needn't show off so. I see you bow gracefully, but I should like to know your names.' The split lips moved and twitched, and the glassy green eyes stared; but they did not speak.

'Well!' said Kotick. 'You're the only people I've ever met uglier than Sea Vitch – and with worse manners.'

Then he remembered in a flash what the Burgomaster Gull had screamed to him when he was a little yearling at Walrus Islet, and he tumbled backward in the water, for he knew that he had found Sea Cow at last.

The sea cows went on schlooping and grazing and chomping in the weed, and Kotick asked them questions in every language that he had picked up in his travels: and the Sea People talk nearly as many languages as human beings. But the Sea Cow did not answer, because Sea Cow cannot talk. He has only six bones in his neck where he ought to have seven, and they say under the sea that that prevents him from speaking even to his companions; but, as you know, he has an extra joint in his fore flipper, and by waving it up and down and about he makes a sort of clumsy telegraphic code.

By daylight Kotick's mane was standing on end and his temper was gone where the dead crabs go. Then the Sea Cow began to travel northward very slowly, stopping to hold absurd bowing councils from time to time, and Kotick followed them, saying to himself: 'People who are such idiots as these are would have been killed long ago if they hadn't found out some safe island; and what is good enough for the Sea Cow is good enough for the Sea Catch. All the same, I wish they'd hurry.'

It was weary work for Kotick. The herd never went more than forty or fifty miles a day, and stopped to feed at night, and kept close to the shore all the time; while Kotick swam round them, and over them, and under them, but he could not hurry them on one half-mile. As they went farther north they held a bowing council every few hours, and Kotick nearly bit off his moustache with impatience till he saw that they were following up a warm current of water, and then he respected them more.

One night they sank through the shiny water – sank like stones – and, for the first time since he had known them, began to swim quickly. Kotick followed, and the pace astonished him, for he never dreamed that Sea Cow was anything of a swimmer. They headed for a cliff by the shore – a cliff that ran down into deep water, and plunged into a dark hole at the foot of it, twenty fathoms under the sea. It was a long, long swim, and Kotick badly wanted fresh air before he was out of the dark tunnel that they led him through.

'My wig!' he said, when he rose, gasping and puffing, into open water at the farther end. 'It was a long dive, but it was worth it.'

The sea cows had separated, and were browsing lazily along the edges of the finest beaches that Kotick had ever seen. There were long stretches of smooth-worn rock running for miles, exactly fitted to make seal-nurseries, and there were playgrounds of hard sand sloping inland behind them, and there were rollers for seals to dance in, and long grass to roll in, and sand-dunes to climb up and down; and, best of all, Kotick knew by the feel of the water, which never deceives a true Sea Catch, that no men had ever come there.

The first thing he did was to assure himself that the fishing was good, and then he swam along the beaches and counted up the delightful low sandy islands half hidden in the beautiful rolling fog. Away to the northward out to sea ran a line of bars and shoals and rocks that would never let a ship come within six miles of the beach; and between the islands and the mainland was a stretch of deep water that ran up to the perpendicular cliffs, and somewhere below the cliffs was the mouth of the tunnel.

'It's Novastoshnah over again, but ten times better,' said Kotick. 'Sea Cow must be wiser than I thought. Men can't come down the cliffs, even if there were any men; and the shoals to seaward would knock a ship to splinters. If any place in the sea is safe, this is it.'

He began to think of the seal he had left behind him, but though he was in a hurry to go back to Novastoshnah, he thoroughly explored the new country, so that he would be able to answer all questions.

Then he dived and made sure of the mouth of the tunnel, and raced through to the southward. No one but a sea cow or a seal would have dreamed of there being such a place, and when he looked back at the cliffs even Kotick could hardly believe that he had been under them.

He was six days going home, though he was not swimming slowly; and when he hauled out just above Sea-Lion's Neck the first person he met was the seal who had been waiting for him, and she saw by the look in his eyes that he had found his island at last.

But the holluschickie and Sea Catch, his father, and all the other seals, laughed at him when he told them what he had discovered, and a young seal about his own age said: 'This is all very well, Kotick, but you can't come from no one knows where and order us off like this. Remember we've been fighting for our nurseries, and that's a thing you never did. You preferred prowling about in the sea.'

The other seals laughed at this, and the young seal began twisting his head from side to side. He had just married that year, and was making a great fuss about it.

'I've no nursery to fight for,' said Kotick. 'I want only to show you all a place where you will be safe. What's the use of fighting?'

'Oh, if you're trying to back out, of course I've no more to say,' said the young seal, with an ugly chuckle.

'Will you come with me if I win?' said Kotick; and a green light came into his eyes, for he was very angry at having to fight at all.

'Very good,' said the young seal carelessly. '*If* you win, I'll come.'

He had no time to change his mind, for Kotick's head darted out and his teeth sank in the blubber of the young seal's neck. Then he threw himself back on his haunches and hauled his enemy down the beach, shook him, and knocked him over. Then Kotick roared to the seals: 'I've done my best for you these five seasons past. I've found you the island where you'll be safe, but unless your heads are dragged off your silly necks you won't believe. I'm going to teach you now. Look out for yourselves!'

Limmershin told me that never in his life – and Limmershin sees ten thousand big seals fighting every year – never in all his little life did he see anything like Kotick's charge into the nurseries. He flung himself at the biggest sea-catch he could find, caught him by the throat, choked him and bumped him and banged him till he grunted for mercy, and then threw him aside and attacked the next. You see, Kotick had never fasted for four months as the big seals did every year, and his deep-sea swimming-trips kept him in perfect condition, and, best of all, he had never fought before. His curly white mane stood up with rage, and his eyes flamed, and his big dogteeth glistened, and he was splendid to look at.

Old Sea Catch, his father, saw him tearing past, hauling the grizzled old seals about as though they had been halibut, and upsetting the young bachelors in all directions; and Sea Catch gave one roar and shouted: 'He may be a fool, but he is the best fighter on the Beaches. Don't tackle your father, my son! He's with you!'

Kotick roared in answer, and old Sea Catch waddled in, his moustache on end, blowing like a locomotive, while Matkah and the seal that was going to marry Kotick cowered down and admired their menfolk. It was a gorgeous fight, for the two fought as long as there was a seal that dared lift up his head, and then they paraded grandly up and down the beach side by side, bellowing.

At night, just as the Northern Lights were winking and flashing through the fog, Kotick climbed a bare rock and looked down on the scattered nurseries and the torn and bleeding seals. 'Now,' he said, 'I've taught you your lesson.'

'My wig!' said old Sea Catch, boosting himself up stiffly, for he was fearfully mauled. 'The Killer Whale himself could not have cut them up worse. Son, I'm proud of you, and what's more, I'll come with you to your island – if there is such a place.'

'Here you, fat pigs of the sea! Who comes with me to the Sea Cow's tunnel? Answer, or I shall teach you again,' roared Kotick.

There was a murmur like the ripple of the tide all up and down the beaches. 'We will come,' said thousands of tired voices. 'We will follow Kotick, the White Seal.'

Then Kotick dropped his head between his shoulders and shut his eyes proudly. He was not a white seal any more, but red from head to tail. All the same, he would have scorned to look at or touch one of his wounds.

A week later he and his army (nearly ten thousand holluschickie and old seals) went away north to the Sea Cow's tunnel, Kotick leading them, and the seals that stayed at Novastoshnah called them idiots. But next spring, when they all met off the fishing-banks of the Pacific, Kotick's seals told such tales of the new beaches beyond Sea Cow's tunnel that more and more seals left Novastoshnah.

Of course it was not all done at once, for the seals need a long time to turn things over in their minds, but year by year more seals went away from Novastoshnah, and Lukannon, and the other nurseries, to the quiet, sheltered beaches where Kotick sits all the summer through, getting bigger and fatter and stronger each year, while the holluschickie play round him, in that sea where no man comes.

Lukannon

This is the great deep-sea song that all the St Paul seals sing when they are heading back to their beaches in the summer. It is a sort of very sad seal national anthem.

I met my mates in the morning (and oh, but I am old!)
Where roaring on the ledges the summer ground-swell rolled;
I heard them lift the chorus that drowned the breakers' song –
The Beaches of Lukannon – two million voices strong!

The song of pleasant stations beside the salt lagoons,
The song of blowing squadrons that shuffled down the dunes,
The song of midnight dances that churned the sea to flame –
The Beaches of Lukannon – before the sealers came!

I met my mates in the morning (I'll never meet them more!);
They came and went in legions that darkened all the shore.
And through the foam-flecked offing as far as voice could reach
We hailed the landing-parties and we sang them up the beach.

The Beaches of Lukannon – the winter-wheat so tall –
The dripping, crinkled lichens, and the sea-fog drenching all!
The platforms of our playground, all shining smooth and worn!
The Beaches of Lukannon – the home where we were born!

I meet my mates in the morning, a broken, scattered band.
Men shoot us in the water and club us on the land;
Men drive us to the Salt House like silly sheep and tame,
And still we sing Lukannon – before the sealers came.

Wheel down, wheel down to southward! Oh, Gooverooska, go!
And tell the Deep-Sea Viceroys the story of our woe;
Ere, empty as the shark's egg the tempest flings ashore,
The Beaches of Lukannon shall know their sons no more!

Rikki-tikki-tavi

At the hole where he went in
Red-Eye called to Wrinkle-Skin.
Hear what little Red-Eye saith:
'Nag, come up and dance with death!'

Eye to eye and head to head,
    (*Keep the measure, Nag.*)
This shall end when one is dead;
    (*At thy pleasure, Nag.*)
Turn for turn and twist for twist –
    (*Run and hide thee, Nag.*)
Hah! The hooded Death has missed!
    (*Woe betide thee, Nag!*)

This is the story of the great war that Rikki-tikki-tavi fought single-handed, through the bathrooms of the big bungalow in Segowlee cantonment. Darzee, the tailor-bird, helped him, and Chuchundra, the musk-rat, who never comes out into the middle of the floor, but always creeps round by the wall, gave him advice; but Rikki-tikki did the real fighting.

He was a mongoose, rather like a little cat in his fur and his tail, but quite like a weasel in his head and his habits. His eyes and the end of his restless nose were pink; he could scratch himself anywhere he pleased, with any leg, front or back, that he chose to use; he could fluff up his tail till it looked like a bottle-brush, and his war-cry, as he scuttled through the long grass, was: '*Rikk-tikk-tikki-tikki-tchk!*'

One day, a high summer flood washed him out of the burrow where he lived with his father and mother, and carried him, kicking and clucking, down a roadside ditch. He found a little wisp of grass floating there, and clung to it till he lost his senses. When he revived, he was lying in the hot sun on the middle of a garden path, very draggled indeed, and a small boy was saying: 'Here's a dead mongoose. Let's have a funeral.'

'No,' said his mother; 'let's take him in and dry him. Perhaps he isn't really dead.'

They took him into the house, and a big man picked him up between his finger and thumb, and said he was not dead but half choked; so they wrapped him in cotton-wool, and warmed him, and he opened his eyes and sneezed.

'Now,' said the big man (he was an Englishman who had just moved into the bungalow); 'don't frighten him, and we'll see what he'll do.'

It is the hardest thing in the world to frighten a mongoose, because he is eaten up from nose to tail with curiosity. The motto of all the mongoose family is, 'Run and find out'; and Rikki-tikki was a true mongoose. He looked at the cotton-wool, decided that it was not good to eat, ran all round the table, sat up and put his fur in order, scratched himself, and jumped on the small boy's shoulder.

Rikki-tikki looked down between the boy's collar and neck,

'Don't be frightened, Teddy,' said his father. 'That's his way of making friends.'

'Ouch! He's tickling under my chin,' said Teddy.

Rikki-tikki looked down between the boy's collar and neck, snuffed at his ear, and climbed down to the floor, where he sat rubbing his nose.

'Good gracious,' said Teddy's mother, 'and that's a wild creature! I suppose he's so tame because we've been kind to him.'

'All mongooses are like that,' said her husband. 'If Teddy doesn't pick him up by the tail, or try to put him in a cage, he'll run in and out of the house all day long. Let's give him something to eat.'

They gave him a little piece of raw meat. Rikki-tikki liked it immensely, and when it was finished he went out into the veranda and sat in the sunshine and fluffed up his fur to make it dry to the roots. Then he felt better.

'There are more things to find out about in this house,' he said to himself, 'than all my family could find out in all their lives. I shall certainly stay and find out.'

He spent all that day roaming over the house. He nearly drowned himself in the bathtubs, put his nose into the ink on a writing-table, and burnt it on the end of the big man's cigar, for he climbed up in the big man's lap to see how writing was done. At nightfall he ran into Teddy's nursery to watch

*He put his nose into the ink on a
writing-table*

how kerosene-lamps were lighted, and when Teddy went to bed Rikki-tikki climbed up too; but he was a restless companion, because he had to get up and attend to every noise all through the night, and find out what made it. Teddy's mother and father came in, the last thing, to look at their boy, and Rikki-tikki was awake on the pillow. 'I don't like that,' said Teddy's mother; 'he may bite the child.' 'He'll do no such thing,' said the father. 'Teddy's safer with that little beast than if he had a bloodhound to watch him. If a snake came into the nursery now –'

But Teddy's mother wouldn't think of anything so awful.

Early in the morning Rikki-tikki came to early breakfast in the veranda riding on Teddy's shoulder, and they gave him banana and some boiled egg; and he sat on all their laps one after the other, because every well-brought-up mongoose always hopes to be a house-mongoose someday and have rooms to run about in, and Rikki-tikki's mother (she used to live in the General's house at Segowlee) had carefully told Rikki what to do if ever he came across white men.

Then Rikki-tikki went out into the garden to see what was to be seen. It was a large garden, only half cultivated, with bushes as big as summerhouses of Marshal Niel roses, lime and orange trees, clumps of bamboos, and thickets of high grass. Rikki-tikki licked his lips. 'This is a splendid hunting-ground,' he said, and his tail grew bottle-brushy at the thought of it, and he scuttled up and down the garden, snuffing here and there till he heard very sorrowful voices in a thornbush.

Rikki-tikki was awake on the pillow

*Rikki-tikki came to breakfast
on Teddy's shoulder*

It was Darzee, the tailor-bird, and his wife. They had made a beautiful nest by pulling two big leaves together and stitching them up the edges with fibres, and had filled the hollow with cotton and downy fluff. The nest swayed to and fro, as they sat on the rim and cried.

'What is the matter?' asked Rikki-tikki.

'We are very miserable,' said Darzee. 'One of our babies fell out of the nest yesterday, and Nag ate him.'

'H'm!' said Rikki-tikki, 'that is very sad – but I am a stranger here. Who is Nag?'

Darzee and his wife only cowered down in the nest without answering, for from the thick grass at the foot of the bush there came a low hiss – a horrid cold sound that made Rikki-tikki jump back two clear feet.

Then inch by inch out of the grass rose up the head and spread hood of Nag, the big black cobra, and he was five feet long from tongue to tail. When he had lifted one-third of himself clear of the ground, he stayed balancing to and fro exactly as a dandelion-tuft balances in the wind, and he looked at Rikki-tikki with the wicked snake's eyes that never change their expression, whatever the snake may be thinking of.

'We are very miserable,' said Darzee.

'I am Nag. Look, and be afraid!'

'Who is Nag?' said he. '*I* am Nag. The great god Brahm put his mark upon all our people when the first cobra spread his hood to keep the sun off Brahm as he slept. Look, and be afraid!'

He spread out his hood more than ever, and Rikki-tikki saw the spectacle-mark on the back of it that looks exactly like the eye part of a hook-and-eye fastening. He was afraid for the minute; but it is impossible for a mongoose to stay frightened for any length of time, and though Rikki-tikki had never met a live cobra before, his mother had fed him on dead ones, and he knew that all a grown mongoose's business in life was to fight and eat snakes. Nag knew that too, and at the bottom of his cold heart he was afraid.

'Well,' said Rikki-tikki, and his tail began to fluff up again, 'marks or no marks, do you think it is right for you to eat fledglings out of a nest?'

Nag was thinking to himself, and watching the least little movement in the grass behind Rikki-tikki. He knew that mongooses in the garden meant death sooner or later for him and his family, but he wanted to get Rikki-tikki off his guard. So he dropped his head a little, and put it on one side.

'Let us talk,' he said. 'You eat eggs. Why should not I eat birds?'

'Behind you! Look behind you!' sang Darzee.

Rikki-tikki knew better than to waste time in staring. He jumped up in the air as high as he could go, and just under him whizzed by the head of Nagaina, Nag's wicked wife. She had crept up behind him as he was talking, to make an end of him; and he heard her savage hiss as the stroke missed. He came down almost across her back, and if he had been an old mongoose he would have known that then was the time to break her back with one bite; but he was

*He jumped up in the air as high as he could go, and just under
him whizzed by the head of Nagaina*

afraid of the terrible lashing return-stroke of the cobra. He bit, indeed, but
did not bite long enough, and he jumped clear of the whisking tail, leaving
Nagaina torn and angry.

'Wicked, wicked Darzee!' said Nag, lashing up as high as he could reach
toward the nest in the thornbush; but Darzee had built it out of reach of
snakes, and it only swayed to and fro.

Rikki-tikki felt his eyes growing red and hot (when a mongoose's eyes
grow red, he is angry), and he sat back on his tail and hind legs like a little
kangaroo, and looked all round him, and chattered with rage. But Nag and
Nagaina had disappeared into the grass. When a snake misses its stroke, it
never says anything or gives any sign of what it means to do next. Rikki-tikki
did not care to follow them, for he did not feel sure that he could manage two
snakes at once. So he trotted off to the gravel path near the house, and sat
down to think. It was a serious matter for him.

If you read the old books of natural history, you will find they say that
when the mongoose fights the snake and happens to get bitten, he runs off
and eats some herb that cures him. That is not true. The victory is only a

matter of quickness of eye and quickness of foot – snake's blow against mongoose's jump – and as no eye can follow the motion of a snake's head when it strikes, that makes things much more wonderful than any magic herb. Rikki-tikki knew he was a young mongoose, and it made him all the more pleased to think that he had managed to escape a blow from behind. It gave him confidence in himself, and when Teddy came running down the path, Rikki-tikki was ready to be petted.

But just as Teddy was stooping, something flinched a little in the dust, and a tiny voice said: 'Be careful. I am death!' It was Karait, the dusty brown snakeling that lies for choice on the dusty earth; and his bite is as dangerous as the cobra's. But he is so small that nobody thinks of him, and so he does the more harm to people.

Rikki-tikki's eyes grew red again, and he danced up to Karait with the peculiar rocking, swaying motion that he had inherited from his family. It looks very funny, but it is so perfectly balanced a gait that you can fly off from it at any angle you please; and in dealing with snakes this is an advantage. If Rikki-tikki had only known, he was doing a much more dangerous thing than fighting Nag, for Karait is so small, and can turn so quickly, that unless Rikki bit him close to the back of the head, he would get the return-stroke in his eye or lip. But Rikki did not know: his eyes were all red, and he rocked back and forth, looking for a good place to hold. Karait struck out. Rikki jumped sideways and tried to run in, but the wicked little dusty grey head lashed within a fraction of his shoulder, and he had to jump over the body, and the head followed his heels close.

Teddy shouted to the house: 'Oh, look here! Our mongoose is killing a snake'; and Rikki-tikki heard a scream from Teddy's mother. His father ran out with a stick, but by the time he came up, Karait had lunged out once too far, and Rikki-tikki had sprung, jumped on the snake's back, dropped his head far between his forelegs, bitten as high up the back as he could get hold, and rolled away. That bite paralysed Karait, and Rikki-tikki was just going to eat him up from the tail, after the custom of his family at dinner, when he remembered that a full meal makes a slow mongoose, and if he wanted all his strength and quickness ready, he must keep himself thin.

He went away for a dust-bath under the castor-oil bushes, while Teddy's father beat the dead Karait. 'What is the use of that?' thought Rikki-tikki. 'I have settled it all'; and then Teddy's mother picked him up from the dust and hugged him, crying that he had saved Teddy from death, and Teddy's father said that he was a providence, and Teddy looked on with big scared eyes. Rikki-tikki was rather amused at all the fuss, which, of course, he did not understand. Teddy's mother might just as well have petted Teddy for playing in the dust. Rikki was thoroughly enjoying himself.

That night, at dinner, walking to and fro among the wineglasses on the table, he could have stuffed himself three times over with nice things; but he remembered Nag and Nagaina, and though it was very pleasant to be patted

In the dark he ran up against Chuchundra, the musk-rat

and petted by Teddy's mother, and to sit on Teddy's shoulder, his eyes would get red from time to time, and he would go off into his long war-cry of '*Rikk-tikk-tikki-tikki-tchk!*'

Teddy carried him off to bed, and insisted on Rikki-tikki sleeping under his chin. Rikki-tikki was too well-bred to bite or scratch, but as soon as Teddy was asleep he went off for his nightly walk round the house, and in the dark he ran up against Chuchundra, the musk-rat, creeping round by the wall. Chuchundra is a broken-hearted little beast. He whimpers and cheeps all the night, trying to make up his mind to run into the middle of the room, but he never gets there.

'Don't kill me,' said Chuchundra, almost weeping. 'Rikki-tikki, don't kill me.'

'Do you think a snake-killer kills musk-rats?' said Rikki-tikki scornfully.

'Those who kill snakes get killed by snakes,' said Chuchundra, more sorrowfully than ever. 'And how am I to be sure that Nag won't mistake me for you some dark night?'

'There's not the least danger,' said Rikki-tikki; 'but Nag is in the garden, and I know you don't go there.'

'My cousin Chua, the rat, told me – ' said Chuchundra, and then he stopped.

'Told you what?'

'H'sh! Nag is everywhere, Rikki-tikki. You should have talked to Chua in the garden.'

'I didn't – so you must tell me. Quick, Chuchundra, or I'll bite you!'

Chuchundra sat down and cried till the tears rolled off his whiskers. 'I am a very poor man,' he sobbed. 'I never had spirit enough to run out into the middle of the room. H'sh! I mustn't tell you anything. Can't you *hear*, Rikki-tikki?'

Rikki-tikki listened. The house was as still as still, but he thought he could just catch the faintest *scratch-scratch* in the world – a noise as faint as that of a wasp walking on a windowpane – the dry scratch of a snake's scales on brickwork.

'That's Nag or Nagaina,' he said to himself; 'and he is crawling into the bathroom sluice. You're right, Chuchundra; I should have talked to Chua.'

He stole off to Teddy's bathroom, but there was nothing there, and then to Teddy's mother's bathroom. At the bottom of the smooth plaster wall there was a brick pulled out to make a sluice for the bath-water, and as Rikki-tikki stole in by the masonry curb where the bath is put, he heard Nag and Nagaina whispering together outside in the moonlight.

'When the house is emptied of people,' said Nagaina to her husband, '*he* will have to go away, and then the garden will be our own again. Go in quietly, and remember that the big man who killed Karait is the first one to bite. Then come out and tell me, and we will hunt for Rikki-tikki together.'

'But are you sure that there is anything to be gained by killing the people?' said Nag.

'Everything. When there were no people in the bungalow, did we have any mongoose in the garden? So long as the bungalow is empty, we are king and queen of the garden; and remember that as soon as our eggs in the melon-bed hatch (as they may tomorrow), our children will need room and quiet.'

'I had not thought of that,' said Nag. 'I will go, but there is no need that we should hunt for Rikki-tikki afterward. I will kill the big man and his wife, and the child if I can, and come away quietly. Then the bungalow will be empty, and Rikki-tikki will go.'

Rikki-tikki tingled all over with rage and hatred at this, and then Nag's head came through the sluice, and his five feet of cold body followed it. Angry as he was, Rikki-tikki was very frightened as he saw the size of the big cobra. Nag coiled himself up, raised his head, and looked into the bathroom in the dark, and Rikki could see his eyes glitter.

'Now, if I kill him here, Nagaina will know; and if I fight him on the open floor, the odds are in his favour. What am I to do?' said Rikki-tikki-tavi.

Nag waved to and fro, and then Rikki-tikki heard him drinking from the biggest water-jar that was used to fill the bath. 'That is good,' said the snake. 'Now, when Karait was killed, the big man had a stick. He may have that stick still, but when he comes in to bathe in the morning he will not have a stick. I shall wait here till he comes. Nagaina – do you hear me? – I shall wait here in the cool till daytime.'

There was no answer from outside, so Rikki-tikki knew Nagaina had gone away. Nag coiled himself down, coil by coil, round the bulge at the bottom of the water-jar, and Rikki-tikki stayed still as death. After an hour he began to move, muscle by muscle, toward the jar. Nag was asleep, and Rikki-tikki looked at his big back, wondering which would be the best place for a good hold. 'If I don't break his back at the first jump,' said Rikki, 'he can still fight; and if he fights – oh, Rikki!' He looked at the thickness of the neck below the hood, but that was too much for him; and a bite near the tail would only make Nag savage.

'It must be the head,' he said at last; 'the head above the hood; and when I am once there, I must not let go.'

Then he jumped. The head was lying a little clear of the water-jar, under the curve of it; and, as his teeth met, Rikki braced his back against the bulge of the red earthenware to hold down the head. This gave him just one second's purchase, and he made the most of it. Then he was battered to and fro as a rat is shaken by a dog – to and fro on the floor, up and down, and round in great circles; but his eyes were red, and he held on as the body cart-whipped over the floor, upsetting the tin dipper and the soap-dish and the flesh-brush, and banged against the tin side of the bath. As he held he closed his jaws tighter and tighter, for he made sure he would be banged to death, and, for the honour of his family, he preferred to be found with his teeth locked. He was dizzy, aching, and felt shaken to pieces when something went off like a thunderclap just behind him; a hot wind knocked him senseless, and red fire singed his fur. The big man had been wakened by the noise, and had fired both barrels of a shotgun into Nag just behind the hood.

Then he was battered to and fro as a rat is shaken by a dog

Rikki-tikki held on with his eyes shut, for now he was quite sure he was dead; but the head did not move, and the big man picked him up and said: 'It's the mongoose again, Alice; the little chap has saved *our* lives now.' Then Teddy's mother came in with a very white face, and saw what was left of Nag, and Rikki-tikki dragged himself to Teddy's bedroom and spent half the rest of the night shaking himself tenderly to find out whether he really was broken into forty pieces, as he fancied.

When morning came he was very stiff, but well pleased with his doings. 'Now I have Nagaina to settle with, and she will be worse than five Nags, and there's no knowing when the eggs she spoke of will hatch. Goodness! I must go and see Darzee,' he said.

Without waiting for breakfast, Rikki-tikki ran to the thornbush where Darzee was singing a song of triumph at the top of his voice. The news of Nag's death was all over the garden, for the sweeper had thrown the body on the rubbish-heap.

'Oh, you stupid tuft of feathers!' said Rikki-tikki angrily. 'Is this the time to sing?'

'Nag is dead – is dead – is dead!' sang Darzee. 'The valiant Rikki-tikki caught him by the head and held fast. The big man brought the bang-stick, and Nag fell in two pieces! He will never eat my babies again.'

'All that's true enough; but where's Nagaina?' said Rikki-tikki, looking carefully round him.

'Nagaina came to the bathroom sluice and called for Nag,' Darzee went on; 'and Nag came out on the end of a stick – the sweeper picked him up on the end of a stick and threw him upon the rubbish-heap. Let us sing about the great, the red-eyed Rikki-tikki!' and Darzee filled his throat and sang.

'If I could get up to your nest, I'd roll all your babies out!' said Rikki-tikki. 'You don't know when to do the right thing at the right time. You're safe enough in your nest there, but it's war for me down here. Stop singing a minute, Darzee.'

'For the great, the beautiful Rikki-tikki's sake I will stop,' said Darzee. 'What is it, O Killer of the terrible Nag?'

'Where is Nagaina, for the third time?'

'On the rubbish-heap by the stables, mourning for Nag. Great is Rikki-tikki with the white teeth.'

'Bother my white teeth! Have you ever heard where she keeps her eggs?'

'In the melon-bed, on the end nearest the wall, where the sun strikes nearly all day. She hid them there weeks ago.'

'And you never thought it worth while to tell me? The end nearest the wall, you said?'

'Rikki-tikki, you are not going to eat her eggs?'

'Not eat exactly; no. Darzee, if you have a grain of sense you will fly off to the stables and pretend that your wing is broken, and let Nagaina chase you away to this bush. I must get to the melon-bed, and if I went there now she'd see me.'

She fluttered in front of Nagaina and cried out: 'Oh, my wing is broken!'

Darzee was a feather-brained little fellow who could never hold more than one idea at a time in his head; and just because he knew that Nagaina's children were born in eggs like his own, he didn't think at first that it was fair to kill them. But his wife was a sensible bird, and she knew that cobras' eggs meant young cobras later on; so she flew off from the nest, and left Darzee to keep the babies warm, and continue his song about the death of Nag. Darzee was very like a man in some ways.

She fluttered in front of Nagaina by the rubbish-heap, and cried out: 'Oh, my wing is broken! The boy in the house threw a stone at me and broke it.' Then she fluttered more desperately than ever.

Nagaina lifted up her head and hissed: 'You warned Rikki-tikki when I would have killed him. Indeed and truly, you've chosen a bad place to be lame in.' And she moved toward Darzee's wife, slipping along over the dust.

'The boy broke it with a stone!' shrieked Darzee's wife.

'Well, it may be some consolation to you when you're dead to know that I shall settle accounts with the boy. My husband lies on the rubbish-heap this morning, but before night the boy in the house will lie very still. What is the use of running away? I am sure to catch you. Little fool, look at me!'

Darzee's wife knew better than to do *that*, for a bird who looks at a snake's eyes gets so frightened that she cannot move. Darzee's wife fluttered on, piping sorrowfully, and never leaving the ground, and Nagaina quickened her pace.

Rikki-tikki heard them going up the path from the stables, and he raced for the end of the melon-patch near the wall. There, in the warm litter about the melons, very cunningly hidden, he found twenty-five eggs, about the size of a bantam's eggs, but with whitish skin instead of shell.

'I was not a day too soon,' he said; for he could see the baby cobras curled up inside the skin, and he knew that the minute they were hatched they could each kill a man or a mongoose. He bit off the tops of the eggs as fast as he could, taking care to crush the young cobras, and turned over the litter from time to time to see whether he had missed any. At last there were only three eggs left, and Rikki-tikki began to chuckle to himself, when he heard Darzee's wife screaming:

'Rikki-tikki, I led Nagaina toward the house, and she has gone into the veranda, and – oh, come quickly – she means killing!'

Rikki-tikki smashed two eggs, and tumbled backward down the melon-bed with the third egg in his mouth, and scuttled to the veranda as hard as he could put foot to the ground. Teddy and his mother and father were there at early breakfast; but Rikki-tikki saw that they were not eating anything. They sat stone-still, and their faces were white. Nagaina was coiled up on the matting by Teddy's chair, within easy striking-distance of Teddy's bare leg, and she was swaying to and fro singing a song of triumph.

'Son of the big man that killed Nag,' she hissed, 'stay still. I am not ready yet. Wait a little. Keep very still, all you three. If you move I strike, and if you do not move I strike. Oh, foolish people, who killed my Nag!'

Teddy's eyes were fixed on his father, and all his father could do was to whisper: 'Sit still, Teddy. You mustn't move. Teddy, keep still.'

Then Rikki-tikki came up and cried: 'Turn round, Nagaina; turn and fight!'

'All in good time,' said she, without moving her eyes. 'I will settle my account with *you* presently. Look at your friends, Rikki-tikki. They are still and white; they are afraid. They dare not move, and if you come a step nearer I strike.'

'Look at your eggs,' said Rikki-tikki, 'in the melon-bed near the wall. Go and look, Nagaina.'

The big snake turned half round, and saw the egg on the veranda. 'Ah-h! Give it to me,' she said.

Rikki-tikki put his paws one on each side of the egg, and his eyes were blood-red. 'What price for a snake's egg? For a young cobra? For a young king-cobra? For the last—the very last of the brood? The ants are eating all the others down by the melon-bed.'

Nagaina spun clear round, forgetting everything for the sake of the one egg; and Rikki-tikki saw Teddy's father shoot out a big hand, catch Teddy by the shoulder, and drag him across the little table with the teacups, safe and out of reach of Nagaina.

'Tricked! Tricked! Tricked! *Rikk-tck-tck!*' chuckled Rikki-tikki. 'The boy is safe, and it was I – I – I that caught Nag by the hood last night in the bathroom.' Then he began to jump up and down, all four feet together, his

head close to the floor. 'He threw me
to and fro, but he could not shake me
off. He was dead before the big man
blew him in two. I did it. *Rikki-tikki-
tck-tck!* Come then, Nagaina. Come
and fight with me. You shall not
be a widow long.'

Nagaina saw that she had lost
her chance of killing
Teddy, and the egg lay
between Rikki-tikki's
paws. 'Give me the
egg, Rikki-tikki.
Give me the last of
my eggs, and I will go
away and never come
back,' she said, lowering
her hood.

'Yes,
you will go
away, and you
will never come
back; for you will go to
the rubbish-heap with Nag.
Fight, widow! The big man
has gone for his gun! Fight!'
Rikki-tikki was bounding all round
Nagaina, keeping just out of reach of her
stroke, his little eyes like hot coals. Nagaina
gathered herself together, and flung out at him.
Rikki-tikki jumped up and backward. Again and again
and again she struck, and each time her head came with a whack on the
matting of the veranda, and she gathered herself together like a watch-spring.
Then Rikki-tikki danced in a circle to get behind her, and Nagaina spun
round to keep her head to his head, so that the rustle of her tail on the matting
sounded like dry leaves blown along by the wind.

He had forgotten the egg. It still lay on the veranda, and Nagaina came
nearer and nearer to it, till at last, while Rikki-tikki was drawing breath, she
caught it in her mouth, turned to the veranda steps, and flew like an arrow
down the path, with Rikki-tikki behind her. When the cobra runs for her life,
she goes like a whiplash flicked across a horse's neck.

Rikki-tikki knew that he must catch her, or all the trouble would begin
again. She headed straight for the long grass by the thornbush, and as he was
running Rikki-tikki heard Darzee still singing his foolish little song of

triumph. But Darzee's wife was wiser. She flew off her nest as Nagaina came along, and flapped her wings about Nagaina's head. If Darzee had helped they might have turned her; but Nagaina only lowered her hood and went on. Still, the instant's delay brought Rikki-tikki up to her, and as she plunged into the rat-hole where she and Nag used to live, his little white teeth were clenched on her tail, and he went down with her – and very few mongooses, however wise and old they may be, care to follow a cobra into its hole. It was dark in the hole; and Rikki-tikki never knew when it might open out and give Nagaina room to turn and strike at him. He held on savagely, and struck out his feet to act as brakes on the dark slope of the hot, moist earth.

Then the grass by the mouth of the hole stopped waving, and Darzee said: 'It is all over with Rikki-tikki! We must sing his death-song. Valiant Rikki-tikki is dead! For Nagaina will surely kill him underground.'

So he sang a very mournful song that he made up on the spur of the minute, and just as he got to the most touching part the grass quivered again, and Rikki-tikki, covered with dirt, dragged himself out of the hole leg by leg, licking his whiskers. Darzee stopped with a little shout. Rikki-tikki shook some of the dust out of his fur and sneezed. 'It is all over,' he said. 'The widow will never come out again.' And the red ants that live between the grass-stems heard him, and began to troop down one after another to see if he had spoken the truth.

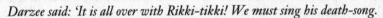

Darzee said: 'It is all over with Rikki-tikki! We must sing his death-song.

Rikki-tikki curled himself up in the grass and slept where he was – slept and slept till it was late in the afternoon, for he had done a hard day's work.

'Now,' he said, when he awoke, 'I will go back to the house. Tell the Coppersmith, Darzee, and he will tell the garden that Nagaina is dead.'

The Coppersmith is a bird who makes a noise exactly like the beating of a little hammer on a copper pot; and the reason he is always making it is because he is the town-crier to every Indian garden, and tells all the news to everybody who cares to listen. As Rikki-tikki went up the path, he heard his 'attention' notes like a tiny dinner-gong; and then the steady '*Ding-dong-tock!* Nag is dead – *dong!* Nagaina is dead! *Ding-dong-tock!*' That set all the birds in the garden singing, and the frogs croaking; for Nag and Nagaina used to eat frogs as well as little birds.

When Rikki got to the house, Teddy and Teddy's mother (she still looked very white, for she had been fainting) and Teddy's father came out and almost cried over him; and that night he ate all that was given him till he could eat no more, and went to bed on Teddy's shoulder, where Teddy's mother saw him when she came to look late at night.

'He saved our lives and Teddy's life,' she said to her husband. 'Just think, he saved all our lives!'

Rikki-tikki woke up with a jump, for all the mongooses are light sleepers.

'Oh, it's you,' said he. 'What are you bothering for? All the cobras are dead; and if they weren't, I'm here.'

Rikki-tikki had a right to be proud of himself; but he did not grow too proud, and he kept that garden as a mongoose should keep it, with tooth and jump and spring and bite, till never a cobra dared show its head inside the walls.

Darzee's Chaunt

SUNG IN HONOUR OF RIKKI-TIKKI-TAVI

Singer and tailor am I –
    Doubled the joys that I know –
Proud of my lilt through the sky,
    Proud of the house that I sew –
Over and under, so weave I my music – so weave
                        I the house that I sew.

Sing to your fledglings again,
    Mother, oh, lift up your head!
Evil that plagues us is slain,
    Death in the garden lies dead.
Terror that hid in the roses is impotent – flung
                      on the dunghill and dead!

Who hath delivered us, who?
    Tell me his nest and his name.
Rikki, the valiant, the true,
    Tikki, with eyeballs of flame,
Rik-tikki-tikki, the ivory-fangèd, the hunter
                    with eyeballs of flame.

Give him the Thanks of the Birds,
    Bowing with tail-feathers spread!
Praise him with nightingale-words –
    Nay, I will praise him instead.
Hear! I will sing you the praise of the bottle-tailed
                    Rikki, with eyeballs of red!

(Here Rikki-tikki interrupted, and the rest of the song is lost.)

Toomai of the Elephants

I will remember what I was. I am sick of rope and chain.
　　I will remember my old strength and all my forest affairs.
I will not sell my back to man for a bundle of sugar-cane,
　　I will go out to my own kind, and the wood-folk in their lairs.

I will go out until the day, until the morning break,
　　Out to the winds' untainted kiss, the waters' clean caress:
I will forget my ankle-ring and snap my picket-stake.
　　I will revisit my lost loves, and playmates masterless!

Kala Nag, which means Black Snake, had served the Indian Government in
every way that an elephant could serve it for forty-seven years, and as he was
fully twenty years old when he was caught, that makes him nearly seventy –
a ripe age for an elephant. He remembered pushing, with a big leather pad
on his forehead, at a gun stuck in deep mud, and that was before the Afghan
War of 1842, and he had not then come to his full strength. His mother,
Radha Pyari – Radha the darling – who had been caught in the same drive
with Kala Nag, told him, before his little milk-tusks had dropped out, that
elephants who were afraid always got hurt; and Kala Nag knew that that
advice was good, for the first time that he saw a shell burst he backed,
screaming, into a stand of piled rifles, and the bayonets pricked him in all his
softest places. So before he was twenty-five he gave up being afraid, and so
he was the best-loved and the best-looked-after elephant in the service of
the Government of India. He had carried tents, twelve hundred pounds'
weight of tents, on the march in Upper India; he had been hoisted into a
ship at the end of a steam-crane and taken for days across the water, and
made to carry a mortar on his back in a strange and rocky country very far
from India, and had seen the Emperor Theodore lying dead in Magdala,
and had come back again in the steamer, entitled, so the soldiers said, to the

Abyssinian War medal. He had seen his fellow-elephants die of cold and epilepsy and starvation and sunstroke up at a place called Ali Musjid, ten years later; and afterwards he had been sent down thousands of miles south to haul and pile big baulks of teak in the timberyards at Moulmein. There he had half killed an insubordinate young elephant who was shirking his fair share of the work.

After that he was taken off timber-hauling, and employed, with a few score other elephants who were trained to the business, in helping to catch wild elephants among the Garo hills. Elephants are very strictly preserved by the Indian Government. There is one whole department which does nothing else but hunt them, and catch them, and break them in, and send them up and down the country as they are needed for work.

Kala Nag stood ten fair feet at the shoulders, and his tusks had been cut off short at five feet, and bound round the ends, to prevent them splitting, with bands of copper; but he could do more with those stumps than any untrained elephant could do with the real sharpened ones.

When, after weeks and weeks of cautious driving of scattered elephants across the hills, the forty or fifty wild monsters were driven into the last stockade, and the big drop-gate, made of tree trunks lashed together, jarred down behind them, Kala Nag, at the word of command, would go into that flaring, trumpeting pandemonium (generally at night, when the flicker of the torches made it difficult to judge distances), and, picking out the biggest and wildest tusker of the mob, would hammer him and hustle him into quiet while the men on the backs of the other elephants roped and tied the smaller ones.

There was nothing in the way of fighting that Kala Nag, the old wise Black Snake, did not know, for he had stood up more than once in his time to the charge of the wounded tiger, and, curling up his soft trunk to be out of harm's way, had knocked the springing brute sideways in mid-air with a quick sickle-cut of his head, that he had invented all by himself; had knocked him over, and kneeled upon him with his huge knees till the life went out with a gasp and a howl, and there was only a fluffy striped thing on the ground for Kala Nag to pull by the tail.

'Yes,' said Big Toomai, his driver, the son of Black Toomai who had taken him to Abyssinia, and grandson of Toomai of the Elephants who had seen him caught, 'there is nothing that the Black Snake fears except me. He has seen three generations of us feed him and groom him, and he will live to see four.'

'He is afraid of *me* also,' said Little Toomai, standing up to his full height of four feet, with only one rag upon him. He was ten years old, the eldest son of Big Toomai, and, according to custom, he would take his father's place on Kala Nag's neck when he grew up, and would handle the heavy iron *ankus*, the elephant-goad that had been worn smooth by his father, and his grandfather, and his great-grandfather. He knew what he was talking of; for he had been born under Kala Nag's shadow, had played with the end of his trunk

'He is afraid of me also,' said Little Toomai

before he could walk, had taken him down to water as soon as he could walk, and Kala Nag would no more have dreamed of disobeying his shrill little orders than he would have dreamed of killing him on that day when Big Toomai carried the little brown baby under Kala Nag's tusks, and told him to salute his master that was to be.

'Yes,' said Little Toomai, 'he is afraid of me,' and he took long strides up to Kala Nag, called him a fat old pig, and made him lift up his feet one after the other.

'Wah!' said Little Toomai, 'thou art a big elephant,' and he wagged his fluffy head, quoting his father. 'The Government may pay for elephants, but they belong to us mahouts. When thou art old, Kala Nag, there will come some rich Rajah, and he will buy thee from the Government, on account of thy size and thy manners, and then thou wilt have nothing to do but to carry gold earrings in thy ears, and a gold howdah on thy back, and a red cloth covered with gold on thy sides, and walk at the head of the processions of the King. Then I shall sit on thy neck, O Kala Nag, with a silver *ankus*, and men will run before us with golden sticks, crying, "Room for the King's elephant!" That will be good, Kala Nag, but not so good as this hunting in the jungles.'

'Umph!' said Big Toomai. 'Thou art a boy, and as wild as a buffalo-calf.

This running up and down among the hills is not the best Government service. I am getting old, and I do not love wild elephants. Give me brick elephant-lines, one stall to each elephant, and big stumps to tie them to safely, and flat, broad roads to exercise upon, instead of this come-and-go camping. Aha, the Cawnpore barracks were good. There was a bazaar close by, and only three hours' work a day.'

Little Toomai remembered the Cawnpore elephant-lines and said nothing. He very much preferred the camp life, and hated those broad, flat roads, with the daily grubbing for grass in the forage-reserve, and the long hours when there was nothing to do except to watch Kala Nag fidgeting in his pickets.

What Little Toomai liked was the scramble up bridle-paths that only an elephant could take; the dip into the valley below; the glimpses of the wild elephants browsing miles away; the rush of the frightened pig and peacock under Kala Nag's feet; the blinding warm rains, when all the hills and valleys smoked; the beautiful misty mornings when nobody knew where they would camp that night; the steady, cautious drive of the wild elephants, and the mad rush and blaze and hullabaloo of the last night's drive, when the elephants poured into the stockade like boulders in a landslide, found that they could not get out, and flung themselves at the heavy posts only to be driven back by yells and flaring torches and volleys of blank cartridge.

Even a little boy could be of use there, and Toomai was as useful as three boys. He would get his torch and wave it, and yell with the best. But the really good time came when the driving out began, and the Keddah – that is, the stockade – looked like a picture of the end of the world, and men had to make signs to one another, because they could not hear themselves speak. Then Little Toomai would climb up to the top of one of the quivering stockade-posts, his sun-bleached brown hair flying loose all over his shoulders, and he looking like a goblin in the torchlight; and as soon as there was a lull you could hear his high-pitched yells of encouragement to Kala Nag, above the trumpeting and crashing, and snapping of ropes, and groans of the tethered elephants. '*Maîl, maîl, Kala Nag!* [Go on, go on, Black Snake!] *Dant do!* [Give him the tusk!] *Somalo! Somalo!* [Careful, careful!] *Maro! Mar!* [Hit him, hit him!] Mind the post! *Arré! Arré! Hai! Yai! Kya-a-ah!*' he would shout, and the big fight between Kala Nag and the wild elephant would sway to and fro across the Keddah, and the old elephant-catchers would wipe the sweat out of their eyes, and find time to nod to Little Toomai wriggling with joy on the top of the posts.

He did more than wriggle. One night he slid down from the post and slipped in between the elephants, and threw up the loose end of a rope, which had dropped, to a driver who was trying to get a purchase on the leg of a kicking young calf (calves always give more trouble than full-grown animals). Kala Nag saw him, caught him in his trunk, and handed him up to Big Toomai, who slapped him then and there, and put him back on the post.

Toomai was as useful as three boys. He would get his torch and wave it,
and yell with the best.

Next morning he gave him a scolding, and said: 'Are not good brick elephant-lines and a little tent-carrying enough, that thou must needs go elephant-catching on thy own account, little worthless? Now those foolish hunters, whose pay is less than my pay, have spoken to Petersen Sahib of the matter.' Little Toomai was frightened. He did not know much of white men, but Petersen Sahib was the greatest white man in the world to him. He was the head of all the Keddah operations – the man who caught all the elephants for the Government of India, and who knew more about the ways of elephants than any living man.

'What – what will happen?' said Little Toomai.

'Happen! the worst that can happen. Petersen Sahib is a madman. Else why should he go hunting these wild devils? He may even require thee to be an elephant-catcher, to sleep anywhere in these fever-filled jungles, and at last to be trampled to death in the Keddah. It is well that this nonsense ends safely. Next week the catching is over, and we of the plains are sent back to our stations. Then we will march on smooth roads, and forget all this hunting. But, son, I am angry that thou shouldst meddle in the business that belongs to these dirty Assamese jungle folk. Kala Nag will obey none but me, so I must go with him into the Keddah; but he is only a fighting elephant, and he does not help to rope them. So I sit at my ease, as befits a mahout – not a mere hunter – a mahout, I say, and a man who gets a pension at the end of his service. Is the family of Toomai of the Elephants to be trodden underfoot in the dirt of a Keddah? Bad one! Wicked one!

Worthless son! Go and wash Kala Nag and attend to his ears, and see that there are no thorns in his feet; or else Petersen Sahib will surely catch thee and make thee a wild hunter – a follower of elephants' foot-tracks, a jungle-bear. Bah! Shame! Go!'

Little Toomai went off without saying a word, but he told Kala Nag all his grievances while he was examining his feet. 'No matter,' said Little Toomai, turning up the fringe of Kala Nag's huge right ear. 'They have said my name to Petersen Sahib, and perhaps – and perhaps – and perhaps – who knows? Hai! That is a big thorn that I have pulled out!'

The next few days were spent in getting the elephants together, in walking the newly caught wild elephants up and down between a couple of tame ones, to prevent them from giving too much trouble on the downward march to the plains, and in taking stock of the blankets and ropes and things that had been worn out or lost in the forest.

Petersen Sahib came in on his clever she-elephant Pudmini. He had been paying off other camps among the hills, for the season was coming to an end, and there was a native clerk sitting at a table under a tree to pay the drivers their wages. As each man was paid he went back to his elephant, and joined the line that stood ready to start. The catchers, and hunters, and beaters, the men of the regular Keddah, who stayed in the jungle year in and year out, sat on the backs of the elephants that belonged to Petersen Sahib's permanent force, or leaned against the trees with their guns across their arms, and made fun of the drivers who were going away, and laughed when the newly caught elephants broke the line and ran about.

Big Toomai went up to the clerk with Little Toomai behind him, and Machua Appa, the head-tracker, said in an undertone to a friend of his, 'There goes one piece of good elephant-stuff at least. 'Tis a pity to send that young jungle-cock to moult in the plains.'

Now Petersen Sahib had ears all over him, as a man must have who listens to the most silent of all living things – the wild elephant. He turned where he was lying all along on Pudmini's back, and said, 'What is that? I did not know of a man among the plains-drivers who had wit enough to rope even a dead elephant.'

'This is not a man, but a boy. He went into the Keddah at the last drive, and threw Barmao there the rope when we were trying to get that young calf with the blotch on his shoulder away from his mother.'

Machua Appa pointed at Little Toomai, and Petersen Sahib looked, and Little Toomai bowed to the earth.

'He throw a rope? He is smaller than a picket-pin. Little one, what is thy name?' said Petersen Sahib.

Little Toomai was too frightened to speak, but Kala Nag was behind him, and Toomai made a sign with his hand, and the elephant caught him up in his trunk and held him level with Pudmini's forehead, in front of the great Petersen Sahib. Then Little Toomai covered his face with his hands, for he

'Not green corn, Protector of the Poor – melons,' said Little Toomai

was only a child, and except where elephants were concerned, he was just as bashful as a child could be.

'Oho!' said Petersen Sahib, smiling underneath his moustache, 'and why didst thou teach thy elephant *that* trick? Was it to help thee steal green corn from the roofs of the houses when the ears are put out to dry?'

'Not green corn, Protector of the Poor – melons,' said Little Toomai, and all the men sitting about broke into a roar of laughter. Most of them had taught their elephants that trick when they were boys. Little Toomai was hanging eight feet up in the air, and he wished very much that he were eight feet under ground.

'He is Toomai, my son, Sahib,' said Big Toomai, scowling. 'He is a very bad boy, and he will end in a jail, Sahib.'

'Of that I have my doubts,' said Petersen Sahib. 'A boy who can face a full Keddah at his age does not end in jails. See, little one, here are four annas to spend in sweetmeats because thou hast a little head under that great thatch of hair. In time thou mayest become a hunter too.' Big Toomai scowled more than ever. 'Remember, though, that Keddahs are not good for children to play in,' Petersen Sahib went on.

'Must I never go there, Sahib?' asked Little Toomai, with a big gasp.

'Yes.' Petersen Sahib smiled again. 'When thou hast seen the elephants dance. That is the proper time. Come to me when thou hast seen the elephants dance, and then I will let thee go into all the Keddahs.'

There was another roar of laughter, for that is an old joke among elephant-catchers, and it means just never. There are great cleared flat places hidden away in the forests that are called elephants' ballrooms, but even these are only found by accident, and no man has ever seen the elephants dance. When a driver boasts of his skill and bravery the other drivers say, 'And when didst *thou* see the elephants dance?'

Kala Nag put Little Toomai down, and he bowed to the earth again and went away with his father, and gave the silver four-anna piece to his mother, who was nursing his baby brother, and they all were put up on Kala Nag's back, and the line of grunting, squealing elephants rolled down the hill-path to the plains. It was a very lively march on account of the new elephants, who gave trouble at every ford, and who needed coaxing or beating every other minute.

Big Toomai prodded Kala Nag spitefully, for he was very angry, but Little Toomai was too happy to speak. Petersen Sahib had noticed him, and given him money, so he felt as a private soldier would feel if he had been called out of the ranks and praised by his commander-in-chief.

'What did Petersen Sahib mean by the elephant-dance?' he said, at last, softly to his mother.

Big Toomai heard him and grunted. 'That thou shouldst never be one of these hill-buffaloes of trackers. *That* was what he meant. Oh, you in front, what is blocking the way?'

An Assamese driver, two or three elephants ahead, turned round angrily, crying: 'Bring up Kala Nag, and knock this youngster of mine into good behaviour. Why should Petersen Sahib have chosen *me* to go down with you donkeys of the rice-fields? Lay your beast alongside, Toomai, and let him prod with his tusks. By all the gods of the Hills, these new elephants are possessed, or else they can smell their companions in the jungle.'

Kala Nag hit the new elephant in the ribs and knocked the wind out of him, as Big Toomai said, 'We have swept the hills of wild elephants at the last catch. It is only your carelessness in driving. Must I keep order along the whole line?'

'Hear him!' said the other driver. '*We* have swept the hills! Ho! ho! You are very wise, you plains-people. Anyone but a mud-head who never saw the jungle would know that *they* know that the drives are ended for the season. Therefore all the wild elephants tonight will – but why should I waste wisdom on a river-turtle?'

'What will they do?' Little Toomai called out.

'*Ohé*, little one. Art thou there? Well, I will tell thee, for thou hast a cool head. They will dance, and it behoves thy father, who has swept *all* the hills of *all* the elephants, to double-chain his pickets tonight.'

'What talk is this?' said Big Toomai. 'For forty years, father and son, we have tended elephants, and we have never heard such moonshine about dances.'

'Yes; but a plainsman who lives in a hut knows only the four walls of his hut. Well, leave thy elephants unshackled tonight and see what comes; as for their dancing, I have seen the place where – *Bapree-Bap!* how many windings has the Dihang River? Here is another ford, and we must swim the calves. Stop still, you behind there.'

And in this way, talking and wrangling and splashing through the rivers, they made their first march to a sort of receiving-camp for the new elephants; but they lost their tempers long before they got there.

Then the elephants were chained by their hind legs to their big stumps of pickets, and extra ropes were fitted to the new elephants, and the fodder was piled before them, and the hill-drivers went back to Petersen Sahib through the afternoon light, telling the plains-drivers to be extra careful that night, and laughing when the plains-drivers asked the reason.

Little Toomai attended to Kala Nag's supper, and as evening fell wandered through the camp, unspeakably happy, in search of a tom-tom. When an Indian child's heart is full, he does not run about and make a noise in an irregular fashion. He sits down to a sort of revel all by himself. And Little Toomai had been spoken to by Petersen Sahib! If he had not found what he wanted, I believe he would have burst. But the sweetmeat-seller in the camp lent him a little tom-tom – a drum beaten with the flat of the hand – and he sat down, cross-legged, before Kala Nag as the stars began to come out, the tom-tom in his lap, and he thumped and he thumped and he thumped, and the more he thought of the great honour that had been done to him, the more he thumped, all alone among the elephant-fodder. There was no tune and no words, but the thumping made him happy.

The new elephants strained at their ropes, and squealed and trumpeted from time to time, and he could hear his mother in the camp hut putting his small brother to sleep with an old, old song about the great God Shiv, who once told all the animals what they should eat. It is a very soothing lullaby, and the first verse says:

Shiv, who poured the harvest and made the winds to blow,
Sitting at the doorways of a day of long ago,
Gave to each his portion, food and toil and fate,
From the King upon the *guddee* to the Beggar at the gate.
  All things made he – Shiva the Preserver.
  Mahadeo! Mahadeo! He made all –
  Thorn for the camel, fodder for the kine,
  And mother's heart for sleepy head, O little son of mine!

Little Toomai came in with a joyous *tunk-a-tunk* at the end of each verse, till he felt sleepy and stretched himself on the fodder at Kala Nag's side.

At last the elephants began to lie down one after another, as is their custom, till only Kala Nag at the right of the line was left standing up; and he rocked slowly from side to side, his ears put forward to listen to the night wind as it blew very slowly across the hills. The air was full of all the night noises that, taken together, make one big silence – the click of one bamboo-stem against the other, the rustle of something alive in the undergrowth, the scratch and squawk of a half-waked bird (birds are awake in the night much more often than we imagine), and the fall of water ever so far away. Little Toomai slept for some time, and when he waked it was brilliant moonlight, and Kala Nag was still standing up with his ears cocked. Little Toomai turned, rustling in the fodder, and watched the curve of his big back against half the stars in heaven; and while he watched he heard, so far away that it sounded no more than a pinhole of noise pricked through the stillness, the 'hoot-toot' of a wild elephant.

All the elephants in the lines jumped up as if they had been shot, and their grunts at last waked the sleeping mahouts, and they came out and drove in the picket-pegs with big mallets, and tightened this rope and knotted that till all was quiet. One new elephant had nearly grubbed up his picket, and Big Toomai took off Kala Nag's leg-chain and shackled that elephant forefoot to hind-foot, but slipped a loop of grass-string round Kala Nag's leg, and told him to remember that he was tied fast. He knew that he and his father and his grandfather had done the very same thing hundreds of times before. Kala Nag did not answer to the order by gurgling, as he usually did. He stood still, looking out across the moonlight, his head a little raised, and his ears spread like fans, up to the great folds of the Garo hills.

'Look to him if he grows restless in the night,' said Big Toomai to Little Toomai, and he went into the hut and slept. Little Toomai was just going to sleep, too, when he heard the coir string snap with a little 'tang', and Kala Nag rolled out of his pickets as slowly and as silently as a cloud rolls out of the mouth of a valley. Little Toomai pattered after him, barefooted, down the road in the moonlight, calling under his breath, 'Kala Nag! Kala Nag! Take me with you, O Kala Nag!' The elephant turned without a sound, took three strides back to the boy in the moonlight, put down his trunk, swung him up to his neck, and almost before Little Toomai had settled his knees slipped into the forest.

There was one blast of furious trumpeting from the lines, and then the silence shut down on everything, and Kala Nag began to move. Sometimes a tuft of high grass washed along his sides as a wave washes along the sides of a ship, and sometimes a cluster of wild-pepper vines would scrape along his back, or a bamboo would creak where his shoulder touched it; but between those times he moved absolutely without any sound, drifting through the thick Garo forest as though it had been smoke. He was going uphill, but though Little Toomai watched the stars in the rifts of the trees, he could not tell in what direction.

Then Kala Nag reached the crest of the ascent and stopped for a minute, and Little Toomai could see the tops of the trees lying all speckled and furry under the moonlight for miles and miles, and the blue-white mist over the river in the hollow. Toomai leaned forward and looked, and he felt that the forest was awake below him – awake and alive and crowded. A big brown fruit-eating bat brushed past his ear; a porcupine's quills rattled in the thicket; and in the darkness between the tree-stems he heard a hog-bear digging hard in the moist, warm earth, and snuffing as it dug.

Then the branches closed over his head again, and Kala Nag began to go slowly down into the valley – not quietly this time, but as a runaway gun goes down a steep bank – in one rush. The huge limbs moved as steadily as pistons, eight feet to each stride, and the wrinkled skin of the elbow-points rustled. The undergrowth on either side of him ripped with a noise like torn canvas, and the saplings that he heaved away right and left with his shoulders sprang back again, and banged him on the flank, and great trails of creepers, all matted together, hung from his tusks as he threw his head from side to side and ploughed out his pathway. Then Little Toomai laid himself down close to the great neck, lest a swinging bough should sweep him to the ground, and he wished that he were back in the lines again.

The grass began to get squashy, and Kala Nag's feet sucked and squelched as he put them down, and the night mist at the bottom of the valley chilled Little Toomai. There was a splash and a trample, and the rush of running water, and Kala Nag strode through the bed of a river, feeling his way at each step. Above the noise of the water, as it swirled round the elephant's legs, Little Toomai could hear more splashing and some trumpeting both up stream and down – great grunts and angry snortings, and all the mist about him seemed to be full of rolling, wavy shadows.

'*Ai!*' he said, half aloud, his teeth chattering. 'The elephant-folk are out tonight. It *is* the dance, then.'

Kala Nag swashed out of the water, blew his trunk clear, and began another climb; but this time he was not alone, and he had not to make his path. That was made already, six feet wide, in front of him, where the bent jungle-grass was trying to recover itself and stand up. Many elephants must

Then Little Toomai laid himself down close to the great neck, lest a swinging bough should sweep him to the ground

have gone that way only a few minutes before. Little Toomai looked back, and behind him a great wild tusker, with his little pig's eyes glowing like hot coals, was just lifting himself out of the misty river. Then the trees closed up again, and they went on and up, with trumpetings and crashings, and the sound of breaking branches on every side of them.

At last Kala Nag stood still between two tree-trunks at the very top of the hill. They were part of a circle of trees that grew round an irregular space of some three or four acres, and in all that space, as Little Toomai could see, the ground had been trampled down as hard as a brick floor. Some trees grew in the centre of the clearing, but their bark was rubbed away, and the white wood beneath showed all shiny and polished in the patches of moonlight. There were creepers hanging from the upper branches, and the bells of the flowers of the creepers, great waxy white things like convolvuluses, hung down fast asleep; but within the limits of the clearing there was not a single blade of green – nothing but the trampled earth.

The moonlight showed it all iron-grey, except where some elephants stood upon it, and their shadows were inky black. Little Toomai looked, holding his breath, with his eyes starting out of his head, and as he looked, more and more and more elephants swung out into the open from between the tree-trunks. Little Toomai could count only up to ten, and he counted again and again on his fingers till he lost count of the tens, and his head began to swim. Outside the clearing he could hear them crashing in the under-growth as they worked their way up the hillside; but as soon as they were within the circle of the tree-trunks they moved like ghosts.

There were white-tusked wild males, with fallen leaves and nuts and twigs lying in the wrinkles of their necks and the folds of their ears; fat, slow-footed she-elephants, with restless little pinky-black calves only three or four feet high running under their stomachs; young elephants with their tusks just beginning to show, and very proud of them; lanky, scraggy old-maid el-ephants, with their hollow, anxious faces, and trunks like rough bark; savage old bull-elephants, scarred from shoulder to flank with great weals and cuts of bygone fights, and the caked dirt of their solitary mud-baths dropping from their shoulders; and there was one with a broken tusk and the marks of the full-stroke, the terrible drawing scrape, of a tiger's claws on his side.

They were standing head to head, or walking to and fro across the ground in couples, or rocking and swaying all by themselves – scores and scores of elephants.

Toomai knew that, so long as he lay still on Kala Nag's neck, nothing would happen to him; for even in the rush and scramble of a Keddah-drive a wild elephant does not reach up with his trunk and drag a man off the neck of a tame elephant; and these elephants were not thinking of men that night. Once they started and put their ears forward when they heard the chinking of a leg-iron in the forest, but it was Pudmini, Petersen Sahib's pet elephant, her chain snapped short off, grunting, snuffling up the hillside. She must have broken her pickets, and come straight from Petersen Sahib's camp; and Little Toomai saw another elephant, one that he did not know, with deep rope-galls on his back and breast. He, too, must have run away from some camp in the hills about.

At last there was no sound of any more elephants moving in the forest, and

Kala Nag rolled out from his station between the trees and went into the middle of the crowd, clucking and gurgling, and all the elephants began to talk in their own tongue, and to move about.

Still lying down, Little Toomai looked down upon scores and scores of broad backs, and wagging ears, and tossing trunks, and little rolling eyes. He heard the click of tusks as they crossed other tusks by accident, and the dry rustle of trunks twined together, and the chafing of enormous sides and shoulders in the crowd, and the incessant flick and *hissh* of the great tails. Then a cloud came over the moon, and he sat in black darkness; but the quiet, steady hustling and pushing and gurgling went on just the same. He knew that there were elephants all round Kala Nag, and that there was no chance of backing him out of the assembly; so he set his teeth and shivered. In a Keddah at least there was torch light and shouting, but here he was all alone in the dark, and once a trunk came up and touched him on the knee.

Then an elephant trumpeted, and they all took it up for five or ten terrible seconds. The dew from the trees above spattered down like rain on the unseen backs, and a dull booming noise began, not very loud at first, and Little Toomai could not tell what it was; but it grew and grew, and Kala Nag lifted up one forefoot and then the other, and brought them down on the ground – one–two, one–two, as steadily as trip-hammers. The elephants were stamping all together now, and it sounded like a war-drum beaten at the mouth of a cave. The dew fell from the trees till there was no more left to fall, and the booming went on, and the ground rocked and shivered, and Little Toomai put his hands up to his ears to shut out the sound. But it was all one gigantic jar that ran through him – this stamp of hundreds of heavy feet on the raw earth. Once or twice he could feel Kala Nag and all the others surge forward a few strides, and the thumping would change to the crushing sound of juicy green things being bruised, but in a minute or two the boom of feet on hard earth began again. A tree was creaking and groaning somewhere near him. He put out his arm and felt the bark, but Kala Nag moved forward, still tramping, and he could not tell where he was in the clearing. There was no sound from the elephants, except once when two or three little calves squeaked together. Then he heard a thump and a shuffle, and the booming went on. It must have lasted fully two hours, and Little Toomai ached in every nerve; but he knew by the smell of the night air that the dawn was coming.

The morning broke in one sheet of pale yellow behind the green hills, and the booming stopped with the first ray, as though the light had been an order. Before Little Toomai had got the ringing out of his head, before even he had shifted his position, there was not an elephant in sight except Kala Nag, Pudmini, and the elephant with the rope-galls, and there was neither sign nor rustle nor whisper down the hillsides to show where the others had gone.

Little Toomai stared again and again. The clearing, as he remembered it, had grown in the night. More trees stood in the middle of it, but the

*Little Toomai looked down upon scores and scores of broad backs, and wagging
ears, and tossing trunks, and little rolling eyes*

undergrowth and the jungle-grass at the sides had been rolled back. Little Toomai stared once more. Now he understood the trampling. The elephants had stamped out more room – had stamped the thick grass and juicy cane to trash, the trash into slivers, the slivers into tiny fibres, and the fibres into hard earth.

'Wah!' said Little Toomai, and his eyes were very heavy. 'Kala Nag, my lord, let us keep by Pudmini and go to Petersen Sahib's camp, or I shall drop from thy neck.'

The third elephant watched the two go away, snorted, wheeled round, and took his own path. He may have belonged to some little native king's establishment, fifty or sixty or a hundred miles away.

Two hours later, as Petersen Sahib was eating early breakfast, the elephants, who had been double-chained that night, began to trumpet, and Pudmini, mired to the shoulders, with Kala Nag, very footsore, shambled into the camp.

Little Toomai's face was grey and pinched, and his hair was full of leaves and drenched with dew; but he tried to salute Petersen Sahib, and cried faintly: 'The dance – the elephant-dance! I have seen it, and – I die!' As Kala Nag sat down, he slid off his neck in a dead faint.

But, since native children have no nerves worth speaking of, in two hours he was lying very contentedly in Petersen Sahib's hammock with Petersen Sahib's shooting-coat under his head, and a glass of warm milk, a little brandy, with a dash of quinine inside of him; and while the old hairy, scarred hunters of the jungles sat three-deep before him, looking at him as though he were a spirit, he told his tale in short words, as a child will, and wound up with – 'Now, if I lie in one word, send men to see, and they will find that the elephant-folk have trampled down more room in their dance-room, and they will find ten and ten, and many times ten, tracks leading to that dance-room. They made more room with their feet. I have seen it. Kala Nag took me, and I saw. Also Kala Nag is very leg-weary!'

Little Toomai lay back and slept all through the long afternoon and into the twilight, and while he slept Petersen Sahib and Machua Appa followed the track of the two elephants for fifteen miles across the hills. Petersen Sahib had spent eighteen years in catching elephants, and he had only once before found such a dance-place. Machua Appa had no need to look twice at the clearing to see what had been done there, or to scratch with his toe in the packed, rammed earth.

'The child speaks truth,' said he. 'All this was done last night, and I have counted seventy tracks crossing the river. See, Sahib, where Pudmini's leg-iron cut the bark off that tree! Yes; she was there too.'

They looked at each other, and up and down, and they wondered; for the ways of elephants are beyond the wit of any man, black or white, to fathom.

'Forty years and five,' said Machua Appa, 'have I followed my lord the elephant, but never have I heard that any child of man had seen what this

The whole line flung up their trunks till the tips touched their foreheads, and broke out into the full salute

child has seen. By all the Gods of the Hills, it is – what can we say?' and he shook his head.

When they got back to camp it was time for the evening meal. Petersen Sahib ate alone in his tent, but he gave orders that the camp should have two sheep and some fowls, as well as a double ration of flour and rice and salt, for he knew that there would be a feast.

Big Toomai had come up hotfoot from the camp in the plains to search for his son and his elephant, and now that he had found them he looked at them as though he were afraid of them both. And there was a feast by the blazing campfires in front of the lines of picketed elephants, and Little Toomai was the hero of it all; and the big brown elephant-catchers, the trackers and drivers and ropers, and the men who know all the secrets of breaking the wildest elephants, passed him from one to the other, and they marked his forehead with blood from the breast of a newly killed jungle-cock, to show that he was a forester, initiated and free of all the jungles.

And at last, when the flames died down, and the red light of the logs made the elephants look as though they had been dipped in blood too, Machua Appa, the head of all the drivers of all the Keddahs – Machua Appa, Petersen Sahib's other self, who had never seen a made road in forty years: Machua Appa, who was so great that he had no other name than Machua Appa –

leaped to his feet, with Little Toomai held high in the air above his head, and shouted: 'Listen, my brothers. Listen, too, you my lords in the lines there, for I, Machua Appa, am speaking! This little one shall no more be called Little Toomai, but Toomai of the Elephants, as his great-grandfather was called before him. What never man has seen he has seen through the long night, and the favour of the elephant-folk and of the Gods of the Jungles is with him. He shall become a great tracker; he shall become greater than I, even I – Machua Appa! He shall follow the new trail, and the stale trail, and the mixed trail, with a clear eye! He shall take no harm in the Keddah when he runs under their bellies to rope the wild tuskers; and if he slips before the feet of the charging bull-elephant, that bull-elephant shall know who he is and shall not crush him. *Aihai!* my lords in the chains' – he whirled up the line of pickets – 'here is the little one that has seen your dances in your hidden places – the sight that never man saw! Give him honour, my lords! *Salaam karo*, my children! Make your salute to Toomai of the Elephants! Gunga Pershad, ahaa! Hira Guj, Birchi Guj, Kuttar Guj, ahaa! Pudmini – thou hast seen him at the dance, and thou too, Kala Nag, my pearl among elephants! – ahaa! Together! To Toomai of the Elephants. *Barrao!*'

And at that last wild yell the whole line flung up their trunks till the tips touched their foreheads, and broke out into the full salute, the crashing trumpet-peal that only the Viceroy of India hears – the Salaamut of the Keddah.

But it was all for the sake of Little Toomai, who had seen what never man had seen before – the dance of the elephants at night and alone in the heart of the Garo hills!

Shiv and the Grasshopper

Shiv, who poured the harvest and made the winds to blow,
Sitting at the doorways of a day of long ago,
Gave to each his portion, food and toil and fate,
From the King upon the *guddee* to the Beggar at the gate.
   All things made he – Shiva the Preserver.
   Mahadeo! Mahadeo! He made all –
   Thorn for the camel, fodder for the kine,
   And mother's heart for sleepy head, O little son of mine!

Wheat he gave to rich folk, millet to the poor,
Broken scraps for holy men that beg from door to door;
Cattle to the tiger, carrion to the kite,
And rags and bones to wicked wolves without the wall at night.
Naught he found too lofty, none he saw too low –
Parbati beside him watched them come and go;
Thought to cheat her husband, turning Shiv to jest –
Stole the little grasshopper and hid it in her breast.
   So she tricked him, Shiva the Preserver.
   Mahadeo! Mahadeo! turn and see.
   Tall are the camels, heavy are the kine,
   But this was least of little things, O little son of mine!

When the dole was ended, laughingly she said,
'Master, of a million mouths is not one unfed?'
Laughing, Shiv made answer, 'All have had their part,
Even he, the little one, hidden next thy heart.'
From her breast she plucked it, Parbati the thief,
Saw the Least of Little Things gnawed a new-grown leaf!
Saw and feared and wondered, making prayer to Shiv,
Who hath surely given meat to all that live.
   All things made he – Shiva the Preserver.
   Mahadeo! Mahedo! He made all –
   Thorn for the camel, fodder for the kine,
   And mother's heart for sleepy head, O little son of mine!

Her Majesty's Servants

You can work it out by Fractions or by simple Rule of Three,
But the way of Tweedledum is not the way of Tweedledee.
You can twist it, you can turn it, you can plait it till you drop,
But the way of Pilly-Winky's not the way of Winkie-Pop!

It had been raining heavily for one whole month – raining on a camp of thirty
thousand men, thousands of camels, elephants, horses, bullocks, and mules,
all gathered together at a place called Rawalpindi, to be reviewed by the
Viceroy of India. He was receiving a visit from the Amir of Afghanistan – a
wild king of a very wild country; and the Amir had brought with him for a
bodyguard eight hundred men and horses who had never seen a camp or a
locomotive before in their lives – savage men and savage horses from
somewhere at the back of Central Asia. Every night a mob of these horses
would be sure to break their heel-ropes, and stampede up and down the camp
through the mud in the dark, or the camels would break loose and run about
and fall over the ropes of the tents, and you can imagine how pleasant that was
for men trying to go to sleep. My tent lay far away from the camel-lines, and
I thought it was safe; but one night a man popped his head in and shouted,
'Get out, quick! They're coming! My tent's gone!'

I knew who 'they' were; so I put on my boots and waterproof and scuttled
out into the slush. Little Vixen, my fox-terrier, went out through the other
side; and then there was a roaring and a grunting and bubbling, and I saw the
tent cave in, as the pole snapped, and begin to dance about like a mad ghost.
A camel had blundered into it, and wet and angry as I was, I could not help
laughing. Then I ran on, because I did not know how many camels might
have got loose, and before long I was out of sight of the camp, ploughing my
way through the mud.

At last I fell over the tail-end of a gun, and by that knew I was somewhere
near the Artillery lines where the cannon were stacked at night. As I did not
want to plowter about any more in the drizzle and the dark, I put my
waterproof over the muzzle of one gun, and made a sort of wigwam with two

or three rammers that I found, and lay along the tail of another gun, wondering where Vixen had got to, and where I might be.

Just as I was getting ready to sleep I heard a jingle of harness and a grunt, and a mule passed me shaking his wet ears. He belonged to a screw-gun battery, for I could hear the rattle of the straps and rings and chains and things on his saddle-pad. The screw-guns are tiny little cannon made in two pieces that are screwed together when the time comes to use them. They are taken up mountains, anywhere that a mule can find a road, and they are very useful for fighting in rocky country.

Behind the mule there was a camel, with his big soft feet squelching and slipping in the mud, and his neck bobbing to and fro like a strayed hen's. Luckily, I knew enough of beast language – not wild-beast language, but camp-beast language, of course – from the natives to know what he was saying.

He must have been the one that flopped into my tent, for he called to the mule, 'What shall I do? Where shall I go? I have fought with a white thing that waved, and it took a stick and hit me on the neck.' (That was my broken tentpole, and I was very glad to know it.) 'Shall we run on?'

'Oh, it was you,' said the mule, 'you and your friends, that have been disturbing the camp? All right. You'll be beaten for this in the morning; but I may as well give you something on account now.'

I heard the harness jingle as the mule backed and caught the camel two kicks in the ribs that rang like a drum. 'Another time,' he said, 'you'll know better than to run through a mule-battery at night, shouting "Thieves and fire!" Sit down, and keep your silly neck quiet.'

The camel doubled up camel-fashion, like a two-foot rule, and sat down whimpering. There was a regular beat of hoofs in the darkness, and a big troop-horse cantered up as steadily as though he were on parade, jumped a gun-tail, and landed close to the mule.

'It's disgraceful,' he said, blowing out his nostrils. 'Those camels have racketed through our lines again – the third time this week. How's a horse to keep his condition if he isn't allowed to sleep. Who's here?'

'I'm the breech-piece mule of Number Two gun of the First Screw Battery,' said the mule, 'and the other's one of your friends. He's waked me up too. Who are you?'

'Number Fifteen, E troop, Ninth Lancers – Dick Cunliffe's horse. Stand over a little, there.'

'Oh, beg your pardon,' said the mule. 'It's too dark to see much. Aren't these camels too sickening for anything? I walked out of my lines to get a little peace and quiet here.'

'My lords,' said the camel humbly, 'we dreamed bad dreams in the night, and we were very much afraid. I am only a baggage-camel of the 39th Native Infantry, and I am not so brave as you are, my lords.'

'Then why the pickets didn't you stay and carry baggage for the 39th Native Infantry, instead of running all round the camp?' said the mule.

'They were such very bad dreams,' said the camel. 'I am sorry. Listen! What is that? Shall we run on again?'

'Sit down,' said the mule, 'or you'll snap your long legs between the guns.' He cocked one ear and listened. 'Bullocks!' he said. 'Gun-bullocks. On my word, you and your friends have waked the camp very thoroughly. It takes a good deal of prodding to put up a gun-bullock.'

I heard a chain dragging along the ground, and a yoke of the great sulky white bullocks that drag the heavy siege-guns when the elephants won't go any nearer to the firing, came shouldering along together; and almost stepping on the chain was another battery-mule, calling wildly for 'Billy'.

'That's one of our recruits,' said the old mule to the troop-horse. 'He's calling for me. Here, youngster, stop squealing. The dark never hurt anybody yet.'

The gun-bullocks lay down together and began chewing the cud, but the young mule huddled close to Billy.

'Things!' he said. 'Fearful and horrible things, Billy! They came into our lines while we were asleep. D'you think they'll kill us?'

'I've a great mind to give you a number-one kicking,' said Billy. 'The idea of a fourteen-hand mule with your training disgracing the battery before this gentleman!'

'Gently, gently!' said the troop-horse. 'Remember they are always like this to begin with. The first time I ever saw a man (it was in Australia when I was a three-year-old) I ran for half a day, and if I'd seen a camel I should have been running still.'

Nearly all our horses for the English cavalry are brought to India from Australia, and are broken in by the troopers themselves.

'True enough,' said Billy. 'Stop shaking, youngster. The first time they put the full harness with all its chains on my back, I stood on my forelegs and kicked every bit of it off. I hadn't learned the real science of kicking then, but the battery said they had never seen anything like it.'

'But this wasn't harness or anything that jingled,' said the young mule. 'You know I don't mind that now, Billy. It was Things like trees, and they fell up and down the lines and bubbled; and my head-rope broke, and I couldn't find my driver, and I couldn't find you, Billy, so I ran off with – with these gentlemen.'

'H'm!' said Billy. 'As soon as I heard the camels were loose I came away on my own account, quietly. When a battery – a screw-gun mule calls gun-bullocks gentlemen, he must be very badly shaken up. Who are you fellows on the ground there?'

The gun-bullocks rolled their cuds, and answered both together: 'The seventh yoke of the first gun of the Big Gun Battery. We were asleep when the camels came, but when we were trampled on we got up and walked away. It is better to lie quiet in the mud than to be disturbed on good bedding. We told your friend here that there was nothing to be afraid of, but he knew so much that he thought otherwise. Wah!'

They went on chewing.

'That comes of being afraid,' said Billy. 'You get laughed at by gun-bullocks. I hope you like it, young un.'

The young mule's teeth snapped, and I heard him say something about not being afraid of any beefy old bullock in the world; but the bullocks only clicked their horns together and went on chewing.

'Now, don't be angry *after* you've been afraid. That's the worst kind of cowardice,' said the troop-horse. 'Anybody can be forgiven for being scared in the night, I think, if they see things they don't understand. We've broken out of our pickets, again and again, four hundred and fifty of us, just because a new recruit got to telling tales of whip-snakes at home in Australia till we were scared to death of the loose ends of our head-ropes.'

'That's all very well in camp,' said Billy; 'I'm not above stampeding myself, for the fun of the thing, when I haven't been out for a day or two; but what do you do on active service?'

'Oh, that's quite another set of new shoes,' said the troop-horse. 'Dick Cunliffe's on my back then, and drives his knees into me, and all I have to do is to watch where I am putting my feet and to keep my hind legs well under me, and be bridle-wise.'

'What's bridle-wise?' said the young mule.

'By the Blue Gums of the Back Blocks,' snorted the troop-horse, 'do you mean to say that you aren't taught to be bridle-wise in your business? How can you do anything, unless you can spin round at once when the rein is pressed on your neck? It means life or death to your man, and of course that's life or death to you. Get round with your hind legs under you the instant you feel the rein on your neck. If you haven't room to swing round, rear up a little and come round on your hind legs. That's being bridle-wise.'

'We aren't taught that way,' said Billy the mule stiffly. 'We're taught to obey the man at our head: step off when he says so, and step in when he says so. I suppose it comes to the same thing. Now, with all this fine fancy business and rearing, which must be very bad for your hocks, what do you *do*?'

'That depends,' said the troop-horse. 'Generally I have to go in among a lot of yelling, hairy men with knives – long shiny knives, worse than the farrier's knives – and I have to take care that Dick's boot is just touching the next man's boot without crushing it. I can see Dick's lance to the right of my right eye, and I know I am safe. I shouldn't care to be the man or horse that stood up to Dick and me when we're in a hurry.'

'Don't the knives hurt?' said the young mule.

'Well, I got one cut across the chest once, but that wasn't Dick's fault – '

'A lot I should have cared whose fault it was, if it hurt!' said the young mule.

'You must,' said the troop-horse. 'If you don't trust your man, you may as well run away at once. That's what some of our horses do, and I don't blame them. As I was saying, it wasn't Dick's fault. The man was lying on the ground, and I stretched myself not to tread on him, and he slashed up at me.

Next time I have to go over a man lying down I shall step on him – hard.'

'H'm!' said Billy; 'it sounds very foolish. Knives are dirty things at any time. The proper thing to do is to climb up a mountain with a well-balanced saddle, hang on by all four feet and your ears too, and creep and crawl and wriggle along, till you come out hundreds of feet above anyone else, on a ledge where there's just room enough for your hoofs. Then you stand still and keep quiet – never ask a man to hold your head, young un – keep quiet while the guns are being put together, and then you watch the little poppy shells drop down into the tree-tops ever so far below.'

'Don't you ever trip?' said the troop-horse.

'They say that when a mule trips you can split a hen's ear,' said Billy. 'Now and again *per–haps* a badly packed saddle will upset a mule, but it's very seldom. I wish I could show you our business. It's beautiful. Why, it took me three years to find out what the men were driving at. The science of the thing is never to show up against the skyline, because, if you do, you may get fired at. Remember that, young un. Always keep hidden as much as possible, even if you have to go a mile out of your way. I lead the battery when it comes to that sort of climbing.'

'Fired at without the chance of running into the people who are firing!' said the troop-horse, thinking hard. 'I couldn't stand that. I should want to charge, with Dick.'

'Oh no, you wouldn't; you know that as soon as the guns are in position *they'll* do all the charging. That's scientific and neat; but knives – pah!'

The baggage-camel had been bobbing his head to and fro for some time past, anxious to get a word in edgeways.

Then I heard him say, as he cleared his throat, nervously: 'I – I – I have fought a little, but not in that climbing way or that running way.'

'No. Now you mention it,' said Billy, 'you don't look as though you were made for climbing or running – much. Well, how was it, old Hay-bales?'

'The proper way,' said the camel. 'We all sat down – '

'Oh, my cropper and breastplate!' said the troop-horse under his breath. 'Sat down?'

'We sat down – a hundred of us,' the camel went on, 'in a big square, and the men piled our packs and saddles outside the square, and they fired over our backs, the men did, on all sides of the square.'

'What sort of men? Any men that came along?' said the troop-horse. 'They teach us in riding-school to lie down and let our masters fire across us, but Dick Cunliffe is the only man I'd trust to do that. It tickles my girths, and, besides, I can't see with my head on the ground.'

'What does it matter who fires across you?' said the camel. 'There are plenty of men and plenty of other camels close by, and a great many clouds of smoke. I am not frightened then. I sit still and wait.'

'And yet,' said Billy, 'you dream bad dreams and upset the camp at night. Well! well! Before I'd lie down, not to speak of sitting down, and let a man fire across me, my heels and his head would have something to say to each other. Did you ever hear anything so awful as that?'

There was a long silence, and then one of the gun-bullocks lifted up his big head and said, 'This is very foolish indeed. There is only one way of fighting.'

'Oh, go on,' said Billy. '*Please* don't mind me. I suppose you fellows fight standing on your tails?'

'Only one way,' said the two together. (They must have been twins.) 'This is that way. To put all twenty yoke of us to the big gun as soon as Two Tails trumpets.' ('Two Tails' is camp slang for the elephants.)

'What does Two Tails trumpet for?' said the young mule.

'To show that he is not going any nearer to the smoke on the other side. Two Tails is a great coward. Then we tug the big gun all together – *Heya* – *Hullah! Heeyah! Hullah! We* do not climb like cats nor run like calves. We go across the level plain, twenty yoke of us, till we are unyoked again, and we graze while the big guns talk across the plain to some town with mud walls, and pieces of the wall fall out, and the dust goes up as though many cattle were coming home.'

'Oh! And you choose that time for grazing, do you?' said the young mule.

'That time or any other. Eating is always good. We eat till we are yoked up again and tug the gun back to where Two Tails is waiting for it. Sometimes there are big guns in the city that speak back, and some of us are killed, and then there is all the more grazing for those that are left. This is Fate – nothing but Fate. None the less, Two Tails is a great coward. That is the proper way to fight. We are brothers from Hapur. Our father was a sacred bull of Shiva. We have spoken.'

'Well, I've certainly learned something tonight,' said the troop-horse. 'Do you gentlemen of the screw-gun battery feel inclined to eat when you are being fired at with big guns, and Two Tails is behind you?'

'About as much as we feel inclined to sit down and let men sprawl all over us, or run into people with knives. I never heard such stuff. A mountain ledge, a well-balanced load, a driver you can trust to let you pick your own way, and I'm your mule; but the other things – no!' said Billy, with a stamp of his foot.

'Of course,' said the troop-horse, 'everyone is not made in the same way, and I can quite see that your family, on your father's side, would fail to understand a great many things.'

'Never you mind my family on my father's side,' said Billy angrily, for every mule hates to be reminded that his father was a donkey. 'My father was a Southern gentleman, and he could pull down and bite and kick into rags every horse he came across. Remember that, you big brown Brumby!'

Brumby means wild horse without any breeding. Imagine the feelings of Sunol if a car-horse called her a 'skate', and you can imagine how the Australian horse felt. I saw the white of his eye glitter in the dark.

'See here, you son of an imported Malaga jackass,' he said between his teeth, 'I'd have you know that I'm related on my mother's side to Carbine, winner of the Melbourne Cup; and where *I* come from we aren't accustomed to being ridden over roughshod by any parrot-mouthed, pig-headed mule in a pop-gun pea-shooter battery. Are you ready?'

'On your hind legs!' squealed Billy. They both reared up facing each other, and I was expecting a furious fight, when a gurgly, rumbly voice called out of the darkness to the right: 'Children, what are you fighting about there? Be quiet.'

Both beasts dropped down with a snort of disgust, for neither horse nor mule can bear to listen to an elephant's voice.

'It's Two Tails!' said the troop-horse. 'I can't stand him. A tail at each end isn't fair!'

'My feelings exactly,' said Billy, crowding into the troop-horse for company. 'We're very alike in some things.'

'I suppose we've inherited them from our mothers,' said the troop-horse. 'It's not worth quarrelling about. Hi! Two Tails, are you tied up?'

'Yes,' said Two Tails, with a laugh all up his trunk. 'I'm picketed for the night. I've heard what you fellows have been saying. But don't be afraid. I'm not coming over.'

The bullocks and the camel said, half aloud: 'Afraid of Two Tails – what nonsense!' And the bullocks went on: 'We are sorry that you heard, but it is true. Two Tails, why are you afraid of the guns when they fire?'

'Well,' said Two Tails, rubbing one hind leg against the other, exactly like a little boy saying poetry, 'I don't quite know whether you'd understand.'

'We don't, but we have to pull the guns,' said the bullocks.

'I know it, and I know you are a good deal braver than you think you are. But it's different with me. My battery captain called me a Pachydermatous Anachronism the other day.'

'That's another way of fighting, I suppose?' said Billy, who was recovering his spirits.

'*You* don't know what that means, of course, but I do. It means betwixt and between, and that is just where I am. I can see inside my head what will happen when a shell bursts; and you bullocks can't.'

'I can,' said the troop-horse. 'At least a little bit. I try not to think about it.'

'I can see more than you, and I *do* think about it. I know there's a great deal of me to take care of, and I know that nobody knows how to cure me when I'm sick. All they can do is to stop my driver's pay till I get well, and I can't trust my driver.'

'Ah!' said the troop-horse. 'That explains it. I can trust Dick.'

'You could put a whole regiment of Dicks on my back without making me feel any better. I know just enough to be uncomfortable, and not enough to go on in spite of it.'

'We do not understand,' said the bullocks.

'I know you don't. I'm not talking to you. You don't know what blood is.'

'We do,' said the bullocks. 'It is red stuff that soaks into the ground and smells.'

The troop-horse gave a kick and a bound and a snort.

'Don't talk of it,' he said. 'I can smell it now, just thinking of it. It makes me want to run – when I haven't Dick on my back.'

'But it is not here,' said the camel and the bullocks. 'Why are you so stupid?'

'It's vile stuff,' said Billy. 'I don't want to run, but I don't want to talk about it.'

'There you are!' said Two Tails, waving his tail to explain.

'Surely. Yes, we have been here all night,' said the bullocks.

Two Tails stamped his foot till the iron ring on it jingled. 'Oh, I'm not talking to *you*. You can't see inside your heads.'

'No. We see out of our four eyes,' said the bullocks. 'We see straight in front of us.'

'If I could do that and nothing else you wouldn't be needed to pull the big guns at all. If I was like my captain – he can see things inside his head before the firing begins, and he shakes all over, but he knows too much to run away – if I was like him I could pull the guns. But if I were as wise as all that I should never be here. I should be a king in the forest, as I used to be, sleeping half the day and bathing when I liked. I haven't had a good bath for a month.'

'That's all very fine,' said Billy; 'but giving a thing a long name doesn't make it any better.'

'H'sh!' said the troop-horse. 'I think I understand what Two Tails means.'

'You'll understand better in a minute,' said Two Tails angrily. 'Now, just you explain to me why you don't like *this*!'

He began trumpeting furiously at the top of his trumpet.

'Stop that!' said Billy and the troop-horse together, and I could hear them stamp and shiver. An elephant's trumpeting is always nasty, especially on a dark night.

'I shan't stop,' said Two Tails. 'Won't you explain that, please? *Hhrrmph! Rrrt! Rrrmph! Rrrhha!*' Then he stopped suddenly, and I heard a little whimper in the dark, and knew that Vixen had found me at last. She knew as well as I did that if there is one thing in the world the elephant is more afraid of than another, it is a little barking dog; so she stopped to bully Two Tails in his pickets, and yapped round his big feet. Two Tails shuffled and squeaked. 'Go away, little dog!' he said. 'Don't snuff at my ankles, or I'll kick at you. Good little dog – nice little doggie, then! Go home, you yelping little beast! Oh, why doesn't someone take her away? She'll bite me in a minute.'

'Seems to me,' said Billy to the troop-horse, 'that our friend Two Tails is afraid of most things. Now, if I had a full meal for every dog I've kicked across the parade-ground, I should be nearly as fat as Two Tails.'

I whistled, and Vixen ran up to me, muddy all over, and licked my nose, and told me a long tale about hunting for me all through the camp. I never let her know that I understood beast talk, or she would have taken all sorts of liberties. So I buttoned her into the breast of my overcoat, and Two Tails shuffled and stamped and growled to himself.

'Extraordinary! Most extraordinary!' he said. 'It runs in our family. Now, where has that nasty little beast gone to?'

I heard him feeling about with his trunk.

'We all seem to be affected in various ways,' he went on, blowing his nose. 'Now, you gentlemen were alarmed, I believe, when I trumpeted.'

'Not alarmed, exactly,' said the troop-horse, 'but it made me feel as though I had hornets where my saddle ought to be. Don't begin again.'

'I'm frightened of a little dog, and the camel here is frightened by bad dreams in the night.'

'It is very lucky for us that we haven't all got to fight in the same way,' said the troop-horse.

'What I want to know,' said the young mule, who had been quiet for a long time – 'what *I* want to know is, why we have to fight at all.'

'Because we're told to,' said the troop-horse, with a snort of contempt.

'Orders,' said Billy the mule; and his teeth snapped.

'*Hukm hai!* [It is an order],' said the camel with a gurgle; and Two Tails and the bullocks repeated, '*Hukm hai!*'

'Yes, but who gives the orders?' said the recruit-mule.

'The man who walks at your head – Or sits on your back – Or holds your nose-rope – Or twists your tail,' said Billy and the troop-horse and the camel and the bullocks one after the other.

'But who gives them the orders?'

'Now you want to know too much, young un,' said Billy, 'and that is one way of getting kicked. All you have to do is to obey the man at your head and ask no questions.'

'He's quite right,' said Two Tails. 'I can't always obey, because I'm betwixt and between; but Billy's right. Obey the man next to you who gives the order, or you'll stop all the battery, besides getting a thrashing.'

The gun-bullocks got up to go. 'Morning is coming,' they said. 'We will go back to our lines. It is true that we see only out of our eyes, and we are not very clever; but still, we are the only people tonight who have not been afraid. Good-night, you brave people.'

Nobody answered, and the troop-horse said, to change the conversation, 'Where's that little dog? A dog means a man somewhere about.'

'Here I am,' yapped Vixen, 'under the gun-tail with my man. You big, blundering beast of a camel, you, you upset our tent. My man's very angry.'

'Phew!' said the bullocks. 'He must be white?'

'Of course he is,' said Vixen. 'Do you suppose I'm looked after by a black bullock-driver?'

'*Huah! Ouach! Ugh!*' said the bullocks. 'Let us get away quickly.'

They plunged forward in the mud, and managed some- how to run their yoke on the pole of an ammunition-waggon, where it jammed.

'Now you *have* done it,' said Billy calmly. 'Don't struggle. You're hung up till daylight. What on earth's the matter?'

The bullocks went off into the long, hissing snorts that Indian cattle give, and pushed and crowded and slewed and stamped and slipped and nearly fell down in the mud, grunting savagely.

'You'll break your necks in a minute,' said the troop-horse. 'What's the matter with white men? I live with 'em.'

'They – eat – us! Pull!' said the near bullock: the yoke snapped with a twang, and they lumbered off together.

I never knew before what made Indian cattle so scared of Englishmen. We eat beef – a thing that no cattle-driver touches – and of course the cattle do not like it.

'May I be flogged with my own pad-chains! Who'd have thought of two big lumps like those losing their heads?' said Billy.

'Never mind. I'm going to look at this man. Most of the white men, I know, have things in their pockets,' said the troop-horse.

'I'll leave you, then. I can't say I'm over fond of 'em myself. Besides, white men who haven't a place to sleep in are more than likely to be thieves, and I've a good deal of Government property on my back. Come along, young un, and we'll go back to our lines. Good-night, Australia! See you on parade tomorrow, I suppose. Good-night old Hay-bales! – try to control your feelings, won't you? Good-night, Two Tails! If you pass us on the ground tomorrow, don't trumpet. It spoils our formation.'

Billy the mule stumped off with the swaggering limp of an old campaigner, as the troop-horse's head came nuzzling into my breast, and I gave him biscuits; while Vixen, who is a most conceited little dog, told him fibs about the scores of horses that she and I kept.

'I'm coming to the parade tomorrow in my dog-cart,' she said. 'Where will you be?'

'On the left hand of the second squadron. I set the time for all my troop, little lady,' he said politely. 'Now I must go back to Dick. My tail's all muddy, and he'll have two hours' hard work dressing me for parade.'

The big parade of all the thirty thousand men was held that afternoon, and Vixen and I had a good place close to the Viceroy and the Amir of Afghanistan, with his high, big black hat of astrakhan wool and the great diamond star in the centre. The first part of the review was all sunshine, and the regiments went by in wave upon wave of legs all moving together, and guns all in a line, till our eyes grew dizzy. Then the cavalry came up, to the beautiful cavalry canter of 'Bonnie Dundee', and Vixen cocked her ear where she sat on the dog-cart. The second squadron of the Lancers shot by, and there was the troop-horse, with his tail like spun silk, his head pulled into his breast, one ear forward and one back, setting the time for all his squadron, his legs going as smoothly as waltz-music. Then the big guns came by, and I saw Two Tails and two other elephants harnessed in line to a forty-pounder siege-gun, while twenty yoke of oxen walked behind. The seventh pair had a new yoke, and they looked rather stiff and tired. Last came the screw-guns, and Billy the mule carried himself as though he commanded all the troops, and his harness was oiled and polished till it winked. I gave a cheer all by myself for Billy the mule, but he never looked right or left.

The rain began to fall again, and for a while it was too misty to see what the troops were doing. They had made a big half-circle across the plain, and were spreading out into a line. That line grew and grew and grew till it was three-quarters of a mile long from wing to wing – one solid wall of men, horses, and guns. Then it came on straight toward the Viceroy and the Amir, and as it got nearer the ground began to shake, like the deck of a steamer when the engines are going fast.

Unless you have been there you cannot imagine what a frightening effect this steady come-down of troops has on the spectators, even when they know it is only a review. I looked at the Amir. Up till then he had not shown the shadow of a sign of astonishment or anything else; but now his eyes began to get bigger and bigger, and he picked up the reins on his horse's neck and looked behind him. For a minute it seemed as though he were going to draw his sword and slash his way out through the English men and women in the carriages at the back. Then the advance stopped dead, the ground stood still, the whole line saluted, and thirty bands began to play all together. That was the end of the review, and the regiments went off to their camps in the rain; and an infantry band struck up:

> The animals went in two by two,
> Hurrah!
> The animals went in two by two,
> The elephant and the battery mu-
> l', and they all got into the Ark
> For to get out of the rain!

Then I heard an old grizzled, long-haired Central Asian chief, who had come down with the Amir, asking questions of a native officer.

'Now,' said he, 'in what manner was this wonderful thing done?'

And the officer answered, 'There was an order, and they obeyed.'

'But are the beasts as wise as the men?' said the chief.

'They obey, as the men do. Mule, horse, elephant, or bullock, he obeys his driver, and the driver his sergeant, and the sergeant his lieutenant, and the lieutenant his captain, and the captain his major, and the major his colonel, and the colonel his brigadier commanding three regiments, and the brigadier his general, who obeys the Viceroy, who is the servant of the Empress. Thus it is done.'

'Would it were so in Afghanistan!' said the chief; 'for there we obey only our own wills.'

'And for that reason,' said the native officer, twirling his moustache, 'your Amir whom you do not obey must come here and take orders from our Viceroy.'

Parade Song of the Camp Animals

Elephants of the Gun-teams

We lent to Alexander the strength of Hercules,
The wisdom of our foreheads, the cunning of our knees;
We bowed our necks to service; they ne'er were loosed again –
Make way there, way for the ten-foot teams
       Of the Forty-Pounder train!

Gun-bullocks

Those heroes in their harnesses avoid a cannonball,
And what they know of powder upsets them one and all;
Then *we* come into action and tug the guns again –
Make way there, way for the twenty yoke
       Of the Forty-Pounder train!

Cavalry Horses

By the brand on my withers, the finest of tunes
Is played by the Lancers, Hussars, and Dragoons,
And it's sweeter than 'Stables' or 'Water' to me,
The Cavalry Canter of 'Bonnie Dundee'!

Then feed us and break us and handle and groom,
And give us good riders and plenty of room,
And launch us in column of squadron and see
The way of the war-horse to 'Bonnie Dundee'!

Screw-gun Mules

As me and my companions were scrambling up a hill,
The path was lost in rolling stones, but we went forward still;
For we can wriggle and climb, my lads, and turn up everywhere,
And it's our delight on a mountain height, with a leg or two to spare!

Good luck to every sergeant, then, that lets us pick our road!
Bad luck to all the driver-men that cannot pack a load!
For we can wriggle and climb, my lads, and turn up everywhere,
And it's our delight on a mountain height, with a leg or two to spare!

Commissariat Camels

We haven't a camelty tune of our own
To help us trollop along,
But every neck is a hair-trombone
(*Rtt-ta-ta-ta!* is a hair-trombone!)
And this is our marching-song:
Can't! Don't! Shan't! Won't!
Pass it along the line!
Somebody's pack has slid from his back,
'Wish it were only mine!
Somebody's load has tipped off in the road –
Cheer for a halt and a row!
Urr! Yarrh! Grr! Arrh!
Somebody's catching it now!

All the Beasts Together

Children of the Camp are we,
Serving each in his degree;
Children of the yoke and goad,
Pack and harness, pad and load.
See our line across the plain,
Like a heel-rope bent again,
Reaching, writhing, rolling far,
Sweeping all away to war!
While the men that walk beside,
Dusty, silent, heavy-eyed,
Cannot tell why we or they
March and suffer day by day.
  Children of the Camp are we,
  Serving each in his degree;
  Children of the yoke and goad,
  Pack and harness, pad and load.

THE SECOND JUNGLE BOOK

Contents

How Fear Came

The stream is shrunk – the pool is dry,
And we be comrades, thou and I;
With fevered jowl and dusty flank
Each jostling each along the bank;
And by one drouthy fear made still,
Forgoing thought of quest or kill.
Now 'neath his dam the fawn may see,
The lean Pack-wolf as cowed as he,
And the tall buck, unflinching, note
The fangs that tore his father's throat.
The pools are shrunk – the streams are dry,
And we be playmates, thou and I,
Till yonder cloud – Good Hunting! – loose
The rain that breaks our Water Truce.

THE LAW OF THE JUNGLE – which is by far the oldest law in the world – has arranged for almost every kind of accident that may befall the Jungle People, till now its code is as perfect as time and custom can make it. You will remember that Mowgli spent a great part of his life in the Seeonee Wolf-Pack, learning the Law from Baloo, the Brown Bear; and it was Baloo who told him, when the boy grew impatient at the constant orders, that the Law was like the Giant Creeper, because it dropped across everyone's back and no one could escape. 'When thou hast lived as long as I have, Little Brother, thou wilt see how all the Jungle obeys at least one Law. And that will be no pleasant sight,' said Baloo.

This talk went in at one ear and out at the other, for a boy who spends his life eating and sleeping does not worry about anything till it actually stares him in the face. But, one year, Baloo's words came true, and Mowgli saw all the Jungle working under the Law.

It began when the winter Rains failed almost entirely, and Ikki, the Porcupine, meeting Mowgli in a bamboo-thicket, told him that the wild yams were drying up. Now everybody knows that Ikki is ridiculously fastidious in his choice of food, and will eat nothing but the very best and ripest. So Mowgli laughed and said, 'What is that to me?'

'Not much *now*,' said Ikki, rattling his quills in a stiff, uncomfortable way, 'but later we shall see. Is there any more diving into the deep rock-pool below the Bee-Rocks, Little Brother?'

'No. The foolish water is going all away, and I do not wish to break my head,' said Mowgli, who, in those days, was quite sure that he knew as much as any five of the Jungle People put together.

'That is thy loss. A small crack might let in some wisdom.' Ikki ducked quickly to prevent Mowgli from pulling his nose-bristles, and Mowgli told Baloo what Ikki had said. Baloo looked very grave, and mumbled half to himself: 'If I were alone I would change my hunting-grounds now, before the others began to think. And yet – hunting among strangers ends in fighting; and they might hurt the Man-cub. We must wait and see how the mohwa blooms.'

That spring the mohwa tree, that Baloo was so fond of, never flowered. The greeny, cream-coloured, waxy blossoms were heat-killed before they were born, and only a few bad-smelling petals came down when he stood on his hind legs and shook the tree. Then, inch by inch, the untempered heat crept into the heart of the Jungle, turning it yellow, brown, and at last black. The green growths in the sides of the ravines burned up to broken wires and curled films of dead stuff; the hidden pools sank down and caked over, keeping the last least footmark on their edges as if it had been cast in iron; the juicy-stemmed creepers fell away from the trees they clung to and died at their feet; the bamboos withered, clanking when the hot winds blew, and the moss peeled off the rocks deep in the Jungle, till they were as bare and as hot as the quivering blue boulders in the bed of the stream.

The birds and the monkey-people went north early in the year, for they knew what was coming; and the deer and the wild pig broke far away to the perished fields of the villages, dying sometimes before the eyes of men too weak to kill them. Chil, the Kite, stayed and grew fat, for there was a great deal of carrion, and evening after evening he brought the news to the beasts, too weak to force their way to fresh hunting-grounds, that the sun was killing the Jungle for three days' flight in every direction.

Mowgli, who had never known what real hunger meant, fell back on stale honey, three years old, scraped out of deserted rock-hives – honey black as a sloe, and dusty with dried sugar. He hunted, too, for deep-boring grubs under the bark of the trees, and robbed the wasps of their new broods. All the game in the jungle was no more than skin and bone, and Bagheera could kill thrice in a night, and hardly get a full meal. But the want of water was the worst, for though the Jungle People drink seldom they must drink deep.

And the heat went on and on, and sucked up all the moisture, till at last the main channel of the Waingunga was the only stream that carried a trickle of water between its dead banks; and when Hathi, the wild elephant, who lives for a hundred years and more, saw a long, lean blue ridge of rock show dry in the very centre of the stream, he knew that he was looking at the Peace Rock, and then and there he lifted up his trunk and proclaimed the Water Truce, as his father before him had proclaimed it fifty years ago. The deer, wild pig, and buffalo took up the cry hoarsely; and Chil, the Kite, flew in great circles far and wide, whistling and shrieking the warning.

By the Law of the Jungle it is death to kill at the drinking-places when once the Water Truce has been declared. The reason of this is that drinking comes before eating. Everyone in the Jungle can scramble along somehow when only game is scarce; but water is water, and when there is but one source of supply, all hunting stops while the Jungle People go there for their needs. In good seasons, when water was plentiful, those who came down to drink at the Waingunga – or anywhere else, for that matter – did so at the risk of their lives, and that risk made no small part of the fascination of the night's doings. To move down so cunningly that never a leaf stirred; to wade knee-deep in the roaring shallows that drown all noise from behind; to drink, looking backward over one shoulder, every muscle ready for the first desperate bound of keen terror; to roll on the sandy margin, and return, wet-muzzled and well plumped out, to the admiring herd, was a thing that all tall-antlered young bucks took a delight in, precisely because they knew that at any moment Bagheera or Shere Khan might leap upon them and bear them down. But now all that life-and-death fun was ended, and the Jungle People came up, starved and weary, to the shrunken river – tiger, bear, deer, buffalo, and pig, all together – drank the fouled waters, and hung above them, too exhausted to move off.

The deer and the pig had tramped all day in search of something better than dried bark and withered leaves. The buffaloes had found no wallows to be cool in, and no green crops to steal. The snakes had left the Jungle and come down to the river in the hope of finding a stray frog. They curled round wet stones, and never offered to strike when the nose of a rooting pig dislodged them. The river-turtles had long ago been killed by Bagheera, cleverest of hunters, and the fish had buried themselves deep in the dry mud. Only the Peace Rock lay across the shallows like a long snake, and the little tired ripples hissed as they dried on its hot side.

It was here that Mowgli came nightly for the cool and the companionship. The most hungry of his enemies would hardly have cared for the boy then, His naked hide made him seem more lean and wretched than any of his fellows. His hair was bleached to tow colour by the sun; his ribs stood out like the ribs of a basket, and the lumps on his knees and elbows, where he was used to tracking on all fours, gave his shrunken limbs the look of knotted grass-stems. But his eye, under his matted forelock, was cool and quiet, for Bagheera was his adviser in this time of trouble, and told him to go quietly, hunt slowly, and never, on any account, to lose his temper.

'It is an evil time,' said the Black Panther, one furnace-hot evening, 'but it will go if we can live till the end. Is thy stomach full, Man-cub?'

'There is stuff in my stomach, but I get no good of it. Think you, Bagheera, the Rains have forgotten us and will never come again?'

'Not I! We shall see the mohwa in blossom yet, and the little fawns all fat with new grass. Come down to the Peace Rock and hear the news. On my back, Little Brother.'

'This is no time to carry weight. I can still stand alone, but – indeed we be no fatted bullocks, we two.'

Bagheera looked along his ragged, dusty flank and whispered. 'Last night I killed a bullock under the yoke. So low was I brought that I think I should not have dared to spring if he had been loose. *Wou!*'

Mowgli laughed. 'Yes, we be great hunters now,' said he. 'I am very bold – to eat grubs,' and the two came down together through the crackling undergrowth to the river-bank and the lacework of shoals that ran out from it in every direction.

'The water cannot live long,' said Baloo, joining them. 'Look across. Yonder are trails like the roads of Man.'

On the level plain of the farther bank the stiff jungle-grass had died standing, and, dying, had mummied. The beaten tracks of the deer and the pig, all heading toward the river, had striped that colourless plain with dusty gullies driven through the ten-foot grass, and, early as it was, each long avenue was full of first-comers hastening to the water. You could hear the does and fawns coughing in the snuff-like dust.

Upstream, at the bend of the sluggish pool round the Peace Rock, and Warden of the Water Truce, stood Hathi, the wild elephant, with his sons, gaunt and grey in the moonlight, rocking to and fro – always rocking. Below him a little were the vanguard of the deer; below these, again, the pig and the wild buffalo; and on the opposite bank, where the tall trees came down to the water's edge, was the place set apart for the Eaters of Flesh – the tiger, the wolves, the panther, the bear, and the others.

'We are under one Law, indeed,' said Bagheera, wading into the water and looking across at the lines of clicking horns and starting eyes where the deer and the pig pushed each other to and fro. 'Good hunting, all you of my blood,' he added, lying own at full length, one flank thrust out of the shallows; and then, between his teeth, 'But for that which is the Law it would be *very* good hunting.'

The quick-spread ears of the deer caught the last sentence, and a frightened whisper ran along the ranks. 'The Truce! Remember the Truce!'

'Peace there, peace!' gurgled Hathi, the wild elephant. 'The Truce holds, Bagheera. This is no time to talk of hunting.'

'Who should know better than I?' Bagheera answered, rolling his yellow eyes upstream. 'I am an eater of turtles – a fisher of frogs. Ngaayah! Would I could get good from chewing branches!'

'*We* wish so, very greatly,' bleated a young fawn, who had only been born that spring, and did not at all like it. Wretched as the Jungle People were, even Hathi could not help chuckling; while Mowgli, lying on his elbows in the warm water, laughed aloud, and beat up the scum with his feet.

'Well spoken, little bud-horn,' Bagheera purred. 'When the Truce ends that shall be remembered in thy favour,' and he looked keenly through the darkness to make sure of recognising the fawn again.

Gradually the talking spread up and down the drinking-places. One could hear the scuffling, snorting pig asking for more room; the buffaloes grunting among themselves as they lurched out across the sand-bars, and the deer telling pitiful stories of their long footsore wanderings in quest of food. Now and again they asked some question of the Eaters of Flesh across the river, but all the news was bad, and the roaring hot wind of the Jungle came and went between the rocks and the rattling branches, and scattered twigs, and dust on the water.

'The menfolk, too, they die beside their ploughs,' said a young sambhur. 'I passed three between sunset and night. They lay still, and their Bullocks with them. We also shall lie still in a little.'

'The river has fallen since last night,' said Baloo. 'O Hathi, hast thou ever seen the like of this drought?'

'It will pass, it will pass,' said Hathi, squirting water along his back and sides.

'We have one here that cannot endure long,' said Baloo; and he looked toward the boy he loved.

'I?' said Mowgli indignantly, sitting up in the water. 'I have no long fur to cover my bones, but – but if *thy* hide were taken off, Baloo – '

Hathi shook all over at the idea, and Baloo said severely:

'Man-cub, that is not seemly to tell a Teacher of the Law. Never have I been seen without my hide.'

'Nay, I meant no harm, Baloo; but only that thou art, as it were, like the coconut in the husk, and I am the same coconut all naked. Now that brown husk of thine – ' Mowgli was sitting cross-legged, and explaining things with his forefinger in his usual way, when Bagheera put out a paddy paw and pulled him over backward into the water.

'Worse and worse,' said the Black Panther, as the boy rose spluttering. 'First Baloo is to be skinned, and now he is a coconut. Be careful that he does not do what the ripe coconuts do.'

'And what is that?' said Mowgli, off his guard for the minute, though that is one of the oldest catches in the Jungle.

'Break thy head,' said Bagheera quietly, pulling him under again.

'It is not good to make a jest of thy teacher,' said the bear, when Mowgli had been ducked for the third time.

'Not good! What would ye have? That naked thing running to and fro makes a monkey-jest of those who have once been good hunters, and pulls the best of us by the whiskers for sport.' This was Shere Khan, the Lame Tiger, limping down to the water. He waited a little to enjoy the sensation he made among the deer on the opposite to lap, growling: 'The Jungle has become a whelping-ground for naked cubs now. Look at me, Man-cub!'

Mowgli looked – stared, rather – as insolently as he knew how, and in a minute Shere Khan turned away uneasily. 'Man-cub this, and Man-cub that,' he rumbled, going on with his drink, 'the cub is neither man nor cub, or he would have been afraid. Next season I shall have to beg his leave for a drink. Augrh!'

'That may come, too,' said Bagheera, looking him steadily between the eyes. 'That may come, too – Faugh, Shere Khan! – what new shame hast thou brought here?'

The Lame Tiger had dipped his chin and jowl in the water, and dark, oily streaks were floating from it downstream.

'Man!' said Shere Khan coolly, 'I killed an hour since.' He went on purring and growling to himself.

The line of beasts shook and wavered to and fro, and a whisper went up that grew to a cry. 'Man! Man! He has killed Man!' Then all looked towards Hathi, the wild elephant, but he seemed not to hear. Hathi never does anything till the time comes, and that is one of the reasons why he lives so long.

'At such a season as this to kill Man! Was no other game afoot?' said Bagheera scornfully, drawing himself out of the tainted water, and shaking each paw, cat-fashion, as he did so.

'I killed for choice – not for food.' The horrified whisper began again, and Hathi's watchful little white eye cocked itself in Shere Khan's direction. 'For choice,' Shere Khan drawled. 'Now come I to drink and make me clean again. Is there any to forbid?'

Bagheera's back began to curve like a bamboo in a high wind, but Hathi lifted up his trunk and spoke quietly.

'Thy kill was from choice?' he asked; and when Hathi asks a question it is best to answer.

'Even so. It was my right and my Night. Thou knowest, O Hathi.' Shere Khan spoke almost courteously.

'Yes, I know,' Hathi answered; and, after a little silence, 'Hast thou drunk thy fill?'

'For tonight, yes.'

'Go, then. The river is to drink, and not to defile. None but the Lame Tiger would so have boasted of his right at this season when – when we suffer together – Man and Jungle People alike.' Clean or unclean, get to thy lair, Shere Khan!'

The last words rang out like silver trumpets, and Hathi's three sons rolled forward half a pace, though there was no need. Shere Khan slunk away, not daring to growl, for he knew – what everyone else knows – that when the last comes to the last, Hathi is the Master of the Jungle.'

'What is this right Shere Khan speaks of?' Mowgli whispered in Bagheera's ear. 'To kill Man is always shameful. The Law says so. And yet Hathi says – '

'Ask him. I do not know, Little Brother. Right or no right, if Hathi had not spoken I would have taught that lame butcher his lesson. To come to the Peace Rock fresh from a kill of Man – and to boast of it – is a jackal's trick. Besides, he tainted the good water.'

Mowgli waited for a minute to pick up his courage, because no one cared to address Hathi directly, and then he cried: 'What is Shere Khan's right, O Hathi?' Both banks echoed his words, for all the People of the Jungle are intensely curious, and they had just seen something that none except Baloo, who looked very thoughtful, seemed to understand.

'It is an old tale,' said Hathi; 'a tale older than the Jungle. Keep silence along the banks and I will tell that tale.'

There was a minute or two of pushing and shouldering among the pigs and the buffalo, and then the leaders of the herds grunted, one after another, 'We wait,' and Hathi strode forward, till he was nearly knee-deep in the pool by the Peace Rock. Lean and wrinkled and yellow-tusked though he was, he looked what the Jungle knew him to be – their master.

'Ye know, children,' he began, 'that of all things ye most fear Man'; and there was a mutter of agreement.

'This tale touches thee, Little Brother,' said Bagheera to Mowgli.

'I? I am of the Pack – a hunter of the Free People,' Mowgli answered. 'What have I to do with Man?'

'And ye do not know why ye fear Man?' Hathi went on. 'This is the reason. In the beginning of the Jungle, and none know when that was, we of the Jungle walked together, having no fear of one another. In those days there was no drought, and leaves and flowers and fruit grew on the same tree, and we ate nothing at all except leaves and flowers and grass and fruit and bark.'

'I am glad I was not born in those days,' said Bagheera. 'Bark is only good to sharpen claws.'

'And the Lord of the Jungle was Tha, the First of the Elephants. He drew the Jungle out of deep waters with his trunk; and where he made furrows in the ground with his tusks, there the rivers ran; and where he struck with his foot, there rose ponds of good water; and when he blew through his trunk – thus – the trees fell. That was the manner in which the Jungle was made by Tha; and so the tale was told to me.'

'It has not lost fat in the telling,' Bagheera whispered, and Mowgli laughed behind his hand.

'In those days there was no corn or melons or pepper or sugar-cane, nor were there any little huts such as ye have all seen; and the Jungle People knew nothing of Man, but lived in the Jungle together, making one people. But presently they began to dispute over their food, though there was grazing enough for all. They were lazy. Each wished to eat where he lay, as sometimes we can do now when the spring rains are good. Tha, the First of the Elephants, was busy making new jungles and leading the rivers in their beds. He could not walk in all places; therefore he made the First of the Tigers the master and the judge of the Jungle, to whom the Jungle People should bring their disputes. In those days the First of the Tigers ate fruit and grass with the others. He was as large as I am, and he was very beautiful, in colour all over like the blossom of the yellow creeper. There was never stripe nor bar upon his hide in those good days when this the Jungle was new. All the Jungle People came before him without fear, and his word was the Law of all the Jungle. We were then, remember ye, one people.

'Yet upon a night there was a dispute between two bucks – a grazing-quarrel such as ye now settle with the horns and the forefeet – and it is said that as the two spoke together before the First of the Tigers lying among the flowers, a buck pushed him with his horns, and the First of the Tigers forgot that he was the master and judge of the Jungle, and, leaping upon that buck, broke his neck.

'Till that night never one of us had died, and the First of the Tigers, seeing what he had done, and being made foolish by the scent of the blood, ran away into the marshes of the North, and we of the Jungle, left without a judge, fell to fighting among ourselves; and Tha heard the noise of it and came back. Then some of us said this and some of us said that, but he saw the dead buck among the flowers, and asked who had killed, and we of the Jungle would not tell because the smell of the blood made us foolish. We ran to and fro in circles, capering and crying out and shaking our heads. Then Tha gave an order to the trees that hang low, and to the trailing creepers of the Jungle, that they should mark the killer of the buck so that he should know him again, and he said, "Who will now be master of the Jungle People?" Then up leaped the Grey Ape who lives in the branches, and said, "I will now be master of the Jungle." At this Tha laughed, and said, "So be it," and went away very angry.

'Children, ye know the Grey Ape. He was then as he is now. At the first he made a wise face for himself, but in a little while he began to scratch and to leap up and down, and when Tha came back he found the Grey Ape hanging, head down, from a bough, mocking those who stood below; and they mocked him again. And so there was no Law in the Jungle – only foolish talk and senseless words.

'Then Tha called us all together and said: "The first of your masters has brought Death into the Jungle, and the second Shame. Now it is time there was a Law, and a Law that ye must not break. Now ye shall know Fear, and when ye have found him ye shall know that he is your master, and the rest shall follow." Then we of the jungle said, "What is Fear?" And Tha said, "Seek till ye find." So we went up and down the Jungle seeking for Fear, and presently the buffaloes – '

'Ugh!' said Mysa, the leader of the buffaloes, from their sandbank.

'Yes, Mysa, it was the buffaloes. They came back with the news that in a cave in the Jungle sat Fear, and that he had no hair, and went upon his hind legs. Then we of the Jungle followed the herd till we came to that cave, and Fear stood at the mouth of it, and he was, as the buffaloes had said, hairless, and he walked upon his hinder legs. When he saw us he cried out, and his voice filled us with the fear that we have now of that voice when we hear it, and we ran away, tramping upon and tearing each other because we were afraid. That night, so it was told to me, we of the Jungle did not lie down together as used to be our custom, but each tribe drew off by itself – the pig with the pig, the deer with the deer; horn to horn, hoof to hoof – like keeping to like, and so lay shaking in the Jungle.

'Only the First of the Tigers was not with us, for he was still hidden in the marshes of the North, and when word was brought to him of the Thing we had seen in the cave, he said. "I will go to this Thing and break his neck." So he ran all the night till he came to the cave; but the trees and the creepers on his path, remembering the order that Tha had given, let down their branches and marked him as he ran, drawing their fingers across his back, his flank, his forehead, and his jowl. Wherever they touched him there was a mark and a stripe upon his yellow hide. *And those stripes do this children wear to this day!* When he came to the cave, Fear, the Hairless One, put out his hand and called him "The Striped One that comes by night", and the First of the Tigers was afraid of the Hairless One, and ran back to the swamps howling.'

Mowgli chuckled quietly here, his chin in the water.

'So loud did he howl that Tha heard him and said, "What is the sorrow?" And the First of the Tigers, lifting up his muzzle to the new-made sky, which is now so old, said: "Give me back my power, O Tha. I am made ashamed before all the Jungle, and I have run away from a Hairless One, and he has called me a shameful name." "And why?" said Tha. "Because I am smeared with the mud of the marshes," said the First of the Tigers. "Swim, then, and roll on the wet grass, and if it be mud it will wash away," said Tha; and the First of the Tigers swam, and rolled and rolled upon the grass, till the Jungle ran round and round before his eyes, but not one little bar upon all his hide was changed, and Tha, watching him, laughed. Then the First of the Tigers said: "What have I done that this comes to me?' Tha said, "Thou hast killed the buck, and thou hast let Death loose in the Jungle, and with Death has come Fear, so that the people of the Jungle are afraid one of the other, as thou art afraid of the Hairless One.' The First of the Tigers said, "They will never fear me, for I knew them since the beginning.' Tha said, "Go and see.' And the First of the Tigers ran to and fro, calling aloud to the deer and the pig and the sambhur and the porcupine and all the Jungle Peoples, and they all ran away from him who had been their judge, because they were afraid.

'Then the First of the Tigers came back, and his pride was broken in him, and, beating his head upon the ground, he tore up the earth with all his feet and said: "Remember that I was once the Master of the Jungle. Do not forget me, O Tha! Let my children remember that I was once without shame or fear!" And Tha said: "This much I will do, because thou and I together saw the Jungle made. For one night in each year it shall be as it was before the buck was killed – for thee and for thy children. In that one night, if ye meet the Hairless One – and his name is Man – ye shall not be afraid of him, but he shall be afraid of you, as though ye were judges of the Jungle and masters of all things. Show him mercy in that night of his fear, for thou hast known what Fear is."

'Then the First of the Tigers answered, "I am content"; but when next he drank he saw the black stripes upon his flank and his side, and he remembered the name that the Hairless One had given him, and he was angry. For a year he lived in the marshes waiting till Tha should keep his promise. And upon a night when the jackal of the Moon [the Evening Star] stood clear of the Jungle, he felt that his Night was upon him, and he went to that cave to meet the Hairless One. Then it happened as Tha promised, for the Hairless One fell down before him and lay along the ground, and the First of the Tigers struck him and broke his back, for he thought that there was but one such Thing in the Jungle, and that he had killed Fear. Then, nosing above the kill, he heard Tha coming down from the woods of the North, and presently the voice of the First of the Elephants, which is the voice that we hear now –'

The thunder was rolling up and down the dry, scarred hills, but it brought no rain – only heat – lightning that flickered along the ridges – and Hathi went on: '*That* was the voice he heard, and it said: "Is this thy mercy?" The First of the Tigers licked his lips and said: "What matter? I have killed Fear." And Tha said: "O blind and foolish! Thou hast untied the feet of Death, and he will follow thy trail till thou diest. Thou hast taught Man to kill!"

'The First of the Tigers, standing stiffly to his kill, said. "He is as the buck was. There is no Fear. Now I will judge the Jungle Peoples once more."

'And Tha said: "Never again shall the Jungle Peoples come to thee. They shall never cross thy trail, nor sleep near thee, nor follow after thee, nor browse by thy lair. Only Fear shall follow thee, and with a blow that thou cannot see he shall bid thee wait his pleasure. He shall make the ground to open under thy feet, and the creeper to twist about thy neck, and the tree-trunks to grow together about thee higher than thou canst leap, and at the last he shall take thy hide to wrap his cubs when they are cold. Thou hast shown him no mercy, and none will he show thee.'

'The First of the Tigers was very bold, for his Night was still on him, and he said: "The Promise of Tha is the Promise of Tha. He will not take away my Night?" And Tha said: "The one Night is thine, as I have said, but there is a price to pay. Thou hast taught Man to kill, and he is no slow learner."

'The First of the Tigers said: "He is here under my foot, and his back is broken. Let the Jungle know I have killed Fear."

'Then Tha laughed, and said: "Thou hast killed one of many, but thou thyself shalt tell the Jungle – for thy Night is ended."

'So the day came; and from the mouth of the cave went out another Hairless One, and he saw the kill in the path, and the First of the Tigers above it, and he took a pointed stick – '

'They throw a thing that cuts now,' said Ikki, rustling down the bank; for Ikki was considered uncommonly good eating by the Gonds – they called him Ho-Igoo – and he knew something of the wicked little Gondee axe that whirls across a clearing like a dragonfly.

'It was a pointed stick, such as they put in the foot of a pit-trap,' said Hathi, 'and throwing it, he struck the First of the Tigers deep in the flank. Thus it happened as Tha said, for the First of the Tigers ran howling up and down the Jungle till he tore out the stick, and all the Jungle knew that the Hairless One could strike from far off, and they feared more than before. So it came about that the First of the Tigers taught the Hairless One to kill – and ye know what harm that has since done to all our peoples – through the noose, and the pitfall, and the hidden trap, and the flying stick and the stinging fly that comes out of white smoke [Hathi meant the rifle], and the Red Flower that drives us into the open. Yet for one night in the year the Hairless One fears the Tiger, as Tha promised, and never has the Tiger given him cause to be less afraid. Where he finds him, there he kills him, remembering how the First of the Tigers was made ashamed. For the rest, Fear walks up and down the Jungle by day and by night.'

'*Ahi! Aoo!*' said the deer, thinking of what it all meant to them.

'And only when there is one great Fear over all, as there is now, can we of the Jungle lay aside our little fears, and meet together in one place as we do now.'

'For one night only does Man fear the Tiger?' said Mowgli.

'For one night only,' said Hathi.

'But I – but we – but all the Jungle knows that Shere Khan kills Man twice and thrice in a moon.'

'Even so. *Then* he springs from behind and turns his head aside as he strikes, for he is full of fear. If Man looked at him he would run. But on his one Night he goes openly down to the village. He walks between the houses and thrusts his head into the doorway, and the men fall on their faces, and there he does his kill. One kill in that Night.'

'Oh!' said Mowgli to himself, rolling over in the water. '*Now* I see why it was Shere Khan bade me look at him! He got no good of it, for he could not hold his eyes steady, and – and I certainly did not fall down at his feet. But then I am not a man, being of the Free People.'

'Umm!' said Bagheera deep in his furry throat. 'Does the Tiger know his Night?'

'Never till the Jackal of the Moon stands clear of the evening mist. Sometimes it falls in the dry summer and sometimes in the wet rains – this one Night of the Tiger. But for the First of the Tigers, this would never have been, nor would any of us have known fear.'

The deer grunted sorrowfully and Bagheera's lips curled in a wicked smile. 'Do men know this – tale?' said he.

'None know it except the tigers, and we, the elephants – the children of Tha. Now ye by the pools have heard it, and I have spoken.'

Hathi dipped his trunk into the water as a sign that he did not wish to talk.

'But – but – but,' said Mowgli, turning to Baloo, 'why did not the First of the Tigers continue to eat grass and leaves and trees? He did but break the buck's neck. He did not *eat*. What led him to the hot meat?'

'The trees and the creepers marked him, Little Brother, and made him the striped thing that we see. Never again would he eat their fruit; but from that day he revenged himself upon the deer, and the others, the Eaters of Grass,' said Baloo.

'Then *thou knowest* the tale. Heh? Why have I never heard?'

'Because the Jungle is full of such tales. If I made a beginning there would never be an end to them. Let go my ear, Little Brother.'

The Law of the Jungle

 UST TO GIVE YOU AN IDEA of the immense variety of the Jungle Law, I have translated into verse (Baloo always recited them in a sort of singsong) a few of the laws that apply to the wolves. There are, of course, hundreds and hundreds more, but these will do for specimens of the simpler rulings.

Now this is the Law of the Jungle – as old and as true as the sky;
And the Wolf that shall keep it may prosper, but the Wolf that
                                                shall break it must die.

As the creeper that girdles the tree-trunk the Law runneth forward
                                                and back –
For the strength of the Pack is the Wolf, and the strength of the
                                                Wolf is the Pack.

Wash daily from nose-tip to tail-tip; drink deeply, but
                                                never too deep;
And remember the night is for hunting, and forget not the
                                                day is for sleep.

The jackal may follow the Tiger, but, Cub, when thy whiskers
                                                are grown,
Remember the Wolf is a hunter – go forth and get food
                                                of thine own.

Keep peace with the Lords of the Jungle – the Tiger,
                                                the Panther, the Bear;
And trouble not Hathi the Silent, and mock not the Boar
                                                in his lair.

When Pack meets with Pack in the Jungle, and neither will
                                                go from the trail,
Lie down till the leaders have spoken – it may be fair words
                                                shall prevail.

When ye fight with a Wolf of the Pack, ye must fight him
                                                alone and afar,

Lest others take part in the quarrel, and the Pack be diminished
                                        by war.

The Lair of the Wolf is his refuge, and where he has made
                                        him his home,
Not even the Head Wolf may enter, not even the Council
                                        may come.

The Lair of the Wolf is his refuge, but where he has digged
                                        it too plain,
The Council shall send him a message, and so he shall
                                        change it again.

If ye kill before midnight, be silent, and wake not the woods
                                        with your bay,
Lest ye frighten the deer from the crops, and the brothers
                                        go empty away.

Ye may kill for yourselves, and your mates, and your cubs
                                        as they need, and ye can;
But kill not for pleasure of killing, and *seven times never kill Man.*

If ye plunder his Kill from a weaker, devour not all in thy pride;
Pack-Right is the right of the meanest; so leave him the
                                        head and the hide.

The Kill of the Pack is the meat of the Pack. Ye must eat
                                        where it lies;
And no one may carry away of that meat to his lair, or he dies.

The Kill of the Wolf is the meat of the Wolf. He may do
                                        what he will,
But, till he has given permission, the Pack may not eat of that Kill.

Cub-Right is the right of the Yearling. From all of his Pack
                                        he may claim
Full-gorge when the killer has eaten; and none may refuse
                                        him the same.

Lair-Right is the right of the Mother. From all of her year
                                        she may claim
One haunch of each kill for her litter, and none may deny
                                        her the same.

Cave-Right is the right of the Father – to hunt by himself
for his own.
He is freed of all calls to the Pack; he is judged by the Council alone.

Because of his age and his cunning, because of his gripe
and his paw,
In all that the Law leaveth open, the word of the Head Wolf
is Law.

Now these are the Laws of the Jungle, and many and mighty are they;
But the head and the hoof of the Law and the haunch and the
hump is – Obey!

The Miracle of Purun Bhagat

The night we felt the earth would move
    We stole and plucked him by the hand,
Because we loved him with the love
    That knows but cannot understand.

And when the roaring hillside broke,
    And all our world fell down in rain,
We saved him, we the Little Folk;
    But lo! he does not come again!

Mourn now, we saved him for the sake
    Of such poor love as wild ones may.
Mourn ye! Our brother will not wake,
    And his own kind drive us away!

Dirge of the Langurs

THERE WAS ONCE A MAN IN INDIA who was Prime Minister of one of the semi-independent native States in the northwestern part of the country. He was a Brahmin, so high-caste that caste ceased to have any particular meaning for him; and his father had been an important official in the gay-coloured rag-tag and bobtail of an old-fashioned Hindu Court. But as Purun Dass grew up he felt that the old order of things was changing, and that if anyone wished to get on in the world he must stand well with the English, and imitate all that the English believed to be good. At the same time a native official must keep his own master's favour. This was a difficult game, but the quiet, close-mouthed young Brahmin, helped by a good English education at a Bombay University, played it coolly, and rose, step by step, to be Prime Minister of the kingdom. That is to say, he held more real power than his master the Maharajah.

When the old king – who was suspicious of the English, their railways and telegraphs – died, Purun Dass stood high with his young successor, who had been tutored by an Englishman; and between them, though he always took care that his master should have the credit, they established schools for little girls, made roads, and started State dispensaries and shows of agricultural implements, and published a yearly blue-book on the 'Moral and Material Progress of the State', and the Foreign Office and the Government of India were delighted. Very few native States take up English progress altogether, for they will not believe, as Purun Dass showed he did, that what was good for the Englishman must be twice as good for the Asiatic. The Prime Minister became the honoured friend of Viceroys, and Governors, and Lieutenant-Governors, and medical missionaries, and common missionaries, and hard-riding English officers who came to shoot in the State preserves, as well as of whole hosts of tourists who travelled up and down India in the cold weather, showing how things ought to be managed. In his spare time he would endow scholarships for the study of medicine and manufactures on strictly English lines, and write letters to the *Pioneer*, the greatest Indian daily paper, explaining his master's aims and objects.

At last he went to England on a visit, and had to pay enormous sums to the priests when he came back; for even so high-caste a Brahmin as Purun Dass lost caste by crossing the Black Sea. In London he met and talked with everyone worth knowing – men whose names go all over the world – and saw a great deal more than he said. He was given honorary degrees by learned universities, and he made speeches and talked of Hindu social reform to English ladies in evening dress, till all London cried, 'This is the most fascinating man we have ever met at dinner since cloths were first laid.'

When he returned to India there was a blaze of glory, for the Viceroy himself made a special visit to confer upon the Maharajah the Grand Cross of the Star of India – all diamonds and ribbons and enamel; and at the same ceremony, while the cannon boomed, Purun Dass was made a Knight Commander of the Order of the Indian Empire; so that his name stood Sir Purun Dass, KCIE.

That evening, at dinner in the big Viceregal tent, he stood up with the badge and the collar of the Order on his breast, and replying to the toast of his master's health, made a speech few Englishmen could have bettered.

Next month, when the city had returned to its sunbaked quiet, he did a thing no Englishman would have dreamed of doing; for, so far as the world's affairs went, he died. The jewelled order of his knighthood went back to the Indian Government, and a new Prime Minister was appointed to the charge of affairs, and a great game of General Post began in all the subordinate appointments. The priests knew what had happened, and the people guessed; but India is the one place in the world where a man can do as he pleases and nobody asks why; and the fact that Dewan Sir Purun Dass, KCIE, had resigned position, palace, and power, and taken up the begging-bowl and ochre-coloured dress of a Sunnyasi, or holy man, was considered nothing extraordinary. He had been, as the Old Law recommends, twenty years a youth, twenty years a fighter – though he had never carried a weapon in his life – and twenty years head of a household. He had used his wealth and his power for what he knew both to be worth; he had taken honour when it came his way; he had seen men and cities far and near, and men and cities had stood up and honoured him. Now he would let those things go, as a man drops the cloak he no longer needs.

Behind him, as he walked through the city gates, an antelope skin and brass-handled crutch under his arm, and a begging-bowl of polished brown *coco-de-mer* in his hand, barefoot, alone, with eyes cast on the ground – behind him they were firing salutes from the bastions in honour of his happy successor. Purun Dass nodded. All that life was ended; and he bore it no more ill will or good will than a man bears to a colourless dream of the night. He was a Sunnyasi – a houseless, wandering mendicant, depending on his neighbours for his daily bread; and so long as there is a morsel to divide in India, neither priest nor beggar starves. He had never in his life tasted meat, and very seldom eaten even fish. A five-pound note would have covered his personal expenses for food through any one of the many years in which he had been absolute master of millions of money. Even when he was being lionised in London he had held before him his dream of peace and quiet – the long, white, dusty Indian road, printed all over with bare feet, the incessant, slow-moving traffic, and the sharp-smelling wood-smoke curling up under the fig trees in the twilight, where the wayfarers sit at their evening meal.

When the time came to make that dream true the Prime Minister took the proper steps, and in three days you might more easily have found a bubble in the trough of the long Atlantic seas, than Purun Dass among the roving, gathering, separating millions of India.

At night his antelope skin was spread where the darkness overtook him – sometimes in a Sunnyasi monastery by the roadside; sometimes by a mud-pillar shrine of Kala Pir, where the Jogis, who are another misty division of holy men, would receive him as they do those who know what castes and divisions are worth; sometimes on the outskirts of a little Hindu village, where the children would steal up with the food their parents had prepared; and sometimes on the pitch of the bare grazing-grounds, where the flame of his stick fire waked the drowsy camels. It was all one to Purun Dass – or Purun Bhagat, as he called himself now. Earth, people, and food were all one. But unconsciously his feet drew him away northward and eastward; from the south to Rohtak; from Rohtak to Kurnool; from Kurnool to ruined Samanah, and then upstream along the dried bed of the Gugger river that fills only when the rain falls in the hills, till one day he saw the far line of the great Himalayas.

Then Purun Bhagat smiled, for he remembered that his mother was of Rajput Brahmin birth, from Kulu way – a Hill-woman, always homesick for the snows – and that the least touch of Hill blood draws a man in the end back to where he belongs.

'Yonder,' said Purun Bhagat, breasting the lower slopes of the Sewaliks, where the cacti stand up like seven-branched candlesticks – 'yonder I shall sit down and get knowledge'; and the cool wind of the Himalayas whistled about his ears as he trod the road that led to Simla.

The last time he had come that way it had been in state, with a clattering cavalry escort, to visit the gentlest and most affable of Viceroys; and the two had talked for an hour together about mutual friends in London, and what the Indian common folk really thought of things. This time Purun Bhagat paid no calls, but leaned on the rail of the Mall, watching that glorious view of the Plains spread out forty miles below, till a native Mohammedan policeman told him he was obstructing traffic; and Purun Bhagat salaamed reverently to the Law, because he knew the value of it, and was seeking for a Law of his own. Then he moved on, and slept that night in an empty hut at Chota Simla, which looks like the very last end of the earth, but it was only the beginning of his journey. He followed the Himalaya–Tibet road, the little ten-foot track that is blasted out of solid rock, or strutted out on timbers over gulfs a thousand feet deep; that dips into warm, wet, shut-in valleys, and climbs out across bare, grassy hill-shoulders where the sun strikes like a burning-glass; or turns through dripping, dark forests where the tree-ferns dress the trunks from head to heel, and the pheasant calls to his mate. And he met Tibetan herdsmen with their dogs and flocks of sheep, each sheep with a little bag of borax on his back, and wandering woodcutters, and cloaked and blanketed Lamas from Tibet, coming into India on pilgrimage, and envoys of little solitary Hill-states, posting furiously on ring-streaked and piebald ponies, or the cavalcade of a Rajah paying a visit; or else for a long, clear day he would see nothing more than a black bear grunting and rooting below in the valley. When he first started, the roar of the world he had left still rang in his ears, as the roar of a tunnel rings long after the train has passed through; but when he had put the Mutteeanee Pass behind him that was all done, and Purun Bhagat was alone with himself, walking, wondering, and thinking, his eyes on the ground, and his thoughts with the clouds.

One evening he crossed the highest pass he had met till then – it had been a two-day climb – and came out on a line of snow-peaks that banded all the horizon – mountains from fifteen to twenty thousand feet high, looking almost near enough to hit with a stone, though they were fifty or sixty miles away. The pass was crowned with dense, dark forest – deodar, walnut, wild cherry, wild olive, and wild pear, but mostly deodar, which is the Himalayan cedar; and under the shadow of the deodars stood a deserted shrine to Kali – who is Durga, who is Sitala, who is sometimes worshipped against the smallpox.

Purun Dass swept the stone floor clean, smiled at the grinning statue, made himself a little mud fireplace at the back of the shrine, spread his antelope skin on a bed of fresh pine-needles, tucked his *bairagi* – his brass-handled crutch – under his armpit, and sat down to rest.

Immediately below him the hillside fell away, clean and cleared for fifteen hundred feet, where a little village of stone-walled houses, with roofs of beaten earth, clung to the steep tilt. All round it the tiny terraced fields lay out like aprons of patchwork on the knees of the mountain, and cows no bigger than beetles grazed between the smooth stone circles of the threshing-floors. Looking across the valley, the eye was deceived by the size of things, and could not at first realise that what seemed to be low scrub, on the opposite mountain-flank, was in truth a forest of hundred-foot pines. Purun Bhagat saw an eagle swoop across the gigantic hollow, but the great bird dwindled to a dot ere it was halfway over. A few bands of scattered clouds strung up and down the valley, catching on a shoulder of the hills, or rising up and dying out when they were level with the head of the pass. And, 'Here shall I find peace,' said Purun Bhagat.

Now, a Hill-man makes nothing of a few hundred feet up or down, and as soon as the villagers saw the smoke in the deserted shrine, the village priest climbed up the terraced hillside to welcome the stranger.

When he met Purun Bhagat's eyes – the eyes of a man used to control thousands – he bowed to the earth, took the begging-bowl without a word, and returned to the village, saying, 'We have at last a holy man. Never have I seen such a man. He is of the Plains – but pale-coloured – a Brahmin of the Brahmins.' Then all the housewives of the village said, 'Think you he will stay with us?' and each did her best to cook the most savoury meal for the Bhagat. Hill-food is very simple, but with buckwheat and Indian corn, and rice and red pepper, and little fish out of the stream in the valley, and honey from the flue-like hives built in the stone walls, and dried apricots, and turmeric, and wild ginger, and bannocks of flour, a devout woman can make good things, and it was a full bowl that the priest carried to the Bhagat. Was he going to stay? asked the priest. Would he need a *chela* – a disciple – to beg for him? Had he a blanket against the cold weather? Was the food good?

Purun Bhagat ate, and thanked the giver. It was in his mind to stay. That was sufficient, said the priest. Let the begging-bowl be placed outside the shrine, in the hollow made by those two twisted roots, and daily should the Bhagat be fed; for the village felt honoured that such a man – he looked timidly into the Bhagat's face – should tarry among them.

That day saw the end of Purun Bhagat's wanderings. He had come to the place appointed for him – the silence and the space. After this, time stopped, and he, sitting at the mouth of the shrine, could not tell whether he were alive or dead; a man with control of his limbs, or a part of the hills, and the clouds, and the shifting rain and sunlight. He would repeat a Name softly to himself a hundred hundred times, till, at each repetition, he seemed to move more and more out of his body, sweeping up to the doors of some tremendous discovery; but, just as the door was opening, his body would drag him back, and, with grief, he felt he was locked up again in the flesh and bones of Purun Bhagat.

Every morning the filled begging-bowl was laid silently in the crutch of the roots outside the shrine. Sometimes the priest brought it; sometimes a Ladakhi trader, lodging in the village, and anxious to get merit, trudged up the path; but, more often, it was the woman who had cooked the meal overnight; and she would murmur, hardly above her breath. 'Speak for me before the gods, Bhagat. Speak for such a one, the wife of so-and-so!' Now and then some bold child would be allowed the honour, and Purun Bhagat would hear him drop the bowl and run as fast as his little legs could carry him, but the Bhagat never came down to the village. It was laid out like a map at his feet. He could see the evening gatherings, held on the circle of the threshing-floors, because that was the only level ground; could see the wonderful unnamed green of the young rice, the indigo blues of the Indian corn, the dock-like patches of buckwheat, and, in its season, the red bloom of the amaranth, whose tiny seeds, being neither grain nor pulse, make a food that can be lawfully eaten by Hindus in time of fasts.

When the year turned, the roofs of the huts were all little squares of purest gold, for it was on the roofs that they laid out their cobs of the corn to dry. Hiving and harvest, rice-sowing and husking, passed before his eyes, all embroidered down there on the many sided plots of fields, and he thought of them all, and wondered what they all led to at the long last.

Even in populated India a man cannot a day sit still before the wild things run over him as though he were a rock; and in that wilderness very soon the wild things, who knew Kali's Shrine well, came back to look at the intruder. The *langurs*, the big grey-whiskered monkeys of the Himalayas, were, naturally, the first, for they are alive with curiosity; and when they had upset the begging-bowl, and rolled it round the floor, and tried their teeth on the brass-handled crutch, and made faces at the antelope skin, they decided that the human being who sat so still was harmless. At evening, they would leap down from the pines, and beg with their hands for things to eat, and then swing off in graceful curves. They liked the warmth of the fire, too, and huddled round it till Purun Bhagat had to push them aside to throw on more fuel; and in the morning, as often as not, he would find a furry ape sharing his blanket. All day long, one or other of the tribe would sit by his side, staring out at the snows, crooning and looking unspeakably wise and sorrowful.

After the monkeys came the *barasingh*, that big deer which is like our red deer, but stronger. He wished to rub off the velvet of his horns against the cold stones of Kali's statue, and stamped his feet when he saw the man at the shrine. But Purun Bhagat never moved, and, little by little, the royal stag edged up and nuzzled his shoulder. Purun Bhagat slid one cool hand along the hot antlers, and the touch soothed the fretted beast, who bowed his head, and Purun Bhagat very softly rubbed and ravelled off the velvet. Afterward, the *barasingh* brought his doe and fawn – gentle things that mumbled on the holy man's blanket – or would come alone at night, his eyes green in the fire-flicker, to take his share of fresh walnuts. At last, the musk-deer, the shyest and almost the smallest of the deerlets, came, too, her big rabbity ears erect; even brindled, silent *mushick-nabha* must needs find out what the light in the shrine meant, and drop out her moose-like nose into Purun Bhagat's lap, coming and going with the shadows of the fire. Purun Bhagat called them all 'my brothers', and his low call of '*Bhai! Bhai!*' would draw them from the forest at noon if they were within ear shot. The Himalayan black bear, moody and suspicious – Sona, who has the V-shaped white mark under his chin – passed that way more than once; and since the Bhagat showed no fear, Sona showed no anger, but watched him, and came closer, and begged a share of the caresses, and a dole of bread or wild berries. Often, in the still dawns, when the Bhagat would climb to the very crest of the pass to watch the red day walking along the peaks of the snows, he would find Sona shuffling and grunting at his heels, thrusting, a curious forepaw under fallen trunks, and bringing it away with a *whoof* of impatience; or his early steps would wake Sona where he lay curled up, and the great brute, rising erect, would think to fight, till he heard the Bhagat's voice and knew his best friend.

Nearly all hermits and holy men who live apart from the big cities have the reputation of being able to work miracles with the wild things, but all the miracle lies in keeping still, in never making a hasty movement, and, for a long time, at least, in never looking directly at a visitor. The villagers saw the outline of the *barasingh* stalking like a shadow through the dark forest behind the shrine; saw the *minaul*, the Himalayan pheasant, blazing in her best colours before Kali's statue; and the *langurs* on their haunches, inside, playing with the walnut shells. Some of the children, too, had heard Sona singing to himself, bear-fashion, behind the fallen rocks, and the Bhagat's reputation as miracle-worker stood firm.

Yet nothing was farther from his mind than miracles. He believed that all things were one big Miracle, and when a man knows that much he knows something to go upon. He knew for a certainty that there was nothing great and nothing little in this world: and day and night he strove to think out his way into the heart of things, back to the place whence his soul had come.

So thinking, his untrimmed hair fell down about his shoulders, the stone slab at the side of the antelope skin was dented into a little hole by the foot of his brass-handled crutch, and the place between the tree-trunks, where the begging-bowl rested day after day, sunk and wore into a hollow almost as smooth as the brown shell itself; and each beast knew his exact place at the fire. The fields changed their colours with the seasons; the threshing-floors filled and emptied, and filled again and again; and again and again, when winter came, the *langurs* frisked among the branches feathered with light snow, till the mother-monkeys brought their sad-eyed little babies up from the warmer valleys with the spring. There were few changes in the village. The priest was older, and many of the little children who used to come with the begging-dish sent their own children now; and when you asked of the villagers how long their holy man had lived in Kali's Shrine at the head of the pass, they answered, 'Always.'

Then came such summer rains as had not been known in the Hills for many seasons. Through three good months the valley was wrapped in cloud and soaking mist – steady, unrelenting downfall, breaking off into thunder-shower after thundershower. Kali's Shrine stood above the clouds, for the most part, and there was a whole month in which the Bhagat never caught a glimpse of his village. It was packed away under a white floor of cloud that swayed and shifted and rolled on itself and bulged upward, but never broke from its piers – the streaming flanks of the valley.

All that time he heard nothing but the sound of a million little waters, overhead from the trees, and underfoot along the ground, soaking through the pine-needles, dripping from the tongues of draggled fern, and spouting in newly-torn muddy channels down the slopes. Then the sun came out, and drew forth the good incense of the deodars and the rhododendrons, and that far-off, clean smell which the Hill people call 'the smell of the snows.' The hot sunshine lasted for a week, and then the rains gathered together for their last downpour, and the water fell in sheets that flayed off the skin of the ground and leaped back in mud. Purun Bhagat heaped his fire high that night, for he was sure his brothers would need warmth; but never a beast came to the shrine, though he called and called till he dropped asleep, wondering what had happened in the woods.

It was in the black heart of the night, the rain drumming like a thousand drums, that he was roused by a plucking at his blanket, and, stretching out, felt the little hand of a *langur*. 'It is better here than in the trees,' he said sleepily, loosening a fold of blanket; 'take it and be warm.' The monkey caught his hand and pulled hard. 'Is it food, then?' said Purun Bhagat. 'Wait awhile, and I will prepare some.' As he knelt to throw fuel on the fire the *langur* ran to the door of the shrine, crooned and ran back again, plucking at the man's knee.

'What is it? What is thy trouble, Brother?' said Purun Bhagat, for the *langur*'s eyes were full of things that he could not tell. 'Unless one of thy caste be in a trap – and none set traps here – I will not go into that weather. Look, Brother, even the *barasingh* comes for shelter!'

The deer's antlers clashed as he strode into the shrine, clashed against the grinning statue of Kali. He lowered them in Purun Bhagat's direction and stamped uneasily, hissing through his half-shut nostrils.

'Hai! Hai! Hai!' said the Bhagat, snapping his fingers, 'Is *this* payment for a night's lodging?' But the deer pushed him toward the door, and as he did so Purun Bhagat heard the sound of something opening with a sigh, and saw two slabs of the floor draw away from each other, while the sticky earth below smacked its lips.

'Now I see,' said Purun Bhagat. 'No blame to my brothers that they did not sit by the fire tonight. The mountain is falling. And yet – why should I go?' His eye fell on the empty begging-bowl, and his face changed. 'They have given me good food daily since – since I came, and, if I am not swift, tomorrow there will not be one mouth in the valley. Indeed, I must go and warn them below. Back there, Brother! Let me get to the fire.'

The *barasingh* backed unwillingly as Purun Bhagat drove a pine torch deep into the flame, twirling it till it was well lit. 'Ah! ye came to warn me,' he said, rising. 'Better than that we shall do; better than that. Out, now, and lend me thy neck, Brother, for I have but two feet.'

He clutched the bristling withers of the *barasingh* with his right hand, held the torch away with his left, and stepped out of the shrine into the desperate night. There was no breath of wind, but the rain nearly drowned the flare as the great deer hurried down the slope, sliding on his haunches. As soon as they were clear of the forest more of the Bhagat's brothers joined them. He heard, though he could not see, the *langurs* pressing about him, and behind them the *uhh! uhh!* of Sona. The rain matted his long white hair into ropes; the water splashed beneath his bare feet, and his yellow robe clung to his frail old body, but he stepped down steadily, leaning against the *barasingh*. He was no longer a holy man, but Sir Purun Dass, KCIE, Prime Minister of no small State, a man accustomed to command, going out to save life. Down the steep, plashy path they poured all together, the Bhagat and his brothers, down and down till the deer's feet clicked and stumbled on the wall of a threshing-floor, and he snorted because he smelt Man. Now they were at the head of the one crooked village street, and the Bhagat beat with his crutch on the barred windows of the blacksmith's house, as his torch blazed up in the shelter of the eaves. 'Up and out!' cried Purun Bhagat; and he did not know his own voice, for it was years since he had spoken aloud to a man. 'The hill falls! The hill is falling! Up and out, oh, you within!'

'It is our Bhagat,' said the blacksmith's wife. He stands among his beasts. Gather the little ones and give the call.'

It ran from house to house, while the beasts, cramped in the narrow way, surged and huddled round the Bhagat, and Sona puffed impatiently.

The people hurried into the street – they were no more than seventy souls all told – and in the glare of the torches they saw their Bhagat holding back the terrified *barasingh*, while the monkeys plucked piteously at his skirts, and Sona sat on his haunches and roared.

'Across the valley and up the next hill!' shouted Purun Bhagat. 'Leave none behind! We follow!'

Then the people ran as only Hill folk can run, for they knew that in a landslip you must climb for the highest ground across the valley. They fled, splashing through the little river at the bottom, and panted up the terraced fields on the far side, while the Bhagat and his brethren followed. Up and up the opposite mountain they climbed, calling to each other by name – the roll-call of the village – and at their heels toiled the big *barasingh*, weighted by the failing strength of Purun Bhagat. At last the deer stopped in the shadow of a deep pinewood, five hundred feet up the hillside. His instinct, that had warned him of the coming slide, told him he would he safe here.

Purun Bhagat dropped fainting by his side, for the chill of the rain and that fierce climb were killing him; but first he called to the scattered torches ahead, 'Stay and count your numbers'; then, whispering to the deer as he saw the lights gather in a cluster: 'Stay with me, Brother. Stay – till – I – go!'

There was a sigh in the air that grew to a mutter, and a mutter that grew to a roar, and a roar that passed all sense of hearing, and the hillside on which the villagers stood was hit in the darkness, and rocked to the blow. Then a note as steady, deep, and true as the deep C of the organ drowned everything for perhaps five minutes, while the very roots of the pines quivered to it. It died away, and the sound of the rain falling on miles of hard ground and grass changed to the muffled drum of water on soft earth. That told its own tale.

Never a villager – not even the priest – was bold enough to speak to the Bhagat who had saved their lives. They crouched under the pines and waited till the day. When it came they looked across the valley and saw that what had been forest, and terraced field, and track-threaded grazing-ground was one raw, red, fan-shaped smear, with a few trees flung head-down on the scarp. That red ran high up the hill of their refuge, damming back the little river, which had begun to spread into a brick-coloured lake. Of the village, of the road to the shrine, of the shrine itself, and the forest behind, there was no trace. For one mile in width and two thousand feet in sheer depth the mountain-side had come away bodily, planed clean from head to heel.

And the villagers, one by one, crept through the wood to pray before their Bhagat. They saw the *barasingh* standing over him, who fled when they came near, and they heard the *langurs* wailing in the branches, and Sona moaning up the hill; but their Bhagat was dead, sitting cross-legged, his back against a tree, his crutch under his armpit, and his face turned to the northeast.

The priest said: 'Behold a miracle after a miracle, for in this very attitude must all Sunnyasis be buried! Therefore where he now is we will build the temple to our holy man.'

They built the temple before a year was ended – a little stone-and-earth shrine – and they called the hill the Bhagat's hill, and they worship there with lights and flowers and offerings to this day. But they do not know that the saint of their worship is the late Sir Purun Dass, KCIE, DCL, PhD, etc., once Prime Minister of the progressive and enlightened State of Mohiniwala, and honorary or corresponding member of more learned and scientific societies than will ever do any good in this world or the next.

A Song of Kabir

H, LIGHT was the world that he weighed in his hands!
Oh, heavy the tale of his fiefs and his lands!
He has gone from the *guddee* and put on the shroud,
And departed in guise of *bairagi* avowed!

Now the white road to Delhi is mat for his feet,
The *sal* and the *kikar* must guard him from heat;
His home is the camp, and the waste, and the crowd –
He is seeking the Way as *bairagi* avowed!

He has looked upon Man, and his eyeballs are clear
(There was One; there is One, and but One, saith Kabir);
The Red Mist of Doing has thinned to a cloud –
He has taken the Path for *bairagi* avowed!

To learn and discern of his brother the clod,
Of his brother the brute, and his brother the God.
He has gone from the council and put on the shroud
('Can ye hear?' saith Kabir), a *bairagi* avowed!

Letting in the Jungle

Veil them, cover them, wall them round –
  Blossom, and creeper, and weed –
Let us forget the sight and the sound,
  The smell and the touch of the breed!

Fat black ash by the altar-stone,
  Here is the white-foot rain,
And the does bring forth in the fields unsown,
  And none shall affright them again;
And the blind walls crumble, unknown, o'erthrown
  And none shall inhabit again!

YOU WILL REMEMBER that after Mowgli had pinned Shere Khan's hide to the Council Rock, he told as many as were left of the Seeonee Pack that henceforward he would hunt in the Jungle alone; and the four children of Mother and Father Wolf said that they would hunt with him. But it is not easy to change one's life all in a minute – particularly in the Jungle. The first thing Mowgli did, when the disorderly Pack had slunk off, was to go to the home-cave, and sleep for a day and a night. Then he told Mother Wolf and Father Wolf as much as they could understand of his adventures among men; and when he made the morning sun flicker up and down the blade of his skinning-knife – the same he had skinned Shere Khan with – they said he had learned something. Then Akela and Grey Brother had to explain their share of the great buffalo-drive in the ravine, and Baloo toiled up the hill to hear all about it, and Bagheera scratched himself all over with pure delight at the way in which Mowgli had managed his war.

It was long after sunrise, but no one dreamed of going to sleep, and from time to time, during the talk, Mother Wolf would throw up her head, and sniff a deep snuff of satisfaction as the wind brought her the smell of the tiger-skin on the Council Rock.

'But for Akela and Grey Brother here,' Mowgli said, at the end, 'I could have done nothing. Oh, mother, mother! if thou hadst seen the black herd-bulls pour down the ravine, or hurry through the gates when the Man-Pack flung stones at me!'

'I am glad I did not see that last,' said Mother Wolf stiffly. 'It is not *my* custom to suffer my cubs to be driven to and fro like jackals. *I* would have taken a price from the Man-Pack; but I would have spared the woman who gave thee the milk. Yes, I would have spared her alone.'

'Peace, peace, Raksha!' said Father Wolf, lazily. 'Our Frog has come back again – so wise that his own father must lick his feet; and what is a cut, more or less, on the head? Leave Men alone.' Baloo and Bagheera both echoed: 'Leave Men alone.'

Mowgli, his head on Mother Wolf's side, smiled contentedly, and said that, for his own part, he never wished to see, or hear, or smell Man again.

'But what,' said Akela, cocking one ear – 'but what if men do not leave thee alone, Little Brother?'

'We be *five*,' said Grey Brother, looking round at the company, and snapping his jaws on the last word.

'We also might attend to that hunting,' said Bagheera, with a little *switch-switch* of his tail, looking at Baloo. 'But why think of men now, Akela?'

'For this reason,' the Lone Wolf answered: 'when that yellow chief's hide was hung up on the rock, I went back along our trail to the village, stepping in my tracks, turning aside, and lying down, to make a mixed trail in case one should follow us. But when I had fouled the trail so that I myself hardly knew it again, Mang, the Bat, came hawking between the trees, and hung up above me. Said Mang, "The village of the Man-Pack, where they cast out the Man-cub, hums like a hornet's nest."'

'It was a big stone that I threw,' chuckled Mowgli, who had often amused himself by throwing ripe pawpaws into a hornet's nest, and racing off to the nearest pool before the hornets caught him.

'I asked of Mang what he had seen. He said that the Red Flower blossomed at the gate of the village, and men sat about it carrying guns. Now *I know*, for I have good cause,' – Akela looked down at the old dry scars on his flank and side – 'that men do not carry guns for pleasure. Presently, Little Brother, a man with a gun follows our trail – if, indeed, he be not already on it.'

'But why should he? Men have cast me out. What more do they need?' said Mowgli angrily.

'Thou art a man, Little Brother,' Akela returned. 'It is not for *us*, the Free Hunters, to tell thee what thy brethren do, or why.'

He had just time to snatch up his paw as the skinning-knife cut deep into the ground below. Mowgli struck quicker than an average human eye could follow but Akela was a wolf; and even a dog, who is very far removed from the wild wolf, his ancestor, can be waked out of deep sleep by a cartwheel touching his flank, and can spring away unharmed before that wheel comes on.

'Another time,' Mowgli said quietly, returning the knife to its sheath, 'speak of the Man-Pack and of Mowgli in *two* breaths – not one.'

'Phff! That is a sharp tooth,' said Akela, snuffing at the blade's cut in the earth, 'but living with the Man-Pack has spoiled thine eye, Little Brother. I could have killed a buck while thou wast striking.'

Bagheera sprang to his feet, thrust up his head as far as he could, sniffed, and stiffened through every curve in his body. Grey Brother followed his example quickly, keeping a little to his left to get the wind that was blowing from the right, while Akela bounded fifty yards upwind, and, half-crouching, stiffened too. Mowgli looked on enviously. He could smell things as very few human beings could, but he had never reached the hair-trigger-like sensitiveness of a Jungle nose; and his three months in the smoky village had set him back sadly. However, he dampened his finger, rubbed it on his nose, and stood erect to catch the upper scent, which, though it is the faintest, is the truest.

'Man!' Akela growled, dropping on his haunches.

'Buldeo!' said Mowgli, sitting down. 'He follows our trail, and yonder is the sunlight on his gun. Look!'

It was no more than a splash of sunlight, for a fraction of a second, on the brass clamps of the old Tower musket, but nothing in the Jungle winks with just that flash, except when the clouds race over the sky. Then a piece of mica, or a little pool, or even a highly-polished leaf will flash like a heliograph. But that day was cloudless and still.

'I knew men would follow,' said Akela triumphantly. 'Not for nothing have I led the Pack.'

The four cubs said nothing, but ran down hill on their bellies, melting into the thorn and under-brush as a mole melts into a lawn.

'Where go ye, and without word?' Mowgli called.

'H'sh! We roll his skull here before midday!' Grey Brother answered.

'Back! Back and wait! Man does not eat Man!' Mowgli shrieked.

'Who was a wolf but now? Who drove the knife at me for thinking he might be Man?' said Akela, as the four wolves turned back sullenly and dropped to heel.

'Am I to give reason for all I choose to, do?' said Mowgli furiously.

'That is Man! There speaks Man!' Bagheera muttered under his whiskers. 'Even so did men talk round the King's cages at Oodeypore. We of the Jungle know that Man is wisest of all. If we trusted our ears we should know that of all things he is most foolish.' Raising his voice, he added, 'The Man-cub is right in this. Men hunt in packs. To kill one, unless we know what the others will do, is bad hunting. Come, let us see what this Man means toward us.'

'We will not come,' Grey Brother growled. 'Hunt alone, Little Brother. *We* know our own minds. The skull would have been ready to bring by now.'

Mowgli had been looking from one to the other of his friends, his chest heaving and his eyes full of tears. He strode forward to the wolves, and, dropping on one knee, said: 'Do I not know my mind? Look at me!'

They looked uneasily, and when their eyes wandered, he called them back again and again, till their hair stood up all over their bodies, and they trembled in every limb, while Mowgli stared and stared.

'Now,' said he, 'of us five, which is leader?'

'Thou art leader, Little Brother,' said Grey Brother, and he licked Mowgli's foot.

'Follow, then,' said Mowgli, and the four followed at his heels with their tails between their legs.

'This comes of living with the Man-Pack,' said Bagheera, slipping down after them. 'There is more in the Jungle now than Jungle Law, Baloo.'

The old bear said nothing, but he thought many things.

Mowgli cut across noiselessly through the Jungle, at right angles to Buldeo's path, till, parting the undergrowth, he saw the old man, his musket on his shoulder, running up the trail of overnight at a dogtrot.

You will remember that Mowgli had left the village with the heavy weight of Shere Khan's raw hide on his shoulders, while Akela and Grey Brother trotted behind, so that the triple trail was very clearly marked. Presently Buldeo came to where Akela, as you know, had gone back and mixed it all up. Then he sat down, and coughed and grunted, and made little casts round and about into the Jungle to pick it up again, and, all the time he could have thrown a stone over those who were watching him. No one can be so silent as a wolf when he does not care to be heard; and Mowgli, though the wolves thought he moved very clumsily, could come and go like a shadow. They ringed the old man as a school of porpoises ring a steamer at full speed, and as they ringed him they talked unconcernedly, for their speech began below the lowest end of the scale that untrained human beings can hear. [The other end is bounded by the high squeak of Mang, the Bat, which very many people cannot catch at all. From that note all the bird and bat and insect talk takes on.]

'This is better than any kill,' said Grey Brother, as Buldeo stooped and peered and puffed. 'He looks like a lost pig in the Jungles by the river. What does he say?' Buldeo was muttering savagely.

Mowgli translated. 'He says that packs of wolves must have danced round me. He says that he never saw such a trail in his life. He says he is tired.'

'He will be rested before he picks it up again,' said Bagheera coolly, as he slipped round a tree-trunk, in the game of blindman's-buff that they were playing. '*Now*, what does the lean thing do?'

'Eat or blow smoke out of his mouth. Men always play with their mouths,' said Mowgli; and the silent trailers saw the old man fill and light and puff at a water-pipe, and they took good note of the smell of the tobacco, so as to be sure of Buldeo in the darkest night, if necessary.

Then a little knot of charcoal-burners came down the path, and naturally halted to speak to Buldeo, whose fame as a hunter reached for at least twenty miles round. They all sat down and smoked, and Bagheera and the others came up and watched while Buldeo began to tell the story of Mowgli, the Devil-child, from one end to another, with additions and inventions. How he himself had really killed Shere Khan; and how Mowgli had turned himself into a wolf, and fought with him all the afternoon, and changed into a boy again and bewitched Buldeo's rifle, so that the bullet turned the corner, when he pointed it at Mowgli, and killed one of Buldeo's own buffaloes; and how the village, knowing him to be the bravest hunter in Seeonee, had sent him out to kill this Devil-child. But meantime the village had got hold of Messua and her husband, who were undoubtedly the father and mother of this Devil-child, and had barricaded them in their own hut, and presently would torture them to make them confess they were witch and wizard, and then they would be burned to death.

'When?' said the charcoal-burners, because they would very much like to be present at the ceremony.

Buldeo said that nothing would be done till he returned, because the village wished him to kill the Jungle Boy first. After that they would dispose of Messua and her husband, and divide their lands and buffaloes among the village. Messua's husband had some remarkably fine buffaloes, too. It was an excellent thing to destroy wizards, Buldeo thought; and people who entertained Wolf-children out of the Jungle were clearly the worst kind of witches.

But, said the charcoal-burners, what would happen if the English heard of it? The English, they had heard, were a perfectly mad people, who would not let honest farmers kill witches in peace.

Why, said Buldeo, the headman of the village would report that Messua and her husband had died of snakebite. *That* was all arranged, and the only thing now was to kill the Wolf-child. They did not happen to have seen anything of such a creature?

The charcoal-burners looked round cautiously, and thanked their stars they had not; but they had no doubt that so brave a man as Buldeo would find him if anyone could. The sun was getting rather low, and they had an idea that they would push on to Buldeo's village and see that wicked witch. Buldeo said that, though it was his duty to kill the Devil-child, he could not think of letting a party of unarmed men go through the Jungle, which might produce the Wolf-demon at any minute, without his escort. He, therefore, would accompany them, and if the sorcerer's child appeared – well, he would show them how the best hunter in Seeonee dealt with such things. The Brahmin, he said, had given him a charm against the creature that made everything perfectly safe.

'What says he? What says he? What says he?' the wolves repeated every few minutes; and Mowgli translated until he came to the witch part of the story, which was a little beyond him, and then he said that the man and woman who had been so kind to him were trapped.

'Does Man trap Man?' said Bagheera.

'So he says. I cannot understand the talk. They are all mad together. What have Messua and her man to do with me that they should be put in a trap; and what is all this talk about the Red Flower? I must look to this. Whatever they would do to Messua they will not do till Buldeo returns. And so – ' Mowgli thought hard, with his fingers playing round the haft of the skinning-knife, while Buldeo and the charcoal-burners went off very valiantly in single file.

'I go hotfoot back to the Man-Pack,' Mowgli said at last.

'And those?' said Grey Brother, looking hungrily after the brown backs of the charcoal-burners.

'Sing them home,' said Mowgli, with a grin; 'I do not wish them to be at the village gates till it is dark. Can ye hold them?'

Grey Brother bared his white teeth in contempt. 'We can head them round and round in circles like tethered goats – if I know Man.'

'That I do not need. Sing to them a little, lest they be lonely on the road, and, Grey Brother, the song need not be of the sweetest. Go with them, Bagheera, and help make that song. When night is shut down, meet me by the village – Grey Brother knows the place.'

'It is no light hunting to work for a Man-cub. When shall I sleep?' said Bagheera, yawning, though his eyes showed that he was delighted with the amusement. 'Me to sing to naked men! But let us try.'

He lowered his head so that the sound would travel, and cried a long, long, 'Good hunting' – a midnight call in the afternoon, which was quite awful enough to begin with. Mowgli heard it rumble, and rise, and fall, and die off in a creepy sort of whine behind him, and laughed to himself as he ran through the Jungle. He could see the charcoal-burners huddled in a knot; old Buldeo's gun-barrel waving, like a banana-leaf, to every point of the compass at once. Then Grey Brother gave the *Ya-la-hi! Yalaha!* call for the buck-driving, when the Pack drives the nilghai, the big blue cow, before them, and it seemed to come from the very ends of the earth, nearer, and nearer, and nearer, till it ended in a shriek snapped off short. The other three answered, till even Mowgli could have vowed that the full Pack was in full cry, and then they all broke into the magnificent Morning-song in the Jungle, with every turn, and flourish, and grace-note that a deep-mouthed wolf of the Pack knows. This is a rough rendering of the song, but you must imagine what it sounds like when it breaks the afternoon hush of the Jungle:

One moment past our bodies cast
   No shadow on the plain;
Now clear and black they stride our track,
   And we run home again.
In morning hush, each rock and bush
   Stands hard, and high, and raw:
Then give the Call: '*Good rest to all*
   That keep The Jungle Law!'

Now horn and pelt our peoples melt
   In covert to abide;
Now, crouched and still, to cave and hill
   Our Jungle Barons glide.
Now, stark and plain, Man's oxen strain,
   That draw the new-yoked plough;
Now, stripped and dread, the dawn is red
   Above the lit *talao*.

Ho! Get to lair! The sun's aflare
   Behind the breathing grass:
And cracking through the young bamboo
   The warning whispers pass.
By day made strange, the woods we range
   With blinking eyes we scan;
While down the skies the wild duck cries,
   '*The Day – the Day to Man!*'

The dew is dried that drenched our hide
   Or washed about our way;
And where we drank, the puddled bank
   Is crisping into clay.
The traitor Dark gives up each mark
   Of stretched or hooded claw;
Then hear the Call: '*Good rest to all*
   That keep the Jungle Law!'

But no translation can give the effect of it, or the yelping scorn the Four threw into every word of it, as they heard the trees crash when the men hastily climbed up into the branches, and Buldeo began repeating incantations and charms. Then they lay down and slept, for, like all who live by their own exertions, they were of a methodical cast of mind; and no one can work well without sleep.

Meantime, Mowgli was putting the miles behind him, nine to the hour, swinging on, delighted to find himself so fit after all his cramped months among men. The one idea in his head was to get Messua and her husband out of the trap, whatever it was; for he had a natural mistrust of traps. Later on, he promised himself, he would pay his debts to the village at large.

It was at twilight when he saw the well-remembered grazing-grounds, and the *dhâk* tree where Grey Brother had waited for him on the morning that he killed Shere Khan. Angry as he was at the whole breed and community of Man, something jumped up in his throat and made him catch his breath when he looked at the village roofs. He noticed that everyone had come in from the fields unusually early, and that, instead of getting to their evening cooking, they gathered in a crowd under the village tree, and chattered, and shouted.

'Men must always he making traps for men, or they are not content,' said Mowgli. 'Last night it was Mowgli – but that night seems many Rains ago. Tonight it is Messua and her man. Tomorrow, and for very many nights after, it will be Mowgli's turn again.'

He crept along outside the wall till be came to Messua's hut, and looked through the window into the room. There lay Messua, gagged, and bound hand and foot, breathing hard, and groaning; her husband was tied to the gaily painted bedstead. The door of the hut that opened into the street was shut fast, and three or four people were sitting with their backs to it.

Mowgli knew the manners and customs of the villagers very fairly. He argued that so long as they could eat, and talk, and smoke, they would not do anything else; but as soon as they had fed they would begin to be dangerous. Buldeo would be coming in before long, and if his escort had done its duty, Buldeo would have a very interesting tale to tell. So he went in through the window, and, stooping over the man and the woman, cut their thongs, pulling out the gags, and looked round the hut for some milk.

Messua was half wild with pain and fear (she had been beaten and stoned all the morning), and Mowgli put his hand over her mouth just in time to stop a scream. Her husband was only bewildered and angry, and sat picking dust and things out of his torn beard.

'I knew – I knew he would come,' Messua sobbed at last. 'Now do I *know* that he is my son!' and she hugged Mowgli to her heart. Up to that time Mowgli had been perfectly steady, but now he began to tremble all over, and that surprised him immensely.

'Why are these thongs? Why have they tied thee?' he asked, after a pause.

'To be put to the death for making a son of thee – what else?' said the man sullenly. 'Look! I bleed.'

Messua said nothing, but it was at *her* wounds that Mowgli looked, and they heard him grit his teeth when he saw the blood.

'Whose work is this?' said he. 'There is a price to pay.'

'The work of all the village. I was too rich. I had too many cattle. *Therefore* she and I are witches, because we gave thee shelter.'

'I do not understand. Let Messua tell the tale.'

'I gave thee milk, Nathoo; dost thou remember?' Messua said timidly. 'Because thou wast my son, whom the tiger took, and because I loved thee very dearly. They said that I was thy mother, the mother of a devil, and therefore worthy of death.'

'And what is a devil?' said Mowgli. 'Death I have seen.'

The man looked up gloomily, but Messua laughed. 'See!' she said to her husband, 'I knew – I said that he was no sorcerer. He is my son – my son!'

'Son or sorcerer, what good will that do us?' the man answered. 'We be as dead already.'

'Yonder is the road to the Jungle' – Mowgli pointed through the window. 'Your hands and feet are free. Go now.'

'We do not know the Jungle, my son, as – as thou knowest,' Messua began. 'I do not think that I could walk far.'

'And the men and women would be upon our backs and drag us here again,' said the husband.

'H'm!' said Mowgli, and he tickled the palm of his hand with the tip of his skinning-knife; 'I have no wish to do harm to anyone of this village – *yet*. But I do not think they will stay thee. In a little while they will have much else to think upon. Ah!' he lifted his head and listened to shouting and trampling outside. 'So they have let Buldeo come home at last?'

'He was sent out this morning to kill thee,' Messua cried. 'Didst thou meet him?'

'Yes – we – I met him. He has a tale to tell and while he is telling it there is time to do much. But first I will learn what they mean. Think where ye would go, and tell me when I come back.'

He bounded through the window and ran along again outside the wall of the village till he came within earshot of the crowd round the peepul tree. Buldeo was lying on the ground, coughing and groaning, and everyone was asking him questions. His hair had fallen about his shoulders; his hands and legs were skinned from climbing up trees, and he could hardly speak, but he felt the importance of his position keenly. From time to time he said something about devils and singing devils, and magic enchantment, just to give the crowd a taste of what was coming. Then he called for water.

'Bah!' said Mowgli. 'Chatter – chatter! Talk, talk! Men are blood-brothers of the *Bandar-log*. Now he must wash his mouth with water; now he must blow smoke; and when all that is done he has still his story to tell. They are very wise people – men. They will leave no one to guard Messua till their ears are stuffed with Buldeo's tales. And – I grow as lazy as they!'

He shook himself and glided back to the hut. Just as he was at the window he felt a touch on his foot.

'Mother,' said he, for he knew that tongue well, 'what dost *thou* here?'

'I heard my children singing through the woods, and I followed the one I loved best. Little Frog, I have a desire to see that woman who gave thee milk,' said Mother Wolf, all wet with the dew.

'They have bound and mean to kill her. I have cut those ties, and she goes with her man through the Jungle.'

'I also will follow. I am old, but not yet toothless.' Mother Wolf reared herself up on end, and looked through the window into the dark of the hut.

In a minute she dropped noiselessly, and all she said was: 'I gave thee thy first milk; but Bagheera speaks truth: Man goes to Man at the last.'

'Maybe,' said Mowgli, with a very unpleasant look on his face; 'but tonight I am very far from that trail. Wait here, but do not let her see.'

'*Thou* wast never afraid of *me*, Little Frog,' said Mother Wolf, backing into the high grass, and blotting herself out, as she knew how.

'And now,' said Mowgli cheerfully, as he swung into the hut again, 'they are all sitting round Buldeo, who is saying that which did not happen. When his talk is finished, they say they will assuredly come here with the Red – with fire and burn you both. And then?'

'I have spoken to my man,' said Messua. 'Khanhiwara is thirty miles from here, but at Khanhiwara we may find the English – '

'And what Pack are they?' said Mowgli.

'I do not know. They be white, and it is said that they govern all the land, and do not suffer people to burn or beat each other without witnesses. If we can get thither tonight, we live. Otherwise we die.'

'Live, then. No man passes the gates tonight. But what does *he* do?' Messua's husband was on his hands and knees digging up the earth in one corner of the hut.

'It is his little money,' said Messua. 'We can take nothing else.'

'Ah, yes. The stuff that passes from hand to hand and never grows warmer. Do they need it outside this place also?' said Mowgli.

The man stared angrily. 'He is a fool, and no devil,' he muttered. 'With the money I can buy a horse. We are too bruised to walk far, and the village will follow us in an hour.'

'I say they will *not* follow till I choose; but a horse is well thought of, for Messua is tired.' Her husband stood up and knotted the last of the rupees into his waist-cloth. Mowgli helped Messua through the window, and the cool night air revived her, but the Jungle in the starlight looked very dark and terrible.

'Ye know the trail to Khanhiwara?' Mowgli whispered.

They nodded.

'Good. Remember, now, not to be afraid. And there is no need to go quickly. Only – only there may be some small singing in the Jungle behind you and before.'

'Think you we would have risked a night in the Jungle through anything less than the fear of burning? It is better to be killed by beasts than by men,' said Messua's husband; but Messua looked at Mowgli and smiled.

'I say,' Mowgli went on, just as though he were Baloo repeating an old Jungle Law for the hundredth time to a foolish cub – 'I say that not a tooth in the Jungle is bared against you; not a foot in the Jungle is lifted against you. Neither man nor beast shall stay you till you come within eyeshot of Khanhiwara. There will be a watch about you.' He turned quickly to Messua, saying, '*He* does not believe, but thou wilt believe?'

'Ay, surely, my son. Man, ghost, or wolf of the Jungle, I believe.'

'*He* will be afraid when he hears my people singing. Thou wilt know and understand. Go now, and slowly, for there is no need of any haste. The gates are shut.'

Messua flung herself sobbing at Mowgli's feet, but he lifted her very quickly with a shiver. Then she hung about his neck and called him every name of blessing she could think of, but her husband looked enviously across his fields, and said: '*If* we reach Khanhiwara, and I get the ear of the English, I will bring such a lawsuit against the Brahmin and old Buldeo and the others as shall eat the village to the bone. They shall pay me twice over for my crops untilled and my buffaloes unfed. I will have a great justice.'

Mowgli laughed. 'I do not know what justice is, but – come next Rains and see what is left.'

They went off toward the Jungle, and Mother Wolf leaped from her place of hiding.

'Follow!' said Mowgli; 'and look to it that all the Jungle knows these two are safe. Give tongue a little. I would call Bagheera.'

The long, low howl rose and fell, and Mowgli saw Messua's husband flinch and turn, half minded to run back to the hut.

'Go on,' Mowgli called cheerfully. 'I said there might be singing. That call will follow up to Khanhiwara. It is Favour of the Jungle.'

Messua urged her husband forward, and the darkness shut down on them and Mother Wolf as Bagheera rose up almost under Mowgli's feet, trembling with delight of the night that drives the Jungle People wild.

'I am ashamed of thy brethren,' he said, purring. 'What? Did they not sing sweetly to Buldeo?' said Mowgli.

'Too well! Too well! They made even *me* forget my pride, and, by the Broken Lock that freed me, I went singing through the Jungle as though I were out wooing in the spring! Didst thou not hear us?'

'I had other game afoot. Ask Buldeo if he liked the song. But where are the Four? I do not wish one of the Man-Pack to leave the gates tonight.'

'What need of the Four, then?' said Bagheera, shifting from foot to foot, his eyes ablaze, and purring louder than ever. 'I can hold them, Little Brother. Is it killing at last? The singing and the sight of the men climbing up the trees have made me very ready. Who is Man that we should care for him – the naked brown digger, the hairless and toothless, the eater of earth? I have followed him all day – at noon – in the white sunlight. I herded him as the wolves herd buck. I am Bagheera! Bagheera! Bagheera! As I dance with my shadow, so danced I with those men. Look!' The great panther leaped as a kitten leaps at a dead leaf whirling overhead, struck left and right into the empty air, that sang under the strokes, landed noiselessly, and leaped again and again, while the half purr, half growl gathered head as steam rumbles in a boiler. 'I am Bagheera – in the Jungle – in the night, and my strength is in me. Who shall stay my stroke? Man-cub, with one blow of my paw I could beat thy head flat as a dead frog in the summer!'

'Strike, then!' said Mowgli, in the dialect of the village, *not* the talk of the Jungle, and the human words brought Bagheera to a full stop, flung back on haunches that quivered under him, his head just at the level of Mowgli's. Once more Mowgli stared, as he had stared at the rebellious cubs, full into the beryl-green eyes till the red glare behind their green went out like the light of a lighthouse shut off twenty miles across the sea; till the eyes dropped, and the big head with them – dropped lower and lower, and the red rasp of a tongue grated on Mowgli's instep.

'Brother – Brother – Brother!' the boy whispered, stroking steadily and lightly from the neck along the heaving back. 'Be still, be still! It is the fault of the night, and no fault of thine.'

'It was the smells of the night,' said Bagheera penitently. 'This air cries aloud to me. But how dost *thou* know?'

Of course the air round an Indian village is full of all kinds of smells, and to any creature who does nearly all his thinking through his nose, smells are as maddening as music and drugs are to human beings. Mowgli gentled the panther for a few minutes longer, and he lay down like a cat before a fire, his paws tucked under his breast, and his eyes half shut.

'Thou art of the Jungle and *not* of the Jungle,' he said at last. 'And I am only a black panther. But I love thee, Little Brother.'

'They are very long at their talk under the tree,' Mowgli said, without noticing the last sentence. 'Buldeo must have told many tales. They should come soon to drag the woman and her man out of the trap and put them into the Red Flower. They will find that trap sprung. Ho! ho!'

'Nay, listen,' said Bagheera. 'The fever is out of my blood now. Let them find *me* there! Few would leave their houses after meeting me. It is not the first time I have been in a cage; and I do not think they will tie *me* with cords.'

'Be wise, then,' said Mowgli, laughing; for he was beginning to feel as reckless as the panther, who had glided into the hut.

'Pah!' Bagheera grunted. 'This place is rank with Man, but here is just such a bed as they gave me to lie upon in the King's cages at Oodeypore. Now I lie down.' Mowgli heard the strings of the cot crack under the great brute's weight. 'By the Broken Lock that freed me, they will think they have caught big game! Come and sit beside me, Little Brother; we will give them "good hunting" together!'

'No; I have another thought in my stomach. The Man-Pack shall not know what share I have in the sport. Make thine own hunt. I do not wish to see them.'

'Be it so,' said Bagheera. 'Ah, now they come!'

The conference under the peepul tree had been growing noisier and noisier, at the far end of the village. It broke in wild yells, and a rush up the street of men and women, waving clubs and bamboos and sickles and knives. Buldeo and the Brahmin were at the head of it, but the mob was close at their heels, and they cried, 'The witch and the wizard! Let us see if hot coins will make them confess! Burn the hut over their heads! We will teach them to shelter wolf-devils! Nay, beat them first! Torches! More torches! Buldeo, heat the gun-barrels!'

Here was some little difficulty with the catch of the door. It had been very firmly fastened, but the crowd tore it away bodily, and the light of the torches streamed into the room where, stretched at full length on the bed, his paws crossed and lightly hung down over one end, black as the Pit, and terrible as a demon, was Bagheera. There was one half-minute of desperate silence, as the front ranks of the crowd clawed and tore their way back from the threshold, and in that minute Bagheera raised his head and yawned – elaborately, carefully, and ostentatiously – as he would yawn when he wished to insult an equal. The fringed lips drew back and up; the red tongue curled; the lower jaw dropped and dropped till you could see halfway down the hot gullet; and the gigantic dogteeth stood clear to the pit of the gums till they rang together, upper and under, with the snick of steel-faced wards shooting home round the edges of a safe. Next instant the street was empty; Bagheera had leaped back through the window, and stood at Mowgli's side, while a yelling, screaming torrent scrambled and tumbled one over another in their panic haste to get to their own huts.

'They will not stir till day comes,' said Bagheera quietly. 'And now?'

The silence of the afternoon sleep seemed to have overtaken the village; but, as they listened, they could hear the sound of heavy grain-boxes being dragged over earthen floors and set down against doors. Bagheera was quite right; the village would not stir till daylight. Mowgli sat still, and thought, and his face grew darker and darker.

'What have I done?' said Bagheera, at last coming to his feet, fawning.

'Nothing but great good. Watch them now till the day. I sleep.' Mowgli ran off into the Jungle, and dropped like a dead man across a rock, and slept and slept the day round, and the night back again.

When he waked, Bagheera was at his side, and there was a newly-killed buck at his feet. Bagheera watched curiously while Mowgli went to work with his skinning-knife, ate and drank, and turned over with his chin in his hands.

'The man and the woman are come safe within eyeshot of Khanhiwara,' Bagheera said. 'Thy lair mother sent the word back by Chil, the Kite. They found a horse before midnight of the night they were freed, and went very quickly. Is not that well?'

'That is well,' said Mowgli.

'And thy Man-Pack in the village did not stir till the sun was high this morning. Then they ate their food and ran back quickly to their houses.'

'Did they, by chance, see thee?'

'It may have been. I was rolling in the dust before the gate at dawn, and I may have made also some small song to myself. Now, Little Brother, there is nothing more to do. Come hunting with me and Baloo. He has new hives that he wishes to show, and we all desire thee back again as of old. Take off that look which makes even me afraid! The man and woman will not be put into the Red Flower, and all goes well in the Jungle. Is it not true? Let us forget the Man-Pack.'

'They shall be forgotten in a little while. Where does Hathi feed tonight?'

'Where he chooses. Who can answer for the Silent One? But why? What is there Hathi can do which we cannot?'

'Bid him and his three sons come here to me.'

'But, indeed, and truly, Little Brother, it is not – it is not seemly to say "Come," and "Go," to Hathi. Remember, he is the Master of the Jungle, and before the Man-Pack changed the look on thy face, he taught thee the Master-words of the Jungle.'

'That is all one. I have a Master-word for him now. Bid him come to Mowgli, the Frog: and if he does not hear at first, bid him come because of the Sack of the Fields of Bhurtpore.'

'The Sack of the Fields of Bhurtpore,' Bagheera repeated two or three times to make sure. 'I go. Hathi can but be angry at the worst, and I would give a moon's hunting to hear a Master-word that compels the Silent One.'

He went away, leaving Mowgli stabbing furiously with his skinning-knife into the earth. Mowgli had never seen human blood in his life before till he had seen, and – what meant much more to him – smelled Messua's blood on the thongs that bound her. And Messua had been kind to him, and, so far as he knew anything about love, he loved Messua as completely as he hated the rest of mankind. But deeply as he loathed them, their talk, their cruelty, and their cowardice, not for anything the Jungle had to offer could he bring himself to take a human life, and have that terrible scent of blood back again in his nostrils. His plan was simpler, but much more thorough; and he laughed to himself when he thought that it was one of old Buldeo's tales told under the peepul tree in the evening that had put the idea into his head.

'It *was* a Master-word,' Bagheera whispered in his ear. 'They were feeding by the river, and they obeyed as though they were bullocks. Look where they come now!'

Hathi and his three sons had arrived, in their usual way, without a sound. The mud of the river was still fresh on their flanks, and Hathi was thought-fully chewing the green stem of a young plantain tree that he had gouged up with his tusks. But every line in his vast body showed to Bagheera, who could see things when he came across them, that it was not the Master of the Jungle speaking to a Man-cub, but one who was afraid coming before one who was not. His three sons rolled side by side, behind their father.

Mowgli hardly lifted his head as Hathi gave him 'Good hunting.' He kept him swinging and rocking, and shifting from one foot to another, for a long time before he spoke; and when he opened his mouth it was to Bagheera, not to the elephants.

'I will tell a tale that was told to me by the hunter ye hunted today,' said Mowgli. 'It concerns an elephant, old and wise, who fell into a trap, and the sharpened stake in the pit scarred him from a little above his heel to the crest of his shoulder, leaving a white mark.' Mowgli threw out his hand, and as Hathi wheeled the moonlight showed a long white scar on his slaty side, as though he had been struck with a red-hot whip. 'Men came to take him from the trap,' Mowgli continued, 'but he broke his ropes, for he was strong, and went away till his wound was healed. Then came he, angry, by night to the fields of those hunters. And I remember now that he had three sons. These things happened many, many Rains ago, and very far away – among the fields of Bhurtpore. What came to those fields at the next reaping, Hathi?'

'They were reaped by me and by my three sons,' said Hathi.

'And to the ploughing that follows the reaping?' said Mowgli.

'There was no ploughing,' said Hathi.

'And to the men that live by the green crops on the ground?' said Mowgli.

'They went away.'

'And to the huts in which the men slept?' said Mowgli.

'We tore the roofs to pieces, and the Jungle swallowed up the walls,' said Hathi.

'And what more?' said Mowgli.

'As much good ground as I can walk over in two nights from the east to the west, and from the north to the south as much as I can walk over in three nights, the Jungle took. We let in the Jungle upon five villages; and in those villages, and in their lands, the grazing-ground and the soft crop-grounds, there is not one man today who takes his food from the ground. That was the Sack of the Fields of Bhurtpore, which I and my three sons did; and now I ask, Man-cub, how the news of it came to thee?' said Hathi.

'A man told me, and now I see even Buldeo can speak truth. It was well done, Hathi with the white mark; but the second time it shall be done better, for the reason that there is a man to direct. Thou knowest the village of the Man-Pack that cast me out? They are idle, senseless, and cruel; they play with their mouths, and they do not kill the weaker for food, but for sport. When they are full-fed they would throw their own breed into the Red Flower. This I have seen. It is not well that they should live here any more. I hate them!'

'Kill, then,' said the youngest of Hathi's three sons, picking up a tuft of grass, dusting it against his forelegs, and throwing it away, while his little red eyes glanced furtively from side to side.

'What good are white bones to me?' Mowgli answered angrily. 'Am I the cub of a wolf to play in the sun with a raw head? I have killed Shere Khan, and his hide rots on the Council Rock; but – but I do not know whither Shere

Khan is gone, and my stomach is still empty. Now I will take that which I can see and touch. Let in the Jungle upon that village, Hathi!'

Bagheera shivered, and cowered down. He could understand, if the worst came to the worst, a quick rush down the village street, and a right and left blow into a crowd, or a crafty killing of men as they ploughed in the twilight; but this scheme for deliberately blotting out an entire village from the eyes of man and beast frightened him. Now he saw why Mowgli had sent for Hathi. No one but the long-lived elephant could plan and carry through such a war.

'Let them run as the men ran from the fields of Bhurtpore, till we have the rainwater for the only plough, and the noise of the rain on the thick leaves for the pattering of their spindles – till Bagheera and I lair in the house of the Brahmin, and the buck drink at the tank behind the temple! Let in the Jungle, Hathi!'

'But I – but we have no quarrel with them, and it needs the red rage of great pain ere we tear down the places where men sleep,' said Hathi doubtfully.

'Are ye the only eaters of grass in the Jungle? Drive in your peoples. Let the deer and the pig and the nilghai look to it. Ye need never show a hand's-breadth of hide till the fields are naked. Let in the Jungle, Hathi!'

'There will be no killing? My tusks were red at the Sack of the Fields of Bhurtpore, and I would not wake that smell again.'

'Nor I. I do not wish even their bones to lie on the clean earth. Let them go and find a fresh lair. They cannot stay here. I have seen and smelled the blood of the woman that gave me food – the woman whom they would have killed but for me. Only the smell of the new grass on their doorsteps can take away that smell. It burns in my mouth. Let in the Jungle, Hathi!'

'Ah!' said Hathi. 'So did the scar of the stake burn on my hide till we watched the villages die under in the spring growth. Now I see. Thy war shall be our war. We will let in the Jungle!'

Mowgli had hardly time to catch his breath – he was shaking all over with rage and hate before the place where the elephants had stood was empty, and Bagheera was looking at him with terror.

'By the Broken Lock that freed me!' said the Black Panther at last. 'Art *thou* the naked thing I spoke for in the Pack when all was young? Master of the Jungle, when my strength goes, speak for me – speak for Baloo – speak for us all! We are cubs before thee! Snapped twigs under foot! Fawns that have lost their doe!'

The idea of Bagheera being a stray fawn upset Mowgli altogether, and he laughed and caught his breath, and sobbed and laughed again, till he had to jump into a pool to make himself stop. Then he swam round and round, ducking in and out of the bars of the moonlight like the frog, his namesake.

By this time Hathi and his three sons had turned, each to one point of the compass, and were striding silently down the valleys a mile away. They went on and on for two days' march – that is to say, a long sixty miles – through the Jungle; and every step they took, and every wave of their trunks, was known and noted and talked over by Mang and Chil and the Monkey People and all the birds. Then they began to feed, and fed quietly for a week or so. Hathi and his sons are like Kaa, the Rock Python. They never hurry till they have to.

At the end of that time – and none knew who had started it – a rumour went through the Jungle that there was better food and water to be found in such and such a valley. The pig – who, of course, will go to the ends of the earth for a full meal – moved first by companies, scuffling over the rocks, and the deer followed, with the small wild foxes that live on the dead and dying of the herds; and the heavy-shouldered nilghai moved parallel with the deer, and the wild buffaloes of the swamps came after the nilghai. The least little thing would have turned the scattered, straggling droves that grazed and sauntered and drank and grazed again; but whenever there was an alarm some one would rise up and soothe them. At one time it would be Ikki the Porcupine, full of news of good feed just a little farther on; at another Mang would cry cheerily and flap down a glade to show it was all empty; or Baloo, his mouth full of roots, would shamble alongside a wavering line and half frighten, half romp it clumsily back to the proper road. Very many creatures broke back or ran away or lost interest, but very many were left to go forward. At the end of another ten days or so the situation was this. The deer and the pig and the nilghai were milling round and round in a circle of eight or ten miles radius, while the Eaters of Flesh skirmished round its edge. And the centre of that circle was the village, and round the village the crops were ripening, and in the crops sat men on what they call *machans* – platforms like pigeon-perches, made of sticks at the top of four poles – to scare away birds and other stealers. Then the deer were coaxed no more. The Eaters of Flesh were close behind them, and forced them forward and inward.

It was a dark night when Hathi and his three sons slipped down from the Jungle, and broke off the poles of the *machans* with their trunks; they fell as a snapped stalk of hemlock in bloom falls, and the men that tumbled from them heard the deep gurgling of the elephants in their ears. Then the vanguard of the bewildered armies of the deer broke down and flooded into the village grazing-grounds and the ploughed fields; and the sharp-hoofed, rooting wild pig came with them, and what the deer left the pig spoiled, and from time to time an alarm of wolves would shake the herds, and they would rush to and fro desperately, treading down the young barley, and cutting flat the banks of the irrigating channels. Before the dawn broke the pressure on the outside of the circle gave way at one point. The Eaters of Flesh had fallen back and left an open path to the south, and drove upon drove of buck fled along it. Others, who were bolder, lay up in the thickets to finish their meal next night.

But the work was practically done. When the villagers looked in the morning they saw their crops were lost. And that meant death if they did not get away, for they lived year in and year out as near to starvation as the Jungle was near to them. When the buffaloes were sent to graze the hungry brutes found that the deer had cleared the grazing-grounds, and so wandered into the Jungle and drifted off with their wild mates; and when twilight fell the three or four ponies that belonged to the village lay in their stables with their heads beaten in. Only Bagheera could have given those strokes, and only Bagheera would have thought of insolently dragging the last carcass to the open street.

The villagers had no heart to make fires in the fields that night, so Hathi and his three sons went gleaning among what was left; and where Hathi gleans there is no need to follow. The men decided to live on their stored seed-corn until the rains had fallen, and then to take work as servants till they could catch up with the lost year; but as the grain-dealer was thinking of his well-filled crates of corn, and the prices he would levy at the sale of it, Hathi's sharp tusks were picking out the corner of his mud-house, and smashing open the big wicker chest, leeped with cow-dung, where the precious stuff lay.

When that last loss was discovered, it was the Brahmin's turn to speak. He had prayed to his own Gods without answer. It might be, he said, that, unconsciously, the village had offended some one of the Gods of the Jungle, for, beyond doubt, the Jungle was against them. So they sent for the headman of the nearest tribe of wandering Gonds – little, wise, and very black hunters, living in the deep Jungle, whose fathers came of the oldest race in India – the aboriginal owners of the land. They made the Gond welcome with what they had, and he stood on one leg, his bow in his hand, and two or three poisoned arrows stuck through his topknot, looking half afraid and half contemptuously at the anxious villagers and their ruined fields. They wished to know whether his Gods – the Old Gods – were angry with them and what sacrifices should be offered. The Gond said nothing, but picked up a trail of the *Karela*, the vine that bears the bitter wild gourd, and laced it to and fro across the temple door in the face of the staring red Hindu image. Then he pushed with his hand in the open air along the road to Khanhiwara, and went back to his Jungle, and watched the Jungle People drifting through it. He knew that when the Jungle moves only white men can hope to turn it aside.

There was no need to ask his meaning. The wild gourd would grow where they had worshipped their God, and the sooner they saved themselves the better.

But it is hard to tear a village from its moorings. They stayed on as long as any summer food was left to them, and they tried to gather nuts in the Jungle, but shadows with glaring eyes watched them, and rolled before them even at midday; and when they ran back afraid to their walls, on the tree-trunks they had passed not five minutes before the bark would be stripped and chiselled with the stroke of some great taloned paw. The more they kept to their village, the bolder grew the wild things that gambolled and bellowed on the grazing-grounds by the Waingunga. They had no time to patch and plaster the rear walls of the empty byres that backed on to the Jungle; the wild pig trampled them down, and the knotty-rooted vines hurried after and threw their elbows over the new-won ground, and the coarse grass bristled behind the vines like the lances of a goblin army following a retreat. The unmarried men ran away first, and carried the news far and near that the village was doomed. Who could fight, they said, against the Jungle, or the Gods of the Jungle, when the very village cobra had left his hole in the platform under the peepul tree? So their little commerce with the outside world shrunk as the trodden paths across the open grew fewer and fainter. At last the nightly trumpetings of Hathi and his three sons ceased to trouble them; for they had no more to be robbed of. The crop on the ground and the seed in the ground had been taken. The outlying fields were already losing their shape, and it was time to throw themselves on the charity of the English at Khanhiwara.

Native fashion, they delayed their departure from one day to another till the first Rains caught them and the unmended roofs let in a flood, and the grazing-ground stood ankle deep, and all life came on with a rush after the heat of the summer. Then they waded out – men, women, and children – through the blinding hot rain of the morning, but turned naturally for one farewell look at their homes.

They heard, as the last burdened family filed through the gate, a crash of falling beams and thatch behind the walls. They saw a shiny, snaky black trunk lifted for an instant, scattering sodden thatch. It disappeared, and there was another crash, followed by a squeal. Hathi had been plucking off the roofs of the huts as you pluck water-lilies, and a rebounding beam had pricked him. He needed only this to unchain his full strength, for of all things in the Jungle the wild elephant enraged is the most wantonly destructive. He kicked backward at a mud wall that crumbled at the stroke, and, crumbling, melted to yellow mud under the torrent of rain. Then he wheeled and squealed, and tore through the narrow streets, leaning against the huts right and left, shivering the crazy doors, and crumpling up the caves; while his three sons raged behind as they had raged at the Sack of the Fields of Bhurtpore.

'The Jungle will swallow these shells,' said a quiet voice in the wreckage. 'It is the outer wall that must lie down,' and Mowgli, with the rain sluicing over his bare shoulders and arms, leaped back from a wall that was settling like a tired buffalo.

'All in good time,' panted Hathi. 'Oh, but my tusks were red at Bhurtpore; To the outer wall, children! With the head! Together! Now!'

The four pushed side by side; the outer wall bulged, split, and fell, and the villagers, dumb with horror, saw the savage, clay-streaked heads of the wreckers in the ragged gap. Then they fled, houseless and foodless, down the valley, as their village, shredded and tossed and trampled, melted behind them.

A month later the place was a dimpled mound, covered with soft, green young stuff; and by the end of the Rains there was the roaring jungle in full blast on the spot that had been under plough not six months before.

Mowgli's Song against People

WILL LET LOOSE against you the fleet-footed vines –
I will call in the Jungle to stamp out your lines!
   The roofs shall fade before it,
     The house-beams shall fall,
   And the *Karela*, the bitter *Karela*,
     Shall cover it all!

In the gates of these your councils my people shall sing,
In the doors of these your garners the Bat-folk shall cling;
   And the snake shall be your watchman,
     By a hearthstone unswept;
   For the *Karela*, the bitter *Karela*,
     Shall fruit where ye slept!

Ye shall not see my strikers; ye shall hear them and guess;
By night, before the moon-rise, I will send for my cess,
   And the wolf shall he your herdsman
     By a landmark removed,
   For the *Karela*, the bitter *Karela*,
     Shall seed where ye loved!

I will reap your fields before you at the hands of a host;
Ye shall glean behind my reapers, for the bread that is lost,
   And the deer shall be your oxen
     By a headland untilled,
   For the *Karela*, the bitter *Karela*,
     Shall leaf where ye build!

I have untied against you the club-footed vines,
I have sent in the Jungle to swamp out your lines.
   The trees – the trees are on you!
     The house-beams shall fall,
   And the *Karela*, the bitter *Karela*,
     Shall cover you all!

The Undertakers

When ye say to Tabaqui, 'My Brother!' when ye call the Hyena to meat,
Ye may cry the Full Truce with Jacala – the Belly that runs on four feet.

Jungle Law

 'RESPECT THE AGED!'
It was a thick voice – a muddy voice that would have made you shudder – a voice like something soft breaking in two. There was a quaver in it, a croak and a whine.

'Respect the aged! O Companions of the River – respect the aged!'

Nothing could be seen on the broad reach of the river except a little fleet of square-sailed, wooden-pinned barges, loaded with building-stone, that had just come under the railway bridge, and were driving downstream. They put their clumsy helms over to avoid the sand-bar made by the scour of the bridge-piers, and as they passed, three abreast, the horrible voice began again: 'O Brahmins of the River – respect the aged and infirm!'

A boatman turned where he sat on the gunwale, lifted up his hand, said something that was not a blessing, and the boats creaked on through the twilight. The broad Indian river, that looked more like a chain of little lakes than a stream, was as smooth as glass, reflecting the sandy-red sky in mid-channel, but splashed with patches of yellow and dusky purple near and under the low banks. Little creeks ran into the river in the wet season, but now their dry mouths hung clear above water-line. On the left shore, and almost under the railway bridge, stood a mud-and-brick and thatch-and-stick village, whose main street, full of cattle going back to their byres, ran straight to the river, and ended in a sort of rude brick pier-head, where people who wanted to wash could wade in step by step. That was the Ghaut of the village of Mugger-Ghaut.

Night was falling fast over the fields of lentils and rice and cotton in the low-lying ground yearly flooded by the river; over the reeds that fringed the elbow of the bend, and the tangled jungle of the grazing-grounds behind the still reeds. The parrots and crows, who had been chattering and shouting over their evening drink, had flown inland to roost, crossing the outgoing battalions of the flying-foxes; and cloud upon cloud of water-birds came whistling and 'honking' to the cover of the reed-beds. There were geese, barrel-headed and black-backed, teal, widgeon, mallard, and sheldrake, with curlews, and here and there a flamingo.

A lumbering Adjutant-crane brought up the rear, flying as though each slow stroke would be his last.

'Respect the aged! Brahmins of the River – respect the aged!'

The Adjutant half turned his head, sheered a little in the direction of the voice, and landed stiffly on the sand-bar below the bridge. Then you saw what a ruffianly brute he really was. His back view was immensely respectable, for he stood nearly six feet high, and looked rather like a very proper bald-headed parson. In front it was different, for his Ally Sloper-like head and neck had not a feather to them, and there was a horrible raw-skin pouch on his neck under his chin – a holdall for the things his pickaxe beak might steal. His legs were long and thin and skinny, but he moved them delicately, and looked at them with pride as he preened down his ashy-grey tail-feathers, glanced over the smooth of his shoulder, and stiffened into 'Stand at attention.'

A mangy little Jackal, who had been yapping hungrily on a low bluff, cocked up his ears and tail, and scuttered across the shallows to join the Adjutant.

He was the lowest of his caste – not that the best of jackals are good for much, but this one was peculiarly low, being half a beggar, half a criminal – a cleaner-up of village rubbish-heaps, desperately timid or wildly bold, ever-lastingly hungry, and full of cunning that never did him any good.

'Ugh!' he said, shaking himself dolefully as he landed. 'May the red mange destroy the dogs of this village! I have three bites for each flea upon me, and all because I looked – only looked, mark you – at an old shoe in a cow-byre. Can I eat mud?' He scratched himself under his left ear.

'I heard,' said the Adjutant, in a voice like a blunt saw going through a thick board – ' I *heard* there was a newborn puppy in that same shoe.'

'To hear is one thing; to know is another,' said the Jackal, who had a very fair knowledge of proverbs, picked up by listening to men round the village fires of an evening.

'Quite true. So, to make sure, I took care of that puppy while the dogs were busy elsewhere.'

'They were *very* busy,' said the Jackal. 'Well, I must not go to the village hunting for scraps yet awhile. And so there truly was a blind puppy in that shoe?'

'It is here,' said the Adjutant, squinting over his beak at his full pouch. 'A small thing, but acceptable now that charity is dead in the world.'

'Ahai! The world is iron in these days,' wailed the Jackal. Then his restless eye caught the least possible ripple on the water, and he went on quickly: 'Life is hard for us all, and I doubt not that even our excellent master, the Pride of the Ghaut and the Envy of the River – '

'A liar, a flatterer, and a Jackal were all hatched out of the same egg,' said the Adjutant to nobody in particular; for he was rather a fine sort of a liar on his own account when he took the trouble.

'Yes, the Envy of the River,' the Jackal repeated, raising his voice. 'Even he, I doubt not, finds that since the bridge has been built good food is more scarce. But on the other hand, though I would by no means say this to his noble face, he is so wise and so virtuous – as I, alas I am not – '

'When the Jackal owns he is grey, how black must the Jackal be!' muttered the Adjutant. He could not see what was coming.

'That *his* food never fails, and in consequence – '

There was a soft grating sound, as though a boat had just touched in shoal water. The Jackal spun round quickly and faced (it is always best to face) the creature he had been talking about. It was a twenty-four-foot crocodile, cased in what looked like treble-riveted boiler plate, studded and keeled and crested; the yellow points of his upper teeth just overhanging his beautifully fluted lower jaw. It was the blunt-nosed Mugger of Mugger-Ghaut, older than any man in the village, who had given his name to the village; the demon of the ford before the railway bridge, came – murderer, man-eater, and local fetish in one. He lay with his chin in the shallows, keeping his place by an almost invisible rippling of his tail, and well the Jackal knew that one stroke of that same tail in the water would carry the Mugger up the bank with the rush of a steam-engine.

'Auspiciously met, Protector of the Poor!' he fawned, backing at every word. 'A delectable voice was heard, and we came in the hopes of sweet conversation. My tailless presumption, while waiting here, led me, indeed, to speak of thee. It is my hope that nothing was overheard.'

Now the Jackal had spoken just to be listened to, for he knew flattery was the best way of getting things to eat, and the Mugger knew that the Jackal had spoken for this end, and the Jackal knew that the Mugger knew, and the Mugger knew that the Jackal knew that the Mugger knew, and so they were all very contented together.

The old brute pushed and panted and grunted up the bank, mumbling, 'Respect the aged and infirm!' and all the time his little eyes burned like coals under the heavy, horny eyelids on the top of his triangular head, as he shoved his bloated barrel-body along between his crutched legs. Then he settled down, and, accustomed as the Jackal was to his ways, he could not help starting, for the hundredth time, when he saw how exactly the Mugger imitated a log adrift on the bar. He had even taken pains to lie at the exact angle a naturally stranded log would make with the water, having regard to the current of the season at the time and place. All this was only a matter of habit, of course, because the Mugger had come ashore for pleasure; but a crocodile is never quite full, and if the Jackal had been deceived by the likeness he would not have lived to philosophise over it.

'My child, I heard nothing,' said the Mugger, shutting one eye. 'The water was in my ears, and also I was faint with hunger. Since the railway bridge was built my people at my village have ceased to love me; and that is breaking my heart.'

'Ah, shame!' said the Jackal. 'So noble a heart, too! But men are all alike, to my mind.'

'Nay, there are very great differences indeed,' the Mugger answered gently. 'Some are as lean as boat-poles. Others again are fat as young ja – dogs. Never would I causelessly revile men. They are of all fashions, but the long years have shown me that, one with another, they are very good. Men, women, and children – I have no fault to find with them. And remember, child, he who rebukes the World is rebuked by the World.'

'Flattery is worse than an empty tin can in the belly. But that which we have just heard is wisdom,' said the Adjutant, bringing down one foot.

'Consider, though, their ingratitude to this excellent one,' began the Jackal tenderly.

'Nay, nay, not ingratitude!' the Mugger said. 'They do not think for others; that is all. But I have noticed, lying at my station below the ford, that the stairs of the new bridge are cruelly hard to climb, both for old people and young children. The old, indeed, are not so worthy of consideration, but I am grieved – I am truly grieved – on account of the fat children. Still, I think, in a little while, when the newness of the bridge has worn away, we shall see my people's bare brown legs bravely splashing through the ford as before. Then the old Mugger will be honoured again.'

'But surely I saw marigold wreaths floating off the edge of the Ghaut only this noon,' said the Adjutant.

Marigold wreaths are a sign of reverence all India over.

'An error – an error. It was the wife of the sweetmeat-seller. She loses her eyesight year by year, and cannot tell a log from me – the Mugger of the Ghaut. I saw the mistake when she threw the garland, for I was lying at the very foot of the Ghaut, and had she taken another step I might have shown her some little difference. Yet she meant well, and we must consider the spirit of the offering.'

'What good are marigold wreaths when one is on the rubbish-heap?' said the Jackal, hunting for fleas, but keeping one wary eye on his Protector of the Poor.

'True, but they have not yet begun to make the rubbish-heap that shall carry *me*. Five times have I seen the river draw back from the village and make new land at the foot of the street. Five times have I seen the village rebuilt on the banks, and I shall see it built yet five times more. I am no faithless, fish-hunting Gavial, I, at Kasi today and Prayag tomorrow, as the saying is, but the true and constant watcher of the ford. It is not for nothing, child, that the village bears my name, and "he who watches long," as the saying is, "shall at last have his reward." '

'*I* have watched long – very long – nearly all my life, and my reward has been bites and blows,' said the Jackal.

'Ho! ho! ho!' roared the Adjutant.

> 'In August was the Jackal born;
> The Rains fell in September;
> "Now such a fearful flood as this,"
> Says he, "I can't remember!" '

There is one very unpleasant peculiarity about the Adjutant. At uncertain times he suffers from acute attacks of the fidgets or cramp in his legs, and though he is more virtuous to behold than any of the cranes, who are all immensely respectable, he flies off into wild, cripple-stilt war-dances, half opening his wings and bobbing his bald head up and down; while for reasons best known to himself he is very careful to time his worst attacks with his nastiest remarks. At the last word of his song he came to attention again, ten times adjutaunter than before.

The Jackal winced, though he was full three seasons old, but you cannot resent an insult from a person with a beak a yard long, and the power of driving it like a javelin. The Adjutant was a most notorious coward, but the Jackal was worse.

'We must live before we can learn,' said the Mugger, 'and there is this to say: Little jackals are very common, child, but such a Mugger as I am is not common. For all that, I am not proud, since pride is destruction; but take notice, it is Fate, and against his Fate no one who swims or walks or runs should say anything at all. I am well contented with Fate. With good luck, a keen eye, and the custom of considering whether a creek or a backwater has an outlet to it ere you ascend, much may be done.'

'Once I heard that even the Protector of the Poor made a mistake,' said the Jackal viciously.

'True; but there my Fate helped me. It was before I had come to my full growth – before the last famine but three (by the Right and Left of Gunga, how full used the streams to be in those days!). Yes, I was young and unthinking, and when the flood came, who so pleased as I? A little made me very happy then. The village was deep in flood, and I swam above the Ghaut and went far inland, up to the rice-fields, and they were deep in good mud. I remember also a pair of bracelets (glass they were, and troubled me not a little) that I found that evening. Yes, glass bracelets; and, if my memory serves me well, a shoe. I should have shaken off both shoes, but I was hungry. I learned better later. Yes. And so I fed and rested me; but when I was ready to go to the river again the flood had fallen, and I walked through the mud of the main street. Who but I? Came out all my people, priests and women and children, and I looked upon them with benevolence. The mud is not a good place to fight in. Said a boatman, "Get axes and kill him, for he is the Mugger of the ford." "Not so," said the Brahmin. "Look, he is driving the flood before him! He is the godling of the village." Then they threw many flowers at me, and by happy thought one led a goat across the road.'

'How good – how very good is goat!' said the Jackal.

'Hairy – too hairy, and when found in the water more than likely to hide a cross-shaped hook. But that goat I accepted, and went down to the Ghaut in great honour. Later, my Fate sent me the boatman who had desired to cut off my tail with an axe. His boat grounded upon an old shoal which you would not remember.'

'We are not *all* jackals here,' said the Adjutant. 'Was it the shoal made where the stone-boats sank in the year of the great drouth – a long shoal that lasted three floods?'

'There were two,' said the Mugger; 'an upper and a lower shoal.'

'Ay, I forgot. A channel divided them, and later dried up again,' said the Adjutant, who prided himself on his memory.

'On the lower shoal my well-wisher's craft grounded. He was sleeping in the bows, and, half awake, leaped over to his waist – no, it was no more than to his knees – to push off. His empty boat went on and touched again below the next reach, as the river ran then. I followed, because I knew men would come out to drag it ashore.'

'And did they do so?' said the Jackal, a little awestricken. This was hunting on a scale that impressed him.

'There and lower down they did. I went no farther, but that gave me three in one day – well-fed *manjis* (boatmen) all, and, except in the case of the last (then I was careless), never a cry to warn those on the bank.'

'Ah, noble sport! But what cleverness and great judgment it requires!' said the Jackal.

'Not cleverness, child, but only thought. A little thought in life is like salt upon rice, as the boatmen say, and I have thought deeply always. The Gavial, my cousin, the fish-eater, has told me how hard it is for him to follow his fish, and how one fish differs from the other, and how he must know them all, both together and apart. I say that is wisdom; but, on the other hand, my cousin, the Gavial, lives among his people. *My* people do not swim in companies, with their mouths out of the water, as Rewa does; nor do they constantly rise to the surface of the water, and turn over on their sides, like Mohoo and little Chapta; nor do they gather in shoals after flood, like Batchua and Chilwa.'

'All are very good eating,' said the Adjutant, clattering his beak.

'So my cousin says, and makes a great to-do over hunting them, but they do not climb the banks to escape his sharp nose. *My* people are otherwise. Their life is on the land, in the houses, among the cattle. I must know what they do, and what they are about to do; and adding the tail to the trunk, as the saying is, I make up the whole elephant. Is there a green branch and an iron ring hanging over a doorway? The old Mugger knows that a boy has been born in that house, and must some day come down to the Ghaut to play. Is a maiden to be married? The old Mugger knows, for he sees the men carry gifts back and forth; and she, too, comes down to the Ghaut to bathe before her wedding, and – he is there. Has the river changed its channel, and made new land where there was only sand before? The Mugger knows.'

'Now, of what use is that knowledge?' said the Jackal. 'The river has shifted even in my little life.' Indian rivers are nearly always moving about in their beds, and will shift, sometimes, as much as two or three miles in a season, drowning the fields on one bank, and spreading good silt on the other.

'There is no knowledge so useful,' said the Mugger, 'for new land means new quarrels. The Mugger knows. Oho! the Mugger knows. As soon as the water has drained off, he creeps up the little creeks that men think would not hide a dog, and there he waits. Presently comes a farmer saying he will plant cucumbers here, and melons there, in the new land that the river has given him. He feels the good mud with his bare toes. Anon comes another, saying he will put onions, and carrots, and sugar-cane in such and such places. They meet as boats adrift meet, and each rolls his eye at the other under the big blue turban. The old Mugger sees and hears. Each calls the other "Brother", and they go to mark out the boundaries of the new land. The Mugger hurries with them from point to point, shuffling very low through the mud. Now they begin to quarrel! Now they say hot words! Now they pull turbans! Now they lift up their *lathis* (clubs), and, at last, one falls backward into the mud, and the other runs away. When he comes back the dispute is settled, as the iron-bound bamboo of the loser witnesses. Yet they are not grateful to the Mugger. No, they cry "Murder!" and their families fight with sticks, twenty a-side. My people are good people – upland Jats – Malwais of the Bet. They do not give blows for sport, and, when the fight is done, the old Mugger waits far down the river, out of sight of the village, behind the *kikar*-scrub yonder. Then come they down, my broad-shouldered Jats – eight or nine together under the stars, bearing the dead man upon a bed. They are old men with grey beards, and voices as deep as mine. They light a little fire – ah! how well I know that fire! – and they drink tobacco, and they nod their heads together forward in a ring, or sideways toward the dead man upon the bank. They say the English Law will come with a rope for this matter, and that such a man's family will be ashamed, because such a man must be hanged in the great square of the Jail. Then say the friends of the dead, "Let him hang!" and the talk is all to do over again – once, twice, twenty times in the long night. Then says one, at last, "The fight was a fair fight. Let us take blood-money, a little more than is offered by the slayer, and we will say no more about it." Then do they haggle over the blood-money, for the dead was a strong man, leaving many sons. Yet before *amratvela* (sunrise) they put the fire to him a little, as the custom is, and the dead man comes to me, and *he* says no more about it.

Aha! my children, the Mugger knows – the Mugger knows – and my Malwah Jats are a good people!'

'They are too close – too narrow in the hand for my crop,' croaked the Adjutant. 'They waste not the polish on the cow's horn, as the saying is; and, again, who can glean after a Malwai?'

'Ah, I – glean – *them*,' said the Mugger.

'Now, in Calcutta of the South, in the old days,' the Adjutant went on, 'everything was thrown into the streets, and we picked and chose. Those wore dainty seasons. But today they keep their streets as clean as the outside of an egg, and my people fly away. To be clean is one thing; to dust, sweep, and sprinkle seven times a day wearies the very Gods themselves.'

'There was a down-country jackal had it from a brother, who told me, that in Calcutta of the South all the jackals were as fat as otters in the Rains,' said the Jackal, his mouth watering at the bare thought of it.

'Ah, but the white-faces are there – the English, and they bring dogs from somewhere down the river in boats – big fat dogs – to keep those same jackals lean,' said the Adjutant.

'They are, then, as hardhearted as these people? I might have known. Neither earth, sky, nor water shows charity to a jackal. I saw the tents of a white-face last season, after the Rains, and I also took a new yellow bridle to eat. The white-faces do not dress their leather in the proper way. It made me very sick.'

'That was better than my case,' said the Adjutant. 'When I was in my third season, a young and a bold bird, I went down to the river where the big boats come in. The boats of the English are thrice as big as this village.'

'He has been as far as Delhi, and says all the people there walk on their heads,' muttered the Jackal. The Mugger opened his left eye, and looked keenly at the Adjutant.

'It is true,' the big bird insisted. 'A liar only lies when he hopes to be believed. No one who had not seen those boats *could* believe this truth.'

'*That* is more reasonable,' said the Mugger. 'And then?'

'From the insides of this boat they were taking out great pieces of white stuff, which, in a little while, turned to water. Much split off, and fell about on the shore, and the rest they swiftly put into a house with thick walls. But a boatman, who laughed, took a piece no larger than a small dog, and threw it to me. I – all my people – swallow without reflection, and that piece I swallowed as is our custom. Immediately I was afflicted with an excessive cold which, beginning in my crop, ran down to the extreme end of my toes, and deprived me even of speech, while the boatmen laughed at me. Never have I felt such cold. I danced in my grief and amazement till I could recover my breath and then I danced and cried out against the falseness of this world; and the boatmen derided me till they fell down. The chief wonder of the matter, setting aside that marvellous coldness, was that there was nothing at all in my crop when I had finished my lamentings!'

The Adjutant had done his very best to describe his feelings after swallowing a seven-pound lump of Wenham Lake ice, off an American ice-ship, in the days before Calcutta made her ice by machinery; but as he did not know what ice was, and as the Mugger and the Jackal knew rather less, the tale missed fire.

'Anything,' said the Mugger, shutting his left eye again – '*anything* is possible that comes out of a boat thrice the size of Mugger-Ghaut. My village is not a small one.'

There was a whistle overhead on the bridge, and the Delhi Mail slid across, all the carriages gleaming with light, and the shadows faithfully following along the river. It clanked away into the dark again; but the Mugger and the Jackal were so well used to it that they never turned their heads.

'Is that anything less wonderful than a boat thrice the size of Mugger-Ghaut?' said the bird, looking up.

'I saw that built, child. Stone by stone I saw the bridge-piers rise, and when the men fell off (they were wondrous sure-footed for the most part – but *when* they fell) I was ready. After the first pier was made they never thought to look down the stream for the body to burn. There, again, I saved much trouble. There was nothing strange in the building of the bridge,' said the Mugger.

'But that which goes across, pulling the roofed carts! That is strange,' the Adjutant repeated. 'It is, past any doubt, a new breed of bullock. Some day it will not be able to keep its foothold up yonder, and will fall as the men did. The old Mugger will then be ready.'

The Jackal looked at the Adjutant and the Adjutant looked at the Jackal. If there was one thing they were more certain of than another, it was that the engine was everything in the wide world except a bullock. The Jackal had watched it time and again from the aloe hedges by the side of the line, and the Adjutant had seen engines since the first locomotive ran in India. But the Mugger had only looked up at the thing from below, where the brass dome seemed rather like a bullock's hump.

'Mm – yes, a new kind of bullock,' the Mugger repeated ponderously, to make himself quite sure in his own mind; and, 'Certainly it is a bullock,' said the Jackal.

'And again it might be – ' began the Mugger pettishly.

'Certainly – most certainly,' said the Jackal, without waiting for the other to finish.

'What?' said the Mugger angrily, for he could feel that the others knew more than he did. 'What might it be? *I* never finished my words. You said it was a bullock.'

'It is anything the Protector of the Poor pleases. I am *his* servant – not the servant of the thing that crosses the river.'

'Whatever it is, it is white-face work,' said the Adjutant; 'and for my own part, I would not lie out upon a place so near to it as this bar.'

'You do not know the English as I do,' said the Mugger. 'There was a white-face here when the bridge was built, and he would take a boat in the evenings and shuffle with his feet on the bottom-boards, and whisper: "Is he here? Is he there? Bring me my gun." I could hear him before I could see him – each sound that he made – creaking and puffing and rattling his gun, up and down the river. As surely as I had picked up one of his workmen, and thus saved great expense in wood for the burning, so surely would he come down to the Ghaut, and shout in a loud voice that he would hunt me, and rid the river of me – the Mugger of Mugger-Ghaut! *Me*! Children, I have swum under the bottom of his boat for hour after hour, and heard him fire his gun at logs; and when I was well sure he was wearied, I have risen by his side and snapped my jaws in his face. When the bridge was finished he went away. All the English hunt in that fashion, except when they are hunted.'

'Who hunts the white-faces?' yapped the Jackal excitedly.

'No one now, but I have hunted them in my time.'

'I remember a little of that Hunting. I was young then,' said the Adjutant, clattering his beak significantly.

'I was well established here. My village was being built for the third time, as I remember, when my cousin, the Gavial, brought me word of rich waters above Benares. At first I would not go, for my cousin, who is a fish-eater, does not always know the good from the bad; but I heard my people talking in the evenings, and what they said made me certain.'

'And what did they say?' the Jackal asked.

'They said enough to make me, the Mugger of Mugger-Ghaut, leave water and take to my feet. I went by night, using the littlest streams as they served me; but it was the beginning of the hot weather, and all streams were low. I crossed dusty roads; I went through tall grass; I climbed hills in the moonlight. Even rocks did I climb, children – consider this well. I crossed the tail of Sirhind, the waterless, before I could find the set of the little rivers that flow Gungaward. I was a month's journey from my own people and the river that I knew. That was very marvellous!'

'What food on the way?' said the Jackal, who kept his soul in his little stomach, and was not a bit impressed by the Mugger's land travels.

'That which I could find – *cousin*,' said the Mugger slowly, dragging each word.

Now you do not call a man a cousin in India unless you think you can establish some kind of blood-relationship, and as it is only in old fairytales that the Mugger ever marries a jackal, the Jackal knew for what reason he had been suddenly lifted into the Mugger's family circle. If they had been alone he would not have cared, but the Adjutant's eyes twinkled with mirth at the ugly jest.

'Assuredly, Father, I might have known,' said the Jackal. A mugger does not care to be called a father of jackals, and the Mugger of Mugger-Ghaut said as much – and a great deal more which there is no use in repeating here.

'The Protector of the Poor has claimed kinship. How can I remember the precise degree? Moreover, we eat the same food. He has said it,' was the Jackal's reply.

That made matters rather worse, for what the Jackal hinted at was that the Mugger must have eaten his food on that land-march fresh, and fresh every day, instead of keeping it by him till it was in a fit and proper condition, as every self-respecting mugger and most wild beasts do when they can. Indeed, one of the worst terms of contempt along the river-bed is 'eater of fresh meat.' It is nearly as bad as calling a man a cannibal.

'That food was eaten thirty seasons ago,' said the Adjutant quietly. 'If we talk for thirty seasons more it will never come back. Tell us, now, what happened when the good waters were reached after thy most wonderful land journey. If we listened to the howling of every jackal the business of the town would stop, as the saying is.'

The Mugger must have been grateful for the interruption, because he went on, with a rush:

'By the Right and Left of Gunga! when I came there never did I see such waters!'

'Were they better, then, than the big flood of last season?' said the Jackal.

'Better! That flood was no more than comes every five years – a handful of drowned strangers, some chickens, and a dead bullock in muddy water with crosscurrents. But the season I think of, the river was low, smooth, and even, and, as the Gavial had warned me, the dead English came down, touching each other. I got my girth in that season – my girth and my depth. From Agra, by Etawah and the broad waters by Allahabad – '

'Oh, the eddy that set under the walls of the fort at Allahabad!' said the Adjutant. 'They came in there like widgeon to the reeds, and round and round they swung – thus!'

He went off into his horrible dance again, while the Jackal looked on enviously. He naturally could not remember the terrible year of the Mutiny they were talking about. The Mugger continued:

'Yes, by Allahabad one lay still in the slack-water and let twenty go by to pick one; and, above all, the English were not cumbered with jewellery and nose-rings and anklets as my women are nowadays. To delight in ornaments is to end with a rope for a necklace, as the saying is. All the muggers of all the rivers grew fat then, but it was my Fate to be fatter than them all. The news was that the English were being hunted into the rivers, and by the Right and Left of Gunga! we believed it was true. So far as I went south I believed it to be true; and I went downstream beyond Monghyr and the tombs that look over the river.'

'I know that place,' said the Adjutant. 'Since those days Monghyr is a lost city. Very few live there now.'

'Thereafter I worked upstream very slowly and lazily, and a little above Monghyr there came down a boatful of white-faces – alive! They were, as I remember, women, lying under a cloth spread over sticks, and crying aloud.

There was never a gun fired at us, the watchers of the fords in those days. All the guns were busy elsewhere. We could hear them day and night inland, coming and going as the wind shifted. I rose up full before the boat, because I had never seen white-faces alive, though I knew them well – otherwise. A naked white child kneeled by the side of the boat, and, stooping over, must needs try to trail his hands in the river. It is a pretty thing to see how a child loves running water. I had fed that day, but there was yet a little unfilled space within me. Still, it was for sport and not for food that I rose at the child's hands. They were so clear a mark that I did not even look when I closed; but they were so small that though my jaws rang true – I am sure of that – the child drew them up swiftly, unhurt. They must have passed between tooth and tooth – those small white hands. I should have caught him crosswise at the elbows; but, as I said, it was only for sport and desire to see new things that I rose at all. They cried out one after another in the boat, and presently I rose again to watch them. The boat was too heavy to push over. They were only women, but he who trusts a woman will walk on duckweed in a pool, as the saying is: and by the Right and Left of Gunga, that is truth!'

'Once a woman gave me some dried skin from a fish,' said the Jackal. 'I had hoped to get her baby, but horse-food is better than the kick of a horse, as the saying is. What did thy woman do?'

'She fired at me with a short gun of a kind I have never seen before or since. Five times, one after another' (the Mugger must have met with an old-fashioned revolver); 'and I stayed open-mouthed and gaping, my head in the smoke. Never did I see such a thing. Five times, as swiftly as I wave my tail – thus!'

The Jackal, who had been growing more and more interested in the story, had just time to leap back as the huge tail swung by like a scythe.

'Not before the fifth shot,' said the Mugger, as though he had never dreamed of stunning one of his listeners – ' not before the fifth shot did I sink, and I rose in time to hear a boatman telling all those white women that I was most certainly dead. One bullet had gone under a neck-plate of mine. I know not if it is there still, for the reason I cannot turn my head. Look and see, child. It will show that my tale is true.'

'I?' said the Jackal. 'Shall an eater of old shoes, a bone-cracker, presume, to doubt the word of the Envy of the River? May my tail be bitten off by blind puppies if the shadow of such a thought has crossed my humble mind! The Protector of the Poor has condescended to inform me, his slave, that once in his life he has been wounded by a woman. That is sufficient, and I will tell the tale to all my children, asking for no proof.'

'Overmuch civility is sometimes no better than overmuch discourtesy, for, as the saying is, one can choke a guest with curds. I do *not* desire that any children of thine should know that the Mugger of Mugger-Ghaut took his only wound from a woman. They will have much else to think of if they get their meat as miserably as does their father.'

'It is forgotten long ago! It was never said! There never was a white woman! There was no boat! Nothing whatever happened at all.'

The Jackal waved his brush to show how completely everything was wiped out of his memory, and sat down with an air.

'Indeed, very many things happened,' said the Mugger, beaten in his second attempt that night to get the better of his friend. (Neither bore malice, however. Eat and be eaten was fair law along the river, and the Jackal came in for his share of plunder when the Mugger had finished a meal.) 'I left that boat and went upstream, and, when I had reached Arrah and the backwaters behind it, there were no more dead English. The river was empty for a while. Then came one or two dead, in red coats, not English, but of one kind all – Hindus and Purbeeahs – then five and six abreast, and at last, from Arrah to the North beyond Agra, it was as though whole villages had walked into the water. They came out of little creeks one after another, as the logs come down in the Rains. When the river rose they rose also in companies from the shoals they had rested upon; and the falling flood dragged them with it across the fields and through the Jungle by the long hair. All night, too, going North, I heard the guns, and by day the shod feet of men crossing fords, and that noise which a heavy cartwheel makes on sand under water; and every ripple brought more dead. At last even I was afraid, for I said: 'If this thing happen to men, how shall the Mugger of Mugger-Ghaut escape?' There were boats, too, that came up behind me without sails, burning continually, as the cotton-boats sometimes burn, but never sinking.'

'Ah!' said the Adjutant. 'Boats like those come to Calcutta of the South. They are tall and black, they beat up the water behind them with a tail, and they –'

'Are thrice as big as my village. *My* boats were low and white; they beat up the water on either side of them and were no larger than the boats of one who speaks truth should be. They made me very afraid, and I left water and went back to this my river, hiding by day and walking by night, when I could not find little streams to help me. I came to my village again, but I did not hope to see any of my people there. Yet they were ploughing and sowing and reaping, and going to and fro in their fields, as quietly as their own cattle.'

'Was there still good food in the river?' said the Jackal.

'More than I had any desire for. Even I – and I do not eat mud – even I was tired, and, as I remember, a little frightened of this constant coming down of the silent ones. I heard my people say in my village that all the English were dead; but those that came, face down, with the current were *not* English, as my people saw. Then my people said that it was best to say nothing at all, but to pay the tax and plough the land. After a long time the river cleared, and those that came down it had been clearly drowned by the floods, as I could well see; and though it was not so easy then to get food, I was heartily glad of it. A little killing here and there is no bad thing – but even the Mugger is sometimes satisfied, as the saying is.'

'Marvellous! Most truly marvellous!' said the Jackal. 'I am become fat through merely hearing about so much good eating. And afterward what, if it be permitted to ask, did the Protector of the Poor do?'

'I said to myself – and by the Right and Left of Gunga! I locked my jaws on that vow – I said I would never go roving any more. So I lived by the Ghaut, very close to my own people, and I watched over them year after year; and they loved me so much that they threw marigold wreaths at my head whenever they saw it lift. Yes, and my Fate has been very kind to me, and the river is good enough to respect my poor and infirm presence; only – '

'No one is all happy from his beak to his tail,' said the Adjutant sympathetically. 'What does the Mugger of Mugger-Ghaut need more?'

'That little white child which I did not get,' said the Mugger, with a deep sigh. 'He was very small, but I have not forgotten. I am old now, but before I die it is my desire to try one new thing. It is true they are a heavy-footed, noisy, and foolish people, and the sport would be small, but I remember the old days above Benares, and, if the child lives, he will remember still. It may be he goes up and down the bank of some river, telling how he once passed his hands between the teeth of the Mugger of Mugger-Ghaut, and lived to make a tale of it. My Fate has been very kind, but that plagues me sometimes in my dreams – the thought of the little white child in the bows of that boat.' He yawned, and closed his jaws. 'And now I will rest and think. Keep silent, my children, and respect the aged.'

He turned stiffly, and shuffled to the top of the sand-bar, while the Jackal drew back with the Adjutant to the shelter of a tree stranded on the end nearest the railway bridge.

'That was a pleasant and profitable life,' he grinned, looking up inquiringly at the bird who towered above him. 'And not once, mark you, did he think fit to tell me where a morsel might have been left along the banks. Yet I have told *him* a hundred times of good things wallowing downstream. How true is the saying, "All the world forgets the Jackal and the Barber when the news has been told!" Now he is going to sleep! *Arrh!*'

'How can a jackal hunt with a Mugger?' said the Adjutant coolly. 'Big thief and little thief; it is easy to say who gets the pickings.'

The Jackal turned, whining impatiently, and was going to curl himself up under the tree-trunk, when suddenly he cowered, and looked up through the draggled branches at the bridge almost above his head.

'What now?' said the Adjutant, opening his wings uneasily.

'Wait till we see. The wind blows from us to them, but they are not looking for us – those two men.'

'Men, is it? My office protects me. All India knows I am holy.' The Adjutant, being a first-class scavenger, is allowed to go where he pleases, and so this one never flinched.

'I am not worth a blow from anything better than an old shoe,' said the Jackal, and listened again. 'Hark to that footfall!' he went on. 'That was no country leather, but the shod foot of a white-face. Listen again! Iron hits iron up there! It is a gun! Friend, those heavy-footed, foolish English are coming to speak with the Mugger.'

'Warn him, then. He was called Protector of the Poor by someone not unlike a starving Jackal but a little time ago.'

'Let my cousin protect his own hide. He has told me again and again there is nothing to fear from the white-faces. They must be white-faces. Not a villager of Mugger-Ghaut would dare to come after him. See, I said it was a gun! Now, with good luck, we shall feed before daylight. He cannot hear well out of water, and – this time it is not a woman!'

A shiny barrel glittered for a minute in the moonlight on the girders. The Mugger was lying on the sand-bar as still as his own shadow, his forefeet spread out a little, his head dropped between them, snoring like a – mugger.

A voice on the bridge whispered: 'It's an odd shot – straight down almost – but as safe as houses. Better try behind the neck. Golly! what a brute! The villagers will be wild if he's shot, though. He's the *deota* [godling] of these parts.'

'Don't care a rap,' another voice answered; 'he took about fifteen of my best coolies while the bridge was building, and it's time he was put a stop to. I've been after him in a boat for weeks. Stand by with the Martini as soon as I've given him both barrels of this.'

'Mind the kick, then. A double four-bore's no joke.'

'That's for him to decide. Here goes!'

There was a roar like the sound of a small cannon (the biggest sort of elephant-rifle is not very different from some artillery), and a double streak of flame, followed by the stinging crack of a Martini, whose long bullet makes nothing of a crocodile's plates. But the explosive bullets did the work. One of them struck just behind the Mugger's neck, a hand's-breadth to the left of the backbone, while the other burst a little lower down, at the beginning of the tail. In ninety-nine cases out of a hundred a mortally-wounded crocodile can scramble to deep water and get away; but the Mugger of Mugger-Ghaut was literally broken into three pieces. He hardly moved his head before the life went out of him, and he lay as flat as the Jackal.

'Thunder and lightning! Lightning and thunder!' said that miserable little beast. 'Has the thing that pulls the covered carts over the bridge tumbled at last?'

'It is no more than a gun,' said the Adjutant, though his very tail-feathers quivered. 'Nothing more than a gun. He is certainly dead. Here come the white-faces.'

The two Englishmen had hurried down from the bridge and across to the sand-bar, where they stood admiring the length of the Mugger. Then a native with an axe cut off the big head, and four men dragged it across the spit.

'The last time that I had my hand in a Mugger's mouth,' said one of the Englishmen, stooping down (he was the man who had built the bridge), 'it was when I was about five years old – coming down the river by boat to Monghyr. I was a Mutiny baby, as they call it. Poor mother was in the boat, too, and she often told me how she fired dad's old pistol at the beast's head.'

'Well, you've certainly had your revenge on the chief of the clan – even if the gun has made your nose bleed. Hi, you boatmen! Haul that head up the bank, and we'll boil it for the skull. The skin's too knocked about to keep. Come along to bed now. This was worth sitting up all night for, wasn't it?'

*   *   *

Curiously enough, the Jackal and the Adjutant made the very same remark not three minutes after the men had left.

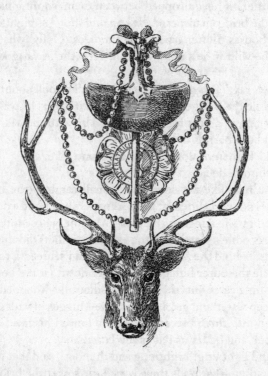

A Ripple Song

NCE A RIPPLE came to land
    In the golden sunset burning –
Lapped against a maiden's hand,
    By the ford returning.

Dainty foot and gentle breast –
    Here, across, be glad and rest.
'Maiden, wait,' the ripple saith.
    'Wait awhile, for I am Death!'

'Where my lover calls I go –
    Shame it were to treat him coldly –
'Twas a fish that circled so,
    Turning over boldly.'

Dainty foot and tender heart,
    Wait the loaded ferry-cart.
'Wait, ah, wait!' the ripple saith;
    'Maiden, wait, for I am Death!'

'When my lover calls I haste –
    Dame Disdain was never wedded!'
Ripple-ripple round her waist,
    Clear the current eddied.

Foolish heart and faithful hand,
    Little feet that touched no land.
Far away the ripple sped,
    Ripple – ripple – running red!

The King Ankus

These are the Four that are never content, that have never
been filled since the Dews began –
Jacala's mouth, and the glut of the Kite, and the hands of the
Ape, and the Eyes of Man.

Jungle Saying

AA, THE BIG ROCK PYTHON, had changed his skin for perhaps the two-hundredth time since his birth; and Mowgli, who never forgot that he owed his life to Kaa for a night's work at Cold Lairs, which you may perhaps remember, went to congratulate him. Skin-changing always makes a snake moody and depressed till the new skin begins to shine and look beautiful. Kaa never made fun of Mowgli any more, but accepted him, as the other Jungle People did, for the Master of the Jungle, and brought him all the news that a python of his size would naturally hear. What Kaa did not know about the Middle Jungle, as they call it – the life that runs close to the earth or under it, the boulder, burrow, and the tree-bole life – might have been written upon the smallest of his scales.

That afternoon Mowgli was sitting in the circle of Kaa's great coils, fingering the flaked and broken old skin that lay all looped and twisted among the rocks just as Kaa had left it. Kaa had very courteously packed himself under Mowgli's broad, bare shoulders, so that the boy was really resting in a living armchair.

'Even to the scales of the eyes it is perfect,' said Mowgli, under his breath, playing with the old skin. 'Strange to see the covering of one's own head at one's own feet!'

'Ay, but I lack feet,' said Kaa; 'and since this is the custom of all my people, I do not find it strange. Does thy skin never feel old and harsh?'

'Then go I and wash, Flathead; but, it is true, in the great heats I have wished I could slough my skin without pain, and run skinless.'

'I wash, and *also* I take off my skin. How looks the new coat?'

Mowgli ran his hand down the diagonal checkerings of the immense back. 'The Turtle is harder-backed, but not so gay,' he said judgematically. 'The Frog, my name-bearer, is more gay, but not so hard. It is very beautiful to see – like the mottling in the mouth of a lily.'

'It needs water. A new skin never comes to full colour before the first bath. Let us go bathe.'

'I will carry thee,' said Mowgli; and he stooped down, laughing, to lift the middle section of Kaa's great body, just where the barrel was thickest. A man might just as well have tried to heave up a two-foot water-main; and Kaa lay still, puffing with quiet amusement. Then the regular evening game began – the Boy in the flush of his great strength, and the Python in his sumptuous new skin, standing up one against the other for a wrestling match – a trial of eye and strength. Of course, Kaa could have crushed a dozen Mowglis if he had let himself go; but he played carefully, and never loosed one-tenth of his power. Ever since Mowgli was strong enough to endure a little rough handling, Kaa had taught him this game, and it suppled his limbs as nothing else could. Sometimes Mowgli would stand lapped almost to his throat in Kaa's shifting coils, striving to get one arm free and catch him by the throat. Then Kaa would give way limply, and Mowgli, with both quick-moving feet, would try to cramp the purchase of that huge tail as it flung backward feeling for a rock or a stump. They would rock to and fro, head to head, each waiting for his chance, till the beautiful, statue-like group melted in a whirl of black-and-yellow coils and struggling legs and arms, to rise up again and again. 'Now! now! now!' said Kaa, making feints with his head that even Mowgli's quick hand could not turn aside. 'Look! I touch thee here, Little Brother! Here, and here! Are thy hands numb? Here again!'

The game always ended in one way – with a straight, driving blow of the head that knocked the boy over and over. Mowgli could never learn the guard for that lightning lunge, and, as Kaa said, there was not the least use in trying.

'Good hunting!' Kaa grunted at last; and Mowgli, as usual, was shot away half a dozen yards, gasping and laughing. He rose with his fingers full of grass, and followed Kaa to the wise snake's pet bathing-place – a deep, pitchy-black pool surrounded with rocks, and made interesting by sunken tree-stumps. The boy slipped in, Jungle-fashion, without a sound, and dived across; rose, too, without a sound, and turned on his back, his arms behind his head, watching the moon rising above the rocks, and breaking up her reflection in the water with his toes. Kaa's diamond-shaped head cut the pool like a razor, and came out to rest on Mowgli's shoulder. They lay still, soaking luxuriously in the cool water.

'It is *very* good,' said Mowgli at last, sleepily. 'Now, in the Man-Pack, at this hour, as I remember, they laid them down upon hard pieces of wood in the inside of a mud-trap, and, having carefully shut out all the clean winds, drew foul cloth over their heavy heads and made evil songs through their noses. It is better in the Jungle.'

A hurrying cobra slipped down over a rock and drank, gave them 'Good hunting!' and went away.

'Sssh!' said Kaa, as though he had suddenly remembered something. 'So the Jungle gives thee all that thou hast ever desired, Little Brother?'

'Not all,' said Mowgli, laughing; 'else there would be a new and strong Shere Khan to kill once a moon. Now, I could kill with my own hands, asking no help of buffaloes. And also I have wished the sun to shine in the middle of the Rains, and the Rains to cover the sun in the deep of summer; and also I have never gone empty but I wished that I had killed a goat; and also I have never killed a goat but I wished it had been buck; nor buck but I wished it had been nilghai. But thus do we feel, all of us.'

'Thou hast no other desire?' the big snake demanded.

'What more can I wish? I have the Jungle, and the favour of the Jungle! Is there more anywhere between sunrise and sunset?'

'Now, the Cobra said – ' Kaa began.

'What cobra? He that went away just now said nothing. He was hunting.'

'It was another.'

'Hast thou many dealings with the Poison People? I give them their own path. They carry death in the fore-tooth, and that is not good – for they are so small. But what hood is this thou hast spoken with?'

Kaa rolled slowly in the water like a steamer in a beam sea. 'Three or four moons since,' said he, 'I hunted in Cold Lairs, which place thou hast not forgotten. And the thing I hunted fled shrieking past the tanks and to that house whose side I once broke for thy sake, and ran into the ground.'

'But the people of Cold Lairs do not live in burrows.' Mowgli knew that Kaa was telling of the Monkey People.

'This thing was not living, but seeking to live,' Kaa replied, with a quiver of his tongue. 'He ran into a burrow that led very far. I followed, and having killed, I slept. When I waked I went forward.'

'Under the earth?'

'Even so, coming at last upon a White Hood [a white cobra], who spoke of things beyond my knowledge, and showed me many things I had never before seen.'

'New game? Was it good hunting?' Mowgli turned quickly on his side.

'It was no game, and would have broken all my teeth; but the White Hood said that a man – he spoke as one that knew the breed – that a man would give the breath under his ribs for only the sight of those things.'

'We will look,' said Mowgli. 'I now remember that I was once a man.'

'Slowly – slowly. It was haste killed the Yellow Snake that ate the sun. We two spoke together under the earth, and I spoke of thee, naming thee as a man. Said the White Hood (and he is indeed as old as the Jungle): "It is long since I have seen a man. Let him come, and he shall see all these things, for the least of which very many men would die." '

'That *must* be new game. And yet the Poison People do not tell us when game is afoot. They are an unfriendly folk.'

'It is *not* game. It is – it is – I cannot say what it is.'

'We will go there. I have never seen a White Hood, and I wish to see the other things. Did he kill them?'

'They are all dead things. He says he is the keeper of them all.'

'Ah! As a wolf stands above meat he has taken to his own lair. Let us go.'

Mowgli swam to bank, rolled on the grass to dry himself, and the two set off for Cold Lairs, the deserted city of which you may have heard. Mowgli was not the least afraid of the Monkey People in those days, but the Monkey People had the liveliest horror of Mowgli. Their tribes, however, were raiding in the Jungle, and so Cold Lairs stood empty and silent in the moonlight. Kaa led up to the ruins of the queens' pavilion that stood on the terrace, slipped over the rubbish, and dived down the half-choked staircase that went underground from the centre of the pavilion. Mowgli gave the snake-call – 'We be of one blood, ye and I,' – and followed on his hands and knees. They crawled a long distance down a sloping passage that turned and twisted several times, and at last came to where the root of some great tree, growing thirty feet overhead, had forced out a solid stone in the wall. They crept through the gap, and found themselves in a large vault, whose domed roof had been also broken away by tree-roots so that a few streaks of light dropped down into the darkness.

'A safe lair,' said Mowgli, rising to his firm feet, 'but over-far to visit daily. And now what do we see?'

'Am I nothing?' said a voice in the middle of the vault; and Mowgli saw something white move till, little by little, there stood up the hugest cobra he had ever set eyes on – a creature nearly eight feet long, and bleached by being in darkness to an old ivory-white. Even the spectacle-marks of his spread hood had faded to faint yellow. His eyes were as red as rubies, and altogether he was most wonderful.

'Good hunting!' said Mowgli, who carried his manners with his knife, and that never left him.

'What of the city?' said the White Cobra, without answering the greeting. 'What of the great, the walled city – the city of a hundred elephants and twenty thousand horses, and cattle past counting – the city of the King of Twenty Kings? I grow deaf here, and it is long since I heard their war-gongs.'

'The Jungle is above our heads,' said Mowgli. 'I know only Hathi and his sons among elephants. Bagheera has slain all the horses in one village, and – what is a King?'

'I told thee,' said Kaa softly to the Cobra – 'I told thee, four moons ago, that thy city was not.'

'The city – the great city of the forest whose gates are guarded by the

King's towers – can never pass. They built it before my father's father came from the egg, and it shall endure when my son's sons are as white as I! Salomdhi, son of Chandrabija, son of Viyeja, son of Yegasuri, made it in the days of Bappa Rawal. Whose cattle are *ye*?'

'It is a lost trail,' said Mowgli, turning to Kaa. 'I know not his talk.'

'Nor I. He is very old. Father of Cobras, there is only the Jungle here, as it has been since the beginning.'

'Then who is *he*,' said the White Cobra, 'sitting down before me, unafraid, knowing not the name of the King, talking our talk through a man's lips? Who is he with the knife and the snake's tongue?'

'Mowgli they call me,' was the answer. 'I am of the Jungle. The wolves are my people, and Kaa here is my brother. Father of Cobras, who art thou?'

'I am the Warden of the King's Treasure. Kurrun Raja built the stone above me, in the days when my skin was dark, that I might teach death to those who came to steal. Then they let down the treasure through the stone, and I heard the song of the Brahmins my masters.'

'Umm!' said Mowgli to himself. 'I have dealt with one Brahmin already, in the Man-Pack, and – I know what I know. Evil comes here in a little.'

'Five times since I came here has the stone been lifted, but always to let down more, and never to take away. There are no riches like these riches – the treasures of a hundred kings. But it is long and long since the stone was last moved, and I think that my city has forgotten.'

'There is no city. Look up. Yonder are roots of the great trees tearing the stones apart. Trees and men do not grow together,' Kaa insisted.

'Twice and thrice have men found their way here,' the White Cobra answered savagely; 'but they never spoke till I came upon them groping in the dark, and then they cried only a little time. But ye come with lies, Man and Snake both, and would have me believe the city is not, and that my wardship ends. Little do men change in the years. But I change never! Till the stone is lifted, and the Brahmins come down singing the songs that I know, and feed me with warm milk, and take me to the light again, I – I – *I*, and no other, am the Warden of the King's Treasure! The city is dead, ye say, and here are the roots of the trees? Stoop down, then, and take what ye will. Earth has no treasure like to these. Man with the snake's tongue, if thou canst go alive by the way that thou hast entered it, the lesser Kings will be thy servants!'

'Again the trail is lost,' said Mowgli coolly. 'Can any jackal have burrowed so deep and bitten this great White Hood? He is surely mad. Father of Cobras, I see nothing here to take away.'

'By the Gods of the Sun and Moon, it is the madness of death upon the boy!' hissed the Cobra. 'Before thine eyes close I will allow thee this favour. Look thou, and see what man has never seen before!'

'They do not well in the Jungle who speak to Mowgli of favours,' said the boy, between his teeth; 'but the dark changes all, as I know. I will look, if that please thee.'

He stared with puckered-up eyes round the vault, and then lifted up from the floor a handful of something that glittered.

'Oho!' said he, 'this is like the stuff they play with in the Man-Pack: only this is yellow and the other was brown.'

He let the gold pieces fall, and move forward. The floor of the vault was buried some five or six feet deep in coined gold and silver that had burst from the sacks it had been originally stored in, and, in the long years, the metal had packed and settled as sand packs at low tide. On it and in it and rising through it, as wrecks lift through the sand, were jewelled elephant-howdahs of embossed silver, studded with plates of hammered gold, and adorned with carbuncles and turquoises. There were palanquins and litters for carrying queens, framed and braced with silver and enamel, with jade-handled poles and amber curtain-rings; there were golden candlesticks hung with pierced emeralds that quivered on the branches; there were studded images, five feet high, of forgotten gods, silver with jewelled eyes; there were coats of mail, gold inlaid on steel, and fringed with rotted and blackened seed-pearls; there were helmets, crested and beaded with pigeon's-blood rubies; there were shields of lacquer, of tortoiseshell and rhinoceros-hide, strapped and bossed with red gold and set with emeralds at the edge; there were sheaves of diamond-hilted swords, daggers, and hunting-knives; there were golden sacrificial bowls and ladles, and portable altars of a shape that never sees the light of day; there were jade cups and bracelets; there were incense-burners, combs, and pots for perfume, henna, and eye-powder, all in embossed gold; there were nose-rings, armlets, headbands, finger-rings, and girdles past any counting; there were belts, seven fingers broad, of square-cut diamonds and rubies, and wooden boxes, trebly clamped with iron, from which the wood had fallen away in powder, showing the pile of uncut star-sapphires, opals, cat's-eyes, sapphires, rubies, diamonds, emeralds, and garnets within.

The White Cobra was right. No mere money would begin to pay the value of this treasure, the sifted pickings of centuries of war, plunder, trade, and taxation. The coins alone were priceless, leaving out of count all the precious stones; and the dead weight of the gold and silver alone might be two or three hundred tons. Every native ruler in India today, however poor, has a hoard to which he is always adding; and though, once in a long while, some enlightened prince may send off forty or fifty bullock-cart loads of silver to be exchanged for Government securities, the bulk of them keep their treasure and the knowledge of it very closely to themselves.

But Mowgli naturally did not understand what these things meant. The knives interested him a little, but they did not balance so well as his own, and so he dropped them. At last he found something really fascinating laid on the front of a howdah half buried in the coins. It was a three-foot ankus, or elephant-goad – something like a small boat hook. The top was one round, shining ruby, and eight inches of the handle below it were studded with rough turquoises close together, giving a most satisfactory grip. Below them was a rim of jade with a flower-pattern running round it – only the leaves were emeralds, and the blossoms were rubies sunk in the cool, green stone. The rest of the handle was a shaft of pure ivory, while the point – the spike and hook – was gold-inlaid steel with pictures of elephant-catching; and the pictures attracted Mowgli, who saw that they had something to do with his friend Hathi the Silent.

The White Cobra had been following him closely.

'Is this not worth dying to behold?' he said. Have I not done thee a great favour?'

'I do not understand,' said Mowgli. 'The things are hard and cold, and by no means good to eat. But this' – he lifted the ankus – 'I desire to take away, that I may see it in the sun. Thou sayest they are all thine? Wilt thou give it to me, and I will bring thee frogs to eat?'

The White Cobra fairly shook with evil delight. 'Assuredly I will give it,' he said. 'All that is here I will give thee – till thou goest away.'

'But I go now. This place is dark and cold, and I wish to take the thorn-pointed thing to the Jungle.'

'Look by thy foot! What is that there?'

Mowgli picked up something white and smooth. 'It is the bone of a man's head,' he said quietly. 'And here are two more.'

'They came to take the treasure away many years ago. I spoke to them in the dark, and they lay still.'

'But what do I need of this that is called treasure? If thou wilt give me the ankus to take away, it is good hunting. If not, it is good hunting none the less. I do not fight with the Poison People, and I was also taught the Master-word of thy tribe.'

'There is but one Master-word here. It is mine!'

Kaa flung himself forward with blazing eyes. 'Who bade me bring the Man?' he hissed.

'I surely,' the old Cobra lisped. 'It is long since I have seen Man, and this Man speaks our tongue.'

'But there was no talk of killing. How can I go to the Jungle and say that I have led him to his death?' said Kaa.

'I talk not of killing till the time. And as to thy going or not going, there is the hole in the wall. Peace, now, thou fat monkey-killer! I have but to touch thy neck, and the Jungle will know thee no longer. Never Man came here that went away with the breath under his ribs. I am the Warden of the Treasure of the King's City!'

'But, thou white worm of the dark, I tell thee there is neither king nor city! The Jungle is all about us!' cried Kaa.

'There is still the Treasure. But this can be done. Wait awhile, Kaa of the Rocks, and see the boy run. There is room for great sport here. Life is good. Run to and fro awhile, and make sport, boy!'

Mowgli put his hand on Kaa's head quietly.

'The white thing has dealt with men of the Man-Pack until now. He does not know me,' he whispered. 'He has asked for this hunting. Let him have it.' Mowgli had been standing with the ankus held point down. He flung it from him quickly and it dropped crossways just behind the great snake's hood, pinning him to the floor. In a flash, Kaa's weight was upon the writhing body, paralysing it from hood to tail. The red eyes burned, and the six spare inches of the head struck furiously right and left.

'Kill!' said Kaa, as Mowgli's hand went to his knife.

'No,' he said, as he drew the blade; 'I will never kill again save for food. But look you, Kaa!' He caught the snake behind the hood, forced the mouth open with the blade of the knife, and showed the terrible poison-fangs of the upper jaw lying black and withered in the gum. The White Cobra had outlived his poison, as a snake will.

'*Thuu*' ('It is dried up' – literally, a rotted out tree-stump), said Mowgli; and motioning Kaa away, he picked up the ankus, setting the White Cobra free.

'The King's Treasure needs a new Warden,' he said gravely. 'Thuu, thou hast not done well. Run to and fro and make sport, Thuu!'

'I am ashamed. Kill me!' hissed the White Cobra.

'There has been too much talk of killing. We will go now. I take the thorn-pointed thing, Thuu, because I have fought and worsted thee.'

'See, then, that the thing does not kill thee at last. It is Death! Remember, it is Death! There is enough in that thing to kill the men of all my city. Not long wilt thou hold it, Jungle Man, nor he who takes it from thee. They will kill, and kill, and kill for its sake! My strength is dried up, but the ankus will do my work. It is Death! It is Death! It is Death!'

Mowgli crawled out through the hole into the passage again, and the last that he saw was the White Cobra striking furiously with his harmless fangs at the stolid golden faces of the gods that lay on the floor, and hissing, 'It is Death!'

They were glad to get to the light of day once more; and when they were back in their own Jungle and Mowgli made the ankus glitter in the morning light, he was almost as pleased as though he had found a bunch of new flowers to stick in his hair.

'This is brighter than Bagheera's eyes,' he said delightedly, as he twirled the ruby. 'I will show it to him; but what did the Thuu mean when he talked of death?'

'I cannot say. I am sorrowful to my tail's tail that he felt not thy knife. There is always evil at Cold Lairs – above ground or below. But now I am hungry. Dost thou hunt with me this dawn?' said Kaa.

'No; Bagheera must see this thing. Good hunting!' Mowgli danced off, flourishing the great ankus, and stopping from time to time to admire it, till he came to that part of the Jungle Bagheera chiefly used, and found him drinking after a heavy kill. Mowgli told him all his adventures from beginning to end, and Bagheera sniffed at the ankus between whiles. When Mowgli came to the White Cobra's last words, the Panther purred approvingly.

'Then the White Hood spoke the thing which is?' Mowgli asked quickly.

'I was born in the King's cages at Oodeypore, and it is in my stomach that I know some little of Man. Very many men would kill thrice in a night for the sake of that one big red stone alone.'

'But the stone makes it heavy to the hand. My little bright knife is better; and – see! the red stone is not good to eat. Then *why* would they kill?'

'Mowgli, go thou and sleep. Thou hast lived among men, and – '

'I remember. Men kill because they are not hunting; – for idleness and pleasure. Wake again, Bagheera. For what use was this thorn-pointed thing made?'

Bagheera half opened his eyes – he was very sleepy – with a malicious twinkle.

'It was made by men to thrust into the head of the sons of Hathi, so that the blood should pour out. I have seen the like in the street of Oodeypore, before our cages. That thing has tasted the blood of many such as Hathi.'

'But why do they thrust into the heads of elephants?'

'To teach them Man's Law. Having neither claws nor teeth, men make these things – and worse.'

'Always more blood when I come near, even to the things the Man-Pack have made,' said Mowgli disgustedly. He was getting a little tired of the weight of the ankus. 'If I had known this, I would not have taken it. First it was Messua's blood on the thongs, and now it is Hathi's. I will use it no more. Look!'

The ankus flew, sparkling, and buried itself point down thirty yards away, between the trees. 'So my hands are clean of Death,' said Mowgli, rubbing his palms on the fresh, moist earth. 'The Thuu said Death would follow me. He is old and white and mad.'

'White or black, or death or life, *I* am going to sleep, Little Brother. I cannot hunt all night and howl all day, as do some folk.'

Bagheera went off to a hunting-lair that he knew, about two miles off. Mowgli made an easy way for himself up a convenient tree, knotted three or four creepers together, and in less time than it takes to tell, was swinging in a hammock fifty feet above ground. Though he had no positive objection to strong daylight, Mowgli followed the custom of his friends, and used it as little as he could. When he waked among the very loud-voiced peoples that live in the trees, it was twilight once more, and he had been dreaming of the beautiful pebbles he had thrown away.

'At least I will look at the thing again,' he said, and slid down a creeper to the earth; but Bagheera was before him. Mowgli could hear him snuffing in the half light.

'Where is the thorn-pointed thing?' cried Mowgli.

'A man has taken it. Here is the trail.'

'Now we shall see whether the Thuu spoke truth. If the pointed thing is Death, that man will die. Let us follow.'

'Kill first,' said Bagheera. 'An empty stomach makes a careless eye. Men go very slowly, and the Jungle is wet enough to hold the lightest mark.'

They killed as soon as they could, but it was nearly three hours before they finished their meat and drink and buckled down to the trail. The Jungle People know that nothing makes up for being hurried over your meals.

'Think you the pointed thing will turn in the man's hand and kill him?' Mowgli asked. 'The Thuu said it was Death.'

'We shall see when we find,' said Bagheera, trotting with his head low. 'It is single-foot' (he meant that there was only one man), 'and the weight of the thing has pressed his heel far into the ground.'

'Hai! This is as clear as summer lightning,' Mowgli answered; and they fell into the quick, choppy trail-trot in and out through the checkers of the moonlight, following the marks of those two bare feet.

'Now he runs swiftly,' said Mowgli. 'The toes are spread apart.' They went on over some wet ground. 'Now why does he turn aside here?'

'Wait!' said Bagheera, and flung himself forward with one superb bound as far as ever he could. The first thing to do when a trail ceases to explain itself is to cast forward without leaving your own confusing footmarks on the ground. Bagheera turned as he landed, and faced Mowgli, crying, 'Here comes another trail to meet him. It is a smaller foot, this second trail, and the toes turn inward.'

Then Mowgli ran up and looked. 'It is the foot of a Gond hunter,' he said. 'Look! Here he dragged his bow on the grass. That is why the first trail turned aside so quickly. Big Foot hid from Little Foot.'

'That is true,' said Bagheera. 'Now, lest by crossing each other's tracks we foul the signs, let each take one trail. I am Big Foot, Little Brother, and thou art Little Foot, the Gond.'

Bagheera leaped back to the original trail, leaving Mowgli stooping above the curious narrow track of the wild little man of the woods.

'Now,' said Bagheera, moving step by step along the chain of footprints, 'I, Big Foot, turn aside here. Now I hide me behind a rock and stand still, not daring to shift my feet. Cry thy trail, Little Brother.'

'Now, I, Little Foot, come to the rock,' said Mowgli, running up his trail. 'Now, I sit down under the rock, leaning upon my right hand, and resting my bow between my toes. I wait long, for the mark of my feet is deep here.'

'I also, said Bagheera, hidden behind the rock. 'I wait, resting the end of the thorn-pointed thing upon a stone. It slips, for here is a scratch upon the stone. Cry thy trail, Little Brother.'

'One, two twigs and a big branch are broken here,' said Mowgli, in an undertone. 'Now, how shall I cry *that*? Ah! It is plain now. I, Little Foot, go away making noises and tramplings so that Big Foot may hear me.' He moved away from the rock pace by pace among the trees, his voice rising in the distance as he approached a little cascade. 'I – go – far – away – to – where – the – noise – of – falling-water – covers – my – noise; and – here – I – wait. Cry thy trail, Bagheera, Big Foot!'

The panther had been casting in every direction to see how Big Foot's trail led away from behind the rock. Then he gave tongue:

'I come from behind the rock upon my knees, dragging the thorn-pointed thing. Seeing no one, I run. I, Big Foot, run swiftly. The trail is clear. Let each follow his own. I run!'

Bagheera swept on along the clearly-marked trail, and Mowgli followed the steps of the Gond. For some time there was silence in the Jungle.

'Where art thou, Little Foot?' cried Bagheera. Mowgli's voice answered him not fifty yards to the right.

'Um!' said the Panther, with a deep cough. 'The two run side by side, drawing nearer!'

They raced on another half-mile, always keeping about the same distance, till Mowgli, whose head was not so close to the ground as Bagheera's, cried: 'They have met. Good hunting – look! Here stood Little Foot, with his knee on a rock – and yonder is Big Foot indeed!'

Not ten yards in front of them, stretched across a pile of broken rocks, lay the body of a villager of the district, a long, small-feathered Gond arrow through his back and breast.

'Was the Thuu so old and so mad, Little Brother?' said Bagheera gently. 'Here is one death, at least.'

'Follow on. But where is the drinker of elephant's blood – the red-eyed thorn?'

'Little Foot has it – perhaps. It is single-foot again now.'

The single trail of a light man who had been running quickly and bearing a burden on his left shoulder held on round a long, low spur of dried grass, where each footfall seemed, to the sharp eyes of the trackers, marked in hot iron.

Neither spoke till the trail ran up to the ashes of a campfire hidden in a ravine.

'Again!' said Bagheera, checking as though he had been turned into stone.

The body of a little wizened Gond lay with its feet in the ashes, and Bagheera looked inquiringly at Mowgli.

'That was done with a bamboo,' said the boy, after one glance. 'I have used such a thing among the buffaloes when I served in the Man-Pack. The Father of Cobras – I am sorrowful that I made a jest of him – knew the breed well, as I might have known. Said I not that men kill for idleness?'

'Indeed, they killed for the sake of the red and blue stones,' Bagheera answered. 'Remember, I was in the King's cages at Oodeypore.'

'One, two, three, four tracks,' said Mowgli, stooping over the ashes. 'Four tracks of men with shod feet. They do not go so quickly as Gonds. Now, what evil had the little woodman done to them? See, they talked together, all five, standing up, before they killed him. Bagheera, let us go back. My stomach is heavy in me, and yet it heaves up and down like an oriole's nest at the end of a branch.'

'It is not good hunting to leave game afoot. Follow!' said the panther. 'Those eight shod feet have not gone far.'

No more was said for fully an hour, as they worked up the broad trail of the four men with shod feet.

It was clear, hot daylight now, and Bagheera said, 'I smell smoke.'

Men are always more ready to eat than to run, Mowgli answered, trotting in and out between the low scrub bushes of the new Jungle they were exploring. Bagheera, a little to his left, made an indescribable noise in his throat.

'Here is one that has done with feeding,' said he. A tumbled bundle of gay-coloured clothes lay under a bush, and round it was some spilt flour.

'That was done by the bamboo again,' said Mowgli. ' See! that white dust is what men eat. They have taken the kill from this one – he carried their food – and given him for a kill to Chil, the Kite.'

'It is the third,' said Bagheera.

'I will go with new, big frogs to the Father of Cobras, and feed him fat,' said Mowgli to himself. 'The drinker of elephant's blood is Death himself – but still I do not understand!'

'Follow!' said Bagheera.

They had not gone half a mile farther when they heard Ko, the Crow, singing the death-song in the top of a tamarisk under whose shade three men were lying. A half-dead fire smoked in the centre of the circle, under an iron plate which held a blackened and burned cake of unleavened bread. Close to the fire, and blazing in the sunshine, lay the ruby-and-turquoise ankus.

'The thing works quickly; all ends here,' said Bagheera. 'How did *these* die, Mowgli? There is no mark on any.'

A Jungle-dweller gets to learn by experience as much as many doctors know of poisonous plants and berries. Mowgli sniffed the smoke that came up from the fire, broke off a morsel of the blackened bread, tasted it, and spat it out again.

'Apple of Death,' he coughed. 'The first must have made it ready in the food for *these*, who killed him, having first killed the Gond.'

'Good hunting, indeed! The kills follow close,' said Bagheera.

'Apple of Death' is what the Jungle call thorn-apple or dhatura, the readiest poison in all India.

'What now?' said the panther. 'Must thou and I kill each other for yonder red-eyed slayer?'

'Can it speak?' said Mowgli in a whisper. Did I do it a wrong when I threw it away? Between us two it can do no wrong, for we do not desire what men desire. If it be left here, it will assuredly continue to kill men one after another as fast as nuts fall in a high wind. I have no love to men, but even I would not have them die six in a night.'

'What matter? They are only men. They killed one another, and were well pleased,' said Bagheera. 'That first little woodman hunted well.'

'They are cubs none the less; and a cub will drown himself to bite the moon's light on the water. The fault was mine,' said Mowgli, who spoke as though he knew all about everything. 'I will never again bring into the Jungle strange things – not though they be as beautiful as flowers. This' – he handled the ankus gingerly – 'goes back to the Father of Cobras. But first we must sleep, and we cannot sleep near these sleepers. Also we must bury *him*, lest he run away and kill another six. Dig me a hole under that tree.'

'But, Little Brother,' said Bagheera, moving off to the spot, 'I tell thee it is no fault of the blood-drinker. The trouble is with the men.'

'All one,' said Mowgli. 'Dig the hole deep. When we wake I will take him up and carry him back.'

                    *   *   *

Two nights later, as the White Cobra sat mourning in the darkness of the vault, ashamed, and robbed, and alone, the turquoise ankus whirled through the hole in the wall, and clashed on the floor of golden coins.

'Father of Cobras,' said Mowgli (he was careful to keep the other side of the wall), 'get thee a young and ripe one of thine own people to help thee guard the King's Treasure, so that no man may come away alive any more.'

'Ah-ha! It returns, then. I said the thing was Death. How comes it that thou art still alive?' the old Cobra mumbled, twining lovingly round the ankus-haft.

'By the Bull that bought me, I do not know! That thing has killed six times in a night. Let him go out no more.'

The Song of the Little Hunter

ERE MOR the Peacock flutters, ere the Monkey People cry,
   Ere Chil the Kite swoops down a furlong sheer,
Through the Jungle very softly flits a shadow and a sigh –
   He is Fear, O Little Hunter, he is Fear!
Very softly down the glade runs a waiting, watching shade,
   And the whisper spreads and widens far and near;
And the sweat is on thy brow, for he passes even now –
   He is Fear, O Little Hunter, he is Fear!

Ere the moon has climbed the mountain, ere the rocks are
                                        ribbed with light,
   When the downward-dipping trails are dank and drear,
Comes a breathing hard behind thee – snuffle-snuffle
                                        through the night –
   It is Fear, O Little Hunter, it is Fear!
On thy knees and draw the bow; bid the shrilling arrow go;
   In the empty, mocking thicket plunge the spear;
But thy hands are loosed and weak, and the blood has
                                        left thy cheek –
   It is Fear, O Little Hunter, it is Fear!

When the heat-cloud sucks the tempest, when the slivered
                                        pine trees fall,
   When the blinding, blaring rain-squalls lash and veer;
Through the war-gongs of the thunder rings a voice more
                                        loud than all –
   It is Fear, O Little Hunter, it is Fear!
Now the spates are banked and deep; now the footless
                                        boulders leap –
   Now the lightning shows each littlest leaf-rib clear –
But thy throat is shut and dried, and thy heart against thy side
   Hammers: Fear, O Little Hunter – this is Fear!

Quiquern

The People of the Eastern Ice, they are melting like the snow –
They beg for coffee and sugar; they go where the white men go.
The People of the Western Ice, they learn to steal and fight;
They sell their furs to the trading-post: they sell their souls
to the white.
The People of the Southern Ice, they trade with the whaler's crew;
Their women have many ribbons, but their tents are torn and few.
But the People of the Elder Ice, beyond the white man's ken –
Their spears are made of the narwhal-horn, and they are the
last of the Men!

Translation

'HE HAS OPENED HIS EYES. LOOK!'

'Put him in the skin again. He will be a strong dog. On the fourth month we will name him.'

'For whom?' said Amoraq.

Kadlu's eye rolled round the skin-lined snow-house till it fell on fourteen-year-old Kotuko sitting on the sleeping-bench, making a button out of walrus ivory. 'Name him for me,' said Kotuko, with a grin. 'I shall need him one day.'

Kadlu grinned back till his eyes were almost buried in the fat of his flat cheeks, and nodded to Amoraq, while the puppy's fierce mother whined to see her baby wriggling far out of reach in the little sealskin pouch hung above the warmth of the blubber-lamp. Kotuko went on with his carving, and Kadlu threw a rolled bundle of leather dog-harnesses into a tiny little room that opened from one side of the house, slipped off his heavy deerskin hunting-suit, put it into a whalebone-net that hung above another lamp, and dropped down on the sleeping-bench to whittle at a piece of frozen seal-meat till Amoraq, his wife, should bring the regular dinner of boiled meat and blood-soup. He had been out since early dawn at the seal-holes, eight miles away, and had come home with three big seal. Halfway down the long, low snow passage or tunnel that led to the inner door of the house you could hear snappings and yelpings, as the dogs of his sleigh-team, released from the day's work, scuffled for warm places.

When the yelpings grew too loud Kotuko lazily rolled off the sleeping-bench, and picked up a whip with an eighteen-inch handle of springy whalebone, and twenty-five feet of heavy, plaited thong. He dived into the passage, where it sounded as though all the dogs were eating him alive; but that was no more than their regular grace before meals. When he crawled out at the far end, half a dozen furry heads followed him with their eyes as he went to a sort of gallows of whale-jawbones, from which the dog's meat was hung; split off the frozen stuff in big lumps with a broad-headed spear; and stood, his whip in one hand and the meat in the other. Each beast was called by name, the weakest first, and woe betide any dog that moved out of his turn; for the tapering lash would shoot out like thonged lightning, and flick away an inch or so of hair and hide. Each beast growled, snapped, choked once over his portion, and hurried back to the protection of the passage, while the boy stood upon the snow under the blazing Northern Lights and dealt out justice. The last to be served was the big black leader of the team, who kept order when the dogs were harnessed; and to him Kotuko gave a double allowance of meat as well as an extra crack of the whip.

'Ah!' said Kotuko, coiling up the lash, 'I have a little one over the lamp that will make a great many howlings. *Sarpok!* Get in!'

He crawled back over the huddled dogs, dusted the dry snow from his furs with the whalebone beater that Amoraq kept by the door, tapped the skin-lined roof of the house to shake off any icicles that might have fallen from the dome of snow above, and curled up on the bench. The dogs in the passage snored and whined in their sleep, the boy-baby in Amoraq's deep fur hood kicked and choked and gurgled, and the mother of the newly-named puppy lay at Kotuko's side, her eyes fixed on the bundle of sealskin, warm and safe above the broad yellow flame of the lamp.

And all this happened far away to the north, beyond Labrador, beyond Hudson's Strait, where the great tides heave the ice about, north of Melville Peninsula – north even of the narrow Fury and Hecla Straits – on the north shore of Baffin Land, where Bylot's Island stands above the ice of Lancaster Sound like a pudding-bowl wrong side up. North of Lancaster Sound there is little we know anything about, except North Devon and Ellesmere Land; but even there live a few scattered people, next door, as it were, to the very Pole.

Kadlu was an Inuit – what you call an Eskimo – and his tribe, some thirty persons all told, belonged to the Tununirmiut – 'the country lying at the back of something.' In the maps that desolate coast is written Navy Board Inlet, but the Inuit name is best, because the country lies at the very back of everything in the world. For nine months of the year there is only ice and snow, and gale after gale, with a cold that no one can realise who has never seen the thermometer even at zero. For six months of those nine it is dark; and that is what makes it so horrible. In the three months of the summer it only freezes every other day and every night, and then the snow begins to weep off on the southerly slopes, and a few ground-willows put out their woolly buds, a tiny stonecrop or so makes believe to blossom, beaches of fine gravel and rounded stones run down to the open sea, and polished boulders and streaked rocks lift up above the granulated snow. But all that is gone in a few weeks, and the wild winter locks down again on the land; while at sea the ice tears up and down the offing, jamming and ramming, and splitting and hitting, and pounding and grounding, till it all freezes together, ten feet thick, from the land outward to deep water.

In the winter Kadlu would follow the seal to the edge of this land-ice, and spear them as they came up to breathe at their blowholes. The seal must have open water to live and catch fish in, and in the deep of winter the ice would sometimes run eighty miles without a break from the nearest shore. In the spring he and his people retreated from the floes to the rocky mainland, where they put up tents of skins, and snared the sea-birds, or speared the young seal basking on the beaches. Later, they would go south into Baffin Land after the reindeer, and to get their year's store of salmon from the hundreds of streams and lakes of the interior; coming back north in September or October for the musk-ox hunting and the regular winter sealery. This travelling was done with dog-sleighs, twenty and thirty miles a day, or sometimes down the coast in big skin 'woman-boats,' when the dogs and the babies lay among the feet of the rowers, and the women sang songs as they glided from cape to cape over the glassy, cold waters. All the luxuries that the Tununirmiut knew came from the south – driftwood for sleigh-runners, rod-iron for harpoon-tips, steel knives, tin kettles that cooked food much better than the old soapstone affairs, flint and steel, and even matches, as well as coloured ribbons for the women's hair, little cheap mirrors, and red cloth for the edging of deerskin dress-jackets. Kadlu traded the rich, creamy, twisted narwhal horn and musk-ox teeth (these are just as valuable as pearls) to the Southern Inuit, and they, in turn, traded with the whalers and the missionary-posts of Exeter and Cumberland Sounds; and so the chain went on, till a kettle picked up by a ship's cook in the Bhendy Bazaar might end its days over a blubber-lamp somewhere on the cool side of the Arctic Circle.

Kadlu, being a good hunter, was rich in iron harpoons, snow-knives, bird-darts, and all the other things that make life easy up there in the great cold; and he was the head of his tribe, or, as they say, 'the man who knows all about it by practice.' This did not give him any authority, except now and then he could advise his friends to change their hunting-grounds; but Kotuko used it to domineer a little, in the lazy, fat Inuit fashion, over the other boys, when they came out at night to play ball in the moonlight, or to sing the Child's Song to the Aurora Borealis.

But at fourteen an Inuit feels himself a man, and Kotuko was tired of making snares for wildfowl and kit-foxes, and most tired of all of helping the women to chew seal- and deer-skins (that supples them as nothing else can) the long day through, while the men were out hunting. He wanted to go into the *quaggi*, the Singing-House, when the hunters gathered there for their mysteries, and the *angekok*, the sorcerer, frightened them into the most delightful fits after the lamps were put out, and you could hear the Spirit of the Reindeer stamping on the roof; and when a spear was thrust out into the open black night it came back covered with hot blood. He wanted to throw his big boots into the net with the tired air of the head of a family, and to gamble with the hunters when they dropped in of an evening and played a sort of home-made roulette with a tin pot and a nail. There were hundreds of things that he wanted to do, but the grown men laughed at him and said, 'Wait till you have been in the buckle, Kotuko. Hunting is not *all* catching.'

Now that his father had named a puppy for him, things looked brighter. An Inuit does not waste a good dog on his son till the boy knows something of dog-driving; and Kotuko was more than sure that he knew more than everything.

If the puppy had not had an iron constitution he would have died from over-stuffing and over-handling. Kotuko made him a tiny harness with a trace to it, and hauled him all over the house-floor, shouting: 'Aua! Ja aua!' (Go to the right.) Choiachoi! Ja choiachoi!' (Go to the left.) 'Ohaha!' (Stop.) The puppy did not like it at all, but being fished for in this way was pure happiness beside being put to the sleigh for the first time. He just sat down on the snow, and played with the seal-hide trace that ran from his harness to the *pitu*, the big thong in the bows of the sleigh. Then the team started, and the puppy found the heavy ten-foot sleigh running up his back, and dragging him along the snow, while Kotuko laughed till the tears ran down his face. There followed days and days of the cruel whip that hisses like the wind over ice, and his companions all bit him because he did not know his work, and the harness chafed him, and he was not allowed to sleep with Kotuko any more, but had to take the coldest place in the passage. It was a sad time for the puppy.

The boy learned, too, as fast as the dog; though a dog-sleigh is a heart-breaking thing to manage. Each beast is harnessed, the weakest nearest to the driver, by his own separate trace, which runs under his left foreleg to the main thong, where it is fastened by a sort of button and loop which can be slipped by a turn of the wrist, thus freeing one dog at a time. This is very necessary, because young dogs often get the trace between their hind legs, where it cuts to the bone. And they one and all *will* go visiting their friends as they run, jumping in and out among the traces. Then they fight, and the result is more mixed than a wet fishing-line next morning. A great deal of trouble can be avoided by scientific use of the whip. Every Inuit boy prides himself as being a master of the long lash; but it is easy to flick at a mark on the ground, and difficult to lean forward and catch a shirking dog just behind the shoulders when the sleigh is going at full speed. If you call one dog's name for 'visiting', and accidentally lash another, the two will fight it out at once, and stop all the others. Again, if you travel with a companion and begin to talk, or by yourself and sing, the dogs will halt, turn round, and sit down to hear what you have to say. Kotuko was run away from once or twice through forgetting to block the sleigh when he stopped; and he broke many lashings, and ruined a few thongs before he could be trusted with a full team of eight and the light sleigh. Then he felt himself a person of consequence, and on smooth, black ice, with a bold heart and a quick elbow, he smoked along over the levels as fast as a pack in full cry. He would go ten miles to the seal-holes, and when he was on the hunting-grounds he would twitch a trace loose from the pitu, and free the big black leader, who was the cleverest dog in the team. As soon as the dog had scented a breathing-hole, Kotuko would reverse the sleigh, driving a couple of sawed-off antlers, that stuck up like perambulator-handles from the back-rest, deep into the snow, so that the team could not get away. Then he would crawl forward inch by inch, and wait till the seal came up to breathe. Then he would stab down swiftly with his spear and running-line, and presently would haul his seal up to the lip of the ice, while the black leader came up and helped to pull the carcass across the ice to the sleigh. That was the time when the harnessed dogs yelled and foamed with excitement, and Kotuko laid the long lash like a red-hot bar across all their faces, till the carcass froze stiff. Going home was the heavy work. The loaded sleigh had to be humoured among the rough ice, and the dogs sat down and looked hungrily at the seal instead of pulling. At last they would strike the well-worn sleigh-road to the village, and toodle-kiyi along the ringing ice, heads down and tails up, while Kotuko struck up the 'An-gutivaun tai-na tau-na-ne taina' (The Song of the Return-ing Hunter), and voices hailed him from house to house under all that dim, star-littern sky.

When Kotuko the dog came to his full growth he enjoyed himself too. He fought his way up the team steadily, fight after fight, till one fine evening, over their food, he tackled the big, black leader (Kotuko the boy saw fair play), and made second dog of him, as they say. So he was promoted to the long thong of the leading dog, running five feet in advance of all the others: it was his bounden duty to stop all fighting, in harness or out of it, and he wore a collar of copper wire, very thick and heavy. On special occasions he was fed with cooked food inside the house, and sometimes was allowed to sleep on the bench with Kotuko. He was a good seal-dog, and would keep a musk-ox at bay by running round him and snapping at his heels. He would even – and this for a sleigh-dog is the last proof of bravery – he would even stand up to the gaunt Arctic wolf, whom all dogs of the North, as a rule, fear beyond anything that walks the snow. He and his master – they did not count the team of ordinary dogs as company – hunted together, day after day and night after night, fur-wrapped boy and savage, long-haired, narrow-eyed, white-fanged, yellow brute. All an Inuit has to do is to get food and skins for himself and his family. The womenfolk make the skins into clothing, and occasionally help in trapping small game; but the bulk of the food – and they eat enormously – must be found by the men. If the supply fails there is no one up there to buy or beg or borrow from. The people must die.

An Inuit does not think of these chances till he is forced to. Kadlu, Kotuko, Amoraq, and the boy-baby who kicked about in Amoraq's fur hood and chewed pieces of blubber all day, were as happy together as any family in the world. They came of a very gentle race – an Inuit seldom loses his temper, and almost never strikes a child – who did not know exactly what telling a real lie meant, still less how to steal. They were content to spear their living out of the heart of the bitter, hopeless cold; to smile oily smiles, and tell queer ghost and fairy tales of evenings, and eat till they could eat no more, and sing the endless woman's song: 'Amna aya, aya amna, ah! ah!' through the long lamp-lighted days as they mended their clothes and their hunting-gear.

But one terrible winter everything betrayed them. The Tununirmiut returned from the yearly salmon-fishing, and made their houses on the early ice to the north of Bylot's Island, ready to go after the seal as soon as the sea froze. But it was an early and savage autumn. All through September there were continuous gales that broke up the smooth seal-ice when it was only four or five feet thick, and forced it inland, and piled a great barrier, some twenty miles broad, of lumped and ragged and needly ice, over which it was impossible to draw the dog-sleighs. The edge of the floe off which the seal were used to fish in winter lay perhaps twenty miles beyond this barrier, and out of reach of the Tununirmiut. Even so, they might have managed to scrape through the winter on their stock of frozen salmon and stored blubber, and what the traps gave them, but in December one of their hunters came across a *tupik* (a skin-tent) of three women and a girl nearly dead, whose men had come down from the far North and been crushed in their little skin hunting-boats while they were out after the long-horned narwhal. Kadlu, of course, could only distribute the women among the huts of the winter village, for no Inuit dare refuse a meal to a stranger. He never knows when his own turn may come to beg. Amoraq took the girl, who was about fourteen, into her own house as a sort of servant. From the cut of her sharp-pointed hood, and the long diamond pattern of her white deerskin leggings, they supposed she came from Ellesmere Land. She had never seen tin cooking-pots or wooden-shod sleighs before; but Kotuko the boy and Kotuko the dog were rather fond of her.

Then all the foxes went south, and even the wolverine, that growling, blunt-headed little thief of the snow, did not take the trouble to follow the line of empty traps that Kotuko set. The tribe lost a couple of their best hunters, who were badly crippled in a fight with a musk-ox, and this threw more work on the others. Kotuko went out, day after day, with a light hunting-sleigh and six or seven of the strongest dogs, looking till his eyes ached for some patch of clear ice where a seal might perhaps have scratched a breathing-hole. Kotuko the dog ranged far and wide, and in the dead stillness of the ice-fields Kotuko the boy could hear his half-choked whine of excitement, above a seal-hole three miles away, as plainly as though he were at his elbow. When the dog found a hole the boy would build himself a little, low snow wall to keep off the worst of the bitter wind, and there he would wait ten, twelve, twenty hours for the seal to come up to breathe, his eyes glued to the tiny mark he had made above the hole to guide the downward thrust of his harpoon, a little sealskin mat under his feet, and his legs tied together in the *tutareang* (the buckle that the old hunters had talked about). This helps to keep a man's legs from twitching as he waits and waits and waits for the quick-eared seal to rise. Though there is no excitement in it, you can easily believe that the sitting still in the buckle with the thermometer perhaps forty degrees below zero is the hardest work an Inuit knows. When a seal was caught, Kotuko the dog would bound forward, his trace trailing behind him, and help to pull the body to the sleigh, where the tired and hungry dogs lay sullenly under the lee of the broken ice.

A seal did not go very far, for each mouth in the little village had a right to be filled, and neither bone, hide, nor sinew was wasted. The dogs' meat was taken for human use, and Amoraq fed the team with pieces of old summer skin-tents raked out from under the sleeping-bench, and they howled and howled again, and waked to howl hungrily. One could tell by the soapstone lamps in the huts that famine was near. In good seasons, when blubber was plentiful, the light in the boat-shaped lamps would be two feet high – cheerful, oily, and yellow. Now it was a bare six inches: Amoraq carefully pricked down the moss wick, when an unwatched flame brightened for a moment, and the eyes of all the family followed her hand. The horror of famine up there in the great cold is not so much dying, as dying in the dark. All the Inuit dread the dark that presses on them without a break for six months in each year; and when the lamps are low in the houses the minds of people begin to be shaken and confused.

But worse was to come.

The underfed dogs snapped and growled in the passages, glaring at the cold stars, and snuffing into the bitter wind, night after night. When they stopped howling the silence fell down again as solid and heavy as a snowdrift against a door, and men could hear the beating of their blood in the thin passages of the ear, and the thumping of their own hearts, that sounded as loud as the noise of sorcerers' drums beaten across the snow. One night Kotuko the dog, who had been unusually sullen in harness, leaped up and pushed his head against Kotuko's knee. Kotuko patted him, but the dog still pushed blindly forward, fawning. Then Kadlu waked, and gripped the heavy wolflike head, and stared into the glassy eyes. The dog whimpered and shivered between Kadlu's knees. The hair rose about his neck, and he growled as though a stranger were at the door; then he barked joyously, and rolled on the ground, and bit at Kotuko's boot like a puppy.

'What is it?' said Kotuko; for he was beginning to be afraid.

'The sickness,' Kadlu answered. 'It is the dog sickness.' Kotuko the dog lifted his nose and howled and howled again.

'I have not seen this before. What will he do?' said Kotuko.

Kadlu shrugged one shoulder a little, and crossed the hut for his short stabbing-harpoon. The big dog looked at him, howled again, and slunk away down the passage, while the other dogs drew aside right and left to give him ample room. When he was out on the snow he barked furiously, as though on the trail of a musk-ox, and, barking and leaping and frisking, passed out of sight. His trouble was not hydrophobia, but simple, plain madness. The cold and the hunger, and, above all, the dark, had turned his head; and when the terrible dog-sickness once shows itself in a team, it spreads like wildfire. Next hunting-day another dog sickened, and was killed then and there by Kotuko as he bit and struggled among the traces. Then the black second dog, who had been the leader in the old days, suddenly gave tongue on an imaginary reindeer-track, and when they slipped him from the *pitu* he flew at the throat of an ice-cliff, and ran away as his leader had done, his harness on his back. After that no one would take the dogs out again. They needed them for something else, and the dogs knew it; and though they were tied down and fed by hand, their eyes were full of despair and fear. To make things worse, the old women began to tell ghost-tales, and to say that they had met the spirits of the dead hunters lost that autumn, who prophesied all sorts of horrible things.

Kotuko grieved more for the loss of his dog than anything else; for though an Inuit eats enormously he also knows how to starve. But the hunger, the darkness, the cold, and the exposure told on his strength, and he began to hear voices inside his head, and to see people who were not there, out of the tail of his eye. One night – he had unbuckled himself after ten hours' waiting above a 'blind' seal-hole, and was staggering back to the village faint and dizzy – he halted to lean his back against a boulder which happened to be supported like a rocking-stone on a single jutting point of ice. His weight disturbed the balance of the thing, it rolled over ponderously, and as Kotuko sprang aside to avoid it, slid after him, squeaking and hissing on the ice-slope.

That was enough for Kotuko. He had been brought up to believe that every rock and boulder had its owner (its *inua*), who was generally a one-eyed kind of a Woman-Thing called a *tornaq*, and that when a tornaq meant to help a man she rolled after him inside her stone house, and asked him whether he would take her for a guardian spirit. (In summer thaws the ice-propped rocks and boulders roll and slip all over the face of the land, so you can easily see how the idea of live stones arose.) Kotuko heard the blood beating in his ears as he had heard it all day, and he thought that was the *tornaq* of the stone speaking to him. Before he reached home he was quite certain that he had held a long conversation with her, and as all his people believed that this was quite possible, no one contradicted him.

'She said to me, "I jump down, I jump down from my place on the snow," ' cried Kotuko, with hollow eyes, leaning forward in the half-lighted hut. 'She said, "I will be a guide." She said, "I will guide you to the good seal-holes." Tomorrow I go out, and the *tornaq* will guide me.'

Then the *angekok*, the village sorcerer, came in, and Kotuko told him the tale a second time. It lost nothing in the telling.

'Follow the *tornait* [the spirits of the stones], and they will bring us food again,' said the angekok.

Now, the girl from the North had been lying near the lamp, eating very little and saying less for days past; but when Amoraq and Kadlu next morning packed and lashed a little hand-sleigh for Kotuko, and loaded it with his hunting-gear and as much blubber and frozen seal-meat as they could spare, she took the pulling-rope, and stepped out boldly at the boy's side.

'Your house is my house,' she said, as the little bone-shod sleigh squeaked and bumped behind them in the awful Arctic night.

'My house is your house,' said Kotuko; 'but *I* think that we shall both go to Sedna together.'

Now, Sedna is the Mistress of the Underworld, and the Inuit believe that everyone who dies must spend a year in her horrible country before going to Quadliparmiut, the Happy Place, where it never freezes and the fat reindeer trot up when you call.

Through the village people were shouting: 'The tornait have spoken to Kotuko. They will show him open ice. He will bring us the seal again!' Their voices were soon swallowed up by the cold, empty dark, and Kotuko and the girl shouldered close together as they strained on the pulling-rope or humoured the sleigh through the ice in the direction of the Polar Sea. Kotuko insisted that the *tornaq* of the stone had told him to go north, and north they went under Tuktuqdjung the Reindeer – those stars that we call the Great Bear.

No European could have made five miles a day over the ice-rubbish and the sharp-edged drifts; but those two knew exactly the turn of the wrist that coaxes a sleigh round a hummock, the jerk that nearly lifts it out of an ice-crack, and the exact strength that goes to the few quiet strokes of the spearhead that make a path possible when everything looks hopeless.

The girl said nothing, but bowed her head, and the long wolverine-fur fringe of her ermine hood blew across her broad, dark face. The sky above them was an intense velvety black, changing to bands of Indian red on the horizon, where the great stars burned like street-lamps. From time to time a greenish wave of the Northern Lights would roll across the hollow of the high heavens, flick like a flag, and disappear; or a meteor would crackle from darkness to darkness, trailing a shower of sparks behind. Then they could see the ridged and furrowed surface of the floe tipped and laced with strange colours – red, copper, and bluish; but in the ordinary starlight everything turned to one frostbitten grey. The floe, as you will remember, had been battered and tormented by the autumn gales till it was one frozen earthquake.

There were gullies and ravines, and holes like gravel-pits, cut in ice; lumps and scattered pieces frozen down to the original floor of the floe; blotches of old black ice that had been thrust under the floe in some gale and heaved up again; roundish boulders of ice; sawlike edges of ice carved by the snow that flies before the wind; and sunken pits where thirty or forty acres lay below the level of the rest of the field. From a little distance you might have taken the lumps for seal or walrus, overturned sleighs or men on a hunting expedition, or even the great Ten-legged White Spirit-Bear himself; but in spite of these fantastic shapes, all on the very edge of starting into life, there was neither sound nor the least faint echo of sound. And through this silence and through this waste, where the sudden lights flapped and went out again, the sleigh and the two that pulled it crawled like things in a nightmare – a nightmare of the end of the world at the end of the world.

When they were tired Kotuko would make what the hunters call a 'half-house', a very small snow hut, into which they would huddle with the travelling-lamp, and try to thaw out the frozen seal-meat. When they had slept, the march began again – thirty miles a day to get ten miles northward. The girl was always very silent, but Kotuko muttered to himself and broke out into songs he had learned in the Singing-House – summer songs, and reindeer and salmon songs – all horribly out of place at that season. He would declare that he heard the *tornaq* growling to him, and would run wildly up a hummock, tossing his arms and speaking in loud, threatening tones. To tell the truth, Kotuko was very nearly crazy for the time being; but the girl was sure that he was being guided by his guardian spirit, and that everything would come right. She was not surprised, therefore, when at the end of the fourth march Kotuko, whose eyes were burning like fireballs in his head, told her that his *tornaq* was following them across the snow in the shape of a two-headed dog. The girl looked where Kotuko pointed, and something seemed to slip into a ravine. It was certainly not human, but everybody knew that the *tornait* preferred to appear in the shape of bear and seal, and such like.

It might have been the Ten-legged White Spirit-Bear himself, or it might have been anything, for Kotuko and the girl were so starved that their eyes were untrustworthy. They had trapped nothing, and seen no trace of game since they had left the village; their food would not hold out for another week, and there was a gale coming. A Polar storm can blow for ten days without a break, and all that while it is certain death to be abroad. Kotuko laid up a snow-house large enough to take in the hand-sleigh (never be separated from your meat), and while he was shaping the last irregular block of ice that makes the keystone of the roof, he saw a Thing looking at him from a little cliff of ice half a mile away. The air was hazy, and the Thing seemed to be forty feet long and ten feet high, with twenty feet of tail and a shape that quivered all along the outlines. The girl saw it too, but instead of crying aloud with terror, said quietly, 'That is Quiquern. What comes after?'

'He will speak to me,' said Kotuko; but the snow-knife trembled in his hand as he spoke, because however much a man may believe that he is a friend of strange and ugly spirits, he seldom likes to be taken quite at his word. Quiquern, too, is the phantom of a gigantic toothless dog without any hair, who is supposed to live in the far North, and to wander about the country just before things are going to happen. They may be pleasant or unpleasant things, but not even the sorcerers care to speak about Quiquern. He makes the dogs go mad. Like the Spirit-Bear, he has several extra pairs of legs – six or eight – and this Thing jumping up and down in the haze had more legs than any real dog needed. Kotuko and the girl huddled into their hut quickly. Of course if Quiquern had wanted them, he could have torn it to pieces above their heads, but the sense of a foot-thick snow-wall between themselves and the wicked dark was great comfort. The gale broke with a shriek of wind like the shriek of a train, and for three days and three nights it held, never varying one point, and never lulling even for a minute. They fed the stone lamp between their knees, and nibbled at the half-warm seal-meat, and watched the black soot gather on the roof for seventy-two long hours. The girl counted up the food in the sleigh; there was not more than two days' supply, and Kotuko looked over the iron heads and the deer-sinew fastenings of his harpoon and his seal-lance and his bird-dart. There was nothing else to do.

'We shall go to Sedna soon – very soon,' the girl whispered. 'In three days we shall lie down and go. Will your *tornaq* do nothing? Sing her an *angekok*'s song to make her come here.'

He began to sing in the high-pitched howl of the magic songs, and the gale went down slowly. In the middle of his song the girl started, laid her mittened hand and then her head to the ice floor of the hut. Kotuko followed her example, and the two kneeled, staring into each other's eyes, and listening with every nerve. He ripped a thin sliver of whalebone from the rim of a bird-snare that lay on the sleigh, and, after straightening, set it upright in a little hole in the ice, firming it down with his mitten. It was almost as delicately adjusted as a compass-needle, and now instead of listening they watched. The thin rod quivered a little – the least little jar in the world; then it vibrated steadily for a few seconds, came to rest, and vibrated again, this time nodding to another point of the compass.

'Too soon!' said Kotuko. 'Some big floe has broken far away outside.'

The girl pointed at the rod, and shook her head. 'It is the big breaking,' she said. 'Listen to the ground-ice. It knocks.'

When they kneeled this time they heard the most curious muffled grunts and knockings, apparently under their feet. Sometimes it sounded as though a blind puppy were squeaking above the lamp; then as if a stone were being ground on hard ice; and again, like muffled blows on a drum; but all dragged out and made small, as though they travelled through a little horn a weary distance away.

'We shall not go to Sedna lying down,' said Kotuko. 'It is the breaking. The *tornaq* has cheated us. We shall die.'

All this may sound absurd enough, but the two were face to face with a very real danger. The three days' gale had driven the deep water of Baffin's Bay southerly, and piled it on to the edge of the far-reaching land-ice that stretches from Bylot's Island to the west. Also, the strong current which sets east out of Lancaster Sound carried with it mile upon mile of what they call pack-ice – rough ice that has not frozen into fields; and this pack was bombarding the floe at the same time that the swell and heave of the storm-worked sea was weakening and undermining it. What Kotuko and the girl had been listening to were the faint echoes of that fight thirty or forty miles away, and the little telltale rod quivered to the shock of it.

Now, as the Inuit say, when the ice once wakes after its long winter sleep, there is no knowing what may happen, for solid floe-ice changes shape almost as quickly as a cloud. The gale was evidently a spring gale sent out of time, and anything was possible.

Yet the two were happier in their minds than before. If the floe broke up there would be no more waiting and suffering. Spirits, goblins, and witch-people were moving about on the racking ice, and they might find themselves stepping into Sedna's country side by side with all sorts of wild Things, the flush of excitement still on them. When they left the hut after the gale, the noise on the horizon was steadily growing, and the tough ice moaned and buzzed all round them.

'It is still waiting,' said Kotuko.

On the top of a hummock sat or crouched the eight-legged Thing that they had seen three days before – and it howled horribly.

'Let us follow,' said the girl. 'It may know some way that does not lead to Sedna'; but she reeled from weakness as she took the pulling-rope. The Thing moved off slowly and clumsily across the ridges, heading always toward the westward and the land, and they followed, while the growling thunder at the edge of the floe rolled nearer and nearer. The floe's lip was split and cracked in every direction for three or four miles inland, and great pans of ten-foot-thick ice, from a few yards to twenty acres square, were jolting and ducking and surging into one another, and into the yet unbroken floe, as the heavy swell took and shook and spouted between them. This battering-ram ice was, so to speak, the first army that the sea was flinging against the floe. The incessant crash and jar of these cakes almost drowned the ripping sound of sheets of pack-ice driven bodily under the floe as cards are hastily pushed under a tablecloth. Where the water was shallow these sheets would be piled one atop of the other till the bottommost touched mud fifty feet down, and the discoloured sea banked behind the muddy ice till the increasing pressure drove all forward again. In addition to the floe and the pack-ice, the gale and the currents were bringing down true bergs, sailing mountains of ice, snapped off from the Greenland side of the water or the north shore of Melville Bay. They pounded in solemnly, the waves breaking white round them, and advanced on the floe like an old-time fleet under full sail. A berg that seemed ready to carry the world before it would ground helplessly in deep water, reel over, and wallow in a lather of foam and mud and flying frozen spray, while a much smaller and lower one would rip and ride into the flat floe, flinging tons of ice on either side, and cutting a track half a mile long before it was stopped. Some fell like swords, shearing a raw-edged canal; and others splintered into a shower of blocks, weighing scores of tons apiece, that whirled and skirted among the hummocks. Others, again, rose up bodily out of the water when they shoaled, twisted as though in pain, and fell solidly on their sides, while the sea threshed over their shoulders. This trampling and crowding and bending and buckling and arching of the ice into every possible shape was going on as far as the eye could reach all along the north line of the floe. From where Kotuko and the girl were, the confusion looked no more than an uneasy, rippling, crawling movement under the horizon; but it came toward them each moment, and they could hear, far away to landward a heavy booming, as it might have been the boom of artillery through a fog. That showed that the floe was being jammed home against the iron cliffs of Bylot's Island, the land to the southward behind them.

'This has never been before,' said Kotuko, staring stupidly. 'This is not the time. How can the floe break *now*?'

'Follow *that*! the girl cried, pointing to the Thing half limping, half running distractedly before them. They followed, tugging at the hand-sleigh, while nearer and nearer came the roaring march of the ice. At last the fields round them cracked and starred in every direction, and the cracks opened and snapped like the teeth of wolves. But where the Thing rested, on a mound of old and scattered ice-blocks some fifty feet high, there was no motion. Kotuko leaped forward wildly, dragging the girl after him, and crawled to the bottom of the mound. The talking of the ice grew louder and louder round them, but the mound stayed fast, and, as the girl looked at him, he threw his right elbow upward and outward, making the Inuit sign for land in the shape of an island. And land it was that the eight-legged, limping Thing had led them to – some granite-tipped, sand-beached islet off the coast, shod and sheathed and masked with ice so that no man could have told it from the floe, but at the bottom solid earth, and not shifting ice! The smashing and rebound of the floes as they grounded and splintered marked the borders of it, and a friendly shoal ran out to the northward, and turned aside the rush of the heaviest ice, exactly as a ploughshare turns over loam. There was danger, of course, that some heavily squeezed ice-field might shoot up the beach, and plane off the top of the islet bodily; but that did not trouble Kotuko and the girl when they made their snow-house and began to eat, and heard the ice hammer and skid along the beach. The Thing had disappeared, and Kotuko was talking excitedly about his power over spirits as he crouched round the lamp. In the middle of his wild sayings the girl began to laugh, and rock herself backward and forward.

Behind her shoulder, crawling into the hut crawl by crawl, there were two heads, one yellow and one black, that belonged to two of the most sorrowful and ashamed dogs that ever you saw. Kotuko the dog was one, and the black leader was the other. Both were now fat, well-looking, and quite restored to their proper minds, but coupled to each other in an extraordinary fashion. When the black leader ran off, you remember, his harness was still on him. He must have met Kotuko the dog, and played or fought with him, for his shoulder-loop had caught in the plaited copper wire of Kotuko's collar, and had drawn tight, so that neither could get at the trace to gnaw it apart, but each was fastened sidelong to his neighbour's neck. That, with the freedom of hunting on their own account, must have helped to cure their madness. They were very sober.

The girl pushed the two shamefaced creatures towards Kotuko, and, sobbing with laughter, cried, 'That is Quiquern, who led us to safe ground. Look at his eight legs and double head!'

Kotuko cut them free, and they fell into his arms, yellow and black together, trying to explain how they had got their senses back again. Kotuko ran a hand down their ribs, which were round and well clothed. 'They have found food,' he said, with a grin. 'I do not think we shall go to Sedna so soon. My *tornaq* sent these. The sickness has left them.'

As soon as they had greeted Kotuko, these two, who had been forced to sleep and eat and hunt together for the past few weeks, flew at each other's throat, and there was a beautiful battle in the snow-house. 'Empty dogs do not fight,' Kotuko said. 'They have found the seal. Let us sleep. We shall find food.'

When they waked there was open water on the north beach of the island, and all the loosened ice had been driven landward. The first sound of the surf is one of the most delightful that the Inuit can hear, for it means that spring is on the road. Kotuko and the girl took hold of hands and smiled, for the clear, full roar of the surge among the ice reminded them of salmon and reindeer time and the smell of blossoming ground-willows. Even as they looked, the sea began to skim over between the floating cakes of ice, so intense was the cold; but on the horizon there was a vast red glare, and that was the light of the sunken sun. It was more like hearing him yawn in his sleep than seeing him rise, and the glare lasted for only a few minutes, but it marked the turn of the year. Nothing, they felt, could alter that.

Kotuko found the dogs fighting over a fresh-killed seal who was following the fish that a gale always disturbs. He was the first of some twenty or thirty seal that landed on the island in the course of the day, and till the sea froze hard there were hundreds of keen black heads rejoicing in the shallow free water and floating about with the floating ice.

It was good to eat seal-liver again; to fill the lamps recklessly with blubber, and watch the flame blaze three feet in the air; but as soon as the new sea-ice bore, Kotuko and the girl loaded the hand-sleigh, and made the two dogs pull as they had never pulled in their lives, for they feared what might have happened in their village. The weather was as pitiless as usual; but it is easier to draw a sleigh loaded with good food than to hunt starving. They left five-and-twenty seal carcasses buried in the ice of the beach, all ready for use, and hurried back to their people. The dogs showed them the way as soon as Kotuko told them what was expected, and though there was no sign of a landmark, in two days they were giving tongue outside Kadlu's house. Only three dogs answered them; the others had been eaten, and the houses were all dark. But when Kotuko shouted, 'Ojo!' (boiled meat), weak voices replied, and when he called the muster of the village name by name, very distinctly, there were no gaps in it.

An hour later the lamps blazed in Kadlu's house; snow-water was heating; the pots were beginning to simmer, and the snow was dripping from the roof, as Amoraq made ready a meal for all the village, and the boy-baby in the hood chewed at a strip of rich nutty blubber, and the hunters slowly and methodically filled themselves to the very brim with seal-meat. Kotuko and the girl told their tale. The two dogs sat between them, and whenever their names came in, they cocked an ear apiece and looked most thoroughly ashamed of themselves. A dog who has once gone mad and recovered, the Inuit say, is safe against all further attacks.

'So the *tornaq* did not forget us,' said Kotuko. 'The storm blew, the ice broke, and the seal swam in behind the fish that were frightened by the storm. Now the new seal-holes are not two days distant. Let the good hunters go tomorrow and bring back the seal I have speared – twenty-five seal buried in the ice. When we have eaten those we will all follow the seal on the floe.'

'What do *you* do?' said the sorcerer in the same sort of voice as he used to Kadlu, richest of the Tununirmiut.

Kadlu looked at the girl from the North, and said quietly, '*We* build a house.' He pointed to the northwest side of Kadlu's house, for that is the side on which the married son or daughter always lives.

The girl turned her hands palm upward, with a little despairing shake of her head. She was a foreigner, picked up starving, and could bring nothing to the housekeeping.

Amoraq jumped from the bench where she sat, and began to sweep things into the girl's lap – stone lamps, iron skin-scrapers, tin kettles, deer-skins embroidered with musk-ox teeth, and real canvas-needles such as sailors use – the finest dowry that has ever been given on the far edge of the Arctic Circle, and the girl from the North bowed her head down to the very floor.

'Also these!' said Kotuko, laughing and signing to the dogs, who thrust their cold muzzles into the girl's face.

'Ah,' said the *angekok*, with an important cough, as though he had been thinking it all over. 'As soon as Kotuko left the village I went to the Singing-House and sang magic. I sang all the long nights, and called upon the Spirit of the Reindeer. *My* singing made the gale blow that broke the ice and drew the two dogs toward Kotuko when the ice would have crushed his bones. *My* song drew the seal in behind the broken ice. My body lay still in the *quaggi*, but my spirit ran about on the ice, and guided Kotuko and the dogs in all the things they did. I did it.'

Everybody was full and sleepy, so no one contradicted; and the *angekok*, by virtue of his office, helped himself to yet another lump of boiled meat, and lay down to sleep with the others in the warm, well-lighted, oil-smelling home.

* * *

Now Kotuko, who drew very well in the Inuit fashion, scratched pictures of all these adventures on a long, flat piece of ivory with a hole at one end. When he and the girl went north to Ellesmere Land in the year of the Wonderful Open Winter, he left the picture-story with Kadlu, who lost it in the shingle when his dog-sleigh broke down one summer on the beach of Lake Netilling at Nikosiring, and there a Lake Inuit found it next spring and sold it to a man at Imigen who was interpreter on a Cumberland Sound whaler, and he sold it to Hans Olsen, who was afterward a quartermaster on board a big steamer that took tourists to the North Cape in Norway. When the tourist season was over, the steamer ran between London and Australia, stopping at Ceylon, and there Olsen sold the ivory to a Cingalese jeweller for two imitation sapphires. I found it under some rubbish in a house at Colombo, and have translated it from one end to the other.

'Angutivaun Taina'

[This is a very free translation of the Song of the Returning Hunter, as the men used to sing it after seal-spearing. The Inuit always repeat things over and over again.]

OUR GLOVES ARE STIFF with the frozen blood,
    Our furs with the drifted snow,
As we come in with the seal – the seal!
    In from the edge of the floe.

Au jana! Aua! Oha! Haq!
    And the yelping dog-teams go,
And the long whips crack, and the men come back,
    Back from the edge of the floe !

We tracked our seal to his secret place,
    We heard him scratch below,
We made our mark, and we watched beside,
    Out on the edge of the floe.

We raised our lance when he rose to breathe,
    We drove it downward – so!
And we played him thus, and we killed him thus,
    Out on the edge of the floe.

Our gloves are glued with the frozen blood,
    Our eyes with the drifting snow;
But we come back to our wives again,
    Back from the edge of the floe!

Au jana! Aua! Oha! Haq!
    And the loaded dog-teams go,
And the wives can hear their men come back,
    Back from the edge of the floe!

Red Dog

For our white and our excellent nights – for the nights of swift running.
Fair ranging, far seeing, good hunting, sure cunning!
For the smells of the dawning, untainted, ere dew has departed!
For the rush through the mist, and the quarry blind-started!
For the cry of our mates when the sambhur has wheeled
and is standing at bay,
For the risk and the riot of night!
For the sleep at the lair-mouth by day,
It is met, and we go to the fight.
Bay! O Bay!

T WAS AFTER the letting in of the Jungle that the pleasantest part of Mowgli's life began. He had the good conscience that comes from paying debts; all the Jungle was his friend, and just a little afraid of him. The things that he did and saw and heard when he was wandering from one people to another, with or without his four companions, would make many many stories, each as long as this one. So you will never be told how he met the Mad Elephant of Mandla, who killed two-and-twenty bullocks drawing eleven carts of coined silver to the Government Treasury, and scattered the shiny rupees in the dust; how he fought Jacala, the Crocodile, all one long night in the Marshes of the North, and broke his skinning-knife on the brute's back-plates; how he found a new and longer knife round the neck of a man who had been killed by a wild boar, and how he tracked that boar and killed him as a fair price for the knife; how he was caught up once in the Great Famine, by the moving of the deer, and nearly crushed to death in the swaying hot herds; how he saved Hathi the Silent from being once more trapped in a pit with a stake at the bottom, and how, next day, he himself fell into a very cunning leopard-trap, and how Hathi broke the thick wooden bars to pieces above him; how he milked the wild buffaloes in the swamp, and how –

But we must tell one tale at a time. Father and Mother Wolf died, and Mowgli rolled a big boulder against the mouth of their cave, and cried the Death Song over them; Baloo grew very old and stiff, and even Bagheera, whose nerves were steel and whose muscles were iron, was a shade slower on the kill than he had been. Akela turned from grey to milky white with pure age; his ribs stuck out, and he walked as though he had been made of wood, and Mowgli killed for him. But the young wolves, the children of the disbanded Seeonee Pack, throve and increased, and when there were about forty of them, masterless, full-voiced, clean-footed five-year-olds, Akela told them that they ought to gather themselves together and follow the Law, and run under one head, as befitted the Free People.

This was not a question in which Mowgli concerned himself, for, as he said, he had eaten sour fruit, and he knew the tree it hung from; but when Phao, son of Phaona (his father was the Grey Tracker in the days of Akela's headship), fought his way to the leadership of the Pack, according to the Jungle Law, and the old calls and songs began to ring under the stars once more, Mowgli came to the Council Rock for memory's sake. When he chose to speak, the Pack waited till he had finished, and he sat at Akela's side on the rock above Phao. Those were days of good hunting and good sleeping. No stranger cared to break into the jungles that belonged to Mowgli's people, as they called the Pack, and the young wolves grew fat and strong, and there were many cubs to bring to the Looking-over. Mowgli always attended a Looking-over, remembering the night when a black panther bought a naked brown baby into the pack, and the long call, 'Look, look well, O Wolves,' made his heart flutter. Otherwise, he would be far away in the Jungle with his four brothers, tasting, touching, seeing, and feeling new things.

One twilight when he was trotting leisurely across the ranges to give Akela the half of a buck that he had killed, while the Four jogged behind him, sparring a little, and tumbling one another over for joy of being alive, he heard a cry that had never been heard since the bad days of Shere Khan. It was what they call in the Jungle the *pheeal*, a hideous kind of shriek that the jackal gives when he is hunting behind a tiger, or when there is a big killing afoot. If you can imagine a mixture of hate, triumph, fear, and despair, with a kind of leer running through it, you will get some notion of the *pheeal* that rose and sank and wavered and quavered far away across the Waingunga. The Four stopped at once, bristling and growling. Mowgli's hand went to his knife, and he checked, the blood in his face, his eyebrows knotted.

'There is no Striped One dare kill here,' he said.

'That is not the cry of the Forerunner,' answered Grey Brother. 'It is some great killing. Listen!'

It broke out again, half sobbing and half chuckling, just as though the jackal had soft human lips. Then Mowgli drew deep breath, and ran to the Council Rock, overtaking on his way hurrying wolves of the Pack. Phao and Akela were on the Rock together, and below them, every nerve strained, sat the others. The mothers and the cubs were cantering off to their lairs; for when the *pheeal* cries it is no time for weak things to be abroad.

They could hear nothing except the Waingunga rushing and gurgling in the dark, and the light evening winds among the treetops, till suddenly across the river a wolf called. It was no wolf of the Pack, for they were all at the Rock. The note changed to a long, despairing bay; and 'Dhole!' it said, 'Dhole! dhole! dhole!' They heard tired feet on the rocks, and a gaunt wolf, streaked with red on his flanks, his right forepaw useless, and his jaws white with foam, flung himself into the circle and lay gasping at Mowgli's feet.

'Good hunting! Under whose Headship?' said Phao gravely.

'Good hunting! Won-tolla am I,' was the answer. He meant that he was a solitary wolf, fending for himself, his mate, and his cubs in some lonely lair, as do many wolves in the south. Won-tolla means an Outlier – one who lies out from any Pack. Then he panted, and they could see his heartbeats shake him backward and forward.

'What moves?' said Phao, for that is the question all the Jungle asks after the *pheeal* cries.

'The dhole, the dhole of the Dekkan – Red Dog, the Killer! They came north from the south saying the Dekkan was empty and killing out by the way. When this moon was new there were four to me – my mate and three cubs. She would teach them to kill on the grass plains, hiding to drive the buck, as we do who are of the open. At midnight I heard them together, full tongue on the trail. At the dawn-wind I found them stiff in the grass – four, Free People, four when this moon was new. Then sought I my Blood-Right and found the dhole.'

'How many?' said Mowgli quickly; the Pack growled deep in their throats.

'I do not know. Three of them will kill no more, but at the last they drove me like the buck; on my three legs they drove me. Look, Free People!'

He thrust out his mangled forefoot, all dark with dried blood. There were cruel bites low down on his side, and his throat was torn and worried.

'Eat,' said Akela, rising up from the meat Mowgli had brought him, and the Outlier flung himself on it.

'This shall be no loss,' he said humbly, when he had taken off the first edge of his hunger. 'Give me a little strength, Free People, and I also will kill. My lair is empty that was full when this moon was new, and the Blood Debt is not all paid.'

Phao heard his teeth crack on a haunch-bone and grunted approvingly.

'We shall need those jaws,' said he. 'Were there cubs with the dhole?'

'Nay, nay. Red Hunters all: grown dogs of their Pack, heavy and strong for all that they eat lizards in the Dekkan.'

What Won-tolla had said meant that the dhole, the red hunting-dog of the Dekkan, was moving to kill, and the Pack knew well that even the tiger will surrender a new kill to the dhole. They drive straight through the Jungle, and what they meet they pull down and tear to pieces. Though they are not as big nor half as cunning as the wolf, they are very strong and very numerous. The dhole, for instance, do not begin to call themselves a pack till they are a hundred strong; whereas forty wolves make a very fair pack indeed. Mowgli's wanderings had taken him to the edge of the high grassy downs of the Dekkan, and he had seen the fearless dholes sleeping and playing and scratching themselves in the little hollows and tussocks that they use for lairs. He despised and hated them because they did not smell like the Free People, because they did not live in caves, and, above all, because they had hair between their toes while he and his friends were clean-footed. But he knew, for Hathi had told him, what a terrible thing a dhole hunting-pack was. Even Hathi moves aside from their line, and until they are killed, or till game is scarce, they will go forward.

Akela knew something of the dholes, too, for he said to Mowgli quietly, 'It is better to die in a Full Pack than leaderless and alone. This is good hunting, and – my last. But, as men live, thou hast very many more nights and days, Little Brother. Go north and lie down, and if any live after the dhole has gone by he shall bring thee word of the fight.'

'Ah,' said Mowgli, quite gravely, 'must I go to the marshes and catch little fish and sleep in a tree, or must I ask help of the *Bandar-log* and crack nuts, while the Pack fight below?'

'It is to the death,' said Akela. 'Thou hast never met the dhole – the Red Killer. Even the Striped One – '

'*Aowa! Aowa!*' said Mowgli pettingly. 'I have killed one striped ape, and sure am I in my stomach that Shere Khan would have left his own mate for meat to the dhole if he had winded a pack across three ranges. Listen now: There was a wolf, my father, and there was a wolf, my mother, and there was an old grey wolf (not too wise: he is white now) was my father and my mother. Therefore I – ' he raised his voice, 'I say that when the dhole come, and if the dhole come, Mowgli and the Free People are of one skin for that hunting; and I say, by the Bull that bought me – by the Bull Bagheera paid for me in the old days which ye of the Pack do not remember – *I* say, that the Trees and the River may hear and hold fast if I forget; *I* say that this my knife shall be as a tooth to the Pack – and I do not think it is so blunt. This is my Word which has gone from me.'

'Thou dost not know the dhole, man with a wolf's tongue,' said Won-tolla. 'I look only to clear the Blood Debt against them ere they have me in many pieces. They move slowly, killing out as they go, but in two days a little strength will come back to me and I turn again for the Blood Debt. But for *ye*, Free People, my word is that ye go north and eat but little for a while till the dhole are gone. There is no meat in this hunting.'

'Hear the Outlier!' said Mowgli with a laugh. 'Free People, we must go north and dig lizards and rats from the bank, lest by any chance we meet the dhole. He must kill out our hunting-grounds, while we lie hid in the north till it please him to give us our own again. He is a dog – and the pup of a dog – red, yellow-bellied, lairless, and haired between every toe! He counts his cubs six and eight at the litter, as though he were Chikai, the little leaping rat. Surely we must run away, Free People, and beg leave of the peoples of the north for the offal of dead cattle! Ye know the saying: "North are the vermin; south are the lice. *We* are the Jungle." Choose ye, O choose. It is good hunting! For the Pack – for the Full Pack – for the lair and the litter; for the in-kill and the out-kill; for the mate that drives the doe and the little, little cub within the cave; it is met! – it is met! – it is met!'

The Pack answered with one deep, crashing bark that sounded in the night like a big tree falling. 'It is met!' they cried.

'Stay with these,' said Mowgli to the Four. 'We shall need every tooth. Phao and Akela must make ready the battle. I go to count the dogs.'

'It is death!' Won-tolla cried, half rising. 'What can such a hairless one do against the Red Dog? Even the Striped One, remember – '

'Thou art indeed an Outlier,' Mowgli called back; 'but we will speak when the dholes are dead. Good hunting all!'

He hurried off into the darkness, wild with excitement, hardly looking where he set foot, and the natural consequence was that he tripped full length over Kaa's great coils where the python lay watching a deer-path near the river.

'*Kssha!*' said Kaa angrily. 'Is this jungle-work, to stamp and tramp and undo a night's hunting – when the game are moving so well, too?'

'The fault was mine,' said Mowgli, picking himself up. 'Indeed I was seeking thee, Flathead, but each time we meet thou art longer and broader by the length of my arm. There is none like thee in the Jungle, wise, old, strong, and most beautiful Kaa.'

'Now whither does *this* trail lead?' Kaa's voice was gentler. 'Not a moon since there was a Manling with a knife threw stones at my head and called me bad little tree-cat names, because I lay asleep in the open.'

'Ay, and turned every driven deer to all the winds, and Mowgli was hunting, and this same Flathead was too deaf to hear his whistle, and leave the deer-roads free,' Mowgli answered composedly, sitting down among the painted coils.

'Now this same Manling comes with soft, tickling words to this same Flathead, telling him that he is wise and strong and beautiful, and this same old Flathead believes and makes a place, thus, for this same stone-throwing Manling, and – Art thou at ease now? Could Bagheera give thee so good a resting-place?'

Kaa had, as usual, made a sort of soft half-hammock of himself under Mowgli's weight. The boy reached out in the darkness, and gathered in the supple cable-like neck till Kaa's head rested on his shoulder, and then he told him all that had happened in the Jungle that night.

'Wise I may be,' said Kaa at the end; 'but deaf I surely am. Else I should have heard the *pheeal*. Small wonder the Eaters of Grass are uneasy. How many be the dhole?'

'I have not yet seen. I came hotfoot to thee. Thou art older than Hathi. But oh, Kaa,' – here Mowgli wriggled with sheer joy – 'it will be good hunting. Few of us will see another moon.'

'Dost *thou* strike in this? Remember thou art a Man; and remember what Pack cast thee out. Let the Wolf look to the Dog. *Thou* art a Man.'

'Last year's nuts are this year's black earth,' said Mowgli. 'It is true that I am a Man, but it is in my stomach that this night I have said that I am a Wolf. I called the River and the Trees to remember. I am of the Free People, Kaa, till the dhole has gone by.'

'Free People,' Kaa grunted. 'Free thieves! And thou hast tied thyself into the death-knot for the sake of the memory of the dead wolves? This is no good hunting.'

'It is my Word which I have spoken. The Trees know, the River knows. Till the dhole have gone by my Word comes not back to me.'

'*Ngssh!* This changes all trails. I had thought to take thee away with me to the northern marshes, but the Word – even the Word of a little, naked, hairless Manling – is the Word. Now I, Kaa, say – '

'Think well, Flathead, lest thou tie thyself into the death-knot also. I need no Word from thee, for well I know – '

'Be it so, then,' said Kaa. 'I will give no Word; but what is in thy stomach to do when the dhole come?'

'They must swim the Waingunga. I thought to meet them with my knife in the shallows, the Pack behind me; and so stabbing and thrusting, we a little might turn them downstream, or cool their throats.'

'The dhole do not turn and their throats are hot,' said Kaa. 'There will be neither Manling nor Wolf-cub when that hunting is done, but only dry bones.'

'*Alala!* If we die, we die. It will be most good hunting. But my stomach is young, and I have not seen many Rains. I am not wise nor strong. Hast thou a better plan, Kaa?'

'I have seen a hundred and a hundred Rains. Ere Hathi cast his milk-tushes my trail was big in the dust. By the First Egg, I am older than many trees, and I have seen all that the Jungle has done.'

'But *this* is new hunting,' said Mowgli. 'Never before have the dhole crossed our trail.'

'What is has been. What will be is no more than a forgotten year striking backward. Be still while I count those my years.'

For a long hour Mowgli lay back among the coils, while Kaa, his head motionless on the ground, thought of all that he had seen and known since the day he came from the egg. The light seemed to go out of his eyes and leave them like stale opals, and now and again he made little stiff passes with his head, right and left, as though he were hunting in his sleep. Mowgli dozed quietly, for he knew that there is nothing like sleep before hunting, and he was trained to take it at any hour of the day or night.

Then he felt Kaa's back grow bigger and broader below him as the huge python puffed himself out, hissing with the noise of a sword drawn from a steel scabbard.

'I have seen all the dead seasons,' Kaa said at last, 'and the great trees and the old elephants, and the rocks that were bare and sharp-pointed ere the moss grew. Art *thou* still alive, Manling?'

'It is only a little after moonset,' said Mowgli. I do not understand – '

'*Hssh!* I am again Kaa. I knew it was but a little time. Now we will go to the river, and I will show thee what is to be done against the dhole.'

He turned, straight as an arrow, for the main stream of the Waingunga, plunging in a little above the pool that hid the Peace Rock, Mowgli at his side.

'Nay, do not swim. I go swiftly. My back, Little Brother.'

Mowgli tucked his left arm round Kaa's neck, dropped his right close to his body, and straightened his feet. Then Kaa breasted the current as he alone could, and the ripple of the checked water stood up in a frill round Mowgli's neck, and his feet were waved to and fro in the eddy under the python's lashing sides. A mile or two above the Peace Rock the Waingunga narrows between a gorge of marble rocks from eighty to a hundred feet high, and the current runs like a millrace between and over all manner of ugly stones. But Mowgli did not trouble his head about the water; little water in the world could have given him a moment's fear. He was looking at the gorge on either side and sniffing uneasily, for there was a sweetish-sourish smell in the air, very like the smell of a big ant-hill on a hot day. Instinctively he lowered himself in the water, only raising his head to breathe from time to time, and Kaa came to anchor with a double twist of his tail round a sunken rock, holding Mowgli in the hollow of a coil, while the water raced on.

'This is the Place of Death,' said the boy. 'Why do we come here?'

'They sleep,' said Kaa. 'Hathi will not turn aside for the Striped One. Yet Hathi and the Striped One together turn aside for the dhole, and the dhole they say turn aside for nothing. And yet for whom do the Little People of the Rocks turn aside? Tell me, Master of the Jungle, who is the Master of the Jungle?'

'These,' Mowgli whispered. 'It is the Place of Death. Let us go.'

'Nay, look well, for they are asleep. It is as it was when I was not the length of thy arm.'

The split and weatherworn rocks of the gorge of the Waingunga had been used since the beginning of the Jungle by the Little People of the Rocks – the busy, furious, black wild bees of India; and, as Mowgli knew well, all trails turned off half a mile before they reached the gorge. For centuries the Little People had hived and swarmed from cleft to cleft, and swarmed again, staining the white marble with stale honey, and made their combs tall and deep in the dark of the inner caves, where neither man nor beast nor fire nor water had ever touched them. The length of the gorge on both sides was hung as it were with black shimmery velvet curtains, and

Mowgli sank as he looked, for those were the clotted millions of the sleeping bees. There were other lumps and festoons and things like decayed tree-trunks studded on the face of the rock, the old combs of past years, or new cities built in the shadow of the windless gorge, and huge masses of spongy, rotten trash had rolled down and stuck among the trees and creepers that clung to the rock-face. As he listened he heard more than once the rustle and slide of a honey-loaded comb turning over or failing away somewhere in the dark galleries; then a booming of angry wings, and the sullen drip, drip, drip, of the wasted honey, guttering along till it lipped over some ledge in the open air and sluggishly trickled down on the twigs. There was a tiny little beach, not five feet broad, on one side of the river, and that was piled high with the rubbish of uncounted years. There were dead bees, drones, sweepings, and stale combs, and wings of marauding moths that had strayed in after honey, all tumbled in smooth piles of the finest black dust. The mere sharp smell of it was enough to frighten anything that had no wings, and knew what the Little People were.

Kaa moved upstream again till he came to a sandy bar at the head of the gorge.

'Here is this season's kill,' said he. 'Look!' On the bank lay the skeletons of a couple of young deer and a buffalo. Mowgli could see that neither wolf nor jackal had touched the bones, which were laid out naturally.

'They came beyond the line;, they did not know the Law,' murmured Mowgli, 'and the Little People killed them. Let us go ere they wake.'

'They do not wake till the dawn,' said Kaa. 'Now I will tell thee. A hunted buck from the south, many, many Rains ago, came hither from the south, not knowing the Jungle, a Pack on his trail. Being made blind by fear, he leaped from above, the Pack running by sight, for they were hot and blind on the trail. The sun was high, and the Little People were many and very angry. Many, too, were those of the Pack who leaped into the Waingunga, but they were dead ere they took water. Those who did not leap died also in the rocks above. But the buck lived.'

'How?'

'Because he came first, running for his life, leaping ere the Little People were aware, and was in the river when they gathered to kill. The Pack, following, was altogether lost under the weight of the Little People.'

'The buck lived?' Mowgli repeated slowly.

'At least he did not die *then*, though none waited his coming down with a strong body to hold him safe against the water, as a certain old fat, deaf, yellow Flathead would wait for a Manling – yea, though there were all the dholes of the Dekkan on his trail. What is in thy stomach?' Kaa's head was close to Mowgli's ear; and it was a little time before the boy answered.

'It is to pull the very whiskers of Death, but – Kaa, thou art, indeed, the wisest of all the Jungle.'

'So many have said. Look now, if the dhole follow thee – '

'As surely they will follow. Ho! ho! I have many little thorns under my tongue to prick into their hides.'

'If they follow thee hot and blind, looking only at thy shoulders, those who do not die up above will take water either here or lower down, for the Little People will rise up and cover them. Now the Waingunga is hungry water, and they will have no Kaa to hold them, but will go down, such as live, to the shallows by the Seeonee Lairs, and there thy Pack may meet them by the throat.'

'*Ahai! Eowawa!* Better could not be till the Rains fall in the dry season. There is now only the little matter of the run and the leap. I will make me known to the dholes, so that they shall follow me very closely.'

'Hast thou seen the rocks above thee? From the landward side?'

'Indeed, no. That I had forgotten.'

'Go look. It is all rotten ground, cut and full of holes. One of thy clumsy feet set down without seeing would end the hunt. See, I leave thee here, and for thy sake only I will carry word to the Pack that they may know where to look for the dhole. For myself, I am not of one skin with *any* wolf.'

When Kaa disliked an acquaintance he could be more unpleasant than any of the Jungle People, except perhaps Bagheera. He swam downstream, and opposite the Rock he came on Phao and Akela listening to the night noises.

'Hssh! Dogs,' he said cheerfully. 'The dholes will come downstream. If ye be not afraid ye can kill them in the shallows.'

'When come they?' said Phao. 'And where is my Man-cub?' said Akela.

'They come when they come,' said Kaa. 'Wait and see. As for *thy* Man-cub, from whom thou hast taken a Word and so laid him open to Death, *thy* Man-cub is with *me*, and if he be not already dead the fault is none of thine, bleached dog! Wait here for the dhole, and be glad that the Man-cub and I strike on thy side.'

Kaa flashed upstream again, and moored himself in the middle of the gorge, looking upward at the line of the cliff. Presently he saw Mowgli's head move against the stars, and then there was a whizz in the air, the keen, clean *schloop* of a body falling feet first, and next minute the boy was at rest again in the loop of Kaa's body.

'It is no leap by night,' said Mowgli quietly. 'I have jumped twice as far for sport; but that is an evil place above – low bushes and gullies that go down very deep, all full of the Little People. I have put big stones one above the other by the side of three gullies. These I shall throw down with my feet in running, and the Little People will rise up behind me, very angry.'

'That is Man's talk and Man's cunning,' said Kaa. 'Thou art wise, but the Little People are always angry.'

'Nay, at twilight all wings near and far rest for a while. I will play with the dhole at twilight, for the dhole hunts best by day. He follows now Won-tolla's blood-trail.'

'Chil does not leave a dead ox, nor the dhole the blood-trail,' said Kaa.

'Then I will make him a new blood-trail, of his own blood, if I can, and give him dirt to eat. Thou wilt stay here, Kaa, till I come again with my dholes?'

'Ay, but what if they kill thee in the Jungle, or the Little People kill thee before thou canst leap down to the river?'

'When tomorrow comes we will kill for tomorrow,' said Mowgli, quoting a Jungle saying; and again, 'When I am dead it is time to sing the Death Song. Good hunting, Kaa!'

He loosed his arm from the python's neck and went down the gorge like a log in a freshet, paddling toward the far bank, where he found slack-water, and laughing aloud from sheer happiness. There was nothing Mowgli liked better than, as he himself said, 'to pull the whiskers of Death,' and make the Jungle know that he was their overlord. He had often, with Baloo's help, robbed bees' nests in single trees, and he knew that the Little People hated the smell of wild garlic. So he gathered a small bundle of it, tied it up with a bark string, and then followed Won-tolla's blood-trail, as it ran southerly from the Lairs, for some five miles, looking at the trees with his head on one side, and chuckling as he looked.

'Mowgli the Frog have I been,' said he to himself; 'Mowgli the Wolf have I said that I am. Now Mowgli the Ape must I be before I am Mowgli the Buck. At the end I shall be Mowgli the Man. Ho!' and he slid his thumb along the eighteen-inch blade of his knife.

Won-tolla's trail, all rank with dark blood-spots, ran under a forest of thick trees that grew close together and stretched away north-eastward, gradually growing thinner and thinner to within two miles of the Bee Rocks. From the last tree to the low scrub of the Bee Rocks was open country, where there was hardly cover enough to hide a wolf. Mowgli trotted along under the trees, judging distances between branch and branch, occasionally climbing up a trunk and taking a trial leap from one tree to another till he came to the open ground, which he studied very carefully for an hour. Then he turned, picked up Won-tolla's trail where he had left it, settled himself in a tree with an outrunning branch some eight feet from the ground, and sat still, sharpening his knife on the sole of his foot and singing to himself.

A little before midday, when the sun was very warm, he heard the patter of feet and smelt the abominable smell of the dhole-pack as they trotted pitilessly along Won-tolla's trail. Seen from above, the red dhole does not look half the size of a wolf, but Mowgli knew how strong his feet and jaws were. He watched the sharp bay head of the leader snuffing along the trail, and gave him 'Good hunting!'

The brute looked up, and his companions halted behind him, scores and scores of red dogs with low-hung tails, heavy shoulders, weak quarters, and bloody mouths. The dholes are a very silent people as a rule, and they have no manners even in their own Jungle. Fully two hundred must have gathered below him, but he could see that the leaders sniffed hungrily on Won-tolla's trail, and tried to drag the Pack forward. That would never do, or they would be at the Lairs in broad daylight, and Mowgli meant to hold them under his tree till dusk.

'By whose leave do ye come here?' said Mowgli.

'All Jungles are our Jungle,' was the reply, and the dhole that gave it bared his white teeth. Mowgli looked down with a smile, and imitated perfectly the sharp chitter-chatter of Chikai, the leaping rat of the Dekkan, meaning the dholes to understand that he considered them no better than Chikai. The Pack closed up round the tree-trunk and the leader bayed savagely, calling Mowgli a tree-ape. For an answer Mowgli stretched down one naked leg and wriggled his bare toes just above the leader's head. That was enough, and more than enough, to wake the Pack to stupid rage. Those who have hair between their toes do not care to be reminded of it. Mowgli caught his foot away as the leader leaped up, and said sweetly: 'Dog, red dog! Go back to the Dekkan and eat lizards. Go to Chikai thy brother – dog, dog – red, red dog! There is hair between every toe!' He twiddled his toes a second time.

'Come down ere we starve thee out, hairless ape!' yelled the Pack, and this was exactly what Mowgli wanted. He laid himself down along the branch, his cheek to the bark, his right arm free, and there he told the Pack what he thought and knew about them, their manners, their customs, their mates, and their puppies. There is no speech in the world so rancorous and so stinging as the language the Jungle People use to show scorn and contempt. When you come to think of it you will see how this must be so. As Mowgli told Kaa, he had many little thorns under his tongue, and slowly and deliberately he drove the dholes from silence to growls, from growls to yells, and from yells to hoarse slavery ravings. They tried to answer his taunts, but a cub might as well have tried to answer Kaa in a rage; and all the while Mowgli's right hand lay crooked at his side, ready for action, his feet locked round the branch. The big bay leader had leaped many times in the air, but Mowgli dared not risk a false blow. At last, made furious beyond his natural strength, he bounded up seven or eight feet clear of the ground. Then Mowgli's hand shot out like the head of a tree-snake, and gripped him by the scruff of his neck, and the branch shook with the jar as his weight fell back, almost wrenching Mowgli to the ground. But he never loosed his grip, and inch by inch he hauled the beast, hanging like a drowned jackal, up on the branch. With his left hand he reached for his knife and cut off the red, bushy tail, flinging the dhole back to earth again. That was all he needed. The Pack would not go forward on Won-tolla's trail now till they had killed Mowgli or Mowgli had killed them. He saw them settle down in circles with a quiver of the haunches that meant they were going to stay, and so he climbed to a higher crotch, settled his back comfortably, and went to sleep.

After three or four hours he waked and counted the Pack. They were all there, silent, husky, and dry, with eyes of steel. The sun was beginning to sink. In half an hour the Little People of the Rocks would be ending their labours, and, as you know, the dhole does not fight best in the twilight.

'I did not need such faithful watchers,' he said politely, standing up on a branch, 'but I will remember this. Ye be true dholes, but to my thinking over much of one kind. For that reason I do not give the big lizard-eater his tail again. Art thou not pleased, Red Dog?'

'I myself will tear out thy stomach!' yelled the leader, scratching at the foot of the tree.

'Nay, but consider, wise rat of the Dekkan. There will now be many litters of little tailless red dogs, yea, with raw red stumps that sting when the sand is hot. Go home, Red Dog, and cry that an ape has done this. Ye will not go? Come, then, with me, and I will make you very wise!'

He moved, *Bandar-log* fashion, into the next tree, and so on into the next and the next, the Pack following with lifted hungry heads. Now and then he would pretend to fall, and the Pack would tumble one over the other in their haste to be at the death. It was a curious sight – the boy with the knife that shone in the low sunlight as it sifted through the upper branches, and the silent Pack with their red coats all aflame, huddling and following below. When he came to the last tree he took the garlic and rubbed himself all over carefully, and the dholes yelled with scorn. 'Ape with a wolf's tongue, dost thou think to cover thy scent?' they said. 'We follow to the death.'

'Take thy tail,' said Mowgli, flinging it back along the course he had taken. The Pack instinctively rushed after it. 'And follow now – to the death.'

He had slipped down the tree-trunk, and headed like the wind in bare feet for the Bee Rocks, before the dholes saw what he would do.

They gave one deep howl, and settled down to the long, lobbing canter that can at the last run down anything that runs. Mowgli knew their pack-pace to be much slower than that of the wolves, or he would never have risked a two-mile run in full sight. They were sure that the boy was theirs at last, and he was sure that he held them to play with as he pleased. All his trouble was to keep them sufficiently hot behind him to prevent their turning off too soon. He ran cleanly, evenly, and springily; the tailless leader not five yards behind him; and the Pack tailing out over perhaps a quarter of a mile of ground, crazy and blind with the rage of slaughter. So he kept his distance by ear, reserving his last effort for the rush across the Bee Rocks.

The Little People had gone to sleep in the early twilight, for it was not the season of late blossoming flowers; but as Mowgli's first foot-falls rang hollow on the hollow ground he heard a sound as though all the earth were humming. Then he ran as he had never run in his life before, spurned aside one – two – three of the piles of stones into the dark, sweet-smelling gullies; heard a roar like the roar of the sea in a cave; saw with the tail of his eye the air grow dark behind him; saw the current of the Waingunga far below, and a flat, diamond-shaped head in the water; leaped outward with all his strength, the tailless dhole snapping at his shoulder in mid-air, and dropped feet first to the safety of the river, breathless and triumphant. There was not a sting upon him, for the smell of the garlic had checked the Little People for just the few seconds that he was among them. When he rose, Kaa's coils were steadying him and things were bounding over the edge of the cliff – great lumps, it seemed, of clustered bees falling like plummets; but before any lump touched water the bees flew upward and the body of a dhole whirled downstream. Overhead they could hear furious short yells that were drowned in a roar like breakers – the roar of the wings of the Little People of the Rocks. Some of the dholes, too, had fallen into the gullies that communicated with the underground caves, and there choked and fought and snapped among the tumbled honeycombs, and at last, borne up, even when they were dead, on the heaving waves of bees beneath them, shot out of some hole in the river-face, to roll over on the black rubbish-heaps. There were dholes who had leaped short into the trees on the cliffs, and the bees blotted out their shapes; but the greater number of them, maddened by the stings, had flung themselves into the river; and, as Kaa said, the Waingunga was hungry water.

Kaa held Mowgli fast till the boy had recovered his breath.

'We may not stay here,' he said. 'The Little People are roused indeed. Come!'

Swimming low and diving as often as he could, Mowgli went down the river, knife in hand.

'Slowly, slowly,' said Kaa. 'One tooth does not kill a hundred unless it be a cobra's, and many of the dholes took water swiftly when they saw the Little People rise.'

'The more work for my knife, then. *Phai!* How the Little People follow!' Mowgli sank again. The face of the water was blanketed with wild bees, buzzing sullenly and stinging all they found.

'Nothing was ever yet lost by silence,' said Kaa – no sting could penetrate his scales – 'and thou hast all the long night for the hunting. Hear them howl!'

Nearly half the pack had seen the trap their fellows rushed into, and turning sharp aside had flung themselves into the water where the gorge broke down in steep banks. Their cries of rage and their threats against the 'tree-ape' who had brought them to their shame mixed with the yells and growls of those who had been punished by the Little People. To remain ashore was death, and every dhole knew it. Their pack was swept along the current, down to the deep eddies of the Peace Pool, but even there the angry Little People followed and forced them to the water again. Mowgli could hear the voice of the tailless leader bidding his people hold on and kill out every wolf in Seeonee. But he did not waste his time in listening.

'One kills in the dark behind us!' snapped a dhole. 'Here is tainted water!'

Mowgli had dived forward like an otter, twitched a struggling dhole under water before he could open his mouth, and dark rings rose as the body plopped up, turning on its side. The dholes tried to turn, but the current prevented them, and the Little People darted at the heads and ears, and they could hear the challenge of the Seeonee Pack growing louder and deeper in the gathering darkness. Again Mowgli dived, and again a dhole went under, and rose dead, and again the clamour broke out at the rear of the pack; some howling that it was best to go ashore, others calling on their leader to lead them back to the Dekkan, and others bidding Mowgli show himself and he killed.

'They come to the fight with two stomachs and several voices,' said Kaa. 'The rest is with thy brethren below yonder, The Little People go back to sleep. They have chased us far. Now I, too, turn back, for I am not of one skin with any wolf. Good hunting, Little Brother, and remember the dhole bites low.'

A wolf came running along the bank on three legs, leaping up and down, laying his head sideways close to the ground, hunching his back, and breaking high into the air, as though he were playing with his cubs. It was Won-tolla, the Outlier, and he said never a word, but continued his horrible sport beside the dholes. They had been long in the water now, and were swimming wearily, their coats drenched and heavy, their bushy tails dragging like sponges, so tired and shaken that they, too, were silent, watching the pair of blazing eyes that moved abreast.

'This is no good hunting,' said one, panting.

'Good hunting!' said Mowgli, as he rose boldly at the brute's side, and sent the long knife home behind the shoulder, pushing hard to avoid his dying snap.

'Art thou there, Man-cub?' said Won-tolla across the water.

'Ask of the dead, Outlier,' Mowgli replied. 'Have none come downstream? I have filled these dogs' mouths with dirt; I have tricked them in the broad daylight, and their leader lacks his tail, but here be some few for thee still. Whither shall I drive them?'

'I will wait,' said Won-tolla. 'The night is before me.'

Nearer and nearer came the bay of the Seeonee wolves. 'For the Pack, for the Full Pack it is met!' and a bend in the river drove the dholes forward among the sands and shoals opposite the Lairs.

Then they saw their mistake. They should have landed half a mile higher up, and rushed the wolves on dry ground. Now it was too late. The bank was lined with burning eyes, and except for the horrible *pheeal* that had never stopped since sundown, there was no sound in the Jungle. It seemed as though Won-tolla were fawning on them to come ashore; and 'Turn and take hold!' said the leader of the dholes. The entire Pack flung themselves at the shore, threshing and squattering through the shoal water, till the face of the Waingunga was all white and torn, and the great ripples went from side to side, like bow-waves from a boat. Mowgli followed the rush, stabbing and slicing as the dholes, huddled together, rushed up the river-beach in one wave.

Then the long fight began, heaving and straining and splitting and scattering and narrowing and broadening along the red, wet sands, and over and between the tangled tree-roots, and through and among the bushes, and in and out of the grass clumps; for even now the dholes were two to one. But they met wolves fighting for all that made the Pack, and not only the short, high, deep-chested, white-tusked hunters of the Pack, but the anxious-eyed lahinis – the she-wolves of the lair, as the saying is – fighting for their litters, with here and there a yearling wolf, his first coat still half woolly, tugging and grappling by their sides. A wolf, you must know, flies at the throat or snaps at the flank, while a dhole, by preference, bites at the belly; so when the dholes were struggling out of the water and had to raise their heads, the odds were with the wolves. On dry land the wolves suffered; but in the water or ashore, Mowgli's knife came and went without ceasing. The Four had worried their way to his side. Grey Brother, crouched between the boy's knees, was protecting his stomach, while the others guarded his back and either side, or stood over him when the shock of a leaping, yelling dhole who had thrown himself full on the steady blade bore him down. For the rest, it was one tangled confusion – a locked and swaying mob that moved from right to left and from left to right along the bank; and also ground round and round slowly on its own centre. Here would be a heaving mound, like a water-blister in a whirlpool, which would break like a water-blister, and throw up four or five mangled dogs, each striving to get back to the centre; here would be a single wolf borne down by two or three dholes, laboriously dragging them forward, and sinking the while; here a yearling cub would he held up by the pressure round him, though he had been killed early, while his mother, crazed with dumb rage, rolled over and over, snapping, and passing on; and in the middle of the thickest press, perhaps, one wolf and one dhole, forgetting everything else, would be manoeuvring for first hold till they were whirled away by a rush of furious fighters. Once Mowgli passed Akela, a dhole on either flank, and his all but toothless jaws closed over the loins of a third; and once he saw Phao, his teeth set in the throat of a dhole, tugging the unwilling beast forward till the yearlings could finish him. But the bulk of the fight was blind flurry and smother in the dark; hit, trip, and tumble, yelp, groan, and worry-worry-worry, round him and behind him and above him. As the night wore on, the quick, giddy-go-round motion increased. The dholes were cowed and afraid to attack the stronger wolves, but did not yet dare to run away. Mowgli felt that the end was coming soon, and contented himself with striking merely to cripple. The yearlings were growing bolder; there was time now and again to breathe, and pass a word to a friend, and the mere flicker of the knife would sometimes turn a dog aside.

'The meat is very near the bone,' Grey Brother yelled. He was bleeding from a score of flesh-wounds.

'But the bone is yet to he cracked,' said Mowgli. '*Eowawa!* Thus do we do in the Jungle!' The red blade ran like a flame along the side of a dhole whose hindquarters were hidden by the weight of a clinging wolf.

'My kill!' snorted the wolf through his wrinkled nostrils. 'Leave him to me.'

'Is thy stomach still empty, Outlier?' said Mowgli. Won-tolla was fearfully punished, but his grip had paralysed the dhole, who could not turn round and reach him.

'By the Bull that bought me,' said Mowgli, with a bitter laugh, 'it is the tailless one!' And indeed it was the big bay-coloured leader.

'It is not wise to kill cubs and lahinis,' Mowgli went on philosophically, wiping the blood out of his eyes, 'unless one has also killed the Outlier; and it is in my stomach that this Won-tolla kills thee.'

A dhole leaped to his leader's aid; but before his teeth had found Won-tolla's flank, Mowgli's knife was in his throat, and Grey Brother took what was left.

'And thus do we do in the Jungle,' said Mowgli.

Won-tolla said not a word, only his jaws were closing and closing on the backbone as his life ebbed. The dhole shuddered, his head dropped, and he lay still, and Won-tolla dropped above him.

'*Huh!* The Blood Debt is paid,' said Mowgli. 'Sing the song, Won-tolla.'

'He hunts no more,' said Grey Brother; 'and Akela, too, is silent this long time.'

'The bone is cracked!' thundered Phao, son of Phaona. 'They go! Kill, kill out, O hunters of the Free People!'

Dhole after dhole was slinking away from those dark and bloody sands to the river, to the thick Jungle, upstream or downstream as he saw the road clear.

'The debt! The debt!' shouted Mowgli. 'Pay the debt! They have slain the Lone Wolf! Let not a dog go!'

He was flying to the river, knife in hand, to check any dhole who dared to take water, when, from under a mound of nine dead, rose Akela's head and forequarters, and Mowgli dropped on his knees beside the Lone Wolf.

'Said I not it would be my last fight?' Akela gasped. 'It is good hunting. And thou, Little Brother?'

'I live, having killed many.'

'Even so. I die, and I would – I would die by thee, Little Brother.'

Mowgli took the terrible scarred head on his knees, and put his arms round the torn neck.

'It is long since the old days of Shere Khan, and a Man-cub that rolled naked in the dust.'

'Nay, nay, I am a wolf. I am of one skin with the Free People,' Mowgli cried. 'It is no will of mine that I am a man.'

'Thou art a man, Little Brother, wolfling of my watching. Thou art a man, or else the Pack had fled before the dhole. My life I owe to thee, and today thou hast saved the Pack even as once I saved thee. Hast thou forgotten? All debts are paid now. Go to thine own people. I tell thee again, eye of my eye, this hunting is ended. Go to thine own people.'

'I will never go. I will hunt alone in the Jungle. I have said it.'

'After the summer come the Rains, and after the Rains comes the spring. Go back before thou art driven.'

'Who will drive me?'

'Mowgli will drive Mowgli. Go back to thy people. Go to Man.'

'When Mowgli drives Mowgli I will go,' Mowgli answered.

'There is no more to say,' said Akela. 'Little Brother, canst thou raise me to my feet? I also was a leader of the Free People.'

Very carefully and gently Mowgli lifted the bodies aside, and raised Akela to his feet, both arms round him, and the Lone Wolf drew a long breath, and began the Death Song that a leader of the Pack should sing when he dies. It gathered strength as he went on, lifting and lifting, and ringing far across the river, till it came to the last 'Good hunting!' and Akela shook himself clear of Mowgli for an instant, and, leaping into the air, fell backward dead upon his last and most terrible kill.

Mowgli sat with his head on his knees, careless of anything else, while the remnant of the flying dholes were being overtaken and run down by the merciless lahinis. Little by little the cries died away, and the wolves returned limping, as their wounds stiffened, to take stock of the losses. Fifteen of the Pack, as well as half a dozen lahinis, lay dead by the river, and of the others not one was unmarked. And Mowgli sat through it all till the cold daybreak, when Phao's wet, red muzzle was dropped in his hand, and Mowgli drew back to show the gaunt body of Akela.

'Good hunting!' said Phao, as though Akela were still alive, and then over his bitten shoulder to the others: 'Howl, dogs! A Wolf has died tonight!'

But of all the Pack of two hundred fighting dholes, whose boast was that all jungles were their Jungle, and that no living thing could stand before them, not one returned to the Dekkan to carry that word.

Chil's Song

[This is the song that Chil sang as the kites dropped down one after another to the river-bed, when the great fight was finished. Chil is good friends with everybody, but he is a cold-blooded kind of creature at heart, because he knows that almost everybody in the Jungle comes to him in the long-run.]

THESE WERE MY COMPANIONS going forth by night –
(*For Chil! Look you, for Chil!*)
Now come I to whistle them the ending of the fight.
(*Chil! Vanguards of Chil!*)
Word they gave me overhead of quarry newly slain,
Word I gave them underfoot of buck upon the plain.
Here's an end of every trail – they shall not speak again!

They that called the hunting-cry – they that followed fast –
(*For Chil! Look you, for Chil!*)
They that bade the sambhur wheel, or pinned him as he passed –
(*Chil! Vanguards of Chil!*)
They that lagged behind the scent – they that ran before,
They that shunned the level horn – they that overbore.
Here's an end of every trail – they shall not follow more.

These were my companions. Pity 'twas they died!
(*For Chil! Look you, for Chil!*)
Now come I to comfort them that knew them in their pride.
(*Chil! Vanguards of Chil!*)
Tattered flank and sunken eye, open mouth and red,
Locked and lank and lone they lie, the dead upon their dead.
Here's an end of every trail – and here my hosts are fed.

The Spring Running

Man goes to Man! Cry the challenge through the Jungle!
    He that was our Brother goes away.
Hear, now, and judge, O ye People of the Jungle –
    Answer, who shall turn him – who shall stay?

Man goes to Man! He is weeping in the Jungle:
    He that was our Brother sorrows sore!
Man goes to Man! (Oh, we loved him in the Jungle!)
    To the Man-Trail where we may not follow more.

THE SECOND YEAR after the great fight with Red Dog and the death of Akela, Mowgli must have been nearly seventeen years old. He looked older, for hard exercise, the best of good eating, and baths whenever he felt in the least hot or dusty, had given him strength and growth far beyond his age. He could swing by one hand from a top branch for half an hour at a time, when he had occasion to look along the tree-roads. He could stop a young buck in mid-gallop and throw him sideways by the head. He could even jerk over the big, blue wild boars that lived in the Marshes of the North. The Jungle People who used to fear him for his wits feared him now for his strength, and when he moved quietly on his own affairs the mere whisper of his coming cleared the wood-paths. And yet the look in his eyes was always gentle. Even when he fought, his eyes never blazed as Bagheera's did. They only grew more and more interested and excited; and that was one of the things that Bagheera himself did not understand.

He asked Mowgli about it, and the boy laughed and said. 'When I miss the kill I am angry. When I must go empty for two days I am very angry. Do not my eyes talk then?'

'The mouth is hungry,' said Bagheera, 'but the eyes say nothing. Hunting, eating, or swimming, it is all one – like a stone in wet or dry weather.' Mowgli looked at him lazily from under his long eyelashes, and, as usual, the panther's head dropped. Bagheera knew his master.

They were lying out far up the side of a hill overlooking the Waingunga, and the morning mists hung below them in bands of white and green. As the sun rose it changed into bubbling seas of red gold, churned off, and let the low rays stripe the dried grass on which Mowgli and Bagheera were resting. It was the end of the cold weather, the leaves and the trees looked worn and faded, and there was a dry, ticking rustle everywhere when the wind blew. A little leaf tap-tap-tapped furiously against a twig, as a single leaf caught in a current will. It roused Bagheera, for he snuffed the morning air with a deep, hollow cough, threw himself on his back, and struck with his forepaws at the nodding leaf above.

'The year turns,' he said. 'The Jungle goes forward. The Time of New Talk is near. That leaf knows. It is very good.'

'The grass is dry,' Mowgli answered, pulling up a tuft. 'Even Eye-of-the-Spring [that is a little trumpet-shaped, waxy red flower that runs in and out among the grasses] – even Eye-of-the Spring is shut, and . . . Bagheera, *is* it well for the Black Panther so to lie on his back and beat with his paws in the air, as though he were the tree-cat?'

'Aowh?' said Bagheera. He seemed to be thinking of other things.

'I say, *is* it well for the Black Panther so to mouth and cough, and howl and roll? Remember, we be the Masters of the Jungle, thou and I.'

'Indeed, yes; I hear, Man-cub.' Bagheera rolled over hurriedly and sat up, the dust on his ragged black flanks. (He was just casting his winter coat.) 'We be surely the Masters of the Jungle! Who is so strong as Mowgli? Who so wise?' There was a curious drawl in the voice that made Mowgli turn to see whether by any chance the Black Panther was making fun of him, for the Jungle is full of words that sound like one thing, but mean another. 'I said we be beyond question the Masters of the Jungle,' Bagheera repeated. 'Have I done wrong? I did not know that the Man-cub no longer lay upon the ground. Does he fly, then?'

Mowgli sat with his elbows on his knees, looking out across the valley at the daylight. Somewhere down in the woods below a bird was trying over in a husky, reedy voice the first few notes of his spring song. It was no more than a shadow of the liquid, tumbling call he would be pouring later, but Bagheera heard it.

'I said the Time of New Talk is near,' growled the panther, switching his tail.

'I hear,' Mowgli answered. 'Bagheera, why dost thou shake all over? The sun is warm.'

'That is Ferao, the scarlet woodpecker,' said Bagheera. '*He* has not forgotten. Now I, too, must remember my song,' and he began purring and crooning to himself, harking back dissatisfied again and again.

'There is no game afoot,' said Mowgli.

'Little Brother, are *both* thine ears stopped? That is no killing-word, but my song that I make ready against the need.'

'I had forgotten. I shall know when the Time of New Talk is here, because then thou and the others all run away and leave me alone.' Mowgli spoke rather savagely.

'But, indeed, Little Brother,' Bagheera began, 'we do not always – '

'I say ye do,' said Mowgli, shooting out his forefinger angrily. 'Ye *do* run away, and I, who am the Master of the Jungle, must needs walk alone. How was it last season, when I would gather sugar-cane from the fields of a Man-Pack? I sent a runner – I sent thee! – to Hathi, bidding him to come upon such a night and pluck the sweet grass for me with his trunk.'

'He came only two nights later,' said Bagheera, cowering a little; 'and of that long, sweet grass that pleased thee so he gathered more than any Man-cub could eat in all the nights of the Rains. That was no fault of mine.'

'He did not come upon the night when I sent him the word. No, he was trumpeting and running and roaring through the valleys in the moonlight. His trail was like the trail of three elephants, for he would not hide among the trees. He danced in the moonlight before the houses of the Man-Pack. I saw him, and yet he would not come to me; and *I* am the Master of the Jungle!'

'It was the Time of New Talk,' said the panther, always very humble. 'Perhaps, Little Brother, thou didst not that time call him by a Master-word? Listen to Ferao, and be glad!'

Mowgli's bad temper seemed to have boiled itself away. He lay back with his head on his arms, his eyes shut. 'I do not know – nor do I care,' he said sleepily. 'Let us sleep, Bagheera. My stomach is heavy in me. Make me a rest for my head.'

The panther lay down again with a sigh, because he could hear Ferao practising and repractising his song against the Springtime of New Talk, as they say.

In an Indian Jungle the seasons slide one into the other almost without division. There seem to be only two – the wet and the dry; but if you look closely below the torrents of rain and the clouds of char and dust you will find all four going round in their regular ring. Spring is the most wonderful, because she has not to cover a clean, bare field with new leaves and flowers, but to drive before her and to put away the hanging-on, over-surviving raffle of half-green things which the gentle winter has suffered to live, and to make the partly-dressed stale earth feel new and young once more. And this she does so well that there is no spring in the world like the Jungle spring.

There is one day when all things are tired, and the very smells, as they drift on the heavy air, are old and used. One cannot explain this, but it feels so. Then there is another day – to the eye nothing whatever has changed – when all the smells are new and delightful, and the whiskers of the Jungle People quiver to their roots, and the winter hair comes away from their sides in long, draggled locks. Then, perhaps, a little rain falls, and all the trees and the bushes and the bamboos and the mosses and the juicy-leaved plants wake with a noise of growing that you can almost hear, and under this noise runs, day and night, a deep hum. *That* is the noise of the spring – a vibrating boom which is neither bees, nor falling water, nor the wind in treetops, but the purring of the warm, happy world.

Up to this year Mowgli had always delighted in the turn of the seasons. It was he who generally saw the first Eye-of-the-Spring deep down among the grasses, and the first bank of spring clouds, which are like nothing else in the Jungle. His voice could be heard in all sorts of wet, star-lighted, blossoming places, helping the big frogs through their choruses, or mocking the little upside-down owls that hoot through the white nights. Like all his people, spring was the season he chose for his flittings – moving, for the mere joy of rushing through the warm air, thirty, forty, or fifty miles between twilight and the morning star, and coming back panting and laughing and wreathed with strange flowers. The Four did not follow him on these wild ringings of the Jungle, but went off to sing songs with other wolves. The Jungle People are very busy in the spring, and Mowgli could hear them grunting and screaming and whistling according to their kind. Their voices then are different from their voices at other times of the year, and that is one of the reasons why spring in the Jungle is called the Time of New Talk.

But that spring, as he told Bagheera, his stomach was changed in him. Ever since the bamboo shoots turned spotty-brown he had been looking forward to the morning when the smells should change. But when the morning came, and Mor the Peacock, blazing in bronze and blue and gold, cried it aloud all along the misty woods, and Mowgli opened his mouth to send on the cry, the words choked between his teeth, and a feeling came over him that began at his toes and ended in his hair – a feeling of pure unhappiness, so that he looked himself over to be sure that he had not trod on a thorn. Mor cried the new smells, the other birds took it over, and from the rocks by the Waingunga he heard Bagheera's hoarse scream – something between the scream of an eagle and the neighing of a horse. There was a yelling and scattering of *Bandar-log* in the new-budding branches above, and there stood Mowgli, his chest, filled to answer Mor, sinking in little gasps as the breath was driven out of it by this unhappiness.

He stared all round him, but he could see no more than the mocking *Bandar-log* scudding through the trees, and Mor, his tail spread in full splendour, dancing on the slopes below.

'The smells have changed,' screamed Mor. 'Good hunting, Little Brother! Where is thy answer?'

'Little Brother, good hunting!' whistled Chil the Kite and his mate, swooping down together. The two baffed under Mowgli's nose so close that a pinch of downy white feathers brushed away.

A light spring rain – elephant-rain they call it – drove across the Jungle in a belt half a mile wide, left the new leaves wet and nodding behind, and died out in a double rainbow and a light roll of thunder. The spring hum broke out for a minute, and was silent, but all the Jungle Folk seemed to be giving tongue at once. All except Mowgli.

'I have eaten good food,' he said to himself. 'I have drunk good water. Nor does my throat burn and grow small, as it did when I bit the blue-spotted root that Oo the Turtle said was clean food. But my stomach is heavy, and I have given very bad talk to Bagheera and others, people of the Jungle and my people. Now, too, I am hot and now I am cold, and now I am neither hot nor cold, but angry with that which I cannot see. Huhu! It is time to make a running! Tonight I will cross the ranges; yes, I will make a spring running to the Marshes of the North, and back again. I have hunted too easily too long. The Four shall come with me, for they grow as fat as white grubs.'

He called, but never one of the Four answered. They were far beyond earshot, singing over the spring songs – the Moon and Sambhur Songs – with the wolves of the pack; for in the springtime the Jungle People make very little difference between the day and the night. He gave the sharp, barking note, but his only answer was the mocking maiou of the little spotted tree-cat winding in and out among the branches for early birds' nests. At this he shook all over with rage, and half drew his knife. Then he became very haughty, though there was no one to see him, and stalked severely down the hillside, chin up and eyebrows down. But never a single one of his people asked him a question, for they were all too busy with their own affairs.

'Yes,' said Mowgli to himself, though in his heart he knew that he had no reason. 'Let the Red Dhole come from the Dekkan, or the Red Flower dance among the bamboos, and all the Jungle runs whining to Mowgli, calling him great elephant-names. But now, because Eye-of-the-Spring is red, and Mor, forsooth, must show his naked legs in some spring dance, the Jungle goes mad as Tabaqui . . . By the Bull that bought me! am I the Master of the Jungle, or am I not? Be silent! What do ye here?'

A couple of young wolves of the Pack were cantering down a path, looking for open ground in which to fight. (You will remember that the Law of the Jungle forbids fighting where the Pack can see.) Their neck-bristles were as stiff as wire, and they bayed furiously, crouching for the first grapple. Mowgli leaped forward, caught one outstretched throat in either hand, expecting to fling the creatures backward as he had often done in games or Pack hunts. But he had never before interfered with a spring fight. The two leaped forward and dashed him aside, and without word to waste rolled over and over close locked.

Mowgli was on his feet almost before he fell, his knife and his white teeth were bared, and at that minute he would have killed both for no reason but that they were fighting when he wished them to be quiet, although every wolf has full right under the Law to fight. He danced round them with lowered shoulders and quivering hand, ready to send in a double blow when the first flurry of the scuffle should be over; but while he waited the strength seemed to ebb from his body, the knife-point lowered, and he sheathed the knife and watched.

'I have surely eaten poison,' he sighed at last. 'Since I broke up the Council with the Red Flower – since I killed Shere Khan – none of the Pack could fling me aside. And these be only tail-wolves in the Pack, little hunters! My strength is gone from me, and presently I shall die. Oh, Mowgli, why dost thou not kill them both?'

The fight went on till one wolf ran away, and Mowgli was left alone on the torn and bloody ground, looking now at his knife, and now at his legs and arms, while the feeling of unhappiness he had never known before covered him as water covers a log.

He killed early that evening and ate but little, so as to be in good fettle for his spring running, and he ate alone because all the Jungle People were away singing or fighting. It was a perfect white night, as they call it. All green things seemed to have made a month's growth since the morning. The branch that was yellow-leaved the day before dripped sap when Mowgli broke it. The mosses curled deep and warm over his feet, the young grass had no cutting edges, and all the voices of the Jungle boomed like one deep harp-string touched by the moon – the Moon of New Talk, who splashed her light full on rock and pool, slipped it between trunk and creeper, and sifted it through a million leaves. Forgetting his unhappiness, Mowgli sang aloud with pure delight as he settled into his stride. It was more like flying than anything else, for he had chosen the long downward slope that leads to the Northern Marshes through the heart of the main Jungle, where the springy ground deadened the fall of his feet. A man-taught man would have picked his way with many stumbles through the cheating moonlight, but Mowgli's muscles, trained by years of experience, bore him up as though he were a feather. When a rotten log or a hidden stone turned under his foot he saved himself, never checking his pace, without effort and without thought. When he tired of ground-going he threw up his hands monkey-fashion to the nearest creeper, and seemed to float rather than to climb up into the thin branches, whence he would follow a tree-road till his mood changed, and he shot downward in a long, leafy curve to the levels again. There were still, hot hollows surrounded by wet rocks where he could hardly breathe for the heavy scents of the night flowers and the bloom along the creeper buds; dark avenues where the moonlight lay in belts as regular as checkered marbles in a church aisle; thickets where the wet young growth stood breast-high about him and threw its arms round his waist; and hilltops crowned with broken rock, where he leaped from stone to stone above the lairs of the frightened little foxes. He would hear, very faint and far off, the *chug-drug* of a boar sharpening his tusks on a bole; and would come across the great grey brute all alone, scribing and rending the bark of a tall tree, his mouth dripping with foam, and his eyes blazing like fire. Or he would turn aside to the sound of clashing horns and hissing grunts, and dash past a couple of furious sambhur, staggering to and fro with lowered heads, striped with blood that showed black in the moonlight. Or at some rushing ford he would hear Jacala the Crocodile bellowing like a bull, or disturb a twined knot of the Poison People, but before they could strike he would be away and across the glistening shingle, and deep in the Jungle again.

So he ran, sometimes shouting, sometimes singing to himself, the happiest thing in all the Jungle that night, till the smell of the flowers warned him that he was near the marshes, and those lay far beyond his farthest hunting-grounds.

Here, again, a man-trained man would have sunk overhead in three strides, but Mowgli's feet had eyes in them, and they passed him from tussock to tussock and clump to quaking clump without asking help from the eyes in his head. He ran out to the middle of the swamp, disturbing the duck as he ran, and sat down on a moss-coated tree-trunk lapped in the black water. The marsh was awake all round him, for in the spring the Bird People sleep very lightly, and companies of them were coming or going the night through. But no one took any notice of Mowgli sitting among the tall reeds humming songs without words, and looking at the soles of his hard brown feet in case of neglected thorns. All his unhappiness seemed to have been left behind in his own Jungle, and he was just beginning a full-throat song when it came back again – ten times worse than before.

This time Mowgli was frightened. 'It is here also!' he said half aloud. 'It has followed me,' and he looked over his shoulder to see whether the It were not standing behind him. 'There is no one here.' The night noises of the marsh went on, but never a bird or beast spoke to him, and the new feeling of misery grew.

'I have surely eaten poison,' he said in an awestricken voice. 'It must be that carelessly I have eaten poison, and my strength is going from me. I was afraid – and yet it was not *I* that was afraid – Mowgli was afraid when the two wolves fought. Akela, or even Phao, would have silenced them; yet Mowgli was afraid. That is true sign I have eaten poison . . . But what do they care in the Jungle? They sing and howl and fight, and run in companies under the moon, and I – *Hai-mai!* – I am dying in the marshes, of that poison which I have eaten.' He was so sorry for himself that he nearly wept. 'And after,' he went on, 'they will find me lying in the black water. Nay, I will go back to my own Jungle, and I will die upon the Council Rock, and Bagheera, whom I love, if he is not screaming in the valley – Bagheera, perhaps, may watch by what is left for a little, lest Chil use me as he used Akela.'

A large, warm tear splashed down on his knee, and, miserable as he was, Mowgli felt happy that he was so miserable, if you can understand that upside-down sort of happiness. 'As Chil the Kite used Akela,' he repeated, 'on the night I saved the Pack from Red Dog.' He was quiet for a little, thinking of the last words of the Lone Wolf, which you, of course, remember. 'Now Akela said to me many foolish things before he died, for when we die our stomachs change. He said . . . None the less, I *am* of the Jungle!'

In his excitement, as he remembered the fight on Waingunga bank, he shouted the last words aloud, and a wild buffalo-cow among the reeds sprang to her knees, snorting, 'Man!'

'Uhh!' said Mysa the Wild Buffalo (Mowgli could hear him turn in his wallow), '*that* is no man. It is only the hairless wolf of the Seeonee Pack. On such nights runs he to and fro.'

'Uhh!' said the cow, dropping her head again to graze, 'I thought it was Man.'

'I say no. Oh, Mowgli, is it danger?' lowed Mysa.

'Oh, Mowgli, is it danger?' the boy called back mockingly. 'That is all Mysa thinks for: Is it danger? But for Mowgli, who goes to and fro in the Jungle by night, watching, what do ye care?'

'How loud he cries!' said the cow.

'Thus do they cry,' Mysa answered contemptuously, 'who, having torn up the grass, know not how to eat it.'

'For less than this,' Mowgli groaned to himself, 'for less than this even last Rains I had pricked Mysa out of his wallow, and ridden him through the swamp on a rush halter.' He stretched a hand to break one of the feathery reeds, but drew it back with a sigh. Mysa went on steadily chewing the cud, and the long grass ripped where the cow grazed. 'I will not die *here*,' he said angrily. 'Mysa, who is of one blood with Jacala and the pig, would see me. Let us go beyond the swamp and see what comes. Never have I run such a spring running – hot and cold together. Up, Mowgli!'

He could not resist the temptation of stealing across the reeds to Mysa and pricking him with the point of his knife. The great dripping bull broke out of his wallow like a shell exploding, while Mowgli laughed till he sat down.

'Say now that the hairless wolf of the Seeonee Pack once herded thee, Mysa,' he called.

'Wolf! *Thou*?' the bull snorted, stamping in the mud. 'All the jungle knows thou wast a herder of tame cattle – such a man's brat as shouts in the dust by the crops yonder. *Thou* of the Jungle! What hunter would have crawled like a snake among the leeches, and for a muddy jest – a jackal's jest – have shamed me before my cow? Come to firm ground, and I will – I will . . . ' Mysa frothed at the mouth, for Mysa has nearly the worst temper of anyone in the Jungle.

Mowgli watched him puff and blow with eyes that never changed. When he could make himself heard through the pattering mud, he said: 'What Man-Pack lair here by the marshes, Mysa? This is new Jungle to me.'

'Go north, then,' roared the angry bull, for Mowgli had pricked him rather sharply. 'It was a naked cowherd's jest. Go and tell them at the village at the foot of the marsh.'

'The Man-Pack do not love jungle-tales, nor do I think, Mysa, that a scratch more or less on thy hide is any matter for a council. But I will go and look at this village. Yes, I will go. Softly now. It is not every night that the Master of the Jungle comes to herd thee.'

He stepped out to the shivering ground on the edge of the marsh, well knowing that Mysa would never charge over it and laughed, as he ran, to think of the bull's anger.

'My strength is not altogether gone,' he said. It may be that the poison is not to the bone. There is a star sitting low yonder.' He looked at it between his half-shut hands. 'By the Bull that bought me, it is the Red Flower – the Red Flower that I lay beside before – before I came even to the first Seeonee Pack! Now that I have seen, I will finish the running.'

The marsh ended in a broad plain where a light twinkled. It was a long time since Mowgli had concerned himself with the doings of men, but this night the glimmer of the Red Flower drew him forward.

'I will look,' said he, 'as I did in the old days, and I will see how far the Man-Pack has changed.'

Forgetting that he was no longer in his own Jungle, where he could do what he pleased, he trod carelessly through the dew-loaded grasses till he came to the hut where the light stood. Three or four yelping dogs gave tongue, for he was on the outskirts of a village.

'Ho!' said Mowgli, sitting down noiselessly, after sending back a deep wolf-growl that silenced the curs. 'What comes will come. Mowgli, what hast thou to do any more with the lairs of the Man-Pack?' He rubbed his mouth, remembering where a stone had struck it years ago when the other Man-Pack had cast him out.

The door of the hut opened, and a woman stood peering out into the darkness. A child cried, and the woman said over her shoulder, 'Sleep. It was but a jackal that waked the dogs. In a little time morning comes.'

Mowgli in the grass began to shake as though he had fever. He knew that voice well, but to make sure he cried softly, surprised to find how man's talk came back, 'Messua! O Messua!'

'Who calls?' said the woman, a quiver in her voice.

'Hast thou forgotten?' said Mowgli. His throat was dry as he spoke.

'If it be *thou*, what name did I give thee? Say!' She had half shut the door, and her hand was clutching at her breast.

'Nathoo! Ohe, Nathoo!' said Mowgli, for, as you remember, that was the name Messua gave him when he first came to the Man-Pack.

'Come, my son,' she called, and Mowgli stepped into the light, and looked full at Messua, the woman who had been good to him, and whose life he had saved from the Man-Pack so long before. She was older, and her hair was grey, but her eyes and her voice had not changed. Woman-like, she expected to find Mowgli where she had left him, and her eyes travelled upward in a puzzled way from his chest to his head, that touched the top of the door.

'My son,' she stammered; and then, sinking to his feet: 'But it is no longer my son. It is a Godling of the Woods! Ahai!'

As he stood in the red light of the oil-lamp, strong, tall, and beautiful, his long black hair sweeping over his shoulders, the knife swinging at his neck, and his head crowned with a wreath of white jasmine, he might easily have been mistaken for some wild god of a jungle legend. The child half asleep on a cot sprang up and shrieked aloud with terror. Messua turned to soothe him, while Mowgli stood still, looking in at the water-jars and the cooking-pots, the grain-bin, and all the other human belongings that he found himself remembering so well.

'What wilt thou eat or drink?' Messua murmured. 'This is all thine. We owe our lives to thee. But art thou him I called Nathoo, or a Godling, indeed?'

'I am Nathoo,' said Mowgli, 'I am very far from my own place. I saw this light, and came hither. I did not know thou wast here.'

'After we came to Khanhiwara,' Messua said timidly, 'the English would have helped us against those villagers that sought to burn us. Rememberest thou?'

'Indeed, I have not forgotten.'

'But when the English Law was made ready, we went to the village of those evil people, and it was no more to be found.'

'That also I remember,' said Mowgli, with a quiver of his nostril.

'My man, therefore, took service in the fields, and at last – for, indeed, he was a strong man – we held a little land here. It is not so rich as the old village, but we do not need much – we two.'

'Where is he, the man that dug in the dirt when he was afraid on that night?'

'He is dead – a year.'

'And he?' Mowgli pointed to the child.

'My son that was born two Rains ago. If thou art a Godling, give him the Favour of the Jungle, that he may be safe among thy – thy people, as we were safe on that night.'

She lifted up the child, who, forgetting his fright, reached out to play with the knife that hung on Mowgli's chest, and Mowgli put the little fingers aside very carefully.

'And if thou art Nathoo whom the tiger carried away,' Messua went on, choking, 'he is then thy younger brother. Give him an elder brother's blessing.'

'Hai-mai! What do I know of the thing called a blessing? I am neither a Godling nor his brother, and – O mother, mother, my heart is heavy in me.' He shivered as he set down the child.

'Like enough,' said Messua, bustling among the cooking-pots. 'This comes of running about the marshes by night. Beyond question, the fever had soaked thee to the marrow.' Mowgli smiled a little at the idea of anything in the Jungle hurting him. 'I will make a fire, and thou shalt drink warm milk. Put away the jasmine wreath: the smell is heavy in so small a place.'

Mowgli sat down, muttering, with his face in his hands. All manner of strange feelings that he had never felt before were running over him, exactly as though he had been poisoned, and he felt dizzy and a little sick. He drank the warm milk in long gulps, Messua patting him on the shoulder from time to time, not quite sure whether he were her son Nathoo of the long ago days, or some wonderful Jungle being, but glad to feel that he was at least flesh and blood.

'Son,' she said at last – her eyes were full of pride – 'have any told thee that thou art beautiful beyond all men?'

'Hah?' said Mowgli, for naturally he had never heard anything of the kind. Messua laughed softly and happily. The look in his face was enough for her.

'I am the first, then? It is right, though it comes seldom, that a mother should tell her son these good things. Thou art very beautiful. Never have I looked upon such a man.'

Mowgli twisted his head and tried to see over his own hard shoulder, and Messua laughed again so long that Mowgli, not knowing why, was forced to laugh with her, and the child ran from one to the other, laughing too.

'Nay, thou must not mock thy brother,' said Messua, catching him to her breast. 'When thou art one-half as fair we will marry thee to the youngest daughter of a king, and thou shalt ride great elephants.'

Mowgli could not understand one word in three of the talk here; the warm milk was taking effect on him after his long run, so he curled up and in a minute was deep asleep, and Messua put the hair back from his eyes, threw a cloth over him, and was happy. Jungle-fashion, he slept out the rest of that night and all the next day; for his instincts, which never wholly slept, warned him there was nothing to fear. He waked at last with a bound that shook the hut, for the cloth over his face made him dream of traps; and there he stood, his hand on his knife, the sleep all heavy in his rolling eyes, ready for any fight.

Messua laughed, and set the evening meal before him. There were only a few coarse cakes baked over the smoky fire, some rice, and a lump of sour preserved tamarinds – just enough to go on with till he could get to his evening kill. The smell of the dew in the marshes made him hungry and restless. He wanted to finish his spring running, but the child insisted on sitting in his arms, and Messua would have it that his long, blue-black hair must be combed out. So she sang, as she combed, foolish little baby-songs, now calling Mowgli her son, and now begging him to give some of his jungle power to the child. The hut door was closed, but Mowgli heard a sound he knew well, and saw Messua's jaw drop with horror as a great grey paw came under the bottom of the door, and Grey Brother outside whined a muffled and penitent whine of anxiety and fear.

'Out and wait! Ye would not come when I called,' said Mowgli in Jungle-talk, without turning his head, and the great grey paw disappeared.

'Do not – do not bring thy – thy servants with thee,' said Messua. 'I – we have always lived at peace with the Jungle.'

'It is peace,' said Mowgli, rising. 'Think of that night on the road to Khanhiwara. There were scores of such folk before thee and behind thee.

But I see that even in springtime the Jungle People do not always forget. Mother, I go.'

Messua drew aside humbly – he was indeed a wood-god, she thought; but as his hand was on the door the mother in her made her throw her arms round Mowgli's neck again and again.

'Come back!' she whispered. 'Son or no son, come back, for I love thee – Look, he too grieves.'

The child was crying because the man with the shiny knife was going away.

'Come back again,' Messua repeated. 'By night or by day this door is never shut to thee.'

Mowgli's throat worked as though the cords in it were being pulled, and his voice seemed to be dragged from it as he answered, 'I will surely come back.'

'And now,' he said, as he put by the head of the fawning wolf on the threshold, 'I have a little cry against thee, Grey Brother. Why came ye not all four when I called so long ago?'

'So long ago? It was but last night. I – we – were singing in the Jungle the new songs, for this is the Time of New Talk. Rememberest thou?'

'Truly, truly.'

'And as soon as the songs were sung,' Grey Brother went on earnestly, 'I followed thy trail. I ran from all the others and followed hotfoot. But, O Little Brother, what hast *thou* done, eating and sleeping with the Man-Pack?'

'If ye had come when I called, this had never been,' said Mowgli, running much faster.

'And now what is to be?' said Grey Brother. Mowgli was going to answer when a girl in a white cloth came down some path that led from the outskirts of the village. Grey Brother dropped out of sight at once, and Mowgli backed noiselessly into a field of high-springing crops. He could almost have touched her with his hand when the warm, green stalks closed before his face and he disappeared like a ghost. The girl screamed, for she thought she had seen a spirit, and then she gave a deep sigh. Mowgli parted the stalks with his hands and watched her till she was out of sight.

'And now I do not know,' he said, sighing in his turn. '*Why* did ye not come when I called?'

'We follow thee – we follow thee,' Grey Brother mumbled, licking at Mowgli's heel. 'We follow thee always, except in the Time of the New Talk.'

'And would ye follow me to the Man-Pack?' Mowgli whispered.

'Did I not follow thee on the night our old Pack cast thee out? Who waked thee lying among the crops?'

'Ay, but again?'

'Have I not followed thee tonight? '

'Ay, but again and again, and it may be again, Grey Brother?'

Grey Brother was silent. When he spoke he growled to himself, 'The Black One spoke truth.'

'And he said?'

'Man goes to Man at the last. Raksha, our mother, said – '

'So also said Akela on the night of Red Dog,' Mowgli muttered.

'So also says Kaa, who is wiser than us all.'

'What dost thou say, Grey Brother?'

'They cast thee out once, with bad talk. They cut thy mouth with stones. They sent Buldeo to slay thee. They would have thrown thee into the Red Flower. Thou, and not I, hast said that they are evil and senseless. Thou, and not I – I follow my own people – didst let in the Jungle upon them. Thou, and not I, didst make song against them more bitter even than our song against Red Dog.'

'I ask thee what *thou* sayest?'

They were talking as they ran. Grey Brother cantered on a while without replying, and then he said – between bound and bound as it were – 'Man-cub – Master of the Jungle – Son of Raksha, Lair-brother to me – though I forget for a little while in the spring, thy trail is my trail, thy lair is my lair, thy kill is my kill, and thy death-fight is my death-fight. I speak for the Three. But what wilt thou say to the Jungle?'

'That is well thought. Between the sight and the kill it is not good to wait. Go before and cry them all to the Council Rock, and I will tell them what is in my stomach. But they may not come – in the Time of New Talk they may forget me.'

'Hast thou, then, forgotten nothing?' snapped Grey Brother over his shoulder, as he laid himself down to gallop, and Mowgli followed, thinking.

At any other season the news would have called all the Jungle together with bristling necks, but now they were busy hunting and fighting and killing and singing. From one to another Grey Brother ran, crying, 'The Master of the Jungle goes back to Man! Come to the Council Rock.' And the happy, eager People only answered, 'He will return in the summer heats. The Rains will drive him to lair. Run and sing with us, Grey Brother.'

'But the Master of the Jungle goes back to Man,' Grey Brother would repeat.

'*Eee – Yoawa?* Is the Time of New Talk any less sweet for that?' they would reply. So when Mowgli, heavy-hearted, came up through the well-remembered rocks to the place where he had been brought into the Council, he found only the Four; Baloo, who was nearly blind with age, and the heavy, cold-blooded Kaa coiled around Akela's empty seat.

'Thy trail ends here, then, Manling?' said Kaa, as Mowgli threw himself down, his face in his hands. 'Cry thy cry. We be of one blood, thou and I – man and snake together.'

'Why did I not die under Red Dog?' the boy moaned. 'My strength is gone from me, and it is not any poison. By night and by day I hear a double step upon my trail. When I turn my head it is as though one had hidden himself from me that instant. I go to look behind the trees and he is not there. I call and none cry again; but it is as though one listened and kept back the answer. I lie down, but I do not rest. I run the spring running, but I am not made still. I bathe, but I am not made cool. The kill sickens me, but I have no heart to fight except I kill. The Red Flower is in my body, my bones are water – and – I know not what I know.'

'What need of talk?' said Baloo slowly, turning his head to where Mowgli lay. 'Akela by the river said it, that Mowgli should drive Mowgli back to the Man-Pack. I said it. But who listens now to Baloo? Bagheera – where is Bagheera this night? – he knows also. It is the Law.'

'When we met at Cold Lairs, Manling, I knew it,' said Kaa, turning a little in his mighty coils. 'Man goes to Man at the last, though the Jungle does not cast him out.'

The Four looked at one another and at Mowgli, puzzled but obedient.

'The Jungle does not cast me out, then?' Mowgli stammered.

Grey Brother and the Three growled furiously, beginning, 'So long as we live none shall dare – ' But Baloo checked them.

'I taught thee the Law. It is for me to speak,' he said; 'and, though I cannot now see the rocks before me, I see far. Little Frog, take thine own trail; make thy lair with thine own blood and pack and people; but when there is need of foot or tooth or eye, or a word carried swiftly by night, remember, Master of the Jungle, the Jungle is thine at call.'

'The Middle Jungle is thine also,' said Kaa. 'I speak for no small people.'

'*Hai-mai*, my brothers,' cried Mowgli, throwing up his arms with a sob. 'I know not what I know! I would not go; but I am drawn by both feet. How shall I leave these nights?'

'Nay, look up, Little Brother,' Baloo repeated. 'There is no shame in this hunting. When the honey is eaten we leave the empty hive.'

'Having cast the skin,' said Kaa, 'we may not creep into it afresh. It is the Law.'

'Listen, dearest of all to me,' said Baloo. 'There is neither word nor will here to hold thee back. Look up! Who may question the Master of the Jungle? I saw thee playing among the white pebbles yonder when thou wast a little frog; and Bagheera, that bought thee for the price of a young bull newly killed, saw thee also. Of that Looking Over we two only remain; for Raksha, thy lair-mother, is dead with thy lair-father; the old Wolf-Pack is long since dead; thou knowest whither Shere Khan went, and Akela died among the dholes, where, but for thy wisdom and strength, the second Seeonee Pack would also have died. There remains nothing but old bones. It is no longer the Man-cub that asks leave of his Pack, but the Master of the Jungle that changes his trail. Who shall question Man in his ways?'

'But Bagheera and the Bull that bought me,' said Mowgli. 'I would not – '

His words were cut short by a roar and a crash in the thicket below, and Bagheera, light, strong, and terrible as always, stood before him.

'*Therefore*,' he said, stretching out a dripping right paw, 'I did not come.

It was a long hunt, but he lies dead in the bushes now – a bull in his second year – the Bull that frees thee, Little Brother. All debts are paid now. For the rest, my word is Baloo's word.' He licked Mowgli's foot. 'Remember, Bagheera loved thee,' he cried, and bounded away. At the foot of the hill he cried again long and loud, 'Good hunting on a new trail, Master of the Jungle! Remember, Bagheera loved thee.'

'Thou hast heard,' said Baloo. 'There is no more. Go now; but first come to me. O wise Little Frog, come to me!'

'It is hard to cast the skin,' said Kaa as Mowgli sobbed and sobbed, with his head on the blind bear's side and his arms round his neck, while Baloo tried feebly to lick his feet.

'The stars are thin,' said Grey Brother, snuffing at the dawn wind. 'Where shall we lair today? for from now, we follow new trails.'

*   *   *

And this is the last of the Mowgli stories.

The Out song

This is the song that Mowgli heard behind him in the Jungle till he came to Messua's door again.

BALOO

OR THE SAKE of him who showed
One wise Frog the Jungle-Road,
Keep the Law the Man-Pack make –
For thy blind old Baloo's sake!
Clean or tainted, hot or stale,
Hold it as it were the Trail,
Through the day and through the night,
Questing neither left nor right.
For the sake of him who loves
Thee beyond all else that moves,
When thy Pack would make thee pain,
Say: 'Tabaqui sings again.'
When thy Pack would work thee ill,
Say: 'Shere Khan is yet to kill.'
When the knife is drawn to slay,
Keep the Law and go thy way.
(Root and honey, palm and spathe,
Guard a cub from harm and scathe!)
Wood and Water, Wind and Tree,
Jungle-Favour go with thee!

KAA

Anger is the egg of Fear –
Only lidless eyes are clear.
Cobra-poison none may leech.
Even so with Cobra-speech.

Open talk shall call to thee
Strength, whose mate is Courtesy.
Send no lunge beyond thy length;
Lend no rotten bough thy strength.
Gauge thy gape with buck or goat,
Lest thine eye should choke thy throat,
After gorging, wouldst thou sleep?
Look thy den is hid and deep,
Lest a wrong, by thee forgot,
Draw thy killer to the spot.
East and West and North and South,
Wash thy hide and close thy mouth.
(Pit and rift and blue pool-brim,
Middle-Jungle follow him!)
Wood and Water, Wind and Tree,
Jungle-Favour go with thee!

BAGHEERA

In the cage my life began;
Well I know the worth of Man.
By the Broken Lock that freed –
Man-cub, 'ware the Man-cub's breed!
Scenting-dew or starlight pale,
Choose no tangled tree-cat trail.
Pack or council, hunt or den,
Cry no truce with Jackal-Men.
Feed them silence when they say:
'Come with us an easy way.'
Feed them silence when they seek
Help of thine to hurt the weak.
Make no *banaar*'s boast of skill;
Hold thy peace above the kill.
Let nor call nor song nor sign
Turn thee from thy hunting-line.
(Morning mist or twilight clear,
Serve him, Wardens of the Deer!)
Wood and Water, Wind and Tree,
Jungle-Favour go with thee!

THE THREE

On the trail that thou must tread
To the thresholds of our dread,
Where the Flower blossoms red;
Through the nights when thou shalt lie
Prisoned from our Mother-sky,
Hearing us, thy loves, go by;
In the dawns when thou shalt wake
To the toil thou canst not break,
Heartsick for the Jungle's sake:
Wood and Water, Wind and Tree,
Wisdom, Strength, and Courtesy,
Jungle-Favour go with thee!

JUST SO STORIES

Contents

How the Whale got his Throat

IN THE SEA, once upon a time, O my Best Beloved, there was a Whale, and he ate fishes. He ate the starfish and the garfish, and the crab and the dab, and the plaice and the dace, and the skate and his mate, and the mackereel and the pickereel, and the really truly twirly-whirly eel. All the fishes he could find in all the sea he ate with his mouth – so! Till at last there was only one small fish left in all the sea, and he was a small 'Stute Fish, and he swam a little behind the Whale's right ear, so as to be out of harm's way. Then the Whale stood up on his tail and said, 'I'm hungry.' And the small 'Stute Fish said in a small 'stute voice, 'Noble and generous Cetacean, have you ever tasted Man?'

'No,' said the Whale. 'What is it like?'

'Nice,' said the small 'Stute Fish. 'Nice but nubbly.'

'Then fetch me some,' said the Whale, and he made the sea froth up with his tail.

'One at a time is enough,' said the 'Stute Fish. 'If you swim to latitude Fifty North, longitude Forty West (that is Magic), you will find, sitting *on* a raft, *in* the middle of the sea, with nothing on but a pair of blue canvas breeches, a pair of suspenders (you must *not* forget the suspenders, Best Beloved), and a jackknife, one shipwrecked Mariner, who, it is only fair to tell you, is a man of infinite-resource-and-sagacity.'

So the Whale swam and swam to latitude Fifty North, longitude Forty West, as fast as he could swim, and *on* a raft, *in* the middle of the sea, *with* nothing to wear except a pair of blue canvas breeches, a pair of suspenders (you must particularly remember the suspenders, Best Beloved), *and* a jackknife, he found one single, solitary shipwrecked Mariner, trailing his toes in the water. (He had his Mummy's leave to paddle, or else he would never have done it, because he was a man of infinite-resource-and-sagacity.)

Then the Whale opened his mouth back and back and back till it nearly touched his tail, and he swallowed the shipwrecked Mariner, and the raft he was sitting on, and his blue canvas breeches, and the suspenders (which you *must* not forget), *and* the jackknife – He swallowed them all down into his warm, dark, inside cupboards, and then he smacked his lips – so, and turned round three times on his tail.

But as soon as the Mariner, who was a man of infinite-resource-and-sagacity, found himself truly inside the Whale's warm, dark, inside cupboards,

This is the picture

of the Whale swallowing the Mariner with his infinite-resource-and-sagacity, and the raft and the jackknife *and* his suspenders, which you must *not* forget. The buttony-things are the Mariner's suspenders, and you can see the knife close by them. He is sitting on the raft, but it has tilted up sideways, so you don't see much of it. The whity thing by the Mariner's left hand is a piece of wood that he was trying to row the raft with when the Whale came along. The piece of wood is called the jaws-of-a-gaff. The Mariner left it outside when he went in. The Whale's name was Smiler, and the Mariner was called Mr Henry Albert Bivvens, a.b. The little 'Stute Fish is hiding under the Whale's tummy, or else I would have drawn him. The reason that the sea looks so ooshy-skooshy is because the Whale is sucking it all into his mouth so as to suck in Mr Henry Albert Bivvens and the raft and the jackknife and the suspenders. You must never forget the suspenders.

he stumped and he jumped and he thumped and he bumped, and he pranced and he danced, and he banged and he clanged, and he hit and he bit, and he leaped and he creeped, and he prowled and he howled, and he hopped and he dropped, and he cried and he sighed, and he crawled and he bawled and he stepped and he lepped, and he danced hornpipes where he shouldn't, and the Whale felt most unhappy indeed. (*Have* you forgotten the suspenders?)

So he said to the 'Stute Fish, 'This man is very nubbly, and besides he is making me hiccough. What shall I do?'

'Tell him to come out,' said the 'Stute Fish.

So the Whale called down his own throat to the shipwrecked Mariner, 'Come out and behave yourself. I've got the hiccoughs.'

'Nay, nay!' said the Mariner. 'Not so, but far otherwise. Take me to my natal-shore and the white-cliffs-of-Albion, and I'll think about it.' And he began to dance more than ever.

'You had better take him home,' said the 'Stute Fish to the Whale. 'I ought to have warned you that he is a man of infinite-resource-and-sagacity.'

So the Whale swam and swam and swam, with both flippers and his tail, as hard as he could for the hiccoughs; and at last he saw the Mariner's natal-shore and the white-cliffs-of-Albion, and he rushed halfway up the beach, and opened his mouth wide and wide and wide, and said, 'Change here for Winchester, Ashuelot, Nashua, Keene, and stations on the *Fitch*burg Road'; and just as he said 'Fitch' the Mariner walked out of his mouth. But while the Whale had been swimming, the Mariner, who was indeed a person of infinite-resource-and-sagacity, had taken his jackknife and cut up the raft into a little square grating all running criss-cross, and he had tied it firm with his suspenders (*now* you know why you were not to forget the suspenders!), and he dragged that grating good and tight into the Whale's throat, and there it stuck! Then he recited the following *Sloka*, which, as you have not heard it, I will now proceed to relate:

> By means of a grating
> I have stopped your ating.

For the Mariner he was also an Hi-ber-ni-an. And he stepped out on the shingle, and went home to his Mother, who had given him leave to trail his toes in the water; and he married and lived happily ever afterward. So did the Whale. But from that day on, the grating in his throat, which he could neither cough up nor swallow down, prevented him eating anything except very, very small fish; and that is the reason why whales nowadays never eat men or boys or little girls.

The small 'Stute Fish went and hid himself in the mud under the Door-sills of the Equator. He was afraid that the Whale might be angry with him.

The Sailor took the jackknife home. He was wearing the blue canvas breeches when he walked out on the shingle. The suspenders were left behind, you see, to tie the grating with; and that is the end of *that* tale.

Here is the Whale

looking for the little 'Stute Fish, who is hiding under the Door-sills of the Equator. The little 'Stute Fish's name was Pingle. He is hiding among the roots of the big seaweed that grows in front of the Doors of the Equator. I have drawn the Doors of the Equator. They are shut. They are always kept shut, because a door ought always to be kept shut. The ropy thing right across is the Equator itself; and the things that look like rocks are the two giants Moar and Koar, that keep the Equator in order. They drew the shadow-pictures on the Doors of the Equator, and they carved all those twisty fishes under the Doors. The beaky-fish are called beaked Dolphins, and the other fish with the queer heads are called Hammer-headed Sharks. The Whale never found the little 'Stute Fish till he got over his temper, and then they became good friends again.

When the cabin port-holes are dark and green
  Because of the seas outside;
When the ship goes *wop* (with a wiggle between)
And the steward falls into the soup-tureen,
  And the trunks begin to slide;
When Nursey lies on the floor in a heap,
And Mummy tells you to let her sleep,
And you aren't waked or washed or dressed,
Why, then you will know (if you haven't guessed)
You're 'Fifty North and Forty West!'

How the Camel got his Hump

NOW THIS IS THE NEXT TALE, and it tells how the Camel got his big hump.

In the beginning of years, when the world was so new-and-all, and the Animals were just beginning to work for Man, there was a Camel, and he lived in the middle of a Howling Desert because he did not want to work; and besides, he was a Howler himself. So he ate sticks and thorns and tamarisks and milkweed and prickles, most 'scruciating idle; and when anybody spoke to him he said 'Humph!' Just 'Humph!' and no more.

Presently the Horse came to him on Monday morning, with a saddle on his back and a bit in his mouth, and said, 'Camel, O Camel, come out and trot like the rest of us.'

'Humph!' said the Camel; and the Horse went away and told the Man.

Presently the Dog came to him, with a stick in his mouth, and said, 'Camel, O Camel, come and fetch and carry like the rest of us.'

'Humph!' said the Camel; and the Dog went away and told the Man.

Presently the Ox came to him, with the yoke on his neck, and said, 'Camel, O Camel, come and plough like the rest of us.'

'Humph!' said the Camel; and the Ox went away and told the Man.

At the end of the day the Man called the Horse and the Dog and the Ox together, and said, 'Three, O Three, I'm very sorry for you (with the world so new-and-all); but that Humph-thing in the Desert can't work, or he would have been here by now, so I am going to leave him alone, and you must work double-time to make up for it.'

That made the Three very angry (with the world so new-and-all), and they held a palaver, and an *indaba*, and a *punchayet*, and a pow-wow on the edge of the Desert; and the Camel came chewing milkweed *most* 'scruciating idle, and laughed at them. Then he said 'Humph!' and went away again.

Presently there came along the Djinn in charge of All Deserts, rolling in a cloud of dust (Djinns always travel that way because it is Magic), and he stopped to palaver and pow-wow with the Three.

'Djinn of All Deserts,' said the Horse, '*is* it right for anyone to be idle, with the world so new-and-all?'

'Certainly not,' said the Djinn.

'Well,' said the Horse, 'there's a thing in the middle of your Howling

Desert (and he's a Howler himself) with a long neck and long legs, and he hasn't done a stroke of work since Monday morning. He won't trot.'

'Whew!' said the Djinn, whistling, 'that's my Camel, for all the gold in Arabia! What does he say about it?'

'He says "Humph!" ' said the Dog; 'and he won't fetch and carry.'

'Does he say anything else?'

'Only "Humph!"; and he won't plough,' said the Ox.

'Very good,' said the Djinn. 'I'll humph him if you will kindly wait a minute.'

The Djinn rolled himself up in his dust-cloak, and took a bearing across the desert, and found the Camel most 'scruciatingly idle, looking at his own reflection in a pool of water.

'My long and bubbling friend,' said the Djinn, 'what's this I hear of your doing no work, with the world so new-and-all?'

'Humph!' said the Camel.

The Djinn sat down, with his chin in his hand, and began to think a Great Magic, while the Camel looked at his own reflection in the pool of water.

'You've given the Three extra work ever since Monday morning, all on account of your 'scruciating idleness,' said the Djinn; and he went on thinking Magics, with his chin in his hand.

'Humph!' said the Camel.

'I shouldn't say that again if I were you,' said the Djinn; 'you might say it once too often. Bubbles, I want you to work.'

And the Camel said 'Humph!' again; but no sooner had he said it than he saw his back, that he was so proud of, puffing up and puffing up into a great big lolloping humph.

'Do you see that?' said the Djinn. 'That's your very own humph that you've brought upon your very own self by not working. Today is Thursday, and you've done no work since Monday, when the work began. Now you are going to work.'

'How can I,' said the Camel, 'with this humph on my back?'

'That's made a-purpose,' said the Djinn, 'all because you missed those three days. You will be able to work now for three days without eating, because you can live on your humph; and don't you ever say I never did anything for you. Come out of the Desert and go to the Three, and behave. Humph yourself!'

And the Camel humphed himself, humph and all, and went away to join the Three. And from that day to this the Camel always wears a humph (we call it 'hump' now, not to hurt his feelings); but he has never yet caught up with the three days that he missed at the beginning of the world, and he has never yet learned how to behave.

> The Camel's hump is an ugly lump
>   Which well you may see at the Zoo;
> But uglier yet is the hump we get
>   From having too little to do.

This is the picture

of the Djinn making the beginnings of the Magic that brought the Humph to the Camel. First he drew a line in the air with his finger, and it became solid; and then he made a cloud, and then he made an egg – you can see them at the bottom of the picture – and then there was a magic pumpkin that turned into a big white flame. Then the Djinn took his magic fan and fanned that flame till the flame turned into a Magic by itself. It was a good Magic and a very kind Magic really, though it had to give the Camel a Humph because the Camel was lazy. The Djinn in charge of All Deserts was one of the nicest of the Djinns, so he would never do anything really unkind.

Here is the picture

of the Djinn in charge of All Deserts guiding the Magic with his magic fan. The Camel is eating a twig of acacia, and he has just finished saying 'humph' once too often (the Djinn told him he would), and so the Humph is coming. The long towelly thing growing out of the thing like an onion is the Magic, and you can see the Humph on its shoulder. The Humph fits on the flat part of the Camel's back. The Camel is too busy looking at his own beautiful self in the pool of water to know what is going to happen to him.

Underneath the truly picture is a picture of the World-so-new-and-all. There are two smoky volcanoes in it, some other mountains and some stones and a lake and a black island and a twisty river and a lot of other things, as well as a Noah's Ark. I couldn't draw all the deserts that the Djinn was in charge of, so I only drew one, but it is a most deserty desert.

Kiddies and grown-ups too–oo–oo,
If we haven't enough to do–oo–oo,
        We get the hump –
        Cameelious hump –
The hump that is black and blue!

We climb out of bed with a frouzly head
    And a snarly-yarly voice.
We shiver and scowl and we grunt and we growl
    At our bath and our boots and our toys;

And there ought to be a corner for me
(And I know there is one for you)
        When we get the hump –
        Cameelious hump –
The hump that is black and blue!

The cure for this ill is not to sit still,
    Or frowst with a book by the fire;
But to take a large hoe and a shovel also,
    And dig till you gently perspire;

And then you will find that the sun and the wind,
And the Djinn of the Garden too,
    Have lifted the hump –
    The horrible hump –
The hump that is black and blue!

I get it as well as you–oo–oo –
If I haven't enough to do–oo–oo!
    We all get hump –
    Cameelious hump –
Kiddies and grown-ups too!

How the Rhinoceros got his Skin

ONCE UPON A TIME, on an uninhabited island on the shores of the Red Sea, there lived a Parsee from whose hat the rays of the sun were reflected in more-than- oriental splendour. And the Parsee lived by the Red Sea with nothing but his hat and his knife and a cooking-stove of the kind that you must particularly never touch. And one day he took flour and water and currants and plums and sugar and things, and made himself one cake which was two feet across and three feet thick. It was indeed a Superior Comestible (*that's* Magic), and he put it on the stove because *he* was allowed to cook on that stove, and he baked it and he baked it till it was all done brown and smelt most sentimental. But just as he was going to eat it there came down to the beach from the Altogether Uninhabited Interior one Rhinoceros with a horn on his nose, two piggy eyes, and few manners. In those days the Rhinoceros's skin fitted him quite tight. There were no wrinkles in it anywhere. He looked exactly like a Noah's Ark Rhinoceros, but of course much bigger. All the same, he had no manners then, and he has no manners now, and he never will have any manners. He said, 'How!' and the Parsee left that cake and climbed to the top of a palm tree with nothing on but his hat, from which the rays of the sun were always reflected in more-than-oriental splendour. And the Rhinoceros upset the oil-stove with his nose, and the cake rolled on the sand, and he spiked that cake on the horn of his nose, and he ate it, and he went away, waving his tail, to the desolate and Exclusively Uninhabited Interior which abuts on the islands of Mazanderan, Socotra, and the Promontories of the Larger Equinox. Then the Parsee came down from his palm tree and put the stove on its legs and recited the following *Sloka*, which, as you have not heard, I will now proceed to relate:

> Them that takes cakes
> Which the Parsee-man bakes
> Makes dreadful mistakes.

And there was a great deal more in that than you would think.
Because, five weeks later, there was a heatwave in the Red Sea, and everybody took off all the clothes they had. The Parsee took off his hat; but

This is the picture

of the Parsee beginning to eat his cake on the Uninhabited Island in the Red Sea on a very hot day; and of the Rhinoceros coming down from the Altogether Uninhabited Interior, which, as you can truthfully see, is all rocky. The Rhinoceros's skin is quite smooth, and the three buttons that button it up are underneath, so you can't see them. The squiggly things on the Parsee's hat are the rays of the sun reflected in more-than-oriental splendour, because if I had drawn real rays they would have filled up all the picture. The cake has currants in it; and the wheel-thing lying on the sand in front belonged to one of Pharaoh's chariots when he tried to cross the Red Sea. The Parsee found it, and kept it to play with. The Parsee's name was Pestonjee Bomonjee, and the Rhinoceros was called Strorks, because he breathed through his mouth instead of his nose. I wouldn't ask anything about the cooking-stove if *I* were you.

the Rhinoceros took off his skin and carried it over his shoulder as he came down to the beach to bathe. In those days it buttoned underneath with three buttons and looked like a waterproof. He said nothing whatever about the Parsee's cake, because he had eaten it all; and he never had any manners, then, since, or henceforward. He waddled straight into the water and blew bubbles through his nose, leaving his skin on the beach.

Presently the Parsee came by and found the skin, and he smiled one smile that ran all round his face two times. Then he danced three times round the skin and rubbed his hands. Then he went to his camp and filled his hat with cake-crumbs, for the Parsee never ate anything but cake, and never swept out his camp. He took that skin, and he shook that skin, and he scrubbed that skin, and he rubbed that skin just as full of old, dry, stale, tickly cake-crumbs and some burned currants as ever it could *possibly* hold. Then he climbed to the top of his palm tree and waited for the Rhinoceros to come out of the water and put it on.

And the Rhinoceros did. He buttoned it up with the three buttons, and it tickled like cake-crumbs in bed. Then he wanted to scratch, but that made it worse; and then he lay down on the sands and rolled and rolled and rolled, and every time he rolled the cake-crumbs tickled him worse and worse and worse. Then he ran to the palm tree and rubbed and rubbed and rubbed himself against it. He rubbed so much and so hard that he rubbed his skin into a great fold over his shoulders, and another fold underneath, where the buttons used to be (but he rubbed the buttons off), and he rubbed some more folds over his legs. And it spoiled his temper, but it didn't make the least difference to the cake-crumbs. They were inside his skin and they tickled. So he went home, very angry indeed and horribly scratchy; and from that day to this every rhinoceros has great folds in his skin and a very bad temper, all on account of the cake-crumbs inside.

But the Parsee came down from his palm tree, wearing his hat, from which the rays of the sun were reflected in more-than-oriental splendour, packed up his cooking-stove, and went away in the direction of Orotavo, Amygdala, the Upland Meadows of Anantarivo, and the Marshes of Sonaput.

This is the Parsee Pestonjee Bomonjee

sitting in his palm tree and watching the Rhinoceros Strorks bathing near the beach of the Altogether Uninhabited Island after Strorks had taken off his skin. The Parsee has rubbed the cake-crumbs into the skin, and he is smiling to think how they will tickle Strorks when Strorks puts it on again. The skin is just under the rocks below the palm tree in a cool place; that is why you can't see it. The Parsee is wearing a new more-than-oriental-splendour hat of the sort that Parsees wear; and he has a knife in his hand to cut his name on palm trees. The black things on the islands out at sea are bits of ships that got wrecked going down the Red Sea; but all the passengers were saved and went home. The black thing in the water close to the shore is not a wreck at all. It is Strorks the Rhinoceros bathing without his skin. He was just as black underneath his skin as he was outside. I wouldn't ask anything about the cooking-stove if *I* were you.

This Uninhabited Island
　　　Is off Cape Gardafui,
By the Beaches of Socotra
　　　And the Pink Arabian Sea:
But it's hot – too hot from Suez
　　　For the likes of you and me
　　　　　Ever to go
　　　　　In a P&O
And call on the Cake-Parsee.

How the Leopard got his Spots

IN THE DAYS when everybody started fair, Best Beloved, the Leopard lived in a place called the High Veldt. 'Member it wasn't the Low Veldt, or the Bush Veldt, or the Sour Veldt, but the 'sclusively bare, hot, shiny High Veldt, where there was sand and sandy-coloured rock and 'sclusively tufts of sandy-yellowish grass. The Giraffe and the Zebra and the Eland and the Koodoo and the Hartebeest lived there; and they were 'sclusively sandy-yellow-brownish all over; but the Leopard, he was the 'sclusivest sandiest-yellowest-brownest of them all – a greyish-yellowish catty-shaped kind of beast, and he matched the 'sclusively yellowish-greyish-brownish colour of the High Veldt to one hair. This was very bad for the Giraffe and the Zebra and the rest of them; for he would lie down by a 'sclusively yellowish-greyish-brownish stone or clump of grass, and when the Giraffe or the Zebra or the Eland or the Koodoo or the Bush-Buck or the Bonte-Buck came by he would surprise them out of their jumpsome lives. He would indeed! And, also, there was an Ethiopian with bows and arrows (a 'sclusively greyish- brownish-yellowish man he was then), who lived on the High Veldt with the Leopard; and the two used to hunt together – the Ethiopian with his bows and arrows, and the Leopard 'sclusively with his teeth and claws – till the Giraffe and the Eland and the Koodoo and the Quagga and all the rest of them didn't know which way to jump, Best Beloved. They didn't indeed!

After a long time – things lived for ever so long in those days – they learned to avoid anything that looked like a Leopard or an Ethiopian; and bit by bit – the Giraffe began it, because his legs were the longest – they went away from the High Veldt. They scuttled for days and days and days till they came to a great forest, 'sclusively full of trees and bushes and stripy, speckly, patchy-blatchy shadows, and there they hid: and after another long time, what with standing half in the shade and half out of it, and what with the slippery-slidy shadows of the trees falling on them, the Giraffe grew blotchy, and the Zebra grew stripy, and the Eland and the Koodoo grew darker, with little wavy grey lines on their backs like bark on a tree trunk; and so, though you could hear them and smell them, you could very seldom see them, and then only when you knew precisely where to look. They had a beautiful time in the 'sclusively speckly-spickly shadows of the forest, while the Leopard and the Ethiopian ran about over the 'sclusively greyish-yellowish-reddish High Veldt outside, wondering where all their breakfasts and their dinners and their teas had gone. At last they were so hungry that they ate rats and beetles and rock-rabbits, the Leopard and the Ethiopian, and then they had the Big Tummyache, both together; and then they met Baviaan – the dog-headed, barking Baboon, who is Quite the Wisest Animal in All South Africa.

Said Leopard to Baviaan (and it was a very hot day), 'Where has all the game gone?'

And Baviaan winked. *He* knew.

Said the Ethiopian to Baviaan, 'Can you tell me the present habitat of the aboriginal Fauna?' (That meant just the same thing, but the Ethiopian always used long words. He was a grown-up.)

And Baviaan winked. *He* knew.

Then said Baviaan, 'The game has gone into other spots; and my advice to you, Leopard, is to go into other spots as soon as you can.'

And the Ethiopian said, 'That is all very fine, but I wish to know whither the aboriginal Fauna has migrated.'

Then said Baviaan, 'The aboriginal Fauna has joined the aboriginal Flora because it was high time for a change; and my advice to you, Ethiopian, is to change as soon as you can.'

That puzzled the Leopard and the Ethiopian, but they set off to look for the aboriginal Flora, and presently, after ever so many days, they saw a great, high, tall forest full of tree trunks all 'sclusively speckled and sprottled and spottled, dotted and splashed and slashed and hatched and cross-hatched with shadows. (Say that quickly aloud, and you will see how *very* shadowy the forest must have been.)

'What is this,' said the Leopard, 'that is so 'sclusively dark, and yet so full of little pieces of light?'

'I don't know,' said the Ethiopian, 'but it ought to be the aboriginal Flora. I can smell Giraffe, and I can hear Giraffe, but I can't see Giraffe.'

'That's curious,' said the Leopard. 'I suppose it is because we have just come in out of the sunshine. I can smell Zebra, and I can hear Zebra, but I can't see Zebra.'

'Wait a bit,' said the Ethiopian. 'It's a long time since we've hunted 'em. Perhaps we've forgotten what they were like.'

'Fiddle!' said the Leopard. 'I remember them perfectly on the High Veldt, especially their marrow- bones. Giraffe is about seventeen feet high, of a 'sclusively fulvous golden-yellow from head to heel; and Zebra is about four and a half feet high, of a 'sclusively grey-fawn colour from head to heel.'

'Umm,' said the Ethiopian, looking into the speckly-spickly shadows of the aboriginal Flora-forest. 'Then they ought to show up in this dark place like ripe bananas in a smoke-house.'

This is Wise Baviaan,

the dog-headed Baboon, who is Quite the Wisest Animal in All
South Africa. I have drawn him from a statue that I made up out of
my own head, and I have written his name on his belt and on his
shoulder and on the thing he is sitting on. I have written it in what
is not called Coptic and Hieroglyphic and Cuneiformic and
Bengalic and Burmic and Hebric, all because he is so wise. He is
not beautiful, but he is very wise; and I should like to paint him
with paintbox colours, but I am not allowed. The umbrella-ish
thing about his head is his Conventional Mane.

But they didn't. The Leopard and the Ethiopian hunted all day; and though they could smell them and hear them, they never saw one of them.

'For goodness' sake,' said the Leopard at teatime, 'let us wait till it gets dark. This daylight hunting is a perfect scandal.'

So they waited till dark, and then the Leopard heard something breathing sniffily in the starlight that fell all stripy through the branches, and he jumped at the noise, and it smelt like Zebra, and it felt like Zebra, and when he knocked it down it kicked like Zebra, but he couldn't see it. So he said, 'Be quiet, O you person without any form. I am going to sit on your head till morning, because there is something about you that I don't understand.'

Presently he heard a grunt and a crash and a scramble, and the Ethiopian called out, 'I've caught a thing that I can't see. It smells like Giraffe, and it kicks like Giraffe, but it hasn't any form.'

'Don't you trust it,' said the Leopard. 'Sit on its head till the morning – same as me. They haven't any form – any of 'em.'

*　　*　　*

So they sat down on them hard till bright morning – time, and then Leopard said, 'What have you at your end of the table, Brother?'

The Ethiopian scratched his head and said, 'It ought to be 'sclusively a rich fulvous orange-tawny from head to heel, and it ought to be Giraffe; but it is covered all over with chestnut blotches. What have you at *your* end of the table, Brother?'

And the Leopard scratched his head and said, 'It ought to be 'sclusively a delicate greyish-fawn, and it ought to be Zebra; but it is covered all over with black and purple stripes. What in the world have you been doing to yourself, Zebra? Don't you know that if you were on the High Veldt I could see you ten miles off? You haven't any form.'

'Yes,' said the Zebra, 'but this isn't the High Veldt. Can't you see?'

'I can now,' said the Leopard. 'But I couldn't all yesterday. How is it done?'

'Let us up,' said the Zebra, 'and we will show you.'

They let the Zebra and the Giraffe get up; and Zebra moved away to some little thorn-bushes where the sunlight fell all stripy, and Giraffe moved off to some tallish trees where the shadows fell all blotchy.

'Now watch,' said the Zebra and the Giraffe. 'This is the way it's done. One – two – three! And where's your breakfast?'

Leopard stared, and Ethiopian stared, but all they could see were stripy shadows and blotched shadows in the forest, but never a sign of Zebra and Giraffe. They had just walked off and hidden themselves in the shadowy forest.

'Hi! Hi!' said the Ethiopian. 'That's a trick worth learning. Take a lesson by it, Leopard. You show up in this dark place like a bar of soap in a coal scuttle.'

'Ho! Ho!' said the Leopard. 'Would it surprise you very much to know that you show up in this dark place like a mustard-plaster on a sack of coals?'

'Well, calling names won't catch dinner,' said the Ethiopian. 'The long

This is the picture

of the Leopard and the Ethiopian after they had taken Wise Baviaan's advice and the Leopard had gone into other spots and the Ethiopian had changed his skin. The Ethiopian was really a negro, and so his name was Sambo. The Leopard was called Spots, and he has been called Spots ever since. They are out hunting in the spickly-speckly forest, and they are looking for Mr One-Two-Three-Where's-your-Breakfast. If you look a little you will see Mr One-Two-Three not far away. The Ethiopian has hidden behind a splotchy-blotchy tree because it matches his skin, and the Leopard is lyingbeside a spickly-speckly bank of stones because it matches his spots. Mr One-Two-Three- Where's-your-Breakfast is standing up eating leaves from a tall tree. This is really a puzzle-picture like 'Find-the-Cat'.

and the little of it is that we don't match our backgrounds. I'm going to take Baviaan's advice. He told me I ought to change; and as I've nothing to change except my skin I'm going to change that.'

'What to?' said the Leopard, tremendously excited.

'To a nice working blackish-brownish colour, with a little purple in it, and touches of slaty-blue. It will be the very thing for hiding in hollows and behind trees.'

So he changed his skin then and there, and the Leopard was more excited than ever; he had never seen a man change his skin before.

'But what about me?' he said, when the Ethiopian had worked his last little finger into his fine new black skin.

'You take Baviaan's advice too. He told you to go into spots.'

'So I did,' said the Leopard. 'I went into other spots as fast as I could. I went into this spot with you, and a lot of good it has done me.'

'Oh,' said the Ethiopian, 'Baviaan didn't mean spots in South Africa. He meant spots on your skin.'

'What's the use of that?' said the Leopard.

'Think of Giraffe,' said the Ethiopian. 'Or if you prefer stripes, think of Zebra. They find their spots and stripes give them per-fect satisfaction.'

'Umm,' said the Leopard. 'I wouldn't look like Zebra – not for ever so.'

'Well, make up your mind,' said the Ethiopian, 'because I'd hate to go hunting without you, but I must if you insist on looking like a sunflower against a tarred fence.'

'I'll take spots, then,' said the Leopard; 'but don't make 'em too vulgar-big. I wouldn't look like Giraffe – not for ever so.'

'I'll make 'em with the tips of my fingers,' said the Ethiopian. 'There's plenty of black left on my skin still. Stand over!'

Then the Ethiopian put his five fingers close together (there was plenty of black left on his new skin still) and pressed them all over the Leopard, and wherever the five fingers touched they left five little black marks, all close together. You can see them on any Leopard's skin you like, Best Beloved. Sometimes the fingers slipped and the marks got a little blurred; but if you look closely at any Leopard now you will see that there are always five spots – off five fat black fingertips.

'Now you *are* a beauty!' said the Ethiopian. 'You can lie out on the bare ground and look like a heap of pebbles. You can lie out on the naked rocks and look like a piece of pudding-stone. You can lie out on a leafy branch and look like sunshine sifting through the leaves; and you can lie right across the centre of a path and look like nothing in particular. Think of that and purr!'

'But if I'm all this,' said the Leopard, 'why didn't you go spotty too?'

'Oh, plain black's best for a nigger,' said the Ethiopian. 'Now come along and we'll see if we can't get even with Mr One-Two-Three-Where's-your-Breakfast!'

*   *   *

So they went away and lived happily ever afterward, Best Beloved. That is all.

Oh, now and then you will hear grown-ups say, 'Can the Ethiopian change his skin or the Leopard his spots?' I don't think even grown-ups would keep on saying such a silly thing if the Leopard and the Ethiopian hadn't done it once – do you? But they will never do it again, Best Beloved. They are quite contented as they are.

I am the Most Wise Baviaan, saying in most wise tones,
'Let us melt into the landscape – just us two by our lones.'
People have come – in a carriage – calling. But Mummy is there . . .
Yes, I can go if you take me – Nurse says *she* don't care.
Let's go up to the pig-sties and sit on the farmyard rails!
Let's say things to the bunnies, and watch 'em skitter their tails!
Let's – oh, *anything*, Daddy, so long as it's you and me,
And going truly exploring, and not being in till tea!
Here's your boots (I've brought 'em), and here's your cap and stick,
And here's your pipe and tobacco. Oh, come along out of it – quick!

The Elephant's Child

 IN THE HIGH AND FAR-OFF TIMES
the Elephant, O Best Beloved, had no trunk.
He had only a blackish, bulgy nose, as big as
a boot, that he could wriggle about from side
to side; but he couldn't pick up things with
it. But there was one Elephant – a new
Elephant – an Elephant's Child – who was
full of 'satiable curiosity, and that means he
asked ever so many questions. *And* he lived
in Africa, and he filled all Africa with his
'satiable curtiosities. He asked his tall aunt,
the Ostrich, why her tail-feathers grew just
so, and his tall aunt the Ostrich spanked him with her hard, hard claw. He
asked his tall uncle, the Giraffe, what made his skin spotty, and his tall uncle,
the Giraffe, spanked him with his hard, hard hoof. And still he was full of
'satiable curtiosity! He asked his broad aunt, the Hippopotamus, why her eyes
were red, and his broad aunt, the Hippopotamus, spanked him with her broad,
broad hoof; and he asked his hairy uncle, the Baboon, why melons tasted just
so, and his hairy uncle, the Baboon, spanked him with his hairy, hairy paw.
And *still* he was full of 'satiable curtiosity! He asked questions about everything that he saw, or heard, or felt, or smelt, or touched, and all his uncles and
his aunts spanked him. And still he was full of 'satiable curtiosity!

One fine morning in the middle of the Precession of the Equinoxes this
'satiable Elephant's Child asked a new fine question that he had never asked
before. He asked, 'What does the Crocodile have for dinner?' Then everybody said, 'Hush!' in a loud and dretful tone, and they spanked him
immediately and directly, without stopping, for a long time.

By and by, when that was finished, he came upon Kolokolo Bird sitting in
the middle of a wait-a-bit thorn-bush, and he said, 'My father has spanked
me, and my mother has spanked me; all my aunts and uncles have spanked me
for my 'satiable curtiosity; and *still* I want to know what the Crocodile has for
dinner!'

Then Kolokolo Bird said, with a mournful cry, 'Go to the banks of the
great grey-green, greasy Limpopo River, all set about with fever trees, and
find out.'

That very next morning, when there was nothing left of the Equinoxes, because the Precession had preceded according to precedent, this 'satiable Elephant's Child took a hundred pounds of bananas (the little short red kind), and a hundred pounds of sugar-cane (the long purple kind), and seventeen melons (the greeny-crackly kind), and said to all his dear families, 'Goodbye. I am going to the great grey-green, greasy Limpopo River, all set about with fever trees, to find out what the Crocodile has for dinner.' And they all spanked him once more for luck, though he asked them most politely to stop.

Then he went away, a little warm, but not at all astonished, eating melons, and throwing the rind about, because he could not pick it up.

He went from Graham's Town to Kimberley, and from Kimberley to Khama's Country, and from Khama's Country he went east by north, eating melons all the time, till at last he came to the banks of the great grey-green, greasy Limpopo River, all set about with fever trees, precisely as Kolokolo Bird had said.

Now you must know and understand, O Best Beloved, that till that very week, and day, and hour, and minute, this 'satiable Elephant's Child had never seen a Crocodile, and did not know what one was like. It was all his 'satiable curtiosity.

The first thing that he found was a Bi-Coloured-Python-Rock-Snake curled round a rock.

' 'Scuse me,' said the Elephant's Child most politely, 'but have you seen such a thing as a Crocodile in these promiscuous parts?'

'*Have* I seen a Crocodile?' said the Bi-Coloured-Python-Rock-Snake, in a voice of dretful scorn. 'What will you ask me next?'

' 'Scuse me,' said the Elephant's Child, 'but could you kindly tell me what he has for dinner?'

Then the Bi-Coloured-Python-Rock-Snake uncoiled himself very quickly from the rock, and spanked the Elephant's Child with his scalesome, flailsome tail.

'That is odd,' said the Elephant's Child, 'because my father and my mother, and my uncle and my aunt, not to mention my other aunt, the Hippopotamus, and my other uncle, the Baboon, have all spanked me for my 'satiable curtiosity – and I suppose this is the same thing.'

So he said goodbye very politely to the Bi-Coloured-Python-Rock-Snake, and helped to coil him up on the rock again, and went on, a little warm, but not at all astonished, eating melons, and throwing the rind about, because he could not pick it up, till he trod on what he thought was a log of wood at the very edge of the great grey-green, greasy Limpopo River, all set about with fever trees.

But it was really the Crocodile, O Best Beloved, and the Crocodile winked one eye – like this!

' 'Scuse me,' said the Elephant's Child most politely, 'but do you happen to have seen a Crocodile in these promiscuous parts?'

Then the Crocodile winked the other eye, and lifted half his tail out of the

This is the Elephant's Child

having his nose pulled by the Crocodile. He is much surprised and astonished and hurt, and he is talking through his nose and saying, 'Led go! You are hurtig be!' He is pulling very hard, and so is the Crocodile; but the Bi-Coloured-Python-Rock-Snake is hurrying through the water to help the Elephant's Child. All that black stuff is the banks of the great grey-green, greasy Limpopo River (but I am not allowed to paint these pictures), and the bottly tree with the twisty roots and the eight leaves is one of the fever trees that grow there.

Underneath the truly picture are shadows of African animals walking into an African ark. There are two lions, two ostriches, two oxen, two camels, two sheep, and two other things that look like rats, but I think they are rock-rabbits. They don't mean anything. I put them in because I thought they looked pretty.

They would look very fine if I were allowed to paint them.

mud; and the Elephant's Child stepped back most politely, because he did not wish to be spanked again.

'Come hither, Little One,' said the Crocodile 'Why do you ask such things?'

' 'Scuse me,' said the Elephant's Child most politely, 'but my father has spanked me, my mother has spanked me, not to mention my tall aunt, the Ostrich, and my tall uncle, the Giraffe, who can kick ever so hard, as well as my broad aunt, the Hippopotamus, and my hairy uncle, the Baboon, *and* including the Bi-Coloured-Python-Rock-Snake, with the scalesome, flailsome tail, just up the bank, who spanks harder than any of them; and *so*, if it's quite all the same to you, I don't want to be spanked any more.'

'Come hither, Little One,' said the Crocodile, 'for I am the Crocodile,' and he wept crocodile-tears to show it was quite true.

Then the Elephant's Child grew all breathless, and panted, and kneeled down on the bank and said, 'You are the very person I have been looking for all these long days. Will you please tell me what you have for dinner?'

'Come hither, Little One,' said the Crocodile, 'and I'll whisper.'

Then the Elephant's Child put his head down close to the Crocodile's musky, tusky mouth, and the Crocodile caught him by his little nose, which up to that very week, day, hour, and minute, had been no bigger than a boot, though much more useful.

'I think,' said the Crocodile – and he said it between his teeth, like this – 'I think today I will begin with Elephant's Child!'

At this, O Best Beloved, the Elephant's Child was much annoyed, and he said, speaking through his nose, like this, 'Led go! You are hurtig be!'

Then the Bi-Coloured-Python-Rock-Snake scuffled down from the bank and said, 'My young friend, if you do not now, immediately and instantly, pull as hard as ever you can, it is my opinion that your acquaintance in the large-pattern leather ulster' (and by this he meant the Crocodile) 'will jerk you into yonder limpid stream before you can say Jack Robinson.'

This is the way Bi-Coloured-Python-Rock-Snakes always talk.

Then the Elephant's Child sat back on his little haunches, and pulled, and pulled, and pulled, and his nose began to stretch. And the Crocodile floundered into the water, making it all creamy with great sweeps of his tail, and *he* pulled, and pulled, and pulled.

And the Elephant's Child's nose kept on stretching; and the Elephant's Child spread all his little four legs and pulled, and pulled, and pulled, and his nose kept on stretching; and the Crocodile threshed his tail like an oar, and *he* pulled, and pulled, and pulled, and at each pull the Elephant's Child's nose grew longer and longer – and it hurt him hijjus!

Then the Elephant's Child felt his legs slipping, and he said through his nose, which was now nearly five feet long, 'This is too butch for be!'

Then the Bi-Coloured-Python-Rock-Snake came down from the bank, and knotted himself in a double-clove-hitch round the Elephant's Child's hind legs, and said, 'Rash and inexperienced traveller, we will now seriously devote ourselves to a little high tension, because if we do not, it is my impression that yonder self-propelling man-of-war with the armour-plated upper deck' (and by this, O Best Beloved, he meant the Crocodile) 'will permanently vitiate your future career.'

That is the way all Bi-Coloured-Python-Rock-Snakes always talk.

So he pulled, and the Elephant's Child pulled, and the Crocodile pulled; but the Elephant's Child and the Bi-Coloured-Python-Rock-Snake pulled hardest; and at last the Crocodile let go of the Elephant's Child's nose with a plop that you could hear all up and down the Limpopo.

Then the Elephant's Child sat down most hard and sudden; but first he was careful to say 'Thank you' to the Bi-Coloured-Python-Rock-Snake; and next he was kind to his poor pulled nose, and wrapped it all up in cool banana leaves, and hung it in the great grey-green, greasy Limpopo to cool.

'What are you doing that for?' said the Bi-Coloured-Python-Rock-Snake.

' 'Scuse me,' said the Elephant's Child, 'but my nose is badly out of shape, and I am waiting for it to shrink.'

'Then you will have to wait a long time,' said the Bi-Coloured-Python-Rock-Snake. 'Some people do not know what is good for them.'

The Elephant's Child sat there for three days waiting for his nose to shrink. But it never grew any shorter, and, besides, it made him squint. For, O Best Beloved, you will see and understand that the Crocodile had pulled it out into a really truly trunk same as all Elephants have today.

At the end of the third day a fly came and stung him on the shoulder, and before he knew what he was doing he lifted up his trunk and hit that fly dead with the end of it.

' 'Vantage number one!' said the Bi-Coloured-Python-Rock-Snake. 'You couldn't have done that with a mere-smear nose. Try and eat a little now.'

Before he thought what he was doing the Elephant's Child put out his trunk and plucked a large bundle of grass, dusted it clean against his forelegs, and stuffed it into his own mouth.

' 'Vantage number two!' said the Bi-Coloured-Python-Rock-Snake. 'You couldn't have done that with a mere-smear nose. Don't you think the sun is very hot here?'

'It is,' said the Elephant's Child, and before he thought what he was doing he schlooped up a schloop of mud from the banks of the great grey-green, greasy Limpopo, and slapped it on his head, where it made a cool schloopy-sloshy mud-cap all trickly behind his ears.

' 'Vantage number three!' said the Bi-Coloured-Python-Rock-Snake. 'You couldn't have done that with a mere-smear nose. Now how do you feel about being spanked again?'

' 'Scuse me,' said the Elephant's Child, 'but I should not like it at all.'

'How would you like to spank somebody?' said the Bi-Coloured-Python-Rock-Snake.

'I should like it very much indeed,' said the Elephant's Child.

'Well,' said the Bi-Coloured-Python-Rock-Snake, 'you will find that new nose of yours very useful to spank people with.'

'Thank you,' said the Elephant's Child, 'I'll remember that; and now I think I'll go home to all my dear families and try.'

So the Elephant's Child went home across Africa frisking and whisking his trunk. When he wanted fruit to eat he pulled fruit down from a tree, instead of waiting for it to fall as he used to do. When he wanted grass he plucked grass up from the ground, instead of going on his knees as he used to do. When the flies bit him he broke off the branch of a tree and used it as a fly-whisk; and he made himself a new, cool, slushy-squshy mud-cap whenever the sun was hot. When he felt lonely walking through Africa he sang to himself down his trunk, and the noise was louder than several brass bands. He went especially out of his way to find a broad Hippopotamus (she was no relation of his), and he spanked her very hard, to make sure that the Bi-Coloured-Python-Rock-Snake had spoken the truth about his new trunk. The rest of the time he picked up the melon rinds that he had dropped on his way to the Limpopo – for he was a Tidy Pachyderm.

One dark evening he came back to all his dear families, and he coiled up his trunk and said, 'How do you do?' They were very glad to see him, and immediately said, 'Come here and be spanked for your 'satiable curtiosity.'

'Pooh,' said the Elephant's Child. 'I don't think you peoples know anything about spanking; but *I* do, and I'll show you.'

Then he uncurled his trunk and knocked two of his dear brothers head over heels.

'O Bananas!' said they, 'where did you learn that trick, and what have you done to your nose?'

'I got a new one from the Crocodile on the banks of the great grey-green, greasy Limpopo River,' said the Elephant's Child. 'I asked him what he had for dinner, and he gave me this to keep.'

'It looks very ugly,' said his hairy uncle, the Baboon.

'It does,' said the Elephant's Child. 'But it's very useful,' and he picked up his hairy uncle, the Baboon, by one hairy leg, and hove him into a hornet's nest.

Then that bad Elephant's Child spanked all his dear families for a long time, till they were very warm and greatly astonished. He pulled out his tall Ostrich aunt's tail-feathers; and he caught his tall uncle, the Giraffe, by the hind leg, and dragged him through a thorn bush; and he shouted at his broad aunt, the Hippopotamus, and blew bubbles into her ear when she was sleeping in the water after meals; but he never let anyone touch Kolokolo Bird.

At last things grew so exciting that his dear families went off one by one in a hurry to the banks of the great grey-green, greasy Limpopo River, all set about with fever trees, to borrow new noses from the Crocodile. When they came back nobody spanked anybody any more; and ever since that day, O Best Beloved, all the Elephants you will ever see, besides all those that you won't, have trunks precisely like the trunk of the 'satiable Elephant's Child.

This is just a picture of the Elephant's Child

going to pull bananas off a banana tree after he had got his fine
new long trunk. I don't think it is a very nice picture; but I couldn't
make it any better, because elephants and bananas are hard to
draw. The streaky things behind the Elephant's Child mean
squoggy marshy country somewhere in Africa. The Elephant's
Child made most of his mud-cakes out of the mud that he found
there. I think it would look better if you painted the banana tree
green and the Elephant's Child red.

I keep six honest serving-men
   (They taught me all I knew);
Their names are What and Why and When
   And How and Where and Who.
I send them over land and sea,
   I send them east and west;
But after they have worked for me,
   I give them all a rest.

I let them rest from nine till five,
   For I am busy then,
As well as breakfast, lunch, and tea,
   For they are hungry men:
But different folk have different views;
   I know a person small –
She keeps ten million serving-men,
   Who get no rest at all!
She sends 'em abroad on her own affairs,
   From the second she opens her eyes –
One million Hows, two million Wheres,
   And seven million Whys!

The Sing-Song of Old Man Kangaroo

NOT ALWAYS WAS THE KANGAROO as now we do behold him, but a Different Animal with four short legs. He was grey and he was woolly, and his pride was inordinate: he danced on an outcrop in the middle of Australia, and he went to the Little God Nqa.

He went to Nqa at six before breakfast, saying, 'Make me different from all other animals by five this afternoon.'

Up jumped Nqa from his seat on the sand-flat and shouted, 'Go away!'

He was grey and he was woolly, and his pride was inordinate; he danced on a rock-ledge in the middle of Australia, and he went to the Middle God Nquing.

He went to Nquing at eight after breakfast, saying, 'Make me different from all other animals; make me, also, wonderfully popular by five this afternoon.'

Up jumped Nquing from his burrow in the spinifex and shouted, 'Go away!'

He was grey and he was woolly, and his pride was inordinate: he danced on a sandbank in the middle of Australia, and he went to the Big God Nqong.

He went to Nqong at ten before dinner-time, saying, 'Make me different from all other animals; make me popular and wonderfully run after by five this afternoon.'

Up jumped Nqong from his bath in the salt-pan and shouted, 'Yes I will!'

Nqong called Dingo – Yellow-Dog Dingo – always hungry, dusty in the sunshine, and showed him Kangaroo. Nqong said, 'Dingo! Wake up, Dingo! Do you see that gentleman dancing on an ashpit? He wants to be popular and very truly run after. Dingo, make him so!'

Up jumped Dingo – Yellow-Dog Dingo – and said, 'What, *that* cat-rabbit?'

Off ran Dingo – Yellow-Dog Dingo – always hungry, grinning like a coal scuttle, ran after Kangaroo.

Off went the proud Kangaroo on his four little legs like a bunny.

This, O Beloved of mine, ends the first part of the tale!

He ran through the desert; he ran through the mountains; he ran through

This is a picture of Old Man Kangaroo

when he was the Different Animal with four short legs. I have drawn him grey and woolly, and you can see that he is very proud because he has a wreath of flowers in his hair. He is dancing on an outcrop (that means a ledge of rock) in the middle of Australia at six o'clock before breakfast. You can see that it is six o'clock, because the sun is just getting up. The thing with the ears and the open mouth is Little God Nqa. Nqa is very much surprised, because he has never seen a Kangaroo dance like that before. Little God Nqa is just saying, 'Go away,' but the Kangaroo is so busy dancing that he has not heard him yet.

The Kangaroo hasn't any real name except Boomer.
He lost it because he was so proud.

the salt-pans; he ran through the reed-beds; he ran through the blue gums; he ran through the spinifex; he ran till his front legs ached.

He had to!

Still ran Dingo – Yellow-Dog Dingo – always hungry, grinning like a rat trap, never getting nearer, never getting farther, ran after Kangaroo.

He had to!

Still ran Kangaroo – Old Man Kangaroo. He ran through the ti trees; he ran through the mulga; he ran through the long grass; he ran through the short grass; he ran through the Tropics of Capricorn and Cancer; he ran till his hind legs ached.

He had to!

Still ran Dingo – Yellow-Dog Dingo – hungrier and hungrier, grinning like a horse-collar, never getting nearer, never getting farther; and they came to the Wollgong River.

Now, there wasn't any bridge, and there wasn't any ferry boat, and Kangaroo didn't know how to get over; so he stood on his legs and hopped.

He had to!

He hopped through the Flinders; he hopped through the Cinders; he hopped through the deserts in the middle of Australia. He hopped like a Kangaroo.

First he hopped one yard; then he hopped three yards; then he hopped five yards; his legs growing stronger; his legs growing longer. He hadn't any time for rest or refreshment, and he wanted them very much.

Still ran Dingo – Yellow-Dog Dingo – very much bewildered, very much hungry, and wondering what in the world or out of it made Old Man Kangaroo hop.

For he hopped like a cricket; like a pea in a saucepan; or a new rubber ball on a nursery floor.

He had to!

He tucked up his front legs; he hopped on his hind legs; he stuck out his tail for a balance-weight behind him; and he hopped through the Darling Downs.

He had to!

Still ran Dingo – Tired-Dog Dingo – hungrier and hungrier, very much bewildered, and wondering when in the world or out of it would Old Man Kangaroo stop.

Then came Nqong from his bath in the salt-pan, and said, 'It's five o'clock.'

Down sat Dingo – Poor-Dog Dingo – always hungry, dusty in the sunshine; hung out his tongue and howled.

Down sat Kangaroo – Old Man Kangaroo – stuck out his tail like a milking-stool behind him, and said, 'Thank goodness *that's* finished!'

Then said Nqong, who is always a gentleman, 'Why aren't you grateful to Yellow-Dog Dingo? Why don't you thank him for all he has done for you?'

This is the picture of Old Man Kangaroo

at five in the afternoon, when he had got his beautiful hind legs just as Big God Nqong had promised. You can see that it is five o'clock, because Big God Nqong's pet tame clock says so. That is Nqong, in his bath, sticking his feet out. Old Man Kangaroo is being rude to Yellow-Dog Dingo. Yellow-Dog Dingo has been trying to catch Kangaroo all across Australia. You can see the marks of Kangaroo's big new feet running ever so far back over the bare hills. Yellow-Dog Dingo is drawn black, because I am not allowed to paint these pictures with real colours out of a paintbox; and besides, Yellow-Dog Dingo got dreadfully black and dusty after running through the Flinders and the Cinders.

I don't know the names of the flowers growing round Nqong's bath. The two little squatty things out in the desert are the other two gods that Old Man Kangaroo spoke to early in the morning. That thing with theletters on it is Old Man Kangaroo's pouch. He had to have a pouch just as he had to have legs.

Then said Kangaroo – Tired Old Kangaroo – 'He's chased me out of the homes of my childhood; he's chased me out of my regular meal-times; he's altered my shape so I'll never get it back; and he's played Old Scratch with my legs.'

Then said Nqong, 'Perhaps I'm mistaken, but didn't you ask me to make you different from all other animals, as well as to make you very truly sought after? And now it is five o'clock.'

'Yes,' said Kangaroo. 'I wish that I hadn't. I thought you would do it by charms and incantations, but this is a practical joke.'

'Joke!' said Nqong, from his bath in the blue gums. 'Say that again and I'll whistle up Dingo and run your hind legs off.'

'No,' said the Kangaroo. 'I must apologise. Legs and legs, and you needn't alter 'em so far as I am concerned. I only meant to explain to Your Lordliness that I've had nothing to eat since morning, and I'm very empty indeed.'

'Yes,' said Dingo – Yellow-Dog Dingo – 'I am just in the same situation. I've made him different from all other animals; but what may I have for my tea?'

Then said Nqong from his bath in the salt-pan, 'Come and ask me about it tomorrow, because I'm going to wash.'

So they were left in the middle of Australia, Old Man Kangaroo and Yellow-Dog Dingo, and each said, 'That's *your* fault.'

This is the mouth-filling song
Of the race that was run by a Boomer,
Run in a single burst – only event of its kind –
Started by Big God Nqong from Warrigaborrigarooma
Old Man Kangaroo first: Yellow-Dog Dingo behind.

Kangaroo bounded away,
His back-legs working like pistons –
Bounded from morning till dark,
Twenty-five feet to a bound.
Yellow-Dog Dingo lay
Like a yellow cloud in the distance –
Much too busy to bark.
My! but they covered the ground!

Nobody knows where they went,
Or followed the track that they flew in,
For that Continent
Hadn't been given a name.
They ran thirty degrees,
From Torres Straits to the Leeuwin
(Look at the Atlas, please),
And they ran back as they came.

S'posing you could trot
From Adelaide to the Pacific,
For an afternoon's run –
Half what these gentlemen did –
You would feel rather hot,
But your legs would develop terrific –
Yes, my importunate son,
You'd be a Marvellous Kid!

The Beginning of the Armadillos

THIS, O BEST BELOVED, is another story of the High and Far-Off Times. In the very middle of those times was a Stickly-Prickly Hedgehog, and he lived on the banks of the turbid Amazon, eating shelly snails and things. And he had a friend, a Slow-Solid Tortoise, who lived on the banks of the turbid Amazon, eating green lettuces and things. And so *that* was all right, Best Beloved. Do you see?

But also, and at the same time, in those High and Far-Off Times, there was a Painted Jaguar, and he lived on the banks of the turbid Amazon too; and he ate everything that he could catch. When he could not catch deer or monkeys he would eat frogs and beetles; and when he could not catch frogs and beetles he went to his Mother Jaguar, and she told him how to eat hedgehogs and tortoises.

She said to him ever so many times, graciously waving her tail, 'My son, when you find a Hedgehog you must drop him into the water and then he will uncoil, and when you catch a Tortoise you must scoop him out of his shell with your paw.' And so that was all right, Best Beloved.

One beautiful night on the banks of the turbid Amazon, Painted Jaguar found Stickly-Prickly Hedgehog and Slow-Solid Tortoise sitting under the trunk of a fallen tree. They could not run away, and so Stickly-Prickly curled himself up into a ball, because he was a Hedgehog, and Slow-Solid Tortoise drew in his head and feet into his shell as far as they would go, because he was a Tortoise; and so *that* was all right, Best Beloved. Do you see?

'Now attend to me,' said Painted Jaguar, 'because this is very important. My mother said that when I meet a Hedgehog I am to drop him into the water and then he will uncoil, and when I meet a Tortoise I am to scoop him out of his shell with my paw. Now which of you is Hedgehog and which is Tortoise? because, to save my spots, I can't tell.'

'Are you sure of what your Mummy told you?' said Stickly-Prickly Hedgehog. 'Are you quite sure? Perhaps she said that when you uncoil a Tortoise you must shell him out of the water with a scoop, and when you paw a Hedgehog you must drop him on the shell.'

'Are you sure of what your Mummy told you?' said Slow-and-Solid Tortoise. 'Are you quite sure? Perhaps she said that when you water a Hedgehog you must drop him into your paw, and when you meet a Tortoise you must shell him till he uncoils.'

'I don't think it was at all like that,' said Painted Jaguar, but he felt a little puzzled; 'but, please, say it again more distinctly.'

'When you scoop water with your paw you uncoil it with a Hedgehog,' said Stickly-Prickly. 'Remember that, because it's important.'

'*But*,' said the Tortoise, 'when you paw your meat you drop it into a Tortoise with a scoop. Why can't you understand?'

'You are making my spots ache,' said Painted Jaguar; 'and besides, I didn't want your advice at all. I only wanted to know which of you is Hedgehog and which is Tortoise.'

'I shan't tell you,' said Stickly-Prickly. 'But you can scoop me out of my shell if you like.'

'Aha!' said Painted Jaguar. 'Now I know you're Tortoise. You thought I wouldn't! Now I will.' Painted Jaguar darted out his paddy-paw just as Stickly-Prickly curled himself up, and of course Jaguar's paddy-paw was just filled with prickles. Worse than that, he knocked Stickly-Prickly away and away into the woods and the bushes, where it was too dark to find him. Then he put his paddy-paw into his mouth, and of course the prickles hurt him worse than ever. As soon as he could speak he said, 'Now I know he isn't Tortoise at all. But' – and then he scratched his head with his un-prickly paw – 'how do I know that this other is Tortoise?'

'But I *am* Tortoise,' said Slow-and-Solid. 'Your mother was quite right. She said that you were to scoop me out of my shell with your paw. Begin.'

'You didn't say she said that a minute ago,' said Painted Jaguar, sucking the prickles out of his paddy-paw. 'You said she said something quite different.'

This is an inciting map

of the Turbid Amazon [originally] done in Red and Black. It hasn't anything to do with the story except that there are two Armadillos in it – up by the top. The inciting part are the adventures that happened to the men who went along the road. I meant to draw Armadillos when I began the map, and I meant to draw manatees and spider-tailed monkeys and big snakes and lots of Jaguars, but it was more inciting to do the map and the venturesome adventures in red. You begin at the bottom left-hand corner and follow the little arrows all about, and then you come quite round again to where the adventuresome people went home in a ship called the *Royal Tiger*. This is a most adventuresome picture, and all the adventuresare told about in writing, so you can be quite sure which is an adventure and which is a tree or a boat.

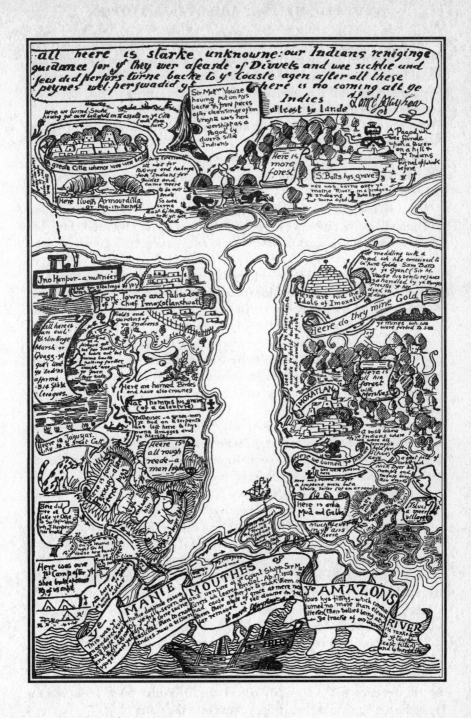

'Well, suppose you say that I said that she said something quite different, I don't see that it makes any difference; because if she said what you said I said she said, it's just the same as if I said what she said she said. On the other hand, if you think she said that you were to uncoil me with a scoop, instead of pawing me into drops with a shell, I can't help that, can I?'

'But you said you wanted to be scooped out of your shell with my paw,' said Painted Jaguar.

'If you'll think again you'll find that I didn't say anything of the kind. I said that your mother said that you were to scoop me out of my shell,' said Slow-and-Solid.

'What will happen if I do?' said the Jaguar most sniffily and most cautious.

'I don't know, because I've never been scooped out of my shell before; but I tell you truly, if you want to see me swim away you've only got to drop me into the water.'

'I don't believe it,' said Painted Jaguar. 'You've mixed up all the things my mother told me to do with the things that you asked me whether I was sure that she didn't say, till I don't know whether I'm on my head or my painted tail; and now you come and tell me something I *can* understand, and it makes me more mixy than before. My mother told me that I was to drop one of you two into the water, and as you seem so anxious to be dropped I think you don't want to be dropped. So jump into the turbid Amazon and be quick about it.'

'I warn you that your Mummy won't be pleased. Don't tell her I didn't tell you,' said Slow-Solid.

'If you say another word about what my mother said – ' the Jaguar answered, but he had not finished the sentence before Slow-and-Solid quietly dived into the turbid Amazon, swam under water for a long way, and came out on the bank where Stickly-Prickly was waiting for him.

'That was a very narrow escape,' said Stickly-Prickly. 'I don't like Painted Jaguar. What did you tell him that you were?'

'I told him truthfully that I was a truthful Tortoise, but he wouldn't believe it, and he made me jump into the river to see if I was, and I was, and he is surprised. Now he's gone to tell his Mummy. Listen to him!'

They could hear Painted Jaguar roaring up and down among the trees and the bushes by the side of the turbid Amazon, till his Mummy came.

'Son, son!' said his mother ever so many times, graciously waving her tail, 'what have you been doing that you shouldn't have done?'

'I tried to scoop something that said it wanted to be scooped out of its shell with my paw, and my paw is full of per-ickles,' said Painted Jaguar.

'Son, son!' said his mother ever so many times, graciously waving her tail, 'by the prickles in your paddy-paw I see that that must have been a Hedgehog. You should have dropped him into the water.'

'I did that to the other thing; and he said he was a Tortoise, and I didn't believe him, and it was quite true, and he has dived under the turbid Amazon, and he won't come up again, and I haven't anything at all to eat, and I think we had better find lodgings somewhere else. They are too clever on the turbid Amazon for poor me!'

'Son, son!' said his mother ever so many times, graciously waving her tail, 'now attend to me and remember what I say. A Hedgehog curls himself up into a ball and his prickles stick out every which way at once. By this you may know the Hedgehog.'

'I don't like this old lady one little bit,' said Stickly-Prickly, under the shadow of a large leaf. 'I wonder what else she knows?'

'A Tortoise can't curl himself up,' Mother Jaguar went on, ever so many times, graciously waving her tail. 'He only draws his head and legs into his shell. By this you may know the Tortoise.'

'I don't like this old lady at all – at all,' said Slow-and-Solid Tortoise. 'Even Painted Jaguar can't forget those directions. It's a great pity that you can't swim, Stickly-Prickly.'

'Don't talk to me,' said Stickly-Prickly. 'Just think how much better it would be if you could curl up. This *is* a mess! Listen to Painted Jaguar.'

Painted Jaguar was sitting on the banks of the turbid Amazon sucking prickles out of his paw and saying to himself –

> 'Can't curl, but can swim –
> Slow-Solid, that's him!
> Curls up, but can't swim –
> Stickly-Prickly, that's him!'

'He'll never forget that this month of Sundays,' said Stickly-Prickly. 'Hold up my chin, Slow-and-Solid. I'm going to try to learn to swim. It may be useful.'

'Excellent!' said Slow-and-Solid; and he held up Stickly-Prickly's chin, while Stickly-Prickly kicked in the waters of the turbid Amazon.

'You'll make a fine swimmer yet,' said Slow-and-Solid. 'Now, if you can unlace my back-plates a little, I'll see what I can do towards curling up. It may be useful.'

Stickly-Prickly helped to unlace Tortoise's back-plates, so that by twisting and straining Slow-and-Solid actually managed to curl up a tiddy wee bit.

'Excellent!' said Stickly-Prickly; 'but I shouldn't do any more just now. It's making you black in the face. Kindly lead me into the water once again and I'll practise that side-stroke which you say is so easy.' And so Stickly-Prickly practised, and Slow-Solid swam alongside.

'Excellent!' said Slow-and-Solid. 'A little more practice will make you a regular whale. Now, if I may trouble you to unlace my back and front plates two holes more, I'll try that fascinating bend that you say is so easy. Won't Painted Jaguar be surprised!'

'Excellent!' said Stickly-Prickly, all wet from the turbid Amazon. 'I declare, I shouldn't know you from one of my own family. Two holes, I think, you said? A little more expression, please, and don't grunt quite so much, or

Painted Jaguar may hear us. When you've finished, I want to try that long dive which you say is so easy. Won't Painted Jaguar be surprised!'

And so Stickly-Prickly dived, and Slow-and-Solid dived alongside.

'Excellent!' said Slow-and-Solid. 'A leetle more attention to holding your breath and you will be able to keep house at the bottom of the turbid Amazon. Now I'll try that exercise of wrapping my hind legs round my ears which you say is so peculiarly comfortable. Won't Painted Jaguar be surprised!'

'Excellent!' said Stickly-Prickly. 'But it's straining your back-plates a little. They are all overlapping now, instead of lying side by side.'

'Oh, that's the result of exercise,' said Slow-and-Solid. 'I've noticed that your prickles seem to be melting into one another, and that you're growing to look rather more like a pine-cone, and less like a chestnut-burr, than you used to.'

'Am I?' said Stickly-Prickly. 'That comes from my soaking in the water. Oh, won't Painted Jaguar be surprised!'

They went on with their exercises, each helping the other, till morning came; and when the sun was high they rested and dried themselves. Then they saw that they were both of them quite different from what they had been.

This is a picture of the whole story

of the Jaguar and the Hedgehog and the Tortoise *and* the Armadillo all in a heap. It looks rather the same any way you turn it. The Tortoise is in the middle, learning how to bend, and that is why the shelly plates on his back are so spread apart. He is standing on the Hedgehog, who is waiting to learn how to swim. The Hedgehog is a Japanesy Hedgehog, because I couldn't find our own Hedgehogs in the garden when I wanted to draw them. (It was daytime, and they had gone to bed under the dahlias.) Painted Jaguar is looking over the edge, with his paddy-paw carefully tied up by his mother, because he pricked himself scooping the Hedgehog. He is much surprised to see what the Tortoise is doing, and his paw is hurting him. The snouty thing with the little eye that Painted Jaguar is trying to climb over is the Armadillo that the Tortoise and the Hedgehog are going to turn into when they have finished bending and swimming. It is all a magic picture, and that is one of the reasons why I haven't drawn the Jaguar's whiskers. The other reason was that he was so young that his whiskers had not grown. The Jaguar's pet name with his Mummy was Doffles.

'Stickly-Prickly,' said Tortoise after breakfast, 'I am not what I was yesterday; but I think that I may yet amuse Painted Jaguar.'

'That was the very thing I was thinking just now,' said Stickly-Prickly. 'I think scales are a tremendous improvement on prickles – to say nothing of being able to swim. Oh, *won't* Painted Jaguar be surprised! Let's go and find him.'

By and by they found Painted Jaguar, still nursing his paddy-paw that had been hurt the night before. He was so astonished that he fell three times backward over his own painted tail without stopping.

'Good-morning!' said Stickly-Prickly. 'And how is your dear gracious Mummy this morning?'

'She is quite well, thank you,' said Painted Jaguar; 'but you must forgive me if I do not at this precise moment recall your name.'

'That's unkind of you,' said Stickly-Prickly, 'seeing that this time yesterday you tried to scoop me out of my shell with your paw.'

'But, you hadn't any shell. It was all prickles,' said Painted Jaguar. 'I know it was. Just look at my paw!'

'You told me to drop into the turbid Amazon and be drowned,' said Slow-Solid. 'Why are you so rude and forgetful today?'

'Don't you remember what your mother told you?' said Stickly-Prickly:

> 'Can't curl, but can swim –
> Stickly-Prickly, that's him!
> Curls up, but can't swim –
> Slow-Solid, that's him!'

Then they both curled themselves up and rolled round and round Painted Jaguar till his eyes turned truly cartwheels in his head.

Then he went to fetch his mother.

'Mother,' he said, 'there are two new animals in the woods today, and the one that you said couldn't swim, swims, and the one that you said couldn't curl up, curls; and they've gone shares in their prickles, I think, because both of them are scaly all over, instead of one being smooth and the other very prickly; and, besides that, they are rolling round and round in circles, and I don't feel comfy.'

'Son, son!' said Mother Jaguar ever so many times, graciously waving her tail, 'a Hedgehog is a Hedgehog, and can't be anything but a Hedgehog; and a Tortoise is a Tortoise, and can never be anything else.'

'But it isn't a Hedgehog, and it isn't a Tortoise. It's a little bit of both, and I don't know its proper name.'

'Nonsense!' said Mother Jaguar. 'Everything has its proper name. I should call it "Armadillo" till I found out the real one. And I should leave it alone.'

So Painted Jaguar did as he was told, especially about leaving them alone; but the curious thing is that from that day to this, O Best Beloved, no one on the banks of the turbid Amazon has ever called Stickly-Prickly and Slow-Solid anything except Armadillo. There are Hedgehogs and Tortoises in other places, of course (there are some in my garden); but the real old and clever kind, with their scales lying lippety-lappety one over the other, like pine-cone scales, that lived on the banks of the turbid Amazon in the High and Far-Off Days, are always called Armadillos, because they were so clever.

So *that's* all right, Best Beloved. Do you see?

I've never sailed the Amazon,
  I've never reached Brazil;
But the *Don* and *Magdalena*,
  They can go there when they will!

          Yes, weekly from Southampton,
          Great steamers, white and gold,
          Go rolling down to Rio
          (Roll down – roll down to Rio!)
          And I'd like to roll to Rio
          Someday before I'm old!

I've never seen a Jaguar,
  Nor yet an Armadill –
O dilloing in his armour,
  And I s'pose I never will,

          Unless I go to Rio
          These wonders to behold –
          Roll down – roll down to Rio –
          Roll really down to Rio!
          Oh, I'd love to roll to Rio
          Someday before I'm old!

How the First Letter was Written

ONCE UPON A MOST EARLY TIME was a Neolithic man. He was not a Jute or an Angle, or even a Dravidian, which he might well have been, Best Beloved, but never mind why. He was a Primitive, and he lived cavily in a Cave, and he wore very few clothes, and he couldn't read and he couldn't write and he didn't want to, and except when he was hungry he was quite happy. His name was Tegumai Bopsulai, and that means, 'Man-who-does-not-put-his-foot-forward-in-a-hurry'; but we, O Best Beloved, will call him Tegumai, for short. And his wife's name was Teshumai Tewindrow, and that means, 'Lady-who-asks-a-very-many-questions'; but we, O Best Beloved, will call her Teshumai, for short. And his little girl-daughter's name was Taffimai Metallumai, and that means, 'Small-person-without-any-manners-who-ought-to-be-spanked'; but I'm going to call her Taffy. And she was Tegumai Bopsulai's Best Beloved and her own Mummy's Best Beloved, and she was not spanked half as much as was good for her; and they were all three very happy. As soon as Taffy could run about she went everywhere with her Daddy Tegumai, and sometimes they would not come home to the Cave till they were hungry, and then Teshumai Tewindrow would say, 'Where in the world have you two been to, to get so shocking dirty? Really, my Tegumai, you're no better than my Taffy.'

Now attend and listen!

One day Tegumai Bopsulai went down through the beaver-swamp to the Wagai river to spear carp-fish for dinner, and Taffy went too. Tegumai's spear was made of wood with shark's teeth at the end, and before he had caught any fish at all he accidentally broke it clean across by jabbing it down too hard on the bottom of the river. They were miles and miles from home (of course they had their lunch with them in a little bag), and Tegumai had forgotten to bring any extra spears.

'Here's a pretty kettle of fish!' said Tegumai. 'It will take me half the day to mend this.'

'There's your big black spear at home,' said Taffy. 'Let me run back to the Cave and ask Mummy to give it me.'

'It's too far for your little fat legs,' said Tegumai. 'Besides, you might fall

into the beaver-swamp and be drowned. We must make the best of a bad job.'
He sat down and took out a little leather mendy-bag, full of reindeer-sinews
and strips of leather, and lumps of beeswax and resin, and began to mend the
spear. Taffy sat down too, with her toes in the water and her chin in her hand,
and thought very hard. Then she said: 'I say, Daddy, it's an awful nuisance
that you and I don't know how to write, isn't it? If we did we could send a
message for the new spear.'

'Taffy,' said Tegumai, 'how often have I told you not to use slang? "Awful"
isn't a pretty word, but it *would* be a convenience, now you mention it, if we
could write home.'

Just then a Stranger-man came along the river, but he belonged to a far
tribe, the Tewaras, and he did not understand one word of Tegumai's
language. He stood on the bank and smiled at Taffy, because he had a little
girl-daughter of his own at home. Tegumai drew a hank of deer-sinews from
his mendy-bag and began to mend his spear.

'Come here,' said Taffy. 'Do you know where my Mummy lives?' And the
Stranger-man said 'Um!' – being, as you know, a Tewara.

'Silly!' said Taffy, and she stamped her foot, because she saw a shoal of very
big carp going up the river just when her Daddy couldn't use his spear.

'Don't bother grown-ups,' said Tegumai, so busy with his spear-mending
that he did not turn round.

'I aren't,' said Taffy. 'I only want him to do what I want him to do, and he
won't understand.'

'Then don't bother me,' said Tegumai, and he went on pulling and
straining at the deer sinews with his mouth full of loose ends. The Stranger-
man – a genuine Tewara he was – sat down on the grass, and Taffy showed
him what her Daddy was doing. The Stranger-man thought, 'This is a very
wonderful child. She stamps her foot at me and she makes faces. She must be
the daughter of that noble Chief who is so great that he won't take any notice
of me.' So he smiled more politely than ever.

'Now,' said Taffy, 'I want you to go to my Mummy, because your legs are
longer than mine, and you won't fall into the beaver-swamp, and ask for
Daddy's other spear – the one with the black handle that hangs over our
fireplace.'

The Stranger-man (*and* he was a Tewara) thought, 'This is a very, very
wonderful child. She waves her arms and she shouts at me, but I don't
understand a word of what she says. But if I don't do what she wants, I greatly
fear that that haughty Chief, Man-who-turns-his-back-on-callers, will be
angry.' He got up and twisted a big flat piece of bark off a birch tree and gave
it to Taffy. He did this, Best Beloved, to show that his heart was as white as
the birch-bark and that he meant no harm; but Taffy didn't quite understand.

'Oh!' said she. 'Now I see! You want my Mummy's living-address? Of
course I can't write, but I can draw pictures if I've anything sharp to scratch
with. Please lend me the shark's tooth off your necklace.'

The Stranger-man (and *he* was a Tewara) didn't say anything, so Taffy put up her little hand and pulled at the beautiful bead and seed and shark-tooth necklace round his neck.

The Stranger-man (and he *was* a Tewara) thought, 'This is a very, very wonderful child. The shark's tooth on my necklace is a magic shark's tooth, and I was always told that if anybody touched it without my leave they would immediately swell up or burst. But this child doesn't swell up or burst, and that important Chief, Man-who-attends-strictly-to-his-business, who has not yet taken any notice of me at all, doesn't seem to be afraid that she will swell up or burst. I had better be more polite.'

So he gave Taffy the shark's tooth, and she lay down flat on her tummy with her legs in the air, like some people on the drawing-room floor when they want to draw pictures, and she said, 'Now I'll draw you some beautiful pictures! You can look over my shoulder, but you mustn't joggle. First I'll draw Daddy fishing. It isn't very like him; but Mummy will know, because I've drawn his spear all broken. Well, now I'll draw the other spear that he wants, the black-handled spear. It looks as if it was sticking in Daddy's back, but that's because the shark's tooth slipped and this piece of bark isn't big enough. That's the spear I want you to fetch; so I'll draw a picture of me myself 'splaining to you. My hair doesn't stand up like I've drawn, but it's easier to draw that way. Now I'll draw you. *I* think you're very nice really, but I can't make you pretty in the picture, so you mustn't be 'fended. Are you 'fended?'

The Stranger-man (and he was *a* Tewara) smiled. He thought, 'There must be a big battle going to be fought somewhere, and this extraordinary child, who takes my magic shark's tooth but who does not swell up or burst, is telling me to call all the great Chief's tribe to help him. He *is* a great Chief, or he would have noticed me.'

'Look,' said Taffy, drawing very hard and rather scratchily, 'now I've drawn you, and I've put the spear that Daddy wants into your hand, just to remind you that you're to bring it. Now I'll show you how to find my Mummy's living-address. You go along till you come to two trees (those are trees), and then you go over a hill (that's a hill), and then you come into a beaver-swamp all full of beavers. I haven't put in all the beavers, because I can't draw beavers, but I've drawn their heads, and that's all you'll see of them when you cross the swamp. Mind you don't fall in! Then our Cave is just beyond the beaver-swamp. It isn't as high as the hills really, but I can't draw things very small. That's my Mummy outside. She is beautiful. She is the most beautifullest Mummy there ever was, but she won't be 'fended when she sees I've drawn her so plain. She'll be pleased of me because I can draw. Now, in case you forget, I've drawn the spear that Daddy wants *outside* our Cave. It's *inside* really, but you show the picture to my Mummy and she'll give it you. I've made her holding up her hands, because I know she'll be so pleased to see you. Isn't it a beautiful picture? And do you quite understand, or shall I 'splain again?'

The Stranger-man (and he was a *Tewara*) looked at the picture and nodded very hard. He said to himself, 'If I do not fetch this great Chief's tribe to help him, he will be slain by his enemies who are coming up on all sides with spears. Now I see why the great Chief pretended not to notice me! He feared that his enemies were hiding in the bushes and would see him deliver a message to me. Therefore he turned his back, and let the wise and wonderful child draw the terrible picture showing me his difficulties. I will away and get help for him from his tribe.' He did not even ask Taffy the road, but raced off into the bushes like the wind, with the birch-bark in his hand, and Taffy sat down most pleased.

Now this is the picture that Taffy had drawn for him!

'What have you been doing, Taffy?' said Tegumai. He had mended his spear and was carefully waving it to and fro.

'It's a little berangement of my own, Daddy dear,' said Taffy. 'If you won't ask me questions, you'll know all about it in a little time, and you'll be surprised. You don't know how surprised you'll be, Daddy! Promise you'll be surprised.'

'Very well,' said Tegumai, and went on fishing.

The Stranger-man – did you know he was a Tewara? – hurried away with the picture and ran for some miles, till quite by accident he found Teshumai Tewindrow at the door of her Cave, talking to some other Neolithic ladies who had come in to a Primitive lunch. Taffy was very like Teshumai, specially about the upper part of the face and the eyes, so the Stranger-man – always a pure Tewara – smiled politely and handed Teshumai the birch-bark. He had run hard, so that he panted, and his legs were scratched with brambles, but he still tried to be polite.

As soon as Teshumai saw the picture she screamed like anything and flew

This is the story of Taffimai Metallumai

carved on an old tusk a very long time ago by the Ancient Peoples. If you read my story, or have it read to you, you can see how it is all told out on the tusk. The tusk was part of an old tribal trumpet that belonged to the Tribe of Tegumai. The pictures were scratched on it with a nail or something, and then the scratches were filled up with black wax, but all the dividing lines and the five little rounds at the bottom were filled with red wax. When it was new there was a sort of network of beads and shells and precious stones at one end of it; but now that has been broken and lost – all except the little bit that you see. The letters round the tusk are magic – Runic magic – and if you can read them you will find out something rather new. The tusk is of ivory – very yellow and scratched. It is two feet long and two feet round, and weighs eleven pounds nine ounces.

at the Stranger-man. The other Neolithic ladies at once knocked him down and sat on him in a long line of six, while Teshumai pulled his hair. 'It's as plain as the nose on this Stranger-man's face,' she said. 'He has stuck my Tegumai all full of spears, and frightened poor Taffy so that her hair stands all on end; and not content with that, he brings me a horrid picture of how it was done. Look!' She showed the picture to all the Neolithic ladies sitting patiently on the Stranger-man. 'Here is my Tegumai with his arm broken; here is a spear sticking into his back; here is a man with a spear ready to throw; here is another man throwing a spear from a Cave, and here are a whole pack of people' (they were Taffy's beavers really, but they did look rather like people) 'coming up behind Tegumai. Isn't it shocking!'

'Most shocking!' said the Neolithic ladies, and they filled the Stranger-man's hair with mud (at which he was surprised), and they beat upon the Reverberating Tribal Drums, and called together all the chiefs of the Tribe of Tegumai, with their Hetmans and Dolmans, all Neguses, Woons, and Akhoonds of the organisation, in addition to the Warlocks, Angekoks, Juju-men, Bonzes, and the rest, who decided that before they chopped the Stranger-man's head off he should instantly lead them down to the river and show them where he had hidden poor Taffy.

By this time the Stranger-man (in spite of being a Tewara) was really annoyed. They had filled his hair quite solid with mud; they had rolled him up and down on knobby pebbles; they had sat upon him in a long line of six; they had thumped him and bumped him till he could hardly breathe; and though he did not understand their language, he was almost sure that the names the Neolithic ladies called him were not ladylike. However, he said nothing till all the Tribe of Tegumai were assembled, and then he led them back to the bank of the Wagai river, and there they found Taffy making daisy-chains, and Tegumai carefully spearing small carp with his mended spear.

'Well, you *have* been quick!' said Taffy. 'But why did you bring so many people? Daddy dear, this is my surprise. *Are* you surprised, Daddy?'

'Very,' said Tegumai; 'but it has ruined all my fishing for the day. Why, the whole dear, kind, nice, clean, quiet Tribe is here, Taffy.'

And so they were. First of all walked Teshumai Tewindrow and the Neolithic ladies, tightly holding on to the Stranger-man, whose hair was full of mud (although he was a Tewara). Behind them came the Head Chief, the Vice-Chief, the Deputy and Assistant Chiefs (all armed to the upper teeth), the Hetmans and Heads of Hundreds, Platoffs with their Platoons, and Dolmans with their Detachments; Woons, Neguses, and Akhoonds ranking in the rear (still armed to the teeth). Behind them was the Tribe in hierarchical order, from owners of four caves (one for each season), a private reindeer-run, and two salmon-leaps, to feudal and prognathous Villeins, semi- entitled to half a bearskin of winter nights, seven yards from the fire, and adscript serfs, holding the reversion of a scraped marrowbone under heriot. (Aren't those beautiful words, Best Beloved?) They were all there, prancing and shouting, and they frightened every fish for twenty miles, and Tegumai thanked them in a fluid Neolithic oration.

Then Teshumai Tewindrow ran down and kissed and hugged Taffy very much indeed; but the Head Chief of the Tribe of Tegumai took Tegumai by the topknot feathers and shook him severely.

'Explain! Explain! Explain!' cried all the Tribe of Tegumai.

'Goodness' sakes alive!' said Tegumai. 'Let go of my topknot. Can't a man break his carp-spear without the whole countryside descending on him? You're a very interfering people.'

'I don't believe you've brought my Daddy's black-handled spear after all,' said Taffy. 'And what *are* you doing to my nice Stranger-man?'

They were thumping him by twos and threes and tens till his eyes turned round and round. He could only gasp and point at Taffy.

'Where are the bad people who speared you, my darling?' said Teshumai Tewindrow.

'There weren't any,' said Tegumai. 'My only visitor this morning was the poor fellow that you are trying to choke. Aren't you well, or are you ill, O Tribe of Tegumai?'

'He came with a horrible picture,' said the Head Chief, 'a picture that showed you were full of spears.'

'Er – um – P'raps I'd better 'splain that I gave him that picture,' said Taffy, but she did not feel quite comfy.

'You!' said the Tribe of Tegumai all together. 'Small-person-with-no-manners-who-ought-to-be-spanked! You?'

'Taffy dear, I'm afraid we're in for a little trouble,' said her Daddy, and put his arm round her, so she didn't care.

'Explain! Explain! Explain!' said the Head Chief of the Tribe of Tegumai, and he hopped on one foot.

'I wanted the Stranger-man to fetch Daddy's spear, so I drawded it,' said Taffy. 'There wasn't lots of spears. There was only one spear. I drawded it three times to make sure. I couldn't help it looking as if it stuck into Daddy's head – there wasn't room on the birch-bark; and those things that Mummy called bad people are my beavers. I drawded them to show him the way through the swamp; and I drawded Mummy at the mouth of the Cave looking pleased because he is a nice Stranger-man, and *I* think you are just the stupidest people in the world,' said Taffy. 'He is a very nice man. Why have you filled his hair with mud? Wash him!'

Nobody said anything at all for a long time, till the Head Chief laughed; then the Stranger-man (who was at least a Tewara) laughed; then Tegumai laughed till he fell down flat on the bank; then all the Tribe laughed more and worse and louder. The only people who did not laugh were Teshumai Tewindrow and all the Neolithic ladies. They were very polite to all their husbands, and said 'idiot!' ever so often.

Then the Head Chief of the Tribe of Tegumai cried and said and sang, 'O

Small-person-without-any-manners-who-ought-to-be-spanked, you've hit upon a great invention!'

'I didn't intend to; I only wanted Daddy's black-handled spear,' said Taffy.

'Never mind. It *is* a great invention, and someday men will call it writing. At present it is only pictures, and, as we have seen today, pictures are not always properly understood. But a time will come, O Babe of Tegumai, when we shall make letters – all twenty-six of 'em – and when we shall be able to read as well as to write, and then we shall always say exactly what we mean without any mistakes. Let the Neolithic ladies wash the mud out of the stranger's hair!'

'I shall be glad of that,' said Taffy, 'because, after all, though you've brought every single other spear in the Tribe of Tegumai, you've forgotten my Daddy's black-handled spear.'

Then the Head Chief cried and said and sang, 'Taffy dear, the next time you write a picture-letter, you'd better send a man who can talk our language with it, to explain what it means. I don't mind it myself, because I am a Head Chief, but it's very bad for the rest of the Tribe of Tegumai, and, as you can see, it surprises the stranger.'

Then they adopted the Stranger-man (a genuine Tewara of Tewar) into the Tribe of Tegumai, because he was a gentleman and did not make a fuss about the mud that the Neolithic ladies had put into his hair. But from that day to this (and I suppose it is all Taffy's fault), very few little girls have ever liked learning to read or write. Most of them prefer to draw pictures and play about with their Daddies – just like Taffy.

There runs a road by Merrow Down –
    A grassy track today it is –
An hour out of Guildford town,
    Above the river Wey it is.

Here, when they heard the horse-bells ring,
    The ancient Britons dressed and rode
To watch the dark Phoenicians bring
    Their goods along the Western Road.

And here, or hereabouts, they met
    To hold their racial talks and such –
To barter beads for Whitby jet,
    And tin for gay shell torques and such.

But long and long before that time
    (When bison used to roam on it)
Did Taffy and her Daddy climb
    That down, and had their home on it.

Then beavers built in Broadstonebrook
    And made a swamp where Bramley stands;
And bears from Shere would come and look
    For Taffimai where Shamley stands.

The Wey, that Taffy called Wagai,
    Was more than six times bigger then;
And all the Tribe of Tegumai
    They cut a noble figure then!

How the Alphabet was Made

THE WEEK AFTER TAFFIMAI METALLUMAI (we will still call her Taffy, Best Beloved) made that little mistake about her Daddy's spear and the Stranger- man and the picture-letter and all, she went carp-fishing again with her Daddy. Her Mummy wanted her to stay at home and help hang up hides to dry on the big drying-poles outside their Neolithic Cave, but Taffy slipped away down to her Daddy quite early, and they fished. Presently she began to giggle, and her Daddy said, 'Don't be silly, child.'

'But wasn't it inciting!' said Taffy. 'Don't you remember how the Head Chief puffed out his cheeks, and how funny the nice Stranger-man looked with the mud in his hair?'

'Well do I,' said Tegumai. 'I had to pay two deer skins – soft ones with fringes – to the Stranger-man for the things we did to him.'

'*We* didn't do anything,' said Taffy. 'It was Mummy and the other Neolithic ladies – and the mud.'

'We won't talk about that,' said her Daddy. 'Let's have lunch.'

Taffy took a marrowbone and sat mousy-quiet for ten whole minutes, while her Daddy scratched on pieces of birch-bark with a shark's tooth. Then she said, 'Daddy, I've thinked of a secret surprise. You make a noise – any sort of noise.'

'Ah!' said Tegumai. 'Will that do to begin with?'

'Yes,' said Taffy. 'You look just like a carp-fish with its mouth open. Say it again, please.'

'Ah! ah! ah!' said her Daddy. 'Don't be rude, my daughter.'

'I'm not meaning rude, really and truly,' said Taffy. 'It's part of my secret-surprise-think. *Do* say *ah*, Daddy, and keep your mouth open at the end, and lend me that tooth. I'm going to draw a carp-fish's mouth wide-open.'

'What for?' said her Daddy.

'Don't you see?' said Taffy, scratching away on the bark. 'That will be our little secret s'prise. When I draw a carp-fish with his mouth open in the smoke at the back of our Cave – if Mummy doesn't mind – it will remind you of that ah-noise. Then we can play that it was me jumped out of the dark and s'prised you with that noise – same as I did in the beaver-swamp last winter.'

'Really?' said her Daddy, in the voice that grown-ups use when they are truly attending. 'Go on, Taffy.'

'Oh bother!' she said. 'I can't draw all of a carp-fish, but I can draw something that means a carp-fish's mouth. Don't you know how they stand on their heads rooting in the mud? Well, here's a pretence carp-fish (we can play that the rest of him is drawn). Here's just his mouth, and that means *ah*.' And she drew this. (1)

(1)

'That's not bad,' said Tegumai, and scratched on his own piece of bark for himself; 'but you've forgotten the feeler that hangs across his mouth.'

'But I can't draw, Daddy.'

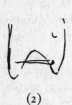

(2)

'You needn't draw anything of him except just the opening of his mouth and the feeler across. Then we'll know he's a carp-fish, 'cause the perches and trouts haven't got feelers. Look here, Taffy.' And he drew this. (2)

'Now I'll copy it,' said Taffy. 'Will you understand *this* when you see it?' And she drew this. (3)

'Perfectly,' said her Daddy. 'And I'll be quite as s'prised when I see it anywhere, as if you had jumped out from behind a tree and said "Ah!" '

(3)

'Now, make another noise,' said Taffy, very proud.

'Yah!' said her Daddy, very loud.

'H'm,' said Taffy. 'That's a mixy noise. The end part is *ah*-carp-fish-mouth; but what can we do about the front part? *Yer-yer-yer* and *ah! Ya!*'

'It's very like the carp-fish-mouth noise. Let's draw another bit of the carp-fish and join 'em,' said her Daddy. *He* was quite incited too.

'No. If they're joined, I'll forget. Draw it separate. Draw his tail. If he's standing on his head the tail will come first. 'Sides, I think I can draw tails easiest,' said Taffy.

(4)

'A good notion,' said Tegumai. 'Here's a carp-fish tail for the *yer*-noise.' And he drew this. (4)

'I'll try now,' said Taffy. ' 'Member I can't draw like you, Daddy. Will it do if I just draw the split part of the tail, and a sticky-down line for where it joins?' And she drew this. (5)

(5)

Her Daddy nodded, and his eyes were shiny bright with 'citement.

'That's beautiful,' she said.

'Now, make another noise, Daddy.'

(6)

'Oh!' said her Daddy, very loud.

'That's quite easy,' said Taffy. 'You make your mouth all round like an egg or a stone. So an egg or a stone will do for that.'

'You can't always find eggs or stones. We'll have to scratch a round something like one.' And he drew this. (6)

'My gracious!' said Taffy, 'what a lot of noise-pictures we've made – carp-mouth, carp-tail and egg! Now, make another noise, Daddy.'

'Ssh!' said her Daddy, and frowned to himself, but Taffy was too incited to notice.

'That's quite easy,' she said, scratching on the bark.

'Eh, what?' said her Daddy. 'I meant I was thinking, and didn't want to be disturbed.'

'It's a noise, just the same. It's the noise a snake makes, Daddy, when it is thinking and doesn't want to be disturbed. Let's make the *ssh*-noise a snake. Will this do?' And she drew this. (7)

'There,' she said. 'That's another s'prise-secret. When you draw a hissy-snake by the door of your little back-cave where you mend the spears, I'll know you're thinking hard; and I'll come in most mousy-quiet. And if you draw it on a tree by the river when you're fishing, I'll know you want me to walk most *most* mousy-quiet, so as not to shake the banks.'

(7)

'Perfectly true,' said Tegumai. 'And there's more in this game than you think. Taffy, dear, I've a notion that your Daddy's daughter has hit upon the finest thing that there ever was since the Tribe of Tegumai took to using shark's teeth instead of flints for their spearheads. I believe we've found out *the* big secret of the world.'

'Why?' said Taffy, and her eyes shone too with incitement.

'I'll show,' said her Daddy. 'What's water in the Tegumai language?'

'*Ya*, of course, and it means river too – like Wagai-*ya* – the Wagai river.'

'What is bad water that gives you fever if you drink it – black water – swamp-water?'   (8)

'*Yo*, of course.'

'Now look,' said her Daddy. 'S'pose you saw this scratched by the side of a pool in the beaver-swamp?' And he drew this. (8)

'Carp-tail and round egg. Two noises mixed! *Yo*, bad water,' said Taffy. ' 'Course I wouldn't drink that water because I'd know you said it was bad.'

'But I needn't be near the water at all. I might be miles away, hunting, and still – '

'And *still* it would be just the same as if you stood there and said, "G'way, Taffy, or you'll get fever." All that in a carp-fish-tail and a round egg! O Daddy, we must tell Mummy, quick!' and Taffy danced all round him.

'Not yet,' said Tegumai; 'not till we've gone a little further. Let's see. *Yo* is bad water, but *so* is food cooked on the fire, isn't it?' And he drew this. (9)

'Yes. Snake and egg,' said Taffy. 'So that means dinner's ready. If you saw that scratched on a tree you'd know it was time to come to the Cave. So'd I.'

(9)

'My Winkie!' said Tegumai. 'That's true too. But wait a minute. I see a difficulty. *So* means "come and have dinner", but *sho* means the drying-poles where we hang our hides.'

'Horrid old drying-poles!' said Taffy. 'I hate helping to hang heavy, hot, hairy hides on them. If you drew the snake and egg, and I thought it meant dinner, and I came in from the wood and found that it meant I was to help Mummy hang the hides on the drying-poles, what *would* I do?'

'You'd be cross. So'd Mummy. We must make a new picture for *sho*. We must draw a spotty snake that hisses *sh-sh*, and we'll play that the plain snake only hisses *ssss*.'

'I couldn't be sure how to put in the spots,' said Taffy. 'And p'raps if *you* were in a hurry you might leave them out, and I'd think it was *so* when it was *sho*, and then Mummy would catch me just the same. *No!* I think we'd better draw a picture of the horrid high drying-poles their very selves, and make *quite* sure. I'll put 'em in just after the hissy-snake. Look!' And she drew this. (10)

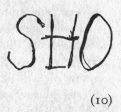

(10)

'P'raps that's safest. It's very like our drying-poles, anyhow,' said her Daddy, laughing. 'Now I'll make a new noise with a snake and drying-pole sound in it. I'll say *shi*. That's Tegumai for spear, Taffy.' And he laughed.

'Don't make fun of me,' said Taffy, as she thought of her picture-letter and the mud in the Stranger-man's hair. '*You* draw it, Daddy.'

'We won't have beavers or hills this time, eh?' said her Daddy. 'I'll just draw a straight line for my spear.' And he drew this. (11)

(11)

'Even Mummy couldn't mistake that for me being killed.'

'*Please* don't, Daddy. It makes me uncomfy. Do some more noises. We're getting on beautifully.'

'Er-hm!' said Tegumai, looking up. 'We'll say *shu*. That means sky.'

Taffy drew the snake and the drying-pole. Then she stopped. 'We must make a new picture for that end sound, mustn't we?'

'*Shu-shu-u-u-u!*' said her Daddy. 'Why, it's just like the round-egg-sound made thin.'

'Then s'pose we draw a thin round egg, and pretend it's a frog that hasn't eaten anything for years.'

(12)

'N-no,' said her Daddy. 'If we drew that in a hurry we might mistake it for the round egg itself. *Shu-shu-shu! I'll* tell you what we'll do. We'll open a little hole at the end of the round egg to show how the O-noise runs out all thin, *ooo–oo–oo*. Like this.' And he drew this. (12)

'Oh, that's lovely! Much better than a thin frog. Go on,' said Taffy, using her shark's tooth.

Her Daddy went on drawing, and his hand shook with incitement. He went on till he had drawn this. (13)

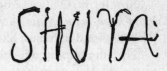

(13)

'Don't look up, Taffy,' he said. 'Try if you can make out what that means in the Tegumai language. If you can, we've found the Secret.'

'Snake – pole – broken-egg – carp-tail and carp-mouth,' said Taffy. '*Shu-ya.* Sky-water (rain).' Just then a drop fell on her hand, for the day had clouded over. 'Why, Daddy, it's raining. Was *that* what you meant to tell me?'

'Of course,' said her Daddy. 'And I told it you without saying a word, didn't I?'

'Well, I *think* I would have known it in a minute, but that raindrop made me quite sure. I'll always remember now. *Shu-ya* means rain, or "it is going to rain". Why, Daddy!' She got up and danced round him. 'S'pose you went out before I was awake, and drawed *shu-ya* in the smoke on the wall, I'd know it was going to rain and I'd take my beaver-skin hood. Wouldn't Mummy be surprised.'

Tegumai got up and danced. (Daddies didn't mind doing those things in those days.) 'More than that! More than that!' he said. 'S'pose I wanted to tell you it wasn't going to rain much and you must come down to the river, what would we draw? Say the words in Tegumai-talk first.'

'*Shu-ya-las, ya maru.* (Sky-water ending. River come to.) *What* a lot of new sounds! *I* don't see how we can draw them.'

'But I do – but I do!' said Tegumai. 'Just attend a minute, Taffy, and we won't do any more today. We've got *shu-ya* all right, haven't we? but this *las* is a teaser. *La-la-la!*' and he waved his shark-tooth.

'There's the hissy-snake at the end and the carp-mouth before the snake – *as-as-as.* We only want *la-la*,' said Taffy.

'I know it, but we have to make *la-la*. And we're the first people in all the world who've ever tried to do it, Taffimai!'

'Well,' said Taffy, yawning, for she was rather tired. '*Las* means breaking or finishing as well as ending, doesn't it?'

'So it does,' said Tegumai. '*Ya-las* means that there's no water in the tank for Mummy to cook with – just when I'm going hunting, too.'

'And *shi-las* means that your spear is broken. If I'd only thought of *that* instead of drawing silly beaver-pictures for the Stranger-man!' (14)

'*La! La! La!*' said Tegumai, waving his stick and frowning. 'Oh bother!'

'I could have drawn *shi* quite easily,' Taffy went on. 'Then I'd have drawn your spear all broken – this way!' And she drew. (14)

(15)

'The very thing,' said Tegumai. 'That's *la* all over. It isn't like any of the other marks, either.' And he drew this. (15)

'Now for *ya*. Oh, we've done that before. Now for *maru*. *Mum-mum-mum*. *Mum* shuts one's mouth up, doesn't it? We'll draw a shut mouth like this.' And he drew. (16)

(16)

'Then the carp-mouth open. That makes *Ma-ma-ma!* But what about this *rrrrr*-thing, Taffy?'

'It sounds all rough and edgy, like your shark-tooth saw when you're cutting out a plank for the canoe,' said Taffy.

(17)

'You mean all sharp at the edges, like this?' said Tegumai. And he drew. (17)

' 'Xactly,' said Taffy. 'But we don't want all those teeth: only put two.'

'I'll only put in one,' said Tegumai. 'If this game of ours is going to be what I think it will, the easier we make our sound-pictures the better for everybody.' And he drew. (18)

(18)

'*Now* we've got it,' said Tegumai, standing on one leg. 'I'll draw 'em all in a string like fish.'

'Hadn't we better put a little bit of stick or something between each word, so's they won't rub up against each other and jostle, same as if they were carps?'

'Oh, I'll leave a space for that,' said her Daddy. And very incitedly he drew them all without stopping, on a big new bit of birch-bark. (19)

(19)

'*Shu-ya-las ya-maru*,' said Taffy, reading it out sound by sound.

'That's enough for today,' said Tegumai. 'Besides, you're getting tired, Taffy. Never mind, dear. We'll finish it all tomorrow, and then we'll be remembered for years and years after the biggest trees you can see are all chopped up for firewood.'

So they went home, and all that evening Tegumai sat on one side of the fire and Taffy on the other, drawing *ya*'s and *yo*'s and *shu*'s and *shi*'s in the smoke on the wall and giggling together till her Mummy said, 'Really, Tegumai, you're worse than my Taffy.'

'Please don't mind,' said Taffy. 'It's only our secret-s'prise, Mummy dear, and we'll tell you all about it the very minute it's done; but *please* don't ask me what it is now, or else I'll have to tell.'

So her Mummy most carefully didn't; and bright and early next morning Tegumai went down to the river to think about new sound-pictures, and when Taffy got up she saw *Ya-las* (water is ending or running out) chalked on the side of the big stone water-tank, outside the Cave.

'Um,' said Taffy. 'These picture-sounds are rather a bother! Daddy's just as good as come here himself and told me to get more water for Mummy to cook with.' She went to the spring at the back of the Cave and filled the tank from a bark bucket, and then she ran down to the river and pulled her Daddy's left ear – the one that belonged to her to pull when she was good.

'Now come along and we'll draw all the left-over sound-pictures,' said her Daddy, and they had a most inciting day of it, and a beautiful lunch in the middle, and two games of romps. When they came to T, Taffy said that as her name, and her Daddy's, and her Mummy's all began with that sound, they should draw a sort of family group of themselves holding hands. That was all very well to draw once or twice; but when it came to drawing it six or seven times, Taffy and Tegumai drew it scratchier and scratchier, till at last the T-sound was only a thin long Tegumai with his arms out to hold Taffy and Teshumai. You can see from these three pictures partly how it happened. (20, 21, 22)

(20) (21) (22)

Many of the other pictures were much too beautiful to begin with, especially before lunch; but as they were drawn over and over again on birch-bark, they became plainer and easier, till at last even Tegumai said he could find no fault with them. They turned the hissy-snake the other way round for the Z-sound, to show it was hissing backwards in a soft and gentle way (23); and they just made a twiddle for E, because it came into the pictures so often (24); and they drew pictures of the sacred Beaver of the Tegumais for the B-sound (25, 26, 27, 28); and because it was a nasty, nosy noise, they just drew

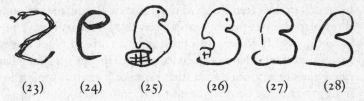

(23)   (24)   (25)   (26)   (27)   (28)

noses for the N-sound, till they were tired (29); and they drew a picture of the big lake-pike's mouth for the greedy Ga-sound (30); and they drew the pike's mouth again with a spear behind it for the scratchy, hurty Ka-sound (31); and they drew pictures of a little bit of the winding Wagai river for the nice windy-windy Wa-sound (32, 33); and so on and so forth and so following till they had done and drawn all the sound-pictures that they wanted, and there was the Alphabet, all complete.

(29)   (30)   (31)   (32)   (33pī)

And after thousands and thousands and thousands of years, and after Hieroglyphics, and Demotics, and Nilotics, and Cryptics, and Cufics, and Runics, and Dorics, and Ionics, and all sorts of other ricks and tricks (because the Woons, and the Neguses, and the Akhoonds, and the Repositories of Tradition would never leave a good thing alone when they saw it), the fine old easy, understandable Alphabet – A, B, C, D, E, and the rest of 'em – got back into its proper shape again for all Best Beloveds to learn when they are old enough.

But *I* remember Tegumai Bopsulai, and Taffimai Metallumai and Teshumai Tewindrow, her dear Mummy, and all the days gone by. And it was so – just so – a long time ago – on the banks of the big Wagai!

One of the first things

that Tegumai Bopsulai did after Taffy and he had made the Alphabet was to make a magic Alphabet-necklace of all the letters, so that it could be put in the Temple of Tegumai and kept for ever and ever. All the Tribe of Tegumai brought their most precious beads and beautiful things, and Taffy and Tegumai spent five whole years getting the necklace in order. This is a picture of the magic Alphabet-necklace. The string was made of the finest and strongest reindeer-sinew, bound round with thin copper wire.

Beginning at the top, the first bead is an old silver one that belonged to the Head Priest of the Tribe of Tegumai; then come three black mussel-pearls; next is a clay bead (blue and grey); next a nubbly gold bead sent as a present by a tribe who got it from Africa (but it must have been Indian really); the next is a long flat-sided glass bead from Africa (the Tribe of Tegumai took it in a fight); then come two clay beads (white and green), with dots on one, and dots and bands on the other; next are three rather chipped amber beads; then three clay beads (red and white), two with dots, and the big one in the middle with a toothed pattern. Then the letters begin, and between each letter is a little whitish clay bead with the letter repeated small. Here are the letters:

A   is scratched on a tooth – an elk-tush, I think.
B   is the Sacred Beaver of Tegumai on a bit of old ivory.
C   is a pearly oyster-shell – inside front.
D   must be a sort of mussel-shell – outside front.
E   is a twist of silver wire.
F   is broken, but what remains of it is a bit of stag's horn.

G is painted black on a piece of wood. (The bead after G is a
   small shell, and not a clay bead. I don't know why they did
   that.)
H is a kind of big brown cowrie-shell.
I is the inside part of a long shell ground down by hand. (It took
   Tegumai three months to grind it down.)
J is a fish-hook in mother-of-pearl.
L is the broken spear in silver. (K ought to follow J, of course;
   but the necklace was broken once and they mended it wrong.)
K is a thin slice of bone scratched and rubbed in black.
M is on a pale grey shell.
N is a piece of what is called porphyry with a nose scratched on it.
   (Tegumai spent five months polishing this stone.)
O is a piece of oyster-shell with a hole in the middle.
P and Q are missing. They were lost, a long time ago, in a great
   war, and the tribe mended the necklace with the dried rattles

of a rattlesnake, but no one ever found P and Q. That is how the saying began, 'You must mind your P's and Q's.'

R   is, of course, just a shark's tooth.

S   is a little silver snake.

T   is the end of a small bone, polished brown and shiny.

U   is another piece of oyster-shell.

W   is a twisty piece of mother-of-pearl that they found inside a big mother-of-pearl shell, and sawed off with a wire dipped in sand and water. It took Taffy a month and a half to polish it and drill the holes.

X   is silver wire joined in the middle with a raw garnet. (Taffy found the garnet.)

Y   is the carp's tail in ivory.

Z   is a bell-shaped piece of agate marked with Z-shaped stripes. They made the Z-snake out of one of the stripes by picking out the soft stone and rubbing in red sand and beeswax. Just in the mouth of the bell you see the clay bead repeating the Z-letter.

These are all the letters.

The next bead is a small round greeny lump of copper ore; the next is a lump of rough turquoise; the next is a rough gold nugget (what they call water-gold); the next is a melon-shaped clay bead (white with green spots). Then come four flat ivory pieces, with dots on them rather like dominoes; then come three stone beads, very badly worn; then two soft iron beads with rust-holes at the edges (they must have been magic, because they look very common); and last is a very very old African bead, like glass – blue, red, white, black, and yellow. Then comes the loop to slip over the big silver button at the other end, and that is all.

I have copied the necklace very carefully. It weighs one pound seven and a half ounces. The black squiggle behind is only put in to make the beads and things look better.

Of all the Tribe of Tegumai
   Who cut that figure, none remain –
On Merrow Down the cuckoos cry –
   The silence and the sun remain.

But as the faithful years return
   And hearts unwounded sing again,
Comes Taffy dancing through the fern
   To lead the Surrey spring again.

Her brows are bound with bracken-fronds
   And golden elf-locks fly above;
Her eyes are bright as diamonds
   And bluer than the sky above.

In moccasins and deer-skin cloak,
   Unfearing, free and fair she flits,
And lights her little damp-wood smoke
   To show her Daddy where she flits.

For far – oh, very far behind,
   So far she cannot call to him,
Comes Tegumai alone to find
   The daughter that was all to him.

The Crab that Played with the Sea

 BEFORE THE HIGH AND FAR-OFF TIMES, O my Best Beloved, came the Time of the Very Beginnings; and that was in the days when the Eldest Magician was getting Things ready. First he got the Earth ready; then he got the Sea ready; and then he told all the Animals that they could come out and play. And the Animals said, 'O Eldest Magician, what shall we play at?' and he said, 'I will show you.' He took the Elephant – All-the-Elephant-there-was – and said, 'Play at being an Elephant,' and All-the-Elephant-there-was played. He took the Beaver – All-the-Beaver-there-was – and said, 'Play at being a Beaver,' and All-the-Beaver-there-was played. He took the Cow – All-the-Cow- there-was – and said, 'Play at being a Cow,' and All-the-Cow-there-was played. He took the Turtle – All- the-Turtle-there-was – and said, 'Play at being a Turtle,' and All-the-Turtle-there-was played. One by one he took all the beasts and birds and fishes and told them what to play at.

But towards evening, when people and things grow restless and tired, there came up the Man (With his own little girl-daughter?) – Yes, with his own best-beloved little girl-daughter sitting upon his shoulder, and he said, 'What is this play, Eldest Magician?' And the Eldest Magician said, 'Ho, Son of Adam, this is the play of the Very Beginning; but you are too wise for this play.' And the Man saluted and said, 'Yes, I am too wise for this play; but see that you make all the Animals obedient to me.'

Now, while the two were talking together, Pau Amma the Crab, who was next in the game, scuttled off sideways and stepped into the sea, saying to himself, 'I will play my play alone in the deep waters, and I will never be obedient to this son of Adam.' Nobody saw him go away except the little girl-daughter where she leaned on the Man's shoulder. And the play went on till there were no more Animals left without orders; and the Eldest Magician wiped the fine dust off his hands and walked about the world to see how the Animals were playing.

He went North, Best Beloved, and he found All-the-Elephant-there-was digging with his tusks and stamping with his feet in the nice new clean earth that had been made ready for him.

'*Kun?*' said All-the-Elephant-there-was, meaning, 'Is this right?'

'*Payah kun*,' said the Eldest Magician, meaning, 'That is quite right'; and he breathed upon the great rocks and lumps of earth that All-the-Elephant-there-was had thrown up, and they became the great Himalayan Mountains, and you can look them out on the map.

He went East, and he found All-the-Cow-there-was feeding in the field that had been made ready for her, and she licked her tongue round a whole forest at a time, and swallowed it and sat down to chew her cud.

'*Kun?*' said All-the-Cow-there-was.

'*Payah kun*,' said the Eldest Magician; and he breathed upon the bare patch where she had eaten, and upon the place where she had sat down, and one became the great Indian Desert, and the other became the Desert of Sahara, and you can look them out on the map.

He went West, and he found All-the-Beaver-there-was making a beaver-dam across the mouths of broad rivers that had been got ready for him.

'*Kun?*' said All-the-Beaver-there-was.

'*Payah kun*,' said the Eldest Magician; and he breathed upon the fallen trees and the still water, and they became the Everglades in Florida, and you may look them out on the map.

Then he went South and found All-the-Turtle-there-was scratching with his flippers in the sand that had been got ready for him, and the sand and the rocks whirled through the air and fell far off into the sea.

'*Kun?*' said All-the-Turtle-there-was.

'*Payah kun*,' said the Eldest Magician; and he breathed upon the sand and the rocks, where they had fallen in the sea, and they became the most beautiful islands of Borneo, Celebes, Sumatra, Java, and the rest of the Malay Archipelago, and you can look *them* out on the map!

By and by the Eldest Magician met the Man on the banks of the Perak River, and said, 'Ho! Son of Adam, are all the Animals obedient to you?'

'Yes,' said the Man.

'Is all the Earth obedient to you?'

'Yes,' said the Man.

'Is all the Sea obedient to you?'

'No,' said the Man. 'Once a day and once a night the Sea runs up the Perak River and drives the sweet-water back into the forest, so that my house is made wet; once a day and once a night it runs down the river and draws all the water after it, so that there is nothing left but mud, and my canoe is upset. Is that the play you told it to play?'

'No,' said the Eldest Magician. 'That is a new and a bad play.'

'Look!' said the Man, and as he spoke the great Sea came up the mouth of the Perak River, driving the river backwards till it overflowed all the dark forests for miles and miles, and flooded the Man's house.

'This is wrong. Lauch your canoe and we will find out who is playing with the Sea,' said the Eldest Magician. They stepped into the canoe; the little girl-daughter came with them; and the man took his *kris* – a curving, wavy dagger with a blade like a flame – and they pushed out on the Perak River. Then the Sea began to run back and back, and the canoe was sucked out of the mouth of the Perak River, past Selangor, past Malacca, past Singapore, out and out to the Island of Bintang, as though it had been pulled by a string.

Then the Eldest Magician stood up and shouted, 'Ho! beasts, birds, and fishes, that I took between my hands at the Very Beginning and taught the play that you should play, which one of you is playing with the Sea?'

Then all the beasts, birds, and fishes said together, 'Eldest Magician, we play the plays that you taught us to play – we and our children's children. But not one of us plays with the Sea.'

Then the Moon rose big and full over the water, and the Eldest Magician said to the hunchbacked old man who sits in the Moon spinning a fishing-line with which he hopes one day to catch the world, 'Ho! Fisher of the Moon, are you playing with the Sea?'

'No,' said the Fisherman, 'I am spinning a line with which I shall someday catch the world; but I do not play with the Sea.' And he went on spinning his line.

Now there is also a Rat up in the Moon who always bites the old Fisherman's line as fast as it is made, and the Eldest Magician said to him, 'Ho! Rat of the Moon, are *you* playing with the Sea?'

And the Rat said, 'I am too busy biting through the line that this old Fisherman is spinning. I do not play with the Sea.' And he went on biting the line.

Then the little girl-daughter put up her little soft brown arms with the beautiful white shell bracelets and said, 'O Eldest Magician! when my father here talked to you at the Very Beginning, and I leaned upon his shoulder while the beasts were being taught their plays, one beast went away naughtily into the Sea before you had taught him his play.'

And the Eldest Magician said, 'How wise are little children who see and are silent! What was that beast like?'

And the little girl-daughter said, 'He was round and he was flat; and his eyes grew upon stalks; and he walked sideways like this; and he was covered with strong armour upon his back.'

And the Eldest Magician said, 'How wise are little children who speak truth! Now I know where Pau Amma went. Give me the paddle!'

So he took the paddle; but there was no need to paddle, for the water flowed steadily past all the islands till they came to the place called Pusat Tasek – the Heart of the Sea – where the great hollow is that leads down to the heart of the world, and in that hollow grows the Wonderful Tree, Pauh Janggi, that bears the magic twin-nuts. Then the Eldest Magician slid his arm up to the shoulder through the deep warm water, and under the roots of the Wonderful Tree he touched the broad back of Pau Amma the Crab. And Pau Amma settled down at the touch, and all the Sea rose up as water rises in a basin when you put your hand into it.

This is a picture of Pau Amma the Crab

running away while the Eldest Magician was talking to the Man
and his Little Girl Daughter. The Eldest Magician is sitting on
his magic throne, wrapped up in his Magic Cloud. The three
flowers in front of him are the three Magic Flowers. On the top of
the hill you can see All-the-Elephant-there-was, and All-the-
Cow-there-was, and All-the-Turtle-there-was going off to play
as the Eldest Magician told them. The Cow has a hump, because
she was All-the-Cow-there-was; so she had to have all there was
for all the cows that were made afterwards. Under the hill there
are Animals who have been taught the game they were to play.
You can see All-the-Tiger-there-was smiling at All-the-Bones-
there-were, and you can see All-the-Elk-there-was, and All-the-
Parrot-there-was, and All-the-Bunnies-there-were on the hill.
The other Animals are on the other side of the hill, so I haven't
drawn them. The little house up the hill is All-the-House-there-
was. The Eldest Magician made it to show the Man how to make
houses when he wanted to. The Snake round that spiky hill is All-
the-Snake-there-was, and he is talking to All-the-Monkey-there-
was, and the Monkey is being rude to the Snake, and the Snake is
being rude to the Monkey. The Man is very busy talking to the
Eldest Magician. The Little Girl Daughter is looking at Pau
Amma as he runs away. That humpy thing in the water in front is
Pau Amma. He wasn't a common Crab in those days. He was a
King Crab. That is why he looks different. The thing that looks
like bricks that the Man is standing in, is the Big Miz-Maze.
When the Man has done talking with the Eldest Magician he will
walk in the Big Miz-Maze, because he has to. The mark on the
stone under the Man's foot is a magic mark; and down underneath
I have drawn the three Magic Flowers all mixed up with the Magic
Cloud. All this picture is Big Medicine and Strong Magic.

'Ah!' said the Eldest Magician. 'Now I know who has been playing with the Sea'; and he called out, 'What are you doing, Pau Amma?'

And Pau Amma, deep down below, answered, 'Once a day and once a night I go out to look for my food. Once a day and once a night I return. Leave me alone.'

Then the Eldest Magician said, 'Listen, Pau Amma. When you go out from your cave the waters of the Sea pour down into Pusat Tasek, and all the beaches of all the islands are left bare, and the little fish die, and Raja Moyang Kaban, the King of the Elephants, his legs are made muddy. When you come back and sit in Pusat Tasek, the waters of the Sea rise, and half the little islands are drowned, and the Man's house is flooded, and Raja Abdullah, the King of the Crocodiles, his mouth is filled with the salt water.'

Then Pau Amma, deep down below, laughed and said, 'I did not know I was so important. Henceforward I will go out seven times a day, and the waters shall never be still.'

And the Eldest Magician said, 'I cannot make you play the play you were meant to play, Pau Amma, because you escaped me at the Very Beginning; but if you are not afraid, come up and we will talk about it.'

'I am not afraid,' said Pau Amma, and he rose to the top of the sea in the moonlight. There was nobody in the world so big as Pau Amma – for he was the King Crab of all Crabs. Not a common Crab, but a King Crab. One side of his great shell touched the beach at Sarawak; the other touched the beach at Pahang; and he was taller than the smoke of three volcanoes! As he rose up through the branches of the Wonderful Tree he tore off one of the great twin-fruits – the magic double-kernelled nuts that make people young – and the little girl-daughter saw it bobbing alongside the canoe, and pulled it in and began to pick out the soft eyes of it with her little golden scissors.

'Now,' said the Magician, 'make a Magic, Pau Amma, to show that you are really important.'

Pau Amma rolled his eyes and waved his legs, but he could only stir up the Sea, because, though he was a King Crab, he was nothing more than a Crab, and the Eldest Magician laughed.

'You are not so important after all, Pau Amma,' he said. 'Now, let *me* try,' and he made a Magic with his left hand – with just the little finger of his left hand – and – lo and behold, Best Beloved, Pau Amma's hard, blue-green-black shell fell off him as a husk falls off a coconut, and Pau Amma was left all soft – soft as the little crabs that you sometimes find on the beach, Best Beloved.

'Indeed, you are very important,' said the Eldest Magician. 'Shall I ask the Man here to cut you with his *kris*? Shall I send for Raja Moyang Kaban, the King of the Elephants, to pierce you with his tusks? or shall I call Raja Abdullah, the King of the Crocodiles, to bite you?'

And Pau Amma said, 'I am ashamed! Give me back my hard shell and let me go back to Pusat Tasek, and I will only stir out once a day and once a night to get my food.'

And the Eldest Magician said, 'No, Pau Amma, I will *not* give you back your shell, for you will grow bigger and prouder and stronger, and perhaps you will forget your promise, and you will play with the Sea once more.'

Then Pau Amma said, 'What shall I do? I am so big that I can only hide in Pusat Tasek, and if I go anywhere else, all soft as I am now, the sharks and the dogfish will eat me. And if I go to Pusat Tasek, all soft as I am now, though I may be safe, I can never stir out to get my food, and so I shall die.' Then he waved his legs and lamented.

'Listen, Pau Amma,' said the Eldest Magician. 'I cannot make you play the play you were meant to play, because you escaped me at the Very Beginning; but if you choose, I can make every stone and every hole and every bunch of weed in all the seas a safe Pusat Tasek for you and your children for always.'

Then Pau Amma said, 'That is good, but I do not choose yet. Look! there is that Man who talked to you at the Very Beginning. If he had not taken up your attention I should not have grown tired of waiting and run away, and all this would never have happened. What will *he* do for me?'

And the Man said, 'If you choose, I will make a Magic, so that both the deep water and the dry ground will be a home for you and your children – so that you shall be able to hide both on the land and in the sea.'

And Pau Amma said, 'I do not choose yet. Look! there is that girl who saw me running away at the Very Beginning. If she had spoken then, the Eldest Magician would have called me back, and all this would never have happened. What will *she* do for me?'

And the little girl-daughter said, 'This is a good nut that I am eating. If you choose, I will make a Magic and I will give you this pair of scissors, very sharp and strong, so that you and your children can eat coconuts like this all day long when you come up from the Sea to the land; or you can dig a Pusat Tasek for yourself with the scissors that belong to you when there is no stone or hole near by; and when the earth is too hard, by the help of these same scissors you can run up a tree.'

And Pau Amma said, 'I do not choose yet, for, all soft as I am, these gifts would not help me. Give me back my shell, O Eldest Magician, and then I will play your play.'

And the Eldest Magician said, 'I will give it back, Pau Amma, for eleven months of the year; but on the twelfth month of every year it shall grow soft again, to remind you and all your children that I can make Magics, and to keep you humble, Pau Amma; for I see that if you can run both under the water and on land, you will grow too bold; and if you can climb trees and crack nuts and dig holes with your scissors, you will grow too greedy, Pau Amma.'

Then Pau Amma thought a little and said, 'I have made my choice. I will take all the gifts.'

Then the Eldest Magician made a Magic with the right hand, with all five fingers of his right hand, and lo and behold, Best Beloved, Pau Amma grew smaller and smaller and smaller, till at last there was only a little green crab

This is the picture of Pau Amma the Crab

rising out of the sea as tall as the smoke of three volcanoes. I haven't drawn the three volcanoes, because Pau Amma was so big. Pau Amma is trying to make a Magic, but he is only a silly old King Crab, and so he can't do anything. You can see he is all legs and claws and empty hollow shell. The canoe is the canoe that the Man and the Girl Daughter and the Eldest Magician sailed from the Perak River in. The Sea is all black and bobbly, because Pau Amma has just risen up out of Pusat Tasek. Pusat Tasek is underneath, so I haven't drawn it. The Man is waving his curvy *kris*-knife at Pau Amma. The Little Girl Daughter is sitting quietly in the middle of the canoe. She knows she is quite safe with her Daddy. The Eldest Magician is standing up at the other end of the canoe beginning to make a Magic. He has left his magic throne on the beach, and he has taken off his clothes so as not to get wet, and he has left the Magic Cloud behind too, so as not to tip the boat over. The thing that looks like another little canoe outside the real canoe is called an out-rigger. It is a piece of wood tied to sticks, and it prevents the canoe from being tipped over.

The canoe is made out of one piece of wood, and there is a paddle at one end of it.

swimming in the water alongside the canoe, crying in a very small voice, 'Give me the scissors!'

And the girl-daughter picked him up on the palm of her little brown hand, and sat him in the bottom of the canoe and gave him her scissors, and he waved them in his little arms, and opened them and shut them and snapped them, and said, 'I can eat nuts. I can crack shells. I can dig holes. I can climb trees. I can breathe in the dry air, and I can find a safe Pusat Tasek under every stone. I did not know I was so important. *Kun?*' (Is this right?)

'*Payah kun,*' said the Eldest Magician, and he laughed and gave him his blessing; and little Pau Amma scuttled over the side of the canoe into the water; and he was so tiny that he could have hidden under the shadow of a dry leaf on land or of a dead shell at the bottom of the sea.

'Was that well done?' said the Eldest Magician.

'Yes,' said the Man. 'But now we must go back to Perak, and that is a weary way to paddle. If we had waited till Pau Amma had gone out of Pusat Tasek and come home, the water would have carried us there by itself.'

'You are lazy,' said the Eldest Magician. 'So your children shall be lazy. They shall be the laziest people in the world. They shall be called the Malazy – the lazy people'; and he held up his finger to the Moon and said, 'O Fisherman, here is this Man too lazy to row home. Pull his canoe home with your line, Fisherman.'

'No,' said the Man. 'If I am to be lazy all my days, let the Sea work for me twice a day for ever. That will save paddling.'

And the Eldest Magician laughed and said, '*Payah kun*' (That is right).

And the Rat of the Moon stopped biting the line; and the Fisherman let his line down till it touched the Sea, and he pulled the whole deep Sea along, past the Island of Bintang, past Singapore, past Malacca, past Selangor, till the canoe whirled into the mouth of the Perak River again.

'*Kun?*' said the Fisherman of the Moon.

'*Payah kun,*' said the Eldest Magician. 'See now that you pull the Sea twice a day and twice a night for ever, so that the Malazy fishermen may be saved paddling. But be careful not to do it too hard, or I shall make a Magic on you as I did to Pau Amma.'

Then they all went up the Perak River and went to bed, Best Beloved.

Now listen and attend!

From that day to this the Moon has always pulled the Sea up and down and made what we call the tides. Sometimes the Fisher of the Sea pulls a little too hard, and then we get spring tides; and sometimes he pulls a little too softly, and then we get what are called neap tides; but nearly always he is careful, because of the Eldest Magician.

And Pau Amma? You can see when you go to the beach, how all Pau Amma's babies make little Pusat Taseks for themselves under every stone and bunch of weed on the sands; you can see them waving their little scissors; and in some parts of the world they truly live on the dry land and run up the palm trees and eat coconuts, exactly as the girl-daughter promised. But once a year all Pau Ammas must shake off their hard armour and be soft – to remind them of what the Eldest Magician could do. And so it isn't fair to kill or hunt Pau Amma's babies just because old Pau Amma was stupidly rude a very long time ago.

Oh yes! And Pau Amma's babies hate being taken out of their little Pusat Taseks and brought home in pickle-bottles. That is why they nip you with their scissors, and it serves you right!

China-going P&O's
Pass Pau Amma's playground close,
And his Pusat Tasek lies
Near the track of most BI's.
NYK and NDL
Know Pau Amma's home as well
As the Fisher of the Sea knows
'Ben's' MM's and Rubattinos.
But (and this is rather queer)
ATL's can *not* come here;
O and O and DOA
Must go round another way.
Orient, Anchor, Bibby, Hall,
Never go that way at all.
UCS would have a fit
If it found itself on it.
And if 'Beavers' took their cargoes
To Penang instead of Lagos,
Or a fat Shaw-Savill bore
Passengers to Singapore,
Or a White Star were to try a
Little trip to Sourabaya,
Or a BSA went on
Past Natal to Cheribon,
Then great Mr Lloyds would come
With a wire and drag them home!

You'll know what my riddle means
When you've eaten mangosteens.

Or if you can't wait till then, ask them to let you have the outside page of *The Times*; turn over to page 2, where it is marked 'Shipping' on the top left hand; then take the Atlas (and that is the finest picture-book in the world) and see how the names of the places that the steamers go to fit into the names of the places on the map. Any steamer-kiddy ought to be able to do that; but if you can't read, ask someone to show it you.

The Cat that Walked by Himself

 Hear and attend and listen; for this befell and behappened and became and was, O my Best Beloved, when the Tame animals were wild. The Dog was wild, and the Horse was wild, and the Cow was wild, and the Sheep was wild, and the Pig was wild – as wild as wild could be – and they walked in the Wet Wild Woods by their wild lones. But the wildest of all the wild animals was the Cat. He walked by himself, and all places were alike to him.

Of course the Man was wild too. He was dreadfully wild. He didn't even begin to be tame till he met the Woman, and she told him that she did not like living in his wild ways. She picked out a nice dry Cave, instead of a heap of wet leaves, to lie down in; and she strewed clean sand on the floor; and she lit a nice fire of wood at the back of the Cave; and she hung a dried wild-horse skin, tail-down, across the opening of the Cave; and she said, 'Wipe your feet, dear, when you come in, and now we'll keep house.'

That night, Best Beloved, they are wild sheep roasted on the hot stones, and flavoured with wild garlic and wild pepper; and wild duck stuffed with wild rice and wild fenugreek and wild coriander; and marrowbones of wild oxen; and wild cherries, and wild grenadillas. Then the Man went to sleep in front of the fire ever so happy; but the Woman sat up, combing her hair. She took the bone of the shoulder of mutton – the big flat blade-bone – and she looked at the wonderful marks on it, and she threw more wood on the fire, and she made a Magic. She made the First Singing Magic in the world.

Out in the Wet Wild Woods all the wild animals gathered together where they could see the light of the fire a long way off, and they wondered what it meant.

Then Wild Horse stamped with his wild foot and said, 'O my Friends and O my Enemies, why have the Man and the Woman made that great light in that great Cave, and what harm will it do us?'

Wild Dog lifted up his wild nose and smelled the smell of the roast mutton, and said, 'I will go up and see and look, and say; for I think it is good. Cat, come with me.'

'Nenni!' said the Cat. 'I am the Cat who walks by himself, and all places are alike to me. I will not come.'

'Then we can never be friends again,' said Wild Dog, and he trotted off to the Cave. But when he had gone a little way the Cat said to himself, 'All places are alike to me. Why should I not go too and see and look and come away at my own liking?' So he slipped after Wild Dog softly, very softly, and hid himself where he could hear everything.

When Wild Dog reached the mouth of the Cave he lifted up the dried horse-skin with his nose and sniffed the beautiful smell of the roast mutton, and the Woman, looking at the blade-bone, heard him, and laughed, and said, 'Here comes the first. Wild Thing out of the Wild Woods, what do you want?'

Wild Dog said, 'O my Enemy and Wife of my Enemy, what is this that smells so good in the Wild Woods?'

Then the Woman picked up a roasted mutton-bone and threw it to Wild Dog, and said, 'Wild Thing out of the Wild Woods, taste and try.' Wild Dog gnawed the bone, and it was more delicious than anything he had ever tasted, and he said, 'O my Enemy and Wife of my Enemy, give me another.'

The Woman said, 'Wild Thing out of the Wild Woods, help my Man to hunt through the day and guard this Cave at night, and I will give you as many roast bones as you need.'

'Ah!' said the Cat, listening. 'This is a very wise Woman, but she is not so wise as I am.'

Wild Dog crawled into the Cave and laid his head on the Woman's lap, and said, 'O my Friend and Wife of my Friend, I will help your Man to hunt through the day, and at night I will guard your Cave.'

'Ah!' said the Cat, listening. 'That is a very foolish Dog.' And he went back through the Wet Wild Woods waving his wild tail, and walking by his wild lone. But he never told anybody.

When the Man waked up he said, 'What is Wild Dog doing here?' And the Woman said, 'His name is not Wild Dog any more, but the First Friend, because he will be our friend for always and always and always. Take him with you when you go hunting.'

Next night the Woman cut great green armfuls of fresh grass from the water-meadows, and dried it before the fire, so that it smelt like new-mown hay, and she sat at the mouth of the Cave and plaited a halter out of horse-hide, and she looked at the shoulder-of-mutton bone – at the big broad blade-bone – and she made a Magic. She made the Second Singing Magic in the world.

Out in the Wild Woods all the wild animals wondered what had happened to Wild Dog, and at last Wild Horse stamped with his foot and said, 'I will go and see and say why Wild Dog has not returned. Cat, come with me.'

'Nenni!' said the Cat. 'I am the Cat who walks by himself, and all places are alike to me. I will not come.' But all the same he followed Wild Horse softly, very softly, and hid himself where he could hear everything.

When the Woman heard Wild Horse tripping and stumbling on his long mane, she laughed and said, 'Here comes the second. Wild Thing out of the Wild Woods, what do you want?'

This is the picture of the Cave

where the Man and the Woman lived first of all. It was really a
very nice Cave, and much warmer than it looks. The Man had a
canoe. It is on the edge of the river, being soaked in water to make
it swell up. The tattery-looking thing across the river is the Man's
salmon-net to catch salmon with. There are nice clean stones
leading up from the river to the mouth of the Cave, so that the
Man and the Woman could go down for water without getting
sand between their toes. The things like black-beetles far down
the beach are really trunks of dead trees that floated down the
river from the Wet Wild Woods on the other bank. The Man and
the Woman used to drag them out and dry them and cut them up
for firewood. I haven't drawn the horse-hide curtain at the mouth
of the Cave, because the Woman has just taken it down to be
cleaned. All those little smudges on the sand between the Cave and
the river are the marks of the Woman's feet and the Man's feet.

The Man and the Woman are both inside the Cave eating their
dinner. They went to another cosier Cave when the Baby came,
because the Baby used to crawl down to the river and
fall in, and the Dog had to pull him out.

Wild Horse said, 'O my Enemy and Wife of my Enemy, where is Wild Dog?'

The Woman laughed, and picked up the blade-bone and looked at it, and said, 'Wild Thing out of the Wild Woods, you did not come here for Wild Dog, but for the sake of this good grass.'

And Wild Horse, tripping and stumbling on his long mane, said, 'That is true; give it me to eat.'

The Woman said, 'Wild Thing out of the Wild Woods, bend your wild head and wear what I give you, and you shall eat the wonderful grass three times a day.'

'Ah!' said the Cat, listening. 'This is a clever Woman, but she is not so clever as I am.'

Wild Horse bent his wild head, and the Woman slipped the plaited-hide halter over it, and Wild Horse breathed on the Woman's feet and said, 'O my Mistress, and Wife of my Master, I will be your servant for the sake of the wonderful grass.'

'Ah!' said the Cat, listening. 'That is a very foolish Horse.' And he went back through the Wet Wild Woods, waving his wild tail and walking by his wild lone. But he never told anybody.

When the Man and the Dog came back from hunting, the Man said, 'What is Wild Horse doing here?' And the Woman said, 'His name is not Wild Horse any more, but the First Servant, because he will carry us from place to place for always and always and always. Ride on his back when you go hunting.'

Next day, holding her wild head high that her wild horns should not catch in the wild trees, Wild Cow came up to the Cave, and the Cat followed, and hid himself just the same as before; and everything happened just the same as before; and the cat said the same things as before; and when Wild Cow had promised to give her milk to the Woman every day in exchange for the wonderful grass, the Cat went back through the Wet Wild Woods waving his wild tail and walking by his wild lone, just the same as before. But he never told anybody. And when the Man and the Horse and the Dog came home from hunting and asked the same questions same as before, the Woman said, 'Her name is not Wild Cow any more, but the Giver of Good Food. She will give us the warm white milk for always and always and always, and I will take care of her while you and the First Friend and the First Servant go hunting.'

Next day the Cat waited to see if any other Wild Thing would go up to the Cave, but no one moved in the Wet Wild Woods, so the Cat walked there by himself; and he saw the Woman milking the Cow, and he saw the light of the fire in the Cave, and he smelt the smell of the warm white milk.

Cat said, 'O my Enemy and Wife of my Enemy, where did Wild Cow go?'

The Woman laughed and said, 'Wild Thing out of the Wild Woods, go back to the Woods again, for I have braided up my hair, and I have put away the magic blade-bone, and we have no more need of either friends or servants in our Cave.'

Cat said, 'I am not a friend, and I am not a servant. I am the Cat who walks by himself, and I wish to come into your Cave.'

Woman said, 'Then why did you not come with First Friend on the first night?'

Cat grew very angry and said, 'Has Wild Dog told tales of me?'

Then the Woman laughed and said, 'You are the Cat who walks by himself, and all places are alike to you. You are neither a friend nor a servant. You have said it yourself. Go away and walk by yourself in all places alike.'

Then Cat pretended to be sorry and said, 'Must I never come into the Cave? Must I never sit by the warm fire? Must I never drink the warm white milk? You are very wise and very beautiful. You should not be cruel even to a Cat.'

Woman said, 'I knew I was wise, but I did not know I was beautiful. So I will make a bargain with you. If ever I say one word in your praise, you may come into the Cave.'

'And if you say two words in my praise?' said the Cat.

'I never shall,' said the Woman, 'but if I say two words in your praise, you may sit by the fire in the Cave.'

'And if you say three words?' said the Cat.

'I never shall,' said the Woman, 'but if I say three words in your praise, you may drink the warm white milk three times a day for always and always and always.'

Then the Cat arched his back and said, 'Now let the Curtain at the mouth of the Cave, and the Fire at the back of the Cave, and the Milk-pots that stand beside the Fire, remember what my Enemy and the Wife of my Enemy has said.' And he went away through the Wet Wild Woods waving his wild tail and walking by his wild lone.

That night when the Man and the Horse and the Dog came home from hunting, the Woman did not tell them of the bargain that she had made with the Cat, because she was afraid that they might not like it.

Cat went far and far away and hid himself in the Wet Wild Woods by his wild lone for a long time till the Woman forgot all about him. Only the Bat – the little upside-down Bat – that hung inside the Cave knew where Cat hid; and every evening Bat would fly to Cat with news of what was happening.

One evening Bat said, 'There is a Baby in the Cave. He is new and pink and fat and small, and the Woman is very fond of him.'

'Ah,' said the Cat, listening, 'but what is the Baby fond of?'

'He is fond of things that are soft and tickle,' said the Bat. 'He is fond of warm things to hold in his arms when he goes to sleep. He is fond of being played with. He is fond of all those things.'

'Ah,' said the Cat, listening, 'then my time has come.'

Next night Cat walked through the Wet Wild Woods and hid very near the Cave till morning-time, and Man and Dog and Horse went hunting. The Woman was busy cooking that morning, and the Baby cried and interrupted.

So she carried him outside the Cave and gave him a handful of pebbles to play with. But still the Baby cried.

Then the Cat put out his paddy paw and patted the Baby on the cheek, and it cooed; and the Cat rubbed against its fat knees and tickled it under its fat chin with his tail. And the Baby laughed; and the Woman heard him and smiled.

Then the Bat – the little upside-down Bat – that hung in the mouth of the Cave said, 'O my Hostess and Wife of my Host and Mother of my Host's Son, a Wild Thing from the Wild Woods is most beautifully playing with your Baby.'

'A blessing on that Wild Thing whoever he may be,' said the Woman, straightening her back, 'for I was a busy woman this morning and he has done me a service.'

That very minute and second, Best Beloved, the dried horse-skin Curtain that was stretched tail-down at the mouth of the Cave fell down – *woosh!* – because it remembered the bargain she had made with the Cat; and when the Woman went to pick it up – lo and behold! – the Cat was sitting quite comfy inside the Cave.

'O my Enemy and Wife of my Enemy and Mother of my Enemy,' said the Cat, 'it is I: for you have spoken a word in my praise, and now I can sit within the Cave for always and always and always. But still I am the Cat who walks by himself, and all places are alike to me.'

The Woman was very angry, and shut her lips tight and took up her spinning-wheel and began to spin.

But the Baby cried because the Cat had gone away, and the Woman could not hush it, for it struggled and kicked and grew black in the face.

'O my Enemy and Wife of my Enemy and Mother of my Enemy,' said the Cat, 'take a strand of the thread that you are spinning and tie it to your spindle-whorl and drag it along the floor, and I will show you a Magic that shall make your Baby laugh as loudly as he is now crying.'

'I will do so,' said the Woman, 'because I am at my wits' end; but I will not thank you for it.'

She tied the thread to the little clay spindle-whorl and drew it across the floor, and the Cat ran after it and patted it with his paws and rolled head over heels, and tossed it backward over his shoulder and chased it between his hind legs and pretended to lose it, and pounced down upon it again, till the Baby laughed as loudly as it had been crying, and scrambled after the Cat and frolicked all over the Cave till it grew tired and settled down to sleep with the Cat in its arms.

'Now,' said Cat, 'I will sing the Baby a song that shall keep him asleep for an hour.' And he began to purr, loud and low, low and loud, till the Baby fell fast asleep. The Woman smiled as she looked down upon the two of them, and said, 'That was wonderfully done. No question but you are very clever, O Cat.'

This is the picture

of the Cat that Walked by Himself, walking by his wild lone through the Wet Wild Woods and waving his wild tail. There is nothing else in the picture except some toadstools. They had to grow there because the woods were so wet. The lumpy thing on the low branch isn't a bird. It is moss that grew there because the Wild Woods were so wet.

Underneath the truly picture is a picture of the cosy Cave that the Man and the Woman went to after the Baby came. It was their summer Cave, and they planted wheat in front of it. The man is riding on the Horse to find the Cow and bring her back to the Cave to be milked. He is holding up his hand to call the Dog, who has swum across to the other side of the river, looking for rabbits.

That very minute and second, Best Beloved, the smoke of the Fire at the back of the Cave came down in clouds from the roof – *puff!* – because it remembered the bargain she had made with the Cat; and when it had cleared away – lo and behold! – the Cat was sitting quite comfy close to the fire.

'O my Enemy and Wife of my Enemy and Mother of my Enemy,' said the Cat, 'it is I: for you have spoken a second word in my praise, and now I can sit by the warm fire at the back of the Cave for always and always and always. But still I am the Cat who walks by himself, and all places are alike to me.'

Then the Woman was very very angry, and let down her hair and put more wood on the fire and brought out the broad blade-bone of the shoulder of mutton and began to make a Magic that should prevent her from saying a third word in praise of the Cat. It was not a Singing Magic, Best Beloved, it was a Still Magic; and by and by the Cave grew so still that a little wee-wee mouse crept out of a corner and ran across the floor.

'O my Enemy and Wife of my Enemy and Mother of my Enemy,' said the Cat, 'is that little mouse part of your Magic?'

'Ouh! Chee! No indeed!' said the Woman, and she dropped the blade-bone and jumped upon the footstool in front of the fire and braided up her hair very quick for fear that the mouse should run up it.

'Ah,' said the Cat, watching, 'then the mouse will do me no harm if I eat it?'

'No,' said the Woman, braiding up her hair, 'eat it quickly and I will ever be grateful to you.'

Cat made one jump and caught the little mouse, and the Woman said, 'A hundred thanks. Even the First Friend is not quick enough to catch little mice as you have done. You must be very wise.'

That very moment and second, O Best Beloved, the Milk-pot that stood by the fire cracked in two pieces – *ffft!* – because it remembered the bargain she had made with the Cat; and when the Woman jumped down from the footstool – lo and behold! – the Cat was lapping up the warm white milk that lay in one of the broken pieces.

'O my Enemy and Wife of my Enemy and Mother of my Enemy,' said the Cat, 'it is I: for you have spoken three words in my praise, and now I can drink the warm white milk three times a day for always and always and always. But *still* I am the Cat who walks by himself, and all places are alike to me.'

Then the Woman laughed and set the Cat a bowl of the warm white milk and said, 'O Cat, you are as clever as a man, but remember that your bargain was not made with the Man or the Dog, and I do not know what they will do when they come home.'

'What is that to me?' said the Cat. 'If I have my place in the Cave by the fire and my warm white milk three times a day I do not care what the Man or the Dog can do.'

That evening when the Man and the Dog came into the Cave, the Woman told them all the story of the bargain, while the Cat sat by the fire and smiled. Then the Man said, 'Yes, but he has not made a bargain, with *me* or with all proper Men after me.' Then he took off his two leather boots and he took up his little stone axe (that makes three) and he fetched a piece of wood and a hatchet (that is five altogether), and he set them out in a row and he said, 'Now we will make *our* bargain. If you do not catch mice when you are in the Cave for always and always and always, I will throw these five things at you whenever I see you, and so shall all proper Men do after me.'

'Ah,' said the Woman, listening, 'this is a very clever Cat, but he is not so clever as my Man.'

The Cat counted the five things (and they looked very knobby) and he said, 'I will catch mice when I am in the Cave for always and always and always; but *still* I am the Cat who walks by himself, and all places are alike to me.'

'Not when I am near,' said the Man. 'If you had not said that last I would have put all these things away for always and always and always; but now I am going to throw my two boots and my little stone axe (that makes three) at you whenever I meet you. And so shall all proper Men do after me.'

Then the Dog said, 'Wait a minute. He has not made a bargain with *me* or with all proper Dogs after me.' And he showed his teeth and said, 'If you are not kind to the Baby while I am in the Cave for always and always and always, I will hunt you till I catch you, and when I catch you I will bite you. And so shall all proper Dogs do after me.'

'Ah,' said the Woman, listening, 'this is a very clever Cat, but he is not so clever as the Dog.'

Cat counted the Dog's teeth (and they looked very pointed) and he said, 'I will be kind to the Baby while I am in the Cave, as long as he does not pull my tail too hard, for always and always and always. But *still* I am the Cat that walks by himself, and all places are alike to me.'

'Not when I am near,' said the Dog. 'If you had not said that last I would have shut my mouth for always and always and always; but *now* I am going to hunt you up a tree whenever I meet you. And so shall all proper Dogs do after me.'

Then the Man threw his two boots and his little stone axe (that makes three) at the Cat, and the Cat ran out of the Cave and the Dog chased him up a tree; and from that day to this, Best Beloved, three proper Men out of five will always throw things at a Cat whenever they meet him, and all proper Dogs will chase him up a tree. But the Cat keeps his side of the bargain too. He will kill mice, and he will be kind to Babies when he is in the house, just as long as they do not pull his tail too hard. But when he has done that, and between times, and when the moon gets up and night comes, he is the Cat that walks by himself, and all places are alike to him. Then he goes out to the Wet Wild Woods or up the Wet Wild Trees or on the Wet Wild Roofs, waving his wild tail and walking by his wild lone.

Pussy can sit by the fire and sing,
    Pussy can climb a tree,
Or play with a silly old cork and string
    To 'muse herself, not me.
But I like *Binkie* my dog, because
    He knows how to behave;
So, *Binkie's* the same as the First Friend was,
    And I am the Man in the Cave.

Pussy will play Man Friday till
    It's time to wet her paw
And make her walk on the window-sill
    (For the footprint Crusoe saw);
Then she fluffles her tail and mews,
    And scratches and won't attend.
But *Binkie* will play whatever I choose,
    And he is my true First Friend.

Pussy will rub my knees with her head
    Pretending she loves me hard;
But the very minute I go to my bed
    Pussy runs out in the yard,
And there she stays till the morning-light;
    So I know it is only pretend;
But *Binkie*, he snores at my feet all night,
    And he is my Firstest Friend!

The Butterfly that Stamped

 THIS, O MY BEST BELOVED, is a story – a new and a wonderful story – a story quite different from the other stories – a story about The Most Wise Sovereign Suleiman-bin-Daoud – Solomon the Son of David.

There are three hundred and fifty-five stories about Suleiman-bin-Daoud; but this is not one of them. It is not the story of the Lapwing who found the Water; or the Hoopoe who shaded Suleiman-bin-Daoud from the heat. It is not the story of the Glass Pavement, or the Ruby with the Crooked Hole, or the Gold Bars of Balkis. It is the story of the Butterfly that Stamped.

Now attend all over again and listen!

Suleiman-bin-Daoud was wise. He understood what the beasts said, what the birds said, what the fishes said, and what the insects said. He understood what the rocks said deep under the earth when they bowed in towards each other and groaned; and he understood what the trees said when they rustled in the middle of the morning. He understood everything, from the bishop on the bench to the hyssop on the wall; and Balkis, his Head Queen, the Most Beautiful Queen Balkis, was nearly as wise as he was.

Suleiman-bin-Daoud was strong. Upon the third finger of his right hand he wore a ring. When he turned it once, Afrits and Djinns came out of the earth to do whatever he told them. When he turned it twice, Fairies came down from the sky to do whatever he told them; and when he turned it three times, the very great angel Azrael of the Sword came dressed as a water-carrier, and told him the news of the three worlds – Above – Below – and Here.

And yet Suleiman-bin-Daoud was not proud. He very seldom showed off, and when he did he was sorry for it. Once he tried to feed all the animals in all the world in one day, but when the food was ready an Animal came out of the deep sea and ate it up in three mouthfuls. Suleiman-bin-Daoud was very surprised and said, 'O Animal, who are you?' And the Animal said, 'O King, live for ever! I am the smallest of thirty thousand brothers, and our home is at the bottom of the sea. We heard that you were going to feed all the animals in all the world, and my brothers sent me to ask when dinner would be ready.' Suleiman-bin-Daoud was more surprised than ever and said, 'O Animal, you have eaten all the dinner that I made ready for all the animals in the world.'

And the Animal said, 'O King, live for ever, but do you really call *that* a dinner? Where I come from we each eat twice as much as that between meals.' Then Suleiman-bin-Daoud fell flat on his face and said, 'O Animal! I gave that dinner to show what a great and rich king I was, and not because I really wanted to be kind to the animals. Now I am ashamed, and it serves me right.' Suleiman-bin-Daoud was a really truly wise man, Best Beloved. After that he never forgot that it was silly to show off; and now the real story part of my story begins.

He married ever so many wives. He married nine hundred and ninety-nine wives, besides the Most Beautiful Balkis; and they all lived in a great golden palace in the middle of a lovely garden with fountains. He didn't really want nine hundred and ninety-nine wives, but in those days everybody married ever so many wives, and of course the King had to marry ever so many more just to show that he was the King.

Some of the wives were nice, but some were simply horrid, and the horrid ones quarrelled with the nice ones and made them horrid too, and then they would all quarrel with Suleiman-bin-Daoud, and that was horrid for him. But Balkis the Most Beautiful never quarrelled with Suleiman-bin-Daoud. She loved him too much. She sat in her rooms in the Golden Palace, or walked in the Palace garden, and was truly sorry for him.

Of course if he had chosen to turn his ring on his finger and call up the Djinns and the Afrits they would have magicked all those nine hundred and ninety-nine quarrelsome wives into white mules of the desert or greyhounds or pomegranate seeds; but Suleiman-bin-Daoud thought that that would be showing off. So, when they quarrelled too much, he only walked by himself in one part of the beautiful Palace gardens and wished he had never been born.

One day, when they had quarrelled for three weeks – all nine hundred and ninety-nine wives together – Suleiman-bin-Daoud went out for peace and quiet as usual; and among the orange trees he met Balkis the Most Beautiful, very sorrowful because Suleiman-bin-Daoud was so worried. And she said to him, 'O my Lord and Light of my Eyes, turn the ring upon your finger and show these Queens of Egypt and Mesopotamia and Persia and China that you are the great and terrible King.' But Suleiman-bin-Daoud shook his head and said, 'O my Lady and Delight of my Life, remember the Animal that came out of the sea and made me ashamed before all the animals in all the world because I showed off. Now, if I showed off before these Queens of Persia and Egypt and Abyssinia and China, merely because they worry me, I might be made even more ashamed than I have been.'

And Balkis the Most Beautiful said, 'O my Lord and Treasure of my Soul, what will you do?'

And Suleiman-bin-Daoud said, 'O my Lady and Content of my Heart, I shall continue to endure my fate at the hands of these nine hundred and ninety-nine Queens who vex me with their continual quarrelling.'

So he went on between the lilies and the loquats and the roses and the

This is the picture of the Animal

that came out of the sea and ate up all the food that Suleiman-bin-Daoud had made ready for all the animals in all the world. He was really quite a nice Animal, and his Mummy was very fond of him and of his twenty-nine thousand nine hundred and ninety-nine other brothers that lived at the bottom of the sea. You know that he was the smallest of them all, and so his name was Small Porgies. He ate up all those boxes and packets and bales and things that had been got ready for all the animals, without ever once taking off the lids or untying the strings, and it did not hurt him at all. The sticky-up masts behind the boxes of food belong to Suleiman-bin-Daoud's ships. They were busy bringing more food when Small Porgies came ashore. He did not eat the ships. They stopped unloading the foods and instantly sailed away to sea till Small Porgies had quite finished eating. You can see some of the ships beginning to sail away by Small Porgies' shoulder. I have not drawn Suleiman-bin-Daoud, but he is just outside the picture, very much astonished. The bundle hanging from the mast of the ship in the corner is really a package of wet dates for parrots to eat. I don't know the names of the ships. That is all there is in that picture.

cannas and the heavy-scented ginger-plants that grew in the garden, till he came to the great camphor tree that was called the Camphor Tree of Suleiman-bin-Daoud. But Balkis hid among the tall irises and the spotted bamboos and the red lilies behind the camphor tree, so as to be near her own true love, Suleiman-bin-Daoud.

Presently two Butterflies flew under the tree, quarrelling.

Suleiman-bin-Daoud heard one say to the other, 'I wonder at your presumption in talking like this to me. Don't you know that if I stamped with my foot all Suleiman-bin-Daoud's Palace and this garden here would immediately vanish in a clap of thunder?'

Then Suleiman-bin-Daoud forgot his nine hundred and ninety-nine bothersome wives, and laughed, till the camphor tree shook, at the Butterfly's boast. And he held out his finger and said, 'Little man, come here.'

The Butterfly was dreadfully frightened, but he managed to fly up to the hand of Suleiman-bin-Daoud, and clung there, fanning himself. Suleiman-bin-Daoud bent his head and whispered very softly, 'Little man, you know that all your stamping wouldn't bend one blade of grass. What made you tell that awful fib to your wife? – for doubtless she is your wife.'

The Butterfly looked at Suleiman-bin-Daoud and saw the most wise King's eyes twinkle like stars on a frosty night, and he picked up his courage with both wings, and he put his head on one side and said, 'O King, live for ever. She *is* my wife; and you know what wives are like.'

Suleiman-bin-Daoud smiled in his beard and said, 'Yes, *I* know, little brother.'

'One must keep them in order somehow,' said the Butterfly, 'and she has been quarrelling with me all the morning. I said that to quiet her.'

And Suleiman-bin-Daoud said, 'May it quiet her. Go back to your wife, little brother, and let me hear what you say.'

Back flew the Butterfly to his wife, who was all of a twitter behind a leaf, and she said, 'He heard you! Suleiman-bin-Daoud himself heard you!'

'Heard me!' said the Butterfly. 'Of course he did. I meant him to hear me.'

'And what did he say? Oh what did he say?'

'Well,' said the Butterfly, fanning himself most importantly, 'between you and me, my dear – of course I don't blame him, because his Palace must have cost a great deal and the oranges are just ripening – he asked me not to stamp, and I promised I wouldn't.'

'Gracious!' said his wife, and sat quite quiet; but Suleiman-bin-Daoud laughed till the tears ran down his face at the impudence of the bad little Butterfly.

Balkis the Most Beautiful stood up behind the tree among the red lilies and smiled to herself, for she had heard all this talk. She thought, 'If I am wise I can yet save my Lord from the persecutions of these quarrelsome Queens,' and she held out her finger and whispered softly to the Butterfly's Wife, 'Little woman, come here.'

Up flew the Butterfly's Wife, very frightened, and clung to Balkis's white hand.

Balkis bent her beautiful head down and whispered, 'Little woman, do you believe what your husband has just said?'

The Butterfly's Wife looked at Balkis, and saw the Most Beautiful Queen's eyes shining like deep pools with starlight on them, and she picked up her courage with both wings and said, 'O Queen, be lovely for ever. *You* know what menfolk are like.'

And the Queen Balkis, the Wise Balkis of Sheba, put her hand to her lips to hide a smile, and said, 'Little sister, *I* know.'

'They get angry,' said the Butterfly's Wife, fanning herself quickly, 'over nothing at all, but we must humour them, O Queen. They never mean half they say. If it pleases my husband to believe that I believe he can make Suleiman-bin-Daoud's Palace disappear by stamping his foot, I'm sure *I* don't care. He'll forget all about it tomorrow.'

'Little sister,' said Balkis, 'you are quite right; but next time he begins to boast, take him at his word. Ask him to stamp, and see what will happen. *We* know what menfolk are like, don't we? He'll be very much ashamed.'

Away flew the Butterfly's Wife to her husband, and in five minutes they were quarrelling worse than ever.

'Remember!' said the Butterfly. 'Remember what I can do if I stamp my foot.'

'I don't believe you one little bit,' said the Butterfly's Wife. 'I should very much like to see it done. Suppose you stamp now.'

'I promised Suleiman-bin-Daoud that I wouldn't,' said the Butterfly, 'and I don't want to break my promise.'

'It wouldn't matter if you did,' said his wife. 'You couldn't bend a blade of grass with your stamping. I dare you to do it,' she said. 'Stamp! Stamp! Stamp!'

Suleiman-bin-Daoud, sitting under the camphor tree, heard every word of this, and he laughed as he had never laughed in his life before. He forgot all about his Queens; he forgot about the Animal that came out of the sea; he forgot about showing off. He just laughed with joy, and Balkis, on the other side of the tree, smiled because her own true love was so joyful.

Presently the Butterfly, very hot and puffy, came whirling back under the shadow of the camphor tree and said to Suleiman, 'She wants me to stamp! She wants to see what will happen, O Suleiman-bin-Daoud! You know I can't do it, and now she'll never believe a word I say. She'll laugh at me to the end of my days!'

'No, little brother,' said Suleiman-bin-Daoud, 'she will never laugh at you again,' and he turned the ring on his finger – just for the little Butterfly's sake, not for the sake of showing off – and, lo and behold, four huge Djinns came out of the earth!

'Slaves,' said Suleiman-bin-Daoud, 'when this gentleman on my finger' (that was where the impudent Butterfly was sitting) 'stamps his left front forefoot you will make my Palace and these gardens disappear in a clap of thunder. When he stamps again you will bring them back carefully.'

'Now, little brother,' he said, 'go back to your wife and stamp all you've a mind to.'

Away flew the Butterfly to his wife, who was crying, 'I dare you to do it! I dare you to do it! Stamp! Stamp now! Stamp!' Balkis saw the four vast Djinns stoop down to the four corners of the gardens with the Palace in the middle, and she clapped her hands softly and said, 'At last Suleiman-bin-Daoud will do for the sake of a Butterfly what he ought to have done long ago for his own sake, and the quarrelsome Queens will be frightened!'

Then the Butterfly stamped. The Djinns jerked the Palace and the gardens a thousand miles into the air: there was a most awful thunderclap, and everything grew inky black. The Butterfly's Wife fluttered about in the dark, crying, 'Oh, I'll be good! I'm so sorry I spoke! Only bring the gardens back, my dear darling husband, and I'll never contradict again.'

The Butterfly was nearly as frightened as his wife, and Suleiman-bin-Daoud laughed so much that it was several minutes before he found breath enough to whisper to the Butterfly, 'Stamp again, little brother. Give me back my Palace, most great magician.'

'Yes, give him back his Palace,' said the Butterfly's Wife, still flying about in the dark like a moth. 'Give him back his Palace, and don't let's have any more horrid magic.'

'Well, my dear,' said the Butterfly as bravely as he could, 'you see what your nagging has led to. Of course it doesn't make any difference to *me* – I'm used to this kind of thing – but as a favour to you and to Suleiman-bin-Daoud I don't mind putting things right.'

So he stamped once more, and that instant the Djinns let down the Palace and the gardens, without even a bump. The sun shone on the dark-green orange-leaves; the fountains played among the pink Egyptian lilies; the birds went on singing; and the Butterfly's Wife lay on her side under the camphor tree waggling her wings and panting, 'Oh, I'll be good! I'll be good!'

Suleiman-bin-Daoud could hardly speak for laughing. He leaned back all weak and hiccoughy, and shook his finger at the Butterfly and said, 'O great wizard, what is the sense of returning to me my Palace if at the same time you slay me with mirth!'

Then came a terrible noise, for all the nine hundred and ninety-nine Queens ran out of the Palace shrieking and shouting and calling for their babies. They hurried down the great marble steps below the fountain, one hundred abreast, and the Most Wise Balkis went statelily forward to meet them and said, 'What is your trouble, O Queens?'

They stood on the marble steps one hundred abreast and shouted, '*What* is our trouble? We were living peacefully in our golden Palace, as is our custom, when upon a sudden the Palace disappeared, and we were left sitting in a thick

This is the picture of

the four gull-winged Djinns lifting up Suleiman-bin-Daoud's Palace
the very minute after the Butterfly had stamped. The Palace and the
gardens and everything came up in one piece like a board, and they
left a big hole in the ground all full of dust and smoke. If you look in
the corner, close to the thing that looks like a lion, you will see
Suleiman-bin-Daoud with his magic stick and the two Butterflies
behind him. The thing that looks like a lion is really a lion carved in
stone, and the thing that looks like a milk-can is really a piece of a
temple or a house or something. Suleiman-bin-Daoud stood there
so as to be out of the way of the dust and the smoke when the Djinns
lifted up the Palace. I don't know the Djinns' names. They were
servants of Suleiman-bin-Daoud's magic ring, and they changed
about every day. They were just common gull-winged Djinns.

The thing at the bottom is a picture of a very friendly Djinn
called Akraig. He used to feed the little fishes in the sea three times
a day, and his wings were made of pure copper. I put him in to show
you what a nice Djinn is like. He did not help to lift the Palace. He
was busy feeding little fishes in the Arabian Sea when it happened.

and noisome darkness; and it thundered, and Djinns and Afrits moved about in the darkness! *That* is our trouble, O Head Queen, and we are most extremely troubled on account of that trouble, for it was a troublesome trouble, unlike any trouble we have known.'

Then Balkis the Most Beautiful Queen – Suleiman-bin-Daoud's Very Best Beloved – Queen that was of Sheba and Sabie and the Rivers of the Gold of the South – from the Desert of Zinn to the Towers of Zimbabwe – Balkis, almost as wise as the Most Wise Suleiman-bin-Daoud himself, said, 'It is nothing, O Queens! A Butterfly has made complaint against his wife because she quarrelled with him, and it has pleased our Lord Suleiman-bin-Daoud to teach her a lesson in low-speaking and humbleness, for that is counted a virtue among the wives of the butterflies.'

Then up and spoke an Egyptian Queen – the daughter of a Pharaoh – and she said, 'Our Palace cannot be plucked up by the roots like a leek for the sake of a little insect. No! Suleiman-bin-Daoud must be dead, and what we heard and saw was the earth thundering and darkening at the news.'

Then Balkis beckoned that bold Queen without looking at her, and said to her and to the others, 'Come and see.'

They came down the marble steps, one hundred abreast, and beneath his camphor tree, still weak with laughing, they saw the Most Wise King Suleiman-bin-Daoud rocking back and forth with a Butterfly on either hand, and they heard him say, 'O wife of my brother in the air, remember after this to please your husband in all things, lest he be provoked to stamp his foot yet again; for he has said that he is used to this Magic, and he is most eminently a great magician – one who steals away the very Palace of Suleiman-bin-Daoud himself. Go in peace, little folk!' And he kissed them on the wings, and they flew away.

Then all the Queens except Balkis – the Most Beautiful and Splendid Balkis, who stood apart smiling – fell flat on their faces, for they said, 'If these things are done when a Butterfly is displeased with his wife, what shall be done to us who have vexed our King with our loud-speaking and open quarrelling through many days?'

Then they put their veils over their heads, and they put their hands over their mouths, and they tiptoed back to the Palace most mousy-quiet.

Then Balkis – the Most Beautiful and Excellent Balkis – went forward through the red lilies into the shade of the camphor tree and laid her hand upon Suleiman-bin-Daoud's shoulder and said, 'O my Lord and Treasure of my Soul, rejoice, for we have taught the Queens of Egypt and Ethiopia and Abyssinia and Persia and India and China with a great and a memorable teaching.'

And Suleiman-bin-Daoud, still looking after the Butterflies where they played in the sunlight, said, 'O my Lady and Jewel of my Felicity, when did this happen? For I have been jesting with a Butterfly ever since I came into the garden.' And he told Balkis what he had done.

Balkis – the Tender and Most Lovely Balkis – said, 'O my Lord and Regent of my Existence, I hid behind the camphor tree and saw it all. It was I who told the Butterfly's Wife to ask the Butterfly to stamp, because I hoped that for the sake of the jest my Lord would make some great Magic and that the Queens would see it and be frightened.' And she told him what the Queens had said and seen and thought.

Then Suleiman-bin-Daoud rose up from his seat under the camphor tree, and stretched his arms and rejoiced and said, 'O my Lady and Sweetener of my Days, know that if I had made a Magic against my Queens for the sake of pride or anger, as I made that feast for all the animals, I should certainly have been put to shame. But by means of your wisdom I made the Magic for the sake of a jest and for the sake of a little Butterfly, and – behold – it has also delivered me from the vexations of my vexatious wives! Tell me, therefore, O my Lady and Heart of my Heart, how did you come to be so wise?'

And Balkis the Queen, beautiful and tall, looked up into Suleiman-bin-Daoud's eyes and put her head a little on one side, just like the Butterfly, and said, 'First, O my Lord, because I loved you; and secondly, O my Lord, because I know what womenfolk are.'

Then they went up to the Palace and lived happily ever afterwards.

But wasn't it clever of Balkis?

There was never a Queen like Balkis,
    From here to the wide world's end;
But Balkis talked to a butterfly
    As you would talk to a friend.

There was never a King like Solomon,
    Not since the world began;
But Solomon talked to a butterfly
    As a man would talk to a man.

She was Queen of Sabaea –
    And *he* was Asia's Lord –
But they both of 'em talked to butterflies
    When they took their walks abroad!

PUCK OF POOK'S HILL

Contents

Hal o' the Draft

'Dymchurch Flit'

The Treasure and the Law

PUCK OF POOK'S HILL

WELAND'S SWORD

Puck's Song

See you the dimpled track that runs,
    All hollow through the wheat?
O that was where they hauled the guns
    That smote King Philip's fleet!

See you our little mill that clacks,
    So busy by the brook?
She has ground her corn and paid her tax
    Ever since Domesday Book.

See you our stilly woods of oak,
    And the dread ditch beside?
O that was where the Saxons broke,
    On the day that Harold died!

See you the windy levels spread
    About the gates of Rye?
O that was where the Northmen fled,
    When Alfred's ships came by!

See you our pastures wide and lone,
    Where the red oxen browse?
O there was a City thronged and known,
    Ere London boasted a house!

And see you, after rain, the trace
    Of mound and ditch and wall?
O that was a Legion's camping-place,
    When Caesar sailed from Gaul!

And see you marks that show and fade,
  Like shadows on the Downs?
O they are the lines the Flint Men made,
  To guard their wondrous towns!

Trackway and Camp and City lost,
  Salt Marsh where now is corn;
Old Wars, old Peace, old Arts that cease,
  And so was England born!

She is not any common Earth,
  Water or Wood or Air,
But Merlin's Isle of Gramarye,
  Where you and I will fare.

Weland's Sword

The children were at the theatre, acting to three cows as much as they could remember of *A Midsummer Night's Dream*. Their father had made them a small play out of the big Shakespeare one, and they had rehearsed it with him and with their mother till they could say it by heart. They began when Nick Bottom the weaver comes out of the bushes with a donkey's head on his shoulders, and finds Titania, Queen of the Fairies, asleep. Then they skipped to the part where Bottom asks three little fairies to scratch his head and bring him honey, and they ended where he falls asleep in Titania's arms. Dan was Puck and Nick Bottom, as well as all three Fairies. He wore a pointy-cloth cap for Puck, and a paper donkey's head out of a Christmas cracker – but it tore if you were not careful – for Bottom. Una was Titania, with a wreath of columbines and a foxglove wand.

The theatre lay in a meadow called the Long Slip. A little millstream, carrying water to a mill two or three fields away, bent round one corner of it, and in the middle of the bend lay a large old Fairy Ring of darkened grass, which was the stage. The millstream banks, overgrown with willow, hazel, and guelder rose, made convenient places to wait in till your turn came; and a grown-up who had seen it said that Shakespeare himself could not have imagined a more suitable setting for his play. They were not, of course, allowed to act on Midsummer Night itself, but they went down after tea on Midsummer Eve, when the shadows were growing, and they took their supper – hard-boiled eggs, Bath Oliver biscuits, and salt in an envelope – with them. Three Cows had been milked and were grazing steadily with a tearing noise that one could hear all down the meadow; and the noise of the mill at work sounded like bare feet running on hard ground. A cuckoo sat on a gatepost singing his broken June tune, 'cuckoo-cuck', while a busy kingfisher crossed from the millstream, to the brook which ran on the other side of the meadow. Everything else was a sort of thick, sleepy stillness smelling of meadowsweet and dry grass.

Their play went beautifully. Dan remembered all his parts – Puck, Bottom, and the three Fairies – and Una never forgot a word of Titania – not even the difficult piece where she tells the Fairies how to feed Bottom with 'apricocks, green figs, and dewberries', and all the lines end in 'ies'. They were both so pleased that they acted it three times over from beginning to end before they sat down in the unthistly centre of the Ring to eat eggs and Bath Olivers. This was when they heard a whistle among the alders on the bank, and they jumped.

The bushes parted. In the very spot where Dan had stood as Puck they saw a small, brown, broad-shouldered, pointy-eared person with a snub nose, slanting blue eyes, and a grin that ran right across his freckled face. He shaded his forehead as though he were watching Quince, Snout, Bottom, and the others rehearsing *Pyramus and Thisbe*, and, in a voice as deep as Three Cows asking to be milked, he began:

> 'What hempen homespuns have we swaggering here,
> So near the cradle of the Fairy Queen?'

He stopped, hollowed one hand round his ear, and, with a wicked twinkle in his eye, went on:

> 'What, a play toward? I'll be an auditor;
> An actor, too, perhaps, if I see cause.'

The children looked and gasped. The small thing – he was no taller than Dan's shoulder – stepped quietly into the Ring.

'I'm rather out of practice,' said he; 'but that's the way my part ought to be played.'

Still the children stared at him – from his dark-blue cap, like a big columbine flower, to his bare, hairy feet. At last he laughed.

'Please don't look like that. It isn't my fault. What else could you expect?' he said.

'We didn't expect anyone,' Dan answered slowly. 'This is our field.'

'Is it?' said their visitor, sitting down. 'Then what on Human Earth made you act *A Midsummer Night's Dream* three times over, *on* Midsummer Eve, *in* the middle of a Ring, and under – right *under* one of my oldest hills in Old England? Pook's Hill – Puck's Hill – Puck's Hill – Pook's Hill! It's as plain as the nose on my face.'

He pointed to the bare, fern-covered slope of Pook's Hill that runs up from the far side of the millstream to a dark wood. Beyond that wood the ground rises and rises for five hundred feet, till at last you climb out on the bare top of Beacon Hill, to look over the Pevensey Levels and the Channel and half the naked South Downs.

'By Oak, Ash, and Thorn!' he cried, still laughing. 'If this had happened a few hundred years ago you'd have had all the People of the Hills out like bees in June!'

'We didn't know it was wrong,' said Dan.

'Wrong!' The little fellow shook with laughter. 'Indeed, it isn't wrong. You've done something that Kings and Knights and Scholars in old days would have given their crowns and spurs and books to find out. If Merlin himself had helped you, you couldn't have managed better! You've broken the Hills – you've broken the Hills! It hasn't happened in a thousand years.'

'We – we didn't mean to,' said Una.

'Of course you didn't! That's just why you did it. Unluckily the Hills are empty now, and all the People of the Hills are gone. I'm the only one left. I'm Puck, the oldest Old Thing in England, very much at your service if – if you care to have anything to do with me. If you don't, of course you've only to say so, and I'll go.'

They saw a small, brown, broad-shouldered, pointy-eared person with a snub nose, slanting blue eyes, and a grin that ran right across his freckled face.

He looked at the children, and the children looked at him for quite half a minute. His eyes did not twinkle any more. They were very kind, and there was the beginning of a good smile on his lips.

Una put out her hand. 'Don't go,' she said. 'We like you.'

'Have a Bath Oliver,' said Dan, and he passed over the squashy envelope with the eggs.

'By Oak, Ash, and Thorn,' cried Puck, taking off his blue cap, 'I like you too. Sprinkle a plenty salt on the biscuit, Dan, and I'll eat it with you. That'll show you the sort of person I am. Some of us' – he went on, with his mouth full – 'couldn't abide Salt, or Horseshoes over a door, or Mountain-ash berries, or Running Water, or Cold Iron, or the sound of Church Bells. But I'm Puck!'

He brushed the crumbs carefully from his doublet and shook hands.

'We always said, Dan and I,' Una stammered, 'that if it ever happened we'd know ex–actly what to do; but – but now it seems all different somehow.'

'She means meeting a fairy,' said Dan. '*I* never believed in 'em – not after I was six, anyhow.'

'I did,' said Una. 'At least, I sort of half believed till we learned "Farewell, Rewards". Do you know "Farewell, Rewards and Fairies"?'

'Do you mean this?' said Puck. He threw his big head back and began at the second line:

> 'Good housewives now may say,
> For now foul sluts in dairies
> Do fare as well as they;
> And though they sweep their hearths no less

('Join in, Una!')

> Than maids were wont to do,
> Yet who of late for cleanliness
> Finds sixpence in her shoe?'

The echoes flapped all along the flat meadow. 'Of course I know it,' he said.

'And then there's the verse about the rings,' said Dan. 'When I was little it always made me feel unhappy in my inside.'

' "Witness those rings and roundelays", do you mean?' boomed Puck, with a voice like a great church organ.

> 'Of theirs which yet remain,
> Were footed in Queen Mary's days
> On many a grassy plain,
> But since of late Elizabeth,
> And, later, James came in,
> Are never seen on any heath
> As when the time hath been.

'It's some time since I heard that sung, but there's no good beating about the bush: it's true. The People of the Hills have all left. I saw them come into Old England and I saw them go. Giants, trolls, kelpies, brownies, goblins, imps; wood, tree, mound, and water spirits; heath-people, hill-watchers, treasure-guards, good people, little people, pishogues, leprechauns, night-riders, pixies, nixies, gnomes, and the rest – gone, all gone! I came into England with Oak, Ash and Thorn, and when Oak, Ash and Thorn are gone I shall go too.'

Dan looked round the meadow – at Una's Oak by the lower gate; at the line of ash trees that overhang Otter Pool where the millstream spills over when the mill does not need it, and at the gnarled old white-thorn where Three Cows scratched their necks.

'It's all right,' he said; and added, 'I'm planting a lot of acorns this autumn too.'

'Then aren't you most awfully old?' said Una.

'Not old – fairly long-lived, as folk say hereabouts. Let me see – my friends used to set my dish of cream for me o' nights when Stonehenge was new. Yes, before the Flint Men made the Dewpond under Chanctonbury Ring.'

Una clasped her hands, cried 'Oh!' and nodded her head.

'She's thought a plan,' Dan explained. 'She always does like that when she thinks a plan.'

'I was thinking – suppose we saved some of our porridge and put it in the attic for you? They'd notice if we left it in the nursery.'

'Schoolroom,' said Dan quickly, and Una flushed, because they had made a solemn treaty that summer not to call the schoolroom the nursery any more.

'Bless your heart o' gold!' said Puck. 'You'll make a fine considering wench some market-day. I really don't want you to put out a bowl for me; but if ever I need a bite, be sure I'll tell you.'

He stretched himself at length on the dry grass, and the children stretched out beside him, their bare legs waving happily in the air. They felt they could not be afraid of him any more than of their particular friend old Hobden the hedger. He did not bother them with grown-up questions, or laugh at the donkey's head, but lay and smiled to himself in the most sensible way.

'Have you a knife on you?' he said at last.

Dan handed over his big one-bladed outdoor knife, and Puck began to carve out a piece of turf from the centre of the Ring.

'What's that for – Magic?' said Una, as he pressed up the square of chocolate loam that cut like so much cheese.

'One of my little magics,' he answered, and cut another. 'You see, I can't let you into the Hills because the People of the Hills have gone; but if you care to take seisin from me, I may be able to show you something out of the common here on Human Earth. You certainly deserve it.'

'What's taking seisin?' said Dan, cautiously.

'It's an old custom the people had when they bought and sold land. They used to cut out a clod and hand it over to the buyer, and you weren't lawfully seised of your land – it didn't really belong to you – till the other fellow had actually given you a piece of it – like this.' He held out the turves.

'But it's our own meadow,' said Dan, drawing back. 'Are you going to magic it away?'

Puck laughed. 'I know it's your meadow, but there's a great deal more in it than you or your father ever guessed. Try!'

He turned his eyes on Una.

'I'll do it,' she said. Dan followed her example at once.

'Now are you two lawfully seised and possessed of all Old England,' began Puck, in a sing-song voice. 'By right of Oak, Ash, and Thorn are you free to come and go and look and know where I shall show or best you please. You shall see What you shall see and you shall hear What you shall hear, though It shall have happened three thousand year; and you shall know neither Doubt nor Fear. Fast! Hold fast all I give you.'

The children shut their eyes, but nothing happened.

'Well?' said Una, disappointedly opening them. 'I thought there would be dragons.'

' "Though It shall have happened three thousand year," ' said Puck, and counted on his fingers. 'No; I'm afraid there were no dragons three thousand years ago.'

'But there hasn't happened anything at all,' said Dan.

'Wait awhile,' said Puck. 'You don't grow an oak in a year – and Old England's older than twenty oaks. Let's sit down again and think. I can do that for a century at a time.'

'Ah, but you're a fairy,' said Dan.

'Have you ever heard me say that word yet?' said Puck quickly.

'No. You talk about "the People of the Hills", but you never say "fairies",' said Una. 'I was wondering at that. Don't you like it?'

'How would you like to be called "mortal" or "human being" all the time?' said Puck; 'or "son of Adam" or "daughter of Eve"?'

'I shouldn't like it at all,' said Dan. 'That's how the Djinns and Afrits talk in the *Arabian Nights*.'

'And that's how I feel about saying – that word that I don't say. Besides, what you call *them* are made-up things the People of the Hills have never heard of – little buzzflies with butterfly wings and gauze petticoats, and shiny stars in their hair, and a wand like a schoolteacher's cane for punishing bad boys and rewarding good ones. *I* know 'em!'

'We don't mean that sort,' said Dan. 'We hate 'em too.'

'Exactly,' said Puck. 'Can you wonder that the People of the Hills don't care to be confused with that painty-winged, wand-waving, sugar-and-shake-your-head set of impostors? Butterfly wings, indeed! I've seen Sir Huon and a troop of his people setting off from Tintagel Castle for Hy-Brasil in the teeth of a sou'-westerly gale, with the spray flying all over the Castle, and the Horses of the Hills wild with fright. Out they'd go in a lull, screaming like gulls, and back they'd be driven five good miles inland before they could come head to wind again. Butterfly-wings! It was Magic – Magic as black as Merlin could make it, and the whole sea was green fire and white foam with singing mermaids in it. And the Horses of the Hills picked their way from one wave to another by the lightning flashes! *That* was how it was in the old days!'

'Splendid,' said Dan, but Una shuddered.

'I'm glad they're gone, then; but what made the People of the Hills go away?' Una asked.

'Different things. I'll tell you one of them some day – the thing that made the biggest flit of any,' said Puck. 'But they didn't all flit at once. They dropped off, one by one, through the centuries. Most of them were foreigners who couldn't stand our climate. *They* flitted early.'

'How early?' said Dan.

'A couple of thousand years or more. The fact is they began as Gods. The Phoenicians brought some over when they came to buy tin; and the Gauls, and the Jutes, and the Danes, and the Frisians, and the Angles brought more when they landed. They were always landing in those days, or being driven back to their ships, and they always brought their Gods with them. England is a bad country for Gods. Now, *I* began as I mean to go on. A bowl of porridge, a dish of milk, and a little quiet fun with the country folk in the lanes was enough for me then, as it is now. I belong here, you see, and I have been mixed up with people all my days. But most of the others insisted on being Gods, and having temples, and altars, and priests, and sacrifices of their own.'

'People burned in wicker baskets?' said Dan. 'Like Miss Blake tells us about?'

'All sorts of sacrifices,' said Puck. 'If it wasn't men, it was horses, or cattle, or pigs, or metheglin – that's a sticky, sweet sort of beer. *I* never liked it. They were a stiff-necked, extravagant set of idols, the Old Things. But what was the result? Men don't like being sacrificed at the best of times; they don't even like sacrificing their farm-horses. After a while, men simply left the Old Things alone, and the roofs of their temples fell in, and the Old Things had to scuttle out and pick up a living as they could. Some of them took to hanging about trees, and hiding in graves and groaning o' nights. If they groaned loud enough and long enough they might frighten a poor country-man into sacrificing a hen, or leaving a pound of butter for them. I remember one Goddess called Belisama. She became a common, wet water spirit somewhere in Lancashire. And there were hundreds of other friends of mine. First they were Gods. Then they were People of the Hills, and then they flitted to other places because they couldn't get on with the English for one reason or another. There was only one Old Thing, I remember, who honestly worked for his living after he came down in the world. He was called Weland, and he was a smith to some Gods. I've forgotten their names, but he used to make them swords and spears. I think he claimed kin with Thor of the Scandinavians.'

'*Heroes of Asgard* Thor?' said Una. She had been reading the book.

'Perhaps,' answered Puck. 'None the less, when bad times came, he didn't beg or steal. He worked; and I was lucky enough to be able to do him a good turn.'

'Tell us about it,' said Dan. 'I think I like hearing of Old Things.'

They rearranged themselves comfortably, each chewing a grass stem. Puck propped himself on one strong arm and went on: 'Let's think! I met Weland first on a November afternoon in a sleet storm, on Pevensey Level – '

'Pevensey? Over the hill, you mean?' Dan pointed south.

'Yes; but it was all marsh in those days, right up to Horsebridge and Hydeneye. I was on Beacon Hill – they called it Brunanburgh then – when I saw the pale flame that burning thatch makes, and I went down to look. Some pirates – I think they must have been Peofn's men – were burning a village on the Levels, and Weland's image – a big, black wooden thing with amber beads round his neck – lay in the bows of a black thirty-two-oar galley that they had just beached. Bitter cold it was! There were icicles hanging from her deck and the oars were glazed over with ice, and there was ice on Weland's lips. When he saw me he began a long chant in his own tongue, telling me how he was going to rule England, and how I should smell the smoke of his altars from Lincolnshire to the Isle of Wight. *I* didn't care! I'd seen too many Gods charging into Old England to be upset about it. I let him sing himself out while his men were burning the village, and then I said (I don't know what put it into my head), "Smith of the Gods," I said, "the time comes when I shall meet you plying your trade for hire by the wayside." '

'What did Weland say?' said Una. 'Was he angry?'

'He called me names and rolled his eyes, and I went away to wake up the people inland. But the pirates conquered the country, and for centuries Weland was a most important God. He had temples everywhere – from Lincolnshire to the Isle of Wight, as he said – and his sacrifices were simply scandalous. To do him justice, he preferred horses to men; but men *or* horses, I knew that presently he'd have to come down in the world – like the other Old Things. I gave him lots of time – I gave him about a thousand years – and at the end of 'em I went into one of his temples near Andover to see how he prospered. There was his altar, and there was his image, and there were his priests, and there were the congregation, and everybody seemed quite happy, except Weland and the priests. In the old days the congregation were unhappy until the priests had chosen their sacrifices; and so would *you* have been. When the service began a priest rushed out, dragged a man up to the altar, pretended to hit him on the head with a little gilt axe, and the man fell down and pretended to die. Then everybody shouted: "A sacrifice to Weland! A sacrifice to Weland!" '

'And the man wasn't really dead?' said Una.

'Not a bit. All as much pretence as a dolls' tea party. Then they brought out a splendid white horse, and the priest cut some hair from its mane and tail and burned it on the altar, shouting, "A sacrifice!" That counted the same as if a man and a horse had been killed. I saw poor Weland's face through the smoke, and I couldn't help laughing. He looked so disgusted and so hungry, and all he had to satisfy himself was a horrid smell of burning hair. Just a dolls' tea party!

'I judged it better not to say anything then ('twouldn't have been fair), and the next time I came to Andover, a few hundred years later, Weland and his temple were gone, and there was a Christian bishop in a church there. None of the People of the Hills could tell me anything about him, and I supposed that he had left England.' Puck turned, lay on his other elbow, and thought for a long time.

'Let's see,' he said at last. 'It must have been some few years later – a year or two before the Conquest, I think – that I came back to Pook's Hill here, and one evening I heard old Hobden talking about Weland's Ford.'

'If you mean old Hobden the hedger, he's only seventy-two. He told me so himself,' said Dan. 'He's an intimate friend of ours.'

'You're quite right,' Puck replied. 'I meant old Hobden's ninth great-grandfather. He was a free man and burned charcoal hereabouts. I've known the family, father and son, so long that I get confused sometimes. Hob of the Dene was my Hobden's name, and he lived at the Forge cottage. Of course, I pricked up my ears when I heard Weland mentioned, and I scuttled through the woods to the Ford just beyond Bog Wood yonder.' He jerked his head westward, where the valley narrows between wooded hills and steep hop-fields.

'Why, that's Willingford Bridge,' said Una. 'We go there for walks often. There's a kingfisher there.'

'It was Weland's Ford then, dearie. A road led down to it from the Beacon on the top of the hill – a shocking bad road it was – and all the hillside was thick, thick oak-forest, with deer in it. There was no trace of Weland, but presently I saw a fat old farmer riding down from the Beacon under the greenwood tree. His horse had cast a shoe in the clay, and when he came to the Ford he dismounted, took a penny out of his purse, laid it on a stone, tied the old horse to an oak, and called out: "Smith, Smith, here is work for you!" Then he sat down and went to sleep. You can imagine how *I* felt when I saw a white-bearded, bent old blacksmith in a leather apron creep out from behind the oak and begin to shoe the horse. It was Weland himself. I was so astonished that I jumped out and said: "What on Human Earth are you doing here, Weland?"'

'Poor Weland!' sighed Una.

'He pushed the long hair back from his forehead (he didn't recognise me at first). Then he said: "*You* ought to know. You foretold it, Old Thing. I'm shoeing horses for hire. I'm not even Weland now," he said. "They call me Wayland-Smith."'

'Poor chap!' said Dan. 'What did you say?'

'What could I say? He looked up, with the horse's foot on his lap, and he said, smiling, "I remember the time when I wouldn't have accepted this old bag of bones as a sacrifice, and now I'm glad enough to shoe him for a penny."

' "Isn't there any way for you to get back to Valhalla, or wherever you come from?" I said.

' "I'm afraid not," he said, rasping away at the hoof. He had a wonderful touch with horses. The old beast was whinnying on his shoulder. "You may remember that I was not a gentle God in my Day and my Time and my Power. I shall never be released till some human being truly wishes me well."

' "Surely," said I, "the farmer can't do less than that. You're shoeing the horse all round for him."

' "Yes," said he, "and my nails will hold a shoe from one full moon to the next. But farmers and Weald clay," said he, "are both uncommon cold and sour."

'Would you believe it, that when that farmer woke and found his horse shod he rode away without one word of thanks? I was so angry that I wheeled his horse right round and walked him back three miles to the Beacon, just to teach the old sinner politeness.'

'Were you invisible?' said Una. Puck nodded, gravely.

'The Beacon was always laid in those days ready to light, in case the French landed at Pevensey; and I walked the horse about and about it that lee-long summer night. The farmer thought he was bewitched – well, he *was*, of course – and began to pray and shout. I didn't care! I was as good a Christian as he any fair-day in the County, and about four o'clock in the morning a young novice came along from the monastery that used to stand on the top of Beacon Hill.'

'What's a novice?' said Dan.

'It really means a man who is beginning to be a monk, but in those days people sent their sons to a monastery just the same as a school. This young fellow had been to a monastery in France for a few months every year, and he was finishing his studies in the monastery close to his home here. Hugh was his name, and he had got up to go fishing hereabouts. His people owned all this valley. Hugh heard the farmer shouting, and asked him what in the world he meant. The old man spun him a wonderful tale about fairies and goblins and witches; and I *know* he hadn't seen a thing except rabbits and red deer all that night. (The People of the Hills are like otters – they don't show except when they choose.) But the novice wasn't a fool. He looked down at the horse's feet, and saw the new shoes fastened as only Weland knew how to fasten 'em. (Weland had a way of turning down the nails that folks called the Smith's Clinch.)

' "H'm!" said the novice. "Where did you get your horse shod?"

'The farmer wouldn't tell him at first, because the priests never liked their people to have any dealings with the Old Things. At last he confessed that the

Smith had done it. "What did you pay him?" said the novice. "Penny," said the farmer, very sulkily. "That's less than a Christian would have charged," said the novice. "I hope you threw a 'thank you' into the bargain." "No," said the farmer; "Wayland-Smith's a heathen." "Heathen or no heathen," said the novice, "you took his help, and where you get help there you must give thanks." "What?" said the farmer – he was in a furious temper because I was walking the old horse in circles all this time – "What, you young jackanapes?" said he. "Then by your reasoning I ought to say 'Thank you' to Satan if he helped me?" "Don't roll about up there splitting reasons with me," said the novice. "Come back to the Ford and thank the Smith, or you'll be sorry."

'Back the farmer had to go. I led the horse, though no one saw me, and the novice walked beside us, his gown swishing through the shiny dew and his fishing-rod across his shoulders, spear-wise. When we reached the Ford again – it was five o'clock and misty still under the oaks – the farmer simply wouldn't say "Thank you". He said he'd tell the Abbot that the novice wanted him to worship heathen Gods. Then Hugh the novice lost his temper. He just cried, "Out!", put his arm under the farmer's fat leg, and heaved him from his saddle on to the turf, and before he could rise he caught him by the back of the neck and shook him like a rat till the farmer growled, "Thank you, Wayland-Smith." '

'Did Weland see all this?' said Dan.

'Oh yes, and he shouted his old war cry when the farmer thudded on to the ground. He was delighted. Then the novice turned to the oak tree and said, "Ho, Smith of the Gods! I am ashamed of this rude farmer; but for all you have done in kindness and charity to him and to others of our people, I thank you and wish you well." Then he picked up his fishing-rod – it looked more like a tall spear than ever – and tramped off down your valley.'

'And what did poor Weland do?' said Una.

'He laughed and he cried with joy, because he had been released at last, and could go away. But he was an honest Old Thing. He had worked for his living and he paid his debts before he left. "I shall give that novice a gift," said Weland. "A gift that shall do him good the wide world over and Old England after him. Blow up my fire, Old Thing, while I get the iron for my last task." Then he made a sword – a dark-grey, wavy-lined sword – and I blew the fire while he hammered. By Oak, Ash and Thorn, I tell you, Weland was a Smith of the Gods! He cooled that sword in running water twice, and the third time he cooled it in the evening dew, and he laid it out in the moonlight and said Runes (that's charms) over it, and he carved Runes of Prophecy on the blade. "Old Thing," he said to me, wiping his forehead, "this is the best blade that Weland ever made. Even the user will never know how good it is. Come to the monastery." '

'We went to the dormitory where the monks slept, we saw the novice fast asleep in his cot, and Weland put the sword into his hand, and I remember the young fellow gripped it in his sleep. Then Weland strode as far as he dared into the Chapel and threw down all his shoeing-tools – his hammers and pincers and rasps – to show that he had done with them for ever. It sounded like suits of armour falling, and the sleepy monks ran in, for they thought the monastery had been attacked by the French. The novice came first of all, waving his new sword and shouting Saxon battle cries. When they saw the shoeing-tools they were very bewildered, till the novice asked leave to speak, and told what he had done to the farmer, and what he had said to Wayland-Smith, and how, though the dormitory light was burning, he had found the wonderful Rune-carved sword in his cot.

'The Abbot shook his head at first, and then he laughed and said to the novice: "Son Hugh, it needed no sign from a heathen God to show me that you will never be a monk. Take your sword, and keep your sword, and go with your sword, and be as gentle as you are strong and courteous. We will hang up the Smith's tools before the Altar," he said, "because, whatever the Smith of the Gods may have been, in the old days, we know that he worked honestly for his living and made gifts to Mother Church." Then they went to bed again, all except the novice, and he sat up in the garth playing with his sword. Then Weland said to me by the stables: "Farewell, Old Thing; you had the right of it. You saw me come to England, and you see me go. Farewell!"

'With that he strode down the hill to the corner of the Great Woods – Woods Corner, you call it now – to the very place where he had first landed – and I heard him moving through the thickets towards Horsebridge for a little, and then he was gone. That was how it happened. I saw it.'

Both children drew a long breath.

'But what happened to Hugh the novice?' said Una.

'And the sword?' said Dan.

Puck looked down the meadow that lay all quiet and cool in the shadow of Pook's Hill. A corncrake jarred in a hayfield near by, and the small trouts of the brook began to jump. A big white moth flew unsteadily from the alders and flapped round the children's heads, and the least little haze of water-mist rose from the brook.

'Do you really want to know?' Puck said.

'We do,' cried the children. 'Awfully!'

'Very good. I promised you that you shall see What you shall see, and you shall hear What you shall hear, though It shall have happened three thousand year; but just now it seems to me that, unless you go back to the house, people will be looking for you. I'll walk with you as far as the gate.'

'Will you be here when we come again?' they asked.

'Surely, sure–ly,' said Puck. 'I've been here some time already. One minute first, please.'

He gave them each three leaves – one of Oak, one of Ash and one of Thorn.

'Bite these,' said he. 'Otherwise you might be talking at home of what

'Then he made a sword – a dark-grey, wavy-lined sword – and
I blew the fire while he hammered.'

you've seen and heard, and – if I know human beings – they'd send for the doctor. Bite!'

They bit hard, and found themselves walking side by side to the lower gate. Their father was leaning over it.

'And how did your play go?' he asked.

'Oh, splendidly,' said Dan. 'Only afterwards, I think, we went to sleep. It was very hot and quiet. Don't you remember, Una?

Una shook her head and said nothing.

'I see,' said her father.

> 'Late – late in the evening Kilmeny came home,
> For Kilmeny had been she could not tell where,
> And Kilmeny had seen what she could not declare.

But why are you chewing leaves at your time of life, daughter? For fun?'

'No. It was for something, but I can't exactly remember,' said Una.

And neither of them could till –

A Tree Song

> Of all the trees that grow so fair,
>   Old England to adorn,
> Greater are none beneath the Sun,
>   Than Oak and Ash and Thorn.
> Sing Oak and Ash and Thorn, good Sirs
>   (All of a Midsummer morn)!
> Surely we sing no little thing,
>   In Oak and Ash and Thorn!
>
> Oak of the Clay lived many a day,
>   Or ever Aeneas began;
> Ash of the Loam was a lady at home,
>   When Brut was an outlaw man;
> Thorn of the Down saw New Troy Town
>   (From which was London born);
> Witness hereby the ancientry
>   Of Oak and Ash and Thorn!

Yew that is old in churchyard mould,
　　He breedeth a mighty bow;
Alder for shoes do wise men choose,
　　And beech for cups also.
But when ye have killed, and your bowl is spilled,
　　And your shoes are clean outworn,
Back ye must speed for all that ye need,
　　To Oak and Ash and Thorn!

Ellum she hateth mankind, and waiteth
　　Till every gust be laid,
To drop a limb on the head of him
　　That anyway trusts her shade:
But whether a lad be sober or sad,
　　Or mellow with ale from the horn,
He will take no wrong when he lieth along
　　'Neath Oak and Ash and Thorn!

Oh, do not tell the Priest our plight,
　　Or he would call it a sin;
But – we have been out in the woods all night,
　　A-conjuring Summer in!
And we bring you news by word of mouth –
　　Good news for cattle and corn –
Now is the Sun come up from the South,
　　With Oak and Ash and Thorn!

Sing Oak and Ash and Thorn, good Sirs
　　(All of a Midsummer morn)!
England shall bide till Judgement Tide,
　　By Oak and Ash and Thorn!

YOUNG MEN AT THE MANOR

They were fishing, a few days later, in the bed of the brook that for centuries had cut deep into the soft valley soil. The trees closing overhead made long tunnels through which the sunshine worked in blobs and patches. Down in the tunnels were bars of sand and gravel, old roots and trunks covered with moss or painted red by the irony water; foxgloves growing lean and pale towards the light; clumps of fern and thirsty shy flowers who could not live away from moisture and shade. In the pools you could see the wave thrown up by the trouts as they charged hither and yon, and the pools were joined to each other – except in flood-time, when all was one brown rush – by sheets of thin broken water that poured themselves chuckling round the darkness of the next bend.

This was one of the children's most secret hunting-grounds, and their particular friend, old Hobden the hedger, had shown them how to use it. Except for the click of a rod hitting a low willow, or a switch and tussle among the young ash leaves as a line hung up for the minute, nobody in the hot pasture could have guessed what game was going on among the trouts below the banks.

'We've got half a dozen,' said Dan, after a warm, wet hour. 'I vote we go up to Stone Bay and try Long Pool.'

Una nodded – most of her talk was by nods – and they crept from the gloom of the tunnels towards the tiny weir that turns the brook into the mill-stream. Here the banks are low and bare, and the glare of the afternoon sun on the Long Pool below the weir makes your eyes ache.

When they were in the open they nearly fell down with astonishment. A huge grey horse, whose tail-hairs crinkled the glassy water, was drinking in the pool, and the ripples about his muzzle flashed like melted gold. On his back sat an old, white-haired man dressed in a loose glimmery gown of chain mail. He was bareheaded, and a nut-shaped iron helmet hung at his saddle-bow. His reins were of red leather five or six inches deep, scalloped at the edges, and his high padded saddle with its red girths was held fore and aft by a red leather breastband and crupper.

'Look!' said Una, as though Dan were not staring his very eyes out. 'It's like the picture in your room – "Sir Isumbras at the Ford".'

The rider turned towards them, and his thin, long face was just as sweet and gentle as that of the knight who carries the children in that picture.

'They should be here now, Sir Richard,' said Puck's deep voice among the willowherb.

'They are here,' the knight said, and he smiled at Dan with the string of trouts in his hand. 'There seems no great change in boys since mine fished this water.'

'If your horse has drunk, we shall be more at ease in the Ring,' said Puck; and he nodded to the children as though he had never magicked away their memories a week before.

The great horse turned and hoisted himself into the pasture with a kick and a scramble that tore the clods down rattling.

'Your pardon!' said Sir Richard to Dan. 'When these lands were mine, I never loved that mounted men should cross the brook except by the paved ford. But my Swallow here was thirsty, and I wished to meet you.'

'We're very glad you've come, sir,' said Dan. 'It doesn't matter in the least about the banks.'

He trotted across the pasture on the sword side of the mighty horse, and it was a mighty iron-handled sword that swung from Sir Richard's belt. Una walked behind with Puck. She remembered everything now.

'I'm sorry about the Leaves,' he said, 'but it would never have done if you had gone home and told, would it?'

'I s'pose not,' Una answered. 'But you said that all the fair – People of the Hills had left England.'

'So they have; but I told you that you should come and go and look and know, didn't I? The knight isn't a fairy. He's Sir Richard Dalyngridge, a very old friend of mine. He came over with William the Conqueror, and he wants to see you particularly.'

'What for?' said Una.

'On account of your great wisdom and learning,' Puck replied, without a twinkle.

'Us?' said Una. 'Why, I don't know my Nine Times – not to say it dodging, and Dan makes the most *awful* mess of fractions. He can't mean *us*!'

'Una!' Dan called back. 'Sir Richard says he is going to tell what happened to Weland's sword. He's got it. Isn't it splendid?'

'Nay – nay,' said Sir Richard, dismounting as they reached the Ring, in the bend of the millstream bank. 'It is you that must tell me, for I hear the youngest child in our England today is as wise as our wisest clerk.' He slipped the bit out of Swallow's mouth, dropped the ruby-red reins over his head, and the wise horse moved off to graze.

Sir Richard (they noticed he limped a little) unslung his great sword.

'That's it,' Dan whispered to Una.

'This is the sword that Brother Hugh had from Wayland-Smith,' Sir Richard said. 'Once he gave it me, but I would not take it; but at the last it became mine after such a fight as never christened man fought. See!' He half drew it from its sheath and turned it before them. On either side just below the handle, where the Runic letters shivered as though they were alive, were two deep gouges in the dull, deadly steel. 'Now, what Thing made those?' said he. 'I know not, but you, perhaps, can say.'

'Tell them all the tale, Sir Richard,' said Puck. 'It concerns their land somewhat.'

'Yes, from the very beginning,' Una pleaded, for the knight's good face and the smile on it more than ever reminded her of 'Sir Isumbras at the Ford'.

They settled down to listen, Sir Richard bareheaded to the sunshine, dandling the sword in both hands, while the grey horse cropped outside the Ring, and the helmet on the saddle-bow clinged softly each time he jerked his head.

'From the beginning, then,' Sir Richard said, 'since it concerns your land, I will tell the tale. When our Duke came out of Normandy to take his England, great knights (have ye heard?) came and strove hard to serve the Duke, because he promised them lands here, and small knights followed the great ones. My folk in Normandy were poor; but a great knight, Engerrard of the Eagle – Engenulf De Aquila – who was kin to my father, followed the Earl of Mortain, who followed William the Duke, and I followed De Aquila. Yes, with thirty men-at-arms out of my father's house and a new sword, I set out to conquer England three days after I was made knight. I did not then know that England would conquer me. We went up to Santlache with the rest – a very great host of us.'

'Does that mean the Battle of Hastings – Ten Sixty-Six?' Una whispered, and Puck nodded, so as not to interrupt.

'At Santlache, over the hill yonder,' – he pointed south-eastward towards Fairlight – 'we found Harold's men. We fought. At the day's end they ran. My men went with De Aquila's to chase and plunder, and in that chase Engerrard of the Eagle was slain, and his son Gilbert took his banner and his men forward. This I did not know till after, for Swallow here was cut in the flank, so I stayed to wash the wound at a brook by a thorn. There a single Saxon cried out to me in French, and we fought together. I should have known his voice, but we fought together. For a long time neither had any advantage, till by pure ill-fortune his foot slipped and his sword flew from his hand. Now I had but newly been made knight, and wished, above all, to be courteous and fameworthy, so I forbore to strike and bade him get his sword again. "A plague on my sword," said he. "It has lost me my first fight. You have spared my life. Take my sword." He held it out to me, but as I stretched my hand the sword groaned like a stricken man, and I leaped back crying, "Sorcery!" '

(The children looked at the sword as though it might speak again.)

'Suddenly a clump of Saxons ran out upon me and, seeing a Norman alone, would have killed me, but my Saxon cried out that I was his prisoner, and beat them off. Thus, see you, he saved my life. He put me on my horse and led me through the woods ten long miles to this valley.'

'To here, d'you mean?' said Una.

'To this very valley. We came in by the Lower Ford under the King's Hill yonder' – he pointed eastward where the valley widens.

'And was that Saxon Hugh the novice?' Dan asked.

'Yes, and more than that. He had been for three years at the monastery at Bec by Rouen, where' – Sir Richard chuckled – 'the Abbot Herluin would not suffer me to remain.'

'Why wouldn't he?' said Dan.

'Because I rode my horse into the refectory, when the scholars were at meat, to show the Saxon boys we Normans were not afraid of an Abbot. It was that very Saxon Hugh tempted me to do it, and we had not met since that day. I thought I knew his voice even inside my helmet, and, for all that our Lords fought, we each rejoiced we had not slain the other. He walked by my side, and he told me how a heathen God, as he believed, had given him his sword, but he said he had never heard it sing before. I remember I warned him to beware of sorcery and quick enchantments.' Sir Richard smiled to himself. 'I was very young – very young!

'When we came to his house here we had almost forgotten that we had been at blows. It was near midnight, and the Great Hall was full of men and women waiting news. There I first saw his sister, the Lady Aelueva, of whom he had spoken to us in France. She cried out fiercely at me, and would have had me hanged in that hour, but her brother said that I had spared his life – he said not how he saved mine from the Saxons – and that our Duke had won the day; and even while they wrangled over my poor body, of a sudden he fell down in a swoon from his wounds.

' "This is *thy* fault," said the Lady Aelueva to me, and she kneeled above him and called for wine and cloths.

' "If I had known," I answered, "he should have ridden and I walked. But he set me on my horse; he made no complaint; he walked beside me and spoke merrily throughout. I pray I have done him no harm."

' "Thou hast need to pray," she said, catching up her underlip. "If he dies, thou shalt hang."

'They bore off Hugh to his chamber; but three tall men of the house bound me and set me under the beam of the Great Hall with a rope round my neck. The end of the rope they flung over the beam, and they sat them down by the fire to wait word whether Hugh lived or died. They cracked nuts with their knife-hilts the while.'

'And how did you feel?' said Dan.

'Very weary; but I did heartily pray for my schoolmate Hugh his health. About noon I heard horses in the valley, and the three men loosed my ropes and fled out, and De Aquila's men rode up. Gilbert de Aquila came with them, for it was his boast that, like his father, he forgot no man that served him. He was little, like his father, but terrible, with a nose like an eagle's nose and yellow eyes like an eagle. He rode tall warhorses – roans, which he bred himself – and he could never abide to be helped into the saddle. He saw the rope hanging from the beam and laughed, and his men laughed, for I was too stiff to rise.

' "This is poor entertainment for a Norman knight," he said, "but, such as it is, let us be grateful. Show me, boy, to whom thou owest most, and we will pay them out of hand." '

'What did he mean? To kill 'em?' said Dan.

'Assuredly. But I looked at the Lady Aeluéva where she stood among her maids, and her brother beside her. De Aquila's men had driven them all into the Great Hall.'

'Was she pretty?' said Una.

'In all my long life I have never seen woman fit to strew rushes before my Lady Aeluéva,' the knight replied, quite simply and quietly. 'As I looked at her I thought I might save her and her house by a jest.

' "Seeing that I came somewhat hastily and without warning," said I to De Aquila, "I have no fault to find with the courtesy that these Saxons have shown me." But my voice shook. It is – it was not good to jest with that little man.

'All were silent awhile, till De Aquila laughed. "Look, men – a miracle," said he. "The fight is scarce sped, my father is not yet buried, and here we find our youngest knight already set down in his Manor, while his Saxons – ye can see it in their fat faces – have paid him homage and service! By the Saints," he said, rubbing his nose, "I never thought England would be so easy won! Surely I can do no less than give the lad what he has taken. This Manor shall be thine, boy," he said, "till I come again, or till thou art slain. Now, mount, men, and ride. We follow our Duke into Kent to make him King of England."

'He drew me with him to the door while they brought his horse – a lean roan, taller than my Swallow here, but not so well girthed.

' "Hark to me," he said, fretting with his great war-gloves. "I have given thee this Manor, which is a Saxon hornets' nest, and I think thou wilt be slain in a month – as my father was slain. Yet if thou canst keep the roof on the hall, the thatch on the barn, and the plough in the furrow till I come back, thou shalt hold the Manor from me; for the Duke has promised our Earl Mortain all the lands by Pevensey, and Mortain will give me of them what he would have given my father. God knows if thou or I shall live till England is won; but remember, boy, that here and now fighting is foolishness and" – he reached for the reins – "craft and cunning is all."

' "Alas, I have no cunning," said I.

' "Not yet," said he, hopping abroad, foot in stirrup, and poking his horse in the belly with his toe. "Not yet, but I think thou hast a good teacher. Farewell! Hold the Manor and live. Lose the Manor and hang," he said, and spurred out, his shield-straps squeaking behind him.

'So, children, here was I, little more than a boy, and Santlache fight not two days old, left alone with my thirty men-at-arms, in a land I knew not, among a people whose tongue I could not speak, to hold down the land which I had taken from them.'

'And that was here at home?' said Una.

'Yes, here. See! From the Upper Ford, Weland's Ford, to the Lower Ford, by the Belle Allée, west and east it ran half a league. From the Beacon of Brunanburgh behind us here, south and north it ran a full league – and all the woods were full of broken men from Santlache, Saxon thieves, Norman plunderers, robbers, and deer-stealers. A hornets' nest indeed!

'When De Aquila had gone, Hugh would have thanked me for saving their lives; but the Lady Aelueva said that I had done it only for the sake of receiving the Manor.

' "How could I know that De Aquila would give it me?" I said. "If I had told him I had spent my night in your halter he would have burned the place twice over by now."

' "If any man had put *my* neck in a rope," she said, "I would have seen his house burned thrice over before *I* would have made terms."

' "But it was a woman," I said; and I laughed, and she wept and said that I mocked her in her captivity.

' "Lady," said I, "there is no captive in this valley except one, and he is not a Saxon."

'At this she cried that I was a Norman thief, who came with false, sweet words, having intended from the first to turn her out in the fields to beg her bread. Into the fields! She had never seen the face of war!

'I was angry, and answered, "This much at least I can disprove, for I swear" – and on my sword-hilt I swore it in that place – "I swear I will never set foot in the Great Hall till the Lady Aelueva herself shall summon me there."

'She went away, saying nothing, and I walked out, and Hugh limped after me, whistling dolorously (that is a custom of the English), and we came upon the three Saxons that had bound me. They were now bound by my men-at-arms, and behind them stood some fifty stark and sullen churls of the House and the Manor, waiting to see what should fall. We heard De Aquila's trumpets blow thin through the woods Kentward.

' "Shall we hang these?" said my men.

' "Then my churls will fight," said Hugh, beneath his breath; but I bade him ask the three what mercy they hoped for. "'None," said they all. "She bade us hang thee if our master died. And we would have hanged thee. There is no more to it."

'As I stood doubting, a woman ran down from the oak wood above the King's Hill yonder, and cried out that some Normans were driving off the swine there.

' "Norman or Saxon," said I, "we must beat them back, or they will rob us every day. Out at them with any arms ye have!" So I loosed those three carles and we ran together, my men-at-arms and the Saxons with bills and axes which they had hidden in the thatch of their huts, and Hugh led them. Half-way up the King's Hill we found a false fellow from Picardy – a sutler that sold wine in the Duke's camp – with a dead knight's shield on his arm, a stolen horse under him, and some ten or twelve wastrels at his tail, all cutting and

'At this she cried that I was a Norman thief . . .'

slashing at the pigs. We beat them off, and saved our pork. One hundred and seventy pigs we saved in that great battle.' Sir Richard laughed.

'That, then, was our first work together, and I bade Hugh tell his folk that so would I deal with any man, knight or churl, Norman or Saxon, who stole as much as one egg from our valley. Said he to me, riding home: "Thou hast gone far to conquer England this evening." I answered: "England must be thine and mine, then. Help me, Hugh, to deal aright with these people. Make them to know that if they slay me De Aquila will surely send to slay them, and he will put a worse man in my place." "That may well be true," said he, and gave me his hand. "Better the devil we know than the devil we know not, till we can pack you Normans home." And so, too, said his Saxons; and they laughed as we drove the pigs downhill. But I think some of them, even then, began not to hate me.'

'I like Brother Hugh,' said Una, softly.

'Beyond question he was the most perfect, courteous, valiant, tender, and wise knight that ever drew breath,' said Sir Richard, caressing the sword. 'He hung up his sword – this sword – on the wall of the Great Hall, because he said it was fairly mine, and never he took it down till De Aquila returned, as I shall presently show. For three months his men and mine guarded the valley, till all robbers and nightwalkers learned there was nothing to get from us save hard tack and a hanging. Side by side we fought against all who came – thrice a week sometimes we fought – against thieves and landless knights looking for good manors. Then we were in some peace, and I made shift by Hugh's help to govern the valley – for all this valley of yours was my Manor – as a knight should. I kept the roof on the hall and the thatch on the barn, but . . . the English are a bold people. His Saxons would laugh and jest with Hugh, and Hugh with them, and – this was marvellous to me – if even the meanest of them said that such and such a thing was the Custom of the Manor, then straightway would Hugh and such old men of the Manor as might be near forsake everything else to debate the matter – I have seen them stop the mill with the corn half ground – and if the custom or usage were proven to be as it was said, why, that was the end of it, even though it were flat against Hugh, his wish and command. Wonderful!'

'Aye,' said Puck, breaking in for the first time. 'The Custom of Old England was here before your Norman knights came, and it outlasted them, though they fought against it cruel.'

'Not I,' said Sir Richard. 'I let the Saxons go their stubborn way, but when my own men-at-arms, Normans not six months in England, stood up and told me what was the custom of the country, *then* I was angry. Ah, good days! Ah, wonderful people! And I loved them all.'

The knight lifted his arms as though he would hug the whole dear valley, and Swallow, hearing the chink of his chain mail, looked up and whinnied softly.

'At last,' he went on, 'after a year of striving and contriving and some little driving, De Aquila came to the valley, alone and without warning. I saw him first at the Lower Ford, with a swineherd's brat on his saddle-bow.

' "There is no need for thee to give any account of thy stewardship," said he. "I have it all from the child here." And he told me how the young thing had stopped his tall horse at the Ford, by waving of a branch, and crying that the way was barred. "And if one bold, bare babe be enough to guard the Ford in these days, thou hast done well," said he, and puffed and wiped his head.

'He pinched the child's cheek, and looked at our cattle in the flat by the river.

' "Both fat," said he, rubbing his nose. "This is craft and cunning such as I love. What did I tell thee when I rode away, boy?"

' "Hold the Manor or hang," said I. I had never forgotten it.

' "True. And thou hast held." He clambered from his saddle and with his sword's point cut out a turf from the bank and gave it me where I knelt.'

Dan looked at Una, and Una looked at Dan.

'That's seisin,' said Puck, in a whisper.

' "Now thou art lawfully seised of the Manor, Sir Richard," said he – 'twas the first time he ever called me that – "thou and thy heirs for ever. This must serve till the King's clerks write out thy title on a parchment. England is all ours – if we can hold it."

' "What service shall I pay?" I asked, and I remember I was proud beyond words.

' "Knight's fee, boy, knight's fee!" said he, hopping round his horse on one foot. (Have I said he was little, and could not endure to be helped to his saddle?) "Six mounted men or twelve archers thou shalt send me whenever I call for them, and – where got you that corn?" said he, for it was near harvest, and our corn stood well. "I have never seen such bright straw. Send me three bags of the same seed yearly, and furthermore, in memory of our last meeting – with the rope round thy neck – entertain me and my men for two days of each year in the Great Hall of thy Manor."

' "Alas!" said I, "then my Manor is already forfeit. I am under vow not to enter the Great Hall." And I told him what I had sworn to the Lady Aelueva.'

'And hadn't you ever been into the house since?' said Una.

'Never,' Sir Richard answered, smiling. 'I had made me a little hut of wood up the hill, and there I did justice and slept . . . De Aquila wheeled aside, and his shield shook on his back. "No matter, boy," said he. "I will remit the homage for a year." '

'He meant Sir Richard needn't give him dinner there the first year,' Puck explained.

'De Aquila stayed with me in the hut, and Hugh, who could read and write and cast accounts, showed him the Roll of the Manor, in which were written all the names of our fields and men, and he asked a thousand questions touching the land, the timber, the grazing, the mill, and the fishponds, and the worth of every man in the valley. But never he named the Lady Aelueva's name, nor went he near the Great Hall. By night he drank with us in the hut. Yes, he sat on the straw like an eagle ruffled in her feathers, his yellow eyes rolling above the cup, and he pounced in his talk like an eagle, swooping from one thing to another, but always binding fast. Yes; he would lie still awhile, and then rustle in the straw, and speak sometimes as though he were King William himself, and anon he would speak in parables and tales, and if at once we saw not his meaning he would yerk us in the ribs with his scabbarded sword.

' "Look you, boys," said he, "I am born out of my due time. Five hundred years ago I would have made all England such an England as neither Dane, Saxon, nor Norman should have conquered. Five hundred years hence I should have been such a counsellor to Kings as the world hath never dreamed of. 'Tis all here," said he, tapping his big head, "but it hath no play in this black age. Now Hugh here is a better man than thou art, Richard." He had made his voice harsh and croaking, like a raven's.

' "Truth," said I. "But for Hugh, his help and patience and long-suffering, I could never have kept the Manor."

' "Nor thy life either," said De Aquila. "Hugh has saved thee not once, but a hundred times. Be still, Hugh!" he said. "Dost thou know, Richard, why Hugh slept, and why he still sleeps, among thy Norman men-at-arms?"

' "To be near me," said I, for I thought this was truth.

' "Fool!" said De Aquila. "It is because his Saxons have begged him to rise against thee, and to sweep every Norman out of the valley. No matter how I know. It is truth. Therefore Hugh hath made himself an hostage for thy life, well knowing that if any harm befell thee from his Saxons thy Normans would slay him without remedy. And this his Saxons know. Is it true, Hugh?"

' "In some sort," said Hugh shamefacedly; "at least, it was true half a year ago. My Saxons would not harm Richard now. I think they know him – but I judged it best to make sure."

'Look, children, what that man had done – and I had never guessed it! Night after night had he lain down among my men-at-arms, knowing that if one Saxon had lifted knife against me, his life would have answered for mine.

' "Yes," said De Aquila. "And he is a swordless man." He pointed to Hugh's belt, for Hugh had put away his sword – did I tell you? – the day after it flew from his hand at Santlache. He carried only the short knife and the longbow. "Swordless and landless art thou, Hugh; and they call thee kin to Earl Godwin." (Hugh was indeed of Godwin's blood.) "The Manor that was thine is given to this boy and to his children for ever. Sit up and beg, for he can turn thee out like a dog, Hugh."

'Hugh said nothing, but I heard his teeth grind, and I bade De Aquila, my own overlord, hold his peace, or I would stuff his words down his throat. Then De Aquila laughed till the tears ran down his face.

' "I warned the King," said he, "what would come of giving England to us Norman thieves. Here art thou, Richard, less than two days confirmed in thy

'There is no need for thee to give any account of thy stewardship,'
said he. 'I have it all from the child here.'

Manor, and already thou hast risen against thy overlord. What shall we do to him, *Sir* Hugh?"

' "I am a swordless man," said Hugh. "Do not jest with me," and he laid his head on his knees and groaned.

' "The greater fool thou," said De Aquila, and all his voice changed; "for I have given thee the Manor of Dallington up the hill this half-hour since," and he yerked at Hugh with his scabbard across the straw.

' "To me?" said Hugh. "I am a Saxon, and, except that I love Richard here, I have not sworn fealty to any Norman."

' "In God's good time, which because of my sins I shall not live to see, there will be neither Saxon nor Norman in England," said De Aquila. "If I know men, thou art more faithful unsworn than a score of Normans I could name. Take Dallington, and join Sir Richard to fight me tomorrow, if it please thee!"

' "Nay," said Hugh. "I am no child. Where I take a gift, there I render service"; and he put his hands between De Aquila's, and swore to be faithful, and, as I remember, I kissed him, and De Aquila kissed us both.

'We sat afterwards outside the hut while the sun rose, and De Aquila marked our churls going to their work in the fields, and talked of holy things, and how we should govern our Manors in time to come, and of hunting and of horse-breeding, and of the King's wisdom and unwisdom; for he spoke to us as though we were in all sorts now his brothers. Anon a churl stole up to me – he was one of the three I had not hanged a year ago – and he bellowed – which is the Saxon for whispering – that the Lady Aelueva would speak to me at the Great House. She walked abroad daily in the Manor, and it was her custom to send me word whither she went, that I might set an archer or two behind and in front to guard her. Very often I myself lay up in the woods and watched on her also.

'I went swiftly, and as I passed the great door it opened from within, and there stood my Lady Aelueva, and she said to me: "Sir Richard, will it please you enter your Great Hall?" Then she wept, but we were alone.'

The knight was silent for a long time, his face turned across the valley, smiling.

'Oh, well done!' said Una, and clapped her hands very softly. 'She was sorry, and she said so.'

'Aye, she was sorry, and she said so,' said Sir Richard, coming back with a little start. 'Very soon – but *he* said it was two full hours later – De Aquila rode to the door, with his shield new scoured (Hugh had cleansed it), and demanded entertainment, and called me a false knight, that would starve his overlord to death. Then Hugh cried out that no man should work in the valley that day, and our Saxons blew horns, and set about feasting and drinking, and running of races, and dancing and singing; and De Aquila climbed upon a horse-block and spoke to them in what he swore was good Saxon, but no man understood it. At night we feasted in the Great Hall, and

'I went swiftly, and as I passed the great door it opened from within,
and there stood my Lady Aelueva.'

when the harpers and the singers were gone we four sat late at the high table. As I remember, it was a warm night with a full moon, and De Aquila bade Hugh take down his sword from the wall again, for the honour of the Manor of Dallington, and Hugh took it gladly enough. Dust lay on the hilt, for I saw him blow it off.

'She and I sat talking a little apart, and at first we thought the harpers had come back, for the Great Hall was filled with a rushing noise of music. De Aquila leaped up; but there was only the moonlight fretty on the floor.

' "Hearken!" said Hugh. "It is my sword," and as he belted it on the music ceased.

' "Over Gods, forbid that I should ever belt blade like that," said De Aquila. "What does it foretell?"

' "The Gods that made it may know. Last time it spoke was at Hastings, when I lost all my lands. Belike it sings now that I have new lands and am a man again," said Hugh.

'He loosed the blade a little and drove it back happily into the sheath, and the sword answered him low and crooningly, as – as a woman would speak to a man, her head on his shoulder.

'Now that was the second time in all my life I heard this Sword sing . . . '

*   *   *

'Look!' said Una. 'There's Mother coming down the Long Slip. What will she say to Sir Richard? She can't help seeing him.'

'And Puck can't magic us this time,' said Dan.

'Are you sure?' said Puck; and he leaned forward and whispered to Sir Richard, who, smiling, bowed his head. 'But what befell the sword and my brother Hugh I will tell on another time,' said he, rising. 'Ohé, Swallow!'

The great horse cantered up from the far end of the meadow, close to Mother.

They heard Mother say: 'Children, Gleason's old horse has broken into the meadow again. Where did he get through?'

'Just below Stone Bay,' said Dan. 'He tore down simple flobs of the bank! We noticed it just now. And we've caught no end of fish. We've been at it all the afternoon.'

And they honestly believed that they had. They never noticed the Oak, Ash and Thorn leaves that Puck had slyly thrown into their laps.

Sir Richard's Song

I followed my Duke ere I was a lover,
    To take from England fief and fee;
But now this game is the other way over –
    But now England hath taken me!

I had my horse, my shield and banner,
    And a boy's heart, so whole and free;
But now I sing in another manner –
    But now England hath taken me!

As for my Father in his tower,
    Asking news of my ship at sea;
He will remember his own hour –
    Tell him England hath taken me!

As for my Mother in her bower,
    That rules my Father so cunningly;
She will remember a maiden's power –
    Tell her England hath taken me!

As for my Brother in Rouen city,
    A nimble and naughty page is he;
But he will come to suffer and pity –
    Tell him England hath taken me!

As for my little Sister waiting
    In the pleasant orchards of Normandie;
Tell her youth is the time of mating –
    Tell her England hath taken me!

As for my Comrades in camp and highway,
    That lift their eyebrows scornfully;
Tell them their way is not my way –
    Tell them England hath taken me!

Kings and Princes and Barons famed,
    Knights and Captains in your degree;
Hear me a little before I am blamed –
    Seeing England hath taken me!

Howso great man's strength be reckoned,
    There are two things he cannot flee;
Love is the first, and Death is the second –
    And Love, in England, hath taken me!

THE KNIGHTS OF THE
JOYOUS VENTURE

Harp Song of the Dane Women

What is a woman that you forsake her,
And the hearth-fire and the home-acre,
To go with the old grey Widow-maker?

She has no house to lay a guest in –
But one chill bed for all to rest in,
That the pale suns and the stray bergs nest in.

She has no strong white arms to fold you,
But the ten-times-fingering weed to hold you
Bound on the rocks where the tide has rolled you.

Yet, when the signs of summer thicken,
And the ice breaks, and the birch-buds quicken,
Yearly you turn from our side, and sicken –

Sicken again for the shouts and the slaughters –
And steal away to the lapping waters,
And look at your ship in her winter quarters.

You forget our mirth, and talk at the tables,
The kine in the shed and the horse in the stables –
To pitch her sides and go over her cables!

Then you drive out where the storm-clouds swallow:
And the sound of your oar-blades falling hollow
Is all we have left through the months to follow.

Ah, what is a Woman that you forsake her,
And the hearth-fire and the home-acre,
To go with the old grey Widow-maker?

The Knights of the Joyous Venture

It was too hot to run about in the open, so Dan asked their friend, old Hobden, to take their own dinghy from the pond and put her on the brook at the bottom of the garden. Her painted name was the *Daisy*, but for exploring expeditions she was the *Golden Hind* or the *Long Serpent*, or some such suitable name. Dan hiked and howked with a boat-hook (the brook was too narrow for sculls), and Una punted with a piece of hop-pole. When they came to a very shallow place (the *Golden Hind* drew quite three inches of water) they disembarked and scuffled her over the gravel by her tow-rope, and when they reached the overgrown banks beyond the garden they pulled themselves upstream by the low branches.

That day they intended to discover the North Cape like 'Othere, the old sea-captain', in the book of verses which Una had brought with her; but on account of the heat they changed it to a voyage up the Amazon and the sources of the Nile. Even on the shaded water the air was hot and heavy with drowsy scents, while outside, through breaks in the trees, the sunshine burned the pasture like fire. The kingfisher was asleep on his watching-branch, and the blackbirds scarcely took the trouble to dive into the next bush. Dragonflies wheeling and clashing were the only things at work, except the moorhens and a big Red Admiral, who flapped down out of the sunshine for a drink.

When they reached Otter Pool the *Golden Hind* grounded comfortably on a shallow, and they lay beneath a roof of close green, watching the water trickle over the floodgates down the mossy brick chute from the millstream to the brook. A big trout – the children knew him well – rolled head and shoulders at some fly that sailed round the bend, while, once in just so often, the brook rose a fraction of an inch against all the wet pebbles, and they watched the slow draw and shiver of a breath of air through the treetops. Then the little voices of the slipping water began again.

'It's like the shadows talking, isn't it?' said Una. She had given up trying to read. Dan lay over the bows, trailing his hands in the current. They heard feet on the gravel-bar that runs half across the pool and saw Sir Richard Dalyngridge standing over them.

'Was yours a dangerous voyage?' he asked, smiling.

'She bumped a lot, sir,' said Dan. 'There's hardly any water this summer.'

'Ah, the brook was deeper and wider when my children played at Danish pirates. Are you pirate-folk?'

'Oh no. We gave up being pirates years ago,' explained Una. 'We're nearly always explorers now. Sailing round the world, you know.'

'Round?' said Sir Richard. He sat him in the comfortable crotch of an old ash-root on the bank. 'How can it be round?'

'Wasn't it in your books?' Dan suggested. He had been doing geography at his last lesson.

'I can neither write nor read,' he replied. 'Canst *thou* read, child?'

'Yes,' said Dan, 'barring the very long words.'

'Wonderful! Read to me, that I may hear for myself.'

Dan flushed, but opened the book and began – gabbling a little – at 'The Discoverer of the North Cape.'

> 'Othere, the old sea-captain,
>   Who dwelt in Helgoland,
> To King Alfred, the lover of truth,
> Brought a snow-white walrus-tooth,
>   Which he held in his brown right hand.'

'But – but – this I know! This is an old song! This I have heard sung! This is a miracle,' Sir Richard interrupted. 'Nay, do not stop!' He leaned forward, and the shadows of the leaves slipped and slid upon his chain mail.

> ' "I ploughed the land with horses,
>   But my heart was ill at ease,
> For the old seafaring men
> Came to me now and then
>   With their sagas of the seas." '

His hand fell on the hilt of the great sword. 'This is truth,' he cried, 'for so did it happen to me,' and he beat time delightedly to the tramp of verse after verse.

> ' "And now the land," said Othere,
>   "Bent southward suddenly,
> And I followed the curving shore,
> And ever southward bore
>   Into a nameless sea." '

'A nameless sea!' he repeated. 'So did I – so did Hugh and I.'

'Where did you go? Tell us,' said Una.

'Wait. Let me hear all first.' So Dan read to the poem's very end.

'Good,' said the knight. 'That is Othere's tale – even so I have heard the men in the Dane ships sing it. Not those same valiant words, but something like to them.'

'Have you ever explored North?' Dan shut the book.

'Nay. My venture was South. Farther South than any man has fared, Hugh and I went down with Witta and his heathen.' He jerked the tall sword forward, and leaned on it with both hands; but his eyes looked long past them.

'I thought you always lived here,' said Una, timidly.

'Yes; while my Lady Aelueva lived. But she died. She died. Then, my eldest son being a man, I asked De Aquila's leave that he should hold the Manor while I went on some journey or pilgrimage – to forget. De Aquila, whom the Second William had made Warden of Pevensey in Earl Mortain's place, was very old then, but still he rode his tall, roan horses, and in the saddle he looked like a little white falcon. When Hugh, at Dallington, over yonder, heard what I did, he sent for my second son, whom being unmarried he had ever looked upon as his own child, and, by De Aquila's leave, gave him the Manor of Dallington to hold till he should return. Then Hugh came with me.'

'When did this happen?' said Dan.

'That I can answer to the very day, for as we rode with De Aquila by Pevensey – have I said that he was Lord of Pevensey and of the Honour of the Eagle? – to the Bordeaux ship that fetched him his wines yearly out of France, a Marsh man ran to us crying that he had seen a great black goat which bore on his back the body of the King, and that the goat had spoken to him. On that same day Red William our King, the Conqueror's son, died of a secret arrow while he hunted in a forest. "This is a cross matter," said De Aquila, "to meet on the threshold of a journey. If Red William be dead I may have to fight for my lands. Wait a little."

'My Lady being dead, I cared nothing for signs and omens, nor Hugh either. We took that wine-ship to go to Bordeaux; but the wind failed while we were yet in sight of Pevensey, a thick mist hid us, and we drifted with the tide along the cliffs to the west. Our company was, for the most part, merchants returning to France, and we were laden with wool and there were three couple of tall hunting dogs chained to the rail. Their master was a knight of Artois. His name I never learned, but his shield bore gold pieces on a red ground, and he limped, much as I do, from a wound which he had got in his youth at Mantes siege. He served the Duke of Burgundy against the Moors in Spain, and was returning to that war with his dogs. He sang us strange Moorish songs that first night, and half persuaded us to go with him. I was on pilgrimage to forget – which is what no pilgrimage brings. I think I would have gone, but . . .

'Look you how the life and fortune of man changes! Towards morning a Dane ship, rowing silently, struck against us in the mist, and while we rolled hither and yon Hugh, leaning over the rail, fell outboard. I leaped after him, and we two tumbled aboard the Dane, and were caught and bound ere we could rise. Our own ship was swallowed up in the mist. I judge the Knight of the Gold Pieces muzzled his dogs with his cloak, lest they should give tongue and betray the merchants, for I heard their baying suddenly stop.

'We lay bound among the benches till morning, when the Danes dragged us to the high deck by the steering-place, and their captain – Witta, he was called – turned us over with his foot. Bracelets of gold from elbow to armpit he wore, and his red hair was long as a woman's, and came down in plaited locks on his shoulder. He was stout, with bowed legs and long arms. He spoiled us of all we had, but when he laid hand on Hugh's sword and saw the

'I leaped after him, and we two tumbled aboard the Dane,
and were caught and bound ere we could rise.'

runes on the blade hastily he thrust it back. Yet his covetousness overcame him and he tried again and again, and the third time the Sword sang loud and angrily, so that the rowers leaned on their oars to listen. Here they all spoke together, screaming like gulls, and a Yellow Man, such as I have never seen, came to the high deck and cut our bonds. He was yellow – not from sickness, but by nature – yellow as honey, and his eyes stood endwise in his head.'

'How do you mean?' said Una, her chin on her hand.

'Thus,' said Sir Richard. He put a finger to the corner of each eye, and pushed it up till his eyes narrowed to slits.

'Why, you look just like a Chinaman!' cried Dan. 'Was the man a Chinaman?'

'I know not what that may be. Witta had found him half dead among ice on the shores of Muscovy. *We* thought he was a devil. He crawled before us and brought food in a silver dish which these sea-wolves had robbed from some rich abbey, and Witta with his own hands gave us wine. He spoke a little in French, a little in South Saxon, and much in the Northman's tongue. We asked him to set us ashore, promising to pay him better ransom than he would get price if he sold us to the Moors – as once befell a knight of my acquaintance sailing from Flushing.

' "Not by my father Guthrum's head," said he. "The Gods sent ye into my ship for a luck-offering."

'At this I quaked, for I knew it was still the Danes' custom to sacrifice captives to their Gods for fair weather.

' "A plague on thy four long bones!" said Hugh. "What profit canst thou make of poor old pilgrims that can neither work nor fight?"

' "Gods forbid I should fight against thee, poor Pilgrim with the Singing Sword," said he. "Come with us and be poor no more. Thy teeth are far apart, which is a sure sign thou wilt travel and grow rich."

' "What if we will not come?" said Hugh.

' "Swim to England or France," said Witta. "We are midway between the two. Unless ye choose to drown yourselves no hair of your head will be harmed here aboard. We think ye bring us luck, and I myself know the runes on that Sword are good." He turned and bade them hoist sail.

'Hereafter all made way for us as we walked about the ship, and the ship was full of wonders.'

'What was she like?' said Dan.

'Long, low, and narrow, bearing one mast with a red sail, and rowed by fifteen oars a side,' the knight answered. 'At her bows was a deck under which men might lie, and at her stern another shut off by a painted door from the rowers' benches. Here Hugh and I slept, with Witta and the Yellow Man, upon tapestries as soft as wool. I remember' – he laughed to himself – 'when first we entered there a loud voice cried, "Out swords! Out swords! Kill, kill!" Seeing us start Witta laughed, and showed us it was but a great-beaked grey bird with a red tail. He sat her on his shoulder, and she called for bread and wine hoarsely, and prayed him to kiss her. Yet she was no more than a silly bird. But – ye knew this?' He looked at their smiling faces.

'We weren't laughing at you,' said Una. 'That must have been a parrot. It's just what Pollies do.'

'So we learned later. But here is another marvel. The Yellow Man, whose name was Kitai, had with him a brown box. In the box was a blue bowl with red marks upon the rim, and within the bowl, hanging from a fine thread, was a piece of iron no thicker than that grass stem, and as long, maybe, as my spur, but straight. In this iron, said Witta, abode an Evil Spirit which Kitai, the Yellow Man, had brought by Art Magic out of his own country that lay three years' journey southward. The Evil Spirit strove day and night to return to his country, and therefore, look you, the iron needle pointed continually to the South.'

'South?' said Dan suddenly, and put his hand into his pocket.

'With my own eyes I saw it. Every day and all day long, though the ship rolled, though the sun and the moon and the stars were hid, this blind Spirit in the iron knew whither it would go, and strained to the South. Witta called it the Wise Iron, because it showed him his way across the unknowable seas.' Again Sir Richard looked keenly at the children. 'How think ye? Was it sorcery?'

'Was it anything like this?' Dan fished out his old brass pocket-compass, that generally lived with his knife and key-ring. 'The glass has got cracked, but the needle waggles all right, sir.'

The knight drew a long breath of wonder. 'Yes, yes! The Wise Iron shook and swung in just this fashion. Now it is still. Now it points to the South.'

'North,' said Dan.

'Nay, South! There is the South,' said Sir Richard. Then they both laughed, for naturally when one end of a straight compass-needle points to the North, the other must point to the South.

'Té,' said Sir Richard, clicking his tongue. 'There can be no sorcery if a child carries it. Wherefore does it point South – or North?'

'Father says that nobody knows,' said Una.

Sir Richard looked relieved. 'Then it may still be magic. It was magic to *us*. And so we voyaged. When the wind served we hoisted sail, and lay all up along the windward rail, our shields on our backs to break the spray. When it failed, they rowed with long oars; the Yellow Man sat by the Wise Iron, and Witta steered. At first I feared the great white-flowering waves, but as I saw how wisely Witta led his ship among them I grew bolder. Hugh liked it well from the first. My skill is not upon the water; and rocks and whirlpools such as we saw by the West Isles of France, where an oar caught on a rock and broke, are much against my stomach. We sailed South across a stormy sea, where by moonlight, between clouds, we saw a Flanders ship roll clean over and sink. Again, though Hugh laboured with Witta all night, I lay under the deck with the Talking Bird, and cared not whether I lived or died. There is a sickness of the sea which for three days is pure death! When we next saw land Witta said it was Spain, and we stood out to sea. That coast was full of ships busy in the Duke's war against the Moors, and we feared to be hanged by the Duke's men or sold into slavery by the Moors. So we put into a small harbour which Witta knew. At night men came down with loaded mules, and Witta exchanged amber out of the North against little wedges of iron and packets of beads in earthen pots. The pots he put under the decks, and the wedges of iron he laid on the bottom of the ship after he had cast out the stones and shingle which till then had been our ballast. Wine, too, he bought for lumps of sweet-smelling grey amber – a little morsel no bigger than a thumbnail purchased a cask of wine. But I speak like a merchant.'

'No, no! Tell us what you had to eat,' cried Dan.

'Meat dried in the sun, and dried fish and ground beans, Witta took in; and corded frails of a certain sweet, soft fruit, which the Moors use, which is like paste of figs, but with thin, long stones. Aha! Dates is the name.

' "Now," said Witta, when the ship was loaded, "I counsel you strangers to pray to your Gods, for, from here on, our road is No Man's road." He and his men killed a black goat for sacrifice on the bows; and the Yellow Man brought out a small, smiling image of dull-green stone and burned incense before it. Hugh and I commended ourselves to God, and Saint Barnabas, and Our Lady of the Assumption, who was specially dear to my Lady. We were not young, but I think no shame to say whenas we drove out of that secret harbour at sunrise over a still sea, we two rejoiced and sang as did the knights of old when they followed our great Duke to England. Yet was our leader an heathen pirate; all our proud fleet but one galley perilously overloaded; for guidance we leaned on a pagan sorcerer; and our port was beyond the world's end. Witta told us that his father Guthrum had once in his life rowed along the shores of Africa to a land where naked men sold gold for iron and beads. There had he bought much gold, and no few elephants' teeth, and thither by help of the Wise Iron would Witta go. Witta feared nothing – except to be poor.

' "My father told me," said Witta, "that a great Shoal runs three days' sail out from that land, and south of the shoal lies a Forest which grows in the sea. South and east of the Forest my father came to a place where the men hid gold in their hair; but all that country, he said, was full of Devils who lived in trees, and tore folk limb from limb. How think ye?"

' "Gold or no gold," said Hugh, fingering his sword, "it is a joyous venture. Have at these Devils of thine, Witta!"

' "Venture!" said Witta sourly. "I am only a poor sea-thief. I do not set my life adrift on a plank for joy, or the venture. Once I beach ship again at Stavanger, and feel the wife's arms round my neck, I'll seek no more ventures. A ship is heavier care than a wife or cattle."

'He leaped down among the rowers, chiding them for their little strength and their great stomachs. Yet Witta was a wolf in fight, and a very fox in cunning.

'We were driven South by a storm, and for three days and three nights he took the stern-oar, and threddled the longship through the sea. When it rose beyond measure he brake a pot of whale's oil upon the water, which wonderfully smoothed it, and in that anointed patch he turned her head to the wind and threw out oars at the end of a rope, to make, he said, an anchor at which we lay rolling sorely, but dry. This craft his father Guthrum had shown him. He knew, too, all the Leech-Book of Bald, who was a wise doctor, and he knew the Ship-Book of Hlaf the Woman, who robbed Egypt. He knew all the care of a ship.

'After the storm we saw a mountain whose top was covered with snow and pierced the clouds. The grasses under this mountain, boiled and eaten, are a good cure for soreness of the gums and swelled ankles. We lay there eight days, till men in skins threw stones at us. When the heat increased Witta spread a cloth on bent sticks above the rowers, for the wind failed between the Island of the Mountain and the shore of Africa, which is east of it. That shore is sandy, and we rowed along it within three bowshots. Here we saw whales, and fish in the shape of shields, but longer than our ship. Some slept, some opened their mouths at us, and some danced on the hot waters. The water was hot to the hand, and the sky was hidden by hot, grey mists, out of which blew a fine dust that whitened our hair and beards of a morning. Here, too, were fish that flew in the air like birds. They would fall on the laps of the rowers, and when we went ashore we would roast and eat them.'

The knight paused to see if the children doubted him, but they only nodded and said, 'Go on.'

'The yellow land lay on our left, the grey sea on our right. Knight though I was, I pulled my oar amongst the rowers. I caught seaweed and dried it, and stuffed it between the pots of beads lest they should break. Knighthood is for the land. At sea, look you, a man is but a spurless rider on a bridleless horse. I learned to make strong knots in ropes – yes, and to join two ropes end to end, so that even Witta could scarcely see where they had been married. But Hugh had tenfold more sea-cunning than I. Witta gave him charge of the rowers of the left side. Thorkild of Borkum, a man with a broken nose, that wore a Norman steel cap, had the rowers of the right, and each side rowed and sang against the other. They saw that no man was idle. Truly, as Hugh said, and Witta would laugh at him, a ship is all more care than a Manor.

'How? Thus. There was water to fetch from the shore when we could find it, as well as wild fruit and grasses, and sand for scrubbing of the decks and benches to keep them sweet. Also we hauled the ship out on low islands and emptied all her gear, even to the iron wedges, and burned off the weed, that had grown on her, with torches of rush, and smoked below the decks with rushes dampened in salt water, as Hlaf the Woman orders in her Ship-Book. Once when we were thus stripped, and the ship lay propped on her keel, the bird cried, "Out swords!" as though she saw an enemy. Witta vowed he would wring her neck.'

'Poor Polly! Did he?' said Una.

'Nay. She was the ship's bird. She could call all the rowers by name . . . Those were good days – for a wifeless man – with Witta and his heathen – beyond the world's end . . . After many weeks we came on the great Shoal which stretched, as Witta's father had said, far out to sea. We skirted it till we were giddy with the sight and dizzy with the sound of bars and breakers, and when we reached land again we found a naked black people dwelling among woods, who for one wedge of iron loaded us with fruits and grasses and eggs. Witta scratched his head at them in sign he would buy gold. They had no gold, but they understood the sign (all the gold-traders hide their gold in their thick hair), for they pointed along the coast. They beat, too, on their chests with their clenched hands, and that, if we had known it, was an evil sign.'

'What did it mean?' said Dan.

'Patience. Ye shall hear. We followed the coast eastward sixteen days (counting time by sword-cuts on the helm-rail) till we came to the Forest in the Sea. Trees grew there out of mud, arched upon lean and high roots, and many muddy waterways ran allwhither into darkness, under the trees. Here we lost the sun. We followed the winding channels between the trees, and where we could not row we laid hold of the crusted roots and hauled ourselves along. The water was foul, and great glittering flies tormented us. Morning and evening a blue mist covered the mud, which bred fevers. Four of our rowers sickened, and were bound to their benches, lest they should leap overboard and be eaten by the monsters of the mud. The Yellow Man lay sick beside the Wise Iron, rolling his head and talking in his own tongue. Only the Bird throve. She sat on Witta's shoulder and screamed in that noisome, silent darkness. Yes; I think it was the silence we most feared.'

He paused to listen to the comfortable home noises of the brook.

'When we had lost count of time among those black gullies and swashes we heard, as it were, a drum beat far off, and following it we broke into a broad, brown river by a hut in a clearing among fields of pumpkins. We thanked God to see the sun again. The people of the village gave the good welcome, and Witta scratched his head at them (for gold), and showed them our iron and beads. They ran to the bank – we were still in the ship – and pointed to our swords and bows, for always when near shore we lay armed. Soon they fetched store of gold in bars and in dust from their huts, and some great blackened elephants' teeth. These they piled on the bank, as though to tempt us, and made signs of dealing blows in battle, and pointed up to the treetops, and to the forest behind. Their captain or chief sorcerer then beat on his chest with his fists, and gnashed his teeth.

'Said Thorkild of Borkum: "Do they mean we must fight for all this gear?" and he half drew sword.

' "Nay," said Hugh. "I think they ask us to league against some enemy."

' "I like this not," said Witta, of a sudden. "Back into midstream."

'So we did, and sat still all, watching the black folk and the gold they piled on the bank. Again we heard drums beat in the forest, and the people fled to their huts, leaving the gold unguarded.

'Then Hugh, at the bows, pointed without speech, and we saw a great Devil come out of the forest. He shaded his brows with his hand, and moistened his pink tongue between his lips – thus.'

'A Devil!' said Dan, delightfully horrified.

'Yea. Taller than a man; covered with reddish hair. When he had well regarded our ship, he beat on his chest with his fists till it sounded like rolling drums, and came to the bank swinging all his body between his long arms, and gnashed his teeth at us. Hugh loosed arrow, and pierced him through the throat. He fell roaring, and three other Devils ran out of the forest and hauled him into a tall tree out of sight. Anon they cast down the blood-stained arrow, and lamented together among the leaves. Witta saw the gold on the bank; he was loath to leave it. "Sirs," said he (no man had spoken till then), "yonder is what we have come so far and so painfully to find, laid out to our very hand. Let us row in while these Devils bewail themselves, and at least bear off what we may."

'Bold as a wolf, cunning as a fox was Witta! He set four archers on the fore-deck to shoot the Devils if they should leap from the tree, which was close to the bank. He manned ten oars a side, and bade them watch his hand to row in or back out, and so coaxed he them toward the bank. But none would set foot ashore, though the gold was within ten pàces. No man is hasty to his hanging! They whimpered at their oars like beaten hounds, and Witta bit his fingers for rage.

'Said Hugh of a sudden, "Hark!" At first we thought it was the buzzing of the glittering flies on the water; but it grew loud and fierce, so that all men heard.'

'What?' said Dan and Una.

'It was the Sword.' Sir Richard patted the smooth hilt. 'It sang as a Dane sings before battle. "I go," said Hugh, and he leaped from the bows and fell among the gold. I was afraid to my four bones' marrow, but for shame's sake I followed, and Thorkild of Borkum leaped after me. None other came. "Blame me not," cried Witta behind us, "I must abide by my ship." We three had no time to blame or praise. We stooped to the gold and threw it back over our shoulders, one hand on our swords and one eye on the tree, which nigh overhung us.

'I know not how the Devils leaped down, or how the fight began. I heard Hugh cry: "Out! out!" as though he were at Santlache again; I saw Thorkild's steel cap smitten off his head by a great hairy hand, and I felt an arrow from the ship whistle past my ear. They say that till Witta took his sword to the rowers he could not bring his ship inshore; and each one of the four archers said afterwards that he alone had pierced the Devil that fought me. I do not know. I went to it in my mail-shirt, which saved my skin. With long-sword and belt-dagger I fought for the life against a Devil whose very feet were hands, and who whirled me back and forth like a dead branch. He had me by the waist, my arms to my side, when an arrow from the ship pierced him between the shoulders, and he loosened grip. I passed my sword twice through him, and he crutched himself away between his long arms, coughing and moaning. Next, as I remember, I saw Thorkild of Borkum, bare-headed and smiling, leaping up and down before a Devil that leaped and gnashed his teeth. Then Hugh passed, his sword shifted to his left hand, and I wondered why I had not known that Hugh was a left-handed man; and thereafter I remembered nothing till I felt spray on my face, and we were in sunshine on the open sea. That was twenty days after.'

'What had happened? Did Hugh die?' the children asked.

'Never was such a fight fought by christened man,' said Sir Richard. 'An arrow from the ship had saved me from my Devil, and Thorkild of Borkum had given back before his Devil, till the bowmen on the ship could shoot it all full of arrows from near by; but Hugh's Devil was cunning, and had kept behind trees, where no arrow could reach. Body to body there, by stark strength of sword and hand, had Hugh slain him, and, dying, the Thing had clenched his teeth on the sword. Judge what teeth they were!'

Sir Richard turned the sword again that the children might see the two great chiselled gouges on either side of the blade.

'Those same teeth met in Hugh's right arm and side,' Sir Richard went on. 'I? Oh, I had no more than a broken foot and a fever. Thorkild's ear was bitten, but Hugh's arm and side clean withered away. I saw him where he lay along, sucking a fruit in his left hand. His flesh was wasted off his bones, his hair was patched with white, and his hand was blue-veined like a woman's. He put his left arm round my neck and whispered, "Take my sword. It has been thine since Hastings, O my brother, but I can never hold hilt again." We lay there on the high deck talking of Santlache, and, I think, of every day since Santlache, and it came so that we both wept. I was weak, and he little more than a shadow.

' "Nay – nay," said Witta, at the helm-rail. "Gold is a good right arm to any man. Look – look at the gold!" He bade Thorkild show us the gold and the elephants' teeth, as though we had been children. He had brought away all the gold on the bank, and twice as much more, that the people of the village gave him for slaying the Devils. They worshipped us as Gods, Thorkild told me: it was one of their old women healed up Hugh's poor arm.'

'How much gold did you get?' asked Dan.

'How can I say? Where we came out with wedges of iron under the rowers' feet we returned with wedges of gold hidden beneath planks. There was dust of gold in packages where we slept and along the side, and cross-wise under the benches we lashed the blackened elephants' teeth.

' "I had sooner have my right arm," said Hugh, when he had seen all.

' "Ahai! That was my fault," said Witta. "I should have taken ransom and landed you in France when first you came aboard, ten months ago."

'The bowmen on the ship could shoot it all full of arrows from near by.'

' "It is over-late now," said Hugh, laughing.

'Witta plucked at his long shoulder-lock. "But think!" said he. "If I had let ye go – which I swear I would never have done, for I love ye more than brothers – if I had let ye go, by now ye might have been horribly slain by some mere Moor in the Duke of Burgundy's war, or ye might have been murdered by land-thieves, or ye might have died of the plague at an inn. Think of this and do not blame me overmuch, Hugh. See! I will only take a half of the gold."

' "I blame thee not at all, Witta," said Hugh. "It was a joyous venture, and we thirty-five here have done what never men have done. If I live till England, I will build me a stout keep over Dallington out of my share."

' "I will buy cattle and amber and warm red cloth for the wife," said Witta, "and I will hold all the land at the head of Stavanger Fiord. Many will fight for me now. But first we must turn North, and with this honest treasure aboard I pray we meet no pirate ships."

'We did not laugh. We were careful. We were afraid lest we should lose one grain of our gold, for which we had fought Devils.

' "Where is the Sorcerer?" said I, for Witta was looking at the Wise Iron in the box, and I could not see the Yellow Man.

' "He has gone to his own country," said he. "He rose up in the night while we were beating out of that forest in the mud, and said that he could see it behind the trees. He leaped out on the mud, and did not answer when we called; so we called no more. He left the Wise Iron, which is all that I care for – and see, the Spirit still points to the South."

'We were troubled for fear that the Wise Iron should fail us now that its Yellow Man had gone, and when we saw the Spirit still served us we grew afraid of too strong winds, and of shoals, and of careless leaping fish, and of all the people on all the shores where we landed.'

'Why?' said Dan.

'Because of the gold – because of our gold. Gold changes men altogether. Thorkild of Borkum did not change. He laughed at Witta for his fears, and at us for our counselling Witta to furl sail when the ship pitched at all.

' "Better be drowned out of hand," said Thorkild of Borkum, "than go tied to a deck-load of yellow dust."

'He was a landless man, and had been slave to some King in the East. He would have beaten out the gold into deep bands to put round the oars, and round the prow.

'Yet, though he vexed himself for the gold, Witta waited upon Hugh like a woman, lending him his shoulder when the ship rolled, and tying of ropes from side to side that Hugh might hold by them. But for Hugh, he said – and so did all his men – they would never have won the gold. I remember Witta made a little, thin gold ring for our Bird to swing in.

'Three months we rowed and sailed and went ashore for fruits or to clean the ship. When we saw wild horsemen, riding among sand dunes, flourishing spears, we knew we were on the Moors' coast, and stood over north to Spain;

'He leaped out on the mud, and did not answer when we called;
so we called no more.'

and a strong south-west wind bore us in ten days to a coast of high red rocks, where we heard a hunting-horn blow among the yellow gorse and knew it was England.

' "Now find ye Pevensey yourselves," said Witta. "I love not these narrow ship-filled seas."

'He set the dried, salted head of the Devil, which Hugh had killed, high on our prow, and all boats fled from us. Yet, for our gold's sake, we were more afraid than they. We crept along the coast by night till we came to the chalk cliffs, and so east to Pevensey. Witta would not come ashore with us, though Hugh promised him wine at Dallington enough to swim in. He was on fire to see his wife, and ran into the Marsh after sunset, and there he left us and our share of gold, and backed out on the same tide. He made no promise; he swore no oath; he looked for no thanks; but to Hugh, an armless man, and to me, an old cripple whom he could have flung into the sea, he passed over wedge upon wedge, packet upon packet of gold and dust of gold, and only ceased when we would take no more. As he stooped from the rail to bid us farewell he stripped off his right-arm bracelets and put them all on Hugh's left, and he kissed Hugh on the cheek. I think when Thorkild of Borkum bade the rowers give way we were near weeping. It is true that Witta was a heathen and a pirate; true it is he held us by force many months in his ship, but I loved that bow-legged, blue-eyed man for his great boldness, his cunning, his skill, and, beyond all, for his simplicity.'

'Did he get home all right?' said Dan.

'I never knew. We saw him hoist sail under the moon-track and stand away. I have prayed that he found his wife and the children.'

'And what did you do?'

'We waited on the Marsh till the day. Then I sat by the gold, all tied in an old sail, while Hugh went to Pevensey, and De Aquila sent us horses.'

Sir Richard crossed hands on his sword-hilt, and stared down stream through the soft warm shadows.

'A whole shipload of gold!' said Una, looking at the little *Golden Hind*. 'But I'm glad I didn't see the Devils.'

'I don't believe they were Devils,' Dan whispered back.

'Eh?' said Sir Richard. 'Witta's father warned him they were unquestionable Devils. One must believe one's father, and not one's children. What were my Devils, then?'

Dan flushed all over. 'I – I only thought,' he stammered; 'I've got a book called *The Gorilla Hunters* – it's a continuation of *Coral Island*, sir – and it says there that the gorillas (they're big monkeys, you know) were always chewing iron up.'

'Not always,' said Una. 'Only twice.' They had been reading *The Gorilla Hunters* in the orchard.

'Well, anyhow, they always drummed on their chests, like Sir Richard's did, before they went for people. And they built houses in trees, too.'

'Ha!' Sir Richard opened his eyes. 'Houses like flat nests did our Devils make, where their imps lay and looked at us. I did not see them (I was sick after the fight), but Witta told me, and, lo, ye know it also? Wonderful! Were our Devils only nest-building apes? Is there no sorcery left in the world?'

'I don't know,' answered Dan, uncomfortably. 'I've seen a man take rabbits out of a hat, and he told us we could see how he did it, if we watched hard. And we did.'

'But we didn't,' said Una, sighing. 'Oh! there's Puck!'

The little fellow, brown and smiling, peered between two stems of an ash, nodded, and slid down the bank into the cool beside them.

'No sorcery, Sir Richard?' he laughed, and blew on a full dandelion head he had picked.

'They tell me that Witta's Wise Iron was a toy. The boy carries such an iron with him. They tell me our Devils were apes, called gorillas!' said Sir Richard, indignantly.

'That is the sorcery of books,' said Puck. 'I warned thee they were wise children. All people can be wise by reading of books.'

'But are the books true?' Sir Richard frowned. 'I like not all this reading and writing.'

'Ye–es,' said Puck, holding the naked dandelion head at arm's length. 'But if we hang all fellows who write falsely, why did De Aquila not begin with Gilbert the Clerk? *He* was false enough.'

'Poor false Gilbert. Yet, in his fashion, he was bold,' said Sir Richard.

'What did he do?' said Dan.

'He wrote,' said Sir Richard. 'Is the tale meet for children, think you?' He looked at Puck; but 'Tell us! Tell us!' cried Dan and Una together.

Thorkild's Song

There's no wind along these seas,
Out oars for Stavanger!
Forward all for Stavanger!
So we must wake the white-ash breeze,
Let fall for Stavanger!
A long pull for Stavanger!

Oh, hear the benches creak and strain!
(A long pull for Stavanger!)
She thinks she smells the Northland rain!
(A long pull for Stavanger!)

She thinks she smells the Northland snow,
And she's as glad as we to go.

She thinks she smells the Northland rime,
And the dear dark nights of winter-time.

Her very bolts are sick for shore,
And we – we want it ten times more!

So all you Gods that love brave men,
Send us a three-reef gale again!

Send us a gale, and watch us come,
With close-cropped canvas slashing home!

But – there's no wind in all these seas.
A long pull for Stavanger!
So we must wake the white-ash breeze,
A long pull for Stavanger!

OLD MEN AT PEVENSEY

'It has naught to do with apes or Devils,' Sir Richard went on, in an undertone. 'It concerns De Aquila, than whom there was never bolder nor craftier, nor more hardy knight born. And remember he was an old, old man at that time.'

'When?' said Dan.

'When we came back from sailing with Witta.'

'What did you do with your gold?' said Dan.

'Have patience. Link by link is chain mail made. I will tell all in its place. We bore the gold to Pevensey on horseback – three loads of it – and then up to the north chamber, above the Great Hall of Pevensey Castle, where De Aquila lay in winter. He sat on his bed like a little white falcon, turning his head swiftly from one to the other as we told our tale. Jehan the Crab, an old sour man-at-arms, guarded the stairway, but De Aquila bade him wait at the stair-foot, and let down both leather curtains over the door. It was Jehan whom De Aquila had sent to us with the horses, and only Jehan had loaded the gold. When our story was told, De Aquila gave us the news of England, for we were as men waked from a year-long sleep. The Red King was dead – slain (ye remember?) the day we set sail – and Henry, his younger brother, had made himself King of England over the head of Robert of Normandy. This was the very thing that the Red King had done to Robert when our Great William died. Then Robert of Normandy, mad, as De Aquila said, at twice missing of this kingdom, had sent an army against England, which army had been well beaten back to their ships at Portsmouth. A little earlier, and Witta's ship would have rowed through them.

' "And now," said De Aquila, "half the great Barons of the North and West are out against the King between Salisbury and Shrewsbury, and half the other half wait to see which way the game shall go. They say Henry is overly English for their stomachs, because he hath married an English wife and she hath coaxed him to give back their old laws to our Saxons. (Better ride a horse on the bit he knows, *I* say!) But that is only a cloak to their falsehood." He cracked his finger on the table, where the wine was spilt, and thus he spoke:

' "William crammed us Norman barons full of good English acres after Santlache. *I* had my share too," he said, and clapped Hugh on the shoulder; "but I warned him – I warned him before Odo rebelled – that he should have bidden the Barons give up their lands and lordships in Normandy if they would be English lords. Now they are all but princes both in England and Normandy – trencher-fed hounds, with a foot in one trough and both eyes on the other! Robert of Normandy has sent them word that if they do not fight for him in England he will sack and harry out their lands in Normandy. Therefore Clare has risen, FitzOsborne has risen, Montgomery has risen – whom our First William made an English Earl. Even D'Arcy is out with his men, whose father I remember – a little hedge-sparrow knight near by Caen. If Henry wins, the Barons can still flee to Normandy, where Robert will welcome them. If Henry loses, Robert, he says, will give them more lands in England. Oh, a pest – a pest on Normandy, for she will be our England's curse this many a long year!"

' "Amen," said Hugh. "But will the war come our ways, think you?"

' "Not from the North," said De Aquila. "But the sea is always open. If the Barons gain the upper hand Robert will send another army into England for sure, and this time I think he will land here – where his father, the Conqueror, landed. Ye have brought your pigs to a pretty market! Half England alight, and gold enough on the ground" – he stamped on the bars beneath the table – "to set every sword in Christendom fighting."

' "What is to do?" said Hugh. "I have no keep at Dallington; and if we buried it, whom could we trust?"

' "Me," said De Aquila. "Pevensey walls are strong. No man but Jehan, who is my dog, knows what is between them." He drew a curtain by the shot-window and showed us the shaft of a well in the thickness of the wall.

' "I made it for a drinking-well," he said, "but we found salt water, and it rises and falls with the tide. Hark!" We heard the water whistle and blow at the bottom. "Will it serve?" said he.

' "Needs must," said Hugh. "Our lives are in thy hands." So we lowered all the gold down except one small chest of it by De Aquila's bed, which we kept as much for his delight in its weight and colour as for any of our needs.

'In the morning, ere we rode to our Manors, he said: "I do not say farewell; because ye will return and bide here. Not for love nor for sorrow, but to be with the gold. Have a care," he said, laughing, "lest I use it to make myself Pope. Trust me not, but return!" '

Sir Richard paused and smiled sadly.

'In seven days, then, we returned from our Manors – from the Manors which had been ours.'

'And were the children quite well?' said Una.

'My sons were young. Land and governance belong by right to young men.' Sir Richard was talking to himself. 'It would have broken their hearts if we had taken back our Manors. They made us great welcome, but we could see – Hugh and I could see – that our day was done. I was a cripple and he a one-armed man. No!' He shook his head. 'And therefore' – he raised his voice – 'we rode back to Pevensey.'

'I'm sorry,' said Una, for the knight seemed very sorrowful.

'Little maid, it all passed long ago. They were young; we were old. We let them rule the Manors. "Aha!" cried De Aquila from his shot-window, when we dismounted. "Back again to earth, old foxes?" but when we were in his chamber above the Hall he puts his arms about us and says, "Welcome, ghosts! Welcome, poor ghosts!" . . . Thus it fell out that we were rich beyond belief, and lonely. And lonely!'

'What did you do?' said Dan.

'We watched for Robert of Normandy,' said the knight. 'De Aquila was like Witta. He suffered no idleness. In fair weather we would ride along between Bexlei on the one side, to Cuckmere on the other – sometimes with hawk, sometimes with hound (there are stout hares both on the Marsh and the Downland), but always with an eye to the sea, for fear of fleets from Normandy. In foul weather he would walk on the top of his tower, frowning against the rain – peering here and pointing there. It always vexed him to think how Witta's ship had come and gone without his knowledge. When the wind ceased and ships anchored, to the wharf's edge he would go and, leaning on his sword among the stinking fish, would call to the mariners for their news from France. His other eye he kept landward for word of Henry's war against the Barons.

'Many brought him news – jongleurs, harpers, pedlars, sutlers, priests and the like; and, though he was secret enough in small things, yet, if their news misliked him, then, regarding neither time nor place nor people, he would curse our King Henry for a fool or a babe. I have heard him cry aloud by the fishing boats: "If I were King of England I would do thus and thus"; and when I rode out to see that the warning-beacons were laid and dry, he hath often called to me from the shot-window: "Look to it, Richard! Do not copy our blind King, but see with thine own eyes and feel with thine own hands." I do not think he knew any sort of fear. And so we lived at Pevensey, in the little chamber above the Hall.

'One foul night came word that a messenger of the King waited below. We were chilled after a long riding in the fog towards Bexlei, which is an easy place for ships to land. De Aquila sent word the man might either eat with us or wait till we had fed. Anon Jehan, at the stair-head, cried that he had called for horse, and was gone. "Pest on him!" said De Aquila. "I have more to do than to shiver in the Great Hall for every gadling the King sends. Left he no word?"

' "None," said Jehan, "except" – he had been with De Aquila at Santlache – "except he said that if an old dog could not learn new tricks it was time to sweep out the kennel."

' "Oho!" said De Aquila, rubbing his nose, "to whom did he say that?"

' "To his beard, chiefly, but some to his horse's flank as he was girthing up. I followed him out," said Jehan the Crab.

' "What was his shield-mark?"

' "Gold horseshoes on black," said the Crab.

' "That is one of Fulke's men," said De Aquila.'

Puck broke in very gently, 'Gold horseshoes on black is *not* the Fulkes' shield. The Fulkes' arms are – '

The knight waved one hand statelily.

'Thou knowest that evil man's true name,' he replied, 'but I have chosen to call him Fulke because I promised him I would not tell the story of his wickedness so that any man might guess it. I have changed *all* the names in my tale. His children's children may be still alive.'

'True – true,' said Puck, smiling softly. 'It is knightly to keep faith – even after a thousand years.'

Sir Richard bowed a little and went on:

' "Gold horseshoes on black?" said De Aquila. "I had heard Fulke had joined the Barons, but if this is true our King must be of the upper hand. No matter, all Fulkes are faithless. Still, I would not have sent the man away empty."

' "He fed," said Jehan. "Gilbert the Clerk fetched him meat and wine from the kitchens. He ate at Gilbert's table."

'This Gilbert was a clerk from Battle Abbey, who kept the accounts of the Manor of Pevensey. He was tall and pale-coloured, and carried those new-fashioned beads for counting of prayers. They were large brown nuts or seeds, and hanging from his girdle with his pen and ink-horn they clashed when he walked. His place was in the great fireplace. There was his table of accounts, and there he lay o' nights. He feared the hounds in the Hall that came nosing after bones or to sleep on the warm ashes, and would slash at them with his beads – like a woman. When De Aquila sat in Hall to do justice, take fines, or grant lands, Gilbert would so write it in the Manor-roll. But it was none of his work to feed our guests, or to let them depart without his lord's knowledge.

'Said De Aquila, after Jehan was gone down the stair: "Hugh, hast thou ever told my Gilbert thou canst read Latin hand-of-write?"

' "No," said Hugh. "He is no friend to me, or to Odo my hound either." "No matter," said De Aquila. "Let him never know thou canst tell one letter from its fellow, and" – there he yerked us in the ribs with his scabbard – "watch him, both of ye. There be devils in Africa, as I have heard, but by the Saints, there be greater devils in Pevensey!" And that was all he would say.

'It chanced, some small while afterwards, a Norman man-at-arms would wed a Saxon wench of the Manor, and Gilbert (we had watched him well since De Aquila spoke) doubted whether her folk were free or slave. Since De Aquila would give them a field of good land, if she were free, the matter came up at the justice in Great Hall before De Aquila. First the wench's father spoke; then her mother; then all together, till the Hall rang and the hounds bayed. De Aquila held up his hands. "Write her free," he called to Gilbert by the fireplace. "A' God's name write her free, before she deafens me! Yes, yes," he said to the wench that was on her knees at him; "thou art Cerdic's sister, and own cousin to the Lady of Mercia, if thou wilt be silent. In fifty years there will be neither Norman nor Saxon, but all English," said he, "and *these* are the men that do our work!" He clapped the man-at-arms that was Jehan's nephew on the shoulder, and kissed the wench, and fretted with his feet

'A' God's name write her free, before she deafens mè!'

among the rushes to show it was finished. (The Great Hall is always bitter cold.) I stood at his side; Hugh was behind Gilbert in the fireplace making to play with wise rough Odo. He signed to De Aquila, who bade Gilbert measure the new field for the new couple. Out then runs our Gilbert between man and maid, his beads clashing at his waist, and the Hall being empty, we three sit by the fire.

'Said Hugh, leaning down to the hearthstones, "I saw this stone move under Gilbert's foot when Odo snuffed at it. Look!" De Aquila digged in the ashes with his sword; the stone tilted; beneath it lay a parchment folden, and the writing atop was: "Words spoken against the King by our Lord of Pevensey – the second part."

'Here was set out (Hugh read it us whispering) every jest De Aquila had made to us touching the King; every time he had called out to me from the shot-window, and every time he had said what he would do if he were King of England. Yes, day by day had his daily speech, which he never stinted, been set down by Gilbert, tricked out and twisted from its true meaning, yet withal so cunningly that none could deny who knew him that De Aquila had in some sort spoken those words. Ye see?'

Dan and Una nodded.

'Yes,' said Una gravely. 'It isn't what you say so much. It's what you mean when you say it. Like calling Dan a beast in fun. Only grown-ups don't always understand.'

' "He hath done this day by day before our very face?" said De Aquila.

' "Nay, hour by hour," said Hugh. "When De Aquila spoke even now, in the Hall, of Saxons and Normans, I saw Gilbert write on a parchment, which he kept beside the Manor-roll, that De Aquila said soon there would be no Normans left in England if his men-at-arms did their work aright."

' "Bones of the Saints!" said De Aquila. "What avail is honour or a sword against a pen? Where did Gilbert hide that writing? He shall eat it."

' "In his breast when he ran out," said Hugh. "Which made me look to see where he kept his finished stuff. When Odo scratched at this stone here, I saw his face change. So I was sure."

' "He is bold," said De Aquila. "Do him justice. In his own fashion, my Gilbert is bold."

' "Overbold," said Hugh. "Hearken here," and he read: "Upon the Feast of St Agatha, our Lord of Pevensey, lying in his upper chamber, being clothed in his second fur gown reversed with rabbit – "

' "Pest on him! He is not my tire-woman!" said De Aquila, and Hugh and I laughed.

' "Reversed with rabbit, seeing a fog over the marshes, did wake Sir Richard Dalyngridge, his drunken cup-mate" (here they laughed at me) "and said, 'Peer out, old fox, for God is on the Duke of Normandy's side.'" '

' "So did I. It was a black fog. Robert could have landed ten thousand men, and we none the wiser. Does he tell how we were out all day riding the Marsh, and how I near perished in a quicksand, and coughed like a sick ewe for ten days after?" cried De Aquila.

' "No," said Hugh. "But here is the prayer of Gilbert himself to his master Fulke."

' "Ah," said De Aquila. "Well I knew it was Fulke. What is the price of my blood?"

' "Gilbert prayeth that when our Lord of Pevensey is stripped of his lands on this evidence which Gilbert hath, with fear and pains, collected – "

' "Fear and pains is a true word," said De Aquila, and sucked in his cheeks. "But how excellent a weapon is a pen! I must learn it."

' "He prays that Fulke will advance him from his present service to that honour in the Church which Fulke promised him. And lest Fulke should forget, he has written below, 'To be Sacristan of Battle'."

'At this De Aquila whistled. "A man who can plot against one lord can plot against another. When I am stripped of my lands Fulke will whip off my Gilbert's foolish head. None the less Battle needs a new Sacristan. They tell me the Abbot Henry keeps no sort of rule there."

' "Let the Abbot wait," said Hugh. "It is our heads and our lands that are in danger. This parchment is the second part of the tale. The first has gone to Fulke, and so to the King, who will hold us traitors."

"Assuredly," said De Aquila. "Fulke's man took the first part that evening when Gilbert fed him, and our King is so beset by his brother and his Barons (small blame, too!) that he is mad with mistrust. Fulke has his ear, and pours poison into it. Presently the King gives him my land and yours. This is old," and he leaned back and yawned.

' "And thou wilt surrender Pevensey without word or blow?" said Hugh. "We Saxons will fight your King then. I will go warn my nephew at Dallington. Give me a horse!"

' "Give thee a toy and a rattle," said De Aquila. "Put back the parchment, and rake over the ashes. If Fulke is given my Pevensey, which is England's gate, what will he do with it? He is Norman at heart, and his heart is in Normandy, where he can kill peasants at his pleasure. He will open England's gate to our sleepy Robert, as Odo and Mortain tried to do, and then there will be another landing and another Santlache. Therefore I cannot give up Pevensey."

' "Good," said we two.

' "Ah, but wait! If my King be made, on Gilbert's evidence, to mistrust me, he will send his men against me here, and while we fight, England's gate is left unguarded. Who will be the first to come through thereby? Even Robert of Normandy. Therefore I cannot fight my King." He nursed his sword – thus.

' "This is saying and unsaying like a Norman," said Hugh. "What of our Manors?"

' "I do not think for myself," said De Aquila, "nor for our King, nor for your lands. I think for England, for whom neither King nor Baron thinks. I am not Norman, Sir Richard, nor Saxon, Sir Hugh. English am I."

' "Saxon, Norman or English," said Hugh, "our lives are thine, however the game goes. When do we hang Gilbert?"

' "Never," said De Aquila. "Who knows, he may yet be Sacristan of Battle, for, to do him justice, he is a good writer. Dead men make dumb witnesses. Wait."

' "But the King may give Pevensey to Fulke. And our Manors go with it," said I. "Shall we tell our sons?"

' "No. The King will not wake up a hornets' nest in the South till he has smoked out the bees in the North. He may hold me a traitor; but at least he sees I am not fighting against him; and every day that I lie still is so much gain to him while he fights the Barons. If he were wise he would wait till that war were over before he made new enemies. But I think Fulke will play upon him to send for me, and if I do not obey the summons, that will, to Henry's mind, be proof of my treason. But mere talk, such as Gilbert sends, is no proof nowadays. We Barons follow the Church, and, like Anselm, we speak what we please. Let us go about our day's dealings, and say naught to Gilbert."

' "Then we do nothing?" said Hugh.

' "We wait," said De Aquila. "I am old, but still I find that the most grievous work I know."

'And so we found it, but in the end De Aquila was right.

'A little later in the year, armed men rode over the hill, the Golden Horseshoes flying behind the King's banner. Said De Aquila, at the window of our chamber: "How did I tell you? Here comes Fulke himself to spy out his new lands which our King hath promised him if he can bring proof of my treason."

' "How dost thou know?" said Hugh.

' "Because that is what I would do if I were Fulke, but *I* should have brought more men. My roan horse to your old shoes," said he, "Fulke brings me the King's Summons to leave Pevensey and join the war." He sucked in his cheeks and drummed on the edge of the well-shaft, where the water sounded all hollow.

' "Shall we go?" said I.

' "Go! At this time of year? Stark madness," said he. "Take *me* from Pevensey to fisk and flyte through fern and forest, and in three days Robert's keels would be lying on Pevensey mud with ten thousand men! Who would stop them – Fulke?"

'The horns blew without, and anon Fulke cried the King's Summons at the great door, that De Aquila with all men and horse should join the King's camp at Salisbury.

' "How did I tell you?" said De Aquila. "There are twenty Barons 'twixt here and Salisbury could give King Henry good land service, but he has been worked upon by Fulke to send South and call me – *me!* – off the Gate of England, when his enemies stand about to batter it in. See that Fulke's men lie in the big south barn," said he. "Give them drink, and when Fulke has eaten we will drink in my chamber. The Great Hall is too cold for old bones."

'As soon as he was off-horse Fulke went to the chapel with Gilbert to give thanks for his safe coming, and when he had eaten – he was a fat man, and rolled his eyes greedily at our good roast Sussex wheat-ears – we led him to the little upper chamber, whither Gilbert had already gone with the Manor-roll. I remember when Fulke heard the tide blow and whistle in the shaft he leaped back, and his long down-turned stirrup-shoes caught in the rushes and he stumbled, so that Jehan behind him found it easy to knock his head against the wall.'

'Did you know it was going to happen?' said Dan.

'Assuredly,' said Sir Richard, with a sweet smile. 'I put my foot on his sword and plucked away his dagger, but he knew not whether it was day or night for awhile. He lay rolling his eyes and bubbling with his mouth, and Jehan roped him like a calf. He was cased all in that newfangled armour which we call lizard mail. Not rings like my hauberk here' – Sir Richard tapped his chest – 'but little pieces of dagger-proof steel overlapping on stout leather. We stripped it off (no need to spoil good harness by wetting it), and in the neck-piece De Aquila found the same folden piece of parchment which we had put back under the hearthstone.

'At this Gilbert would have run out. I laid my hand on his shoulder. It sufficed. He fell to trembling and praying on his beads.

' "Gilbert," said De Aquila, "here be more notable sayings and doings of our Lord of Pevensey for thee to write down. Take pen and ink-horn, Gilbert. We cannot all be Sacristans of Battle."

'Said Fulke from the floor, "Ye have bound a King's messenger. Pevensey shall burn for this."

' "Maybe. I have seen it besieged once," said De Aquila, "but heart up, Fulke. I promise thee that thou shalt be hanged in the middle of the flames at the end of that siege, if I have to share my last loaf with thee; and that is more than Odo would have done when we starved out him and Mortain."

'Then Fulke sat up and looked long and cunningly at De Aquila.

' "By the Saints," said he, "why didst thou not say thou wast on the Duke Robert's side at the first?"

' "Am I?" said De Aquila.

'Fulke laughed and said, "No man who serves King Henry dare do this much to his messenger. When didst thou come over to the Duke? Let me up and we can smooth it out together." And he smiled and becked and winked.

' "Yes, we will smooth it out," said De Aquila. He nodded to me, and Jehan and I heaved up Fulke – he was a heavy man – and lowered him into the shaft by a rope, not so as to stand on our gold, but dangling by his shoulders a little above. It was turn of ebb, and the water came to his knees. He said nothing, but shivered somewhat.

'Then Jehan of a sudden beat down Gilbert's wrist with his sheathed dagger. "Stop!" he said. "He swallows his beads."

' "Poison, belike," said De Aquila. "It is good for men who know too much. I have carried it these thirty years. Give me!"

'Then Gilbert wept and howled. De Aquila ran the beads through his fingers. The last one – I have said they were large nuts – opened in two halves on a pin, and there was a small folded parchment within. On it was written: *The Old Dog goes to Salisbury to be beaten. I have his Kennel. Come quickly.*"

' "This is worse than poison," said De Aquila very softly, and sucked in his cheeks. Then Gilbert grovelled in the rushes, and told us all he knew. The letter, as we guessed, was from Fulke to the Duke (and not the first that had passed between them); Fulke had given it to Gilbert in the chapel, and Gilbert thought to have taken it by morning to a certain fishing boat at the wharf, which trafficked between Pevensey and the French shore. Gilbert was a false fellow, but he found time between his quakings and shakings to swear that the master of the boat knew nothing of the matter.

' "He hath called me shaved-head," said Gilbert, "and he hath thrown haddock-guts at me; but for all that, he is no traitor."

' "I will have no clerk of mine mishandled or miscalled," said De Aquila. "That seaman shall be whipped at his own mast. Write me first a letter, and thou shalt bear it, with the order for the whipping, tomorrow to the boat."

'At this Gilbert would have kissed De Aquila's hand – he had not hoped to live until the morning – and when he trembled less he wrote a letter as from Fulke to the Duke, saying that the Kennel, which signified Pevensey, was shut, and that the Old Dog (which was De Aquila) sat outside it, and, moreover, that all had been betrayed.

' "Write to any man that all is betrayed," said De Aquila, "and even the Pope himself would sleep uneasily. Eh, Jehan? If one told thee all was betrayed, what wouldst thou do?"

' "I would run away," said Jehan. "it might be true."

' "Well said," quoth De Aquila. "Write, Gilbert, that Montgomery, the great Earl, hath made his peace with the King, and that little D'Arcy, whom I hate, hath been hanged by the heels. We will give Robert full measure to chew upon. Write also that Fulke himself is sick to death of a dropsy."

' "Nay!" cried Fulke, hanging in the well-shaft. "Drown me out of hand, but do not make a jest of me."

' "Jest? I?" said De Aquila. "I am but fighting for life and lands with a pen, as thou hast shown me, Fulke."

'Then Fulke groaned, for he was cold, and, "Let me confess," said he.

' "Now, this is right neighbourly," said De Aquila, leaning over the shaft. "Thou hast read my sayings and doings – or at least the first part of them – and thou art minded to repay me with thy own doings and sayings. Take pen and inkhorn, Gilbert. Here is work that will not irk thee."

' "Let my men go without hurt, and I will confess my treason against the King," said Fulke.

' "Now, why has he grown so tender of his men of a sudden?" said Hugh to me; for Fulke had no name for mercy to his men. Plunder he gave them, but pity, none.

' "Té! Té!" said De Aquila. "Thy treason was all confessed long ago by Gilbert. It would be enough to hang Montgomery himself."

' "Nay; but spare my men," said Fulke; and we heard him splash like a fish in a pond, for the tide was rising.

' "All in good time," said De Aquila. "The night is young; the wine is old; and we need only the merry tale. Begin the story of thy life since when thou wast a lad at Tours. Tell it nimbly!"

' "Ye shame me to my soul," said Fulke.

' "Then I have done what neither King nor Duke could do," said De Aquila. "But begin, and forget nothing."

' "Send thy man away," said Fulke.

' "That much can I do," said De Aquila. "But, remember, I am like the Danes' King. I cannot turn the tide."

' "How long will it rise?" said Fulke, and splashed anew.

' "For three hours," said De Aquila. "Time to tell all thy good deeds. Begin, and, Gilbert, – I have heard thou art somewhat careless – do not twist his words from his true meaning."

'So – fear of death in the dark being upon him – Fulke began, and Gilbert, not knowing what his fate might be, wrote it word by word. I have heard many tales, but never heard I aught to match the tale of Fulke his black life, as Fulke told it hollowly, hanging in the shaft.'

'Was it bad?' said Dan, awestruck.

'Beyond belief,' Sir Richard answered. 'None the less, there was that in it which forced even Gilbert to laugh. We three laughed till we ached. At one place his teeth so chattered that we could not well hear, and we reached him down a cup of wine. Then he warmed to it, and smoothly set out all his shifts, malices, and treacheries, his extreme boldnesses (he was desperate bold); his retreats, shufflings, and counterfeitings (he was also inconceivably a coward); his lack of gear and honour; his despair at their loss; his remedies, and well-coloured contrivances. Yes, he waved the filthy rags of his life before us, as though they had been some proud banner. When he ceased, we saw by torches that the tide stood at the corners of his mouth, and he breathed strongly through his nose.

'We had him out, and rubbed him; we wrapped him in a cloak, and gave him wine, and we leaned and looked upon him, the while he drank. He was shivering, but shameless.

'Of a sudden we heard Jehan at the stairway wake, but a boy pushed past him, and stood before us, the Hall-rushes in his hair, all slubbered with sleep. "My father! My father! I dreamed of treachery," he cried, and babbled thickly.

' "There is no treachery here," said Fulke. "Go!" and the boy turned, even then not fully awake, and Jehan led him by the hand to the Great Hall.

' "Thy only son!" said De Aquila. "Why didst thou bring the child here?"

' "He is my heir. I dared not trust him to my brother," said Fulke, and now he was ashamed. De Aquila said nothing, but sat weighing a wine-cup in his two hands – thus. Anon, Fulke touched him on the knee.

' "Let the boy escape to Normandy," said he, "and do with me at thy pleasure. Yea, hang me tomorrow, with my letter to Robert round my neck, but let the boy go."

' "Be still," said De Aquila. "I think for England."

'So we waited what our Lord of Pevensey should devise; and the sweat ran down Fulke's forehead.

'At last said De Aquila: "I am too old to judge, or to trust any man. I do not covet thy lands, as thou hast coveted mine; and whether thou art any better or any worse than any other black Angevin thief, it is for thy King to find out. Therefore, go back to thy King, Fulke."

' "And thou wilt say nothing of what has passed?" said Fulke.

' "Why should I? Thy son will stay with me. If the King calls me again to leave Pevensey, which I must guard against England's enemies; if the King sends his men against me for a traitor; or if I hear that the King in his bed thinks any evil of me or my two knights, thy son will be hanged from out this window, Fulke." '

'But it hadn't anything to do with his son,' cried Una, startled.

'How could we have hanged Fulke?' said Sir Richard. 'We needed him to make our peace with the King. He would have betrayed half England for the boy's sake. Of that we were sure.'

'I don't understand,' said Una. 'But I think it was simply awful.'

'So did not Fulke. He was well pleased.'

'What? Because his son was going to be killed?'

'Nay. Because De Aquila had shown him how he might save the boy's life and his own lands and honours. "I will do it," he said. "I swear I will do it. I will tell the King thou art no traitor, but the most excellent, valiant, and perfect of us all. Yes, I will save thee."

'De Aquila looked still into the bottom of the cup, rolling the wine-dregs to and fro.

' "Ay," he said. "If I had a son, I would, I think, save him. But do not by any means tell me how thou wilt go about it."

' "Nay, nay," said Fulke, nodding his bald head wisely. "That is my secret. But rest at ease, De Aquila, no hair of thy head nor rood of thy land shall be forfeited," and he smiled like one planning great good deeds.

' "And henceforward," said De Aquila, "I counsel thee to serve one master – not two."

' "What?" said Fulke. "Can I work no more honest trading between the two sides these troublous times?"

' "Serve Robert or the King – England or Normandy," said De Aquila. "I care not which it is, but make thy choice here and now."

' "The King, then," said Fulke, "for I see he is better served than Robert. Shall I swear it?"

' "No need," said De Aquila, and he laid his hand on the parchments which Gilbert had written. "It shall be some part of my Gilbert's penance to copy out the savoury tale of thy life, till we have made ten, twenty, an hundred, maybe, copies. How many cattle, think you, would the Bishop of Tours give for that tale? Or thy brother? Or the Monks of Blois? Minstrels will turn it into songs which thy own Saxon serfs shall sing behind their plough-stilts, and men-at-arms riding through thy Norman towns. From here to Rome, Fulke, men will make very merry over that tale, and how Fulke told it, hanging in a well, like a drowned puppy. This shall be thy punishment, if ever I find thee double-dealing with thy King any more. Meantime, the parchments stay here with thy son. Him I will return to thee when thou hast made my peace with the King. The parchments never."

'Fulke hid his face and groaned.

' "Bones of the Saints!" said De Aquila, laughing. "The pen cuts deep. I could never have fetched that grunt out of thee with any sword."

' "But so long as I do not anger thee, my tale will be secret?" said Fulke.

' "Just so long. Does that comfort thee, Fulke?" said De Aquila.

' "What other comfort have ye left me?" he said, and of a sudden he wept hopelessly like a child, dropping his face on his knees.'

'Poor Fulke,' said Una.

'I pitied him also,' said Sir Richard.

' "After the spur, corn," said De Aquila, and he threw Fulke three wedges of gold that he had taken from our little chest by the bedplace.

' "If I had known this," said Fulke, catching his breath, "I would never have lifted hand against Pevensey. Only lack of this yellow stuff has made me so unlucky in my dealings."

'It was dawn then, and they stirred in the Great Hall below. We sent down Fulke's mail to be scoured, and when he rode away at noon under his own and the King's banner, very splendid and stately did he show. He smoothed his long beard, and called his son to his stirrup and kissed him. De Aquila rode with him as far as the New Mill landward. We thought the night had been all a dream.'

'But did he make it right with the King?' Dan asked. 'About your not being traitors, I mean.'

Sir Richard smiled. 'The King sent no second summons to Pevensey, nor did he ask why De Aquila had not obeyed the first. Yes, that was Fulke's work. I know not how he did it, but it was well and swiftly done.'

'Then you didn't do anything to his son?' said Una.

'The boy? Oh, he was an imp! He turned the keep doors out of dortoirs while we had him. He sang foul songs, learned in the Barons' camps – poor fool; he set the hounds fighting in Hall; he lit the rushes to drive out, as he said, the fleas; he drew his dagger on Jehan, who threw him down the stairway for it; and he rode his horse through crops and among sheep. But when we had beaten him, and showed him wolf and deer, he followed us old men like a young, eager hound, and called us "uncle". His father came the summer's end to take him away, but the boy had no lust to go, because of the otter-hunting, and he stayed on till the fox-hunting. I gave him a bittern's claw to bring him good luck at shooting. An imp, if ever there was!'

'And what happened to Gilbert?' said Dan.

'Not even a whipping. De Aquila said he would sooner a clerk, however false, that knew the Manor-roll than a fool, however true, that must be taught his work afresh. Moreover, after that night I think Gilbert loved as much as he feared De Aquila. At least he would not leave us – not even when Vivian, the King's Clerk, would have made him Sacristan of Battle Abbey. A false fellow, but, in his fashion, bold.'

'Did Robert ever land in Pevensey after all?' Dan went on.

'We guarded the coast too well while Henry was fighting his Barons; and three or four years later, when England had peace, Henry crossed to Normandy and showed his brother some work at Tenchebrai that cured Robert of fighting. Many of Henry's men sailed from Pevensey to that war. Fulke came, I remember, and we all four lay in the little chamber once again, and drank together. De Aquila was right. One should not judge men. Fulke was merry. Yes, always merry – with a catch in his breath.'

'And what did you do afterwards?' said Una.

'We talked together of times past. That is all men can do when they grow old, little maid.'

*   *   *

The bell for tea rang faintly across the meadows. Dan lay in the bows of the *Golden Hind*; Una in the stern, the book of verses open in her lap, was reading from 'The Slave's Dream':

> 'Again, in the mist and shadow of sleep,
> He saw his native land.'

'I don't know when you began that,' said Dan, sleepily.

On the middle thwart of the boat, beside Una's sun-bonnet, lay an Oak leaf, an Ash leaf, and a Thorn leaf, that must have dropped down from the trees above; and the brook giggled as though it had just seen some joke.

'He drew his dagger on Jehan, who threw him down the stairway for it.'

The Runes on Weland's Sword

A Smith makes me
To betray my Man
In my first fight.

To gather Gold
At the world's end
I am sent.

The Gold I gather
Comes into England
Out of deep Water.

Like a shining Fish
Then it descends
Into deep Water.

It is not given
For goods or gear,
But for The Thing.

The Gold I gather
A King covets
For an ill use.

The Gold I gather
Is drawn up
Out of deep Water.

Like a shining Fish
Then it descends
Into deep Water.

It is not given
For goods or gear,
But for The Thing.

A CENTURION OF THE THIRTIETH

Cities and Thrones and Powers

Cities and Thrones and Powers
   Stand in Time's eye,
Almost as long as flowers,
   Which daily die.
But, as new buds put forth
   To glad new men,
Out of the spent and unconsidered Earth
   The Cities rise again.

This season's Daffodil,
   She never hears
What change, what chance, what chill,
   Cut down last year's:
But with bold countenance,
   And knowledge small,
Esteems her seven days' continuance
   To be perpetual.

So Time that is o'er-kind
   To all that be,
Ordains us e'en as blind,
   As bold as she:
That in our very death,
   And burial sure,
Shadow to shadow, well persuaded, smith,
   'See how our works endure!'

A Centurion of the Thirtieth

Dan had come to grief over his Latin, and was kept in; so Una went alone to Far Wood. Dan's big catapult and the lead bullets that Hobden had made for him were hidden in an old hollow beech-stub on the west of the wood. They had named the place out of the verse in *Lays of Ancient Rome*:

> From lordly Volaterrae,
>> Where scowls the far-famed hold
> Piled by the hands of giants
>> For Godlike Kings of old.

They were the 'Godlike Kings', and when old Hobden piled some comfortable brushwood between the big wooden knees of Volaterrae, they called him 'Hands of Giants'.

Una slipped through their private gap in the fence, and sat still awhile, scowling as scowlily and lordlily as she knew how; for Volaterrae is an important watchtower that juts out of Far Wood just as Far Wood juts out of the hillside. Pook's Hill lay below her and all the turns of the brook as it wanders out of the Willingford Woods, between hop-gardens, to old Hobden's cottage at the Forge. The sou'-west wind (there is always a wind by Volaterrae) blew from the bare ridge where Cherry Clack Windmill stands.

Now, wind prowling through woods sounds like exciting things going to happen, and that is why on blowy days you stand up in Volaterrae and shout bits of the *Lays* to suit its noises.

Una took Dan's catapult from its secret place, and made ready to meet Lars Porsena's army stealing through the wind-whitened aspens by the brook. A gust boomed up the valley, and Una chanted sorrowfully:

> 'Verbenna down to Ostia
>> Hath wasted all the plain:
> Astur hath stormed Janiculum,
>> And the stout guards are slain.'

But the wind, not charging fair to the wood, started aside and shook a single oak in Gleason's pasture. Here it made itself all small and crouched among the grasses, waving the tips of them as a cat waves the tip of her tail before she springs.

'Now welcome – welcome, Sextus,' sang Una, loading the catapult –

> 'Now welcome to thy home!
> Why dost thou stay, and turn away?
>> Here lies the road to Rome.'

She fired into the face of the lull, to wake up the cowardly wind, and heard a grunt from behind a thorn in the pasture.

'Oh, my Winkie!' she said aloud, and that was something she had picked up from Dan. 'I b'lieve I've tickled up a Gleason cow.'

'You little painted beast!' a voice cried. 'I'll teach you to sling your masters!'

She looked down most cautiously, and saw a young man covered with hoopy bronze armour all glowing among the late broom. But what Una admired beyond all was his great bronze helmet with a red horse-tail that flicked in the wind. She could hear the long hairs rasp on his shimmery shoulder-plates.

'What does the Faun mean,' he said, half aloud to himself, 'by telling me that the Painted People have changed?' He caught sight of Una's yellow head. 'Have you seen a painted lead-slinger?' he called.

'No–o,' said Una. 'But if you've seen a bullet – '

'Seen?' cried the man. 'It passed within a hair's-breadth of my ear.'

'Well, that was me. I'm most awfully sorry.'

'Didn't the Faun tell you I was coming?' He smiled.

'Not if you mean Puck. I thought you were a Gleason cow. I – I didn't know you were a – a – What are you?'

He laughed outright, showing a set of splendid teeth. His face and eyes were dark, and his eyebrows met above his big nose in one bushy black bar.

'They call me Parnesius. I have been a Centurion of the Seventh Cohort of the Thirtieth Legion – the Ulpia Victrix. Did you sling that bullet?'

'I did. I was using Dan's catapult,' said Una.

'Catapults!' said he. 'I ought to know something about them. Show me!'

He leaped the rough fence with a rattle of spear, shield, and armour, and hoisted himself into Volaterrae as quickly as a shadow.

'A sling on a forked stick. *I* understand!' he cried, and pulled at the elastic. 'But what wonderful beast yields this stretching leather?'

'It's laccy – elastic. You put the bullet into that loop, and then you pull hard.'

The man pulled, and hit himself square on his thumbnail.

'Each to his own weapon,' he said gravely, handing it back. 'I am better with the bigger machine, little maiden. But it's a pretty toy. A wolf would laugh at it. Aren't you afraid of wolves?'

'There aren't any,' said Una.

'Never believe it! A wolf's like a Winged Hat. He comes when he isn't expected. Don't they hunt wolves here?'

'We don't hunt,' said Una, remembering what she had heard from grown-ups. 'We preserve – pheasants. Do you know them?'

'I ought to,' said the young man, smiling again, and he imitated the cry of the cock-pheasant so perfectly that a bird answered out of the wood.

'What a big painted clucking fool is a pheasant!' he said. 'Just like some Romans.'

'But you're a Roman yourself, aren't you?' said Una.

'Ye–es and no. I'm one of a good few thousands who have never seen Rome except in a picture. My people have lived at Vectis for generations. Vectis – that island West yonder that you can see from so far in clear weather.'

'Do you mean the Isle of Wight? It lifts up just before rain, and you see it from the Downs.'

'Very likely. Our villa's on the south edge of the Island, by the Broken Cliffs. Most of it is three hundred years old, but the cow-stables, where our first ancestor lived, must be a hundred years older. Oh, quite that, because the founder of our family had his land given him by Agricola at the Settlement. It's not a bad little place for its size. In springtime violets grow down to the very beach. I've gathered seaweeds for myself and violets for my Mother many a time with our old nurse.'

'Was your nurse a – a Romaness too?'

'No, a Numidian. Gods be good to her! A dear, fat, brown thing with a tongue like a cowbell. She was a free woman. By the way, are you free, maiden?'

'Oh, quite,' said Una. 'At least, till teatime; and in summer our governess doesn't say much if we're late.'

The young man laughed again – a proper understanding laugh.

'I see,' said he. 'That accounts for your being in the wood. *We* hid among the cliffs.'

'Did *you* have a governess, then?'

'Did we not? A Greek, too. She had a way of clutching her dress when she hunted us among the gorse bushes that made us laugh. Then she'd say she'd get us whipped. She never did, though, bless her! Aglaia was a thorough sportswoman, for all her learning.'

'But what lessons did you do – when – when you were little?'

'Ancient history, the Classics, arithmetic and so on,' he answered. 'My sister and I were thickheads, but my two brothers (I'm the middle one) liked those things, and, of course, Mother was clever enough for any six. She was nearly as tall as I am, and she looked like the new statue on the Western Road – the Demeter of the Baskets, you know. And funny! Roma Dea! How Mother could make us laugh!'

'What at?'

'Little jokes and sayings that every family has. Don't you know?'

'I know *we* have, but I didn't know other people had them too,' said Una. 'Tell me about all your family, please.'

'Good families are very much alike. Mother would sit spinning of evenings while Aglaia read in her corner, and Father did accounts, and we four romped about the passages. When our noise grew too loud the Pater would say, "Less tumult! Less tumult! Have you never heard of a Father's right over his children? He can slay them, my loves – slay them dead, and the Gods highly approve of the action!" Then Mother would prim up her dear mouth over the

'You put the bullet into that loop, and then you pull hard.'

wheel and answer: "H'm! I'm afraid there can't be much of the Roman Father about you!" Then the Pater would roll up his accounts, and say, "I'll show you!" and then – then, he'd be worse than any of us!'

'Fathers can – if they like,' said Una, her eyes dancing.

'Didn't I say all good families are very much the same?'

'What did you do in summer?' said Una. 'Play about, like us?'

'Yes, and we visited our friends. There are no wolves in Vectis. We had many friends, and as many ponies as we wished.'

'It must have been lovely,' said Una. 'I hope it lasted for ever.'

'Not quite, little maid. When I was about sixteen or seventeen, the Father felt gouty, and we all went to the Waters.'

'What waters?'

'At Aquae Sulis. Everyone goes there. You ought to get your Father to take you someday.'

'But where? I don't know,' said Una.

The young man looked astonished for a moment. 'Aquae Sulis,' he repeated. 'The best baths in Britain. Just as good, I'm told, as Rome. All the old gluttons sit in hot water, and talk scandal and politics. And the Generals come through the streets with their guards behind them; and the magistrates come in their chairs with their stiff guards behind them; and you meet fortune-tellers, and goldsmiths, and merchants, and philosophers, and feather-sellers, and ultra-Roman Britons, and ultra-British Romans, and tame tribesmen pretending to be civilised, and Jew lecturers, and – oh, everybody interesting. We young people, of course, took no interest in politics. We had not the gout. There were many of our age like us. We did not find life sad.

'But while we were enjoying ourselves without thinking, my sister met the son of a magistrate in the West – and a year afterwards she was married to him. My young brother, who was always interested in plants and roots, met the First Doctor of a Legion from the City of the Legions, and he decided that he would be an Army doctor. I do not think it is a profession for a well-born man, but then – I'm not my brother. He went to Rome to study medicine, and now he's First Doctor of a Legion in Egypt – at Antinoë, I think, but I have not heard from him for some time.

'My eldest brother came across a Greek philosopher, and told my Father that he intended to settle down on the estate as a farmer and a philosopher. You see,' – the young man's eyes twinkled – 'his philosopher was a long-haired one!'

'I thought philosophers were bald,' said Una.

'Not all. She was very pretty. I don't blame him. Nothing could have suited me better than my eldest brother's doing this, for I was only too keen to join the Army. I had always feared I should have to stay at home and look after the estate while my brother took *this*.'

He rapped on his great glistening shield that never seemed to be in his way.

'So we were well contented – we young people – and we rode back to Clausentum along the Wood Road very quietly. But when we reached home, Aglaia, our governess, saw what had come to us. I remember her at the door, the torch over her head, watching us climb the cliff-path from the boat. "Aie! Aie!" she said. "Children you went away. Men and a woman you return!" Then she kissed Mother, and Mother wept. Thus our visit to the Waters settled our fates for each of us, maiden.'

He rose to his feet and listened, leaning on the shield-rim.

'I think that's Dan – my brother,' said Una.

'Yes; and the Faun is with him,' he replied, as Dan with Puck stumbled through the copse.

'We should have come sooner,' Puck called, 'but the beauties of your native tongue, O Parnesius, have enthralled this young citizen.'

Parnesius looked bewildered, even when Una explained.

'Dan said the plural of "dominus" was "dominoes", and when Miss Blake said it wasn't he said he supposed it was "backgammon", and so he had to write it out twice – for cheek, you know.'

Dan had climbed into Volaterrae, hot and panting.

'I've run nearly all the way,' he gasped, 'and then Puck met me. How do you do, sir?'

'I am in good health,' Parnesius answered. 'See! I have tried to bend the bow of Ulysses, but – ' He held up his thumb.

'I'm sorry. You must have pulled off too soon,' said Dan. 'But Puck said you were telling Una a story.'

'Continue, O Parnesius,' said Puck, who had perched himself on a dead branch above them. 'I will be chorus. Has he puzzled you much, Una?'

'Not a bit, except – I didn't know where Ak–Ak something was,' she answered.

'Oh, Aquae Sulis. That's Bath, where the buns come from. Let the hero tell his own tale.'

Parnesius pretended to thrust his spear at Puck's legs, but Puck reached down, caught at the horse-tail plume, and pulled off the tall helmet.

'Thanks, jester,' said Parnesius, shaking his curly dark head. 'That is cooler. Now hang it up for me . . .

'I was telling your sister how I joined the Army,' he said to Dan.

'Did you have to pass an Exam?' Dan asked eagerly.

'No. I went to my Father, and said I should like to enter the Dacian Horse (I had seen some at Aquae Sulis); but he said I had better begin service in a regular Legion from Rome. Now, like many of our youngsters, I was not too fond of anything Roman. The Roman-born officers and magistrates looked down on us British-born as though we were barbarians. I told my Father so.

' "I know they do," he said; "but remember, after all, we are the people of the Old Stock, and our duty is to the Empire."

' "To which Empire?" I asked. "We split the Eagle before I was born."

' "What thieves' talk is that?" said my Father. He hated slang.

' "Well, sir," I said, "we've one Emperor in Rome, and I don't know how many Emperors the outlying Provinces have set up from time to time. Which am I to follow?"

' "Gratian," said he. "At least he's a sportsman."

' "He's all that," I said. "Hasn't he turned himself into a raw-beef-eating Scythian?"

' "Where did you hear of it?" said the Pater.

' "At Aquae Sulis," I said. It was perfectly true. This precious Emperor Gratian of ours had a bodyguard of fur-cloaked Scythians, and he was so crazy about them that he dressed like them. In Rome of all places in the world! It was as bad as if my own Father had painted himself blue!

' "No matter for the clothes," said the Pater. "They are only the fringe of the trouble. It began before your time or mine. Rome has forsaken her Gods, and must be punished. The great war with the Painted People broke out in the very year the temples of our Gods were destroyed. We beat the Painted People in the very year our temples were rebuilt. Go back further still . . . " He went back to the time of Diocletian; and to listen to him you would have thought Eternal Rome herself was on the edge of destruction, just because a few people had become a little large-minded.

'*I* knew nothing about it. Aglaia never taught us the history of our own country. She was so full of her ancient Greeks.

' "There is no hope for Rome," said the Pater, at last. "She has forsaken her Gods, but if the Gods forgive *us* here, we may save Britain. To do that, we must keep the Painted People back. Therefore, I tell you, Parnesius, as a Father, that if your heart is set on service, your place is among men on the Wall – and not with women among the cities." '

'What Wall?' asked Dan and Una at once.

'Father meant the one we call Hadrian's Wall. I'll tell you about it later. It was built long ago, across North Britain, to keep out the Painted People – Picts, you call them. Father had fought in the great Pict War that lasted more than twenty years, and he knew what fighting meant. Theodosius, one of our great Generals, had chased the little beasts back far into the North before I was born. Down at Vectis, of course, we never troubled our heads about them. But when my Father spoke as he did, I kissed his hand, and waited for orders. We British-born Romans know what is due to our parents.'

'If I kissed my Father's hand, he'd laugh,' said Dan.

'Customs change; but if you do not obey your Father, the Gods remember it. You may be quite sure of *that*.

'After our talk, seeing I was in earnest, the Pater sent me over to Clausentum to learn my foot-drill in a barrack full of foreign Auxiliaries – as unwashed and unshaved a mob of mixed barbarians as ever scrubbed a breastplate. It was your stick in their stomachs and your shield in their faces to push them into any sort of formation. When I had learned my work the Instructor gave me a handful – and they were a handful! – of Gauls and Iberians to polish up till they were sent to their stations up-country. I did my best, and one night a villa in the suburbs caught fire, and I had my handful out and at work before any of the other troops. I noticed a quiet-looking man on the lawn, leaning on a stick. He watched us passing buckets from the pond, and at last he said to me: "Who are you?"

' "A probationer, waiting for a command," I answered. *I* didn't know who he was from Deucalion!

' "Born in Britain?" he said.

' "Yes, if you were born in Spain," I said, for he neighed his words like an Iberian mule.

' "And what might you call yourself when you are at home?" he said, laughing.

' "That depends," I answered; "sometimes one thing and sometimes another. But now I'm busy."

'He said no more till we had saved the family Gods (they were respectable householders), and then he grunted across the laurels: "Listen, young sometimes-one-thing-and-sometimes-another. In future call yourself Centurion of the Seventh Cohort of the Thirtieth, the Ulpia Victrix. That will help me to remember you. Your Father and a few other people call me Maximus."

'He tossed me the polished stick he was leaning on, and went away. You might have knocked me down with it!'

'Who was he?' said Dan.

'Maximus himself, our great General! *The* General of Britain who had been Theodosius's right hand in the Pict War! Not only had he given me my Centurion's stick direct, but three steps in a good Legion as well! A new man generally begins in the Tenth Cohort of his Legion, and works up.'

'And were you pleased?' said Una.

'Very. I thought Maximus had chosen me for my good looks and fine style in marching, but, when I went home, the Pater told me he had served under Maximus in the great Pict War, and had asked him to befriend me.'

'A child you were!' said Puck, from above.

'I was,' said Parnesius. 'Don't begrudge it me, Faun. Afterwards – the Gods know I put aside the games!' And Puck nodded, brown chin on brown hand, his big eyes still.

'The night before I left we sacrificed to our ancestors – the usual little Home Sacrifice – but I never prayed so earnestly to all the Good Shades, and then I went with my Father by boat to Regnum, and across the chalk eastwards to Anderida yonder.'

'Regnum? Anderida?' The children turned their faces to Puck.

'Regnum's Chichester,' he said, pointing towards Cherry Clack, 'and' – he threw his arm South behind him – 'Anderida's Pevensey.'

'Pevensey again!' said Dan. 'Where Weland landed?'

'Weland and a few others,' said Puck. 'Pevensey isn't young – even compared to me!'

'The headquarters of the Thirtieth lay at Anderida in summer, but my own Cohort, the Seventh, was on the Wall up North. Maximus was inspecting Auxiliaries – the Abulci, I think – at Anderida, and we stayed with him, for he and my Father were very old friends. I was only there ten days when I was ordered to go up with thirty men to my Cohort.' He laughed merrily. 'A man never forgets his first march. I was happier than any Emperor when I led my handful through the North Gate of the Camp, and we saluted the guard and the Altar of Victory there.'

'How? How?' said Dan and Una.

Parnesius smiled, and stood up, flashing in his armour.

'So!' said he; and he moved slowly through the beautiful movements of the Roman Salute, that ends with a hollow clang of the shield coming into its place between the shoulders.

'Hai!' said Puck. 'That sets one thinking!'

'We went out fully armed,' said Parnesius, sitting down; 'but as soon as the road entered the Great Forest, my men expected the packhorses to hang their shields on. "No!" I said; you can dress like women in Anderida, but while you're with me you will carry your own weapons and armour."

' "But it's hot," said one of them, "and we haven't a doctor. Suppose we get sunstroke, or a fever?"

' "Then die," I said, "and a good riddance to Rome! Up shield – up spears, and tighten your footwear!"

' "Don't think yourself Emperor of Britain already," a fellow shouted. I knocked him over with the butt of my spear, and explained to these Roman-born Romans that, if there were any further trouble, we should go on with one man short. And, by the Light of the Sun, I meant it too! My raw Gauls at Clausentum had never treated me so.

'Then, quietly as a cloud, Maximus rode out of the fern (my Father behind him), and reined up across the road. He wore the Purple, as though he were already Emperor; his leggings were of white buckskin laced with gold.

'My men dropped like – like partridges.

'He said nothing for some time, only looked, with his eyes puckered. Then he crooked his forefinger, and my men walked – crawled, I mean – to one side.

' "Stand in the sun, children," he said, and they formed up on the hard road.

' "What would you have done," he said to me, "if I had not been here?"

' "I should have killed that man," I answered.

' "Kill him now," he said. "He will not move a limb."

' "No," I said. "You've taken my men out of my command. I should only be your butcher if I killed him now." Do you see what I meant?' Parnesius turned to Dan.

'Yes,' said Dan. 'It wouldn't have been fair, somehow.'

'That was what I thought,' said Parnesius. 'But Maximus frowned. "You'll never be an Emperor," he said. "Not even a General will you be."

'I was silent, but my Father seemed pleased.

' "I came here to see the last of you," he said.

' "You have seen it," said Maximus. "I shall never need your son any more. He will live and he will die an officer of a Legion – and he might have been Prefect of one of my Provinces. Now eat and drink with us," he said. "Your men will wait till you have finished."

'My miserable thirty stood like wine-skins glistening in the hot sun, and Maximus led us to where his people had set a meal. Himself he mixed the wine.

' "A year from now," he said, "you will remember that you have sat with the Emperor of Britain – and Gaul."

' "Yes," said the Pater, "you can drive two mules – Gaul and Britain."

' "Five years hence you will remember that you have drunk" – he passed me the cup and there was blue borage in it – "with the Emperor of Rome!"

' "No; you can't drive three mules. They will tear you in pieces," said my Father.

' "And you on the Wall, among the heather, will weep because your notion of justice was more to you than the favour of the Emperor of Rome."

'I sat quite still. One does not answer a General who wears the Purple.

' "I am not angry with you," he went on; "I owe too much to your Father – "

' "You owe me nothing but advice that you never took," said the Pater.

' " – to be unjust to any of your family. Indeed, I say you may make a good Tribune, but, so far as I am concerned, on the Wall you will live, and on the Wall you will die," said Maximus.

' "Very like," said my Father. "But we shall have the Picts *and* their friends breaking through before long. You cannot move all troops out of Britain to make you Emperor, and expect the North to sit quiet."

' "I follow my destiny," said Maximus.

' "Follow it, then," said my Father, pulling up a fern root; "and die as Theodosius died."

' "Ah!" said Maximus. "My old General was killed because he served the Empire too well. *I* may be killed, but not for that reason," and he smiled a little pale grey smile that made my blood run cold.

' "Then I had better follow my destiny," I said, "and take my men to the Wall."

'He looked at me a long time, and bowed his head slanting like a Spaniard. "Follow it, boy," he said. That was all. I was only too glad to get away, though I had many messages for home. I found my men standing as they had been put – they had not even shifted their feet in the dust, and off I marched, still feeling that terrific smile like an east wind up my back. I never halted them till sunset, and' – he turned about and looked at Pook's Hill below him – 'then I halted yonder.' He pointed to the broken, bracken-covered shoulder of the Forge Hill behind old Hobden's cottage.

'There? Why, that's only the old Forge – where they made iron once,' said Dan.

'Very good stuff it was too,' said Parnesius calmly. 'We mended three shoulder-straps here and had a spear-head riveted. The Forge was rented from the Government by a one-eyed smith from Carthage. I remember we called him Cyclops. He sold me a beaver-skin rug for my sister's room.'

'But it couldn't have been here,' Dan insisted.

'But it was! From the Altar of Victory at Anderida to the First Forge in the Forest here is twelve miles seven hundred paces. It is all in the Road Book. A man doesn't forget his first march. I think I could tell you every station between this and – ' He leaned forward, but his eye was caught by the setting sun.

It had come down to the top of Cherry Clack Hill, and the light poured in between the tree trunks so that you could see red and gold and black deep into the heart of Far Wood; and Parnesius in his armour shone as though he had been afire.

'Wait!' he said, lifting a hand, and the sunlight jinked on his glass bracelet. 'Wait! I pray to Mithras!'

He rose and stretched his arms westward, with deep, splendid-sounding words.

Then Puck began to sing too, in a voice like bells tolling, and as he sang he slipped from Volaterrae to the ground, and beckoned the children to follow. They obeyed; it seemed as though the voices were pushing them along; and through the goldy-brown light on the beech leaves they walked, while Puck between them chanted something like this:

> 'Cur mundus militat sub vana gloria
> Cujus prosperitas est transitoria?
> Tam cito labitur ejus potentia
> Quam vasa figuli quae sunt fragilia.'

They found themselves at the little locked gates of the wood.

> 'Quo Caesar abiit celsus imperil?
> Vel Dives splendidus totus in prandio?
> Dic ubi Tullius – '

Still singing, he took Dan's hand and wheeled him round to face Una as she came out of the gate. It shut behind her, at the same time as Puck threw the memory-magicking Oak, Ash and Thorn leaves over their heads.

'Well, you *are* jolly late,' said Una. 'Couldn't you get away before?'

'I did,' said Dan. 'I got away in lots of time, but – but I didn't know it was so late. Where've you been?'

'In Volaterrae – waiting for you.'

'Sorry,' said Dan. 'It was all that beastly Latin.'

A British-Roman Song

(AD 406)

My father's father saw it not,
    And I, belike, shall never come
To look on that so-holy spot –
        The very Rome –

Crowned by all Time, all Art, all Might,
    The equal work of Gods and Man,
City beneath whose oldest height –
        The Race began!

Soon to send forth again a brood,
    Unshakeable, we pray, that clings
To Rome's thrice-hammered hardihood –
        In arduous things.

Strong heart with triple armour bound,
    Beat strongly, for Thy life-blood runs,
Age after Age, the Empire round –
        In us Thy Sons,

Who, distant from the Seven Hills,
    Loving and serving much, require Thee –
Thee to guard 'gainst home-born ills
        The Imperial Fire!

ON THE GREAT WALL

'When I left Rome for Lalage's sake
    By the Legions' Road to Rimini,
She vowed her heart was mine to take
    With me and my shield to Rimini –
    (Till the Eagles flew from Rimini!)
        And I've tramped Britain, and I've tramped Gaul,
        And the Pontic shore where the snowflakes fall
As white as the neck of Lalage –
    (As cold as the heart of Lalage!)
    And I've lost Britain, and I've lost Gaul,'

[the voice seemed very cheerful about it]

'And I've lost Rome, and, worst of all,
    I've lost Lalage!'

They were standing by the gate to Far Wood when they heard this song. Without a word they hurried to their private gap and wriggled through the hedge almost atop of a jay that was feeding from Puck's hand.

'Gently!' said Puck. 'What are you looking for?'

'Parnesius, of course,' Dan answered. 'We've only just remembered yesterday. It isn't fair.'

Puck chuckled as he rose. 'I'm sorry, but children who spend the afternoon with me and a Roman Centurion need a little settling dose of Magic before they go to tea with their governess. Ohe, Parnesius!' he called.

'Here, Faun!' came the answer from Volaterrae. They could see the shimmer of bronze armour in the beech-crotch, and the friendly flash of the great shield uplifted.

'I have driven out the Britons.' Parnesius laughed like a boy. 'I occupy their high forts. But Rome is merciful! You may come up.' And up they three all scrambled.

'What was the song you were singing just now?' said Una, as soon as she had settled herself.

'That? Oh, *Rimini*. It's one of the tunes that are always being born somewhere in the Empire. They run like a pestilence for six months or a year, till another one pleases the Legions, and then they march to *that*.'

'Tell them about the marching, Parnesius. Few people nowadays walk from end to end of this country,' said Puck.

'The greater their loss. I know nothing better than the Long March when your feet are hardened. You begin after the mists have risen, and you end, perhaps, an hour after sundown.'

'And what do you have to eat?' Dan asked promptly.

'Fat bacon, beans, and bread, and whatever wine happens to be in the rest-houses. But soldiers are born grumblers. Their very first day out, my men complained of our water-ground British corn. They said it wasn't so filling as the rough stuff that is ground in the Roman ox-mills. However, they had to fetch and eat it.'

'Fetch it? Where from?' said Una.

'From that newly invented water-mill below the Forge.'

'That's Forge Mill – *our* mill!' Una looked at Puck.

'Yes; yours,' Puck put in. 'How old did you think it was?'

'I don't know. Didn't Sir Richard Dalyngridge talk about it?'

'He did, and it was old in his day,' Puck answered. 'Hundreds of years old.'

'It was new in mine,' said Parnesius. 'My men looked at the flour in their helmets as though it had been a nest of adders. They did it to try my patience. But I – addressed them, and we became friends. To tell the truth, they taught me the Roman Step. You see, I'd only served with quick-marching Auxiliaries. A Legion's pace is altogether different. It is a long, slow stride, that never varies from sunrise to sunset. "Rome's Race – Rome's Pace," as the proverb says. Twenty-four miles in eight hours, neither more nor less. Head and spear up, shield on your back, cuirass-collar open one hand's-breadth – and that's how you take the Eagles through Britain.'

'And did you meet any adventures?' said Dan.

'There are no adventures South the Wall,' said Parnesius. 'The worst thing that happened me was having to appear before a magistrate up North, where a wandering philosopher had jeered at the Eagles. I was able to show that the old man had deliberately blocked our road; and the magistrate told him, out of his own Book, I believe, that, whatever his Gods might be, he should pay proper respect to Caesar.'

'What did you do?' said Dan.

'Went on. Why should *I* care for such things, my business being to reach my station? It took me twenty days.

'Of course, the farther North you go the emptier are the roads. At last you fetch clear of the forests and climb bare hills, where wolves howl in the ruins of our cities that have been. No more pretty girls; no more jolly magistrates who knew your Father when he was young, and invite you to stay with them; no news at the temples and way-stations except bad news of wild beasts. There's where you meet hunters, and trappers for the Circuses, prodding along chained bears and muzzled wolves. Your pony shies at them, and your men laugh.

'The houses change from gardened villas to shut forts with watchtowers of grey stone, and great stone-walled sheepfolds, guarded by armed Britons of the North Shore. In the naked hills beyond the naked houses, where the shadows of the clouds play like cavalry charging, you see puffs of black smoke from the mines. The hard road goes on and on – and the wind sings through your helmet-plume – past altars to Legions and Generals forgotten, and broken statues of Gods and Heroes, and thousands of graves where the mountain foxes and hares peep at you. Red-hot in summer, freezing in winter, is that big, purple heather country of broken stone.

'Just when you think you are at the world's end, you see a smoke from East to West as far as the eye can turn, and then, under it, also as far as the eye can stretch, houses and temples, shops and theatres, barracks and granaries, trickling along like dice behind – always behind – one long, low, rising and falling, and hiding and showing line of towers. And that is the Wall!'

'Ah!' said the children, taking breath.

'You may well,' said Parnesius. 'Old men who have followed the Eagles since boyhood say nothing in the Empire is more wonderful than first sight of the Wall!'

'Is it just *a* Wall? Like the one round the kitchen garden?' said Dan.

'No, no! It is *the* Wall. Along the top are towers with guardhouses, small towers, between. Even on the narrowest part of it three men with shields can walk abreast, from guardhouse to guardhouse. A little curtain wall, no higher than a man's neck, runs along the top of the thick wall, so that from a distance you see the helmets of the sentries sliding back and forth like beads. Thirty feet high is the Wall, and on the Picts' side, the North, is a ditch, strewn with blades of old swords and spearheads set in wood, and tyres of wheels joined by chains. The Little People come there to steal iron for their arrowheads.

'But the Wall itself is not more wonderful than the town behind it. Long ago there were great ramparts and ditches on the South side, and no one was allowed to build there. Now the ramparts are partly pulled down and built over, from end to end of the Wall; making a thin town eighty miles long. Think of it! One roaring, rioting, cock-fighting, wolf-baiting, horse-racing town, from Ituna on the West to Segedunum on the cold eastern beach! On one side heather, woods and ruins where Picts hide, and on the other, a vast town – long like a snake, and wicked like a snake. Yes, a snake basking beside a warm wall!

'My Cohort, I was told, lay at Hunno, where the Great North Road runs through the Wall into the Province of Valentia.' Parnesius laughed scornfully. 'The Province of Valentia! We followed the road, therefore, into Hunno town, and stood astonished. The place was a fair – a fair of peoples from every corner of the Empire. Some were racing horses: some sat in wine-shops: some watched dogs baiting bears, and many gathered in a ditch to see cocks fight. A boy not much older than myself, but I could see he was an officer, reined up before me and asked what I wanted.

' "My station," I said, and showed him my shield.' Parnesius held up his broad shield with its three Xs like letters on a beer-cask.

' "Lucky omen!" said he. "Your Cohort's the next tower to us, but they're all at the cock-fight. This is a happy place. Come and wet the Eagles." He meant to offer me a drink.

' "When I've handed over my men," I said. I felt angry and ashamed.

' "Oh, you'll soon outgrow that sort of nonsense," he answered. "But don't let me interfere with your hopes. Go on to the Statue of Roma Dea. You can't miss it. The main road into Valentia!" and he laughed and rode off. I could see the statue not a quarter of a mile away, and there I went. At some time or other the Great North Road ran under it into Valentia; but the far end had been blocked up because of the Picts, and on the plaster a man had scratched, "Finish!" It was like marching into a cave. We grounded spears together, my little thirty, and it echoed in the barrel of the arch, but none came. There was a door at one side painted with our number. We prowled in, and I found a cook asleep, and ordered him to give us food. Then I climbed to the top of the Wall, and looked out over the Pict country, and I – thought,' said Parnesius. 'The bricked-up arch with "Finish!" on the plaster was what shook me, for I was not much more than a boy.'

'What a shame!' said Una. 'But did you feel happy after you'd had a good –' Dan stopped her with a nudge.

'Happy?' said Parnesius. 'When the men of the Cohort I was to command came back unhelmeted from the cock-fight, their birds under their arms, and asked me who I was? No, I was not happy; but I made my new Cohort unhappy too . . . I wrote my Mother I was happy, but, oh, my friends' – he stretched arms over bare knees – 'I would not wish my worst enemy to suffer as I suffered through my first months on the Wall. Remember this: among the officers was scarcely one, except myself (and I thought I had lost the favour of Maximus, my General), scarcely one who had not done something of wrong or folly. Either he had killed a man, or taken money, or insulted the magistrates, or blasphemed the Gods, and so had been sent to the Wall as a hiding place from shame or fear. And the men were as the officers. Remember, also, that the Wall was manned by every breed and race in the Empire. No two towers spoke the same tongue, or worshipped the same Gods. In one thing only we were all equal. No matter what arms we had used before we came to the Wall, *on* the Wall we were all archers, like the Scythians. The Pict cannot run away from the arrow, or crawl under it. He is a bowman himself. *He* knows!'

'I suppose you were fighting Picts all the time,' said Dan.

'Picts seldom fight. I never saw a fighting Pict for half a year. The tame Picts told us they had all gone North.'

'What is a tame Pict?' said Dan.

'A Pict – there were many such – who speaks a few words of our tongue, and slips across the Wall to sell ponies and wolfhounds. Without a horse and a dog, *and* a friend, man would perish. The Gods gave me all three, and there is no gift like friendship. Remember this' – Parnesius turned to Dan – 'when you become a young man. For your fate will turn on the first true friend you make.'

'*And that is the Wall!*'

'He means,' said Puck, grinning, 'that if you try to make yourself a decent chap when you're young, you'll make rather decent friends when you grow up. If you're a beast, you'll have beastly friends. Listen to the Pious Parnesius on Friendship!'

'I am not pious,' Parnesius answered, 'but I know what goodness means; and my friend, though he was without hope, was ten thousand times better than I. Stop laughing, Faun!'

'Oh, Youth Eternal and All-believing,' cried Puck, as he rocked on the branch above. 'Tell them about your Pertinax.'

'He was that friend the Gods sent me – the boy who spoke to me when I first came. Little older than myself, commanding the Augusta Victoria Cohort on the tower next to us and the Numidians. In virtue he was far my superior.'

'Then why was he on the Wall?' Una asked, quickly. 'They'd all done something bad. You said so yourself.'

'He was the nephew, his father had died, of a great rich man in Gaul who was not always kind to his mother. When Pertinax grew up, he discovered this, and so his uncle shipped him off, by trickery and force, to the Wall. We came to know each other at a ceremony in our Temple in the dark. It was the Bull-Killing,' Parnesius explained to Puck.

'*I* see,' said Puck, and turned to the children. 'That's something you wouldn't quite understand. Parnesius means he met Pertinax in church.'

'Yes – in the Cave we first met, and we were both raised to the Degree of Gryphons together.' Parnesius lifted his hand towards his neck for an instant. 'He had been on the Wall two years, and knew the Picts well. He taught me first how to take Heather.'

'What's that?' said Dan.

'Going out hunting in the Pict country with a tame Pict. You are quite safe so long as you are his guest, and wear a sprig of heather where it can be seen. If you went alone you would surely be killed, if you were not smothered first in the bogs. Only the Picts know their way about those black and hidden bogs. Old Allo, the one-eyed, withered little Pict from whom we bought our ponies, was our special friend. At first we went only to escape from the terrible town, and to talk together about our homes. Then he showed us how to hunt wolves and those great red deer with horns like Jewish candlesticks. The Roman-born officers rather looked down on us for doing this, but we preferred the heather to their amusements. Believe me,' Parnesius turned again to Dan, 'a boy is safe from all things that really harm when he is astride a pony or after a deer. Do you remember, O Faun,' – he turned to Puck – 'the little altar I built to the Sylvan Pan by the pine forest beyond the brook?'

'Which? The stone one with the line from Xenophon?' said Puck, in quite a new voice.

'No! What do *I* know of Xenophon? That was Pertinax – after he had shot his first mountain-hare with an arrow – by chance! Mine I made of round

pebbles, in memory of my first bear. It took me one happy day to build.'
Parnesius faced the children quickly.

'And that was how we lived on the Wall for two years – a little scuffling with the Picts, and a great deal of hunting with old Allo in the Pict country. He called us his children sometimes, and we were fond of him and his barbarians, though we never let them paint us Pict-fashion. The marks endure till you die.'

'How's it done?' said Dan. 'Anything like tattooing?'

'They prick the skin till the blood runs, and rub in coloured juices. Allo was painted blue, green, and red from his forehead to his ankles. He said it was part of his religion. He told us about his religion (Pertinax was always interested in such things), and as we came to know him well, he told us what was happening in Britain behind the Wall. Many things took place behind us in those days. And by the Light of the Sun,' said Parnesius, earnestly, 'there was not much that those little people did not know! He told me when Maximus crossed over to Gaul, after he had made himself Emperor of Britain, and what troops and emigrants he had taken with him. We did not get the news on the Wall till fifteen days later. He told me what troops Maximus was taking out of Britain every month to help him to conquer Gaul; and I always found the numbers were as he said. Wonderful! And I tell another strange thing!'

He joined his hands across his knees, and leaned his head on the curve of the shield behind him.

'Late in the summer, when the first frosts begin and the Picts kill their bees, we three rode out after wolf with some new hounds. Rutilianus, our General, had given us ten days' leave, and we had pushed beyond the Second Wall – beyond the Province of Valentia – into the higher hills, where there are not even any of old Rome's ruins. We killed a she-wolf before noon, and while Allo was skinning her he looked up and said to me, "When you are Captain of the Wall, my child, you won't be able to do this any more!"

'I might as well have been made Prefect of Lower Gaul, so I laughed and said, "Wait till I am Captain." "No, don't wait," said Allo. "Take my advice and go home – both of you." "We have no homes," said Pertinax. "You know that as well as we do . We're finished men – thumbs down against both of us. Only men without hope would risk their necks on your ponies." The old man laughed one of those short Pict laughs – like a fox barking on a frosty night. "I'm fond of you two," he said. "Besides, I've taught you what little you know about hunting. Take my advice and go home."

' "We can't," I said. "I'm out of favour with my General, for one thing; and for another, Pertinax has an uncle."

' "I don't know about his uncle," said Allo, "but the trouble with you, Parnesius, is that your General thinks well of you."

' "Roma Dea!" said Pertinax, sitting up. "What, can you guess what Maximus thinks, you old horse-coper?"

'Just then (you know how near the brutes creep when one is eating?) a great dog-wolf jumped out behind us, and away our rested hounds tore after him, with us at their tails. He ran us far out of any country we'd ever heard of, straight as an arrow till sunset, towards the sunset. We came at last to long capes stretching into winding waters, and on a grey beach below us we saw ships drawn up. Forty-seven we counted – not Roman galleys but the raven-winged ships from the North where Rome does not rule. Men moved in the ships, and the sun flashed on their helmets – winged helmets of the red-haired men from the North where Rome does not rule. We watched, and we counted, and we wondered, for though we had heard rumours concerning these Winged Hats, as the Picts called them, never before had we looked upon them.

' "Come away! come away!" said Allo. "My Heather won't protect you here. We shall all be killed!" His legs trembled like his voice. Back we went – back across the heather under the moon, till it was nearly morning, and our poor beasts stumbled on some ruins.

'When we woke, very stiff and cold, Allo was mixing the meal and water. One does not light fires in the Pict country except near a village. The little men are always signalling to each other with smokes, and a strange smoke brings them out buzzing like bees. They can sting, too!

' "What we saw last night was a trading-station," said Allo. "Nothing but a trading-station."

' "I do not like lies on an empty stomach," said Pertinax. "I suppose" (he had eyes like an eagle's) – "I suppose *that* is a trading-station also?" He pointed to a smoke far off on a hilltop, ascending in what we call the Picts' Call: – Puff – double-puff: double-puff – puff! They make it by raising and dropping a wet hide on a fire.

' "No," said Allo, pushing the platter back into the bag. "That is for you and me. Your fate is fixed. Come."

'We came. When one takes Heather, one must obey one's Pict – but that wretched smoke was twenty miles distant, well over on the East coast, and the day was as hot as a bath.

' "Whatever happens," said Allo, while our ponies grunted along, "I want you to remember me."

' "I shall not forget," said Pertinax. "You have cheated me out of my breakfast."

"What is a handful of crushed oats to a Roman?" he said. Then he laughed his laugh that was not a laugh. "What would *you* do if *you* were a handful of oats being crushed between the upper and lower stones of a mill?"

' "I'm Pertinax, not a riddle-guesser," said Pertinax.

' "You're a fool," said Allo. "Your Gods and my Gods are threatened by strange Gods, and all you can do is to laugh."

' "Threatened men live long," I said.

' "I pray the Gods that may be true," he said. "But I ask you again not to forget me."

'We climbed the last hot hill and looked out on the eastern sea, three or four miles off. There was a small sailing-galley of the North Gaul pattern at anchor, her landing-plank down and her sail half up; and below us, alone in a hollow, holding his pony, sat Maximus, Emperor of Britain! He was dressed like a hunter, and he leaned on his little stick; but I knew that back as far as I could see it, and I told Pertinax.

' "You're madder than Allo!" he said. "It must be the sun!"

'Maximus never stirred till we stood before him. Then he looked me up and down, and said: "Hungry again? It seems to be my destiny to feed you whenever we meet. I have food here. Allo shall cook it."

' "No," said Allo. "A Prince in his own land does not wait on wandering Emperors. I feed my two children without asking your leave." He began to blow up the ashes.

' "I was wrong," said Pertinax. "We are all mad. Speak up, O Madman called Emperor!"

'Maximus smiled his terrible tight-lipped smile, but two years on the Wall do not make a man afraid of mere looks. So I was not afraid.

' "I meant you, Parnesius, to live and die a Centurion of the Wall," said Maximus. "But it seems from these," – he fumbled in his breast – "you can think as well as draw." He pulled out a roll of letters I had written to my people, full of drawings of Picts, and bears, and men I had met on the Wall. Mother and my sister always liked my pictures.

'He handed me one that I had called "Maximus's Soldiers". It showed a row of fat wine-skins, and our old Doctor of the Hunno hospital snuffing at them. Each time that Maximus had taken troops out of Britain to help him to conquer Gaul, he used to send the garrisons more wine – to keep them quiet, I suppose. On the Wall, we always called a wine-skin a "Maximus". Oh, yes; and I had drawn them in Imperial helmets.

' "Not long since," he went on, "men's names were sent up to Caesar for smaller jokes than this."

' "True, Caesar," said Pertinax; "but you forget that was before I, your friend's friend, became such a good spear-thrower."

'He did not actually point his hunting-spear at Maximus, but balanced it on his palm – so!

' "I was speaking of time past," said Maximus, never fluttering an eyelid. "Nowadays one is only too pleased to find boys who can think for themselves, *and* their friends." He nodded at Pertinax. "Your Father lent me the letters, Parnesius, so you run no risk from me."

' "None whatever," said Pertinax, and rubbed the spear-point on his sleeve.

' "I have been forced to reduce the garrisons in Britain, because I need troops in Gaul. Now I come to take troops from the Wall itself," said he.

' "I wish you joy of us," said Pertinax. "We're the last sweepings of the Empire – the men without hope. Myself, I'd sooner trust condemned criminals."

' "You think so?" he said, quite seriously. "But it will only be till I win

Gaul. One must always risk one's life, or one's soul, or one's peace – or some little thing."

'Allo passed round the fire with the sizzling deer's meat. He served us two first.

' "Ah!" said Maximus, waiting his turn. "I perceive you are in your own country. Well, you deserve it. They tell me you have quite a following among the Picts, Parnesius."

' "I have hunted with them," I said. "Maybe I have a few friends among the heather."

' "He is the only armoured man of you all who understands us," said Allo, and he began a long speech about our virtues, and how we had saved one of his grandchildren from a wolf the year before.'

'Had you?' said Una.

'Yes; but that was neither here nor there. The little green man orated like a – like Cicero. He made us out to be magnificent fellows. Maximus never took his eyes off our faces.

' "Enough," he said. "I have heard Allo on you. I wish to hear you on the Picts."

'I told him as much as I knew, and Pertinax helped me out. There is never harm in a Pict if you but take the trouble to find out what he wants. Their real grievance against us came from our burning their heather. The whole garrison of the Wall moved out twice a year, and solemnly burned the heather for ten miles North. Rutilianus, our General, called it clearing the country. The Picts, of course, scampered away, and all we did was to destroy their bee-bloom in the summer, and ruin their sheep-food in the spring.

' "True, quite true," said Allo. "How can we make our holy heather-wine, if you burn our bee-pasture?"

'We talked long, Maximus asking keen questions that showed he knew much and had thought more about the Picts. He said presently to me: "If I gave you the old Province of Valentia to govern, could you keep the Picts contented till I won Gaul? Stand away, so that you do not see Allo's face; and speak your own thoughts."

' "No," I said. "You cannot remake that Province. The Picts have been free too long."

' "Leave them their village councils, and let them furnish their own soldiers," he said. "You, I am sure, would hold the reins very lightly."

"Even then, no," I said. "At least not now. They have been too oppressed by us to trust anything with a Roman name for years and years."

'I heard old Allo behind me mutter: "Good child!"

' "Then what do you recommend," said Maximus, "to keep the North quiet till I win Gaul?"

' "Leave the Picts alone," I said. "Stop the heather-burning at once, and – they are improvident little animals – send them a shipload or two of corn now and then."

' ' "Their own men must distribute it – not some cheating Greek accountant," said Pertinax.

' "Yes, and allow them to come to our hospitals when they are sick," I said.

' "Surely they would die first," said Maximus.

' "Not if Parnesius brought them in," said Allo. "I could show you twenty wolf-bitten, bear-clawed Picts within twenty miles of here. But Parnesius must stay with them in hospital, else they would go mad with fear."

' "*I* see," said Maximus. "Like everything else in the world, it is one man's work. You, I think, are that one man."

' "Pertinax and I are one," I said.

' "As you please, so long as you work. Now, Allo, you know that I mean your people no harm. Leave us to talk together," said Maximus.

' "No need!" said Allo. "I am the corn between the upper and lower millstones. I must know what the lower millstone means to do. These boys have spoken the truth as far as they know it. I, a Prince, will tell you the rest. I am troubled about the Men of the North." He squatted like a hare in the heather, and looked over his shoulder.

' "I also," said Maximus, "or I should not be here."

' "Listen," said Allo. "Long and long ago the Winged Hats" – he meant the Northmen – "came to our beaches and said, 'Rome falls! Push her down!' We fought you. You sent men. We were beaten. After that we said to the Winged Hats, 'You are liars! Make our men alive that Rome killed, and we will believe you.' They went away ashamed. Now they come back bold, and they tell the old tale, which we begin to believe – that Rome falls!"

' "Give me three years' peace on the Wall," cried Maximus, "and I will show you and all the ravens how they lie!"

' "Ah, I wish it too! I wish to save what is left of the corn from the millstones. But you shoot us Picts when we come to borrow a little iron from the Iron Ditch; you burn our heather, which is all our crop; you trouble us with your great catapults. Then you hide behind the Wall, and scorch us with Greek fire. How can I keep my young men from listening to the Winged Hats – in winter especially, when we are hungry? My young men will say, 'Rome can neither fight nor rule. She is taking her men out of Britain. The Winged Hats will help us to push down the Wall. Let us show them the secret roads across the bogs.' Do *I* want that? No!" He spat like an adder. "I would keep the secrets of my people though I were burned alive. My two children here have spoken truth. Leave us Picts alone. Comfort us, and cherish us, and feed us from far off – with the hand behind the back. Parnesius understands us. Let *him* have rule on the Wall, and I will hold my young men quiet for," – he ticked it off on his fingers – "one year easily: the next year not so easily: the third year, perhaps! See, I give you three years. If then you do not show us that Rome is strong in men and terrible in arms, the Winged Hats, I tell you, will sweep down the Wall from either sea till they meet in the middle, and you will go. *I* shall not grieve over that, but well I know tribe never helps tribe except for one price. We Picts will go too. The Winged Hats will grind us to this!" He tossed a handful of dust in the air.

' "Oh, Roma Dea!" said Maximus, half aloud. "It is always one man's work – always and everywhere!"

"And one man's life," said Allo. "You are Emperor, but not a God. You may die."

' "I have thought of that too," said he. "Very good. If this wind holds, I shall be at the East end of the Wall by morning. Tomorrow, then, I shall see you two when I inspect, and I will make you Captains of the Wall for this work."

' "One instant, Caesar," said Pertinax. "All men have their price. I am not bought yet."

' "Do *you* also begin to bargain so early?" said Maximus. "Well?"

' "Give me justice against my uncle Icenus, the Duumvir of Divio in Gaul," he said.

' "Only a life? I thought it would be money or an office. Certainly you shall have him. Write his name on these tablets – on the red side; the other is for the living!" and Maximus held out his tablets.

' "He is of no use to me dead," said Pertinax. "My mother is a widow. I am far off. I am not sure he pays her all her dowry."

' "No matter. My arm is reasonably long. We will look through your uncle's accounts in due time. Now, farewell till tomorrow, O Captains of the Wall!"

'We saw him grow small across the heather as he walked to the galley. There were Picts, scores, each side of him, hidden behind stones. He never looked left or right. He sailed away southerly, full spread before the evening breeze, and when we had watched him out to sea, we were silent. We understood that Earth bred few men like to this man.

'Presently Allo brought the ponies and held them for us to mount – a thing he had never done before.

' "Wait awhile," said Pertinax, and he made a little altar of cut turf, and strewed heather-bloom atop, and laid upon it a letter from a girl in Gaul.

' "What do you do, O my friend?" I said.

' "I sacrifice to my dead youth," he answered, and, when the flames had consumed the letter, he ground them out with his heel. Then we rode back to that Wall of which we were to be Captains.'

Parnesius stopped. The children sat still, not even asking if that were all the tale. Puck beckoned, and pointed the way out of the wood. 'Sorry,' he whispered, 'but you must go now.'

'We haven't made him angry, have we?' said Una. 'He looks so far off, and – and – thinky.'

'Bless your heart, no. Wait till tomorrow. It won't be long. Remember, you've been playing *Lays of Ancient Rome*.'

And as soon as they had scrambled through their gap where Oak, Ash and Thorn grew, that was all they remembered.

A Song to Mithras

Mithras, God of the Morning, our trumpets waken the Wall!
'Rome is above the Nations, but Thou art over all!'
Now as the names are answered, and the guards are marched away,
Mithras, also a soldier, give us strength for the day!

Mithras, God of the Noontide, the heather swims in the heat,
Our helmets scorch our foreheads, our sandals burn our feet.
Now in the ungirt hour, now ere we blink and drowse,
Mithras, also a soldier, keep us true to our vows!

Mithras, God of the Sunset, low on the Western main,
Thou descending immortal, immortal to rise again!
Now when the watch is ended, now when the wine is drawn,
Mithras, also a soldier, keep us pure till the dawn!

Mithras, God of the Midnight, here where the great bull dies,
Look on Thy children in darkness. Oh, take our sacrifice!
Many roads Thou hast fashioned: all of them lead to the Light!
Mithras, also a soldier, teach us to die aright!

THE WINGED HATS

The next day happened to be what they called a Wild Afternoon. Father and Mother went out to pay calls; Miss Blake went for a ride on her bicycle, and they were left all alone till eight o'clock.

When they had seen their dear parents and their dear preceptress politely off the premises they got a cabbage-leaf full of raspberries from the gardener, and a Wild Tea from Ellen. They ate the raspberries to prevent their squashing, and they meant to divide the cabbage-leaf with Three Cows down at the theatre, but they came across a dead hedgehog which they simply *had* to bury, and the leaf was too useful to waste.

Then they went on to the Forge and found old Hobden the hedger at home with his son, the Bee Boy, who is not quite right in his head, but who can pick up swarms of bees in his naked hands; and the Bee Boy told them the rhyme about the slow-worm:

> 'If I had eyes as I could see,
> No mortal man would trouble me.'

They all had tea together by the hives, and Hobden said the loaf-cake which Ellen had given them was almost as good as what his wife used to make, and he showed them how to set a wire at the right height for hares. They knew about rabbits already.

Then they climbed up Long Ditch into the lower end of Far Wood. This is sadder and darker than the Volaterrae end because of an old marl-pit full of black water, where weepy, hairy moss hangs round the stumps of the willows and alders. But the birds come to perch on the dead branches, and Hobden says that the bitter willow-water is a sort of medicine for sick animals.

They sat down on a felled oak-trunk in the shadows of the beech undergrowth, and were looping the wires Hobden had given them, when they saw Parnesius.

'How quietly you came!' said Una, moving up to make room. 'Where's Puck?'

'The Faun and I have disputed whether it is better that I should tell you all my tale, or leave it untold,' he replied.

'I only said that if he told it as it happened you wouldn't understand it,' said Puck, jumping up like a squirrel from behind the log.

'I don't understand all of it,' said Una, 'but I like hearing about the little Picts.'

'What *I* can't understand,' said Dan, 'is how Maximus knew all about the Picts when he was over in Gaul.'

'He who makes himself Emperor anywhere must know everything, everywhere,' said Parnesius. 'We had this much from Maximus's mouth after the Games.'

'Games? What Games?' said Dan.

Parnesius stretched his arm out stiffly, thumb pointed to the ground. 'Gladiators! *That* sort of game,' he said. 'There were two days' Games in his honour when he landed all unexpected at Segedunum on the East end of the Wall. Yes, the day after we had met him we held two days' Games; but I think the greatest risk was run, not by the poor wretches on the sand, but by Maximus. In the old days the Legions kept silence before their Emperor. So did not we! You could hear the solid roar run West along the Wall as his chair was carried rocking through the crowds. The garrison beat round him – clamouring, clowning, asking for pay, for change of quarters, for anything that came into their wild heads. That chair was like a little boat among waves, dipping and falling, but always rising again after one had shut the eyes.' Parnesius shivered.

'Were they angry with him?' said Dan.

'No more angry than wolves in a cage when their trainer walks among them. If he had turned his back an instant, or for an instant had ceased to hold their eyes, there would have been another Emperor made on the Wall that hour. Was it not so, Faun?'

'So it was. So it always will be,' said Puck.

'Late in the evening his messenger came for us, and we followed to the Temple of Victory, where he lodged with Rutilianus, the General of the Wall. I had hardly seen the General before, but he always gave me leave when I wished to take Heather. He was a great glutton, and kept five Asian cooks, and he came of a family that believed in oracles. We could smell his good dinner when we entered, but the tables were empty. He lay snorting on a couch. Maximus sat apart among long rolls of accounts. Then the doors were shut.

' "These are your men," said Maximus to the General, who propped his eye-corners open with his gouty fingers, and stared at us like a fish.

' "I shall know them again, Caesar," said Rutilianus.

"Very good," said Maximus. "Now hear! You are not to move man or shield on the Wall except as these boys shall tell you. You will do nothing, except eat, without their permission. They are the head and arms. You are the belly!"

' "As Caesar pleases," the old man grunted. "If my pay and profits are not cut, you may make my Ancestors' Oracle my master. Rome has been! Rome has been!" Then he turned on his side to sleep.

' "He has it," said Maximus. "We will get to what *I* need."

'He unrolled full copies of the number of men and supplies on the Wall – down to the sick that very day in Hunno Hospital. Oh, but I groaned when his pen marked off detachment after detachment of our best – of our least worthless men! He took two towers of our Scythians, two of our North

'You could hear the solid roar run West along the Wall as
his chair was carried rocking through the crowds.'

British auxiliaries, two Numidian cohorts, the Dacians all, and half the Belgians. It was like an eagle pecking a carcass.

' "And now, how many catapults have you?" He turned up a new list, but Pertinax laid his open hand there.

' "No, Caesar," said he. "Do not tempt the Gods too far. Take men, or engines, but not both; else we refuse." '

'Engines?' said Una.

'The catapults of the Wall – huge things forty feet high to the head – firing nets of raw stone or forged bolts. Nothing can stand against them. He left us our catapults at last, but he took a Caesar's half of our men without pity. We were a shell when he rolled up the lists!

' "Hail, Caesar! We, about to die, salute you!" said Pertinax, laughing. "If any enemy even leans against the Wall now, it will tumble."

' "Give me the three years Allo spoke of," he answered, "and you shall have twenty thousand men of your own choosing up here. But now it is a gamble – a game played against the Gods, and the stakes are Britain, Gaul, and perhaps Rome. You play on my side?"

' "We will play, Caesar," I said, for I had never met a man like this man.

' "Good. Tomorrow," said he, "I proclaim you Captains of the Wall before the troops."

'So we went into the moonlight, where they were cleaning the ground after the Games. We saw great Roma Dea atop of the Wall, the frost on her helmet, and her spear pointed towards the North Star. We saw the twinkle of night-fires all along the guard-towers, and the line of the black catapults growing smaller and smaller in the distance. All these things we knew till we were weary; but that night they seemed very strange to us, because the next day we knew we were to be their masters.

'The men took the news well; but when Maximus went away with half our strength, and we had to spread ourselves into the emptied towers, and the townspeople complained that trade would be ruined, and the autumn gales blew – it was dark days for us two. Here Pertinax was more than my right hand. Being born and bred among the great country houses in Gaul, he knew the proper words to address to all – from Roman-born Centurions to those dogs of the Third – the Libyans. And he spoke to each as though that man were as high-minded as himself. Now *I* saw so strongly what things were needed to be done, that I forgot things are only accomplished by means of men. That was a mistake.

'I feared nothing from the Picts, at least for that year, but Allo warned me that the Winged Hats would soon come in from the sea at each end of the Wall to prove to the Picts how weak we were. So I made ready in haste, and none too soon. I shifted our best men to the ends of the Wall, and set up screened catapults by the beach. The Winged Hats would drive in before the snow-squalls – ten or twenty boats at a time – on Segedunum or Ituna, according as the wind blew.

'Now, a ship coming in to land men must furl her sail. If you wait till you see her men gather up the sail's foot, your catapults can jerk a net of loose stones (bolts only cut through the cloth) into the bag of it. Then she turns over, and the sea makes everything clean again. A few men may come ashore, but very few . . . It was not hard work, except the waiting on the beach in blowing sand and snow. And that was how we dealt with the Winged Hats that winter.

'Early in the spring, when the East winds blow like skinning-knives, they gathered again off Segedunum with many ships. Allo told me they would never rest till they had taken a tower in open fight. Certainly they fought in the open. We dealt with them thoroughly through a long day: and when all was finished, one man dived clear of the wreckage of his ship, and swam towards shore. I waited, and a wave tumbled him at my feet.

'As I stooped, I saw he wore such a medal as I wear.' Parnesius raised his hand to his neck. 'Therefore, when he could speak, I addressed him a certain Question which can only be answered in a certain manner. He answered with the necessary Word – the Word that belongs to the Degree of Gryphons in the science of Mithras my God. I put my shield over him till he could stand up. You see I am not short, but he was a head taller than I. He said: "What now?" I said: "At your pleasure, my brother, to stay or go."

'He looked out across the surf. There remained one ship unhurt, beyond range of our catapults . I checked the catapults and he waved her in. She came as a hound comes to a master. When she was yet a hundred paces from the beach, he flung back his hair, and swam out. They hauled him in, and went away. I knew that those who worship Mithras are many and of all races, so I did not think much more upon the matter.

'A month later I saw Allo with his horses – by the Temple of Pan, O Faun – and he gave me a great necklace of gold studded with coral.

'At first I thought it was a bribe from some tradesman in the town – meant for old Rutilianus. "Nay," said Allo. "This is a gift from Amal, that Winged Hat whom you saved on the beach. He says you are a Man."

' "He is a Man, too. Tell him I can wear his gift," I answered.

' "Oh, Amal is a young fool; but, speaking as sensible men, your Emperor is doing such great things in Gaul that the Winged Hats are anxious to be his friends, or, better still, the friends of his servants. They think you and Pertinax could lead them to victories." Allo looked at me like a one-eyed raven.

' "Allo," I said, "you are the corn between the two millstones. Be content if they grind evenly, and don't thrust your hand between them."

' "I?" said Allo. "I hate Rome and the Winged Hats equally; but if the Winged Hats thought that some day you and Pertinax might join them against Maximus, they would leave you in peace while you considered. Time is what we need – you and I and Maximus. Let me carry a pleasant message back to the Winged Hats – something for them to make a council over. We barbarians are all alike. We sit up half the night to discuss anything a Roman says. Eh?"

' "We have no men. We must fight with words," said Pertinax. "Leave it to Allo and me."

'So Allo carried word back to the Winged Hats that we would not fight them if they did not fight us; and they (I think they were a little tired of losing men in the sea) agreed to a sort of truce. I believe Allo, who being a horse-dealer loved lies, also told them we might some day rise against Maximus as Maximus had risen against Rome.

'Indeed, they permitted the corn-ships which I sent to the Picts to pass North that season without harm. Therefore the Picts were well fed that winter, and since they were in some sort my children, I was glad of it. We had only two thousand men on the Wall, and I wrote many times to Maximus and begged – prayed – him to send me only one cohort of my old North British troops. He could not spare them. He needed them to win more victories in Gaul.

'Then came news that he had defeated and slain the Emperor Gratian, and thinking he must now be secure, I wrote again for men. He answered: "You will learn that I have at last settled accounts with the pup Gratian. There was no need that he should have died, but he became confused and lost his head, which is a bad thing to befall any Emperor. Tell your Father I am content to drive two mules only; for unless my old General's son thinks himself destined to destroy me, I shall rest Emperor of Gaul and Britain, and then you, my two children, will presently get all the men you need. just now I can spare none." '

'What did he mean by his General's son?' said Dan.

'He meant Theodosius Emperor of Rome, who was the son of Theodosius the General under whom Maximus had fought in the old Pict War. The two men never loved each other, and when Gratian made the younger Theo-dosius Emperor of the East (at least, so I've heard), Maximus carried on the war to the second generation. It was his fate, and it was his fall. But Theodosius the Emperor is a good man. As I know.' Parnesius was silent for a moment and then continued.

'I wrote back to Maximus that, though we had peace on the Wall, I should be happier with a few more men and some new catapults. He answered: "You must live a little longer under the shadow of my victories, till I can see what young Theodosius intends. He may welcome me as a brother-Emperor, or he may be preparing an army. In either case I cannot spare men just now." '

'But he was always saying that,' cried Una.

'It was true. He did not make excuses; but thanks, as he said, to the news of his victories, we had no trouble on the Wall for a long, long time. The Picts grew fat as their own sheep among the heather, and as many of my men as lived were well exercised in their weapons. Yes, the Wall looked strong. For myself, I knew how weak we were. I knew that if even a false rumour of any defeat to Maximus broke loose among the Winged Hats, they might come down in earnest, and then – the Wall must go! For the Picts I never cared, but

'We dealt with them thoroughly through a long day.'

in those years I learned something of the strength of the Winged Hats. They increased their strength every day, but I could not increase my men. Maximus had emptied Britain behind us, and I felt myself to be a man with a rotten stick standing before a broken fence to turn bulls.

'Thus, my friends, we lived on the Wall, waiting – waiting – waiting for the men that Maximus never sent.

'Presently he wrote that he was preparing an army against Theodosius. He wrote – and Pertinax read it over my shoulder in our quarters: "Tell your Father that my destiny orders me to drive three mules or be torn in pieces by them. I hope within a year to finish with Theodosius, son of Theodosius, once and for all. Then you shall have Britain to rule, and Pertinax, if he chooses, Gaul. Today I wish strongly you were with me to beat my Auxiliaries into shape. Do not, I pray you, believe any rumour of my sickness. I have a little evil in my old body which I shall cure by riding swiftly into Rome."

'Said Pertinax: "It is finished with Maximus. He writes as a man without hope. I, a man without hope, can see this. What does he add at the bottom of the roll? 'Tell Pertinax I have met his late Uncle, the Duumvir of Divio, and that he accounted to me quite truthfully for all his Mother's monies. I have sent her with a fitting escort, for she is the mother of a hero, to Nicaea, where the climate is warm.'

' "That is proof," said Pertinax. "Nicaea is not far by sea from Rome. A woman there could take ship and fly to Rome in time of war. Yes, Maximus foresees his death, and is fulfilling his promises one by one. But I am glad my uncle met him." '

' "You think blackly today?" I asked.

' "I think truth. The Gods weary of the play we have played against them. Theodosius will destroy Maximus. It is finished!"

' "Will you write him that?" I said.

' "See what I shall write," he answered, and he took pen and wrote a letter cheerful as the light of day, tender as a woman's and full of jests. Even I, reading over his shoulder, took comfort from it till – I saw his face!

' "And now," he said, sealing it, "we be two dead men, my brother. Let us go to the Temple."

'We prayed awhile to Mithras, where we had many times prayed before. After that, we lived day by day among evil rumours till winter came again.

'It happened one morning that we rode to the East shore, and found on the beach a fair-haired man, half frozen, bound to some broken planks. Turning him over, we saw by his belt-buckle that he was a Goth of an Eastern Legion. Suddenly he opened his eyes and cried loudly, "He is dead! The letters were with me, but the Winged Hats sank the ship." So saying, he died between our hands.

'We asked not who was dead. We knew! We raced before the driving snow to Hunno, thinking perhaps Allo might be there. We found him already at our stables, and he saw by our faces what we had heard.

' "It was in a tent by the sea," he stammered. "He was beheaded by Theodosius. He sent a letter to you, written while he waited to be slain. The Winged Hats met the ship and took it. The news is running through the heather like fire. Blame me not! I cannot hold back my young men any more."

' "I would we could say as much for our men," said Pertinax, laughing. "But, Gods be praised, they cannot run away."

' "What do you do?" said Allo. "I bring an order – a message – from the Winged Hats that you join them with your men, and march South to plunder Britain."

' "It grieves me," said Pertinax, "but we are stationed here to stop that thing."

' "If I carry back such an answer they will kill me," said Allo. "I always promised the Winged Hats that you would rise when Maximus fell. I – I did not think he could fall."

' "Alas! my poor barbarian," said Pertinax, still laughing. "Well, you have sold us too many good ponies to be thrown back to your friends. We will make you a prisoner, although you are an ambassador."

' "Yes, that will be best," said Allo, holding out a halter. We bound him lightly, for he was an old man.

' "Presently the Winged Hats may come to look for you, and that will give us more time. See how the habit of playing for time sticks to a man!" said Pertinax, as he tied the rope.

' "No," I said. "Time may help. If Maximus wrote us a letter while he was a prisoner, Theodosius must have sent the ship that brought it. If he can send ships, he can send men."

' "How will that profit us?" said Pertinax. "We serve Maximus, not Theodosius. Even if by some miracle of the Gods Theodosius down South sent and saved the Wall, we could not expect more than the death Maximus died."

' "It concerns us to defend the Wall, no matter what Emperor dies, or makes die," I said.

' "That is worthy of your brother the philosopher," said Pertinax. "Myself I am without hope, so I do not say solemn and stupid things! Rouse the Wall!"

'We armed the Wall from end to end; we told the officers that there was a rumour of Maximus's death which might bring down the Winged Hats, but we were sure, even if it were true, that Theodosius, for the sake of Britain, would send us help. Therefore, we must stand fast . . . My friends, it is above all things strange to see how men bear ill news! Often the strongest till then become the weakest, while the weakest, as it were, reach up and steal strength from the Gods. So it was with us. Yet my Pertinax by his jests and his courtesy and his labours had put heart and training into our poor numbers during the past years – more than I should have thought possible. Even our Libyan Cohort – the Third – stood up in their padded cuirasses and did not whimper.

'In three days came seven chiefs and elders of the Winged Hats. Among them was that tall young man, Amal, whom I had met on the beach, and he smiled when he saw my necklace. We made them welcome, for they were ambassadors. We showed them Allo, alive but bound. They thought we had killed him, and I saw it would not have vexed them if we had. Allo saw it too, and it vexed him. Then in our quarters at Hunno we came to council.

'They said that Rome was falling, and that we must join them. They offered me all South Britain to govern after they had taken a tribute out of it.

'I answered, "Patience. This Wall is not weighed off like plunder. Give me proof that my General is dead."

' "Nay," said one elder, "prove to us that he lives"; and another said cunningly, "What will you give us if we read you his last words?"

' "We are not merchants to bargain," cried Amal. "Moreover, I owe this man my life. He shall have his proof." He threw across to me a letter (well I knew the seal) from Maximus.

' "We took this out of the ship we sank," he cried. "I cannot read, but I know one sign, at least, which makes me believe. " He showed me a dark stain on the outer roll that my heavy heart perceived was the valiant blood of Maximus.

' "Read!" said Amal. "Read, and then let us hear whose servants you are!"

'Said Pertinax, very softly, after he had looked through it: "I will read it all. Listen, barbarians!" He read that which I have carried next my heart ever since.'

Parnesius drew from his neck a folded and spotted piece of parchment, and began in a hushed voice: ' "To Parnesius and Pertinax, the not unworthy Captains of the Wall, from Maximus, once Emperor of Gaul and Britain, now prisoner waiting death by the sea in the camp of Theodosius – Greeting and Goodbye!"

' "Enough," said young Amal; "there is your proof! You must join us now!"

'Pertinax looked long and silently at him, till that fair man blushed like a girl. Then read Pertinax: "I have joyfully done much evil in my life to those who have wished me evil, but if ever I did any evil to you two I repent, and I ask your forgiveness. The three mules which I strove to drive have torn me in pieces as your Father prophesied. The naked swords wait at the tent door to give me the death I gave to Gratian. Therefore I, your General and your emperor, send you free and honourable dismissal from my service, which you entered, not for money or office, but, as it makes me warm to believe, because you loved me!"

' "By the Light of the Sun," Amal broke in. "This was in some sort a Man! We may have been mistaken in his servants!"

'And Pertinax read on: "You gave me the time for which I asked. If I have failed to use it, do not lament. We have gambled very splendidly against the Gods, but they hold weighted dice, and I must pay the forfeit. Remember, I have been; but Rome is; and Rome will be. Tell Pertinax his Mother is in safety at Nicaea, and her monies are in charge of the Prefect at Antipolis.

Make my remembrances to your Father and to your Mother, whose friend-ship was great gain to me. Give also to my little Picts and to the Winged Hats such messages as their thick heads can understand. I would have sent you three Legions this very day if all had gone aright. Do not forget me. We have worked together. Farewell! Farewell! Farewell!"

'Now, that was my Emperor's last letter.' (The children heard the parchment crackle as Parnesius returned it to its place.)

' "I was mistaken," said Amal. "The servants of such a man will sell nothing except over the sword. I am glad of it." He held out his hand to me.

' "But Maximus has given you your dismissal," said an elder. "You are certainly free to serve – or to rule – whom you please. Join – do not follow – join us!"

' "We thank you," said Pertinax. "But Maximus tells us to give you such messages as – pardon me, but I use his words – your thick heads can understand." He pointed through the door to the foot of a catapult wound up.

' "We understand," said an elder. "The Wall must be won at a price?"

' "It grieves me," said Pertinax, laughing, "but so it must be won," and he gave them of our best Southern wine.

'They drank, and wiped their yellow beards in silence till they rose to go.

'Said Amal, stretching himself (for they were barbarians): "We be a goodly company; I wonder what the ravens and the dogfish will make of some of us before this snow melts."

' "Think rather what Theodosius may send," I answered; and though they laughed, I saw that my chance shot troubled them.

'Only old Allo lingered behind a little.

' "You see," he said, winking and blinking, "I am no more than their dog. When I have shown their men the secret short ways across our bogs, they will kick me like one."

' "Then I should not be in haste to show them those ways," said Pertinax, "till I was sure that Rome could not save the Wall."

' "You think so? Woe is me!" said the old man. "I only wanted peace for my people," and he went out stumbling through the snow behind the tall Winged Hats.

'In this fashion then, slowly, a day at a time, which is very bad for doubting troops, the War came upon us. At first the Winged Hats swept in from the sea as they had done before, and there we met them as before – with the catapults; and they sickened of it. Yet for a long time they would not trust their duck-legs on land, and I think, when it came to revealing the secrets of the tribe, the little Picts were afraid or ashamed to show them all the roads across the heather. I had this from a Pict prisoner. They were as much our spies as our enemies, for the Winged Hats oppressed them, and took their winter stores. Ah, foolish Little People!

'Then the Winged Hats began to roll us up from each end of the Wall. I sent runners Southward to see what the news might be in Britain, but the

'The Wall must be won at a price?'

wolves were very bold that winter, among the deserted stations where the troops had once been, and none came back. We had trouble, too, with the forage for the ponies along the Wall. I kept ten, and so did Pertinax. We lived and slept in the saddle, riding east or west, and we ate our worn-out ponies. The people of the town also made us some trouble till I gathered them all in one quarter behind Hunno. We broke down the Wall on either side of it to make as it were a citadel. Our men fought better in close order.

'By the end of the second month we were deep in the War as a man is deep in a snowdrift, or in a dream. I think we fought in our sleep. At least I know I have gone on the Wall and come off again, remembering nothing between, though my throat was harsh with giving orders, and my sword, I could see, had been used.

'The Winged Hats fought like wolves – all in a pack. Where they had suffered most, there they charged in most hotly. This was hard for the defenders, but it held them from sweeping on into Britain.

'In those days Pertinax and I wrote on the plaster of the bricked archway into Valentia the names of the towers, and the days on which they fell one by one. We wished for some record.

'And the fighting? The fight was always hottest to left and right of the great statue of Roma Dea, near to Rutilianus's house. By the Light of the Sun, that old fat man, whom we had not considered at all, grew young again among the trumpets! I remember he said his sword was an oracle! "Let us consult the Oracle," he would say, and put the handle against his ear, and shake his head wisely. "And *this* day is allowed Rutilianus to live," he would say, and, tucking up his cloak, he would puff and pant and fight well. Oh, there were jests in plenty on the Wall to take the place of food!

'We endured for two months and seventeen days – always being pressed from three sides into a smaller space. Several times Allo sent in word that help was at hand. We did not believe it, but it cheered our men.

'The end came not with shootings of joy, but, like the rest, as in a dream. The Winged Hats suddenly left us in peace for one night and the next day; which is too long for spent men. We slept at first lightly, expecting to be roused, and then like logs, each where he lay. May you never need such sleep! When I waked our towers were full of strange, armed men, who watched us snoring. I roused Pertinax, and we leaped up together.

' "What?" said a young man in clean armour. "Do you fight against Theodosius? Look!"

'North we looked over the red snow. No Winged Hats were there. South we looked over the white snow, and behold there were the Eagles of two strong Legions encamped. East and west we saw flame and fighting, but by Hunno all was still.

' "Trouble no more," said the young man. "Rome's arm is long. Where are the Captains of the Wall?"

'We said we were those men.

' "But you are old and grey-haired," he cried. "Maximus said that they were boys."

' "Yes, that was true some years ago," said Pertinax. "What is our fate to be, you fine and well-fed child?"

' "I am called Ambrosius, a secretary of the Emperor," he answered. "Show me a certain letter which Maximus wrote from a tent at Aquileia, and perhaps I will believe."

'I took it from my breast, and when he had read it he saluted us, saying: "Your fate is in your own hands. If you choose to serve Theodosius, he will give you a Legion. If it suits you to go to your homes, we will give you a Triumph."

' "I would like better a bath, wine, food, razors, soaps, oils, and scents," said Pertinax, laughing.

' "Oh, I see you are a boy," said Ambrosius. "And you?" turning to me.

' "We bear no ill-will against Theodosius, but in War – " I began.

' "In War it is as it is in Love," said Pertinax. "Whether she be good or bad, one gives one's best once, to one only. That given, there remains no second worth giving or taking."

' "That is true," said Ambrosius. "I was with Maximus before he died. He warned Theodosius that you would never serve him, and frankly I say I am sorry for my Emperor."

' "He has Rome to console him," said Pertinax. "I ask you of your kindness to let us go to our homes and get this smell out of our nostrils."

'None the less they gave us a Triumph!'

*   *   *

'It was well earned,' said Puck, throwing some leaves into the still water of the marlpit. The black, oily circles spread dizzily as the children watched them.

'I want to know, oh, ever so many things,' said Dan. 'What happened to old Allo? Did the Winged Hats ever come back? And what did Amal do?'

'And what happened to the fat old General with the five cooks?' said Una. 'And what did your Mother say when you came home . . . ?'

'She'd say you're settin' too long over this old pit, so late as 'tis already,' said old Hobden's voice behind them. 'Hst!' he whispered.

He stood still, for not twenty paces away a magnificent dog-fox sat on his haunches and looked at the children as though he were an old friend of theirs.

'Oh, Mus' Reynolds, Mus' Reynolds!' said Hobden, under his breath. 'If I knowed all was inside your head, I'd know something wuth knowin'. Mus' Dan an' Miss Una, come along o' me while I lock up my liddle henhouse.'

'*There they charged in most hotly . . .*'

A Pict Song

Rome never looks where she treads,
    Always her heavy hooves fall
On our stomachs, our hearts or our heads;
    And Rome never heeds when we bawl.
Her sentries pass on – that is all,
    And we gather behind them in hordes,
And plot to reconquer the Wall,
    With only our tongues for our swords.

We are the Little Folk – we!
    Too little to love or to hate.
Leave us alone and you'll see
    How we can drag down the Great!
We are the worm in the wood!
    We are the rot in the root!
We are the germ in the blood!
    We are the thorn in the foot!

Mistletoe killing an oak –
    Rats gnawing cables in two –
Moths making holes in a cloak –
    How they must love what they do!
Yes – and we Little Folk too,
    We are as busy as they –
Working our works out of view –
    Watch, and you'll see it some day!

No indeed! We are not strong,
    But we know Peoples that are.
Yes, and we'll guide them along,
    To smash and destroy you in War!
We shall be slaves just the same?
    Yes, we have always been slaves,
But you – you will die of the shame,
    And then we shall dance on your graves!

We are the Little Folk, we, etc.

HAL O' THE DRAFT

Prophets have honour all over the Earth,
   Except in the village where they were born,
Where such as knew them boys from birth
   Nature-ally hold 'em in scorn.

When Prophets are naughty and young and vain,
   They make a won'erful grievance of it;
(You can see by their writings how they complain),
   But Oh, 'tis won'erful good for the Prophet!

There's nothing Nineveh Town can give
   (Nor being swallowed by whales between),
Makes up for the place where a man's folk live,
   That don't care nothing what he has been.
He might ha' been that, or he might ha' been this,
But they love and they hate him for what he is.

Hal o' the Draft

A rainy afternoon drove Dan and Una over to play pirates in the Little Mill. If you don't mind rats on the rafters and oats in your shoes, the mill-attic, with its trapdoors and inscriptions on beams about floods and sweethearts, is a splendid place. It is lighted by a foot-square window, called Duck Window, that looks across to Little Lindens Farm, and the spot where Jack Cade was killed.

When they had climbed the attic ladder (they called it 'the mainmast tree', out of the ballad of Sir Andrew Barton, and Dan 'swarved it with might and main', as the ballad says) they saw a man sitting on Duck Window-sill. He was dressed in a plum-coloured doublet and tight plum-coloured hose, and he drew busily in a red-edged book.

'Sit ye! Sit ye!' Puck cried from a rafter overhead. 'See what it is to be beautiful! Sir Harry Dawe – pardon, Hal – says I am the very image of a head for a gargoyle.'

The man laughed and raised his dark velvet cap to the children, and his grizzled hair bristled out in a stormy fringe. He was old – forty at least – but his eyes were young, with funny little wrinkles all round them. A satchel of embroidered leather hung from his broad belt, which looked interesting.

'May we see?' said Una, coming forward.

'Surely – sure–ly!' he said, moving up on the window-seat, and returned to his work with a silver-pointed pencil. Puck sat as though the grin were fixed for ever on his broad face, while they watched the quick, certain fingers that copied it. Presently the man took a reed pen from his satchel, and trimmed it with a little ivory knife, carved in the semblance of a fish.

'Oh, what a beauty!' cried Dan.

' 'Ware fingers! That blade is perilous sharp. I made it myself of the best Low Country cross-bow steel. And so, too, this fish. When his back-fin travels to his tail – so – he swallows up the blade, even as the whale swallowed Gaffer Jonah . . . Yes, and that's my ink-horn. I made the four silver saints round it. Press Barnabas's head. It opens, and then – ' He dipped the trimmed pen, and with careful boldness began to put in the essential lines of Puck's rugged face, that had been but faintly revealed by the silver point.

The children gasped, for it fairly leaped from the page.

As he worked, and the rain fell on the tiles, he talked – now clearly, now muttering, now breaking off to frown or smile at his work. He told them he was born at Little Lindens Farm, and his father used to beat him for drawing things instead of doing things, till an old priest called Father Roger, who drew illuminated letters in rich people's books, coaxed the parents to let him take the boy as a sort of painter's apprentice. Then he went with Father Roger to Oxford, where he cleaned plates and carried cloaks and shoes for the scholars of a College called Merton.

'Didn't you hate that?' said Dan after a great many other questions.

'I never thought on't. Half Oxford was building new colleges or beautifying the old, and she had called to her aid the master-craftsmen of all Christendie – kings in their trade and honoured of Kings. I knew them. I worked for them: that was enough. No wonder – ' He stopped and laughed.

'You became a great man, Hal,' said Puck.

'They said so, Robin. Even Bramante said so.'

'Why? What did you do?' Dan asked.

The artist looked at him queerly. 'Things in stone and such, up and down England. You would not have heard of 'em. To come nearer home, I rebuilt this little St Barnabas' church of ours. It cost me more trouble and sorrow than aught I've touched in my life. But 'twas a sound lesson.'

'Um,' said Dan. 'We've had lessons this morning.'

'I'll not afflict ye, lad,' said Hal, while Puck roared. 'Only 'tis strange to think how that little church was rebuilt, re-roofed, and made glorious, thanks to some few godly Sussex ironmasters, a Bristow sailor lad, a proud ass called Hal o' the Draft because, d'you see, he was always drawing and drafting; and' – he dragged the words slowly – '*and* a Scotch pirate.'

'Pirate?' said Dan. He wriggled like a hooked fish.

'Even that Andrew Barton you were singing of on the stair just now.' He dipped again in the inkwell, and held his breath over a sweeping line, as though he had forgotten everything else.

'Pirates don't build churches, do they?' said Dan. 'Or *do* they?'

'They help mightily,' Hal laughed. 'But you were at your lessons this morn, Jack Scholar.'

'Oh, pirates aren't lessons. It was only Bruce and his silly old spider,' said Una. 'Why did Sir Andrew Barton help you?'

'I question if he ever knew it,' said Hal, twinkling. 'Robin, how a' mischief's name am I to tell these innocents what comes of sinful pride?'

'Oh, we know all about *that*,' said Una pertly. 'If you get too beany – that's cheeky – you get sat upon, of course.'

Hal considered a moment, pen in air, and Puck said some long words.

'Aha! that was my case too,' he cried. 'Beany – you say – but certainly I did not conduct myself well. I was proud of – of such things as porches – a Galilee porch at Lincoln for choice – proud of one Torrigiano's arm on my shoulder, proud of my knighthood when I made the gilt scroll-work for the *Sovereign* – our King's ship. But Father Roger sitting in Merton College Library, he did not forget me. At the top of my pride, when I and no other should have builded the porch at Lincoln, he laid it on me with a terrible forefinger to go back to my Sussex clays and rebuild, at my own charges, my own church, where us Dawes have been buried for six generations. "Out! Son of my Art!"

said he. "Fight the Devil at home ere you call yourself a man and a craftsman." And I quaked, and I went . . . How's yon, Robin?' He flourished the finished sketch before Puck.

'Me! Me past peradventure,' said Puck, smirking like a man at a mirror. 'Ah, see! The rain has took off! I hate housen in daylight.'

'Whoop! Holiday!' cried Hal, leaping up. 'Who's for my Little Lindens? We can talk there.'

They tumbled downstairs, and turned past the dripping willows by the sunny mill-dam.

'Body o' me,' said Hal, staring at the hop-garden, where the hops were just ready to blossom. 'What are these? Vines? No, not vines, and they twine the wrong way to beans.' He began to draw in his ready book.

'Hops. New since your day,' said Puck. 'They're a herb of Mars, and their flowers dried flavour ale. We say –

> 'Turkeys, Heresy, Hops, and Beer
> Came into England all in one year.'

'Heresy I know. I've seen Hops – God be praised for their beauty! What is your Turkis?'

The children laughed. They knew the Lindens turkeys, and as soon as they reached Lindens orchard on the hill the full flock charged at them.

Out came Hal's book at once. 'Hoity-toity!' he cried. 'Here's Pride in purple feathers! Here's wrathy contempt and the Pomps of the Flesh! How d'you call *them*?'

'Turkeys! Turkeys!' the children shouted, as the old gobbler raved and flamed against Hal's plum-coloured hose.

' 'Save Your Magnificence!' he said. 'I've drafted two good new things today.' And he doffed his cap to the bubbling bird.

Then they walked through the grass to the knoll where Little Lindens stands. The old farmhouse, weather-tiled to the ground, took almost the colour of a blood-ruby in the afternoon light. The pigeons pecked at the mortar in the chimney-stacks; the bees that had lived under the tiles since it was built filled the hot August air with their booming; and the smell of the box-tree by the dairy window mixed with the smell of earth after rain, bread after baking, and a tickle of wood-smoke.

The farmer's wife came to the door, baby on arm, shaded her brows against the sun, stooped to pluck a sprig of rosemary, and turned down the orchard. The old spaniel in his barrel barked once or twice to show he was in charge of the empty house. Puck clicked back the garden-gate.

'D'you marvel that I love it?' said Hal, in a whisper. 'What can townfolk know of the nature of housen – or land?'

They perched themselves arow on the old hacked oak bench in Lindens garden, looking across the valley of the brook at the fern-covered dimples and hollows of the Forge behind Hobden's cottage. The old man was cutting a faggot in his garden by the hives. It was quite a second after his chopper fell that the chump of the blow reached their lazy ears.

'Eh – yeh!' said Hal. 'I mind when where that old gaffer stands was Nether Forge – Master John Collins's foundry. Many a night has his big trip-hammer shook me in my bed here. *Boom-bitty*! *Boom-bitty*! If the wind was east, I could hear Master Tom Collins's forge at Stockens answering his brother, *Boom-oop*! *Boom-oop*! and midway between, Sir John Pelham's sledgehammers at Brightling would strike in like a pack o' scholars, and "*Hic-haec-hoc*" they'd say, "*Hic-haec-hoc*," till I fell asleep. Yes. The valley was as full o' forges and fineries as a May shaw o' cuckoos. All gone to grass now!'

'What did they make?' said Dan.

'Guns for the King's ships – and for others. Serpentines and cannon mostly. When the guns were cast, down would come the King's Officers, and take our plough-oxen to haul them to the coast. Look! Here's one of the first and finest craftsmen of the Sea!'

He fluttered back a page of his book, and showed them a young man's head. Underneath was written: 'Sebastianus.'

'He came down with a King's Order on Master John Collins for twenty serpentines (wicked little cannon they be!) to furnish a venture of ships. I drafted him thus sitting by our fire telling Mother of the new lands he'd find the far side the world. And he found them, too! There's a nose to cleave through unknown seas! Cabot was his name – a Bristol lad – half a foreigner. I set a heap by him. He helped me to my church-building.'

'I thought that was Sir Andrew Barton,' said Dan.

'Ay, but foundations before roofs,' Hal answered. 'Sebastian first put me in the way of it. I had come down here, not to serve God as a craftsman should, but to show my people how great a craftsman I was. They cared not, and it served me right, one split straw for my craft or my greatness. What a murrain call had I, they said, to mell with old St Barnabas'? Ruinous the church had been since the Black Death, and ruinous she would remain; and I could hang myself in my new scaffold-ropes! Gentle and simple, high and low – the Hayes, the Fowles, the Fenners, the Collinses – they were all in a tale against me. Only Sir John Pelham up yonder at Brightling bade me heart-up and go on. Yet how could I? Did I ask Master Collins for his timber-tug to haul beams? The oxen had gone to Lewes after lime. Did he promise me a set of iron cramps or ties for the roof? They never came to hand, or else they were spaulty or cracked. So with everything. Nothing said, but naught done except I stood by them, and then done amiss. I thought the countryside was fair bewitched.'

'It was, surely,' said Puck, knees under chin. 'Did you never suspect ary one?'

'Not till Sebastian came for his guns, and John Collins played him the same dog's tricks as he'd played me with my ironwork. Week in, week out, two of three serpentines would be flawed in the casting, and only fit, they said, to be re-melted. Then John Collins would shake his head, and vow he could pass no cannon for the King's service that were not perfect. Saints! How Sebastian stormed! *I* know, for we sat on this bench sharing our sorrows inter-common.

'When Sebastian had fumed away six weeks at Lindens and gotten just six serpentines, Dirk Brenzett, Master of the *Cygnet* hoy, sends me word that the block of stone he was fetching me from France for our new font he'd hove overboard to lighten his ship, chased by Andrew Barton up to Rye Port.'

'Ah! The pirate!' said Dan.

'Yes. And while I am tearing my hair over this, Ticehurst Will, my best mason, comes to me shaking, and vowing that the Devil, horned, tailed, and chained, has run out on him from the church-tower, and the men would work there no more. So I took 'em off the foundations, which we were strengthening, and went into the Bell Tavern for a cup of ale. Says Master John Collins: "Have it your own way, lad; but if I was you, I'd take the sinnification o' the sign, and leave old Barnabas' Church alone!" And they all wagged their sinful heads, and agreed. Less afraid of the Devil than of me – as I saw later.

'When I brought my sweet news to Lindens, Sebastian was limewashing the kitchen-beams for Mother. He loved her like a son.

' "Cheer up, lad," he says. "God's where He was. Only you and I chance to be pure pute asses. We've been tricked, Hal, and more shame to me, a sailor, that I did not guess it before! You must leave your belfry alone, forsooth, because the Devil is adrift there; and I cannot get my serpentines because John Collins cannot cast them aright. Meantime Andrew Barton hawks off the Port of Rye. And why? To take those very serpentines which poor Cabot must whistle for; the said serpentines, I'll wager my share of new continents, being now hid away in St Barnabas' church-tower. Clear as the Irish coast at noonday!"

' "They'd sure never dare to do it," I said; "and, for another thing, selling cannon to the King's enemies is black treason – hanging and fine."

' "It is sure, large profit. Men'll dare any gallows for that. I have been a trader myself," says he. "We must be upsides with 'em for the honour of Bristol."

'Then he hatched a plot, sitting on the limewash bucket. We gave out to ride o' Tuesday to London and made a show of taking farewells of our friends – especially of Master John Collins. But at Wadhurst Woods we turned; rode home to the water-meadows; hid our horses in a willow-tot at the foot of the glebe, and, come night, stole a-tiptoe uphill to Barnabas' church again. A thick mist, and a moon striking through.

'I had no sooner locked the tower door behind us than over goes Sebastian full length in the dark.

' "Pest!" he says. "Step high and feel low, Hal. I've stumbled over guns before."

'I groped, and one by one – the tower was pitchy dark – I counted the lither barrels of twenty serpentines laid out on pease straw. No conceal at all!

' "There's two demi-cannon my end," says Sebastian, slapping metal. "They'll be for Andrew Barton's lower deck. Honest – honest John Collins! So this is his warehouse, his arsenal, his armoury! Now see you why your pokings and pryings have raised the Devil in Sussex? You've hindered John's lawful trade for months," and he laughed where he lay.

'A clay-cold tower is no fireside at midnight, so we climbed the belfry stairs, and there Sebastian trips over a cow-hide with its horns and tail.

' "Aha! Your Devil has left his doublet! Does it become me, Hal?" He draws it on and capers in the shafts of window-moonlight – won'erful devilish-like. Then he sits on the stairs, rapping with his tail on a board, and his back-aspect was dreader than his front, and a howlet lit in, and screeched at the horns of him.

' "If you'd keep out the Devil, shut the door," he whispered. "And that's another false proverb, Hal, for I can hear your tower door opening."

' "I locked it. Who a-plague has another key, then?" I said.

' "All the congregation, to judge by their feet," he says, and peers into the blackness. "Still! Still, Hal! Hear 'em grunt! That's more o' my serpentines, I'll be bound. One – two – three – four they bear in! Faith, Andrew equips himself like an Admiral! Twenty-four serpentines in all!"

'As if it had been an echo, we heard John Collins's voice come up all hollow: "Twenty-four serpentines and two demi-cannon. That's the full tally for Sir Andrew Barton."

' "Courtesy costs naught," whispers Sebastian. "Shall I drop my dagger on his head?"

' "They go over to Rye o' Thursday in the wool-wains, hid under the wool-packs. Dirk Brenzett meets them at Udimore, as before," says John.

' "Lord! What a worn, handsmooth trade it is!" says Sebastian. "I lay we are the sole two babes in the village that have not our lawful share in the venture."

'There was a full score folk below, talking like all Robertsbridge Market. We counted them by voice.

'Master John Collins pipes: "The guns for the French carrack must lie here next month. Will, when does your young fool" (me, so please you!) "come back from Lunnon?"

' "No odds," I heard Ticehurst Will answer. "Lay 'em just where you've a mind, Mus' Collins. We're all too afraid o' the Devil to mell with the tower now." And the long knave laughed.

' "Ah! 'tis easy enow for you to raise the Devil, Will," says another – Ralph Hobden of the Forge.

' "Aaa–men!" roars Sebastian, and ere I could hold him, he leaps down the stairs – won'erful devilish-like – howling no bounds. He had scarce time to lay out for the nearest than they ran. Saints, how they ran! We heard them pound on the door of the Bell Tavern, and then we ran too.

' "What's next?" says Sebastian, looping up his cow-tail as he leaped the briars. "I've broke honest John's face."

' "Ride to Sir John Pelham's," I said. "He is the only one that ever stood by me."

'We rode to Brightling, and past Sir John's lodges, where the keepers would have shot at us for deer-stealers, and we had Sir John down into his Justice's chair, and when we had told him our tale and showed him the cow-hide which Sebastian wore still girt about him, he laughed till the tears ran.

' "Wel–a–well!" he says. "I'll see justice done before daylight. What's your complaint? Master Collins is my old friend."

' "He's none of mine," I cried. "When I think how he and his likes have baulked and dozened and cozened me at every turn over the church" – and I choked at the thought.

' "Ah, but ye see now they needed it for another use," says he smoothly.

' "So they did my serpentines," Sebastian cries. "I should be half across the Western Ocean by now if my guns had been ready. But they're sold to a Scotch pirate by your old friend."

' "Where's your proof?" says Sir John, stroking his beard.

' "I broke my shins over them not an hour since, and I heard John give order where they were to be taken," says Sebastian.

' "Words! Words only," says Sir John. "Master Collins is somewhat of a liar at best."

'He carried it so gravely that, for the moment, I thought he was dipped in this secret traffick too, and that there was not an honest ironmaster in Sussex.

' "Name o' Reason!" says Sebastian, and raps with his cow-tail on the table, "whose guns are they, then?"

' "Yours, manifestly," says Sir John. "You come with the King's Order for 'em, and Master Collins casts them in his foundry. If he chooses to bring them up from Nether Forge and lay 'em out in the church-tower, why, they are e'en so much the nearer to the main road and you are saved a day's hauling. What a coil to make of a mere act of neighbourly kindness, lad!"

' "I fear I have requited him very scurvily," says Sebastian, looking at his knuckles. "But what of the demi-cannon? I could do with 'em well, but *they* are not in the King's Order."

' "Kindness – loving-kindness," says Sir John. "Questionless, in his zeal for the King and his love for you, John adds those two cannon as a gift. 'Tis plain as this coming daylight, ye stockfish!"

' "So it is," says Sebastian. "Oh, Sir John, Sir John, why did you never use the sea? You are lost ashore." And he looked on him with great love.

' "I do my best in my station." Sir John strokes his beard again and rolls forth his deep drumming Justice's voice thus: "But – suffer me! – you two lads, on some midnight frolic into which I probe not, roystering around the taverns, surprise Master Collins at his" – he thinks a moment – "at his good deeds done by stealth. Ye surprise him, I say, cruelly."

' "Truth, Sir John. If you had seen him run!" says Sebastian.

' "On this you ride breakneck to me with a tale of pirates, and wool-wains, and cow-hides, which, though it hath moved my mirth as a man, offendeth my reason as a magistrate. So I will e'en accompany you back to the tower with, perhaps, some few of my own people, and three-four wagons, and I'll be your warrant that Master John Collins will freely give you your guns and your demi-cannon, Master Sebastian." He breaks into his proper voice – "I warned the old tod and his neighbours long ago that they'd come to trouble with their side-sellings and bye-dealings; but we cannot have half Sussex hanged for a little gun-running. Are ye content, lads?"

' "I'd commit any treason for two demi-cannon, said Sebastian, and rubs his hands.

' "Ye have just compounded with rank treason-felony for the same bribe," says Sir John. "Wherefore to horse, and get the guns." '

'But Master Collins meant the guns for Sir Andrew Barton all along, didn't he?' said Dan.

'Questionless, that he did,' said Hal. 'But he lost them. We poured into the village on the red edge of dawn, Sir John horsed, in half-armour, his pennon flying; behind him thirty stout Brightling knaves, five abreast; behind them four wool-wains, and behind them four trumpets to triumph over the jest, blowing: *Our King went forth to Normandie*. When we halted and rolled the ringing guns out of the tower, 'twas for all the world like Friar Roger's picture of the French siege in the Queen's Missal-book.'

'And what did we – I mean, what did our village do?' said Dan.

'Oh! Bore it nobly – nobly,' cried Hal. 'Though they had tricked me, I was proud of them. They came out of their housen, looked at that little army as though it had been a post, and went their shut-mouthed way. Never a sign! Never a word! They'd ha' perished sooner than let Brightling overcrow us. Even that villain, Ticehurst Will, coming out of the Bell for his morning ale, he all but runs under Sir John's horse.

' " 'Ware, Sirrah Devil!" cries Sir John, reining back.

' "Oh!" says Will. "Market-day, is it? And all the bullocks from Brightling here?"

'I spared him his belting for that – the brazen knave!

'But John Collins was our masterpiece! He happened along-street (his jaw tied up where Sebastian had clouted him) when we were trundling the first demi-cannon through the lychgate.

' "I reckon you'll find her middlin' heavy," he says. "If you've a mind to pay, I'll loan ye my timber-tug. She won't lie easy on ary wool-wain."

'That was the one time I ever saw Sebastian taken flat aback. He opened and shut his mouth, fishy-like.

' "No offence," says Master John. "You've got her reasonable good cheap. I thought ye might not grudge me a groat if I helped move her." Ah, he was a masterpiece! They say that morning's work cost our John two hundred

'I reckon you'll find her middlin' heavy,' he says.

pounds, and he never winked an eyelid, not even when he saw the guns all carted off to Lewes.'

'Neither then nor later?' said Puck.

'Once. 'Twas after he gave St Barnabas' the new chime of bells. (Oh, there was nothing the Collinses, or the Hayes, or the Fowles, or the Fenners would not do for the church then! "Ask and have" was their song.) We had rung 'em in, and he was in the tower with Black Nick Fowle, that gave us our rood-screen. The old man pinches the bell-rope one hand and scratches his neck with t'other. "Sooner she was pulling yon clapper than my neck," he says. That was all! That was Sussex – seely Sussex for everlastin'!'

'And what happened after?' said Una.

'I went back into England,' said Hal, slowly. 'I'd had my lesson against pride. But they tell me I left St Barnabas' a jewel – justabout a jewel! Wel–a–well! 'Twas done for and among my own people, and – Father Roger was right – I never knew such trouble or such triumph since. That's the nature o' things. A dear – dear land.' He dropped his chin on his chest.

'There's your Father at the Forge. What's he talking to old Hobden about?' said Puck, opening his hand with three leaves in it.

Dan looked towards the cottage.

'Oh, I know. It's that old oak lying across the brook. Pater always wants it grubbed.'

In the still valley they could hear old Hobden's deep tones.

'Have it *as* you've a mind to,' he was saying. 'But the vivers of her roots they hold the bank together. If you grub her out, the bank she'll all come tearin' down, an' next floods the brook'll swarve up. But have it *as* you've a mind. The Mistuss she sets a heap by the ferns on her trunk.'

'Oh! I'll think it over,' said the Pater.

Una laughed a little bubbling chuckle.

'What Devil's in *that* belfry?' said Hal, with a lazy laugh. 'That should be a Hobden by his voice.'

'Why, the oak is the regular bridge for all the rabbits between the Three Acre and our meadow. The best place for wires on the farm, Hobden says. He's got two there now,' Una answered. '*He* won't ever let it be grubbed!'

'Ah, Sussex! Seely Sussex for everlastin',' murmured Hal; and the next moment their Father's voice calling across to Little Lindens broke the spell as little St Barnabas' clock struck five.

A Smugglers' Song

If you wake at midnight, and hear a horse's feet,
Don't go drawing back the blind, or looking in the street,
Them that asks no questions isn't told a lie.
Watch the wall, my darling, while the Gentlemen go by!
        Five-and-twenty ponies,
        Trotting through the dark –
        Brandy for the Parson,
        'Baccy for the Clerk;
        Laces for a lady; letters for a spy,
And watch the wall, my darling, while the Gentlemen go by!
Running round the woodlump if you chance to find
Little barrels, roped and tarred, all full of brandy-wine;
Don't you shout to come and look, nor take 'em for your play;
Put the brushwood back again, – and they'll be gone next day!

If you see the stable-door setting open wide;
If you see a tired horse lying down inside;
If your mother mends a coat cut about and tore;
If the lining's wet and warm – don't you ask no more!

If you meet King George's men, dressed in blue and red,
You be careful what you say, and mindful what is said.
If they call you 'pretty maid', and chuck you 'neath the chin,
Don't you tell where no one is, nor yet where no one's been!

Knocks and footsteps round the house – whistles after dark –
You've no call for running out till the house-dogs bark.
Trusty's here, and Pincher's here, and see how dumb they lie –
They don't fret to follow when the Gentlemen go by!

If you do as you've been told, likely there's a chance
You'll be give a dainty doll, all the way from France,
With a cap of Valenciennes, and a velvet hood –
A present from the Gentlemen, along o' being good!
        Five-and-twenty ponies,
        Trotting through the dark –
        Brandy for the Parson,
        'Baccy for the Clerk.
Them that asks no questions isn't told a lie –
Watch the wall, my darling, while the Gentlemen go by!

'DYMCHURCH FLIT'

The Bee Boy's Song

Bees! Bees! Hark to your bees!
'Hide from your neighbours as much as you please,
But all that has happened, to us you must tell,
Or else we will give you no honey to sell!'

A Maiden in her glory,
   Upon her wedding-day,
Must tell her Bees the story,
   Or else they'll fly away.
      Fly away – die away –
         Dwindle down and leave you!
      But if you don't deceive your Bees,
         Your Bees will not deceive you.

Marriage, birth or buryin',
   News across the seas,
All you're sad or merry in,
   You must tell the Bees.
      Tell 'em coming in an' out,
         Where the Fanners fan,
      'Cause the Bees are justabout
         As curious as a man!

Don't you wait where trees are,
   When the lightnings play;
Nor don't you hate where Bees are,
   Or else they'll pine away.
      Pine away – dwine away –
         Anything to leave you!
      But if you never grieve your Bees,
         Your Bees'll never grieve you!

'Dymchurch Flit'

Just at dusk, a soft September rain began to fall on the hop-pickers. The mothers wheeled the bouncing perambulators out of the gardens; bins were put away, and tally-books made up. The young couples strolled home, two to each umbrella, and the single men walked behind them laughing. Dan and Una, who had been picking after their lessons, marched off to roast potatoes at the oast house, where old Hobden, with Blue-eyed Bess, his lurcher dog, lived all the month through, drying the hops.

They settled themselves, as usual, on the sack-strewn cot in front of the fires, and, when Hobden drew up the shutter, stared, as usual, at the flameless bed of coals spouting its heat up the dark well of the old-fashioned roundel. Slowly he cracked off a few fresh pieces of coal, packed them, with fingers that never flinched, exactly where they would do most good; slowly he reached behind him till Dan tilted the potatoes into his iron scoop of a hand; carefully he arranged them round the fire, and then stood for a moment, black against the glare. As he closed the shutter, the oast house seemed dark before the day's end, and he lit the candle in the lanthorn. The children liked all these things because they knew them so well.

The Bee Boy, Hobden's son, who is not quite right in his head, though he can do anything with bees, slipped in like a shadow. They only guessed it when Bess's stump-tail wagged against them.

A big voice began singing outside in the drizzle:

'Old Mother Laidinwool had nigh twelve months been dead,
She heard the hops were doin' well, and then popped up her head.'

'There can't be two people made to holler like that!' cried old Hobden, wheeling round.

'For, says she, "The boys I've picked with when I was young and fair,
They're bound to be at hoppin', and I'm – " '

A man showed at the doorway.

'Well, well! They do say hoppin' 'll draw the very deadest, and now I belieft 'em. You, Tom? Tom Shoesmith?' Hobden lowered his lanthorn.

'You're a hem of a time makin' your mind to it, Ralph!' The stranger strode in – three full inches taller than Hobden, a grey-whiskered, brown-faced giant with clear blue eyes. They shook hands, and the children could hear the hard palms rasp together.

'You ain't lost none o' your grip,' said Hobden. 'Was it thirty or forty year back you broke my head at Peasmarsh Fair?'

'Only thirty, an' no odds 'tween us regardin' heads, neither. You had it back at me with a hop-pole. How did we get home that night? Swimmin'?'

'Same way the pheasant come into Gubbs's pocket – by a little luck an' a deal o' conjurin'.' Old Hobden laughed in his deep chest.

'I see you've not forgot your way about the woods. D'ye do any o' *this* still?' The stranger pretended to look along a gun.

Hobden answered with a quick movement of the hand as though he were pegging down a rabbit-wire.

'No. *That's* all that's left me now. Age she must as Age she can. An' what's your news since all these years?'

> 'Oh, I've bin to Plymouth, I've bin to Dover –
> I've bin ramblin', boys, the wide world over,'

the man answered cheerily. 'I reckon I know as much of Old England as most.' He turned towards the children and winked boldly.

'I lay they told you a sight o' lies, then. I've been into England fur as Wiltsheer once. I was cheated proper over a pair of hedgin'-gloves,' said Hobden.

'There's fancy-talkin' everywhere. You've cleaved to your own parts pretty middlin' close, Ralph.'

'Can't shift an old tree 'thout it dyin',' Hobden chuckled. 'An' I be no more anxious to die than you look to be to help me with my hops tonight.'

The great man leaned against the brickwork of the roundel, and swung his arms abroad. 'Hire me!' was all he said, and they stumped upstairs laughing.

The children heard their shovels rasp on the cloth where the yellow hops lie drying above the fires, and all the oast house filled with the sweet, sleepy . smell as they were turned.

'Who is it?' Una whispered to the Bee Boy.

'Dunno, no more'n you – if *you* dunno,' said he, and smiled.

The voices on the drying-floor talked and chuckled together, and the heavy footsteps moved back and forth. Presently a hop-pocket dropped through the press-hole overhead, and stiffened and fattened as they shovelled it full. 'Clank!' went the press, and rammed the loose stuff into tight cake.

'Gentle!' they heard Hobden cry. 'You'll bust her crop if you lay on so. You be as careless as Gleason's bull, Tom. Come an' sit by the fires. She'll do now.'

They came down, and as Hobden opened the shutter to see if the potatoes were done Tom Shoesmith said to the children, 'Put a plenty salt on 'em. That'll show you the sort o' man *I* be.' Again he winked, and again the Bee Boy laughed and Una stared at Dan.

'*I* know what sort o' man you be,' old Hobden grunted, groping for the potatoes round the fire.

'Do ye?' Tom went on behind his back. 'Some of us can't abide Horseshoes, or Church Bells, or Running Water; an', talkin' o' runnin' water' – he turned to Hobden, who was backing out of the roundel – 'd'you mind the great floods at Robertsbridge, when the miller's man was drowned in the street?'

'I know what sort o' man you be,' old Hobden grunted, groping
for the potatoes round the fire.

'Middlin' well.' Old Hobden let himself down on the coals by the fire-door. 'I was courtin' my woman on the Marsh that year. Carter to Mus' Plum I was, gettin' ten shillin's week. Mine was a Marsh woman.'

'Won'erful odd-gates place – Romney Marsh,' said Tom Shoesmith. 'I've heard say the world's divided like into Europe, Ashy, Afriky, Ameriky, Australy, an' Romney Marsh.'

'The Marsh folk think so,' said Hobden. 'I had a hem o' trouble to get my woman to leave it.'

'Where did she come out of? I've forgot, Ralph.'

'Dymchurch under the Wall,' Hobden answered, a potato in his hand.

'Then she'd be a Pett – or a Whitgift, would she?'

'Whitgift.' Hobden broke open the potato and ate it with the curious neatness of men who make most of their meals in the blowy open. 'She growed to be quite reasonable-like after livin' in the Weald awhile, but our first twenty year or two she was odd-fashioned, no bounds. And she was a won'erful hand with bees.' He cut away a little piece of potato and threw it out to the door.

'Ah! I've heard say the Whitgifts could see further through a millstone than most,' said Shoesmith. 'Did she, now?'

'She was honest-innocent of any nigromancin',' said Hobden. 'Only she'd read signs and sinnifications out o' birds flyin', stars fallin', bees hivin', and such. An, she'd lie awake – listenin' for calls, she said.'

'That don't prove naught,' said Tom. 'All Marsh folk has been smugglers since time everlastin'. 'Twould be in her blood to listen out o' nights.'

'Nature-ally,' old Hobden replied, smiling. 'I mind when there was smugglin' a sight nearer us than what the Marsh be. But that wasn't my woman's trouble. 'Twas a passel o' no-sense talk' – he dropped his voice – 'about Pharisees.'

'Yes. I've heard Marsh men belief in 'em.' Tom looked straight at the wide-eyed children beside Bess.

'Pharisees,' cried Una. 'Fairies? Oh, I see!'

'People o' the Hills,' said the Bee Boy, throwing half of his potato towards the door.

'There you be!' said Hobden, pointing at him. 'My boy – he has her eyes and her out-gate senses. That's what *she* called 'em!'

'And what did you think of it all?'

'Um – um,' Hobden rumbled. 'A man that uses fields an' shaws after dark as much as I've done, he don't go out of his road excep' for keepers.'

'But settin' that aside?' said Tom, coaxingly. 'I saw ye throw the Good Piece out-at-doors just now. Do ye believe or – *do* ye?'

'There was a great black eye to that tater,' said Hobden indignantly.

'My liddle eye didn't see un, then. It looked as if you meant it for – for anyone that might need it. But settin' that aside, d'ye believe or – *do* ye?'

'I ain't sayin' nothin', because I've heard naught, an' I've see naught. But if you was to say there was more things after dark in the shaws than men, or fur, or feather, or fin, I dunno as I'd go far about to call you a liar. Now turn again, Tom. What's your say?'

'I'm like you. I say nothin'. But I'll tell you a tale, an' you can fit it *as* how you please.'

'Passel o' no-sense stuff,' growled Hobden, but he filled his pipe.

'The Marsh men they call it Dymchurch Flit,' Tom went on slowly. 'Hap you have heard it?'

'My woman she've told it me scores o' times. Dunno as I didn't end by belieftin' it – sometimes.'

Hobden crossed over as he spoke, and sucked with his pipe at the yellow lanthorn flame. Tom rested one great elbow on one great knee, where he sat among the coal.

'Have you ever bin in the Marsh?' he said to Dan.

'Only as far as Rye, once,' Dan answered.

'Ah, that's but the edge. Back behind of her there's steeples settin' beside churches, an' wise women settin' beside their doors, an' the sea settin' above the land, an' ducks herdin' wild in the diks' (he meant ditches). 'The Marsh is justabout riddled with diks an' sluices, an' tide-gates an' water-lets. You can hear 'em bubblin' an' grummelin' when the tide works in 'em, an' then you hear the sea rangin' left and right-handed all up along the Wall. You've seen how flat she is – the Marsh? You'd think nothin' easier than to walk eend-on acrost her? Ah, but the diks an' the water-lets, they twists the roads about as ravelly as witch-yarn on the spindles. So ye get all turned round in broad daylight.'

'That's because they've dreened the waters into the diks,' said Hobden. 'When I courted my woman the rushes was green – Eh me! the rushes was green – an' the Bailiff o' the Marshes he rode up and down as free as the fog.'

'Who was he?' said Dan.

'Why, the Marsh fever an' ague. He've clapped me on the shoulder once or twice till I shook proper. But now the dreenin' off of the waters have done away with the fevers; so they make a joke, like, that the Bailiff o' the Marshes broke his neck in a dik. A won'erful place for bees an' ducks 'tis too.'

'An' old,' Tom went on. 'Flesh an' Blood have been there since Time Everlastin' Beyond. Well, now, speakin' among themselves, the Marsh men say that from Time Everlastin' Beyond, the Pharisees favoured the Marsh above the rest of Old England. I lay the Marsh men ought to know. They've been out after dark, father an' son, smugglin' some one thing or t'other, since ever wool grew to sheep's backs. They say there was always a middlin' few Pharisees to be seen on the Marsh. Impident as rabbits, they was. They'd dance on the nakid roads in the nakid daytime; they'd flash their liddle green lights along the diks, comin' an' goin', like honest smugglers. Yes, an' times they'd lock the church doors against parson an' clerk of Sundays.'

'That 'ud be smugglers layin' in the lace or the brandy till they could run it out o' the Marsh. I've told my woman so,' said Hobden.

'I'll lay she didn't belieft it, then – not if she was a Whitgift. A won'erful choice place for Pharisees, the Marsh, by all accounts, till Queen Bess's father he come in with his Reformatories.'

'Would that be a Act of Parliament like?' Hobden asked.

'Sure–ly. Can't do nothing in Old England without Act, Warrant an' Summons. He got his Act allowed him, an', they say, Queen Bess's father he used the parish churches something shameful. Justabout tore the gizzards out of I dunnamany. Some folk in England they held with 'en; but some they saw it different, an' it eended in 'em takin' sides an' burnin' each other no bounds, accordin' which side was top, time bein'. That tarrified the Pharisees: for Goodwill among Flesh an' Blood is meat an' drink to 'em, an' ill-will is poison.'

'Same as bees,' said the Bee Boy. 'Bees won't stay by a house where there's hating.'

'True,' said Tom. 'This Reformatories tarrified the Pharisees same as the reaper goin' round a last stand o' wheat tarrifies rabbits. They packed into the Marsh from all parts, and they says, "Fair or foul, we must flit out o' this, for Merry England's done with, an' we're reckoned among the Images." '

'Did they *all* see it that way?' said Hobden.

'All but one that was called Robin – if you've heard of him. What are you laughin' at?' Tom turned to Dan. 'The Pharisees's trouble didn't tech Robin, because he'd cleaved middlin' close to people, like. No more he never meant to go out of Old England – not he; so he was sent messagin' for help among Flesh an' Blood. But Flesh an' Blood must always think of their own concerns, an' Robin couldn't get *through* at 'em, ye see. They thought it was tide-echoes off the Marsh.'

'What did you – what did the fai – Pharisees want?' Una asked.

'A boat, to be sure. Their liddle wings could no more cross Channel than so many tired butterflies. A boat an' a crew they desired to sail 'em over to France, where yet awhile folks hadn't tore down the Images. They couldn't abide cruel Canterbury Bells ringin' to Bulverhithe for more pore men an' women to be burnded, nor the King's proud messenger ridin' through the land givin' orders to tear down the Images. They couldn't abide it no shape. Nor yet they couldn't get their boat an' crew to flit by without Leave an' Goodwill from Flesh an' Blood; an' Flesh an' Blood came an' went about its own business the while the Marsh was swarvin' up, an' swarvin' up with Pharisees from all England over, strivin' all means to get *through* at Flesh an' Blood to tell 'em their sore need . . . I don't know as you've ever heard say Pharisees are like chickens?'

'My woman used to say that too,' said Hobden, folding his brown arms.

'They be. You run too many chickens together, an' the ground sickens, like, an' you get a squat, an' your chickens die. Same way, you crowd

Pharisees all in one place – *they* don't die, but Flesh an' Blood walkin' among 'em is apt to sick up an' pine off. *They* don't mean it, an' Flesh an' Blood don't know it, but that's the truth – as I've heard. The Pharisees through bein' all stenched up an' frighted, an' trying' to come *through* with their supplications, they nature-ally changed the thin airs an' humours in Flesh an' Blood. It lay on the Marsh like thunder. Men saw their churches ablaze with the wildfire in the windows after dark; they saw their cattle scatterin' an' no man scarin'; their sheep flockin' an' no man drivin'; their horses latherin' an' no man leadin'; they saw the liddle low green lights more than ever in the dik-sides; they heard the liddle feet patterin' more than ever round the houses; an' night an' day, day an' night, 'twas all as though they were bein' creeped up on, an' hinted at by Some One or other that couldn't rightly shape their trouble. Oh, I lay they sweated! Man an' maid, woman an' child, their nature done 'em no service all the weeks while the Marsh was swarvin' up with Pharisees. But they was Flesh an' Blood, an' Marsh men before all. They reckoned the signs sinnified trouble for the Marsh. Or that the sea 'ud rear up against Dymchurch Wall an' they'd be drownded like Old Winchelsea; or that the Plague was comin'. So they looked for the meanin' in the sea or in the clouds – far an' high up. They never thought to look near an' knee-high, where they could see naught.

'Now there was a poor widow at Dymchurch under the Wall, which, lacking man or property, she had the more time for feeling; and she come to feel there was a Trouble outside her doorstep bigger an' heavier than aught she'd ever carried over it. She had two sons – one born blind, an' t'other struck dumb through fallin' off the Wall when he was liddle. They was men grown, but not wage-earnin', an' she worked for 'em, keepin' bees and answerin' Questions.'

'What sort of questions?' said Dan.

'Like where lost things might be found, an' what to put about a crooked baby's neck, an' how to join parted sweethearts. She felt the Trouble on the Marsh same as eels feel thunder. She was a wise woman.'

'My woman was won'erful weather-tender, too,' said Hobden. 'I've seen her brish sparks like off an anvil out of her hair in thunderstorms. But she never laid out to answer Questions.'

'This woman was a Seeker, like, an' Seekers they sometimes find. One night, while she lay abed, hot an' achin', there come a Dream an' tapped at her window, an' "Widow Whitgift," it said, "Widow Whitgift!"

'First, by the wings an' the whistlin', she thought it was peewits, but last she arose an' dressed herself, an' opened her door to the Marsh, an' she felt the Trouble an' the Groanin' all about her, strong as fever an' ague, an' she calls: "What is it? Oh, what is it?"

'Then 'twas all like the frogs in the diks peepin'; then 'twas all like the reeds in the diks clip-clappin'; an' then the great Tide-wave rummelled along the Wall, an' she couldn't hear proper.

'Three times she called, an' three times the Tide-wave did her down. But she catched the quiet between, an' she cries out, "What is the Trouble on the Marsh that's been lying down with my heart an' arising with my body this month gone?" She felt a liddle hand lay hold on her gown-hem, an' she stooped to the pull o' that liddle hand.'

Tom Shoesmith spread his huge fist before the fire and smiled at it as he went on.

' "Will the sea drown the Marsh?" she says. She was a Marsh woman first an' foremost.

' "No," says the liddle voice. "Sleep sound for all o' that."

' "Is the Plague comin' to the Marsh?" she says. Them was all the ills she knowed.

' "No. Sleep sound for all o' that," says Robin.

'She turned about, half mindful to go in, but the liddle voices grieved that shrill an' sorrowful she turns back, an' she cries: "If it is not a Trouble of Flesh an' Blood, what can I do?"

'The Pharisees cried out upon her from all round to fetch them a boat to sail to France, an' come back no more.

' "There's a boat on the Wall," she says, "but I can't push it down to the sea, nor sail it when 'tis there."

' "Lend us your sons," says all the Pharisees. "Give 'em Leave an' Good-will to sail it for us, Mother – O Mother!"

' "One's dumb, an' t'other's blind," she says. "But all the dearer me for that; and you'll lose them in the big sea." The voices justabout pierced through her; an' there was children's voices too. She stood out all she could, but she couldn't rightly stand against *that*. So she says: "If you can draw my sons for your job, I'll not hinder 'em. You can't ask no more of a Mother."

'She saw them liddle green lights dance an' cross till she was dizzy; she heard them liddle feet patterin' by the thousand; she heard cruel Canterbury Bells ringing to Bulverhithe, an' she heard the great Tide-wave ranging along the Wall. That was while the Pharisees was workin' a Dream to wake her two sons asleep: an' while she bit on her fingers she saw them two she'd bore come out an' pass her with never a word. She followed 'em, cryin' pitiful, to the old boat on the Wall, an' that they took an' runned down to the sea.

'When they'd stepped mast an' sail the blind son speaks: "Mother, we're waitin' your Leave an' Goodwill to take Them over." '

Tom Shoesmith threw back his head and half shut his eyes.

'Eh, me!' he said. 'She was a fine, valiant woman, the Widow Whitgift. She stood twistin' the ends of her long hair over her fingers, an' she shook like a poplar, makin' up her mind. The Pharisees all about they hushed their children from cryin' an' they waited dumb-still. She was all their dependence. 'Thout her Leave an' Goodwill they could not pass; for she was the Mother. So she shook like a aps-tree makin' up her mind. 'Last she drives the word past her teeth, an' "Go!" she says. "Go with my Leave an' Goodwill."

'Then I saw – then, they say, she had to brace back same as if she was wadin' in tide-water; for the Pharisees just about flowed past her – down the beach to the boat, I dunnamany of 'em – with their wives an' childern an' valooables, all escapin' out of cruel Old England. Silver you could hear chinkin', an' liddle bundles hove down dunt on the bottom-boards, an' passels o' liddle swords an' shields raklin', an' liddle fingers an' toes scratchin' on the boatside to board her when the two sons pushed her off. That boat she sunk lower an' lower, but all the Widow could see in it was her boys movin' hampered-like to get at the tackle. Up sail they did, an' away they went, deep as a Rye barge, away into the off-shore mists, an' the Widow Whitgift she sat down an' eased her grief till mornin' light.'

'I never heard she was *all* alone,' said Hobden.

'I remember now. The one called Robin, he stayed with her, they tell. She was all too grievious to listen to his promises.'

'Ah! She should ha' made her bargain beforehand. I allus told my woman so!' Hobden cried.

'No. She loaned her sons for a pure love-loan, bein' as she sensed the Trouble on the Marshes, an' was simple good-willin' to ease it.' Tom laughed softly. 'She done that. Yes, she done that! From Hithe to Bulverhithe, fretty man an' maid, ailin' woman an' wailin' child, they took the advantage of the change in the thin airs just about as soon as the Pharisees flitted. Folks come out fresh an' shinin' all over the Marsh like snails after wet. An' that while the Widow Whitgift sat grievin' on the Wall. She might have belieft us – she might have trusted her sons would be sent back! She fussed, no bounds, when their boat come in after three days.'

'And, of course, the sons were both quite cured?' said Una.

'No–o. That would have been out o' nature. She got 'em back *as* she sent 'em. The blind man he hadn't seen naught of anythin', an' the dumb man nature-ally he couldn't say aught of what he'd seen. I reckon that was why the Pharisees pitched on 'em for the ferryin' job.'

'But what did you – what did Robin promise the Widow?' said Dan.

'What *did* he promise, now?' Tom pretended to think. 'Wasn't your woman a Whitgift, Ralph? Didn't she ever say?'

'She told me a passel o' no-sense stuff when he was born.' Hobden pointed at his son. 'There was always to be one of 'em that could see further into a millstone than most.'

'Me! That's me!' said the Bee Boy so suddenly that they all laughed.

'I've got it now!' cried Tom, slapping his knee. 'So long as Whitgift blood lasted, Robin promised there would allers be one o' her stock that – that no Trouble 'ud lie on, no Maid 'ud sigh on, no Night could frighten, no Fright could harm, no Harm could make sin, an' no Woman could make a fool of.'

'Well, ain't that just me?' said the Bee Boy, where he sat in the silver square of the great September moon that was staring into the oast house door.

'They was the exact words she told me when we first found he wasn't like others. But it beats me how you known 'em,' said Hobden.

'Aha! There's more under my hat besides hair!' Tom laughed and stretched himself. 'When I've seen these two young folk home, we'll make a night of old days, Ralph, with passin' old tales – eh? An' where might you live?' he said, gravely, to Dan. 'An' do you think your Pa 'ud give me a drink for takin' you there, Missy?'

They giggled so at this that they had to run out. Tom picked them both up, set one on each broad shoulder, and tramped across the ferny pasture where the cows puffed milky puffs at them in the moonlight.

'Oh, Puck! Puck! I guessed you right from when you talked about the salt. How could you ever do it?' Una cried, swinging along delighted.

'Do what?' he said, and climbed the stile by the pollard oak.

'Pretend to be Tom Shoesmith,' said Dan, and they ducked to avoid the two little ashes that grow by the bridge over the brook. Tom was almost running.

'Yes. That's my name, Mus' Dan,' he said, hurrying over the silent shining lawn, where a rabbit sat by the big white-thorn near the croquet ground. 'Here you be.' He strode into the old kitchen yard, and slid them down as Ellen came to ask questions.

'I'm helping in Mus' Spray's oast house,' he said to her. 'No, I'm no foreigner. I knowed this country 'fore your mother was born; an' – yes, it's dry work oastin', Miss. Thank you.'

Ellen went to get a jug, and the children went in – magicked once more by Oak, Ash, and Thorn!

A Three-Part Song

I'm just in love with all these three,
The Weald an' the Marsh an' the Down countrie;
Nor I don't know which I love the most,
The Weald or the Marsh or the white chalk coast!

I've buried my heart in a ferny hill,
Twix' a liddle low shaw an' a great high gill.
Oh, hop-bine yaller an' wood-smoke blue,
I reckon you'll keep her middling true!

I've loosed my mind for to out an' run
On a Marsh that was old when Kings begun:
Oh, Romney level an' Brenzett reeds,
I reckon you know what my mind needs!

I've given my soul to the Southdown grass,
An' sheep-bells tinkled where you pass.
Oh, Firle an' Ditchling an' sails at sea,
I reckon you keep my soul for me!

THE TREASURE AND THE LAW

Song of the Fifth River

When first by Eden Tree
The Four Great Rivers ran,
To each was appointed a Man
Her Prince and Ruler to be.

But after this was ordained,
(The ancient legends tell),
There came dark Israel,
For whom no River remained.

Then He That is Wholly
Just Said to him: 'Fling on the ground
A handful of yellow dust,
And a Fifth Great River shall run,
Mightier than these four,
In secret the Earth around;
And Her secret evermore
Shall be shown to thee and thy Race.'

So it was said and done.
And, deep in the veins of Earth,
And, fed by a thousand springs
That comfort the market-place,
Or sap the power of Kings,
The Fifth Great River had birth,
Even as it was oretold –
The Secret River of Gold!

And Israel laid down
His sceptre and his crown,
To brood on that River-bank,
Where the waters flashed and sank,
And burrowed in earth and fell,

And bided a season below;
For reason that none might know,
Save only Israel.

He is Lord of the Last –
The Fifth, most wonderful, Flood.
He hears Her thunder past
And Her song is in his blood.
He can foresay: 'She will fall,'
For he knows which fountain dries
Behind which desert-belt
A thousand leagues to the South.
He can foresay: 'She will rise.'
He knows what far snows melt
Along what mountain-wall
A thousand leagues to the North.
He snuffs the coming drouth
As he snuffs the coming rain,
He knows what each will bring forth,
And turns it to his gain.

A Prince without a Sword,
A Ruler without a Throne;
Israel follows his quest.
In every land a guest,
Of many lands a lord,
In no land King is he.
But the Fifth Great River keeps
The secret of Her deeps
For Israel alone,
As it was ordered to be.

The Treasure and the Law

Now it was the third week in November, and the woods rang with the noise of pheasant-shooting. No one hunted that steep, cramped country except the village beagles, who, as often as not, escaped from their kennels and made a day of their own. Dan and Una found a couple of them towling round the kitchen garden after the laundry cat. The little brutes were only too pleased to go rabbiting, so the children ran them all along the brook pastures and into Little Lindens farmyard, where the old sow vanquished them – and up to the quarry-hole, where they started a fox. He headed for Far Wood, and there they frightened out all the Pheasants, who were sheltering from a big beat across the valley. Then the cruel guns began again, and they grabbed the beagles lest they should stray and get hurt.

'I wouldn't be a pheasant – in November – for a lot,' Dan panted, as he caught Folly by the neck. 'Why did you laugh that horrid way?'

'I didn't,' said Una, sitting on Flora, the fat lady-dog. 'Oh, look! The silly birds are going back to their own woods instead of ours, where they would be safe.'

'Safe till it pleased you to kill them.' An old man, so tall he was almost a giant, stepped from behind the clump of hollies by Volaterrae. The children jumped, and the dogs dropped like setters. He wore a sweeping gown of dark thick stuff, lined and edged with yellowish fur, and he bowed a bent-down bow that made them feel both proud and ashamed. Then he looked at them steadily, and they stared back without doubt or fear.

'You are not afraid?' he said, running his hands through his splendid grey beard. 'Not afraid that those men yonder' – he jerked his head towards the incessant pop-pop of the guns from the lower woods – 'will do you hurt?'

'We–ell' – Dan liked to be accurate, especially when he was shy – 'old Hobd – a friend of mine told me that one of the beaters got peppered last week – hit in the leg, I mean. You see, Mr Meyer *will* fire at rabbits. But he gave Waxy Garnett a quid – sovereign, I mean – and Waxy told Hobden he'd have stood both barrels for half the money.'

'He doesn't understand,' Una cried, watching the pale, troubled face. 'Oh, I wish – '

She had scarcely said it when Puck rustled out of the hollies and spoke to the man quickly in foreign words. Puck wore a long cloak too – the afternoon was just frosting down – and it changed his appearance altogether.

'Nay, nay!' he said at last. 'You did not understand the boy. A freeman was a little hurt, by pure mischance, at the hunting.'

'I know that mischance! What did his lord do? Laugh and ride over him?' the old man sneered.

'It was one of your own people did the hurt, Kadmiel.' Puck's eyes twinkled maliciously. 'So he gave the freeman a piece of gold, and no more was said.'

'A Jew drew blood from a Christian and no more was said?' Kadmiel cried. 'Never! When did they torture him?'

'No man may be bound, or fined, or slain till he has been judged by his peers,' Puck insisted. 'There is but one Law in Old England for Jew or Christian – the Law that was signed at Runnymede.'

'Why, that's Magna Carta!' Dan whispered. It was one of the few history dates that he could remember. Kadmiel turned on him with a sweep and a whirr of his spicy-scented gown.

'Dost *thou* know of that, babe?' he cried, and lifted his hands in wonder.

'Yes,' said Dan firmly.

'Magna Charta was signed by John,
That Henry the Third put his heel upon.

And old Hobden says that if it hadn't been for *her* (he calls everything "her", you know), the keepers would have him clapped in Lewes jail all the year round.'

Again Puck translated to Kadmiel in the strange, solemn-sounding language, and at last Kadmiel laughed.

'Out of the mouths of babes do we learn,' said he. 'But tell me now, and I will not call you a babe but a Rabbi, *why* did the King sign the roll of the New Law at Runnymede? For he was a King.'

Dan looked sideways at his sister. It was her turn.

'Because he jolly well had to,' said Una softly. 'The Barons made him.'

'Nay,' Kadmiel answered, shaking his head. 'You Christians always forget that gold does more than the sword. Our good King signed because he could not borrow more money from us bad Jews.' He curved his shoulders as he spoke. 'A King without gold is a snake with a broken back, and' – his nose sneered up and his eyebrows frowned down – 'it is a good deed to break a snake's back. That was my work,' he cried, triumphantly, to Puck. 'Spirit of Earth, bear witness that that was *my* work!' He shot up to his full towering height, and his words rang like a trumpet. He had a voice that changed its tone almost as an opal changes colour – sometimes deep and thundery, sometimes thin and waily, but always it made you listen.

'Many people can bear witness to that,' Puck answered. 'Tell these babes how it was done. Remember, Master, they do not know Doubt or Fear.'

'So I saw in their faces when we met,' said Kadmiel. 'Yet surely, surely they are taught to spit upon Jews?'

'Are they?' said Dan, much interested. 'Where at?'

Puck fell back a pace, laughing. 'Kadmiel is thinking of King John's reign,' he explained. 'His people were badly treated then.'

'Oh, we know *that*,' they answered, and (it was very rude of them, but they could not help it) they stared straight at Kadmiel's mouth to see if his teeth were all there. It stuck in their lesson-memory that King John used to pull out Jews' teeth to make them lend him money.

Kadmiel understood the look and smiled bitterly.

'No. Your King never drew my teeth: I think, perhaps, I drew his. Listen! I was not born among Christians, but among Moors – in Spain – in a little white town under the mountains. Yes, the Moors are cruel, but at least their learned men dare to think. It was prophesied of me at my birth that I should be a Lawgiver to a People of a strange speech and a hard language. We Jews are always looking for the Prince and the Lawgiver to come. Why not? My people in the town (we were very few) set me apart as a child of the prophecy – the Chosen of the Chosen. We Jews dream so many dreams. You would never guess it to see us slink about the rubbish-heaps in our quarter; but at the day's end – doors shut, candles lit – aha! *then* we became the Chosen again.'

He paced back and forth through the wood as he talked. The rattle of the shotguns never ceased, and the dogs whimpered a little and lay flat on the leaves.

'I was a Prince. Yes! Think of a little Prince who had never known rough words in his own house handed over to shouting, bearded Rabbis, who pulled his ears and filliped his nose, all that he might learn – learn – learn to be King when his time came. Hé! Such a little Prince it was! One eye he kept on the stone-throwing Moorish boys, and the other it roved about the streets looking for his Kingdom. Yes, and he learned to cry softly when he was hunted up and down those streets. He learned to do all things without noise. He played beneath his father's table when the Great Candle was lit, and he listened as children listen to the talk of his father's friends above the table. They came across the mountains, from out of all the world, for my Prince's father was their counsellor. They came from behind the armies of Sala-ud-Din: from Rome: from Venice: from England. They stole down our alley, they tapped secretly at our door, they took off their rags, they arrayed themselves, and they talked to my father at the wine. All over the world the heathen fought each other. They brought news of these wars, and while he played beneath the table, my Prince heard these meanly dressed ones decide between themselves how, and when, and for how long King should draw sword against King, and People rise up against People. Why not? There can be no war without gold, and we Jews know how the earth's gold moves with the seasons, and the crops, and the winds; circling and looping and rising and sinking away like a river – a wonderful underground river. How should the foolish Kings know *that* while they fight and steal and kill?'

The children's faces showed that they knew nothing at all as, with open eyes, they trotted and turned beside the long-striding old man. He twitched his gown over his shoulders, and a square plate of gold, studded with jewels, gleamed for an instant through the fur, like a star through flying snow.

'No matter,' he said. 'But, credit me, my Prince saw peace or war decided not once, but many times, by the fall of a coin spun between a Jew from Bury and a Jewess from Alexandria, in his father's house, when the Great Candle was lit. Such power had we Jews among the Gentiles. Ah, my little Prince! Do you wonder that he learned quickly? Why not?' He muttered to himself and went on: 'My trade was that of a physician. When I had learned it in Spain I went to the East to find my Kingdom. Why not? A Jew is as free as a sparrow – or a dog. He goes where he is hunted. In the East I found libraries where men dared to think – schools of medicine where they dared to learn. I was diligent in my business. Therefore I stood before Kings. I have been a brother to Princes and a companion to beggars, and I have walked between the living and the dead. There was no profit in it. I did not find my Kingdom. So, in the tenth year of my travels, when I had reached the Uttermost Eastern Sea, I returned to my father's house. God had wonderfully preserved my people. None had been slain, none even wounded, and only a few scourged. I became once more a son in my father's house. Again the Great Candle was lit; again the meanly apparelled ones tapped on our door after dusk; and again I heard them weigh out peace and war, as they weighed out the gold on the table. But I was not rich – not very rich. Therefore, when those that had power and knowledge and wealth talked together, I sat in the shadow. Why not?

'Yet all my wanderings had shown me one sure thing, which is, that a King without money is like a spear without a head. He cannot do much harm. I said, therefore, to Elias of Bury, a great one among our people: "Why do our people lend any more to the Kings that oppress us?" "Because," said Elias, "if we refuse they stir up their people against us, and the People are tenfold more cruel than Kings. If thou doubtest, come with me to Bury in England and live as I live."

'I saw my mother's face across the candle flame, and I said, "I will come with thee to Bury. Maybe my Kingdom shall be there."

'So I sailed with Elias to the darkness and the cruelty of Bury in England, where there are no learned men. How can a man be wise if he hate? At Bury I kept his accounts for Elias, and I saw men kill Jews there by the tower. No – none laid hands on Elias. He lent money to the King, and the King's favour was about him. A King will not take the life so long as there is any gold. This King – yes, John – oppressed his people bitterly because they would not give him money. Yet his land was a good land. If he had only given it rest he might have cropped it as a Christian crops his beard. But even that little he did not know, for God had deprived him of all understanding, and had multiplied pestilence, and famine, and despair upon the people. Therefore his people turned against us Jews, who are all people's dogs. Why not? Lastly the Barons and the people rose together against the King because of his cruelties. Nay – nay – the Barons did not love the people, but they saw that if the King cut up and destroyed the common people, he would presently destroy the Barons. They joined then, as cats and pigs will join to slay a

'But at the day's end – doors shut, candles lit . . . '

snake. I kept the accounts, and I watched all these things, for I remembered the Prophecy.

'A great gathering of Barons (to most of whom we had lent money) came to Bury, and there, after much talk and a thousand runnings-about, they made a roll of the New Laws that they would force on the King. If he swore to keep those Laws, they would allow him a little money. That was the King's God – Money – to waste. They showed us the roll of the New Laws. Why not? We had lent them money. We knew all their counsels – we Jews shivering behind our doors in Bury.' He threw out his hands suddenly. 'We did not seek to be paid *all* in money. We sought Power – Power – Power! That is *our* God in our captivity. Power to use!

'I said to Elias: "These New Laws are good. Lend no more money to the King: so long as he has money he will lie and slay the people."

' "Nay," said Elias. "I know this people. They are madly cruel. Better one King than a thousand butchers. I have lent a little money to the Barons, or they would torture us, but my most I will lend to the King. He hath promised me a place near him at Court, where my wife and I shall be safe."

' "But if the King be made to keep these New Laws," I said, "the land will have peace, and our trade will grow. If we lend he will fight again."

' "Who made thee a Lawgiver in England?" said Elias. "*I* know this people. Let the dogs tear one another! I will lend the King ten thousand pieces of gold, and he can fight the Barons at his pleasure."

' "There are not two thousand pieces of gold in all England this summer," I said, for I kept the accounts, and I knew how the earth's gold moved – that wonderful underground river. Elias barred home the windows, and, his hands about his mouth, he told me how, when he was trading with small wares in a French ship, he had come to the Castle of Pevensey.'

'Oh!' said Dan. 'Pevensey again!' and looked at Una, who nodded and skipped.

'There, after they had scattered his pack up and down the Great Hall, some young knights carried him to an upper room, and dropped him into a well in a wall, that rose and fell with the tide. They called him Joseph, and threw torches at his wet head. Why not?'

'Why, of course!' cried Dan. 'Didn't you know it was – ' Puck held up his hand to stop him, and Kadmiel, who never noticed, went on.

'When the tide dropped he thought he stood on old armour, but feeling with his toes, he raked up bar on bar of soft gold. Some wicked treasure of the old days put away, and the secret cut off by the sword. I have heard the like before.'

'So have we,' Una whispered. 'But it wasn't wicked a bit.'

'Elias took a little of the stuff with him, and thrice yearly he would return to Pevensey as a chapman, selling at no price or profit, till they suffered him to sleep in the empty room, where he would plumb and grope, and steal away a few bars. The great store of it still remained, and by long brooding he had come to look on it as his own. Yet when we thought how we should lift and convey it, we saw no way. This was before the Word of the Lord had come to me. A walled fortress possessed by Normans; in the midst a forty-foot tide-well out of which to remove secretly many horse-loads of gold! Hopeless! So Elias wept. Adah, his wife, wept too. She had hoped to stand beside the Queen's Christian tiring-maids at Court when the King should give them that place at Court which he had promised. Why not? She was born in England – an odious woman.

'The present evil to us was that Elias, out of his strong folly, had, as it were, promised the King that he would arm him with more gold. Wherefore the King in his camp stopped his ears against the Barons and the people. Wherefore men died daily. Adah so desired her place at Court, she besought Elias to tell the King where the treasure lay, that the King might take it by force, and – they would trust in his gratitude. Why not? This Elias refused to do, for he looked on the gold as his own. They quarrelled, and they wept at the evening meal, and late in the night came one Langton – a priest, almost learned – to borrow more money for the Barons. Elias and Adah went to their chamber.'

Kadmiel laughed scornfully in his beard. The shots across the valley stopped as the shooting party changed their ground for the last beat.

'So it was I, not Elias,' he went on quietly, 'that made terms with Langton touching the fortieth of the New Laws.'

'What terms?' said Puck quickly. 'The Fortieth of the Great Charter says: "To none will we sell, refuse, or delay right or justice." '

'True, but the Barons had written first: *To no free man*. It cost me two hundred broad pieces of gold to change those narrow words. Langton, the priest, understood. "Jew though thou art," said he, "the change is just, and if ever Christian and Jew came to be equal in England thy people may thank thee." Then he went out stealthily, as men do who deal with Israel by night. I think he spent my gift upon his altar. Why not? I have spoken with Langton. He was such a man as I might have been if – if we Jews had been a people. But yet, in many things, a child.

'I heard Elias and Adah abovestairs quarrel, and, knowing the woman was the stronger, I saw that Elias would tell the King of the gold and that the King would continue in his stubbornness. Therefore I saw that the gold must be put away from the reach of any man. Of a sudden, the Word of the Lord came to me saying, "The Morning is come, O thou that dwellest in the land." '

Kadmiel halted, all black against the pale green sky beyond the wood – a huge robed figure, like the Moses in the picture-Bible.

'I rose. I went out, and as I shut the door on that House of Foolishness, the woman looked from the window and whispered, "I have prevailed on my husband to tell the King!" I answered: "There is no need. The Lord is with me."

'In that hour the Lord gave me full understanding of all that I must do; and His Hand covered me in my ways. First I went to London, to a physician of our people, who sold me certain drugs that I needed. You shall see why. Thence I went swiftly to Pevensey. Men fought all around me, for there were neither rulers nor judges in the abominable land. Yet when I walked by them they cried out that I was one Ahasuerus, a Jew, condemned, as they believe, to live for ever, and they fled from me everyways. Thus the Lord saved me for my work, and at Pevensey I bought me a little boat and moored it on the mud beneath the Marsh-gate of the Castle. That also God showed me.'

He was as calm as though he were speaking of some stranger, and his voice filled the little bare wood with rolling music.

'I cast' – his hand went to his breast, and again the strange jewel gleamed – 'I cast the drugs which I had prepared into the common well of the Castle. Nay, I did no harm. The more we physicians know, the less do we do. Only the fool says: "I dare." I caused a blotched and itching rash to break out upon their skins, but I knew it would fade in fifteen days. I did not stretch out my hand against their life. They in the Castle thought it was the Plague, and they ran out, taking with them their very dogs.

'A Christian physician, seeing that I was a Jew and a stranger, vowed that I had brought the sickness from London. This is the one time I have ever heard a Christian leech speak truth of any disease. Thereupon the people beat me, but a merciful woman said: "Do not kill him now. Push him into our Castle with his Plague, and if, as he says, it will abate on the fifteenth day, we can kill him then." Why not? They drove me across the drawbridge of the Castle, and fled back to their booths. Thus I came to be alone with the treasure.'

'But did you know this was all going to happen just right?' said Una.

'My Prophecy was that I should be a Lawgiver to a People of a strange land and a hard speech. I knew I should not die. I washed my cuts. I found the tide-well in the wall, and from Sabbath to Sabbath I dove and dug there in that empty, Christian-smelling fortress. Hé! I spoiled the Egyptians! Hé! If they had only known! I drew up many good loads of gold, which I loaded by night into my boat. There had been gold dust too, but that had been washed out by the tides.'

'Didn't you ever wonder who had put it there?' said Dan, stealing a glance at Puck's calm, dark face under the hood of his gown. Puck shook his head and pursed his lips.

'Often; for the gold was new to me,' Kadmiel replied. 'I know the Golds. I can judge them in the dark; but this was heavier and redder than any we deal in. Perhaps it was the very gold of Parvaim. Eh, why not? It went to my heart to heave it on to the mud, but I saw well that if the evil thing remained, or if even the hope of finding it remained, the King would not sign the New Laws, and the land would perish.'

'Oh, Marvel!' said Puck, beneath his breath, rustling in the dead leaves.

'When the boat was loaded I washed my hands seven times, and pared beneath my nails, for I would not keep one grain. I went out by the little gate where the Castle's refuse is thrown. I dared not hoist sail lest men should see

'They drove me across the drawbridge of the Castle, and fled back to their booths.'

me; but the Lord commanded the tide to bear me carefully, and I was far from land before the morning.'

'Weren't you afraid?' said Una.

'Why? There were no Christians in the boat. At sunrise I made my prayer, and cast the gold – all – all that gold – into the deep sea! A King's ransom – no, the ransom of a People! When I had loosed hold of the last bar, the Lord commanded the tide to return me to a haven at the mouth of a river, and thence I walked across a wilderness to Lewes, where I have brethren. They opened the door to me, and they say – I had not eaten for two days – they say that I fell across the threshold, crying: "I have sunk an army with horsemen in the sea!" '

'But you hadn't,' said Una. 'Oh, yes! I see! You meant that King John might have spent it on that?'

'Even so,' said Kadmiel.

The firing broke out again close behind them. The pheasants poured over the top of a belt of tall firs. They could see young Mr Meyer, in his new yellow gaiters, very busy and excited at the end of the line, and they could hear the thud of the falling birds.

'But what did Elias of Bury do?' Puck demanded. 'He had promised money to the King.'

Kadmiel smiled grimly. 'I sent him word from London that the Lord was on my side. When he heard that the Plague had broken out in Pevensey, and that a Jew had been thrust into the Castle to cure it, he understood my word was true. He and Adah hurried to Lewes and asked me for an accounting. He still looked on the gold as his own. I told them where I had laid it, and I gave them full leave to pick it up . . . Eh, well! The curses of a fool and the dust of a journey are two things no wise man can escape . . . But I pitied Elias! The King was wroth with him because he could not lend; the Barons were wroth too because they heard that he would have lent to the King; and Adah was wroth with him because she was an odious woman. They took ship from Lewes to Spain. That was wise!'

'And you? Did you see the signing of the Law at Runnymede?' said Puck, as Kadmiel laughed noiselessly.

'Nay. Who am I to meddle with things too high for me? I returned to Bury, and lent money on the autumn crops. Why not?'

There was a crackle overhead. A cock-pheasant that had sheered aside after being hit spattered down almost on top of them, driving up the dry leaves like a shell. Flora and Folly threw themselves at it; the children rushed forward, and when they had beaten them off and smoothed down the plumage Kadmiel had disappeared.

'Well,' said Puck calmly, 'what did you think of it? Weland gave the Sword! The Sword gave the Treasure, and the Treasure gave the Law. It's as natural as an oak growing.'

'I don't understand. Didn't he know it was Sir Richard's old treasure?' said

Dan. 'And why did Sir Richard and Brother Hugh leave it lying about? And – and – '

'Never mind,' said Una politely. 'He'll let us come and go and look and know another time. Won't you, Puck?'

'Another time maybe,' Puck answered. 'Brr! It's cold – and late. I'll race you towards home!'

They hurried down into the sheltered valley. The sun had almost sunk behind Cherry Clack, the trodden ground by the cattle-gates was freezing at the edges, and the new-waked north wind blew the night on them from over the hills. They picked up their feet and flew across the browned pastures, and when they halted, panting in the steam of their own breath, the dead leaves whirled up behind them. There was Oak and Ash and Thorn enough in that year-end shower to magic away a thousand memories.

So they trotted to the brook at the bottom of the lawn, wondering why Flora and Folly had missed the quarry-hole fox.

Old Hobden was just finishing some hedge-work. They saw his white smock glimmer in the twilight where he faggoted the rubbish.

'Winter, he's come, I reckon, Mus' Dan,' he called. 'Hard times now till Heffle Cuckoo Fair. Yes, we'll all be glad to see the Old Woman let the Cuckoo out o' the basket for to start lawful Spring in England.'

They heard a crash, and a stamp and a splash of water as though a heavy old cow were crossing almost under their noses.

Hobden ran forward angrily to the ford.

'Gleason's bull again, playin' Robin all over the Farm! Oh, look, Mus' Dan – his great footmark as big as a trencher. No bounds to his impidence! He might count himself to be a man or – or Somebody – '

A voice the other side of the brook boomed:

> 'I wonder who his cloak would turn
>   When Puck had led him round,
>   Or where those walking fires would burn – '

Then the children went in singing 'Farewell, Rewards and Fairies' at the tops of their voices. They had forgotten that they had not even said good-night to Puck.

The Children's Song

Land of our Birth, we pledge to thee
Our love and toil in the years to be;
When we are grown and take our place
As men and women with our race.

Father in Heaven Who lovest all,
Oh, help Thy children when they call;
That they may build from age to age
An undefiled heritage.

Teach us to bear the yoke in youth,
With steadfastness and careful truth;
That, in our time, Thy Grace may give
The Truth whereby the Nations live.

Teach us to rule ourselves alway,
Controlled and cleanly night and day;
That we may bring, if need arise,
No maimed or worthless sacrifice.

Teach us to look in all our ends,
On Thee for judge, and not our friends;
That we, with Thee, may walk uncowed
By fear or favour of the crowd.

Teach us the Strength that cannot seek,
By deed or thought, to hurt the weak;
That, under Thee, we may possess
Man's strength to comfort man's distress.

Teach us Delight in simple things,
And Mirth that has no bitter springs;
Forgiveness free of evil done,
And Love to all men 'neath the sun!

Land of our Birth, our faith, our pride,
For whose dear sake our fathers died;
O Motherland, we pledge to thee
Head, heart and hand through the years to be!

REWARDS AND FAIRIES

Contents

A Charm

Take of English earth as much
As either hand may rightly clutch.
In the taking of it breathe
A prayer for all who lie beneath –
Not the great nor well-bespoke,
But the mere uncounted folk
Of whose life and death is nought
Of lamentations or report.
   Lay that earth upon thy heart,
   And thy sickness shall depart!

It shall sweeten and make whole
Fevered breath and festered soul;
It shall mightily restrain
Over-busy hand and brain;
It shall ease thy mortal strife
'Gainst the immortal woe of life,
   Till thyself restored shall prove
   By what grace the heavens do move.

Take of English flowers these –
Spring's full-faced primroses,
Summer's wild wide-hearted rose,
Autumn's wallflower of the close,
And, thy darkness to illume,
Winter's bee-thronged ivy-bloom.
Seek and serve them where they bide
From Candlemas to Christmastide,
   For these simples used aright
   Shall restore a failing sight.

These shall cleanse and purify
Webbed and inward-turning eye;
These shall show thee treasure hid,
Thy familiar fields amid,
At thy threshold, on thy hearth,
Or about thy daily path;
   And reveal (which is thy need)
   Every man a king indeed!

Introduction

Once upon a time, Dan and Una, brother and sister, living in the English country, had the good fortune to meet with Puck, *alias* Robin Goodfellow, *alias* Nick o' Lincoln, *alias* Lob-lie-by-the-Fire, the last survivor in England of those whom mortals call fairies. Their proper name, of course, is the 'People of the Hills'. This Puck, by means of the magic of oak, ash and thorn, gave the children power

> To see what they should see and hear what they should hear,
> Though it should have happened three thousand year.

The result was that from time to time, and in different places on the farm and in the fields and in the country about, they saw and talked to some rather interesting people. One of these, for instance, was a knight of the Norman Conquest, another a young centurion of a Roman legion stationed in England, another a builder and decorator of King Henry VII's time; and so on and so forth, as I have tried to explain in a book called *Puck of Pook's Hill*.

A year or so later, the children met Puck once more, and though they were then older and wiser, and wore boots regularly instead of going barefooted when they got the chance, Puck was as kind to them as ever, and introduced them to more people of the old days.

He was careful, of course, to take away their memory of their walks and conversations afterwards, but otherwise he did not interfere; and Dan and Una would find the strangest sort of persons in their gardens or woods.

In the stories that follow I am trying to tell something about those people.

COLD IRON

When Dan and Una had arranged to go out before breakfast, they did not remember that it was Midsummer Morning. They only wanted to see the otter which, old Hobden said, had been fishing their brook for weeks; and early morning was the time to surprise him. As they tiptoed out of the house into the wonderful stillness, the church clock struck five. Dan took a few steps across the dew-blobbed lawn, and looked at his black footprints.

'I think we ought to be kind to our poor boots,' he said. 'They'll get horrid wet.'

It was their first summer in boots, and they hated them, so they took them off, and slung them round their necks, and paddled joyfully over the dripping turf where the shadows lay the wrong way, like evening in the East.

The sun was well up and warm, but by the brook the last of the night mist still fumed off the water. They picked up the chain of otter's footprints on the mud, and followed it from the bank, between the weeds and the drenched mowing, while the birds shouted with surprise. Then the track left the brook and became a smear, as though a log had been dragged along.

They traced it into Three Cows Meadow, over the mill-sluice to the forge, round Hobden's garden, and then up the slope till it ran out on the short turf and fern of Pook's Hill, and they heard the cock-pheasants crowing in the woods behind them.

'No use!' said Dan, questing like a puzzled hound. 'The dew's drying off, and old Hobden says otters'll travel for miles.'

'I'm sure we've travelled miles.' Una fanned herself with her hat. 'How still it is! It's going to be a regular roaster.' She looked down the valley, where no chimney yet smoked.

'Hobden's up!' Dan pointed to the open door of the forge cottage. 'What d'you suppose he has for breakfast?'

'One of *them*. He says they eat good all times of the year.' Una jerked her head at some stately pheasants going down to the brook for a drink.

A few steps farther on a fox broke almost under their bare feet, yapped, and trotted off.

'Ah, Mus' Reynolds – Mus' Reynolds' – Dan was quoting from old Hobden – 'if I knowed all you knowed, I'd know something.'*

'I say,' Una lowered her voice, 'you know that funny feeling of things having happened before. I felt it when you said "Mus' Reynolds". '

* See 'The Winged Hats' in *Puck of Pook's Hill*.

'So did I,' Dan began. 'What is it?'

They faced each other, stammering with excitement.

'Wait a shake! I'll remember in a minute. Wasn't it something about a fox – last year? Oh, I nearly had it then!' Dan cried.

'Be quiet!' said Una, prancing excitedly. 'There was something happened before we met the fox last year. Hills! Broken Hills – the play at the theatre – see what you see – '

'I remember now,' Dan shouted. 'It's as plain as the nose on your face – Pook's Hill – Puck's Hill – Puck!'

'I remember, too,' said Una. 'And it's Midsummer Day again!' The young fern on a knoll rustled, and Puck walked out, chewing a green-topped rush.

'Good Midsummer Morning to you! Here's a happy meeting,' said he. They shook hands all round, and asked questions.

'You've wintered well,' he said after a while, and looked them up and down. 'Nothing much wrong with you, seemingly.'

'They've put us into boots,' said Una. 'Look at my feet – they're all pale white, and my toes are squidged together awfully.'

'Yes – boots make a difference.' Puck wriggled his brown, square, hairy foot, and cropped a dandelion flower between the big toe and the next.

'I could do that – last year,' Dan said dismally, as he tried and failed. 'And boots simply ruin one's climbing.'

'There must be some advantage to them, I suppose,' said Puck, 'or folk wouldn't wear them. Shall we come this way?'

They sauntered along side by side till they reached the gate at the far end of the hillside. Here they halted, just like cattle, and let the sun warm their backs while they listened to the flies in the wood.

'Little Lindens is awake,' said Una, as she hung with her chin on the top rail. 'See the chimney smoke?'

'Today's Thursday, isn't it?' Puck turned to look at the old pink farmhouse across the little valley. 'Mrs Vincey's baking day. Bread should rise well this weather.' He yawned, and that set them both yawning.

The bracken about rustled and ticked and shook in every direction. They felt that little crowds were stealing past.

'Doesn't that sound like – er – the People of the Hills?' said Una.

'It's the birds and wild things drawing up to the woods before people get about,' said Puck, as though he were Ridley the keeper.

'Oh, we know that. I only said it sounded like.'

'As I remember 'em, the People of the Hills used to make more noise. They'd settle down for the day rather like small birds settling down for the night. But that was in the days when they carried the high hand. Oh, me! The deeds that I've had act and part in, you'd scarcely believe!'

'I like that!' said Dan. 'After all you told us last year, too!'

'Only, the minute you went away, you made us forget everything,' said Una.

Puck laughed and shook his head. 'I shall this year, too. I've given you seisin of Old England, and I've taken away your doubt and fear, but your memory and remembrance between whiles I'll keep where old Billy Trott kept his night-lines – and that's where he could draw 'em up and hide 'em at need. Does that suit?' He twinkled mischievously.

'It's got to suit,' said Una, and laughed. 'We can't magic back at you.' She folded her arms and leaned against the gate. 'Suppose, now, you wanted to magic me into something – an otter? Could you?'

'Not with those boots round your neck.'

'I'll take them off.' She threw them on the turf. Dan's followed immediately. 'Now!' she said.

'Less than ever now you've trusted me. Where there's true faith, there's no call for magic.' Puck's slow smile broadened all over his face.

'But what have boots to do with it?' said Una, perching on the gate.

'There's Cold Iron in them,' said Puck, and settled beside her. 'Nails in the soles, I mean. It makes a difference.'

'How?'

'Can't you feel it does? You wouldn't like to go back to bare feet again, same as last year, would you? Not really?'

'No–o. I suppose I shouldn't – not for always. I'm growing up, you know,' said Una.

'But you told us last year, in the Long Slip – at the theatre – that you didn't mind Cold Iron,' said Dan.

'*I* don't; but folks in housen, as the People of the Hills call them, must be ruled by Cold Iron. Folk in housen are born on the near side of Cold Iron – there's iron in every man's house, isn't there? They handle Cold Iron every day of their lives, and their fortune's made or spoilt by Cold Iron in some shape or other. That's how it goes with flesh and blood, and one can't prevent it.'

'I don't quite see. How do you mean?' said Dan.

'It would take me some time to tell you.'

'Oh, it's ever so long to breakfast,' said Dan. 'We looked in the larder before we came out.' He unpocketed one big hunk of bread and Una another, which they shared with Puck.

'That's Little Lindens' baking,' he said, as his white teeth sank in it. 'I know Mrs Vincey's hand.' He ate with a slow sideways thrust and grind, just like old Hobden, and, like Hobden, hardly dropped a crumb. The sun flashed on Little Lindens' windows, and the cloudless sky grew stiller and hotter in the valley.

'Ah – Cold Iron,' he said at last to the impatient children. 'Folk in housen, as the People of the Hills say, grow careless about Cold Iron. They'll nail the horseshoe over the front door, and forget to put it over the back. Then, some time or other, the People of the Hills slip in, find the cradle-babe in the corner, and – '

'Oh, I know. Steal it and leave a changeling,' Una cried.

'No,' said Puck firmly. 'All that talk of changelings is people's excuse for their own neglect. Never believe 'em. I'd whip 'em at the cart-tail through three parishes if I had my way.'

'But they don't do it now,' said Una.

'Whip, or neglect children? Umm! Some folks and some fields never alter. But the People of the Hills didn't work any changeling tricks. They'd tiptoe in and whisper and weave round the cradle-babe in the chimney-corner – a fag-end of a charm here, or half a spell there – like kettles singing; but when the babe's mind came to bud out afterwards, it would act differently from other people in its station. That's no advantage to man or maid. So I wouldn't allow it with my folks' babies here. I told Sir Huon so once.'

'Who was Sir Huon?' Dan asked, and Puck turned on him in quiet astonishment.

'Sir Huon of Bordeaux – he succeeded King Oberon. He had been a bold knight once, but he was lost on the road to Babylon, a long while back. Have you ever heard "How many miles to Babylon?" '

'Of course,' said Dan, flushing.

'Well, Sir Huon was young when that song was new. But about tricks on mortal babies. I said to Sir Huon in the fern here, on just such a morning as this: "If you crave to act and influence on folk in housen, which I know is your desire, why don't you take some human cradle-babe by fair dealing, and bring him up among yourselves on the far side of Cold Iron – as Oberon did in time past? Then you could make him a splendid fortune, and send him out into the world."

' "Time past is past time," says Sir Huon. "I doubt if we could do it. For one thing, the babe would have to be taken without wronging man, woman, or child. For another, he'd have to be born on the far side of Cold Iron – in some house where no Cold Iron ever stood; and for yet the third, he'd have to be kept from Cold Iron all his days till we let him find his fortune. No, it's not easy," he said, and he rode off, thinking. You see, Sir Huon had been a man once.

'I happened to attend Lewes Market next Woden's Day even, and watched the slaves being sold there – same as pigs are sold at Robertsbridge Market nowadays. Only, the pigs have rings in their noses, and the slaves had rings round their necks.'

'What sort of rings?' said Dan.

'A ring of Cold Iron, four fingers wide, and a thumb thick, just like a quoit, but with a snap to it for to snap round the slave's neck. They used to do a big trade in slave-rings at the forge here, and ship them to all parts of Old England, packed in oak sawdust. But, as I was saying, there was a farmer out of the Weald who had bought a woman with a babe in her arms, and he didn't want any encumbrances to her driving his beasts home for him.'

'Beast himself!' said Una, and kicked her bare heel on the gate.

'So he blamed the auctioneer. "It's none o' my baby," the wench puts in. "I took it off a woman in our gang who died on Terrible Down yesterday." "I'll take it off to the church then," says the farmer. "Mother Church'll make a monk of it, and we'll step along home." '

'It was dusk then. He slipped down to St Pancras' Church, and laid the babe at the cold chapel door. I breathed on the back of his stooping neck – and – I've *heard* he never could be warm at any fire afterwards. I should have been surprised if he could! Then I whipped up the babe, and came flying home here like a bat to his belfry.

'On the dewy break of morning of Thor's own day – just such a day as this – I laid the babe outside the hill here, and the people flocked up and wondered at the sight.

' "You've brought him, then?" Sir Huon said, staring like any mortal man.

' "Yes, and he's brought his mouth with him, too," I said. The babe was crying loud for his breakfast.

' " What is he?" says Sir Huon, when the womenfolk had drawn him under to feed him.

' "Full Moon and Morning Star may know," I says. "*I* don't. By what I could make out of him in the moonlight, he's without brand or blemish. I'll answer for it that he's born on the far side of Cold Iron, for he was born under a shaw on Terrible Down, and I've wronged neither man, woman nor child in taking him, for he is the son of a dead slave-woman.

' " All to the good, Robin," Sir Huon said. "He'll be the less anxious to leave us. Oh, we'll give him a splendid fortune, and we shall act and influence on folk in housen as we have always craved." His lady came up then, and drew him under to watch the babe's wonderful doings.'

'Who was his lady?' said Dan.

'The Lady Esclairmonde. She had been a woman once, till she followed Sir Huon across the fern, as we say. Babies are no special treat to me – I've watched too many of them – so I stayed on the hill. Presently I heard hammering down at the forge there.' Puck pointed towards Hobden's cottage. 'It was too early for any workmen, but it passed through my mind that the breaking day was Thor's own day. A slow north-east wind blew up and set the oaks sawing and fretting in a way I remembered; so I slipped over to see what I could see.'

'And what did you see?'

'A smith forging something or other out of Cold Iron. When it was finished, he weighed it in his hand (his back was towards me), and tossed it from him a longish quoit-throw down the valley. I saw Cold Iron flash in the sun, but I couldn't quite make out where it fell. *That* didn't trouble me. I knew it would be found sooner or later by someone.'

'How did you know?' Dan went on.

'Because I knew the smith that made it,' said Puck quietly.

'Wayland Smith?'* Una suggested.

---

* See 'Weland's Sword' in *Puck of Pook's Hill.*

'No. I should have passed the time o' day with Wayland Smith, of course. This other was different. So' – Puck made a queer crescent in the air with his finger – 'I counted the blades of grass under my nose till the wind dropped and he had gone – he and his hammer.'

'Was it Thor then?' Una murmured under her breath.

'Who else? It was Thor's own day.' Puck repeated the sign. 'I didn't tell Sir Huon or his lady what I'd seen. Borrow trouble for yourself if that's your nature, but don't lend it to your neighbours. Moreover, I might have been mistaken about the smith's work. He might have been making things for mere amusement, though it wasn't like him, or he might have thrown away an old piece of made iron. One can never be sure. So I held my tongue and enjoyed the babe. He was a wonderful child – and the People of the Hills were so set on him, they wouldn't have believed me. He took to me wonderfully. As soon as he could walk he'd putter forth with me all about my hill here. Fern makes soft falling! He knew when day broke on earth above, for he'd thump, thump, thump, like an old buck-rabbit in a bury, and I'd hear him say "Opy!" till someone who knew the charm let him out, and then it would be "Robin! Robin!" all round Robin Hood's barn, as we say, till he'd found me.'

'The dear!' said Una. 'I'd like to have seen him!'

'Yes, he was a boy. And when it came to learning his words – spells and suchlike – he'd sit on the hill in the long shadows, worrying out bits of charms to try on passers-by. And when the bird flew to him, or the tree bowed to him for pure love's sake (like everything else on my hill), he'd shout, "Robin! Look – see! Look, see, Robin!" and sputter out some spell or other that they had taught him, *all* wrong end first, till I hadn't the heart to tell him it was his own dear self and not the words that worked the wonder. When he got more abreast of his words, and could cast spells for sure, as we say, he took more and more notice of things and people in the world. People, of course, always drew him, for he was mortal all through.

'Seeing that he was free to move among folk in housen, under or over Cold Iron, I used to take him along with me, night-walking, where he could watch folk, and I could keep him from touching Cold Iron. That wasn't so difficult as it sounds, because there are plenty of things besides Cold Iron in housen to catch a boy's fancy. He *was* a handful, though! I shan't forget when I took him to Little Lindens – his first night under a roof. The smell of the rush-lights and the bacon on the beams – they were stuffing a feather-bed too, and it was a drizzling warm night – got into his head. Before I could stop him – we were hiding in the bakehouse – he'd whipped up a storm of wildfire, with flashlights and voices, which sent the folk shrieking into the garden, and a girl overset a hive there, and – of course *he* didn't know till then such things could touch him – he got badly stung, and came home with his face looking like kidney potatoes!

'You can imagine how angry Sir Huon and Lady Esclairmonde were with poor Robin! They said the boy was never to be trusted with me night-walking any more – and he took about as much notice of their order as he did of the bee-stings. Night after night, as soon as it was dark, I'd pick up his whistle in the wet fern, and off we'd flit together among folk in housen till break of day – he asking questions, and I answering according to my knowledge. Then we fell into mischief again!' Puck shook till the gate rattled.

'We came across a man up at Brightling who was beating his wife with a bat in the garden. I was just going to toss the man over his own woodlump when the boy jumped the hedge and ran at him. Of course the woman took her husband's part, and while the man beat him, the woman scratted his face. It wasn't till I danced among the cabbages like Brightling Beacon all ablaze that they gave up and ran indoors. The boy's fine green-and-gold clothes were torn all to pieces, and he had been welted in twenty places with the man's bat, and scratted by the woman's nails to pieces. He looked like a Robertsbridge hopper on a Monday morning.

' "Robin," said he, while I was trying to clean him down with a bunch of hay, "I don't quite understand folk in housen. I went to help that old woman, and she hit me, Robin!"

' "What else did you expect?" I said. "That was the one time when you might have worked one of your charms, instead of running into three times your weight."

' "I didn't think," he says. "But I caught the man one on the head that was as good as any charm. Did you see it work, Robin?"

' "Mind your nose," I said. "Bleed it on a dockleaf – not your sleeve, for pity's sake." I knew what the Lady Esclairmonde would say.

'*He* didn't care. He was as happy as a gypsy with a stolen pony, and the front part of his gold coat, all blood and grass stains, looked like ancient sacrifices.

'Of course the People of the Hills laid the blame on me. The boy could do nothing wrong, in their eyes.

' "You are bringing him up to act and influence on folk in housen, when you're ready to let him go," I said. "Now he's begun to do it, why do you cry shame on me? That's no shame. It's his nature drawing him to his kind."

' "But we don't want him to begin *that* way," the Lady Esclairmonde said. "We intend a splendid fortune for him – not your flitter-by-night, hedge-jumping, gypsy-work."

' "I don't blame you, Robin," says Sir Huon, "but I *do* think you might look after the boy more closely."

' "I've kept him away from Cold Iron these sixteen years," I said. "You know as well as I do, the first time he touches Cold Iron he'll find his own fortune, in spite of everything you intend for him. You owe me something for that."

'Sir Huon, having been a man, was going to allow me the right of it, but the Lady Esclairmonde, being the Mother of all Mothers, over-persuaded him.

' "We're very grateful," Sir Huon said, "but we think that just for the present you are about too much with him on the hill."

' "Though you have said it," I said, "I will give you a second chance." I did not like being called to account for my doings on my own hill. I wouldn't have stood it even that far except I loved the boy.

' "No! No!" says the Lady Esclairmonde. "He's never any trouble when he's left to me and himself. It's your fault."

' "You have said it," I answered. "Hear me! From now on till the boy has found his fortune, whatever that may be, I vow to you all on my hill, by oak and ash and thorn, *and* by the hammer of Asa Thor" ' – again Puck made that curious double-cut in the air – ' "that you may leave me out of all your counts and reckonings." Then I went out' – he snapped his fingers – 'like the puff of a candle, and though they called and cried, they made nothing by it. I didn't promise not to keep an eye on the boy, though. I watched him close – close – close!

'When he found what his people had forced me to do, he gave them a piece of his mind, but they all kissed and cried round him, and being only a boy, he came over to their way of thinking (I don't blame him), and called himself unkind and ungrateful; and it all ended in fresh shows and plays, and magics to distract him from folk in housen. Dear heart alive! How he used to call and call on me, and I couldn't answer, or even let him know that I was near!'

'Not even once?' said Una. 'If he was very lonely?'

'No, he couldn't,' said Dan, who had been thinking. 'Didn't you swear by the hammer of Thor that you wouldn't, Puck?'

'By that hammer!' was the deep rumbled reply. Then he came back to his soft speaking voice. 'And the boy *was* lonely, when he couldn't see me any more. He began to try to learn all learning (he had good teachers), but I saw him lift his eyes from the big black books towards folk in housen all the time. He studied song-making (good teachers he had too!), but he sang those songs with his back toward the hill, and his face toward folk. *I* know! I have sat and grieved over him grieving within a rabbit's jump of him. Then he studied the High, Low and Middle Magic. He had promised the Lady Esclairmonde he would never go near folk in housen; so he had to make shows and shadows for his mind to chew on.'

'What sort of shows?' said Dan.

'Just boy's magic as we say. I'll show you some, sometime. It pleased him for the while, and it didn't hurt anyone in particular except a few men coming home late from the taverns. But I knew what it was a sign of, and I followed him like a weasel follows a rabbit. As good a boy as ever lived! I've seen him with Sir Huon and the Lady Esclairmonde stepping just as they stepped to avoid the track of Cold Iron in a furrow, or walking wide of some old ash-tot because a man had left his swop-hook or spade there; and all his heart aching to go straightforward among folk in housen all the time. Oh, a good boy! They always intended a fine fortune for him – but they could never find it in their heart to let him begin. I've heard that many warned them, but they wouldn't be warned. So it happened *as* it happened.

'One hot night I saw the boy roving about here wrapped in his flaming discontents. There was flash on flash against the clouds, and rush on rush of shadows down the valley till the shaws were full of his hounds giving tongue, and the woodways were packed with his knights in armour riding down into the water-mists – all his own magic, of course. Behind them you could see great castles lifting slow and splendid on arches of moonshine, with maidens waving their hands at the windows, which all turned into roaring rivers; and then would come the darkness of his own young heart wiping out the whole slateful. But boy's magic doesn't trouble me – or Merlin's either for that matter. I followed the boy by the flashes and the whirling wildfire of his discontent, and oh, but I grieved for him! Oh, but I grieved for him! He pounded back and forth like a bullock in a strange pasture – sometimes alone – sometimes waist-deep among his shadow-hounds – sometimes leading his shadow-knights on a hawk-winged horse to rescue his shadow-girls. I never guessed he had such magic at his command; but it's often that way with boys.

'Just when the owl comes home for the second time, I saw Sir Huon and the lady ride down my hill, where there's not much magic allowed except mine. They were very pleased at the boy's magic – the valley flared with it – and I heard them settling his splendid fortune when they should find it in their hearts to let him go to act and influence among folk in housen. Sir Huon was for making him a great king somewhere or other, and the lady was for making him a marvellous wise man whom all should praise for his skill and kindness. She was very kind-hearted.

'Of a sudden we saw the flashes of his discontents turned back on the clouds, and his shadow-hounds stopped baying.

' "There's magic fighting magic over yonder," the Lady Esclairmonde cried, reigning up. "Who is against him?"

'I could have told her, but I did not count it any of my business to speak of Asa Thor's comings and goings.'

'How did you know?' said Una.

'A slow north-east wind blew up, sawing and fretting through the oaks in a way I remembered. The wildfire roared up, one last time in one sheet, and snuffed out like a rushlight, and a bucketful of stinging hail fell. We heard the boy walking in the Long Slip – where I first met you.

' "Here, oh, come here!" said the Lady Esclairmonde, and stretched out her arms in the dark.

'He was coming slowly, but he stumbled in the footpath, being, of course, mortal man.

' "Why, what's this?" he said to himself. We three heard him.

' "Hold, lad, hold! 'Ware Cold Iron!" said Sir Huon, and they two swept down like nightjars, crying as they rode.

'I ran at their stirrups, but it was too late. We felt that the boy had touched Cold Iron somewhere in the dark, for the horses of the hill shied off, and whipped round, snorting.

'Then I judged it was time for me to show myself in my own shape; so I did.

' "Whatever it is," I said, "he has taken hold of it. Now we must find out whatever it *is* that he has taken hold of, for that will be his fortune."

' "Come here, Robin," the boy shouted, as soon as he heard my voice. "I don't know what I've hold of."

' "It is in your hands," I called back. "Tell us if it is hard and cold, with jewels atop. For that will be a king's sceptre."

' "Not by a furrow-long," he said, and stooped and tugged in the dark. We heard him.

' "Has it a handle and two cutting edges?" I called. "For that'll be a knight's sword."

' "No, it hasn't," he says. "It's neither ploughshare, whittle, hook nor crook, nor aught I've yet seen men handle." By this time he was scratting in the dirt to prise it up.

' "Whatever it is, you know who put it there, Robin," said Sir Huon to me, "or you would not ask those questions. You should have told me as soon as you knew."

' "What could you or I have done against the smith that made it and laid it for him to find?" I said, and I whispered Sir Huon what I had seen at the forge on Thor's Day, when the babe was first brought to the hill.

' "Oh, goodbye, our dreams!" said Sir Huon. "It's neither sceptre, sword nor plough! Maybe yet it's a bookful of learning, bound with iron clasps. There's a chance for a splendid fortune in that sometimes."

'But we knew we were only speaking to comfort ourselves, and the Lady Esclairmonde, having been a woman, said so.

' "Thur aie! Thor help us!" the boy called. "It is round, without end, Cold Iron, four fingers wide and a thumb thick, and there is writing on the breadth of it."

' "Read the writing if you have the learning," I called. The darkness had lifted by then, and the owl was out over the fern again.

'He called back, reading the runes on the iron:

> "Few can see
> Further forth
> Than when the child
> Meets the Cold Iron."

And there he stood, in clear starlight, with a new, heavy, shining slave-ring round his proud neck.

' "Is this how it goes?" he asked, while the Lady Esclairmonde cried.

' "That is how it goes," I said. He hadn't snapped the catch home yet, though.

' "What fortune does it mean for him?" said Sir Huon, while the boy fingered the ring. "You who walk under Cold Iron, you must tell us and teach us."

' "Tell I can, but teach I cannot," I said. "The virtue of the ring is only that he must go among folk in housen henceforward, doing what they want done, or what he knows they need, all Old England over. Never will he be his own master, nor yet ever any man's. He will get half he gives, and give twice what he gets, till his life's last breath; and if he lays aside his load before he draws that last breath, all his work will go for naught."

' "Oh, cruel, wicked Thor!" cried the Lady Esclairmonde. "Ah, look see, all of you! The catch is still open! He hasn't locked it. He can still take it off. He can still come back. Come back!" She went as near as she dared, but she could not lay hands on Cold Iron. The boy could have taken it off, yes. We waited to see if he would, but he put up his hand, and the snap locked home.

' "What else could I have done?" said he.

' "Surely, then, you will do," I said. "Morning's coming, and if you three have any farewells to make, make them now, for, after sunrise, Cold Iron must be your master."

'So the three sat down, cheek by wet cheek, telling over their farewells till morning light. As good a boy as ever lived, he was.'

'And what happened to him?' asked Dan.

'When morning came, Cold Iron was master of him and his fortune, and he went to work among folk in housen. Presently he came across a maid like-minded with himself, and they were wedded, and had bushels of children, as the saying is. Perhaps you'll meet some of his breed, this year.'

'Thank you,' said Una. 'But what did the poor Lady Esclairmonde do?'

'What *can* you do when Asa Thor lays the Cold Iron in a lad's path? She and Sir Huon were comforted to think they had given the boy a good store of learning to act and influence on folk in housen. For he *was* a good boy! Isn't it getting on for breakfast-time? I'll walk with you a piece.'

When they were well in the centre of the bone-dry fern, Dan nudged Una, who stopped and put on a boot as quickly as she could.

'Now,' she said, 'you can't get any oak, ash and thorn leaves from here, and' – she balanced wildly on one leg – 'I'm standing on Cold Iron. What'll you do if we don't go away?'

'E–eh? Of all mortal impudence!' said Puck, as Dan, also in one boot, grabbed his sister's hand to steady himself. He walked round them, shaking with delight. 'You think I can only work with a handful of dead leaves? This comes of taking away your doubt and fear! I'll show you!'

* * *

A minute later they charged into old Hobden at his simple breakfast of cold roast pheasant, shouting that there was a wasps' nest in the fern which they had nearly stepped on, and asking him to come and smoke it out.

'It's too early for wops-nestës, an' I don't go diggin' in the hill, not for shillin's,' said the old man placidly. 'You've a thorn in your foot, Miss Una. Sit down, and put on your t'other boot. You're too old to be caperin' barefoot on an empty stomach. Stay it with this chicken o' mine.'

Cold Iron

'Gold is for the mistress – silver for the maid!
Copper for the craftsman cunning at his trade.'
'Good!' said the baron, sitting in his hall,
'But iron – Cold Iron – is master of them all!'

So he made rebellion 'gainst the king his liege,
Camped before his citadel and summoned it to siege –
'Nay!' said the cannoneer on the castle wall,
'But iron – Cold Iron – shall be master of you all!'

Woe for the baron and his knights so strong,
When the cruel cannon-balls laid 'em all along!
He was taken prisoner, he was cast in thrall,
And iron – Cold Iron – was master of it all!

Yet his king spake kindly (oh, how kind a lord!):
'What if I release thee now and give thee back thy sword?'
'Nay!' said the baron, 'mock not at my fall,
For iron – Cold Iron – is master of men all.'

'Tears are for the craven, prayers are for the clown –
Halters for the silly neck that cannot keep a crown.'
'As my loss is grievous, so my hope is small,
For iron – Cold Iron – must be master of men all!'

Yet his king made answer (few such kings there be!):
'Here is bread and here is wine – sit and sup with me.
Eat and drink in Mary's name, the whiles I do recall
How iron – Cold Iron – can be master of men all!'

He took the wine and blessed it; he blessed and brake the bread.
With his own hands he served them, and presently he said:
'Look! These hands they pierced with nails outside my city wall
Show iron – Cold Iron – to be master of men all!

'Wounds are for the desperate, blows are for the strong,
Balm and oil for weary hearts all cut and bruised with wrong.
I forgive thy treason – I redeem thy fall –
For iron – Cold Iron – must be master of men all!'

'Crowns are for the valiant – sceptres for the bold!
Thrones and powers for mighty men who dare to take and hold.'
'Nay!' said the baron, kneeling in his hall,
'But iron – Cold Iron – is master of man all!
    Iron, out of Calvary, is master of man all!'

GLORIANA

The Two Cousins

Valour and Innocence
Have latterly gone hence
To certain death by certain shame attended.
Envy – ah! even to tears! –
The fortune of their years
Which, though so few, yet so divinely ended.

Scarce had they lifted up
Life's full and fiery cup,
Than they had set it down untouched before them.
Before their day arose
They beckoned it to close –
Close in destruction and confusion o'er them.

They did not stay to ask
What prize should crown their task,
Well sure that prize was such as no man strives for;
But passed into eclipse,
Her kiss upon their lips –
Even Belphoebe's, whom they gave their lives for!

Gloriana

Willow Shaw, the little fenced wood where the hop-poles are stacked like Indian wigwams, had been given to Dan and Una for their very own kingdom when they were quite small. As they grew older, they contrived to keep it most particularly private. Even Phillips, the gardener, told them every time that he came in to take a hop-pole for his beans, and old Hobden would no more have thought of setting his rabbit-wires there without leave, given fresh each spring, than he would have torn down the calico and marking-ink notice on the big willow which said: GROWN-UPS NOT ALLOWED IN THE KINGDOM UNLESS BROUGHT.

Now you can understand their indignation when, one blowy July afternoon, as they were going up for a potato-roast, they saw somebody moving among the trees. They hurled themselves over the gate, dropping half the potatoes, and while they were picking them up Puck came out of a wigwam.

'Oh, it's you, is it?' said Una. 'We thought it was people.'

'I saw you were angry – from your legs,' he answered with a grin.

'Well, it's our own kingdom – not counting you, of course.'

'That's rather why I came. A lady here wants to see you.'

'What about?' said Dan cautiously.

'Oh, just kingdoms and things. She knows about kingdoms.'

There was a lady near the fence dressed in a long dark cloak that hid everything except her high red-heeled shoes. Her face was half covered by a black silk-fringed mask, without goggles. And yet she did not look in the least as if she motored.

Puck led them up to her and bowed solemnly. Una made the best dancing-lesson curtsy she could remember. The lady answered with a long, deep, slow, billowy one.

'Since it seems that you are a queen of this kingdom,' she said, 'I can do no less than acknowledge your sovereignty.' She turned sharply on staring Dan. 'What's in your head, lad? Manners?'

'I was thinking how wonderfully you did that curtsy,' he answered.

She laughed a rather shrill laugh. 'You're a courtier already. Do you know anything of dances, wench – or queen, must I say?'

'I've had some lessons, but I can't really dance a bit,' said Una.

'You should learn, then.' The lady moved forward as though she would teach her at once. 'It gives a woman alone among men or her enemies time to think how she shall win or – lose. A woman can only work in man's playtime. Heigho!' She sat down on the bank.

Old Middenboro, the lawnmower pony, stumped across the paddock and hung his sorrowful head over the fence.

'A pleasant kingdom,' said the lady, looking round. 'Well enclosed. And how does your majesty govern it? Who is your minister?'

Una did not quite understand. 'We don't play that,' she said.

'Play?' The lady threw up her hands and laughed.

'We have it for our own, together,' Dan explained.

'And d'you never quarrel, young Burleigh?'

'Sometimes, but then we don't tell.'

The lady nodded. 'I've no brats of my own, but I understand keeping a secret between queens and their ministers. *Ay de mi!* But with no disrespect to present majesty, methinks your realm is small, and therefore likely to be coveted by man and beast. For example' – she pointed to Middenboro – 'yonder old horse, with the face of a Spanish friar – does he never break in?'

'He can't. Old Hobden stops all our gaps for us,' said Una, 'and we let Hobden catch rabbits in the Shaw.'

The lady laughed like a man. 'I see! Hobden catches conies – rabbits – for himself, and guards your defences for you. Does he make a profit out of his coney-catching?'

'We never ask,' said Una. 'Hobden's a particular friend of ours.'

'Hoity-toity!' the lady began angrily. Then she laughed. 'But I forget. It is your kingdom. I knew a maid once that had a larger one than this to defend, and so long as her men kept the fences stopped, she asked 'em no questions either.'

'Was she trying to grow flowers?' said Una.

'No, trees – perdurable trees. Her flowers all withered.' The lady leaned her head on her hand.

'They do if you don't look after them. We've got a few. Would you like to see? I'll fetch you some.' Una ran off to the rank grass in the shade behind the wigwam, and came back with a handful of red flowers. 'Aren't they pretty?' she said. 'They're Virginia stock.'

'Virginia?' said the lady, and lifted them to the fringe of her mask.

'Yes. They come from Virginia. Did your maid ever plant any?'

'Not herself – but her men adventured all over the earth to pluck or to plant flowers for her crown. They judged her worthy of them.'

'And was she?' said Dan cheerfully.

'*Quien sabe?* (who knows?) But, at least, while her men toiled abroad she toiled in England, that they might find a safe home to come back to.'

'And what was she called?'

'Gloriana – Belphoebe – Elizabeth of England.' Her voice changed at each word.

'You mean Queen Bess?' The lady bowed her head a little towards Dan.

'You name her lightly enough, young Burleigh. What might you know of her?' said she.

'Well, I – I've seen the little green shoes she left at Brickwall House – down the road, you know. They're in a glass case – awfully tiny things.'

'Oh, Burleigh, Burleigh!' she laughed. 'You are a courtier too soon.'

'But they are,' Dan insisted. 'As little as dolls' shoes. Did you really know her well?'

'Well. She was a – woman. I've been at her court all my life. Yes, I remember when she danced after the banquet at Brickwall. They say she danced Philip of Spain out of a brand-new kingdom that day. Worth the price of a pair of old shoes – hey?'

She thrust out one foot, and stooped forward to look at its broad flashing buckle.

'You've heard of Philip of Spain – long-suffering Philip,' she said, her eyes still on the shining stones. 'Faith, what some men will endure at some women's hands passes belief! If I had been a man, and a woman had played with me as Elizabeth played with Philip, I would have – ' She nipped off one of the Virginia stocks and held it up between finger and thumb. 'But for all that' – she began to strip the leaves one by one – 'they say – and I am persuaded – that Philip loved her.' She tossed her head sideways.

'I don't quite understand,' said Una.

'The high heavens forbid that you should, wench!' She swept the flowers from her lap and stood up in the rush of shadows that the wind chased through the wood.

'I should like to know about the shoes,' said Dan.

'So ye shall, Burleigh. So ye shall, if ye watch me. 'Twill be as good as a play.'

'We've never been to a play,' said Una.

The lady looked at her and laughed. 'I'll make one for you. Watch! You are to imagine that she – Gloriana, Belphoebe, Elizabeth – has gone on a progress to Rye to comfort her sad heart (maids are often melancholic), and while she halts at Brickwall House, the village – what was its name?' She pushed Puck with her foot.

'Norgem,' he croaked, and squatted by the wigwam.

'Norgem village loyally entertains her with a masque or play, and a Latin oration spoken by the parson, for whose false quantities, if I'd made 'em in my girlhood, I should have been whipped.'

'You whipped?' said Dan.

'Soundly, sirrah, soundly! She stomachs the affront to her scholarship, makes her grateful, gracious thanks from the teeth outwards, thus' – (the lady yawned) – 'oh, a queen may love her subjects in her heart, and yet be dog-wearied of 'em in body and mind – and so sits down' – her skirts foamed about her as she sat – 'to a banquet beneath Brickwall Oak. Here for her sins she is waited upon by – What were the young cockerels' names that served Gloriana at table?'

'Frewens, Courthopes, Fullers, Husseys – ' Puck began.

She held up her long jewelled hand. 'Spare the rest! They were the best blood of Sussex, and by so much the more clumsy in handling the dishes and plates. Wherefore' – she looked funnily over her shoulder – 'you are to think of Gloriana in a green and gold-laced habit, dreadfully expecting that the jostling youths behind her would, of pure jealousy or devotion, spatter it with sauces and wines. The gown was Philip's gift, too! At this happy juncture a queen's messenger, mounted and mired, spurs up the Rye road and delivers her a letter' – she giggled – 'a letter from a good, simple, frantic Spanish gentleman called – Don Philip.'

'That wasn't Philip, King of Spain?' Dan asked.

'Truly, it was. 'Twixt you and me and the bedpost, young Burleigh, these kings and queens are very like men and women, and I've heard they write each other fond, foolish letters that none of their ministers should open.'

'Did her ministers ever open Queen Elizabeth's letters?' said Una.

'Faith, yes! But she'd have done as much for theirs, any day. You are to think of Gloriana, then (they say she had a pretty hand), excusing herself thus to the company – for the queen's time is never her own – and, while the music strikes up, reading Philip's letter, as I do.' She drew a real letter from her pocket, and held it out almost at arm's length, like the old postmistress in the village when she reads telegrams.

'*Hm! Hm! Hm!* Philip writes as ever most lovingly. He says his Gloriana is cold, for which reason he burns for her through a fair written page.' She turned it with a snap. 'What's here? Philip complains that certain of her gentlemen have fought against his generals in the Low Countries. He prays her to hang 'em when they re-enter her realms. (Hm, that's as may be.) Here's a list of burnt shipping slipped between two vows of burning adoration. Oh, poor Philip! His admirals at sea – no less than three of 'em – have been boarded, sacked and scuttled on their lawful voyages by certain English mariners (gentlemen, he will not call them), who are now at large and working more piracies in *his* American ocean, which the Pope gave him. (He and the Pope should guard it, then!) Philip hears, but his devout ears will not credit it, that Gloriana in some fashion countenances these villains' misdeeds, shares in their booty, and – oh, shame! – has even lent them ships royal for their sinful thefts. Therefore he requires (which is a word Gloriana loves not), *requires* that she shall hang 'em when they return to England, and afterwards shall account to him for all the goods and gold they have plundered. A most loving request! If Gloriana will not be Philip's bride, she shall be his broker and his butcher! Should she still be stiff-necked, he writes – see where the pen digged the innocent paper! – that he hath both the means and the intention to be revenged on her. Aha! Now we come to the Spaniard in his shirt!' (She waved the letter merrily.) 'Listen here! Philip will prepare for Gloriana a destruction from the West – a destruction from the West – far exceeding that which Pedro de Avila wrought upon the Huguenots. And he rests and remains, kissing her feet and her hands, her slave, her enemy, or her conqueror, as he shall find that she uses him.'

She thrust back the letter under her cloak and went on acting, but in a softer voice. 'All this while – hark to it – the wind blows through Brickwall Oak, the music plays, and, with the company's eyes upon her, the Queen of England must think what this means. She cannot remember the name of Pedro de Avila, nor what he did to the Huguenots, nor when, nor where. She can only see darkly some dark motion moving in Philip's dark mind, for he hath never written before in this fashion. She must smile above the letter as though it were good news from her ministers – the smile that tires the mouth and the poor heart. What shall she do?' Again her voice changed.

'You are to fancy that the music of a sudden wavers away. Chris Hatton, captain of her bodyguard, quits the table all red and ruffled, and Gloriana's virgin ear catches the clash of swords at work behind a wall. The mothers of Sussex look round to count their chicks – I mean those young game-cocks that waited on her. Two dainty youths have stepped aside into Brickwall garden with rapier and dagger on a private point of honour. They are haled out through the gate, disarmed and glaring – the lively image of a brace of young Cupids transformed into pale, panting Cains. Ahem! Gloriana beckons awfully – thus! They come up for judgement. Their lives and estates lie at her mercy whom they have doubly offended, both as queen and woman. But la! what will foolish young men not do for a beautiful maid?'

'Why? What did she do? What had they done?' said Una.

'Hsh! You mar the play! Gloriana had guessed the cause of the trouble. They were handsome lads. So she frowns a while and tells 'em not to be bigger fools than their mothers had made 'em, and warns 'em, if they do not kiss and be friends on the instant, she'll have Chris Hatton horse and birch 'em in the style of the new school at Harrow. (Chris looks sour at that.) Lastly, because she needed time to think on Philip's letter burning in her pocket, she signifies her pleasure to dance with 'em and teach 'em better manners. Whereat the revived company call down heaven's blessing on her gracious head; Chris and the others prepare Brickwall House for a dance; and she walks in the clipped garden between those two lovely young sinners who are both ready to sink for shame. They confess their fault. It appears that midway in the banquet the elder – they were cousins – conceived that the queen looked upon him with special favour. The younger, taking the look to himself, after some words gives the elder the lie. Hence, as she guessed, the duel.'

'And which had she really looked at?' Dan asked.

'Neither – except to wish them farther off. She was afraid all the while they'd spill dishes on her gown. She tells 'em this, poor chicks – and it completes their abasement. When they had grilled long enough, she says: "And so you would have fleshed your maiden swords for me – for me?" Faith, they would have been at it again if she'd egged 'em on! but their swords – oh, prettily they said it! – had been drawn for her once or twice already.

' "And where?" says she. "On your hobby-horses before you were breeched?"

' "On my own ship," says the elder. "My cousin was vice-admiral of our venture in his pinnace. We would not have you think of us as brawling children."

' "No, no," says the younger, and flames like a very Tudor rose. "At least the Spaniards know us better."

' "Admiral Boy – Vice-Admiral Babe," says Gloriana, "I cry your pardon. The heat of these present times ripens childhood to age more quickly than I can follow. But we are at peace with Spain. Where did you break your queen's peace?"

' "On the sea called the Spanish Main, though 'tis no more Spanish than my doublet," says the elder. Guess how that warmed Gloriana's already melting heart! She would never suffer any sea to be called Spanish in her private hearing.

' "And why was I not told? What booty got you, and where have you hid it? Disclose," says she. "You stand in some danger of the gallows for pirates."

' "The axe, most gracious lady," says the elder, "for we are gentle born." He spoke truth, but no woman can brook contradiction. "Hoity-toity!" says she, and, but that she remembered that she was queen, she'd have cuffed the pair of 'em. "It shall be gallows, hurdle and dung-cart if I choose."

' "Had our queen known of our going beforehand, Philip might have held her to blame for some small things we did on the seas," the younger lisps.

' "As for treasure," says the elder, "we brought back but our bare lives. We were wrecked on the Gascons' Graveyard, where our sole company for three months was the bleached bones of De Avila's men."

'Gloriana's mind jumped back to Philip's last letter.

' "De Avila that destroyed the Huguenots? What d'you know of him?" she says. The music called from the house here, and they three turned back between the yews.

' "Simply that De Avila broke in upon a plantation of Frenchmen on that coast, and very Spaniardly hung them all for heretics – eight hundred or so. The next year Dominique de Gorgues, a Gascon, broke in upon De Avila's men, and very justly hung 'em all for murderers – five hundred or so. No Christians inhabit there now, says the elder lad, "though 'tis a goodly land north of Florida."

' "How far is it from England?" asks prudent Gloriana.

' "With a fair wind, six weeks. They say that Philip will plant it again soon." This was the younger, and he looked at her out of the corner of his innocent eye.

'Chris Hatton, fuming, meets and leads her into Brickwall Hall, where she dances – thus. A woman can think while she dances – can think. I'll show you. Watch!'

She took off her cloak slowly, and stood forth in dove-coloured satin, worked over with pearls that trembled like running water in the running shadows of the trees. Still talking – more to herself than to the children – she swam into a majestical dance of the stateliest balancings, the naughtiest wheelings and turnings aside, the most dignified sinkings, the gravest risings, all joined together by the elaboratest interlacing steps and circles.

They leaned forward breathlessly to watch the splendid acting.

'Would a Spaniard,' she began, looking on the ground, 'speak of his revenge till his revenge were ripe? No. Yet a man who loved a woman might threaten her in the hope that his threats would make her love him. Such things have been.' She moved slowly across a bar of sunlight. 'A destruction from the West may signify that Philip means to descend on Ireland. But then my Irish spies would have had some warning. The Irish keep no secrets. No – it is not Ireland. Now why – why – why' – the red shoes clicked and paused – 'does Philip name Pedro Melendez de Avila, a general in his Americas, unless' – she turned more quickly – 'unless he intends to work his destruction from the Americas? Did he say De Avila only to put her off her guard, or for this once has his black pen betrayed his black heart? We' – she raised herself to her full height – 'England must forestall Master Philip. But not openly' – she sank again – 'we cannot fight Spain openly – not yet – not yet.' She stepped three paces as though she were pegging down some snare with her twinkling shoe-buckles. 'The queen's mad gentlemen may fight Philip's poor admirals where they find 'em, but England, Gloriana, Harry's daughter, must keep the peace. Perhaps, after all, Philip loves her – as many men and boys do. That may help England. Oh, what shall help England?'

She raised her head – the masked head that seemed to have nothing to do with the busy feet – and stared straight at the children.

'I think this is rather creepy,' said Una with a shiver. 'I wish she'd stop.'

The lady held out her jewelled hand as though she were taking someone else's hand in the Grand Chain.

'Can a ship go down into the Gascons' Graveyard and wait there?' she asked into the air, and passed on rustling.

'She's pretending to ask one of the cousins, isn't she?' said Dan, and Puck nodded.

Back she came in the silent, swaying, ghostly dance. They saw she was smiling beneath the mask, and they could hear her breathing hard.

'I cannot lend you any of my ships for the venture; Philip would hear of it,' she whispered over her shoulder; 'but as much guns and powder as you ask, if you do not ask too –' Her voice shot up and she stamped her foot thrice. 'Louder! Louder, the music in the gallery! Oh, me, but I have burst out of my shoe!'

She gathered her skirts in each hand, and began a curtsy. 'You will go at your own charges,' she whispered straight before her. 'Oh, enviable and adorable age of youth!' Her eyes shone through the mask-holes. 'But I warn you you'll repent it. Put not your trust in princes – or queens. Philip's ships'll blow you out of the water. You'll not be frightened? Well, we'll talk on it again, when I return from Rye, dear lads.'

The wonderful curtsy ended. She stood up. Nothing stirred on her except the rush of the shadows.

'And so it was finished,' she said to the children. 'Why d'you not applaud?'

'What was finished?' said Una.

'The dance,' the lady replied offendedly. 'And a pair of green shoes.'

'I don't understand a bit,' said Una.

'Eh? What did *you* make of it, young Burleigh?'

'I'm not quite sure,' Dan began, 'but – '

'You never can be – with a woman. But – '

'But I thought Gloriana meant the cousins to go back to the Gascons' Graveyard, wherever that was.'

' 'Twas Virginia afterwards. Her plantation of Virginia.'

'Virginia afterwards, and stop Philip from taking it. Didn't she say she'd lend 'em guns?'

'Right so. But not ships – *then*.'

'And I thought you meant they must have told her they'd do it off their own bat, without getting her into a row with Philip. Was I right?'

'Near enough for a minister of the queen. But remember she gave the lads full time to change their minds. She was three long days at Rye Royal – knighting of fat mayors. When she came back to Brickwall, they met her a mile down the road, and she could feel their eyes burn through her riding-mask. Chris Hatton, poor fool, was vexed at it.

' "You would not birch them when I gave you the chance," says she to Chris. "Now you must get me half an hour's private speech with 'em in Brickwall garden. Eve tempted Adam in a garden. Quick, man, or I may repent!" '

'She was a queen. Why did she not send for them herself?' said Una.

The lady shook her head. 'That was never her way. I've seen her walk to her own mirror by bye-ends, and the woman that cannot walk straight *there* is past praying for. Yet I would have you pray for her! What else – what else in England's name could she have done?' She lifted her hand to her throat for a moment. 'Faith,' she cried, 'I'd forgotten the little green shoes! She left 'em at Brickwall – so she did. And I remember she gave the Norgem parson – John Withers, was he? – a text for his sermon – "Over Edom have I cast out my shoe." Neat, if he'd understood!'

'I don't understand,' said Una. 'What about the two cousins?'

'You are as cruel as a woman,' the lady answered. '*I* was not to blame. I told you I gave 'em time to change their minds. On my honour (*ay de mi*!), she asked no more of 'em at first than to wait a while off that coast – the Gascons' Graveyard – to hover a little if their ships chanced to pass that way – they had only one tall ship and a pinnace – only to watch and bring me word of Philip's doings. One must watch Philip always. What a murrain right had he to make any plantation there, a hundred leagues north of his Spanish Main, and only six weeks from England? By my dread father's soul, I tell you he had none – none!' She stamped her red foot again, and the two children shrank back for a second.

'Nay, nay. You must not turn from me too! She laid it all fairly before the lads in Brickwall garden between the yews. I told 'em that if Philip sent a fleet (and to make a plantation he could not well send less), their poor little cock-boats could not sink it. They answered that, with submission, the fight would be their own concern. She showed 'em again that there could be only one end to it – quick death on the sea, or slow death in Philip's prisons. They asked no more than to embrace death for my sake. Many men have prayed to me for life. I've refused 'em, and slept none the worse after; but when my men, my tall, fantastical young men, beseech me on their knees for leave to die for me, it shakes me – ah, it shakes me to the marrow of my old bones.'

Her chest sounded like a board as she hit it. 'She showed 'em all. I told 'em that this was no time for open war with Spain. If by miracle inconceivable they prevailed against Philip's fleet, Philip would hold me accountable. For England's sake, to save war, I should e'en be forced (I told 'em so) to give him up their young lives. If they failed, and again by some miracle escaped Philip's hand, and crept back to England with their bare lives, they must lie – oh, I told 'em all – under my sovereign displeasure. She could not know them, see them, nor hear their names, nor stretch out a finger to save them from the gallows, if Philip chose to ask it.

' "Be it the gallows, then," says the elder. (I could have wept, but that my face was made for the day.)

' "Either way – any way – this venture is death, which I know you fear not. But it is death with assured dishonour," I cried.

' "Yet our queen will know in her heart what we have done," says the younger.

' "Sweetheart," I said. "A queen has no heart."

' "But she is a woman, and a woman would not forget," says the elder. "We will go!" They knelt at my feet.

' "Nay, dear lads – but here!" I said, and I opened my arms to them and I kissed them.

' "Be ruled by me," I said. "We'll hire some ill-featured old tarry-breeks of an admiral to watch the Graveyard, and you shall come to court."

' "Hire whom you please," says the elder; "we are ruled by you, body and soul;" and the younger, who shook most when I kissed 'em, says between his white lips, "I think you have power to make a god of a man."

' "Come to court and be sure of it," I said.

'They shook their heads and I knew – I knew, that go they would. If I had not kissed them – perhaps I might have prevailed.'

'Then why did you do it?' said Una. 'I don't think you knew really what you wanted done.'

'May it please your majesty' – the lady bowed her head low – 'this Gloriana whom I have represented for your pleasure was a woman and a queen. Remember her when you come to your kingdom.'

'But did the cousins go to the Gascons' Graveyard?' said Dan, as Una frowned.

'They went,' said the lady.

'Did they ever come back?' Una began; but – 'Did they stop King Philip's fleet?' Dan interrupted.

The lady turned to him eagerly.

'D'you think they did right to go?' she asked.

'I don't see what else they could have done,' Dan replied, after thinking it over.

'D'you think she did right to send 'em?' The lady's voice rose a little.

'Well,' said Dan, 'I don't see what else she could have done, either – do you? How did they stop King Philip from getting Virginia?'

'There's the sad part of it. They sailed out that autumn from Rye Royal, and there never came back so much as a single rope-yarn to show what had befallen them. The winds blew, and they were not. Does that make you alter your mind, young Burleigh?'

'I expect they were drowned, then. Anyhow, Philip didn't score, did he?'

'Gloriana wiped out her score with Philip later. But if Philip had won, would you have blamed Gloriana for wasting those lads' lives?'

'Of course not. She was bound to try to stop him.'

The lady coughed. 'You have the root of the matter in you. Were I queen, I'd make you minister.'

'We don't play that game,' said Una, who felt that she disliked the lady as much as she disliked the noise the high wind made tearing through Willow Shaw.

'Play!' said the lady with a laugh, and threw up her hands affectedly. The sunshine caught the jewels on her many rings and made them flash till Una's eyes dazzled, and she had to rub them. Then she saw Dan on his knees picking up the potatoes they had spilled at the gate.

'There wasn't anybody in the Shaw, after all,' he said. 'Didn't you think you saw someone?'

'I'm most awfully glad there isn't,' said Una. Then they went on with the potato-roast.

The Looking-Glass

Queen Bess was Harry's daughter!

The Queen was in her chamber, and she was middling old,
Her petticoat was satin and her stomacher was gold.
Backwards and forwards and sideways did she pass,
Making up her mind to face the cruel looking-glass.
   The cruel looking-glass that will never show a lass
   As comely or as kindly or as young as once she was!

The Queen was in her chamber, a-combing of her hair,
There came Queen Mary's spirit and it stood behind her chair,
Singing, 'Backwards and forwards and sideways you may pass,
But I will stand behind you till you face the looking-glass.
   The cruel looking-glass that will never show a lass
   As lovely or unlucky or as lonely as I was!'

The Queen was in her chamber, a-weeping very sore,
There came Lord Leicester's spirit and it scratched upon the door,
Singing, 'Backwards and forwards and sideways may you pass,
But I will walk beside you till you face the looking-glass.
   The cruel looking-glass that will never show a lass
   As hard and unforgiving or as wicked as you was!'

The Queen was in her chamber; her sins were on her head;
She looked the spirits up and down and statelily she said:
'Backwards and forwards and sideways though I've been,
Yet I am Harry's daughter and I am England's queen!'
   And she faced the looking-glass (and whatever else there was),
   And she saw her day was over and she saw her beauty pass
   In the cruel looking-glass that can always hurt a lass
   More hard than any ghost there is or any man there was!

THE WRONG THING

A Truthful Song

THE BRICKLAYER:

I tell this tale, which is strictly true,
  Just by way of convincing you
How very little since things were made
  Have things altered in the building trade.

A year ago, come the middle o' March,
We was building flats near the Marble Arch,
When a thin young man with coal-black hair
Came up to watch us working there.

Now there wasn't a trick in brick or stone
That this young man hadn't seen or known;
Nor there wasn't a tool, from trowel to maul,
But this young man could use 'em all!

Then up and spoke the plumbyers bold,
Which was laying the pipes for the hot and cold:
'Since you with us have made so free,
Will you kindly say what your name might be?'

The young man kindly answered them:
'It might be Lot or Methusalem,
Or it might be Moses (a man I hate),
Whereas it is Pharaoh surnamed the Great.

'Your glazing is new and your plumbing's strange,
But otherwise I perceive no change,
And in less than a month, if you do as I bid,
I'd learn you to build me a Pyramid.'

THE SAILOR:

> *I tell this tale, which is stricter true,*
> *   Just by way of convincing you*
> *How very little since things was made*
> *   Have things altered in the shipwright's trade.*

In Blackwall Basin yesterday
A China barque re-fitting lay,
When a fat old man with snow-white hair
Came up to watch us working there.

Now there wasn't a knot which the riggers knew
But the old man made it – and better too;
Nor there wasn't a sheet, or a lift, or a brace,
But the old man knew its lead and place.

Then up and spake the caulkyers bold,
Which was packing the pump in the after-hold:
'Since you with us have made so free,
Will you kindly tell what your name might be?'

The old man kindly answered them:
'It might be Japhet, it might be Shem,
Or it might be Ham (though his skin was dark),
Whereas it is Noah, commanding the Ark.

'Your wheel is new and your pumps are strange,
But otherwise I perceive no change,
And in less than a week, if she did not ground,
I'd sail this hooker the wide world round!'

BOTH:

> *We tell these tales, which are strictest true, etc.*

The Wrong Thing

Dan had gone in for building model boats; but after he had filled the schoolroom with chips, which he expected Una to clear away, they turned him out of doors and he took all his tools up the hill to Mr Springett's yard, where he knew he could make as much mess as he chose. Old Mr Springett was a builder, contractor and sanitary engineer, and his yard, which opened off the village street, was always full of interesting things. At one end of it was a long loft, reached by a ladder, where he kept his iron-bound scaffold-planks, tins of paints, pulleys, and odds and ends he had found in old houses. He would sit here by the hour watching his carts as they loaded or unloaded in the yard below, while Dan gouged and grunted at the carpenter's bench near the loft window. Mr Springett and Dan had always been particular friends, for Mr Springett was so old he could remember when railways were being made in the southern counties of England, and people were allowed to drive dogs in carts.

One hot, still afternoon – the tar-paper on the roof smelt like ships – Dan, in his shirt-sleeves, was smoothing down a new schooner's bow, and Mr Springett was talking of barns and houses he had built. He said he never forgot any stick or stone he had ever handled, or any man, woman or child he had ever met. Just then he was very proud of the village hall at the entrance of the village, which he had finished a few weeks before.

'An' I don't mind tellin' you, Mus' Dan,' he said, 'that the hall will be my last job top of this mortal earth. I didn't make ten pounds – no, nor yet five – out o' the whole contrac', but my name's lettered on the foundation stone – *Ralph Springett, Builder* – and the stone she's bedded in four foot of good concrete. If she shifts any time these five hundred years, I'll sure–ly turn in my grave. I told the Lunnon architec' so when he come down to oversee my work.'

'What did he say?' Dan was sandpapering the schooner's port bow.

'Nothing. The hall ain't more than one of his small jobs for *him*, but 'tain't small to me, an' my name is cut and lettered, frontin' the village street, I do hope an' pray, for time everlastin'. You'll want the little round file for that holler in her bow. Who's there?' Mr Springett turned stiffly in his chair.

A long pile of scaffold-planks ran down the centre of the loft. Dan looked, and saw Hal of the Draft's touzled head beyond them.*

'Be you the builder of the village hall?' he asked of Mr Springett.

'I be,' was the answer. 'But if you want a job – '

---

* See 'Hal o' the Draft' in *Puck of Pook's Hill*.

Hal laughed. 'No, faith!' he said. 'Only the hall is as good and honest a piece of work as I've ever run a rule over. So, being born hereabouts, and being reckoned a master among masons, and accepted as a master mason, I made bold to pay my brotherly respects to the builder.'

'Aa – um!' Mr Springett looked important. 'I be a bit rusty, but I'll try ye!'

He asked Hal several curious questions, and the answers must have pleased him, for he invited Hal to sit down. Hal moved up, always keeping behind the pile of planks so that only his head showed, and sat down on a trestle in the dark corner at the back of Mr Springett's desk. He took no notice of Dan, but talked at once to Mr Springett about bricks and cement and lead and glass, and after a while Dan went on with his work. He knew Mr Springett was pleased, because he tugged his white sandy beard, and smoked his pipe in short puffs. The two men seemed to agree about everything, but when grown-ups agree they interrupt each other almost as much as if they were quarrelling. Hal said something about workmen.

'Why, that's what *I* always say,' Mr Springett cried. 'A man who can only do one thing, he's but next-above-fool to the man that can't do nothing. That's where the unions make their mistake.'

'My thought to the very dot.' Dan heard Hal slap his tight-hosed leg. 'I've suffered in my time from these same guilds – unions, d'you call 'em? All their precious talk of the mysteries of their trades – why, what does it come to?'

'Nothin'! You've just about hit it,' said Mr Springett, and rammed his hot tobacco with his thumb.

'Take the art of wood-carving,' Hal went on. He reached across the planks, grabbed a wooden mallet, and moved his other hand as though he wanted something. Mr Springett without a word passed him one of Dan's broad chisels. 'Ah! Wood-carving, for example. If you can cut wood and have a fair draft of what ye mean to do, in heaven's name take chisel and maul and let drive at it, say I! You'll soon find all the mystery, forsooth, of wood-carving under your proper hand!' Whack came the mallet on the chisel and a sliver of wood curled up in front of it. Mr Springett watched like an old raven.

'All art is one, man – one!' said Hal between whacks; 'and to wait on another man to finish out – '

'To finish out your work ain't no sense,' Mr Springett cut in. 'That's what I'm always saying to the boy here.' He nodded towards Dan. 'That's what I said when I put the new wheel into Brewster's Mill in 1872. I reckoned I was millwright enough for the job 'thout bringin' a man from Lunnon. An' besides, dividin' work eats up profits, no bounds.'

Hal laughed his beautiful deep laugh, and Mr Springett joined in till Dan laughed too.

'You handle your tools, I can see,' said Mr Springett. 'I reckon, if you're any way like me, you've found yourself hindered by those – guilds, did you call 'em? – unions, we say.'

'You may say so!' Hal pointed to a white scar on his cheekbone. 'This is a remembrance from the master watching-foreman of masons on Magdalen Tower, because, please you, I dared to carve stone without their leave. They said a stone had slipped from the cornice by accident.'

'I know them accidents. There's no way to disprove 'em. An' stones ain't the only things that slip,' Mr Springett grunted.

Hal went on: 'I've seen a scaffold-plank keckle and shoot a too-clever workman thirty foot on to the cold chancel floor below. And a rope can break – '

'Yes, natural as nature; an' lime'll fly up in a man's eyes without any breath o' wind sometimes,' said Mr Springett. 'But who's to show 'twasn't an accident?'

'Who do these things?' Dan asked, and straightened his back at the bench as he turned the schooner end-for-end in the vice to get at her counter.

'Them which don't wish other men to work no better nor quicker than they do,' growled Mr Springett. 'Don't pinch her so hard in the vice, Mus' Dan. Put a piece o' rag in the jaws, or you'll bruise her. More than that' – he turned towards Hal – 'if a man has his private spite laid up against you, the unions give him his excuse for working it off.'

'Well I know it,' said Hal.

'They never let you go, them spiteful ones. I knowed a plasterer in 1861 – down to the Wells. He was a Frenchy – a bad enemy he was.'

'I had mine too. He was an Italian, called Benedetto. I met him first at Oxford on Magdalen Tower when I was learning my trade – or trades, I should say. A bad enemy he was, as you say, but he came to be my singular good friend,' said Hal, as he put down the mallet and settled himself comfortably.

'What might his trade have been – plasterin'?' Mr Springett asked.

'Plastering of a sort. He worked in stucco – fresco we call it. Made pictures on plaster. Not but what he had a fine sweep of the hand in drawing. He'd take the long sides of a cloister, trowel on his stuff, and roll out his great all-abroad pictures of saints and croppy-topped trees quick as a webster unrolling cloth almost. Oh, Benedetto could draw, but he was a little-minded man, professing to be full of secrets of colour or plaster – common tricks, all of 'em – and his one single talk was how Tom, Dick or Harry had stole this or t'other secret art from him.'

'I know that sort,' said Mr Springett. 'There's no keeping peace or making peace with such. An' they're mostly born an' bone idle.'

'True. Even his fellow-countrymen laughed at his jealousy. We two came to loggerheads early on Magdalen Tower. I was a youngster then. Maybe I spoke my mind about his work.'

'You shouldn't never do that.' Mr Springett shook his head. 'That sort lay it up against you.'

'True enough. This Benedetto did most specially. Body o' me, the man lived to hate me! But I always kept my eyes open on a plank or a scaffold. I was mighty glad to be shut of him when he quarrelled with his guild foreman, and went off, nose in air, and paints under his arm. But' – Hal leaned forward – 'if you hate a man or a man hates you – '

'*I* know. You're everlastin' running acrost him,' Mr Springett interrupted. 'Excuse me, sir.' He leaned out of the window, and shouted to a carter who was loading a cart with bricks.

'Ain't you no more sense than to heap 'em up that way?' he said. 'Take an' throw a hundred of 'em off. It's more than the team can compass. Throw 'em off, I tell you, and make another trip for what's left over. Excuse me, sir. You was saying – '

'I was saying that before the end of the year I went to Bury to strengthen the lead-work in the great abbey east window there.'

'Now that's just one of the things I've never done. But I mind there was a cheap excursion to Chichester in 1879, an' I went an' watched 'em leading a won'erful fine window in Chichester Cathedral. I stayed watchin' till 'twas time for us to go back. Dunno as I had two drinks p'raps, all that day.'

Hal smiled. 'At Bury, then, sure enough, I met my enemy Benedetto. He had painted a picture in plaster on the south wall of the refectory – a noble place for a noble thing – a picture of Jonah.'

'Ah! Jonah an' his whale. I've never been as far as Bury. You've worked about a lot,' said Mr Springett, with his eyes on the carter below.

'No. Not the whale. This was a picture of Jonah and the pompion that withered. But all that Benedetto had shown was a peevish grey-beard huggled up in angle-edged drapery beneath a pompion on a wooden trellis. This last, being a dead thing, he'd drawn it as 'twere to the life. But fierce old Jonah, bared in the sun, angry even to death that his cold prophecy was disproven – Jonah, ashamed, and already hearing the children of Nineveh running to mock him – ah, that was what Benedetto had *not* drawn!'

'He better ha' stuck to his whale, then,' said Mr Springett.

'He'd ha' done no better with that. He draws the damp cloth off the picture, an' shows it to me. I was a craftsman too, d'ye see?'

' " 'Tis good," I said, "but it goes no deeper than the plaster."

' "What?" he said in a whisper.

' "Be thy own judge, Benedetto," I answered. "Does it go deeper than the plaster?"

'He reeled against a piece of dry wall. "No," he says, "and I know it. I could not hate thee more than I have done these five years, but if I live, I will try, Hal. I will try." Then he goes away. I pitied him, but I had spoken the truth. His picture went no deeper than the plaster.'

'Ah!' said Mr Springett, who had turned quite red. 'You was talkin' so fast I didn't understand what you was drivin' at. I've seen men – good workmen they was – try to do more than they could do, and – and they couldn't compass it. They knowed it, and it nigh broke their hearts like. You was in your right, o' course, sir, to say what you thought o' his work; but if you'll excuse me, was you in your duty?'

'I was wrong to say it,' Hal replied. 'God forgive me – I was young! He was workman enough himself to know where he failed. But it all came evens in the long run. By the same token, did ye ever hear o' one Torrigiano – Torrisany we called him?'

'I can't say I ever did. Was he a Frenchy like?'

'No, a hectoring, hard-mouthed, long-sworded Italian builder, as vain as a peacock and as strong as a bull, but, mark you, a master workman. More than that – he could get his best work out of the worst men.'

'Which it's a gift. I had a foreman-bricklayer like him once,' said Mr Springett. 'He used to prod 'em in the back like with a pointing-trowel, and they did wonders.'

'I've seen our Torrisany lay a 'prentice down with one buffet and raise him with another – to make a mason of him. I worked under him at building a chapel in London – a chapel and a tomb for the king.'

'I never knew kings went to chapel much,' said Mr Springett. 'But I always hold with a man, don't care who he be, seein' about his own grave before he dies. 'Tisn't the sort of thing to leave to your family after the will's read. I reckon 'twas a fine vault?'

'None finer in England. This Torrigiano had the contract for it, as you'd say. He picked master craftsmen from all parts – England, France, Italy, the Low Countries – no odds to him so long as they knew their work, and he drove them like – like pigs at Brightling Fair. He called us English all pigs. We suffered it because he was a master in his craft. If he misliked any work that a man had done, with his own great hands he'd rive it out and tear it down before us all. "Ah, you pig – you English pig!" he'd scream in the dumb wretch's face. "You answer me? You look at me? You think at me? Come out with me into the cloisters. I will teach you carving myself. I will gild you all over!" But when his passion had blown out, he'd slip his arm round the man's neck, and impart knowledge worth gold. 'Twould have done your heart good, Mus' Springett, to see the two hundred of us – masons, jewellers, carvers, gilders, iron-workers and the rest – all toiling like cock-angels, and this mad Italian hornet fleeing from one to the next up and down the chapel. Done your heart good, it would!'

'I believe you,' said Mr Springett. 'In 1854, I mind, the railway was bein' made into Hastin's. There was two thousand navvies on it – all young – all strong – an' I was one of 'em. Oh, dearie me! Excuse me, sir, but was your enemy workin' with you?'

'Benedetto? Be sure he was. He followed me like a lover. He painted pictures on the chapel ceiling – slung from a chair. Torrigiano made us promise not to fight till the work should be finished. We were both master craftsmen, do ye see, and he needed us. None the less, I never went aloft to carve 'thout testing all my ropes and knots each morning. We were never far from each other. Benedetto 'ud sharpen his knife on his sole while he waited for his plaster to dry – *wheet, wheet, wheet*. I'd hear it where I hung chipping round a pillar-head, and we'd nod to each other friendly-like. Oh, he was a craftsman, was Benedetto, but his hate spoiled his eye and his hand. I mind the night I had finished the models for the bronze saints round the tomb; Torrigiano embraced me before all the chapel, and bade me to supper. I met Benedetto when I came out. He was slavering in the porch like a mad dog.'

'Workin' himself up to it?' said Mr Springett. 'Did he have it in at ye that night?'

'No, no. That time he kept his oath to Torrigiano. But I pitied him. Eh, well! Now I come to my own follies. I had never thought too little of myself; but after Torrisany had put his arm round my neck, I – I' – Hal broke into a laugh – 'I lay there was not much odds 'twixt me and a cock-sparrow in his pride.'

'I was pretty middlin' young once on a time,' said Mr Springett.

'Then ye know that a man can't drink and dice and dress fine, and keep company above his station, but his work suffers for it, Mus' Springett.'

'I never held much with dressin' up, but – you're right! The worst mistakes *I* ever made they was made of a Monday morning,' Mr Springett answered. 'We've all been one sort of fool or t'other. Mus' Dan, Mus' Dan, take the smallest gouge or you'll be spluttin' her stern works clean out. Can't ye see the grain of the wood don't favour a chisel?'

'I'll spare you some of my follies. But there was a man called Brygandyne – Bob Brygandyne – Clerk of the King's Ships, a little, smooth, bustling atomy, as clever as a woman to get work done for nothin' – a won'erful smooth-tongued pleader. He made much o' me, and asked me to draft him out a drawing, a piece of carved and gilt scrollwork for the bows of one of the king's ships – the *Sovereign* was her name.'

'Was she a man-of-war?' asked Dan.

'She was a warship, and a woman called Catherine of Castile desired the king to give her the ship for a pleasure-ship of her own. I did not know at the time, but she'd been at Bob to get this scrollwork done and fitted that the king might see it. I made him the picture, in an hour, all of a heat after supper – one great heaving play of dolphins, and a Neptune or so reining in webby-footed sea-horses, and Arion with his harp high atop of them. It was twenty-three foot long, and maybe nine foot deep – painted and gilt.'

'It must ha' just about looked fine,' said Mr Springett.

'That's the curiosity of it. 'Twas bad – rank bad. In my conceit I must needs show it to Torrigiano, in the chapel. He straddles his legs, hunches his knife behind him, and whistles like a storm-cock through a sleet-shower. Benedetto was behind him. We were never far apart, I've told you.

' "That is pig's work," says our master. "Swine's work. You make any more such things, even after your fine court suppers, and you shall be sent away."

'Benedetto licks his lips like a cat. "It is so bad then, master?" he says. "What a pity!"

' "Yes," says Torrigiano. "Scarcely *you* could do things so bad. I will condescend to show."

'He talks to me then and there. No shouting, no swearing (it was too bad for that); but good, memorable counsel, bitten in slowly. Then he sets me to draft out a pair of iron gates, to take, as he said, the taste of my naughty dolphins out of my mouth. Iron's sweet stuff, if you don't torture her, and hammered work is all pure, truthful line, with a reason and a support for every curve and bar of it. A week at that settled my stomach handsomely, and the master let me put the work through the smithy, where I sweated out more of my foolish pride.'

'Good stuff is good iron,' said Mr Springett. 'I done a pair of lodge gates once in 1863.'

'Oh, I forgot to say that Bob Brygandyne whipped away my draft of the ship's scrollwork, and would not give it back to me to redraw. He said 'twould do well enough. Howsoever, my lawful work kept me too busied to remember him. Body o' me, but I worked that winter upon the gates and the bronzes for the tomb as I'd never worked before! I was leaner than a lath, but I lived – I lived then!' Hal looked at Mr Springett with his wise, crinkled-up eyes, and the old man smiled back.

'Ouch!' Dan cried. He had been hollowing out the schooner's after-deck and the little gouge had slipped and gashed the ball of his left thumb – an ugly, triangular tear.

'That came of not steadying your wrist,' said Hal calmly. 'Don't bleed over the wood. Do your work with your heart's blood, but no need to let it show.' He rose and peered into a corner of the loft.

Mr Springett had risen too, and swept down a ball of cobwebs from a rafter.

'Clap that on,' was all he said, 'and put your handkerchief atop. 'Twill cake over in a minute. It don't hurt now, do it?'

'No,' said Dan indignantly. 'You know it has happened lots of times. I'll tie it up myself. Go on, sir.'

'And it'll happen hundreds of times more,' said Hal with a friendly nod as he sat down again. But he did not go on till Dan's hand was tied up properly. Then he said: 'One dark December day – too dark to judge colour – we was all sitting and talking round the fires in the chapel (you heard good talk there), when Bob Brygandyne bustles in and – "Hal, you're sent for," he squeals. I was at Torrigiano's feet on a pile of put-locks, as I might be here, toasting a herring on my knife's point. 'Twas the one English thing our master liked – salt herring.

' "I'm busy, about my art," I calls.

' "Art?" says Bob. "What's art compared to your scrollwork for the *Sovereign*? Come."

' "Be sure your sins will find you out," says Torrigiano. "Go with him and see." As I followed Bob out I was aware of Benedetto, like a black spot when the eyes are tired, sliddering up behind me.

'Bob hurries through the streets in the raw fog, slips into a doorway, up stairs, along passages, and at last thrusts me into a little cold room vilely hung with Flemish tapestries, and no furnishing except a table and my draft of the *Sovereign*'s scrollwork. Here he leaves me. Presently comes in a dark, long-nosed man in a fur cap.

' "Master Harry Dawe?" said he.

' "The same," I says. "Where a plague has Bob Brygandyne gone?"

'His thin eyebrows surged up in a piece and came down again in a stiff bar. "He went to the king," he says.

' "All one. Where's your pleasure with me?" I says, shivering, for it was mortal cold.

'He lays his hand flat on my draft. "Master Dawe," he says, "do you know the present price of gold leaf for all this wicked gilding of yours?"

'By that I guessed he was some cheese-paring clerk or other of the king's ships, so I gave him the price. I forget it now, but it worked out to thirty pounds – carved, gilt, and fitted in place.

' "Thirty pounds!" he said, as though I had pulled a tooth of him. "You talk as though thirty pounds was to be had for the asking. None the less," he says, "your draft's a fine piece of work."

'I'd been looking at it ever since I came in, and 'twas viler even than I judged it at first. My eye and hand had been purified the past months, d'ye see, by my ironwork.

' "I could do it better now," I said. The more I studied my squabby Neptunes the less I liked 'em; and Arion was a pure flaming shame atop of the unbalanced dolphins.

' "I doubt it will be fresh expense to draft it again," he says.

' "Bob never paid me for the first draft. I lay he'll never pay me for the second. 'Twill cost the king nothing if I redraw it," I says.

' "There's a woman wishes it to be done quickly," he says. "We'll stick to your first drawing, Master Dawe. But thirty pounds is thirty pounds. You must make it less.'

'And all the while the faults in my draft fair leaped out and hit me between the eyes. At any cost, I thinks to myself, I must get it back and redraft it. He grunts at me impatiently, and a splendid thought comes to me, which shall save me. By the same token, 'twas quite honest.'

'They ain't always,' says Mr Springett. 'How did you get out of it?'

'By the truth. I says to Master Fur Cap, as I might to you here, I says, "I'll tell you something, since you seem a knowledgeable man. Is the *Sovereign* to lie in Thames river all her days, or will she take the high seas?"

' "Oh," he says quickly, "the king keeps no cats that don't catch mice. She must sail the seas, Master Dawe. She'll be hired to merchants for the trade. She'll be out in all shapes o' weathers. Does that make any odds?"

' "Why, then," says I, "the first heavy sea she sticks her nose into'll claw off half that scrollwork, and the next will finish it. If she's meant for a pleasure-ship give me my draft again, and I'll porture you a pretty, light piece of scrollwork, good, cheap. If she's meant for the open sea, pitch the draft into the fire. She can never carry that weight on her bows.

'He looks at me squintlings and plucks his underlip.

' "Is this your honest, unswayed opinion?" he says.

' "Body o' me! Ask about!" I says. "Any seaman could tell you 'tis true. I'm advising you against my own profit, but why I do so is my own concern.

' "Not altogether," he says. "It's some of mine. You've saved me thirty pounds, Master Dawe, and you've given me good arguments to use against a wilful woman that wants my fine new ship for her own toy. We'll not have any scrollwork." His face shined with pure joy.

' "Then see that the thirty pounds you've saved on it are honestly paid the king," I says, "and keep clear o' womenfolk." I gathered up my draft and crumpled it under my arm. "If that's all you need of me, I'll be gone," I says, "for I'm pressed."

'He turns him round and fumbles in a corner. "Too pressed to be made a knight, Sir Harry?" he says, and comes at me smiling, with three-quarters of a rusty sword.

'I pledge you my mark I never guessed it was the king till that moment. I kneeled, and he tapped me on the shoulder.

' "Rise up, Sir Harry Dawe," he says, and, in the same breath, "I'm pressed, too," and slips through the tapestries, leaving me like a stuck calf.

'It come over me, in a bitter wave like, that here was I, a master craftsman, who had worked no bounds, soul or body, to make the king's tomb and chapel a triumph and a glory for all time; and here, d'ye see, I was made knight, not for anything I'd slaved over, or given my heart and guts to, but expressedly because I'd saved him thirty pounds and a tongue-lashing from Catherine of Castille – she that had asked for the ship. That thought shrivelled me withinsides while I was folding away my draft. On the heels of it – maybe you'll see why – I began to grin to myself. I thought of the earnest simplicity of the man – the king, I should say – because I'd saved him the money; his smile as though he'd won half France! I thought of my own silly pride and foolish expectations that someday he'd honour me as a master craftsman. I thought of the broken-tipped sword he'd found behind the hangings; the dirt of the cold room, and his cold eye, wrapped up in his own concerns, scarcely resting on me. Then I remembered the solemn chapel roof and the bronzes about the stately tomb he'd lie in, and – d'ye see? – the unreason of it all – the mad high humour of it all – took hold on me till I sat me down on a dark stairhead in a passage, and laughed till I could laugh no more. What else could I have done?

'I never heard his feet behind me – he always walked like a cat – but his arm slid round my neck, pulling me back where I sat, till my head lay on his chest, and his left hand held the knife plumb over my heart – Benedetto! Even so I laughed – the fit was beyond my holding – laughed while he ground his teeth in my ear. He was stark crazed for the time.

' "Laugh," he said. "Finish the laughter. I'll not cut ye short. Tell me now" – he wrenched at my head – "why the king chose to honour you – you – you – you lickspittle Englishman? I am full of patience now. I have waited so long." Then he was off at score about his Jonah in Bury refectory, and what I'd said of it, and his pictures in the chapel which all men praised and none looked at twice (as if that was my fault!), and a whole parcel of words and looks treasured up against me through years.

' "Ease off your arm a little," I said. "I cannot die by choking, for I am just dubbed knight, Benedetto."

' "Tell me, and I'll confess ye, Sir Harry Dawe, Knight. There's a long night before ye. Tell," says he.

'So I told him – his chin on my crown – told him all; told it as well and with as many words as I have ever told a tale at a supper with Torrigiano. I knew Benedetto would understand, for, mad or sad, he was a craftsman. I believed it to be the last tale I'd ever tell top of mortal earth, and I would not put out bad work before I left the lodge. All art's one art, as I said. I bore Benedetto no malice. My spirits, d'ye see, were catched up in a high, solemn exaltation, and I saw all earth's vanities foreshortened and little, laid out below me like a town from a cathedral scaffolding. I told him what befell, and what I thought of it. I gave him the king's very voice at "Master Dawe, you've saved me thirty pounds!"; his peevish grunt while he looked for the sword; and how the badger-eyed figures of Glory and Victory leered at me from the Flemish hangings. Body o' me, 'twas a fine, noble tale, and, as I thought, my last work on earth.

' "That is how I was honoured by the king," I said. "They'll hang ye for killing me, Benedetto. And, since you've killed in the king's palace, they'll draw and quarter you; but you're too mad to care. Grant me, though, ye never heard a better tale."

'He said nothing, but I felt him shake. My head on his chest shook; his right arm fell away, his left dropped the knife, and he leaned with both hands on my shoulder – shaking – shaking! I turned me round. No need to put my foot on his knife. The man was speechless with laughter – honest craftsman's mirth. The first time I'd ever seen him laugh. You know the mirth that cuts off the very breath, while ye stamp and snatch at the short ribs? That was Benedetto's case.

'When he began to roar and bay and whoop in the passage, I haled him out into the street, and there we leaned against the wall and had it all over again – waving our hands and wagging our heads – till the watch came to know if we were drunk.

'Benedetto says to 'em, solemn as an owl: "You have saved me thirty pounds, Mus' Dawe," and off he pealed. In some sort we were mad-drunk – I because dear life had been given back to me, and he because, as he said afterwards, because the old crust of hatred round his heart was broke up and carried away by laughter. His very face had changed too.

' "Hal," he cries, "I forgive thee. Forgive me too, Hal. Oh, you English, you English! Did it gall thee, Hal, to see the rust on the dirty sword? Tell me again, Hal, how the king grunted with joy. Oh, let us tell the master."

'So we reeled back to the chapel, arms round each other's necks, and when we could speak – he thought we'd been fighting – we told the master. Yes, we told Torrigiano, and he laughed till he rolled on the new cold pavement. Then he knocked our heads together.

' "Ah, you English!" he cried. "You are more than pigs. You are English. Now you are well punished for your dirty fishes. Put the draft in the fire, and never do so any more. You are a fool, Hal, and you are a fool, Benedetto, but I need your works to please this beautiful English king."

' "And I meant to kill Hal," says Benedetto. "Master, I meant to kill him because the English king had made him a knight."

' "Ah!" says the master, shaking his finger. "Benedetto, if you had killed my Hal, I should have killed you – in the cloister. But you are a craftsman too, so I should have killed you like a craftsman, very, very slowly – in an hour, if I could spare the time!" That was Torrigiano – the master!'

Mr Springett sat quite still for some time after Hal had finished. Then he turned dark red; then he rocked to and fro; then he coughed and wheezed till the tears ran down his face. Dan knew by this that he was laughing, but it surprised Hal at first.

'Excuse me, sir,' said Mr Springett, 'but I was thinkin' of some stables I built for a gentleman in 1874. They was stables in blue brick – very particular work. Dunno as they weren't the best job which ever I'd done. But the gentleman's lady – she'd come from Lunnon, new married – she was all for buildin' what was called a haw-haw – what you an' me 'ud call a dike – right acrost his park. A middlin' big job which I'd have had the contract of, for she spoke to me in the library about it. But I told her there was a line o' springs just where she wanted to dig her ditch, an' she'd flood the park if she went on.'

'Were there any springs at all?' said Hal.

'Bound to be springs everywhere if you dig deep enough, ain't there? But what I said about the springs put her out o' conceit o' diggin' haw-haws, an' she took an' built a white-tile dairy instead. But when I sent in my last bill for the stables, the gentleman he paid it 'thout even lookin' at it, and I hadn't forgotten nothin', I do assure you. More than that, he slips two five-pound notes into my hand in the library, an' "Ralph," he says – he allers called me by name – "Ralph," he says, "you've saved me a heap of expense an' trouble this autumn." I didn't say nothin', o' course. I knowed he didn't want any haws-haws digged acrost his park no more'n *I* did, but I never said nothin'. No more he didn't say nothin' about my blue-brick stables, which was really the best an' honestest piece o' work I'd done in quite a while. He give me ten pounds for savin' him a deal o' trouble at home. I reckon things are pretty much alike, all times, in all places.'

Hal and he laughed together. Dan couldn't quite understand what they thought so funny, and went on with his work for some time without speaking.

When he looked up, Mr Springett, alone, was wiping his eyes with his green-and-yellow pocket-handkerchief.

'Bless me, Mus' Dan, I've been asleep,' he said. 'An' I've dreamed a dream which has made me laugh – laugh as I ain't laughed in a long day. I can't remember what 'twas all about, but they do say that when old men take to laughin' in their sleep, they're middlin' ripe for the next world. Have you been workin' honest, Mus' Dan?'

'Ra–ather,' said Dan, unclamping the schooner from the vice. 'And look how I've cut myself with the small gouge.'

'Ye–es. You want a lump o' cobwebs to that,' said Mr Springett. 'Oh, I see you've put it on already. That's right, Mus' Dan.'

King Henry VII and the Shipwrights

Harry our king in England from London town is gone,
And comen to Hamull on the Hoke in the countie of Suthampton.
For there lay the *Mary of the Tower*, his ship of war so strong,
And he would discover, certaynely, if his shipwrights did him wrong.

He told not none of his setting forth, nor yet where he would go
(But only my Lord of Arundel), and meanly did he show,
In an old jerkin and patched hose that no man might him mark;
With his frieze hood and cloak about, he looked like any clerk.

He was at Hamull on the Hoke about the hour of the tide,
And saw the *Mary* haled into dock, the winter to abide,
With all her tackle and habiliments which are the king his own;
But then ran on his false shipwrights and stripped her to the bone.

They heaved the mainmast overboard, that was of a trusty tree,
And they wrote down it was spent and lost by force of weather at sea.
But they sawen it into planks and strakes as far as it might go,
To maken beds for their own wives and little children also.

There was a knave called Slingawai, he crope beneath the deck,
Crying: 'Good felawes, come and see! The ship is nigh a wreck!
For the storm that took our tall mainmast, it blew so fierce and fell,
Alack! it hath taken the kettles and pans, and this brass pott as well!'

With that he set the pott on his head and hied him up the hatch,
While all the shipwrights ran below to find what they might snatch;
All except Bob Brygandyne and he was a yeoman good,
He caught Slingawai round the waist and threw him on to the mud.

'I have taken plank and rope and nail, without the king his leave,
After the custom of Portesmouth, but I will not suffer a thief.
Nay, never lift up thy hand at me! There's no clean hands in the trade.
Steal in measure,' quo' Brygandyne. 'There's measure in all
                                                    things made!'

'Gramercy, yeoman!' said our king. 'Thy counsel liketh me.'
And he pulled a whistle out of his neck and whistled whistles three.
Then came my Lord of Arundel, pricking across the down,
And behind him the mayor and burgesses of merry Suthampton town.

They drew the naughty shipwrights up, with the kettles in their hands,
And bound them round the forecastle to wait the king's commands.
But, 'Since ye have made your beds,' said the king, 'ye needs must
                                                    lie thereon.
For the sake of your wives and little ones – felawes, get you gone!'

When they had beaten Slingawai, out of his own lips
Our king appointed Brygandyne to be clerk of all his ships.
'Nay, never lift up thy hands to me – there's no clean hands in the trade.
But steal in measure,' said Harry our king. 'There's measure in
                                                    all things made!'

God speed the Mary of the Tower, *the* Sovereign *and* Grace Dieu,
The Sweepstakes *and the* Mary Fortune *and the* Henry of Bristol *too!*
All tall ships that sail on the sea, or in our harbours stand,
That they may keep measure with Harry our king and peace
                                                    in Engeland!

MARKLAKE WITCHES

The Way Through the Woods

They shut the road through the woods
   Seventy years ago.
Weather and rain have undone it again,
   And now you would never know
There was once a road through the woods
   Before they planted the trees.
It is underneath the coppice and heath,
   And the thin anemones.
   Only the keeper sees
That where the ring-dove broods
   And the badgers roll at ease
There was once a road through the woods.

Yet if you enter the woods
   Of a summer evening late,
When the night-air cools on the trout-ringed pools
   Where the otter whistles his mate
(They fear not men in the woods
   Because they see so few),
You will hear the beat of a horse's feet
   And the swish of a skirt in the dew,
   Steadily cantering through
The misty solitudes,
   As though they perfectly knew
The old lost road through the woods . . .
But there is no road through the woods!

Marklake Witches

When Dan took up boat-building, Una coaxed Mrs Vincey, the farmer's wife at Little Lindens, to teach her to milk. Mrs Vincey milks in the pasture in summer, which is different from milking in the shed, because the cows are not tied up, and until they know you they will not stand still. After three weeks Una could milk Red Cow or Kitty Shorthorn quite dry, without her wrists aching, and then she allowed Dan to look. But milking did not amuse him, and it was pleasanter for Una to be alone in the quiet pastures with quiet-spoken Mrs Vincey. So, evening after evening, she slipped across to Little Lindens, took her stool from the fern-clump beside the fallen oak, and went to work, her pail between her knees, and her head pressed hard into the cow's flank. As often as not, Mrs Vincey would be milking cross Pansy at the other end of the pasture, and would not come near till it was time to strain and pour off.

Once, in the middle of a milking, Kitty Shorthorn boxed Una's ear with her tail.

'You old pig!' said Una, nearly crying, for a cow's tail can hurt.

'Why didn't you tie it down, child?' said a voice behind her.

'I meant to, but the flies are so bad I let her off – and this is what she's done!' Una looked round, expecting Puck, and saw a curly-haired girl, not much taller than herself, but older, dressed in a curious high-waisted, lavender-coloured riding-habit, with a high hunched collar and a deep cape and a belt fastened with a steel clasp. She wore a yellow velvet cap and tan gauntlets, and carried a real hunting-crop. Her cheeks were pale except for two pretty pink patches in the middle, and she talked with little gasps at the end of her sentences, as though she had been running.

'You don't milk so badly, child,' she said, and when she smiled her teeth showed small and even and pearly.

'Can you milk?' Una asked, and then flushed, for she heard Puck's chuckle.

He stepped out of the fern and sat down, holding Kitty Shorthorn's tail. 'There isn't much,' he said, 'that Miss Philadelphia doesn't know about milk – or, for that matter, butter and eggs. She's a great housewife.'

'Oh,' said Una. 'I'm sorry I can't shake hands. Mine are all milky; but Mrs Vincey is going to teach me butter-making this summer.'

'Ah! I'm going to London this summer,' the girl said, 'to my aunt in Bloomsbury.' She coughed as she began to hum, ' "Oh, what a town! What a wonderful metropolis!" '

'You've got a cold,' said Una.

'No. Only my stupid cough. But it's vastly better than it was last winter. It will disappear in London air. Everyone says so. D'you like doctors, child?'

'I don't know any,' Una replied. 'But I'm sure I shouldn't.'

'Think yourself lucky, child. I beg your pardon,' the girl laughed, for Una frowned.

'I'm not a child, and my name's Una,' she said.

'Mine's Philadelphia. But everybody except René calls me Phil. I'm Squire Bucksteed's daughter – over at Marklake yonder.' She jerked her little round chin towards the south behind Dallington. 'Sure–ly you know Marklake?'

'We went a picnic to Marklake Green once,' said Una. 'It's awfully pretty. I like all those funny little roads that don't lead anywhere.'

'They lead over our land,' said Philadelphia stiffly, 'and the coach road is only four miles away. One can go anywhere from the Green. I went to the Assize Ball at Lewes last year.' She spun round and took a few dancing steps, but stopped with her hand to her side.

'It gives me a stitch,' she explained. 'No odds. 'Twill go away in London air. That's the latest French step, child. René taught it me. D'you hate the French, chi— Una?'

'Well, I hate French, of course, but I don't mind Mam'selle. She's rather decent. Is René your French governess?'

Philadelphia laughed till she caught her breath again.

'Oh no! René's a French prisoner – on parole. That means he's promised not to escape till he has been properly exchanged for an Englishman. He's only a doctor, so I hope they won't think him worth exchanging. My uncle captured him last year in the *Ferdinand* privateer, off Belle Isle, and he cured my uncle of a r–r–raging toothache. Of course, after *that* we couldn't let him lie among the common French prisoners at Rye, and so he stays with us. He's of very old family – a Breton, which is nearly next door to being a true Briton, my father says – and he wears his hair clubbed – not powdered. *Much* more becoming, don't you think?'

'I don't know what you're – ' Una began, but Puck, the other side of the pail, winked, and she went on with her milking.

'He's going to be a great French physician when the war is over. He makes me bobbins for my lace-pillow now – he's very clever with his hands; but he'd doctor our people on the Green if they would let him. Only our doctor, Dr Break, says he's an *emp* – or *imp* – something, worse than imposter. But my nurse says – '

'Nurse! You're ever so old. What have you got a nurse for?' Una finished milking, and turned round on her stool as Kitty Shorthorn grazed off.

'Because I can't get rid of her. Old Cissie nursed my mother, and she says she'll nurse me till she dies. The idea! She never lets me alone. She thinks I'm delicate. She has grown infirm in her understanding, you know. Mad – quite mad, poor Cissie!'

'Really mad?' said Una. 'Or just silly?'

'Crazy, I should say – from the things she does. Her devotion to me is terribly embarrassing. You know I have all the keys of the Hall except the brewery and the tenants' kitchen. I give out all stores and the linen and plate.'

'How jolly! I love store-rooms and giving out things.'

'Ah, it's a great responsibility, you'll find, when you come to my age. Last year Dad said I was fatiguing myself with my duties, and he actually wanted me to give up the keys to old Amoore, our housekeeper. I wouldn't. I hate her. I said, "No, sir. I am mistress of Marklake Hall just as long as I live, because I'm never going to be married, and I shall give out stores and linen till I die!"'

'And what did your father say?'

'Oh, I threatened to pin a dishclout to his coat-tail. He ran away. Everyone's afraid of Dad, except me.' Philadelphia stamped her foot. 'The idea! If I can't make my own father happy in his own house, I'd like to meet the woman that can, and – and – I'd have the living hide off her!'

She cut with her long-thonged whip. It cracked like a pistol-shot across the still pasture. Kitty Shorthorn threw up her head and trotted away.

'I beg your pardon,' Philadelphia said; 'but it makes me furious. Don't you hate those ridiculous old quizzes with their feathers and fronts, who come to dinner and call you "child" in your own chair at your own table?'

'I don't always come to dinner,' said Una, 'but I hate being called "child". Please tell me about store-rooms and giving out things.'

'Ah, it's a great responsibility – particularly with that old cat Amoore looking at the lists over your shoulder. And such a shocking thing happened last summer! Poor crazy Cissie, my nurse that I was telling you of, she took three solid silver tablespoons.'

'Took! But isn't that stealing?' Una cried.

'Hsh!' said Philadelphia, looking round at Puck. 'All I say is she took them without my leave. I made it right afterwards. So, as Dad says – and he's a magistrate – it wasn't a legal offence; it was only compounding a felony.'

'It sounds awful,' said Una.

'It was. My dear, I was furious! I had had the keys for ten months, and I'd never lost anything before. I said nothing at first, because a big house offers so many chances of things being mislaid, and coming to hand later. "Fetching up in the lee-scuppers", my uncle calls it. But next week I spoke to old Cissie about it when she was doing my hair at night, and she said I wasn't to worry my heart for trifles!'

'Isn't it like 'em?' Una burst out. 'They see you're worried over something that really matters, and they say, "Don't worry"; as if that did any good!'

'I quite agree with you, my dear; quite agree with you! I told Ciss the spoons were solid silver, and worth forty shillings, so if the thief were found, he'd be tried for his life.'

'Hanged, do you mean?' Una said.

'They ought to be; but Dad says no jury will hang a man nowadays for a forty-shilling theft. They transport 'em into penal servitude at the uttermost ends of the earth beyond the seas, for the term of their natural life. I told Cissie that, and I saw her tremble in my mirror. Then she cried, and caught hold of my knees, and I couldn't for my life understand what it was all about – she cried so. *Can* you guess, my dear, what that poor crazy thing had done? It was midnight before I pieced it together. She had given the spoons to Jerry Gamm, the witchmaster on the Green, so that he might put a charm on me! Me!'

'Put a charm on you? Why?'

'That's what *I* asked; and then I saw how mad poor Cissie was! You know this stupid little cough of mine? It will disappear as soon as I go to London. She was troubled about *that*, and about my being so thin, and she told me Jerry had promised her, if she would bring him three silver spoons, that he'd charm my cough away and make me plump – "flesh up", she said. I couldn't help laughing; but it was a terrible night! I had to put Cissie into my own bed, and stroke her hand till she cried herself to sleep. What else could I have done? When she woke, and I coughed – I suppose I *can* cough in my own room if I please – she said that she'd killed me, and asked me to have her hanged at Lewes sooner than send her to the uttermost ends of the earth away from me.'

'How awful! What did you do, Phil?'

'Do? I rode off at five in the morning to talk to Master Jerry, with a new lash on my whip. Oh, I was *furious*! Witchmaster or no witchmaster, I meant to –'

'Ah! what's a witchmaster?'

'A master of witches, of course. *I* don't believe there are witches; but people say every village has a few, and Jerry was the master of all ours at Marklake. He has been a smuggler, and a man-of-war's man, and now he pretends to be a carpenter and joiner – he can make almost anything – but he really is a white wizard. He cures people by herbs and charms. He can cure them after Dr Break has given them up, and that's why Dr Break hates him so. He used to make me toy carts, and charm off my warts when I was a child.' Philadelphia spread out her hands with the delicate shiny little nails. 'It isn't counted lucky to cross him. He has his ways of getting even with you, they say. But *I* wasn't afraid of Jerry!

'I saw him working in his garden, and I leaned out of my saddle and double-thonged him between the shoulders, over the hedge. Well, my dear, for the first time since Dad gave him to me, my Troubadour (I wish you could see the sweet creature!) shied across the road, and I spilled out into the hedge-top. *Most* undignified! Jerry pulled me through to his side and brushed the leaves off me. I was horribly pricked, but I didn't care. "Now, Jerry," I said, "I'm going to take the hide off you first, and send you to Lewes afterwards. You well know why." "Oh!" he said, and he sat down among his beehives. "Then I reckon you've come about old Cissie's business, my dear." "I reckon I just about have," I said. "Stand away from these hives. I can't get at you there." "That's why I be where I be," he said. "If you'll excuse me, Miss Phil, I don't hold with bein' flogged before breakfast, at my time o' life." He's a huge big man, but he looked so comical squatting among the hives that – I know I oughtn't to – I laughed, and he laughed. I always laugh at the wrong time. But I soon recovered my dignity, and I said, "Then give me back what you made poor Cissie steal!"

' "Your pore Cissie," he said. "She's a hatful o' trouble. But you shall have 'em, Miss Phil. They're all ready put by for you." And, would you believe it, the old sinner pulled my three silver spoons out of his dirty pocket, and polished them on his cuff. "Here they be," he says, and he gave them to me, just as cool as though I'd come to have my warts charmed. That's the worst of people having known you when you were young. But I preserved my composure.

"Jerry," I said, "what in the world are we to do? If you'd been caught with these things on you, you'd have been hanged."

' "I know it," he said. "But they're yours now."

' "But you made my Cissie steal them," I said.

' "That I didn't," he said. "Your Cissie, she was pickin' at me an' tarrifyin' me all the long day an' every day for weeks to put a charm on you, Miss Phil, an' take away your little spitty cough."

' "Yes. I knew that, Jerry, and to make me flesh-up!" I said. "I'm much obliged to you, but I'm not one of your pigs!"

' "Ah! I reckon she've been talking to you, then," he said. "Yes, she give me no peace, and bein' tarrified – for I don't hold with old women – I laid a task on her which I thought 'ud silence her. *I* never reckoned the old scrattle 'ud risk her neckbone at Lewes Assizes for your sake, Miss Phil. But she did. She up an' stole, I tell ye, as cheerful as a tinker. You might ha' knocked me down with any one of them liddle spoons when she brung 'em in her apron."

' "Do you mean to say, then, that you did it to try my poor Cissie?" I screamed at him.

' "What else for, dearie?" he said. "I don't stand in need of hedge-stealings. I'm a freeholder, with money in the bank; and now I won't trust women no more! Silly old besom! I do beleft she'd ha' stole the squire's big fob-watch, if I'd required her."

' "Then you're a wicked, wicked old man," I said, and I was so angry that I couldn't help crying, and of course that made me cough.

'Jerry was in a fearful taking. He picked me up and carried me into his cottage – it's full of foreign curiosities – and he got me something to eat and drink, and he said he'd be hanged by the neck any day if it pleased me. He said he'd even tell old Cissie he was sorry. That's a great comedown for a witchmaster, you know.

'I was ashamed of myself for being so silly, and I dabbed my eyes and said, "The least you can do now is to give poor Ciss some sort of a charm for me."

' "Yes, that's only fair dealings," he said. "You know the names of the Twelve Apostles, dearie? You say them names, one by one, before your open window, rain or storm, wet or shine, five times a day fasting. But mind you, 'twixt every name you draw in your breath through your nose, right down to your pretty liddle toes, as long and as deep as you can, and let it out slow through your pretty liddle mouth. There's virtue for your cough in those names spoke that way. And I'll give you something you can see, moreover. Here's a stick of maple, which is the warmest tree in the wood." '

'That's true,' Una interrupted. 'You can feel it almost as warm as yourself when you touch it.'

' "It's cut one inch long for your every year," Jerry said. "That's sixteen inches. You set it in your window so that it holds up the sash, and thus you keep it, rain or shine, or wet or fine, day and night. I've said words over it which will have virtue on your complaints."

"I haven't any complaints, Jerry," I said. "It's only to please Cissie."

' "I know that as well as you do, dearie," he said. And – and that was all that came of my going to give him a flogging. I wonder whether he made poor Troubadour shy when I lashed at him? Jerry has his ways of getting even with people.'

'I wonder,' said Una. 'Well, did you try the charm? Did it work?'

'What nonsense! I told René about it, of course, because he's a doctor. He's going to be a most famous doctor. That's why our doctor hates him. René said, "Oho! Your Master Gamm, he is worth knowing," and he put up his eyebrows – like this. He made a joke of it all. He can see my window from the carpenter's shed, where he works, and if ever the maple stick fell down, he pretended to be in a fearful taking till I propped the window up again. He used to ask me whether I had said my Apostles properly, and how I took my deep breaths. Oh yes, and the next day, though he had been there ever so many times before, he put on his new hat and paid Jerry Gamm a visit of state – as a fellow-physician. Jerry never guessed René was making fun of him, and so he told René about the sick people in the village, and how he cured them with herbs after Dr Break had given them up. Jerry could talk smugglers' French, of course, and I had taught René plenty of English, if only he wasn't so shy. They called each other Monsieur Gamm and Mosheur Lanark, just like gentlemen. I suppose it amused poor René. He hasn't much to do, except to fiddle about in the carpenter's shop. He's like all the French prisoners – always making knick-knacks; and Jerry had a little lathe at his cottage, and so – and so – René took to being with Jerry much more than I approved of. The Hall is so big and empty when Dad's away, and I will *not* sit with old Amoore – she talks so horridly about everyone – specially about René.

'I was rude to René, I'm afraid; but I was properly served out for it. One always is. You see, Dad went down to Hastings to pay his respects to the general who commanded the brigade there, and to bring him to the Hall afterwards. Dad told me he was a very brave soldier from India – he was colonel of Dad's regiment, the Thirty-third Foot, after Dad left the army, and then he changed his name from Wesley to Wellesley, or else the other way about; and Dad said I was to get out all the silver for him, and I knew that meant a big dinner. So I sent down to the sea for early mackerel, and had such a morning in the kitchen and the store-rooms. Old Amoore nearly cried.

'However, my dear, I made all my preparations in ample time, but the fish didn't arrive – it never does – and I wanted René to ride to Pevensey and bring it himself. He had gone over to Jerry, of course, as he always used, unless I requested his presence beforehand. *I* can't send for René every time I want him. He should be there. Now, don't you ever do what I did, child, because it's in the highest degree unladylike; but – but one of our woods runs up to Jerry's garden, and if you climb – it's ungenteel, but I can climb like a kitten – there's an old hollow oak just above the pigsty where you can hear and see everything below. Truthfully, I only went to tell René about the mackerel, but I saw him and Jerry sitting on the seat playing with wooden toy trumpets. So I slipped into the hollow, and choked down my cough, and listened. René had never shown *me* any of these trumpets.'

'Trumpets? Aren't you too old for trumpets?' said Una.

'They weren't real trumpets, because Jerry opened his short-collar, and René put one end of his trumpet against Jerry's chest, and put his ear to the other. Then Jerry put his trumpet against René's chest, and listened while René breathed and coughed. I was afraid *I* would cough too.

' "This holly-wood one is the best," said Jerry. "'Tis won'erful like hearin' a man's soul whisperin' in his innards; but unless I've a buzzin' in my ears, Mosheur Lanark, you make much about the same kind o' noises as old Gaffer Macklin – but not quite so loud as young Copper. It sounds like breakers on a reef – a long way off. Comprenny?"

' "Perfectly," said René. "I drive on the breakers. But before I strike, I shall save hundreds, thousands, millions perhaps, by my little trumpets. Now tell me what sounds the old Gaffer Macklin have made in his chest, and what the young Copper also."

'Jerry talked for nearly a quarter of an hour about sick people in the village, while René asked questions. Then he sighed, and said, "You explain very well, Monsieur Gamm, but if only I had your opportunities to listen for myself! Do you think these poor people would let me listen to them through my trumpet – for a little money? No?" – René's as poor as a church mouse.

' "They'd kill you, Mosheur. It's all I can do to coax 'em to abide it, and I'm Jerry Gamm," said Jerry. He's very proud of his attainments.

' "Then these poor people are alarmed – No?" said René.

' "They've had it in at me for some time back because o' my tryin' your trumpets on their sick; and I reckon by the talk at the alehouse they won't stand much more. Tom Dunch an' some of his kidney was drinkin' themselves riot-ripe when I passed along after noon. Charms an' mutterin's an' bits o' red wool an' black hens is in the way o' nature to these fools, Mosheur; but anything likely to do 'em real service is devil's work by their estimation. If I was you, I'd go home before they come." Jerry spoke quite quietly, and René shrugged his shoulders.

' "I am prisoner on parole, Monsieur Gamm," he said. "I have no home."

'Now that was unkind of René. He's often told me that he looked on England as his home. I suppose it's French politeness.

' "Then we'll talk o' something that matters," said Jerry. "Not to name no names, Mosheur Lanark, what might be your own opinion o' someone who ain't old Gaffer Macklin nor young Copper? Is that person better or worse?"

' "Better – for time that is," said René. He meant for the time being, but I never could teach him some phrases.

' "I thought so too," said Jerry. "But how about time to come?"

René shook his head, and then he blew his nose. You don't know how odd a man looks blowing his nose when you are sitting directly above him.

' "I've thought that too," said Jerry. He rumbled so deep I could scarcely catch. "It don't make much odds to me, because I'm old. But you're young, Mosheur – you're young," and he put his hand on René's knee, and René covered it with his hand. I didn't know they were such friends.

' "Thank you, *mon ami*," said René. "I am much oblige. Let us return to our trumpet-making. But I forget" – he stood up – "it appears that you receive this afternoon!"

'You can't see into Gamm's Lane from the oak, but the gate opened, and fat little Dr Break stumped in, mopping his head, and half a dozen of our people following him, very drunk.

'You ought to have seen René bow; he does it beautifully.

' "A word with you, Laennec," said Dr Break. "Jerry has been practising some devilry or other on these poor wretches, and they've asked me to be arbiter."

' "Whatever that means, I reckon it's safer than asking you to be doctor," said Jerry, and Tom Dunch, one of our carters, laughed.

' "That ain't right feeling of you, Tom," Jerry said, "seeing how clever Dr Break put away your thorn in the flesh last winter." Tom's wife had died at Christmas, though Dr Break bled her twice a week. Dr Break danced with rage.

' "This is all beside the mark," he said. "These good people are willing to testify that you've been impudently prying into God's secrets by means of some papistical contrivance which this person" – he pointed to poor René – "has furnished you with. Why, here are the things themselves!" René was holding a trumpet in his hand.

'Then all the men talked at once. They said old Gaffer Macklin was dying from stitches in his side where Jerry had put the trumpet – they called it the devil's ear-piece; and they said it left round red witch-marks on people's skins, and dried up their lights, and made 'em spit blood, and threw 'em into sweats. Terrible things they said. You never heard such a noise. I took advantage of it to cough.

'René and Jerry were standing with their backs to the pigsty. Jerry fumbled in his big flap pockets and fished up a pair of pistols. You ought to have seen the men give back when he cocked his. He passed one to René.

' "Wait! Wait!" said René. "I will explain to the doctor if he permits." He waved a trumpet at him, and the men at the gate shouted, "Don't touch it, doctor! Don't lay a hand to the thing."

' "Come, come!" said René. "You are not so big fool as you pretend. No?"

'Dr Break backed toward the gate, watching Jerry's pistol, and René followed him with his trumpet, like a nurse trying to amuse a child, and put the ridiculous thing to his ear to show how it was used, and talked of *la Gloire* and *l'Humanité* and *la Science*, while Doctor Break watched Jerry's pistol and swore. I nearly laughed aloud.

' "Now listen! Now listen!" said René. "This will be moneys in your pockets, my dear *confrère*. You will become rich."

'Then Dr Break said something about adventurers who could not earn an honest living in their own country creeping into decent houses and taking advantage of gentlemen's confidence to enrich themselves by base intrigues.

'René dropped his absurd trumpet and made one of his best bows. I knew he was angry from the way he rolled his r's.

' "Ver-r-ry good," said he. "For that I shall have much pleasure to kill you now and here. Monsieur Gamm" – another bow to Jerry – "you will please lend him your pistol, or he shall have mine. I give you my word I know not which is best; and if he will choose a second from his friends over there" – another bow to our drunken yokels at the gate – "we will commence."

' "That's fair enough," said Jerry. "Tom Dunch, you owe it to the doctor to be his second. Place your man."

' "No," said Tom. "No mixin' in gentry's quarrels for me." And he shook his head and went out, and the others followed him.

' "Hold on," said Jerry. "You've forgot what you set out to do up at the alehouse just now. You was goin' to search me for witch-marks; you was goin' to duck me in the pond; you was goin' to drag all my bits o' sticks out o' my little cottage here. What's the matter with you? Wouldn't you like to be with your old woman tonight, Tom?"

'But they didn't even look back, much less come. They ran to the village alehouse like hares.

' "No matter for these *canaille*," said René, buttoning up his coat so as not to show any linen. All gentlemen do that before a duel, Dad says – and he's been out five times. "You shall be his second, Monsieur Gamm. Give him the pistol."

'Dr Break took it as if it was red-hot, but he said that if René resigned his pretensions in certain quarters he would pass over the matter. René bowed deeper than ever.

' "As for that," he said, "if you were not the ignorant which you are, you would have known long ago that the subject of your remarks is not for any living man."

'I don't know what the subject of his remarks might have been, but he spoke in a simply dreadful voice, my dear, and Dr Break turned quite white, and said René was a liar; and then René caught him by the throat, and choked him black.

'Well, my dear, as if this wasn't deliciously exciting enough, just exactly at that minute I heard a strange voice on the other side of the hedge say, "What's this? What's this, Bucksteed?" and there was my father and Sir Arthur Wesley on horseback in the lane; and there was René kneeling on Dr Break, and there was I up in the oak, listening with all my ears.

'I must have leaned forward too much, and the voice gave me such a start that I slipped. I had only time to make one jump on to the pigsty roof – another, before the tiles broke, on to the pigsty wall – and then I bounced down into the garden, just behind Jerry, with my hair full of bark. Imagine the situation!'

'Oh, I can!' Una laughed till she nearly fell off the stool.

'Dad said, "Phil–a–del–phia!" and Sir Arthur Wesley said, "Good Ged!" and Jerry put his foot on the pistol René had dropped. But René was splendid. He never even looked at me. He began to untwist Dr Break's neckcloth as fast as he'd twisted it, and asked him if he felt better.

' "What's happened? What's happened?" said Dad.

' "A fit!" said René. "I fear my *confrère* has had a fit. Do not be alarmed. He recovers himself. Shall I bleed you a little, my dear doctor?" Dr Break was very good too. He said, "I am vastly obliged, Monsieur Laennec, but I am restored now." And as he went out of the gate he told Dad it was a syncope – I think. Then Sir Arthur said, "Quite right, Bucksteed. Not another word! They are both gentlemen." And he took off his cocked hat to Dr Break and René.

'But poor Dad wouldn't let well alone. He kept saying, "Philadelphia, what does all this mean?"

' "Well, sir," I said, "I've only just come down. As far as I could see, it looked as though Dr Break had had a sudden seizure." That was quite true – if you'd seen René seize him. Sir Arthur laughed. "Not much change there, Bucksteed," he said. "She's a lady – a thorough lady."

' "Heaven knows she doesn't look like one," said poor Dad. "Go home, Philadelphia."

'So I went home, my dear – don't laugh so! – right under Sir Arthur's nose – a most enormous nose – feeling as though I were twelve years old, going to be whipped. Oh, I *beg* your pardon, child!'

'It's all right,' said Una. 'I'm getting on for thirteen. I've never been whipped, but I know how you felt. All the same, it must have been funny!'

'Funny! If you'd heard Sir Arthur jerking out, "Good Ged, Bucksteed!" every minute as they rode behind me; and poor Dad saying, ' "'Pon my honour, Arthur, I can't account for it!" Oh, how my cheeks tingled when I reached my room! But Cissie had laid out my very best evening dress, the white satin one, vandyked at the bottom with spots of morone foil, and the pearl knots, you know, catching up the drapery from the left shoulder. I had poor mother's lace tucker and her coronet comb.'

'Oh, you lucky!' Una murmured. '*And* gloves?'

'French kid, my dear' – Philadelphia patted her shoulder – 'and morone satin shoes and a morone and gold crape fan. That restored my calm. Nice

592 RUDYARD KIPLING: CHILDREN'S STORIES

things always do. I wore my hair banded on my forehead with a little curl over the left ear. And when I descended the stairs, *en grande tenue*, old Amoore curtsied to me without my having to stop and look at her, which, alas! is too often the case. Sir Arthur highly approved of the dinner, my dear: the mackerel *did* come in time. We had all the Marklake silver out, and he toasted my health, and he asked me where my little bird's-nesting sister was. I *know* he did it to quiz me, so I looked him straight in the face, my dear, and I said, "I always send her to the nursery, Sir Arthur, when I receive guests at Marklake Hall." '

'Oh, how chee— clever of you. What did he say?' Una cried.

'He said, "Not much change there, Bucksteed. Ged, I deserved it," and he toasted me again. They talked about the French and what a shame it was that Sir Arthur only commanded a brigade at Hastings, and he told Dad of a battle in India at a place called Assaye. Dad said it was a terrible fight, but Sir Arthur described it as though it had been a whist-party – I suppose because a lady was present.'

'Of course you were the lady. I wish I'd seen you,' said Una.

'I wish you had, child. I had such a triumph after dinner. René and Dr Break came in. They had quite made up their quarrel, and they told me they had the highest esteem for each other, and I laughed and said, "I heard every word of it up in the tree." You never saw two men so frightened in your life, and when I said, "What was 'the subject of your remarks', René?" neither of them knew where to look. Oh, I quizzed them unmercifully. They'd seen me jump off the pigsty roof, remember.'

'But what *was* the subject of their remarks?' said Una.

'Oh, Dr Break said it was a professional matter, so the laugh was turned on me. I was horribly afraid it might have been something unladylike and indelicate. But that wasn't my triumph. Dad asked me to play on the harp. Between just you and me, child, I had been practising a new song from London – I don't always live in trees – for weeks; and I gave it them for a surprise.'

'What was it?' said Una. 'Sing it.'

' "I have given my heart to a flower". Not very difficult fingering, but r–r– ravishing sentiment.'

Philadelphia coughed and cleared her throat.

'I've a deep voice for my age and size,' she explained. 'Contralto, you know, but it ought to be stronger,' and she began, her face all dark against the last of the soft pink sunset:

'I have given my heart to a flower,
Though I know it is fading away,
Though I know it will live but an hour
And leave me to mourn its decay!

'Isn't that touchingly sweet? Then the last verse – I wish I had my harp, dear – goes as low as my register will reach.' She drew in her chin, and took a deep breath:

> 'Ye desolate whirlwinds that rave,
> I charge you be good to my dear!
> She is all – she is all that I have,
> And the time of our parting is near!'

'Beautiful!' said Una. 'And did they like it?'

'Like it? They were overwhelmed – *accablés*, as René says. My dear, if I hadn't seen it, I shouldn't have believed that I could have drawn tears, genuine tears, to the eyes of four grown men. But I did! René simply couldn't endure it! He's all French sensibility. He hid his face and said, "*Assez, Mademoiselle! C'est plus fort que moi! Assez!*" And Sir Arthur blew his nose and said, "Good Ged! This is worse than Assaye!" While Dad sat with the tears simply running down his cheeks.'

'And what did Dr Break do?'

'He got up and pretended to look out of the window, but I saw his little fat shoulders jerk as if he had the hiccups. That was a triumph. I never suspected him of sensibility.'

'Oh, I wish I'd seen! I wish I'd been you,' said Una, clasping her hands. Puck rustled and rose from the fern, just as a big blundering cock-chafer flew smack against Una's cheek.

When she had finished rubbing the place, Mrs Vincey called to her that Pansy had been fractious, or she would have come long before to help her strain and pour off.

'It didn't matter,' said Una; 'I just waited. Is that old Pansy barging about the lower pasture now?'

'No,' said Mrs Vincey, listening. 'It sounds more like a horse being galloped middlin' quick through the woods; but there's no road there. I reckon it's one of Gleason's colts loose. Shall I see you up to the house, Miss Una?'

'Gracious, no! thank you. What's going to hurt me?' said Una, and she put her stool away behind the oak, and strolled home through the gaps that old Hobden kept open for her.

Brookland Road

I was very well pleased with what I knowed,
   I reckoned myself no fool –
Till I met with a maid on the Brookland Road
   That turned me back to school.

   Low down – low down!
   Where the liddle green lanterns shine –
   Oh! maids, I've done with 'ee all but one,
   And she can never be mine!

'Twas right in the middest of a hot June night,
   With thunder duntin' round,
And I seed her face by the fairy light
   That beats from off the ground.

She only smiled and she never spoke,
   She smiled and went away;
But when she'd gone my heart was broke,
   And my wits was clean astray.

Oh! Stop your ringing and let me be –
   Let be, O Brookland bells!
You'll ring Old Goodman* out of the sea,
   Before I wed one else!

Old Goodman's farm is rank sea sand,
   And was this thousand year;
But it shall turn to rich ploughland
   Before I change my dear!

Oh! Fairfield Church is water-bound
   From autumn to the spring;
But it shall turn to high hill ground
   Before my bells do ring!

   * Earl Godwin of the Goodwin Sands(?)

Oh! leave me walk on the Brookland Road,
  In the thunder and warm rain –
Oh! leave me look where my love goed
  And p'raps I'll see her again!

  Low down – low down!
  Where the liddle green lanterns shine –
  Oh! maids, I've done with 'ee all but one,
  And she can never be mine!

THE KNIFE AND THE NAKED CHALK

The Run of the Downs

The Weald is good, the Downs are best –
I'll give you the run of 'em, east to west.
Beachy Head and Winddoor Hill,
They were once and they are still.
Firle, Mount Caburn and Mount Harry
Go back as far as sums'll carry.
Ditchling Beacon and Chanctonbury Ring,
They have looked on many a thing;
And what those two have missed between 'em
I reckon Truleigh Hill has seen 'em.
Highden, Bignor and Duncton Down
Knew Old England before the Crown.
Linch Down, Treyford and Sunwood
Knew Old England before the Flood.
And when you end on the Hampshire side –
Butser's old as Time and Tide.
   The Downs are sheep, the Weald is corn,
   You be glad you are Sussex born!

The Knife and the Naked Chalk

The children went to the seaside for a month, and lived in a flint village on the bare windy chalk downs, quite thirty miles away from home. They made friends with an old shepherd, called Mr Dudeney, who had known their father when their father was little. He did not talk like their own people in the Weald of Sussex, and he used different names for farm things, but he understood how they felt, and let them go with him. He had a tiny cottage about half a mile from the village, where his wife made mead from thyme honey, and nursed sick lambs in front of a coal fire, while Old Jim, who was Mr Dudeney's sheep-dog's father, lay at the door. They brought up beef bones for Old Jim (you must never give a sheep-dog mutton bones), and if Mr Dudeney happened to be far in the Downs, Mrs Dudeney would tell the dog to take them to him, and he did.

One August afternoon when the village water-cart had made the street smell specially townified, they went to look for their shepherd as usual, and, as usual, Old Jim crawled over the doorstep and took them in charge. The sun was hot, the dry grass was very slippery, and the distances were very distant.

'It's just like the sea,' said Una, when Old Jim halted in the shade of a lonely flint barn on a bare rise. 'You see where you're going, and – you go there, and there's nothing between.'

Dan slipped off his shoes. 'When we get home I shall sit in the woods all day,' he said.

'Whuff!' said Old Jim, to show he was ready, and struck across a long rolling stretch of turf. Presently he asked for his beef bone.

'Not yet,' said Dan. 'Where's Mr Dudeney? Where's master?' Old Jim looked as if he thought they were mad, and asked again.

'Don't you give it him,' Una cried. 'I'm not going to be left howling in a desert.'

'Show, boy! Show!' said Dan, for the downs seemed as bare as the palm of your hand.

Old Jim sighed, and trotted forward. Soon they spied the blob of Mr Dudeney's hat against the sky a long way off.

'Right! All right!' said Dan. Old Jim wheeled round, took his bone carefully between his blunted teeth, and returned to the shadow of the old barn, looking just like a wolf. The children went on. Two kestrels hung bivvering and squealing above them. A gull flapped lazily along the white edge of the cliffs. The curves of the downs shook a little in the heat, and so did Mr Dudeney's distant head.

They walked towards it very slowly and found themselves staring into a horseshoe-shaped hollow a hundred feet deep, whose steep sides were laced with tangled sheep-tracks. The flock grazed on the flat at the bottom, under charge of Young Jim. Mr Dudeney sat comfortably knitting on the edge of the slope, his crook between his knees. They told him what Old Jim had done.

'Ah, he thought you could see my head as soon as he did. The closeter you be to the turf the more you see things. You look warm-like,' said Mr Dudeney.

'We be,' said Una, flopping down. '*And* tired.'

'Set beside o' me here. The shadow'll begin to stretch out in a little while, and a heat-shake o' wind will come up with it that'll overlay your eyes like so much wool.'

'We don't want to sleep,' said Una indignantly; but she settled herself, as she spoke, in the first strip of early afternoon shade.

'O' course not. You come to talk with me same as your father used. *He* didn't need no dog to guide him to Norton Pit.'

'Well, he belonged here,' said Dan, and laid himself down at length on the turf.

'He did. And what beats me is why he went off to live among them messy trees in the Weald, when he might ha' stayed here and looked all about him. There's no profit to trees. They draw the lightning, and sheep shelter under 'em, and *so*, like as not, you'll lose a half-score ewes struck dead in one storm. Tck! Your father knew that.'

'Trees aren't messy.' Una rose on her elbow. 'And what about firewood? I don't like coal.'

'Eh? You lie a piece more uphill and you'll lie more natural,' said Mr Dudeney, with his provoking deaf smile. 'Now press your face down and smell to the turf. That's Southdown thyme which makes our Southdown mutton beyond compare, and, my mother told me, 'twill cure anything except broken necks, or hearts. I forget which.'

They sniffed, and somehow forgot to lift their cheeks from the soft thymy cushions.

'You don't get nothing like that in the Weald. Watercress, maybe?' said Mr Dudeney.

'But we've water – brooks full of it – where you paddle in hot weather,' Una replied, watching a yellow-and-violet-banded snail-shell close to her eye.

'Brooks flood. Then you must shift your sheep – let alone foot-rot afterward. I put more dependence on a dew-pond any day.'

'How's a dew-pond made?' said Dan, and tilted his hat over his eyes. Mr Dudeney explained.

The air trembled a little as though it could not make up its mind whether to slide into the pit or move across the open. But it seemed easiest to go downhill, and the children felt one soft puff after another slip and sidle down the slope in fragrant breaths that baffed on their eyelids. The little whisper of the sea by the cliffs joined with the whisper of the wind over the grass, the hum of insects in the thyme, the ruffle and rustle of the flock below, and a thickish mutter deep in the very chalk beneath them. Mr Dudeney stopped explaining, and went on with his knitting. They were roused by voices. The shadow had crept halfway down the steep side of Norton Pit, and on the edge of it, his back to them, Puck sat beside a half-naked man who seemed busy at some work. The wind had dropped, and in that funnel of ground every least noise and movement reached them like whispers up a water-pipe.

'That is clever,' said Puck, leaning over. 'How truly you shape it!'

'Yes, but what does the beast care for a brittle flint tip? Bah!' The man flicked something contemptuously over his shoulder. It fell between Dan and Una – a beautiful dark-blue flint arrow-head still hot from the maker's hand.

The man reached for another stone, and worked away like a thrush with a snail-shell.

'Flint work is fool's work,' he said at last. 'One does it because one always did it; but when it comes to dealing with the beast – no good!' He shook his shaggy head.

'The beast was dealt with long ago. He has gone,' said Puck.

'He'll be back at lambing time. *I* know him.' He chipped very carefully, and the flints squeaked.

'Not he. Children can lie out on the chalk now all day through and go home safe.'

'Can they? Well, call the beast by his true name, and I'll believe it,' the man replied.

'Surely!' Puck leaped to his feet, curved his hands round his mouth and shouted: 'Wolf! Wolf!'

Norton Pit threw back the echo from its dry sides – 'Wuff!' Wuff!' like Young Jim's bark.

'You see? You hear?' said Puck. 'Nobody answers. Grey Shepherd is gone. Feet-in-the-Night has run off. There are no more wolves.'

'Wonderful!' The man wiped his forehead as though he were hot. 'Who drove him away? You?'

'Many men through many years, each working in his own country. Were you one of them?' Puck answered.

The man slid his sheepskin cloak to his waist and without a word pointed to his side, which was all seamed and blotched with scars. His arms, too, were dimpled from shoulder to elbow with horrible white dimples.

'I see,' said Puck. 'It is the beast's mark. What did you use against him?'

'Hand, hammer and spear, as our fathers did before us.'

'So? Then how' – Puck twitched aside the man's dark-brown cloak – 'how did a flint-worker come by *that*? Show, man, show!' He held out his little hand.

The man slipped a long dark iron knife, almost a short sword, from his belt, and after breathing on it, handed it hilt-first to Puck, who took it with his head on one side, as you should when you look at the works of a watch, squinted down the dark blade, and very delicately rubbed his forefinger from the point to the hilt.

'Good!' said he, in a surprised tone.

'It should be. The Children of the Night made it,' the man answered.

'So I see by the iron. What might it have cost you?'

'This!' The man raised his hand to his cheek. Puck whistled like a Weald starling.

'By the Great Rings of the Chalk!' he cried. 'Was *that* your price? Turn sunward that I may see better, and shut your eye.'

He slipped his hand beneath the man's chin and swung him till he faced the children up the slope. They saw that his right eye was gone, and the eyelid lay shrunk. Quickly Puck turned him round again, and the two sat down.

'It was for the sheep. The sheep are the people,' said the man, in an ashamed voice. 'What else could I have done? *You* know, Old One.'

Puck sighed a little fluttering sigh. 'Take the knife. I listen.'

The man bowed his head, drove the knife into the turf, and while it still quivered said: 'This is witness between us that I speak the thing that has been. Before my knife and the naked chalk I speak. Touch!'

Puck laid a hand on the hilt. It stopped shaking. The children wriggled a little nearer.

'I am of the People of the Worked Flint. I am the one son of the priestess who sells the winds to the Men of the Sea. I am the Buyer of the Knife – the Keeper of the People,' the man began, in a sort of singing shout. 'These are my names in this country of the naked chalk, between the trees and the sea.'

'Yours was a great country. Your names are great too,' said Puck.

'One cannot feed some things on names and songs.' The man hit himself on the chest. 'It is better – always better – to count one's children safe round the fire, their mother among them.'

'Ahai!' said Puck. 'I think this will be a very old tale.'

'I warm myself and eat at any fire that I choose, but there is no *one* to light me a fire or cook my meat. I sold all that when I bought the magic knife for my people. It was not right that the beast should master man. What else could I have done?'

'I hear. I know. I listen,' said Puck.

'When I was old enough to take my place in the sheepguard, the beast gnawed all our country like a bone between his teeth. He came in behind the flocks at watering-time, and watched them round the dew-ponds; he leaped into the folds between our knees at the shearing; he walked out alongside the grazing flocks, and chose his meat on the hoof while our boys threw flints at him; he crept by night into the huts, and licked the babe from between the mother's hands; he called his companions and pulled down men in broad daylight on the naked chalk. No – not always did he do so! *This* was his cunning! He would go away for a while to let us forget him. A year – two years perhaps – we neither smelt, nor heard, nor saw him. When our flocks had increased; when our men did not always look behind them; when children strayed from the fenced places; when our women walked alone to draw water – back, back, back came the Curse of the Chalk, Grey Shepherd, Feet-in-the-Night – the beast, the beast, the beast!

'He laughed at our little brittle arrows and our poor blunt spears. He learned to run in under the stroke of the hammer. I think he knew when there was a flaw in the flint. Often it does not show till you bring it down on his snout. Then – *Pouf!* – the false flint falls all to flinders, and you are left with the hammer-handle in your fist, and his teeth in your flank! I have felt them. At evening, too, in the dew, or when it has misted and rained, your spearhead lashings slack off, though you have kept them beneath your cloak all day. You are alone – but so close to the home ponds that you stop to tighten the sinews with hands, teeth, and a piece of driftwood. You bend over and pull – so! That is the minute for which he has followed you since the stars went out. "Aarh!" he says. "Wurr-aarh!" he says.' (Norton Pit gave back the growl like a pack of real wolves.) 'Then he is on your right shoulder feeling for the vein in your neck, and – perhaps your sheep run on without you. To fight the beast is nothing, but to be despised by the beast when he fights you – that is like his teeth in the heart! Old One, why is it that men desire so greatly, and can do so little?'

'I do not know. Did you desire so much?' said Puck.

'I desired to master the beast. It is not right that the beast should master man. But my people were afraid. Even, my mother, the priestess, was afraid when I told her what I desired. We were accustomed to be afraid of the beast. When I was made a man, and a maiden – she was a priestess – waited for me at the dew-ponds, the beast flitted from off the chalk. Perhaps it was a sickness; perhaps he had gone to his gods to learn how to do us new harm. But he went, and we breathed more freely. The women sang again; the children were not so much guarded; our flocks grazed far out. I took mine yonder' – he pointed inland to the hazy line of the Weald – 'where the new grass was best. They grazed north. I followed till we were close to the trees' – he lowered his voice – 'close *there* where the Children of the Night live.' He pointed north again.

'Ah, now I remember a thing,' said Puck. 'Tell me, why did your people fear the trees so extremely?'

'Because the gods hate the trees and strike them with lightning. We can see them burning for days all along the chalk's edge. Besides, all the chalk knows that the Children of the Night, though they worship our gods, are magicians. When a man goes into their country, they change his spirit; they put words into his mouth; they make him like talking water. But a voice in my heart told me to go towards the north. While I watched my sheep there I saw three beasts chasing a man, who ran toward the trees. By this I knew he was a Child of the Night. We flint-workers fear the trees more than we fear the beast. He had no hammer. He carried a knife like this one. A beast leaped at him. He stretched out his knife. The beast fell dead. The other beasts ran away howling, which they would never have done from a fllint-worker. The man went in among the trees. I looked for the dead beast. He had been killed in a new way – by a single deep, clean cut, without bruise or tear, which had split his bad heart. Wonderful! So I saw that the man's knife was magic, and I thought how to get it – thought strongly how to get it.

'When I brought the flocks to the shearing, my mother the priestess asked me, "What is the new thing which you have seen and I see in your face?" I said, "It is a sorrow to me;" and she answered, "All new things are sorrow. Sit in my place, and eat sorrow." I sat down in her place by the fire, where she talks to the ghosts in winter, and two voices spoke in my heart.

'One voice said, "Ask the Children of the Night for the magic knife. It is not fit that the beast should master man." I listened to that voice.

'One voice said, "If you go among the trees, the Children of the Night will change your spirit. Eat and sleep here."

'The other voice said, "Ask for the Knife." I listened to that voice.

'I said to my mother in the morning, "I go away to find a thing for the people, but I do not know whether I shall return in my own shape." She answered, "Whether you live or die, or are made different, I am your mother." '

'True,' said Puck. 'The Old Ones themselves cannot change men's mothers even if they would.'

'Let us thank the Old Ones! I spoke to my maiden, the priestess who waited for me at the dew-ponds. She promised fine things too.' The man laughed. 'I went away to that place where I had seen the magician with the knife. I lay out two days on the short grass before I ventured among the trees. I felt my way before me with a stick. I was afraid of the terrible talking trees. I was afraid of the ghosts in the branches; of the soft ground underfoot; of the red and black waters. I was afraid, above all, of the change. It came!'

They saw him wipe his forehead once again, and his strong back-muscles quivered till he laid his hand on the knife-hilt.

'A fire without a flame burned in my head; an evil taste grew in my mouth; my eyelids shut hot over my eyes; my breath was hot between my teeth, and my hands were like the hands of a stranger. I was made to sing songs and to mock the trees, though I was afraid of them. At the same time I saw myself laughing, and I was very sad for this fine young man, who was myself. Ah! The Children of the Night know magic.'

'I think that is done by the Spirits of the Mist. They change a man, if he sleeps among them,' said Puck. 'Had you slept in any mists?'

'Yes – but I know it was the Children of the Night. After three days I saw a red light behind the trees, and I heard a heavy noise. I saw the Children of the Night dig red stones from a hole, and lay them in fires. The stones melted like tallow, and the men beat the soft stuff with hammers. I wished to speak to these men, but the words were changed in my mouth, and all I could say was, "Do not make that noise. It hurts my head." By this I knew that I was bewitched, and I clung to the trees, and prayed the Children of the Night to take off their spells. They were cruel. They asked me many questions which they would never allow me to answer. They changed my words between my teeth till I wept. Then they led me into a hut and covered the floor with hot stones and dashed water on the stones, and sang charms till the sweat poured off me like water. I slept. When I waked, my own spirit – not the strange, shouting thing – was back in my body, and I was like a cool bright stone on the shingle between the sea and the sunshine. The magicians came to hear me – women and men – each wearing a magic knife. Their priestess was their ears and their mouth.

'I spoke. I spoke many words that went smoothly along like sheep in order when their shepherd, standing on a mound, can count those coming, and those far off getting ready to come. I asked for magic knives for my people. I said that my people would bring meat, and milk, and wool, and lay them in the short grass outside the trees, if the Children of the Night would leave magic knives for our people to take away. They were pleased. Their priestess said, "For whose sake have you come?" I answered, "The sheep are the people. If the beast kills our sheep, our people die. So I come for a magic knife to kill the beast."

'She said, "We do not know if our god will let us trade with the People of the Naked Chalk. Wait till we have asked."

'When they came back from the question-place (their gods are our gods), their priestess said, "The god needs a proof that your words are true." I said, "What is the proof?" She said, "The god says that if you have come for the sake of your people you will give him your right eye to be put out; but if you have come for any other reason you will not give it. This proof is between you and the god. We ourselves are sorry."

'I said, "This is a hard proof. Is there no other road?"

'She said, "Yes. You can go back to your people with your two eyes in your head if you choose. But then you will not get any magic knives for your people."

'I said, "It would be easier if I knew that I were to be killed."

'She said, "Perhaps the god knew this too. See! I have made my knife hot."

'I said, "Be quick, then!" With her knife heated in the flame she put out my right eye. She herself did it. I am the son of a priestess. She was a priestess. It was not work for any common man.'

'True! Most true,' said Puck. 'No common man's work that. And, afterwards?'

'Afterwards I did not see out of that eye any more. I found also that a one eye does not tell you truly where things are. Try it!'

At this Dan put his hand over one eye, and reached for the flint arrow-head on the grass. He missed it by inches. 'It's true,' he whispered to Una. 'You can't judge distances a bit with only one eye.'

Puck was evidently making the same experiment, for the man laughed at him.

'I know it is so,' said he. 'Even now I am not always sure of my blow. I stayed with the Children of the Night till my eye healed. They said I was the son of Tyr, the god who put his right hand in a beast's mouth. They showed me how they melted their red stone and made the magic knives of it. They told me the charms they sang over the fires and at the beatings. I can sing many charms.' Then he began to laugh like a boy.

'I was thinking of my journey home,' he said, 'and of the surprised beast. He had come back to the chalk. I saw him – I smelt his lairs as soon as ever I left the trees. He did not know I had the magic knife – I hid it under my cloak – the knife that the priestess gave me. Ho! Ho! That happy day was too short! See! A beast would wind me. "Wow!" he would say. "Here is my flint-worker!" He would come leaping, tail in air; he would roll; he would lay his head between his paws out of merriness of heart at his warm, waiting meal. He would leap – and, oh, his eye in mid-leap when he saw – when he saw the knife held ready for him! It pierced his hide as a rush pierces curdled milk. Often he had no time to howl. I did not trouble to flay any beasts I killed. Sometimes I missed my blow. Then I took my little flint hammer and beat out his brains as he cowered. He made no fight. He knew the knife! But the beast is very cunning. Before evening all the beasts had smelt the blood on my knife, and were running from me like hares. *They* knew! Then I walked as a man should – the master of the beast!

'So came I back to my mother's house. There was a lamb to be killed. I cut it in two halves with my knife, and I told her all my tale. She said, "This is the work of a god." I kissed her and laughed. I went to my maiden who waited for me at the dew-ponds. There was a lamb to be killed. I cut it in two halves with my knife, and told her all my tale. She said, "It is the work of a God." I laughed, but she pushed me away, and being on my blind side, ran off before I could kiss her. I went to the Men of the Sheepguard at watering-time. There was a sheep to be killed for their meat. I cut it in two halves with my knife, and told them all my tale. They said, "It is the work of a god." I said, "We talk too much about gods. Let us eat and be happy, and tomorrow I will take you to the Children of the Night, and each man will find a magic knife. "

'I was glad to smell our sheep again; to see the broad sky from edge to edge, and to hear the sea. I slept beneath the stars in my cloak. The men talked among themselves.

'I led them, the next day, to the trees, taking with me meat, wool, and curdled milk, as I had promised. We found the magic knives laid out on the grass, as the Children of the Night had promised. They watched us from among the trees. Their priestess called to me and said, "How is it with your people?" I said "Their hearts are changed. I cannot see their hearts as I used to." She said, "That is because you have only one eye. Come to me and I will be both your eyes." But I said, "I must show my people how to use their knives against the beast, as you showed me how to use my knife." I said this because the magic knife does not balance like the flint. She said, "What you have done, you have done for the sake of a woman, and not for the sake of your people." I asked of her, "Then why did the god accept my right eye, and why are you so angry?" She answered, "Because any man can lie to a god, but no man can lie to a woman. And I am not angry with you. I am only very sorrowful for you. Wait a little, and you will see out of your one eye why I am sorry." So she hid herself.

'I went back with my people, each one carrying his knife, and making it sing in the air – *tssee–sssse*. The flint never sings. It mutters – *ump–ump*. The beast heard. The beast saw. He knew! Everywhere he ran away from us. We all laughed. As we walked over the grass my mother's brother – the chief on the men's side – he took off his chief's necklace of yellow sea-stones.'

'How? Eh? Oh, I remember! Amber,' said Puck.

'And would have put them on my neck. I said, "No, I am content. What does my one eye matter if my other eye sees fat sheep and fat children running about safely?" My mother's brother said to them, "I told you he would never take such things." Then they began to sing a song in the old tongue – *The Song of Tyr*. I sang with them, but my mother's brother said, "This is your song, O Buyer of the Knife. Let *us* sing it, Tyr."

'Even then I did not understand, till I saw that – that no man stepped on my shadow; and I knew that they thought me to be a god, like the god Tyr, who gave his right hand to conquer a great beast.'

'By the Fire in the Belly of the Flint was that so?' Puck rapped out.

'By my Knife and the Naked Chalk, so it was! They made way for my shadow as though it had been a priestess walking to the Barrows of the Dead. I was afraid. I said to myself, "My mother and my maiden will know I am not Tyr." But *still* I was afraid, with the fear of a man who falls into a steep flint-pit while he runs, and feels that it will be hard to climb out.

'When we came to the dew-ponds all our people were there. The men showed their knives and told their tale. The sheep-guards also had seen the beast flying from us. The beast went west across the river in packs – howling! He knew the knife had come to the naked chalk at last – at last! *He* knew! So my work was done. I looked for my maiden among the priestesses. She looked at me, but she did not smile. She made the sign to me that our priestesses must make when they sacrifice to the Old Dead in the Barrows. I would have spoken, but my mother's brother made himself my mouth, as though I had been one of the Old Dead in the Barrows for whom our priests speak to the people on midsummer mornings.'

'I remember. Well I remember those midsummer mornings!' said Puck.

'Then I went away angrily to my mother's house. She would have knelt before me. Then I was more angry, but she said, "Only a god would have spoken to me thus, a priestess. A man would have feared the punishment of the gods." I looked at her and I laughed. I could not stop my unhappy laughing. They called me from the door by the name of Tyr himself. A young man with whom I had watched my first flocks, and chipped my first arrow, and fought my first beast, called me by that name in the old tongue. He asked my leave to take my maiden. His eyes were lowered, his hands were on his forehead. He was full of the fear of a god, but of me, a man, he had no fear when he asked. I did not kill him. I said, "Call the maiden." She came also without fear – this very one that had waited for me, that had talked with me, by our dew-ponds. Being a priestess, she lifted her eyes to me. As I look on a hill or a cloud, so she looked at me. She spoke in the old tongue which priestesses use when they make prayers to the Old Dead in the Barrows. She asked leave that she might light the fire in my companion's house – and that I should bless their children. I did not kill her. I heard my own voice, little and cold, say, "Let it be as you desire," and they went away hand in hand. My heart grew little and cold; a wind shouted in my ears; my eye darkened. I said to my mother, "Can a god die?" I heard her say, "What is it? What is it, my son?" and I fell into darkness full of hammer-noises. I was not.'

'Oh, poor – poor god!' said Puck. 'And your wise mother?'

'*She* knew. As soon as I dropped she knew. When my spirit came back I heard her whisper in my ear, "Whether you live or die, or are made different, I am your mother." That was good – better even than the water she gave me and the going away of the sickness. Though I was ashamed to have fallen down, yet I was very glad. She was glad too. Neither of us wished to lose the other. There is only the one mother for the one son. I heaped the fire for her, and barred the doors, and sat at her feet as before I went away, and she combed my hair, and sang.

'I said at last, "What is to be done to the people who say that I am Tyr?"

'She said, "He who has done a godlike thing must bear himself like a god. I see no way out of it. The people are now your sheep till you die. You cannot drive them off."

'I said, "This is a heavier sheep than I can lift." She said, "In time it will grow easy. In time perhaps you will not lay it down for any maiden anywhere. Be wise – be very wise, my son, for nothing is left you except the words, and the songs, and the worship of a god."

'Oh, poor god!' said Puck. 'But those are not altogether bad things.'

'I know they are not; but I would sell them all – all – all for one small child of my own, smearing himself with the ashes of our own house-fire.'

He wrenched his knife from the turf, thrust it into his belt and stood up.

'And yet, what else could I have done?' he said. 'The sheep are the people.'

'It is a very old tale,' Puck answered. 'I have heard the like of it not only on the naked chalk, but also among the trees – under oak and ash and thorn.'

The afternoon shadows filled all the quiet emptiness of Norton Pit. The children heard the sheep-bells and Young Jim's busy bark above them, and they scrambled up the slope to the level.

'We let you have your sleep out,' said Mr Dudeney, as the flock scattered before them. 'It's making for teatime now.'

'Look what I've found,' said Dan, and held up a little blue flint arrow-head as fresh as though it had been chipped that very day.

'Oh,' said Mr Dudeney, 'the closeter you be to the turf the more you're apt to see things. I've found 'em often. Some says the fairies made 'em, but I says they was made by folks like ourselves – only a goodish time back. They're lucky to keep. Now, you couldn't ever have slept – not to any profit – among your father's trees same as you've laid out on naked chalk – could you?'

'One doesn't want to sleep in the woods,' said Una.

'Then what's the good of 'em?' said Mr Dudeney. 'Might as well set in the barn all day. Fetch 'em 'long, Jim boy!'

The downs, that looked so bare and hot when they came, were full of delicious little shadow-dimples; the smell of the thyme and the salt mixed together on the south-west drift from the still sea; their eyes dazzled with the low sun, and the long grass under it looked golden. The sheep knew where their fold was, so Young Jim came back to his master, and they all four strolled home, the scabious-heads swishing about their ankles, and their shadows streaking behind them like the shadows of giants.

Song of the Men's Side

Once we feared the beast – when he followed us we ran,
   Ran very fast though we knew
It was not right that the beast should master man;
   But what could we flint-workers do?
The beast only grinned at our spears round his ears –
   Grinned at the hammers that we made;
But now we will hunt him for the life with the knife –
   And this is the Buyer of the Blade!

    Room for his shadow on the grass – let it pass!
      To left and right – stand clear!
    This is the Buyer of the Blade – be afraid!
      This is the great god Tyr!

Tyr thought hard till he hammered out a plan,
    For he knew it was not right
(And it *is* not right) that the beast should master man;
    So he went to the Children of the Night.
He begged a magic knife of their make for our sake.
    When he begged for the knife they said:
'The price of the knife you would buy is an eye!'
    And that was the price he paid.

        Tell it to the Barrows of the Dead – run ahead!
          Shout it so the women's side can hear!
        This is the Buyer of the Blade – be afraid!
          This is the great god Tyr!

Our women and our little ones may walk on the chalk,
    As far as we can see them and beyond.
We shall not be anxious for our sheep when we keep
    Tally at the shearing-pond.
We can eat with both our elbows on our knees, if we please,
    We can sleep after meals in the sun;
For Shepherd-of-the-Twilight is dismayed at the blade,
    Feet-in-the-Night has run!
Dog-without-a-Master goes away (Hai, Tyr aie!),
    Devil-in-the-Dusk has run!

    THEN:
        Room for his shadow on the grass – let it pass!
          To left and right – stand clear!
        This is the Buyer of the Blade – be afraid!
          This is the great god Tyr!

BROTHER SQUARE-TOES

Philadelphia

If you're off to Philadelphia in the morning,
    You mustn't take my stories for a guide.
There's little left indeed of the city you will read of,
    And all the folk I write about have died.
Now few will understand if you mention Talleyrand,
    Or remember what his cunning and his skill did.
And the cabmen at the wharf do not know Count Zinnendorf,
    Nor the church in Philadelphia he builded.

        It is gone, gone, gone with lost Atlantis
           (Never say I didn't give you warning).
        In 1793 'twas there for all to see,
           But it's not in Philadelphia this morning,

If you're off to Philadelphia in the morning,
    You mustn't go by everything I've said.
Bob Bicknell's Southern Stages have been laid aside for ages,
    But the Limited will take you there instead.
Toby Hirte can't be seen at one hundred and eighteen,
    North Second Street – no matter when you call;
And I fear you'll search in vain for the wash-house down the lane
    Where Pharaoh played the fiddle at the ball.

        It is gone, gone, gone with Thebes the Golden
           (Never say I didn't give you warning).
        In 1794 'twas a famous dancing-floor –
           But it's not in Philadelphia this morning.

If you're off to Philadelphia in the morning,
    You must telegraph for rooms at some hotel.
You needn't try your luck at Epply's or the Buck,
    Though the Father of his Country liked them well.

It is not the slightest use to enquire for Adam Goos,
  Or to ask where Pastor Meder has removed – so
You must treat as out-of-date the story I relate
  Of the church in Philadelphia he loved so.

        He is gone, gone, gone with Martin Luther
          (Never say I didn't give you warning).
        In 1795 he was (rest his soul!) alive,
          But he's not in Philadelphia this morning.

If you're off to Philadelphia this morning,
  And wish to prove the truth of what I say,
I pledge my word you'll find the pleasant land behind
  Unaltered since Red Jacket rode that way.
Still the pine woods scent the noon; still the cat-bird sings his tune;
  Still autumn sets the maple-forest blazing.
Still the grape-vine through the dusk flings her
                            soul-compelling musk;
  Still the fireflies in the corn make night amazing.

        They are there, there, there with earth immortal
          (Citizens, I give you friendly warning).
        The things that truly last when men and times
                            have passed,
        They are all in Pennsylvania this morning!

Brother Square-Toes

It was almost the end of their visit to the seaside. They had turned themselves out of doors while their trunks were being packed, and strolled over the downs towards the dull evening sea. The tide was dead low under the chalk cliffs, and the little wrinkled waves grieved along the sands up the coast to New-haven and down the coast to long, grey Brighton, whose smoke trailed out across the Channel.

They walked to The Gap, where the cliff is only a few feet high. A windlass for hoisting shingle from the beach below stands at the edge of it. The coastguard cottages are a little farther on, and an old ship's figurehead of a Turk in a turban stared at them over the wall.

'This time tomorrow we shall be at home, thank goodness,' said Una. 'I hate the sea!'

'I believe it's all right in the middle,' said Dan. 'The edges are the sorrowful parts.'

Cordery, the coastguard, came out of the cottage, levelled his telescope at some fishing-boats, shut it with a click and walked away. He grew smaller and smaller along the edge of the cliff, where neat piles of white chalk every few yards show the path even on the darkest night. 'Where's Cordery going?' said Una.

'Half-way to Newhaven,' said Dan. 'Then he'll meet the Newhaven coastguard and turn back. He says if coastguards were done away with, smuggling would start up at once.'

A voice on the beach under the cliff began to sing:

'The moon she shined on Telscombe Tye –
On Telscombe Tye at night it was –
She saw the smugglers riding by,
A very pretty sight it was!'

Feet scrabbled on the flinty path. A dark, thin-faced man in very neat brown clothes and broad-toed shoes came up, followed by Puck. 'Three Dunkirk boats was standin' in!' the man went on.

'Hssh!' said Puck. 'You'll shock these nice young people.'

'Oh! Shall I? *Mille pardons!*' He shrugged his shoulders almost up to his ears – spread his hands abroad, and jabbered in French. 'No comprenny?' he said. 'I'll give it you in Low German.' And he went off in another language, changing his voice and manner so completely that they hardly knew him for the same person. But his dark beady-brown eyes still twinkled merrily in his lean face, and the children felt that they did not suit the straight, plain, snuffy-brown coat, brown knee-breeches and broad-brimmed hat. His hair was tied in a short pigtail which danced wickedly when he turned his head.

'Ha' done!' said Puck, laughing. 'Be one thing or t'other, Pharaoh – French or English or German – no great odds which.'

'Oh, but it is, though,' said Una quickly. 'We haven't begun German yet, and – and we're going back to our French next week.'

'Aren't you English?' said Dan. 'We heard you singing just now.'

'Aha! That was the Sussex side o' me. Dad he married a French girl out o' Boulogne, and French she stayed till her dyin' day. She was an Aurette, of course. We Lees mostly marry Aurettes. Haven't you ever come across the saying:

> Aurettes and Lees,
> Like as two peas.
> What they can't smuggle,
> They'll run overseas?'

'Then, are you a smuggler?' Una cried; and, 'Have you smuggled much?' said Dan.

Mr Lee nodded solemnly.

'Mind you,' said he, 'I don't uphold smuggling for the generality o' mankind – mostly they can't make a do of it – but I was brought up to the trade, d'ye see, in a lawful line o' descent on' – he waved across the Channel – 'on both sides the water. 'Twas all in the families, same as fiddling. The Aurettes used mostly to run the stuff across from Boulogne, and we Lees landed it here and ran it up to London town, by the safest road.'

'Then where did you live?' said Una.

'You mustn't ever live too close to your business in our trade. We kept our little fishing smack at Shoreham, but otherwise we Lees was all honest cottager folk – at Warminghurst under Washington – Bramber way – on the old Penn estate.'

'Ah!' said Puck, squatted by the windlass. 'I remember a piece about the Lees at Warminghurst, I do:

> There was never a Lee to Warminghurst
> That wasn't a gypsy last and first.

I reckon that's truth, Pharaoh.'

Pharaoh laughed. 'Admettin' that's true,' he said, 'my gypsy blood must be wore pretty thin, for I've made and kept a worldly fortune.'

'By smuggling?' Dan asked.

'No, in the tobacco trade.'

'You don't mean to say you gave up smuggling just to go and be a tobacconist!' Dan looked so disappointed they all had to laugh.

'I'm sorry; but there's all sorts of tobacconists,' Pharaoh replied. 'How far out, now, would you call that smack with the patch on her foresail?' He pointed to the fishing-boats.

'A scant mile,' said Puck after a quick look.

'Just about. It's seven fathom under her – clean sand. That was where Uncle Aurette used to sink his brandy kegs from Boulogne, and we fished 'em up and rowed 'em into The Gap here for the ponies to run inland. One thickish night in January of '93, Dad and Uncle Lot and me came over from Shoreham in the smack, and we found Uncle Aurette and the L'Estranges, my cousins, waiting for us in their lugger with New Year's presents from Mother's folk in Boulogne. I remember Aunt Cécile she'd sent me a fine new red knitted cap, which I put on then and there, for the French was having their Revolution in those days, and red caps was all the fashion. Uncle Aurette tells us that they had cut off their King Louis's head, and, moreover, the Brest forts had fired on an English man-o'-war. The news wasn't a week old.

' "That means war again, when we was only just getting used to the peace," says Dad. "Why can't King George's men and King Louis's men do up their uniforms and fight it out over our heads?"

' "Me too, I wish that," says Uncle Aurette. "But they'll be pressing better men than themselves to fight for 'em. The press-gangs are out already on our side. You look out for yours."

' "I'll have to bide ashore and grow cabbages for a while, after I've run this cargo; but I do wish" – Dad says, going over the lugger's side with our New Year presents under his arm and young L'Estrange holding the lantern – "I just do wish that those folk which make war so easy had to run one cargo a month all this winter. It 'ud show 'em what honest work means."

' "Well, I've warned ye," says Uncle Aurette. "I'll be slipping off now before your Revenue cutter comes. Give my love to Sister and take care o' the kegs. It's thicking to southward."

'I remember him waving to us and young Stephen L'Estrange blowing out the lantern. By the time we'd fished up the kegs the fog came down so thick Dad judged it risky for me to row 'em ashore, even though we could hear the ponies stamping on the beach. So he and Uncle Lot took the dinghy and left me in the smack playing on my fiddle to guide 'em back.

'Presently I heard guns. Two of 'em sounded mighty like Uncle Aurette's three-pounders. *He* didn't go naked about the seas after dark. Then come more, which I reckoned was Captain Giddens in the Revenue cutter. He was open-handed with his compliments, but he *would* lay his guns himself. I stopped fiddling to listen, and I heard a whole skyful o' French up in the fog – and a high bow come down on top o' the smack. I hadn't time to call or think. I remember the smack heeling over, and me standing on the gunwale pushing against the ship's side as if I hoped to bear her off. Then the square of an open port, with a lantern in it, slid by in front of my nose. I kicked back on our gunwale as it went under and slipped through that port into the French ship – me and my fiddle.'

'Gracious!' said Una. 'What an adventure!'

'Didn't anybody see you come in?' said Dan.

'There wasn't anyone there. I'd made use of an orlop-deck port – that's the next deck below the gun-deck, which by rights should not have been open at all. The crew was standing by their guns up above. I rolled on to a pile of dunnage in the dark and I went to sleep. When I woke, men was talking all round me, telling each other their names and sorrows just like Dad told me pressed men used to talk in the last war. Pretty soon I made out they'd all been hove aboard together by the press-gangs, and left to sort 'emselves. The ship she was the *Embuscade*, a thirty-six-gun Republican frigate, Captain Jean Baptiste Bompard, two days out of Le Havre, going to the United States with a Republican French ambassador of the name of Genêt. They had been up all night clearing for action on account of hearing guns in the fog. Uncle Aurette and Captain Giddens must have been passing the time o' day with each other off Newhaven, and the frigate had drifted past 'em. She never knew she'd run down our smack. Seeing so many aboard was total strangers to each other, I thought one more mightn't be noticed; so I put Aunt Cécile's red cap on the back of my head, and my hands in my pockets like the rest, and, as we French say, I circulated till I found the galley.

' "What! Here's one of 'em that isn't sick!" says a cook. "Take his breakfast to Citizen Bompard."

'I carried the tray to the cabin, but I didn't call this Bompard "citizen". Oh no! "mon capitaine" was my little word, same as Uncle Aurette used to answer in King Louis's navy. Bompard, he liked it. He took me on for cabin servant, and after that no one asked questions; and thus I got good victuals and light work all the way across to America. He talked a heap of politics, and so did his officers, and when this Ambassador Genêt got rid of his land-stomach and laid down the law after dinner, a rooks' parliament was nothing compared to their cabin. I learned to know most of the men which had worked the French Revolution, through waiting at table and hearing talk about 'em. One of our forecas'le six-pounders was called Danton and t'other Marat. I used to play the fiddle between 'em, sitting on the capstan. Day in and day out Bompard and Monsieur Genêt talked o' what France had done, and how the United States was going to join her to finish off the English in this war. Monsieur Genêt said he'd just about make the United States fight for France. He was a rude common man. But I liked listening. I always helped drink any healths that was proposed – specially Citizen Danton's who'd cut off King Louis's head. An all-Englishman might have been shocked – but that's where my French blood saved me.

'It didn't save me from getting a dose of ship's fever though, the week before we put Monsieur Genêt ashore at Charleston; and what was left of me after bleeding and pills took the dumb horrors from living 'tween decks. The surgeon, Karaguen his name was, kept me down there to help him with his plasters – I was too weak to wait on Bompard. I don't remember much of any account for the next few weeks, till I smelled lilacs, and I looked out of the port, and we was moored to a wharf-edge and there was a town o' fine gardens and red-brick houses and all the green leaves o' God's world waiting for me outside.

' "What's this?" I said to the sick-bay man – Old Pierre Tiphaigne he was. "Philadelphia," says Pierre. "You've missed it all. We're sailing next week."

'I just turned round and cried for longing to be amongst the laylocks.

' "If that's your trouble," says old Pierre, "you go straight ashore. None'll hinder you. They're all gone mad on these coasts – French and American together. 'Tisn't *my* notion o' war." Pierre was an old King Louis man.

'My legs was pretty tottly, but I made shift to go on deck, which it was like a fair. The frigate was crowded with fine gentlemen and ladies pouring in and out. They sang and they waved French flags, while Captain Bompard and his officers – yes, and some of the men – speechified to all and sundry about war with England. They shouted, "Down with England!" – "Down with Washington!" – "Hurrah for France and the Republic!" *I* couldn't make sense of it. I wanted to get out from that crunch of swords and petticoats and sit in a field. One of the gentlemen said to me, "Is that a genuine cap o' Liberty you're wearing?" 'Twas Aunt Cécile's red one, and pretty near wore out. "Oh yes!" I says, "straight from France." "I'll give you a shilling for it," he says, and with that money in my hand and my fiddle under my arm I squeezed past the entry-port and went ashore. It was like a dream – meadows, trees, flowers, birds, houses, and people *all* different! I sat me down in a meadow and fiddled a bit, and then I went in and out the streets, looking and smelling and touching, like a little dog at a fair. Fine folk was setting on the white stone doorsteps of their houses, and a girl threw me a handful of laylock sprays, and when I said "*Merci*" without thinking, she said she loved the French. They all was the fashion in the city. I saw more tricolour flags in Philadelphia than ever I'd seen in Boulogne, and everyone was shouting for war with England. A crowd o' folk was cheering after our French ambassador – that same Monsieur Genêt which we'd left at Charleston. He was a-horseback behaving as if the place belonged to him – and commanding all and sundry to fight the British. But I'd heard that before. I got into a long straight street as wide as the Broyle, where gentlemen was racing horses. I'm fond o' horses. Nobody hindered 'em, and a man told me it was called Race Street o' purpose for that. Then I followed some black niggers, which I'd never seen close before; but I left them to run after a great, proud, copper-faced man with feathers in his hair and a red blanket trailing behind him. A man told me he was a real Red Indian called Red Jacket, and I followed him into an alley-way off Race Street by Second Street, where there was a fiddle playing. I'm fond o' fiddling. The Indian stopped at a baker's shop – Conrad Gerhard's it was – and bought some sugary cakes. Hearing what the price was I was going to have some too, but the Indian asked me in English if I was hungry. "Oh yes!" I says. I must have looked a sore scrattel. He opens a door on to a staircase and leads the way up. We walked into a dirty little room full of flutes and fiddles and a fat man fiddling by the window, in a smell of cheese and medicines fit to knock you down. I was knocked down too, for the fat man jumped up and hit me a smack in the face. I fell against an old spinet covered with pill-boxes and the pills rolled about the floor. The Indian never moved an eyelid.

' "Pick up the pills! Pick up the pills!" the fat man screeches.

'I started picking 'em up – hundreds of 'em – meaning to run out under the Indian's arm, but I came on giddy all over and I sat down. The fat man went back to his fiddling.

' "Toby!" says the Indian after quite a while. "I brought the boy to be fed, not hit."

' "What?" says Toby, "I thought it was Gert Schwankfelder." He put down his fiddle and took a good look at me. "*Himmel!*" he says. "I have hit the wrong boy. It is not the new boy. Why are you not the new boy? Why are you not Gert Schwankfelder?"

' "I don't know," I said. "The gentleman in the pink blanket brought me."

'Says the Indian, "He is hungry, Toby. Christians always feed the hungry. So I bring him."

' "You should have said that first," said Toby. He pushed plates at me and the Indian put bread and pork on them, and a glass of Madeira wine. I told him I was off the French ship, which I had joined on account of my mother being French. That was true enough when you think of it, and besides I saw that the French was all the fashion in Philadelphia. Toby and the Indian whispered and I went on picking up the pills.

' "You like pills – eh?" says Toby.

' "No," I says. "I've seen our ship's doctor roll too many of 'em.'

' "Ho!" he says, and he shoves two bottles at me. "What's those?"

' "Calomel," I says. "And t'other's senna."

' "Right," he says. "One week have I tried to teach Gert Schwankfelder the difference between them, yet he cannot tell. You like to fiddle?" he says. He'd just seen my kit on the floor.

' "Oh yes!" says I,

' "Oho!" he says. "What note is this?" drawing his bow across.

'He meant it for A, so I told him it was.

' "My brother," he says to the Indian. "I think this is the hand of Providence! I warned that Gert if he went to play upon the wharves any more he would hear from me. Now look at this boy and say what you think."

'The Indian looked me over whole minutes – there was a musical clock on the wall and dolls came out and hopped while the hour struck. He looked me over all the while they did it.

' "Good," he says at last. "This boy is good."

' "Good, then," says Toby. "Now I shall play my fiddle and you shall sing your hymn, brother. Boy, go down to the bakery and tell them you are young Gert Schwankfelder that was. The horses are in Davy Jones's locker. If you ask any questions you shall hear from me."

'I left 'em singing hymns and I went down to old Conrad Gerhard. He wasn't at all surprised when I told him I was young Gert Schwankfelder that was. He knew Toby. His wife she walked me into the back-yard without a word, and she washed me and she cut my hair to the edge of a basin, and she put me to bed, and oh! how I slept – how I slept in that little room behind the oven looking on the flower garden! I didn't know Toby went to the *Embuscade* that night and bought me off Dr Karaguen for twelve dollars and a dozen bottles of Seneca oil. Karaguen wanted a new lace to his coat, and he reckoned I hadn't long to live; so he put me down as "discharged sick".'

'I like Toby,' said Una.

'Who was he?' said Puck.

'Apothecary Tobias Hirte,' Pharaoh replied. 'One hundred and eighteen, Second Street – the famous Seneca oil man, that lived half of every year among the Indians. But let me tell my tale my own way, same as his brown mare used to go to Lebanon.'

'Then why did he keep her in Davy Jones's locker?' Dan asked.

'That was his joke. He kept her under David Jones's hat shop in the Buck tavern yard, and his Indian friends kept their ponies there when they visited him. I looked after the horses when I wasn't rolling pills on top of the old spinet, while he played his fiddle and Red Jacket sang hymns. I liked it. I had good victuals, light work, a suit o' clean clothes, a plenty music, and quiet, smiling German folk all around that let me sit in their gardens. My first Sunday, Toby took me to his church in Moravian Alley; and that was in a garden too. The women wore long-eared caps and handkerchiefs. They came in at one door and the men at another, and there was a brass chandelier you could see your face in, and a nigger-boy to blow the organ bellows. I carried Toby's fiddle, and he played pretty much as he chose all against the organ and the singing. He was the only one they let do it, for they was a simple-minded folk. They used to wash each other's feet up in the attic to keep 'emselves humble: which Lord knows they didn't need.'

'How very queer!' said Una.

Pharaoh's eyes twinkled. 'I've met many and seen much,' he said; 'but I haven't yet found any better or quieter or forbearinger people than the Brethren and Sistern of the Moravian Church in Philadelphia. Nor will I ever forget my first Sunday – the service was in English that week – with the smell of the flowers coming in from Pastor Meder's garden where the big peach tree is, and me looking at all the clean strangeness and thinking of 'tween decks on the *Embuscade* only six days ago. Being a boy, it seemed to me it had lasted for ever, and was going on for ever. But I didn't know Toby then. As soon as the dancing clock struck midnight that Sunday – I was lying under the spinet – I heard Toby's fiddle. He'd just done his supper, which he always took late and heavy. "Gert," says he, "get the horses. Liberty and Independence for ever! The flowers appear upon the earth, and the time of the singing of birds is come. We are going to my country seat in Lebanon."

'I rubbed my eyes, and fetched 'em out of the Buck stables. Red Jacket was there saddling his, and when I'd packed the saddle-bags we three rode up Race Street to the ferry by starlight. So we went travelling. It's a kindly, softly country there, back of Philadelphia among the German towns, Lancaster way. Little houses and bursting big barns, fat cattle, fat women, and all as peaceful as heaven might be if they farmed there. Toby sold medicines out of his saddlebags, and gave the French war-news to folk along the roads. Him and his long-hilted umberell was as well known as the stage-coaches. He took orders for that famous Seneca oil which he had the secret of from Red Jacket's Indians, and he slept in friends' farmhouses, but he *would* shut all the windows; so Red Jacket and me slept outside. There's nothing to hurt except snakes – and they slip away quick enough if you thrash in the bushes.'

'I'd have liked that!' said Dan.

'I'd no fault to find with those days. In the cool o' the morning the cat-bird sings. He's something to listen to. And there's a smell of wild grape-vine growing in damp hollows which you drop into, after long rides in the heat, which is beyond compare for sweetness. So's the puffs out of the pine woods of afternoons. Come sundown, the frogs strike up, and later on the fireflies dance in the corn. Oh me, the fireflies in the corn! We were a week or ten days on the road, tacking from one place to another – such as Lancaster, Bethlehem-Ephrata – "thou Bethlehem-Ephrata". No odds – I loved the going about. And so we jogged into dozy little Lebanon by the Blue Mountains, where Toby had a cottage and a garden of all fruits. He come north every year for this wonderful Seneca oil the Seneca Indians made for him. They'd never sell to anyone else, and he doctored 'em with von Swieten pills, which they valued more than their own oil. He could do what he chose with them, and, of course, he tried to make them Moravians. The Senecas are a seemly, quiet people, and they'd had trouble enough from white men – American and English – during the wars, to keep 'em in that walk. They lived on a Reservation by themselves away off by their lake. Toby took me up there, and they treated me as if I was their own blood brother. Red Jacket said the mark of my bare feet in the dust was just like an Indian's and my style of walking was similar. I know I took to their ways all over.'

'Maybe the gypsy drop in your blood helped you?' said Puck.

'Sometimes I think it did,' Pharaoh went on. 'Anyhow, Red Jacket and Cornplanter, the other Seneca chief, they let me be adopted into the tribe. It's only a compliment, of course, but Toby was angry when I showed up with my face painted. They gave me a side-name which means "Two Tongues", because, d'ye see, I talked French and English.

'They had their own opinions (I've heard 'em) about the French and the

English, and the Americans. They'd suffered from all of 'em during the wars, and they only wished to be left alone. But they thought a heap of the president of the United States. Cornplanter had had dealings with him in some French wars out West when General Washington was only a lad. His being president afterwards made no odds to 'em. They always called him Big Hand, for he was a large-fisted man, and he was all of their notion of a white chief. Cornplanter 'ud sweep his blanket round him, and after I'd filled his pipe he'd begin – "In the old days, long ago, when braves were many and blankets were few, Big Hand said – " If Red Jacket agreed to the say-so he'd trickle a little smoke out of the corners of his mouth. If he didn't, he'd blow through his nostrils. Then Cornplanter 'ud stop and Red Jacket 'ud take on. Red Jacket was the better talker of the two. I've laid and listened to 'em for hours. Oh! they knew General Washington well. Cornplanter used to meet him at Epply's – the great dancing-place in the city before District Marshal William Nichols bought it. They told me he was always glad to see 'em, and he'd hear 'em out to the end if they had anything on their minds. They had a good deal in those days. I came at it by degrees, after I was adopted into the tribe. The talk up in Lebanon and everywhere else that summer was about the French war with England and whether the United States 'ud join in with France or make a peace treaty with England. Toby wanted peace so as he could go about the Reservation buying his oils. But most of the white men wished for war, and they was angry because the president wouldn't give the sign for it. The newspaper said men was burning Guy Fawkes images of General Washington and yelling after him in the streets of Philadelphia. You'd have been astonished what those two fine old chiefs knew of the ins and outs of such matters. The little I've learned of politics I picked up from Cornplanter and Red Jacket on the Reservation. Toby used to read the *Aurora* newspaper. He was what they call a "Democrat", though our church is against the Brethren concerning themselves with politics.'

'I hate politics, too,' said Una, and Pharaoh laughed.

'I might ha' guessed it,' he said. 'But here's something that isn't politics. One hot evening late in August, Toby was reading the newspaper on the stoop and Red Jacket was smoking under a peach tree and I was fiddling. Of a sudden Toby drops his *Aurora*.

' "I am an oldish man, too fond of my own comforts," he says. "I will go to the church which is in Philadelphia. My brother, lend me a spare pony. I must be there tomorrow night."

' "Good!" says Red Jacket, looking at the sun. "My brother shall be there. I will ride with him and bring back the ponies.

'I went to pack the saddle-bags. Toby had cured me of asking questions. He stopped my fiddling if I did. Besides, Indians don't ask questions much and I wanted to be like 'em.

'When the horses were ready I jumped up.

' "Get off," says Toby. "Stay and mind the cottage till I come back. The Lord has laid this on me, not on you. I wish He hadn't."

'He powders off down the Lancaster road, and I sat on the doorstep wondering after him. When I picked up the paper to wrap his fiddle-strings in, I spelled out a piece about the yellow fever being in Philadelphia so dreadful everyone was running away. I was scared, for I was fond of Toby. We never said much to each other, but we fiddled together, and music's as good as talking to them that understand.'

'Did Toby die of yellow fever?' Una asked.

'Not him! There's justice left in the world still. He went down to the city and bled 'em well again in heaps. He sent back word by Red Jacket that, if there was war or he died, I was to bring the oils along to the city, but till then I was to go on working in the garden and Red Jacket was to see me do it. Down at heart all Indians reckon digging a squaw's business, and neither him nor Cornplanter, when he relieved watch, was a hard taskmaster. We hired a nigger-boy to do our work, and a lazy grinning runagate he was. When I found Toby didn't die the minute he reached town, why, boylike, I took him off my mind and went with my Indians again. Oh! those days up north at Canasedago, running races and gambling with the Senecas, or bee-hunting in the woods, or fishing in the lake.' Pharaoh sighed and looked across the water. 'But it's best,' he went on suddenly, 'after the first frosts. You roll out o' your blanket and find every leaf left green overnight turned red and yellow, not by trees at a time, but hundreds and hundreds of miles of 'em, like sunsets splattered upside down. On one of such days – the maples was flaming scarlet and gold, and the sumach bushes were redder – Cornplanter and Red Jacket came out in full war-dress, making the very leaves look silly: feathered war-bonnets, yellow doeskin leggings, fringed and tasselled, red horse-blankets, and their bridles feathered and shelled and beaded no bounds. I thought it was war against the British till I saw their faces weren't painted, and they only carried wrist-whips. Then I hummed "Yankee Doodle" at 'em. They told me they was going to visit Big Hand and find out for sure whether he meant to join the French in fighting the English or make a peace treaty with England. I reckon those two would ha' gone out on the war-path at a nod from Big Hand, but they knew well, if there was war 'twixt England and the United States, their tribe 'ud catch it from both parties same as in all the other wars. They asked me to come along and hold the ponies. That puzzled me, because they always put their ponies up at the Buck or Epply's when they went to see General Washington in the city, and horse-holding is a nigger's job. Besides, I wasn't exactly dressed for it.'

'D'you mean you were dressed like an Indian?' Dan demanded.

Pharaoh looked a little abashed. 'This didn't happen at Lebanon,' he said, 'but a bit farther north, on the Reservation; and at that particular moment of time, so far as blanket, hair-band, moccasins, and sunburn went, there wasn't much odds 'twix' me and a young Seneca buck. You may laugh' – he smoothed down his long-skirted brown coat – 'but I told you I took to their ways all over. I said nothing, though I was bursting to let out the war-whoop like the young men had taught me.'

'No, and you don't let out one here, either,' said Puck before Dan could ask. 'Go on, Brother Square-Toes.'

'We went on.' Pharaoh's narrow dark eyes gleamed and danced. 'We went on – forty, fifty miles a day, for days on end – we three braves. And how a great tall Indian a-horseback can carry his war-bonnet at a canter through thick timber without brushing a feather beats *me*! My silly head was banged often enough by low branches, but they slipped through like running elk. We had evening hymn-singing every night after they'd blown their pipe-smoke to the quarters of heaven. Where did we go? I'll tell you, but don't blame me if you're no wiser. We took the old war-trail from the end of the lake along the East Susquehanna through the Nantego country, right down to Fort Shamokin on the Senachse river. We crossed the Juniata by Fort Granville, got into Shippensberg over the hills by the Ochwick trail, and then to Williams Ferry (it's a bad one). From Williams Ferry, across the Shanedore, over the Blue Mountains, through Ashby's Gap, and so south-east by south from there, till we found the president at the back of his own plantations. I'd hate to be trailed by Indians in earnest. They caught him like a partridge on a stump. After we'd left our ponies, we scouted forward through a woody piece, and, creeping slower and slower, at last if my moccasins even slipped Red Jacket 'ud turn and frown. I heard voices – Monsieur Genêt's for choice – long before I saw anything, and we pulled up at the edge of a clearing where some niggers in grey-and-red liveries were holding horses, and half a dozen gentlemen – but one was Genêt – were talking among felled timber. I fancy they'd come to see Genêt a piece on his road, for his portmantle was with him. I hid in between two logs as near to the company as I be to that old windlass there. I didn't need anybody to show me Big Hand. He stood up, very still, his legs a little apart, listening to Genêt, that French ambassador, which never had more manners than a Bosham tinker. Genêt was as good as ordering him to declare war on England at once. I had heard that clack before on the *Embuscade*. He said he'd stir up the whole United States to have war with England, whether Big Hand liked it or not.

'Big Hand heard him out to the last end. I looked behind me, and my two chiefs had vanished like smoke. Says Big Hand, "That is very forcibly put, Monsieur Genêt – " "Citizen – citizen!" the fellow spits in. "*I*, at least, am a Republican!" "Citizen Genêt," he says, "you may be sure it will receive my fullest consideration." This seemed to take Citizen Genêt back a piece. He rode off grumbling, and never gave his nigger a penny. No gentleman!

'The others all assembled round Big Hand then, and, in their way, they said pretty much what Genêt had said. They put it to him, here was France and England at war, in a manner of speaking, right across the United States' stomach, and paying no regards to anyone. The French was searching

American ships on pretence they was helping England, but really for to steal the goods. The English was doing the same, only t'other way round, and besides searching, they was pressing American citizens into their navy to help them fight France, on pretence that those Americans was lawful British subjects. His gentlemen put this very clear to Big Hand. It didn't look to them, they said, as though the United States trying to keep out of the fight was any advantage to her, because she only catched it from both French and English. They said that nine out of ten good Americans was crazy to fight the English then and there. They wouldn't say whether that was right or wrong; they only wanted Big Hand to turn it over in his mind. He did – for a while. I saw Red Jacket and Cornplanter watching him from the far side of the clearing, and how they had slipped round there was another mystery. Then Big Hand drew himself up, and he let his gentlemen have it.'

'Hit 'em?' Dan asked.

'No, nor yet was it what you might call swearing. He – he blasted 'em with his natural speech. He asked them half a dozen times over whether the United States had enough armed ships for any shape or sort of war with anyone. He asked 'em, if they thought she had those ships, to give him those ships, and they looked on the ground, as if they expected to find 'em there. He put it to 'em whether, setting ships aside, their country – I reckon he gave 'em good reasons – whether the United States was ready or able to face a new big war; she having but so few years back wound up one against England, and being all holds full of her own troubles. As I said, the strong way he laid it all before 'em blasted 'em, and when he'd done it was like a still in the woods after a storm. A little man – but they all looked little – pipes up like a young rook in a blowed-down nest, "Nevertheless, general, it seems you will be compelled to fight England." Quick Big Hand wheeled on him, "And is there anything in my past which makes you think I am averse to fighting Great Britain?"

'Everybody laughed except him. "Oh, General, you mistake us entirely!" they says. "I trust so," he says. "But I know my duty. We must have peace with England."

' "At any price?" says the man with the rook's voice.

' "At any price," says he, word by word. "Our ships will be searched – our citizens will be pressed, but – "

' "Then what about the Declaration of Independence?" says one.

' "Deal with facts, not fancies," says Big Hand. "The United States are in no position to fight England."

' "But think of public opinion," another one starts up. "The feeling in Philadelphia alone is at fever heat."

'He held up one of his big hands. "Gentlemen," he says – slow he spoke, but his voice carried far – "I have to think of our country. Let me assure you that the treaty with Great Britain will be made though every city in the Union burn me in effigy."

' "At any price?" the actor-like chap keeps on croaking.

' "The treaty must be made on Great Britain's own terms. What else can I do?"

'He turns his back on 'em and they looked at each other and slinked off to the horses, leaving him alone: and then I saw he was an old man. Then Red Jacket and Cornplanter rode down the clearing from the far end as though they had just chanced along. Back went Big Hand's shoulders, up went his head, and he stepped forward one single pace with a great deep Hough! so pleased he was. That was a statelified meeting to behold – three big men, and two of 'em looking like jewelled images among the spattle of gay-coloured leaves. I saw my chiefs' war-bonnets sinking together, down and down. Then they made the sign which no Indian makes outside of the medicine lodges – a sweep of the right hand just clear of the dust and an inbend of the left knee at the same time, and those proud eagle feathers almost touched his boot-top.'

'What did it mean?' said Dan.

'Mean!' Pharaoh cried. 'Why it's what you – what we – it's the Sachems' way of sprinkling the sacred corn-meal in front of – oh! it's a piece of Indian compliment really, and it signifies that you are a very big chief.'

'Big Hand looked down on 'em. First he says quite softly, "My brothers know it is not easy to be a chief." Then his voice grew. "My children," says he, "what is in your minds?"

'Says Cornplanter, "We came to ask whether there will be war with King George's men, but we have heard what our father has said to his chiefs. We will carry away that talk in our hearts to tell to our people."

' "No," says Big Hand. "Leave all that talk behind – it was between white men only – but take this message from *me* to your people – 'There will be no war.' " '

'His gentlemen were waiting, so they didn't delay him-, only Cornplanter says, using his old side-name, "Big Hand, did you see us among the timber just now?"

' "Surely," says he. "*You* taught me to look behind trees when we were both young." And with that he cantered off.

'Neither of my chiefs spoke till we were back on our ponies again and a half-hour along the home-trail. Then Cornplanter says to Red Jacket, "We will have the corn-dance this year. There will be no war." And that was all there was to it.'

Pharaoh stood up as though he had finished.

'Yes,' said Puck, rising too. 'And what came out of it in the long run?'

'Let me get at my story my own way,' was the answer. 'Look! it's later than I thought. That Shoreham smack's thinking of her supper.' The children looked across the darkening Channel. A smack had hoisted a lantern and slowly moved west where Brighton pier lights ran out in a twinkling line. When they turned round The Gap was empty behind them.

'I expect they've packed our trunks by now,' said Dan. 'This time tomorrow we'll be home.'

If –

If you can keep your head when all about you
Are losing theirs and blaming it on you;
If you can trust yourself when all men doubt you,
But make allowance for their doubting too;
If you can wait and not be tired by waiting,
Or being lied about, don't deal in lies,
Or being hated, don't give way to hating,
And yet don't look too good, nor talk too wise;

If you can dream – and not make dreams your master;
If you can think – and not make thoughts your aim,
If you can meet with Triumph and Disaster
And treat those two impostors just the same;
If you can bear to hear the truth you've spoken
Twisted by knaves to make a trap for fools,
Or watch the things you gave your life to, broken,
And stoop and build 'em up with worn-out tools;

If you can make one heap of all your winnings
And risk it on one turn of pitch-and-toss,
And lose, and start again at your beginnings
And never breathe a word about your loss;
If you can force your heart and nerve and sinew
To serve your turn long after they are gone,
And so hold on when there is nothing in you
Except the will which says to them: 'Hold on!'

If you can talk with crowds and keep your virtue,
Or walk with kings – nor lose the common touch,
If neither foes nor loving friends can hurt you,
If all men count with you, but none too much;
If you can fill the unforgiving minute
With sixty seconds' worth of distance run,
Yours is the earth and everything that's in it,
And – which is more – you'll be a man, my son!

A PRIEST IN SPITE OF HIMSELF

A St Helena Lullaby

How far is St Helena from a little child at play?
What makes you want to wander there with all the world between?
Oh, mother, call your son again or else he'll run away.
   (*No one thinks of winter when the grass is green!*)

How far is St Helena from a fight in Paris street?
I haven't time to answer now – the men are falling fast.
The guns begin to thunder, and the drums begin to beat.
   (*If you take the first step you will take the last!*)

How far is St Helena from the field at Austerlitz?
You couldn't hear me if I told – so loud the cannons roar.
But not so far for people who are living by their wits.
   ('*Gay go up*' means '*gay go down*' the wide world o'er!)

How far is St Helena from an Emperor of France?
I cannot see – I cannot tell – the crowns they dazzle so.
The kings sit down to dinner, and the queens stand up to dance.
   (*After open weather you may look for snow!*)

How far is St Helena from the Capes of Trafalgar?
A longish way – a longish way – with ten year more to run.
It's south across the water underneath a setting star.
   (*What you cannot finish you must leave undone!*)

How far is St Helena from the Beresina ice?
   An ill way – a chill way – the ice begins to crack.
But not so far for gentlemen who never took advice.
   (*When you can't go forward you must needs come back!*)

How far is St Helena from the field of Waterloo?
   A near way – a clear way – the ship will take you soon.
A pleasant place for gentlemen with little left to do.
   (*Morning never tries you till the afternoon!*)

How far from St Helena to the Gate of Heaven's Grace?
That no one knows – that no one knows – and no one ever will.
But fold your hands across your heart and cover up your face,
And after all your trapesings, child, lie still!

A Priest in Spite of Himself

The day after they came home from the seaside they set out on a tour of inspection to make sure everything was as they had left it. Soon they discovered that old Hobden had blocked their best hedge-gaps with stakes and thorn-bundles, and had trimmed up the hedges where the blackberries were setting.

'It can't be time for the gypsies to come along,' said Una. 'Why, it was summer only the other day!'

'There's smoke in Low Shaw!' said Dan, sniffing. 'Let's make sure!'

They crossed the fields towards the thin line of blue smoke that leaned above the hollow of Low Shaw which lies beside the King's Hill road. It used to be an old quarry till somebody planted it, and you can look straight down into it from the edge of Banky Meadow.

'I thought so,' Dan whispered, as they came up to the fence at the edge of the larches. A gypsy-van – not the showman's sort, but the old black kind, with little windows high up and a baby-gate across the door – was getting ready to leave. A man was harnessing the horses; an old woman crouched over the ashes of a fire made out of broken fence-rails; and a girl sat on the van-steps singing to a baby on her lap. A wise-looking, thin dog snuffed at a patch of fur on the ground till the old woman put it carefully in the middle of the fire. The girl reached back inside the van and tossed her a paper parcel. This was laid on the fire too, and they smelt singed feathers.

'Chicken feathers!' said Dan. 'I wonder if they are old Hobden's.'

Una sneezed. The dog growled and crawled to the girl's feet, the old woman fanned the fire with her hat, while the man led the horses up to the shafts. They all moved as quickly and quietly as snakes over moss.

'Ah!' said the girl. 'I'll teach you!' She beat the dog, who seemed to expect it.

'Don't do that,' Una called down. 'It wasn't his fault.'

'How do you know what I'm beating him for?' she answered.

'For not seeing us,' said Dan. 'He was standing right in the smoke, and the wind was wrong for his nose, anyhow.'

The girl stopped beating the dog, and the old woman fanned faster than ever.

'You've fanned some of your feathers out of the fire,' said Una. 'There's a tail-feather by that chestnut-tot.'

'What of it?' said the old woman, as she grabbed it.

'Oh, nothing!' said Dan. 'Only I've heard say that tail-feathers are as bad as the whole bird, sometimes.'

That was a saying of Hobden's about pheasants. Old Hobden always burned all feather and fur before he sat down to eat.

'Come on, mother,' the man whispered. The old woman climbed into the van, and the horses drew it out of the deep-rutted shaw on to the hard road.

The girl waved her hands and shouted something they could not catch.

'That was gypsy for "Thank you kindly, brother and sister," ' said Pharaoh Lee.

He was standing behind them, his fiddle under his arm.

'Gracious, you startled me!' said Una.

'*You* startled old Priscilla Savile,' Puck called from below them. 'Come and sit by their fire. She ought to have put it out before they left.'

They dropped down the ferny side of the shaw. Una raked the ashes together, Dan found a dead wormy oak branch that burns without flame, and they watched the smoke while Pharaoh played a curious wavery air.

'That's what the girl was humming to the baby,' said Una.

'I know it,' he nodded, and went on: 'Ai Lumai, Lumai, Lumai! Luludia! Ai Luludia!'

He passed from one odd tune to another, and quite forgot the children. At last Puck asked him to go on with his adventures in Philadelphia and among the Seneca Indians.

'I'm telling it,' he said, staring straight in front of him as he played. 'Can't you hear?'

'Maybe, but *they* can't. Tell it aloud,' said Puck.

Pharaoh shook himself, laid his fiddle beside him, and began:

'I'd left Red Jacket and Cornplanter riding home with me after Big Hand had said that there wouldn't be any war. That's all there was to it. We believed Big Hand and we went home again – we three braves. When we reached Lebanon we found Toby at the cottage with his waistcoat a foot too big for him – so hard he had worked amongst the yellow-fever people. He beat me for running off with the Indians, but 'twas worth it – I was glad to see him – and when we went back to Philadelphia for the winter, and I was told how he'd sacrificed himself over sick people in the yellow fever, I thought the world and all of him. No, I didn't neither. I'd thought that all along. That yellow fever must have been something dreadful. Even in December people had no more than begun to trinkle back to town. Whole houses stood empty and the niggers was robbing them out. But I can't call to mind that any of the Moravian Brethren had died. It seemed like they had just kept on with their own concerns, and the good Lord He'd just looked after 'em. That was the winter – yes, winter of '93 – the Brethren bought a stove for the church. Toby spoke in favour of it because the cold spoiled his fiddle hand, but many thought stove-heat not in the Bible, and there was yet a third party which always brought hickory coal foot-warmers to service and wouldn't speak either way. They ended by casting the lot for it, which is like pitch-and-toss. After my summer with the Senecas, church-stoves didn't highly interest me, so I took to haunting round among the French *émigrés* which Philadelphia was full of. My French and my fiddling helped me there, d'ye see. They come over in shiploads from France, where, by what I made out, everyone was killing everyone else by any means, and they spread 'emselves about the city – mostly in Drinker's Alley and Elfrith's Alley – and they did odd jobs till times should mend. But whatever they stooped to, they were gentry and kept a cheerful countenance, and after an evening's fiddling at one of their poor little proud parties, the Brethren seemed old-fashioned. Pastor Meder and Brother Adam Goos didn't like my fiddling for hire, but Toby said it was lawful in me to earn my living by exercising my talents. He never let me be put upon.

'In February of '94 – No, March it must have been, because a new ambassador called Fauchet had come from France, with no more manners than Genêt the old one – in March, Red Jacket came in from the Reservation bringing news of all kind friends there. I showed him round the city, and we saw General Washington riding through a crowd of folk that shouted for war with England. They gave him quite rough music, but he looked 'twixt his horse's ears and made out not to notice. His stirrup brished Red Jacket's elbow, and Red Jacket whispered up, "My brother knows it is not easy to be a chief." Big Hand shot just one look at him and nodded. Then there was a scuffle behind us over someone who wasn't hooting at Washington loud enough to please the people. We went away to be out of the fight. Indians won't risk being hit.'

'What do they do if they are?' Dan asked.

'Kill, of course. That's why they have such proper manners. Well, then, coming home by Drinker's Alley to get a new shirt which a French vicomte's lady was washing to take the stiff out of (I'm always choice in my body-linen) a lame Frenchman pushes a paper of buttons at us. He hadn't long landed in the United States, and please would we buy. He sure–ly was a pitiful scrattel – his coat half torn off, his face cut, but his hands steady; so I knew it wasn't drink. He said his name was Peringuey, and he'd been knocked about in the crowd round the Stadt – Independence Hall. One thing leading to another we took him up to Toby's rooms, same as Red Jacket had taken me the year before. The compliments he paid to Toby's Madeira wine fairly conquered the old man, for he opened a second bottle and he told this Monsieur Peringuey all about our great stove dispute in the church. I remember Pastor Meder and Brother Adam Goos dropped in, and although they and Toby were direct opposite sides regarding stoves, yet this Monsieur Peringuey he made 'em feel as if he thought each one was in the right of it. He said he had been a clergyman before he had to leave France. He admired at Toby's fiddling, and he asked if Red Jacket, sitting by the spinet, was a simple Huron. Senecas aren't Hurons, they're Iroquois, of course, and Toby told him so. Well, then, in due time he arose and left in a style which made us feel he'd been favouring us, instead of us feeding him. I've never seen that so strong before – in a man. We all talked him over but couldn't make head or tail of him, and Red Jacket come out to walk with me to the French quarter where I was due to fiddle at a party. Passing Drinker's Alley again we saw a naked window with a light in it, and there sat our button-selling Monsieur Peringuey throwing dice all alone, right hand against left.

'Says Red Jacket, keeping back in the dark, "Look at his face!"

'I was looking. I protest to you I wasn't frightened like I was when Big Hand talked to his gentlemen. I – I only looked, and I wondered that even those dead dumb dice 'ud dare to fall different from what that face wished. It – it *was* a face!

' "He is bad," says Red Jacket. "But he is a great chief. The French have sent away a great chief. I thought so when he told us his lies. Now I know."

'I had to go on to the party, so I asked him to call round for me afterwards and we'd have hymn-singing at Toby's as usual.

"No," he says. "Tell Toby I am not Christian tonight. All Indian." He had those fits sometimes. I wanted to know more about Monsieur Peringuey, and the *émigré* party was the very place to find out. It's neither here nor there, of course, but those French *émigré* parties they almost make you cry. The men that you bought fruit of in Market Street, the hairdressers and fencing-masters and French teachers, they turn back again by candlelight to what they used to be at home, and you catch their real names. There wasn't much room in the wash-house, so I sat on top of the copper and played 'em the tunes they called for – "*Si le Roi m'avait donné*", and such nursery stuff. They cried sometimes. It hurt me to take their money afterwards, indeed it did. And there I found out about Monsieur Peringuey. He was a proper rogue too! None of 'em had a good word for him except the marquise that kept the French boarding-house on Fourth Street. I made out that his real name was the Count Talleyrand de Périgord – a priest right enough, but sorely come down in the world. He'd been King Louis's ambassador to England a year or two back, before the French had cut off King Louis's head; and, by what I heard, that head wasn't hardly more than hanging loose before he'd run back to Paris and prevailed on Danton, the very man which did the murder, to send him back to England again as ambassador of the French Republic! That was too much for the English, so they kicked him out by Act of Parliament, and he'd fled to the Americas without money or friends or prospects. I'm telling you the talk in the wash-house. Some of 'em was laughing over it. Says the French marquise, "My friends, you laugh too soon. That man will be on the winning side before any of us."

' "I did not know you were so fond of priests, marquise," says the vicomte. His lady did my washing, as I've told you.

' "I have my reasons," says the marquise. "He sent my uncle and my two brothers to heaven by the little door" – that was one of the *émigré* names for the guillotine. "He will be on the winning side if it costs him the blood of every friend he has in the world."

' "Then what does he want here?" says one of 'em. "We have all lost our game."

' "My faith!" says the marquise. "He will find out, if anyone can, whether this *canaille* of a Washington means to help us to fight England. Genêt" (that was my ambassador in the *Embuscade*) "has failed and gone off disgraced; Fauchet" (he was the new man) "hasn't done any better, but our abbé will find out, and he will make his profit out of the news. Such a man does not fail."

' "He begins unluckily," says the vicomte. "He was set upon today in the street for not hooting your Washington." They all laughed again, and one remarks, "How does the poor devil keep himself?"

'He must have slipped in through the wash-house door, for he flits past me and joins 'em, cold as ice.

' "One does what one can," he says. "I sell buttons. And you, marquise?"

' "I?" – she waves her poor white hands all burned – "I am a cook – a very bad one – at your service, abbé. We were just talking about you."

They didn't treat him like they talked of him. They backed off and stood still.

' "I have missed something, then," he says. "But I spent this last hour playing – only for buttons, marquise – against a noble savage, the veritable Huron himself."

' "You had your usual luck, I hope?" she says.

' "Certainly," he says. "I cannot afford to lose even buttons in these days."

' "Then I suppose the child of nature does not know that your dice are usually loaded, Father Tout-à-tous," she continues. I don't know whether she meant to accuse him of cheating. He only bows.

' "Not yet, Mademoiselle Cunégonde," he says, and goes on to make himself agreeable to the rest of the company. And that was how I found out our Monsieur Peringuey was Count Charles Maurice Talleyrand de Périgord.'

Pharaoh stopped, but the children said nothing.

'You've heard of him?' said Pharaoh.

Una shook her head.

'Was Red Jacket the Indian he played dice with?' Dan asked.

'He was. Red Jacket told me the next time we met. I asked if the lame man had cheated. Red Jacket said no – he had played quite fair and was a master player. I allow Red Jacket knew. I've seen him, on the Reservation, play himself out of everything he had and in again. Then I told Red Jacket all I'd heard at the party concerning Talleyrand.

' "I was right," he says. "I saw the man's war-face when he thought he was alone. That's why I played him. I played him face to face. He's a great chief. Do they say why he comes here?"

' "They say he comes to find out if Big Hand makes war against the English," I said.

'Red Jacket grunted. "Yes," he says. "He asked me that too. If he had been a small chief I should have lied. But he is a great chief. He knew I was a chief, so I told him the truth. I told him what Big Hand said to Cornplanter and me in the clearing – 'There will be no war.' I could not see what he thought. I could not see behind his face. But he is a great chief. He will believe."

' "Will he believe that Big Hand can keep his people back from war?" I said, thinking of the crowds that hooted Big Hand whenever he rode out.

' "He is as bad as Big Hand is good, but he is not as strong as Big Hand," says Red Jacket. "When he talks with Big Hand he will feel this in his heart. The French have sent away a great chief. Presently he will go back and make them afraid."

'Now wasn't that comical? The French woman that knew him and owed all her losses to him; the Indian that picked him up, cut and muddy on the street, and played dice with him; they neither of 'em doubted that Talleyrand was something by himself – appearances notwithstanding.'

'And was he something by himself?' asked Una.

Pharaoh began to laugh, but stopped. 'The way *I* look at it,' he said, 'Talleyrand was one of just three men in this world who are quite by themselves. Big Hand I put first, because I've seen him.'

'Ay,' said Puck. 'I'm sorry we lost him out of Old England. Who d'you put second?'

'Talleyrand: maybe because I've seen him too,' said Pharaoh.

'Who's third?' said Puck.

'Boney – even though I've seen him.'

'Whew!' said Puck. 'Every man has his own weights and measures, but that's queer reckoning.' 'Boney?' said Una. 'You don't mean you've ever met Napoleon Bonaparte?'

'There, I knew you wouldn't have patience with the rest of my tale after hearing that! But wait a minute. Talleyrand he come round to hundred and eighteen in a day or two to thank Toby for his kindness. I didn't mention the dice-playing, but I could see that Red Jacket's doings had made Talleyrand highly curious about Indians – though he would call him the Huron. Toby, as you may believe, was all holds full of knowledge concerning their manners and habits. He only needed a listener. The Brethren don't study Indians much till they join the church, but Toby knew 'em wild. So evening after evening Talleyrand crossed his sound leg over his game one and Toby poured forth. Having been adopted into the Senecas I, naturally, kept still, but Toby 'ud call on me to back up some of his remarks, and by that means, and a habit he had of drawing you on in talk, Talleyrand saw I knew something of his noble savages too. Then he tried a trick. Coming back from an *émigré* party he turns into his little shop and puts it to me, laughing like, that I'd gone with the two chiefs on their visit to Big Hand. *I* hadn't told. Red Jacket hadn't told, and Toby, of course, didn't know. 'Twas just Talleyrand's guess. "Now," he says, "my English and Red Jacket's French was so bad that I am not sure I got the rights of what the president really said to the unsophisticated Huron. Do me the favour of telling it again." I told him every word Red Jacket had told him and not one word more. I had my suspicions, having just come from an *émigré* party where the marquise was hating and praising him as usual.

' "Much obliged," he said. "But I couldn't gather from Red Jacket exactly what the president said to Monsieur Genêt, or to his American gentlemen after Monsieur Genêt had ridden away."

'I saw Talleyrand was guessing again, for Red Jacket hadn't told him a word about the white men's pow-wow.'

'Why hadn't he?' Puck asked.

'Because Red Jacket was a chief. He told Talleyrand what the president had said to him and Cornplanter; but he didn't repeat the talk, between the white men, that Big Hand ordered him to leave behind.

'Oh!' said Puck. 'I see. What did *you* do?'

'First I was going to make some sort of tale round it, but Talleyrand was a chief too. So I said, "As soon as I get Red Jacket's permission to tell that part of the tale, I'll be delighted to refresh your memory, abbé." What else could I have done?

' "Is that all?" he says, laughing. "Let me refresh your memory. In a month from now I can give you a hundred dollars for your account of the conversation."

' "Make it five hundred, abbé," I says.

' "Five, then," says he.

' "That will suit me admirably," I says. "Red Jacket will be in town again by then, and the moment he gives me leave I'll claim the money."

'He had a hard fight to be civil, but he come out smiling.

' "Monsieur," he says, "I beg your pardon as sincerely as I envy the noble Huron your loyalty. Do me the honour to sit down while I explain."

'There wasn't another chair, so I sat on the button-box.

'He was a clever man. He had got hold of the gossip that the president meant to make a peace treaty with England at any cost. He had found out – from Genêt, I reckon, who was with the president on the day the two chiefs met him. He'd heard that Genêt had had a huff with the president and had ridden off leaving his business at loose ends. What he wanted – what he begged and blustered to know – was just the very words which the president had said to his gentlemen after Genêt had left, concerning the peace treaty with England. He put it to me that in helping him to those very words I'd be helping three great countries as well as mankind. The room was as bare as the palm of your hand, but I couldn't laugh at him.

' "I'm sorry," I says, when he wiped his forehead. "As soon as Red Jacket gives permission – "

' "You don't believe me, then?" he cuts in.

' "Not one little, little word, abbé," I says; "except that you mean to be on the winning side. Remember, I've been fiddling to all your old friends for months."

'Well, then his temper fled him and he called me names.

' "Wait a minute, *ci-devant*," I says at last. "I *am* half English and half French, but I am not the half of a man. I will tell thee something the Indian told me. Has thee seen the president?"

' "Oh yes!" he sneers. "I had letters from the Lord Lansdowne to that estimable old man."

' "Then," I says, "thee will understand. The Red Skin said that when thee has met the president thee will feel in thy heart he is a stronger man than thee."

' "Go!" he whispers. "Before I kill thee, go."

'He looked like it. So I left him.'

'Why did he want to know so badly?' said Dan.

'The way I look at it is that if he *had* known for certain that Washington meant to make the peace treaty with England at any price, he'd ha' left old Fauchet fumbling about in Philadelphia while he went straight back to France and told old Danton – "It's no good your wasting time and hopes on the United States, because she won't fight on our side – that I've proof of!" Then Danton might have been grateful and given Talleyrand a job, because a whole mass of things hang on knowing for sure who's your friend and who's your enemy. Just think of us poor shopkeepers, for instance.'

'Did Red Jacket let you tell, when he came back?' Una asked.

'Of course not. He said, "When Cornplanter and I ask you what Big Hand said to the whites you can tell the Lame Chief. All that talk was left behind in the timber, as Big Hand ordered. Tell the Lame Chief there will be no war. He can go back to France with that word."

'Talleyrand and me hadn't met for a long time except at *émigré* parties. When I give him the message he just shook his head. He was sorting buttons in the shop.

'I cannot return to France with nothing better than the word of an unsophisticated savage," he says.

' "Hasn't the president said anything to you?" I asked him.

' "He has said everything that one in his position ought to say, but – but if only I had what he said to his cabinet after Genêt rode off I believe I could change Europe – the world, maybe."

' "I'm sorry," I says. "Maybe you'll do that without my help."

'He looked at me hard. "Either you have unusual observation for one so young, or you choose to be insolent," he says.

' "It was intended for a compliment," I says. "But no odds. We're off in a few days for our summer trip, and I've come to make my goodbyes."

' "I go on my travels too," he says. "If ever we meet again you may be sure I will do my best to repay what I owe you."

' "Without malice, abbé, I hope," I says.

' "None whatever," says he. "Give my respects to your adorable Dr Pangloss" (that was one of his side-names for Toby) "and the Huron." I never *could* teach him the difference betwixt Hurons and Senecas.

'Then Sister Haga came in for a paper of what we call "pilly buttons", and that was the last I saw of Talleyrand in those parts.'

'But after that you met Napoleon, didn't you?' said Una.

'Wait just a little, dearie. After that, Toby and I went to Lebanon and the Reservation, and, being older and knowing better how to manage him, I enjoyed myself well that summer with fiddling and fun. When we came back, the Brethren got after Toby because I wasn't learning any lawful trade, and he had hard work to save me from being apprenticed to Helmbold and Geyer the printers. 'Twould have ruined our music together, indeed it would. And when we escaped that, old Mattes Roush, the leather-breeches maker round the corner, took a notion I was cut out for skin-dressing. But we were rescued. Along towards Christmas there comes a big sealed letter from the bank saying that a Monsieur Talleyrand had put five hundred dollars – a hundred pounds – to my credit there to use as I pleased. There was a little note from him inside – he didn't give any address – to thank me for past kindnesses and my believing in his future, which he said was pretty cloudy at the time of writing. I wished Toby to share the money. *I* hadn't done more than bring Talleyrand up to hundred and eighteen. The kindnesses were Toby's. But Toby said, "No! Liberty and Independence for ever. I have all my wants, my son." So I gave him a set of new fiddle-strings, and the Brethren didn't advise us any more. Only Pastor Meder he preached about the deceitfulness of riches, and Brother Adam Goos said if there was war the English 'ud surely shoot down the bank. *I* knew there wasn't going to be any war, but I drew the money out and on Red Jacket's advice I put it into horseflesh, which I sold to Bob Bicknell for the Baltimore stage-coaches. That way, I doubled my money inside the twelvemonth.'

'You gypsy! You proper gypsy!' Puck shouted.

'Why not? 'Twas fair buying and selling. Well, one thing leading to another, in a few years I had made the beginning of a worldly fortune and was in the tobacco trade.'

'Ah!' said Puck, suddenly. 'Might I enquire if you'd ever sent any news to your people in England – or in France?'

'O' course I had. I wrote regular every three months after I'd made money in the horse trade. We Lees don't like coming home empty-handed. If it's only a turnip or an egg, it's something. Oh yes, I wrote good and plenty to Uncle Aurette, and – Dad don't read very quickly – Uncle used to slip over Newhaven way and tell Dad what was going on in the tobacco trade.'

'I see –

> Aurettes and Lees –
> Like as two peas.

Go on, Brother Square-Toes,' said Puck. Pharaoh laughed and went on.

'Talleyrand he'd gone up in the world same as me. He'd sailed to France again, and was a great man in the government there awhile, but they had to turn him out on account of some story about bribes from American shippers. All our poor *émigrés* said he was surely finished this time, but Red Jacket and me we didn't think it likely, not unless he was quite dead. Big Hand had made his peace treaty with Great Britain, just as he said he would, and there was a roaring trade 'twixt England and the United States for such as 'ud take the risk of being searched by British and French men-o'-war. Those two was fighting, and – just as his gentlemen told Big Hand 'ud happen – the United States was catching it from both. If an English man-o'-war met an American ship he'd press half the best men out of her, and swear they was British subjects. Most of 'em was! If a Frenchman met her he'd, likely, have the cargo out of her, swearing it was meant to aid and comfort the English; and if a Spaniard or a Dutchman met her – they was hanging on to England's coat-tails too – Lord only knows what *they* wouldn't do! It came over me that what I wanted in my tobacco trade was a fast-sailing ship and a man who could be French, English or American at a pinch. Luckily I could lay my hands on both articles. So along towards the end of September in the year '99 I sailed from Philadelphia with a hundred and eleven hogshead o' good Virginia tobacco, in the brig *Berthe Aurette*, named after Mother's maiden name, hoping 'twould bring me luck, which she didn't – and yet she did.'

'Where was you bound for?' Puck asked.

'Er – any port I found handiest. I didn't tell Toby or the Brethren. They don't understand the ins and outs of the tobacco trade.'

Puck coughed a small cough as he shifted a piece of wood with his bare foot.

'It's easy for you to sit and judge,' Pharaoh cried. 'But think o' what we had to put up with! We spread our wings and run across the broad Atlantic like a hen through a horse-fair. Even so, we was stopped by an English frigate, three days out. He sent a boat alongside and pressed seven able seamen. I remarked it was hard on honest traders, but the officer said they was fighting all creation and hadn't time to argue. The next English frigate we escaped with no more than a shot in our quarter. Then we was chased two days and a night by a French privateer, firing between squalls, and the dirty little English ten-gun brig which made him sheer off had the impudence to press another five of our men. That's how we reached to the chops of the Channel. Twelve good men pressed out of thirty-five; an eighteen-pound shot-hole close beside our rudder; our mainsail looking like spectacles where the Frenchman had hit us – and the Channel crawling with short-handed British cruisers. Put *that* in your pipe and smoke it next time you grumble at the price of tobacco!

'Well, then, to top it off, while we was trying to get at our leaks, a French lugger come swooping at us out o' the dusk. We warned him to keep away, but he fell aboard us, and up climbed his jabbering red-caps. We couldn't endure any more – indeed we couldn't. We went at 'em with all we could lay hands on.

It didn't last long. They was fifty odd to our twenty-three. Pretty soon I heard the cutlasses thrown down and someone bellowed for the *sacré* captain.

' "Here I am!" I says. "I don't suppose it makes any odds to you thieves, but this is the United States brig *Berthe Aurette*."

' "My aunt!" the man says, laughing. "Why is she named that?"

' "Who's speaking?" I said. 'Twas too dark to see, but I thought I knew the voice.

' "Enseigne de Vaisseau Estèphe L'Estrange," he sings out, and then I was sure.

' "Oh!" I says. "It's all in the family, I suppose, but you *have* done a fine day's work, Stephen."

'He whips out the binnacle-light and holds it to my face. He was young L'Estrange, my full cousin, that I hadn't seen since the night the smack sank off Telscombe Tye – six years before.

' "Whew!" he says. "That's why she was named for Aunt Berthe, is it? What's your share in her, Pharaoh?"

' "Only half owner, but the cargo's mine."

' "That's bad," he says. "I'll do what I can, but you shouldn't have fought us."

' "Steve," I says, "you aren't ever going to report our little fall-out as a fight! Why, a Revenue cutter 'ud laugh at it!"

' "So'd I if I wasn't in the Republican navy," he says. "But two of our men are dead, d'ye see, and I'm afraid I'll have to take you to the Prize Court at Le Havre."

' "Will they condemn my 'baccy?" I asks.

' "To the last ounce. But I was thinking more of the ship. She'd make a sweet little craft for the navy if the Prize Court 'ud let me have her," he says.

'Then I knew there was no hope. I don't blame him – a man must consider his own interests, but nigh every dollar I had was in ship or cargo, and Steve kept on saying, "You shouldn't have fought us."

'Well, then, the lugger took us to Le Havre, and that being the one time we *did* want a British ship to rescue us, why, o' course, we never saw one. My cousin spoke his best for us at the Prize Court. He owned he'd no right to rush alongside in the face o' the United States flag, but we couldn't get over those two men killed, d'ye see, and the court condemned both ship and cargo. They was kind enough not to make us prisoners – only beggars – and young L'Estrange was given the *Berthe Aurette* to re-arm into the French navy.

' "I'll take you round to Boulogne," he says. "Mother and the rest'll be glad to see you, and you can slip over to Newhaven with Uncle Aurette. Or you can ship with me, like most o' your men, and take a turn at King George's loose trade. There's plenty pickings," he says.

'Crazy as I was, I couldn't help laughing.

' "I've had my allowance of pickings and stealings," I says. "Where are they taking my tobacco?" 'Twas being loaded on to a barge.

' "Up the Seine to be sold in Paris," he says. "Neither you nor I will ever touch a penny of that money."

' "Get me leave to go with it," I says. "I'll see if there's justice to be gotten out of our American ambassador."

' "There's not much justice in this world," he says, "without a navy." But he got me leave to go with the barge and he gave me some money. That tobacco was all I had, and I followed it like a hound follows a snatched bone. Going up the river I fiddled a little to keep my spirits up, as well as to make friends with the guard. They was only doing their duty. Outside o' that they were the reasonablest o' God's creatures. They never even laughed at me. So we come to Paris, by river, along in November, which the French had christened Brumaire. They'd given new names to all the months, and after such an outrageous silly piece o' business as *that*, they wasn't likely to trouble 'emselves with my rights and wrongs. They didn't. The barge was laid up below Notre Dame church in charge of a caretaker, and he let me sleep aboard after I'd run about all day from office to office, seeking justice and fair dealing, and getting speeches concerning liberty. None heeded me. Looking back on it I can't rightly blame 'em. I'd no money, my clothes was filthy mucked; I hadn't changed my linen in weeks, and I'd no proof of my claims except the ship's papers, which, they said, I might have stolen. The thieves! The doorkeeper to the American ambassador – for I never saw even the secretary – he swore I spoke French a sight too well for an American citizen. Worse than that – I had spent my money, d'ye see, and I – I took to fiddling in the streets for my keep; and – and, a ship's captain with a fiddle under his arm – well, I *don't* blame 'em that they didn't believe me.

'I come back to the barge one day – late in this month Brumaire it was – fair beazled out. Old Maingon, the caretaker, he'd lit a fire in a bucket and was grilling a herring.

' "*Courage, mon ami*," he says. "Dinner is served."

' "I can't eat," I says. "I can't do any more. It's stronger than I am."

' "Bah!" he says. "Nothing's stronger than a man. Me, for example! Less than two years ago I was blown up in the *Orient* in Aboukir Bay, but I descended again and hit the water like a fairy. Look at me now," he says. He wasn't much to look at, for he'd only one leg and one eye, but the cheerfullest soul that ever trod shoe-leather. "That's worse than a hundred and eleven hogshead of 'baccy," he goes on. "You're young, too! What wouldn't I give to be young in France at this hour! There's nothing you couldn't do," he says. "The ball's at your feet – kick it!" he says. He kicks the old fire-bucket with his peg-leg. "General Bonaparte, for example!" he goes on. "That man's a babe compared to me, and see what he's done already. He's conquered Egypt and Austria and Italy – oh! half Europe!" he says, "and now he sails back to Paris, and he sails out to St Cloud down the river here – *don't* stare at the river, you young fool! – and all in front of these pig-jobbing lawyers and citizens he makes himself consul, which is as good as a king. He'll *be* king, too, in the next three turns of the capstan – King of France, England, and the world! Think o' that!" he shouts, "and eat your herring."

'I says something about Boney. If he hadn't been fighting England I shouldn't have lost my 'baccy – should I?

' "Young fellow," says Maingon, "you don't understand."

'We heard cheering. A carriage passed over the bridge with two in it.

' "That's the man himself," says Maingon. "He'll give 'em something to cheer for soon." He stands at the salute.

' "Who's t'other in black beside him?" I asks, fairly shaking all over.

' "Ah! he's the clever one. You'll hear of him before long. He's that scoundrel-bishop, Talleyrand."

' "It is!" I said, and up the steps I went with my fiddle, and run after the carriage calling, "Abbé, abbé!"

'A soldier knocked the wind out of me with the back of his sword, but I had sense to keep on following till the carriage stopped – and there just was a crowd round the house-door! I must have been half-crazy else I wouldn't have struck up "*Si le Roi m'avait donné Paris la grande ville!*" I thought it might remind him.

' "That is a good omen!" he says to Boney sitting all hunched up; and he looks straight at me.

' "Abbé – oh, abbé!" I says. "Don't you remember Toby and hundred and eighteen, Second Street?"

'He said not a word. He just crooked his long white finger to the guard at the door while the carriage steps were let down, and I skipped into the house, and they slammed the door in the crowd's face.

' "You go there," says a soldier, and shoves me into an empty room, where I catched my first breath since I'd left the barge. Presently I heard plates rattling next door – there were only folding doors between – and a cork drawn. "I tell you," someone shouts with his mouth full, "it was all that sulky ass Sieyés' fault. Only my speech to the Five Hundred saved the situation."

' "Did it save your coat?" says Talleyrand. "I hear they tore it when they threw you out. Don't gasconade to me. You may be in the road of victory, but you aren't there yet."

'Then I guessed t'other man was Boney. He stamped about and swore at Talleyrand.

' "You forget yourself, consul," says Talleyrand, "or rather you remember yourself – Corsican."

' "Pig!" says Boney, and worse.

' "Emperor!" says Talleyrand, but, the way he spoke, it sounded worst of all. Someone must have backed against the folding doors, for they flew open and showed me in the middle of the room. Boney whipped out his pistol before I could stand up.

"General," says Talleyrand to him, "this gentleman has a habit of catching us *canaille en déshabillé*. Put that thing down."

'Boney laid it on the table, so I guessed which was master. Talleyrand takes my hand – "Charmed to see you again, Candide," he says. "How is the adorable Dr Pangloss and the noble Huron?"

' "They were doing very well when I left," I said. "But I'm not."

' "Do *you* sell buttons now?" he says, and fills me a glass of wine off the table. "Madeira," says he. "Not so good as some I have drunk."

' "You mountebank!" Boney roars. "Turn that out." (He didn't even say "man", but Talleyrand, being gentle born, just went on.)

' "Pheasant is not so good as pork," he says. "You will find some at that table if you will do me the honour to sit down. Pass him a clean plate, general." And, as true as I'm here, Boney slid a plate along just like a sulky child. He was a lanky-haired, yellow-skinned little man, as nervous as a cat – and as dangerous. I could feel that.

' "And now," said Talleyrand, crossing his game leg over his sound one, "will you tell me your story?"

'I was in a fluster, but I told him nearly everything from the time he left me the five hundred dollars in Philadelphia, up to my losing ship and cargo at Le Havre. Boney began by listening, but after a bit he dropped into his own thoughts and looked at the crowd sideways through the front-room curtains. Talleyrand called to him when I'd done.

' "Eh? What we need now," says Boney, "is peace for the next three or four years."

' "Quite so," says Talleyrand. "Meantime I want the consul's order to the Prize Court at Le Havre to restore my friend here his ship."

' "Nonsense!" says Boney. "Give away an oak-built brig of two hundred and seven tons for sentiment? Certainly not! She must be armed into my navy with ten – no, fourteen twelve-pounders and two long fours. Is she strong enough to bear a long twelve forward?"

'Now I could ha' sworn he'd paid no heed to my talk, but that wonderful head-piece of his seemingly skimmed off every word of it that was useful to him.

' "Ah, general!" says Talleyrand. "You are a magician – a magician without morals. But the brig is undoubtedly American, and we don't want to offend them more than we have."

' "Need anybody talk about the affair?" he says. He didn't look at me, but I knew what was in his mind – just cold murder because I worried him; and he'd order it as easy as ordering his carriage.

' "You can't stop 'em," I said. "There's twenty-two other men besides me." I felt a little more 'ud set me screaming like a wired hare.

' "Undoubtedly American," Talleyrand goes on. "You would gain something if you returned the ship – with a message of fraternal goodwill – published in the *Moniteur*" (that's a French paper like the Philadelphia *Aurora*).

' "A good idea!" Boney answers. "One could say much in a message."

' "It might be useful," says Talleyrand. "Shall I have the message prepared?" He wrote something in a little pocket ledger.

' "Yes – for me to embellish this evening. The *Moniteur* will publish it tonight."

' "Certainly. Sign, please," says Talleyrand, tearing the leaf out.

' "But that's the order to return the brig," says Boney. "Is that necessary? Why should I lose a good ship? Haven't I lost enough ships already?"

'Talleyrand didn't answer any of those questions. Then Boney sidled up to the table and jabs his pen into the ink. Then he shies at the paper again: "My signature alone is useless," he says. "You must have the other two consuls as well. Sieyès and Roger Ducos must sign. We must preserve the laws."

' "By the time my friend presents it," says Talleyrand, still looking out of window, "only one signature will be necessary."

'Boney smiles. "It's a swindle," says he, but he signed and pushed the paper across.

' "Give that to the president of the Prize Court at Le Havre," says Talleyrand, "and he will give you back your ship. I will settle for the cargo myself. You have told me how much it cost. What profit did you expect to make on it?"

'Well, then, as man to man, I was bound to warn him that I'd set out to run it into England without troubling the Revenue, and so I couldn't rightly set bounds to my profits.'

'I guessed that all along,' said Puck.

> 'There was never a Lee to Warminghurst –
> That wasn't a smuggler last and first.'

The children laughed.

'It's comical enough now,' said Pharaoh. 'But I didn't laugh then. Says Talleyrand after a minute, "I am a bad accountant and I have several calculations on hand at present. Shall we say twice the cost of the cargo?"

'Say? I couldn't say a word. I sat choking and nodding like a China image while he wrote an order to his secretary to pay me, I won't say how much, because you wouldn't believe it.

' "Oh! Bless you, abbé! God bless you!" I got it out at last.

' "Yes," he says, "I am a priest in spite of myself, but they call me bishop now. Take this for my episcopal blessing," and he hands me the paper.

' "He stole all that money from me," says Boney over my shoulder. "A Bank of France is another of the things we must make. Are you mad?" he shouts at Talleyrand.

' "Quite," says Talleyrand, getting up. "But be calm. The disease will never attack you. It is called gratitude. This gentleman found me in the street and fed me when I was hungry."

' "I see; and he has made a fine scene of it, and you have paid him, I suppose. Meantime, France waits."

' "Oh! poor France!" says Talleyrand. "Goodbye, Candide," he says to me. "By the way," he says, "have you yet got Red Jacket's permission to tell me what the president said to his cabinet after Monsieur Genêt rode away?"

'I couldn't speak, I could only shake my head, and Boney – so impatient was he to go on with his doings – he ran at me and fair pushed me out of the room. And that was all there was to it.' Pharaoh stood up and slid his fiddle into one of his big skirt-pockets as though it were a dead hare.

'Oh! but we want to know lots and lots more,' said Dan. 'How you got home – and what old Maingon said on the barge – and wasn't your cousin surprised when he had to give back the *Berthe Aurette*, and – '

'Tell us more about Toby!' cried Una.

'Yes, and Red Jacket,' said Dan.

'Won't you tell us any more?' they both pleaded.

Puck kicked the oak branch on the fire, till it sent up a column of smoke that made them sneeze. When they had finished the shaw was empty except for old Hobden stamping through the larches.

'They gypsies have took two,' he said. "My black pullet and my liddle gingy-speckled cockrel.'

'I thought so,' said Dan, picking up one tail-feather that the old woman had overlooked.

'Which way did they go? Which way did the runagates go?' said Hobden.

'Hobby!' said Una. 'Would you like it if we told Keeper Ridley all your goings and comings?'

Poor Honest Men

Your jar of Virginny
Will cost you a guinea,
Which you reckon too much by five shilling or ten;
But light your churchwarden
And judge it accordin'
When I've told you the troubles of poor honest men.

From the Capes of the Delaware,
As you are well aware,
We sail with tobacco for England – but then
Our own British cruisers,
They watch us come through, sirs,
And they press half a score of us poor honest men.

Or if by quick sailing
(Thick weather prevailing)
We leave them behind (as we do now and then),
We are sure of a gun from
Each frigate we run from,
Which is often destruction to poor honest men!

Broadsides the Atlantic
We tumble short-handed,
With shot-holes to plug and new canvas to bend,
And off the Azores,
Dutch, Dons and Monsieurs
Are waiting to terrify poor honest men!

Napoleon's embargo
Is laid on all cargo
Which comfort or aid to King George may intend;
And since roll, twist and leaf,
Of all comforts is chief,
They try for to steal it from poor honest men!

With no heart for fight,
We take refuge in flight,
But fire as we run, our retreat to defend,
Until our stern-chasers
Cut up her fore-braces,
And she flies off the wind from us poor honest men!

'Twix' the forties and fifties,
South-eastward the drift is,
And so, when we think we are making Land's End,
Alas, it is Ushant
With half the king's navy,
Blockading French ports against poor honest men!

But they may not quit station
(Which is our salvation),
So swiftly we stand to the nor'ard again;
And finding the tail of
A homeward-bound convoy,
We slip past the Scillies like poor honest men.

'Twix' the Lizard and Dover,
We hand our stuff over,
Though I may not inform how we do it, nor when;
But a light on each quarter
Low down on the water
Is well understood by poor honest men.

Even then we have dangers
From meddlesome strangers,
Who spy on our business and are not content
To take a smooth answer,
Except with a handspike . . .
And they say they are murdered by poor honest men!

To be drowned or be shot
Is our natural lot,
Why should we, moreover, be hanged in the end –
After all our great pains
For to dangle in chains,
As though we were smugglers, not poor honest men?

THE CONVERSION OF ST WILFRID

Eddi's Service

Eddi, priest of St Wilfrid
In the chapel at Manhood End,
Ordered a midnight service
For such as cared to attend.

But the Saxons were keeping Christmas,
And the night was stormy as well.
Nobody came to service
Though Eddi rang the bell.

'Wicked weather for walking,'
Said Eddi of Manhood End.
'But I must go on with the service
For such as care to attend.'

The altar candles were lighted –
An old marsh donkey came,
Bold as a guest invited,
And stared at the guttering flame.

The storm beat on at the windows,
The water splashed on the floor,
And a wet yoke-weary bullock
Pushed in through the open door.

'How do I know what is greatest,
How do I know what is least?
That is My Father's business,'
Said Eddi, Wilfrid's priest.

'But, three are gathered together –
Listen to me and attend.
I bring good news, my brethren!'
Said Eddi, of Manhood End.

And he told the ox of a manger
And a stall in Bethlehem,
And he spoke to the ass of a rider
That rode to Jerusalem.

They steamed and dripped in the chancel,
They listened and never stirred,
While, just as though they were bishops,
Eddi preached to them The Word.

Till the gale blew off on the marshes
And the windows showed the day,
And the ox and the ass together
Wheeled and clattered away.

And when the Saxons mocked him,
Said Eddi of Manhood End,
'I dare not shut His chapel
On such as care to attend.'

The Conversion of St Wilfrid

They had bought peppermints up at the village, and were coming home past little St Barnabas' Church, when they saw Jimmy Kidbrooke, the carpenter's baby, kicking at the churchyard gate, with a shaving in his mouth and the tears running down his cheeks.

Una pulled out the shaving and put in a peppermint. Jimmy said he was looking for his grand-daddy – he never seemed to take much notice of his father – so they went up between the old graves, under the leaf-dropping limes, to the porch, where Jim trotted in, looked about the empty church, and screamed like a gate-hinge.

Young Sam Kidbrooke's voice came from the bell-tower and made them jump.

'Why, Jimmy,' he called, 'what are you doin' here? Fetch him, Father!'

Old Mr Kidbrooke stumped downstairs, jerked Jimmy on to his shoulder, stared at the children beneath his brass spectacles, and stumped back again. They laughed: it was so exactly like Mr Kidbrooke.

'It's all right,' Una called up the stairs. 'We found him, Sam. Does his mother know?'

'He's come off by himself. She'll be just about crazy,' Sam answered.

'Then I'll run down street and tell her.' Una darted off.

'Thank you, Miss Una. Would you like to see how we're mendin' the bell-beams, Mus' Dan?'

Dan hopped up, and saw young Sam lying on his stomach in a most delightful place among beams and ropes, close to the five great bells. Old Mr Kidbrooke on the floor beneath was planing a piece of wood, and Jimmy was eating the shavings as fast as they came away. He never looked at Jimmy; Jimmy never stopped eating; and the broad gilt-bobbed pendulum of the church clock never stopped swinging across the whitewashed wall of the tower.

Dan winked through the sawdust that fell on his upturned face. 'Ring a bell,' he called.

'I mustn't do that, but I'll buzz one of 'em a bit for you,' said Sam. He pounded on the sound-bow of the biggest bell, and waked a hollow groaning boom that ran up and down the tower like creepy feelings down your back. Just when it almost began to hurt, it died away in a hurry of beautiful sorrowful cries, like a wineglass rubbed with a wet finger. The pendulum clanked – one loud clank to each silent swing.

Dan heard Una return from Mrs Kidbrooke's, and ran down to fetch her. She was standing by the font staring at someone who knelt at the altar-rail.

'Is that the lady who practises the organ?' she whispered.

'No. She's gone into the organ-place. Besides, she wears black,' Dan replied.

The figure rose and came down the nave. It was a white-haired man in a long white gown with a sort of scarf looped low on the neck, one end hanging over his shoulder. His loose long sleeves were embroidered with gold, and a deep strip of gold embroidery waved and sparkled round the hem of his gown.

'Go and meet him,' said Puck's voice behind the font. 'It's only Wilfrid.'

'Wilfrid who?' said Dan. 'You come along too.'

'Wilfrid – Saint of Sussex, and Archbishop of York. *I* shall wait till he asks me.' He waved them forward. Their feet squeaked on the old grave-slabs in the centre aisle. The archbishop raised one hand with a pink ring on it, and said something in Latin. He was very handsome, and his thin face looked almost as silvery as his thin circle of hair.

'Are you alone?' he asked.

'Puck's here, of course,' said Una. 'Do you know him?'

'I know him better now than I used to.' He beckoned over Dan's shoulder, and spoke again in Latin. Puck pattered forward, holding himself as straight as an arrow. The archbishop smiled.

'Be welcome,' said he. 'Be very welcome.'

'Welcome to you also, O prince of the church,' Puck replied.

The archbishop bowed his head and passed on, till he glimmered like a white moth in the shadow by the font.

'He does look awfully princely,' said Una. 'Isn't he coming back?'

'Oh yes. He's only looking over the church. He's very fond of churches,' said Puck. 'What's that?'

The lady who practises the organ was speaking to the blower-boy behind the organ-screen. 'We can't very well talk here,' Puck whispered. 'Let's go to Panama Corner.'

He led them to the end of the south aisle, where there is a slab of iron which says in queer, long-tailed letters: *Orate p. annema Jhone Coline*. The children always called it Panama Corner.

The archbishop moved slowly about the little church, peering at the old memorial tablets and the new glass windows. The lady who practises the organ began to pull out stops and rustle hymn-books behind the screen.

'I hope she'll do all the soft lacey tunes – like treacle on porridge,' said Una.

'I like the trumpety ones best,' said Dan. 'Oh, look at Wilfrid! He's trying to shut the altar-gates!'

'Tell him he mustn't,' said Puck, quite seriously.

He can't, anyhow,' Dan muttered, and tiptoed out of Panama Corner while the archbishop patted and patted at the carved gates that always sprang open again beneath his hand.

'That's no use, sir,' Dan whispered. 'Old Mr Kidbrooke says altar-gates are just the one pair of gates which no man can shut. He made 'em so himself.'

The archbishop's blue eyes twinkled. Dan saw that he knew all about it.

'I beg your pardon,' Dan stammered – very angry with Puck.

'Yes, I know! He made them so Himself.' The archbishop smiled, and crossed to Panama Corner, where Una dragged up a certain padded armchair for him to sit on.

The organ played softly. 'What does that music say?' he asked.

Una dropped into the chant without thinking: ' "O all ye works of the Lord, bless ye the Lord; praise him and magnify him for ever." We call it the Noah's Ark, because it's all lists of things – beasts and birds and whales, you know.'

'Whales?' said the archbishop quickly.

'Yes – "O ye whales, and all that move in the waters," ' Una hummed – ' "Bless ye the Lord." It sounds like a wave turning over, doesn't it?'

'Holy father,' said Puck with a demure face, 'is a little seal also "one who moves in the water"?'

'Eh? Oh yes – yess!' he laughed. 'A seal moves wonderfully in the waters. Do the seal come to my island still?'

Puck shook his head. 'All those little islands have been swept away.'

'Very possible. The tides ran fiercely down there. Do you know the land of the sea-calf, maiden?'

'No – but we've seen seals – at Brighton.'

'The archbishop is thinking of a little farther down the coast. He means Seal's Eye – Selsey – down Chichester way – where he converted the South Saxons,' Puck explained.

'Yes – yess; if the South Saxons did not convert me,' said the archbishop, smiling. 'The first time I was wrecked was on that coast. As our ship took ground and we tried to push her off, an old fat fellow of a seal, I remember, reared breast-high out of the water, and scratched his head with his flipper as if he were saying: "What *does* that excited person with the pole think he is doing?" I was very wet and miserable, but I could not help laughing, till the natives came down and attacked us.'

'What did you do?' Dan asked.

'One couldn't very well go back to France, so one tried to make them go back to the shore. All the South Saxons are born wreckers, like my own Northumbrian folk. I was bringing over a few things for my old church at York, and some of the natives laid hands on them, and – and I'm afraid I lost my temper.'

'It is said,' Puck's voice was wickedly meek – 'that there was a great fight.'

'Eh, but I must ha' been a silly lad.' Wilfrid spoke with a sudden thick burr in his voice. He coughed, and took up his silvery tones again. 'There was no fight really. My men thumped a few of them, but the tide rose half an hour before its time, with a strong wind, and we backed off. What I wanted to say, though, was, that the seas about us were full of sleek seals watching the scuffle. My good Eddi – my chaplain – insisted that they were demons. Yes – yess! That was my first acquaintance with the South Saxons and their seals.'

'But not the only time you were wrecked, was it?' said Dan.

'Alas, no! On sea and land my life seems to have been one long shipwreck.' He looked at the Jhone Coline slab as old Hobden sometimes looks into the fire. 'Ah, well!'

'But did you ever have any more adventures among the seals?" said Una, after a little.

'Oh, the seals! I beg your pardon. They are the important things. Yes – yess! I went back to the South Saxons after twelve – fifteen – years. No, I did not come by water, but overland from my own Northumbria, to see what I could do. It's little one can do with that class of native except make them stop killing each other and themselves – '

'Why did they kill themselves?' Una asked, her chin in her hand.

'Because they were heathen. When they grew tired of life (as if *they* were the only people!) they would jump into the sea. They called it going to Wotan. It wasn't want of food always – by any means. A man would tell you that he felt grey in the heart, or a woman would say that she saw nothing but long days in front of her; and they'd saunter away to the mud-flats and – that would be the end of them, poor souls, unless one headed them off. One had to run quick, but one can't allow people to lay hands on themselves because they happen to feel grey. Yes – yess – Extraordinary people, the South Saxons. Disheartening, sometimes . . . What does that say now?' The organ had changed tune again.

'Only a hymn for next Sunday,' said Una. ' "The Church's One Foundation". Go on, please, about running over the mud. I should like to have seen you.'

'I dare say you would, and I really *could* run in those days. Ethelwalch the king gave me some five or six muddy parishes by the sea, and the first time my good Eddi and I rode there we saw a man slouching along the slob, among the seals at Manhood End. My good Eddi disliked seals – but he swallowed his objections and ran like a hare.'

'Why?' said Dan.

'For the same reason that I did. We thought it was one of our people going to drown himself. As a matter of fact, Eddi and I were nearly drowned in the pools before we overtook him. To cut a long story short, we found ourselves very muddy, very breathless, being quietly made fun of in good Latin by a very well-spoken person. No – he'd no idea of going to Wotan. He was fishing on his own beaches, and he showed us the beacons and turf-heaps that divided his land from the church property. He took us to his own house, gave us a good dinner, some more than good wine, sent a guide with us into Chichester, and became one of my best and most refreshing friends. He was a Meon by descent, from the west edge of the kingdom; a scholar educated, curiously enough, at Lyons, my old school; had travelled the world over, even to Rome, and was a brilliant talker. We found we had scores of acquaintances in common. It seemed he was a small chief under King

Ethelwalch, and I fancy the king was somewhat afraid of him. The South Saxons mistrust a man who talks too well. Ah! Now, I've left out the very point of my story. He kept a great grey-muzzled old dog-seal that he had brought up from a pup. He called it Padda – after one of my clergy. It was rather like fat, honest old Padda. The creature followed him everywhere, and nearly knocked down my good Eddi when we first met him. Eddi loathed it. It used to sniff at his thin legs and cough at him. I can't say I ever took much notice of it (I was not fond of animals), till one day Eddi came to me with a circumstantial account of some witchcraft that Meon worked. He would tell the seal to go down to the beach the last thing at night, and bring him word of the weather. When it came back, Meon might say to his slaves, "Padda thinks we shall have wind tomorrow. Haul up the boats!" I spoke to Meon casually about the story, and he laughed.

'He told me he could judge by the look of the creature's coat and the way it sniffed what weather was brewing. Quite possible. One need not put down everything one does not understand to the work of bad spirits – or good ones, for that matter.' He nodded towards Puck, who nodded gaily in return.

'I say so,' he went on, 'because to a certain extent I have been made a victim of that habit of mind. Some while after I was settled at Selsea, King Ethelwalch and Queen Ebba ordered their people to be baptised. I fear I'm too old to believe that a whole nation can change its heart at the king's command, and I had a shrewd suspicion that their real motive was to get a good harvest. No rain had fallen for two or three years, but as soon as we had finished baptising, it fell heavily, and they all said it was a miracle.'

'And was it?' Dan asked.

'Everything in life is a miracle, but' – the archbishop twisted the heavy ring on his finger – 'I should be slow – ve–ry slow should I be – to assume that a certain sort of miracle happens whenever lazy and improvident people say they are going to turn over a new leaf if they are paid for it. My friend Meon had sent his slaves to the font, but he had not come himself, so the next time I rode over – to return a manuscript – I took the liberty of asking why. He was perfectly open about it. He looked on the king's action as a heathen attempt to curry favour with the Christians' God through me the archbishop, and he would have none of it. "My dear man," I said, "admitting that that is the case, surely you, as an educated person, don't believe in Wotan and all the other hobgoblins any more than Padda here?" The old seal was hunched up on his oxhide behind his master's chair.

' "Even if I don't," he said, "why should I insult the memory of my fathers' gods? I have sent you a hundred and three of my rascals to christen. Isn't that enough?"

' "By no means," I answered. "I want *you*."

' "He wants us! What do you think of that, Padda?" He pulled the seal's whiskers till it threw back its head and roared, and he pretended to interpret. "No! Padda says he won't be baptised yet awhile. He says you'll stay to dinner and come fishing with me tomorrow, because you're over-worked and need a rest."

' "I wish you'd keep yon brute in its proper place," I said, and Eddi, my chaplain, agreed.

' "I do," said Meon. "I keep him just next my heart. He can't tell a lie, and he doesn't know how to love anyone except me. It 'ud be the same if I were dying on a mudbank, wouldn't it, Padda?"

' "Augh! Augh!" said Padda, and put up his head to be scratched.

'Then Meon began to tease Eddi: "Padda says, if Eddi saw his archbishop dying on a mudbank Eddi would tuck up his gown and run. Padda knows Eddi can run too! Padda came into Wittering Church last Sunday – all wet – to hear the music, and Eddi ran out."

'My good Eddi rubbed his hands and his shins together, and flushed. "Padda is a child of the Devil, who is the father of lies!" he cried, and begged my pardon for having spoken. I forgave him.

' "Yes. You are just about stupid enough for a musician," said Meon. "But here he is. Sing a hymn to him, and see if he can stand it. You'll find my small harp beside the fireplace."

'Eddi, who is really an excellent musician, played and sang for quite half an hour. Padda shuffled off his oxhide, hunched himself on his flippers before him, and listened with his head thrown back. Yes – yess! A rather funny sight! Meon tried not to laugh, and asked Eddi if he were satisfied.

'It takes some time to get an idea out of my good Eddi's head. He looked at me.

' "Do you want to sprinkle him with holy water, and see if he flies up the chimney? Why not baptise him?" said Meon.

'Eddi was really shocked. I thought it was bad taste myself.

' "That's not fair," said Meon. "You call him a demon and a familiar spirit because he loves his master and likes music, and when I offer you a chance to prove it you won't take it. Look here! I'll make a bargain. I'll be baptised if you'll baptise Padda too. He's more of a man than most of my slaves."

' "One doesn't bargain – or joke – about these matters," I said. He was going altogether too far.

' "Quite right," said Meon; "I shouldn't like anyone to joke about Padda. Padda, go down to the beach and bring us tomorrow's weather!"

'My good Eddi must have been a little overtired with his day's work. "I am a servant of the church," he cried. "My business is to save souls, not to enter into fellowships and understandings with accursed beasts."

' "Have it your own narrow way," said Meon. "Padda, you needn't go." The old fellow flounced back to his oxhide at once.

' "Man could learn obedience at least from that creature," said Eddi, a little ashamed of himself. Christians should not curse.

' "Don't begin to apologise Just when I am beginning to like you," said Meon. "We'll leave Padda behind tomorrow – out of respect to your feelings. Now let's go to supper. We must be up early tomorrow for the whiting."

'The next was a beautiful crisp autumn morning – a weather-breeder, if I had taken the trouble to think; but it's refreshing to escape from kings and converts for half a day. We three went by ourselves in Meon's smallest boat, and we got on the whiting near an old wreck, a mile or so offshore. Meon knew the marks to a yard, and the fish were keen. Yes – yess! A perfect morning's fishing! If a bishop can't be a fisherman, who can?' He twiddled his ring again. 'We stayed there a little too long, and while we were getting up our stone, down came the fog. After some discussion, we decided to row for the land. The ebb was just beginning to make round the point, and sent us all ways at once like a coracle.'

'Selsey Bill,' said Puck under his breath. 'The tides run something furious there.'

'I believe you,' said the archbishop. 'Meon and I have spent a good many evenings arguing as to where exactly we drifted. All I know is we found ourselves in a little rocky cove that had sprung up round us out of the fog, and a swell lifted the boat on to a ledge, and she broke up beneath our feet. We had just time to shuffle through the weed before the next wave. The sea was rising.

' "It's rather a pity we didn't let Padda go down to the beach last night," said Meon. "He might have warned us this was coming."

' "Better fall into the hands of God than the hands of demons," said Eddi, and his teeth chattered as he prayed. A nor'-west breeze had just got up – distinctly cool.

' "Save what you can of the boat," said Meon; "we may need it," and we had to drench ourselves again, fishing out stray planks.'

'What for?' said Dan.

'For firewood. We did not know when we should get off. Eddi had flint and steel, and we found dry fuel in the old gulls' nests and lit a fire. It smoked abominably, and we guarded it with boat-planks up-ended between the rocks. One gets used to that sort of thing if one travels. Unluckily I'm not so strong as I was. I fear I must have been a trouble to my friends. It was blowing a full gale before midnight. Eddi wrung out his cloak, and tried to wrap me in it, but I ordered him on his obedience to keep it. However, he held me in his arms all the first night, and Meon begged his pardon for what he'd said the night before – about Eddi, running away if he found me on a sandbank, you remember.

' "You are right in half your prophecy," said Eddi. "I have tucked up my gown, at any rate." (The wind had blown it over his head.) "Now let us thank God for His mercies."

' "Hum!" said Meon. "If this gale lasts, we stand a very fair chance of dying of starvation."

' "If it be God's will that we survive, God will provide," said Eddi. "At least help me to sing to Him." The wind almost whipped the words out of his mouth, but he braced himself against a rock and sang psalms.

'I'm glad I never concealed my opinion – from myself – that Eddi was a better man than I. Yet I have worked hard in my time – very hard! Yes – yess! So the morning and the evening were our second day on that islet. There was rainwater in the rock-pools, and, as a churchman, I knew how to fast, but I admit we were hungry. Meon fed our fire chip by chip to eke it out, and they made me sit over it, the dear fellows, when I was too weak to object. Meon held me in his arms the second night, just like a child. My good Eddi was a little out of his senses, and imagined himself teaching a York choir to sing. Even so, he was beautifully patient with them.

'I heard Meon whisper, "If this keeps up we shall go to our gods. I wonder what Wotan will say to me. He must know I don't believe in him. On the other hand, I can't do what Ethelwalch finds so easy – curry favour with your God at the last minute, in the hope of being saved – as you call it. How do you advise, bishop?"

' "My dear man," I said, "if that is your honest belief, I take it upon myself to say you had far better not curry favour with any god. But if it's only your Jutish pride that holds you back, lift me up, and I'll baptise you even now."

' "Lie still," said Meon. "I could judge better if I were in my own hall. But to desert one's fathers' gods – even if one doesn't believe in them – in the middle of a gale, isn't quite – What would you do yourself?"

'I was lying in his arms, kept alive by the warmth of his big, steady heart. It did not seem to me the time or the place for subtle arguments, so I answered, "No, I certainly should not desert my God." I don't see even now what else I could have said.

' "Thank you. I'll remember that, if I live," said Meon, and I must have drifted back to my dreams about Northumbria and beautiful France, for it was broad daylight when I heard him calling on Wotan in that high, shaking heathen yell that I detest so.

' "Lie quiet. I'm giving Wotan his chance," he said. Our dear Eddi ambled up, still beating time to his imaginary choir.

' "Yes. Call on your gods," he cried, "and see what gifts they will send you. They are gone on a journey, or they are hunting."

'I assure you the words were not out of his mouth when old Padda shot from the top of a cold wrinkled swell, drove himself over the weedy ledge, and landed fair in our laps with a rock-cod between his teeth. I could not help smiling at Eddi's face. "A miracle! A miracle!" he cried, and kneeled down to clean the cod.

' "You've been a long time finding us, my son," said Meon. "Now fish – fish for all our lives. We're starving, Padda."

'The old fellow flung himself quivering like a salmon backward into the boil of the currents round the rocks, and Meon said, "We're safe. I'll send him to fetch help when this wind drops. Eat and be thankful."

'I never tasted anything so good as those rock-codlings we took from Padda's mouth and half roasted over the fire. Between his plunges Padda would hunch up and purr over Meon with the tears running down his face. I never knew before that seals could weep for joy – as I have wept.

' "Surely," said Eddi, with his mouth full, "God has made the seal the loveliest of His creatures in the water. Look how Padda breasts the current! He stands up against it like a rock; now watch the chain of bubbles where he dives; and now – there is his wise head under that rock-ledge! Oh, a blessing be on thee, my little brother Padda!"

' "You *said* he was a child of the Devil!" Meon laughed.

' "There I sinned," poor Eddi answered. "Call him here, and I will ask his pardon. God sent him out of the storm to humble me, a fool."

' "I won't ask you to enter into fellowships and understandings with any accursed brute," said Meon, rather unkindly. "Shall we say he was sent to our bishop as the ravens were sent to your prophet Elijah?"

' "Doubtless that is so," said Eddi. "I will write it so if I live to get home."

' "No – no!" I said. "Let us three poor men kneel and thank God for His mercies."

'We kneeled, and old Padda shuffled up and thrust his head under Meon's elbows. I laid my hand upon it and blessed him. So did Eddi.

' "And now, my son," I said to Meon, "shall I baptise thee?"

' "Not yet," said he. "Wait till we are well ashore and at home. No God in any heaven shall say that I came to him or left him because I was wet and cold. I will send Padda to my people for a boat. Is that witchcraft, Eddi?"

' "Why, no. Surely Padda will go and pull them to the beach by the skirts of their gowns as he pulled me in Wittering Church to ask me to sing. Only then I was afraid, and did not understand," said Eddi.

' "You are understanding now," said Meon, and at a wave of his arm off went Padda to the mainland, making a wake like a war-boat till we lost him in the rain. Meon's people could not bring a boat across for some hours; even so it was ticklish work among the rocks in that tideway. But they hoisted me aboard, too stiff to move, and Padda swam behind us, barking and turning somersaults all the way to Manhood End!'

'Good old Padda!' murmured Dan.

'When we were quite rested and reclothed, and his people had been summoned – not an hour before – Meon offered himself to be baptised.'

'Was Padda baptised too?' Una asked.

'No, that was only Meon's joke. But he sat blinking on his oxhide in the middle of the hall. When Eddi (who thought I wasn't looking) made a little cross in holy water on his wet muzzle, he kissed Eddi's hand. A week before Eddi wouldn't have touched him. That was a miracle, if you like! But seriously, I was more glad than I can tell you to get Meon. A rare and splendid soul that never looked back – never looked back!' The archbishop half closed his eyes.

'But, sir,' said Puck, most respectfully, 'haven't you left out what Meon said afterwards?' Before the bishop could speak he turned to the children and went on: 'Meon called all his fishers and ploughmen and herdsmen into the hall and he said: "Listen, men! Two days ago I asked our bishop whether it was fair for a man to desert his fathers' gods in a time of danger. Our bishop said it was not fair. You needn't shout like that, because you are all Christians now. My red war-boat's crew will remember how near we all were to death when Padda fetched them over to the bishop's islet. You can tell your mates that even in that place, at that time, hanging on the wet, weedy edge of death, our bishop, a Christian, counselled me, a heathen, to stand by my fathers' gods. I tell you now that a faith which takes care that every man shall keep faith, even though he may save his soul by breaking faith, is the faith for a man to believe in. So I believe in the Christian God, and in Wilfrid His bishop, and in the church that Wilfrid rules. You have been baptised once by the king's orders. I shall not have you baptised again; but if I find any more old women being sent to Wotan, or any girls dancing on the sly before Balder, or any men talking about Thun or Lok or the rest, I will teach you with my own hands how to keep faith with the Christian God. Go out quietly; you'll find a couple of beefs on the beach." Then of course they shouted "Hurrah!" which meant "Thor help us!" and – I think you laughed, sir?'

'I think you remember it all too well,' said the archbishop, smiling. 'It was a joyful day for me. I had learned a great deal on that rock where Padda found us. Yes – yess! One should deal kindly with all the creatures of God, and gently with their masters. But one learns late.'

He rose, and his gold-embroidered sleeves rustled thickly.

The organ cracked and took deep breaths.

'Wait a minute,' Dan whispered. 'She's going to do the trumpety one. It takes all the wind you can pump. It's in Latin, sir.'

'There is no other tongue,' the archbishop answered.

'It's not a real hymn,' Una explained. 'She does it as a treat after her exercises. She isn't a real organist, you know. She just comes down here sometimes, from the Albert Hall.'

'Oh, what a miracle of a voice!' said the archbishop.

It rang out suddenly from a dark arch of lonely noises – every word spoken to the very end:

> 'Dies Irae, dies illa,
> Solvet soeclum in favilla,
> Teste David cum Sibylla.'

The archbishop caught his breath and moved forward.

The music carried on by itself a while.

'Now it's calling all the light out of the windows,' Una whispered to Dan.

'I think it's more like a horse neighing in battle,' he whispered back. The voice continued:

'Tuba mirum spargens sonum
Per sepulchre regionum.'

Deeper and deeper the organ dived down, but far below its deepest note
they heard Puck's voice joining in the last line:

'Coget omnes ante thronum.'

As they looked in wonder, for it sounded like the dull jar of one of the very
pillars shifting, the little fellow turned and went out through the south door.

'Now's the sorrowful part, but it's very beautiful.' Una found herself
speaking to the empty chair in front of her.

'What are you doing that for?' Dan said behind her. 'You spoke so politely
too.'

'I don't know . . . I thought . . . ' said Una. 'Funny!'

' 'Tisn't. It's the part you like best,' Dan grunted.

The music had turned soft – full of little sounds that chased each other on
wings across the broad gentle flood of the main tune. But the voice was ten
times lovelier than the music.

'Recordare Jesu pie,
Quod sum causa Tuae viae,
Ne me perdas illa die!'

There was no more. They moved out into the centre aisle.

'That you?' the lady called as she shut the lid. 'I thought I heard you, and
I played it on purpose.'

'Thank you awfully,' said Dan. 'We hoped you would, so we waited. Come
on, Una, it's pretty nearly dinner-time.'

Song of the Red War-Boat

Shove off from the wharf-edge! Steady!
　　Watch for a smooth! Give way!
If she feels the lop already
　　She'll stand on her head in the bay.
It's ebb – it's dusk – it's blowing,
　　The shoals are a mile of white,
But (snatch her along!) we're going
　　To find our master tonight.

For we hold that in all disaster
　　Of shipwreck, storm, or sword,
A man must stand by his master
　　When once he has pledged his word!

Raging seas have we rowed in,
　　But we seldom saw them thus;
Our master is angry with Odin –
　　Odin is angry with us!
Heavy odds have we taken,
　　But never before such odds.
The gods know they are forsaken,
　　We must risk the wrath of the gods!

Over the crest she flies from,
　　Into its hollow she drops,
Crouches and clears her eyes from
　　The wind-torn breaker-tops,
Ere out on the shrieking shoulder
　　Of a hill-high surge she drives.
Meet her! Meet her and hold her!
　　Pull for your scoundrel lives!

The thunders bellow and clamour
　　The harm that they mean to do;
There goes Thor's own hammer
　　Cracking the dark in two!

Close! But the blow has missed her,
  Here comes the wind of the blow!
Row or the squall'll twist her
  Broadside on to it! – *Row!*

Hearken, Thor of the Thunder!
  We are not here for a jest –
For wager, warfare, or plunder,
  Or to put your power to test.
This work is none of our wishing –
  We would stay at home if we might –
But our master is wrecked out fishing,
  We go to find him tonight.

  For we hold that in all disaster –
    As the gods themselves have said –
  A man must stand by his master
    Till one of the two is dead.

That is our way of thinking,
  Now you can do as you will,
While we try to save her from sinking,
  And hold her head to it still.
Bale her and keep her moving,
  Or she'll break her back in the trough . . .
Who said the weather's improving,
  And the swells are taking off?

*   *   *

Sodden, and chafed and aching,
  Gone in the loins and knees –
No matter – the day is breaking,
  And there's far less weight to the seas!
Up mast, and finish baling –
  In oars, and out with the mead –
The rest will be two-reef sailing . . .
  That was a night indeed!

  But we hold that in all disaster
    (And faith, we have found it true!)
  If only you stand by your master,
    The gods will stand by you!

A DOCTOR OF MEDICINE

An Astrologer's Song

To the heavens above us,
Oh, look, and behold
The planets that love us
All harnessed in gold!
What chariots, what horses,
Against us shall bide
While the stars in their courses
Do fight on our side?

All thought, all desires,
That are under the sun,
Are one with their fires,
As we also are one;
All matter, all spirit,
All fashion, all frame,
Receive and inherit
Their strength from the same.

(Oh, man that deniest
All power save thine own,
Their power in the highest
Is mightily shown.
Not less in the lowest
That power is made clear.
Oh, man, if thou knowest,
What treasure is here!)

Earth quakes in her throes
And we wonder for why!
But the blind planet knows
When her ruler is nigh;
And, attuned since Creation,
To perfect accord,

She thrills in her station
And yearns to her lord.

The waters have risen,
The springs are unbound –
The floods break their prison,
And ravin around.
No rampart withstands 'em,
Their fury will last,
Till the sign that commands 'em
Sinks low or swings past.

Through abysses unproven,
And gulfs beyond thought,
Our portion is woven,
Our burden is brought.
Yet they that prepare it,
Whose nature we share,
Make us who must bear it
Well able to bear.

Though terrors o'ertake us
We'll not be afraid,
No power can unmake us
Save that which has made.
Nor yet beyond reason
Nor hope shall we fall –
All things have their season,
And mercy crowns all.

Then, doubt not, ye fearful –
The eternal is king –
Up, heart, and be cheerful,
And lustily sing:
What chariots, what horses,
Against us shall bide
While the stars in their courses
Do fight on our side?

A Doctor of Medicine

They were playing hide-and-seek with bicycle lamps after tea. Dan had hung his lamp on the apple tree at the end of the hellebore bed in the walled garden, and was crouched by the gooseberry bushes ready to dash off when Una should spy him. He saw her lamp come into the garden and disappear as she hid it under her cloak. While he listened for her footsteps, somebody (they both thought it was Phillips the gardener) coughed in the corner of the herb-beds.

'All right,' Una shouted across the asparagus; 'we aren't hurting your old beds, Phippsey!'

She flashed her lantern towards the spot, and in its circle of light they saw a Guy Fawkes-looking man in a black cloak and a steeple-crowned hat, walking down the path beside Puck. They ran to meet him, and the man said something to them about *rooms* in their head. After a time they understood he was warning them not to catch colds.

'You've a bit of a cold yourself, haven't you?' said Una, for he ended all his sentences with a consequential cough. Puck laughed.

'Child,' the man answered, 'if it hath pleased heaven to afflict me with an infirmity – '

'Nay, nay,' Puck struck in, 'the maid spoke out of kindness. *I* know that half your cough is but a catch to trick the vulgar; and that's a pity. There's honesty enough in you, Nick, without rasping and hawking.'

'Good people' – the man shrugged his lean shoulders – 'the vulgar crowd love not truth unadorned. Wherefore we philosophers must needs dress her to catch their eye or – ahem! – their ear.'

'And what d'you think of *that*?' said Puck solemnly to Dan.

'I don't know,' he answered. 'It sounds like lessons.'

'Ah – well! There have been worse men than Nick Culpeper to take lessons from. Now, where can we sit that's not indoors?'

'In the hay-mow, next to old Middenboro,' Dan suggested. '*He* doesn't mind.'

'Eh?' Mr Culpeper was stooping over the pale hellebore blooms by the light of Una's lamp. 'Does Master Middenboro need my poor services, then?'

'Save him, no!' said Puck. 'He is but a horse – next door to an ass, as you'll see presently. Come!'

Their shadows jumped and slid on the fruit-tree walls. They filed out of the garden by the snoring pig-pound and the crooning hen-house, to the shed where Middenboro the old lawnmower pony lives. His friendly eyes showed green in the light as they set their lamps down on the chickens' drinking-trough outside, and pushed past to the hay-mow. Mr Culpeper stooped at the door.

'Mind where you lie,' said Dan. 'This hay's full of hedge-brishings.'

'In! in!' said Puck. 'You've lain in fouler places than this, Nick. Ah! Let us keep touch with the stars!' He kicked open the top of the half-door, and pointed to the clear sky. 'There be the planets you conjure with! What does your wisdom make of that wandering and variable star behind those apple boughs?'

The children smiled. A bicycle that they knew well was being walked down the steep lane.

'Where?' Mr Culpeper leaned forward quickly. 'That? Some country-man's lantern.'

'Wrong, Nick,' said Puck. ' 'Tis a singular bright star in Virgo, declining towards the house of Aquarius the water-carrier, who hath lately been afflicted by Gemini. Aren't I right, Una?' Mr Culpeper snorted contemptuously.

'No. It's the village nurse going down to the mill about some fresh twins that came there last week. Nurse,' Una called, as the light stopped on the flat, 'when can I see the Morris twins? And how are they?'

'Next Sunday, perhaps. Doing beautifully,' the nurse called back, and with a *ping-ping-ping* of the bell brushed round the corner.

'Her uncle's a vetinary surgeon near Banbury,' Una explained, and if you ring her bell at night, it rings right beside her bed – not downstairs at all. Then she jumps up – she always keeps a pair of dry boots in the fender, you know – and goes anywhere she's wanted. We help her bicycle through gaps sometimes. Most of her babies do beautifully. She told us so herself.'

'I doubt not, then, that she reads in my books,' said Mr Culpeper quietly. 'Twins at the mill!' he muttered half aloud. ' "And again He sayeth, Return, ye children of men." '

'Are you a doctor or a rector?' Una asked, and Puck with a shout turned head over heels in the hay. But Mr Culpeper was quite serious. He told them that he was a physician-astrologer – a doctor who knew all about the stars as well as all about herbs for medicine. He said that the sun, the moon, and five planets, called Jupiter, Mars, Mercury, Saturn and Venus, governed every-body and everything in the world. They all lived in houses – he mapped out some of them against the dark with a busy forefinger – and they moved from house to house like pieces at draughts; and they went loving and hating each other all over the skies. If you knew their likes and dislikes, he said, you could make them cure your patient and hurt your enemy, and find out the secret causes of things. He talked of these five planets as though they belonged to him, or as though he were playing long games against them. The children burrowed in the hay up to their chins, and looked out over the half-door at the solemn, star-powdered sky till they seemed to be falling upside down into it, while Mr Culpeper talked about 'trines' and 'oppositions' and 'conjunctions' and 'sympathies' and 'antipathies' in a tone that just matched things.

A rat ran between Middenboro's feet, and the old pony stamped.

'Mid hates rats,' said Dan, and passed him over a lock of hay. 'I wonder why.'

'Divine astrology tells us,' said Mr Culpeper. 'The horse, being a martial beast that beareth man to battle, belongs naturally to the red planet Mars – the Lord of War. I would show you him, but he's too near his setting. Rats and mice, doing their businesses by night, come under the dominion of Our Lady the Moon. Now between Mars and Luna, the one red, t'other white, the one hot t'other cold and so forth, stands, as I have told you, a natural antipathy, or, as you say, hatred. Which antipathy their creatures do inherit. Whence, good people, you may both see and hear your cattle stamp in their stalls for the self-same causes as decree the passages of the stars across the unalterable face of heaven! Ahem!'

Puck lay along chewing a leaf. They felt him shake with laughter, and Mr Culpeper sat up stiffly.

'I myself,' said he, 'have saved men's lives, and not a few neither, by observing at the proper time – there is a time, mark you, for all things under the sun – by observing, I say, so small a beast as a rat in conjunction with so great a matter as this dread arch above us.' He swept his hand across the sky. 'Yet there are those,' he went on sourly, 'who have years without knowledge.'

'Right,' said Puck. 'No fool like an old fool.'

Mr Culpeper wrapped his cloak round him and sat still while the children stared at the Great Bear on the hilltop.

'Give him time,' Puck whispered behind his hand. 'He turns like a timber-tug – all of a piece.'

'Ahem!' Mr Culpeper said suddenly. 'I'll prove it to you. When I was physician to Saye's Horse, and fought the king – or rather the man Charles Stuart – in Oxfordshire (I had *my* learning at Cambridge), the plague was very hot all around us. I saw it at close hand. He who says I am ignorant of the plague, for example, is altogether beside the bridge.'

'We grant it,' said Puck solemnly. 'But why talk of the plague this rare night?'

'To prove my argument. This Oxfordshire plague, good people, being generated among rivers and ditches, was of a werish, watery nature. Therefore it was curable by drenching the patient in cold water, and laying him in wet cloths; or at least, so I cured some of them. Mark this. It bears on what shall come after.'

'Mark also, Nick,' said Puck, 'that we are not your College of Physicians, but only a lad and a lass and a poor lubberkin. Therefore be plain, old Hyssop on the Wall!'

'To be plain and in order with you, I was shot in the chest while gathering of betony from a brookside near Thame, and was took by the king's men before their colonel, one Blagg or Bragge, whom I warned honestly that I had spent the week past among our plague-stricken. He flung me off into a cowshed, much like this here, to die, as I supposed; but one of their priests crept in by night and dressed my wound. He was a Sussex man like myself.'

'Who was that?' said Puck suddenly. 'Zack Tutshom?'

'No, Jack Marget,' said Mr Culpeper.

'Jack Marget of New College? The little merry man that stammered so? Why a plague was stuttering Jack at Oxford then?' said Puck.

'He had come out of Sussex in hope of being made a bishop when the king should have conquered the rebels, as he styled us Parliament men. His college had lent the king some monies too, which they never got again, no more than simple Jack got his bishopric. When we met he had had a bitter bellyful of king's promises, and wished to return to his wife and babes. This came about beyond expectation, for, so soon as I could stand of my wound, the man Blagge made excuse that I had been among the plague, and Jack had been tending me, to thrust us both out from their camp. The king had done with Jack now that Jack's college had lent the money, and Blagge's physician could not abide me because I would not sit silent and see him butcher the sick. (He was a College of Physicians man!) So Blagge, I say, thrust us both out, with many vile words, for a pair of pestilent, prating, pragmatical rascals.'

'Ha! Called *you* pragmatical, Nick?' Puck started up. 'High time Oliver came to purge the land! How did you and honest Jack fare next?'

'We were in some sort constrained to each other's company. I was for going to my house in Spitalfields, he would go to his parish in Sussex; but the plague was broke out and spreading through Wiltshire, Berkshire and Hampshire, and he was so mad distracted to think that it might even then be among his folk at home that I bore him company. He had comforted me in my distress. I could not have done less; and I remembered that I had a cousin at Great Wigsell, near by Jack's parish. Thus we footed it from Oxford, cassock and buff coat together, resolute to leave wars on the left side henceforth; and either through our mean appearances, or the plague making men less cruel, we were not hindered. To be sure, they put us in the stocks one half-day for rogues and vagabonds at a village under St Leonard's forest, where, as I have heard, nightingales never sing; but the constable very honestly gave me back my *Astrological Almanac*, which I carry with me.' Mr Culpeper tapped his thin chest. 'I dressed a whitlow on his thumb. So we went forward.

'Not to trouble you with impertinences, we fetched over against Jack Marget's parish in a storm of rain about the day's end. Here our roads divided, for I would have gone on to my cousin at Great Wigsell, but while Jack was pointing me out his steeple, we saw a man lying drunk, as he conceived, athwart the road. He said it would be one Hebden, a parishioner, and till then a man of good life; and he accused himself bitterly for an unfaithful shepherd, that had left his flock to follow princes. But I saw it was the plague, and not the beginnings of it neither. They had set out the plague-stone, and the man's head lay on it.'

'What's a plague-stone?' Dan whispered.

'When the plague is so hot in a village that the neighbours shut the roads against 'em, people set a hollowed stone, pot or pan where such as would purchase victual from outside may lay money and the paper of their wants, and depart. Those that would sell come later – what will a man not do for gain? – snatch the money forth, and leave in exchange such goods as their conscience reckons fair value. I saw a silver groat in the water, and the man's list of what he would buy was rain-pulped in his wet hand.

' "My wife! Oh, my wife and babes!" says Jack of a sudden, and makes uphill – I with him.

'A woman peers out from behind a barn, crying out that the village is stricken with the plague, and that for our lives' sake we must avoid it.

' "Sweetheart!" says Jack. "Must I avoid thee?" and she leaps at him and says the babes are safe. She was his wife.

'When he had thanked God, even to tears, he tells me this was not the welcome he had intended, and presses me to flee the place while I was clean.

' "Nay! The Lord do so to me and more also if I desert thee now," I said. "These affairs are, under God's leave, in some fashion my strength."

' "Oh, sir," she says, "are you a physician? We have none."

' "Then, good people," said I, "I must e'en justify myself to you by my works."

' "Look – look ye," stammers Jack, "I took you all this time for a crazy Roundhead preacher." He laughs, and she, and then I – all three together in the rain are overtook by an unreasonable gust or clap of laughter, which none the less eased us. We call it in medicine the hysterical passion. So I went home with 'em.'

'Why did you not go on to your cousin at Great Wigsell, Nick?' Puck suggested. ' 'tis barely seven mile up the road.'

'But the plague was here,' Mr Culpeper answered, and pointed up the hill. 'What else could I have done?'

'What were the parson's children called?' said Una.

'Elizabeth, Alison, Stephen and Charles – a babe. I scarce saw them at first, for I separated to live with their father in a cart-lodge. The mother we put – forced – into the house with her babes. She had done enough.

'And now, good people, give me leave to be particular in this case. The plague was worst on the north side of the street, for lack, as I showed 'em, of sunshine; which, proceeding from the *prime mobile*, or source of life (I speak astrologically), is cleansing and purifying in the highest degree. The plague was hot too by the corn-chandler's, where they sell forage to the carters, extreme hot in both mills, along the river, and scatteringly in other places, except, mark you, at the smithy. Mark here, that all forges and smith shops belong to Mars, even as corn and meat and wine shops acknowledge Venus for their mistress. There was no plague in the smithy at Munday's Lane – '

'Munday's Lane? You mean our village? I thought so when you talked about the two mills,' cried Dan. 'Where did we put the plague-stone? I'd like to have seen it.'

'Then look at it now,' said Puck, and pointed to the chickens' drinking-trough where they had set their bicycle lamps. It was a rough, oblong stone pan, rather like a small kitchen sink, which Phillips, who never wastes anything, had found in a ditch and had used for his precious hens.

'That?' said Dan and Una, and stared, and stared, and stared. Mr Culpeper made impatient noises in his throat and went on.

'I am at these pains to be particular, good people, because I would have you follow, so far as you may, the operations of my mind. That plague which I told you I had handled outside Wallingford in Oxfordshire was of a watery nature, conformable to the brookish riverine country it bred in, and curable, as I have said, by drenching in water. This plague of ours here, for all that it flourished along watercourses – every soul at both mills died of it – could not be so handled. Which brought me to a stand. Ahem!'

'And your sick people in the meantime?' Puck demanded.

'We persuaded them on the north side of the street to lie out in Hitheram's field. Where the plague had taken one, or at most two, in a house, folk would not shift for fear of thieves in their absence. They cast away their lives to die among their goods.'

'Human nature,' said Puck. 'I've seen it time and again. How did your sick do in the fields?'

'They died not near so thick as those that kept within doors, and even then they died more out of distraction and melancholy than plague. But I confess, good people, I could not in any sort master the sickness, or come at a glimmer of its nature or governance. To be brief, I was flat bewildered at the brute malignity of the disease, and so – did what I should have done before – dismissed all conjectures and apprehensions that had grown up within me, chose a good hour by my *Almanac*, clapped my vinegar-cloth to my face, and entered some empty houses, resigned to wait upon the stars for guidance.'

'At night? Were you not horribly frightened?' said Puck.

'I dared to hope that the God who hath made man so nobly curious to search out his mysteries might not destroy a devout seeker. In due time – there's a time, as I have said, for everything under the sun – I spied a whitish rat, very puffed and scabby, which sat beneath the dormer of an attic through which shined Our Lady the Moon. Whilst I looked on him – and her – she was moving towards old cold Saturn, her ancient ally – the rat creeped languishingly into her light, and there, before my eyes, died. Presently his mate or companion came out, laid him down beside there, and in like fashion died too. Later – an hour or less to midnight – a third rat did e'en the same; always choosing the moonlight to die in. This threw me into an amaze, since, as we know, the moonlight is favourable, not hurtful, to the creatures of the Moon; and Saturn, being friends with her, as you would say, was hourly strengthening her evil influence. Yet these three rats had been stricken dead in very moonlight. I leaned out of the window to see which of heaven's host might be on our side, and there beheld I good trusty Mars, very red and heated, bustling about his setting. I straddled the roof to see better.

'Jack Marget came up street going to comfort our sick in Hitheram's field. A tile slipped under my foot. Says he, heavily enough, "Watchman, what of the night?"

' "Heart up, Jack," says I. "Methinks there's one fighting for us that, like a fool, I've forgot all this summer." My meaning was naturally the planet Mars.

' "Pray to him then," says he. "I forgot him too this summer."

'He meant God, whom he always bitterly accused himself of having forgotten up in Oxfordshire, among the king's men. I called down that he had made amends enough for his sin by his work among the sick, but he said he would not believe so till the plague was lifted from 'em. He was at his strength's end – more from melancholy than any just cause. I have seen this before among priests and over-cheerful men. I drenched him then and there with a half-cup of waters, which I do not say cure the plague, but are excellent against heaviness of the spirits.'

'What were they?' said Dan.

'White brandy rectified, camphor, cardamoms, ginger, two sorts of pepper, and aniseed.'

'Whew!' said Puck. 'Waters you call 'em!'

'Jack coughed on it valiantly, and went downhill with me. I was for the Lower Mill in the valley, to note the aspect of the heavens. My mind had already shadowed forth the reason, if not the remedy, for our troubles, but I would not impart it to the vulgar till I was satisfied. That practice may be perfect, judgement ought to be sound, and to make judgement sound is required an exquisite knowledge. Ahem! I left Jack and his lantern among the sick in Hitheram's field. He still maintained the prayers of the so-called church, which were rightly forbidden by Cromwell.'

'You should have told your cousin at Wigsell,' said Puck, 'and Jack would have been fined for it, and you'd have had half the money. How did you come so to fail in your duty, Nick?'

Mr Culpeper laughed – his only laugh that evening – and the children jumped at the loud neigh of it.

'We were not fearful of *men's* judgement in those days,' he answered. 'Now mark me closely, good people, for what follows will be to you, though not to me, remarkable. When I reached the empty mill, old Saturn, low down in the House of the Fishes, threatened the Sun's rising-place. Our Lady the Moon was moving towards the help of him (understand, I speak astrologically). I looked abroad upon the high heavens, and I prayed the maker of 'em for guidance. Now Mars sparkingly withdrew himself below the sky. On the instant of his departure, which I noted, a bright star or vapour leaped forth above his head (as though he had heaved up his sword), and broke all about in fire. The cocks crowed midnight through the valley, and I sat me down by the mill-wheel, chewing spearmint (though that's a herb of Venus), and calling myself all the asses' heads in the world! 'Twas plain enough *now*!'

'What was plain?' said Una.

'The true cause and cure of the plague. Mars, good fellow, had fought for us to the uttermost. Faint though he had been in the heavens, and this had made me overlook him in my computations, he more than any of the other planets had kept the heavens – which is to say, had been visible some part of each night well-nigh throughout the year. Therefore his fierce and cleansing influence, warring against the Moon, had stretched out to kill those three rats under my nose, and under the nose of their natural mistress, the Moon. I had known Mars lean half across heaven to deal Our Lady the Moon some shrewd blow from under his shield, but I had never before seen his strength displayed so effectual.'

'I don't understand a bit. Do you mean Mars killed the rats because he hated the Moon?' said Una.

'*That* is as plain as the pikestaff with which Blagge's men pushed me forth,' Mr Culpeper answered. 'I'll prove it. Why had the plague not broken out at the blacksmith's shop in Munday's Lane? Because, as I've shown you, forges and smithies belong naturally to Mars, and, for his honour's sake, Mars 'ud keep 'em clean from the creatures of the Moon. But was it like, think you, that he'd come down and rat-catch in general for lazy, ungrateful mankind? That were working a willing horse to death. So, then, you can see that the meaning of the blazing star above him when he set was simply this: "Destroy and burn the creatures of the Moon, for they are the root of your trouble. And thus, having shown you a taste of my power, good people, adieu." '

'Did Mars really say all that?' Una whispered.

'Yes, and twice so much as that to anyone who had ears to hear. Briefly, he enlightened me that the plague was spread by the creatures of the Moon. The Moon, Our Lady of Ill-Aspect, was the offender. My own poor wits showed me that I, Nick Culpeper, had the people in my charge, God's good providence aiding me, and no time to lose neither.

'I posted up the hill, and broke into Hitheram's field amongst 'em all at prayers.

' "Eureka, good people!" I cried, and cast down a dead mill-rat which I'd found. "Here's your true enemy, revealed at last by the stars."

' "Nay, but I'm praying," says Jack. His face was as white as washed silver.

' "There's a time for everything under the sun," says I. "If you would stay the plague, take and kill your rats."

' "Oh, mad, stark mad!" says he, and wrings his hands.

'A fellow lay in the ditch beside him, who bellows that he'd as soon die mad hunting rats as be preached to death on a cold fallow. They laughed round him at this, but Jack Marget falls on his knees, and very presumptuously petitions that he may be appointed to die to save the rest of his people. This was enough to thrust 'em back into their melancholy.

' "You are an unfaithful shepherd, Jack," I says. "Take a bat" (which we call a stick in Sussex) "and kill a rat if you die before sunrise. 'Twill save your people."

' "Aye, aye. Take a bat and kill a rat," he says ten times over, like a child, which moved 'em to ungovernable motions of that hysterical passion before mentioned, so that they laughed all, and at least warmed their chill bloods at that very hour – one o'clock or a little after – when the fires of life burn lowest. Truly there is a time for everything; and the physician must work with it – ahem! – or miss his cure. To be brief with you, I persuaded 'em, sick or sound, to have at the whole generation of rats throughout the village. And there's a reason for all things too, though the wise physician need not blab 'em all. *Imprimis*, or firstly, the mere sport of it, which lasted ten days, drew 'em most markedly out of their melancholy. I'd defy sorrowful Job himself to lament or scratch while he's routing rats from a rick. *Secundo*, or secondly, the vehement act and operation of this chase or war opened their skins to generous transpiration – more vulgarly, sweated 'em handsomely; and this further drew off their black bile – the mother of sickness. Thirdly, when we came to burn the bodies of the rats, I sprinkled sulphur on the faggots, whereby the onlookers were as handsomely suffumigated. This I could not have compassed if I had made it a mere physician's business; they'd have thought it some conjuration. Yet more, we cleansed, limed, and burned out a hundred foul poke-holes, sinks, slews and corners of unvisited filth in and about the houses in the village, and by good fortune (mark here that Mars was in opposition to Venus) burned the corn-handler's shop to the ground. Mars loves not Venus. Will Noakes the saddler dropped his lantern on a truss of straw while he was rat-hunting there.'

'Had ye given Will any of that gentle cordial of yours, Nick, by any chance?' said Puck.

'A glass – or two glasses – not more. But as I would say, in fine, when we had killed the rats, I took ash, slag and charcoal from the smithy, and burnt earth from the brickyard (I reason that a brickyard belongs to Mars), and rammed it with iron crowbars into the rat-runs and buries, and beneath all the house floors. The Creatures of the Moon hate all that Mars hath used for his own clean ends. For example – rats bite not iron.'

'And how did poor stuttering Jack endure it?' said Puck.

'He sweated out his melancholy through his skin, and catched a loose cough, which I cured with electuaries, according to art. It is noteworthy, were I speaking among my equals, that the venom of the plague translated, or turned itself into, and evaporated, or went away as, a very heavy hoarseness and thickness of the head, throat and chest. (Observe from my books which planets govern these portions of man's body, and your darkness, good people, shall be illuminated – ahem!) None the less, the plague, *qua* plague, ceased and took off (for we only lost three more, and two of 'em had it already on 'em) from the morning of the day that Mars enlightened me by the Lower Mill.' He coughed – almost trumpeted – triumphantly.

'It is proved,' he jerked out. 'I say I have proved my contention, which is that by divine astrology and humble search into the veritable causes of things – at the proper time – the sons of wisdom may combat even the plague.'

'H'm!' Puck replied. 'For my own part I hold that a simple soul – '

'Mine? – simple, forsooth?' said Mr Culpeper.

'A very simple soul, a high courage tempered with sound and stubborn conceit, is stronger than all the stars in their courses. So I confess truly that you saved the village, Nick.'

'I stubborn? I stiff-necked? I ascribed all my poor success, under God's good providence, to divine astrology. Not to me the glory! You talk as that dear weeping ass Jack Marget preached before I went back to my work in Red Lion House, Spitalfields.'

'Oh! Stammering Jack preached, did he? They say he loses his stammer in the pulpit.'

'And his wits with it. He delivered a most idolatrous discourse when the plague was stayed. He took for his text: "The wise man that delivered the city." I could have given him a better, such as: "There is a time for –" '

'But what made you go to church to hear him?' Puck interrupted. 'Wail Attersole was your lawfully appointed preacher, and a dull dog he was!'

Mr Culpeper wriggled uneasily.

'The vulgar,' said he, 'the old crones and – ahem! – the children, Alison and the others, they dragged me to the House of Rimmon by the hand. I was in two minds to inform on Jack for maintaining the mummeries of the falsely-called church, which, I'll prove to you, are founded merely on ancient fables – '

'Stick to your herbs and planets,' said Puck, laughing. 'You should have told the magistrates, Nick, and had Jack fined. Again, why did you neglect your plain duty?'

'Because – because I was kneeling, and praying, and weeping with the rest of 'em at the altar-rails. In medicine this is called the hysterical passion. It may be – it may be.'

'That's as may be,' said Puck. They heard him turn the hay. 'Why, your hay is half hedge-brishings,' he said. 'You don't expect a horse to thrive on oak and ash and thorn leaves, do you?'

Ping-ping-ping went the bicycle bell round the corner. The nurse was coming back from the mill.

'Is it all right?' Una called.

'All quite right,' the nurse called back. 'They're to be christened next Sunday.'

'What? What?' They both leaned forward across the half-door. It could not have been properly fastened, for it opened, and tilted them out with hay and leaves sticking all over them.

'Come on! We must get those twins' names,' said Una, and they charged uphill shouting over the hedge, till the nurse slowed up and told them. When they returned, old Middenboro had got out of his stall, and they spent a lively ten minutes chasing him in again by starlight.

Our Fathers of Old

Excellent herbs had our fathers of old –
  Excellent herbs to ease their pain –
Alexanders and marigold,
  Eyebright, orris and elecampane,
Basil, rocket, valerian, rue
  (Almost singing themselves they run)
Vervain, dittany, call-me-to-you –
  Cowslip, melilot, rose of the sun.
    Anything green that grew out of the mould
    Was an excellent herb to our fathers of old.

Wonderful tales had our fathers of old –
  Wonderful tales of the herbs and the stars –
The sun was lord of the marigold,
  Basil and rocket belonged to Mars.
Pat as a sum in division it goes
  (Every plant had a star bespoke) –
Who but Venus should govern the rose?
  Who but Jupiter own the oak?
    Simply and gravely the facts are told
    In the wonderful books of our fathers of old.

Wonderful little, when all is said,
  Wonderful little our fathers knew.
Half their remedies cured you dead –
  Most of their teaching was quite untrue –
'Look at the stars when a patient is ill
  (Dirt has nothing to do with disease),
Bleed and blister as much as you will,
  Blister and bleed him as oft as you please.'
    Whence enormous and manifold
    Errors were made by our fathers of old.

Yet when the sickness was sore in the land,
  And neither planet nor herb assuaged,
They took their lives in their lancet-hand
  And, oh, what a wonderful war they waged!

Yes, when the crosses were chalked on the door –
   Yes, when the terrible dead-cart rolled,
Excellent courage our fathers bore –
   Excellent heart had our fathers of old.
      Not too learned, but nobly bold,
      Into the fight went our fathers of old.

If it be certain, as Galen says –
   And sage Hippocrates holds as much –
That those afflicted by doubts and dismays
   Are mightily helped by a dead man's touch,
Then, be good to us, stars above!
   Then, be good to us, herbs below!
We are afflicted by what we can prove;
   We are distracted by what we know – So – ah, so!
      Down from your heaven or up from your mould,
      Send us the hearts of our fathers of old!

SIMPLE SIMON

The Thousandth Man

One man in a thousand, Solomon says,
  Will stick more close than a brother.
And it's worth while seeking him half your days
  If you find him before the other.
Nine hundred and ninety-nine depend
  On what the world sees in you
But the Thousandth Man will stand your friend
  With the whole round world agin you.

'Tis neither promise nor prayer nor show
  Will settle the finding for 'ee.
Nine hundred and ninety-nine of 'em go
  By your looks or your acts or your glory.
But if he finds you and you find him,
  The rest of the world don't matter;
For the Thousandth Man will sink or swim
  With you in any water.

You can use his purse with no more shame
  Than he uses yours for his spendings;
And laugh and mention it just the same
  As though there had been no lendings.
Nine hundred and ninety-nine of 'em call
  For silver and gold in their dealings;
But the Thousandth Man he's worth 'em all,
  Because you can show him your feelings!

His wrong's your wrong, and his right's your right,
  In season or out of season.
Stand up and back it in all men's sight –
  With *that* for your only reason!
Nine hundred and ninety-nine can't bide
  The shame or mocking or laughter,
But the Thousandth Man will stand by your side
  To the gallows-foot – and after!

Simple Simon

Cattiwow came down the steep lane with his five-horse timber-tug. He stopped by the wood-lump at the back gate to take off the brakes. His real name was Brabon, but the first time the children met him, years and years ago, he told them he was 'carting wood', and it sounded so exactly like 'cattiwow' that they never called him anything else.

'Hi!' Una shouted from the top of the wood-lump, where they had been watching the lane. 'What are you doing? Why weren't we told?'

'They've just sent for me,' Cattiwow answered. 'There's a middlin' big log stacked in the dirt at Rabbit Shaw, and' – he flicked his whip back along the line – 'so they've sent for us all.'

Dan and Una threw themselves off the wood-lump almost under black Sailor's nose. Cattiwow never let them ride the big beam that makes the body of the timber-tug, but they hung on behind while their teeth thuttered.

The wood road beyond the brook climbs at once into the woods, and you see all the horses' backs rising, one above another, like moving stairs. Cattiwow strode ahead in his sackcloth woodman's petticoat, belted at the waist with a leather strap; and when he turned and grinned, his red lips showed under his sackcloth-coloured beard. His cap was sackcloth too, with a flap behind, to keep twigs and bark out of his neck. He navigated the tug among pools of heather-water that splashed in their faces, and through clumps of young birches that slashed at their legs, and when they hit an old toadstooled stump they never knew whether it would give way in showers of rotten wood or jar them back again.

At the top of Rabbit Shaw half a dozen men and a team of horses stood round a forty-foot oak log in a muddy hollow. The ground about was poached and stoached with sliding hoof-marks, and a wave of dirt was driven up in front of the butt.

'What did you want to bury her for this way?' said Cattiwow. He took his broad-axe and went up the log tapping it.

'She's sticked fast,' said 'Bunny' Lewknor, who managed the other team.

Cattiwow unfastened the five wise horses from the tug. They cocked their ears forward, looked, and shook themselves.

'I believe Sailor knows,' Dan whispered to Una.

'He do,' said a man behind them. He was dressed in flour sacks like the others, and he leaned on his broad-axe, but the children, who knew all the wood-gangs, knew he was a stranger. In his size and oily hairiness he might have been Bunny Lewknor's brother, except that his brown eyes were as soft as a spaniel's, and his rounded black beard, beginning close up under them, reminded Una of the walrus in 'The Walrus and the Carpenter'.

'Don't he justabout know?' he said shyly, and shifted from one foot to the other.

'Yes. "What Cattiwow can't get out of the woods must have roots growing to her." ' Dan had heard old Hobden say this a few days before.

At that minute Puck pranced up, picking his way through the pools of black water in the ling.

'Look *out*!' cried Una, jumping forward. 'He'll see you, Puck!'

'Me and Mus' Robin are pretty middlin' well acquainted,' the man answered with a smile that made them forget all about walruses.

'This is Simon Cheyneys,' Puck began, and cleared his throat. 'Shipbuilder of Rye Port; burgess of the said town, and the only – '

'Oh, look! Look ye! That's a knowing one,' said the man. Cattiwow had fastened his team to the thin end of the log, and was moving them about with his whip till they stood at right angles to it, heading downhill. Then he grunted. The horses took the strain, beginning with Sailor next the log, like a tug-of-war team, and dropped almost to their knees. The log shifted a nail's breadth in the clinging dirt, with the noise of a giant's kiss.

'You're getting her!' Simon Cheyneys slapped his knee. 'Hing on! Hing on, lads, or she'll master ye! Ah!'

Sailor's left hind hoof had slipped on a heather-tuft. One of the men whipped off his sack apron and spread it down. They saw Sailor feel for it, and recover. Still the log hung, and the team grunted in despair.

'Hai!' shouted Cattiwow, and brought his dreadful whip twice across Sailor's loins with the crack of a shotgun. The horse almost screamed as he pulled that extra last ounce which he did not know was in him. The thin end of the log left the dirt and rasped on dry gravel. The butt ground round like a buffalo in his wallow. Quick as an axe-cut, Lewknor snapped on his five horses, and sliding, trampling, jingling and snorting they had the whole thing out on the heather.

'Dat's the very first time I've knowed you lay into Sailor – to hurt him,' said Lewknor.

'It is,' said Cattiwow, and passed his hand over the two wheals. 'But I'd ha' laid my own brother open at that pinch. Now we'll twitch her down the hill a piece – she lies just about right – and get her home by the low road. My team'll do it, Bunny; you bring the tug along. Mind out!'

He spoke to the horses, who tightened the chains. The great log half rolled over, and slowly drew itself out of sight downhill, followed by the wood-gang and the timber-tug. In half a minute there was nothing to see but the deserted hollow of the torn-up dirt, the birch undergrowth still shaking, and the water draining back into the hoofprints.

'Ye heard him?' Simon Cheyneys asked. 'He cherished his horse, but he'd ha' laid him open at that pinch.'

'Not for his own advantage,' said Puck quickly. ' 'Twas only to shift the log.'

'I reckon every man born of woman has his log to shift in the world – if so be you're hintin' at any o' Frankie's doings. *He* never hit beyond reason or without reason,' said Simon.

'*I* never said a word against Frankie,' Puck retorted, with a wink at the children. 'An' if I did, do it lie in your mouth to contest my say-so, seeing how you – '

'Why don't it lie in my mouth, seeing I was the first which knowed Frankie for all he was?' The burly sack-clad man puffed down at cool little Puck.

'Yes, and the first which set out to poison him – Frankie – on the high seas – '

Simon's angry face changed to a sheepish grin. He waggled his immense hands, but Puck stood off and laughed mercilessly.

'But let me tell you, Mus' Robin – ' he pleaded.

'I've heard the tale. Tell the children here. Look, Dan! Look, Una!' – Puck's straight brown finger levelled like an arrow. 'There's the only man that ever tried to poison Sir Francis Drake!'

'Oh, Mus' Robin! 'Tisn't fair. You've the 'vantage of us all in your upbringin's by hundreds o' years. Stands to nature you know all the tales against everyone.'

He turned his soft eyes so helplessly on Una that she cried, 'Stop ragging him, Puck! You know he didn't really.'

'I do. But why are you so sure, little maid?'

'Because – because he doesn't look like it,' said Una stoutly.

'I thank you,' said Simon to Una. 'I – I was always trustable-like with children if you let me alone, you double handful o' mischief.' He pretended to heave up his axe on Puck; and then his shyness overtook him afresh.

'Where did you know Sir Francis Drake?' said Dan, not liking being called a child.

'At Rye Port, to be sure,' said Simon, and seeing Dan's bewilderment, repeated it.

'Yes, but look here,' said Dan. ' "Drake he was a Devon man". The song says so.'

' "*And* ruled the Devon seas",' Una went on. 'That's what I was thinking – if you don't mind.'

Simon Cheyneys seemed to mind very much indeed, for he swelled in silence while Puck laughed.

'Hutt!' he burst out at last, 'I've heard that talk too. If you listen to them West Country folk, you'll listen to a pack o' lies. I believe Frankie was born somewhere out west among the shires, but his father had to run for it when Frankie was a baby, because the neighbours was wishful to kill him, d'ye see? He run to Chatham, old Parson Drake did, an' Frankie was brought up in an old hulks of a ship moored in the Medway river, same as it might ha' been the Rother. Brought up *at* sea, you might say, before he could walk *on* land – nigh Chatham in Kent. And ain't Kent back-door to Sussex? And don't that make

Frankie Sussex? O' course it do. Devon man! Bah! Those West Country boats they're always fishin' in other folks' water.'

'I beg your pardon,' said Dan. 'I'm sorry .

'No call to be sorry. You've been misled. I met Frankie at Rye Port when my uncle, that was the shipbuilder there, pushed me off his wharf-edge on to Frankie's ship. Frankie had put in from Chatham with his rudder splutted, and a man's arm – Moon's that 'ud be – broken at the tiller. "Take this boy aboard an' drown him," says my uncle, "and I'll mend your rudder-piece for love." '

'What did your uncle want you drowned for?' said Una.

'That was only his fashion of say-so, same as Mus' Robin. I'd a foolishness in my head that ships could be builded out of iron. Yes – iron ships! I'd made me a liddle toy one of iron plates beat out thin – and she floated a wonder! But my uncle, bein' a burgess of Rye, and a shipbuilder, he 'prenticed me to Frankie in the fetchin' trade, to cure this foolishness.'

'What was the fetchin' trade?' Dan interrupted.

'Fetchin' poor Flemishers and Dutchmen out o' the Low Countries into England. The King o' Spain, d'ye see, he was burnin' 'em in those parts, for to make 'em Papishers, so Frankie he fetched 'em away to *our* parts, and a risky trade it was. His master wouldn't never touch it while he lived, but he left his ship to Frankie when he died, and Frankie turned her into this fetchin' trade. Outrageous cruel hard work – on besom-black nights bulting back and forth off they Dutch roads with shoals on all sides, and having to hark out for the *frish-frish-frish*-like of a Spanish galliwopses' oars creepin' up on ye. Frankie 'ud have the tiller and Moon he'd peer forth at the bows, our lantern under his skirts, till the boat we was lookin' for 'ud blurt up out o' the dark, and we'd lay hold and haul aboard whoever 'twas – man, woman or babe – an' round we'd go again, the wind bewling like a kite in our riggin's, and they'd drop into the hold and praise God for happy deliverance till they was all sick.

'I had nigh a year at it, an' we must have fetched off – oh, a hundred pore folk, I reckon. Outrageous bold, too, Frankie growed to be. Outrageous cunning he was. Once we was as near as nothing nipped by a tall ship off Tergo Sands in a snowstorm. She had the wind of us, and spooned straight before it, shooting all bow guns. Frankie fled inshore smack for the beach, till he was atop of the first breakers. Then he hove his anchor out, which nigh tore our bows off, but it twitched us round end-for-end into the wind, d'ye see, an' we clawed off them sands like a drunk man rubbin' along a tavern bench. When we could see, the Spanisher was laid flat along in the breakers with the snows whitening on his wet belly. He thought he could go where Frankie went.'

'What happened to the crew?' said Una.

'We didn't stop,' Simon answered. 'There was a very liddle new baby in our hold, and the mother she wanted to get to some dry bed middlin' quick. We runned into Dover, and said nothing.'

'Was Sir Francis Drake very much pleased?'

'Heart alive, maid, he'd no head to his name in those days. He was just an outrageous, valiant, crop-haired, tutt-mouthed boy, roarin' up an' down the narrer seas, with his beard not yet quilted out. He made a laughing-stock of everything all day, and he'd hold our lives in the bight of his arm all the besom-black night among they Dutch sands; and we'd ha' jumped overside to behove him any one time, all of us.'

'Then why did you try to poison him?' Una asked wickedly, and Simon hung his head like a shy child.

'Oh, that was when he set me to make a pudden, for because our cook was hurted. *I* done my uttermost, but she all fetched adrift like in the bag, an' the more I biled the bits of her, the less she favoured any fashion o' pudden. Moon he chawed and chammed his piece, and Frankie chawed and chammed his'n, and – no words to it – he took me by the ear an' walked me out over the bow-end, an' him an' Moon hove the pudden at me on the bowsprit gub by gub, something cruel hard!' Simon rubbed his hairy cheek.

' "Nex' time you bring me anything," says Frankie, "you bring me cannon-shot an' I'll know what I'm getting." But as for poisoning – ' He stopped, the children laughed so.

'Of course you didn't,' said Una. 'Oh, Simon, we *do* like you!'

'I was always likeable with children.' His smile crinkled up through the hair round his eyes. 'Simple Simon they used to call me through our yard gates.'

'Did Sir Francis mock you?' Dan asked.

'Ah, no. He was gentle-born. Laugh he did – he was always laughing – but not so as to hurt a feather. An' I loved 'en. I loved 'en before England knew 'en, or Queen Bess she broke his heart.'

'But he hadn't really done anything when you knew him, had he?' Una insisted. 'Armadas and those things, I mean.'

Simon pointed to the scars and scrapes left by Cattiwow's great log. 'You tell me that that good ship's timber never done nothing against winds and weathers since her up-springing, and I'll confess ye that young Frankie never done nothing neither. Nothing? He adventured and suffered and made shift on they Dutch sands as much in any one month as ever he had occasion for to do in a half-year on the high seas afterwards. An' what was his tools? A coaster boat – a liddle box o' walty plankin' an' some few fathom feeble rope held together an' made able by *him* sole. He drawed our spirits up in our bodies same as a chimney-towel draws a fire. 'Twas in him, and it comed out all times and shapes.'

'I wonder did he ever 'magine what he was going to be? Tell himself stories about it?' said Dan with a flush.

'I expect so. We mostly do – even when we're grown. But bein' Frankie, he took good care to find out beforehand what his fortune might be. Had I rightly ought to tell 'em this piece?' Simon turned to Puck, who nodded.

'My mother, she was just a fair woman, but my aunt, her sister, she had gifts by inheritance laid up in her,' Simon began.

'Oh, that'll never do,' cried Puck, for the children stared blankly. 'Do you remember what Robin promised to the Widow Whitgift so long as her blood and get lasted?'*

'Yes. There was always to be one of them that could see farther through a millstone than most,' Dan answered promptly.

'Well, Simon's aunt's mother,' said Puck slowly, 'married the widow's blind son on the marsh, and Simon's aunt was the one chosen to see farthest through millstones. Do you understand?'

'That was what I was gettin' at,' said Simon, 'but you're so desperate quick. My aunt she knew what was coming to people. My uncle being a burgess of Rye, he counted all such things odious, and my aunt she couldn't be got to practise her gifts hardly at all, because it hurted her head for a week afterwards; but when Frankie heard she had 'em, he was all for nothing till she foretold on him – till she looked in his hand to tell his fortune, d'ye see? One time we was at Rye she come aboard with my other shirt and some apples, and he fair beazled the life out of her about it.

' "Oh, you'll be twice wed, and die childless," she says, and pushes his hand away.

' "That's the woman's part," he says. "What'll come to me – to me?" an' he thrusts it back under her nose.

' "Gold – gold, past belief or counting," she says. "Let go o' me, lad."

' "Sink the gold!" he says. "What'll I do, mother?" He coaxed her like no woman could well withstand. I've seen him with 'em – even when they were seasick.

' "If you *will* have it," she says at last, 'you shall have it. You'll do a many things, and eating and drinking with a dead man beyond the world's end will be the least of them. For you'll open a road from the East unto the West, and back again, and you'll bury your heart with your best friend by that roadside, and the road you open none shall shut so long as you're let lie quiet in your grave."†

' "And if I'm not?" he says.

' "Why, then," she says, "Sim's iron ships will be sailing on dry land. Now ha' done with this foolishness. Where's Sim's shirt?"

'He couldn't fetch no more out of her, and when we come up from the cabin, he stood mazed like by the tiller, playing with an apple.

' "My sorrow!" says my aunt; "d'ye see that? The great world lying in his hand, liddle and round like an apple."

---

* See 'Dymchurch Flit' in *Puck of Pook's Hill*.
† The old lady's prophecy is in a fair way to come true, for now the Panama Canal is finished, one end of it opens into the very bay where Sir Francis Drake was buried. So ships are taken through the Canal, and the road round Cape Horn which Sir Francis opened is very little used.

' "Why, 'tis one you gived him," I says.

' "To be sure," she says. " 'Tis just an apple," and she went ashore with her hand to her head. It always hurted her to show her gifts.

'Him and me puzzled over that talk plenty. It sticked in his mind quite extravagant. The very next time we slipped out for some fetchin' trade, we met Mus' Stenning's boat over by Calais sands; and he warned us that the Spanishers had shut down all their Dutch ports against us English, and their galliwopses was out picking up our boats like flies off hogs' backs. Mus' Stenning he runs for Shoreham, but Frankie held on a piece, knowin' that Mus Stenning was jealous of our good trade. Over by Dunkirk a great gor-bellied Spanisher, with the Cross on his sails, came rampin' at us. We left him. We left him all they bare seas to conquest in.

' "Looks like this road was going to be shut pretty soon," says Frankie, humouring her at the tiller. "I'll have to open that other one your aunt foretold of."

' "The Spanisher's crowdin' down on us middlin' quick," I says.

' "No odds," says Frankie, "he'll have the inshore tide against him. Did your aunt say I was to be quiet in my grave for ever?"

' "Till my iron ships sailed dry land," I says.

' "That's foolishness," he says. "Who cares where Frankie Drake makes a hole in the water now or twenty years from now?"

'The Spanisher kept muckin' on more and more canvas. I told him so.

' "He's feelin' the tide," was all he says. "If he was among Tergoes Sands with this wind, we'd be picking his bones proper. I'd give my heart to have all their tall ships there some night before a north gale, and me to windward. There'd be gold in my hands then. Did your aunt say she saw the world settin' in my hand, Sim?"

' "Yes, but 'twas an apple," says I, and he laughed like he always did at me.

' "Do you ever feel minded to jump overside and be done with every-thing?" he asks after a while.

' "No. What water comes aboard is too wet as 'tis," I says. "The Spanisher's going about."

' "I told you," says he, never looking back. "He'll give us the Pope's blessing as he swings. Come down off that rail. There's no knowin' where stray shots may hit." So I came down off the rail, and leaned against it, and the Spanisher he ruffled round in the wind, and his port-lids opened all red inside.

' "Now what'll happen to my road if they don't let me lie quiet in my grave?" he says. "Does your aunt mean there's two roads to be found and kept open – or what does she mean? I don't like that talk about t'other road. D'you believe in your iron ships, Sim?"

'He knowed I did, so I only nodded, and he nodded back again.

' "Anybody but me 'ud call you a fool, Sim," he says. "Lie down. Here comes the Pope's blessing!"

'The Spanisher gave us his broadside as he went about. They all fell short except one that smack-smooth hit the rail behind my back, an' I felt most won'erful cold.

' "Be you hit anywhere to signify?" he says. "Come over to me."

' "Oh, lord, Mus' Drake," I says, "my legs won't move," and that was the last I spoke for months.'

'Why? What had happened?' cried Dan and Una together.

'The rail had jarred me in here like.' Simon reached behind him clumsily. 'From my shoulders down I didn't act no shape. Frankie carried me piggyback to my aunt's house, and I lay bed-rid and tongue-tied while she rubbed me day and night, month in and month out. She had faith in rubbing with the hands. P'raps she put some of her gifts into it, too. Last of all, something loosed itself in my pore back, and lo! I was whole restored again, but kitten-feeble.

' "Where's Frankie?" I says, thinking I'd been a longish while abed.

' "Down-wind amongst the Dons – months ago," says my aunt.

' "When can I go after 'en?" I says.

' "Your duty's to your town and trade now," says she. "Your uncle he died last Michaelmas and he've left you and me the yard. So no more iron ships, mind ye."

' "What?" I says. "And you the only one that beleft in 'em!"

' "Maybe I do still," she says, "but I'm a woman before I'm a Whitgift, and wooden ships is what England needs us to build. I lay on ye to do so."

'That's why I've never teched iron since that day – not to build a toy ship of. I've never even drawed a draft of one for my pleasure of evenings.' Simon smiled down on them all.

'Whitgift blood is terrible resolute – on the she-side,' said Puck.

'Didn't you ever see Sir Francis Drake again?' Dan asked.

'With one thing and another, and my being made a burgess of Rye, I never clapped eyes on him for the next twenty years. Oh, I had the news of his mighty doings the world over. They was the very same bold, cunning shifts and passes he'd worked with beforetimes off they Dutch sands, but, naturally, folk took more note of them. When Queen Bess made him knight, he sent my aunt a dried orange stuffed with spiceries to smell to. She cried outrageous on it. She blamed herself for her foretellings, having set him on his won'erful road; but I reckon he'd ha' gone that way all withstanding. Curious how close she foretelled it! The world in his hand like an apple, an' he burying his best friend, Mus' Doughty – '

'Never mind for Mus' Doughty,' Puck interrupted. 'Tell us where you met Sir Francis next.'

'Oh, ha! That was the year I was made a burgess of Rye – the same year which King Philip sent his ships to take England without Frankie's leave.'

'The Armada!' said Dan contentedly. 'I was hoping that would come.'

'I knowed Frankie would never let 'em smell London smoke, but plenty good men in Rye was two-three minded about the upshot. 'Twas the noise of the gunfire terrified us. The wind favoured it our way from off behind the Isle of Wight. It made a mutter like, which growed and growed, and by the end of a week women was shruckin' in the streets. Then *they* come sliddering past Fairlight in a great smoky pat vambrished with red gunfire, and our ships flying forth and ducking in again. The smoke-pat sliddered over to the French shore, so I knowed Frankie was edging the Spanishers toward they Dutch sands where he was master. I says to my aunt, "The smoke's thinning out. I lay Frankie's just about scrapin' his hold for a few last rounds shot. 'Tis time for me to go."

' "Never in them clothes," she says. "Do on the doublet I bought you to be made burgess in, and don't you shame this day."

'So I mucked it on, and my chain, and my stiffed Dutch breeches and all.

' "I be comin', too," she says from her chamber, and forth she come pavisandin' like a peacock – stuff, ruff, stomacher and all. She was a notable woman.'

'But how did you go? You haven't told us,' said Una.

'In my own ship – but half-share was my aunt's. In the *Antony of Rye*, to be sure; and not empty-handed. I'd been loadin' her for three days with the pick of our yard. We was ballasted on cannon-shot of all three sizes; and iron rods and straps for his carpenters; and a nice passel of clean three-inch oak planking and hide breech-ropes for his cannon, and gubs of good oakum, and bolts o' canvas, and all the sound rope in the yard. What else could I ha' done? *I* knowed what he'd need most after a week's such work. I'm a shipbuilder, little maid.

'We'd a fair slant o' wind off Dungeness, and we crept on till it fell light airs and puffed out. The Spanishers was all in a huddle over by Calais, and our ships was strawed about mending 'emselves like dogs lickin' bites. Now and then a Spanisher would fire from a low port, and the ball 'ud troll across the flat swells, but both sides was finished fightin' for that tide.

'The first ship we foreslowed on, her breastworks was crushed in, an' men was shorin' 'em up. She said nothing. The next was a black pinnace, his pumps clackin' middling quick, and he said nothing. But the third, mending shot-holes, he spoke out plenty. I asked him where Mus' Drake might be, and a shiny-suited man on the poop looked down into us, and saw what we carried.

' "Lay alongside, you!" he says. "We'll take that all."

' "'Tis for Mus' Drake," I says, keeping away lest his size should lee the wind out of my sails.

' "Hi! Ho! Hither! We're Lord High Admiral of England! Come along-side, or we'll hang ye," he says.

' 'Twas none of my affairs who he was if he wasn't Frankie, and while he talked so hot I slipped behind a green-painted ship with her top-sides splintered. We was all in the middest of 'em then.

' "Hi! Hoi!" the green ship says. "Come alongside, honest man, and I'll buy your load. I'm Fenner that fought the seven Portugals – clean out of shot or bullets. Frankie knows me."

' "Ay, but I don't," I says, and I slacked nothing.

'He was a masterpiece. Seein' I was for goin' on, he hails a Bridport hoy beyond us and shouts, "George! Oh, George! Wing that duck. He's fat!" An' true as we're all here, that squatty Bridport boat rounds to acrost our bows, intending to stop us by means o' shooting.

'My aunt looks over our rail. "George," she says, "you finish with your enemies afore you begin on your friends."

'Him that was laying the liddle swivel-gun at us sweeps off his hat an' calls her Queen Bess, and asks if she was selling liquor to pore dry sailors. My aunt answered him quite a piece. She was a notable woman.

'Then *he* come up – his long pennant trailing overside – his waistcloths and netting tore all to pieces where the Spanishers had grappled, and his sides black-smeared with their gun-blasts like candle-smoke in a bottle. We hooked on to a lower port and hung.

' "Oh, Mus' Drake! Mus' Drake!" I calls up.

'He stood on the great anchor cathead, his shirt open to the middle, and his face shining like the sun.

' "Why, Sim!" he says. Just like that – after twenty year! "Sim," he says, "what brings you?"

' "Pudden," I says, not knowing whether to laugh or cry. ' "You told me to bring cannon-shot next time, an' I've brought 'em."

'He saw we had. He ripped out a fathom and a half o' brimstone Spanish, and he swung down on our rail, and he kissed me before all his fine young captains. His men was swarming out of the lower ports ready to unload us. When he saw how I'd considered all his likely wants, he kissed me again.

' "Here's a friend that sticketh closer than a brother!" he says. "Mistress," he says to my aunt, "all you foretold on me was true. I've opened that road from the East to the West, and I've buried my heart beside it."

' "I know," she says. "That's why I be come."

' "But ye never foretold this" – he points to both they great fleets.

' "This don't seem to me to make much odds compared to what happens *to* a man," she says. "Do it?"

' "Certain sure a man forgets to remember when he's proper mucked up with work. Sim," he says to me, "we must shift every living Spanisher round Dunkirk corner on to our Dutch sands before morning. The wind'll come out of the north after this calm – same as it used – and then they're our meat."

' "Amen," says I. "I've brought you what I could scutchel up of odds and ends. Be you hit anywhere to signify?"

' "Oh, our folk'll attend to all that when we've time," he says. He turns to talk to my aunt, while his men flew the stuff out of our hold. I think I saw old Moon amongst 'em, but he was too busy to more than nod like. Yet the Spanishers was going to prayers with their bells and candles before we'd cleaned out the *Antony*. Twenty-two ton o' useful stuff I'd fetched him.

' "Now, Sim," says my aunt, "no more devouring of Mus' Drake's time.

He's sending us home in the Bridport hoy. I want to speak to them young springalds again."

' "But here's our ship all ready and swept," I says.

' "Swep' an' garnished," says Frankie. "I'm going to fill her with devils in the likeness o' pitch and sulphur. We must shift the Dons round Dunkirk corner, and if shot can't do it, we'll send down fireships."

' "I've given him my share of the *Antony*," says my aunt. "What do you reckon to do about yours?"

' "She offered it," said Frankie, laughing.

' "She wouldn't have if I'd overheard her," I says; "because I'd have offered my share first." Then I told him how the *Antony*'s sails was best trimmed to drive before the wind, and seeing he was full of occupations we went acrost to that Bridport hoy, and left him.

'But Frankie was gentle-born, d'ye see, and that sort they never overlook any folks' dues.

'When the hoy passed under his stern, he stood bare-headed on the poop same as if my aunt had been his queen, and his musicianers played "Mary Ambree" on their silver trumpets quite a long while. Heart alive, little maid! I never meaned to make you look sorrowful – '

Bunny Lewknor in his sackcloth petticoats burst through the birch scrub wiping his forehead.

'We've got the stick to rights now! She've been a whole hatful o' trouble. You come an' ride her home, Mus' Dan and Miss Una!'

They found the proud wood-gang at the foot of the slope, with the log double-chained on the tug.

'Cattiwow, what are you going to do with it?' said Dan, as they straddled the thin part.

'She's going down to Rye to make a keel for a Lowestoft fishin' boat, I've heard. Hold tight!'

Cattiwow cracked his whip, and the great log dipped and tilted, and leaned and dipped again, exactly like a stately ship upon the high seas.

Frankie's Trade

Old Horn to All Atlantic said:
   (*A-hay O! To me O!*)
'Now where did Frankie learn his trade?
For he ran me down with a three-reef mains'le.'
   (*All round the Horn!*)

Atlantic answered: 'Not from me!
You'd better ask the cold North Sea,
For he ran me down under all plain canvas.'
   (*All round the Horn!*)

The North Sea answered: 'He's my man,
For he came to me when he began –
Frankie Drake in an open coaster.
   (*All round the Sands!*)

I caught him young and I used him sore,
So you never shall startle Frankie more,
Without capsizing Earth and her waters.
   (*All round the Sands!*)

I did not favour him at all,
I made him pull and I made him haul –
And stand his trick with the common sailors.
   (*All round the Sands!*)

I froze him stiff and I fogged him blind,
And kicked him home with his road to find
By what he could see of a three-day snowstorm.
   (*All round the Sands!*)

I learned him his trade o' winter nights,
'Twixt Mardyk Fort and Dunkirk lights
On a five-knot tide with the forts a-firing.
   (*All round the Sands!*)

Before his beard began to shoot,
I showed him the length of the Spaniard's foot –
And I reckon he clapped the boot on it later.
    (*All round the Sands!*)

If there's a risk which you can make
That's worse than he was used to take
Nigh every week in the way of his business
    (*All round the Sands!*);

If there's a trick that you can try
Which he hasn't met in time gone by,
Not once or twice, but ten times over
    (*All round the Sands!*);

If you can teach him aught that's new
    (*A-hay O! To me O!*),
I'll give you Bruges and Niewport too,
And the ten tall churches that stand between 'em.'
    Storm along, my gallant captains!
    (*All round the Horn!*)

THE TREE OF JUSTICE

The Ballad of Minepit Shaw

About the time that taverns shut
   And men can buy no beer,
Two lads went up by the keepers' hut
   To steal Lord Pelham's deer.

Night and the liquor was in their heads –
   They laughed and talked no bounds,
Till they waked the keepers on their beds,
   And the keepers loosed the hounds.

They had killed a hart, they had killed a hind,
   Ready to carry away,
When they heard a whimper down the wind
   And they heard a bloodhound bay.

They took and ran across the fern,
   Their crossbows in their hand,
Till they met a man with a green lantern
   That called and bade 'em stand.

'What are you doing, O Flesh and Blood,
   And what's your foolish will,
That you must break into Minepit Wood
   And wake the Folk of the Hill?'

'Oh, we've broke into Lord Pelham's park,
   And killed Lord Pelham's deer,
And if ever you heard a little dog bark
   You'll know why we come here!'

'We ask you let us go our way,
   As fast as we can flee,
For if ever you heard a bloodhound bay,
   You'll know how pressed we be.'

'Oh, lay your crossbows on the bank
  And drop the knife from your hand,
And though the hounds are at your flank
  I'll save you where you stand!'

They laid their crossbows on the bank,
  They threw their knives in the wood,
And the ground before them opened and sank
  And saved 'em where they stood.

'Oh, what's the roaring in our ears
  That strikes us well-nigh dumb?'
'Oh, that is just how things appears
  According as they come.'

'What are the stars before our eyes
  That strike us well-nigh blind?'
'Oh, that is just how things arise
  According as you find.'

'And why's our bed so hard to the bones
  Excepting where it's cold?'
'Oh, that's because it is precious stones
  Excepting where 'tis gold.

Think it over as you stand
  For I tell you without fail,
If you haven't got into Fairyland
  You're not in Lewes Gaol.'

All night long they thought of it,
  And, come the dawn, they saw
They'd tumbled into a great old pit,
  At the bottom of Minepit Shaw.

And the keepers' hound had followed 'em close
  And broke her neck in the fall;
So they picked up their knives and their crossbows
  And buried the dog. That's all.

But whether the man was a poacher too
  Or a Pharisee so bold –
I reckon there's more things told than are true,
  And more things true than are told.

The Tree of Justice

It was a warm, dark winter day with the sou'-west wind singing through Dallington Forest, and the woods below the Beacon. The children set out after dinner to find old Hobden, who had a three months' job in the Rough at the back of Pound's Wood. He had promised to get them a dormouse in its nest. The bright leaf still clung to the beech coppice; the long chestnut leaves lay orange on the ground, and the rides were speckled with scarlet-lipped sprouting acorns. They worked their way by their own short cuts to the edge of Pound's Wood, and heard a horse's feet just as they came to the beech where Ridley the keeper hangs up the vermin. The poor little fluffy bodies dangled from the branches – some perfectly good, but most of them dried to twisted strips.

'Three more owls,' said Dan, counting. 'Two stoats, four jays, and a kestrel. That's ten since last week. Ridley's a beast.'

'In my time this sort of tree bore heavier fruit.' Sir Richard Dalyngridge* reined up his grey horse, Swallow, in the ride behind them. 'What play do you make?' he asked.

'Nothing, sir. We're looking for old Hobden,' Dan replied. 'He promised to get us a sleeper.'

'Sleeper? A *dormeuse*, do you say?'

'Yes, a dormouse, sir.'

'I understand. I passed a woodman on the low grounds. Come!'

He wheeled up the ride again, and pointed through an opening to the patch of beech-stubs, chestnut, hazel and birch that old Hobden would turn into firewood, hop-poles, pea-boughs and house-faggots before spring. The old man was as busy as a beaver.

Something laughed beneath a thorn, and Puck stole out, his finger on his lip.

'Look!' he whispered. 'Along between the spindle-trees. Ridley has been there this half-hour.'

The children followed his point, and saw Ridley the keeper in an old dry ditch, watching Hobden as a cat watches a mouse.

'Huhh!' cried Una. 'Hobden always 'tends to his wires before breakfast. He puts his rabbits into the faggots he's allowed to take home. He'll tell us about 'em tomorrow.'

* This is the Norman knight they met the year before in *Puck of Pook's Hill*. See 'Young Men at the Manor', 'The Knights of the Joyous Venture' and 'Old Men at Pevensey' in that book.

'We had the same breed in my day,' Sir Richard replied, and moved off quietly, Puck at his bridle, the children on either side between the close-trimmed beech stuff.

'What did you do to them?' said Dan, as they repassed Ridley's terrible tree.

'That!' Sir Richard jerked his head toward the dangling owls.

'Not he!' said Puck. 'There was never enough brute Norman in you to hang a man for taking a buck.'

'I – I cannot abide to hear their widows screech. But why am I on horseback while you are afoot?' He dismounted lightly, tapped Swallow on the chest, so that the wise thing backed instead of turning in the narrow ride, and put himself at the head of the little procession. He walked as though all the woods belonged to him. 'I have often told my friends,' he went on, 'that Red William the king was not the only Norman found dead in a forest while he hunted.'

'D'you mean William Rufus?' said Dan.

'Yes,' said Puck, kicking a clump of red toadstools off a dead log.

'For example, there was a knight new from Normandy,' Sir Richard went on, 'to whom Henry our king granted a manor in Kent near by. He chose to hang his forester's son the day before a deer-hunt that he gave to pleasure the king.'

'Now when would that be?' said Puck, and scratched an ear thoughtfully.

'The summer of the year King Henry broke his brother Robert of Normandy at Tenchebrai fight. Our ships were even then at Pevensey loading for the war.'

'What happened to the knight?' Dan asked.

'They found him pinned to an ash, three arrows through his leather coat. *I* should have worn mail that day.'

'And did you see him all bloody?' Dan continued.

'Nay, I was with De Aquila at Pevensey, counting horseshoes and arrow-sheaves and ale-barrels into the holds of the ships. The army only waited for our king to lead them against Robert in Normandy, but he sent word to De Aquila that he would hunt with him here before he set out for France.'

'Why did the king want to hunt so particularly?' Una demanded.

'If he had gone straight to France after the Kentish knight was killed, men would have said he feared being slain like the knight. It was his duty to show himself debonair to his English people as it was De Aquila's duty to see that he took no harm while he did it. But it was a great burden! De Aquila, Hugh and I ceased work on the ships, and scoured all the Honour of the Eagle – all De Aquila's lands – to make a fit, and, above all, a safe sport for our king. Look!'

The ride twisted, and came out on the top of Pound's Hill Wood. Sir Richard pointed to the swells of beautiful, dappled Dallington that showed like a woodcock's breast up the valley. 'Ye know the forest?' said he.

'You ought to see the bluebells there in spring!' said Una. 'I have seen,' said Sir Richard, gazing, and stretched out his hand. 'Hugh's work and mine was first to move the deer gently from all parts into Dallington yonder, and there to hold them till the king came. Next, we must choose some three hundred beaters to drive the deer to the stands within bowshot of the king. Here was our trouble! In the mêlée of a deer-drive a Saxon peasant and a Norman king may come over-close to each other. The conquered do not love their conquerors all at once. So we needed sure men, for whom their village or kindred would answer in life, cattle and land if any harm come to the king. Ye see?'

'If one of the beaters shot the king,' said Puck, 'Sir Richard wanted to be able to punish that man's village. Then the village would take care to send a good man.'

'So! So it was. But, lest our work should be too easy, the king had done such a dread justice over at Salehurst, for the killing of the Kentish knight (twenty-six men he hanged, as I heard), that our folk were half mad with fear before we began. It is easier to dig out a badger gone to earth than a Saxon gone dumb-sullen. And atop of their misery the old rumour waked that Harold the Saxon was alive and would bring them deliverance from us Normans. This has happened every autumn since Senlac fight.'

'But King Harold was killed at Hastings,' said Una.

'So it was said, and so it was believed by us Normans, but our Saxons always believed he would come again. *That* rumour did not make our work any more easy.'

Sir Richard strode on down the far slope of the wood, where the trees thin out. It was fascinating to watch how he managed his long spurs among the lumps of blackened ling.

'But we did it!' he said. 'After all, a woman is as good as a man to beat the woods, and the mere word that deer are afoot makes cripples and crones young again. De Aquila laughed when Hugh told him over the list of beaters. Half were women; and many of the rest were clerks – Saxon and Norman priests.

'Hugh and I had not time to laugh for eight days, till De Aquila, as Lord of Pevensey, met our king and led him to the first shooting-stand – by the mill on the edge of the forest. Hugh and I – it was no work for hot heads or heavy hands – lay with our beaters on the skirts of Dallington to watch both them and the deer. When De Aquila's great horn blew we went forward, a line half a league long. Oh, to see the fat clerks, their gowns tucked up, puffing and roaring, and the sober millers dusting the undergrowth with their staves; and, like as not, between them a Saxon wench, hand in hand with her man, shrilling like a kite as she ran, and leaping high through the fern, all for joy of the sport.'

'*Ah! How! Ah! How! How–ah! Sa–how–ah!*' Puck bellowed without warning, and Swallow bounded forward, ears cocked and nostrils cracking.

'*Hal–lal–lal–lal–la–hai–ie!*' Sir Richard answered in a high clear shout.

The two voices joined in swooping circles of sound, and a heron rose out of a red osier-bed below them, circling as though he kept time to the outcry. Swallow quivered and swished his glorious tail. They stopped together on the same note.

A hoarse shout answered them across the bare woods.

'That's old Hobden,' said Una.

'Small blame to him. It is in his blood,' said Puck. 'Did your beaters cry so, Sir Richard?'

'My faith, they forgot all else. (Steady, Swallow, steady!) They forgot where the king and his people waited to shoot. They followed the deer to the very edge of the open till the first flight of wild arrows from the stands flew fair over them.

'I cried, " 'Ware shot! 'Ware shot!" and a knot of young knights new from Normandy, that had strayed away from the grand stand, turned about, and in mere sport loosed off at our line shouting: " 'Ware Senlac arrows! 'Ware Senlac arrows!" A jest, I grant you, but too sharp. One of our beaters answered in Saxon: " 'Ware New Forest arrows! 'Ware Red William's arrow!" so I judged it time to end the jests, and when the boys saw my old mail gown (for to shoot with strangers *I* count the same as war), they ceased shooting. So *that* was smoothed over, and we gave our beaters ale to wash down their anger. They were excusable! We – they had sweated to show our guests good sport, and our reward was a flight of hunting-arrows which no man loves, and worse, a churl's jibe over hard-fought, fair-lost Hastings fight. So, before the next beat, Hugh and I assembled and called the beaters over by name, to steady them. The greater part we knew, but among the Netherfield men I saw an old, old man, in the dress of a pilgrim.

'The Clerk of Netherfield said he was well known by repute for twenty years as a witless man that journeyed without rest to all the shrines of England. The old man sits, Saxon fashion, head between fists. We Normans rest the chin on the left palm.

' "Who answers for him?" said I. "If he fails in his duty, who will pay his fine?"

' "Who will pay my fine?" the pilgrim said. "I have asked that of all the saints in England these forty years, less three months and nine days! They have not answered!" When he lifted his thin face I saw he was one-eyed, and frail as a rush.

' "Nay, but, father," I said, "to whom hast thou commended thyself?" He shook his head, so I spoke in Saxon: "Whose man art thou?"

' "I think I have a writing from Rahere, the king's jester," said he after a while. "I am, as I suppose, Rahere's man."

'He pulled a writing from his scrip, and Hugh, coming up, read it.

'It set out that the pilgrim was Rahere's man, and that Rahere was the king's jester. There was Latin writ at the back.

' "What a plague conjuration's here?" said Hugh, turning it over. "*Pumquum-sum oc-occ.* Magic?"

' "Black Magic," said the Clerk of Netherfield (he had been a monk at Battle). "They say Rahere is more of a priest than a fool and more of a wizard than either. Here's Rahere's name writ, and there's Rahere's red cockscomb mark drawn below for such as cannot read." He looked slyly at me.

' "Then read it," said I, "and show thy learning." He was a vain little man, and he gave it us after much mouthing.

' "The charm, which I think is from Virgilius the Sorcerer, says: 'When thou art once dead, and Minos' (which is a heathen judge) 'has doomed thee, neither cunning, nor speechcraft, nor good works will restore thee!' A terrible thing! It denies any mercy to a man's soul!"

' "Does it serve?" said the pilgrim, plucking at Hugh's cloak. "Oh, man of the king's blood, does it cover me?"

'Hugh was of Earl Godwin's blood, and all Sussex knew it, though no Saxon dared call him kingly in a Norman's hearing. There can be but one king.

' "It serves," said Hugh. "But the day will be long and hot. Better rest here. We go forward now."

' "No, I will keep with thee, my kinsman," he answered like a child. He was indeed childish through great age.

'The line had not moved a bowshot when De Aquila's great horn blew for a halt, and soon young Fulke – our false Fulke's son – yes, the imp that lit the straw in Pevensey Castle* – came thundering up a woodway.

' "Uncle," said he (though he was a man grown, he called me uncle), "those young Norman fools who shot at you this morn are saying that your beaters cried treason against the king. It has come to Harry's long ears, and he bids you give account of it. There are heavy fines in his eye, but I am with you to the hilt, uncle!"

'When the boy had fled back, Hugh said to me: "It was Rahere's witless man that cried, ' 'Ware Red William's arrow!' I heard him, and so did the Clerk of Netherfield."

' "Then Rahere must answer to the king for his man," said I. "Keep him by you till I send," and I hastened down.

'The king was with De Aquila in the grand stand above Welansford down in the valley yonder. His court – knights and dames – lay glittering on the edge of the glade. I made my homage, and Henry took it coldly.

' "How came your beaters to shout threats against me?" said he.

' "The tale has grown," I answered. "One old witless man cried out, ' 'Ware Red William's arrow,' when the young knights shot at our line. We had two beaters hit."

' "I will do justice on that man," he answered. "Who is his master?"

' "He's Rahere's man," said I.

' "Rahere's?" said Henry. "Has my fool a fool?"

'I heard the bells jingle at the back of the stand, and a red leg waved over it; then a black one. So, very slowly, Rahere the king's jester straddled the edge of the planks, and looked down on us, rubbing his chin. Loose-knit, with cropped hair, and a sad priest's face, under his cockscomb cap, that he could

* See 'Old Men at Pevensey' in *Puck of Pook's Hill*.

twist like a strip of wet leather. His eyes were hollow-set.

' "Nay, nay, brother," said he. "If I suffer you to keep your fool, you must e'en suffer me to keep mine."

'This he delivered slowly into the king's angry face! My faith, a king's jester must be bolder than lions!

' "Now we will judge the matter," said Rahere. "Let these two brave knights go hang my fool because he warned King Henry against running after Saxon deer through woods full of Saxons. 'Faith, brother, if *thy* brother, Red William, now among the saints as we hope, had been timely warned against a certain arrow in New Forest, one fool of us four would not be crowned fool of England this morning. Therefore, hang the fool's fool, knights!"

'Mark the fool's cunning! Rahere had himself given us order to hang the man. No king dare confirm a fool's command to such a great baron as De Aquila; and the helpless king knew it.

' "What? No hanging?" said Rahere, after a silence. "A' God's gracious name, kill something, then! Go forward with the hunt!"

'He splits his face ear to ear in a yawn like a fish-pond. "Henry," says he, "the next time I sleep, do not pester me with thy fooleries." Then he throws himself out of sight behind the back of the stand.

'I have seen courage with mirth in De Aquila and Hugh, but stark mad courage of Rahere's sort I had never even guessed at.'

'What did the king say?' cried Dan.

'He had opened his mouth to speak, when young Fulke, who had come into the stand with us, laughed, and, boy-like, once begun, could not check himself. He kneeled on the instant for pardon, but fell sideways, crying: "His legs! Oh, his long, waving red legs as he went backward!"

'Like a storm breaking, our grave king laughed – stamped and reeled with laughter till the stand shook. So, like a storm, this strange thing passed!

'He wiped his eyes, and signed to De Aquila to let the drive come on.

'When the deer broke, we were pleased that the king shot from the shelter of the stand, and did not ride out after the hurt beasts as Red William would have done. Most vilely his knights and barons shot!

De Aquila kept me beside him, and I saw no more of Hugh till evening. We two had a little hut of boughs by the camp, where I went to wash me before the great supper, and in the dusk I heard Hugh on the couch.

' "Wearied, Hugh?" said I.

' "A little," he says. "I have driven Saxon deer all day for a Norman king, and there is enough of Earl Godwin's blood left in me to sicken at the work. Wait awhile with the torch."

'I waited then, and I thought I heard him sob.'

'Poor Hugh! Was he so tired?' said Una. 'Hobden says beating is hard work sometimes.'

'I think this tale is getting like the woods,' said Dan, 'darker and twistier every minute.'

Sir Richard had walked as he talked, and though the children thought they knew the woods well enough, they felt a little lost.

'A dark tale enough,' says Sir Richard, 'but the end was not all black. When we had washed, we went to wait on the king at meat in the great pavilion. Just before the trumpets blew for the entry – all the guests upstanding – long Rahere comes posturing up to Hugh, and strikes him with his bauble-bladder.

' "Here's a heavy heart for a joyous meal!" he says. "But each man must have his black hour or where would be the merit of laughing? Take a fool's advice, and sit it out with my man. I'll make a jest to excuse you to the king if he remember to ask for you. That's more than I would do for Archbishop Anselm."

'Hugh looked at him heavy-eyed. "Rahere?" said he. "The king's jester? Oh, saints, what punishment for my king!" and smites his hands together.

' "Go – go fight it out in the dark," says Rahere, "and thy Saxon saints reward thee for thy pity to my fool." He pushed him from the pavilion, and Hugh lurched away like one drunk.'

'But why?' said Una. 'I don't understand.'

'Ah, why indeed? Live you long enough, maiden, and you shall know the meaning of many whys.' Sir Richard smiled. 'I wondered too, but it was my duty to wait on the king at the high table in all that glitter and stir.

'He spoke me his thanks for the sport I had helped show him, and he had learned from De Aquila enough of my folk and my castle in Normandy graciously to feign that he knew and had loved my brother there. (This, also, is part of a king's work.) Many great men sat at the high table – chosen by the king for their wits, not for their birth. I have forgotten their names, and their faces I only saw that one night. But' – Sir Richard turned in his stride – 'but Rahere, flaming in black and scarlet among our guests, the hollow of his dark cheek flushed with wine – long, laughing Rahere, and the stricken sadness of his face when he was not twisting it about – Rahere I shall never forget.

'At the king's outgoing De Aquila bade me follow him, with his great bishops and two great barons, to the little pavilion. We had devised jugglers and dances for the court's sport; but Henry loved to talk gravely to grave men, and De Aquila had told him of my travels to the world's end. We had a fire of apple-wood, sweet as incense – and the curtains at the door being looped up, we could hear the music and see the lights shining on mail and dresses.

'Rahere lay behind the king's chair. The questions he darted forth at me were as shrewd as the flames. I was telling of our fight with the apes, as ye called them, at the world's end.*

' "But where is the Saxon knight that went with you?" said Henry. "He must confirm these miracles."

' "He is busy," said Rahere, "confirming a new miracle."

* See 'The Knights of the Joyous Venture' in *Puck of Pook's Hill*.

' "Enough miracles for today," said the king. "Rahere, you have saved your long neck. Fetch the Saxon knight."

' "Pest on it," said Rahere. "Who would be a king's jester? I'll bring him, brother, if you'll see that none of your home-brewed bishops taste my wine while I am away." So he jingled forth between the men-at-arms at the door.

'Henry had made many bishops in England without the Pope's leave. I know not the rights of the matter, but only Rahere dared jest about it. We waited on the king's next word.

' "I think Rahere is jealous of you," said he, smiling, to Nigel of Ely. He was one bishop; and William of Exeter, the other – Wal-wist the Saxons called him – laughed long. "Rahere is a priest at heart. Shall I make him a bishop, De Aquila?" says the king.

' "There might be worse," said our Lord of Pevensey. "Rahere would never do what Anselm has done."

'This Anselm, Archbishop of Canterbury, had gone off raging to the Pope at Rome, because Henry would make bishops without his leave either. I knew not the rights of it, but De Aquila did, and the king laughed.

' "Anselm means no harm. He should have been a monk, not a bishop," said the king. "I'll never quarrel with Anselm or his Pope till they quarrel with my England. If we can keep the king's peace till my son comes to rule, no man will lightly quarrel with our England."

' "Amen," said De Aquila. "But the king's peace ends when the king dies."

'That is true. The king's peace dies with the king. The custom then is that all laws are outlaw, and men do what they will till the new king is chosen.

' "I will amend that," said the king hotly. "I will have it so that though king, son and grandson were all slain in one day, *still* the king's peace should hold over all England! What is a man that his mere death must upheave a people? We must have the law."

' "Truth," said William of Exeter; but that he would have said to any word of the king.

'The two great barons behind said nothing. This teaching was clean against their stomachs, for when the king's peace ends, the great barons go to war and increase their lands. At that instant we heard Rahere's voice returning, in a scurril Saxon rhyme against William of Exeter:

' "Well wist Wal-wist where lay his fortune
When that he fawned on the king for his crozier,"

and amid our laughter he burst in, with one arm round Hugh, and one round the old pilgrim of Netherfield.

' "Here is your knight, brother," said he, "and for the better disport of the company, here is my fool. Hold up, Saxon Samson, the gates of Gaza are clean carried away!"

'Hugh broke loose, white and sick, and staggered to my side; the old man blinked upon the company.

'We looked at the king, but he smiled.

' "Rahere promised he would show me some sport after supper to cover his morning's offence," said he to De Aquila. "So this is thy man, Rahere?"

' "Even so," said Rahere. "My man he has been, and my protection he has taken, ever since I found him under the gallows at Stamford Bridge telling the kites atop of it that he was – Harold of England!"

'There was a great silence upon these last strange words, and Hugh hid his face on my shoulder, woman-fashion.

' "It is most cruel true," he whispered to me. "The old man proved it to me at the beat after you left, and again in our hut even now. It is Harold, my king!"

'De Aquila crept forward. He walked about the man and swallowed.

' "Bones of the Saints!" said he, staring.

' "Many a stray shot goes too well home," said Rahere.

'The old man flinched as at an arrow. "Why do you hurt me still?" he said in Saxon. "It was on some bones of some saints that I promised I would give my England to the Great Duke." He turns on us all crying, shrilly: "Thanes, he had caught me at Rouen – a lifetime ago. If I had not promised, I should have lain there all my life. What else could I have done? I have lain in a strait prison all my life none the less. There is no need to throw stones at me." He guarded his face with his arms, and shivered.

"Now his madness will strike him down," said Rahere. "Cast out the evil spirit, one of you new bishops."

'Said William of Exeter: "Harold was slain at Senlac fight. All the world knows it."

' "I think this man must have forgotten," said Rahere. "Be comforted, father. Thou wast well slain at Hastings forty years gone, less three months and nine days. Tell the king."

'The man uncovered his face. "I thought they would stone me," he said. "I did not know I spoke before a king." He came to his full towering height – no mean man, but frail beyond belief.

'The king turned to the tables, and held him out his own cup of wine. The old man drank, and beckoned behind him, and, before all the Normans, my Hugh bore away the empty cup, Saxon-fashion, upon the knee.

' "It is Harold!" said De Aquila. "His own stiff-necked blood kneels to serve him." '

' "Be it so," said Henry. "Sit, then, thou that hast been Harold of England."

'The madman sat, and hard, dark Henry looked at him between half-shut eyes. We others stared like oxen, all but De Aquila, who watched Rahere as I have seen him watch a far sail on the sea.

'The wine and the warmth cast the old man into a dream. His white head bowed; his hands hung. His eye indeed was opened, but the mind was shut. When he stretched his feet, they were scurfed and road-cut like a slave's.

' "Ah, Rahere," cried Hugh, "why hast thou shown him thus? Better have let him die than shame him – and me!"

' "Shame thee?" said the king. "Would any baron of mine kneel to me if I were witless, discrowned and alone and Harold had my throne?"

' "No," said Rahere. "I am the sole fool that might do it, brother, unless" – he pointed at De Aquila, whom he had only met that day – "yonder tough Norman crab kept me company. But, Sir Hugh, I did not mean to shame him. He hath been somewhat punished through, maybe, little fault of his own."

' "Yet he lied to my father, the Conqueror," said the king, and the old man flinched in his sleep.

' "Maybe," said Rahere, "but thy brother Robert, whose throat we purpose soon to slit with our own hands – "

' "Hutt!" said the king, laughing. "I'll keep Robert at my table for a life's guest when I catch him. Robert means no harm. It is all his cursed barons."

' "None the less," said Rahere, "Robert may say that thou hast not always spoken the stark truth to him about England. I should not hang too many men on *that* bough, brother."

' "And it is certain," said Hugh, "that" – he pointed to the old man – "Harold was forced to make his promise to the Great Duke."

' "Very strongly, forced," said De Aquila. He had never any pride in the Duke William's dealings with Harold before Hastings. Yet, as he said, one cannot build a house all of straight sticks.

' "No matter how he was forced," said Henry, "England was promised to my father William by Edward the Confessor. Is it not so?" William of Exeter nodded. "Harold confirmed that promise to my father on the bones of the saints. Afterwards he broke his oath and would have taken England by the strong hand."

' "Oh! La! La!" Rahere rolled up his eyes like a girl. "That ever England should be taken by the strong hand!"

'Seeing that Red William and Henry after him had each in just that fashion snatched England from Robert of Normandy, we others knew not where to look. But De Aquila saved us quickly.

' "Promise kept or promise broken," he said, "Harold came near enough to breaking us Normans at Senlac. "

"Was it so close a fight, then?" said Henry.

"A hair would have turned it either way," De Aquila answered. "His house-carles stood like rocks against rain. Where wast thou, Hugh, in it?"

' "Among Godwin's folk beneath the Golden Dragon till your front gave back, and we broke our ranks to follow," said Hugh.

"But I bade you stand! I bade you stand! I knew it was all a deceit!" Harold had waked, and leaned forward as one crying from the grave.

' "Ah, now we see how the traitor himself was betrayed!" said William of Exeter, and looked for a smile from the king.

' "I made thee bishop to preach at my bidding," said Henry; and turning to

Harold, "Tell us here how thy people fought us?" said he. "Their sons serve me now against my brother Robert!"

'The old man shook his head cunningly. "Na – Na – Na!" he cried. "I know better. Every time I tell my tale men stone me. But, thanes, I will tell you a greater thing. Listen!" He told us how many paces it was from some Saxon saint's shrine to another shrine, and how many more back to the Abbey of the Battle.

' "Ay," said he. "I have trodden it too often to be out even ten paces. I move very swiftly. Harold of Norway knows that, and so does Tostig my brother. They lie at ease at Stamford Bridge, and from Stamford Bridge to the Battle Abbey it is—" he muttered over many numbers and forgot us.

' "Ay," said De Aquila, all in a muse. "That man broke Harold of Norway at Stamford Bridge, and came near to breaking us at Senlac – all within one month."

' "But how did he come alive from Senlac fight?" asked the king. "Ask him! Hast thou heard it, Rahere?"

' "Never. He says he has been stoned too often for telling the tale. But he can count you off Saxon and Norman shrines till daylight," said Rahere and the old man nodded proudly.

' "My faith!" said Henry after a while. "I think even my father the Great Duke would pity if he could see him.

' "How if he *does* see?" said Rahere.

'Hugh covered his face with his sound hand. "Ah, why hast thou shamed him?" he cried again to Rahere.

' "No – no," says the old man, reaching to pluck at Rahere's cape. "I am Rahere's man. None stone me now," and he played with the bells on the scollops of it.

' "How if he had been brought to me when you found him?" said the king to Rahere.

' "You would have held him prisoner again – as the Great Duke did," Rahere answered.

' "True," said our king. "He is nothing except his name. Yet that name might have been used by stronger men to trouble my England. Yes. I must have made him my life's guest – as I shall make Robert."

' "I knew it," said Rahere. "But while this man wandered mad by the wayside, none cared what he called himself."

' "I learned to cease talking before the stones flew," says the old man, and Hugh groaned.

' "Ye have heard!" said Rahere. "Witless, landless, nameless, and, but for my protection, masterless, he can still make shift to bide his doom under the open sky."

' "Then wherefore didst thou bring him here for a mock and a shame?" cried Hugh, beside himself with woe.

' "A right mock and a just shame!" said William of Exeter.

' "Not to me," said Nigel of Ely. "I see and I tremble, but I neither mock nor judge."

' "Well spoken, Ely." Rahere falls into the pure fool again. "I'll pray for thee when I turn monk. Thou hast given thy blessing on a war between two most Christian brothers." He meant the war forward 'twixt Henry and Robert of Normandy. "I charge you, brother," he says, wheeling on the king, "dost thou mock my fool?"

The king shook his head, and so then did smooth William of Exeter.

' "De Aquila, does thou mock him?" Rahere jingled from one to another, and the old man smiled.

' "By the Bones of the Saints, not I," said our Lord of Pevensey. "I know how dooms near he broke us at Senlac."

' "Sir Hugh, you are excused the question. But you, valiant, loyal, honourable, and devout barons, Lords of Man's justice in your own bounds, do *you* mock my fool?"

'He shook his bauble in the very faces of those two barons whose names I have forgotten. "Na – Na!" they said, and waved him back foolishly enough.

'He hies him across to staring, nodding Harold, and speaks from behind his chair.

' "No man mocks thee. Who here judges this man? Henry of England – Nigel – De Aquila! On your souls, swift with the answer!" he cried.

'None answered. We were all – the king not least – overborne by that terrible scarlet-and-black wizard-jester.

' "Well for your souls," he said, wiping his brow. Next, shrill like a woman: "Oh, come to me!" and Hugh ran forward to hold Harold, that had slidden down in the chair.

' "Hearken," said Rahere, his arm round Harold's neck. "The king – his bishops – the knights – all the world's crazy chessboard neither mock nor judge thee. Take that comfort with thee, Harold of England!"

'Hugh heaved the old man up and he smiled.

' "Good comfort," said Harold. "Tell me again! I have been somewhat punished."

'Rahere hallooed it once more into his ear as the head rolled. We heard him sigh, and Nigel of Ely stood forth, praying aloud.

' "Out! I will have no Norman!" Harold said as clearly as I speak now, and he refuged himself on Hugh's sound shoulder, and stretched out, and lay all still.'

'Dead?' said Una, turning up a white face in the dusk.

'That was his good fortune. To die in the king's presence, and on the breast of the most gentlest, truest knight of his own house. Some of us envied him,' said Sir Richard, and fell back to take Swallow's bridle.

'Turn left here,' Puck called ahead of them from under an oak. They ducked down a narrow path through close ash plantation.

The children hurried forward, but cutting a corner charged full-abreast into the thorn-faggot that old Hobden was carrying home on his back. 'My! My!' said he. 'Have you scratted your face, Miss Una?'

'Sorry! It's all right,' said Una, rubbing her nose. 'How many rabbits did you get today?'

'That's tellin's,' the old man grinned as he re-hoisted his faggot. 'I reckon Mus' Ridley he've got rheumatism along o' lyin' in the ditch to see I didn't snap up any. Think o' that now!'

They laughed a good deal while he told them the tale.

'An' just as he crawled away I heard someone hollerin' to the hounds in our woods,' said he. 'Didn't you hear? You must ha' been asleep sure–ly.'

'Oh, what about the sleeper you promised to show us?' Dan cried.

' 'Ere he be – house an' all!' Hobden dived into the prickly heart of the faggot and took out a dormouse's wonderfully woven nest of grass and leaves. His blunt fingers parted it as if it had been precious lace, and tilting it toward the last of the light he showed the little, red, furry chap curled up inside, his tail between his eyes that were shut for their winter sleep.

'Let's take him home. Don't breathe on him,' said Una. 'It'll make him warm and he'll wake up and die straight off. Won't he, Hobby?'

'That's a heap better by my reckonin' than wakin' up and findin' himself in a cage for life. No! We'll lay him into the bottom o' this hedge. Dat's jus' right! No more trouble for him till come spring. An' now we'll go home.'

A Carol

Our Lord who did the ox command
To kneel to Judah's king, he binds
His frost upon the land
To ripen it for spring –
To ripen it for spring, good sirs,
According to his word;
Which well must be as ye can see –
And who shall judge the Lord?

When we poor fenmen skate the ice
Or shiver on the wold,
We hear the cry of a single tree
That breaks her heart in the cold –
That breaks her heart in the cold, good sirs,
And rendeth by the board;
Which well must be as ye can see –
And who shall judge the Lord?

Her wood is crazed and little worth
Excepting as to burn,
That we may warm and make our mirth
Until the spring return –
Until the spring return, good sirs,
When people walk abroad;
Which well must be as ye can see –
And who shall judge the Lord?

God bless the master of this house,
And all that sleep therein!
And guard the fens from pirate folk,
And keep us all from sin,
To walk in honesty, good sirs,
Of thought and deed and word!
Which shall befriend our latter end –
And who shall judge the Lord?

STALKY & CO.

TO
CORMELL PRICE
Headmaster, United Sevices College
Westward Ho!, Bideford, North Devon
1874–1894

A School Song

'Let us now praise famous men' –
  Men of little showing –
For their work continueth,
And their work continueth,
  Greater than their knowing.

Western wind and open surge
  Took us from our mothers;
Flung us on a naked shore
(Twelve bleak houses by the shore!
Seven summers by the shore!)
  'Mid two hundred brothers.

There we met with famous men
  Set in office o'er us.
And they beat on us with rods –
Faithfully with many rods –
Daily beat us on with rods –
  For the love they bore us!

Out of Egypt unto Troy –
  Over Himalaya –
Far and sure our bands have gone –
Hy-Brasil or Babylon,
Islands of the Southern Run,
  And cities of Cathaia!

And we all praise famous men –
  Ancients of the college;
For they taught us common sense –
Tried to teach us common sense –
Truth and God's Own Common Sense
  Which is more than knowledge!

Each degree of Latitude
  Strung about Creation
Seeth one (or more) of us
(Of one muster all of us –
Of one master all of us)
  Keen in his vocation.

This we learned from famous men,
  Knowing not its uses,
When they showed in daily work
Man must finish off his work –
Right or wrong, his daily work –
  And without excuses.

Servants of the staff and chain,
  Mine and fuse and grapnel –
Some before the face of kings,
Stand before the face of kings;
Bearing gifts to divers kings –
  Gifts of case and shrapnel.

This we learned from famous men
  Teaching in our borders.
Who declare'd it was best,
Safest, easiest and best –
Expeditious, wise and best –
  To obey your orders.

Some beneath the further stars
  Bear the greater burden:
Set to serve the lands they rule
(Save he serve no man may rule),
Serve and love the lands they rule;
  Seeking praise nor guerdon.

This we learned from famous men
  Knowing not we learned it.
Only, as the years went by –
Lonely, as the years went by –
Far from help as years went by,
  Plainer we discerned it.

Wherefore praise we famous men
   From whose bays we borrow –
They that put aside Today –
All the joys of their Today –
And with toil of their Today
   Bought for us Tomorrow!

Bless and praise we famous men
   Men of little showing!
For their work continueth,
And their work continueth,
Broad and deep continueth,
   Great beyond their knowing!

Contents

In summer all right-minded boys built huts in the furze-hill behind the college – little lairs whittled out of the heart of the prickly bushes, full of stumps, odd root-ends, and spikes, but, since they were strictly forbidden, palaces of delight. And for the fifth summer in succession, Stalky, McTurk, and Beetle (this was before they reached the dignity of a study) had built like beavers a place of retreat and meditation, where they smoked.

Now, there was nothing in their characters as known to Mr Prout, their housemaster, at all commanding respect; nor did Foxy, the subtle red-haired school sergeant, trust them. His business was to wear tennis-shoes, carry binoculars, and swoop hawklike upon evil boys. Had he taken the field alone, that hut would have been raided, for Foxy knew the manners of his quarry; but providence moved Mr Prout, whose school-name, derived from the size of his feet, was Hoofer, to investigate on his own account; and it was the cautious Stalky who found the track of his pugs on the very floor of their lair one peaceful afternoon when Stalky would fain have forgotten Prout and his works in a volume of Surtees and a new briar-wood pipe. Crusoe, at sight of the footprint, did not act more swiftly than Stalky. He removed the pipes, swept up all loose match-ends, and departed to warn Beetle and McTurk.

But it was characteristic of the boy that he did not approach his allies till he had met and conferred with little Hartopp, president of the Natural History Society, an institution which Stalky held in contempt. Hartopp was more than surprised when the boy, meekly as he knew how, begged to propose himself, Beetle, and McTurk as candidates; confessed to a long-smothered interest in first-flowerings, early butterflies, and new arrivals, and volunteered, if Mr Hartopp saw fit, to enter on the new life at once. Being a master, Hartopp was suspicious; but he was also an enthusiast, and his gentle little soul had been galled by chance-heard remarks from the three, and specially Beetle. So he was gracious to that repentant sinner, and entered the three names in his book.

Then, and not till then, did Stalky seek Beetle and McTurk in their house form-room. They were stowing away books for a quiet afternoon in the furze, which they called the 'wuzzy'.

'All up,' said Stalky, serenely. 'I spotted Heffy's fairy feet round our hut after dinner. Blessing they're so big.'

'Con–found! Did you hide our pipes?' said Beetle.

'Oh, no. Left 'em in the middle of the hut, of course. What a blind ass you are, Beetle! D'you think nobody thinks but yourself? Well, we can't use the hut any more. Hoofer will be watchin' it.'

'Bother! Likewise blow!' said McTurk thoughtfully, unpacking the volumes with which his chest was cased. The boys carried their libraries between their belt and their collar. 'Nice job! This means we're under suspicion for the rest of the term.'

'Why? All that Heffy has found is a hut. He and Foxy will watch it. It's nothing to do with us; only we mustn't be seen that way for a bit.'

'Yes, and where else are we to go?' said Beetle. 'You chose that place, too – an' – an' I wanted to read this afternoon.'

Stalky sat on a desk drumming his heels on the form.

'You're a despondin' brute, Beetle. Sometimes I think I shall have to drop you altogether. Did you ever know your Uncle Stalky forget you yet? *His rebus infectis* – after I'd seen Heffy's man-tracks marchin' round our hut, I found little Hartopp – *destricto ense* – wavin' a butterfly net. I conciliated Hartopp. Told him that you'd read papers to the Bug-hunters if he'd let you join, Beetle. Told him you liked butterflies, Turkey. Anyhow, I soothed the Hartoffles, and we're Bug-hunters now.'

'What's the good of that?' said Beetle.

'Oh, Turkey, kick him!'

In the interests of science, bounds were largely relaxed for the members of the Natural History Society. They could wander, if they kept clear of all houses, practically where they chose; Mr Hartopp holding himself responsible for their good conduct.

Beetle began to see this as McTurk began the kicking.

'I'm an ass, Stalky!' he said, guarding the afflicted part. '*Pax*, Turkey. I'm an ass.'

'Don't stop, Turkey. Isn't your Uncle Stalky a great man?'

'Great man,' said Beetle.

'All the same, bug huntin's a filthy business,' said McTurk. 'How the deuce does one begin?'

'This way,' said Stalky, turning to some fags' lockers behind him. 'Fags are dabs at Natural History. Here's young Braybrooke's botany case.' He flung out a tangle of decayed roots and adjusted the slide. 'Gives one no end of a professional air, I think. Here's Clay minor's geological hammer. Beetle can carry that. Turkey, you'd better covet a butterfly net from somewhere.'

'I'm blowed if I do,' said McTurk, simply, with immense feeling. 'Beetle, give me the hammer.'

'All right. I'm not proud. Chuck us down that net on top of the lockers, Stalky.'

'That's all right. It's a collapsible jamboree, too. Beastly luxurious dogs these fags are. Built like a fishin'-rod. 'Pon my sainted Sam, but we look the complete bug-hunters! Now, listen to your Uncle Stalky! We're goin' along the cliffs after butterflies. Very few chaps come there. We're goin' to leg it, too. You'd better leave your book behind.'

'Not much!' said Beetle, firmly. 'I'm not goin' to be done out of my fun for a lot of filthy butterflies.'

'Then you'll sweat horrid. You'd better carry my Jorrocks. 'Twon't make you any hotter.'

They all sweated; for Stalky led them at a smart trot west away along the cliffs under the furze-hills, crossing combe after gorsy combe. They took no heed to flying rabbits or fluttering fritillaries, and all that Turkey said of geology was utterly unquotable.

'Are we going to Clovelly?' he puffed at last, and they flung themselves down on the short, springy turf between the drone of the sea below and the light summer wind among the inland trees. They were looking into a combe half full of old, high furze in gay bloom that ran up to a fringe of brambles and a dense wood of mixed timber and hollies. It was as though one-half the combe were filled with golden fire to the cliff's edge. The side nearest to them was open grass, and fairly bristled with noticeboards.

'Fee–rocious old cove, this,' said Stalky, reading the nearest. ' "*Prosecuted with the utmost rigour of the law. G. M. Dabney, Col., JP*", an' all the rest of it. Don't seem to me that any chap in his senses would trespass here, does it?'

'You've got to prove damage 'fore you can prosecute for anything! Can't prosecute for trespass,' said McTurk, whose father held many acres in Ireland. 'That's all rot!'

'Glad of that, 'cause this looks like what we wanted. Not straight across, Beetle, you blind lunatic! Anyone could spot us half a mile off. This way; and furl up your beastly butterfly net.'

Beetle disconnected the ring, thrust the net into a pocket, shut up the handle to a two-foot stave, and slid the cane-ring round his waist. Stalky led inland to the wood, which was, perhaps, a quarter of a mile from the sea, and reached the fringe of the brambles.

'*Now* we can get straight down through the furze, and never show up at all,' said the tactician. 'Beetle, go ahead and explore. Snf! Snf! Beastly stink of fox somewhere!'

On all fours, save when he clung to his spectacles, Beetle wormed into the gorse, and presently announced between grunts of pain that he had found a very fair fox-track. This was well for Beetle, since Stalky pinched him *a tergo*. Down that tunnel they crawled. It was evidently a highway for the inhabitants of the combe; and, to their inexpressible joy, ended at the very edge of the cliff, in a few square feet of dry turf walled and roofed with impenetrable gorse.

'By gum! There isn't a single thing to do except lie down,' said Stalky, returning a knife to his pocket. 'Look here!'

He parted the tough stems before him, and it was as a window opened on a far view of Lundy, and the deep sea sluggishly nosing the pebbles a couple of hundred feet below. They could hear young jackdaws squawking on the ledges, the hiss and jabber of a nest of hawks somewhere out of sight; and, with great deliberation, Stalky spat on to the back of a young rabbit sunning himself far down where only a cliff-rabbit could have found foothold. Great grey and black gulls screamed against the jackdaws; the heavy-scented acres of bloom round them were alive with low-nesting birds, singing or silent as the shadow of the wheeling hawks passed and returned; and on the naked turf across the combe, rabbits thumped and frolicked.

'Whew! What a place! Talk of natural history; this is it,' said Stalky, filling himself a pipe. 'Isn't it scrumptious? Good old sea!' He spat again approvingly, and was silent.

McTurk and Beetle had taken out their books and were lying on their stomachs, chin in hand. The sea snored and gurgled; the birds, scattered for the moment by these new animals, returned to their businesses, and the boys read on in the rich, warm, sleepy silence.

'Hullo, here's a keeper,' said Stalky, shutting *Handley Cross* cautiously, and peering through the jungle. A man with a gun appeared on the skyline to the east. 'Confound him, he's going to sit down.'

'He'd swear we were poachin', too,' said Beetle. 'What's the good of pheasants' eggs? They're always addled, too.'

'Might as well get up to the wood, I think,' said Stalky. 'We don't want G. M. Dabney, Col., JP, to be bothered about us so soon. Up the wuzzy and keep quiet! He may have followed us, you know.'

Beetle was already far up the tunnel. They heard him gasp indescribably: there was the crash of a heavy body leaping through the furze.

'Aie! yeou little red rascal. I see yeou!' The keeper threw the gun to his shoulder, and fired both barrels in their direction. The pellets dusted the dry stems round them as a big fox plunged between Stalky's legs, and ran over the cliff-edge.

They said nothing till they reached the wood – torn, dishevelled, hot, but unseen.

'Narrow squeak,' said Stalky. 'I'll swear some of the pellets went through my hair.'

'Did you see him?' said Beetle. 'I almost put my hand on him. Wasn't he a whopper! Didn't he stink! Hullo, Turkey, what's the matter? Are you hit?'

McTurk's lean face had turned pearly white; his mouth, generally half open, was tight shut, and his eyes blazed. They had never seen him like this save once in a sad time of civil war.

'Do you know that that was just as bad as murder?' he said, in a grating voice, as he brushed prickles from his head.

'Well, he didn't hit us,' said Stalky. 'I think it was rather a lark. Here, where are you going?'

'I'm going up to the house, if there is one,' said McTurk, pushing through the hollies. 'I am going to tell this Colonel Dabney.'

'Are you crazy? He'll swear it served us jolly well right. He'll report us. It'll be a public lickin'. Oh, Turkey, don't be an ass! Think of us!'

'You fool!' said McTurk, turning savagely. 'D'you suppose I'm thinkin' of *us*? It's the keeper.'

'He's cracked,' said Beetle, miserably, as they followed. Indeed, this was a new Turkey – a haughty, angular, nose-lifted Turkey – whom they accompanied through a shrubbery on to a lawn, where a white-whiskered old gentleman with a cleek was alternately putting and blaspheming vigorously.

'Are you Colonel Dabney?' McTurk began in this new creaking voice of his.

'I – I am, and – ' his eyes travelled up and down the boy – 'who – what the devil d'you want? Ye've been disturbing my pheasants. Don't attempt to deny it. Ye needn't laugh at it.' (McTurk's not too lovely features had twisted themselves into a horrible sneer at the word pheasant.) 'You've been birds'-nesting. You needn't hide your hat. I can see that you belong to the college. Don't attempt to deny it. Ye do! Your name and number at once, sir. Ye want to speak to me – Eh? You saw my noticeboards? Must have. Don't attempt to deny it. Ye did! Damnable, oh damnable!'

He choked with emotion. McTurk's heel tapped the lawn and he stuttered a little – two sure signs that he was losing his temper. But why should he, the offender, be angry?

'Lo–look here, sir. Do – do you shoot foxes? Because, if you don't, your keeper does. We've seen him! I do – don't care what you call us – but it's an awful thing. It's the ruin of good feelin' among neighbours. A ma–man ought to say once and for all how he stands about preservin'. It's worse than murder, because there's no legal remedy.' McTurk was quoting confusedly from his father, while the old gentleman made noises in his throat.

'Do you know who I am?' he gurgled at last; Stalky and Beetle quaking.

'No, sorr, nor do I care if ye belonged to the Castle itself. Answer me now, as one gentleman to another. Do ye shoot foxes or do ye not?'

And four years before, Stalky and Beetle had carefully kicked McTurk out of his Irish dialect! Assuredly he had gone mad or taken a sunstroke, and as assuredly he would be slain – once by the old gentleman and once by the head. A public licking for the three was the least they could expect. Yet – if their eyes and ears were to be trusted – the old gentleman had collapsed. It might be a lull before the storm, but –

'I do not.' He was still gurgling.

'Then you must sack your keeper. He's not fit to live in the same county with a God-fearin' fox. An' a vixen, too – at this time o' year!'

'Did ye come up on purpose to tell me this?'

'Of course I did, ye silly man,' with a stamp of the foot. 'Would you not have done as much for me if you'd seen that thing happen on my land, now?'

Forgotten – forgotten was the college and the decency due to elders!

McTurk was treading again the barren purple mountains of the rainy west coast, where in his holidays he was viceroy of four thousand naked acres, only son of a three-hundred-year-old house, lord of a crazy fishing-boat, and the idol of his father's shiftless tenantry. It was the landed man speaking to his equal – deep calling to deep – and the old gentleman acknowledged the cry.

'I apologise,' said he. 'I apologise unreservedly – to you, and to the old country. Now, will you be good enough to tell me your story?'

'We were in your combe,' McTurk began, and he told his tale alternately as a schoolboy and, when the iniquity of the thing overcame him, as an indignant squire; concluding: 'So you see he must be in the habit of it. I – we – one never wants to accuse a neighbour's man; but I took the liberty in this case – '

'I see. Quite so. For a reason ye had. Infamous – oh, infamous!' The two had fallen into step beside each other on the lawn, and Colonel Dabney was talking as one man to another. 'This comes of promoting a fisherman – a fisherman – from his lobster-pots. It's enough to ruin the reputation of an archangel. Don't attempt to deny it. It is! Your father has brought you up well. He has. I'd much like the pleasure of his acquaintance. Very much, indeed. And these young gentlemen? English they are. Don't attempt to deny it. They came up with you, too? Extraordinary! Extraordinary, now! In the present state of education I shouldn't have thought any three boys would be well enough grounded . . . But out of the mouths of – No – no! Not that by any odds. Don't attempt to deny it. Ye're not! Sherry always catches me under the liver, but – beer, now? Eh? What d'you say to beer, and something to eat? It's long since I was a boy – abominable nuisances; but exceptions prove the rule. And a vixen, too!'

They were fed on the terrace by a grey-haired housekeeper. Stalky and Beetle merely ate, but McTurk with bright eyes continued a free and lofty discourse; and ever the old gentleman treated him as a brother.

'My dear man, of *course* ye can come again. Did I not say exceptions prove the rule? The lower combe? Man, dear, anywhere ye please, so long as you do not disturb my pheasants. The two are not incompatible. Don't attempt to deny it. They're not! I'll never allow another gun, though. Come and go as ye please. I'll not see you, and ye needn't see me. Ye've been well brought up. Another glass of beer, now? I tell you a fisherman he was and a fisherman he shall be tonight again. He shall! Wish I could drown him. I'll convoy you to the Lodge. My people are not precisely – ah – broke to boy, but they'll know *you* again.'

He dismissed them with many compliments by the high Lodge-gate in the split-oak park palings and they stood still; even Stalky, who had played second, not to say a dumb, fiddle, regarding McTurk as one from another world. The two glasses of strong home-brewed had brought a melancholy upon the boy, for, slowly strolling with his hands in his pockets, he crooned: 'Oh, Paddy dear, and did ye hear the news that's goin' round?'

Under other circumstances Stalky and Beetle would have fallen upon him, for that song was barred utterly – anathema – the sin of witchcraft. But seeing what he had wrought, they danced round him in silence, waiting till it pleased him to touch earth.

The tea-bell rang when they were still half a mile from college. McTurk shivered and came out of dreams. The glory of his holiday estate had left him. He was a colleger of the college, speaking English once more.

'Turkey, it was immense!' said Stalky, generously. 'I didn't know you had it in you. You've got us a hut for the rest of the term, where we simply *can't* be collared. Fids! Fids! Oh, Fids! I gloat! Hear me gloat!'

They spun wildly on their heels, yodelling after the accepted manner of a 'gloat', which is not unremotely allied to the primitive man's song of triumph, and dropped down the hill by the path from the gasometer just in time to meet their housemaster, who had spent the afternoon watching their abandoned hut in the 'wuzzy'.

Unluckily, all Mr Prout's imagination leaned to the darker side of life, and he looked on those young-eyed cherubims most sourly. Boys that he understood attended house-matches and could be accounted for at any moment. But he had heard McTurk openly deride cricket – even house-matches; Beetle's views on the honour of the house he knew were incendiary; and he could never tell when the soft and smiling Stalky was laughing at him. Consequently – since human nature is what it is – those boys had been doing wrong somewhere. He hoped it was nothing very serious, but . . .

'*Ti-ra-ra-la-i-tu!* I gloat! Hear me!' Stalky, still on his heels, whirled like a dancing dervish to the dining-hall.

'*Ti-ra-la-la-i-tu!* I gloat! Hear me!' Beetle spun behind him with outstretched arms.

'*Ti-ra-la-la-i-tu!* I gloat! Hear me!' McTurk's voice cracked.

Now was there or was there not a distinct flavour of beer as they shot past Mr Prout?

He was unlucky in that his conscience as a housemaster impelled him to consult his associates. Had he taken his pipe and his troubles to little Hartopp's rooms he would, perhaps, have been saved confusion, for Hartopp believed in boys, and knew something about them. His fate led him to King, a fellow housemaster, no friend of his, but a zealous hater of Stalky & Co.

'Ah–haa!' said King, rubbing his hands when the tale was told. 'Curious! Now *my* house never dream of doing these things.'

'But you see I've no proof, exactly.'

'Proof? With the egregious Beetle! As if one wanted it! I suppose it is not impossible for the sergeant to supply it? Foxy is considered at least a match for any evasive boy in my house. Of course they were smoking and drinking somewhere. That type of boy always does. They think it manly.'

'But they've no following in the school, and they are distinctly – er – brutal to their juniors,' said Prout, who had from a distance seen Beetle return, with interest, his butterfly net to a tearful fag.

'Ah! They consider themselves superior to ordinary delights. Self-sufficient little animals! There's something in McTurk's Hibernian sneer that would make me a little annoyed. And they are so careful to avoid all overt acts, too. It's sheer calculated insolence. I am strongly opposed, as you know, to interfering with another man's house; but they need a lesson, Prout. They need a sharp lesson, if only to bring down their overweening self-conceit. Were I you, I should devote myself for a week to their little performances. Boys of that order – and I may flatter myself, but I think I know boys – don't join the Bug-hunters for love. Tell the sergeant to keep his eye open; and, of course, in my peregrinations I may casually keep mine open, too.'

'*Ti-ra-la-la-i-tu!* I gloat! Hear me!' far down the corridor.

'Disgusting!' said King. 'Where do they pick up these obscene noises? One sharp lesson is what they want.'

The boys did not concern themselves with lessons for the next few days. They had all Colonel Dabney's estate to play with, and they explored it with the stealth of Red Indians and the accuracy of burglars. They could enter either by the Lodge-gates on the upper road – they were careful to ingratiate themselves with the Lodge-keeper and his wife – drop down into the combe, and return along the cliffs; or they could begin at the combe and climb up into the road.

They were careful not to cross the Colonel's path – he had served his turn, and they would not outwear their welcome – nor did they show up on the skyline when they could move in cover. The shelter of the gorse by the cliff-edge was their chosen retreat. Beetle christened it the Pleasant Isle of Aves, for the peace and the shelter of it; and here, the pipes and tobacco once cached in a convenient ledge an arm's length down the cliff, their position was legally unassailable.

For, observe, Colonel Dabney had not invited them to enter his house. Therefore, they did not need to ask specific leave to go visiting; and school rules were strict on that point. He had merely thrown open his grounds to them; and, since they were lawful Bug-hunters, their extended bounds ran up to his noticeboards in the combe and his Lodge-gates on the hill.

They were amazed at their own virtue.

'And even if it wasn't,' said Stalky, flat on his back, staring into the blue. 'Even suppose we were miles out of bounds, no one could get at us through this wuzzy, unless he knew the tunnel. Isn't this better than lyin' up just behind the coll. – in a blue funk every time we had a smoke? Isn't your Uncle Stalky – ?'

'No,' said Beetle – he was stretched at the edge of the cliff spitting thoughtfully. 'We've got to thank Turkey for this. Turkey is the Great Man. Turkey, dear, you're distressing Heffles.'

'Gloomy old ass!' said McTurk, deep in a book.

'They've got us under suspicion,' said Stalky. 'Hoophats *is* so suspicious somehow; and Foxy always makes every stalk he does a sort of – sort of – '

'Scalp,' said Beetle. 'Foxy's a giddy Chingangook.'

'Poor Foxy,' said Stalky. 'He's goin' to catch us one of these days. Said to me in the gym last night, "I've got my eye on you, Mr Corkran. I'm only warning you for your good." Then I said: "Well, you jolly well take it off again, or you'll get into trouble. I'm only warnin' you for your good." Foxy was wrath.'

'Yes, but it's only fair sport for Foxy,' said Beetle. 'It's Hefflelinga that has the evil mind. Shouldn't wonder if he thought we got tight.'

'I never got squiffy but once – that was in the holidays,' said Stalky, reflectively; 'an' it made me horrid sick. 'Pon my sacred Sam, though, it's enough to drive a man to drink, havin' an animal like Hoof for housemaster.'

'If we attended the matches an' yelled, "Well hit, sir," an' stood on one leg an' grinned every time Heffy said, "So ho, my sons. Is it thus?" an' said, "Yes, sir", an' "No, sir", an' "O, sir", an' "Please, sir", like a lot o' filthy fa–ags, Heffy 'ud think no end of us,' said McTurk with a sneer.

'Too late to begin that.'

'It's all right. The Hefflelinga means well. *But* he is an ass. *And* we show him that we think he's an ass. An' *so* Heffy don't love us. Told me last night after prayers that he was *in loco parentis*,' Beetle grunted.

'The deuce he did!' cried Stalky. 'That means he's maturin' something unusual dam' mean. Last time he told me that he gave me three hundred lines for dancin' the cachucha in number ten dormitory. *Loco parentis*, by gum! But what's the odds as long as you're 'appy? We're all right.'

They were, and their very rightness puzzled Prout, King, and the sergeant. Boys with bad consciences show it. They slink out past the fives court in haste, and smile nervously when questioned. They return, disordered, in bare time to save a call-over. They nod and wink and giggle one to the other, scattering at the approach of a master. But Stalky and his allies had long outlived these manifestations of youth. They strolled forth unconcernedly, and returned in excellent shape after a light refreshment of strawberries and cream at the Lodge.

The Lodge-keeper had been promoted to keeper, *vice* the murderous fisherman, and his wife made much of the boys. The man, too, gave them a squirrel, which they presented to the Natural History Society; thereby checkmating little Hartopp, who wished to know what they were doing for science. Foxy faithfully worked some deep Devon lanes behind a lonely crossroads inn; and it was curious that Prout and King, members of common-room seldom friendly, walked together in the same direction – that is to say, northeast. Now, the pleasant Isle of Aves lay due southwest.

'They're deep – day–vilish deep,' said Stalky. 'Why are they drawin' those covers?'

'Me,' said Beetle sweetly. 'I asked Foxy if he had ever tasted the beer there. That was enough for Foxy, and it cheered him up a little. He and Heffy were sniffin' round our old hut so long I thought they'd like a change.'

'Well, it can't last for ever,' said Stalky. 'Heffy's bankin' up like a thundercloud, an' King goes rubbin' his beastly hands, an' grinnin' like a hyena. It's shockin' demoralisin' for King. He'll burst some day.'

That day came a little sooner than they expected – came when the sergeant, whose duty it was to collect defaulters, did not attend an afternoon call-over.

'Tired of pubs, eh? He's gone up to the top of the bill with his binoculars to spot us,' said Stalky. 'Wonder he didn't think of that before. Did you see old Heffy cock his eye at us when we answered our names? Heffy's in it, too. *Ti-ra-la-la-i-tu!* I gloat! Hear me! Come on!'

'Aves?' said Beetle.

'Of course, but I'm not smokin' *aujourd'hui. Parce que je* jolly well *pense* that we'll be *suivi*. We'll go along the cliffs, slow, an' give Foxy lots of time to parallel us up above.'

They strolled towards the swimming-baths, and presently overtook King. 'Oh, don't let *me* interrupt you,' he said. 'Engaged in scientific pursuits, of course? I trust you will enjoy yourselves, my young friends.'

'You see!' said Stalky, when they were out of earshot. 'He can't keep a secret. He's followin' to cut off our line of retreat. He'll wait at the baths till Heffy comes along. They've tried every blessed place except along the cliffs, and now they think they've bottled us. No need to hurry.'

They walked leisurely over the combes till they reached the line of noticeboards.

'Listen a shake. Foxy's upwind comin' down hill like beans. When you hear him move in the bushes, go straight across to Aves. They want to catch us *flagrante delicto*.'

They dived into the gorse at right angles to the tunnel, openly crossing the grass, and lay still in Aves.

'What did I tell you?' Stalky carefully put away the pipes and tobacco. The sergeant, out of breath, was leaning against the fence, raking the furze with his binoculars, but he might as well have tried to see through a sandbag. Anon, Prout and King appeared behind him. They conferred.

'Aha! Foxy don't like the noticeboards, and he don't like the prickles either. Now we'll cut up the tunnel and go to the lodge. Hullo! They've sent Foxy into cover.'

The sergeant was waist-deep in crackling, swaying furze, his ears filled with the noise of his own progress. The boys reached the shelter of the wood and looked down through a belt of hollies.

'Hellish noise!' said Stalky, critically. 'Don't think Colonel Dabney will like it. I move we go into the Lodge and get something to eat. We might as well see the fun out.'

Suddenly the keeper passed them at a trot. 'Who'm they to combe-bottom for Lard's sake? Master'll be crazy,' he said.

'Poachers simly,' Stalky replied in the broad Devon that was the boy's *langue de guerre*.

'I'll poach 'em to raights!' He dropped into the funnel-like combe, which presently began to fill with noises, notably King's voice crying: 'Go on, sergeant! Leave him alone, you, sir. He is executing my orders.'

'Who'm yeou to give arders here, gingy whiskers? Yeou come up to the master. Come out o' that wuzzy! [This is to the sergeant.] Yiss, I reckon us knows the boys yeou'm after. They've tu long ears an' vuzzy bellies, an' you nippies they in yeour pockets when they'm dead. Come on up to master! He'll boy yeou all you're a mind to. Yeou other folk bide your side fence.'

'Explain to the proprietor. You can explain, sergeant,' shouted King. Evidently the sergeant had surrendered to the major force.

Beetle lay at full length on the turf behind the Lodge, literally biting the earth in spasms of joy. Stalky kicked him upright. There was nothing of levity about Stalky or McTurk save a stray muscle twitching on the cheek.

They tapped at the Lodge door, where they were always welcome. 'Come yeou right in an' set down, my little dearrs,' said the woman. 'They'll niver touch my man. He'll poach 'em to rights. Iss fai! Fresh berries an' cream. Us Dartymoor folk niver forget their friends. But them Bidevor poachers, they've no hem to their garments. Sugar? My man he've digged a badger for yeou, my dearrs. 'Tis in the linhay in a box.'

'Us'll take un with us when we'm finished here. I reckon yeou'm busy. We'll bide here an' – 'tis washin' day with yeou, simly,' said Stalky. 'We'm no company to make all vitty for. Never yeou mind us. Yiss. There's plenty cream.'

The woman withdrew, wiping her pink hands on her apron, and left them in the parlour. There was a scuffle of feet on the gravel outside the heavily leaded diamond panes, and then the voice of Colonel Dabney, something clearer than a bugle.

'Ye can read? You've eyes in your head? Don't attempt to deny it. Ye have!'

Beetle snatched a crochet-work antimacassar from the shiny horsehair sofa, stuffed it into his mouth, and rolled out of sight.

'You saw my noticeboards. Your duty? Curse your impudence, sir. Your duty was to keep off my grounds. Talk of duty to *me*! Why – why – why, ye misbegotten poacher, ye'll be teaching me my A B C next! Roarin' like a bull in the bushes down there! Boys? Boys? Boys? Keep your boys at home, then! I'm not responsible for your boys! But I don't believe it – I don't believe a word of it. Ye've a furtive look in your eye – a furtive, sneakin', poachin' look in your eye, that 'ud ruin the reputation of an archangel! Don't attempt to deny it! Ye have! A sergeant? More shame to you, then, an' the worst bargain Her Majesty ever made! A sergeant, to run about the country poachin' – on your pension! Damnable! Oh, damnable! But I'll be considerate. I'll be merciful. By gad, I'll be the very essence o' humanity! Did ye, or did ye not, see my noticeboards? Don't attempt to deny it! Ye did. Silence, sergeant!'

Twenty-one years in the army had left their mark on Foxy. He obeyed.

'Now. March!' The high Lodge-gate shut with a clang. 'My duty! A sergeant to tell me my duty!' puffed Colonel Dabney. 'Good Lard! more sergeants!'

'It's King! It's King!' gulped Stalky, his head on the horsehair pillow. McTurk was eating the rag-carpet before the speckless hearth, and the sofa heaved to the emotions of Beetle. Through the thick glass the figures without showed blue, distorted, and menacing.

'I – I protest against this outrage.' King had evidently been running up hill. 'The man was entirely within his duty. Let – let me give you my card.'

'He's in flannels!' Stalky buried his head again.

'Unfortunately – most unfortunately – I have not one with me, but my name is King, sir, a housemaster of the college, and you will find me prepared – fully prepared – to answer for this man's action. We've seen three – '

'Did ye see my noticeboards?'

'I admit we did; but under the circumstances – '

'I stand *in loco parentis*.' Prout's deep voice was added to the discussion. They could hear him pant.

'F'what?' Colonel Dabney was growing more and more Irish.

'I'm responsible for the boys under my charge.'

'Ye are, are ye? Then all I can say is that ye set them a very bad example – a dam' bad example, if I may say so. I do not own your boys. I've not seen your boys, an' I tell you that if there was a boy grinnin' in every bush on the place, *still* ye've no shadow of a right here, comin' up from the combe that way, an' frightenin' everything in it. Don't attempt to deny it. Ye did. Ye should have come to the Lodge an' seen me like Christians, instead of chasin' your dam' boys through the length and breadth of my covers. *In loco parentis* ye are? Well, I've not forgotten my Latin either, an' I'll say to you: "*Quis custodiet ipsos custodes*." If the masters trespass, how can we blame the boys?'

'But if I could speak to you privately,' said Prout.

'I'll have nothing private with you! Ye can be as private as ye please on the other side o' that gate an' – I wish ye a very good afternoon.'

A second time the gate clanged. They waited till Colonel Dabney had returned to the house, and fell into one another's arms, crowing for breath.

'Oh, my Soul! Oh, my King! Oh, my Heffy! Oh, my Foxy! Zeal, all zeal, Mr Simple.' Stalky wiped his eyes. 'Oh! Oh! Oh! – "I *did* boil the exciseman!" We must get out of this or we'll be late for tea.'

'Ge–Ge–get the badger and make little Hartopp happy. Ma–ma–make 'em all happy,' sobbed McTurk, groping for the door and kicking the prostrate Beetle before him.

They found the beast in an evil-smelling box, left two half-crowns for payment, and staggered home. Only the badger grunted most marvellous like Colonel Dabney, and they dropped him twice or thrice with shrieks of helpless laughter. They were but imperfectly recovered when Foxy met them by the fives court with word that they were to go up to their dormitory and wait till sent for.

'Well, take this box to Mr Hartopp's rooms, then. We've done something for the Natural History Society, at any rate,' said Beetle.

' 'Fraid that won't save you, young gen'elmen,' Foxy answered, in an awful voice. He was sorely ruffled in his mind.

'All sereno, Foxibus.' Stalky had reached the extreme stage of hiccups. 'We – we'll never desert you, Foxy. Hounds choppin' foxes in cover is more a proof of vice, ain't it? . . . No, you're right. I'm – I'm not quite well.'

'They've gone a bit too far this time,' Foxy thought to himself. 'Very far gone, I'd say, excep' there was no smell of liquor. An' yet it isn't like 'em – somehow. King and Prout, they 'ad their dressin'-down same as me. That's one comfort.'

'Now, we must pull up,' said Stalky, rising from the bed on which he had thrown himself. 'We're injured innocence – as usual. *We* don't know what we've been sent up here for, do we?'

'No explanation. Deprived of tea. Public disgrace before the house,' said McTurk, whose eyes were running over. 'It's dam' serious.'

'Well, hold on, till King loses his temper,' said Beetle. 'He's a libellous old rip, an' he'll be in a ravin' paddywhack. Prout's too beastly cautious. Keep your eye on King, and, if he gives us a chance, appeal to the head. That always makes 'em sick.'

They were summoned to their housemaster's study, King and Foxy supporting Prout, and Foxy had three canes under his arm. King leered triumphantly, for there were tears, undried tears of mirth, on the boys' cheeks. Then the examination began.

Yes, they had walked along the cliffs. Yes, they had entered Colonel Dabney's grounds. Yes, they had seen the noticeboards (at this point Beetle sputtered hysterically). For what purpose had they entered Colonel Dabney's grounds? 'Well, sir, there was a badger.'

Here King, who loathed the Natural History Society because he did not like Hartopp, could no longer be restrained. He begged them not to add mendacity to open insolence. But the badger was in Mr Hartopp's rooms, sir. The sergeant had kindly taken it up for them. That disposed of the badger, and the temporary check brought King's temper to boiling point. They could hear his foot on the floor while Prout prepared his lumbering enquiries. They had settled into their stride now. Their eyes ceased to sparkle; their faces were blank; their hands hung beside them without a twitch. They were learning, at the expense of a fellow-countryman, the lesson of their race, which is to put away all emotion and entrap the alien at the proper time.

So far good. King was importing himself more freely into the trial, being vengeful where Prout was grieved. They knew the penalties of trespassing? With a fine show of irresolution, Stalky admitted that he had gathered some information vaguely bearing on this head, but he thought – The sentence was dragged out to the uttermost: Stalky did not wish to play his trump with such an opponent. Mr King desired no buts, nor was he interested in Stalky's evasions. They, on the other hand, might be interested in his poor views. Boys who crept – who sneaked – who lurked – out of bounds, even the generous bounds of the Natural History Society, which they had falsely joined as a cloak for their misdeeds – their vices – their villainies – their immoralities –

'He'll break cover in a minute,' said Stalky to himself. 'Then we'll run into him before he gets away.'

Such boys, scabrous boys, moral lepers – the current of his words was carrying King off his feet – evil-speakers, liars, slow-bellies – yea, incipient drunkards . . .

He was merely working up to a peroration, and the boys knew it; but McTurk cut through the frothing sentence, the others echoing:

'I appeal to the head, sir.'

'I appeal to the head, sir.'

'I appeal to the head, sir.'

It was their unquestioned right. Drunkenness meant expulsion after a public flogging. They had been accused of it. The case was the head's, and the head's alone.

'Thou hast appealed unto Caesar: unto Caesar shalt thou go.' They had heard that sentence once or twice before in their careers. 'None the less,' said King, uneasily, 'you would be better advised to abide by our decision, my young friends.'

'Are we allowed to associate with the rest of the school till we see the head, sir?' said McTurk to his housemaster, disregarding King. This at once lifted the situation to its loftiest plane. Moreover, it meant no work, for moral leprosy was strictly quarantined, and the head never executed judgment till twenty-four cold hours later.

'Well – er – if you persist in your defiant attitude,' said King, with a loving look at the canes under Foxy's arm. 'There is no alternative.'

Ten minutes later the news was over the whole school. Stalky and Co. had fallen at last – fallen by drink. They had been drinking. They had returned blind-drunk from a hut. They were even now lying hopelessly intoxicated on the dormitory floor. A few bold spirits crept up to look, and received boots about the head from the criminals.

'We've got him – got him on the Caudine Toasting-fork!' said Stalky, after those hints were taken. 'King'll have to prove his charges up to the giddy hilt.'

'Too much ticklee, him bust,' Beetle quoted from a book of his reading. 'Didn't I say he'd go pop if we lat un bide?'

'No prep, either, O ye incipient drunkards,' said McTurk, 'and it's trig night, too. Hullo! Here's our dear friend Foxy. More tortures, Foxibus?'

'I've brought you something to eat, young gentlemen,' said the sergeant from behind a crowded tray. Their wars had ever been waged without malice, and a suspicion floated in Foxy's mind that boys who allowed themselves to be tracked so easily might, perhaps, hold something in reserve. Foxy had served through the Mutiny, when early and accurate information was worth much.

'I – I noticed you 'adn't 'ad anything to eat, an' I spoke to Gumbly, an' he said you wasn't exactly cut off from supplies. So I brought up this. It's your potted 'am tin, ain't it, Mr Corkran?'

'Why, Foxibus, you're a brick,' said Stalky. 'I didn't think you had this much – what's the word, Beetle?'

'Bowels,' Beetle replied, promptly. 'Thank you, sergeant. That's young Carter's potted ham, though.'

'There was a C on it. I thought it was Mr Corkran's. This is a very serious business, young gentlemen. That's what it is. I didn't know, perhaps, but there might be something on your side which you hadn't said to Mr King or Mr Prout, maybe.'

'There is. Heaps, Foxibus.' This from Stalky through a full mouth.

'Then you see, if that was the case, it seemed to me I might represent it, quiet so to say, to the 'ead when he asks me about it. I've got to take 'im the charges tonight, an' – it looks bad on the face of it.'

' 'Trocious bad, Foxy. Twenty-seven cuts in the gym before all the school, and public expulsion. "Wine is a mocker, strong drink is ragin'," ' quoth Beetle.

'It's nothin' to make fun of, young gentlemen. I 'ave to go to the 'ead with the charges. An' – an' you mayn't be aware, per'aps, that I was followin' you this afternoon; havin' my suspicions.'

'Did ye see the noticeboards?' croaked McTurk, in the very brogue of Colonel Dabney.

'Ye've eyes in your head. Don't attempt to deny it. Ye did!' said Beetle.

'A sergeant! To run about poachin' on your pension! Damnable, O damnable!' said Stalky, without pity.

'Good Lord!' said the sergeant, sitting heavily upon a bed. 'Where – where the devil *was* you? I might ha' known it was a do – somewhere.'

'Oh, you clever maniac!' Stalky resumed. 'We mayn't be aware you were followin' us this afternoon, mayn't we? Thought you were stalkin' us, eh? Why, we led you bung into it, of course. Colonel Dabney – don't you think he's a nice man, Foxy? – Colonel Dabney's our pet particular friend. We've been goin' there for weeks and weeks, he invited us. You and your duty! Curse your duty, sir! Your duty was to keep off his covers.'

'You'll never be able to hold up your head again, Foxy. The fags'll hoot at you,' said Beetle.

'Think of your giddy prestige!' The sergeant was thinking – hard.

'Look 'ere, young gentlemen,' he said, earnestly. 'You aren't surely ever goin' to tell, are you? Wasn't Mr Prout and Mr King in – in it too?'

'Foxibusculus, they *was*. They was – singular horrid. Caught it worse than you. We heard every word of it. You got off easy, considerin'. If I'd been Dabney I swear I'd ha' quodded you. I think I'll suggest it to him tomorrow.'

'An' it's all goin' up to the 'ead. Oh, Good Lord!'

'Every giddy word of it, my Chingangook,' said Beetle, dancing. 'Why shouldn't it? *We've* done nothing wrong. *We* ain't poachers. *We* didn't cut about blastin' the characters of poor, innocent boys – saying they were drunk.'

'That I didn't,' said Foxy. 'I – I only said that you be'aved uncommon odd when you come back with that badger. Mr King may have taken the wrong hint from that.'

' 'Course he did; an' he'll jolly well shove all the blame on you when he finds out he's wrong. We know King, if you don't. I'm ashamed of you. You ain't fit to be a sergeant,' said McTurk.

'Not with three thorough-goin' young devils like you, I ain't. I've been had. I've been ambuscaded. Horse, foot, an' guns, I've been had, an' – an' there'll be no holdin' the junior forms after this. M'rover, the 'ead will send me with a note to Colonel Dabney to ask if what you say about bein' invited was true.'

'Then you'd better go in by the Lodge-gates this time, instead of chasin' your dam' boys – oh, that was the Epistle to King – so it was. We–el, Foxy?' Stalky put his chin on his hands and regarded the victim with deep delight.

'*Ti-ra-la-la-i-tu!* I gloat! Hear me!' said McTurk. 'Foxy brought us tea when we were moral lepers. Foxy has a heart. Foxy has been in the army, too.'

'I wish I'd ha' had you in my company, young gentlemen,' said the sergeant from the depths of his heart; 'I'd ha' given you something.'

'Silence at drumhead court martial,' McTurk went on. 'I'm advocate for the prisoner; and, besides, this is much too good to tell all the other brutes in the coll. They'd *never* understand. They play cricket, and say: "Yes sir", and "O, sir", and "No, sir". '

'Never mind that. Go ahead,' said Stalky.

'Well, Foxy's a good little chap when he does not esteem himself so as to be clever.'

' "Take not out your 'ounds on a werry windy day",' Stalky struck in. '*I* don't care if you let him off.'

'Nor me,' said Beetle. 'Heffy is my only joy – Heffy and King.'

'I 'ad to do it,' said the sergeant, plaintively.

'Right, O! Led away by bad companions in the execution of his duty or – or words to that effect. You're dismissed with a reprimand, Foxy. *We* won't tell about *you*. I swear we won't,' McTurk concluded. 'Bad for the discipline of the school. Horrid bad.'

'Well,' said the sergeant, gathering up the tea-things, 'knowin' what I know o' the young dev – gentlemen of the college, I'm very glad to 'ear it. But what am I to tell the 'ead?'

'Anything you jolly well please, Foxy. We aren't the criminals.'

To say that the head was annoyed when the sergeant appeared after dinner with the day's crime-sheet would be putting it mildly.

'Corkran, McTurk, and Co., I see. Bounds as usual. Hullo! What the deuce is this? Suspicion of drinking. Whose charge?'

'Mr King's, sir. I caught 'em out of bounds, sir: at least that was 'ow it looked. But there's a lot be'ind, sir.' The sergeant was evidently troubled.

'Go on,' said the head. 'Let us have your version.' He and the sergeant had dealt with one another for some seven years; and the head knew that Mr King's statements depended very largely on Mr King's temper.

'I thought they were out of bounds along the cliffs. But it come out they wasn't, sir. I saw them go into Colonel Dabney's woods, and – Mr King and Mr Prout come along – and the fact was, sir, we was mistook for poachers by Colonel Dabney's people – Mr King and Mr Prout and me. There were some words, sir, on both sides. The young gentlemen slipped 'ome somehow, and they seemed 'ighly humorous, sir. Mr King was mistook by Colonel Dabney himself – Colonel Dabney bein' strict. Then they preferred to come straight to you, sir, on account of what – what Mr King may 'ave said about their 'abits afterwards in Mr Prout's study. I only said they was 'ighly humorous, laughin' an' gigglin', an' a bit above 'emselves. They've since told me, sir, in a humorous way, that they was invited by Colonel Dabney to go into 'is woods.'

'I see. They didn't tell their housemaster that, of course?'

'They took up Mr King on appeal just as soon as he spoke about their – 'abits. Put in the appeal at once, sir, an' asked to be sent to the dormitory waitin' for you. I've since gathered, sir, in their humorous way, sir, that some'ow or other they've 'eard about every word Colonel Dabney said to Mr King and Mr Prout when he mistook 'em for poachers. I – I might ha' known when they led me on so that they 'eld the inner line of communications. It's – it's a plain do, sir, if you ask me; an' they're gloatin' over it in the dormitory.'

The head saw – saw even to the uttermost farthing – and his mouth twitched a little under his moustache.

'Send them to me at once, sergeant. This case needn't wait over.'

'Good evening,' said he when the three appeared under escort. 'I want your undivided attention for a few minutes. You've known me for five years, and I've known you for – twenty-five. I think we understand one another perfectly. I am now going to pay you a tremendous compliment (the brown one, please, sergeant. Thanks. You needn't wait). I'm going to execute you without rhyme, Beetle, or reason. I know you went to Colonel Dabney's covers because you were invited. I'm not even going to send the sergeant with a note to ask if your statement is true; because I am convinced that on this occasion you have adhered strictly to the truth. I know, too, that you were not drinking. (You can take off that virtuous expression, McTurk, or I shall begin to fear you don't understand me.) There is not a flaw in any of your characters. And that is why I am going to perpetrate a howling injustice. Your reputations have been injured, haven't they? You have been disgraced before the house, haven't you? You have a peculiarly keen regard for the honour of your house, haven't you? Well, now I am going to lick you.'

Six apiece was their portion upon that word.

'And this I think' – the head replaced the cane, and flung the written charge into the wastepaper basket – 'covers the situation. When you find a variation from the normal – this will be useful to you in later life – always meet him in an abnormal way. And that reminds me. There are a pile of paperbacks on that shelf. You can borrow them if you put them back. I don't think they'll take any harm from being read in the open. They smell of tobacco rather. You will go to prep this evening as usual. Good-night,' said that amazing man.

'Good-night, and thank you, sir.'

'I swear I'll pray for the head tonight,' said Beetle. 'Those last two cuts were just flicks on my collar. There's a *Monte Cristo* in that lower shelf. I saw it. Bags I, next time we go to Aves!'

'Dear man!' said McTurk. 'No gating. No impots. No beastly questions. All settled. Hullo! what's King goin' in to him for – King and Prout?'

Whatever the nature of that interview, it did not improve either King's or Prout's ruffled plumes, for, when they came out of the head's house, eyes noted that the one was red and blue with emotion as to his nose, and that the other was sweating profusely. That sight compensated them amply for the Imperial Jaw with which they were favoured by the two. It seems – and who so astonished as they? – that they had held back material facts; were guilty both of *suppressio veri* and *suggestio falsi* (well-known gods against whom they often offended); further, that they were malignant in their dispositions, untrustworthy in their characters, pernicious and revolutionary in their influences, abandoned to the devils of wilfulness, pride, and a most intolerable conceit. Ninthly, and lastly, they were to have a care and to be very careful.

They were careful, as only boys can be when there is a hurt to be inflicted. They waited through one suffocating week till Prout and King were their royal selves again; waited till there was a house-match – their own house, too – in which Prout was taking part; waited, further, till he had his pads in the pavilion and stood ready to go forth. King was scoring at the window, and the three sat on a bench without.

Said Stalky to Beetle: 'I say, Beetle, *quis custodiet ipsos custodes*?'

'Don't ask me,' said Beetle. 'I'll have nothin' private with you. Ye can be as private as ye please the other end of the bench; and I wish ye a very good afternoon.'

McTurk yawned.

'Well, ye should ha' come up to the lodge like Christians instead o' chasin' your – a–hem – boys through the length an' breadth of my covers. *I* think these house-matches are all rot. Let's go over to Colonel Dabney's an' see if he's collared any more poachers.'

That afternoon there was joy in Aves.

Slaves of the Lamp – Part One

The music room on the top floor of number five was filled with the 'Aladdin' company at rehearsal. Dickson Quartus, commonly known as Dick Four, was Aladdin, stage manager, ballet master, half the orchestra, and largely librettist, for the 'book' had been rewritten and filled with local allusions. The pantomime was to be given next week, in the downstairs study occupied by Aladdin, Abanazar, and the Emperor of China. The Slave of the Lamp, with the Princess Badroulbadour and the Widow Twankey, owned number five study across the same landing, so that the company could be easily assembled. The floor shook to the stamp-and-go of the ballet, while Aladdin, in pink cotton tights, a blue and tinsel jacket, and a plumed hat, banged alternately on the piano and his banjo. He was the moving spirit of the game, as befitted a senior who had passed his army preliminary and hoped to enter Sandhurst next spring.

Aladdin came to his own at last, Abanazar lay poisoned on the floor, the Widow Twankey danced her dance, and the company decided it would 'come all right on the night'.

'What about the last song, though?' said the Emperor, a tallish, fair-headed boy with a ghost of a moustache, at which he pulled manfully. 'We need a rousing old tune.'

' "John Peel"? "Drink, Puppy, Drink"?' suggested Abanazar, smoothing his baggy lilac pyjamas. 'Pussy' Abanazar never looked more than one-half awake, but he owned a soft, slow smile which well suited the part of the Wicked Uncle.

'Stale,' said Aladdin. 'Might as well have "Grandfather's Clock". What's that thing you were humming at prep last night, Stalky?'

Stalky, the Slave of the Lamp, in black tights and doublet, a black silk half-mask on his forehead, whistled lazily where he lay on the top of the piano. It was a catchy music-hall tune.

Dick Four cocked his head critically, and squinted down a large red nose. 'Once more, and I can pick it up,' he said, strumming. 'Sing the words.'

'Arrah, Patsy, mind the baby! Arrah, Patsy, mind the child!
Wrap him in an overcoat, he's surely going wild!
Arrah, Patsy, mind the baby! just you mind the child awhile!
He'll kick and bite and cry all night! Arrah, Patsy, mind the child!'

'Rippin'! Oh, rippin'!' said Dick Four. 'Only we shan't have any piano on the night. We must work it with the banjoes – play an' dance at the same time. You try, Tertius.'

The Emperor pushed aside his pea-green sleeves of state, and followed Dick Four on a heavy nickel-plated banjo.

'Yes, but I'm dead all this time. Bung in the middle of the stage, too,' said Abanazar.

'Oh, that's Beetle's biznai,' said Dick Four. 'Vamp it up, Beetle. Don't keep us waiting all night. You've got to get Pussy out of the light somehow, and bring us all in dancin' at the end.'

'All right. You two play it again,' said Beetle, who, in a grey skirt and a wig of chestnut sausage-curls, set slantwise above a pair of spectacles mended with an old bootlace, represented the Widow Twankey. He waved one leg in time to the hammered refrain, and the banjoes grew louder.

'Um! Ah! Er – "Aladdin now has won his wife",' he sang, and Dick Four repeated it.

' "Your Emperor is appeased." ' Tertius flung out his chest as he delivered his line.

'Now jump up, Pussy! Say, "I think I'd better come to life!" Then we all take hands and come forward: "We hope you've all been pleased." *Twiggez-vous?*'

'*Nous twiggons.* Good enough. What's the chorus for the final ballet? It's four kicks and a turn,' said Dick Four.

'Oh! Er!

> John Short will ring the curtain down.
>   And ring the prompter's bell;
> We hope you know before you go
>   That we all wish you well.'

'Rippin'! Rippin'! Now for the Widow's scene with the Princess. Hurry up, Turkey.'

McTurk, in a violet silk skirt and a coquettish blue turban, slouched forward as one thoroughly ashamed of himself. The Slave of the Lamp climbed down from the piano, and dispassionately kicked him. 'Play up, Turkey,' he said; 'this is serious.' But there fell on the door the knock of authority. It happened to be King, in gown and mortarboard, enjoying a Saturday evening prowl before dinner.

'Locked doors! Locked doors!' he snapped with a scowl. 'What's the meaning of this; and what, may I ask, is the intention of this – this epicene attire?'

'Pantomime, sir. The head gave us leave,' said Abanazar, as the only member of the Sixth concerned. Dick Four stood firm in the confidence born of well-fitting tights, but Beetle strove to efface himself behind the piano. A grey princess-skirt borrowed from a day-boy's mother and a spotted cotton bodice unsystematically padded with imposition-paper make one ridiculous. And in other regards Beetle had a bad conscience.

'As usual!' sneered King. 'Futile foolery just when your careers, such as they may be, are hanging in the balance. I see! Ah, I see! The old gang of criminals – allied forces of disorder – Corkran' – the Slave of the Lamp smiled politely – 'McTurk' – the Irishman scowled – 'and, of course, the unspeakable Beetle, our friend Gigadibs.' Abanazar, the Emperor, and Aladdin had more or less of characters, and King passed them over. 'Come forth, my inky buffoon, from behind yonder instrument of music! You supply, I presume, the doggerel for this entertainment. Esteem yourself to be, as it were, a poet?'

'He's found one of 'em,' thought Beetle, noting the flush on King's cheekbone.

'I have just had the pleasure of reading an effusion of yours to my address, I believe – an effusion intended to rhyme. So – so you despise me, Master Gigadibs, do you? I am quite aware – you need not explain – that it was ostensibly not intended for my edification. I read it with laughter – yes, with laughter. These paper pellets of inky boys – still a boy we are, Master Gigadibs – do not disturb my equanimity.'

'Wonder which it was,' thought Beetle. He had launched many lampoons on an appreciative public ever since he discovered that it was possible to convey reproof in rhyme.

In sign of his unruffled calm, King proceeded to tear Beetle, whom he called Gigadibs, slowly asunder. From his untied shoestrings to his mended spectacles (the life of a poet at a big school is hard) he held him up to the derision of his associates – with the usual result. His wild flowers of speech – King had an unpleasant tongue – restored him to good humour at the last. He drew a lurid picture of Beetle's latter end as a scurrilous pamphleteer dying in an attic, scattered a few compliments over McTurk and Corkran, and, reminding Beetle that he must come up for judgement when called upon, went to common room, where he triumphed anew over his victims.

'And the worst of it,' he explained in a loud voice over his soup, 'is that I waste such gems of sarcasm on their thick heads. It's miles above them, I'm certain.'

'We–ell,' said the school chaplain slowly, 'I don't know what Corkran's appreciation of your style may be, but young McTurk reads Ruskin for his amusement.'

'Nonsense! He does it to show off. I mistrust the dark Celt.'

'He does nothing of the kind. I went into their study the other night, unofficially, and McTurk was gluing up the back of four odd numbers of *Fors Clavigera*.'

'I don't know anything about their private lives,' said a mathematical master hotly, 'but I've learned by bitter experience that number five study are best left alone. They are utterly soulless young devils.'

He blushed as the others laughed.

But in the music room there were wrath and bad language. Only Stalky, Slave of the Lamp, lay on the piano unmoved.

'That little swine Manders minor must have shown him your stuff. He's always suckin' up to King. Go and kill him,' he drawled. 'Which one was it, Beetle?'

'Dunno,' said Beetle, struggling out of the skirt. 'There was one about his hunting for popularity with the small boys, and the other one was one about him in hell, tellin' the Devil he was a Balliol man. I swear both of 'em rhymed all right. By gum! P'raps Manders minor showed him both! *I'll* correct his caesuras for him.'

He disappeared down two flights of stairs, flushed a small pink and white boy in a form-room next door to King's study, which, again, was immediately below his own, and chased him up the corridor into a form-room sacred to the revels of the Lower Third. Thence he came back, greatly disordered, to find McTurk, Stalky, and the others of the company, in his study enjoying an unlimited 'brew' – coffee, cocoa, buns, new bread hot and steaming, sardine, sausage, ham-and-tongue paste, pilchards, three jams, and at least as many pounds of Devonshire cream.

'My hat!' said he, throwing himself upon the banquet. 'Who stumped up for this, Stalky?' It was within a month of term end, and blank starvation had reigned in the studies for weeks.

'You,' said Stalky, serenely.

'Confound you! You haven't been popping my Sunday bags, then?'

'Keep your hair on. It's only your watch.'

'Watch! I lost it – weeks ago. Out on the Burrows, when we tried to shoot the old ram – the day our pistol burst.'

'It dropped out of your pocket (you're so beastly careless, Beetle), and McTurk and I kept it for you. I've been wearing it for a week, and you never noticed. Took it into Bideford after dinner today. Got thirteen and sevenpence. Here's the ticket.'

'Well, that's pretty average cool,' said Abanazar behind a slab of cream and jam, as Beetle, reassured upon the safety of his Sunday trousers, showed not even surprise, much less resentment. Indeed, it was McTurk who grew angry, saying: 'You gave him the ticket, Stalky? You pawned it? You unmitigated beast! Why, last month you and Beetle sold mine! Never got a sniff of any ticket.'

'Ah, that was because you locked your trunk, and we wasted half the afternoon hammering it open. We might have pawned it if you'd behaved like a Christian, Turkey.'

'My Aunt!' said Abanazar, 'you chaps are communists. Vote of thanks to Beetle, though.'

'That's beastly unfair,' said Stalky, 'when I took all the trouble to pawn it. Beetle never knew he had a watch. Oh, I say, Rabbits-Eggs gave me a lift into Bideford this afternoon.'

Rabbits-Eggs was the local carrier – an outcrop of the early Devonian formation. It was Stalky who had invented his unlovely name. 'He was pretty average drunk, or he wouldn't have done it. Rabbits-Eggs is a little shy of me, somehow. But I swore it was *pax* between us, and gave him a bob. He stopped at two pubs on the way in, so he'll be howling drunk tonight. Oh, don't begin reading, Beetle; there's a council of war on. What the deuce is the matter with your collar?'

'Chivvied Manders minor into the Lower Third box room. Had all his beastly little friends on top of me,' said Beetle from behind a jar of pilchards and a book.

'You ass! Any fool could have told you where Manders would bunk to,' said McTurk.

'I didn't think,' said Beetle, meekly, scooping out pilchards with a spoon.

' 'Course you didn't. You never do.' McTurk adjusted Beetle's collar with a savage tug. 'Don't drop oil all over my *Fors* or I'll scrag you!'

'Shut up, you – you Irish biddy! 'Tisn't your beastly *Fors*. It's one of mine.'

The book was a fat, brown-backed volume of the later sixties, which King had once thrown at Beetle's head that Beetle might see whence the name Gigadibs came. Beetle had quietly annexed the book, and had seen – several things. The quarter-comprehended verses lived and ate with him, as the bedropped pages showed. He removed himself from all that world, drifting at large with wondrous men and women, till McTurk hammered the pilchard spoon on his head and he snarled.

'Beetle! You're oppressed and insulted and bullied by King. Don't you feel it?'

'Let me alone! I can write some more poetry about him if I am, I suppose.'

'Mad! Quite mad!' said Stalky to the visitors, as one exhibiting strange beasts. 'Beetle reads an ass called Brownin', and McTurk reads an ass called Ruskin, and – '

'Ruskin isn't an ass,' said McTurk. 'He's almost as good as the Opium Eater. He says "we're children of noble races trained by surrounding art". That means *me*, and the way I decorated the study when you two badgers would have stuck up brackets and Christmas cards. Child of a noble race, trained by surrounding art, stop reading, or I'll shove a pilchard down your neck!'

'It's two to one,' said Stalky, warningly, and Beetle closed the book, in obedience to the law under which he and his companions had lived for six checkered years.

The visitors looked on delighted. Number five study had a reputation for more variegated insanity than the rest of the school put together; and so far as its code allowed friendship with outsiders it was polite and open-hearted to its neighbours on the same landing.

'What rot do you want now?' said Beetle.

'King! War!' said McTurk, jerking his head toward the wall, where hung a small wooden West African war drum, a gift to McTurk from a naval uncle.

'Then we shall be turned out of the study again,' said Beetle, who loved his fleshpots. 'Mason turned us out for – just warbling on it.' Mason was the mathematical master who had testified in common room.

'Warbling? – O Lord!' said Abanazar. 'We couldn't hear ourselves speak in our study when you played the infernal thing. What's the good of getting turned out of your study, anyhow?'

'We lived in the form-rooms for a week, too,' said Beetle, tragically. 'And it was beastly cold.'

'Ye–es, but Mason's rooms were filled with rats every day we were out. It took him a week to draw the inference,' said McTurk. 'He loathes rats. Minute he let us go back the rats stopped. Mason's a little shy of us now, but there was no evidence.'

'Jolly well there wasn't,' said Stalky, 'when I got out on the roof and dropped the beastly things down his chimney. But, look here – question is, are our characters good enough just now to stand a study row?'

'Never mind mine,' said Beetle. 'King swears I haven't any.'

'I'm not thinking of you,' Stalky returned scornfully. 'You aren't going up for the army, you old bat. I don't want to be expelled – and the head's getting rather shy of us, too.'

'Rot!' said McTurk. 'The head never expels except for beastliness or stealing. But I forgot; you and Stalky *are* thieves – regular burglars.'

The visitors gasped, but Stalky interpreted the parable with large grins.

'Well, you know, that little beast Manders minor saw Beetle and me hammerin' McTurk's trunk open in the dormitory when we took his watch last month. Of course Manders sneaked to Mason, and Mason solemnly took it up as a case of theft, to get even with us about the rats.'

'That just put Mason into our giddy hands,' said McTurk, blandly. 'We were nice to him, because he was a new master and wanted to win the confidence of the boys. Pity he draws inferences, though. Stalky went to his study and pretended to blub, and told Mason he'd lead a new life if Mason would let him off this time, but Mason wouldn't. Said it was his duty to report him to the head.'

'Vindictive swine!' said Beetle. 'It was all those rats! Then *I* blubbed, too, and Stalky confessed that he'd been a thief in regular practice for six years, ever since he came to the school; and that I'd taught him – *à la* Fagin. Mason turned white with joy. He thought he had us on toast.'

'Gorgeous! Gorgeous!' said Dick Four. 'We never heard of this.'

' 'Course not. Mason kept it jolly quiet. He wrote down all our statements on impot-paper. There wasn't anything he wouldn't believe,' said Stalky.

'And handed it all up to the head, *with* an extempore prayer. It took about forty pages,' said Beetle. 'I helped him a lot.'

'And then, you crazy idiots?' said Abanazar.

'Oh, we were sent for; and Stalky asked to have the "depositions" read out, and the head knocked him spinning into a wastepaper basket. Then he gave us eight cuts apiece – welters – for – for – takin' unheard-of liberties with a new master. I saw his shoulders shaking when we went out. Do you know,' said Beetle, pensively, 'that Mason can't look at us now in second lesson without blushing? We three stare at him sometimes till he regularly trickles. He's an awfully sensitive beast.'

'He read *Eric, or Little by Little*,' said McTurk; 'so we gave him *St Winifred's, or the World of School*. They spent all their spare time stealing at St Winifred's, when they weren't praying or getting drunk at pubs. Well, that was only a week ago, and the head's a little bit shy of us. He called it constructive devilry. Stalky invented it all.'

'Not the least good having a row with a master unless you can make an ass of him,' said Stalky, extended at ease on the hearthrug. 'If Mason didn't know number five – well, he's learnt, that's all. Now, my dearly beloved 'earers' – Stalky curled his legs under him and addressed the company – 'we've got that strong, perseverin' man King on our hands. He went miles out of his way to provoke a conflict.' (Here Stalky snapped down the black silk domino and assumed the air of a judge.) 'He has oppressed Beetle, McTurk, and me, *privatim et seriatim*, one by one, as he could catch us. But now, he has insulted number five up in the music room, and in the presence of these – these ossifers of the Ninety-third, wot look like hairdressers. Binjimin, we must make him cry, "*Capivi!*" '

Stalky's reading did not include Browning or Ruskin.

'And, besides,' said McTurk, 'he's a Philistine, a basket-hanger. He wears a tartan tie. Ruskin says that any man who wears a tartan tie will, without doubt, be damned everlastingly.'

'Bravo, McTurk,' said Tertius; 'I thought he was only a beast.'

'He's that, too, of course, but he's worse. He has a china basket with blue ribbons and a pink kitten on it, hung up in his window to grow musk in. You know when I got all that old oak carvin' out of Bideford Church, when they were restoring it (Ruskin says that any man who'll restore a church is an unmitigated sweep), and stuck it up here with glue? Well, King came in and wanted to know whether we'd done it with a fretsaw! Yah! He is the King of basket-hangers!'

Down went McTurk's inky thumb over an imaginary arena full of bleeding Kings. '*Placete*, child of a generous race!' he cried to Beetle.

'Well,' began Beetle, doubtfully, 'he comes from Balliol, but I'm going to give the beast a chance. You see I can always make him hop with some more poetry. He can't report me to the head, because it makes him ridiculous. (Stalky's quite right.) But he shall have his chance.'

Beetle opened the book on the table, ran his finger down a page, and began at random:

> 'Or who in Moscow toward the Czar
> With the demurest of footfalls,
> Over the Kremlin's pavement white
> With serpentine and syenite,
> Steps with five other generals –'

'That's no good. Try another,' said Stalky.

'Hold on a shake; I know what's coming.' McTurk was reading over Beetle's shoulder.

> 'That simultaneously take snuff,
> For each to have pretext enough
> And kerchiefwise unfold his sash,
> Which – softness' self – is yet the stuff

(Gummy! What a sentence!)

> To hold fast where a steel chain snaps
> And leave the grand white neck no gash.

(Full stop.)

'Don't understand a word of it,' said Stalky.

'More fool you! Construe,' said McTurk. 'Those six bargees scragged the Czar, and left no evidence. *Actum est* with King.'

'He gave me that book, too,' said Beetle, licking his lips:

> 'There's a great text in Galatians,
>   Once you trip on it entails
> Twenty-nine distinct damnations,
>   One sure if another fails.'

Then irrelevantly:

> 'Setebos! Setebos! and Setebos!
> Thinketh he liveth in the cold of the moon.'

'He's just come in from dinner,' said Dick Four, looking through the window. 'Manders minor is with him.'

'Safest place for Manders minor just now,' said Beetle.

'Then you chaps had better clear out,' said Stalky politely to the visitors. ' 'Tisn't fair to mix you up in a study row. Besides, we can't afford to have evidence.'

'Are you going to begin at once?' said Aladdin.

'Immediately, if not sooner,' said Stalky, and turned out the gas. 'Strong, perseverin' man – King. Make him cry, "*Capivi!*" G'way, Binjimin.'

The company retreated to their own neat and spacious study with expectant souls.

'When Stalky blows out his nostrils like a horse,' said Aladdin to the Emperor of China, 'he's on the warpath. Wonder what King will get.'

'Beans,' said the Emperor. 'Number five generally pays in full.'

'Wonder if I ought to take any notice of it officially,' said Abanazar, who had just remembered he was a prefect.

'It's none of your business, Pussy. Besides, if you did, we'd have them hostile to us; and we shouldn't be able to do any work,' said Aladdin. 'They've begun already.'

Now, that West African war drum had been made to signal across estuaries and deltas. Number five was forbidden to wake the engine within earshot of the school. But a deep, devastating drone filled the passages as McTurk and Beetle scientifically rubbed its top. Anon it changed to the blare of trumpets – of savage pursuing trumpets. Then, as McTurk slapped one side, smooth with the blood of ancient sacrifice, the roar broke into short coughing howls such as the wounded gorilla throws in his native forest. These were followed by the wrath of King – three steps at a time, up the staircase, with a dry whirr of the gown. Aladdin and company, listening, squeaked with excitement as the door crashed open. King stumbled into the darkness, and cursed those performers by the gods of Balliol and quiet repose.

'Turned out for a week,' said Aladdin, holding the study door on the crack. 'Key to be brought down to his study in five minutes. "Brutes! Barbarians! Savages! Children!" He's rather agitated. "Arrah, Patsy, mind the baby",' he sang in a whisper as he clung to the doorknob, dancing a noiseless war-dance.

King went downstairs again, and Beetle and McTurk lit the gas to confer with Stalky. But Stalky had vanished.

'Looks like no end of a mess,' said Beetle, collecting his books and mathematical instrument case. 'A week in the form-rooms isn't any advantage to us.'

'Yes, but don't you see that Stalky isn't here, you owl!' said McTurk. 'Take down the key, and look sorrowful. King'll only jaw you for half an hour. I'm going to read in the lower form-room.'

'But it's always me,' mourned Beetle.

'Wait till we see,' said McTurk, hopefully. 'I don't know any more than you do what Stalky means, but it's something. Go down and draw King's fire. You're used to it.'

No sooner had the key turned in the door than the lid of the coal-box, which was also the window seat, lifted cautiously. It had been a tight fit, even for the lithe Stalky, his head between his knees, and his stomach under his right ear. From a drawer in the table he took a well-worn catapult, a handful of buckshot, and a duplicate key of the study; noiselessly he raised the window and kneeled by it, his face turned to the road, the wind-sloped trees, the dark levels of the Burrows, and the white line of breakers falling nine-deep along the Pebbleridge. Far down the steep-banked Devonshire lane he heard the husky hoot of the carrier's horn. There was a ghost of melody in it, as it might have been the wind in a gin bottle essaying to sing, 'It's a way we have in the army.'

Stalky smiled a tight-lipped smile, and at extreme range opened fire: the old horse half wheeled in the shafts.

'Where he gwaine tu?' hiccoughed Rabbits-Eggs. Another buckshot tore through the rotten canvas tilt with a vicious zipp.

'*Habet!*' murmured Stalky, as Rabbits-Eggs swore into the patient night, protesting that he saw the 'dommed colleger' who was assaulting him.

*   *   *

'And so,' King was saying in a high head voice to Beetle, whom he had kept to play with before Manders minor, well knowing that it hurts a Fifth-form boy to be held up to a fag's derision, 'and so, Master Beetle, in spite of all our verses, which we are so proud of, when we presume to come into direct conflict with even so humble a representative of authority as myself, for instance, we are turned out of our studies, are we not?'

'Yes, sir,' said Beetle, with a sheepish grin on his lips and murder in his heart. Hope had nearly left him, but he clung to a well-established faith that never was Stalky so dangerous as when he was invisible.

'You are *not* required to criticise, thank you. Turned out of our studies, we are, just as if we were no better than little Manders minor. Only inky schoolboys we are, and must be treated as such.'

Beetle pricked up his ears, for Rabbits-Eggs was swearing savagely on the road, and some of the language entered at the upper sash. King believed in ventilation. He strode to the window gowned and majestic, very visible in the gaslight. 'I zee 'un! I zee 'un!' roared Rabbits-Eggs, now that he had found a visible foe – another shot from the darkness above. 'Yiss, yeou, yeou long-nosed, fower-eyed, gingy-whiskered beggar! Yeu'm tu old for such goin's on. Aie! Poultice yeour nose, I tall 'ee! Poultice yeour long nose!'

Beetle's heart leaped up within him. Somewhere, somehow, he knew, Stalky moved behind these manifestations. There were hope and the prospect of revenge. He would embody the suggestion about the nose in deathless verse. King threw up the window, and sternly rebuked Rabbits-Eggs. But the carrier was beyond fear or fawning. He had descended from the cart, and was stooping by the roadside.

It all fell swiftly as a dream. Manders minor raised his hand to his head with a cry, as a jagged flint cannoned on to some rich tree-calf bindings in the bookshelf. Another quoited along the writing table. Beetle made zealous feint to stop it, and in that endeavour overturned a student's lamp, which dripped, *via* King's papers and some choice books, greasily on to a Persian rug. There was much broken glass on the window seat; the china basket – McTurk's aversion – cracked to flinders, had dropped her musk plant and its earth over the red rep cushions; Manders minor was bleeding profusely from a cut on the cheekbone; and King, using strange words, every one of which Beetle treasured, ran forth to find the school-sergeant, that Rabbits-Eggs might be instantly cast into jail.

'Poor chap!' said Beetle, with a false, feigned sympathy. 'Let it bleed a little. That'll prevent apoplexy,' and he held the blind head skilfully over the table, and the papers on the table, as he guided the howling Manders to the door.

Then did Beetle, alone with the wreckage, return good for evil. How, in that office, a complete set of 'Gibbon' was scarred all along the back as by a flint; how so much black and copying ink came to be mingled with Manders's gore on the tablecloth; why the big gum bottle, unstoppered, had rolled semicircularly across the floor; and in what manner the white china doorknob grew to be painted with yet more of Manders's young blood, were matters which Beetle did not explain when the rabid King returned to find him standing politely over the reeking hearthrug.

'You never told me to go, sir,' he said, with the air of Casabianca, and King consigned him to the outer darkness.

But it was to a boot cupboard under the staircase on the ground floor that he hastened, to loose the mirth that was destroying him. He had not drawn breath for a first whoop of triumph when two hands choked him dumb.

'Go to the dormitory and get me my things. Bring 'em to number five lavatory. I'm still in tights,' hissed Stalky, sitting on his head. 'Don't run. Walk.'

But Beetle staggered into the form-room next door, and delegated his duty to the yet unenlightened McTurk, with an hysterical precis of the campaign thus far. So it was McTurk, of the wooden visage, who brought the clothes from the dormitory while Beetle panted on a form. Then the three buried themselves in number five lavatory, turned on all the taps, filled the place with steam, and dropped weeping into the baths, where they pieced out the war.

'*Moi! Je! Ich! Ego!*' gasped Stalky. 'I waited till I couldn't hear myself think, while you played the drum! Hid in the coal-locker – and tweaked Rabbits-Eggs – and Rabbits-Eggs rocked King. Wasn't it beautiful? Did you hear the glass?'

'Why, he – he – he,' shrieked McTurk, one trembling finger pointed at Beetle.

'Why, I – I – I was through it all,' Beetle howled; 'in his study, being jawed.'

'Oh, my soul!' said Stalky with a yell, disappearing under water.

'The – the glass was nothing. Manders minor's head's cut open. La – la – lamp upset all over the rug. Blood on the books and papers. The gum! The gum! The gum! The ink! The ink! The ink! Oh, Lord!'

Then Stalky leaped out, all pink as he was, and shook Beetle into some sort of coherence; but his tale prostrated them afresh.

'I bunked for the boot cupboard the second I heard King go downstairs.

Beetle tumbled in on top of me. The spare key's hid behind the loose board. There isn't a shadow of evidence,' said Stalky. They were all chanting together.

'And he turned us out himself – himself – himself!' This from McTurk. 'He can't begin to suspect us. Oh, Stalky, it's the loveliest thing we've ever done.'

'Gum! Gum! Dollops of gum!' shouted Beetle, his spectacles gleaming through a sea of lather. 'Ink and blood all mixed. I held the little beast's head all over the Latin proses for Monday. Golly, how the oil stunk! And Rabbits-Eggs told King to poultice his nose! Did you hit Rabbits-Eggs, Stalky?'

'Did I jolly well not? Tweaked him all over. Did you hear him curse? Oh, I shall be sick in a minute if I don't stop.'

But dressing was a slow process, because McTurk was obliged to dance when he heard that the musk basket was broken, and, moreover, Beetle retailed all King's language with emendations and purple insets.

'Shockin'!' said Stalky, collapsing in a helpless welter of half-hitched trousers. 'So dam' bad, too, for innocent boys like us! Wonder what they'd say at *St Winifred's, or the World of School*. By gum! That reminds me, we owe the Lower Third one for assaultin' Beetle when he chivvied Manders minor. Come on! It's an alibi, Samivel; and, besides, if we let 'em off they'll be worse next time.'

The Lower Third had set a guard upon their form-room for the space of a full hour, which to a boy is a lifetime. Now they were busy with their Saturday evening businesses – cooking sparrows over the gas with rusty nibs; brewing unholy drinks in gallipots; skinning moles with pocketknives; attending to paper trays full of silkworms, or discussing the iniquities of their elders with a freedom, fluency, and point that would have amazed their parents. The blow fell without warning. Stalky upset a form crowded with small boys among their own cooking utensils, McTurk raided the untidy lockers as a terrier digs at a rabbit-hole, while Beetle poured ink upon such heads as he could not appeal to with a Smith's *Classical Dictionary*. Three brisk minutes accounted for many silkworms, pet larvae, French exercises, school caps, half-prepared bones and skulls, and a dozen pots of home-made sloe jam. It was a great wreckage, and the form-room looked as though three conflicting tempests had smitten it.

'Phew!' said Stalky, drawing breath outside the door (amid groans of 'Oh, you beastly ca–ads! You think yourselves awful funny,' and so forth). '*That's* all right. Never let the sun go down upon your wrath. Rummy little devils, fags. Got no notion o' combinin'.'

'Six of 'em sat on my head when I went in after Manders minor,' said Beetle. 'I warned 'em what they'd get, though.'

'Everybody paid in full – beautiful feelin',' said McTurk absently, as they strolled along the corridor. 'Don't think we'd better say much about King, though, do you, Stalky?'

'Not much. Our line is injured innocence, of course – same as when the sergeant reported us on suspicion of smoking in the bunkers. If I hadn't thought of buyin' the pepper and spillin' it all over our clothes, he'd have smelt us. King was gha–astly facetious about that. Called us bird-stuffers in form for a week.'

'Ah, King hates the Natural History Society because little Hartopp is president. Mustn't do anything in the coll. without glorifyin' King,' said McTurk. 'But he must be a putrid ass, you know, to suppose at our time o' life we'd go and stuff birds like fags.'

'Poor old King!' said Beetle. 'He's unpopular in common room, and they'll chaff his head off about Rabbits-Eggs. Golly! How lovely! How beautiful! How holy! But you should have seen his face when the first rock came in! *And* the earth from the basket!'

So they were all stricken helpless for five minutes.

They repaired at last to Abanazar's study, and were received reverently.

'What's the matter?' said Stalky, quick to realise new atmospheres.

'You know jolly well,' said Abanazar. 'You'll be expelled if you get caught. King is a gibbering maniac.'

'Who? Which? What? Expelled for how? We only played the war drum. We've got turned out for that already.'

'Do you chaps mean to say you didn't make Rabbits-Eggs drunk and bribe him to rock King's rooms?'

'Bribe him? No, that I'll swear we didn't,' said Stalky, with a relieved heart, for he loved not to tell lies. 'What a low mind you've got, Pussy! We've been down having a bath. Did Rabbits-Eggs rock King? Strong, perseverin' man King? Shockin'!'

'Awf'ly. King's frothing at the mouth. There's bell for prayers. Come on.'

'Wait a sec,' said Stalky, continuing the conversation in a loud and cheerful voice, as they descended the stairs. 'What did Rabbits-Eggs rock King for?'

'I know,' said Beetle, as they passed King's open door. 'I was in his study.'

'Hush, you ass!' hissed the Emperor of China.

'Oh, he's gone down to prayers,' said Beetle, watching the shadow of the housemaster on the wall. 'Rabbits-Eggs was only a bit drunk, swearin' at his horse, and King jawed him through the window, and then, of course, he rocked King.'

'Do you mean to say,' said Stalky, 'that King began it?'

King was behind them, and every well-weighed word went up the staircase like an arrow. 'I can only swear,' said Beetle, 'that King cursed like a bargee. Simply disgustin'. I'm goin' to write to my father about it.'

'Better report it to Mason,' suggested Stalky. 'He knows our tender consciences. Hold on a shake. I've got to tie my bootlace.'

The other study hurried forward. They did not wish to be dragged into stage asides of this nature. So it was left to McTurk to sum up the situation beneath the guns of the enemy.

'You see,' said the Irishman, hanging on the banister, 'he begins by bullying little chaps; then he bullies the big chaps; then he bullies someone who isn't connected with the college, and then catches it. Serves him jolly well right . . . I beg your pardon, sir. I didn't see you were coming down the staircase.'

The black gown tore past like a thunderstorm, and in its wake, three abreast, arms linked, the Aladdin company rolled up the big corridor to prayers, singing with most innocent intention:

'Arrah, Patsy, mind the baby! Arrah, Patsy, mind the child!
Wrap him up in an overcoat, he's surely goin' wild!
Arrah, Patsy, mind the baby; just ye mind the child awhile!
He'll kick an' bite an' cry all night! Arrah, Patsy, mind the child!'

An Unsavoury Interlude

It was a maiden aunt of Stalky who sent him both books, with the inscription, 'To dearest Artie, on his sixteenth birthday'; it was McTurk who ordered their hypothecation; and it was Beetle, returned from Bideford, who flung them on the window sill of number five study with news that Bastable would advance but ninepence on the two; *Eric, or, Little by Little*, being almost as great a drug as *St Winifred's*. 'An' I don't think much of your aunt. We're nearly out of cartridges, too – Artie, dear.'

Whereupon Stalky rose up to grapple with him, but McTurk sat on Stalky's head, calling him a 'pure-minded boy' till peace was declared. As they were grievously in arrears with a Latin prose, as it was a blazing July afternoon, and as they ought to have been at a house cricket match, they began to renew their acquaintance, intimate and unholy, with the volumes.

'Here we are!' said McTurk. ' "Corporal punishment produced on Eric the worst effects. He burned *not* with remorse or regret" – make a note o' that, Beetle – "but with shame and violent indignation. He glared" – oh, naughty Eric! Let's get to where he goes in for drink.'

'Hold on half a shake. Here's another sample. "The Sixth," he says, "is the palladium of all public schools." But this lot – Stalky rapped the gilded book – 'can't prevent fellows drinkin' and stealin', an' lettin' fags out the window at night, an' – an' doin' what they please. Golly, what we've missed – not goin' to St Winifred's! . . . '

'I'm sorry to see any boys of my house taking so little interest in their matches.'

Mr Prout could move very silently if he pleased, though that is no merit in a boy's eyes. He had flung open the study door without knocking – another sin – and looked at them suspiciously. 'Very sorry, indeed, I am to see you frowsting in your studies.'

'We've been out ever since dinner, sir,' said McTurk wearily. One house-match is just like another, and their 'ploy' of that week happened to be rabbit-shooting with saloon-pistols.

'I can't see a ball when it's coming, sir,' said Beetle. 'I've had my gig-lamps smashed at the Nets till I got excused. I wasn't any good even as a fag, then, sir.'

'Tuck is probably your form. Tuck and brewing. Why can't you three take any interest in the honour of your house?'

They had heard that phrase till they were wearied. The 'honour of the house' was Prout's weak point, and they knew well how to flick him on the raw.

'If you order us to go down, sir, of course we'll go,' said Stalky, with maddening politeness. But Prout knew better than that. He had tried the experiment once at a big match, when the three, self-isolated, stood to attention for half an hour in full view of all the visitors, to whom fags, subsidised for that end, pointed them out as victims of Prout's tyranny. And Prout was a sensitive man.

In the infinitely petty confederacies of the common room, King and Macrea, fellow housemasters, had borne it in upon him that by games, and games alone, was salvation wrought. Boys neglected were boys lost. They must be disciplined. Left to himself, Prout would have made a sympathetic housemaster; but he was never so left, and with the devilish insight of youth, the boys knew to whom they were indebted for his zeal.

'Must we go down, sir?' said McTurk.

'I don't want to order you to do what a right-thinking boy should do gladly. I'm sorry.' And he lurched out with some hazy impression that he had sown good seed on poor ground.

'Now what does he suppose is the use of that?' said Beetle.

'Oh, he's cracked. King jaws him in common room about not keepin' us up to the mark, an' Macrea burbles about "dithcipline", an' old Heffy sits between 'em sweatin' big drops. I heard Oke (the common room butler) talking to Richards (Prout's house-servant) about it down in the basement the other day when I went down to bag some bread,' said Stalky.

'What did Oke say?' demanded McTurk, throwing *Eric* into a corner.

'Oh,' he said, 'They make more nise nor a nest full o' jackdaws, an' half of it like we'd no ears to our heads that waited on 'em. They talks over old Prout – what he've done an' left undone about his boys. An' how their boys be fine boys, an' his'n be dom bad.' Well, Oke talked like that, you know, and Richards got awf'ly wrathy. He has a down on King for something or other. Wonder why?'

'Why, King talks about Prout in form-room – makes allusions, an' all that – only half the chaps are such asses they can't see what he's drivin' at. And d'you remember what he said about the 'Casual House' last Tuesday? He meant us. They say he says perfectly beastly things to his own house, making fun of Prout's,' said Beetle.

'Well, we didn't come here to mix up in their rows,' McTurk said wrathfully. 'Who'll bathe after call-over? King's takin' it in the cricket field. Come on.' Turkey seized his straw and led the way.

They reached the sun-blistered pavilion over against the grey Pebbleridge just before roll-call, and, asking no questions, gathered from King's voice and manner that his house was on the road to victory.

'Ah, ha!' said he, turning to show the light of his countenance. 'Here we have the ornaments of the Casual House at last. You consider cricket beneath you, I believe,' – the flannelled crowd sniggered, 'and from what I have seen this afternoon, I fancy many others of your house hold the same view. And may I ask what you purpose to do with your noble selves till teatime?'

'Going down to bathe, sir,' said Stalky.

'And whence this sudden zeal for cleanliness? There is nothing about you that particularly suggests it. Indeed, so far as I remember – I may be at fault – but a short time ago – '

'Five years, sir,' said Beetle hotly.

King scowled. '*One* of you was that thing called a water-funk. Yes, a water-funk. So now you wish to wash? It is well. Cleanliness never injured a boy or – a house. We will proceed to business,' and he addressed himself to the call-over board.

'What the deuce did you say anything to him for, Beetle?' said McTurk angrily, as they strolled towards the big, open sea-baths.

' 'Twasn't fair – remindin' one of bein' a water-funk. My first term, too. Heaps of chaps are – when they can't swim.'

'Yes, you ass; but he saw he'd fetched you. You ought never to answer King.'

'But it wasn't fair, Stalky.'

'My hat! You've been here six years, and you expect fairness. Well, you are a dithering idiot.'

A knot of King's boys, also bound for the baths, hailed them, beseeching them to wash – for the honour of their house.

'That's what comes of King's jawin' and messin'. Those young animals wouldn't have thought of it unless he'd put it into their heads. Now they'll be funny about it for weeks,' said Stalky. 'Don't take any notice.'

The boys came nearer, shouting an opprobrious word. At last they moved to windward, ostentatiously holding their noses.

'That's pretty,' said Beetle. 'They'll be sayin' our house stinks next.'

When they returned from the baths, damp-headed, languid, at peace with the world, Beetle's forecast came only too true. They were met in the corridor by a fag – a common, Lower-Second fag – who at arm's length handed them a carefully wrapped piece of soap 'with the compliments of King's House'.

'Hold on,' said Stalky, checking immediate attack. 'Who put you up to this, Nixon? Rattray and White? (Those were two leaders in King's house.) Thank you. There's no answer.'

'Oh, it's too sickening to have this kind o' rot shoved on to a chap. What's the sense of it? What's the fun of it?' said McTurk.

'It will go on to the end of the term, though,' Beetle wagged his head sorrowfully. He had worn many jests threadbare on his own account.

In a few days it became an established legend of the school that Prout's house did not wash and were therefore noisome. Mr King was pleased to smile succulently in form when one of his boys drew aside from Beetle with certain gestures.

'There seems to be some disability attaching to you, my Beetle, or else why should Burton major withdraw, so to speak, the hem of his garments? I confess I am still in the dark. Will someone be good enough to enlighten me?'

Naturally, he was enlightened by half the form.

'Extraordinary! Most extraordinary! However, each house has its traditions, with which I would not for the world interfere. *We* have a prejudice in favour of washing. Go on, Beetle – from *jugurtha tamen* – and, if you can, avoid the more flagrant forms of guessing.'

Prout's house was furious because Macrea's and Hartopp's houses joined King's to insult them. They called a house-meeting after dinner – an excited and angry meeting of all save the prefects, whose dignity, though they sympathised, did not allow them to attend. They read ungrammatical resolutions, and made speeches beginning, 'Gentlemen, we have met on this occasion,' and ending with, 'It's a beastly shame,' precisely as houses have done since time and schools began.

Number five study attended, with its usual air of bland patronage. At last McTurk, of the lanthorn jaws, delivered himself:

'You jabber and jaw and burble, and that's about all you can do. What's the good of it? King's house'll only gloat because they've drawn you, and King will gloat, too. Besides, that resolution of Orrin's is chock-full of bad grammar, and King'll gloat over that.'

'I thought you an' Beetle would put it right, an' – an' we'd post it in the corridor,' said the composer meekly.

'*Par si je le connai.* I'm not goin' to meddle with the biznai,' said Beetle. 'It's a gloat for King's house. Turkey's quite right.'

'Well, won't Stalky, then?'

But Stalky puffed out his cheeks and squinted down his nose in the style of Panurge, and all he said was, 'Oh, you abject burblers!'

'You're three beastly scabs!' was the instant retort of the democracy, and they went out amid execrations.

'This is piffling,' said McTurk. 'Let's get our sallies, and go and shoot bunnies.'

Three saloon-pistols, with a supply of bulleted breech-caps, were stored in Stalky's trunk, and this trunk was in their dormitory, and their dormitory was a three-bed attic one, opening out of a ten-bed establishment, which, in turn, communicated with the great range of dormitories that ran practically from one end of the college to the other. Macrea's house lay next to Prout's, King's next to Macrea's, and Hartopp's beyond that again. Carefully locked doors divided house from house, but each house, in its internal arrangements – the college had originally been a terrace of twelve large houses – was a replica of the next; one straight roof covering all.

They found Stalky's bed drawn out from the wall to the left of the dormer window, and the latter end of Richards protruding from a two-foot-square cupboard in the wall.

'What's all this? I've never noticed it before. What are you tryin' to do, Fatty?'

'Fillin' basins, Muster Corkran.' Richards's voice was hollow and muffled. 'They've been savin' me trouble. Yiss.'

'Looks like it,' said McTurk. 'Hi! You'll stick if you don't take care.'

Richards backed puffing.

'I can't rache un. Yiss, 'tess a turncock, Muster McTurk. They've took an' runned all the watter pipes a storey higher in the houses – runned 'em all along under the 'ang of the heaves, like. Runned 'em in last holidays. *I* can't rache the turncock.'

'Let me try,' said Stalky, diving into the aperture.

'Slip 'ee to the left, then, Muster Corkran. Slip 'ee to the left, an' feel in the dark.'

To the left Stalky wriggled, and saw a long line of lead pipe disappearing up a triangular tunnel, whose roof was the rafters and boarding of the college roof, whose floor was sharp-edged joists, and whose side was the rough studding of the lath and plaster wall under the dormer.

'Rummy show. How far does it go?'

'Right along, Muster Corkran – right along from end to end. Her runs under the 'ang of the heaves. Have 'ee rached the stopcock yet? Mr King got un put in to save us carryin' watter from downstairs to fill the basins. No place for a lusty man like old Richards. I'm tu thickabout to go ferritin'. Thank 'ee, Muster Corkran.'

The water squirted through the tap just inside the cupboard, and, having filled the basins, the grateful Richards waddled away.

The boys sat round-eyed on their beds considering the possibilities of this trove. Two floors below them they could hear the hum of the angry house; for nothing is so still as a dormitory in mid-afternoon of a midsummer term.

'It has been papered over till now.' McTurk examined the little door. 'If we'd only known before!'

'I vote we go down and explore. No one will come up this time o' day. We needn't keep *cave*.'

They crawled in, Stalky leading, drew the door behind them, and on all fours embarked on a dark and dirty road full of plaster, odd shavings, and all the raffle that builders leave in the waste room of a house. The passage was perhaps three feet wide, and, except for the struggling light round the edges of the cupboards (there was one to each dormer), almost pitchy dark.

'Here's Macrea's house,' said Stalky, his eye at the crack of the third cupboard. 'I can see Barnes's name on his trunk. Don't make such a row, Beetle! We can get right to the end of the coll. Come on! . . . We're in King's house now – I can see a bit of Rattray's trunk. How these beastly boards hurt one's knees!' They heard his nails scraping on plaster.

'That's the ceiling below. Look out! If we smashed that the plaster 'ud fall down in the lower dormitory,' said Beetle.

'Let's,' whispered McTurk.

'An' be collared first thing? Not much. Why, I can shove my hand ever so far up between these boards.'

Stalky thrust an arm to the elbow between the joists.

'No good stayin' here. I vote we go back and talk it over. It's a crummy place. Must say I'm grateful to King for his waterworks.'

They crawled out, brushed one another clean, slid the saloon-pistols down a trouser leg, and hurried forth to a deep and solitary Devonshire lane in whose flanks a boy might sometimes slay a young rabbit. They threw themselves down under the rank elder bushes, and began to think aloud.

'You know,' said Stalky at last, sighting at a distant sparrow, 'we could hide our sallies in there like anything.'

'Huh!' Beetle snorted, choked, and gurgled. He had been silent since they left the dormitory. 'Did you ever read a book called *The History of a House* or something? I got it out of the library the other day. A French woman wrote it – Violet somebody. But it's translated, you know; and it's very interestin'. Tells you how a house is built.'

'Well, if you're in a sweat to find out that, you can go down to the new cottages they're building for the coastguard.'

'My hat! I will.' He felt in his pockets. 'Give me tuppence, someone.'

'Rot! Stay here, and don't mess about in the sun.'

'Gi' me tuppence.'

'I say, Beetle, you aren't stuffy about anything, are you?' said McTurk, handing over the coppers. His tone was serious, for though Stalky often, and McTurk occasionally, manoeuvred on his own account, Beetle had never been known to do so in all the history of the confederacy.

'No, I'm not. I'm thinking.'

'Well, we'll come, too,' said Stalky, with a general's suspicion of his aides.

'Don't want you.'

'Oh, leave him alone. He's been taken worse with a poem,' said McTurk. 'He'll go burbling down to the Pebbleridge and spit it all up in the study when he comes back.'

'Then why did he want the tuppence, Turkey? He's gettin' too beastly independent. Hi! There's a bunny. No, it ain't. It's a cat, by Jove! You plug first.'

Twenty minutes later a boy with a straw hat at the back of his head, and his hands in his pockets, was staring at workmen as they moved about a half-finished cottage. He produced some ferocious tobacco, and was passed from the forecourt into the interior, where he asked many questions.

'Well, let's have your beastly epic,' said Turkey, as they burst into the study, to find Beetle deep in Viollet-le-Duc and some drawings. 'We've had no end of a lark.'

'Epic? What epic? I've been down to the coastguard.'

'No epic? Then we will slay you, O Beetle,' said Stalky, moving to the attack. 'You've got something up your sleeve. *I* know, when you talk in that tone!'

'Your Uncle Beetle' – with an attempt to imitate Stalky's war-voice – 'is a great man.'

'Oh, no; he jolly well isn't anything of the kind. You deceive yourself, Beetle. Scrag him, Turkey!'

'A great man,' Beetle gurgled from the floor. '*You* are futile – look out for my tie! – futile burblers. I am the Great Man. I gloat. Ouch! Hear me!'

'Beetle, de–ah' – Stalky dropped unreservedly on Beetle's chest – 'we love you, an' you're a poet. If I ever said you were a doggaroo, I apologise; but you know as well as we do that you can't do anything by yourself without mucking it.'

'I've got a notion.'

'And you'll spoil the whole show if you don't tell your Uncle Stalky. Cough it up, ducky, and we'll see what we can do. Notion, you fat impostor – I knew you had a notion when you went away! Turkey said it was a poem.'

'I've found out how houses are built. Le' me get up. The floor-joists of one room are the ceiling-joists of the room below.'

'Don't be so filthy technical.'

'Well, the man told me. The floor is laid on top of those joists – those boards on edge that we crawled over – but the floor stops at a partition. Well, if you get behind a partition, same as you did in the attic, don't you see that you can shove anything you please under the floor between the floorboards and the lath and plaster of the ceiling below? Look here. I've drawn it.'

He produced a rude sketch, sufficient to enlighten the allies. There is no part of the modern school curriculum that deals with architecture, and none of them had yet reflected whether floors and ceilings were hollow or solid. Outside his own immediate interests the boy is as ignorant as the savage he so admires; but he has also the savage's resource.

'I see,' said Stalky. 'I shoved my hand there. An' then?'

'An' then They've been calling us stinkers, you know. We might shove somethin' under – sulphur, or something that stunk pretty bad – an' stink 'em out. I know it can be done somehow.' Beetle's eyes turned to Stalky handling the diagrams.

'Stinks?' said Stalky interrogatively. Then his face grew luminous with delight. 'By gum! I've got it. Horrid stinks! Turkey!' He leaped at the Irishman. 'This afternoon – just after Beetle went away! *She's* the very thing!'

'Come to my arms, my beamish boy,' carolled McTurk, and they fell into each other's arms dancing. 'Oh, frabjous day! Calloo, callay! She will! She will!'

'Hold on,' said Beetle. 'I don't understand.'

'Dearr man! It shall, though. Oh, Artie, my pure-souled youth, let us tell our darling Reggie about Pestiferous Stinkadores.'

'Not until after call-over. Come on!'

'I say,' said Orrin, stiffly, as they fell into their places along the walls of the gymnasium. 'The house are goin' to hold another meeting.'

'Hold away, then.' Stalky's mind was elsewhere.

'It's about you three this time.'

'All right, give 'em my love . . . *Here, sir*,' and he tore down the corridor.

Gambolling like kids at play, with bounds and side starts, with caperings and curvetings, they led the almost bursting Beetle to the rabbit-lane, and from under a pile of stones drew forth the new-slain corpse of a cat. Then did Beetle see the inner meaning of what had gone before, and lifted up his voice in thanksgiving for that the world held warriors so wise as Stalky and McTurk.

'Well-nourished old lady, ain't she?' said Stalky. 'How long d'you suppose it'll take her to get a bit whiff in a confined space?'

'Bit whiff! What a coarse brute you are!' said McTurk. 'Can't a poor pussy-cat get under King's dormitory floor to die without your pursuin' her with your foul innuendoes?'

'What did she die under the floor for?' said Beetle, looking to the future.

'Oh, they won't worry about that when they find her,' said Stalky.

'A cat may look at a king.' McTurk rolled down the bank at his own jest. 'Pussy, you don't know how useful you're goin' to be to three pure-souled, high-minded boys.'

'They'll have to take up the floor for her, same as they did in number nine when the rat croaked. Big medicine – heap big medicine! Phew! Oh, Lord, I wish I could stop laughin',' said Beetle.

'Stinks! Hi, stinks! Clammy ones!' McTurk gasped as he regained his place. 'And' – the exquisite humour of it brought them sliding down together in a tangle – 'it's all for the honour of the house, too!'

'An' they're holdin' another meeting – on us,' Stalky panted, his knees in the ditch and his face in the long grass. 'Well, let's get the bullet out of her and hurry up. The sooner she's bedded out the better.'

Between them they did some grisly work with a penknife; between them (ask not who buttoned her to his bosom) they took up the corpse and hastened back, Stalky arranging their plan of action at the full trot.

The afternoon sun, lying in broad patches on the bed-rugs, saw three boys and an umbrella disappear into a dormitory wall. In five minutes they emerged, brushed themselves all over, washed their hands, combed their hair, and descended.

'Are you sure you shoved her far enough under?' said McTurk suddenly.

'Hang it, man, I shoved her the full length of my arm and Beetle's brolly. That must be about six feet. She's bung in the middle of King's big upper ten-bedder. Eligible central situation, *I* call it. She'll stink out his chaps, and Hartopp's and Macrea's, when she really begins to fume. I swear your Uncle Stalky is a great man. Do you realise what a great man he is, Beetle?'

'Well, I had the notion first, hadn't I – ? Only – '

'You couldn't do it without your Uncle Stalky, could you?'

'They've been calling us stinkers for a week now,' said McTurk. 'Oh, *won't* they catch it!'

'Stinker! Yah! Stink–ah!' rang down the corridor.

'And she's there,' said Stalky, a hand on either boy's shoulder. 'She – is – there, gettin' ready to surprise 'em. Presently she'll begin to whisper to 'em in their dreams. Then she'll whiff. Golly, how she'll whiff! Oblige me by thinkin' of it for two minutes.'

They went to their study in more or less of silence. There they began to laugh – laugh as only boys can. They laughed with their foreheads on the tables, or on the floor; laughed at length, curled over the backs of chairs or clinging to a bookshelf; laughed themselves limp.

And in the middle of it Orrin entered on behalf of the house. 'Don't mind us, Orrin; sit down. You don't know how we respect and admire you. There's something about your pure, high young forehead, full of the dreams of innocent boyhood, that's no end fetchin'. It is, indeed.'

'The house sent me to give you this.' He laid a folded sheet of paper on the table and retired with an awful front.

'It's the resolution! Oh, read it, someone. I'm too silly-sick with laughin' to see,' said Beetle. Stalky jerked it open with a precautionary sniff. 'Phew! Phew! Listen. "*The house notices with pain and contempt the attitude of indifference*" – how many f's in indifference, Beetle?'

'Two for choice.'

'Only one here – "*adopted by the occupants of number five study in relation to the insults offered to Mr Prout's house at the recent meeting in number twelve form-room, and the house hereby pass a vote of censure on the said study*". That's all.'

'And she bled all down my shirt, too!' said Beetle.

'An' I'm catty all over,' said McTurk, 'though I washed twice.'

'An' I nearly broke Beetle's brolly plantin' her where she would blossom!'

The situation was beyond speech, but not laughter. There was some attempt that night to demonstrate against the three in their dormitory; so they came forth.

'You see,' Beetle began suavely as he loosened his braces, 'the trouble with you is that you're a set of unthinkin' asses. You've no more brains than spidgers. We've told you that heaps of times, haven't we?'

'We'll give the three of you a dormitory lickin'. You always jaw at us as if you were prefects,' cried one.

'Oh, no, you won't,' said Stalky, 'because you know that if you did you'd get the worst of it sooner or later. *We* aren't in any hurry. We can afford to wait for our little revenges. You've made howlin' asses of yourselves, and just as soon as King gets hold of your precious resolutions tomorrow you'll find that out. If you aren't sick an' sorry by tomorrow night, I'll – I'll eat my hat.'

But when the dinner-bell rang the next day Prout's were sadly aware of their error. King received stray members of that house with an exaggerated attitude of fear. Did they purpose to cause him to be dismissed from the college by unanimous resolution? What were their views concerning the government of the school, that he might hasten to give effect to them? He would not offend them for worlds; but he feared – he sadly feared – that his own house, who did not pass resolutions (but washed), might somewhat deride.

King was a happy man, and his house, basking in the favour of his smile, made that afternoon a long penance to the misled Prout's. And Prout himself, with a dull and lowering visage, tried to think out the rights and wrongs of it all, only plunging deeper into bewilderment. Why should his house be called 'Stinkers'? Truly, it was a small thing, but he had been trained to believe that straws show which way the wind blows, and that there is no smoke without fire. He approached King in common room with a sense of injustice, but King was pleased to be full of airy persiflage that tide, and brilliantly danced dialectical rings round Prout.

'Now,' said Stalky at bedtime, making pilgrimage through the dormitories before the prefects came by, '*now* what have you got to say for yourselves? Foster, Carton, Finch, Longbridge, Marlin, Brett! I heard you chaps catchin' it from King – he made hay of you – an' all you could do was to wriggle an' grin an' say, "Yes, sir", an' "No, sir", an' "O, sir", an' "Please, sir"! You an' your resolution! Urh!'

'Oh, shut up, Stalky.'

'Not a bit of it. You're a gaudy lot of resolutionists, you are! You've made a sweet mess of it. Perhaps you'll have the decency to leave us alone next time.'

Here the house grew angry, and in many voices pointed out how this blunder would never have come to pass if number five study had helped them from the first.

'But you chaps are so beastly conceited, an' – an' you swaggered into the meetin' as if we were a lot of idiots,' growled Orrin of the resolution.

'That's precisely what you are! That's what we've been tryin' to hammer into your thick heads all this time,' said Stalky. 'Never mind, we'll forgive you. Cheer up. You can't help bein' asses, you know,' and, the enemy's flank deftly turned, Stalky hopped into bed.

That night was the first of sorrow among the jubilant King's. By some accident of underfloor drafts the cat did not vex the dormitory beneath which she lay, but the next one to the right; stealing on the air rather as a pale-blue sensation than as any poignant offence. But the mere adumbration of an odour is enough for the sensitive nose and clean tongue of youth. Decency demands that we draw several carbolised sheets over what the dormitory said to Mr King and what Mr King replied. He was genuinely proud of his house and fastidious in all that concerned their well-being. He came; he sniffed; he said things. Next morning a boy in that dormitory confided to his bosom friend, a fag of Macrea's, that there was trouble in their midst which King would fain keep secret.

But Macrea's boy had also a bosom friend in Prout's, a shock-headed fag of malignant disposition, who, when he had wormed out the secret, told – told it in a high-pitched treble that rang along the corridor like a bat's squeak.

'An' – an' they've been calling us "stinkers" all this week. Why, Harland minor says they simply can't sleep in his dormitory for the stink. Come on!'

'With one shout and with one cry' Prout's juniors hurled themselves into the war, and through the interval between first and second lesson some fifty twelve-year-olds were embroiled on the gravel outside King's windows to a tune whose *leit-motif* was the word 'stinker.'

'Hark to the minute-gun at sea!' said Stalky. They were in their study collecting books for second lesson – Latin, with King. 'I thought his azure brow was a bit cloudy at prayers.

> She is comin', sister Mary.
> She is – '

'If they make such a row now, what will they do when she really begins to look up an' take notice?'

'Well, no vulgar repartee, Beetle. All we want is to keep out of this row like gentlemen.'

' " 'Tis but a little faded flower." Where's my Horace? Look here, I don't understand what she means by stinkin' out Rattray's dormitory first. We holed in under White's, didn't we?' asked McTurk, with a wrinkled brow.

'Skittish little thing. She's rompin' about all over the place, I suppose.'

'My aunt! King'll be a cheerful customer at second lesson. I haven't prepared my Horace one little bit, either,' said Beetle. 'Come on!'

They were outside the form-room door now. It was within five minutes of the bell, and King might arrive at any moment.

Turkey elbowed into a cohort of scuffling fags, cut out Thornton tertius (he that had been Harland's bosom friend), and bade him tell his tale.

It was a simple one, interrupted by tears. Many of King's house trod already battered him for libel.

'Oh, it's nothing,' McTurk cried. 'He says that King's house stinks. That's all.'

'Stale!' Stalky shouted. 'We knew that years ago, only we didn't choose to run about shoutin' "stinker". We've got some manners, if they haven't. Catch a fag, Turkey, and make sure of it.'

Turkey's long arm closed on a hurried and anxious ornament of the Lower Second.

'Oh, McTurk, please let me go. I don't stink – I swear I don't!'

'Guilty conscience!' cried Beetle. 'Who said you did?'

'What d'you make of it?' Stalky punted the small boy into Beetle's arms.

'Snf! Snf! He does, though. I think it's leprosy – or thrush. P'raps it's both. Take it away.'

'Indeed, Master Beetle' – King generally came to the house-door for a minute or two as the bell rang – 'we are vastly indebted to you for your diagnosis, which seems to reflect almost as much credit on the natural unwholesomeness of your mind as it does upon your pitiful ignorance of the diseases of which you discourse so glibly. We will, however, test your knowledge in other directions.'

That was a merry lesson, but, in his haste to scarify Beetle, King clean neglected to give him an imposition, and since at the same time he supplied him with many priceless adjectives for later use, Beetle was well content, and applied himself most seriously throughout third lesson (algebra with little Hartopp) to composing a poem entitled 'The Lazar-house.'

After dinner King took his house to bathe in the sea off the Pebbleridge. It was an old promise; but he wished he could have evaded it, for all Prout's lined up by the fives court and cheered with intention. In his absence, not less than half the school invaded the infected dormitory to draw their own conclusions. The cat had gained in the last twelve hours, but a battlefield of the fifth day could not have been so flamboyant as the spies reported.

'My word, she *is* doin' herself proud,' said Stalky. 'Did you ever smell anything like it? Ah, an' she isn't under White's dormitory at all yet.'

'But she will be. Give her time,' said Beetle. 'She'll twine like a giddy honeysuckle. What howlin' Lazarites they are! No house is justified in makin' itself a stench in the nostrils of decent – '

'High-minded, pure-souled boys. Do you burn with remorse and regret?' said McTurk, as they hastened to meet the house coming up from the sea. King had deserted it, so speech was unfettered. Round its front played a crowd of skirmishers – all houses mixed – flying, reforming, shrieking insults. On its tortured flanks marched the Hoplites, seniors hurling jests one after another – simple and primitive jests of the Stone Age. To these the three added themselves, dispassionately, with an air of aloofness, almost sadly.

'And they look all right, too,' said Stalky. 'It can't be Rattray, can it? Rattray?'

No answer.

'Rattray, dear? He seems stuffy about something or other. Look here, old man, we don't bear any malice about your sending that soap to us last week, do we? Be cheerful, Rat. You can live this down all right. I dare say it's only a few fags. Your house is so beastly slack, though.'

'You aren't going back to the house, are you?' said McTurk. The victims desired nothing better. 'You've simply no conception of the reek up there. Of course, frowzin' as you do, you wouldn't notice it; but, after this nice wash and the clean, fresh air, even you'd be upset. Much better camp on the Burrows. We'll get you some straw. Shall we?' The house hurried in to the tune of 'John Brown's body', sung by loving schoolmates, and barricaded themselves in their form-room. Straightway Stalky chalked a large cross, with 'Lord, have mercy upon us', on the door, and left King to find it.

The wind shifted that night and wafted a carrion-reek into Macrea's dormitories; so that boys in nightgowns pounded on the locked door between the houses, entreating King's to wash. Number five study went to second lesson with not more than half a pound of camphor apiece in their clothing; and King, too wary to ask for explanations, gibbered a while and hurled them forth. So Beetle finished yet another poem at peace in the study.

'They're usin' carbolic now. Malpas told me,' said Stalky. 'King thinks it's the drains.'

'She'll need a lot o' carbolic,' said McTurk. 'No harm tryin', I suppose. It keeps King out of mischief.'

'I swear I thought he was goin' to kill me when I sniffed just now. He didn't mind Burton major sniffin' at me the other day, though. He never stopped Alexander howlin' "Stinker!" into our form-room before – before we doctored 'em. He just grinned,' said Stalky. 'What was he frothing over you for, Beetle?'

'Aha! That, was my subtle jape. I had him on toast. You know he always jaws about the learned Lipsius.'

' "Who at the age of four" – that chap?' said McTurk.

'Yes. Whenever he hears I've written a poem. Well, just as I was sittin' down, I whispered, "How is our learned Lipsius?" to Burton major. Old Butt grinned like an owl. *He* didn't know what I was drivin' at; but King jolly well did. That was really why he hove us out. Ain't you grateful? Now shut up. I'm goin' to write the *Ballad of the Learned Lipsius*.'

'Keep clear of anything coarse, then,' said Stalky. 'I shouldn't like to be coarse on this happy occasion.'

'Not for wo–orlds. What rhymes to "stenches", someone?'

In common room at lunch King discoursed acridly to Prout of boys with prurient minds, who perverted their few and baleful talents to sap discipline and corrupt their equals, to deal in foul imagery and destroy reverence.

'But you didn't seem to consider this when your house called us – ah – stinkers. If you hadn't assured me that you never interfere with another man's house, I should almost believe that it was a few casual remarks of yours that started all this nonsense.'

Prout had endured much, for King always took his temper to meals.

'You spoke to Beetle yourself, didn't you? Something about not bathing, and being a water-funk?' the school chaplain put in. 'I was scoring in the pavilion that day.'

'I may have – jestingly. I really don't pretend to remember every remark I let fall among small boys; and full well I know the Beetle has no feelings to be hurt.'

'Maybe; but he, or they – it comes to the same thing – have the fiend's own knack of discovering a man's weak place. I confess I rather go out of my way to conciliate number five study. It may be soft, but so far, I believe, I am the only man here whom they haven't maddened by their – well – attentions.'

'That is all beside the point. I flatter myself I can deal with them alone as occasion arises. But if they feel themselves morally supported by those who should wield an absolute and open-handed justice, then I say that my lot is indeed a hard one. Of all things I detest, I admit that anything verging on disloyalty among ourselves is the first.'

The common room looked at one another out of the corners of their eyes, and Prout blushed.

'I deny it absolutely,' he said. 'Er – in fact, I own that I personally object to all three of them. It is not fair, therefore, to – '

'How long do you propose to allow it?' said King.

'But surely,' said Macrea, deserting his usual ally, 'the blame, if there be any, rests with you, King. You can't hold them responsible for the – you prefer the good old Anglo-Saxon, I believe – stink in your house. My boys are complaining of it now.'

'What can you expect? You know what boys are. Naturally they take advantage of what to them is a heaven-sent opportunity,' said little Hartopp. 'What *is* the trouble in your dormitories, King?'

Mr King explained that as he had made it the one rule of his life never to interfere with another man's house, so he expected not to be too patently interfered with. They might be interested to learn – here the chaplain heaved a weary sigh – that he had taken all steps that, in his poor judgement, would meet the needs of the case. Nay, further, he had himself expended, with no thought of reimbursement, sums, the amount of which he would not specify, on disinfectants. This he had done because he knew by bitter – by most bitter – experience that the management of the college was slack, dilatory, and inefficient. He might even add, almost as slack as the administration of certain houses which now thought fit to sit in judgement on his actions. With a short summary of his scholastic career, and a precis of his qualifications, including his degrees, he withdrew, slamming the door.

'Heigho!' said the chaplain. 'Ours is a dwarfing life – a belittling life, my brethren. God help all schoolmasters! They need it.'

'I don't like the boys, I own' – Prout dug viciously with his fork into the tablecloth – 'and I don't pretend to be a strong man, as you know. But I confess I can't see any reason why I should take steps against Stalky and the others because King happens to be annoyed by – by – '

'Falling into the pit he has digged,' said little Hartopp. 'Certainly not, Prout. No one accuses you of setting one house against another through sheer idleness.'

'A belittling life – a belittling life.' The chaplain rose. 'I go to correct French exercises. By dinner King will have scored off some unlucky child of thirteen; he will repeat to us every word of his brilliant repartees, and all will be well.'

'But about those three. Are they so prurient-minded?'

'Nonsense,' said little Hartopp. 'If you thought for a minute, Prout, you would see that the "precocious flow of fetid imagery", that King complains of, is borrowed wholesale from King. He "nursed the pinion that impelled the steel". Naturally he does not approve. Come into the smoking-room for a minute. It isn't fair to listen to boys; but they should be now rubbing it into King's house outside. Little things please little minds.'

The dingy den off the common room was never used for anything except gowns. Its windows were ground glass; one could not see out of it, but one could hear almost every word on the gravel outside. A light and wary footstep came up from number five.

'Rattray!' in a subdued voice – Rattray's study fronted that way. 'D'you know if Mr King's anywhere about? I've got a –.' McTurk discreetly left the end of the sentence open.

'No; he's gone out,' said Rattray unguardedly.

'Ah! The learned Lipsius is airing himself, is he? His Royal Highness has gone to fumigate.' McTurk climbed on the railings, where he held forth like the never-wearied rook.

'Now in all the coll. there was no stink like the stink of King's house, for it stank vehemently and none knew what to make of it. Save King. And he washed the fags *privatim et seriatim*. In the fishpools of Hesbon washed he them, with an apron about his loins.'

'Shut up, you mad Irishman!' There was the sound of a golf ball spurting up gravel.

'It's no good getting wrathy, Rattray. We've come to jape with you. Come on, Beetle. They're all at home. You can wind 'em.'

'Where's the Pomposo Stinkadore? 'Tisn't safe for a pure-souled, high-minded boy to be seen round his house these days. Gone out, has he? Never mind. I'll do the best I can, Rattray. I'm *in loco parentis* just now.'

('One for you, Prout,' whispered Macrea, for this was Mr Prout's pet phrase.)

'I have a few words to impart to you, my young friend. We will discourse together a while.'

Here the listening Prout sputtered: Beetle, in a strained voice, had chosen a favourite gambit of King's.

'I repeat, Master Rattray, we will confer, and the matter of our discourse shall not be stinks, for that is a loathsome and obscene word. We will, with your good leave – granted, I trust, Master Rattray, granted, I trust – study this – this scabrous upheaval of latent demoralisation. What impresses me most is not so much the blatant indecency with which you swagger abroad under your load of putrescence' (you must imagine this discourse punctuated with golf balls, but old Rattray was ever a bad shot) 'as the cynical immorality with which you revel in your abhorrent aromas. Far be it from me to interfere with another's house –'

('Good Lord!' said Prout, 'but this is King.'

'Line for line, letter for letter; listen,' said little Hartopp.)

'But to say that you stink, as certain lewd fellows of the baser sort aver, is to say nothing – less than nothing. In the absence of your beloved housemaster, for whom no one has a higher regard than myself, I will, if you will allow me, explain the grossness – the unparalleled enormity – the appalling fetor of the stenches (I believe in the good old Anglo-Saxon word), stenches, sir, with which you have seen fit to infect your house ... Oh, bother! I've forgotten the rest, but it was very beautiful. Aren't you grateful to us for labourin' with you this way, Rattray? Lots of chaps 'ud never have taken the trouble, but we're grateful, Rattray.'

'Yes, we're horrid grateful,' grunted McTurk. 'We don't forget that soap. We're polite. Why ain't you polite, Rat?'

'Hullo!' Stalky cantered up, his cap over one eye. 'Exhortin' the Whiffers, eh? I'm afraid they're too far gone to repent. Rattray! White! Perowne! Malpas! No answer. This is distressin'. This is truly distressin'. Bring out your dead, you glandered lepers!'

'You think yourself funny, don't you?' said Rattray, stung from his dignity by this last. 'It's only a rat or something under the floor. We're going to have it up tomorrow.'

'Don't try to shuffle it off on a poor dumb animal, and dead, too. I loathe prevarication. 'Pon my soul, Rattray – '

'Hold on. The Hartoffles never said " 'Pon my soul" in all his little life,' said Beetle critically.

('Ah!' said Prout to little Hartopp.)

'Upon my word, sir, upon my word, sir, I expected better things of you, Rattray. Why can you not own up to your misdeeds like a man? Have *I* ever shown any lack of confidence in *you*?'

('It's not brutality,' murmured little Hartopp, as though answering a question no one had asked. 'It's boy; only boy.')

'And this was the house,' Stalky changed from a pecking, fluttering voice to tragic earnestness. 'This was the – the – open cesspit that dared to call us "stinkers". And now – and now, it tries to shelter itself behind a dead rat. You annoy me, Rattray. You disgust me! You irritate me unspeakably! Thank heaven, I am a man of equable temper – '

('This is to your address, Macrea,' said Prout.

'I fear so, I fear so.')

'Or I should scarcely be able to contain myself before your mocking visage.'

'*Cave!*' in an undertone. Beetle had spied King sailing down the corridor.

'And what may you be doing here, my little friends?' the housemaster began. 'I had a fleeting notion – correct me if I am wrong' (the listeners with one accord choked) – 'that if I found you outside my house I should visit you with dire pains and penalties.'

'We were just goin' for a walk, sir,' said Beetle.

'And you stopped to speak to Rattray *en route*?'

'Yes, sir. We've been throwing golf balls,' said Rattray, coming out of the study.

('Old Rat is more of a diplomat than I thought. So far he is strictly within the truth,' said little Hartopp. 'Observe the ethics of it, Prout.')

'Oh, you were sporting with them, were you? I must say I do not envy you your choice of associates. I fancied they might have been engaged in some of the prurient discourse with which they have been so disgustingly free of late. I should strongly advise you to direct your steps most carefully in the future. Pick up those golf balls.' He passed on.

* * *

Next day Richards, who had been a carpenter in the Navy, and to whom odd jobs were confided, was ordered to take up a dormitory floor; for Mr King held that something must have died there.

'We need not neglect all our work for a trumpery incident of this nature; though I am quite aware that little things please little minds. Yes, I have decreed the boards to be taken up after lunch under Richards's auspices. I have no doubt it will be vastly interesting to a certain type of so-called intellect; but any boy of my house or another's found on the dormitory stairs will *ipso facto* render himself liable to three hundred lines.'

The boys did not collect on the stairs, but most of them waited outside King's. Richards had been bound to cry the news from the attic window, and, if possible, to exhibit the corpse.

' 'Tis a cat, a dead cat!' Richards's face showed purple at the window. He had been in the chamber of death and on his knees for some time.

'Cat be blowed!' cried McTurk. 'It's a dead fag left over from last term. Three cheers for King's dead fag!'

They cheered lustily.

'Show it, show it! Let's have a squint at it!' yelled the juniors. 'Give her to the Bug-hunters.' (This was the Natural History Society.) 'The cat looked at the King – and died of it! Hoosh! Yai! Yaow! Maiow! Ftzz!' were some of the cries that followed.

Again Richards appeared.

'She've been' – he checked himself suddenly – 'dead a long taime.'

The school roared.

'Well, come on out for a walk,' said Stalky in a well-chosen pause. 'It's all very disgustin', and I do hope the Lazar-house won't do it again.'

'Do what?' a King's boy cried furiously.

'Kill a poor innocent cat every time you want to get off washing. It's awfully hard to distinguish between you as it is. I prefer the cat, I must say. She isn't quite so whiff. What are you goin' to do, Beetle?'

'*Je vais gloater. Je vais gloater tout le* blessed afternoon. *Jamais j'ai gloaté comme je gloaterai aujourd'hui. Nous bunkerons aux* bunkers.'

And it seemed good to them so to do.

* * *

Down in the basement, where the gas flickers and the boots stand in racks, Richards, amid his blacking-brushes, held forth to Oke of the common room, Gumbly of the dining-halls, and fair Lena of the laundry.

'Yiss. Her were in a shockin' staate an' condition. Her nigh made me sick, I tal 'ee. But I rowted un out, and I rowted un out, an' I made all shipshape, though her smelt like to bilges.'

'Her died mousin', I reckon, poor thing,' said Lena.

'Then her moused different to any made cat o' God's world, Lena. I up with the top-board, an' she were lying on her back, an' I turned un ovver with the brume-handle, an' 'twas her back was all covered with the plaster from 'twixt the lathin'. Yiss, I tal 'ee. An' under her head there lay, like, so's to say, a little pillow o' plaster druv up in front of her by raison of her slidin' along on her back. No cat niver went mousin' on her back, Lena. Some one had shoved her along right underneath, so far as they could shove un. Cats don't make theyselves pillows for to die on. Shoved along, she were, when she was settin' for to be cold, laike.'

'Oh, yeou'm too clever to live, Fatty. Yeou go get wed an' taught some sense,' said Lena, the affianced of Gumbly.

'Larned a little 'fore iver some maidens was born. Sarved in the Queen's Navy, I have, where yeou'm taught to use your eyes. Yeou go 'tend your own business, Lena.'

'Do 'ee mean what you'm been tellin' us?' said Oke.

'Ask me no questions, I'll give 'ee no lies. Bullethole clane thru from side to side, an' tu heart-ribs broke like withies. I seed un when I turned un ovver. They're clever, oh, they'm clever, but they'm not too clever for old Richards! 'Twas on the born tip o' my tongue to tell, tu, but . . . he said us niver washed, he did. Let his dom boys call us "stinkers", he did. Sarve un dom well raight, I say!'

Richards spat on a fresh boot and fell to his work, chuckling.

The Impressionists

They had dropped into the chaplain's study for a Saturday night smoke – all four housemasters – and the three briars and the one cigar reeking in amity proved the Revd John Gillett's good generalship. Since the discovery of the cat, King had been too ready to see affront where none was meant, and the Revd John, buffer-state and general confidant, had worked for a week to bring about a good understanding. He was fat, clean-shaven, except for a big moustache, of an imperturbable good temper, and, those who loved him least said, a guileful Jesuit. He smiled benignantly upon his handiwork – four sorely tried men talking without very much malice.

'Now remember,' he said, when the conversation turned that way, 'I impute nothing. But every time that heaven has taken direct steps against number five study, the issue has been more or less humiliating to the taker.'

'I can't admit that. I pulverise the egregious Beetle daily for his soul's good; and the others with him,' said King.

'Well, take your own case, King, and go back a couple of years. Do you remember when Prout and you were on their track for hutting and trespass, wasn't it? Have you forgotten Colonel Dabney?'

The others laughed. King did not care to be reminded of his career as a poacher.

'That was one instance. Again, when you had rooms below them – I always said that that was entering the lion's den – you turned them out.'

'For making disgusting noises. Surely, Gillett, you don't excuse – '

'All I say is that you turned them out. That same evening your study was wrecked.'

'By Rabbits-Eggs – most beastly drunk – from the road,' said King. 'What has that?'

The Revd John went on.

'Lastly, they conceive that aspersions are cast upon their personal cleanliness – a most delicate matter with all boys. Ve–ry good. Observe how, in each case, the punishment fits the crime. A week after your house calls them "stinkers", King, your house is, not to put too fine a point on it, stunk out by a dead cat who chooses to die in the one spot where she can annoy you most. Again the long arm of coincidence! *Summa*. You accuse them of trespass. Through some absurd chain of circumstances – they may or may not be at the other end of it – you and Prout are made to appear as trespassers. You evict them. For a time your study is made untenable. I have drawn the parallel in the last case. Well?'

'She was under the centre of White's dormitory,' said King. 'There are double floorboards there to deaden noise. No boy, even in my own house, could possibly have pried up the boards without leaving some trace – and Rabbits-Eggs was phenomenally drunk that other night.'

'They are singularly favoured by fortune. That is all I ever said. Personally, I like them immensely, and I believe I have a little of their confidence. I confess I like being called "padre". They are at peace with me; consequently I am not treated to bogus confessions of theft.'

'You mean Mason's case?' said Prout heavily. 'That always struck me as peculiarly scandalous. I thought the head should have taken up the matter more thoroughly. Mason may be misguided, but at least he is thoroughly sincere and means well.'

'I confess I cannot agree with you, Prout,' said the Revd John. 'He jumped at some silly tale of theft on their part; accepted another boy's evidence without, so far as I can see, any enquiry; and – frankly, I think he deserved all he got.'

'They deliberately outraged Mason's best feelings,' said Prout. 'A word to me on their part would have saved the whole thing. But they preferred to lure him on; to play on his ignorance of their characters – '

'That may be,' said King, 'but I don't like Mason. I dislike him for the very reason that Prout advances to his credit. He means well.'

'Our criminal tradition is not theft – among ourselves, at least,' said little Hartopp.

'For the head of a house that raided seven head of cattle from the innocent pot-wallopers of Northam, isn't that rather a sweeping statement?' said Macrae.

'Precisely so,' said Hartopp, unabashed. 'That, with gate-lifting, and a little poaching and hawk-hunting on the cliffs, is our salvation.'

'It does us far more harm as a school – ' Prout began.

'Than any hushed-up scandal could? Quite so. Our reputation among the farmers is most unsavoury. But I would much sooner deal with any amount of ingenious crime of that nature than – some other offences.'

'They may be all right, but they are unboylike, abnormal, and, in my opinion, unsound,' Prout insisted. 'The moral effect of their performances must pave the way for greater harm. It makes me doubtful how to deal with them. I might separate them.'

'You might, of course; but they have gone up the school together for six years. *I* shouldn't care to do it,' said Macrae.

'They use the editorial "we",' said King, irrelevantly. 'It annoys me. "Where's your prose, Corkran?" "Well, sir, we haven't quite done it yet". "We'll bring it in a minute", and so on. And the same with the others.'

'There's great virtue in that "we",' said little Hartopp. 'You know I take them for trig. McTurk may have some conception of the meaning of it; but Beetle is as the brutes that perish about sines and cosines. He copies serenely from Stalky, who positively rejoices in mathematics.'

'Why don't you stop it?' said Prout.

'It rights itself at the exams. Then Beetle shows up blank sheets, and trusts to his 'English' to save him from a fall. I fancy he spends most of his time with me in writing verse.'

'I wish to heaven he would transfer a little of his energy in that direction to elegiacs.' King jerked himself upright. 'He is, with the single exception of Stalky, the very vilest manufacturer of "barbarous hexameters" that I have ever dealt with.'

'The work is combined in that study,' said the chaplain. 'Stalky does the mathematics, McTurk the Latin, and Beetle attends to their English and French. At least, when he was in the sick-house last month – '

'Malingering,' Prout interjected.

'Quite possibly. I found a very distinct falling off in their *Roman d'un Jeune Homme Pauvre* translations.'

'I think it is profoundly immoral,' said Prout. 'I've always been opposed to the study system.'

'It would be hard to find any study where the boys don't help each other; but in number five the thing has probably been reduced to a system,' said little Hartopp. 'They have a system in most things.'

'They confess as much,' said the Revd John. 'I've seen McTurk being hounded up the stairs to elegise the 'Elegy in a Churchyard', while Beetle and Stalky went to punt-about.'

'It amounts to systematic cribbing,' said Prout, his voice growing deeper and deeper.

'No such thing,' little Hartopp returned. 'You can't teach a cow the violin.'

'In intention it is cribbing.'

'But we spoke under the seal of the confessional, didn't we?' said the Revd John.

'You say you've heard them arranging their work in this way, Gillett,' Prout persisted.

'Good heavens! Don't make me Queen's evidence, my dear fellow. Hartopp is equally incriminated. If they ever found out that I had sneaked, our relations would suffer – and I value them.'

'I think your attitude in this matter is weak,' said Prout, looking round for support. 'It would be really better to break up the study – for a while – wouldn't it?'

'Oh, break it up by all means,' said Macrae. 'We shall see then if Gillett's theory holds water.'

'Be wise, Prout. Leave them alone, or calamity will overtake you; and what is much more important, they will be annoyed with me. I am too fat, alas! to be worried by bad boys. Where are you going?'

'Nonsense! They would not dare – but I am going to think this out,' said Prout. 'It needs thought. In intention they cribbed, and I must think out my duty.'

'He's perfectly capable of putting the boys on their honour. It's *I* that am a fool.' The Revd John looked round remorsefully. 'Never again will I forget that a master is not a man. Mark my words,' said the Revd John. 'There will be trouble.'

* * *

But by the yellow Tiber
Was tumult and affright.

Out of the blue sky (they were still rejoicing over the cat war) Mr Prout had dropped into number five, read them a lecture on the enormity of cribbing, and bidden them return to the form-rooms on Monday. They had raged, solo and chorus, all through the peaceful Sabbath, for their sin was more or less the daily practice of all the studies.

'What's the good of cursing?' said Stalky at last. 'We're all in the same boat. We've got to go back and consort with the house. A locker in the form-room, and a seat at prep in number twelve.' (He looked regretfully round the cosy study which McTurk, their leader in matters of Art, had decorated with a dado, a stencil, and cretonne hangings.)

'Yes! Heffy lurchin' into the form-rooms like a frowzy old retriever, to see if we aren't up to something. You know he never leaves his house alone, these days,' said McTurk. 'Oh, it will be giddy!'

'Why aren't you down watchin' cricket? I like a robust, healthy boy. You mustn't frowst in a form-room. Why don't you take an interest in your house? Yah!' quoted Beetle.

'Yes, why don't we? Let's! We'll take an interest in the house. We'll take no end of interest in the house! He hasn't had us in the form-rooms for a year. We've learned a lot since then. Oh, we'll make it a be–autiful house before we've done! 'Member that chap in *Eric* or *St Winifred's* – Belial somebody? I'm goin' to be Belial,' said Stalky, with an ensnaring grin.

'Right O,' said Beetle, 'and I'll be Mammon. I'll lend money at usury – that's what they do at all schools accordin' to the *Boys' Own Paper*. Penny a week on a shillin'. That'll startle Heffy's weak intellect. You can be Lucifer, Turkey.'

'What have I got to do?' McTurk also smiled.

'Head conspiracies – and cabals – and boycotts. Go in for that "stealthy intrigue" that Heffy is always talkin' about. Come on!'

The house received them on their fall with the mixture of jest and sympathy always extended to boys turned out of their study. The known aloofness of the three made them more interesting.

'Quite like old times, ain't it?' Stalky selected a locker and flung in his books. 'We've come to sport with you, my young friends, for a while, because our beloved housemaster has hove us out of our diggin's.'

'Serve you jolly well right,' said Orrin, 'you cribbers!'

'This will never do,' said Stalky. 'We can't maintain our giddy prestige, Orrin, de–ah, if you make these remarks.'

They wrapped themselves lovingly about the boy, thrust him to the opened window, and drew down the sash to the nape of his neck. With an equal swiftness they tied his thumbs together behind his back with a piece of twine, and then, because he kicked furiously, removed his shoes. There Mr Prout happened to find him a few minutes later, guillotined and helpless, surrounded by a convulsed crowd who would not assist.

Stalky, in an upper form-room, had gathered himself allies against vengeance. Orrin presently tore up at the head of a boarding party, and the form-room grew one fog of dust through which boys wrestled, stamped, shouted, and yelled. A desk was carried away in the tumult, a knot of warriors reeled into and split a door-panel, a window was broken, and a gas-jet fell. Under cover of the confusion the three escaped to the corridor, whence they called in and sent up passers-by to the fray.

'Rescue, Kings! Kings! Kings! Number twelve form-room! Rescue, Prouts – Prouts! Rescue, Macraes! Rescue, Hartopps!'

The juniors hurried out like bees aswarm, asking no questions, clattered up the staircase, and added themselves to the embroilment.

'Not bad for the first evening's work,' said Stalky, rearranging his collar. 'I fancy Prout'll be somewhat annoyed. We'd better establish an alibi.' So they sat on Mr King's railings till prep.

'You see,' quoth Stalky, as they strolled up to prep with the ignoble herd, 'if you get the houses well mixed up an' scufflin', it's even bettin' that some ass will start a real row. Hullo, Orrin, you look rather metagrobolised.'

'It was all your fault, you beast! You started it. We've got two hundred lines apiece, and Heffy's lookin' for you. Just see what that swine Malpas did to my eye!'

'I like your saying we started it. Who called us cribbers? Can't your infant mind connect cause and effect yet? Some day you'll find out that it don't pay to jest with number five.'

'Where's that shillin' you owe me?' said Beetle suddenly.

Stalky could not see Prout behind him, but returned the lead without a quaver. 'I only owed you ninepence, you old usurer.'

'You've forgotten the interest,' said McTurk. 'A halfpenny a week per bob is Beetle's charge. You must be beastly rich, Beetle.'

'Well, Beetle lent me sixpence.' Stalky came to a full stop and made as to work it out on his fingers. 'Sixpence on the nineteenth, didn't he?'

'Yes; hut you've forgotten you paid no interest on the other bob – the one I lent you before.'

'But you took my watch as security.' The game was developing itself almost automatically.

'Never mind. Pay me my interest, or I'll charge you interest on interest. Remember, I've got your note-of-hand!' shouted Beetle.

'You are a cold-blooded Jew,' Stalky groaned.

'Hush!' said McTurk very loudly indeed, and started as Prout came upon them.

'I didn't see you in that disgraceful affair in the form-room just now,' said he.

'What, sir? We're just come up from Mr King's,' said Stalky. 'Please, sir, what am I to do about prep? They've broken the desk you told me to sit at, and the form's just swimming with ink.'

'Find another seat – find another seat. D'you expect me to dry-nurse you? I wish to know whether you are in the habit of advancing money to your associates, Beetle?'

'No, sir; not as a general rule, sir.'

'It is a most reprehensible habit. I thought that my house, at least, would be free from it. Even with my opinion of you, I hardly thought it was one of your vices.'

'There's no harm in lending money, sir, is there?'

'I am not going to bandy words with you on your notions of morality. How much have you lent Corkran?'

'I – I don't quite know,' said Beetle. It is difficult to improvise a going concern on the spur of the minute.

'You seemed certain enough just now.'

'I think it's two and fourpence,' said McTurk, with a glance of cold scorn at Beetle. In the hopelessly involved finances of the study there was just that sum to which both McTurk and Beetle laid claim, as their share in the pledging of Stalky's second-best Sunday trousers. But Stalky had maintained for two terms that the money was his 'commission' for effecting the pawn; and had, of course, spent it on a study 'brew'.

'Understand this, then. You are not to continue your operations as a moneylender. Two and fourpence, you said, Corkran?'

Stalky had said nothing, and continued so to do.

'Your influence for evil is quite strong enough without buying a hold over your companions.' He felt in his pockets, and (oh joy!) produced a florin and fourpence. 'Bring me what you call Corkran's note-of-hand, and be thankful that I do not carry the matter any further. The money is stopped from your pocket money, Corkran. The receipt to my study, at once!'

Little they cared! Two and fourpence in a lump is worth six weekly sixpences any hungry day of the week.

'But what the deuce is a note-of-hand?' said Beetle. 'I only read about it in a book.'

'Now you've jolly well got to make one,' said Stalky.

'Yes – but our ink don't turn black till next day. S'pose he'll spot that?'

'Not him. He's too worried,' said McTurk. 'Sign your name on a bit of impot-paper, Stalky, and write, "IOU two and fourpence." Aren't you grateful to me for getting that out of Prout? Stalky'd never have paid . . . Why, you ass!'

Mechanically Beetle had handed over the money to Stalky as treasurer of the study. The custom of years is not lightly broken. In return for the document, Prout expounded to Beetle the enormity of moneylending, which, like everything except compulsory cricket, corrupted houses and destroyed good feeling among boys, made youth cold and calculating, and opened the door to all evil. Finally, did Beetle know of any other cases? If so, it was his duty as proof of repentance to let his housemaster know. No names need be mentioned.

Beetle did not know – at least, he was not quite sure, sir. How could he give evidence against his friends? The house might, of course – here he feigned an anguished delicacy – be full of it. He was not in a position to say. He had not met with any open competition in his trade; but if Mr Prout considered it was a matter that affected the honour of the house (Mr Prout did consider it precisely that), perhaps the house-prefects would be better . . .

He spun it out till halfway through prep.

'And,' said the amateur Shylock, returning to the form-room and dropping at Stalky's side, 'if he don't think the house is putrid with it, I'm several Dutchmen – that's all . . . I've been to Mr Prout's study, sir.' This to the prepmaster. 'He said I could sit where I liked, sir . . . Oh, he is just tricklin' with emotion . . . Yes, sir, I'm only askin' Corkran to let me have a dip in his ink.'

After prayers, on the road to the dormitories, Harrison and Craye, senior house-prefects, zealous in their office, waylaid them with great anger. 'What have you been doing to Heffy this time, Beetle? He's been jawing us all the evening.'

'What has His Serene Transparency been vexin' you for?' said McTurk.

'About Beetle lendin' money to Stalky,' began Harrison; 'and then Beetle went and told him that there was any amount of money lendin' in the house.'

'No, you don't,' said Beetle, sitting on a boot-basket. 'That's just what I didn't tell him. I spoke the giddy truth. He asked me if there was much of it in the house; and I said I didn't know.'

'He thinks you're a set of filthy Shylocks,' said McTurk. 'It's just as well for you he don't think you're burglars. You know he never gets a notion out of his conscientious old head.'

'Well-meanin' man. Did it all for the best.' Stalky curled gracefully round the stair-rail. 'Head in a drainpipe. Full confession in the left boot. Bad for the honour of the house – very.'

'Shut up,' said Harrison. 'You chaps always behave as if you were jawin' us when we come to jaw you.'

'You're a lot too cheeky,' said Craye.

'I don't quite see where the cheek comes in, except on your part, in interferin' with a private matter between me an' Beetle after it has been settled by Prout.' Stalky winked cheerfully at the others.

'That's the worst of clever little swots,' said McTurk, addressing the gas. 'They get made prefects before they have any tact, and then they annoy chaps who could really help 'em to look after the honour of the house.'

'We won't trouble you to do that!' said Craye hotly.

'Then what are you badgerin' us for?' said Beetle. 'On your own showing, you've been so beastly slack, looking after the house, that Prout believes it's a nest of moneylenders. I've told him that I've lent money to Stalky, and no one else. I don't know whether he believes me, but that finishes my case. The rest is your business.'

'Now we find out,' Stalky's voice rose, 'that there is apparently an organised conspiracy throughout the house. For aught we know, the fags may be lendin' and borrowin' far beyond their means. We aren't responsible for it. We're only the rank and file.'

'Are you surprised we don't wish to associate with the house?' said McTurk, with dignity. 'We've kept ourselves to ourselves in our study till we were turned out, and now we find ourselves let in for this sort of thing. It's simply disgraceful.'

'Then you hector and bullyrag us on the stairs,' said Stalky, 'about matters that are your business entirely. You know we aren't prefects.'

'You threatened us with a prefect's lickin' just now,' said Beetle, boldly inventing as he saw the bewilderment in the faces of the enemy. 'And if you expect you'll gain anything from us by your way of approachin' us, you're jolly well mistaken. That's all. Good-night.'

They clattered upstairs, injured virtue on every inch of their backs.

'But – but what the dickens have we done?' said Harrison, amazedly, to Craye.

'I don't know. Only – it always happens that way when one has anything to do with them. They're so beastly plausible.'

And Mr Prout called the good boys into his study anew, and succeeded in sinking both his and their innocent minds ten fathoms deeper in blindfolded bedazement. He spoke of steps and measures, of tone and loyalty in the house and to the house, and urged them to take up the matter tactfully.

So they demanded of Beetle whether he had any connection with any other establishment. Beetle promptly went to his housemaster, and wished to know by what right Harrison and Craye had reopened a matter already settled between him and his housemaster. In injured innocence no boy excelled Beetle.

Then it occurred to Prout that he might have been unfair to the culprit, who had not striven to deny or palliate his offence. He sent for Harrison and Craye, reprehending them very gently for the tone they had adopted to a repentant sinner, and when they returned to their study, they used the language of despair. They then made headlong inquisition through the house, driving the fags to the edge of hysterics, and unearthing, with tremendous pomp and parade, the natural and inevitable system of small loans that prevails among small boys.

'You see, Harrison, Thornton minor lent me a penny last Saturday, because I was fined for breaking the window; and I spent it at Keyte's. I didn't know there was any harm in it. And Wray major borrowed twopence from me when my uncle sent me a post-office order – I cashed it at Keyte's – for five bob; but he'll pay me back before the holidays. We didn't know there was anything wrong in it.'

They waded through hours of this kind of thing, but found no usury, or anything approaching to Beetle's gorgeous scale of interest. The seniors – for the school had no tradition of deference to prefects outside compulsory games – told them succinctly to go about their business. They would not give evidence on any terms. Harrison was one idiot, and Craye was another; but the greatest of all, they said, was their housemaster.

When a house is thoroughly upset, however good its conscience, it breaks into knots and coteries – small gatherings in the twilight, box-room committees, and groups in the corridor. And when from group to group, with an immense affectation of secrecy, three wicked boys steal, crying '*Cave*' when there is no need of caution, and whispering 'Don't tell!' on the heels of trumpery confidences that instant invented, a very fine air of plot and intrigue can be woven round such a house.

At the end of a few days, it dawned on Prout that he moved in an atmosphere of perpetual ambush. Mysteries hedged him on all sides, warnings ran before his heavy feet, and countersigns were muttered behind his attentive back. McTurk and Stalky invented many absurd and idle phrases – catchwords that swept through the house as fire through stubble. It was a rare jest, and the only practical outcome of the Usury Commission, that one boy should say to a friend, with awful gravity, 'Do you think there's much of it going on in the house?' The other would reply, 'Well, one can't be too careful, you know.' The effect on a housemaster of humane conscience and good intent may be imagined. Again, a man who has sincerely devoted himself to gaining the esteem of his charges does not like to hear himself described, even at a distance, as 'Popularity Prout' by a dark and scowling Celt with a fluent tongue. A rumour that stories – unusual stories – are told in the form-rooms, between the lights, by a boy who does not command his confidence, agitates such a man; and even elaborate and tender politeness – for the courtesy wise-grown men offer to a bewildered child was the courtesy that Stalky wrapped round Prout – restores not his peace of mind.

'The tone of the house seems changed – changed for the worse,' said Prout to Harrison and Craye. 'Have you noticed it? I don't for an instant impute – '

He never imputed anything; but, on the other hand, he never did anything else, and, with the best intentions in the world, he had reduced the house-prefects to a state as nearly bordering on nervous irritation as healthy boys can know. Worst of all, they began at times to wonder whether Stalky & Co. had not some truth in their often-repeated assertions that Prout was a gloomy ass.

'As you know, I am not the kind of man who puts himself out for every little thing he hears. I believe in letting the house work out their own salvation – with a light guiding hand on the reins, of course. But there is a perceptible lack of reverence – a lower tone in matters that touch the honour of the house, a sort of hardness.'

> 'Oh, Prout he is a nobleman, a nobleman, a nobleman!
> Our Heffy is a nobleman –
> He does an awful lot,
> Because his popularity
> Oh, pop–u–pop–u–larity –
> His giddy popularity
> Would suffer did he not!'

The study door stood ajar; and the song, borne by twenty clear voices, came faint from a form-room. The fags rather liked the tune; the words were Beetle's.

'That's a thing no sensible man objects to,' said Prout with a lopsided smile; 'but you know straws show which way the wind blows. Can you trace it to any direct influence? I am speaking to you now as heads of the house.'

'There isn't the least doubt of it,' said Harrison angrily. 'I know what you mean, sir. It all began when number five study came to the form-rooms. There's no use blinkin' it, Craye. You know that, too.'

'They make things rather difficult for us, sometimes,' said Craye. 'It's more their manner than anything else, that Harrison means.'

'Do they hamper you in the discharge of your duties, then?'

'Well, no, sir. They only look on and grin – and turn up their noses generally.'

'Ah,' said Prout sympathetically.

'I think, sir,' said Craye, plunging into the business boldly, 'it would be a great deal better if they wore sent back to their study – better for the house. They are rather old to be knocking about the form-rooms.'

'They are younger than Orrin, or Flint, and a dozen others that I can think of.'

'Yes, sir; but that's different, somehow. They're rather influential. They have a knack of upsettin' things in a quiet way that one can't take hold of. At least, if one does – '

'And you think they would be better in their own study again?'

Emphatically Harrison and Craye were of that opinion. As Harrison said to Craye, afterwards, 'They've weakened our authority. They're too big to lick; they've made an exhibition of us over this usury business, and we're a laughing stock to the rest of the school. I'm going up (for Sandhurst, understood) next term. They've managed to knock me out of half my work already with their – their lunacy. If they go back to their study we may have a little peace.'

'Hullo, Harrison.' McTurk ambled round the corner, with a roving eye on all possible horizons. 'Bearin' up, old man? That's right. Live it down! Live it down!'

'What d'you mean?'

'You look a little pensive,' said McTurk. 'Exhaustin' job superintendin' the honour of the house, ain't it? By the way, how are you off for mares'-nests?'

'Look here,' said Harrison, hoping for instant reward. 'We've recommended Prout to let you go back to your study.'

'The deuce you have! And who under the sun are *you* to interfere between us and our housemaster?. Upon my Sam, you two try us very hard – you do, indeed. Of course we don't know how far you abuse your position to prejudice us with Mr Prout; but when you deliberately stop me to tell me you've been makin' arrangements behind our back – in secret – with Prout – I – I don't know really what we ought to do.'

'That's beastly unfair! 'cried Craye.

'It is.' McTurk had adopted a ghastly solemnity that sat well on his long, lean face. 'Hang it all! A prefect's one thing and an usher's another; but you seem to combine 'em. You recommend this – you recommend that! *You* say how and when we go back to our study!'

'But – but – we thought you'd like it, Turkey. We did, indeed. You know you'll be ever so much more comfortable there.' Harrison's voice was almost tearful.

McTurk turned away as though to hide his emotions.

'They're broke!' He hunted up Stalky and Beetle in a boxroom. 'They're sick! They've been beggin' Heffy to let us go back to number five. Poor devils! Poor little devils!'

'It's the olive branch,' was Stalky's comment. 'It's the giddy white flag, by gum! Come to think of it, we *have* metagrobolised 'em.'

Just after tea that day, Mr Prout sent for them to say that if they chose to ruin their future by neglecting their work, it was entirely their own affair. He wished them, however, to understand that their presence in the form-rooms could not be tolerated one hour longer. He personally did not care to think of the time he must spend in eliminating the traces of their evil influences. How far Beetle had pandered to the baser side of youthful imagination he would ascertain later; and Beetle might be sure that if Mr Prout came across any soul-corrupting consequences –

'Consequences of what, sir?' said Beetle, genuinely bewildered this time; and McTurk quietly kicked him on the ankle for being 'fetched' by Prout. Beetle, the housemaster continued, knew very well what was intended. Evil and brief had been their careers under his eye; and as one standing *in loco parentis* to their yet uncontaminated associates, he was bound to take his precautions. The return of the study key closed the sermon.

'But what was the baser-side-of-imagination business?' said Beetle on the stairs.

'I never knew such an ass as you are for justifyin' yourself,' said McTurk. 'I hope I jolly well skinned your ankle. Why do you let yourself be drawn by everybody?'

'Drawn be blowed! I must have tickled him up in some way I didn't know about. If I'd had a notion of that before, of course I could have rubbed it in better. It's too late now. What a pity! "Baser side." What *was* he drivin' at?'

'Never mind,' said Stalky. 'I knew we could make it a happy little house. I said so, remember – but I swear I didn't think we'd do it so soon.'

'No,' said Prout most firmly in common room. 'I maintain that Gillett is wrong. True, I let them return to their study.'

'With your known views on cribbing, too?' purred little Hartopp. 'What an immoral compromise!'

'One moment,' said the Revd John. 'I – we – all of us have exercised an absolutely heartbreaking discretion for the last ten days. Now we want to know. Confess – have you known a happy minute since – '

'As regards my house, I have not,' said Prout. 'But you are entirely wrong in your estimate of those boys. In justice to the others – in self-defence – '

'Ha! I said it would come to that,' murmured the Revd John.

' – I was forced to send them back. Their moral influence was unspeakable – simply unspeakable.'

And bit by bit he told his tale, beginning with Beetle's usury, and ending with the house-prefects' appeal.

'Beetle in the role of Shylock is new to me,' said King, with twitching lips. 'I heard rumours of it – '

'Before?' said Prout.

'No, after you had dealt with them; but I was careful not to enquire. I never interfere with – '

'I myself,' said Hartopp, 'would cheerfully give him five shillings if he could work out one simple sum in compound interest without three gross errors.'

'Why – why – why!' Mason, the mathematical master, stuttered, a fierce joy on his face, 'you've been had – precisely the same as me!'

'And so you held an enquiry?' Little Hartopp's voice drowned Mason's ere Prout caught the import of the sentence.

'The boy himself hinted at the existence of a deal of it in the house,' said Prout.

'He is past master in that line,' said the chaplain. 'But, as regards the honour of the house – '

'They lowered it in a week. I have striven to build it up for years. My own house-prefects – and boys do not willingly complain of each other –

besought me to get rid of them. You say you have their confidence, Gillett: they may tell you another tale. As far as I am concerned, they may go to the devil in their own way. I'm sick and tired of them,' said Prout bitterly.

But it was the Revd John, with a smiling countenance, who went to the devil just after number five had cleared away a very pleasant little brew (it cost them two and fourpence) and was settling down to prep.

'Come in, padre, come in,' said Stalky, thrusting forward the best chair. 'We've only met you official-like these last ten days.'

'You were under sentence,' said the Revd John. 'I do not consort with malefactors.'

'Ah, but we're restored again,' said McTurk. 'Mr Prout has relented.'

'Without a stain on our characters,' said Beetle. 'It was a painful episode, padre, most painful.'

'Now, consider for a while, and perpend, *mes enfants*. It is about your characters that I've called tonight. In the language of the schools, what the deuce *have* you been up to in Mr Prout's house? It isn't anything to laugh over. He says that you so lowered the tone of the house he had to pack you back to your studies. Is that true?'

'Every word of it, padre.'

'Don't be flippant, Turkey. Listen to me. I've told you very often that no boys in the school have a greater influence for good or evil than you have. You know I don't talk about ethics and moral codes, because I don't believe that the young of the human animal realises what they mean for some years to come. All the same, I don't want to think you've been perverting the juniors. Don't interrupt, Beetle. Listen to me. Mr Prout has a notion that you have been corrupting your associates somehow or other.'

'Mr Prout has so many notions, padre,' said Beetle wearily. 'Which one is this?'

'Well, he tells me that he heard you telling a story in the twilight in the form-room, in a whisper. And Orrin said, just as he opened the door, "Shut up, Beetle, it's too beastly." Now then?'

'You remember Mrs Oliphant's "Beleaguered City" that you lent me last term?' said Beetle.

The padre nodded.

'I got the notion out of that. Only, instead of a city, I made it the coll. in a fog – besieged by ghosts of dead boys, who hauled chaps out of their beds in the dormitory. All the names are quite real. You tell it in a whisper, you know with the names. Orrin didn't like it one little bit. None of 'em have ever let me finish it. It gets just awful at the end part.'

'But why in the world didn't you explain to Mr Prout, instead of leaving him under the impression – ?'

'Padre sahib,' said McTurk, 'it isn't the least good explainin' to Mr Prout. If he hasn't one impression, he's bound to have another.'

'He'd do it with the best o' motives. He's *in loco parentis*,' purred Stalky.

'You young demons!' the Revd John replied. 'And am I to understand that the – the usury business was another of your housemaster's impressions?'

'Well – we helped a little in that,' said Stalky. 'I did owe Beetle two and fourpence. At least, Beetle says I did, but I never intended to pay him. Then we started a bit of an argument on the stairs, and – and Mr Prout dropped into it accidental. That was how it was, padre. He paid me cash down like a giddy Dook (stopped it out of my pocket money just the same), and Beetle gave him my note-of-hand all correct. I don't know what happened after that.'

'I was too truthful,' said Beetle. 'I always am. You see, he was under an impression, padre, and I suppose I ought to have corrected that impression; but of course I couldn't be *quite* certain that his house wasn't given over to money lendin', could I? I thought the house-prefects might know more about it than I did. They ought to. They're giddy palladiums of public schools.'

'They did, too – by the time they'd finished,' said McTurk. 'As nice a pair of conscientious, well-meanin', upright, pure-souled boys as you'd ever want to meet, padre. They turned the house upside down – Harrison and Craye – with the best motives in the world.'

'They said so.

> They said it very loud and clear.
> They went and shouted in our ear,'

said Stalky.

'My own private impression is that all three of you will infallibly be hanged,' said the Revd John.

'Why, we didn't do anything,' McTurk replied. 'It was all Mr Prout. Did you ever read a book about Japanese wrestlers? My uncle – he's in the navy – gave me a beauty once.'

'Don't try to change the subject, Turkey.'

'I'm not, sir. I'm givin' an illustration – same as a sermon. These wrestler-chaps have got some sort of trick that lets the other chap do all the work. Than they give a little wriggle, and he upsets himself. It's called *shibbuwichee* or *tokonoma*, or somethin'. Mr Prout's a *shibbuwicher*. It isn't our fault.'

'Did you suppose we went round corruptin' the minds of the fags?' said Beetle. 'They haven't any, to begin with; and if they had, they're corrupted long ago. I've been a fag, padre.'

'Well, I fancied I knew the normal range of your iniquities; but if you take so much trouble to pile up circumstantial evidence against yourselves, you can't blame any one if – '

'We don't blame any one, padre. We haven't said a word against Mr Prout, have we?' Stalky looked at the others. 'We love him. He hasn't a notion how we love him.'

'H'm! You dissemble your love very well. Have you ever thought who got you turned out of your study in the first place?'

'It was Mr Prout turned us out,' said Stalky, with significance.

'Well, I was that man. I didn't mean it; but some words of mine, I'm afraid, gave Mr Prout the impression – '

Number five laughed aloud.

'You see it's just the same thing with you, padre,' said McTurk. 'He is quick to get an impression, ain't he? But you mustn't think we don't love him, 'cause we do. There isn't an ounce of vice about him.'

A double knock fell on the door.

'The head to see number five study in his study at once,' said the voice of Foxy, the school sergeant.

'Whew!' said the Revd John. 'It seems to me that there is a great deal of trouble coming for some people.'

'My word! Mr Prout's gone and told the head,' said Stalky. 'He's a moral double-ender. Not fair, luggin' the head into a house-row.'

'I should recommend a copybook on a – h'm – safe and certain part,' said the Revd John disinterestedly.

'Huh! He licks across the shoulders, an' it would slam like a beastly barn-door,' said Beetle. 'Good-night, padre. We're in for it.'

Once more they stood in the presence of the head – Belial, Mammon, and Lucifer. But they had to deal with a man more subtle than them all. Mr Prout had talked to him, heavily and sadly, for half an hour; and the head had seen all that was hidden from the housemaster.

'You've been bothering Mr Prout,' he said pensively. 'Housemasters aren't here to be bothered by boys more than is necessary. I don't like being bothered by these things. You are bothering *me*. That is a very serious offence. You see it?'

'Yes, sir.'

'Well, now, I purpose to bother you, on personal and private grounds, because you have broken into my time. You are much too big to lick, so I suppose I shall have to mark my displeasure in some other way. Say, a thousand lines apiece, a week's gating, and a few things of that kind. Much too big to lick, aren't you?'

'Oh, no, sir,' said Stalky cheerfully; for a week's gating in the summer term is serious.

'Ve–ry good. Then we will do what we can. I wish you wouldn't bother me.'

It was a fair, sustained, equable stroke, with a little draw to it, but what they felt most was his unfairness in stopping to talk between executions. Thus: 'Among the – lower classes this would lay me open to a charge of – assault. You should be more grateful for your – privileges than you are. There is a limit – one finds it by experience, Beetle – beyond which it is never safe to pursue private vendettas, because – don't move – sooner or later one comes – into collision with the – higher authority, who has studied the animal. *Et ego* – McTurk, please – *in Arcadia vixi*. There's a certain flagrant injustice about this that ought to appeal to – your temperament. And that's all! You will tell your housemaster that you have been formally caned by me.'

'My word!' said McTurk, wriggling his shoulder-blades all down the corridor. 'That was business! The Prooshian Bates has an infernal straight eye.'

'Wasn't it wily of me to ask for the lickin',' said Stalky, 'instead of those impots?'

'Rot! We were in for it from the first. I knew the look of his old eye,' said Beetle. 'I was within an inch of blubbing.'

'Well, I didn't exactly smile,' Stalky confessed.

'Let's go down to the lavatory and have a look at the damage. One of us can hold the glass and t'others can squint.'

They proceeded on these lines for some ten minutes. The weals were very red and very level. There was not a penny to choose between any of them for thoroughness, efficiency, and a certain clarity of outline that stamps the work of the artist.

'What are you doing down there?' Mr Prout was at the head of the lavatory stairs, attracted by the noise of splashing.

'We've only been caned by the head, sir, and we're washing off the blood. The head said we were to tell you. We were coming to report ourselves in a minute, sir. (*Sotto voce*.) That's a score for Heffy!'

'Well, he deserves to score something, poor devil,' said McTurk, putting on his shirt. 'We've sweated a stone and a half off him since we began.'

'But look here, why aren't we wrathy with the head? He said it was a flagrant injustice. So it is!' said Beetle.

'Dear man,' said McTurk, and vouchsafed no further answer.

It was Stalky who laughed till he had to hold on by the edge of a basin.

'You *are* a funny ass! What's that for?' said Beetle.

'I'm – I'm thinking of the flagrant injustice of it!'

The Moral Reformers

There was no disguising the defeat. The victory was to Prout, but they grudged it not. If he had broken the rules of the game by calling in the head, they had had a good run for their money.

The Revd John sought the earliest opportunity of talking things over. Members of a bachelor common room, of a school where masters' studies are designedly dotted among studies and form-rooms, can, if they choose, see a great deal of their charges. Number five had spent some cautious years in testing the Revd John. He was emphatically a gentleman. He knocked at a study door before entering; he comported himself as a visitor and not a strayed lictor; he never prosed, and he never carried over into official life the confidences of idle hours. Prout was ever an unmitigated nuisance; King came solely as an avenger of blood; even little Hartopp, talking natural history, seldom forgot his office; but the Revd John was a guest desired and beloved by number five.

Behold him, then, in their only armchair, a bent briar between his teeth, chin down in three folds on his clerical collar, and blowing like an amiable whale, while number five discoursed of life as it appeared to them, and specially of that last interview with the head – in the matter of usury.

'One licking once a week would do you an immense amount of good,' he said, twinkling and shaking all over; 'and, as you say, you were entirely in the right.'

'Ra–ather, padre! We could have proved it if he'd let us talk,' said Stalky; 'but he didn't. The head's a downy bird.'

'He understands you perfectly. Ho! ho! Well, you worked hard enough for it.'

'But he's awfully fair. He doesn't lick a chap in the morning an' preach at him in the afternoon,' said Beetle.

'He can't; he ain't in Orders, thank goodness,' said McTurk. Number five held the very strongest views on clerical headmasters, and were ever ready to meet their pastor in argument.

'Almost all other schools have clerical heads,' said the Revd John gently.

'It isn't fair on the chaps,' Stalky replied. 'Makes 'em sulky. Of course it's different with you, sir. You belong to the school – same as we do. I mean ordinary clergymen.'

'Well, I am a most ordinary clergyman; and Mr Hartopp's in Orders, too.'

'Ye–es, but he took 'em after he came to the coll. We saw him go up for his exam. That's all right,' said Beetle. 'But just think if the head went and got ordained!'

'What would happen, Beetle?'

'Oh, the coll. 'ud go to pieces in a year, sir. There's no doubt o' that.'

'How d'you know?' The Revd John was smiling.

'We've been here nearly six years now. There are precious few things about the coll. we don't know,' Stalky replied. 'Why, even you came the term after I did, sir. I remember your asking our names in form your first lesson. Mr King, Mr Prout, and the head, of course, are the only masters senior to us – in that way.'

'Yes, we've changed a good deal – in common room.'

'Huh!' said Beetle with a grunt. 'They came here, an' they went away to get married. Jolly good riddance, too!'

'Doesn't our Beetle hold with matrimony?'

'No, padre; don't make fun of me. I've met chaps in the holidays who've got married housemasters. It's perfectly awful! They have babies and teething and measles and all that sort of thing right bung *in* the school; and the masters' wives give tea parties – tea parties, padre! – and ask the chaps to breakfast.'

'That don't matter so much,' said Stalky. 'But the housemasters let their houses alone, and they leave everything to the prefects. Why, in one school, a chap told me, there were big baize doors and a passage about a mile long between the house and the master's house. They could do just what they pleased.'

'Satan rebuking sin with a vengeance.'

'Oh, larks are right enough; but you know what we mean, padre. After a bit it gets worse an' worse. Then there's a big bust-up and a row that gets into the papers, and a lot of chaps are expelled, you know.'

'Always the wrong uns; don't forget that. Have a cup of cocoa, padre?' said McTurk with the kettle.

'No, thanks; I'm smoking. Always the wrong 'uns? Pro–ceed, my Stalky.'

'And then' – Stalky warmed to the work – 'everybody says, "Who'd ha' thought it? Shockin' boys! Wicked little kids!" It all comes of havin' married housemasters, *I* think.'

'A Daniel come to judgment.'

'But it does,' McTurk interrupted. 'I've met chaps in the holidays, an' they've told me the same thing. It looks awfully pretty for one's people to see – a nice separate house with a nice lady in charge, an' all that. But it isn't. It takes the housemasters off their work, and it gives the prefects a heap too much power, an' – an' – it rots up everything. You see, it isn't as if we were just an ordinary school. We take crammers' rejections as well as good little boys like Stalky. We've got to do that to make our name, of course, and we get 'em into Sandhurst somehow or other, don't we?'

'True, O Turk. Like a book thou talkest, Turkey.'

'And so we want rather different masters, don't you think so, to other places? We aren't like the rest of the schools.'

'It leads to all sorts of bullyin', too, a chap told me,' said Beetle.

'Well, you *do* need most of a single man's time, I must say.' The Revd John considered his hosts critically. 'But do you never feel that the world – the common room – is too much with you sometimes?'

'Not exactly – in summer, anyhow.' Stalky's eye roved contentedly to the window. 'Our bounds are pretty big, too, and they leave us to ourselves a good deal.'

'For example, here am I sitting in your study, very much in your way, eh?'

'Indeed you aren't, padre. Sit down. Don't go, sir. You know we're glad whenever you come.'

There was no doubting the sincerity of the voices. The Revd John flushed a little with pleasure and refilled his briar.

'And we generally know where the common room are,' said Beetle triumphantly. 'Didn't you come through our lower dormitories last night after ten, sir?'

'I went to smoke a pipe with your housemaster. No, I didn't give him any impressions. I took a short cut through your dormitories.'

'I sniffed a whiff of baccy, this mornin'. Yours is stronger than Mr Prout's. *I* knew,' said Beetle, wagging his head.

'Good heavens!' said the Revd John absently. It was some years before Beetle perceived that this was rather a tribute to innocence than observation. The long, light, blindless dormitories, devoid of inner doors, were crossed at all hours of the night by masters visiting one another; for bachelors sit up later than married folk. Beetle had never dreamed that there might be a purpose in this steady policing.

'Talking about bullying,' the Revd John resumed, 'you all caught it pretty hot when you were fags, didn't you?'

'Well, we must have been rather awful little beasts,' said Beetle, looking serenely over the gulf between eleven and sixteen. 'My hat, what bullies they were then – Fairburn, "Gobby" Maunsell, and all that gang!'

'Member when "Gobby" called us the Three Blind Mice; and we had to get up on the lockers and sing while he buzzed inkpots at us?' said Stalky. 'They *were* bullies if you like!'

'But there isn't any of it now,' said McTurk soothingly.

'That's where you make a mistake. We're all inclined to say that everything is all right as long we aren't ourselves hurt. I sometimes wonder if it is extinct – bullying.'

'Fags bully each other horrid; but the upper forms are supposed to be swottin' for exams. They've got something else to think about,' said Beetle.

'Why? What do you think?' Stalky was watching the chaplain's face.

'I have my doubts.' Then, explosively, 'On my word, for three moderately intelligent boys you aren't very observant. I suppose you were too busy making things warm for your housemaster to see what lay under your noses when you were in the form-rooms last week?'

'What, sir? I – I swear we didn't see anything,' said Beetle.

'Then I'd advise you to look. When a little chap is whimpering in a corner and wears his clothes like rags, and never does any work, and is notoriously the dirtiest little "corridor-caution" in the coll., something's wrong somewhere.'

'That's Clewer,' said McTurk under his breath.

'Yes, Clewer. He comes to me for his French. It's his first term, and he's almost as complete a wreck as you were, Beetle. He's not naturally clever, but he has been hammered till he's nearly an idiot.'

'Oh, no. They sham silly to get off more tickings,' said Beetle. '*I* know that.'

'I've never actually seen him knocked about,' said the Revd John.

'The genuine article don't do that in public,' said Beetle. 'Fairburn never touched me when any one was looking on.'

'You needn't swagger about it, Beetle,' said McTurk. 'We all caught it in our time.'

'But I got it worse than anyone,' said Beetle. 'If you want an authority on bullyin', padre, come to me. Corkscrews – brush-drill – keys – head-knucklin' – arm-twistin' – rockin' – Ag Ags – and all the rest of it.'

'Yes. I do want you as an authority, or rather I want your authority to stop it – all of you.'

'What about Abana and Pharpar, padre – Harrison and Craye? They are Mr Prout's pets,' said McTurk a little bitterly. 'We aren't even sub-prefects.'

'I've considered that, but on the other hand, since most bullying is mere thoughtlessness – '

'Not one little bit of it, padre,' said McTurk. 'Bullies like bullyin'. They mean it. They think it up in lesson and practise it in the quarters.'

'Never mind. If the thing goes up to the prefects it may make another house-row. You've had one already. Don't laugh. Listen to me. I ask you – my own Tenth Legion – to take the thing up quietly. I want little Clewer made to look fairly clean and decent – '

'Blowed if *I* wash him!' whispered Stalky.

'Decent and self-respecting. As for the other boy, whoever he is, you can use your influence' – a purely secular light flickered in the chaplain's eye – 'in any way you please to – to dissuade him. That's all. I'll leave it to you. Good-night, *mes enfants*.'

*   *   *

'Well, what are we goin' to do?' Number five stared at each other.

'Young Clewer would give his eyes for a place to be quiet in. *I* know that,' said Beetle. 'If we made him a study-fag, eh?'

'No!' said McTurk firmly. 'He's a dirty little brute, and he'd mess up everything. Besides, we ain't goin' to have any beastly Erickin'. D'you want to walk about with your arm round his neck?'

'He'd clean out the jam-pots, anyhow; an' the burnt-porridge saucepan – it's filthy now.'

'Not good enough,' said Stalky, bringing up both heels with a crash on the table. 'If we find the merry jester who's been bullyin' him an' make him happy, that'll be all right. Why didn't we spot him when we were in the form-rooms, though?'

'Maybe a lot of fags have made a dead set at Clewer. They do that sometimes.'

'Then we'll have to kick the whole of the lower school in our house – on spec. Come on,' said McTurk.

'Keep your hair on! We mustn't make a fuss about the biznai. Whoever it is he's kept quiet or we'd have seen him,' said Stalky. 'We'll walk round and sniff about till we're sure.'

They drew the house form-rooms, accounting for every junior and senior against whom they had suspicions; investigated, at Beetle's suggestion, the lavatories and box rooms, but without result. Everybody seemed to be present save Clewer.

'Rum!' said Stalky, pausing outside a study door. 'Golly!'

A thin piping mixed with tears came muffled through the panels. 'As beautiful Kitty one morning was tripping – '

'Louder, you young devil, or I'll buzz a book at you!'

'With a pitcher of milk – '

'Oh, Campbell, *please* don't!'

'To the fair of – '

A book crashed on something soft, and squeals arose.

'Well, I never thought it was a study-chap, anyhow. That accounts for our not spotting him,' said Beetle. 'Sefton and Campbell are rather hefty chaps to tackle. Besides, one can't go into their study like a form-room.'

'What swine!' McTurk listened. 'Where's the fun of it? I suppose Clewer's faggin' for them.'

'They aren't prefects. That's one good job,' said Stalky, with his war-grin. 'Sefton and Campbell! Um! Campbell and Sefton! Ah! One of 'em's a crammer's pup.'

The two were precocious hairy youths between seventeen and eighteen, sent to the school in despair by parents who hoped that six months' steady cram might, perhaps, jockey them into Sandhurst. Nominally they were in Mr Prout's house; actually they were under the head's eye; and since he was very careful never to promote strange new boys to prefectships, they considered they had a grievance against the school. Sefton had spent three months with a London crammer, and the tale of his adventures there lost nothing in the telling. Campbell, who had a fine taste in clothes and a fluent vocabulary, followed his lead in looking down loftily on the rest of the world.

This was only their second term, and the school, used to what it profanely called 'crammers' pups', had treated them with rather galling reserve. But their whiskers – Sefton owned a real razor – and their moustaches were beyond question impressive.

'Shall we go in an' dissuade 'em?' McTurk asked. 'I've never had much to do with 'em, but I'll bet my hat Campbell's a funk.'

'No – o! That's *oratio directa*,' said Stalky, shaking his head. 'I like *oratio obliqua*. 'Sides, where'd our moral influence be then? Think o' that!'

'Rot! What are you goin' to do?' Beetle turned into lower number nine form-room, next door to the study.

'Me?' The lights of war flickered over Stalky's face. 'Oh, I want to jape with 'em. Shut up a bit!'

He drove his hands into his pockets and stared out of window at the sea, whistling between his teeth. Then a foot tapped the floor; one shoulder lifted; he wheeled, and began the short quick double-shuffle – the war-dance of Stalky in meditation. Thrice he crossed the empty form-room, with compressed lips and expanded nostrils, swaying to the quickstep. Then he halted before the dumb Beetle and softly knuckled his bead, Beetle bowing to the strokes. McTurk nursed one knee and rocked to and fro. They could hear Clewer howling as though his heart would break.

'Beetle is the sacrifice,' Stalky said at last, 'I'm sorry for you, Beetle. 'Member Galton's *Art of Travel* [one of the forms had been studying that pleasant work] an' the kid whose bleatin' excited the tiger?'

'Oh, curse!' said Beetle uneasily. It was not his first season as a sacrifice. 'Can't you get on without me?'

' 'Fraid not, Beetle, dear. You've got to be bullied by Turkey an' me. The more you howl, o' course, the better it'll be. Turkey, go an' covet a stump and a box-rope from somewhere. We'll tie him up for a kill – *à la* Galton. 'Member when "Molly" Fairburn made us cockfight with our shoes off, an' tied up our knees?'

'But that hurt like sin.'

' 'Course it did. What a clever chap you are, Beetle! Turkey'll knock you all over the place. 'Member we've had a big row all round, an' I've trapped you into doin' this. Lend us your wipe.' Beetle was trussed for cockfighting; but, in addition to the transverse stump between elbow and knee, His knees were bound with a box-rope. In this posture, at a push from Stalky he rolled over sideways, covering himself with dust.

'Ruffle his hair, Turkey. Now you get down, too. "The bleatin' of the kid excites the tiger." You two are in such a sweatin' wax with me that you only curse. 'Member that. I'll tickle you up with a stump. You'll have to blub, Beetle.'

'Right O! I'll work up to it in half a shake,' said Beetle.

'Now begin – and remember the bleatin' o' the kid.'

'Shut up, you brutes! Let me up! You've nearly cut my knees off. Oh, you *are* beastly cads! *Do* shut up. ''Tisn't a joke!' Beetle's protest was, in tone, a work of art.

'Give it to him, Turkey! Kick him! Roll him over! Kill him! Don't funk, Beetle, you brute. Kick him again, Turkey.'

'He's not blubbin' really. Roll up, Beetle, or I'll kick you into the fender,' roared McTurk. They made a hideous noise among them, and the bait allured their quarry.

'Hullo! What's the giddy jest?' Sefton and Campbell entered to find Beetle on his side, his head against the fender, weeping copiously, while McTurk prodded him in the back with his toes.

'It's only Beetle,' Stalky explained. 'He's shammin' hurt. I can't get Turkey to go for him properly.' Sefton promptly kicked both boys, and his face lighted. 'All right, I'll attend to 'em. Get up an' cockfight, you two. Give me the stump. I'll tickle 'em. Here's a giddy jest! Come on, Campbell. Let's cook 'em.'

Then McTurk turned on Stalky and called him very evil names.

'You said you were goin' to cockfight too, Stalky. Come on!'

'More ass you for believin' me, then!' shrieked Stalky.

'Have you chaps had a row?' said Campbell.

'Row?' said Stalky. 'Huh! I'm only educatin' them. D'you know anythin' about cockfighting, Seffy?'

'Do I know? Why, at Maclagan's, where I was crammin' in town, we used to cockfight in his drawing-room, and little Maclagan daren't say anything. But we were just the same as men there, of course. Do I know? *I'll* show you.'

'Can't I get up?' moaned Beetle, as Stalky sat on his shoulder.

'Don't jaw, you fat piffler. You're going to fight Seffy.'

'He'll slay me!'

'Oh, lug 'em into our study,' said Campbell. 'It's nice an' quiet in there. I'll cockfight Turkey. This is an improvement on young Clewer.'

'Right O! I move it's shoes-off for them an' shoes-on for us,' said Sefton joyously, and the two were flung down on the study floor. Stalky rolled them behind an armchair. 'Now I'll tie you two up an' direct the bullfight. Golly, what wrists you have, Seffy. They're too thick for a wipe; got a box-rope?' said he.

'Lots in the corner,' Sefton replied. 'Hurry up! Stop blubbin', you brute, Beetle. We're goin' to have a giddy campaign. Losers have to sing for the winners – sing odes in honour of the conqueror. You call yourself a beastly poet, don't you, Beetle? I'll poet you.'

He wriggled into position by Campbell's side. Swiftly and scientifically the stumps were thrust through the natural crooks, and the wrists tied with well-stretched box-ropes to an accompaniment of insults from McTurk, bound, betrayed, and voluble behind the chair. Stalky set away Campbell and Sefton, and strode over to his allies, locking the door on the way.

'And that's all right,' said he in a changed voice.

'What the devil – ?' Sefton began. Beetle's false tears had ceased; McTurk, smiling, was on his feet. Together they bound the knees and ankles of the enemy even more straitly.

Stalky took the armchair and contemplated the scene with his blandest smile. A man trussed for cock-fighting is, perhaps, the most helpless thing in the world.

' "The bleatin' of the kid excites the tiger." Oh, you frabjous asses!' He lay back and laughed till he could no more. The victims took in the situation but slowly. 'We'll give you the finest lickin' you ever had in your young lives when we get up!' thundered Sefton from the floor. 'You'll laugh the other side of your mouth before you've done. What the deuce d'you mean by this?'

'You'll see in two shakes,' said McTurk. 'Don't swear like that. What we want to know is, why you two hulkin' swine have been bullyin' Clewer?'

'It's none of your business.'

'What did you bully Clewer for?' The question was repeated with maddening iteration by each in turn. They knew their work.

'Because we jolly well chose!' was the answer at last. 'Let's get up.' Even then they could not realise the game.

'Well, now we're goin' to bully you because we jolly well choose. We're goin' to be just as fair to you as you were to Clewer. He couldn't do anything against you. You can't do anything to us. Odd, ain't it?'

'Can't we? You wait an' see.'

'Ah,' said Beetle reflectively, 'that shows you've never been properly jested with. A public lickin' ain't in it with a gentle jape. Bet a bob you'll weep an' promise anything.'

'Look here, young Beetle, we'll half kill you when we get up. I'll promise you that, at any rate.'

'You're going to be half killed first, though. Did you give Clewer head-knuckles?'

'Did you give Clewer head-knuckles?' McTurk echoed. At the twentieth repetition – no boy can stand the torture of one unvarying query, which is the essence of bullying – came confession.

'We did, confound you!'

'Then you'll be knuckled;' and knuckled they were, according to ancient experience. Head-knuckling is no trifle; 'Molly' Fairburn of the old days could not have done better.

'Did you give Clewer brush-drill?' This time the question was answered sooner, and brush-drill was dealt out for the space of five minutes by Stalky's watch. They could not even writhe in their bonds. No brush is employed in brush-drill.

'Did you give Clewer the key?'

'No; we didn't. I swear we didn't!' from Campbell, rolling in agony.

'Then we'll give it to you, so you can see what it would be like if you had.'

The torture of the key – which has no key at all – hurts excessively. They endured several minutes of it, and their language necessitated the gag.

'Did you give Clewer corkscrews?'

'Yes. Oh, curse your silly souls! Let us alone, you cads.'

They were corkscrewed, and the torture of the corkscrew – this has nothing to do with corkscrews – is keener than the torture of the key.

The method and silence of the attacks was breaking their nerves. Between each new torture came the pitiless, dazing rain of questions, and when they did not answer to the point, Isabella-coloured handkerchiefs were thrust into their mouths.

'Now are those all the things you did to Clewer? Take out the gag, Turkey, and let 'em answer.'

'Yes, I swear that was all. Oh, you're killing us, Stalky!' cried Campbell.

'Pre–cisely what Clewer said to you. I heard him. Now we're goin' to show you what real bullyin' is. What I don't like about you, Sefton, is, you come to the coll. with your stick-up collars an' patent-leather boots, an' you think you can teach us something about bullying. Do you think you can teach us anything about bullying? Take out the gag and let him answer.'

'No!' – ferociously.

'He says no. Rock him to sleep. Campbell can watch.'

It needs three boys and two boxing-gloves to rock a boy to sleep. Again the operation has nothing to do with its name. Sefton was 'rocked' till his eyes set in his head and he gasped and crowed for breath, sick and dizzy.

'My aunt!' said Campbell, appalled, from his corner, and turned white.

'Put him away,' said Stalky. 'Bring on Campbell. Now this is bullyin'. Oh, I forgot! I say, Campbell, what did you bully Clewer for? Take out his gag and let him answer.'

'I – I don't know. Oh, let me off! I swear I'll make it *pax*. Don't "rock" me!'

' "The bleatin' of the kid excites the tiger." He says he don't know. Set him up, Beetle. Give me the glove an' put in the gag.'

In silence Campbell was 'rocked' sixty-four times.

'I believe I'm goin' to die!' he gasped.

'He says he is goin' to die. Put him away. Now, Sefton! Oh, I forgot! Sefton, what did you bully Clewer for?'

The answer is unprintable; but it brought not the faintest flush to Stalky's downy cheek.

'Make him an Ag Ag, Turkey!'

And an Ag Ag was he made, forthwith. The hard-bought experience of nearly eighteen years was at his disposal, but he did not seem to appreciate it.

'He says we are sweeps. Put him away! Now, Campbell! Oh, I forgot! I say, Campbell, what did you bully Clewer for?'

Then came the tears – scalding tears; appeals for mercy and abject promises of peace. Let them cease the tortures and Campbell would never lift hand against them. The questions began again – to an accompaniment of small persuasions.

'You seem hurt, Campbell. Are you hurt?'

'Yes. Awfully!'

'He says he is hurt. Are you broke?'

'Yes, yes! I swear I am. Oh, stop!'

'He says he is broke. Are you humble?'

'Yes!'

'He says he is humble. Are you devilish humble?'

'Yes!'

'He says he is devilish humble. Will you bully Clewer any more?'

'No. No – ooh!'

'He says he won't bully Clewer. Or any one else?'

'No. I swear I won't.'

'Or anyone else. What about that lickin' you and Sefton were goin' to give us?'

'I won't! I won't! I swear I won't!'

'He says he won't lick us. Do you esteem yourself to know anything about bullyin'?'

'No, I don't!'

'He says he doesn't know anything about bullyin'. Haven't we taught you a lot?'

'Yes – yes!'

'He says we've taught him a lot. Aren't you grateful?'

'Yes!'

'He says he is grateful. Put him away. Oh, I forgot! I say, Campbell, what did you bully Clewer for?'

He wept anew; his nerves being raw. 'Because I was a bully. I suppose that's what you want me to say?'

'He says he is a bully. Right he is. Put him in the corner. No more japes for Campbell. Now, Sefton!'

'You devils! You young devils!' This and much more as Sefton was punted across the carpet by skilful knees.

' "The bleatin' of the kid excites the tiger." We're goin' to make you beautiful. Where does he keep his shaving things? [Campbell told.] Beetle, get some water. Turkey, make the lather. We're goin' to shave you, Seffy, so you'd better lie jolly still, or you'll get cut. I've never shaved anyone before.'

'Don't! Oh, don't! Please don't!'

'Gettin' polite, eh? I'm only goin' to take off one ducky little whisker – '

'I'll – I'll make it *pax*, if you don't. I swear I'll let you off your lickin' when I get up!'

'*And* half that moustache we're so proud of. He says he'll let us off our lickin'. Isn't he kind?'

McTurk laughed into the nickel-plated shaving-cup, and settled Sefton's head between Stalky's vice-like knees.

'Hold on a shake,' said Beetle, 'you can't shave long hairs. You've got to cut all that moustache short first, an' then scrape him.'

'Well, I'm not goin' to hunt about for scissors. Won't a match do? Chuck us the matchbox. He *is* a hog, you know; we might as well singe him. Lie still!' He lit a vesta, but checked his hand. 'I only want to take off half, though.'

'That's all right.' Beetle waved the brush. 'I'll lather up to the middle – see? and you can burn off the rest.'

The thin-haired first moustache of youth fluffed off in flame to the lather-line in the centre of the lip, and Stalky rubbed away the burnt stumpage with his thumb. It was not a very gentle shave, but it abundantly accomplished its purpose.

'Now the whisker on the other side. Turn him over!' Between match and razor this, too, was removed. 'Give him his shaving-glass. Take the gag out. I want to hear what he'll say.'

But there were no words. Sefton gazed at the lopsided wreck in horror and despair. Two fat tears rolled down his cheek.

'Oh, I forgot! I say, Sefton, what did you bully Clewer for?'

'Leave me alone! Oh, you infernal bullies, leave me alone! Haven't I had enough?'

'He says we must leave him alone,' said McTurk.

'He says we are bullies, an' we haven't even begun yet,' said Beetle. 'You're ungrateful, Seffy. Golly! You do look an atrocity and a half!'

'He says he has had enough,' said Stalky. 'He errs!'

'Well, to work, to work!' chanted McTurk, waving a stump. 'Come on, my giddy Narcissus. Don't fall in love with your own reflection!'

'Oh, let him off,' said Campbell from his corner; 'he's blubbing, too.'

Sefton cried like a twelve-year-old with pain, shame, wounded vanity, and utter helplessness.

'You'll make it *pax*, Sefton, won't you? You can't stand up to those young devils – '

'Don't be rude, Campbell, de-ah,' said McTurk, 'or you'll catch it again!'

'You *are* devils, you know,' said Campbell.

'What? for a little bullyin' – same as you've been givin' Clewer! How long have you been jestin' with him?' said Stalky. 'All this term?'

'We didn't always knock him about, though!'

'You did when you could catch him,' said Beetle, cross-legged on the floor, dropping a stump from time to time across Sefton's instep. 'Don't I know it!'

'I – perhaps we did.'

'And you went out of your way to catch him? Don't I know it! Because he was an awful little beast, eh? Don't I know it! Now, you see, *you*'re awful beasts, and you're gettin' what he got – for bein' a beast. Just because we choose.'

'We never really bullied him – like you've done us.'

'Yah!' said Beetle. 'They never really bully – "Molly" Fairburn didn't. Only knock 'em about a little bit. That's what they say. Only kick their souls out of 'em, and they go and blub in the box rooms. Shove their heads into the ulsters an' blub. Write home three times a day – yes, you brute, I've done that – askin' to be taken away. You've never been bullied properly, Campbell I'm sorry you made *pax*.'

'I'm not!' said Campbell, who was a humorist in a way. 'Look out, you're slaying Sefton!'

In his excitement Beetle had used the stump unreflectingly, and Sefton was now shouting for mercy.

'An' you!' he cried, wheeling where he sat. 'You've never been bullied, either. Where were you before you came here?'

'I – I had a tutor.'

'Yah! You would. You never blubbed in your life. But you're blubbin' now, by gum. Aren't you blubbin'?'

'Can't you see, you blind beast?' Sefton fell over sideways, tear-tracks furrowing the dried lather. Crack came the cricket-stump on the curved latter-end of him.

'Blind, am I,' said Beetle, 'and a beast? Shut up, Stalky. I'm goin' to jape a bit with our friend, *à la* "Molly" Fairburn. *I* think I can see. Can't I see, Sefton?'

'The point is well taken,' said McTurk, watching the strap at work. 'You'd better say that he sees, Seffy.'

'You do – you can! I swear you do!' yelled Sefton, for strong arguments were coercing him.

'Aren't my eyes lovely?' The stump rose and fell steadily throughout this catechism.

'Yes.'

'A gentle hazel, aren't they?'

'Yes – oh, yes!'

'What a liar you are! They're sky-blue. Ain't they sky-blue?'

'Yes – oh, yes!'

'You don't know your mind from one minute to another. You must learn – you must learn.'

'What a bate you're in!' said Stalky. 'Keep your hair on, Beetle.'

'I've had it done to me,' said Beetle. 'Now – about my being a beast.'

'*Pax* – oh, *pax*!' cried Sefton; 'make it *pax*. I'll give up! Let me off! I'm broke! I can't stand it!'

'Ugh! Just when we were gettin' our hand in!' grunted McTurk.

'They didn't let Clewer off, I'll swear.'

'Confess – apologise – quick!' said Stalky.

From the floor Sefton made unconditional surrender, more abjectly even than Campbell. He would never touch anyone again. He would go softly all the days of his life.

'We've got to take it, I suppose?' said Stalky. 'All right, Sefton. You're broke? Very good. Shut up, Beetle! But before we let you up, you an' Campbell will kindly oblige us with "Kitty of Coleraine" – *à la* Clewer.'

'That's not fair,' said Campbell; 'we've surrendered.'

' 'Course you have. Now you're goin' to do what we tell you – same as Clewer would. If you hadn't surrendered you'd ha' been really bullied. Havin' surrendered – do you follow, Seffy? – you sing odes in honour of the conquerors. Hurry up!'

They dropped into chairs luxuriously. Campbell and Sefton looked at each other, and, neither taking comfort from that view, struck up 'Kitty of Coleraine'.

'Vile bad,' said Stalky, as the miserable wailing ended. 'If you hadn't surrendered it would have been our painful duty to buzz books at you for singin' out o' tune. Now then.'

He freed them from their bonds, but for several minutes they could not rise. Campbell was first on his feet, smiling uneasily. Sefton staggered to the table, buried his head in his arms, and shook with sobs. There was no shadow of fight in either – only amazement, distress, and shame.

'Ca–can't he shave clean before tea, please?' said Campbell. 'It's ten minutes to bell.'

Stalky shook his head. He meant to escort the half-shaved one to the meal.

McTurk yawned in his chair and Beetle mopped his face. They were all dripping with excitement and exertion.

'If I knew anything about it, I swear I'd give you a moral lecture,' said Stalky severely.

'Don't jaw; they've surrendered,' said McTurk. 'This moral 'suasion biznai takes it out of a chap.'

'Don't you see how gentle we've been? We might have called Clewer in to look at you,' said Stalky. ' "The bleatin' of the tiger excites the kid." But we didn't. We've only got to tell a few chaps in coll. about this and you'd be hooted all over the shop. Your life wouldn't be worth havin'. But we aren't goin' to do that, either. We're strictly moral 'suasers, Campbell; so, unless you or Seffy split about this, no one will.'

'I swear you're a brick,' said Campbell. 'I suppose I was rather a brute to Clewer.'

'It looked like it,' said Stalky. 'But I don't think Seffy need come into hall with cockeyed whiskers. Horrid bad for the fags if they saw him. He can shave. Ain't you grateful, Sefton?'

The head did not lift. Sefton was deeply asleep.

'That's rummy,' said McTurk, as a snore mixed with a sob. 'Cheek, *I* think; or else he's shammin'.'

'No, 'tisn't,' said Beetle. 'When "Molly" Fairburn had attended to me for an hour or so I used to go bung off to sleep on a form sometimes. Poor devil! But he called me a beastly poet, though.'

'Well, come on.' Stalky lowered his voice. 'Goodbye, Campbell. 'Member, if you don't talk, nobody will.'

There should have been a war-dance, but that all three were so utterly tired that they almost went to sleep above the teacups in their study, and slept till prep.

*   *   *

'A most extraordinary letter. Are all parents incurably mad? What do you make of it?' said the head, handing a closely written eight pages to the Revd John.

' "The only son of his mother, and she a widow." That is the least reasonable sort.' The chaplain read with pursed lips. 'If half those charges are true he should be in the sick-house; whereas he is disgustingly well. Certainly he has shaved. I noticed that.'

'Under compulsion, as his mother points out. How delicious! How salutary!'

'You haven't to answer her. It isn't often I don't know what has happened in the school; but this is beyond me.'

'If you asked me I should say seek not to propitiate. When one is forced to take crammers' pups – '

'He was perfectly well at extra-tuition – with me – this morning,' said the head, absently. 'Unusually well behaved, too.'

' – they either educate the school, or the school, as in this case, educates them. I prefer our own methods,' the chaplain concluded.

'You think it was that?' A lift of the head's eyebrow.

'I'm sure of it! And nothing excuses his trying to give the college a bad name.'

'That's the line I mean to take with him,' the head answered.

The Augurs winked.

*   *   *

A few days later the Revd John called on number five. 'Why haven't we seen you before, padre?' said they.

'I've been watching times and seasons and events and men – and boys,' he replied. 'I am pleased with my Tenth Legion. I make them my compliments. Clewer was throwing ink balls in form this morning, instead of doing his work. He is now doing fifty lines for – unheard-of audacity.'

'You can't blame us, sir,' said Beetle. 'You told us to remove the – er – pressure. That's the worst of a fag.'

'I've known boys five years his senior throw ink balls, Beetle. To such a one have I given two hundred lines – not so long ago. And now I come to think of it, were those lines ever shown up?'

'Were they, Turkey?' said Beetle unblushingly.

'Don't you think Clewer looks a little cleaner, padre?' Stalky interrupted.

'We're no end of moral reformers,' said McTurk.

'It was all Stalky, but it was a lark,' said Beetle.

'I have noticed the moral reform in several quarters. Didn't I tell you you had more influence than any boys in the coll. if you cared to use it?'

'It's a trifle exhaustin' to use frequent – our kind of moral 'suasion. Besides, you see, it only makes Clewer cheeky.'

'I wasn't thinking of Clewer; I was thinking of – the other people, Stalky.'

'Oh, we didn't bother much about the other people,' said McTurk. 'Did we?'

'But *I* did – from the beginning.'

'Then you knew, sir?'

A downward puff of smoke. 'Boys educate each other, they say, more than we can or dare. If I had used one half of the moral 'suasion you may or may not have employed – '

'With the best motives in the world. Don't forget our pious motives, padre,' said McTurk.

'I suppose I should be now languishing in Bideford jail, shouldn't I? Well, to quote the head, in a little business which we have agreed to forget, that strikes me as flagrant injustice . . . What are you laughing at, you young sinners? Isn't it true? I will not stay to be shouted at. What I looked into this den of iniquity for was to find out if anyone cared to come down for a bathe off the Ridge. But I see you won't.'

'Won't we, though! Half a shake, padre sahib, till we get our towels, and *nous sommes avec vous!*'

A Little Prep

Qui procul hinc – the legend's writ,
   The frontier grave is far away;
Qui ante diem periit,
   Sed miles, sed pro patria.

HENRY NEWBOLT

Easter term was but a month old when Stettson major, a day boy, contracted diphtheria, and the head was very angry. He decreed a new and narrower set of bounds – the infection had been traced to an outlying farmhouse – urged the prefects severely to lick all trespassers, and promised extra attentions from his own hand. There were no words bad enough for Stettson major, quarantined at his mother's house, who had lowered the school-average of health. This he said in the gymnasium after prayers. Then he wrote some two hundred letters to as many anxious parents and guardians, and bade the school carry on. The trouble did not spread, but, one night, a dog-cart drove to the head's door, and in the morning the head had gone, leaving all things in charge of Mr King, senior housemaster. The head often ran up to town, where the school devoutly believed he bribed officials for early proofs of the army examination papers; but this absence was unusually prolonged.

'Downy old bird!' said Stalky to the allies one wet afternoon in the study. 'He must have gone on a bend and been locked up under a false name.'

'What for?' Beetle entered joyously into the libel.

'Forty shillin's or a month for hackin' the chucker-out of the Pavvy on the shins. Bates always has a spree when he goes to town. Wish he was back, though. I'm about sick o' King's "whips an' scorpions" an' lectures on public-school spirit – yah! – and scholarship!'

' "Crass an' materialised brutality of the middle classes – readin' solely for marks. Not a scholar in the whole school," ' McTurk quoted, pensively boring holes in the mantelpiece with a hot poker.

'That's rather a sickly way of spending an afternoon. Stinks too. Let's come out an' smoke. Here's a treat.' Stalky held up a long Indian cheroot. 'Bagged it from my pater last holidays. I'm a bit shy of it though; it's heftier than a pipe. We'll smoke it palaver-fashion. Hand it round, eh? Let's lie up behind the old harrow on the Monkey-farm Road.'

'Out of bounds. Bounds beastly strict these days, too. Besides, we shall cat.'
Beetle sniffed the cheroot critically. 'It's a regular Pomposo Stinkadore.'

'You can; I shan't. What d'you say, Turkey?'

'Oh, may's well, I s'pose.'

'Chuck on your cap, then. It's two to one. Beetle, out you come!'

They saw a group of boys by the noticeboard in the corridor; little Foxy,
the school sergeant, among them.

'More bounds, I expect,' said Stalky. 'Hullo, Foxibus, who are you in
mournin' for?' There was a broad band of crape round Foxy's arm.

'He was in my old regiment,' said Foxy, jerking his head towards the
notices, where a newspaper cutting was thumb-tacked between callover lists.

'By gum!' quoth Stalky, uncovering as he read. 'It's old Duncan – Fat-Sow
Duncan – killed on duty at something or other Kotal. "*Rallyin' his men with
conspicuous gallantry.*" He would, of course. "*The body was recovered.*" That's all
right. They cut 'em up sometimes, don't they, Foxy?'

'Horrid,' said the sergeant briefly.

'Poor old Fat-Sow! I was a fag when he left. How many does that make to
us, Foxy?'

'Mr Duncan, he is the ninth. He come here when he was no bigger than
little Grey tertius. My old regiment, too. Yiss, nine to us, Mr Corkran, up to
date.'

The boys went out into the wet, walking swiftly.

'Wonder how it feels – to be shot and all that,' said Stalky, as they splashed
down a lane. 'Where did it happen, Beetle?'

'Oh, out in India somewhere. We're always rowin' there. But look here,
Stalky, what *is* the good o' sittin' under a hedge an' cattin'? It's be–eastly cold.
It's be–eastly wet, and we'll be collared as sure as a gun.'

'Shut up! Did you ever know your Uncle Stalky get you into a mess yet?' Like
many other leaders, Stalky did not dwell on past defeats. They pushed through
a dripping hedge, landed among waterlogged clods, and sat down on a rust-
coated harrow. The cheroot burned with sputterings of saltpetre. They smoked
it gingerly, each passing to the other between closed forefinger and thumb.

'Good job we hadn't one apiece, ain't it?' said Stalky, shivering through set
teeth. To prove his words he immediately laid all before them, and they
followed his example . . .

'I told you,' moaned Beetle, sweating clammy drops. 'Oh, Stalky, you are a
fool!'

'*Je cat, tu cat, il cat. Nous cattons!*' McTurk handed up his contribution and
lay hopelessly on the cold iron.

'Something's wrong with the beastly thing. I say, Beetle, have you been
droppin' ink on it?'

But Beetle was in no case to answer. Limp and empty, they sprawled across
the harrow, the rust marking their ulsters in red squares and the abandoned
cheroot-end reeking under their very cold noses. Then – they had heard

nothing – the head himself stood before them – the head who should have been in town bribing examiners – the head fantastically attired in old tweeds and a deerstalker!

'Ah,' he said, fingering his moustache. 'Very good. I might have guessed who it was. You will go back to the college and give my compliments to Mr King and ask him to give you an extra-special licking. You will then do me five hundred lines. I shall be back tomorrow. Five hundred lines by five o'clock tomorrow. You are also gated for a week. This is not exactly the time for breaking bounds. Extra-special, please.'

He disappeared over the hedge as lightly as he had come. There was a murmur of women's voices in the deep lane.

'Oh, you Prooshian brute!' said McTurk as the voices died away. 'Stalky, it's all your silly fault.'

'Kill him! Kill him!' gasped Beetle.

'I ca–an't. I'm going to cat again . . . I don't mind that, but King'll gloat over us horrid. Extra-special, ooh!'

Stalky made no answer – not even a soft one. They went to college and received that for which they had been sent. King enjoyed himself most thoroughly, for by virtue of their seniority the boys were exempt from his hand, save under special order. Luckily, he was no expert in the gentle art.

' "Strange, how desire doth outrun performance",' said Beetle irreverently, quoting from some Shakespeare play that they were cramming that term. They regained their study and settled down to the imposition.

'You're quite right, Beetle.' Stalky spoke in silky and propitiating tones. 'Now, if the head had sent us up to a prefect, we'd have got something to remember!'

'Look here,' McTurk began with cold venom, 'we aren't goin' to row you about this business, because it's too bad for a row; but we want you to understand you're jolly well excommunicated, Stalky. You're a plain ass.'

'How was I to know that the head 'ud collar us? What was he doin' in those ghastly clothes, too?'

'Don't try to raise a side issue,' Beetle grunted severely.

'Well, it was all Stettson major's fault. If he hadn't gone an' got diphtheria 'twouldn't have happened. But don't you think it rather rummy – the head droppin' on us that way?'

'Shut up! You're dead!' said Beetle. 'We've chopped your spurs off your beastly heels. We've cocked your shield upside down and – and I don't think you ought to be allowed to brew for a month.'

'Oh, stop jawin' at me. I want – '

'Stop? Why – why, we're gated for a week.' McTurk almost howled as the agony of the situation overcame him. 'A lickin' from King, five hundred lines, *and* a gatin'. D'you expect us to kiss you, Stalky, you beast?'

'Drop rottin' for a minute. I want to find out about the head bein' where he was.'

'Well, you have. You found him quite well and fit. Found him makin' love to Stettson major's mother. That was her in the lane – I heard her. And so we were ordered a lickin' before a day boy's mother. Bony old widow, too,' said McTurk. 'Anything else you'd like to find out?'

'I don't care. I swear I'll get even with him some day,' Stalky growled.

'Looks like it,' said McTurk. 'Extra-special, week's gatin' and five hundred . . . and now you're goin' to row about it! Help scrag him, Beetle!' Stalky had thrown his Virgil at them.

The head returned next day without explanation, to find the lines waiting for him and the school a little relaxed under Mr King's vice-royalty. Mr King had been talking at and round and over the boys' heads, in a lofty and promiscuous style, of public-school spirit and the traditions of ancient seats; for he always improved an occasion. Beyond waking in two hundred and fifty young hearts a lively hatred of all other foundations, he accomplished little – so little, indeed, that when, two days after the head's return, he chanced to come across Stalky & Co., gated but ever resourceful, playing marbles in the corridor, he said that he was not surprised – not in the least surprised. This was what he had expected from persons of their *morale*.

'But there isn't any rule against marbles, sir. Very interestin' game,' said Beetle, his knees white with chalk and dust. Then he received two hundred lines for insolence, besides an order to go to the nearest prefect for judgement and slaughter.

This is what happened behind the closed doors of Flint's study, and Flint was then head of the games: 'Oh, I say, Flint. King has sent me to you for playin' marbles in the corridor an' shoutin' "alley tor" an' "knuckle down".'

'What does he suppose I have to do with that?' was the answer.

'Dunno. Well?' Beetle grinned wickedly. 'What am I to tell him? He's rather wrathy about it.'

'If the head chooses to put a notice in the corridor forbiddin' marbles, I can do something; but I can't move on a housemaster's report. He knows that as well as I do.'

The sense of this oracle Beetle conveyed, all unsweetened, to King, who hastened to interview Flint.

Now Flint had been seven and a half years at the college, counting six months with a London crammer, from whose roof he had returned, homesick, to the head for the final army polish. There were four or five other seniors who had gone through much the same mill, not to mention boys, rejected by other establishments on account of a certain overwhelmingness, whom the head had wrought into very fair shape. It was not a Sixth to be handled without gloves, as King found.

'Am I to understand it is your intention to allow board-school games under your study windows, Flint? If so, I can only say – ' He said much, and Flint listened politely.

'Well, sir, if the head sees fit to call a prefects' meeting we are bound to take the matter up. But the tradition of the school is that the prefects can't move in any matter affecting the whole school without the head's direct order.'

Much more was then delivered, both sides a little losing their temper.

After tea, at an informal gathering of prefects in his study, Flint related the adventure.

'He's been playin' for this for a week, and now he's got it. You know as well as I do that if he hadn't been gassing at us the way he has, that young devil Beetle wouldn't have dreamed of marbles.'

'We know that,' said Perowne, 'but that isn't the question. On Flint's showin' King has called the prefects names enough to justify a first-class row. Crammers' rejections, ill-regulated hobbledehoys, wasn't it? Now it's impossible for prefects –'

'Rot,' said Flint. 'King's the best classical cram we've got; and 'tisn't fair to bother the head with a row. He's up to his eyes with extra-tuition and army work as it is. Besides, as I told King, we *aren't* a public school. We're a limited liability company payin' four per cent. My father's a shareholder, too.'

'What's that got to do with it?' said Venner, a red-headed boy of nineteen.

'Well, seems to me that we should be interferin' with ourselves. We've got to get into the army or – get out, haven't we? King's hired by the council to teach us. All the rest's gumdiddle. Can't you see?'

It might have been because he felt the air was a little thunderous that the head took his after-dinner cheroot to Flint's study; but he so often began an evening in a prefect's room that nobody suspected when he drifted in pensively, after the knocks that etiquette demanded.

'Prefects' meeting?' A cock of one wise eyebrow.

'Not exactly, sir; we're just talking things over. Won't you take the easy chair?'

'Thanks. Luxurious infants, you are.' He dropped into Flint's big half-couch and puffed for a while in silence. 'Well, since you're all here, I may confess that I'm the mute with the bowstring.'

The young faces grew serious. The phrase meant that certain of their number would be withdrawn from all further games for extra-tuition. It might also mean future success at Sandhurst; but it was present ruin for the 1st XV.

'Yes, I've come for my pound of flesh. I ought to have had you out before the Exeter match; but it's our sacred duty to beat Exeter.'

'Isn't the old boys' match sacred, too, sir?' said Perowne. The old boys' match was the event of the Easter term.

'We'll hope they aren't in training. Now for the list. First I want Flint. It's the Euclid that does it. You must work deductions with me. Perowne, extra mechanical drawing. Dawson goes to Mr King for extra Latin, and Venner to me for German. Have I damaged the 1st XV much?' He smiled sweetly.

'Ruined it, I'm afraid, sir,' said Flint. 'Can't you let us off till the end of the term?'

'Impossible. It will be a tight squeeze for Sandhurst this year.'

'And all to be cut up by those vile Afghans, too,' said Dawson. 'Wouldn't think there'd be so much competition, would you?'

'Oh, that reminds me. Crandall is coming down with the old boys – I've asked twenty of them, but we shan't get more than a weak team. I don't know whether he'll be much use, though. He was rather knocked about, recovering poor old Duncan's body.'

'Crandall major – the Gunner?' Perowne asked.

'No, the minor – "Toffee" Crandall – in a native infantry regiment. He was almost before your time, Perowne.'

'The papers didn't say anything about him. We read about Fat-Sow, of course. What's Crandall done, sir?'

'I've brought over an Indian paper that his mother sent me. It was rather a – hefty, I think you say – piece of work. Shall I read it?' The head knew how to read. When he had finished the quarter-column of close type everybody thanked him politely.

'Good for the old coll.!' said Perowne. 'Pity he wasn't in time to save Fat-Sow, though. That's nine to us, isn't it, in the last three years?'

'Yes . . . And I took old Duncan off all games for extra-tuition five years ago this term,' said the head. 'By the way, who do you hand over the Games to, Flint?'

'Haven't thought yet. Who'd you recommend, sir?'

'No, thank you. I've heard it casually hinted behind my back that the Prooshian Bates is a downy bird, but he isn't going to make himself responsible for a new head of the games. Settle it among yourselves. Good-night.'

'And that's the man,' said Flint, when the door shut, 'that you want to bother with a dame's school row.'

'I was only pullin' your fat leg,' Perowne returned, hastily. 'You're so easy to draw, Flint.'

'Well, never mind that. The head's knocked the 1st XV to bits, and we've got to pick up the pieces, or the old boys will have a walkover. Let's promote all the 2nd XV and make big side play up. There's heaps of talent somewhere that we can polish up between now and the match.'

The case was represented so urgently to the school that even Stalky and McTurk, who affected to despise football, played one big-side game seriously. They were forthwith promoted ere their ardour had time to cool, and the dignity of their caps demanded that they should keep some show of virtue. The match-team was worked at least four days out of seven, and the school saw hope ahead.

With the last week of the term the old boys began to arrive, and their welcome was nicely proportioned to their worth. Gentlemen cadets from Sandhurst and Woolwich, who had only left a year ago, but who carried enormous side, were greeted with a cheerful 'Hullo! What's the Shop like?' from those who had shared their studies. Militia subalterns had more consideration, but it was understood they were not precisely of the true metal. Recreants who, failing for the army, had gone into business or banks were received for old sake's sake, but in no way made too much of. But when the real subalterns, officers and gentlemen full-blown – who had been to the ends of the earth and back again and so carried no side – came on the scene strolling about with the head, the school divided right and left in admiring silence. And when one laid hands on Flint, even upon the head of the games crying, 'Good heavens! What do you mean by growing in this way? You were a beastly little fag when I left,' visible haloes encircled Flint. They would walk to and fro in the corridor with the little red school-sergeant, telling news of old regiments; they would burst into form-rooms sniffing the well-remembered smells of ink and whitewash; they would find nephews and cousins in the lower forms and present them with enormous wealth; or they would invade the gymnasium and make Foxy show off the new stock on the bars.

Chiefly, though, they talked with the head, who was father-confessor and agent-general to them all; for what they shouted in their unthinking youth, they proved in their thoughtless manhood – to wit, that the Prooshian Bates was 'a downy bird'. Young blood who had stumbled into an entanglement with a pastry-cook's daughter at Plymouth; experience who had come into a small legacy but mistrusted lawyers; ambition halting at crossroads, anxious to take the one that would lead him farthest; extravagance pursued by the moneylender; arrogance in the thick of a regimental row – each carried his trouble to the head; and Chiron showed him, in language quite unfit for little boys, a quiet and safe way round, out, or under. So they overflowed his house, smoked his cigars, and drank his health as they had drunk it all the earth over when two or three of the old school had foregathered.

'Don't stop smoking for a minute,' said the head. 'The more you're out of training the better for us. I've demoralised the 1st XV with extra-tuition.'

'Ah, but we're a scratch lot. Have you told 'em we shall need a substitute even if Crandall can play?' said a lieutenant of engineers with a DSO to his credit.

'He wrote me he'd play, so he can't have been much hurt. He's coming down tomorrow morning.'

'Crandall minor that was, and brought off poor Duncan's body?' The head nodded. 'Where are you going to put him? We've turned you out of house and home already, head sahib.' This was a squadron commander of Bengal Lancers, home on leave.

'I'm afraid he'll have to go up to his old dormitory. You know old boys can claim that privilege. Yes, I think little Crandall minor must bed down there once more.'

'Bates sahib,' – a gunner flung a heavy arm round the head's neck – 'you've got something up your sleeve. Confess! I know that twinkle.'

'Can't you see, you cuckoo?' a submarine miner interrupted. 'Crandall goes up to the dormitory as an object-lesson, for moral effect and so forth. Isn't that true, head sahib?'

'It is. You know too much, Purvis. I licked you for that in '79.'

'You did, sir, and it's my private belief you chalked the cane.'

'N—no. But I've a very straight eye. Perhaps that misled you.'

That opened the floodgates of fresh memories, and they all told tales out of school.

When Crandall minor that was – Lieutenant R. Crandall of an ordinary Indian regiment – arrived from Exeter on the morning of the match, he was cheered along the whole front of the college, for the prefects had repeated the sense of that which the head had read them in Flint's study. When Prout's house understood that he would claim his old boy's right to a bed for one night, Beetle ran into King's house next door and executed a public 'gloat' up and down the enemy's big form-room, departing in a haze of inkpots.

'What d'you take any notice of those rotters for?' said Stalky, playing substitute for the old boys, magnificent in black jersey, white knickers, and black stockings. 'I talked to *him* up in the dormitory when he was changin'. Pulled his sweater down for him. He's cut about all over the arms – horrid purply ones. He's goin' to tell us about it tonight. I asked him to when I was lacin' his boots.'

'Well, you *have* got cheek,' said Beetle, enviously.

'Slipped out before I thought. But he wasn't a bit angry. He's no end of a chap. I swear, I'm goin' to play up like beans. Tell Turkey!'

The technique of that match belongs to a bygone age. Scrimmages were tight and enduring; hacking was direct and to the purpose; and around the scrimmage stood the school, crying, 'Put down your heads and shove!' Toward the end everybody lost all sense of decency, and mothers of day boys too close to the touchline heard language not included in the bills. No one was actually carried off the field, but both sides felt happier when time was called, and Beetle helped Stalky and McTurk into their overcoats. The two had met in the many-legged heart of things, and, as Stalky said, had 'done each other proud.' As they swaggered woodenly behind the teams – substitutes do not rank as equals of hairy men – they passed a pony-carriage near the wall, and a husky voice cried, 'Well played. Oh, played indeed!' It was Stettson major, white-cheeked and hollow-eyed, who had fought his way to the ground under escort of an impatient coachman.

'Hullo, Stettson,' said Stalky, checking. 'Is it safe to come near you yet?'

'Oh, yes. I'm all right. They wouldn't let me out before, but I had to come to the match. Your mouth looks pretty plummy.'

'Turkey trod on it accidental-done-a-purpose. Well, I'm glad you're better, because we owe you something. You and your membranes got us into a sweet mess, young man.'

'I heard of that,' said the boy, giggling. 'The head told me.'

'Deuce he did! When?'

'Oh, come on up to coll. My shin'll stiffen if we stay jawin' here.'

'Shut up, Turkey. I want to find out about this. Well?'

'He was stayin' at our house all the time I was ill.'

'What for? Neglectin' the coll. that way? Thought he was in town.'

'I was off my head, you know, and they said I kept on callin' for him.'

'Cheek! You're only a day boy.'

'He came just the same, and he about saved my life. I was all bunged up one night – just goin' to croak, the doctor said – and they stuck a tube or somethin' in my throat, and the head sucked out the stuff.'

'Ugh! Shot if *I* would!'

'He ought to have got diphtheria himself, the doctor said. So he stayed on at our house instead of going back. I'd ha' croaked in another twenty minutes, the doctor says.'

Here the coachman, being under orders, whipped up and nearly ran over the three.

'My hat!' said Beetle. 'That's pretty average heroic.'

'Pretty average!' McTurk's knee in the small of his back cannoned him into Stalky, who punted him back. 'You ought to be hung!'

'And the head ought to get the VC,' said Stalky. 'Why, he might have been dead *and* buried by now. But he wasn't. But he didn't. Ho! ho! He just nipped through the hedge like a lusty old blackbird. Extra-special, five hundred lines, an' gated for a week – all sereno!'

'I've read o' somethin' like that in a book,' said Beetle. 'Gummy, what a chap! Just think of it!'

'I'm thinking,' said McTurk; and he delivered a wild Irish yell that made the team turn round.

'Shut your fat mouth,' said Stalky, dancing with impatience. 'Leave it to your Uncle Stalky, and he'll have the head on toast. If you say a word, Beetle, till I give you leave, I swear I'll slay you. *Habeo Capitem crinibus minimis*. I've got him by the short hairs! Now look as if nothing had happened.'

There was no need of guile. The school was too busy cheering the drawn match. It hung round the lavatories regardless of muddy boots while the team washed. It cheered Crandall minor whenever it caught sight of him, and it cheered more wildly than ever after prayers, because the old boys in evening dress, openly twirling their moustaches, attended, and instead of standing with the masters, ranged themselves along the wall immediately before the prefects; and the head called them over, too – majors, minors, and tertiuses, after their old names.

'Yes, it's all very fine,' he said to his guests after dinner, 'but the boys are getting a little out of hand. There will be trouble and sorrow later, I'm afraid. You'd better turn in early, Crandall. The dormitory will be sitting up for you. I don't know to what dizzy heights you may climb in your profession, but I do know you'll never get such absolute adoration as you're getting now.'

'Confound the adoration. I want to finish my cigar, sir.'

'It's all pure gold. Go where glory waits, Crandall – minor.'

The setting of that apotheosis was a ten-bed attic dormitory, communicating through doorless openings with three others. The gas flickered over the raw pine washstands. There was an incessant whistling of draughts, and outside the naked windows the sea beat on the Pebbleridge.

'Same old bed – same old mattress, I believe,' said Crandall, yawning. 'Same old everything. Oh, but I'm lame! I'd no notion you chaps could play like this.' He caressed a battered shin. 'You've given us all something to remember you by.'

It needed a few minutes to put them at their ease; and, in some way they could not understand, they were more easy when Crandall turned round and said his prayers – a ceremony he had neglected for some years.

'Oh, I *am* sorry. I've forgotten to put out the gas.'

'Please don't bother,' said the prefect of the dormitory. 'Worthington does that.'

A nightgowned twelve-year-old, who had been waiting to show off, leaped from his bed to the bracket and back again, by way of a washstand.

'How d'you manage when he's asleep?' said Crandall, chuckling.

'Shove a cold cleek down his neck.'

'It was a wet sponge when I was junior in the dormitory . . . Hullo! What's happening?'

The darkness had filled with whispers, the sound of trailing rugs, bare feet on bare boards, protests, giggles, and threats such as:

'Be quiet, you ass! . . . *Squattez-vous* on the floor, then! . . . I swear you aren't going to sit on *my* bed! . . . Mind the tooth-glass,' etc.

'Sta – Corkran said,' the prefect began, his tone showing his sense of Stalky's insolence, 'that perhaps you'd tell us about that business with Duncan's body.'

'Yes – yes – yes,' ran the keen whispers. 'Tell us'

'There's nothing to tell. What on earth are you chaps hoppin' about in the cold for?'

'Never mind us,' said the voices. 'Tell about Fat-Sow.'

So Crandall turned on his pillow and spoke to the generation he could not see.

'Well, about three months ago he was commanding a treasure-guard – a cart full of rupees to pay troops with – five thousand rupees in silver. He was comin' to a place called Fort Pearson, near Kalabagh.'

'I was born there,' squeaked a small fag. 'It was called after my uncle.'

'Shut up – you and your uncle! Never mind him, Crandall.'

'Well, ne'er mind. The Afridis found out that this treasure was on the move, and they ambushed the whole show a couple of miles before he got to the fort, and cut up the escort. Duncan was wounded, and the escort hooked it. There weren't more than twenty Sepoys all told, and there were any amount of Afridis. As things turned out, I was in charge at Fort Pearson. Fact was, I'd heard the firing and was just going to see about it, when Duncan's men came up. So we all turned back together. They told me something about an officer, but I couldn't get the hang of things till I saw a chap under the wheels of the cart out in the open, propped up on one arm, blazing away with a revolver. You see, the escort had abandoned the cart, and the Afridis – they're an awfully suspicious gang – thought the retreat was a trap – sort of draw, you know – and the cart was the bait. So they had left poor old Duncan alone. Minute they spotted how few we were, it was a race across the flat who should reach old Duncan first. We ran, and they ran, and we won, and after a little hackin' about they pulled off. I never knew it was one of us till I was right on top of him. There are heaps of Duncans in the service, and of course the name didn't remind me. He wasn't changed at all hardly. He'd been shot through the lungs, poor old man, and he was pretty thirsty. I gave him a drink and sat down beside him, and – funny thing, too – he said, "Hullo, Toffee!" and I said, "Hullo, Fat-Sow! Hope you aren't hurt," or something of the kind. But he died in a minute or two – never lifted his head off my knees . . . I say, you chaps out there will get your death of cold. Better go to bed.'

'All right. In a minute. But your cuts – your cuts. How did you get wounded?'

'That was when we were taking the body back to the Fort. They came on again, and there was a bit of a scrimmage.'

'Did you kill anyone?'

'Yes. Shouldn't wonder. Good-night.'

'Good-night. Thank you, Crandall. Thanks awf'ly, Crandall. Good-night.'

The unseen crowds withdrew. His own dormitory rustled into bed and lay silent for a while.

'I say, Crandall' – Stalky's voice was tuned to a wholly foreign reverence.

'Well, what?'

'Suppose a chap found another chap croaking with diphtheria – all bunged up with it – and they stuck a tube in his throat and the chap sucked the stuff out, what would you say?'

'Um,' said Crandall, reflectively. 'I've only heard of one case, and that was a doctor. He did it for a woman.'

'Oh, this wasn't a woman. It was just a boy.'

'Makes it all the finer, then. It's about the bravest thing a man can do. Why?'

'Oh, I heard of a chap doin' it. That's all.'

'Then he's a brave man.'

'Would *you* funk it?'

'Ra–ather. Anybody would. Fancy dying of diphtheria in cold blood.'

'Well – ah! Er! Look here!' The sentence ended in a grunt, for Stalky had leaped out of bed and with McTurk was sitting on the head of Beetle, who would have sprung the mine there and then.

Next day, which was the last of the term and given up to a few wholly unimportant examinations, began with wrath and war. Mr King had discovered that nearly all his house – it lay, as you know, next door but one to Prout's in the long range of buildings – had unlocked the doors between the dormitories and had gone in to listen to a story told by Crandall. He went to the head, clamorous, injured, appealing; for he never approved of allowing so-called young men of the world to contaminate the morals of boyhood. Very good, said the head, he would attend to it.

'Well, I'm awf'ly sorry,' said Crandall guiltily. 'I don't think I told 'em anything they oughtn't to hear. Don't let them get into trouble on my account.'

'Tck!' the head answered, with the ghost of a wink. 'It isn't the boys that make trouble; it's the masters. However, Prout and King don't approve of dormitory gatherings on this scale, and one must back up the housemasters. Moreover, it's hopeless to punish two houses only, so late in the term. We must be fair and include everybody. Let's see. They have a holiday task for the Easters, which, of course, none of them will ever look at. We will give the whole school, except prefects and study-boys, regular prep tonight; and the common room will have to supply a master to take it. We must be fair to all.'

'Prep on the last night of the term. Whew!' said Crandall, thinking of his own wild youth. 'I fancy there will be larks.'

The school, frolicking among packed trunks, whooping down the corridor, and 'gloating' in form-rooms, received the news with amazement and rage. No school in the world did prep on the last night of the term. This thing was monstrous, tyrannical, subversive of law, religion, and morality. They would go into the form-rooms, and they would take their degraded holiday task with them, but – here they smiled and speculated what manner of man the common room would send up against them. The lot fell on Mason, credulous and enthusiastic, who loved youth. No other master was anxious to take that 'prep', for the school lacked the steadying influence of tradition; and men accustomed to the ordered routine of ancient foundations found it occasionally insubordinate. The four long form-rooms, in which all below the rank of study-boys worked, received him with thunders of applause. Ere he had coughed twice they favoured him with a metrical summary of the marriage laws of Great Britain, as recorded by the high priest of the Israelites and commented on by the leader of the host. The lower forms reminded him that it was the last day, and that therefore he must 'take it all in play'. When he dashed off to rebuke them, the Lower Fourth and Upper Third began with one accord to be sick, loudly and realistically. Mr Mason tried, of all vain things under heaven, to argue with them, and a bold soul at a back desk bade him 'take fifty lines for not 'olding up 'is 'and before speaking'. As one who prided himself upon the perfection of his English this cut Mason to the quick, and while he was trying to discover the offender, the Upper and Lower Second, three form-rooms away, turned out the gas and threw inkpots. It was a pleasant and stimulating 'prep'. The study-boys and prefects heard the echoes of it far off, and the common room at dessert smiled.

Stalky waited, watch in hand, till half-past eight. 'If it goes on much longer the head will come up,' said he. 'We'll tell the studies first, and then the dorm-rooms. Look sharp!'

He allowed no time for Beetle to be dramatic or McTurk to drawl. They poured into study after study, told their tale, and went again so soon as they saw they were understood, waiting for no comment; while the noise of that unholy 'prep' grew and deepened. By the door of Flint's study they met Mason flying towards the corridor.

'He's gone to fetch the head. Hurry up! Come on!' They broke into number twelve form-room abreast and panting.

'The head! The head! The head!' That call stilled the tumult for a minute, and Stalky, leaping to a desk, shouted, 'He went and sucked the diphtheria stuff out of Stettson major's throat when we thought he was in town. Stop rotting, you asses! Stettson major would have croaked if the head hadn't done it. The head might have died himself. Crandall says it's the bravest thing any livin' man can do, and – ' his voice cracked – 'the head don't know we know!'

McTurk and Beetle, jumping from desk to desk, drove the news home among the junior forms. There was a pause, and then, Mason behind him, the head entered. It was in the established order of things that no boy should speak or move under his eye. He expected the hush of awe. He was received with cheers – steady, ceaseless cheering. Being a wise man, he went away, and the forms were silent and a little frightened.

'It's all right,' said Stalky. 'He can't do much. 'Tisn't as if you'd pulled the desks up like we did when old Carleton took prep once. Keep it up! Hear 'em cheering in the studies!' He rocketed out with a yell, to find Flint and the prefects lifting the roof off the corridor.

When the head of a limited liability company, paying four per cent, is cheered on his saintly way to prayers, not only by four form-rooms of boys waiting punishment, but by his trusted prefects, he can either ask for an explanation or go his road with dignity, while the senior housemaster glares like an excited cat and points out to a white and trembling mathematical master that certain methods – not his, thank God – usually produce certain results. Out of delicacy the old boys did not attend that call-over; and it was to the school drawn up in the gymnasium that the head spoke icily.

'It is not often that I do not understand you; but I confess I do not tonight. Some of you, after your idiotic performances at prep, seem to think me a fit person to cheer. I am going to show you that I am not.'

Crash – crash – crash – came the triple cheer that disproved it, and the head glowered under the gas. 'That is enough. You will gain nothing. The little boys' (the Lower School did not like that form of address) 'will do me three hundred lines apiece in the holidays. I shall take no further notice of them.

The Upper School will do me one thousand lines apiece in the holidays, to be shown up the evening of the day they come back. And further – '

'Gummy, what a glutton!' Stalky whispered.

'For your behaviour towards Mr Mason I intend to lick the whole of the Upper School tomorrow when I give you your journey-money. This will include the three study-boys I found dancing on the form-room desks when I came up. Prefects will stay after call-over.'

The school filed out in silence, but gathered in groups by the gymnasium door waiting what might befall.

'And now, Flint,' said the head, 'will you be good enough to give me some explanation of your conduct?'

'Well, sir,' said Flint desperately, 'if you save a chap's life at the risk of your own when he's dyin' of diphtheria, and the coll. finds it out, wha–what can you expect, sir?'

'Um, I see. Then that noise was not meant for – ah, cheek. I can connive at immorality, but I cannot stand impudence. However, it does not excuse their insolence to Mr Mason. I'll forego the lines this once, remember; but the lickings hold good.'

When this news was made public, the school, lost in wonder and admiration, gasped at the head as he went to his house. Here was a man to be reverenced. On the rare occasions when he caned he did it very scientifically, and the execution of a hundred boys would be epic – immense.

'It's all right, head sahib. *We* know,' said Crandall, as the head slipped off his gown with a grunt in his smoking-room. 'I found out just now from our substitute. He was gettin' my opinion of your performance last night in the dormitory. I didn't know then that it was you he was talkin' about. Crafty young animal. Freckled chap with eyes – Corkran, I think his name is.'

'Oh, I know *him*, thank you,' said the head, and reflectively. 'Ye–es, I should have included them even if I hadn't seen 'em.'

'If the old coll. weren't a little above themselves already, we'd chair you down the corridor,' said the Engineer. 'Oh, Bates, how could you? You might have caught it yourself, and where would we have been, then?'

'I always knew you were worth twenty of us any day. Now I'm sure of it,' said the Squadron Commander, looking round for contradictions.

'He isn't fit to manage a school, though. Promise you'll never do it again, Bates sahib. We – we can't go away comfy in our minds if you take these risks,' said the Gunner.

'Bates sahib, you aren't ever goin' to cane the whole Upper School, are you?' said Crandall.

'I can connive at immorality, as I said, but I can't stand impudence. Mason's lot is quite hard enough even when I back him. Besides, the men at the golf club heard them singing "Aaron and Moses". I shall have complaints about that from the parents of day-boys. Decency must be preserved.'

'We're coming to help,' said all the guests.

The Upper School were caned one after the other, their overcoats over their arms, the brakes waiting in the road below to take them to the station, their journey-money on the table. The head began with Stalky, McTurk, and Beetle. He dealt faithfully by them.

'And here's your journey-money. Goodbye, and pleasant holidays.'

'Goodbye. Thank you, sir. Goodbye.'

They shook hands. 'Desire don't outrun performance – much – this mornin'. We got the cream of it,' said Stalky. 'Now wait till a few chaps come out, and we'll really cheer him.'

'Don't wait on our account, please,' said Crandall, speaking for the old boys. 'We're going to begin now.'

It was very well so long as the cheering was confined to the corridor, but when it spread to the gymnasium, when the boys awaiting their turn cheered, the head gave it up in despair, and the remnant flung themselves upon him to shake hands. Then they seriously devoted themselves to cheering till the brakes were hustled off the premises in dumbshow.

'Didn't I say I'd get even with him?' said Stalky on the box-seat, as they swung into the narrow Northam Street. 'Now all together – takin' time from your Uncle Stalky:

> It's a way we have in the army,
> It's a way we have in the navy,
> It's a way we have at the public schools,
>   Which nobody can deny!'

The Flag of Their Country

It was winter and bitter cold of mornings. Consequently Stalky and Beetle – McTurk being of the offensive type that makes ornate toilet under all circumstances – drowsed till the last moment before turning out to call-over in the gaslit gymnasium. It followed that they were often late; and since every unpunctuality earned them a black mark, and since three black marks a week meant defaulters' drill, equally it followed that they spent hours under the sergeant's hand. Foxy drilled the defaulters with all the pomp of his old parade ground.

'Don't think it's any pleasure to me' (his introduction never varied). 'I'd much sooner be smoking a quiet pipe in my own quarters – but I see we 'ave the old brigade on our 'ands this afternoon. If I only 'ad you regular, Muster Corkran,' said he, dressing the line.

'You've had me for nearly six weeks, you old glutton. Number off from the right!'

'Not *quite* so previous, please. I'm taking this drill. Left, half – turn! Slow – march.' Twenty-five sluggards, all old offenders, filed into the gymnasium. 'Quietly provide yourselves with the requisite dumbbells; returnin' quietly to your place. Number off from the right, in a low voice. Odd numbers one pace to the front. Even numbers stand fast. Now, leanin' forward from the 'ips, takin' your time from me.'

The dumbbells rose and fell, clashed and were returned as one. The boys were experts at the weary game.

'Ve–ry good. I shall be sorry when any of you resume your 'abits of punctuality. Quietly return dumbbells. We will now try some simple drill.'

'Ugh! I know that simple drill.'

'It would be 'ighly to your discredit if you did not, Muster Corkran. *At* the same time, it is not so easy as it looks.'

'Bet you a bob, I can drill as well as you, Foxy.'

'We'll see later. Now try to imagine you ain't defaulters at all, but an 'arf company on parade, me bein' your commandin' officer. There's no call to laugh. If you're lucky, most of you will 'ave to take drills 'arf your life. Do me a little credit. You've been at it long enough, goodness knows.'

They were formed into fours, marched, wheeled, and countermarched, the spell of ordered motion strong on them. As Foxy said, they had been at it a long time.

The gymnasium door opened, revealing McTurk in charge of an old gentleman.

The sergeant, leading a wheel, did not see. 'Not so bad,' he murmured. 'Not 'arf so bad. The pivot-man of the wheel *honly* marks time, Muster Swayne. Now, Muster Corkran, you say you know the drill? Oblige me by takin' over the command and, reversin' my words step by step, relegate them to their previous formation.'

'What's this? What's this?' cried the visitor authoritatively.

'A – a little drill, sir,' stammered Foxy, saying nothing of first causes.

'Excellent – excellent. I only wish there were more of it,' he chirruped. 'Don't let me interrupt. You were just going to hand over to someone, weren't you?'

He sat down, breathing frostily in the chill air.

'I shall muck it. I know I shall,' whispered Stalky uneasily; and his discomfort was not lightened by a murmur from the rear rank that the old gentleman was General Collinson, a member of the college Board of Council.

'Eh – what?' said Foxy.

'Collinson, KCB – he commanded the Pompadours – my father's old regiment,' hissed Swayne major.

'Take your time,' said the visitor. '*I* know how it feels. Your first drill – eh?'

'Yes, sir.' He drew an unhappy breath. ' 'Tention. Dress!' The echo of his own voice restored his confidence.

The wheel was faced about, flung back, broken into fours, and restored to line without a falter. The official hour of punishment was long passed, but no one thought of that. They were backing up Stalky – Stalky in deadly fear lest his voice should crack.

'He does you credit, sergeant,' was the visitor's comment. 'A good drill – and good material to drill. Now, it's an extraordinary thing: I've been lunching with your headmaster and he never told me you had a cadet corps in the college.'

'We 'aven't, sir. This is only a little drill,' said the sergeant.

'But aren't they keen on it?' said McTurk, speaking for the first time, with a twinkle in his deep-set eyes.

'Why aren't you in it, though, Willy?'

'Oh, I'm not punctual enough,' said McTurk. 'The sergeant only takes the pick of us.'

'Dismiss! Break off!' cried Foxy, fearing an explosion in the ranks. 'I – I ought to have told you, sir, that – '

'But you should have a cadet corps.' The general pursued his own line of thought. 'You *shall* have a cadet corps, too, if my recommendation in council is any use. I don't know when I've been so pleased. Boys animated by a spirit like yours should set an example to the whole school.'

'They do,' said McTurk.

'Bless my soul! Can it be so late? I've kept my fly waiting half an hour. Well, I must run away. Nothing like seeing things for one's self. Which end of the buildings does one get out at? Will you show me, Willy? Who was that boy who took the drill?'

'Corkran, I think his name is.'

'You ought to know him. That's the kind of boy you should cultivate. Evidently an unusual sort. A wonderful sight. Five and twenty boys, who, I dare say, would much sooner be playing cricket – ' (it was the depth of winter; but grown people, especially those who have lived long in foreign parts, make these little errors, and McTurk did not correct him) – 'drilling for the sheer love of it. A shame to waste so much good stuff; but I think I can carry my point.'

'An' who's your friend with the white whiskers?' demanded Stalky, on McTurk's return to the study.

'General Collinson. He comes over to shoot with my father sometimes. Rather a decent old bargee, too. He said I ought to cultivate your acquaintance, Stalky.'

'Did he tip you?'

McTurk exhibited a blessed whole sovereign.

'Ah,' said Stalky, annexing it, for he was treasurer. 'We'll have a hefty brew. You'd pretty average cool cheek, Turkey, to jaw about our keenness an' punctuality.'

'Didn't the old boy know we were defaulters?' said Beetle.

'Not him. He came down to lunch with the head. I found him pokin' about the place on his own hook afterwards, an' I thought I'd show him the giddy drill. When I found he was so pleased, I wasn't goin' to damp his giddy ardour. He mightn't ha' given me the quid if I had.'

'Wasn't old Foxy pleased? Did you see him get pink behind the ears?' said Beetle. 'It was an awful score for him. Didn't we back him up beautifully? Let's go down to Keyte's and get some cocoa and sassingers.'

They overtook Foxy, speeding down to retail the adventure to Keyte, who in his time had been troop sergeant-major in a cavalry regiment, and now, war-worn veteran, was local postmaster and confectioner.

'You owe us something,' said Stalky, with meaning.

'I'm 'ighly grateful, Muster Corkran. I've 'ad to run against you pretty hard in the way o' business, now and then, but I will say that outside o' business – bounds an' smokin', an' such like – I don't wish to have a more trustworthy young gentleman to 'elp me out of a hole. The way you 'andled the drill was beautiful, though I say it. Now, if you come regular henceforward – '

'But he'll have to be late three times a week,' said Beetle. 'You can't expect a chap to do that – just to please you, Foxy.'

'Ah, that's true. Still, if you could manage it – and you, Muster Beetle – it would give you a big start when the cadet corps is formed. I expect the general will recommend it.'

They raided Keyte's very much at their own sweet will, for the old man, who knew them well, was deep in talk with Foxy.

'I make what we've taken seven and six,' Stalky called at last over the counter; 'but you'd better count for yourself.'

'No – no. I'd take your word any day, Muster Corkran. – In the Pompadours, was he, sergeant? We lay with them once at Umballa, I think it was.'

'I don't know whether this ham-and-tongue tin is eighteen pence or one an' four.'

'Say one an' fourpence, Muster Corkran . . . Of course, sergeant, if it was any use to give my time, I'd be pleased to do it, but I'm too old. I'd like to see a drill again.'

'Oh, come on, Stalky,' cried McTurk. 'He isn't listenin' to you. Chuck over the money.'

'I want the quid changed, you ass. Keyte! Private Keyte! Corporal Keyte! Terroop-Sergeant-Major Keyte, will you give me change for a quid?'

'Yes – yes, of course. Seven an' six.' He stared abstractedly, pushed the silver over, and melted away into the darkness of the back room.

'Now those two'll jaw about the mutiny till teatime,' said Beetle.

'Old Keyte was at Sobraon,' said Stalky. 'Hear him talk about that sometimes! Beats Foxy hollow.'

* * *

The head's face, inscrutable as ever, was bent over a pile of letters.

'What do you think?' he said at last to the Revd John Gillett.

'It's a good idea. There's no denying that – an estimable idea.'

'We concede that much. Well?'

'I have my doubts about it – that's all. The more I know of boys, the less do I profess myself capable of following their moods; but I own I shall be very much surprised if the scheme takes. It – it isn't the temper of the school. We prepare for the army.'

'My business – in *this* matter – is to carry out the wishes of the council. They demand a volunteer cadet corps. A volunteer cadet corps will be furnished. I have suggested, however, that we need not embark upon the expense of uniforms till we are drilled. General Collinson is sending us fifty lethal weapons – cut-down Sniders, he calls them – all carefully plugged.'

'Yes, that is necessary in a school that uses loaded saloon-pistols to the extent we do.' The Revd John smiled.

'Therefore there will be no outlay except the sergeant's time.'

'But if he fails you will be blamed.'

'Oh, assuredly. I shall post a notice in the corridor this afternoon, and –'

'I shall watch the result.'

* * *

'Kindly keep your 'ands off the new arm-rack.' Foxy wrestled with a turbulent crowd in the gymnasium. 'Nor it won't do even a condemned Snider any good to be continual snappin' the lock, Mr Swayne. – Yiss, the uniforms will come later, when we're more proficient; at present we will confine ourselves to drill. I am 'ere for the purpose o' takin' the names o' those willin' to join. – Put down that Snider, Muster Hogan!'

'What are you goin' to do, Beetle?' said a voice.

'I've had all the drill *I* want, thank you.'

'What! After all you've learned? Come on! Don't be a scab! They'll make you corporal in a week,' cried Stalky.

'I'm not goin' up for the army.' Beetle touched his spectacles.

'Hold on a shake, Foxy,' said Hogan. 'Where are you goin' to drill us?'

'Here – in the gym – till you are fit an' capable to be taken out on the road.' The sergeant threw a chest.

'For all the Northam cads to look at? Not good enough, Foxibus.'

'Well, we won't make a point of it. You learn your drill first, an' later we'll see.'

'Hullo,' said Ansell of Macrea's, shouldering through the mob. 'What's all this about a giddy cadet corps?'

'It will save you a lot o' time at Sandhurst,' the sergeant replied promptly. 'You'll be dismissed your drills early if you go up with a good groundin' before'and.'

'Hm! Don't mind learnin' my drill, but I'm not goin' to ass about the country with a toy Snider. Perowne, what are you goin' to do? Hogan's joinin'.'

'Don't know whether I've the time,' said Perowne. 'I've got no end of extra-tuition as it is.'

'Well, call this extra-tuition,' said Ansell. ' 'Twon't take us long to mug up the drill.'

'Oh, that's right enough, but what about marchin' in public?' said Hogan, not foreseeing that three years later he should die in the Burmese sunlight outside Minhla Fort.

'Afraid the uniform won't suit your creamy complexion?' McTurk asked with a villainous sneer.

'Shut up, Turkey. You aren't goin' up for the army.'

'No, but I'm goin' to send a substitute. Hi! Morrell an' Wake! You two fags by the arm-rack, you've got to volunteer.'

Blushing deeply – they had been too shy to apply before – the youngsters sidled towards the sergeant.

'But I don't want the little chaps – not at first,' said the sergeant disgustedly. 'I want – I'd like some of the old brigade the defaulters – to stiffen 'em a bit.'

'Don't be ungrateful, sergeant. They're nearly as big as you get 'em in the army now.' McTurk read the papers of those years and could be trusted for general information, which he used as he used his 'tweaker'. Yet he did not know that Wake minor would be a bimbashi of the Egyptian army ere his thirtieth year.

Hogan, Swayne, Stalky, Perowne, and Ansell were deep in consultation by the vaulting-horse, Stalky as usual laying down the law. The sergeant watched them uneasily, knowing that many waited on their lead.

'Foxy don't like my recruits,' said McTurk, in a pained tone, to Beetle. 'You get him some.'

Nothing loath, Beetle pinioned two more fags – each no taller than a carbine. 'Here you are, Foxy. Here's food for powder. Strike for your hearths an' homes, you young brutes – an' be jolly quick about it.'

'Still he isn't happy,' said McTurk.

> 'For the way we have with our army
> Is the way we have with our navy.'

Here Beetle joined in. They had found the poem in an old volume of *Punch*, and it seemed to cover the situation:

> 'An' both of 'em lead to adversity,
> Which nobody can deny!'

'You be quiet, young gentlemen. If you can't 'elp – don't 'inder.' Foxy's eye was still on the council by the horse. Carter, White, and Tyrrell, all boys of influence, had joined it. The rest fingered the rifles irresolutely. 'Wait a shake,' cried Stalky. 'Can't we turn out those rotters before we get to work?'

'Certainly,' said Foxy. 'Any one wishful to join will stay 'ere. Those who do not so intend will go out, quietly closin' the door be'ind 'em.'

Half a dozen of the earnest-minded rushed at them, and they had just time to escape into the corridor.

'Well, why don't you join?' Beetle asked, resetting his collar.

'Why didn't you?'

'What's the good? We aren't goin' up for the army. Besides, I know the drill – all except the manual, of course. Wonder what they're doin' inside?'

'Makin' a treaty with Foxy. Didn't you hear Stalky say: "That's what we'll do – an' if he don't like it he can lump it"? They'll use Foxy for a cram. Can't you see, you idiot? They're goin' up for Sandhurst or the Shop in less than a year. They'll learn their drill an' then they'll drop it like a shot. D'you suppose chaps with their amount of extra-tuition are takin' up volunteerin' for fun?'

'Well, I don't know. I thought of doin' a poem about it – rottin' 'em, you know – 'The Ballad of the Dogshooters' – eh?'

'I don't think you can, because King'll be down on the corps like a cartload o' bricks. He hasn't been consulted, he's sniffin' round the noticeboard now. Let's lure him.' They strolled up carelessly towards the housemaster – a most meek couple.

'How's this?' said King with a start of feigned surprise. 'Methought you would be learning to fight for your country.'

'I think the company's full, sir,' said McTurk.

'It's a great pity,' sighed Beetle.

'Forty valiant defenders, have we, then? How noble! What devotion! I presume that it is possible that a desire to evade their normal responsibilities may be at the bottom of this zeal. Doubtless they will be accorded special privileges, like the choir and the Natural History Society – one must not say bug-hunters.'

'Oh, I suppose so, sir,' said McTurk, cheerily. 'The head hasn't said anything about it yet, but he will, of course.'

'Oh, sure to.'

'It is just possible, my Beetle,' King wheeled on the last speaker, 'that the housemasters – a necessary but somewhat neglected factor in our humble scheme of existence – may have a word to say on the matter. Life, for the young at least, is not all weapons and munitions of war. Education is incidentally one of our aims.'

'What a consistent pig he is,' cooed McTurk, when they were out of earshot. 'One always knows where to have him. Did you see how he rose to that draw about the head and special privileges?'

'Confound him, he might have had the decency to have backed the scheme. I could do such a lovely ballad, rottin' it; and now I'll have to be a giddy enthusiast. It don't bar our pulling Stalky's leg in the study, does it?'

'Oh, no; but in the coll. we must be pro-cadet corps like anything. Can't you make up a giddy epigram, *à la* Catullus, about King objectin' to it?' Beetle was at this noble task when Stalky returned all hot from his first drill.

'Hullo, my ramrod-bunger!' began McTurk. 'Where's your dead dog? Is it defence or defiance?'

'Defiance,' said Stalky, and leaped on him at that word. 'Look here, Turkey, you mustn't rot the corps. We've arranged it beautifully. Foxy swears he won't take us out into the open till we say we want to go.'

'*Dis*–gustin' exhibition of immature infants apin' the idiosyncrasies of their elders. Snff!'

'Have you drawn King, Beetle?' Stalky asked in a pause of the scuffle.

'Not exactly; but that's his genial style.'

'Well, listen to your Uncle Stalky – who is a great man. Moreover and subsequently, Foxy's goin' to let us drill the corps in turn – *privatim et seriatim* – so that we'll all know how to handle a half company anyhow. *Ergo*, an' *propter hoc*, when we go to the shop we shall be dismissed drill early; thus, my beloved 'earers, combinin' education with wholesome amusement.'

'I knew you'd make a sort of extra-tuition of it, you cold-blooded brute,' said McTurk. 'Don't you want to die for your giddy country?'

'Not if I can jolly well avoid it. So you mustn't rot the corps.'

'We'd decided on that, years ago,' said Beetle, scornfully. 'King'll do the rottin'.'

'Then you've got to rot King, my giddy poet. Make up a good catchy limerick, and let the fags sing it.'

'Look here, you stick to volunteerin', and don't jog the table.'

'He won't have anything to take hold of,' said Stalky, with dark significance.

They did not know what that meant till, a few days later, they proposed to watch the corps at drill. They found the gymnasium door locked and a fag on guard. 'This is sweet cheek,' said McTurk, stooping.

'Mustn't look through the keyhole,' said the sentry.

'I like that. Why, Wake, you little beast, I made you a volunteer.'

'Can't help it. My orders are not to allow any one to look.'

'S'pose we do?' said McTurk. 'S'pose we jolly well slay you?'

'My orders are, I am to give the name of anybody who interfered with me on my post, to the corps, an' they'd deal with him after drill, accordin' to martial law.'

'What a brute Stalky is!' said Beetle. They never doubted for a moment who had devised that scheme.

'You esteem yourself a giddy centurion, don't you?' said Beetle, listening to the crash and rattle of grounded arms within.

'My orders are, not to talk except to explain my orders – they'll lick me if I do.'

McTurk looked at Beetle. The two shook their heads and turned away.

'I swear Stalky *is* a great man,' said Beetle after a long pause. 'One consolation is that this sort of secret-society biznai will drive King wild.'

It troubled many more than King, but the members of the corps were muter than oysters. Foxy, being bound by no vow, carried his woes to Keyte.

'I never come across such nonsense in my life. They've tiled the lodge, inner and outer guard, all complete, and then they get to work, keen as mustard.'

'But what's it all for?' asked the ex-troop sergeant-major.

'To learn their drill. You never saw anything like it. They begin after I've dismissed 'em – practisin' tricks; but out into the open they will *not* come – not for ever so. The 'ole thing is pre–posterous. If you're a cadet corps, *I* say, be a cadet corps, instead o' hidin' be'ind locked doors.'

'And what do the authorities say about it?'

'That beats me again.' The sergeant spoke fretfully. 'I go to the 'ead an' 'e gives me no help. There's times when I think he's makin' fun o' me. I've never been a volunteer-sergeant, thank god – but I've always had the consideration to pity 'em. I'm glad o' that.'

'I'd like to see 'em,' said Keyte. 'From your statements, sergeant, I can't get at what they're after.'

'Don't ask me, major! Ask that freckle-faced young Corkran. He's their generalissimo.'

One does not refuse a warrior of Sobraon, or deny the only pastry cook within bounds. So Keyte came, by invitation, leaning upon a stick, tremulous with old age, to sit in a corner and watch.

'They shape well. They shape uncommon well,' he whispered between evolutions.

'Oh, this isn't what they're after. Wait till I dismiss 'em.'

At the 'break-off' the ranks stood fast. Perowne fell out, faced them, and, refreshing his memory by glimpses at a red-bound, metal-clasped book, drilled them for ten minutes. (This is that Perowne who was shot in Equatorial Africa by his own men.) Ansell followed him, and Hogan followed Ansell. All three were implicitly obeyed. Then Stalky laid aside his Snider, and, drawing a long breath, favoured the company with a blast of withering invective.

' 'Old 'ard, Muster Corkran. That ain't in any drill,' cried Foxy.

'All right, sergeant. You never know what you may have to say to your men. – For pity's sake, try to stand up without leanin' against each other, you blear-eyed, herrin'-gutted guttersnipes. It's no pleasure to me to comb you out. That ought to have been done before you came here, you – you militia broom-stealers.'

'The old touch – the old touch. *We* know it,' said Keyte, wiping his rheumy eyes. 'But where did he pick it up?'

'From his father – or his uncle. Don't ask me! Half of 'em must have been born within earshot o' the barracks.' (Foxy was not far wrong in his guess.) 'I've heard more back-talk since this volunteerin' nonsense began than I've heard in a year in the service.'

'There's a rear-rank man lookin' as though his belly were in the pawnshop. Yes, you, Private Ansell,' and Stalky tongue-lashed the victim for three minutes, in gross and in detail.

'Hullo!' He returned to his normal tone. 'First blood to me. You flushed, Ansell. You wriggled.'

'Couldn't help flushing,' was the answer. 'Don't think I wriggled, though.'

'Well, it's your turn now.' Stalky resumed his place in the ranks.

'Lord, Lord! It's as good as a play,' chuckled the attentive Keyte. Ansell, too, had been blessed with relatives in the service, and slowly, in a lazy drawl – his style was more reflective than Stalky's – descended the abysmal depths of personality.

'Blood to me!' he shouted triumphantly. 'You couldn't stand it, either.' Stalky was a rich red, and his Snider shook visibly.

'I didn't think I would,' he said, struggling for composure, 'but after a bit I got in no end of a bate. Curious, ain't it?'

'Good for the temper,' said the slow-moving Hogan, as they returned arms to the rack.

'Did you ever?' said Foxy, hopelessly, to Keyte.

'I don't know much about volunteers, but it's the rummiest show I ever saw. I can see what they're gettin' at, though. Lord! how often I've been told off an' dressed down in my day! They shape well – extremely well they shape.'

'If I could get 'em out into the open, there's nothing I couldn't do with 'em, major. Perhaps when the uniforms come down, they'll change their mind.'

Indeed it was time that the corps made some concession to the curiosity of the school. Thrice had the guard been maltreated and thrice had the corps dealt out martial law to the offender. The school raged. What was the use, they asked, of a cadet corps which none might see? Mr King congratulated them on their invisible defenders, and they could not parry his thrusts. Foxy was growing sullen and restive. A few of the corps expressed openly doubts as to the wisdom of their course; and the question of uniforms loomed on the near horizon. If these were issued, they would be forced to wear them.

But, as so often happens in this life, the matter was suddenly settled from without.

The head had duly informed the council that their recommendation had been acted upon, and that, so far as he could learn, the boys were drilling. He said nothing of the terms on which they drilled. Naturally, General Collinson was delighted and told his friends. One of his friends rejoiced in a friend, a Member of Parliament – a zealous, an intelligent, and, above all, a patriotic person, anxious to do the most good in the shortest possible time. But we cannot answer, alas! for the friends of our friends. If Collinson's friend had introduced him to the general, the latter would have taken his measure and saved much. But the friend merely spoke of his friend; and since no two people in the world see eye to eye, the picture conveyed to Collinson was inaccurate. Moreover, the man was an MP, an impeccable Conservative, and the general had the English soldier's lurking respect for any member of the Court of Last Appeal. He was going down into the West Country, to spread light in somebody's benighted constituency. Wouldn't it be a good idea if, armed with the general's recommendation, he, taking the admirable and newly established cadet corps for his text, spoke a few words – 'Just talked to the boys a little – eh? You know the kind of thing that would be acceptable; and he'd be the very man to do it. The sort of talk that boys understand, you know.'

'They didn't talk to 'em much in my time,' said the general, suspiciously.

'Ah! but times change – with the spread of education and so on. The boys of today are the men of tomorrow. An impression in youth is likely to be permanent. And in these times, you know, with the country going to the dogs?'

'You're quite right.' The island was then entering on five years of Mr Gladstone's rule; and the general did not like what he had seen of it. He would certainly write to the head, for it was beyond question that the boys of today made the men of tomorrow. That, if he might say so, was uncommonly well put.

In reply, the head stated that he should be delighted to welcome Mr Raymond Martin, MP, of whom he had heard so much; to put him up for the night, and to allow him to address the school on any subject that he conceived would interest them. If Mr Martin had not yet faced an audience of this particular class of British youth, the head had no doubt that he would find it an interesting experience.

'And I don't think I am very far wrong in that last,' he confided to the Revd John. 'Do you happen to know anything of one Raymond Martin?'

'I was at college with a man of that name,' the chaplain replied. 'He was without form and void, so far as I remember, but desperately earnest.'

'He will address the coll. on "Patriotism" next Saturday.'

'If there is one thing our boys detest more than another it is having their Saturday evenings broken into. Patriotism has no chance beside "brewing".'

'Nor art either. D'you remember our "Evening with Shakespeare"?' The head's eyes twinkled. 'Or the humorous gentleman with the magic lantern?'

* * *

'An' who the deuce is this Raymond Martin, MP?' demanded Beetle, when he read the notice of the lecture in the corridor. 'Why do the brutes always turn up on a Saturday?'

'Ouh! Reomeo, Reomeo. Wherefore art thou Reomeo?' said McTurk over his shoulder, quoting the Shakespeare artiste of last term. 'Well, he won't be as bad as *her*, I hope. Stalky, are you properly patriotic? Because if you ain't, this chap's goin' to make you.'

'Hope he won't take up the whole of the evening. I suppose we've got to listen to him.'

'Wouldn't miss him for the world,' said McTurk. 'A lot of chaps thought that Romeo-Romeo woman was a bore. *I* didn't. I liked her! 'Member when she began to hiccough in the middle of it? P'raps he'll hiccough. Whoever gets into the gym first, bags seats for the other two.'

* * *

There was no nervousness, but a brisk and cheery affability about Mr Raymond Martin, MP, as he drove up, watched by many eyes, to the head's house.

'Looks a bit of a bargee,' was McTurk's comment. 'Shouldn't be surprised if he was a Radical. He rowed the driver about the fare. I heard him.'

'That was his giddy patriotism,' Beetle explained. After tea they joined the rush for seats, secured a private and invisible corner, and began to criticise. Every gas-jet was lit. On the little dais at the far end stood the head's official desk, whence Mr Martin would discourse, and a ring of chairs for the masters.

Entered then Foxy, with official port, and leaned something like a cloth rolled round a stick against the desk. No one in authority was yet present, so the school applauded, crying: 'What's that, Foxy? What are you stealin' the gentleman's brolly for? – We don't birch here. We cane! Take away that bauble! – Number off from the right' – and so forth, till the entry of the head and the masters ended all demonstrations.

'One good job – the common room hate this as much as we do. Watch King wrigglin' to get out of the draught.'

'Where's the Raymondiferous Martin? Punctuality, my beloved 'earers, is the image o' war –'

'Shut up. Here's the giddy duke. Golly, what a dewlap!' Mr Martin, in evening dress, was undeniably throaty – a tall, generously designed, pink-and-white man. Still, Beetle need not have been coarse.

'Look at his back while he's talkin' to the head. Vile bad form to turn your back on the audience! He's a Philistine – a Bopper – a Jebusite – an' a Hivite.' McTurk leaned back and sniffed contemptuously.

In a few colourless words, the head introduced the speaker and sat down amid applause. When Mr Martin took the applause to himself, they naturally applauded more than ever. It was some time before be could begin. He had no knowledge of the school – its tradition or heritage. He did not know that the last census showed that eighty per cent of the boys had been born abroad – in camp, cantonment, or upon the high seas; or that seventy-five per cent were sons of officers in one or other of the services – Willoughbys, Paulets, De Castros, Maynes, Randalls, after their kind – looking to follow their fathers' profession. The head might have told him this, and much more; but, after an hour-long dinner in his company, the head decided to say nothing whatever. Mr Raymond Martin seemed to know so much already.

He plunged into his speech with a long-drawn, rasping 'Well, boys,' that, though they were not conscious of it, set every young nerve ajar. He supposed they knew – hey? – what he had come down for? It was not often that he had an opportunity to talk to boys. He supposed that boys were very much the same kind of persons – some people thought them rather funny persons – as they had been in his youth.

'This man,' said McTurk, with conviction, 'is *the* Gadarene swine.'

But they must remember that they would not always be boys. They would grow up into men, because the boys of today made the men of tomorrow, and upon the men of tomorrow the fair fame of their glorious native land depended.

'If this goes on, my beloved 'earers, it will be my painful duty to rot this bargee.' Stalky drew a long breath through his nose.

'Can't do that,' said McTurk. 'He ain't chargin' anything for his Romeo.'

And so they ought to think of the duties and responsibilities of the life that was opening before them. Life was not all – he enumerated a few games, and, that nothing might be lacking to the sweep and impact of his fall, added 'marbles'. 'Yes, life was not,' he said, 'all marbles.'

There was one tense gasp – among the juniors almost a shriek – of quivering horror, he was a heathen – an outcast – beyond the extremest pale of toleration – self-damned before all men. Stalky bowed his head in his hands. McTurk, with a bright and cheerful eye, drank in every word, and Beetle nodded solemn approval.

Some of them, doubtless, expected in a few years to have the honour of a commission from the Queen, and to wear a sword. Now, he himself had had some experience of these duties, as a major in a volunteer regiment, and he was glad to learn that they had established a volunteer corps in their midst. The establishment of such an establishment conduced to a proper and healthy spirit, which, if fostered, would be of great benefit to the land they loved and were so proud to belong to. Some of those now present expected, he had no doubt – some of them anxiously looked forward to leading their men against the bullets of England's foes; to confronting the stricken field in all the pride of their youthful manhood.

Now the reserve of a boy is tenfold deeper than the reserve of a maid, she being made for one end only by blind Nature, but man for several. With a large and healthy hand, he tore down these veils, and trampled them under the well-intentioned feet of eloquence. In a raucous voice, he cried aloud little matters, like the hope of honour and the dream of glory, that boys do not discuss even with their most intimate equals, cheerfully assuming that, till he spoke, they had never considered these possibilities. He pointed them to shining goals, with fingers which smudged out all radiance on all horizons. He profaned the most secret places of their souls with outcries and gesticulations, he bade them consider the deeds of their ancestors in such a fashion that they were flushed to their tingling ears. Some of them – the rending voice cut a frozen stillness – might have had relatives who perished in defence of their country. They thought, not a few of them, of an old sword in a passage, or above a breakfast-room table, seen and fingered by stealth since they could walk. He adjured them to emulate those illustrious examples; and they looked all ways in their extreme discomfort.

Their years forbade them even to shape their thoughts clearly to themselves. They felt savagely that they were being outraged by a fat man who considered marbles a game.

And so he worked towards his peroration – which, by the way, he used later with overwhelming success at a meeting of electors – while they sat, flushed and uneasy, in sour disgust. After many, many words, he reached for the cloth-wrapped stick and thrust one hand in his bosom. This – this was the concrete symbol of their land – worthy of all honour and reverence! Let no boy look on this flag who did not purpose to worthily add to its imperishable lustre. He shook it before them – a large calico Union Jack, staring in all three colours, and waited for the thunder of applause that should crown his effort.

They looked in silence. They had certainly seen the thing before – down at the coastguard station, or through a telescope, half-mast high when a brig went ashore on Braunton Sands; above the roof of the golf club, and in Keyte's window, where a certain kind of striped sweetmeat bore it in paper on each box. But the college never displayed it; it was no part of the scheme of their lives; the head had never alluded to it; their fathers had not declared it unto them. It was a matter shut up, sacred and apart. What, in the name of everything caddish, was he driving at, who waved that horror before their eyes? Happy thought! Perhaps he was drunk.

The head saved the situation by rising swiftly to propose a vote of thanks, and at his first motion, the school clapped furiously, from a sense of relief.

'And I am sure,' he concluded, the gaslight full on his face, 'that you will all join me in a very hearty vote of thanks to Mr Raymond Martin for the most enjoyable address he has given us.'

To this day we shall never know the rights of the case. The head vows that he did no such thing; or that, if he did, it must have been something in his eye; but those who were present are persuaded that he winked, once, openly and solemnly, after the word 'enjoyable'. Mr Raymond Martin got his applause full tale. As he said, 'Without vanity, I think my few words went to their hearts. I never knew boys could cheer like that.'

He left as the prayer-bell rang, and the boys lined up against the wall. The flag lay still unrolled on the desk, Foxy regarding it with pride, for he had been touched to the quick by Mr Martin's eloquence. The head and the common room, standing back on the dais, could not see the glaring offence, but a prefect left the line, rolled it up swiftly, and as swiftly tossed it into a glove and foil locker.

Then, as though he had touched a spring, broke out the low murmur of content, changing to quick-volleyed hand-clapping.

They discussed the speech in the dormitories. There was not one dissentient voice. Mr Raymond Martin, beyond question, was born in a gutter, and bred in a board-school, where they played marbles. He was further (I give the barest handful from great store) a flopshus cad, an outrageous stinker, a jelly-bellied flag-flapper (this was Stalky's contribution), and several other things which it is not seemly to put down.

The volunteer cadet corps fell in next Monday, depressedly, with a face of shame. Even then, judicious silence might have turned the corner.

Said Foxy: 'After a fine speech like what you 'eard night before last, you ought to take 'old of your drill with *re*-newed activity. I don't see how you can avoid comin' out an' marchin' in the open now.'

'Can't we get out of it, then, Foxy?' Stalky's fine old silky tone should have warned him.

'No, not with his giving the flag so generously. He told me before he left this morning that there was no objection to the corps usin' it as their own. It's a handsome flag.'

Stalky returned his rifle to the rack in dead silence, and fell out. His example was followed by Hogan and Ansell.

Perowne hesitated. 'Look here, oughtn't we – ?' he began.

'I'll get it out of the locker in a minute,' said the sergeant, his back turned. 'Then we can – '

'Come on!' shouted Stalky. 'What the devil are you waiting for? Dismiss! Break off.'

'Why – what the – where the – ?'

The rattle of Sniders, slammed into the rack, drowned his voice, as boy after boy fell out.

'I – I don't know that I shan't have to report this to the head,' he stammered.

'Report, then, and be damned to you,' cried Stalky, white to the lips, and ran out.

*   *   *

'Rummy thing!' said Beetle to McTurk. 'I was in the study, doin' a simply lovely poem about the jelly-bellied flag-flapper, an' Stalky came in, an' I said "Hullo!" an' he cursed me like a bargee, and then he began to blub like anything. Shoved his head on the table and howled. Hadn't we better do something?'

McTurk was troubled. 'P'raps he's smashed himself up somehow.'

They found him, with very bright eyes, whistling between his teeth.

'Did I take you in, Beetle? I thought I would. Wasn't it a good draw? Didn't you think I was blubbin'? Didn't I do it well? Oh, you fat old ass!' And he began to pull Beetle's ears and cheeks, in the fashion that was called 'milking'.

'I knew you were blubbin',' Beetle replied, composedly. 'Why aren't you at drill?'

'Drill! What drill?'

'Don't try to be a clever fool. Drill in the gym.'

' 'Cause there isn't any. The volunteer cadet corps is broke up – disbanded – dead – putrid – corrupt – stinkin'. An' if you look at me like that, Beetle, I'll slay you too . . . Oh, yes, an' I'm goin' to be reported to the head for swearin'.'

The Last Term

It was within a few days of the holidays, the term-end examinations, and, more important still, the issue of the college paper which Beetle edited. He had been cajoled into that office by the blandishments of Stalky and McTurk and the extreme rigor of study law. Once installed, he discovered, as others have done before him, that his duty was to do the work while his friends criticised. Stalky christened it the *Swillingford Patriot*, in pious memory of Sponge – and McTurk compared the output unfavourably with Ruskin and De Quincey. Only the head took an interest in the publication, and his methods were peculiar. He gave Beetle the run of his brown-bound, tobacco-scented library; prohibiting nothing, recommending nothing. There Beetle found a fat armchair, a silver inkstand, and unlimited pens and paper. There were scores and scores of ancient dramatists; there were Hakluyt, his voyages; French translations of Muscovite authors called Pushkin and Lermontoff; little tales of a heady and bewildering nature, interspersed with unusual songs – Peacock was that writer's name; there was Borrow's *Lavengro*; an odd theme, purporting to be a translation of something, called a 'Ruba'iyat', which the head said was a poem not yet come to its own; there were hundreds of volumes of verse – Crashaw; Dryden; Alexander Smith; L. E. L.; Lydia Sigourney; Fletcher and a purple island; Donne; Marlowe's *Faust*; and – this made McTurk (to whom Beetle conveyed it) sheer drunk for three days – Ossian; *The Earthly Paradise*; *Atalanta in Calydon*; and Rossetti – to name only a few. Then the head, drifting in under pretence of playing censor to the paper, would read here a verse and here another of these poets, opening up avenues. And, slow breathing, with half-shut eyes above his cigar, would he speak of great men living, and journals, long dead, founded in their riotous youth; of years when all the planets were little new-lit stars trying to find their places in the uncaring void, and he, the head, knew them as young men know one another. So the regular work went to the dogs, Beetle being full of other matters and meters, hoarded in secret and only told to McTurk of an afternoon, on the sands, walking high and disposedly round the wreck of the armada galleons, shouting and declaiming against the long-ridged seas.

Thanks in large part to their housemaster's experienced distrust, the three for three consecutive terms had been passed over for promotion to the rank of prefect – an office that went by merit, and carried with it the honour of the ground-ash, and liberty, under restrictions, to use it.

'*But,*' said Stalky, 'come to think of it, we've done more giddy jesting with the sixth since we've been passed over than anyone else in the last seven years.'

He touched his neck proudly. It was encircled by the stiffest of stick-up collars, which custom decreed could be worn only by the Sixth. And the Sixth saw those collars and said no word. 'Pussy', Abanazar, or Dick Four of a year ago would have seen them discarded in five minutes or . . . But the Sixth of that term was made up mostly of young but brilliantly clever boys, pets of the housemasters, too anxious for their dignity to care to come to open odds with the resourceful three. So they crammed their caps at the extreme back of their heads, instead of a trifle over one eye as the Fifth should, and rejoiced in patent-leather boots on weekdays, and marvellous made-up ties on Sundays – no man rebuking. McTurk was going up for Cooper's Hill, and Stalky for Sandhurst, in the spring; and the head had told them both that, unless they absolutely collapsed during the holidays, they were safe. As a trainer of colts, the head seldom erred in an estimate of form.

He had taken Beetle aside that day and given him much good advice, not one word of which did Beetle remember when he dashed up to the study, white with excitement, and poured out the wondrous tale. It demanded a great belief.

'You begin on a hundred a year?' said McTurk unsympathetically. 'Rot!'

'And my passage out! It's all settled. The head says he's been breaking me in for this for ever so long, and I never knew – I never knew. One don't begin with writing straight off, y'know. Begin by filling in telegrams and cutting things out o' papers with scissors.'

'Oh, scissors! What an ungodly mess you'll make of it,' said Stalky. 'But, anyhow, this will be your last term, too. Seven years, my dearly beloved 'earers – though not prefects.'

'Not half bad years, either,' said McTurk. 'I shall be sorry to leave the old coll.; shan't you?'

They looked out over the sea creaming along the Pebbleridge in the clear winter light. 'Wonder where we shall all be this time next year?' said Stalky absently.

'This time five years,' said McTurk.

'Oh,' said Beetle, 'my leavin's between ourselves. The head hasn't told any one. I know he hasn't, because Prout grunted at me today that if I were more reasonable – yah! – I might be a prefect next term. I s'pose he's hard up for his prefects.'

'Let's finish up with a row with the Sixth,' suggested McTurk.

'Dirty little schoolboys!' said Stalky, who already saw himself a Sandhurst cadet. 'What's the use?'

'Moral effect,' quoth McTurk. 'Leave an imperishable tradition, and all the rest of it.'

'Better go into Bideford an' pay up our debts,' said Stalky. 'I've got three quid out of my father – *ad hoc*. Don't owe more than thirty bob, either. Cut along, Beetle, and ask the head for leave. Say you want to correct the *Swillingford Patriot*.'

'Well, I do,' said Beetle. 'It'll be my last issue, and I'd like it to look decent. I'll catch him before he goes to his lunch.'

Ten minutes later they wheeled out in line, by grace released from five o'clock call-over, and all the afternoon lay before them. So also unluckily did King, who never passed without witticisms. But brigades of Kings could not have ruffled Beetle that day.

'Aha! Enjoying the study of light literature, my friends,' said he, rubbing his hands. 'Common mathematics are not for such soaring minds as yours, are they?'

('One hundred a year,' thought Beetle, smiling into vacancy.)

'Our open incompetence takes refuge in the flowery paths of inaccurate fiction. But a day of reckoning approaches, Beetle mine. I myself have prepared a few trifling foolish questions in Latin prose which can hardly be evaded even by your practised acts of deception. Ye–es, Latin prose. I think, if I may say so – but we shall see when the papers are set – "Ulpian serves your need." Aha! "*Elucescebat*, quoth our friend." We shall see! We shall see!'

Still no sign from Beetle. He was on a steamer, his passage paid into the wide and wonderful world – a thousand leagues beyond Lundy Island.

King dropped him with a snarl.

'He doesn't know. He'll go on correctin' exercises an' jawin' an' showin' off before the little boys next term – and next.' Beetle hurried after his companions up the steep path of the furze-clad hill behind the college.

They were throwing pebbles on the top of the gasometer, and the grimy gasman in change bade them desist. They watched him oil a turncock sunk in the ground between two furze-bushes.

'Cokey, what's that for?' said Stalky.

'To turn the gas on to the kitchens,' said Cokey. 'If so be I didn't turn her on, yeou young gen'lemen 'ud be larnin' your book by candlelight.'

'Um!' said Stalky, and was silent for at least a minute.

'Hullo! Where are you chaps going?' A bend of the lane brought them face to face with Tulke, senior prefect of King's house – a smallish, white-haired boy, of the type that must be promoted on account of its intellect, and ever afterwards appeals to the head to support its authority when zeal has outrun discretion.

The three took no sort of notice. They were on lawful pass. Tulke repeated his question hotly, for he had suffered many slights from number five study, and fancied that he had at last caught them tripping.

'What the devil is that to you?' Stalky replied with his sweetest smile.

'Look here, I'm not goin' – I'm not goin' to be sworn at by the Fifth!' sputtered Tulke.

'Then cut along and call a prefects' meeting,' said McTurk, knowing Tulke's weakness.

The prefect became inarticulate with rage.

'Mustn't yell at the Fifth that way,' said Stalky. 'It's vile bad form.'

'Cough it up, ducky!' McTurk said calmly.

'I – I want to know what you chaps are doing out of bounds?' This with an important flourish of his ground-ash.

'Ah,' said Stalky. 'Now we're gettin' at it. Why didn't you ask that before?'

'Well, I ask it now. What are you doing?'

'We're admiring you, Tulke,' said Stalky. 'We think you're no end of a fine chap, don't we?'

'We do! We do!' A dog-cart with some girls in it swept round the corner, and Stalky promptly kneeled before Tulke in the attitude of prayer; so Tulke turned a colour.

'I've reason to believe – ' he began.

'Oyez! Oyez! Oyez!' shouted Beetle, after the manner of Bideford's town crier, 'Tulke has reason to believe! Three cheers for Tulke!'

They were given. 'It's all our giddy admiration,' said Stalky. 'You know how we love you, Tulke. We love you so much we think you ought to go home and die. You're too good to live, Tulke.'

'Yes,' said McTurk. 'Do oblige us by dyin'. Think how lovely you'd look stuffed!'

Tulke swept up the road with an unpleasant glare in his eye.

'That means a prefects' meeting – sure pop,' said Stalky. 'Honour of the Sixth involved, and all the rest of it. Tulke'll write notes all this afternoon, and Carson will call us up after tea. They daren't overlook that.'

'Bet you a bob he follows us!' said McTurk. 'He's King's pet, and it's scalps to both of 'em if we're caught out. We must be virtuous.'

'Then I move we go to Mother Yeo's for a last gorge. We owe her about ten bob, and Mary'll weep sore when she knows we're leaving,' said Beetle.

'She gave me an awful wipe on the head last time – Mary,' said Stalky.

'She does if you don't duck,' said McTurk. 'But she generally kisses one back. Let's try Mother Yeo.'

They sought a little bottle-windowed half dairy, half restaurant, a dark-brewed, two-hundred-year-old house, at the head of a narrow side street. They had patronised it from the days of their fagdom, and were very much friends at home.

'We've come to pay our debts, mother,' said Stalky, sliding his arm round the fifty-six-inch waist of the mistress of the establishment. 'To pay our debts and say goodbye – and – and we're awf'ly hungry.'

'Aie!' said Mother Yeo, 'makkin' love to me! I'm shaamed of 'ee.'

' 'Rackon us wouldn't du no such thing if Mary was here,' said McTurk, lapsing into the broad North Devon that the boys used on their campaigns.

'Who'm takin' my name in vain?' The inner door opened, and Mary, fair-haired, blue-eyed, and apple-checked, entered with a bowl of cream in her bands. McTurk kissed her. Beetle followed suit, with exemplary calm. Both boys were promptly cuffed.

'Niver kiss the maid when 'e can kiss the mistress,' said Stalky, shamelessly winking at Mother Yeo, as he investigated a shelf of jams.

'Glad to see one of 'ee don't want his head slapped no more?' said Mary invitingly, in that direction.

'Neu! Reckon I can get 'em give me,' said Stalky, his back turned.

'Not by me – yeou little masterpiece!'

'Niver asked 'ee. There's maids to Northam. Yiss – an' Appledore.' An unreproducible sniff, half contempt, half reminiscence, rounded the retort.

'Aie! Yeou won't niver come to no good end. Whutt be 'baout, smellin' the cream?'

' 'Tees bad,' said Stalky. 'Zmell 'un.'

Incautiously Mary did as she was bid.

'Bidevoor kiss.'

'Niver amiss,' said Stalky, taking it without injury.

'Yeou – yeou – yeou – ' Mary began, bubbling with mirth.

'They'm better to Northam – more rich, laike an' us gets them give back again,' he said, while McTurk solemnly waltzed Mother Yeo out of breath, and Beetle told Mary the sad news, as they sat down to clotted cream, jam, and hot bread.

'Yiss. Yeou'll niver zee us no more, Mary. We're goin' to be passons an' missioners.'

'Steady the Buffs!' said McTurk, looking through the blind. 'Tulke has followed us. He's comin' up the street now.'

'They've niver put us out o' bounds,' said Mother Yeo. 'Bide yeou still, my little dearrs.' She rolled into the inner room to make the score.

'Mary,' said Stalky, suddenly, with tragic intensity. 'Do 'ee lov' me, Mary?'

'Iss – fai! Talled 'ee zo since yeou was zo high!' the damsel replied.

'Zee 'un comin' up street, then?' Stalky pointed to the unconscious Tulke. 'He've niver been kissed by no sort or manner o' maid in hees borned laife, Mary. Oh, 'tees shaamful!'

'Whutt's to do with me? 'Twill come to 'un in the way o' nature, I rackon.' She nodded her head sagaciously. 'You niver want me to kiss un – sure–*ly*?'

'Give 'ee half a crown if 'ee will,' said Stalky, exhibiting the coin.

Half a crown was much to Mary Yeo, and a jest was more; but –

'Yeu'm afraid,' said McTurk, at the psychological moment.

'Aie!' Beetle echoed, knowing her weak point. 'There's not a maid to Northam 'ud think twice. An' yeou such a fine maid, tu!'

McTurk planted one foot firmly against the inner door lest Mother Yeo should return inopportunely, for Mary's face was set. It was then that Tulke found his way blocked by a tall daughter of Devon – that county of easy kisses, the pleasantest under the sun. He dodged aside politely. She reflected a moment, and laid a vast hand upon his shoulder.

'Where be 'ee gwaine tu, my dearr?' said she.

Over the handkerchief he had crammed into his mouth Stalky could see the boy turn scarlet.

'Gie I a kiss! Don't they larn 'ee manners to college?'

Tulke gasped and wheeled. Solemnly and conscientiously Mary kissed him twice, and the luckless prefect fled.

She stepped into the shop, her eyes full of simple wonder. 'Kissed 'un?' said Stalky, handing over the money.

'Iss, fai! But, oh, my little body, he'm no colleger. Zeemed tu-minded to cry, like.'

'Well, we won't. You couldn't make us cry that way,' said McTurk. 'Try.'

Whereupon Mary cuffed them all round.

As they went out with tingling cars, said Stalky generally, 'Don't think there'll be much of a prefects' meeting.'

'Won't there, just!' said Beetle. 'Look here. If he kissed her – which is our tack – he is a cynically immoral hog, and his conduct is blatant indecency. *Confer orationes Regis furiosissimi*, when he collared me readin' *Don Juan*.'

' 'Course he kissed her,' said McTurk. 'In the middle of the street. With his house-cap on!'

'Time, 3.57 p.m. Make a note o' that. What d'you mean, Beetle?' said Stalky.

'Well! He's a truthful little beast. He may say he was kissed.'

'And then?'

'Why, then!' Beetle capered at the mere thought of it. 'Don't you see? The corollary to the giddy proposition is that the Sixth can't protect 'emselves from outrages an' ravishin's. Want nursemaids to look after 'em! We've only got to whisper that to the coll. Jam for the Sixth! Jam for us! Either way it's jammy!'

'By gum!' said Stalky. 'Our last term's endin' well. Now you cut along an' finish up your old rag, and Turkey and me will help. We'll go in the back way. No need to bother Randall.'

'Don't play the giddy garden-goat, then?' Beetle knew what help meant, though he was by no means averse to showing his importance before his allies. The little loft behind Randall's printing office was his own territory, where he saw himself already controlling *The Times*. Here, under the guidance of the inky apprentice, he had learned to find his way more or less circuitously about the case, and considered himself an expert compositor.

The school paper in its locked formes lay on a stone-topped table, a proof by the side; but not for worlds would Beetle have corrected from the mere proof. With a mallet and a pair of tweezers, he knocked out mysterious wedges of wood that released the forme, picked a letter here and inserted a letter there, reading as he went along and stopping much to chuckle over his own contributions.

'You won't show off like that,' said McTurk, 'when you've got to do it for your living. Upside down and backwards, isn't it? Let's see if I can read it.'

'Get out!' said Beetle. 'Go and read those formes in the rack there, if you think you know so much.'

'Formes in a rack! What's that? Don't be so beastly professional.'

McTurk drew off with Stalky to prowl about the office. They left little unturned.

'Come here a shake, Beetle. What's this thing?' aid Stalky, in a few minutes. 'Looks familiar.'

Said Beetle, after a glance: 'It's King's Latin prose exam paper. *In – In Varrem: actio prima*. What a lark!'

'Think o' the pure-souled, high-minded boys who'd give their eyes for a squint at it!' said McTurk.

'No, Willie dear,' said Stalky; 'that would be wrong and painful to our kind teachers. You wouldn't crib, Willie, would you?'

'Can't read the beastly stuff, anyhow,' was the reply. 'Besides, we're leavin' at the end o' the term, so it makes no difference to us.'

' 'Member what the Considerate Bloomer did to Spraggon's account of the Puffin'ton Hounds? We must sugar Mr King's milk for him,' said Stalky, all lighted from within by a devilish joy. 'Let's see what Beetle can do with those forceps he's so proud of.'

'Don't see now you can make Latin prose much more cockeye than it is, but we'll try,' said Beetle, transposing an *aliud* and *Asiae* from two sentences. 'Let's see! We'll put that full stop a little further on, and begin the sentence with the next capital. Hurrah! Here's three lines that can move up all in a lump.'

' "One of those scientific rests for which this eminent huntsman is so justly celebrated".' Stalky knew the Puffington run by heart.

'Hold on! Here's a *vol – voluntate quidnam* all by itself,' said McTurk.

'I'll attend to her in a shake. *Quidnam* goes after *Dolabella*.'

'Good old Dolabella,' murmured Stalky. 'Don't break him. Vile prose Cicero wrote, didn't he? He ought to be grateful for – '

'Hullo!' said McTurk, over another forme. 'What price a giddy ode? *Qui – quis –* oh, it's *Quis multa gracilis*, o' course.'

'Bring it along. We've sugared the milk here,' said Stalky, after a few minutes' zealous toil. 'Never thrash your hounds unnecessarily.'

'*Quis munditiis*? I swear that's not bad,' began Beetle, plying the tweezers. 'Don't that interrogation look pretty? *Heu quoties fidem!* That sounds as if the chap were anxious an' excited. *Cui flavam religas in rosa* – Whose flavour is relegated to a rose. *Mutatosque Deos flebit in antro*.'

'Mute gods weepin' in a cave,' suggested Stalky. ' 'Pon my Sam, Horace needs as much lookin' after as – Tulke.'

They edited him faithfully till it was too dark to see.

*   *   *

' "Aha! *Elucescebat*, quoth our friend." Ulpian serves my need, does it? If King can make anything out of *that*, I'm a blue-eyed squatteroo,' said Beetle, as they slid out of the loft window into a back alley of old acquaintance and started on a three-mile trot to the college. But the revision of the classics had detained them too long. They halted, blown and breathless, in the furze at the back of the gasometer, the college lights twinkling below, ten minutes at least late for tea and lockup.

'It's no good,' puffed McTurk. 'Bet a bob Foxy is waiting for defaulters under the lamp by the fives court. It's a nuisance, too, because the head gave us long leave, and one doesn't like to break it.'

' "Let me now from the bonded ware'ouse of my knowledge",' began Stalky.

'Oh, rot! Don't Jorrock. Can we make a run for it?' snapped McTurk.

'Bishops' boots Mr Radcliffe also condemned, an' spoke 'ighly in favour of tops cleaned with champagne an' abricot jam. Where's that thing Cokey was twiddlin' this afternoon?'

They heard him groping in the wet, and presently beheld a great miracle. The lights of the coastguard cottages near the sea went out; the brilliantly illuminated windows of the golf-club disappeared, and were followed by the frontages of the two hotels. Scattered villas dulled, twinkled, and vanished. Last of all, the college lights died also. They were left in the pitchy darkness of a windy winter's night.

'Blister my kidneys. It *is* a frost. The dahlias are dead!' said Stalky. 'Bunk!'

They squattered through the dripping gorse as the college hummed like an angry hive and the dining-rooms chorused, 'Gas! gas! gas!' till they came to the edge of the sunk path that divided them from their study. Dropping that ha-ha like bullets, and rebounding like boys, they dashed to their study, in less than two minutes had changed into dry trousers and coat, and, ostentatiously slippered, joined the mob in the dining-hall, which resembled the storm-centre of a South American revolution.

' "Hellish dark and smells of cheese".' Stalky elbowed his way into the press, howling lustily for gas. 'Cokey must have gone for a walk. Foxy'll have to find him.'

Prout, as the nearest housemaster, was trying to restore order, for rude boys were flicking butter-pats across chaos, and McTurk had turned on the fags' tea-urn, so that many were parboiled and wept with an unfeigned dolour. The Fourth and Upper Third broke into the school song, the '*Vive la Compagnie*', to the accompaniment of drumming knife-handles; and the junior forms shrilled batlike shrieks and raided one another's victuals. Two hundred and fifty boys in high condition, seeking for more light, are truly earnest enquirers.

When a most vile smell of gas told them that supplies had been renewed, Stalky, waistcoat unbuttoned, sat gorgedly over what might have been his fourth cup of tea. 'And that's all right,' he said. 'Hullo! 'Ere's Pomponius Ego!'

It was Carson, the head of the school, a simple, straight-minded soul, and a pillar of the 1st XV, who crossed over from the prefects' table and in a husky, official voice invited the three to attend in his study in half an hour. 'Prefects' meetin'! Prefects' meetin'!' hissed the tables, and they imitated barbarically the actions and effects of the ground-ash.

'How are we goin' to jest with 'em?' said Stalky, turning half-face to Beetle. 'It's your play this time!'

'Look here,' was the answer, 'all I want you to do is not to laugh. I'm goin' to take charge o' young Tulke's immorality – *à la* King, and it's goin' to be serious. If you can't help laughin' don't look at me, or I'll go pop.'

'I see. All right,' said Stalky.

McTurk's lank frame stiffened in every muscle and his eyelids dropped half over his eyes. That last was a war-signal.

The eight or nine seniors, their faces very set and sober, were ranged in chairs round Carson's severely Philistine study. Tulke was not popular among them, and a few who had had experience of Stalky and Company doubted that he might, perhaps, have made an ass of himself. But the dignity of the Sixth was to be upheld. So Carson began hurriedly: 'Look here, you chaps, I've – we've sent for you to tell you you're a good deal too cheeky to the Sixth – have been for some time – and – and we've stood about as much as we're goin' to, and it seems you've been cursin' and swearin' at Tulke on the Bideford road this afternoon, and we're goin' to show you you can't do it. That's all.'

'Well, that's awfully good of you,' said Stalky, 'but we happen to have a few rights of our own, too. You can't, just because you happen to be made prefects, haul up seniors and jaw 'em on spec., like a housemaster. We aren't fags, Carson. This kind of thing may do for Davies tertius, but it won't do for us.'

'It's only old Prout's lunacy that we weren't prefects long ago. You know that,' said McTurk. 'You haven't any tact.'

'Hold on,' said Beetle. 'A prefects' meetin' has to be reported to the head. I want to know if the head backs Tulke in this business?'

'Well – well, it isn't exactly a prefects' meeting,' said Carson. 'We only called you in to warn you.'

'But all the prefects are here,' Beetle insisted. 'Where's the difference?'

'My gum!' said Stalky. 'Do you mean to say you've just called us in for a jaw – after comin' to us before the whole school at tea an' givin' 'em the impression it was a prefects' meeting? 'Pon my Sam, Carson, you'll get into trouble, you will.'

'Hole-an'-corner business – hole-an'-corner business,' said McTurk, wagging his head. 'Beastly suspicious.'

The Sixth looked at each other uneasily. Tulke had called three prefects' meetings in two terms, till the head had informed the Sixth that they were expected to maintain discipline without the recurrent menace of his authority. Now, it seemed that they had made a blunder at the outset, but any right-minded boy would have sunk the legality and been properly impressed by the court. Beetle's protest was distinct 'cheek'.

'Well, you chaps deserve a lickin',' cried one Naughten incautiously. Then was Beetle filled with a noble inspiration.

'For interferin' with Tulke's amours, eh?' Tulke turned a rich sloe colour. 'Oh, no, you don't! 'Beetle went on. 'You've had your innings. We've been sent up for cursing and swearing at you, and we're goin' to be let off with a warning! *Are* we? Now then, you're going to catch it.'

'I – I – I – ' Tulke began. 'Don't let that young devil start jawing.'

'If you've anything to say you must say it decently,' said Carson.

'Decently? I will. Now look here. When we went into Bideford we met this ornament of the Sixth – is that decent enough? – hanging about on the road with a nasty look in his eye. We didn't know *then* why he was so anxious to stop us, *but* at five minutes to four, when we were in Yeo's shop, we saw Tulke in broad daylight, with his house-cap on, kissin' an' huggin' a woman on the pavement. Is that decent enough for you?'

'I didn't – I wasn't.'

'We saw you!' said Beetle. 'And now – I'll be decent, Carson – you sneak back with her kisses' (not for nothing had Beetle perused the later poets) 'hot on your lips and call prefects' meetings, which aren't prefects' meetings, to uphold the honour of the Sixth.' A new and heaven-cleft path opened before him that instant. 'And how do we know,' he shouted – 'how do we know how many of the Sixth are mixed up in this abominable affair?'

'Yes, that's what we want to know,' said McTurk, with simple dignity.

'We meant to come to you about it quietly, Carson, but you would have the meeting,' said Stalky sympathetically.

The Sixth were too taken aback to reply. So, carefully modelling his rhetoric on King, Beetle followed up the attack, surpassing and surprising himself, 'It – it isn't so much the cynical immorality of the biznai, as the blatant indecency of it, that's so awful. As far as we can see, it's impossible for us to go into Bideford without runnin' up against some prefect's unwholesome amours. There's nothing to snigger over, Naughten. I don't pretend to know much about these things – but it seems to me a chap must be pretty far dead in sin' (that was a quotation from the school chaplain) 'when he takes to embracing his paramours' (that was Hakluyt) 'before all the city' (a reminiscence of Milton). 'He might at least have the decency – you're authorities on decency, I believe – to wait till dark. But he didn't. You didn't! Oh, Tulke. You – you incontinent little animal!'

'Here, shut up a minute. What's all this about, Tulke?' said Carson.

'I – look here. I'm awfully sorry. I never thought Beetle would take this line.'

'Because – you've – no decency – you – thought – I hadn't,' cried Beetle all in one breath.

'Tried to cover it all up with a conspiracy, did you?' said Stalky.

'Direct insult to all three of us,' said McTurk. 'A most filthy mind you have, Tulke.'

'I'll shove you fellows outside the door if you go on like this,' said Carson angrily.

'That proves it's a conspiracy,' said Stalky, with the air of a virgin martyr.

'I – I was goin' along the street – I swear I was,' cried Tulke, 'and – and I'm awfully sorry about it – a woman came up and kissed me. I swear I didn't kiss her.'

There was a pause, filled by Stalky's long, liquid whistle of contempt, amazement, and derision.

'On my honour,' gulped the persecuted one. 'Oh, do stop him jawing.'

'Very good,' McTurk interjected. 'We are compelled, of course, to accept your statement.'

'Confound it!' roared Naughten. 'You aren't head-prefect here, McTurk.'

'Oh, well,' returned the Irishman, 'you know Tulke better than we do. I am only speaking for ourselves. *We* accept Tulke's word. But all I can say is that if I'd been collared in a similarly disgustin' situation, and had offered the same explanation Tulke has, I – I wonder what you'd have said. However, it seems on Tulke's word of honour – '

'And Tulkus – beg pardon – *kiss*, of course – Tulkiss is an honourable man,' put in Stalky.

' – that the Sixth can't protect 'emselves from bein' kissed when they go for a walk!' cried Beetle, taking up the running with a rush. 'Sweet business, isn't it? Cheerful thing to tell the fags, ain't it? We aren't prefects, of course, but we aren't kissed very much. Don't think that sort of thing ever enters our heads; does it, Stalky?'

'Oh, no!' said Stalky, turning aside to hide his emotions. McTurk's face merely expressed lofty contempt and a little weariness.

'Well, you seem to know a lot about it,' interposed a prefect.

'Can't help it – when you chaps shove it under our noses.' Beetle dropped into a drawling parody of King's most biting colloquial style – the gentle rain after the thunderstorm. 'Well, it's all very sufficiently vile and disgraceful, isn't it? I don't know who comes out of it worst: Tulke, who happens to have been caught; or the other fellows who haven't. And we – ' here he wheeled fiercely on the other two – 'we've got to stand up and be jawed by them because we've disturbed their intrigues.'

'Hang it! I only wanted to give you a word of warning,' said Carson, thereby handing himself bound to the enemy.

'Warn? You?' This with the air of one who finds loathsome gifts in his locker. 'Carson, would you be good enough to tell us what conceivable thing there is that you are entitled to warn us about after this exposure? Warn? Oh, it's a little too much! Let's go somewhere where it's clean.'

The door banged behind their outraged innocence.

'Oh, Beetle! Beetle! Beetle! Golden Beetle!' sobbed Stalky, hurling himself on Beetle's panting bosom as soon as they reached the study. 'However did you do it?'

'Dear–r man' said McTurk, embracing Beetle's head with both arms, while he swayed it to and fro on the neck, in time to this ancient burden –

'Pretty lips – sweeter than – cherry or plum.
Always look – jolly and – never look glum;
Seem to say – Come away. Kissy! – come, come!
Yummy-yum! Yummy-yum! Yummy-yum-yum!'

'Look out. You'll smash my gig-lamps,' puffed Beetle, emerging. 'Wasn't it glorious? Didn't I *Eric* 'em splendidly? Did you spot my cribs from King? Oh, blow!' His countenance clouded. 'There's one adjective I didn't use – obscene. Don't know how I forgot that. It's one of King's pet ones, too.'

'Never mind. They'll be sendin' ambassadors round in half a shake to beg us not to tell the school. It's a deuced serious business for them,' said McTurk. 'Poor Sixth – poor old Sixth!'

'Immoral young rips,' Stalky snorted. 'What an example to pure-souled boys like you and me!'

And the Sixth in Carson's study sat aghast, glowering at Tulke, who was on the edge of tears. 'Well,' said the head-prefect acidly. 'You've made a pretty average ghastly mess of it, Tulke.'

'Why – why didn't you lick that young devil Beetle before he began jawing?' Tulke wailed.

'I knew there'd be a row,' said a prefect of Prout's house. 'But you would insist on the meeting, Tulke.'

'Yes, and a fat lot of good it's done us,' said Naughten. 'They come in here and jaw our heads off when we ought to be jawin' them. Beetle talks to us as if we were a lot of blackguards and – and all that. And when they've hung us up to dry, they go out and slam the door like a housemaster. All your fault, Tulke.'

'But I didn't kiss her.'

'You ass! If you'd said you *had* and stuck to it, it would have been ten times better than what you did,' Naughten retorted. 'Now they'll tell the whole school – and Beetle'll make up a lot of beastly rhymes and nicknames.'

'But, hang it, she kissed me!' Outside of his work, Tulke's mind moved slowly.

'I'm not thinking of you. I'm thinking of us. I'll go up to their study and see if I can make 'em keep quiet!'

'Tulke's awf'ly cut up about this business,' Naughten began, ingratiatingly, when he found Beetle.

'Who's kissed him this time?'

' – and I've come to ask you chaps, and especially you, Beetle, not to let the thing be known all over the school. Of course, fellows as senior as you are can easily see why.'

'Um!' said Beetle, with the cold reluctance of one who foresees an unpleasant public duty. 'I suppose I must go and talk to the Sixth again.'

'Not the least need, my dear chap, I assure you,' said Naughten hastily. 'I'll take any message you care to send.'

But the chance of supplying the missing adjective was too tempting. So Naughten returned to that still undissolved meeting, Beetle, white, icy, and aloof, at his heels.

'There seems,' he began, with laboriously crisp articulation, 'there seems to be a certain amount of uneasiness among you as to the steps we may think fit to take in regard to this last revelation of the – ah – obscene. If it is any consolation to you to know that we have decided – for the honour of the school, you understand – to keep our mouths shut as to these – ah – obscenities, you – ah – have it.'

He wheeled, his head among the stars, and strode statelily back to his study, where Stalky and McTurk lay side by side upon the table wiping their tearful eyes – too weak to move.

*   *   *

The Latin prose paper was a success beyond their wildest dreams. Stalky and McTurk were, of course, out of all examinations (they did extra-tuition with the head), but Beetle attended with zeal.

'This, I presume, is a par-ergon on your part,' said King, as he dealt out the papers. 'One final exhibition ere you are translated to loftier spheres? A last attack on the classics? It seems to confound you already.'

Beetle studied the print with knit brows. 'I can't make head or tail of it,' he murmured. 'What does it mean?'

'No, no!' said King, with scholastic coquetry. 'We depend upon you to give us the meaning. This is an examination, Beetle mine, not a guessing-competition. You will find your associates have no difficulty in – '

Tulke left his place and laid the paper on the desk. King looked, read, and turned a ghastly green.

'Stalky's missing a heap,' thought Beetle. 'Wonder how King'll get out of it!'

'There seems,' King began with a gulp, 'a certain modicum of truth in our Beetle's remark. I am – er – inclined to believe that the worthy Randall must have dropped this in form – if you know what that means. Beetle, you purport to be an editor. Perhaps you can enlighten the form as to formes.'

'What, sir! Whose form! I don't see that there's any verb in this sentence at all, an' – an' – the Ode is all different, somehow.'

'I was about to say, before you volunteered your criticism, that an accident must have befallen the paper in type, and that the printer reset it by the light of nature. No – ' he held the thing at arm's length – 'our Randall is not an authority on Cicero or Horace.'

'Rather mean to shove it off on Randall,' whispered Beetle to his neighbour. 'King must ha' been as screwed as an owl when he wrote it out.'

'But we can amend the error by dictating it.'

'No, sir.' The answer came pat from a dozen throats at once. 'That cuts the time for the exam. Only two hours allowed, sir. 'Tisn't fair. It's a printed-paper exam. How're we goin' to be marked for it! It's all Randall's fault. It isn't our fault, anyhow. An exam's an exam,' etc., etc.

Naturally Mr King considered this was an attempt to undermine his authority, and, instead of beginning dictation at once, delivered a lecture on the spirit in which examinations should be approached. As the storm subsided, Beetle fanned it afresh.

'Eh? What? What was that you were saying to MacLagan?'

'I only said I thought the papers ought to have been looked at before they were given out, sir.'

'Hear, hear!' from a back bench. Mr King wished to know whether Beetle took it upon himself personally to conduct the traditions of the school. His zeal for knowledge ate up another fifteen minutes, during which the prefects showed unmistakable signs of boredom.

'Oh, it was a giddy time,' said Beetle, afterwards, in dismantled number five. 'He gibbered a bit, and I kept him on the gibber, and then he dictated about a half of Dolabella & Co.'

'Good old Dolabella! Friend of mine. Yes?' said Stalky, pensively.

'Then we had to ask him how every other word was spelt, of course, and he gibbered a lot more. He cursed me and MacLagan (Mac played up like a trump) and Randall, and the "materialised ignorance of the unscholarly middle classes", "lust for mere marks", and all the rest. It was what you might call a final exhibition – a last attack – a giddy par–ergon.'

'But o' course he was blind squiffy when he wrote the paper. I hope you explained that?' said Stalky.

'Oh, yes. I told Tulke so. I said an immoral prefect an' a drunken housemaster were legitimate inferences. Tulke nearly blubbed. He's awfully shy of us since Mary's time.'

Tulke preserved that modesty till the last moment – till the journey-money had been paid, and the boys were filling the brakes that took them to the station. Then the three tenderly constrained him to wait a while.

'You see, Tulke, you may be a prefect,' said Stalky, 'but I've left the coll. Do you see, Tulke, dear?'

'Yes, I see. Don't bear malice, Stalky.'

'Stalky? Curse your impudence, you young cub,' shouted Stalky, magnificent in top hat, stiff collar, spats, and high-waisted, snuff-coloured ulster. 'I want you to understand that *I'm* Mr Corkran, an' you're a dirty little schoolboy.'

'Besides bein' frabjously immoral,' said McTurk. 'Wonder you aren't ashamed to foist your company on pure-minded boys like us.'

'Come on, Tulke,' cried Naughten, from the prefects' brake.

'Yes, we're comin'. Shove up and make room, you collegers. You've all got to be back next term, with your "Yes, sir", and "Oh, sir", an' "No sir" an' "Please sir"; but before we say goodbye we're going to tell you a little story. Go on, Dickie' (this to the driver); 'we're quite ready. Kick that hatbox under the seat, an' don't crowd your Uncle Stalky.'

'As nice a lot of high-minded youngsters as you'd wish to see,' said McTurk, gazing round with bland patronage. 'A trifle immoral, but then – boys will be boys. It's no good tryin' to look stuffy, Carson. *Mr* Corkran will now oblige with the story of Tulke an' Mary Yeo!'

Slaves of the Lamp – Part Two

That very Infant who told the story of the capture of Boh Na Ghee ['A Conference of the Powers', *Many Inventions*] to Eustace Cleaver, novelist, inherited an estateful baronetcy, with vast revenues, resigned the service, and became a landholder, while his mother stood guard over him to see that he married the right girl. But, new to his position, he presented the local volunteers with a full-sized magazine-rifle range, two miles long, across the heart of his estate, and the surrounding families, who lived in savage seclusion among woods full of pheasants, regarded him as an erring maniac. The noise of the firing disturbed their poultry, and Infant was cast out from the society of JPs and decent men till such time as a daughter of the county might lure him back to right thinking. He took his revenge by filling the house with choice selections of old schoolmates home on leave – affable detrimentals, at whom the bicycle-riding maidens of the surrounding families were allowed to look from afar. I knew when a troopship was in port by the Infant's invitations. Sometimes he would produce old friends of equal seniority; at others, young and blushing giants whom I had left small fags far down in the Lower Second; and to these Infant and the elders expounded the whole duty of man in the army.

'I've had to cut the service,' said the Infant; 'but that's no reason why my vast stores of experience should be lost to posterity.' He was just thirty, and in that same summer an imperious wire drew me to his baronial castle: 'Got good haul; ex *Tamar*. Come along.'

It was an unusually good haul, arranged with a single eye to my benefit. There was a baldish, broken-down captain of native infantry, shivering with ague behind an indomitable red nose – and they called him Captain Dickson. There was another captain, also of native infantry, with a fair moustache; his face was like white glass, and his hands were fragile, but he answered joyfully to the cry of Tertius. There was an enormously big and well-kept man, who had evidently not campaigned for years, clean-shaved, soft-voiced, and catlike, but still Abanazar for all that he adorned the Indian Political Service; and there was a lean Irishman, his face tanned blue-black with the suns of the Telegraph Department. Luckily the baize doors of the bachelors' wing fitted tight, for we dressed promiscuously in the corridor or in each other's rooms, talking, calling, shouting, and anon waltzing by pairs to songs of Dick Four's own devising.

There were sixty years of mixed work to be sifted out between us, and since we had met one another from time to time in the quick scene-shifting of India – a dinner, camp, or a race-meeting here; a dak-bungalow or railway station up country somewhere else – we had never quite lost touch. Infant sat on the banisters, hungrily and enviously drinking it in. He enjoyed his baronetcy, but his heart yearned for the old days.

It was a cheerful babel of matters personal, provincial, and imperial, pieces of old call-over lists, and new policies, cut short by the roar of a Burmese gong, and we went down not less than a quarter of a mile of stairs to meet Infant's mother, who had known us all in our schooldays and greeted us as if those had ended a week ago. But it was fifteen years since, with tears of laughter, she had lent me a grey princess-skirt for amateur theatricals.

That was a dinner from the *Arabian Nights*,'served in an eighty-foot hall full of ancestors and pots of flowering roses, and, what was more impressive, heated by steam. When it was ended and the little mother had gone away – ('You boys want to talk, so I shall say good-night now') – we gathered about an apple-wood fire, in a gigantic polished steel grate, under a mantelpiece ten feet high, and the Infant compassed us about with curious liqueurs and that kind of cigarette which serves best to introduce your own pipe.

'Oh, bliss!' grunted Dick Four from a sofa, where he had been packed with a rug over him. 'First time I've been warm since I came home.'

We were all nearly on top of the fire, except Infant, who had been long enough at home to take exercise when he felt chilled. This is a grisly diversion, but much affected by the English of the Island.

'If you say a word about cold tubs and brisk walks,' drawled McTurk, 'I'll kill you, Infant. I've got a liver, too. 'Member when we used to think it a treat to turn out of our beds on a Sunday morning – thermometer fifty-seven degrees if it was summer – and bathe off the Pebbleridge? Ugh!'

'Thing I don't understand,' said Tertius, 'was the way we chaps used to go down into the lavatories, boil ourselves pink, and then come up with all our pores open into a young snowstorm or a black frost. Yet none of our chaps died, that I can remember.'

'Talkin' of baths,' said McTurk, with a chuckle, ' 'member our bath in number five, Beetle, the night Rabbits-Eggs rocked King? What wouldn't I give to see old Stalky now! He is the only one of the two studies not here.'

'Stalky is the great man of his century,' said Dick Four.

'How d'you know?' I asked.

'How do I know?' said Dick Four, scornfully. 'If you've ever been in a tight place with Stalky you wouldn't ask.'

'I haven't seen him since the camp at Pindi in '87,' I said. 'He was goin' strong then – about seven feet high and four feet through.'

'Adequate chap. Infernally adequate,' said Tertius, pulling his moustache and staring into the fire.

'Got dam' near court-martialled and broke in Egypt in '84,' the Infant volunteered. 'I went out in the same trooper with him – as raw as he was. Only *I* showed it, and Stalky didn't.'

'What was the trouble?' said McTurk, reaching forward absently to twitch my dress-tie into position.

'Oh, nothing. His colonel trusted him to take twenty Tommies out to wash, or groom camels, or something at the back of Suakin, and Stalky got embroiled with Fuzzies five miles in the interior. He conducted a masterly retreat and wiped up eight of 'em. He knew jolly well he'd no right to go out so far, so he took the initiative and pitched in a letter to his colonel, who was frothing at the mouth, complaining of the "paucity of support accorded to him in his operations". Gad, it might have been one fat brigadier slangin' another! Then he went into the Staff Corps.'

'That – is – entirely – Stalky,' said Abanazar from his armchair.

'You've come across him, too?' I said.

'Oh, yes,' he replied in his softest tones. 'I was at the tail of that – that epic. Don't you chaps know?'

We did not – Infant, McTurk, and I; and we called for information very politely.

' 'Twasn't anything,' said Tertius. 'We got into a mess up in the Khye-Kheen Hills a couple o' years ago, and Stalky pulled us through. That's all.'

McTurk gazed at Tertius with all an Irishman's contempt for the tongue-tied Saxon.

'Heavens!' he said. 'And it's you and your likes govern Ireland. Tertius, aren't you ashamed?'

'Well, I can't tell a yarn. I can chip in when the other fellow starts. Ask him.' He pointed to Dick Four, whose nose gleamed scornfully over the rug.

'I knew you wouldn't,' said Dick Four. 'Give me a whisky and soda. I've been drinking lemon squash and ammoniated quinine while you chaps were bathin' in champagne, and my head's singin' like a top.'

He wiped his ragged moustache above the drink; and, his teeth chattering in his head, began: 'You know the Khye-Kheen-Malôt expedition, when we scared the souls out of 'em with a field force they daren't fight against? Well, both tribes – there was a coalition against us – came in without firing a shot; and a lot of hairy villains, who had no more power over their men than I had, promised and vowed all sorts of things. On that very slender evidence, Pussy dear – '

'I was at Simla,' said Abanazar, hastily.

'Never mind, you're tarred with the same brush. On the strength of those tuppenny-ha'penny treaties, your asses of politicals reported the country as pacified, and the Government, being a fool, as usual, began road-makin' – dependin' on local supply for labour. 'Member *that*, Pussy? Rest of our chaps who'd had no look-in during the campaign didn't think there'd be any more of it, and were anxious to get back to India. But I'd been in two of these little rows before, and I had my suspicions. I engineered myself, *summa ingenio*, into command of a road patrol – no shovellin', only marching up and down genteelly with a guard. They'd withdrawn all the troops they could, but I nucleused about forty Pathans, recruits chiefly, of my regiment, and sat tight at the base-camp while the road-parties went to work, as per political survey.'

'Had some rippin' singsongs in camp, too,' said Tertius.

'My pup' – thus did Dick Four refer to his subaltern – 'was a pious little beast. He didn't like the singsongs, and so he went down with pneumonia. I rootled round the camp, and found Tertius gassing about as a DAQMG, which, God knows, he isn't cut out for. There were six or eight of the old coll. at base-camp (we're always in force for a frontier row), but I'd heard of Tertius as a steady old hack, and I told him he had to shake off his DAQMG breeches and help *me*. Tertius volunteered like a shot, and we settled it with the authorities, and out we went – forty Pathans, Tertius, and me, looking up the road-parties. Macnamara's – 'member old Mac, the sapper, who played the fiddle so damnably at Umballa? – Mac's party was the last but one. The last was Stalky's. He was at the head of the road with some of his pet Sikhs. Mac said he believed he was all right.'

'Stalky *is* a Sikh,' said Tertius. 'He takes his men to pray at the Durbar sahib at Amritsar, regularly as clockwork, when he can.'

'Don't interrupt, Tertius. It was about forty miles beyond Mac's before I found him; and my men pointed out gently, but firmly, that the country was risin'. What kind o' country, Beetle? Well, *I'm* no word-painter, thank goodness, but *you* might call it a hellish country! When we weren't up to our necks in snow, we were rolling down the khud. The well-disposed inhabitants, who were to supply labour for the road-making (don't forget that, Pussy dear), sat behind rocks and took pot-shots at us. Old, old story! We all legged it in search of Stalky. I had a feeling that he'd be in good cover, and about dusk we found him and his road-party, as snug as a bug in a rug, in an old Malôt stone fort, with a watchtower at one corner. It overhung the road they had blasted out of the cliff fifty feet below; and under the road things went down pretty sheer, for five or six hundred feet, into a gorge about half a mile wide and two or three miles long. There were chaps on the other side of the gorge scientifically gettin' our range. So I hammered on the gate and nipped in, and tripped over Stalky in a greasy, bloody old poshteen, squatting on the ground, eating with his men. I'd only seen him for half a minute about three months before, but I might have met him yesterday. He waved his hand all sereno.

' "Hullo, Aladdin! Hullo, Emperor!" he said. "You're just in time for the performance".'

'I saw his Sikhs looked a bit battered. "Where's your command? Where's your subaltern?" I said.'

' "Here – all there is of it," said Stalky. "If you want young Everett, he's dead, and his body's in the watchtower. They rushed our road-party last

week, and got him and seven men. We've been besieged for five days. I
suppose they let you through to make sure of you. The whole country's up.
Strikes me you've walked into a first-class trap." He grinned, but neither
Tertius nor I could see where the deuce the fun was. We hadn't any grub for
our men, and Stalky had only four days' whack for his. That came of
dependin' upon your asinine politicals, Pussy dear, who told us that the
inhabitants were friendly.

'To make us *quite* comfy, Stalky took us up to the watchtower to see poor
Everett's body, lyin' in a foot o' drifted snow. It looked like a girl of fifteen –
not a hair on the little fellow's face. He'd been shot through the temple, but
the Malôts had left their mark on him. Stalky unbuttoned the tunic, and
showed it to us – a rummy sickle-shaped cut on the chest. 'Member the snow
all white on his eyebrows, Tertius? 'Member when Stalky moved the lamp
and it looked as if he was alive?'

'Ye–es,' said Tertius, with a shudder. ' 'Member the beastly look on
Stalky's face, though, with his nostrils all blown out, same as he used to look
when he was bullyin' a fag? That was a lovely evening.'

'We held a council of war up there over Everett's body. Stalky said the
Malôts and Khye-Kheens were up together; havin' sunk their blood feuds
to settle us. The chaps we'd seen across the gorge were Khye-Kheens. It
was about half a mile from them to us as a bullet flies, and they'd made a line
of sungars under the brow of the hill to sleep in and starve us out. The
Malôts, he said, were in front of us promiscuous. There wasn't good cover
behind the fort, or they'd have been there, too. Stalky didn't mind the
Malôts half as much as he did the Khye-Kheens. He said the Malôts were
treacherous curs. What I couldn't understand was, why in the world the
two gangs didn't join in and rush us. There must have been at least five
hundred of 'em. Stalky said they didn't trust each other very well, because
they were ancestral enemies when they were at home; and the only time
they'd tried a rush he'd hove a couple of blasting-charges among 'em, and
that had sickened 'em a bit.

'It was dark by the time we finished, and Stalky, always serene, said: "You
command now. I don't suppose you mind my taking any action I may
consider necessary to reprovision the fort?" I said, "Of course not," and then
the lamp blew out. So Tertius and I had to climb down the tower steps (we
didn't want to stay with Everett) and got back to our men. Stalky had gone
off – to count the stores, I supposed. Anyhow, Tertius and I sat up in case of
a rush (they were plugging at us pretty generally, you know), relieving each
other till the mornin'.

'Mornin' came. No Stalky. Not a sign of him. I took counsel with his
senior native officer – a grand, white-whiskered old chap – Rutton Singh,
from Jullunder-way. He only grinned, and said it was all right. Stalky had
been out of the fort twice before, somewhere or other, accordin' to him. He
said Stalky 'ud come back unchipped, and gave me to understand that Stalky

was an invulnerable *guru* of sorts. All the same, I put the whole command on half rations, and set 'em to pickin' out loopholes.

'About noon there was no end of a snowstorm, and the enemy stopped firing. We replied gingerly, because we were awfully short of ammunition. Don't suppose we fired five shots an hour, but we generally got our man. Well, while I was talking with Rutton Singh I saw Stalky coming down from the watchtower, rather puffy about the eyes, his poshteen coated with claret-coloured ice.

' "No trustin' these snowstorms," he said. "Nip out quick and snaffle what you can get. There's a certain amount of friction between the Khye-Kheens and the Malôts just now."

'I turned Tertius out with twenty Pathans, and they bucked about in the snow for a bit till they came on to a sort of camp about eight hundred yards away, with only a few men in charge and half a dozen sheep by the fire. They finished off the men, and snaffled the sheep and as much grain as they could carry, and came back. No one fired a shot at 'em. There didn't seem to be anybody about, but the snow was falling pretty thick.

' "That's good enough," said Stalky when we got dinner ready and he was chewin' mutton-kebabs off a cleanin' rod. "There's no sense riskin' men. They're holding a pow-wow between the Khye-Kheens and the Malôts at the head of the gorge. I don't think these so-called coalitions are much good."

'Do you know what that maniac had done? Tertius and I shook it out of him by instalments. There was an underground granary cellar-room below the watchtower, and in blasting the road Stalky had blown a hole into one side of it. Being no one else *but* Stalky, he'd kept the hole open for his own ends; and laid poor Everett's body slap over the well of the stairs that led down to it from the watchtower. He'd had to move and replace the corpse every time he used the passage. The Sikhs wouldn't go near the place, of course. Well, he'd got out of this hole, and dropped on to the road. Then, in the night *and* a howling snowstorm, he'd dropped over the edge of the khud, made his way down to the bottom of the gorge, forded the nullah, which was half frozen, climbed up on the other side along a track he'd discovered, and come out on the right flank of the Khye-Kheens. He had then – listen to this! – crossed over a ridge that paralleled their rear, walked half a mile behind that, and come out on the left of their line where the gorge gets shallow and where there was a regular track between the Malôt and the Khye-Kheen camps. That was about two in the morning, and, as it turned out, a man spotted him – a Khye-Kheen. So Stalky abolished him quietly, and left him – *with* the Malôt mark on his chest, same as Everett had.

' "I was just as economical as I could be," Stalky said to us. "If he'd shouted I should have been slain. I'd never had to do that kind of thing but once before, and that was the first time I tried that path. It's perfectly practicable for infantry, you know."

' "What about your first man?" I said.

' "Oh, that was the night after they killed Everett, and I went out lookin' for a line of retreat for my men. A man found me. I abolished him – *privatim* – scragged him. But on thinkin' it over it occurred to me that if I could find the body (I'd hove it down some rocks) I might decorate it with the Malôt mark and leave it to the Khye-Kheens to draw inferences. So I went out again the next night and did. The Khye-Kheens are shocked at the Malôts perpetratin' these two dastardly outrages after they'd sworn to sink all blood feuds. I lay up behind their sungars early this morning and watched 'em. They all went to confer about it at the head of the gorge. Awf'ly annoyed they are. Don't wonder." You know the way Stalky drops out his words, one by one.'

'My God!' said the Infant, explosively, as the full depth of the strategy dawned on him.

'Dear-r man!' said McTurk, purring rapturously.

'Stalky stalked,' said Tertius. 'That's all there is to it.'

'No, he didn't,' said Dick Four. 'Don't you remember how he insisted that he had only applied his luck? Don't you remember how Rutton Singh grabbed his boots and grovelled in the snow, and how our men shouted?'

'None of our Pathans believed that was luck,' said Tertius. 'They swore Stalky ought to have been born a Pathan, and – 'member we nearly had a row in the fort when Rutton Singh said Stalky was a Pathan? Gad, how furious the old chap was with my Jemadar! But Stalky just waggled his finger and they shut up.

'Old Rutton Singh's sword was half out, though, and he swore he'd cremate every Khye-Kheen and Malôt he killed. That made the Jemadar pretty wild, because he didn't mind fighting against his own creed, but he wasn't going to crab a fellow Mussulman's chances of Paradise. Then Stalky jabbered Pushtu and Punjabi in alternate streaks. Where the deuce did he pick up his Pushtu from, Beetle?'

'Never mind his language, Dick,' said I. 'Give us the gist of it.'

'I flatter myself I can address the wily Pathan on occasion, but, hang it all, I can't make puns in Pushtu, or top off my arguments with a smutty story, as he did. He played on those two old dogs o' war like a – like a concertina. Stalky said – and the other two backed up his knowledge of Oriental nature – that the Khye-Kheens and the Malôts between 'em would organise a combined attack on us that night, as a proof of good faith. They wouldn't drive it home, though, because neither side would trust the other on account, as Rutton Singh put it, of the little accidents. Stalky's notion was to crawl out at dusk with his Sikhs, manoeuvre 'em along this ungodly goat-track that he'd found, to the back of the Khye-Kheen position, and then lob in a few long shots at the Malôts when the attack was well on. "That'll divert their minds and help to agitate 'em,' he said. "Then you chaps can come out and sweep up the pieces, and we'll rendezvous at the head of the gorge. After that, I move we get back to Mac's camp and have something to eat." '

'*You* were commandin'?' the Infant suggested.

'I was about three months senior to Stalky, and two months Tertius's senior,' Dick Four replied. '*But* we were all from the same old coll. I should say ours was the only little affair on record where some one wasn't jealous of someone else.'

'*We* weren't,' Tertius broke in, 'but there was another row between Gul Sher Khan and Rutton Singh. Our Jemadar said – he was quite right – that no Sikh living could stalk worth a damn; and that Koran sahib had better take out the Pathans, who understood that kind of mountain work. Rutton Singh said that Koran sahib jolly well knew every Pathan was a born deserter, and every Sikh was a gentleman, even if he couldn't crawl on his belly. Stalky struck in with some woman's proverb or other, that had the effect of doublin' both men up with a grin. He said the Sikhs and the Pathans could settle their claims on the Khye-Kheens and Malôts later on, but he was going to take his Sikhs along for this mountain-climbing job, because Sikhs could shoot. They can, too. Give 'em a mule-load of ammunition apiece, and they're perfectly happy.'

'And out he gat,' said Dick Four. 'As soon as it was dark, and he'd had a bit of a snooze, him and thirty Sikhs went down through the staircase in the tower, every mother's son of 'em salutin' little Everett where It stood propped up against the wall. The last I heard him say was, "Kubbadar! tumbleinga!" [Look out; you'll fall!] and they tumbleingaed over the black edge of nothing. Close upon 9 P.M. the combined attack developed; Khye-Kheens across the valley, and Malôts in front of us, pluggin' at long range and yellin' to each other to come along and cut our infidel throats. Then they skirmished up to the gate, and began the old game of calling our Pathans renegades, and invitin' 'em to join the holy war. One of our men, a young fellow from Dera Ismail, jumped on the wall to slang 'em back, and jumped down, blubbing like a child. He'd been hit smack in the middle of the hand. Never saw a man yet who could stand a hit in the hand without weepin' bitterly. It tickles up all the nerves. So Tertius took his rifle and smote the others on the head to keep them quiet at the loopholes. The dear children wanted to open the gate and go in at 'em generally, but that didn't suit our book.

'At last, near midnight, I heard the wop, wop, wop, of Stalky's Martinis across the valley, and some general cursing among the Malôts, whose main body was hid from us by a fold in the hillside. Stalky was brownin' 'em at a great rate, and very naturally they turned half right and began to blaze at their faithless allies, the Khye-Kheens – regular volley firin'. In less than ten minutes after Stalky opened the diversion they were going it hammer and tongs, both sides the valley. When we could see, the valley was rather a mixed-up affair. The Khye-Kheens had streamed out of their sungars above the gorge to chastise the Malôts, and Stalky – I was watching him through my glasses – had slipped in behind 'em. Very good. The Khye-Kheens had to leg it along the hillside up to where the gorge got shallow and they could cross over to the Malôts, who were awfully cheered to see the Khye-Kheens taken in the rear.

'Then it occurred to me to comfort the Khye-Kheens. So I turned out the whole command, and we advanced *à la pas de charge*, doublin' up what, for the sake of argument, we'll call the Malôts' left flank. Even then, if they'd sunk their differences, they could have eaten us alive; but they'd been firin' at each other half the night, and they went on firin'. Queerest thing you ever saw in your born days! As soon as our men doubled up to the Malôts, they'd blaze at the Khye-Kheens more zealously than ever, to show they were on our side, run up the valley a few hundred yards, and halt to fire again. The moment Stalky saw our game he duplicated it his side the gorge; and, by Jove! the Khye-Kheens did just the same thing.'

'Yes, but,' said Tertius, 'you've forgot him playin' "Arrah, Patsy, mind the baby' on the bugle to hurry us up." '

'Did he?' roared McTurk. Somehow we all began to sing it, and there was an interruption.

'Rather,' said Tertius, when we were quiet. No one of the Aladdin company could forget that tune. 'Yes, he played "Patsy". Go on, Dick.'

'Finally,' said Dick Four, 'we drove both mobs into each other's arms on a bit of level ground at the head of the valley, and saw the whole crew whirl off, fightin' and stabbin' and swearin' in a blindin' snowstorm. They were a heavy, hairy lot, and we didn't follow 'em.

'Stalky had captured one prisoner – an old pensioned Sepoy of twenty-five years' service, who produced his discharge – an awf'ly sportin' old card. He had been tryin' to make his men rush us early in the day. He was sulky – angry with his own side for their cowardice, and Rutton Singh wanted to bayonet him – Sikhs don't understand fightin' against the Government after you've served it honestly – but Stalky rescued him, and froze on to him tight – with ulterior motives, I believe. When we got back to the fort, we buried young Everett – Stalky wouldn't hear of blowin' up the place – and bunked. We'd only lost ten men, all told.'

'Only ten, out of seventy. How did you lose 'em?' I asked.

'Oh, there was a rush on the fort early in the night, and a few Malôts got over the gate. It was rather a tight thing for a minute or two, but the recruits took it beautifully. Lucky job we hadn't any badly wounded men to carry, because we had forty miles to Macnamara's camp. By Jove, how we legged it! Halfway in, old Rutton Singh collapsed, so we slung him across four rifles and Stalky's overcoat; and Stalky, his prisoner, and a couple of Sikhs were his bearers. After that I went to sleep. You can, you know, on the march, when your legs get properly numbed. Mac swears we all marched into his camp snoring and dropped where we halted. His men lugged us into the tents like gram-bags. I remember wakin' up and seeing Stalky asleep with his head on old Rutton Singh's chest. *He* slept twenty-four hours. I only slept seventeen, but then I was coming down with dysentery.'

'Coming down? What rot! He had it on him before we joined Stalky in the fort,' said Tertius.

'Well, *you* needn't talk! You hove your sword at Macnamara and demanded a drumhead court martial every time you saw him. The only thing that soothed you was putting you under arrest every half- hour. You were off your head for three days.'

'Don't remember a word of it,' said Tertius, placidly. 'I remember my orderly giving me milk, though.'

'How did Stalky come out?' McTurk demanded, puffing hard over his pipe.

'Stalky? Like a serene Brahmini bull. Poor old Mac was at his Royal Engineers' wits' end to know what to do. You see I was putrid with dysentery, Tertius was ravin', half the men had frostbite, and Macnamara's orders were to break camp and come in before winter. So Stalky, who hadn't turned a hair, took half his supplies to save him the bother o' luggin' 'em back to the plains, and all the ammunition he could get at, and, *consilio et auxilio* Rutton Singhi, tramped back to his fort with all his Sikhs and his precious prisoners, and a lot of dissolute hangers-on that he and the prisoner had seduced into service. He had sixty men of sorts – and his brazen cheek. Mac nearly wept with joy when he went. You see there weren't any explicit orders to Stalky to come in before the passes were blocked: Mac is a great man for orders, and Stalky's a great man for orders – when they suit his book.'

'He told me he was goin' to the Engadine,' said Tertius. 'Sat on my cot smokin' a cigarette, and makin' me laugh till I cried. Macnamara bundled the whole lot of us down to the plains next day. We were a walkin' hospital.'

'Stalky told me that Macnamara was a simple godsend to him,' said Dick Four. 'I used to see him in Mac's tent listenin' to Mac playin' the fiddle, and, between the pieces, wheedlin' Mac out of picks and shovels and dynamite cartridges hand over fist. Well, that was the last we saw of Stalky. A week or so later the passes were shut with snow, and I don't think Stalky wanted to be found particularly just then.'

'He didn't,' said the fair and fat Abanazar. 'He didn't. Ho, ho!'

Dick Four threw up his thin, dry hand with the blue veins at the back of it. 'Hold on a minute, Pussy; I'll let you in at the proper time. I went down to my regiment, and that spring, five months later, I got off with a couple of companies on detachment: nominally to look after some friends of ours across the border; actually, of course, to recruit. It was a bit unfortunate, because an ass of a young Naick carried a frivolous blood feud he'd inherited from his aunt into those hills, and the local gentry wouldn't volunteer into my corps. Of course, the Naick had taken short leave to manage the business; that was all regular enough; *but* he'd stalked my pet orderly's uncle. It was an infernal shame, because I knew Harris of the Ghuznees would be covering that ground three months later, and he'd snaffle all the chaps I had my eyes on. Everybody was down on the Naick, because they felt he ought to have had the decency to postpone his – his disgustful amours till our companies were full strength.

'Still the beast had a certain amount of professional feeling left. He sent one of his aunt's clan by night to tell me that, if I'd take safeguard, he'd put me on to a batch of beauties. I nipped over the border like a shot, and about ten miles the other side, in a nullah, my rapparee-in-charge showed me about seventy men variously armed, but standing up like a Queen's company. Then one of 'em stepped out and lugged round an old bugle, just like – who's the man? – Bancroft, ain't it? – feeling for his eyeglass in a farce, and played "Arrah, Patsy, mind the baby. Arrah, Patsy, mind" – that was as far as he could get.'

That, also, was as far as Dick Four could get, because we had to sing the old song through twice, again and once more, and subsequently, in order to repeat it.

'He explained that if I knew the rest of the song he had a note for me from the man the song belonged to. Whereupon, my children, I finished that old tune on that bugle, and *this* is what I got. I knew you'd like to look at it. Don't grab.' (We were all struggling for a sight of the well-known unformed handwriting.) 'I'll read it aloud.

Fort Everett, February 19

Dear Dick or Tertius – The bearer of this is in charge of seventy-five recruits, all pukka devils, but desirous of leading new lives. They have been slightly polished, and after being boiled may shape well. I want you to give thirty of them to my adjutant, who, though God's own ass, will need men this spring. The rest you can keep. You will be interested to learn that I have extended my road to the end of the Malôt country. All headmen and priests concerned in last September's affair worked one month each, supplying road metal from their own houses. Everett's grave is covered by a forty-foot mound, which should serve well as a base for future triangulations. Rutton Singh sends his best salaams. I am making some treaties, and have given my prisoner – who also sends his salaams – local rank of Khan Bahadur.

A. L. Cockran

'Well, that was all,' said Dick Four, when the roaring, the shouting, the laughter, and, I think, the tears, had subsided. 'I chaperoned the gang across the border as quick as I could. They were rather homesick, but they cheered up when they recognised some of my chaps, who had been in the Khye-Kheen row, and they made a rippin' good lot. It's rather more than three hundred miles from Fort Everett to where I picked 'em up. Now, Pussy, tell 'em the latter end o' Stalky as you saw it.'

Abanazar laughed a little nervous, misleading, official laugh.

'Oh, it wasn't much. I was at Simla in the spring, when our Stalky, out of his snows, began corresponding direct with the Government.'

'After the manner of a king,' suggested Dick Four.

'My turn now, Dick. He'd done a whole lot of things he shouldn't have done, and constructively pledged the Government to all sorts of action.'

'Pledged the State's ticker, eh?' said McTurk, with a nod to me.

'About that; but the embarrassin' part was that it was all so thunderin' convenient, so well reasoned, don't you know? Came in as pat as if he'd had access to all sorts of information – which he couldn't, of course.'

'Pooh!' said Tertius, 'I back Stalky against the Foreign Office any day.'

'He'd done pretty nearly everything he could think of, except strikin' coins in his own image and superscription, all under cover of buildin' this infernal road and bein' blocked by the snow. His report was simply amazin'. Von Lennaert tore his hair over it at first, and then he gasped, "Who the deuce is this unknown Warren Hastings? He must be slain. He must be slain officially! The Viceroy'll never stand it. It's unheard of. He must be slain by his Excellency in person. Order him up here and pitch in a stinger." Well, I sent him no end of an official stinger, and I pitched in an unofficial telegram at the same time.'

'You!' This with amazement from the Infant, for Abanazar resembled nothing so much as a fluffy Persian cat.

'Yes – me,' said Abanazar. ' 'Twasn't much, but after what you've said, Dicky, it was rather a coincidence, because I wired:

> Aladdin now has got his wife,
> Your Emperor is appeased.
> I think you'd better come to life:
> We hope you've all been pleased.

'Funny how that old song came up in my head. That was fairly non-committal and encouragin'. The only flaw was that his Emperor wasn't appeased by very long chalks. Stalky extricated himself from his mountain fastnesses and leafed up to Simla at his leisure, to be offered up on the horns of the altar.'

'But,' I began, 'surely the Commander-in-Chief is the proper – '

'His Excellency had an idea that if he blew up one single junior captain – same as King used to blow us up – he was holdin' the reins of empire, and, of course, as long as he had that idea, Von Lennaert encouraged him. I'm not sure Von Lennaert didn't put that notion into his head.'

'They've changed the breed, then, since my time,' I said.

'P'r'aps. Stalky was sent up for his wiggin' like a bad little boy. I've reason to believe that His Excellency's hair stood on end. He walked into Stalky for one hour – Stalky at attention in the middle of the floor, and (so he vowed) Von Lennaert pretending to soothe down His Excellency's topknot in dumb show in the background. Stalky didn't dare to look up, or he'd have laughed.'

'Now, wherefore was Stalky not broken publicly?' said the Infant, with a large and luminous leer.

'Ah, wherefore?' said Abanazar. 'To give him a chance to retrieve his blasted career, and not to break his father's heart. Stalky hadn't a father, but that didn't matter. He behaved like a – like the Sanawar Orphan Asylum, and His Excellency graciously spared him. Then he came round to my office and sat opposite me for ten minutes, puffing out his nostrils. Then he said, "Pussy, if I thought that basket-hanger – " '

'Hah! He remembered that,' said McTurk.

' "That two-anna basket-hanger governed India, I swear I'd become a naturalised Muscovite tomorrow. I'm a *femme incomprise*. This thing's broken my heart. It'll take six months' shootin'-leave in India to mend it. Do you think I can get it, Pussy?"

'He got it in about three minutes and a half, and seventeen days later he was back in the arms of Rutton Singh – horrid disgraced – with orders to hand over his command, etc., to Cathcart MacMonnie.'

'Observe!' said Dick Four. 'One colonel of the Political Department in charge of thirty Sikhs, on a hilltop. Observe, my children!'

'Naturally, Cathcart not being a fool, even if he *is* a Political, let Stalky do his shooting within fifteen miles of Fort Everett for the next six months, and I always understood they and Rutton Singh and the prisoner were as thick as thieves. Then Stalky loafed back to his regiment, I believe. I've never seen him since.'

'I have, though,' said McTurk, swelling with pride.

We all turned as one man. 'It was at the beginning of this hot weather. I was in camp in the Jullunder doab and stumbled slap on Stalky in a Sikh village; sitting on the one chair of state, with half the population grovellin' before him, a dozen Sikh babies on his knees, an old harridan clappin' him on the shoulder, and a garland o' flowers round his neck. Told me he was recruitin'. We dined together that night, but he never said a word of the business at the Fort. Told me, though, that if I wanted any supplies I'd better say I was Koran sahib's *bhai*; and I did, and the Sikhs wouldn't take my money.'

'Ah! That must have been one of Rutton Singh's villages,' said Dick Four; and we smoked for some time in silence.

'I say,' said McTurk, casting back through the years, 'did Stalky ever tell you *how* Rabbits-Eggs came to rock King that night?'

'No,' said Dick Four. Then McTurk told. 'I see,' said Dick Four, nodding. 'Practically he duplicated that trick over again. There's nobody like Stalky.'

'That's just where you make the mistake,' I said. 'India's full of Stalkies – Cheltenham and Haileybury and Marlborough chaps – that we don't know anything about, and the surprises will begin when there is really a big row on.'

'Who will be surprised?' said Dick Four.

'The other side. The gentlemen who go to the front in first-class carriages. Just imagine Stalky let loose on the south side of Europe with a sufficiency of Sikhs and a reasonable prospect of loot. Consider it quietly.'

'There's something in that, but you're too much of an optimist, Beetle,' said the Infant.

'Well, I've a right to be. Ain't I responsible for the whole thing? You needn't laugh. Who wrote "Aladdin now has got his wife" – eh?'

'What's that got to do with it?' said Tertius.

'Everything,' said I.

'Prove it,' said the Infant.

And I have.